W9-AEI-256

KATHERINE ANNE PORTER

KATHERINE ANNE PORTER

COLLECTED STORIES
AND OTHER WRITINGS

THE LIBRARY OF AMERICA

The paper used in this publication meets the
minimum requirements of the American National Standard for
Information Sciences—Permanence of Paper for Printed
Library Materials, ANSI Z39.48—1984.

Distributed to the trade in the United States
by Penguin Putnam Inc.
and in Canada by Penguin Books Canada Ltd.

Library of Congress Catalog Number: 2008927625
ISBN 978-1-59853-029-2

———

First Printing
The Library of America—186

Manufactured in the United States of America

DARLENE HARBOUR UNRUE
IS THE EDITOR OF THIS VOLUME

Contents

THE COLLECTED STORIES
OF KATHERINE ANNE PORTER

Go Little Book . . .

THIS collection of stories has been floating around the world
in many editions, countries and languages, in three small volumes, for many years. There are four stories added which have
never been collected before, and it is by mere hazard they are
here at all. "The Fig Tree," now in its right place in the sequence called *The Old Order*, simply disappeared at the time
The Leaning Tower was published, in 1944, and reappeared
again from a box of otherwise unfinished manuscripts in
another house, another city and a different state, in 1961.
"Holiday" represents one of my prolonged struggles, not with
questions of form or style, but my own moral and emotional
collision with a human situation I was too young to cope with
at the time it occurred; yet the story haunted me for years and
I made three separate versions, with a certain spot in all three
where the thing went off track. So I put it away and it disappeared also, and I forgot it. It rose from one of my boxes of
papers, after a quarter of a century, and I sat down in great excitement to read all three versions. I saw at once that the first
was the right one, and as for the vexing question which had
stopped me short long ago, it had in the course of living
settled itself so slowly and deeply and secretly I wondered why
I had ever been distressed by it. I changed one short paragraph
and a line or two at the end and it was done. "María Concepción" was my first published story. It was followed by "Virgin
Violeta" and "The Martyr," all stories of Mexico, my much-
loved second country, and they were each in turn accepted and
published in the old *Century Magazine*, now vanished, by
good generous sympathetic Carl Van Doren. He was the first
editor—indeed, the first person—to read a story of mine, and
I remember how unhesitatingly and warmly he said, "I believe
you are a writer!" This was in 1923.

Several writers or persons connected with literature in some
way or another, from time to time in published reminiscences,
have done me the honor to mention that they had, so to speak,
"discovered" me.

3

There is no reason to name them, but I shall only say here and now, to have the business straight, it was Carl Van Doren, gifted writer, editor and resourceful friend to young writers, who just lightly tossed my stories into print and started me on my long career, with such an air of it being all in the day's work, which it was, I went away in a dazzle of joy, not in the least thinking of myself as "discovered"—I had known where I was all along—nor looking towards the future as a "career." What unpleasant words they are in this context. "Virgin Violeta" and "The Martyr" were left out of the first edition, I forget why, possibly oversight. A friend fished them out of the ancient *Century* files, got them re-published, after forty-odd years, and so they join their fellows. Every story I ever finished and published is here. I beg of the reader one gentle favor for which he may be sure of my perpetual gratitude: please do not call my short novels *Novelettes*, or even worse, *Novellas*. Novelette is classical usage for a trivial, dime-novel sort of thing; Novella is a slack, boneless, affected word that we do not need to describe anything. Please call my works by their right names: we have four that cover every division: short stories, long stories, short novels, novels. I now have examples of all four kinds under these headings, and they seem very clear, sufficient, and plain English.

To part is to die a little, it is said (in every language I can read), but my farewell to these stories is a happy one, a renewal of their life, a prolonging of their time under the sun, which is what any artist most longs for—to be read, and remembered.

Go little book. . . .

KATHERINE ANNE PORTER
14 June 1965

Contents

FLOWERING JUDAS AND OTHER STORIES

María Concepción

M ARÍA CONCEPCIÓN walked carefully, keeping to the
middle of the white dusty road, where the maguey
thorns and the treacherous curved spines of organ cactus had
not gathered so profusely. She would have enjoyed resting for
a moment in the dark shade by the roadside, but she had no
time to waste drawing cactus needles from her feet. Juan and
his chief would be waiting for their food in the damp trenches
of the buried city.

She carried about a dozen living fowls slung over her right
shoulder, their feet fastened together. Half of them fell upon
the flat of her back, the balance dangled uneasily over her
breast. They wriggled their benumbed and swollen legs against
her neck, they twisted their stupefied eyes and peered into her
face inquiringly. She did not see them or think of them. Her
left arm was tired with the weight of the food basket, and she
was hungry after her long morning's work.

Her straight back outlined itself strongly under her clean
bright blue cotton rebozo. Instinctive serenity softened her
black eyes, shaped like almonds, set far apart, and tilted a bit
endwise. She walked with the free, natural, guarded ease of the
primitive woman carrying an unborn child. The shape of her
body was easy, the swelling life was not a distortion, but the
right inevitable proportions of a woman. She was entirely contented. Her husband was at work and she was on her way to
market to sell her fowls.

Her small house sat half-way up a shallow hill, under a
clump of pepper-trees, a wall of organ cactus enclosing it on
the side nearest to the road. Now she came down into the valley, divided by the narrow spring, and crossed a bridge of loose
stones near the hut where María Rosa the beekeeper lived with
her old godmother, Lupe the medicine woman. María Concepción had no faith in the charred owl bones, the singed rabbit fur, the cat entrails, the messes and ointments sold by Lupe
to the ailing of the village. She was a good Christian, and drank
simple herb teas for headache and stomachache, or bought her
remedies bottled, with printed directions that she could not

9

read, at the drugstore near the city market, where she went almost daily. But she often bought a jar of honey from young María Rosa, a pretty, shy child only fifteen years old.

María Concepción and her husband, Juan Villegas, were each a little past their eighteenth year. She had a good reputation with the neighbors as an energetic religious woman who could drive a bargain to the end. It was commonly known that if she wished to buy a new rebozo for herself or a shirt for Juan, she could bring out a sack of hard silver coins for the purpose.

She had paid for the license, nearly a year ago, the potent bit of stamped paper which permits people to be married in the church. She had given money to the priest before she and Juan walked together up to the altar the Monday after Holy Week. It had been the adventure of the villagers to go, three Sundays one after another, to hear the banns called by the priest for Juan de Dios Villegas and María Concepción Manríquez, who were actually getting married in the church, instead of behind it, which was the usual custom, less expensive, and as binding as any other ceremony. But María Concepción was always as proud as if she owned a hacienda.

She paused on the bridge and dabbled her feet in the water, her eyes resting themselves from the sun-rays in a fixed gaze to the far-off mountains, deeply blue under their hanging drift of clouds. It came to her that she would like a fresh crust of honey. The delicious aroma of bees, their slow thrilling hum, awakened a pleasant desire for a flake of sweetness in her mouth.

"If I do not eat it now, I shall mark my child," she thought, peering through the crevices in the thick hedge of cactus that sheered up nakedly, like bared knife blades set protectingly around the small clearing. The place was so silent she doubted if María Rosa and Lupe were at home.

The leaning jacal of dried rush-withes and corn sheaves, bound to tall saplings thrust into the earth, roofed with yellowed maguey leaves flattened and overlapping like shingles, hunched drowsy and fragrant in the warmth of noonday. The hives, similarly made, were scattered towards the back of the clearing, like small mounds of clean vegetable refuse. Over each mound there hung a dusty golden shimmer of bees.

A light gay scream of laughter rose from behind the hut; a man's short laugh joined in. "Ah, hahahaha!" went the voices together high and low, like a song.

"So María Rosa has a man!" María Concepción stopped short, smiling, shifted her burden slightly, and bent forward shading her eyes to see more clearly through the spaces of the hedge.

María Rosa ran, dodging between beehives, parting two stunted jasmine bushes as she came, lifting her knees in swift leaps, looking over her shoulder and laughing in a quivering, excited way. A heavy jar, swung to her wrist by the handle, knocked against her thighs as she ran. Her toes pushed up sudden spurts of dust, her half-raveled braids showered around her shoulders in long crinkled wisps.

Juan Villegas ran after her, also laughing strangely, his teeth set, both rows gleaming behind the small soft black beard growing sparsely on his lips, his chin, leaving his brown cheeks girl-smooth. When he seized her, he clenched so hard her chemise gave way and ripped from her shoulder. She stopped laughing at this, pushed him away and stood silent, trying to pull up the torn sleeve with one hand. Her pointed chin and dark red mouth moved in an uncertain way, as if she wished to laugh again; her long black lashes flickered with the quick-moving lights in her hidden eyes.

María Concepción did not stir nor breathe for some seconds. Her forehead was cold, and yet boiling water seemed to be pouring slowly along her spine. An unaccountable pain was in her knees, as if they were broken. She was afraid Juan and María Rosa would feel her eyes fixed upon them and would find her there, unable to move, spying upon them. But they did not pass beyond the enclosure, nor even glance towards the gap in the wall opening upon the road.

Juan lifted one of María Rosa's loosened braids and slapped her neck with it playfully. She smiled softly, consentingly. Together they moved back through the hives of honey-comb. María Rosa balanced her jar on one hip and swung her long full petticoats with every step. Juan flourished his wide hat back and forth, walking proudly as a game-cock.

María Concepción came out of the heavy cloud which enwrapped her head and bound her throat, and found herself walking onward, keeping the road without knowing it, feeling her way delicately, her ears strumming as if all María Rosa's bees had hived in them. Her careful sense of duty kept her moving toward the buried city where Juan's chief, the American archaeologist, was taking his midday rest, waiting for his food.

Juan and María Rosa! She burned all over now, as if a layer of tiny fig-cactus bristles, as cruel as spun glass, had crawled under her skin. She wished to sit down quietly and wait for her death, but not until she had cut the throats of her man and that girl who were laughing and kissing under the cornstalks. Once when she was a young girl she had come back from market to find her jacal burned to a pile of ash and her few silver coins gone. A dark empty feeling had filled her; she kept moving about the place, not believing her eyes, expecting it all to take shape again before her. But it was gone, and though she knew an enemy had done it, she could not find out who it was, and could only curse and threaten the air. Now here was a worse thing, but she knew her enemy. María Rosa, that sinful girl, shameless! She heard herself saying a harsh, true word about María Rosa, saying it aloud as if she expected someone to agree with her: "Yes, she is a whore! She has no right to live."

At this moment the gray untidy head of Givens appeared over the edges of the newest trench he had caused to be dug in his field of excavations. The long deep crevasses, in which a man might stand without being seen, lay crisscrossed like orderly gashes of a giant scalpel. Nearly all of the men of the community worked for Givens, helping him to uncover the lost city of their ancestors. They worked all the year through and prospered, digging every day for those small clay heads and bits of pottery and fragments of painted walls for which there was no good use on earth, being all broken and encrusted with clay. They themselves could make better ones, perfectly stout and new, which they took to town and peddled to foreigners for real money. But the unearthly delight of the chief in finding these worn-out things was an endless puzzle. He would fairly roar for joy at times, waving a shattered pot or a human skull above his head, shouting for his photographer to come and make a picture of this!

Now he emerged, and his young enthusiast's eyes welcomed

María Concepción from his old-man face, covered with hard
wrinkles and burned to the color of red earth. "I hope you've
brought me a nice fat one." He selected a fowl from the bunch
dangling nearest him as María Concepción, wordless, leaned
over the trench. "Dress it for me, there's a good girl. I'll
broil it."

María Concepción took the fowl by the head, and silently,
swiftly drew her knife across its throat, twisting the head off
with the casual firmness she might use with the top of a beet.

"Good God, woman, you do have nerve," said Givens,
watching her. "I can't do that. It gives me the creeps."

"My home country is Guadalajara," explained María Concepción, without bravado, as she picked and gutted the fowl.

She stood and regarded Givens condescendingly, that di-
verting white man who had no woman of his own to cook for
him, and moreover appeared not to feel any loss of dignity in
preparing his own food. He squatted now, eyes squinted, nose
wrinkled to avoid the smoke, turning the roasting fowl busily
on a stick. A mysterious man, undoubtedly rich, and Juan's
chief, therefore to be respected, to be placated.

"The tortillas are fresh and hot, señor," she murmured gently. "With your permission I will now go to market."

"Yes, yes, run along; bring me another of these tomorrow."
Givens turned his head to look at her again. Her grand manner
sometimes reminded him of royalty in exile. He noticed her
unnatural paleness. "The sun is too hot, eh?" he asked.

"Yes, sir. Pardon me, but Juan will be here soon?"

"He ought to be here now. Leave his food. The others will
eat it."

She moved away; the blue of her rebozo became a dancing
spot in the heat waves that rose from the gray-red soil. Givens
liked his Indians best when he could feel a fatherly indulgence
for their primitive childish ways. He told comic stories of Juan's
escapades, of how often he had saved him, in the past five
years, from going to jail, and even from being shot, for his varied and always unexpected misdeeds.

"I am never a minute too soon to get him out of one pickle
or another," he would say. "Well, he's a good worker, and I
know how to manage him."

After Juan was married, he used to twit him, with exactly the right shade of condescension, on his many infidelities to María Concepción. "She'll catch you yet, and God help you!" he was fond of saying, and Juan would laugh with immense pleasure.

It did not occur to María Concepción to tell Juan she had found him out. During the day her anger against him died, and her anger against María Rosa grew. She kept saying to herself, "When I was a young girl like María Rosa, if a man had caught hold of me so, I would have broken my jar over his head." She forgot completely that she had not resisted even so much as María Rosa, on the day that Juan had first taken hold of her. Besides she had married him afterwards in the church, and that was a very different thing.

Juan did not come home that night, but went away to war and María Rosa went with him. Juan had a rifle at his shoulder and two pistols at his belt. María Rosa wore a rifle also, slung on her back along with the blankets and the cooking pots. They joined the nearest detachment of troops in the field, and María Rosa marched ahead with the battalion of experienced women of war, which went over the crops like locusts, gathering provisions for the army. She cooked with them, and ate with them what was left after the men had eaten. After battles she went out on the field with the others to salvage clothing and ammunition and guns from the slain before they should begin to swell in the heat. Sometimes they would encounter the women from the other army, and a second battle as grim as the first would take place.

There was no particular scandal in the village. People shrugged, grinned. It was far better that they were gone. The neighbors went around saying that María Rosa was safer in the army than she would be in the same village with María Concepción.

María Concepción did not weep when Juan left her; and when the baby was born, and died within four days, she did not weep. "She is mere stone," said old Lupe, who went over and offered charms to preserve the baby.

"May you rot in hell with your charms," said María Concepción.

If she had not gone so regularly to church, lighting candles before the saints, kneeling with her arms spread in the form of a cross for hours at a time, and receiving holy communion every month, there might have been talk of her being devil-possessed, her face was so changed and blind-looking. But this was impossible when, after all, she had been married by the priest. It must be, they reasoned, that she was being punished for her pride. They decided that this was the true cause for everything: she was altogether too proud. So they pitied her.

During the year that Juan and María Rosa were gone María Concepción sold her fowls and looked after her garden and her sack of hard coins grew. Lupe had no talent for bees, and the hives did not prosper. She began to blame María Rosa for running away, and to praise María Concepción for her behavior. She used to see María Concepción at the market or at church, and she always said that no one could tell by looking at her now that she was a woman who had such a heavy grief.

"I pray God everything goes well with María Concepción from this out," she would say, "for she has had her share of trouble."

When some idle person repeated this to the deserted woman, she went down to Lupe's house and stood within the clearing and called to the medicine woman, who sat in her doorway stirring a mess of her infallible cure for sores: "Keep your prayers to yourself, Lupe, or offer them for others who need them. I will ask God for what I want in this world."

"And will you get it, you think, María Concepción?" asked Lupe, tittering cruelly and smelling the wooden mixing spoon. "Did you pray for what you have now?"

Afterward everyone noticed that María Concepción went oftener to church, and even seldomer to the village to talk with the other women as they sat along the curb, nursing their babies and eating fruit, at the end of the market-day.

"She is wrong to take us for enemies," said old Soledad, who was a thinker and a peace-maker. "All women have these troubles. Well, we should suffer together."

But María Concepción lived alone. She was gaunt, as if something were gnawing her away inside, her eyes were sunken, and she would not speak a word if she could help it. She worked harder than ever, and her butchering knife was scarcely ever out of her hand.

*

Juan and María Rosa, disgusted with military life, came home
one day without asking permission of anyone. The field of war
had unrolled itself, a long scroll of vexations, until the end had
frayed out within twenty miles of Juan's village. So he and
María Rosa, now lean as a wolf, burdened with a child daily expected, set out with no farewells to the regiment and walked
home.

They arrived one morning about daybreak. Juan was picked
up on sight by a group of military police from the small barracks on the edge of town, and taken to prison, where the
officer in charge told him with impersonal cheerfulness that he
would add one to a catch of ten waiting to be shot as deserters
the next morning.

María Rosa, screaming and falling on her face in the road,
was taken under the armpits by two guards and helped briskly
to her jacal, now sadly run down. She was received with professional importance by Lupe, who helped the baby to be born
at once.

Limping with foot soreness, a layer of dust concealing his
fine new clothes got mysteriously from somewhere, Juan appeared before the captain at the barracks. The captain recognized him as head digger for his good friend Givens, and
dispatched a note to Givens saying: "I am holding the person
of Juan Villegas awaiting your further disposition."

When Givens showed up Juan was delivered to him with the
urgent request that nothing be made public about so humane
and sensible an operation on the part of military authority.

Juan walked out of the rather stifling atmosphere of the
drumhead court, a definite air of swagger about him. His
hat, of unreasonable dimensions and embroidered with silver
thread, hung over one eyebrow, secured at the back by a cord
of silver dripping with bright blue tassels. His shirt was of a
checkerboard pattern in green and black, his white cotton
trousers were bound by a belt of yellow leather tooled in red.
His feet were bare, full of stone bruises, and sadly ragged as to
toenails. He removed his cigarette from the corner of his full-
lipped wide mouth. He removed the splendid hat. His black
dusty hair, pressed moistly to his forehead, sprang up suddenly
in a cloudy thatch on his crown. He bowed to the officer, who
appeared to be gazing at a vacuum. He swung his arm wide in

a free circle upsoaring towards the prison window, where for-lorn heads poked over the window sill, hot eyes following after the lucky departing one. Two or three of the heads nodded, and a half dozen hands were flipped at him in an effort to imi-tate his own casual and heady manner.

Juan kept up this insufferable pantomime until they rounded the first clump of fig-cactus. Then he seized Givens' hand and burst into oratory. "Blessed be the day your servant Juan Ville-gas first came under your eyes. From this day my life is yours without condition, ten thousand thanks with all my heart!"

"For God's sake stop playing the fool," said Givens irritably. "Some day I'm going to be five minutes too late."

"Well, it is nothing much to be shot, my chief—certainly you know I was not afraid—but to be shot in a drove of de-serters, against a cold wall, just in the moment of my home-coming, by order of that . . ."

Glittering epithets tumbled over one another like explosions of a rocket. All the scandalous analogies from the animal and vegetable worlds were applied in a vivid, unique and personal way to the life, loves, and family history of the officer who had just set him free. When he had quite cursed himself dry, and his nerves were soothed, he added: "With your permission, my chief!"

"What will María Concepción say to all this?" asked Givens. "You are very informal, Juan, for a man who was married in the church."

Juan put on his hat.

"Oh, María Concepción! That's nothing. Look, my chief, to be married in the church is a great misfortune for a man. After that he is not himself any more. How can that woman com-plain when I do not drink even at fiestas enough to be really drunk? I do not beat her; never, never. We were always at peace. I say to her, Come here, and she comes straight. I say, Go there, and she goes quickly. Yet sometimes I looked at her and thought, Now I am married to that woman in the church, and I felt a sinking inside, as if something were lying heavy on my stomach. With María Rosa it is all different. She is not silent; she talks. When she talks too much, I slap her and say, Silence, thou simpleton! and she weeps. She is just a girl with whom I do as I please. You know how she used to keep those clean little bees in their hives? She is like their honey to me. I swear it. I would not harm María Concepción because I am married to her in the church; but also, my chief, I will not leave María Rosa, because she pleases me more than any other woman."

"Let me tell you, Juan, things haven't been going as well as you think. You be careful. Some day María Concepción will just take your head off with that carving knife of hers. You keep that in mind."

Juan's expression was the proper blend of masculine triumph and sentimental melancholy. It was pleasant to see himself in the rôle of hero to two such desirable women. He had just escaped from the threat of a disagreeable end. His clothes were new and handsome, and they had cost him just nothing. María Rosa had collected them for him here and there after battles. He was walking in the early sunshine, smelling the good smells of ripening cactus-figs, peaches, and melons, of pungent berries dangling from the pepper-trees, and the smoke of his cigarette under his nose. He was on his way to civilian life with his patient chief. His situation was ineffably perfect, and he swallowed it whole.

"My chief," he addressed Givens handsomely, as one man of the world to another, "women are good things, but not at this moment. With your permission, I will now go to the village and eat. My God, *how* I shall eat! Tomorrow morning very early I will come to the buried city and work like seven men. Let us forget María Concepción and María Rosa. Each one in her place. I will manage them when the time comes."

News of Juan's adventure soon got abroad, and Juan found many friends about him during the morning. They frankly commended his way of leaving the army. It was in itself the act of a hero. The new hero ate a great deal and drank somewhat, the occasion being better than a feast-day. It was almost noon before he returned to visit María Rosa.

He found her sitting on a clean straw mat, rubbing fat on her three-hour-old son. Before this felicitous vision Juan's emotions so twisted him that he returned to the village and invited every man in the "Death and Resurrection" pulque shop to drink with him.

Having thus taken leave of his balance, he started back to

María Rosa, and found himself unaccountably in his own house, attempting to beat María Concepción by way of reëstablishing himself in his legal household.

María Concepción, knowing all the events of that unhappy day, was not in a yielding mood, and refused to be beaten. She did not scream nor implore; she stood her ground and resisted; she even struck at him. Juan, amazed, hardly knowing what he did, stepped back and gazed at her inquiringly through a leisurely whirling film which seemed to have lodged behind his eyes. Certainly he had not even thought of touching her. Oh, well, no harm done. He gave up, turned away, half-asleep on his feet. He dropped amiably in a shadowed corner and began to snore.

María Concepción, seeing that he was quiet, began to bind the legs of her fowls. It was market-day and she was late. She fumbled and tangled the bits of cord in her haste, and set off across the plowed fields instead of taking the accustomed road. She ran with a crazy panic in her head, her stumbling legs. Now and then she would stop and look about her, trying to place herself, then go on a few steps, until she realized that she was not going towards the market.

At once she came to her senses completely, recognized the thing that troubled her so terribly, was certain of what she wanted. She sat down quietly under a sheltering thorny bush and gave herself over to her long devouring sorrow. The thing which had for so long squeezed her whole body into a tight dumb knot of suffering suddenly broke with shocking violence. She jerked with the involuntary recoil of one who receives a blow, and the sweat poured from her skin as if the wounds of her whole life were shedding their salt ichor. Drawing her rebozo over her head, she bowed her forehead on her updrawn knees, and sat there in deadly silence and immobility. From time to time she lifted her head where the sweat formed steadily and poured down her face, drenching the front of her chemise, and her mouth had the shape of crying, but there were no tears and no sound. All her being was a dark confused memory of grief burning in her at night, of deadly baffled anger eating at her by day, until her very tongue tasted bitter, and her feet were as heavy as if she were mired in the muddy roads during the time of rains.

After a great while she stood up and threw the rebozo off her face, and set out walking again.

Juan awakened slowly, with long yawns and grumblings, alternated with short relapses into sleep full of visions and clamors. A blur of orange light seared his eyeballs when he tried to unseal his lids. There came from somewhere a low voice weeping without tears, saying meaningless phrases over and over. He began to listen. He tugged at the leash of his stupor, he strained to grasp those words which terrified him even though he could not quite hear them. Then he came awake with frightening suddenness, sitting up and staring at the long sharpened streak of light piercing the corn-husk walls from the level disappearing sun.

María Concepción stood in the doorway, looming colossally tall to his betrayed eyes. She was talking quickly, and calling his name. Then he saw her clearly.

"God's name!" said Juan, frozen to the marrow, "here I am facing my death!" for the long knife she wore habitually at her belt was in her hand. But instead, she threw it away, clear from her, and got down on her knees, crawling toward him as he had seen her crawl many times toward the shrine at Guadalupe Villa. He watched her approach with such horror that the hair of his head seemed to be lifting itself away from him. Falling forward upon her face, she huddled over him, lips moving in a ghostly whisper. Her words became clear, and Juan understood them all.

For a second he could not move nor speak. Then he took her head between both his hands, and supported her in this way, saying swiftly, anxiously reassuring, almost in a babble:

"Oh, thou poor creature! Oh, madwoman! Oh, my María Concepción, unfortunate! Listen. . . . Don't be afraid. Listen to me! I will hide thee away, I thy own man will protect thee! Quiet! Not a sound!"

Trying to collect himself, he held her and cursed under his breath for a few moments in the gathering darkness. María Concepción bent over, face almost on the ground, her feet folded under her, as if she would hide behind him. For the first time in his life Juan was aware of danger. This was danger. María Concepción would be dragged away between two gendarmes, with him following helpless and unarmed, to spend the rest of her days in Belén Prison, maybe. Danger! The night swarmed with threats. He stood up and dragged her up with him. She was silent and perfectly rigid, holding to him with resistless strength, her hands stiffened on his arms.

"Get me the knife," he told her in a whisper. She obeyed, her feet slipping along the hard earth floor, her shoulders straight, her arms close to her side. He lighted a candle. María Concepción held the knife out to him. It was stained and dark even to the handle with drying blood.

He frowned at her harshly, noting the same stains on her chemise and hands.

"Take off thy clothes and wash thy hands," he ordered. He washed the knife carefully, and threw the water wide of the doorway. She watched him and did likewise with the bowl in which she had bathed.

"Light the brasero and cook food for me," he told her in the same peremptory tone. He took her garments and went out. When he returned, she was wearing an old soiled dress, and was fanning the fire in the charcoal burner. Seating himself cross-legged near her, he stared at her as at a creature unknown to him, who bewildered him utterly, for whom there was no possible explanation. She did not turn her head, but kept silent and still, except for the movements of her strong hands fanning the blaze which cast sparks and small jets of white smoke, flaring and dying rhythmically with the motion of the fan, lighting her face and darkening it by turns.

Juan's voice barely disturbed the silence: "Listen to me carefully, and tell me the truth, and when the gendarmes come here for us, thou shalt have nothing to fear. But there will be something for us to settle between us afterward."

The light from the charcoal burner shone in her eyes; a yellow phosphorescence glimmered behind the dark iris.

"For me everything is settled now," she answered, in a tone so tender, so grave, so heavy with suffering, that Juan felt his vitals contract. He wished to repent openly, not as a man, but as a very small child. He could not fathom her, nor himself, nor the mysterious fortunes of life grown so instantly confused where all had seemed so gay and simple. He felt too that she had become invaluable, a woman without equal among a million women, and he could not tell why. He drew an enormous sigh that rattled in his chest.

"Yes, yes, it is all settled. I shall not go away again. We must stay here together."

Whispering, he questioned her and she answered whispering, and he instructed her over and over until she had her lesson by heart. The hostile darkness of the night encroached upon them, flowing over the narrow threshold, invading their hearts. It brought with it sighs and murmurs, the pad of secretive feet in the near-by road, the sharp staccato whimper of wind through the cactus leaves. All these familiar, once friendly cadences were now invested with sinister terrors; a dread, formless and uncontrollable, took hold of them both.

"Light another candle," said Juan, loudly, in too resolute, too sharp a tone. "Let us eat now."

They sat facing each other and ate from the same dish, after their old habit. Neither tasted what they ate. With food halfway to his mouth, Juan listened. The sound of voices rose, spread, widened at the turn of the road along the cactus wall. A spray of lantern light shot through the hedge, a single voice slashed the blackness, ripped the fragile layer of silence suspended above the hut.

"Juan Villegas!"

"Pass, friends!" Juan roared back cheerfully.

They stood in the doorway, simple cautious gendarmes from the village, mixed-bloods themselves with Indian sympathies, well known to all the community. They flashed their lanterns almost apologetically upon the pleasant, harmless scene of a man eating supper with his wife.

"Pardon, brother," said the leader. "Someone has killed the woman María Rosa, and we must question her neighbors and friends." He paused, and added with an attempt at severity, "Naturally!"

"Naturally," agreed Juan. "You know that I was a good friend of María Rosa. This is bad news."

They all went away together, the men walking in a group, María Concepción following a few steps in the rear, near Juan. No one spoke.

*

The two points of candlelight at María Rosa's head fluttered uneasily; the shadows shifted and dodged on the stained darkened walls. To María Concepción everything in the smothering enclosing room shared an evil restlessness. The watchful faces of those called as witnesses, the faces of old friends, were made alien by the look of speculation in their eyes. The ridges of the rose-colored rebozo thrown over the body varied continually, as though the thing it covered was not perfectly in repose. Her eyes swerved over the body in the open painted coffin, from the candle tips at the head to the feet, jutting up thinly, the small scarred soles protruding, freshly washed, a mass of crooked, half-healed wounds, thorn-pricks and cuts of sharp stones. Her gaze went back to the candle flame, to Juan's eyes warning her, to the gendarmes talking among themselves. Her eyes would not be controlled.

With a leap that shook her her gaze settled upon the face of María Rosa. Instantly her blood ran smoothly again: there was nothing to fear. Even the restless light could not give a look of life to that fixed countenance. She was dead. María Concepción felt her muscles give way softly; her heart began beating steadily without effort. She knew no more rancor against that pitiable thing, lying indifferently in its blue coffin under the fine silk rebozo. The mouth drooped sharply at the corners in a grimace of weeping arrested half-way. The brows were distressed; the dead flesh could not cast off the shape of its last terror. It was all finished. María Rosa had eaten too much honey and had had too much love. Now she must sit in hell, crying over her sins and her hard death forever and ever.

Old Lupe's cackling voice arose. She had spent the morning helping María Rosa, and it had been hard work. The child had spat blood the moment it was born, a bad sign. She thought then that bad luck would come to the house. Well, about sunset she was in the yard at the back of the house grinding tomatoes and peppers. She had left mother and babe asleep. She heard a strange noise in the house, a choking and smothered calling, like someone wailing in sleep. Well, such a thing is only natural. But there followed a light, quick, thudding sound—

"Like the blows of a fist?" interrupted an officer.

"No, not at all like such a thing."

"How do you know?"

"I am well acquainted with that sound, friends," retorted Lupe. "This was something else."

She was at a loss to describe it exactly. A moment later, there came the sound of pebbles rolling and slipping under feet; then she knew someone had been there and was running away.

"Why did you wait so long before going to see?"

"I am old and hard in the joints," said Lupe. "I cannot run after people. I walked as fast as I could to the cactus hedge, for it is only by this way that anyone can enter. There was no one in the road, sir, no one. Three cows, with a dog driving them; nothing else. When I got to María Rosa, she was lying all tangled up, and from her neck to her middle she was full of knife-holes. It was a sight to move the Blessed Image Himself! Her eyes were—"

"Never mind. Who came oftenest to her house before she went away? Did you know her enemies?"

Lupe's face congealed, closed. Her spongy skin drew into a network of secretive wrinkles. She turned withdrawn and expressionless eyes upon the gendarmes.

"I am an old woman. I do not see well. I cannot hurry on my feet. I know no enemy of María Rosa. I did not see anyone leave the clearing."

"You did not hear splashing in the spring near the bridge?"

"No, sir."

"Why, then, do our dogs follow a scent there and lose it?"

"God only knows, my friend. I am an old wo—"

"Yes. How did the footfalls sound?"

"Like the tread of an evil spirit!" Lupe broke forth in a swelling oracular tone that startled them. The Indians stirred uneasily, glanced at the dead, then at Lupe. They half expected her to produce the evil spirit among them at once.

The gendarme began to lose his temper.

"No, poor unfortunate; I mean, were they heavy or light? The footsteps of a man or of a woman? Was the person shod or barefoot?"

A glance at the listening circle assured Lupe of their thrilled attention. She enjoyed the dangerous importance of her situation. She could have ruined that María Concepción with a word, but it was even sweeter to make fools of these gendarmes who went about spying on honest people. She raised her voice again. What she had not seen she could not describe, thank God! No one could harm her because her knees were stiff and she could not run even to seize a murderer. As for knowing the difference between footfalls, shod or bare, man or woman, nay, between devil and human, who ever heard of such madness?

"My eyes are not ears, gentlemen," she ended grandly, "but upon my heart I swear those footsteps fell as the tread of the spirit of evil!"

"Imbecile!" yapped the leader in a shrill voice. "Take her away, one of you! Now, Juan Villegas, tell me—"

Juan told his story patiently, several times over. He had returned to his wife that day. She had gone to market as usual. He had helped her prepare her fowls. She had returned about midafternoon, they had talked, she had cooked, they had eaten, nothing was amiss. Then the gendarmes came with the news about María Rosa. That was all. Yes, María Rosa had run away with him, but there had been no bad blood between him and his wife on this account, nor between his wife and María Rosa. Everybody knew that his wife was a quiet woman.

María Concepción heard her own voice answering without a break. It was true at first she was troubled when her husband went away, but after that she had not worried about him. It was the way of men, she believed. She was a church-married woman and knew her place. Well, he had come home at last. She had gone to market, but had come back early, because now she had her man to cook for. That was all.

Other voices broke in. A toothless old man said: "She is a woman of good reputation among us, and María Rosa was not." A smiling young mother, Anita, baby at breast, said: "If no one thinks so, how can you accuse her? It was the loss of her child and not of her husband that changed her so." Another: "María Rosa had a strange life, apart from us. How do we know who might have come from another place to do her evil?" And old Soledad spoke up boldly: "When I saw María Concepción in the market today, I said, 'Good luck to you, María Concepción, this is a happy day for you!'" and she gave María Concepción a long easy stare, and the smile of a born wise-woman.

María Concepción suddenly felt herself guarded, surrounded, upborne by her faithful friends. They were around
her, speaking for her, defending her, the forces of life were
ranged invincibly with her against the beaten dead. María Rosa
had thrown away her share of strength in them, she lay for-
feited among them. María Concepción looked from one to the
other of the circling, intent faces. Their eyes gave back reassurance, understanding, a secret and mighty sympathy.

The gendarmes were at a loss. They, too, felt that sheltering
wall cast impenetrably around her. They were certain she had
done it, and yet they could not accuse her. Nobody could
be accused; there was not a shred of true evidence. They
shrugged their shoulders and snapped their fingers and shuffled their feet. Well, then, good night to everybody. Many par-
dons for having intruded. Good health!

A small bundle lying against the wall at the head of the coffin squirmed like an eel. A wail, a mere sliver of sound, issued.
María Concepción took the son of María Rosa in her arms.

"He is mine," she said clearly, "I will take him with me."

No one assented in words, but an approving nod, a bare
breath of complete agreement, stirred among them as they
made way for her.

María Concepción, carrying the child, followed Juan from the
clearing. The hut was left with its lighted candles and a crowd
of old women who would sit up all night, drinking coffee and
smoking and telling ghost stories.

Juan's exaltation had burned out. There was not an ember
of excitement left in him. He was tired. The perilous adventure
was over. María Rosa had vanished, to come no more forever.
Their days of marching, of eating, of quarreling and making
love between battles, were all over. Tomorrow he would go
back to dull and endless labor, he must descend into the
trenches of the buried city as María Rosa must go into her
grave. He felt his veins fill up with bitterness, with black unendurable melancholy. Oh, Jesus! what bad luck overtakes a man!

Well, there was no way out of it now. For the moment he
craved only to sleep. He was so drowsy he could scarcely guide
his feet. The occasional light touch of the woman at his elbow
was as unreal, as ghostly as the brushing of a leaf against his

face. He did not know why he had fought to save her, and now he forgot her. There was nothing in him except a vast blind hurt like a covered wound.

He entered the jacal, and without waiting to light a candle, threw off his clothing, sitting just within the door. He moved with lagging, half-awake hands, to strip his body of its heavy finery. With a long groaning sigh of relief he fell straight back on the floor, almost instantly asleep, his arms flung up and outward.

María Concepción, a small clay jar in her hand, approached the gentle little mother goat tethered to a sapling, which gave and yielded as she pulled at the rope's end after the farthest reaches of grass about her. The kid, tied up a few feet away, rose bleating, its feathery fleece shivering in the fresh wind. Sitting on her heels, holding his tether, she allowed him to suckle a few moments. Afterward—all her movements very deliberate and even—she drew a supply of milk for the child.

She sat against the wall of her house, near the doorway. The child, fed and asleep, was cradled in the hollow of her crossed legs. The silence overfilled the world, the skies flowed down evenly to the rim of the valley, the stealthy moon crept slantwise to the shelter of the mountains. She felt soft and warm all over; she dreamed that the newly born child was her own, and she was resting deliciously.

María Concepción could hear Juan's breathing. The sound vapored from the low doorway, calmly; the house seemed to be resting after a burdensome day. She breathed, too, very slowly and quietly, each inspiration saturating her with repose. The child's light, faint breath was a mere shadowy moth of sound in the silver air. The night, the earth under her, seemed to swell and recede together with a limitless, unhurried, benign breathing. She drooped and closed her eyes, feeling the slow rise and fall within her own body. She did not know what it was, but it eased her all through. Even as she was falling asleep, head bowed over the child, she was still aware of a strange, wakeful happiness.

New York 1922

Virgin Violeta

VIOLETA, nearly fifteen years old, sat on a hassock, hugging her knees and watching Carlos, her cousin, and her sister Blanca, who were reading poetry aloud by turns at the long table.

Occasionally she glanced down at her own feet, clad in thick-soled brown sandals, the toes turned in a trifle. Their ugliness distressed her, and she pulled her short skirt over them until the beltline sagged under her loose, dark blue woolen blouse. Then she straightened up, with a full, silent breath, uncovering the sandals again. Each time her eyes moved under shy lids to Carlos, to see if he had noticed; he never did notice. Disappointed, a little troubled, Violeta would sit very still for a while, listening and watching.

> "'This torment of love which is in my heart:
> I know that I suffer it, but I do not know why.'"

Blanca's voice was thin, with a whisper in it. She seemed anxious to keep the poetry all for Carlos and herself. Her shawl, embroidered in yellow on gray silk, slipped from her shoulders whenever she inclined toward the lamp. Carlos would lift the tassel of fringe nearest him between finger and thumb and toss it deftly into place. Blanca's nod, her smile, were the perfection of amiable indifference. But her voice wavered, caught on the word. She had always to begin again the line she was reading.

Carlos would slant his pale eyes at Blanca; then he would resume his pose, gaze fixed on a small painting on the white-paneled wall over Violeta's head. "Pious Interview between the Most Holy Virgin Queen of Heaven and Her Faithful Servant St. Ignatius Loyola," read the thin metal plate on the carved and gilded frame. The Virgin, with enameled face set in a detached simper, forehead bald of eyebrows, extended one hand remotely over the tonsured head of the saint, who groveled in a wooden posture of ecstasy. Very ugly and old-fashioned, thought Violeta, but a perfectly proper picture; there was nothing to stare at. But Carlos kept squinting his eyelids at it mysteriously, and never moved his eyes from it save to glance at Blanca. His furry, golden eyebrows were knotted sternly, resembling a tangle of crochet wool. He never seemed to be interested except when it was his turn to read. He read in a thrilling voice. Violeta thought his mouth and chin were very beautiful. A tiny spot of light on his slightly moistened under-lip disturbed her, she did not know why.

Blanca stopped reading, bowed her head and sighed lightly, her mouth half open. It was one of her habits. As the sound of voices had lulled Mamacita to sleep beside her sewing basket, now the silence roused her. She looked about her with a viva-cious smile on her whole face, except her eyes, which were drowsed and weary.

"Go on with your reading, dear children. I heard every word. Violeta, don't fidget, please, sweet little daughter. Car-los, what is the hour?"

Mamacita liked being chaperon to Blanca. Violeta won-dered why Mamacita considered Blanca so very attractive, but she did. She was always saying to Papacito, "Blanquita blooms like a lily!" And Papacito would say, "It is better if she con-ducts herself like one!" And Mamacita said once to Carlos, "Even if you are my nephew, still you must go home at a rea-sonable hour!"

"The hour is early, Doña Paz." St. Anthony himself could not have exceeded in respect the pose of Carlos' head toward his aunt. She smiled and relapsed into a shallow nap, as a cat rises from the rug, turns and lies down again.

Violeta did not move, or answer Mamacita. She had the si-lence and watchfulness of a young wild animal, but no native wisdom. She was at home from the convent in Tacubaya for the first time in almost a year. There they taught her modesty, chastity, silence, obedience, with a little French and music and some arithmetic. She did as she was told, but it was all very confusing, because she could not understand why the things that happen outside of people were so different from what she felt inside of her. Everybody went about doing the same things every day, precisely as if there were nothing else going to hap-pen, ever; and all the time she was certain there was something simply tremendously exciting waiting for her outside the con-vent. Life was going to unroll itself like a long, gay carpet for her to walk upon. She saw herself wearing a long veil, and it would trail and flutter over this carpet as she came out of church. There would be six flower girls and two pages, the way there had been at Cousin Sancha's wedding.

Of course she didn't mean a wedding. Silly! Cousin Sancha had been quite old, almost twenty-four, and Violeta meant for life to begin at once—next year, anyway. It would be more like a festival. She wanted to wear red poppies in her hair and dance. Life would always be very gay, with no one about telling you that almost everything you said and did was wrong. She would be free to read poetry, too, and stories about love, without having to hide them in her copybooks. Even Carlos did not know that she had learned nearly all his poems by heart. She had for a year been cutting them from magazines, keeping them in the pages of her books, in order to read them during study hours.

Several shorter ones were concealed in her missal, and the thrilling music of strange words drowned the chorus of bell and choir. There was one about the ghosts of nuns returning to the old square before their ruined convent, dancing in the moonlight with the shades of lovers forbidden them in life, treading with bared feet on broken glass as a penance for their loves. Violeta would shake all over when she read this, and lift swimming eyes to the delicate spears of candlelight on the altar.

She was certain she would be like those nuns someday. She would dance for joy over shards of broken glass. But where begin? She had sat here in this room, on this very hassock, comfortingly near Mamacita, through the summer evenings of vacation, ever since she could remember. Sometimes it was a happiness to be assured that nothing was expected of her but to follow Mamacita about and be a good girl. It gave her time to dream about life—that is, the future. For of course every-thing beautiful and unexpected would happen later on, when she grew as tall as Blanca and was allowed to come home from the convent for good and all. She would then be miraculously lovely—Blanca would look perfectly dull beside her—and she would dance with fascinating young men like those who rode by on Sunday mornings, making their horses prance in the bright, shallow street on their way to the *paseo* in Chapultepec

Park. She would appear on the balcony above, wearing a blue dress, and everyone would ask who that enchanting girl could be. And Carlos, Carlos! He would understand at last that she had read and loved his poems always.

> *"The nuns are dancing with bare feet*
> *On broken glass in the cobbled street."*

That one above all the rest. She felt it had been written for her. She was even one of the nuns, the youngest and best-loved one, ghostly silent, dancing forever and ever under the moonlight to the shivering tune of old violins.

Mamacita moved her knee uneasily, so that Violeta's head slipped from it, and she almost lost her balance. She sat up, prickling all over with shyness for fear the others would know why she had hidden her face on Mamacita's lap. But no one saw. Mamacita was always lecturing her about things. At such moments it was hard to believe that Blanca was not the favorite child. "You must not run through the house so." "You must brush your hair more smoothly." "And what is this I hear about your using your sister's face powder?"

Blanca, listening, would eye her with superior calm and say nothing. It was really very hard, knowing that Blanca was nicer only because she was allowed to powder and perfume herself and still gave herself such airs about it. Carlos, who used to bring her sugared limes and long strips of dried *membrillo* from the markets, calling her his dear, amusing, modest Violeta, now simply did not know she was present. There were times when Violeta wished to cry, passionately, so everyone could hear her. But what about? And how explain to Mamacita? She would say, "What have you to cry for? And besides, consider the feelings of others in this house and control your moods."

Papacito would say, "What you need is a good renovating." That was his word for a spanking. He would say sternly to Mamacita, "I think her moral nature needs repairment." He and Mamacita seemed to have some mysterious understanding about things. Mamacita's eyes were always perfectly clear when she looked at Papacito, and she would answer: "You are right. I will look after this." Then she would be very severe with Violeta. Papacito always said to the girls: "It is your fault without exception when Mamacita is annoyed with you. So be careful."

But Mamacita never stayed annoyed for long, and afterward it was beautiful to curl up near her, snuggling into her shoulder, and smell the nice, crinkled, perfumed hair at the nape of her neck. But when she was angry her eyes had a considering expression, as if one were a stranger, and she would say, "You are the greatest of my problems." Violeta had often been a problem and it was very humiliating.

¡Ay de mi! Violeta gave a sharp sigh and sat up straight. She wanted to stretch her arms up and yawn, not because she was sleepy but because something inside her felt as if it were enclosed in a cage too small for it, and she could not breathe. Like those poor parrots in the markets, stuffed into tiny wicker cages so that they bulged through the withes, gasping and panting, waiting for someone to come and rescue them.

Church was a terrible, huge cage, but it seemed too small. "Oh, my, I always laugh, to keep from crying!" A silly verse Carlos used to say. Through her eyelashes his face looked suddenly pale and soft, as if he might have tears on his cheeks. Oh, Carlos! But of course he would never cry for anything. She was frightened to find that her own eyes were steeped in tears; they were going to run down her face; she couldn't stop them. Her head bowed over and her chin seemed to be curling up. Where on earth was her handkerchief? A huge, clean, white linen one, almost like a boy's handkerchief. How horrid! The folded corner scratched her eyelids. Sometimes she cried in church when the music wailed terribly and the girls sat in veiled rows, all silent except for the clinking of their beads slipping through their fingers. They were all strangers to her then; what if they knew her thoughts? Suppose she should say aloud, "I love Carlos!" The idea made her blush all over, until her forehead perspired and her hands turned red. She would begin praying frantically, "Oh, Mary! Oh, Mary! Queen Mother of mercy!" while deep underneath her words her thoughts were rushing along in a kind of trance: Oh, dear God, that's my secret; that's a secret between You and me. I should die if anybody knew!

She turned her eyes again to the pair at the long table just in time to see once more the shawl beginning to slip, ever so little, from Blanca's shoulder. A tight shudder of drawn threads played along Violeta's skin, and grew quite intolerable when Carlos reached out to take the fringe in his long fingers. His wrist turned with a delicate toss, the shawl settled into place, Blanca smiled and stammered and bit her lip.

Violeta could not bear to see it. No, no. She wanted to hold her hands over her heart tightly, to quell the slow, burning ache. It felt like a little jar filled with flames, which she could not smother down. It was cruel of Blanca and Carlos to sit there and read and be so pleased with each other without once thinking of her! Yet what could she say if they noticed her? They never did notice.

Blanca rose.

"I am tired of the old poetry. It is all too sad. What else shall we read?"

"Let's have a great deal of gay, modern poetry," suggested Carlos, whose own verses were considered extremely gay and modern. Violeta was always shocked when he called them amusing. He couldn't mean it. It was only his way of pretending he wasn't sad when he wrote them.

"Read me all your new ones again." Blanca was always appreciating Carlos. You could hear it in her voice underneath, like a little trickle of sugar. And Carlos let her do it. He seemed always to be condescending to Blanca a little. But Blanca could never see it, because she really didn't think of anything but the way she had her hair fixed or whether people thought she was pretty. Violeta longed to make a naughty face at Blanca, who posed ridiculously, leaning over the table.

Above the red silk lamp shade her face was not sallow as usual. The thin nose and small lips cast shadows on her cheek. She hated being pale, and had the habit, while reading, of smoothing her cheeks round and round with two fingers, first one cheek and then the other, until deep red spots would burn in them for a long while. Violeta wished to shriek after watching Blanca do this for hours at a time. Why did not Mamacita speak to her about it? It was the worst sort of fidgeting.

"I haven't the new ones with me," said Carlos.

"Then let it be the old ones," agreed Blanca gaily.

She moved to the bookshelves, Carlos beside her. They could not find his book. Their hands touched as fingers sought titles. Something in the intimate murmur of their voices wounded Violeta acutely. Sharing some delightful secret, they were purposely shutting her out. She spoke.

"If you want your book, Carlos, I can find it." At the sound of her own voice she felt calm and firm and equal to anything. By her tone she tried to shut Blanca out.

They turned and regarded her without interest.

"And where may it be, infant?" Carlos' voice always had that chilling edge on it when he was not reading aloud, and his eyes explored. With a glance he seemed to see all one's faults. Violeta remembered her feet and drew down her skirts. The sight of Blanca's narrow, gray satin slippers was hateful.

"I have it. I have had it for a whole week." She eyed the tip of Blanca's nose, hoping they would understand she wished to say, "You see, I have treasured it!"

She got up, feeling a little clumsy, and walked away with a curious imitation of Blanca's grown-up gait. It made her dreadfully aware of her long, straight legs in their ribbed stockings.

"I will help you search," called Carlos, as if he had thought of something interesting, and he followed. Over his suddenly near shoulder she saw Blanca's face. It looked very vague and faraway, like a distressed doll's. Carlos' eyes were enormous, and he smiled steadily. She wished to run away. He said something in a low voice. She could not understand him at all, and it was impossible to find the lamp cord in the narrow, dark hallway. She was frightened at the soft *pad-pad* of his rubber heels so close behind her as they went without speaking through the chill dining room, full of the odor of fruit that has been all day in a closed place. When they entered the small, open sunroom over the entrance of the patio, the moonlight seemed almost warm, it was so radiant after the shadows of the house. Violeta turned over a huddle of books on the small table, but she did not see them clearly; and her hand shook so, she could not take hold of anything.

Carlos' hand came up in a curve, settled upon hers and held fast. His roundish, smooth cheek and blond eyebrows hovered, swooped. His mouth touched hers and made a tiny smacking sound. She felt herself wrench and twist away as if a hand pushed her violently. And in that second his hand was over her

mouth, soft and warm, and his eyes were staring at her, fearfully close. Violeta opened her eyes wide also and peered up at
him. She expected to sink into a look warm and gentle, like the
touch of his palm. Instead, she felt suddenly, sharply hurt, as if
she had collided with a chair in the dark. His eyes were bright
and shallow, almost like the eyes of Pepe, the macaw. His pale,
fluffy eyebrows were arched; his mouth smiled tightly. A sick
thumping began in the pit of her stomach, as it always did
when she was called up to explain things to Mother Superior.
Something was terribly wrong. Her heart pounded until she
seemed about to smother. She was angry with all her might,
and turned her head aside in a hard jerk.

"Keep your hand off my mouth!"

"Then be quiet, you silly child!" The words were astounding,
but the way he said them was more astounding still, as if they
were allies in some shameful secret. Her teeth rattled with chill.

"I will tell my mother! Shame on you for kissing me!"

"I did not kiss you except a little brotherly kiss, Violeta, precisely as I kiss Blanca. Don't be absurd!"

"You do not kiss Blanca. I heard her tell my mother she has
never been kissed by a man!"

"But I do kiss her—as a cousin, nothing more. It does not
count. We are relatives just the same. What did you think?"

Oh, she had made a hideous mistake. She knew she was
blushing until her forehead throbbed. Her breath was gone,
but she must explain. "I thought—a kiss—meant—meant—"
She could not finish.

"Ah, you're so young, like a little newborn calf," said Carlos. His voice trembled in a strange way. "You smell like a nice
baby, freshly washed with white soap! Imagine such a baby
being angry at a kiss from her cousin! Shame on you, Violeta!"

He was loathsome. She saw herself before him, almost as if
his face were a mirror. Her mouth was too large; her face was
simply a moon; her hair was ugly in the tight convent braids.

"Oh, I'm so sorry!" she whispered.

"For what?" His voice had the cutting edge again. "Come,
where is the book?"

"I don't know," she said, trying not to cry.

"Well, then, let us go back, or Mamacita will scold you."

"Oh, no, no. I can't go in there. Blanca will see—Mamacita

will ask questions. I want to stay here. I want to run away—to kill myself!"

"Nonsense!" said Carlos. "Come with me this minute. What did you expect when you came out here alone with me?"

He turned and started away. She was shamefully, incredibly in the wrong. She had behaved like an immodest girl. It was all bitterly real and unbelievable, like a nightmare that went on and on and no one heard you calling to be waked up. She followed, trying to hold up her head.

Mamacita nodded, shining, crinkled hair stiffly arranged, chin on white collar. Blanca sat like a stone in her deep chair, holding a small gray-and-gold book in her lap. Her angry eyes threw out a look that coiled back upon itself like a whiplash, and the pupils became suddenly blank and bright as Carlos' had.

Violeta folded down on her hassock and gathered up her knees. She stared at the carpet to hide her reddened eyes, for it terrified her to see the way eyes could give away such cruel stories about people.

"I found the book here, where it belonged," said Blanca. "I am tired now. It is very late. We shall not read."

Violeta wished to cry in real earnest now. It was the last blow that Blanca should have found the book. A kiss meant nothing at all, and Carlos had walked away as if he had forgotten her. It was all mixed up with the white rivers of moonlight and the smell of warm fruit and a cold dampness on her lips that made a tiny, smacking sound. She trembled and leaned over until her forehead touched Mamacita's lap. She could not look up, ever, ever again.

The low voices sounded contentious; thin metal wires twanged in the air around them.

"But I do not care to read any more, I tell you."

"Very well, I shall go at once. But I am leaving for Paris on Wednesday, and shall not see you again until the fall."

"It would be like you to go without even stopping in to say good-by."

Even when they were angry they still talked to each other like two grown-up people wrapped together in a secret. The sound of his soft, padding rubber heels came near.

"Good night, my dearest Doña Paz. I have had an enchanting evening."

Mamacita's knees moved; she meant to rise.

"What—asleep, Violeta? Well, let us hear often from you, my dear nephew. Your little cousins and I will miss you greatly."

Mamacita was wide-awake and smiling, holding Carlos' hands. They kissed. Carlos turned to Blanca and bent to kiss her. She swept him into the folds of the gray shawl, but turned her cheek for his salute. Violeta rose, her knees trembling. She turned her head from side to side to close out the sight of the macaw eyes coming closer and closer, the tight, smiling mouth ready to swoop. When he touched her, she wavered for a moment, then slid up and back against the wall. She heard herself screaming uncontrollably.

Mamacita sat upon the side of the bed and patted Violeta's cheek. Her curved hand was warm and gentle and so were her eyes. Violeta choked a little and turned her face away.

"I have explained to Papacito that you quarreled with your cousin Carlos and were very rude to him. Papacito says you need a good renovating." Mamacita's voice was soft and reassuring. Violeta lay without a pillow, the ruffled collar of her nightgown standing up about her chin. She did not answer. Even to whisper hurt her.

"We are going to the country this week and you shall live in the garden all summer. Then you won't be so nervous. You are quite a young lady now, and you must learn to control your nerves."

"Yes, Mamacita." The look on Mamacita's face was very hard to bear. She seemed to be asking questions about very hidden thoughts—those thoughts that were not true at all and could never be talked about with anyone. Everything she could remember in her whole life seemed to have melted together in a confusion and misery that could not be explained because it was all changed and uncertain.

She wanted to sit up, take Mamacita around the neck and say, "Something dreadful happened to me—I don't know what," but her heart closed up hard and aching, and she sighed with all her breath. Even Mamacita's breast had become a cold, strange place. Her blood ran back and forth in her, crying terribly, but when the sound came up to her lips it was only a small whimper, like a puppy's.

"You must not cry any more," said Mamacita after a long pause. Then: "Good night, my poor child. This impression will pass." Mamacita's kiss felt cold on Violeta's cheek.

Whether the impression passed or not, no word of it was spoken again. Violeta and the family spent the summer in the country. She refused to read Carlos' poetry, though Mamacita encouraged her to do so. She would not even listen to his letters from Paris. She quarreled on more equal terms with her sister Blanca, feeling that there was no longer so great a difference of experience to separate them. A painful unhappiness possessed her at times, because she could not settle the questions brooding in her mind. Sometimes she amused herself making ugly caricatures of Carlos.

In the early autumn she returned to school, weeping and complaining to her mother that she hated the convent. There was, she declared as she watched her boxes being tied up, nothing to be learned there.

1923

The Martyr

Ruʙén, the most illustrious painter in Mexico, was deeply in love with his model Isabel, who was in turn romantically attached to a rival artist whose name is of no importance.

Isabel used to call Rubén her little "Churro," which is a sort of sweet cake, and is, besides, a popular pet name among the Mexicans for small dogs. Rubén thought it a very delightful name, and would say before visitors to the studio, "And now she calls me 'Churro!' Ha! ha!" When he laughed, he shook in the waistcoat, for he was getting fat.

Then Isabel, who was tall and thin, with long, keen fingers, would rip her hands through a bouquet of flowers Rubén had brought her and scatter the petals, or she would cry, "Yah! yah!" derisively, and flick the tip of his nose with paint. She had been observed also to pull his hair and ears without mercy.

When earnest-minded people made pilgrimages down the narrow, cobbled street, picked their way carefully over puddles in the patio, and clattered up the uncertain stairs for a glimpse of the great and yet so simple personage, she would cry, "Here come the pretty sheep!" She enjoyed their gaze of wonder at her daring.

Often she was bored, for sometimes she would stand all day long, braiding and unbraiding her hair while Rubén made sketches of her, and they would forget to eat until late; but there was no place for her to go until her lover, Rubén's rival, should sell a painting, for everyone declared Rubén would kill on sight the man who even attempted to rob him of Isabel. So Isabel stayed, and Rubén made eighteen different drawings of her for his mural, and she cooked for him occasionally, quarreled with him, and put out her long, red tongue at visitors she did not like. Rubén adored her.

He was just beginning the nineteenth drawing of Isabel when his rival sold a very large painting to a rich man whose decorator told him he must have a panel of green and orange on a certain wall of his new house. By a felicitous chance, this painting was prodigiously green and orange. The rich man

39

paid him a huge price, but was happy to do it, he explained, because it would cost six times as much to cover the space with tapestry. The rival was happy, too, though he neglected to explain why. The next day he and Isabel went to Costa Rica, and that is the end of them so far as we are concerned.

Rubén read her farewell note:

"Poor old Churro! It is a pity your life is so very dull, and I cannot live it any longer. I am going away with someone who will never allow me to cook for him, but will make a mural with fifty figures of me in it, instead of only twenty. I am also to have red slippers, and a gay life to my heart's content.

"Your old friend,

"ISABEL."

When Rubén read this, he felt like a man drowning. His breath would not come, and he thrashed his arms about a great deal. Then he drank a large bottle of *tequila*, without lemon or salt to take the edge off, and lay down on the floor with his head in a palette of freshly mixed paint and wept vehemently.

After this, he was altogether a changed man. He could not talk unless he was telling about Isabel, her angelic face, her pretty little tricks and ways. "She used to kick my shins black and blue," he would say, fondly, and the tears would flow into his eyes. He was always eating crisp sweet cakes from a bag near his easel. "See," he would say, holding one up before taking a mouthful, "she used to call me 'Churro,' like this!"

His friends were all pleased to see Isabel go, and said among themselves he was lucky to lose the lean she-devil. They set themselves to help him forget. But Rubén could not be distracted. "There is no other woman like that woman," he would say, shaking his head stubbornly. "When she went, she took my life with her. I have no spirit even for revenge." Then he would add, "I tell you, my poor little angel Isabel is a murderess, for she has broken my heart."

At times he would roam anxiously about the studio, kicking his felt slippers into the shuffles of drawings piled about, gathering dust, or he would grind colors for a few minutes, saying in a dolorous voice: "She once did all this for me. Imagine her goodness!" But always he came back to the window, and ate sweets and fruits and almond cakes from the bag. When his friends took him out for dinner, he would sit quietly and eat huge platefuls of every sort of food, and wash it down with sweet wine. Then he would begin to weep, and talk about Isabel.

His friends agreed it was getting rather stupid. Isabel had been gone for nearly six months, and Rubén refused even to touch the nineteenth figure of her, much less to begin the twentieth, and the mural was getting nowhere.

"Look, my dear friend," said Ramón, who did caricatures, and heads of pretty girls for the magazines, "even I, who am not a great artist, know how women can spoil a man's work for him. Let me tell you, when Trinidad left me, I was good for nothing for a week. Nothing tasted properly, I could not tell one color from another, I positively was tone deaf. That shameless cheat-by-night almost ruined me. But you, *amigo*, rouse yourself, and finish your great mural for the world, for the future, and remember Isabel only when you give thanks to God that she is gone."

Rubén would shake his head as he sat collapsed upon his couch munching sugared almonds, and would cry:

"I have a pain in my heart that will kill me. There is no woman like that one."

His collars suddenly refused to meet under his chin. He loosened his belt three notches, and explained: "I sit still; I cannot move any more. My energy has gone to grief." The layers of fat piled insidiously upon him, he bulged until he became strange even to himself. Ramón, showing his new caricature of Rubén to his friends, declared: "I could as well have drawn it with a compass, I swear. The buttons are bursting from his shirt. It is positively unsafe."

But still Rubén sat, eating moodily in solitude, and weeping over Isabel after his third bottle of sweet wine at night.

His friends talked it over, concluded that the affair was growing desperate; it was high time someone should tell him the true cause of his pain. But everyone wished the other would be the one chosen. And it came out there was not a person in the group, possibly not one in all Mexico, indelicate enough to do such a thing. They decided to shift the responsibility upon a physician from the faculty of the university. In the mind of such a one would be combined a sufficiently refined sentiment with the highest degree of technical knowledge. This was the diplomatic, the discreet, the fastidious thing to do. It was done.

The doctor found Rubén seated before his easel, facing the half-finished nineteenth figure of Isabel. He was weeping, and between sobs he ate spoonfuls of soft Toluca cheese, with spiced mangos. He hung in all directions over his painting-stool, like a mound of kneaded dough. He told the doctor first about Isabel. "I do assure you faithfully, my friend, not even I could capture in paint the line of beauty in her thigh and instep. And, besides, she was an angel for kindness." Later he said the pain in his heart would be the death of him. The doctor was profoundly touched. For a great while he sat offering consolation without courage to prescribe material cures for a man of such delicately adjusted susceptibilities.

"I have only crass and vulgar remedies"—with a graceful gesture he seemed to offer them between thumb and forefinger—"but they are all the world of flesh may contribute toward the healing of the wounded spirit." He named them one at a time. They made a neat, but not impressive, row: a diet, fresh air, long walks, frequent violent exercise, preferably on the cross-bar, ice showers, almost no wine.

Rubén seemed not to hear him. His sustained, oblivious murmur flowed warmly through the doctor's solemnly rounded periods:

"The pains are most unendurable at night, when I lie in my lonely bed and gaze at the empty heavens through my narrow window, and I think to myself, 'Soon my grave shall be narrower than that window, and darker than that firmament,' and my heart gives a writhe. Ah, Isabelita, my executioner!"

The doctor tiptoed out respectfully, and left him sitting there eating cheese and gazing with wet eyes at the nineteenth figure of Isabel.

The friends grew hopelessly bored and left him more and more alone. No one saw him for some weeks except the proprietor of a small café called "The Little Monkeys" where

Rubén was accustomed to dine with Isabel and where he now went alone for food.

Here one night quite suddenly Rubén clasped his heart with violence, rose from his chair, and upset the dish of tamales and pepper gravy he had been eating. The proprietor ran to him. Rubén said something in a hurried whisper, made rather an impressive gesture over his head with one arm, and, to say it as gently as possible, died.

His friends hastened the next day to see the proprietor, who gave them a solidly dramatic version of the lamentable episode. Ramón was even then gathering material for an intimate biography of his country's most eminent painter, to be illustrated with large numbers of his own character portraits. Already the dedication was composed to his "Friend and Master, Inspired and Incomparable Genius of Art on the American Continent."

"But what did he say to you," insisted Ramón, "at the final stupendous moment? It is most important. The last words of a great artist, they should be very eloquent. Repeat them precisely, my dear fellow! It will add splendor to the biography, nay, to the very history of art itself, if they are eloquent."

The proprietor nodded his head with the air of a man who understands everything.

"I know, I know. Well, maybe you will not believe me when I tell you that his very last words were a truly sublime message to you, his good and faithful friends, and to the world. He said, gentlemen: 'Tell them I am a martyr to love. I perish in a cause worthy the sacrifice. I die of a broken heart!' and then he said, 'Isabelita, my executioner!' That was all, gentlemen," ended the proprietor, simply and reverently. He bowed his head. They all bowed their heads.

"That was truly magnificent," said Ramón, after the correct interval of silent mourning. "I thank you. It is a superb epitaph. I am most gratified."

"He was also supremely fond of my tamales and pepper gravy," added the proprietor in a modest tone. "They were his final indulgence."

"That shall be mentioned in its place, never fear, my good friend," cried Ramón, his voice crumbling with generous emotion, "with the name of your café, even. It shall be a shrine for artists when this story is known. Trust me faithfully to preserve for the future every smallest detail in the life and character of this great genius. Each episode has its own sacred, its precious and peculiar interest. Yes, truly, I shall mention the tamales."

1923

Magic

AND, Madame Blanchard, believe that I am happy to be here with you and your family because it is so serene, everything, and before this I worked for a long time in a fancy house—maybe you don't know what is a fancy house? Naturally . . . everyone must have heard sometime or other. Well, Madame, I work always where there is work to be had, and so in this place I worked very hard all hours, and saw too many things, things you wouldn't believe, and I wouldn't think of telling you, only maybe it will rest you while I brush your hair. You'll excuse me too but I could not help hearing you say to the laundress maybe someone had bewitched your linens, they fall away so fast in the wash. Well, there was a girl there in that house, a poor thing, thin, but well-liked by all the men who called, and you understand she could not get along with the woman who ran the house. They quarreled, the madam cheated her on her checks: you know, the girl got a check, a brass one, every time, and at the week's end she gave those back to the madam, yes, that was the way, and got her percentage, a very small little of her earnings: it is a business, you see, like any other—and the madam used to pretend the girl had given back only so many checks, you see, and really she had given many more, but after they were out of her hands, what could she do? So she would say, I will get out of this place, and curse and cry. Then the madam would hit her over the head. She always hit people over the head with bottles, it was the way she fought. My good heavens, Madame Blanchard, what confusion there would be sometimes with a girl running raving downstairs, and the madam pulling her back by the hair and smashing a bottle on her forehead.

It was nearly always about the money, the girls got in debt so, and if they wished to go they could not without paying every sou marqué. The madam had full understanding with the police; the girls must come back with them or go to the jails. Well, they always came back with the policemen or with another kind of man friend of the madam: she could make men work for her too, but she paid them very well for all, let

me tell you: and so the girls stayed on unless they were sick; if
so, if they got too sick, she sent them away again.

Madame Blanchard said, "You are pulling a little here," and
eased a strand of hair: "and then what?"

Pardon—but this girl, there was a true hatred between her
and the madam. She would say many times, I make more
money than anybody else in the house, and every week were
scenes. So at last she said one morning, Now I will leave this
place, and she took out forty dollars from under her pillow and
said, Here's your money! The madam began to shout, Where
did you get all that, you——? and accused her of robbing the
men who came to visit her. The girl said, Keep your hands off
or I'll brain you: and at that the madam took hold of her
shoulders, and began to lift her knee and kick this girl most
terribly in the stomach, and even in her most secret place,
Madame Blanchard, and then she beat her in the face with
a bottle, and the girl fell back again into her room where I
was making clean. I helped her to the bed, and she sat there
holding her sides with her head hanging down, and when she
got up again there was blood everywhere she had sat. So then
the madam came in once more and screamed, Now you can
get out, you are no good for me any more: I don't repeat all,
you understand it is too much. But she took all the money she
could find, and at the door she gave the girl a great push in the
back with her knee, so that she fell again in the street, and then
got up and went away with the dress barely on her.

After this the men who knew this girl kept saying, Where is
Ninette? And they kept asking this in the next days, so that the
madam could not say any longer, I put her out because she is a
thief. No, she began to see she was wrong to send this Ninette
away, and then she said, She will be back in a few days, don't
trouble yourself.

And now, Madame Blanchard, if you wish to hear, I come to
the strange part, the thing recalled to me when you said your
linens were bewitched. For the cook in that place was a woman,
colored like myself, like myself with much French blood just
the same, like myself living always among people who worked
spells. But she had a very hard heart, she helped the madam in
everything, she liked to watch all that happened, and she gave
away tales on the girls. The madam trusted her above every-

thing, and she said, Well, where can I find that slut? because she had gone altogether out of Basin Street before the madam began to ask the police to bring her again. Well, the cook said, I know a charm that works here in New Orleans, colored women do it to bring back their men: in seven days they come again very happy to stay and they cannot say why: even your enemy will come back to you believing you are his friend. It is a New Orleans charm for sure, for certain, they say it does not work even across the river. . . . And then they did it just as the cook said. They took the chamber pot of this girl from under her bed, and in it they mixed with water and milk all the relics of her they found there: the hair from her brush, and the face powder from the puff, and even little bits of her nails they found about the edges of the carpet where she sat by habit to cut her finger- and toe-nails; and they dipped the sheets with her blood into the water, and all the time the cook said something over it in a low voice; I could not hear all, but at last she said to the madam, Now spit in it: and the madam spat, and the cook said, When she comes back she will be dirt under your feet.

Madame Blanchard closed her perfume bottle with a thin click: "Yes, and then?"

Then in seven nights the girl came back and she looked very sick, the same clothes and all, but happy to be there. One of the men said, Welcome home, Ninette! and when she started to speak to the madam, the madam said, Shut up and get upstairs and dress yourself. So Ninette, this girl, she said, I'll be down in just a minute. And after that she lived there quietly.

1924

Rope

O N the third day after they moved to the country he came walking back from the village carrying a basket of groceries and a twenty-four-yard coil of rope. She came out to meet him, wiping her hands on her green smock. Her hair was tumbled, her nose was scarlet with sunburn; he told her that already she looked like a born country woman. His gray flannel shirt stuck to him, his heavy shoes were dusty. She assured him he looked like a rural character in a play.

Had he brought the coffee? She had been waiting all day long for coffee. They had forgot it when they ordered at the store the first day.

Gosh, no, he hadn't. Lord, now he'd have to go back. Yes, he would if it killed him. He thought, though, he had everything else. She reminded him it was only because he didn't drink coffee himself. If he did he would remember it quick enough. Suppose they ran out of cigarettes? Then she saw the rope. What was that for? Well, he thought it might do to hang clothes on, or something. Naturally she asked him if he thought they were going to run a laundry? They already had a fifty-foot line hanging right before his eyes? Why, hadn't he noticed it, really? It was a blot on the landscape to her.

He thought there were a lot of things a rope might come in handy for. She wanted to know what, for instance. He thought a few seconds, but nothing occurred. They could wait and see, couldn't they? You need all sorts of strange odds and ends around a place in the country. She said, yes, that was so; but she thought just at that time when every penny counted, it seemed funny to buy more rope. That was all. She hadn't meant anything else. She hadn't just seen, not at first, why he felt it was necessary.

Well, thunder, he had bought it because he wanted to, and that was all there was to it. She thought that was reason enough, and couldn't understand why he hadn't said so, at first. Undoubtedly it would be useful, twenty-four yards of rope, there were hundreds of things, she couldn't think of any at the moment, but it would come in. Of course. As he had said, things always did in the country.

But she was a little disappointed about the coffee, and oh, look, look, look at the eggs! Oh, my, they're all running! What had he put on top of them? Hadn't he known eggs mustn't be squeezed? Squeezed, who had squeezed them, he wanted to know. What a silly thing to say. He had simply brought them along in the basket with the other things. If they got broke it was the grocer's fault. He should know better than to put heavy things on top of eggs.

She believed it was the rope. That was the heaviest thing in the pack, she saw him plainly when he came in from the road, the rope was a big package on top of everything. He desired the whole wide world to witness that this was not a fact. He had carried the rope in one hand and the basket in the other, and what was the use of her having eyes if that was the best they could do for her?

Well, anyhow, she could see one thing plain: no eggs for breakfast. They'd have to scramble them now, for supper. It was too damned bad. She had planned to have steak for supper. No ice, meat wouldn't keep. He wanted to know why she couldn't finish breaking the eggs in a bowl and set them in a cool place.

Cool place! if he could find one for her, she'd be glad to set them there. Well, then, it seemed to him they might very well cook the meat at the same time they cooked the eggs and then warm up the meat for tomorrow. The idea simply choked her. Warmed-over meat, when they might as well have had it fresh. Second best and scraps and makeshifts, even to the meat! He rubbed her shoulder a little. It doesn't really matter so much, does it, darling? Sometimes when they were playful, he would rub her shoulder and she would arch and purr. This time she hissed and almost clawed. He was getting ready to say that they could surely manage somehow when she turned on him and said, if he told her they could manage somehow she would certainly slap his face.

He swallowed the words red hot, his face burned. He picked up the rope and started to put it on the top shelf. She would not have it on the top shelf, the jars and tins belonged there;

positively she would not have the top shelf cluttered up with a lot of rope. She had borne all the clutter she meant to bear in the flat in town, there was space here at least and she meant to keep things in order.

Well, in that case, he wanted to know what the hammer and nails were doing up there? And why had she put them there when she knew very well he needed that hammer and those nails upstairs to fix the window sashes? She simply slowed down everything and made double work on the place with her insane habit of changing things around and hiding them.

She was sure she begged his pardon, and if she had had any reason to believe he was going to fix the sashes this summer she would have left the hammer and nails right where he put them; in the middle of the bedroom floor where they could step on them in the dark. And now if he didn't clear the whole mess out of there she would throw them down the well.

Oh, all right, all right—could he put them in the closet? Naturally not, there were brooms and mops and dustpans in the closet, and why couldn't he find a place for his rope outside her kitchen? Had he stopped to consider there were seven God-forsaken rooms in the house, and only one kitchen?

He wanted to know what of it? And did she realize she was making a complete fool of herself? And what did she take him for, a three-year-old idiot? The whole trouble with her was she needed something weaker than she was to heckle and tyrannize over. He wished to God now they had a couple of children she could take it out on. Maybe he'd get some rest.

Her face changed at this, she reminded him he had forgot the coffee and had bought a worthless piece of rope. And when she thought of all the things they actually needed to make the place even decently fit to live in, well, she could cry, that was all. She looked so forlorn, so lost and despairing he couldn't believe it was only a piece of rope that was causing all the racket. What *was* the matter, for God's sake?

Oh, would he please hush and go away, and *stay* away, if he could, for five minutes? By all means, yes, he would. He'd stay away indefinitely if she wished. Lord, yes, there was nothing he'd like better than to clear out and never come back. She couldn't for the life of her see what was holding him, then. It was a swell time. Here she was, stuck, miles from a railroad, with a half-empty house on her hands, and not a penny in her pocket, and everything on earth to do; it seemed the God-sent moment for him to get out from under. She was surprised he hadn't stayed in town as it was until she had come out and done the work and got things straightened out. It was his usual trick.

It appeared to him that this was going a little far. Just a touch out of bounds, if she didn't mind his saying so. Why the hell had he stayed in town the summer before? To do a half-dozen extra jobs to get the money he had sent her. That was it. She knew perfectly well they couldn't have done it otherwise. She had agreed with him at the time. And that was the only time so help him he had ever left her to do anything by herself.

Oh, he could tell that to his great-grandmother. She had her notion of what had kept him in town. Considerably more than a notion, if he wanted to know. So, she was going to bring all that up again, was she? Well, she could just think what she pleased. He was tired of explaining. It may have looked funny but he had simply got hooked in, and what could he do? It was impossible to believe that she was going to take it seriously. Yes, yes, she knew how it was with a man: if he was left by himself a minute, some woman was certain to kidnap him. And naturally he couldn't hurt her feelings by refusing!

Well, what was she raving about? Did she forget she had told him those two weeks alone in the country were the happiest she had known for four years? And how long had they been married when she said that? All right, shut up! If she thought that hadn't stuck in his craw.

She hadn't meant she was happy because she was away from him. She meant she was happy getting the devilish house nice and ready for him. That was what she had meant, and now look! Bringing up something she had said a year ago simply to justify himself for forgetting her coffee and breaking the eggs and buying a wretched piece of rope they couldn't afford. She really thought it was time to drop the subject, and now she wanted only two things in the world. She wanted him to get that rope from underfoot, and go back to the village and get her coffee, and if he could remember it, he might bring a metal mitt for the skillets, and two more curtain rods, and if there were any rubber gloves in the village, her hands were simply raw, and a bottle of milk of magnesia from the drugstore.

He looked out at the dark blue afternoon sweltering on the slopes, and mopped his forehead and sighed heavily and said, if only she could wait a minute for *anything*, he was going back. He had said so, hadn't he, the very instant they found he had overlooked it?

Oh, yes, well . . . run along. She was going to wash windows. The country was so beautiful! She doubted they'd have a moment to enjoy it. He meant to go, but he could not until he had said that if she wasn't such a hopeless melancholiac she might see that this was only for a few days. Couldn't she remember anything pleasant about the other summers? Hadn't they ever had any fun? She hadn't time to talk about it, and now would he please not leave that rope lying around for her to trip on? He picked it up, somehow it had toppled off the table, and walked out with it under his arm.

Was he going this minute? He certainly was. She thought so. Sometimes it seemed to her he had second sight about the precisely perfect moment to leave her ditched. She had meant to put the mattresses out to sun, if they put them out this minute they would get at least three hours, he must have heard her say that morning she meant to put them out. So of course he would walk off and leave her to it. She supposed he thought the exercise would do her good.

Well, he was merely going to get her coffee. A four-mile walk for two pounds of coffee was ridiculous, but he was perfectly willing to do it. The habit was making a wreck of her, but if she wanted to wreck herself there was nothing he could do about it. If he thought it was coffee that was making a wreck of her, she congratulated him: he must have a damned easy conscience.

Conscience or no conscience, he didn't see why the mattresses couldn't very well wait until tomorrow. And anyhow, for God's sake, were they living *in* the house, or were they going to let the house ride them to death? She paled at this, her face grew livid about the mouth, she looked quite dangerous, and reminded him that housekeeping was no more her work than it was his: she had other work to do as well, and when did he think she was going to find time to do it at this rate?

Was she going to start on that again? She knew as well as he did that his work brought in the regular money, hers was only occasional, if they depended on what *she* made—and she might as well get straight on this question once for all!

That was positively not the point. The question was, when both of them were working on their own time, was there going to be a division of the housework, or wasn't there? She merely wanted to know, she had to make her plans. Why, he thought that was all arranged. It was understood that he was to help. Hadn't he always, in summers?

Hadn't he, though? Oh, just hadn't he? And when, and where, and doing what? Lord, what an uproarious joke!

It was such a very uproarious joke that her face turned slightly purple, and she screamed with laughter. She laughed so hard she had to sit down, and finally a rush of tears spurted from her eyes and poured down into the lifted corners of her mouth. He dashed towards her and dragged her up to her feet and tried to pour water on her head. The dipper hung by a string on a nail and he broke it loose. Then he tried to pump water with one hand while she struggled in the other. So he gave it up and shook her instead.

She wrenched away, crying out for him to take his rope and go to hell, she had simply given him up: and ran. He heard her high-heeled bedroom slippers clattering and stumbling on the stairs.

He went out around the house and into the lane; he suddenly realized he had a blister on his heel and his shirt felt as if it were on fire. Things broke so suddenly you didn't know where you were. She could work herself into a fury about simply nothing. She was terrible, damn it: not an ounce of reason. You might as well talk to a sieve as that woman when she got going. Damned if he'd spend his life humoring her! Well, what to do now? He would take back the rope and exchange it for something else. Things accumulated, things were mountainous, you couldn't move them or sort them out or get rid of them. They just lay and rotted around. He'd take it back. Hell, why should he? He wanted it. What was it anyhow? A piece of rope. Imagine anybody caring more about a piece of rope than about a man's feelings. What earthly right had she to say a word about it? He remembered all the useless, meaningless things she bought for herself: Why? because I wanted it, that's why! He stopped and selected a large stone by the road. He would put the rope behind it. He would put it in the tool-box when he got back. He'd heard enough about it to last him a life-time.

When he came back she was leaning against the post box beside the road waiting. It was pretty late, the smell of broiled steak floated nose high in the cooling air. Her face was young and smooth and fresh-looking. Her unmanageable funny black hair was all on end. She waved to him from a distance, and he speeded up. She called out that supper was ready and waiting, was he starved?

You bet he was starved. Here was the coffee. He waved it at her. She looked at his other hand. What was that he had there?

Well, it was the rope again. He stopped short. He had meant to exchange it but forgot. She wanted to know why he should exchange it, if it was something he really wanted. Wasn't the air sweet now, and wasn't it fine to be here?

She walked beside him with one hand hooked into his leather belt. She pulled and jostled him a little as he walked, and leaned against him. He put his arm clear around her and patted her stomach. They exchanged wary smiles. Coffee, coffee for the Ootsum-Wootsums! He felt as if he were bringing her a beautiful present.

He was a love, she firmly believed, and if she had had her coffee in the morning, she wouldn't have behaved so funny . . . There was a whippoorwill still coming back, imagine, clear out of season, sitting in the crab-apple tree calling all by himself. Maybe his girl stood him up. Maybe she did. She hoped to hear him once more, she loved whippoorwills . . . He knew how she was, didn't he?

Sure, he knew how she was.

He

LIFE was very hard for the Whipples. It was hard to feed all the hungry mouths, it was hard to keep the children in flannels during the winter, short as it was: "God knows what would become of us if we lived north," they would say: keeping them decently clean was hard. "It looks like our luck won't never let up on us," said Mr. Whipple, but Mrs. Whipple was all for taking what was sent and calling it good, anyhow when the neighbors were in earshot. "Don't ever let a soul hear us complain," she kept saying to her husband. She couldn't stand to be pitied. "No, not if it comes to it that we have to live in a wagon and pick cotton around the country," she said, "nobody's going to get a chance to look down on us."

Mrs. Whipple loved her second son, the simple-minded one, better than she loved the other two children put together. She was forever saying so, and when she talked with certain of her neighbors, she would even throw in her husband and her mother for good measure.

"You needn't keep on saying it around," said Mr. Whipple, "you'll make people think nobody else has any feelings about Him but you."

"It's natural for a mother," Mrs. Whipple would remind him. "You know yourself it's more natural for a mother to be that way. People don't expect so much of fathers, some way."

This didn't keep the neighbors from talking plainly among themselves. "A Lord's pure mercy if He should die," they said. "It's the sins of the fathers," they agreed among themselves. "There's bad blood and bad doings somewhere, you can bet on that." This behind the Whipples' backs. To their faces everybody said, "He's not so bad off. He'll be all right yet. Look how He grows!"

Mrs. Whipple hated to talk about it, she tried to keep her mind off it, but every time anybody set foot in the house, the subject always came up, and she had to talk about Him first, before she could get on to anything else. It seemed to ease her mind. "I wouldn't have anything happen to Him for all the world, but it just looks like I can't keep Him out of mischief.

55

He's so strong and active, He's always into everything; He was
like that since He could walk. It's actually funny sometimes,
the way He can do anything; it's laughable to see Him up to
His tricks. Emly has more accidents; I'm forever tying up her
bruises, and Adna can't fall a foot without cracking a bone.
But He can do anything and not get a scratch. The preacher
said such a nice thing once when he was here. He said, and I'll
remember it to my dying day, 'The innocent walk with God—
that's why He don't get hurt.'" Whenever Mrs. Whipple repeated these words, she always felt a warm pool spread in her
breast, and the tears would fill her eyes, and then she could
talk about something else.

He did grow and He never got hurt. A plank blew off the
chicken house and struck Him on the head and He never
seemed to know it. He had learned a few words, and after this
He forgot them. He didn't whine for food as the other children did, but waited until it was given Him; He ate squatting
in the corner, smacking and mumbling. Rolls of fat covered
Him like an overcoat, and He could carry twice as much wood
and water as Adna. Emly had a cold in the head most of the
time—"she takes that after me," said Mrs. Whipple—so in bad
weather they gave her the extra blanket off His cot. He never
seemed to mind the cold.

Just the same, Mrs. Whipple's life was a torment for fear
something might happen to Him. He climbed the peach trees
much better than Adna and went skittering along the branches
like a monkey, just a regular monkey. "Oh, Mrs. Whipple, you
hadn't ought to let Him do that. He'll lose His balance sometime. He can't rightly know what He's doing."

Mrs. Whipple almost screamed out at the neighbor. "He
does know what He's doing! He's as able as any other child!
Come down out of there, you!" When He finally reached the
ground she could hardly keep her hands off Him for acting
like that before people, a grin all over His face and her worried
sick about Him all the time.

"It's the neighbors," said Mrs. Whipple to her husband.
"Oh, I do mortally wish they would keep out of our business.
I can't afford to let Him do anything for fear they'll come
nosing around about it. Look at the bees, now. Adna can't
handle them, they sting him up so; I haven't got time to do

everything, and now I don't dare let Him. But if He gets a sting He don't really mind."

"It's just because He ain't got sense enough to be scared of anything," said Mr. Whipple.

"You ought to be ashamed of yourself," said Mrs. Whipple, "talking that way about your own child. Who's to take up for Him if we don't, I'd like to know? He sees a lot that goes on, He listens to things all the time. And anything I tell Him to do He does it. Don't never let anybody hear you say such things. They'd think you favored the other children over Him."

"Well, now I don't, and you know it, and what's the use of getting all worked up about it? You always think the worst of everything. Just let Him alone, He'll get along somehow. He gets plenty to eat and wear, don't He?" Mr. Whipple suddenly felt tired out. "Anyhow, it can't be helped now."

Mrs. Whipple felt tired too, she complained in a tired voice. "What's done can't never be undone, I know that as good as anybody; but He's my child, and I'm not going to have people say anything. I get sick of people coming around saying things all the time."

In the early fall Mrs. Whipple got a letter from her brother saying he and his wife and two children were coming over for a little visit next Sunday week. "Put the big pot in the little one," he wrote at the end. Mrs. Whipple read this part out loud twice, she was so pleased. Her brother was a great one for saying funny things. "We'll just show him that's no joke," she said, "we'll just butcher one of the sucking pigs."

"It's a waste and I don't hold with waste the way we are now," said Mr. Whipple. "That pig'll be worth money by Christmas."

"It's a shame and a pity we can't have a decent meal's vittles once in a while when my own family comes to see us," said Mrs. Whipple. "I'd hate for his wife to go back and say there wasn't a thing in the house to eat. My God, it's better than buying up a great chance of meat in town. There's where you'd spend the money!"

"All right, do it yourself then," said Mr. Whipple. "Christa-mighty, no wonder we can't get ahead!"

The question was how to get the little pig away from his ma, a great fighter, worse than a Jersey cow. Adna wouldn't try it:

"That sow'd rip my insides out all over the pen." "All right, old fraidy," said Mrs. Whipple, "*He's* not scared. Watch *Him* do it." And she laughed as though it was all a good joke and gave Him a little push towards the pen. He sneaked up and snatched the pig right away from the teat and galloped back and was over the fence with the sow raging at His heels. The little black squirming thing was screeching like a baby in a tantrum, stiffening its back and stretching its mouth to the ears. Mrs. Whipple took the pig with her face stiff and sliced its throat with one stroke. When He saw the blood He gave a great jolting breath and ran away. "But He'll forget and eat plenty, just the same," thought Mrs. Whipple. Whenever she was thinking, her lips moved making words. "He'd eat it all if I didn't stop Him. He'd eat up every mouthful from the other two if I'd let Him."

She felt badly about it. He was ten years old now and a third again as large as Adna, who was going on fourteen. "It's a shame, a shame," she kept saying under her breath, "and Adna with so much brains!"

She kept on feeling badly about all sorts of things. In the first place it was the man's work to butcher; the sight of the pig scraped pink and naked made her sick. He was too fat and soft and pitiful-looking. It was simply a shame the way things had to happen. By the time she had finished it up, she almost wished her brother would stay at home.

Early Sunday morning Mrs. Whipple dropped everything to get Him all cleaned up. In an hour He was dirty again, with crawling under fences after a possum, and straddling along the rafters of the barn looking for eggs in the hayloft. "My Lord, look at you now after all my trying! And here's Adna and Emly staying so quiet. I get tired trying to keep you decent. Get off that shirt and put on another, people will say I don't half dress you!" And she boxed Him on the ears, hard. He blinked and blinked and rubbed His head, and His face hurt Mrs. Whipple's feelings. Her knees began to tremble, she had to sit down while she buttoned His shirt. "I'm just all gone before the day starts."

The brother came with his plump healthy wife and two great roaring hungry boys. They had a grand dinner, with the pig roasted to a crackling in the middle of the table, full of dressing, a pickled peach in his mouth and plenty of gravy for the sweet potatoes.

"This looks like prosperity all right," said the brother; "you're going to have to roll me home like I was a barrel when I'm done."

Everybody laughed out loud; it was fine to hear them laughing all at once around the table. Mrs. Whipple felt warm and good about it. "Oh, we've got six more of these; I say it's as little as we can do when you come to see us so seldom."

He wouldn't come into the dining room, and Mrs. Whipple passed it off very well. "He's timider than my other two," she said, "He'll just have to get used to you. There isn't everybody He'll make up with, you know how it is with some children, even cousins." Nobody said anything out of the way.

"Just like my Alfy here," said the brother's wife. "I sometimes got to lick him to make him shake hands with his own grandmammy."

So that was over, and Mrs. Whipple loaded up a big plate for Him first, before everybody. "I always say He ain't to be slighted, no matter who else goes without," she said, and carried it to Him herself.

"He can chin Himself on the top of the door," said Emly, helping along.

"That's fine, He's getting along fine," said the brother.

They went away after supper. Mrs. Whipple rounded up the dishes, and sent the children to bed and sat down and unlaced her shoes. "You see?" she said to Mr. Whipple. "That's the way my whole family is. Nice and considerate about everything. No out-of-the-way remarks—they *have* got refinement. I get awfully sick of people's remarks. Wasn't that pig good?"

Mr. Whipple said, "Yes, we're out three hundred pounds of pork, that's all. It's easy to be polite when you come to eat. Who knows what they had in their minds all along?"

"Yes, that's like you," said Mrs. Whipple. "I don't expect anything else from you. You'll be telling me next that my own brother will be saying around that we made Him eat in the kitchen! Oh, my God!" She rocked her head in her hands, a hard pain started in the very middle of her forehead. "Now it's all spoiled, and everything was so nice and easy. All right, you don't like them and you never did—all right, they'll not come here again soon, never you mind! But they *can't* say He wasn't dressed every lick as good as Adna—oh, honest, sometimes I wish I was dead!"

"I wish you'd let up," said Mr. Whipple. "It's bad enough as it is."

It was a hard winter. It seemed to Mrs. Whipple that they hadn't ever known anything but hard times, and now to cap it all a winter like this. The crops were about half of what they had a right to expect; after the cotton was in it didn't do much more than cover the grocery bill. They swapped off one of the plow horses, and got cheated, for the new one died of the heaves. Mrs. Whipple kept thinking all the time it was terrible to have a man you couldn't depend on not to get cheated. They cut down on everything, but Mrs. Whipple kept saying there are things you can't cut down on, and they cost money. It took a lot of warm clothes for Adna and Emly, who walked four miles to school during the three-months session. "He sets around the fire a lot, He won't need so much," said Mr. Whipple. "That's so," said Mrs. Whipple, "and when He does the out-door chores He can wear your tarpaullion coat. I can't do no better, that's all."

In February He was taken sick, and lay curled up under His blanket looking very blue in the face and acting as if He would choke. Mr. and Mrs. Whipple did everything they could for Him for two days, and then they were scared and sent for the doctor. The doctor told them they must keep Him warm and give Him plenty of milk and eggs. "He isn't as stout as He looks, I'm afraid," said the doctor. "You've got to watch them when they're like that. You must put more cover onto Him, too."

"I just took off His big blanket to wash," said Mrs. Whipple, ashamed. "I can't stand dirt."

"Well, you'd better put it back on the minute it's dry," said the doctor, "or He'll have pneumonia."

Mr. and Mrs. Whipple took a blanket off their own bed and put His cot in by the fire. "They can't say we didn't do everything for Him," she said, "even to sleeping cold ourselves on His account."

When the winter broke He seemed to be well again, but He walked as if His feet hurt Him. He was able to run a cotton planter during the season.

"I got it all fixed up with Jim Ferguson about breeding the cow next time," said Mr. Whipple. "I'll pasture the bull this summer and give Jim some fodder in the fall. That's better than paying out money when you haven't got it."

"I hope you didn't say such a thing before Jim Ferguson," said Mrs. Whipple. "You oughtn't to let him know we're so down as all that."

"Godamighty, that ain't saying we're down. A man is got to look ahead sometimes. He can lead the bull over today. I need Adna on the place."

At first Mrs. Whipple felt easy in her mind about sending Him for the bull. Adna was too jumpy and couldn't be trusted. You've got to be steady around animals. After He was gone she started thinking, and after a while she could hardly bear it any longer. She stood in the lane and watched for Him. It was nearly three miles to go and a hot day, but He oughtn't to be so long about it. She shaded her eyes and stared until colored bubbles floated in her eyeballs. It was just like everything else in life, she must always worry and never know a moment's peace about anything. After a long time she saw Him turn into the side lane, limping. He came on very slowly, leading the big hulk of an animal by a ring in the nose, twirling a little stick in His hand, never looking back or sideways, but coming on like a sleepwalker with His eyes half shut.

Mrs. Whipple was scared sick of bulls; she had heard awful stories about how they followed on quietly enough, and then suddenly pitched on with a bellow and pawed and gored a body to pieces. Any second now that black monster would come down on Him, my God, He'd never have sense enough to run.

She mustn't make a sound nor a move; she mustn't get the bull started. The bull heaved his head aside and horned the air at a fly. Her voice burst out of her in a shriek, and she screamed at Him to come on, for God's sake. He didn't seem to hear her clamor, but kept on twirling His switch and limping on, and the bull lumbered along behind him as gently as a calf. Mrs. Whipple stopped calling and ran towards the house, praying under her breath: "Lord, don't let anything happen to Him. Lord, you *know* people will say we oughtn't to have sent Him. You *know* they'll say we didn't take care of Him. Oh, get Him home, safe home, safe home, and I'll look out for Him better! Amen."

She watched from the window while He led the beast in, and tied him up in the barn. It was no use trying to keep up, Mrs. Whipple couldn't bear another thing. She sat down and rocked and cried with her apron over her head.

From year to year the Whipples were growing poorer and poorer. The place just seemed to run down of itself, no matter how hard they worked. "We're losing our hold," said Mrs. Whipple. "Why can't we do like other people and watch for our best chances? They'll be calling us poor white trash next."

"When I get to be sixteen I'm going to leave," said Adna. "I'm going to get a job in Powell's grocery store. There's money in that. No more farm for me."

"I'm going to be a schoolteacher," said Emly. "But I've got to finish the eighth grade, anyhow. Then I can live in town. I don't see any chances here."

"Emly takes after my family," said Mrs. Whipple. "Ambitious every last one of them, and they don't take second place for anybody."

When fall came Emly got a chance to wait on table in the railroad eating-house in the town near by, and it seemed such a shame not to take it when the wages were good and she could get her food too, that Mrs. Whipple decided to let her take it, and not bother with school until the next session. "You've got plenty of time," she said. "You're young and smart as a whip."

With Adna gone too, Mr. Whipple tried to run the farm with just Him to help. He seemed to get along fine, doing His work and part of Adna's without noticing it. They did well enough until Christmas time, when one morning He slipped on the ice coming up from the barn. Instead of getting up He thrashed round and round, and when Mr. Whipple got to Him, He was having some sort of fit.

They brought Him inside and tried to make Him sit up, but He blubbered and rolled, so they put Him to bed and Mr.

Whipple rode to town for the doctor. All the way there and back he worried about where the money was to come from: it sure did look like he had about all the troubles he could carry.

From then on He stayed in bed. His legs swelled up double their size, and the fits kept coming back. After four months, the doctor said, "It's no use, I think you'd better put Him in the County Home for treatment right away. I'll see about it for you. He'll have good care there and be off your hands."

"We don't begrudge Him any care, and I won't let Him out of my sight," said Mrs. Whipple. "I won't have it said I sent my sick child off among strangers."

"I know how you feel," said the doctor. "You can't tell me anything about that, Mrs. Whipple. I've got a boy of my own. But you'd better listen to me. I can't do anything more for Him, that's the truth."

Mr. and Mrs. Whipple talked it over a long time that night after they went to bed. "It's just charity," said Mrs. Whipple, "that's what we've come to, charity! I certainly never looked for this."

"We pay taxes to help support the place just like everybody else," said Mr. Whipple, "and I don't call that taking charity. I think it would be fine to have Him where He'd get the best of everything . . . and besides, I can't keep up with these doctor bills any longer."

"Maybe that's why the doctor wants us to send Him—he's scared he won't get his money," said Mrs. Whipple.

"Don't talk like that," said Mr. Whipple, feeling pretty sick, "or we won't be able to send Him."

"Oh, but we won't keep Him there long," said Mrs. Whipple. "Soon's He's better, we'll bring Him right back home."

"The doctor has told you and told you time and again He can't ever get better, and you might as well stop talking," said Mr. Whipple.

"Doctors don't know everything," said Mrs. Whipple, feeling almost happy. "But anyhow, in the summer Emly can come home for a vacation, and Adna can get down for Sundays: we'll all work together and get on our feet again, and the children will feel they've got a place to come to."

All at once she saw it full summer again, with the garden

going fine, and new white roller shades up all over the house, and Adna and Emly home, so full of life, all of them happy together. Oh, it could happen, things would ease up on them.

They didn't talk before Him much, but they never knew just how much He understood. Finally the doctor set the day and a neighbor who owned a double-seated carryall offered to drive them over. The hospital would have sent an ambulance, but Mrs. Whipple couldn't stand to see Him going away looking so sick as all that. They wrapped Him in blankets, and the neighbor and Mr. Whipple lifted Him into the back seat of the carryall beside Mrs. Whipple, who had on her black shirt waist. She couldn't stand to go looking like charity.

"You'll be all right, I guess I'll stay behind," said Mr. Whipple. "It don't look like everybody ought to leave the place at once."

"Besides, it ain't as if He was going to stay forever," said Mrs. Whipple to the neighbor. "This is only for a little while."

They started away, Mrs. Whipple holding to the edges of the blankets to keep Him from sagging sideways. He sat there blinking and blinking. He worked His hands out and began rubbing His nose with His knuckles, and then with the end of the blanket. Mrs. Whipple couldn't believe what she saw; He was scrubbing away big tears that rolled out of the corners of His eyes. He sniveled and made a gulping noise. Mrs. Whipple kept saying, "Oh, honey, you don't feel so bad, do you? You don't feel so bad, do you?" for He seemed to be accusing her of something. Maybe He remembered that time she boxed His ears, maybe He had been scared that day with the bull, maybe He had slept cold and couldn't tell her about it; maybe He knew they were sending Him away for good and all because they were too poor to keep Him. Whatever it was, Mrs. Whipple couldn't bear to think of it. She began to cry, frightfully, and wrapped her arms tight around Him. His head rolled on her shoulder: she had loved Him as much as she possibly could, there were Adna and Emly who had to be thought of too, there was nothing she could do to make up to Him for His life. Oh, what a mortal pity He was ever born.

They came in sight of the hospital, with the neighbor driving very fast, not daring to look behind him.

Theft

SHE had the purse in her hand when she came in. Standing in the middle of the floor, holding her bathrobe around her and trailing a damp towel in one hand, she surveyed the immediate past and remembered everything clearly. Yes, she had opened the flap and spread it out on the bench after she had dried the purse with her handkerchief.

She had intended to take the Elevated, and naturally she looked in her purse to make certain she had the fare, and was pleased to find forty cents in the coin envelope. She was going to pay her own fare, too, even if Camilo did have the habit of seeing her up the steps and dropping a nickel in the machine before he gave the turnstile a little push and sent her through it with a bow. Camilo by a series of compromises had managed to make effective a fairly complete set of smaller courtesies, ignoring the larger and more troublesome ones. She had walked with him to the station in a pouring rain, because she knew he was almost as poor as she was, and when he insisted on a taxi, she was firm and said, "You know it simply will not do." He was wearing a new hat of a pretty biscuit shade, for it never occurred to him to buy anything of a practical color; he had put it on for the first time and the rain was spoiling it. She kept thinking, "But this is dreadful, where will he get another?" She compared it with Eddie's hats that always seemed to be precisely seven years old and as if they had been quite purposely left out in the rain, and yet they sat with a careless and incidental rightness on Eddie. But Camilo was far different; if he wore a shabby hat it would be merely shabby on him, and he would lose his spirits over it. If she had not feared Camilo would take it badly, for he insisted on the practice of his little ceremonies up to the point he had fixed for them, she would have said to him as they left Thora's house, "Do go home. I can surely reach the station by myself."

"It is written that we must be rained upon tonight," said Camilo, "so let it be together."

At the foot of the platform stairway she staggered slightly—they were both nicely set up on Thora's cocktails—and said:

"At least, Camilo, do me the favor not to climb these stairs in your present state, since for you it is only a matter of coming down again at once, and you'll certainly break your neck."

He made three quick bows, he was Spanish, and leaped off through the rainy darkness. She stood watching him, for he was a very graceful young man, thinking that tomorrow morning he would gaze soberly at his spoiled hat and soggy shoes and possibly associate her with his misery. As she watched, he stopped at the far corner and took off his hat and hid it under his overcoat. She felt she had betrayed him by seeing, because he would have been humiliated if he thought she even suspected him of trying to save his hat.

Roger's voice sounded over her shoulder above the clang of the rain falling on the stairway shed, wanting to know what she was doing out in the rain at this time of night, and did she take herself for a duck? His long, imperturbable face was streaming with water, and he tapped a bulging spot on the breast of his buttoned-up overcoat: "Hat," he said. "Come on, let's take a taxi."

She settled back against Roger's arm which he laid around her shoulders, and with the gesture they exchanged a glance full of long amiable associations, then she looked through the window at the rain changing the shapes of everything, and the colors. The taxi dodged in and out between the pillars of the Elevated, skidding slightly on every curve, and she said: "The more it skids the calmer I feel, so I really must be drunk."

"You must be," said Roger. "This bird is a homicidal maniac, and I could do with a cocktail myself this minute."

They waited on the traffic at Fortieth Street and Sixth Avenue, and three boys walked before the nose of the taxi. Under the globes of light they were cheerful scarecrows, all very thin and all wearing very seedy snappy-cut suits and gay neckties. They were not very sober either, and they stood for a moment wobbling in front of the car, and there was an argument going on among them. They leaned toward each other as if they were getting ready to sing, and the first one said: "When I get married it won't be jus' for getting married, I'm gonna marry for *love*, see?" and the second one said, "Aw, gwan and tell that stuff to *her*, why n't yuh?" and the third one gave a kind of hoot, and said, "Hell, dis guy? Wot the hell's he got?" and the first one said: "Aaah, shurrup yuh mush, I got plenty." Then they all squealed and scrambled across the street beating the first one on the back and pushing him around.

"Nuts," commented Roger, "pure nuts."

Two girls went skittering by in short transparent raincoats, one green, one red, their heads tucked against the drive of the rain. One of them was saying to the other, "Yes, I know all about *that*. But what about me? You're always so sorry for *him* . . ." and they ran on with their little pelican legs flashing back and forth.

The taxi backed up suddenly and leaped forward again, and after a while Roger said: "I had a letter from Stella today, and she'll be home on the twenty-sixth, so I suppose she's made up her mind and it's all settled."

"I had a sort of letter today too," she said, "making up my mind for me. I think it is time for you and Stella to do something definite."

When the taxi stopped on the corner of West Fifty-third Street, Roger said, "I've just enough if you'll add ten cents," so she opened her purse and gave him a dime, and he said, "That's beautiful, that purse."

"It's a birthday present," she told him, "and I like it. How's your show coming?"

"Oh, still hanging on, I guess. I don't go near the place. Nothing sold yet. I mean to keep right on the way I'm going and they can take it or leave it. I'm through with the argument."

"It's absolutely a matter of holding out, isn't it?"

"Holding out's the tough part."

"Good night, Roger."

"Good night, you should take aspirin and push yourself into a tub of hot water, you look as though you're catching cold."

"I will."

With the purse under her arm she went upstairs, and on the first landing Bill heard her step and poked his head out with his hair tumbled and his eyes red, and he said: "For Christ's sake, come in and have a drink with me. I've had some bad news."

"You're perfectly sopping," said Bill, looking at her drenched feet. They had two drinks, while Bill told how the director had thrown his play out after the cast had been picked over twice, and had gone through three rehearsals. "I said to him, 'I didn't say it was a masterpiece, I said it would make a good show.' And he said, 'It just doesn't *play*, do you see? It needs a doctor.' So I'm stuck, absolutely stuck," said Bill, on the edge of weeping again. "I've been crying," he told her, "in my cups." And he went on to ask her if she realized his wife was ruining him with her extravagance. "I send her ten dollars every week of my unhappy life, and I don't really have to. She threatens to jail me if I don't, but she can't do it. God, let her try it after the way she treated me! She's no right to alimony and she knows it. She keeps on saying she's got to have it for the baby and I keep on sending it because I can't bear to see anybody suffer. So I'm way behind on the piano and the victrola, both—"

"Well, this is a pretty rug, anyhow," she said.

Bill stared at it and blew his nose. "I got it at Ricci's for ninety-five dollars," he said. "Ricci told me it once belonged to Marie Dressler, and cost fifteen hundred dollars, but there's a burnt place on it, under the divan. Can you beat that?"

"No," she said. She was thinking about her empty purse and that she could not possibly expect a check for her latest review for another three days, and her arrangement with the basement restaurant could not last much longer if she did not pay something on account. "It's no time to speak of it," she said, "but I've been hoping you would have by now that fifty dollars you promised for my scene in the third act. Even if it doesn't play. You were to pay me for the work anyhow out of your advance."

"Weeping Jesus," said Bill, "you, too?" He gave a loud sob, or hiccough, in his moist handkerchief. "Your stuff was no better than mine, after all. Think of that."

"But you got something for it," she said. "Seven hundred dollars."

Bill said, "Do me a favor, will you? Have another drink and forget about it. I can't, you know I can't, I would if I could, but you know the fix I'm in."

"Let it go, then," she found herself saying almost in spite of herself. She had meant to be quite firm about it. They drank again without speaking, and she went to her apartment on the floor above.

There, she now remembered distinctly, she had taken the letter out of the purse before she spread the purse out to dry.

She had sat down and read the letter over again: but there were phrases that insisted on being read many times, they had a life of their own separate from the others, and when she tried to read past and around them, they moved with the movement of her eyes, and she could not escape them . . . "thinking about you more than I mean to . . . yes, I even talk about you . . . why were you so anxious to destroy . . . even if I could see you now I would not . . . not worth all this abominable . . . the end . . ."

Carefully she tore the letter into narrow strips and touched a lighted match to them in the coal grate.

Early the next morning she was in the bathtub when the janitress knocked and then came in, calling out that she wished to examine the radiators before she started the furnace going for the winter. After moving about the room for a few minutes, the janitress went out, closing the door very sharply.

She came out of the bathroom to get a cigarette from the package in the purse. The purse was gone. She dressed and made coffee, and sat by the window while she drank it. Certainly the janitress had taken the purse, and certainly it would be impossible to get it back without a great deal of ridiculous excitement. Then let it go. With this decision of her mind, there rose coincidentally in her blood a deep almost murderous anger. She set the cup carefully in the center of the table, and walked steadily downstairs, three long flights and a short hall and a steep short flight into the basement, where the janitress, her face streaked with coal dust, was shaking up the furnace. "Will you please give me back my purse? There isn't any money in it. It was a present, and I don't want to lose it."

The janitress turned without straightening up and peered at her with hot flickering eyes, a red light from the furnace reflected in them. "What do you mean, your purse?"

"The gold cloth purse you took from the wooden bench in my room," she said. "I must have it back."

"Before God I never laid eyes on your purse, and that's the holy truth," said the janitress.

"Oh, well then, keep it," she said, but in a very bitter voice; "keep it if you want it so much." And she walked away.

She remembered how she had never locked a door in her life, on some principle of rejection in her that made her uncomfortable in the ownership of things, and her paradoxical boast before the warnings of her friends, that she had never lost a penny by theft; and she had been pleased with the bleak humility of this concrete example designed to illustrate and justify a certain fixed, otherwise baseless and general faith which ordered the movements of her life without regard to her will in the matter.

In this moment she felt that she had been robbed of an enormous number of valuable things, whether material or intangible: things lost or broken by her own fault, things she had forgotten and left in houses when she moved: books borrowed from her and not returned, journeys she had planned and had not made, words she had waited to hear spoken to her and had not heard, and the words she had meant to answer with; bitter alternatives and intolerable substitutes worse than nothing, and yet inescapable: the long patient suffering of dying friendships and the dark inexplicable death of love—all that she had had, and all that she had missed, were lost together, and were twice lost in this landslide of remembered losses.

The janitress was following her upstairs with the purse in her hand and the same deep red fire flickering in her eyes. The janitress thrust the purse towards her while they were still a half dozen steps apart, and said: "Don't never tell on me. I musta been crazy. I get crazy in the head sometimes, I swear I do. My son can tell you."

She took the purse after a moment, and the janitress went on: "I got a niece who is going on seventeen, and she's a nice girl and I thought I'd give it to her. She needs a pretty purse. I musta been crazy; I thought maybe you wouldn't mind, you leave things around and don't seem to notice much."

She said: "I missed this because it was a present to me from someone . . ."

The janitress said: "He'd get you another if you lost this one. My niece is young and needs pretty things, we oughta give the young ones a chance. She's got young men after her maybe will want to marry her. She oughta have nice things. She needs them bad right now. You're a grown woman, you've had your chance, you ought to know how it is!"

She held the purse out to the janitress saying: "You don't know what you're talking about. Here, take it, I've changed my mind. I really don't want it."

The janitress looked up at her with hatred and said: "I don't want it either now. My niece is young and pretty, she don't need fixin' up to be pretty, she's young and pretty anyhow! I guess you need it worse than she does!"

"It wasn't really yours in the first place," she said, turning away. "You mustn't talk as if I had stolen it from you."

"It's not from me, it's from her you're stealing it," said the janitress, and went back downstairs.

She laid the purse on the table and sat down with the cup of chilled coffee, and thought: I was right not to be afraid of any thief but myself, who will end by leaving me nothing.

That Tree

H E had really wanted to be a cheerful bum lying under a tree in a good climate, writing poetry. He wrote bushel basketsful of poetry and it was all no good and he knew it, even while he was writing it. Knowing his poetry was no good did not take away much from his pleasure in it. He would have enjoyed just that kind of life: no respectability, no responsibility, no money to speak of, wearing worn-out sandals and a becoming, if probably ragged, blue shirt, lying under a tree writing poetry. That was why he had come to Mexico in the first place. He had felt in his bones that it was the country for him. Long after he had become quite an important journalist, an authority on Latin-American revolutions and a best seller, he confessed to any friends and acquaintances who would listen to him—he enjoyed this confession, it gave him a chance to talk about the thing he believed he loved best, the idle free romantic life of a poet—that the day Miriam kicked him out was the luckiest day of his life. She had left him, really, packing up suddenly in a cold quiet fury, stabbing him with her elbows when he tried to get his arms around her, now and again cutting him to the bone with a short sentence expelled through her clenched teeth; but he felt that he had been, as he always explained, kicked out. She had kicked him out and it had served him right.

The shock had brought him to himself as if he had been surprised out of a long sleep. He had sat quite benumbed in the bare clean room, among the straw mats and the painted Indian chairs Miriam hated, in the sudden cold silence, his head in his hands, nearly all night. It hadn't even occurred to him to lie down. It must have been almost daylight when he got up stiff in every joint from sitting still so long, and though he could not say he had been thinking yet he had formed a new resolution. He had started out, you might almost say that very day, to make a career for himself in journalism. He couldn't say why he had hit on that, except that the word would impress his wife, the work was just intellectual enough to save his self-respect, such as it was, and even to him it seemed a suitable occupation for a man such as he had suddenly become, bent on getting on in the world of affairs. Nothing ever happens suddenly to anyone, he observed, as if the thought had just occurred to him; it had been coming on probably for a long time, sneaking up on him when he wasn't looking. His wife had called him "Parasite!" She had said "Ne'er-do-well!" and as she repeated these things for what proved to be the last time, it struck him she had said them often before, when he had not listened to her with the ear of his mind. He translated these relatively harmless epithets instantly into their proper synonyms of Loafer! and Bum! Miriam had been a school-teacher, and no matter what her disappointments and provocations may have been, you could not expect her easily to forget such discipline. She had got into a professional habit of primness; besides, she was a properly brought-up girl, not a prissy bore, not at all, but a—well, there you are, a nicely brought-up Middle-Western girl, who took life seriously. And what can you do about that? She was sweet and gay and full of little crazy notions, but she never gave way to them honestly, or at least never at the moment when they might have meant something. She was never able to see the amusing side of a threatening situation which, taken solemnly, would ruin everything. No, her sense of humor never worked for salvation. It was just an extra frill on what would have been a good time anyhow.

He wondered if anybody had ever thought—oh, well, of course everybody else had, he was always making marvelous discoveries that other people had known all along—how impossible it is to explain or to make other eyes see the special qualities in the person you love. There was such a special kind of beauty in Miriam. In certain lights and moods he simply got a clutch in the pit of his stomach when he looked at her. It was something that could happen at any hour of the day, in the midst of the most ordinary occupations. He thought there was something to be said for living with one person day and night the year round. It brings out the worst, but it brings out the best, too, and Miriam's best was pretty damn swell. He couldn't describe it. It was easy to talk about her faults. He remembered all of them, he could add them up against her like rows of figures in a vast unpaid debt. He had lived with her for four years, and even now sometimes he woke out of a sound sleep

in a sweating rage with himself, asking himself again why he
had ever wasted a minute on her. She wasn't beautiful in his
style. He confessed to a weakness for the kind that knocks your
eye out. Her notion of daytime dress was a tailored suit with a
round-collared blouse and a little felt hat like a bent shovel
pulled down over her eyes. In the evening she put on a black
dinner dress, positively disappeared into it. But she did her hair
well and had the most becoming nightgowns he ever saw. You
could have put her mind in a peanut shell. She hadn't temperament of the kind he had got used to in the Mexican girls.
She did not approve of his use of the word temperament,
either. She thought it was a kind of occupational disease among
artists, or a trick they practiced to make themselves interesting.
In any case, she distrusted artists and she distrusted temperament. But there was something about her. In cold blood he
could size her up to himself, but it made him furious if anyone
even hinted a criticism against her. His second wife had made a
point of being catty about Miriam. In the end he could almost
be willing to say this had led to his second divorce. He could
not bear hearing Miriam called a mousy little nit-wit—at least
not by *that* woman . . .

They both jumped nervously at an explosion in the street,
the backfire of an automobile.

"Another revolution," said the fat scarlet young man in the
tight purplish suit, at the next table. He looked like a parboiled
sausage ready to burst from its skin. It was the oldest joke since
the Mexican Independence, but he was trying to look as if
he had invented it. The journalist glanced back at him over a
sloping shoulder. "Another of those smart-cracking newspaper
guys," he said in a tough voice, too loudly on purpose, "sitting
around the Hotel Regis lobby wearing out the spittoons."

The smart-cracker swelled visibly and turned a darker red.
"Who do you think you're talking about, you banjo-eyed
chinless wonder, you?" he asked explicitly, spreading his chest
across the table.

"Somebody way up, no doubt," said the journalist, in his
natural voice, "somebody in with the government, I'll bet."

"Dyuhwana fight?" asked the newspaper man, trying to un-
wedge himself from between the table and his chair, which sat
against the wall.

"Oh, I don't mind," said the journalist, "if you don't."

The newspaper man's friends laid soothing paws all over him and held him down. "Don't start anything with that shrimp," said one of them, his wet pink eyes trying to look sober and responsible. "For crisesake, Joe, can't you see he's about half your size and a feeb to boot? You wouldn't hit a feeb, now, Joe, would you?"

"I'll feeb him," said the newspaper man, wiggling faintly under restraint.

"*Señores'n, señores'n,*" urged the little Mexican waiter, "there are respectable ladies and gentlemen present. Please, a little silence and correct behavior, please."

"Who the hell are *you*, anyhow?" the newspaper man asked the journalist, from under his shelter of hands, around the thin form of the waiter.

"Nobody you'd wanta know, Joe," said another of his pawing friends. "Pipe down now before these greasers turn in a general alarm. You know how liable they are to go off when you least expect it. Pipe down, now, Joe, now you just remember what happened the last time, Joe. Whaddayah *care,* anyhow?"

"*Señores'n,*" said the little waiter, working his thin outspread mahogany-colored hands up and down alternately as if they were on sticks, "it is necessary it must cease or the *señores'n* must remove themselves."

It did cease. It seemed to evaporate. The four newspaper men at the next table subsided, cluttered in a circle with their heads together, muttering into their highballs. The journalist turned back, ordered another round of drinks, and went on talking, in a low voice.

He had never liked this café, never had any luck in it. Something always happened here to spoil his evening. If there was one brand of bum on earth he despised, it was a newspaper bum. Or anyhow the drunken illiterates the United Press and Associated Press seemed to think were good enough for Mexico and South America. They were always getting mixed up in affairs that were none of their business, and they spent their time trying to work up trouble somewhere so they could get a story out of it. They were always having to be thrown out on their ears by the government. He just happened to know that the bum at the next table was about due to be deported. It had been pretty safe to make that crack about how he was no doubt way up in Mexican official esteem. . . . He thought that would remind him of something, all right.

One evening he had come here with Miriam for dinner and dancing, and at the very next table sat four fat generals from the North, with oxhorn mustaches and big bellies and big belts full of cartridges and pistols. It was in the old days just after Obregón had taken the city, and the town was crawling with generals. They infested the steam baths, where they took off their soiled campaign harness and sweated away the fumes of tequila and fornication, and they infested the cafés to get drunk again on champagne, and pick up the French whores who had been imported for the festivities of the presidential inauguration. These four were having an argument very quietly, their mean little eyes boring into each other's faces. He and his wife were dancing within arm's length of the table when one of the generals got up suddenly, tugging at his pistol, which stuck, and the other three jumped and grabbed him, all without a word; everybody in the place saw it at once. So far there was nothing unusual. The point was, every right-minded Mexican girl just seized her man firmly by the waist and spun him around until his back was to the generals, holding him before her like a shield, and there the whole roomful had stood frozen for a second, the music dead. His wife Miriam had broken from him and hidden under a table. He had to drag her out by the arm before everybody. "Let's have another drink," he said, and paused, looking around him as if he saw again the place as it had been on that night nearly ten years before. He blinked, and went on. It had been the most utterly humiliating moment of his whole blighted life. He had thought he couldn't survive to pick up their things and get her out of there. The generals had all sat down again and everybody went on dancing as though nothing had happened. . . . Indeed, nothing had happened to anyone except himself.

He tried, for hours that night and on and on for nearly a year, to explain to her how he felt about it. She could not understand at all. Sometimes she said it was all perfect nonsense. Or she remarked complacently that it had never occurred to her to save her life at his expense. She thought such tricks were all very well for the Mexican girls who had only one idea in their heads, and any excuse would do to hold a man closer than they should, but she could not, could *not*, see why he should expect her to imitate them. Besides, she had felt safer under the table. It was her first and only thought. He told her a bullet might very well have gone through the wood; a plank was no protection at all, a human torso was as good as a feather pillow to stop a bullet. She kept saying it simply had not occurred to her to do anything else, and that it really had nothing at all to do with him. He could never make her see his point of view for one moment. It should have had something to do with him. All those Mexican girls were born knowing what they should do and they did it instantly, and Miriam had merely proved once for all that her instincts were out of tune. When she tightened her mouth to bite her lip and say "Instincts!" she could make it sound like the most obscene word in any language. It was a shocking word. And she did not stop there. At last she said, she hadn't the faintest interest in what Mexican girls were born for, but she had no intention of wasting her life flattering male vanity. "Why should I trust you in anything?" she asked. "What reason have you given me to trust you?"

He was surprised at the change in her since he had first met her in Minneapolis. He chose to believe this change had been caused by her teaching school. He told her he thought it the most deadly occupation there was and a law should be passed prohibiting pretty women under thirty-five years of age from taking it up. She reminded him they were living on the money she had earned at it. They had been engaged for three years, a chaste long-distance engagement which he considered morbid and unnatural. Of course he had to do something to wear away the time, so while she was in Minneapolis saving her money and filling a huge trunk with household linen, he had been living in Mexico City with an Indian girl who posed for a set of painters he knew. He had a job teaching English in one of the technical schools—damned odd, he had been a schoolteacher too, but he never thought of it just that way until this minute—and he lived very comfortably with the Indian girl on his wages, for naturally the painters did not pay her for posing. The Indian girl divided her time cheerfully between the

painters, the cooking pot, and his bed, and she managed to
have a baby without interrupting any of these occupations for
more than a few days. Later on she was taken up by one of the
more famous and successful painters, and grew very sophisticated and a "character," but at that time she was still simple
and nice. She took, later on, to wearing native art-jewelry and
doing native dances in costume, and learned to paint almost as
well as a seven-year-old child; "you know," he said, "the primitive style." Well, by that time, he was having troubles of his
own. When the time came for Miriam to come out and marry
him—the whole delay, he realized afterward, was caused by
Miriam's expansive notions of what a bride's outfit should
be—the Indian girl had gone away very cheerfully, too cheerfully, in fact, with a new man. She had come back in three days
to say she was at last going to get married honestly, and she felt
he should give her the furniture for a dowry. He had helped
her pile the stuff on the backs of two Indian carriers, and the
girl had walked away with the baby's head dangling out of her
shawl. For just a moment when he saw the baby's face, he had
an odd feeling. "That's mine," he said to himself, and added at
once, "perhaps." There was no way of knowing, and it certainly looked like any other little shock-haired Indian baby.
Of course the girl had not got married; she had never even
thought of it.

When Miriam arrived, the place was almost empty, because
he had not been able to save a peso. He had a bed and a stove,
and the walls were decorated with drawings and paintings by
his Mexican friends, and there was a litter of painted gourds
and carved wood and pottery in beautiful colors. It didn't
seem so bad to him, but Miriam's face, when she stepped into
the first room, was, he had to admit, pretty much of a study.
She said very little, but she began to be unhappy about a number of things. She cried intermittently for the first few weeks,
for the most mysterious and farfetched causes. He would wake
in the night and find her crying hopelessly. When she sat down
to coffee in the morning she would lean her head on her hands
and cry. "It's nothing, nothing really," she would tell him. "I
don't know what is the matter. I just want to cry." He knew
now what was the matter. She had come all that way to marry
after three years' planning, and she couldn't see herself going

back and facing the music at home. This mood had not lasted, but it made a fairly dreary failure of their honeymoon. She knew nothing about the Indian girl, and believed, or professed to believe, that he was virgin as she was at their marriage. She hadn't much curiosity and her moral standards were severe, so it was impossible for him ever to take her into his confidence about his past. She simply took it for granted in the most irritating way that he hadn't any past worth mentioning except the three years they were engaged, and that, of course, they shared already. He had believed that all virgins, however austere their behavior, were palpitating to learn about life, were you might say hanging on by an eyelash until they arrived safely at initiation within the secure yet libertine advantages of marriage. Miriam upset this theory as in time she upset most of his theories. His intention to play the rôle of a man of the world educating an innocent but interestingly teachable bride was nipped in the bud. She was not at all teachable and she took no trouble to make herself interesting. In their most intimate hours her mind seemed elsewhere, gone into some darkness of its own, as if a prior and greater shock of knowledge had forestalled her attention. She was not to be won, for reasons of her own which she would not or could not give. He could not even play the rôle of a poet. She was not interested in his poetry. She preferred Milton, and she let him know it. She let him know also that she believed their mutual sacrifice of virginity was the most important act of their marriage, and this sacred rite once achieved, the whole affair had descended to a pretty low plane. She had a terrible phrase about "walking the chalk line" which she applied to all sorts of situations. One walked, as never before, the chalk line in marriage; there seemed to be a chalk line drawn between them as they lay together. . . .

The thing that finally got him down was Miriam's devilish inconsistency. She spent three mortal years writing him how dull and dreadful and commonplace her life was, how sick and tired she was of petty little conventions and amusements, how narrowminded everybody around her was, how she longed to live in a beautiful dangerous place among interesting people who painted and wrote poetry, and how his letters came into her stuffy little world like a breath of free mountain air, and all

that. "For God's sake," he said to his guest, "let's have
another drink." Well, he had something of a notion he was
freeing a sweet bird from a cage. Once freed, she would perch
gratefully on his hand. He wrote a poem about a caged bird
set free, dedicated it to her and sent her a copy. She forgot to
mention it in her next letter. Then she came out with a two-
hundred-pound trunk of linen and enough silk underwear to
last her a lifetime, you might have supposed, expecting to settle
down in a modern steam-heated flat and have nice artistic
young couples from the American colony in for dinner Wednesday evenings. No wonder her face had changed at the first
glimpse of her new home. His Mexican friends had scattered
flowers all over the place, tied bunches of carnations on the
door knobs, almost carpeted the floor with red roses, pinned
posies of small bright blooms on the sagging cotton curtains,
spread a coverlet of gardenias on the lumpy bed, and had disappeared discreetly, leaving gay reassuring messages scribbled
here and there, even on the white plastered walls. . . . She
had walked through with a vague look of terror in her eyes,
pushing back the wilting flowers with her advancing feet. She
swept the gardenias aside to sit on the edge of the bed, and she
had said not a word. Hail, Hymen! What next?

He had lost his teaching job almost immediately. The Minister of Education, who was a patron of the school superin-
tendent, was put out of office suddenly, and naturally every
soul in his party down to the school janitors went out with
him, and there you were. After a while you learn to take such
things calmly. You wait until your man gets back in the saddle
or you work up an alliance with the new one. . . . Whichever
. . . Meanwhile the change and movement made such a good
show you almost forgot the effect it had on your food supply.
Miriam was not interested in politics or the movement of local
history. She could see nothing but that he had lost his job.
They lived on Miriam's savings eked out with birthday checks
and Christmas checks from her father, who threatened constantly to come for a visit, in spite of Miriam's desperate letters
warning him that the country was appalling, and the climate
would most certainly ruin his health. Miriam went on holding
her nose when she went to the markets, trying to cook wholesome civilized American food over a charcoal brasier, and doing

the washing in the patio over a stone tub with a cold water tap; and everything that had seemed so jolly and natural and inexpensive with the Indian girl was too damnifying and costly for words with Miriam. Her money melted away and they got nothing for it.

She would not have an Indian servant near her: they were dirty and besides how could she afford it? He could not see why she despised and resented housework so, especially since he offered to help. He had thought it rather a picnic to wash a lot of gayly colored Indian crockery outdoors in the sunshine, with the bougainvillea climbing up the wall and the heaven tree in full bloom. Not Miriam. She despised him for thinking it a picnic. He remembered for the first time his mother doing the housework when he was a child. There were half a dozen assorted children, her work was hard and endless, but she went about it with a quiet certainty, a happy absorbed look on her face, as if her hands were working automatically while her imagination was away playing somewhere. "Ah, your mother," said his wife, without any particular emphasis. He felt horribly injured, as if she were insulting his mother and calling down a curse on her head for bringing such a son into the world. No doubt about it, Miriam had force. She could make her personality, which no one need really respect, felt in a bitter, sinister way. She had a background, and solid earth under her feet, and a point of view and a strong spine: even when she danced with him he could feel her tense controlled hips and her locked knees, which gave her dancing a most attractive strength and lightness without any yielding at all. She had her points, all right, like a good horse, but she had missed being beautiful. It wasn't in her. He began to cringe when she reminded him that if he were an invalid she would cheerfully work for him and take care of him, but he appeared to be in the best of health, he was not even looking for a job, and he was still writing that poetry, which was the last straw. She called him a failure. She called him worthless and shiftless and trifling and faithless. She showed him her ruined hands and asked him what she had to look forward to, and told him again, and again, that she was not used to associating with the simply indescribably savage and awful persons who kept streaming through the place. Moreover, she had no intention of getting used to it. He tried to tell her that these persons were the best painters and poets and what-alls in Mexico, that she should try to appreciate them; these were the artists he had told her about in his letters. She wanted to know why Carlos never changed his shirt. "I told her," said the journalist, "it was because probably he hadn't got any other shirt." And why was Jaime such a glutton, leaning over his plate and wolfing his food? Because he was famished, no doubt. It was precisely that she could not understand. Why didn't they go to work and make a living? It was no good trying to explain to her his Franciscan notions of holy Poverty as being the natural companion for the artist. She said, "So you think they're being poor on purpose? Nobody but you would be such a fool." Really, the things that girl said. And his general impression of her was that she was silent as a cat. He went on in his pawky way trying to make clear to her his mystical faith in these men who went ragged and hungry because they had chosen once for all between what he called in all seriousness their souls, and this world. Miriam knew better. She knew they were looking for the main chance. "She was abominably, obscenely right. How I hate that woman, I hate her as I hate no one else. She assured me they were not so stupid as I thought; and I lived to see Jaime take up with a rich old woman, and Ricardo decide to turn film actor, and Carlos sitting easy with a government job, painting revolutionary frescoes to order, and I asked myself, Why shouldn't a man survive in any way he can?" But some fixed point of feeling in him refused to be convinced, he had a sackful of romantic notions about artists and their destiny and he was left holding it. Miriam had seen through them with half an eye, and how he wished he might have thought of a trick to play on her that would have finished her for life. But he had not. They all in turn ran out on him and in the end he had run out too. "So you see, I don't feel any better about doing what I did finally do, but I can say I am not unusual. That I can say. The trouble was that Miriam was right, damn her. I am not a poet, my poetry is filthy, and I had notions about artists that I must have got out of books. . . . You know, a race apart, dedicated men much superior to common human needs and ambitions. . . . I mean I thought art was a religion. . . . I mean that when Miriam kept saying . . ."

What he meant was that all this conflict began to damage him seriously. Miriam had become an avenging fury, yet he could not condemn her. Hate her, yes, that was almost too simple. His old-fashioned respectable middle-class hard-working American ancestry and training rose up in him and fought on Miriam's side. He felt he had broken about every bone in him to get away from them and live them down, and here he had been overtaken at last and beaten into resignation that had nothing to do with his mind or heart. It was as if his blood stream had betrayed him. The prospect of taking a job and being a decent little clerk with shiny pants and elbows—for he couldn't think of a job in any other terms—seemed like a kind of premature death which would not even compensate him with loss of memory. He didn't do anything about it at all. He did odd jobs and picked up a little money, but never enough. He could see her side of it, at least he tried hard to see it. When it came to a showdown, he hadn't a single argument in favor of his way of life that would hold water. He had been trying to live and think in a way that he hoped would end by making a poet of him, but it hadn't worked. That was the long and short of it. So he might have just gone on to some unimaginably sordid end if Miriam, after four years: four years? yes, good God, four years and one month and eleven days, had not written home for money, packed up what was left of her belongings, called him a few farewell names, and left. She had been shabby and thin and wild-looking for so long he could not remember ever having seen her any other way, yet all at once her profile in the doorway was unrecognizable to him.

So she went, and she did him a great favor without knowing it. He had fallen into the cowardly habit of thinking their marriage was permanent, no matter how evil it might be, that they loved each other, and so it did not matter what cruelties they committed against each other, and he had developed a real deafness to her words. He was unable, towards the end, either to see her or hear her. He realized this afterward, when remembered phrases and expressions of her eyes and mouth began to eat into his marrow. He was grateful to her. If she had not gone, he might have loitered on, wasting his time trying to write poetry, hanging around dirty picturesque little cafés with a fresh set of clever talkative poverty-stricken young Mexicans who were painting or writing or talking about getting ready to paint or write. His faith had renewed itself; these fellows were pure artists—they would never sell out. They were not bums, either. They worked all the time at something to do with Art. "Sacred Art," he said, "our glasses are empty again."

But try telling anything of the kind to Miriam. Somehow he had never got to that tree he meant to lie down under. If he had, somebody would certainly have come around and collected rent for it, anyhow. He had spent a good deal of time lying under tables at Dinty Moore's or the Black Cat with a gang of Americans like himself who were living a free life and studying the native customs. He was rehearsing, he explained to Miriam, hoping for once she would take a joke, for lying under a tree later on. It didn't go over. She would have died with her boots on before she would have cracked a smile at that. So then . . . He had gone in for a career in the hugest sort of way. It had been easy. He hardly could say now just what his first steps were, but it had been easy. Except for Miriam, he would have been a lousy failure, like those bums at Dinty Moore's, still rolling under the tables, studying the native customs. He had gone in for a career in journalism and he had made a good thing of it. He was a recognized authority on revolutions in twenty-odd Latin-American countries, and his sympathies happened to fall in exactly right with the high-priced magazines of a liberal humanitarian slant which paid him well for telling the world about the oppressed peoples. He could really write, too; if he did say so, he had a prose style of his own. He had made the kind of success you can clip out of newspapers and paste in a book, you can count it and put it in the bank, you can eat and drink and wear it, and you can see it in other people's eyes at tea and dinner parties. Fine, and now what? On the strength of all this he had got married again. Twice, in fact, and divorced twice. That made three times, didn't it? That was plenty. He had spent a good deal of time and energy doing all sorts of things he didn't care for in the least to prove to his first wife, who had been a twenty-three-year-old schoolteacher in Minneapolis, Minnesota, that he was not just merely a bum, fit for nothing but lying under a tree—if he had ever been able to locate that ideal tree he had in his mind's eye—writing poetry and enjoying his life.

Now he had done it. He smoothed out the letter he had been turning in his hands and stroked it as if it were a cat. He said, "I've been working up to the climax all this time. You know, good old surprise technique. Now then, get ready."

Miriam had written to him, after these five years, asking him to take her back. And would you believe it, he was going to break down and do that very thing. Her father was dead, she was terribly lonely, she had had time to think everything over, she believed herself to blame for a great many things, she loved him truly and she always had, truly; she regretted, oh, everything, and hoped it was not too late for them to make a happy life together once more. . . . She had read everything she could find of his in print, and she loved all of it. He had that very morning sent by cable the money for her to travel on, and he was going to take her back. She was going to live again in a Mexican house without any conveniences and she was not going to have a modern flat. She was going to take whatever he chose to hand her, and like it. And he wasn't going to marry her again, either. Not he. If she wanted to live with him on these terms, well and good. If not, she could just go back once more to that school of hers in Minneapolis. If she stayed, she would walk a chalk line, all right, one she hadn't drawn for herself. He picked up a cheese knife and drew a long sharp line in the checkered table-cloth. She would, believe him, walk *that*.

The hands of the clock pointed half past two. The journalist swallowed the last of his drink and went on drawing more cross-hatches on the table-cloth with a relaxed hand. His guest wished to say, "Don't forget to invite me to your wedding," but thought better of it. The journalist raised his twitching lids and swung his half-focused eyes upon the shadow opposite and said, "I suppose you think I don't know—"

His guest moved to the chair edge and watched the orchestra folding up for the night. The café was almost empty. The journalist paused, not for an answer, but to give weight to the important statement he was about to make.

"I don't know what's happening, this time," he said, "don't deceive yourself. This time, I know." He seemed to be admonishing himself before a mirror.

The Jilting of Granny Weatherall

SHE flicked her wrist neatly out of Doctor Harry's pudgy careful fingers and pulled the sheet up to her chin. The brat ought to be in knee breeches. Doctoring around the country with spectacles on his nose! "Get along now, take your schoolbooks and go. There's nothing wrong with me."

Doctor Harry spread a warm paw like a cushion on her forehead where the forked green vein danced and made her eyelids twitch. "Now, now, be a good girl, and we'll have you up in no time."

"That's no way to speak to a woman nearly eighty years old just because she's down. I'd have you respect your elders, young man."

"Well, Missy, excuse me." Doctor Harry patted her cheek. "But I've got to warn you, haven't I? You're a marvel, but you must be careful or you're going to be good and sorry."

"Don't tell me what I'm going to be. I'm on my feet now, morally speaking. It's Cornelia. I had to go to bed to get rid of her."

Her bones felt loose, and floated around in her skin, and Doctor Harry floated like a balloon around the foot of the bed. He floated and pulled down his waistcoat and swung his glasses on a cord. "Well, stay where you are, it certainly can't hurt you."

"Get along and doctor your sick," said Granny Weatherall. "Leave a well woman alone. I'll call for you when I want you. . . . Where were you forty years ago when I pulled through milk-leg and double pneumonia? You weren't even born. Don't let Cornelia lead you on," she shouted, because Doctor Harry appeared to float up to the ceiling and out. "I pay my own bills, and I don't throw my money away on nonsense!"

She meant to wave good-by, but it was too much trouble. Her eyes closed of themselves, it was like a dark curtain drawn around the bed. The pillow rose and floated under her, pleasant as a hammock in a light wind. She listened to the leaves rustling outside the window. No, somebody was swishing newspapers: no, Cornelia and Doctor Harry were whispering together. She leaped broad awake, thinking they whispered in her ear.

"She was never like this, *never* like this!" "Well, what can we expect?" "Yes, eighty years old. . . ."

Well, and what if she was? She still had ears. It was like Cornelia to whisper around doors. She always kept things secret in such a public way. She was always being tactful and kind. Cornelia was dutiful; that was the trouble with her. Dutiful and good: "So good and dutiful," said Granny, "that I'd like to spank her." She saw herself spanking Cornelia and making a fine job of it.

"What'd you say, Mother?"

Granny felt her face tying up in hard knots.

"Can't a body think, I'd like to know?"

"I thought you might want something."

"I do. I want a lot of things. First off, go away and don't whisper."

She lay and drowsed, hoping in her sleep that the children would keep out and let her rest a minute. It had been a long day. Not that she was tired. It was always pleasant to snatch a minute now and then. There was always so much to be done, let me see: tomorrow.

Tomorrow was far away and there was nothing to trouble about. Things were finished somehow when the time came; thank God there was always a little margin over for peace: then a person could spread out the plan of life and tuck in the edges orderly. It was good to have everything clean and folded away, with the hair brushes and tonic bottles sitting straight on the white embroidered linen: the day started without fuss and the pantry shelves laid out with rows of jelly glasses and brown jugs and white stone-china jars with blue whirligigs and words painted on them: coffee, tea, sugar, ginger, cinnamon, allspice: and the bronze clock with the lion on top nicely dusted off. The dust that lion could collect in twenty-four hours! The box in the attic with all those letters tied up, well, she'd have to go through that tomorrow. All those letters—George's letters and John's letters and her letters to them both—lying around for the children to find afterwards made her uneasy. Yes, that would be tomorrow's business. No use to let them know how silly she had been once.

While she was rummaging around she found death in her mind and it felt clammy and unfamiliar. She had spent so much time preparing for death there was no need for bringing it up again. Let it take care of itself now. When she was sixty she had felt very old, finished, and went around making farewell trips to see her children and grandchildren, with a secret in her mind: This is the very last of your mother, children! Then she made her will and came down with a long fever. That was all just a notion like a lot of other things, but it was lucky too, for she had once for all got over the idea of dying for a long time. Now she couldn't be worried. She hoped she had better sense now. Her father had lived to be one hundred and two years old and had drunk a noggin of strong hot toddy on his last birthday. He told the reporters it was his daily habit, and he owed his long life to that. He had made quite a scandal and was very pleased about it. She believed she'd just plague Cornelia a little.

"Cornelia! Cornelia!" No footsteps, but a sudden hand on her cheek. "Bless you, where have you been?"

"Here, Mother."

"Well, Cornelia, I want a noggin of hot toddy."

"Are you cold, darling?"

"I'm chilly, Cornelia. Lying in bed stops the circulation. I must have told you that a thousand times."

Well, she could just hear Cornelia telling her husband that Mother was getting a little childish and they'd have to humor her. The thing that most annoyed her was that Cornelia thought she was deaf, dumb, and blind. Little hasty glances and tiny gestures tossed around her and over her head saying, "Don't cross her, let her have her way, she's eighty years old," and she sitting there as if she lived in a thin glass cage. Sometimes Granny almost made up her mind to pack up and move back to her own house where nobody could remind her every minute that she was old. Wait, wait, Cornelia, till your own children whisper behind your back!

In her day she had kept a better house and had got more work done. She wasn't too old yet for Lydia to be driving eighty miles for advice when one of the children jumped the track, and Jimmy still dropped in and talked things over: "Now, Mammy, you've a good business head, I want to know what you think of this? . . ." Old. Cornelia couldn't change the furniture around without asking. Little things, little things! They had been so sweet when they were little. Granny wished the old days were back again with the children young and everything to be done over. It had been a hard pull, but not too much for her. When she thought of all the food she had cooked, and all the clothes she had cut and sewed, and all the gardens she had made—well, the children showed it. There they were, made out of her, and they couldn't get away from that. Sometimes she wanted to see John again and point to them and say, Well, I didn't do so badly, did I? But that would have to wait. That was for tomorrow. She used to think of him as a man, but now all the children were older than their father, and he would be a child beside her if she saw him now. It seemed strange and there was something wrong in the idea. Why, he couldn't possibly recognize her. She had fenced in a hundred acres once, digging the post holes herself and clamping the wires with just a negro boy to help. That changed a woman. John would be looking for a young woman with the peaked Spanish comb in her hair and the painted fan. Digging post holes changed a woman. Riding country roads in the winter when women had their babies was another thing: sitting up nights with sick horses and sick negroes and sick children and hardly ever losing one. John, I hardly ever lost one of them! John would see that in a minute, that would be something he could understand, she wouldn't have to explain anything!

It made her feel like rolling up her sleeves and putting the whole place to rights again. No matter if Cornelia was determined to be everywhere at once, there were a great many things left undone on this place. She would start tomorrow and do them. It was good to be strong enough for everything, even if all you made melted and changed and slipped under your hands, so that by the time you finished you almost forgot what you were working for. What was it I set out to do? she asked herself intently, but she could not remember. A fog rose over the valley, she saw it marching across the creek swallowing the trees and moving up the hill like an army of ghosts. Soon it would be at the near edge of the orchard, and then it was time to go in and light the lamps. Come in, children, don't stay out in the night air.

Lighting the lamps had been beautiful. The children huddled up to her and breathed like little calves waiting at the bars
in the twilight. Their eyes followed the match and watched the
flame rise and settle in a blue curve, then they moved away
from her. The lamp was lit, they didn't have to be scared and
hang on to mother any more. Never, never, never more. God,
for all my life I thank Thee. Without Thee, my God, I could
never have done it. Hail, Mary, full of grace.

I want you to pick all the fruit this year and see that nothing
is wasted. There's always someone who can use it. Don't let
good things rot for want of using. You waste life when you
waste good food. Don't let things get lost. It's bitter to lose
things. Now, don't let me get to thinking, not when I am tired
and taking a little nap before supper. . . .

The pillow rose about her shoulders and pressed against her
heart and the memory was being squeezed out of it: oh, push
down the pillow, somebody: it would smother her if she tried
to hold it. Such a fresh breeze blowing and such a green day
with no threats in it. But he had not come, just the same. What
does a woman do when she has put on the white veil and set
out the white cake for a man and he doesn't come? She tried to
remember. No, I swear he never harmed me but in that. He
never harmed me but in that . . . and what if he did? There
was the day, the day, but a whirl of dark smoke rose and covered it, crept up and over into the bright field where everything was planted so carefully in orderly rows. That was hell,
she knew hell when she saw it. For sixty years she had prayed
against remembering him and against losing her soul in the
deep pit of hell, and now the two things were mingled in one
and the thought of him was a smoky cloud from hell that
moved and crept in her head when she had just got rid of Doctor Harry and was trying to rest a minute. Wounded vanity,
Ellen, said a sharp voice in the top of her mind. Don't let your
wounded vanity get the upper hand of you. Plenty of girls get
jilted. You were jilted, weren't you? Then stand up to it. Her
eyelids wavered and let in streamers of blue-gray light like tissue paper over her eyes. She must get up and pull the shades
down or she'd never sleep. She was in bed again and the
shades were not down. How could that happen? Better turn
over, hide from the light, sleeping in the light gave you night-

mares. "Mother, how do you feel now?" and a stinging wet-ness on her forehead. But I don't like having my face washed in cold water!

Hapsy? George? Lydia? Jimmy? No, Cornelia, and her fea-tures were swollen and full of little puddles. "They're coming, darling, they'll all be here soon." Go wash your face, child, you look funny.

Instead of obeying, Cornelia knelt down and put her head on the pillow. She seemed to be talking but there was no sound. "Well, are you tongue-tied? Whose birthday is it? Are you going to give a party?"

Cornelia's mouth moved urgently in strange shapes. "Don't do that, you bother me, daughter."

"Oh, no, Mother. Oh, no. . . ."

Nonsense. It was strange about children. They disputed your every word. "No what, Cornelia?"

"Here's Doctor Harry."

"I won't see that boy again. He just left five minutes ago."

"That was this morning, Mother. It's night now. Here's the nurse."

"This is Doctor Harry, Mrs. Weatherall. I never saw you look so young and happy!"

"Ah, I'll never be young again—but I'd be happy if they'd let me lie in peace and get rested."

She thought she spoke up loudly, but no one answered. A warm weight on her forehead, a warm bracelet on her wrist, and a breeze went on whispering, trying to tell her something. A shuffle of leaves in the everlasting hand of God, He blew on them and they danced and rattled. "Mother, don't mind, we're going to give you a little hypodermic." "Look here, daughter, how do ants get in this bed? I saw sugar ants yesterday." Did you send for Hapsy too?

It was Hapsy she really wanted. She had to go a long way back through a great many rooms to find Hapsy standing with a baby on her arm. She seemed to herself to be Hapsy also, and the baby on Hapsy's arm was Hapsy and himself and herself, all at once, and there was no surprise in the meeting. Then Hapsy melted from within and turned flimsy as gray gauze and the baby was a gauzy shadow, and Hapsy came up close and said, "I thought you'd never come," and looked at her very searchingly and said, "You haven't changed a bit!" They leaned forward to kiss, when Cornelia began whispering from a long way off, "Oh, is there anything you want to tell me? Is there anything I can do for you?"

Yes, she had changed her mind after sixty years and she would like to see George. I want you to find George. Find him and be sure to tell him I forgot him. I want him to know I had my husband just the same and my children and my house like any other woman. A good house too and a good husband that I loved and fine children out of him. Better than I hoped for even. Tell him I was given back everything he took away and more. Oh, no, oh, God, no, there was something else besides the house and the man and the children. Oh, surely they were not all? What was it? Something not given back. . . . Her breath crowded down under her ribs and grew into a monstrous frightening shape with cutting edges; it bored up into her head, and the agony was unbelievable: Yes, John, get the Doctor now, no more talk, my time has come.

When this one was born it should be the last. The last. It should have been born first, for it was the one she had truly wanted. Everything came in good time. Nothing left out, left over. She was strong, in three days she would be as well as ever. Better. A woman needed milk in her to have her full health.

"Mother, do you hear me?"

"I've been telling you—"

"Mother, Father Connolly's here."

"I went to Holy Communion only last week. Tell him I'm not so sinful as all that."

"Father just wants to speak to you."

He could speak as much as he pleased. It was like him to drop in and inquire about her soul as if it were a teething baby, and then stay on for a cup of tea and a round of cards and gossip. He always had a funny story of some sort, usually about an Irishman who made his little mistakes and confessed them, and the point lay in some absurd thing he would blurt out in the confessional showing his struggles between native piety and original sin. Granny felt easy about her soul. Cornelia, where are your manners? Give Father Connolly a chair. She had her secret comfortable understanding with a few favorite saints who cleared a straight road to God for her. All as surely signed and

sealed as the papers for the new Forty Acres. Forever . . .
heirs and assigns forever. Since the day the wedding cake was
not cut, but thrown out and wasted. The whole bottom
dropped out of the world, and there she was blind and sweating
with nothing under her feet and the walls falling away. His
hand had caught her under the breast, she had not fallen, there
was the freshly polished floor with the green rug on it, just as
before. He had cursed like a sailor's parrot and said, "I'll kill
him for you." Don't lay a hand on him, for my sake leave
something to God. "Now, Ellen, you must believe what I tell
you. . . ."

So there was nothing, nothing to worry about any more, except sometimes in the night one of the children screamed in a
nightmare, and they both hustled out shaking and hunting for
the matches and calling, "There, wait a minute, here we are!"
John, get the doctor now, Hapsy's time has come. But there
was Hapsy standing by the bed in a white cap. "Cornelia, tell
Hapsy to take off her cap. I can't see her plain."

Her eyes opened very wide and the room stood out like a
picture she had seen somewhere. Dark colors with the shadows
rising towards the ceiling in long angles. The tall black dresser
gleamed with nothing on it but John's picture, enlarged from
a little one, with John's eyes very black when they should have
been blue. You never saw him, so how do you know how he
looked? But the man insisted the copy was perfect, it was very
rich and handsome. For a picture, yes, but it's not my husband. The table by the bed had a linen cover and a candle and
a crucifix. The light was blue from Cornelia's silk lampshades.
No sort of light at all, just frippery. You had to live forty years
with kerosene lamps to appreciate honest electricity. She felt
very strong and she saw Doctor Harry with a rosy nimbus
around him.

"You look like a saint, Doctor Harry, and I vow that's as
near as you'll ever come to it."

"She's saying something."

"I heard you, Cornelia. What's all this carrying-on?"

"Father Connolly's saying—"

Cornelia's voice staggered and bumped like a cart in a bad
road. It rounded corners and turned back again and arrived
nowhere. Granny stepped up in the cart very lightly and

reached for the reins, but a man sat beside her and she knew him by his hands, driving the cart. She did not look in his face, for she knew without seeing, but looked instead down the road where the trees leaned over and bowed to each other and a thousand birds were singing a Mass. She felt like singing too, but she put her hand in the bosom of her dress and pulled out a rosary, and Father Connolly murmured Latin in a very solemn voice and tickled her feet. My God, will you stop that nonsense? I'm a married woman. What if he did run away and leave me to face the priest by myself? I found another a whole world better. I wouldn't have exchanged my husband for anybody except St. Michael himself, and you may tell him that for me with a thank you in the bargain.

Light flashed on her closed eyelids, and a deep roaring shook her. Cornelia, is that lightning? I hear thunder. There's going to be a storm. Close all the windows. Call the children in. . . . "Mother, here we are, all of us." "Is that you, Hapsy?" "Oh, no, I'm Lydia. We drove as fast as we could." Their faces drifted above her, drifted away. The rosary fell out of her hands and Lydia put it back. Jimmy tried to help, their hands fumbled together, and Granny closed two fingers around Jimmy's thumb. Beads wouldn't do, it must be something alive. She was so amazed her thoughts ran round and round. So, my dear Lord, this is my death and I wasn't even thinking about it. My children have come to see me die. But I can't, it's not time. Oh, I always hated surprises. I wanted to give Cornelia the amethyst set—Cornelia, you're to have the amethyst set, but Hapsy's to wear it when she wants, and, Doctor Harry, do shut up. Nobody sent for you. Oh, my dear Lord, do wait a minute. I meant to do something about the Forty Acres, Jimmy doesn't need it and Lydia will later on, with that worthless husband of hers. I meant to finish the altar cloth and send six bottles of wine to Sister Borgia for her dyspepsia. I want to send six bottles of wine to Sister Borgia, Father Connolly, now don't let me forget.

Cornelia's voice made short turns and tilted over and crashed. "Oh, Mother, oh, Mother, oh, Mother. . . ."

"I'm not going, Cornelia. I'm taken by surprise. I can't go."

You'll see Hapsy again. What about her? "I thought you'd never come." Granny made a long journey outward, looking for Hapsy. What if I don't find her? What then? Her heart sank down and down, there was no bottom to death, she couldn't come to the end of it. The blue light from Cornelia's lampshade drew into a tiny point in the center of her brain, it flickered and winked like an eye, quietly it fluttered and dwindled. Granny lay curled down within herself, amazed and watchful, staring at the point of light that was herself; her body was now only a deeper mass of shadow in an endless darkness and this darkness would curl around the light and swallow it up. God, give a sign!

For the second time there was no sign. Again no bridegroom and the priest in the house. She could not remember any other sorrow because this grief wiped them all away. Oh, no, there's nothing more cruel than this—I'll never forgive it. She stretched herself with a deep breath and blew out the light.

Flowering Judas

BRAGGIONI sits heaped upon the edge of a straight-backed chair much too small for him, and sings to Laura in a furry, mournful voice. Laura has begun to find reasons for avoiding her own house until the latest possible moment, for Braggioni is there almost every night. No matter how late she is, he will be sitting there with a surly, waiting expression, pulling at his kinky yellow hair, thumbing the strings of his guitar, snarling a tune under his breath. Lupe the Indian maid meets Laura at the door, and says with a flicker of a glance towards the upper room, "He waits."

Laura wishes to lie down, she is tired of her hairpins and the feel of her long tight sleeves, but she says to him, "Have you a new song for me this evening?" If he says yes, she asks him to sing it. If he says no, she remembers his favorite one, and asks him to sing it again. Lupe brings her a cup of chocolate and a plate of rice, and Laura eats at the small table under the lamp, first inviting Braggioni, whose answer is always the same: "I have eaten, and besides, chocolate thickens the voice."

Laura says, "Sing, then," and Braggioni heaves himself into song. He scratches the guitar familiarly as though it were a pet animal, and sings passionately off key, taking the high notes in a prolonged painful squeal. Laura, who haunts the markets listening to the ballad singers, and stops every day to hear the blind boy playing his reed-flute in Sixteenth of September Street, listens to Braggioni with pitiless courtesy, because she dares not smile at his miserable performance. Nobody dares to smile at him. Braggioni is cruel to everyone, with a kind of specialized insolence, but he is so vain of his talents, and so sensitive to slights, it would require a cruelty and vanity greater than his own to lay a finger on the vast cureless wound of his self-esteem. It would require courage, too, for it is dangerous to offend him, and nobody has this courage.

Braggioni loves himself with such tenderness and amplitude and eternal charity that his followers—for he is a leader of men, a skilled revolutionist, and his skin has been punctured in honorable warfare—warm themselves in the reflected glow, and say to each other: "He has a real nobility, a love of humanity raised above mere personal affections." The excess of this self-love has flowed out, inconveniently for her, over Laura, who, with so many others, owes her comfortable situation and her salary to him. When he is in a very good humor, he tells her, "I am tempted to forgive you for being a *gringa. Gringita!*" and Laura, burning, imagines herself leaning forward suddenly, and with a sound back-handed slap wiping the suety smile from his face. If he notices her eyes at these moments he gives no sign.

She knows what Braggioni would offer her, and she must resist tenaciously without appearing to resist, and if she could avoid it she would not admit even to herself the slow drift of his intention. During these long evenings which have spoiled a long month for her, she sits in her deep chair with an open book on her knees, resting her eyes on the consoling rigidity of the printed page when the sight and sound of Braggioni singing threaten to identify themselves with all her remembered afflictions and to add their weight to her uneasy premonitions of the future. The gluttonous bulk of Braggioni has become a symbol of her many disillusions, for a revolutionist should be lean, animated by heroic faith, a vessel of abstract virtues. This is nonsense, she knows it now and is ashamed of it. Revolution must have leaders, and leadership is a career for energetic men. She is, her comrades tell her, full of romantic error, for what she defines as cynicism in them is merely "a developed sense of reality." She is almost too willing to say, "I am wrong, I suppose I don't really understand the principles," and afterward she makes a secret truce with herself, determined not to surrender her will to such expedient logic. But she cannot help feeling that she has been betrayed irreparably by the disunion between her way of living and her feeling of what life should be, and at times she is almost contented to rest in this sense of grievance as a private store of consolation. Sometimes she wishes to run away, but she stays. Now she longs to fly out of this room, down the narrow stairs, and into the street where the houses lean together like conspirators under a single mottled lamp, and leave Braggioni singing to himself.

Instead she looks at Braggioni, frankly and clearly, like a good child who understands the rules of behavior. Her knees

cling together under sound blue serge, and her round white
collar is not purposely nun-like. She wears the uniform of an
idea, and has renounced vanities. She was born Roman Catholic, and in spite of her fear of being seen by someone who
might make a scandal of it, she slips now and again into some
crumbling little church, kneels on the chilly stone, and says a
Hail Mary on the gold rosary she bought in Tehuantepec. It is
no good and she ends by examining the altar with its tinsel
flowers and ragged brocades, and feels tender about the battered doll-shape of some male saint whose white, lace-trimmed
drawers hang limply around his ankles below the hieratic dignity of his velvet robe. She has encased herself in a set of principles derived from her early training, leaving no detail of
gesture or of personal taste untouched, and for this reason she
will not wear lace made on machines. This is her private heresy,
for in her special group the machine is sacred, and will be the
salvation of the workers. She loves fine lace, and there is a tiny
edge of fluted cobweb on this collar, which is one of twenty
precisely alike, folded in blue tissue paper in the upper drawer
of her clothes chest.

Braggioni catches her glance solidly as if he had been waiting
for it, leans forward, balancing his paunch between his spread
knees, and sings with tremendous emphasis, weighing his
words. He has, the song relates, no father and no mother, nor
even a friend to console him; lonely as a wave of the sea he
comes and goes, lonely as a wave. His mouth opens round and
yearns sideways, his balloon cheeks grow oily with the labor of
song. He bulges marvelously in his expensive garments. Over
his lavender collar, crushed upon a purple necktie, held by a
diamond hoop: over his ammunition belt of tooled leather
worked in silver, buckled cruelly around his gasping middle:
over the tops of his glossy yellow shoes Braggioni swells with
ominous ripeness, his mauve silk hose stretched taut, his ankles
bound with the stout leather thongs of his shoes.

When he stretches his eyelids at Laura she notes again that
his eyes are the true tawny yellow cat's eyes. He is rich, not in
money, he tells her, but in power, and this power brings with it
the blameless ownership of things, and the right to indulge his
love of small luxuries. "I have a taste for the elegant refine-
ments," he said once, flourishing a yellow silk handkerchief

before her nose. "Smell that? It is Jockey Club, imported from New York." Nonetheless he is wounded by life. He will say so presently. "It is true everything turns to dust in the hand, to gall on the tongue." He sighs and his leather belt creaks like a saddle girth. "I am disappointed in everything as it comes. Everything." He shakes his head. "You, poor thing, you will be disappointed too. You are born for it. We are more alike than you realize in some things. Wait and see. Some day you will remember what I have told you, you will know that Braggioni was your friend."

Laura feels a slow chill, a purely physical sense of danger, a warning in her blood that violence, mutilation, a shocking death, wait for her with lessening patience. She has translated this fear into something homely, immediate, and sometimes hesitates before crossing the street. "My personal fate is nothing, except as the testimony of a mental attitude," she reminds herself, quoting from some forgotten philosophic primer, and is sensible enough to add, "Anyhow, I shall not be killed by an automobile if I can help it."

"It may be true I am as corrupt, in another way, as Braggioni," she thinks in spite of herself, "as callous, as incomplete," and if this is so, any kind of death seems preferable. Still she sits quietly, she does not run. Where could she go? Uninvited she has promised herself to this place; she can no longer imagine herself as living in another country, and there is no pleasure in remembering her life before she came here.

Precisely what is the nature of this devotion, its true motives, and what are its obligations? Laura cannot say. She spends part of her days in Xochimilco, near by, teaching Indian children to say in English, "The cat is on the mat." When she appears in the classroom they crowd about her with smiles on their wise, innocent, clay-colored faces, crying, "Good morning, my titcher!" in immaculate voices, and they make of her desk a fresh garden of flowers every day.

During her leisure she goes to union meetings and listens to busy important voices quarreling over tactics, methods, internal politics. She visits the prisoners of her own political faith in their cells, where they entertain themselves with counting cockroaches, repenting of their indiscretions, composing their memoirs, writing out manifestoes and plans for their comrades

who are still walking about free, hands in pockets, sniffing
fresh air. Laura brings them food and cigarettes and a little
money, and she brings messages disguised in equivocal phrases
from the men outside who dare not set foot in the prison for
fear of disappearing into the cells kept empty for them. If the
prisoners confuse night and day, and complain, "Dear little
Laura, time doesn't pass in this infernal hole, and I won't
know when it is time to sleep unless I have a reminder," she
brings them their favorite narcotics, and says in a tone that
does not wound them with pity, "Tonight will really be night
for you," and though her Spanish amuses them, they find her
comforting, useful. If they lose patience and all faith, and curse
the slowness of their friends in coming to their rescue with
money and influence, they trust her not to repeat everything,
and if she inquires, "Where do you think we can find money,
or influence?" they are certain to answer, "Well, there is Braggioni, why doesn't he do something?"

She smuggles letters from headquarters to men hiding from
firing squads in back streets in mildewed houses, where they sit
in tumbled beds and talk bitterly as if all Mexico were at their
heels, when Laura knows positively they might appear at the
band concert in the Alameda on Sunday morning, and no one
would notice them. But Braggioni says, "Let them sweat a
little. The next time they may be careful. It is very restful to have
them out of the way for a while." She is not afraid to knock on
any door in any street after midnight, and enter in the darkness, and say to one of these men who is really in danger:
"They will be looking for you—seriously—tomorrow morning
after six. Here is some money from Vicente. Go to Vera Cruz
and wait."

She borrows money from the Roumanian agitator to give
to his bitter enemy the Polish agitator. The favor of Braggioni
is their disputed territory, and Braggioni holds the balance
nicely, for he can use them both. The Polish agitator talks love
to her over café tables, hoping to exploit what he believes is her
secret sentimental preference for him, and he gives her misinformation which he begs her to repeat as the solemn truth to
certain persons. The Roumanian is more adroit. He is generous with his money in all good causes, and lies to her with an
air of ingenuous candor, as if he were her good friend and con-

fidant. She never repeats anything they may say. Braggioni never asks questions. He has other ways to discover all that he wishes to know about them.

Nobody touches her, but all praise her gray eyes, and the soft, round under lip which promises gayety, yet is always grave, nearly always firmly closed: and they cannot understand why she is in Mexico. She walks back and forth on her errands, with puzzled eyebrows, carrying her little folder of drawings and music and school papers. No dancer dances more beautifully than Laura walks, and she inspires some amusing, unexpected ardors, which cause little gossip, because nothing comes of them. A young captain who had been a soldier in Zapata's army attempted, during a horseback ride near Cuernavaca, to express his desire for her with the noble simplicity befitting a rude folk-hero: but gently, because he was gentle. This gentleness was his defeat, for when he alighted, and removed her foot from the stirrup, and essayed to draw her down into his arms, her horse, ordinarily a tame one, shied fiercely, reared and plunged away. The young hero's horse careered blindly after his stable-mate, and the hero did not return to the hotel until rather late that evening. At breakfast he came to her table in full charro dress, gray buckskin jacket and trousers with strings of silver buttons down the leg, and he was in a humorous, careless mood. "May I sit with you?" and "You are a wonderful rider. I was terrified that you might be thrown and dragged. I should never have forgiven myself. But I cannot admire you enough for your riding!"

"I learned to ride in Arizona," said Laura.

"If you will ride with me again this morning, I promise you a horse that will not shy with you," he said. But Laura remembered that she must return to Mexico City at noon.

Next morning the children made a celebration and spent their playtime writing on the blackboard, "We lov ar ticher," and with tinted chalks they drew wreaths of flowers around the words. The young hero wrote her a letter: "I am a very foolish, wasteful, impulsive man. I should have first said I love you, and then you would not have run away. But you shall see me again." Laura thought, "I must send him a box of colored crayons," but she was trying to forgive herself for having spurred her horse at the wrong moment.

A brown, shock-haired youth came and stood in her patio one night and sang like a lost soul for two hours, but Laura could think of nothing to do about it. The moonlight spread a wash of gauzy silver over the clear spaces of the garden, and the shadows were cobalt blue. The scarlet blossoms of the Judas tree were dull purple, and the names of the colors repeated themselves automatically in her mind, while she watched not the boy, but his shadow, fallen like a dark garment across the fountain rim, trailing in the water. Lupe came silently and whispered expert counsel in her ear: "If you will throw him one little flower, he will sing another song or two and go away." Laura threw the flower, and he sang a last song and went away with the flower tucked in the band of his hat. Lupe said, "He is one of the organizers of the Typographers Union, and before that he sold corridos in the Merced market, and before that, he came from Guanajuato, where I was born. I would not trust any man, but I trust least those from Guanajuato."

She did not tell Laura that he would be back again the next night, and the next, nor that he would follow her at a certain fixed distance around the Merced market, through the Zócalo, up Francisco I. Madero Avenue, and so along the Paseo de la Reforma to Chapultepec Park, and into the Philosopher's Footpath, still with that flower withering in his hat, and an indivisible attention in his eyes.

Now Laura is accustomed to him, it means nothing except that he is nineteen years old and is observing a convention with all propriety, as though it were founded on a law of nature, which in the end it might well prove to be. He is beginning to write poems which he prints on a wooden press, and he leaves them stuck like handbills in her door. She is pleasantly disturbed by the abstract, unhurried watchfulness of his black eyes which will in time turn easily towards another object. She tells herself that throwing the flower was a mistake, for she is twenty-two years old and knows better; but she refuses to regret it, and persuades herself that her negation of all external events as they occur is a sign that she is gradually perfecting herself in the stoicism she strives to cultivate against that disaster she fears, though she cannot name it.

She is not at home in the world. Every day she teaches children who remain strangers to her, though she loves their tender round hands and their charming opportunist savagery. She knocks at unfamiliar doors not knowing whether a friend or a stranger shall answer, and even if a known face emerges from the sour gloom of that unknown interior, still it is the face of a stranger. No matter what this stranger says to her, nor what her message to him, the very cells of her flesh reject knowledge and kinship in one monotonous word. No. No. No. She draws her strength from this one holy talismanic word which does not suffer her to be led into evil. Denying everything, she may walk anywhere in safety, she looks at everything without amazement.

No, repeats this firm unchanging voice of her blood; and she looks at Braggioni without amazement. He is a great man, he wishes to impress this simple girl who covers her great round breasts with thick dark cloth, and who hides long, invaluably beautiful legs under a heavy skirt. She is almost thin except for the incomprehensible fullness of her breasts, like a nursing mother's, and Braggioni, who considers himself a judge of women, speculates again on the puzzle of her notorious virginity, and takes the liberty of speech which she permits without a sign of modesty, indeed, without any sort of sign, which is disconcerting.

"You think you are so cold, *gringita!* Wait and see. You will surprise yourself some day! May I be there to advise you!" He stretches his eyelids at her, and his ill-humored cat's eyes waver in a separate glance for the two points of light marking the opposite ends of a smoothly drawn path between the swollen curve of her breasts. He is not put off by that blue serge, nor by her resolutely fixed gaze. There is all the time in the world. His cheeks are bellying with the wind of song. "O girl with the dark eyes," he sings, and reconsiders. "But yours are not dark. I can change all that. O girl with the green eyes, you have stolen my heart away!" then his mind wanders to the song, and Laura feels the weight of his attention being shifted elsewhere. Singing thus, he seems harmless, he is quite harmless, there is nothing to do but sit patiently and say "No," when the moment comes. She draws a full breath, and her mind wanders also, but not far. She dares not wander too far.

Not for nothing has Braggioni taken pains to be a good

revolutionist and a professional lover of humanity. He will never die of it. He has the malice, the cleverness, the wickedness, the sharpness of wit, the hardness of heart, stipulated for loving the world profitably. *He will never die of it.* He will live to see himself kicked out from his feeding trough by other hungry world-saviors. Traditionally he must sing in spite of his life which drives him to bloodshed, he tells Laura, for his father was a Tuscany peasant who drifted to Yucatan and married a Maya woman: a woman of race, an aristocrat. They gave him the love and knowledge of music, thus: and under the rip of his thumbnail, the strings of the instrument complain like exposed nerves.

Once he was called Delgadito by all the girls and married women who ran after him; he was so scrawny all his bones showed under his thin cotton clothing, and he could squeeze his emptiness to the very backbone with his two hands. He was a poet and the revolution was only a dream then; too many women loved him and sapped away his youth, and he could never find enough to eat anywhere, anywhere! Now he is a leader of men, crafty men who whisper in his ear, hungry men who wait for hours outside his office for a word with him, emaciated men with wild faces who waylay him at the street gate with a timid, "Comrade, let me tell you . . ." and they blow the foul breath from their empty stomachs in his face.

He is always sympathetic. He gives them handfuls of small coins from his own pocket, he promises them work, there will be demonstrations, they must join the unions and attend the meetings, above all they must be on the watch for spies. They are closer to him than his own brothers, without them he can do nothing—until tomorrow, comrade!

Until tomorrow. "They are stupid, they are lazy, they are treacherous, they would cut my throat for nothing," he says to Laura. He has good food and abundant drink, he hires an automobile and drives in the Paseo on Sunday morning, and enjoys plenty of sleep in a soft bed beside a wife who dares not disturb him; and he sits pampering his bones in easy billows of fat, singing to Laura, who knows and thinks these things about him. When he was fifteen, he tried to drown himself because he loved a girl, his first love, and she laughed at him. "A thousand women have paid for that," and his tight little mouth turns down at the corners. Now he perfumes his hair with Jockey Club, and confides to Laura: "One woman is really as good as another for me, in the dark. I prefer them all."

His wife organizes unions among the girls in the cigarette factories, and walks in picket lines, and even speaks at meetings in the evening. But she cannot be brought to acknowledge the benefits of true liberty. "I tell her I must have my freedom, net. She does not understand my point of view." Laura has heard this many times. Braggioni scratches the guitar and meditates. "She is an instinctively virtuous woman, pure gold, no doubt of that. If she were not, I should lock her up, and she knows it."

His wife, who works so hard for the good of the factory girls, employs part of her leisure lying on the floor weeping because there are so many women in the world, and only one husband for her, and she never knows where nor when to look for him. He told her: "Unless you can learn to cry when I am not here, I must go away for good." That day he went away and took a room at the Hotel Madrid.

It is this month of separation for the sake of higher principles that has been spoiled not only for Mrs. Braggioni, whose sense of reality is beyond criticism, but for Laura, who feels herself bogged in a nightmare. Tonight Laura envies Mrs. Braggioni, who is alone, and free to weep as much as she pleases about a concrete wrong. Laura has just come from a visit to the prison, and she is waiting for tomorrow with a bitter anxiety as if tomorrow may not come, but time may be caught immovably in this hour, with herself transfixed, Braggioni singing on forever, and Eugenio's body not yet discovered by the guard.

Braggioni says: "Are you going to sleep?" Almost before she can shake her head, he begins telling her about the May-day disturbances coming on in Morelia, for the Catholics hold a festival in honor of the Blessed Virgin, and the Socialists celebrate their martyrs on that day. "There will be two independent processions, starting from either end of town, and they will march until they meet, and the rest depends . . ." He asks her to oil and load his pistols. Standing up, he unbuckles his ammunition belt, and spreads it laden across her knees. Laura sits with the shells slipping through the cleaning cloth dipped in oil, and he says again he cannot understand why she works so hard for the revolutionary idea unless she loves some man who is in it. "Are you not in love with someone?" "No," says Laura. "And no one is in love with you?" "No." "Then it is your own fault. No woman need go begging. Why, what is the matter with you? The legless beggar woman in the Alameda has a perfectly faithful lover. Did you know that?"

Laura peers down the pistol barrel and says nothing, but a long, slow faintness rises and subsides in her; Braggioni curves his swollen fingers around the throat of the guitar and softly smothers the music out of it, and when she hears him again he seems to have forgotten her, and is speaking in the hypnotic voice he uses when talking in small rooms to a listening, close-gathered crowd. Some day this world, now seemingly so composed and eternal, to the edges of every sea shall be merely a tangle of gaping trenches, of crashing walls and broken bodies. Everything must be torn from its accustomed place where it has rotted for centuries, hurled skyward and distributed, cast down again clean as rain, without separate identity. Nothing shall survive that the stiffened hands of poverty have created for the rich and no one shall be left alive except the elect spirits destined to procreate a new world cleansed of cruelty and injustice, ruled by benevolent anarchy: "Pistols are good, I love them, cannon are even better, but in the end I pin my faith to good dynamite," he concludes, and strokes the pistol lying in her hands. "Once I dreamed of destroying this city, in case it offered resistance to General Ortíz, but it fell into his hands like an overripe pear."

He is made restless by his own words, rises and stands waiting. Laura holds up the belt to him: "Put that on, and go kill somebody in Morelia, and you will be happier," she says softly. The presence of death in the room makes her bold. "Today, I found Eugenio going into a stupor. He refused to allow me to call the prison doctor. He had taken all the tablets I brought him yesterday. He said he took them because he was bored."

"He is a fool, and his death is his own business," says Braggioni, fastening his belt carefully.

"I told him if he had waited only a little while longer, you would have got him set free," says Laura. "He said he did not want to wait."

"He is a fool and we are well rid of him," says Braggioni, reaching for his hat.

He goes away. Laura knows his mood has changed, she will not see him any more for a while. He will send word when he needs her to go on errands into strange streets, to speak to the strange faces that will appear, like clay masks with the power of human speech, to mutter their thanks to Braggioni for his help. Now she is free, and she thinks, I must run while there is time. But she does not go.

Braggioni enters his own house where for a month his wife has spent many hours every night weeping and tangling her hair upon her pillow. She is weeping now, and she weeps more at the sight of him, the cause of all her sorrows. He looks about the room. Nothing is changed, the smells are good and familiar, he is well acquainted with the woman who comes toward him with no reproach except grief on her face. He says to her tenderly: "You are so good, please don't cry any more, you dear good creature." She says, "Are you tired, my angel? Sit here and I will wash your feet." She brings a bowl of water, and kneeling, unlaces his shoes, and when from her knees she raises her sad eyes under her blackened lids, he is sorry for everything, and bursts into tears. "Ah, yes, I am hungry, I am tired, let us eat something together," he says, between sobs. His wife leans her head on his arm and says, "Forgive me!" and this time he is refreshed by the solemn, endless rain of her tears.

Laura takes off her serge dress and puts on a white linen nightgown and goes to bed. She turns her head a little to one side, and lying still, reminds herself that it is time to sleep. Numbers tick in her brain like little clocks, soundless doors close of themselves around her. If you would sleep, you must not remember anything, the children will say tomorrow, good morning, my teacher, the poor prisoners who come every day bringing flowers to their jailor. 1-2-3-4-5—it is monstrous to confuse love with revolution, night with day, life with death—ah, Eugenio!

The tolling of the midnight bell is a signal, but what does it mean? Get up, Laura, and follow me: come out of your sleep, out of your bed, out of this strange house. What are you doing in this house? Without a word, without fear she rose and reached for Eugenio's hand, but he eluded her with a sharp, sly smile and drifted away. This is not all, you shall see—Murderer, he said, follow me, I will show you a new country, but it is far away and we must hurry. No, said Laura, not unless you take my hand, no; and she clung first to the stair rail, and then to the topmost branch of the Judas tree that bent down slowly and set her upon the earth, and then to the rocky ledge of a cliff, and then to the jagged wave of a sea that was not water but a desert of crumbling stone. Where are you taking me, she asked in wonder but without fear. To death, and it is a long way off, and we must hurry, said Eugenio. No, said Laura, not unless you take my hand. Then eat these flowers, poor prisoner, said Eugenio in a voice of pity, take and eat: and from the Judas tree he stripped the warm bleeding flowers, and held them to her lips. She saw that his hand was fleshless, a cluster of small white petrified branches, and his eye sockets were without light, but she ate the flowers greedily for they satisfied both hunger and thirst. Murderer! said Eugenio, and Cannibal! This is my body and my blood. Laura cried No! and at the sound of her own voice, she awoke trembling, and was afraid to sleep again.

The Cracked Looking-Glass

DENNIS heard Rosaleen talking in the kitchen and a man's voice answering. He sat with his hands dangling over his knees, and thought for the hundredth time that sometimes Rosaleen's voice was company to him, and other days he wished all day long she didn't have so much to say about everything. More and more the years put a quietus on a man; there was no earthly sense in saying the same things over and over. Even thinking the same thoughts grew tiresome after a while. But Rosaleen was full of talk as ever. If not to him, to whatever passer-by stopped for a minute, and if nobody stopped, she talked to the cats and to herself. If Dennis came near she merely raised her voice and went on with whatever she was saying, so it was nothing for her to shout suddenly, "Come out of that, now—how often have I told ye to keep off the table?" and the cats would scatter in all directions with guilty faces. "It's enough to make a man lep out of his shoes," Dennis would complain. "It's not meant for you, darlin'," Rosaleen would say, as if that cured everything, and if he didn't go away at once, she would start some kind of story. But today she kept shooing him out of the place and hadn't a kind word in her mouth, and Dennis in exile felt that everything and everybody was welcome in the place but himself. For the twentieth time he approached on tiptoe and listened at the parlor keyhole.

Rosaleen was saying: "Maybe his front legs might look a little stuffed for a living cat, but in the picture it's no great matter. I said to Kevin, 'You'll never paint that cat alive,' but Kevin did it, with house paint mixed in a saucer, and a small brush the way he could put in all them fine lines. His legs look like that because I wanted him pictured on the table, but it wasn't so, he was on my lap the whole time. He was a wonder after the mice, a born hunter bringing them in from morning till night—"

Dennis sat on the sofa in the parlor and thought: "There it is. There she goes telling it again." He wondered who the man was, a strange voice, but a loud and ready gabbler as if maybe he was trying to sell something. "It's a fine painting, Miz O'Toole," he said, "and who did you say the artist was?"

"A lad named Kevin, like my own brother he was, who went away to make his fortune," answered Rosaleen. "A house painter by trade."

"The spittin' image of a cat!" roared the voice.

"It is so," said Rosaleen. "The Billy-cat to the life. The Nelly-cat here is own sister to him, and the Jimmy-cat and the Annie-cat and the Mickey-cat is nephews and nieces, and there's a great family look between all of them. It was the strangest thing happened to the Billy-cat, Mr. Pendleton. He sometimes didn't come in for his supper till after dark, he was so taken up with the hunting, and then one night he didn't come at all, nor the next day neither, nor the next, and me with him on my mind so I didn't get a wink of sleep. Then at midnight on the third night I did go to sleep, and the Billy-cat came into my room and lep upon my pillow and said: 'Up beyond the north field there's a maple tree with a great scar where the branch was taken away by the storm, and near to it is a flat stone, and there you'll find me. I was caught in a trap,' he says; 'wasn't set for me,' he says, 'but it got me all the same. And now be easy in your mind about me,' he says, 'for it's all over.' Then he went away, giving me a look over his shoulder like a human crea-ture, and I woke up Dennis and told him. Surely as we live, Mr. Pendleton, it was all true. So Dennis went beyond the north field and brought him home and we buried him in the garden and cried over him." Her voice broke and lowered and Dennis shuddered for fear she was going to shed tears before this stranger.

"For God's *sake*, Miz O'Toole," said the loud-mouthed man, "you can't get around that now, can you? Why, that's the most remarkable thing I ever heard!"

Dennis rose, creaking a little, and hobbled around to the east side of the house in time to see a round man with a flabby red face climbing into a rusty old car with a sign painted on the door. "Always something, now," he commented, putting his head in at the kitchen door. "Always telling a tall tale!"

"Well," said Rosaleen, without the least shame, "he wanted a story so I gave him a good one. That's the Irish in me."

"Always making a thing more than it is," said Dennis. "That's the way it goes."

Rosaleen turned a little edgy. "Out with ye!" she cried, and the cats never budged a whisker. "The kitchen's no place for a man! How often must I tell ye?"

"Well, hand me my hat, will you?" said Dennis, for his hat hung on a nail over the calendar and had hung there within easy reach ever since they had lived in the farmhouse. A few minutes later he wanted his pipe, lying on the lamp shelf where he always kept it. Next he had to have his barn boots at once, though he hadn't seen them for a month. At last he thought of something to say, and opened the door a few inches.

"Wherever have I been sitting unmolested for the past ten years?" he asked, looking at his easy chair with the pillow freshly plumped, sideways to the big table. "And today it's no place for me?"

"If ye grumble ye'll be sorry," said Rosaleen gayly, "and now clear out before I hurl something at ye!"

Dennis put his hat on the parlor table and his boots under the sofa, and sat on the front steps and lit his pipe. It would soon be cold weather, and he wished he had his old leather jacket off the hook on the kitchen door. Whatever was Rosaleen up to now? He decided that Rosaleen was always doing the Irish a great wrong by putting her own faults off on them. To be Irish, he felt, was to be like him, a sober, practical, thinking man, a lover of truth. Rosaleen couldn't see it at all. "It's just your head is like a stone!" she said to him once, pretending she was joking, but she meant it. She had never appreciated him, that was it. And neither had his first wife. Whatever he gave them, they always wanted something else. When he was young and poor his first wife wanted money. And when he was a steady man with money in the bank, his second wife wanted a young man full of life. "They're all born ingrates one way or another," he decided, and felt better at once, as if at last he had something solid to stand on. In September a man could get his death sitting on the steps like this, and little she cared! He clacked his teeth together and felt how they didn't fit any more, and his feet and hands seemed tied on him with strings.

All the while Rosaleen didn't look to be a year older. She

might almost be doing it to spite him, except that she wasn't
the spiteful kind. He'd be bound to say that for her. But she
couldn't forget that her girlhood had been a great triumph in
Ireland, and she was forever telling him tales about it, and
telling them again. This youth of hers was clearer in his mind
than his own. He couldn't remember one thing over another
that had happened to him. His past lay like a great lump within
him; there it was, he knew it all at once, when he thought of it,
like a chest a man has packed away, knowing all that is in it
without troubling to name or count the objects. All in a lump
it had not been an easy life being named Dennis O'Toole in
Bristol, England, where he was brought up and worked sooner
than he was able at the first jobs he could find. And his English
wife had never forgiven him for pulling her up by the roots
and bringing her to New York, where his brothers and sisters
were, and a better job. All the long years he had been first a
waiter and then head waiter in a New York hotel had tele-
scoped in his mind, somehow. It wasn't the best of hotels, to
be sure, but still he was head waiter and there was good money
in it, enough to buy this farm in Connecticut and have a little
steady money coming in, and what more could Rosaleen ask?

He was not unhappy over his first wife's death a few years
after they left England, because they had never really liked
each other, and it seemed to him now that even before she was
dead he had made up his mind, if she did die, never to marry
again. He had held out on this until he was nearly fifty, when
he met Rosaleen at a dance in the County Sligo hall far over on
East 86th Street. She was a great tall rosy girl, a prize dancer,
and the boys were fairly fighting over her. She led him a dance
then for two years before she would have him. She said there
was nothing against him except he came from Bristol, and
the outland Irish had the name of people you couldn't trust.
She couldn't say why—it was just a name they had, worse than
Dublin people itself. No decent Sligo girl would marry a Dublin
man if he was the last man on earth. Dennis didn't believe this,
he'd never heard any such thing against the Dubliners; he
thought a country girl would lep at the chance to marry a city
man whatever. Rosaleen said, "Maybe," but he'd see whether
she would lep to marry Bristol Irish. She was chambermaid in
a rich woman's house, a fiend of darkness if there ever was one,

said Rosaleen, and at first Dennis had been uneasy about the whole thing, fearing a young girl who had to work so hard might be marrying an older man for his money, but before the two years were up he had got over that notion.

It wasn't long after they were married Dennis began almost to wish sometimes he had let one of those strong-armed boys have her, but he had been fond of her, she was a fine good girl, and after she cooled down a little, he knew he could have never done better. The only thing was, he wished it had been Rosaleen he had married that first time in Bristol, and now they'd be settled together, nearer an age. Thirty years was too much difference altogether. But he never said any such thing to Rosaleen. A man owes something to himself. He knocked out his pipe on the foot scraper and felt a real need to go in the kitchen and find a pipe cleaner.

Rosaleen said, "Come in and welcome!" He stood peering around wondering what she had been making. She warned him: "I'm off to milk now, and mind ye keep your eyes in your pocket. The cow now—the creature! Pretty soon she'll be jumping the stone walls after the apples, and running wild through the fields roaring, and it's all for another calf only, the poor deceived thing!" Dennis said, "I don't see what deceit there is in that." "Oh, don't you now?" said Rosaleen, and gathered up her milk pails.

The kitchen was warm and Dennis felt at home again. The kettle was simmering for tea, the cats lay curled or sprawled as they chose, and Dennis sat within himself smiling a sunken smile, cleaning his pipe. In the barn Rosaleen looped up her purple gingham skirts and sat with her forehead pressed against the warm, calm side of the cow, drawing two thick streams of milk into the pail. She said to the cow: "It's no life, no life at all. A man of his years is no comfort to a woman," and went on with a slow murmur that was not complaining about the things of her life.

She wished sometimes they had never come to Connecticut where there was nobody to talk to but Rooshans and Polacks and Wops no better than Black Protestants when you come right down to it. And the natives were worse even. A picture of her neighbors up the hill came into her mind: a starved-looking woman in a blackish gray dress, and a jaundiced man with red-rimmed eyes, and their mizzle-witted boy. On Sundays they shambled by in their sad old shoes, walking to the meeting-house, but that was all the religion they had, thought Rosaleen, contemptuously. On week days they beat the poor boy and the animals, and fought between themselves. Never a feast-day, nor a bit of bright color in their clothes, nor a Christian look out of their eyes for a living soul. "It's just living in mortal sin from one day to the next," said Rosaleen. But it was Dennis getting old that took the heart out of her. And him with the grandest head of hair she had ever seen on a man. A fine man, oh, a fine man Dennis was in those days! Dennis rose before her eyes in his black suit and white gloves, a knowledgeable man who could tell the richest people the right things to order for a good dinner, such a gentleman in his stiff white shirt front, managing the waiters on the one hand and the customers on the other, and making good money at it. And now. No, she couldn't believe it was Dennis any more. Where was Dennis now? and where was Kevin? She was sorry now she had spited Kevin about his girl. It had been all in fun, really, no harm meant. It was strange if you couldn't speak your heart out to a good friend. Kevin had showed her the picture of his girl, like a clap of thunder it came one day when Rosaleen hadn't even heard there was one. She was a waitress in New York, and if ever Rosaleen had laid eyes on a brassy, bold-faced hussy, the kind the boys make jokes about at home, the kind that comes out to New York and goes wrong, this was the one. "You're never never keeping steady with her, are you?" Rosaleen had cried out and the tears came into her eyes. "And why not?" asked Kevin, his chin square as a box. "We've been great now for three years. Who says a word against her says it against me." And there they were, not exactly quarreling, but not friends for the moment, certainly, with Kevin putting the picture back in his pocket, saying: "There's the last of it between us. I was greatly wrong to tell ye!"

That night he was packing up his clothes before he went to bed, but came down and sat on the steps with them awhile, and they made it up by saying nothing, as if nothing had happened. "A man must do something with his life," Kevin explained. "There's always a place to be made in the world, and I'm off to New York, or Boston, maybe." Rosaleen said,

"Write me a letter, don't forget, I'll be waiting." "The very day I know where I'll be," he promised her. They had parted with false wide smiles on their faces, arms around each other to the very gate. There had come a postcard from New York of the Woolworth building, with a word on it: "This is my hotel. Kevin." And never another word for these five years. The wretch, the stump! After he had disappeared down the road with his suitcase strapped on his shoulders, Rosaleen had gone back in the house and had looked at herself in the square looking-glass beside the kitchen window. There was a ripple in the glass and a crack across the middle, and it was like seeing your face in water. "Before God I don't look like that," she said, hanging it on the nail again. "If I did, it's no wonder he was leaving. But I don't." She knew in her heart no good would come of him running off after that common-looking girl; but it was likely he'd find her out soon, and come back, for Kevin was nobody's fool. She waited and watched for Kevin to come back and confess she had been right, and he would say, "I'm sorry I hurt your feelings over somebody not fit to look at you!" But now it was five years. She hung a drapery of crochet lace over the frame on the Billy-cat's picture, and propped it up on a small table in the kitchen, and sometimes it gave her an excuse to mention Kevin's name again, though the sound of it was a crack on the eardrums to Dennis. "Don't speak of him," said Dennis, more than once. "He owed it to send us word. It's ingratitude I can't stand." Whatever was she going to do with Dennis now, she wondered, and sighed heavily into the flank of the cow. It wasn't being a wife at all to wrap a man in flannels like a baby and put hot water bottles to him. She got up sighing and kicked back the stool. "There you are now," she said to the cow.

She couldn't help feeling happy all at once at the sight of the lamp and the fire making everything cozy, and the smell of vanilla reminded her of perfume. She set the table with a white-fringed cloth while Dennis strained the milk.

"Now, Dennis, today's a big day, and we're having a feast for it."

"Is it All-Saints?" asked Dennis, who never looked at a calendar any more. What's a day, more or less?

"It is not," said Rosaleen; "draw up your chair now."

Dennis made another guess it was Christmas, and Rosaleen said it was a better day than Christmas, even.

"I can't think what," said Dennis, looking at the glossy baked goose. "It's nobody's birthday that I mind."

Rosaleen lifted the cake like a mound of new snow blooming with candles. "Count them and see what day is this, will you?" she urged him.

Dennis counted them with a waggling forefinger. "So it is, Rosaleen, so it is."

They went on bandying words. It had slipped his mind entirely. Rosaleen wanted to know when hadn't it slipped his mind? For all he ever thought of it, they might never have had a wedding day at all. "That's not so," said Dennis. "I mind well I married you. It's the date that slips me."

"You might as well be English," said Rosaleen, "you might just as well."

She glanced at the clock, and reminded him it was twenty-five years ago that morning at ten o'clock, and tonight the very hour they had sat down to their first married dinner together. Dennis thought maybe it was telling people what to eat and then watching them eat it all those years that had taken away his wish for food. "You know I can't eat cake," he said. "It upsets my stomach."

Rosaleen felt sure her cake wouldn't upset the stomach of a nursing child. Dennis knew better, any kind of cake sat on him like a stone. While the argument went on, they ate nearly all the goose which fairly melted on the tongue, and finished with wedges of cake and floods of tea, and Dennis had to admit he hadn't felt better in years. He looked at her sitting across the table from him and thought she was a very fine woman, noticed again her red hair and yellow eyelashes and big arms and strong big teeth, and wondered what she thought of him now he was no human good to her. Here he was, all gone, and he had been so for years, and he felt guilt sometimes before Rosaleen, who couldn't always understand how there comes a time when a man is finished, and there is no more to be done that way. Rosaleen poured out two small glasses of home-made cherry brandy.

"I could feel like dancing itself this night, Dennis," she told him. "Do you remember the first time we met in Sligo Hall with the band playing?" She gave him another glass of brandy and took one herself and leaned over with her eyes shining as if she was telling him something he had never heard before.

"I remember a boy in Ireland was a great step-dancer, the best, and he was wild about me and I was a devil to him. Now what makes a girl like that, Dennis? He was a fine match, too, all the girls were glad of a chance with him, but I wasn't. He said to me a thousand times, 'Rosaleen, why won't ye dance with me just once?' And I'd say, 'Ye've plenty to dance with ye without my wasting my time.' And so it went for the summer long with him not dancing at all and everybody plaguing the living life out of him, till in the end I danced with him. Afterwards he walked home with me and a crowd of them, and there was a heaven full of stars and the dogs barking far off. Then I promised to keep steady with him, and was sorry for it the minute I promised. I was like that. We used to be the whole day getting ready for the dances, washing our hair and curling it and trying on our dresses and trimming them, laughing fit to kill about the boys and making up things to say to them. When my sister Honora was married they took me for the bride, Dennis, with my white dress ruffled to the heels and my hair with a wreath. Everybody drank my health for the belle of the ball, and said I would surely be the next bride. Honora said for me to save my blushes or I'd have none left for my own wedding. She was always jealous, Dennis, she's jealous of me to this day, you know that."

"Maybe so," said Dennis.

"There's no maybe about it," said Rosaleen. "But we had grand times together when we was little. I mind the time when my great-grandfather was ninety years old on his deathbed. We watched by turns the night—"

"And he was a weary time on it," said Dennis, to show his interest. He was so sleepy he could hardly hold up his head.

"He was," said Rosaleen, "so this night Honora and me was watching, and we was yawning our hearts out of us, for there had been a great ball the night before. Our mother told us, 'Feel his feet from time to time, and when you feel the chill rising, you'll know he's near the end. He can't last out the night,' she said, 'but stay by him.' So there we was drinking tea and laughing together in whispers to keep awake, and the old man lying there with his chin propped on the quilt. 'Wait a minute,' says Honora, and she felt his feet. 'They're getting cold,' she says, and went on telling me what she had said to Shane at the ball, how he was jealous of Terence and asks her can he trust her out of his sight. And Honora says to Shane, 'No, you cannot,' and oh, but he was roaring mad with anger! Then Honora stuffs her fist in her mouth to keep down the giggles. I felt great-grandfather's feet and legs and they was like clay to the knees, and I says, 'Maybe we'd better call somebody'; but Honora says, 'Oh, there's a power of him left to get cold yet!' So we poured out tea and began to comb and braid each other's hair, and fell to whispering our secrets and laughing more. Then Honora put her hand under the quilt and said, 'Rosaleen, his stomach's cold, it's gone he must be by now.' Then great-grandfather opened the one eye full of rage and says, 'It's nothing of the kind, and to hell with ye!' We let out a great scream, and the others came flying in, and Honora cried out, 'Oh, he's dead and gone surely, God rest him!' And would you believe it, it was so. He was gone. And while the old women were washing him Honora and me sat down laughing and crying in the one breath . . . and it was six months later to the very day great-grandfather came to me in the dream, the way I told you, and he was still after Honora and me for laughing in the watch. 'I've a great mind to thrash ye within an inch of your life,' he told me, 'only I'm wailing in Purgatory this minute for them last words to ye. Go and have an extra Mass said for the repose of me soul because it's by your misconduct I'm here at all,' he says to me. 'Get a move on now,' he said. 'And be damned to ye!'"

"And you woke up in a sweat," said Dennis, "and was off to Mass before daybreak."

Rosaleen nodded her head. "Ah, Dennis, if I'd set my heart on that boy I need never have left Ireland. And when I think how it all came out with him. With me so far away, him struck on the head and left for dead in a ditch."

"You dreamed that," said Dennis.

"Surely I dreamed it, and it is so. When I was crying and crying over him—" Rosaleen was proud of her crying—"I didn't know then what good luck I would find here."

Dennis couldn't think what good luck she was talking about.

"Let it pass, then," said Rosaleen. She went to the corner shelves again. "The man today was selling pipes," she said, "and I bought the finest he had." It was an imitation meerschaum pipe carved with a crested lion glaring out of a jungle and it was as big as a man's fist.

Dennis said, "You must have paid a pretty penny for that."

"It doesn't concern ye," said Rosaleen. "I wanted to give ye a pipe."

Dennis said, "It's grand carving, I wonder if it'll draw at all." He filled it and lit it and said there wasn't much taste on a new one, for he was tired holding it up.

"It is such a pipe as my father had once," Rosaleen said to encourage him. "And in no time it was fit to knock ye off your feet, he said. So it will be a fine pipe some day."

"And some day I'll be in my tomb," thought Dennis, bitterly, "and she'll find a man can keep her quiet."

When they were in bed Rosaleen took his head on her shoulder. "Dennis, I could cry for the wink of an eyelash. When I think how happy we were that wedding day."

"From the way you carried on," said Dennis, feeling very sly all of a sudden on that brandy, "I thought different."

"Go to sleep," said Rosaleen, prudishly. "That's no way to talk."

Dennis's head fell back like a bag of sand on the pillow. Rosaleen could not sleep, and lay thinking about marriage: not about her own, for once you've given your word there's nothing to think about it, but all other kinds of marriages, unhappy ones: where the husband drinks, or won't work, or mistreats his wife and the children. Where the wife runs away from home, or spoils the children or neglects them, or turns a perfect strumpet and flirts with other men: where a woman marries a man too young for her, and he feels cheated and strays after other women till it's just a disgrace: or take when a young girl marries an old man, even if he has money she's bound to be disappointed in some way. If Dennis hadn't been such a good man, God knows what might have come out of it. She was lucky. It would break your heart to dwell on it. Her black mood closed down on her and she wanted to walk the floor holding her head and remembering every unhappy thing in the world. She had had nothing but disasters, one after another, and she couldn't get over them, no matter how long ago they happened. Once she had let entirely the wrong man kiss her, she had almost got into bad trouble with him, and even now her heart stopped on her when she thought how near she'd come to being a girl with no character. There was the Billy-cat and his good heart and his sad death, and it was mixed up with the time her father had been knocked down, by a runaway horse, when the drink was in him, and the time when she had to wear mended stockings to a big ball because that sneaky Honora had stolen the only good ones.

She wished now she'd had a dozen children instead of the one that died in two days. This half-forgotten child suddenly lived again in her, she began to weep for him with all the freshness of her first agony; now he would be a fine grown man and the dear love of her heart. The image of him floated before her eyes plain as day, and became Kevin, painting the barn and the pig sty all colors of the rainbow, the brush swinging in his hand like a bell. He would work like a wild man for days and then lie for days under the trees, idle as a tramp. The darling, the darling lad like her own son. A painter by trade was a nice living, but she couldn't bear the thought of him boarding around the country with the heathen Rooshans and Polacks and Wops with their liquor stills and their outlandish lingo. She said as much to Kevin.

"It's not a Christian way to live, and you a good County Sligo boy."

So Kevin started to make jokes at her like any other Sligo boy. "I said to myself, that's a County Mayo woman if ever I clapped eyes on one."

"Hold your tongue," said Rosaleen softly as a dove. "You're talking to a Sligo woman as if you didn't know it!"

"Is it so?" said Kevin in great astonishment. "Well, I'm glad of the mistake. The Mayo people are too proud for me."

"And for me, too," said Rosaleen. "They beat the world for holding up their chins about nothing."

"They do so," said Kevin, "but the Sligo people have a right to be proud."

"And you've a right to live in a good Irish house," said Rosaleen, "so you'd best come with us."

"I'd be proud of that as if I came from Mayo," said Kevin,

and he went on slapping paint on Rosaleen's front gate. They stood there smiling at each other, feeling they had agreed enough, it was time to think of how to get the best of each other in the talk from now on. For more than a year they had tried to get the best of each other in the talk, and sometimes it was one and sometimes another, but a gay easy time and such a bubble of joy like a kettle singing. "You've been a sister to me, Rosaleen, I'll not forget ye while I have breath," he had said that the last night.

Dennis muttered and snored a little. Rosaleen wanted to mourn about everything at the top of her voice, but it wouldn't do to wake Dennis. He was sleeping like the dead after all that goose.

Rosaleen said, "Dennis, I dreamed about Kevin in the night. There was a grave, an old one, but with fresh flowers on it, and a name on the headstone cut very clear but as if it was in another language and I couldn't make it out some way. You came up then and I said, 'Dennis, what grave is this?' and you answered me, 'That's Kevin's grave, don't you remember? And you put those flowers there yourself.' Then I said, 'Well, a grave it is then, and let's not think of it any more.' Now isn't it strange to think Kevin's been dead all this time and I didn't know it?"

Dennis said, "He's not fit to mention, going off as he did after all our kindness to him, and not a word from him."

"It was because he hadn't the power any more," said Rosaleen. "And ye mustn't be down on him now. I was wrong to put my judgment on him the way I did. Ah, but to think! Kevin dead and gone, and all these natives and foreigners living on, with the paint still on their barns and houses where Kevin put it! It's very bitter."

Grieving for Kevin, she drifted into thinking of the natives and foreigners who owned farms all around her. She was afraid for her life of them, she said, the way they looked at you out of their heathen faces, the foreigners bold as brass, the natives sly and mean. "The way they do be selling the drink to all, and burning each other in their beds and splitting each other's heads with axes," she complained. "The decent people aren't safe in their houses."

Yesterday she had seen that native Guy Richards going by wild-drunk again, fit to do any crime. He was a great offense to Rosaleen, with his shaggy mustaches and his shirt in rags till the brawny skin showed through; a shame to the world, staring around with his sneering eyes; living by himself in a shack and having his cronies in for drink until you could hear them shouting at all hours and careering round the country-side like the devils from hell. He would pass by the house driving his bony gray horse at top speed, standing up in the rackety buggy singing in a voice like a power of scrap-iron falling, drunk as a lord before breakfast. Once when Rosaleen was standing in her doorway, wearing a green checkerboard dress, he yelled at her: "Hey, Rosie, want to come for a ride?"

"The bold stump!" said Rosaleen to Dennis. "If ever he lays a finger on me I'll shoot him dead."

"If you mind your business by day," said Dennis in a shriv-eled voice, "and bar the doors well by night, there'll be no call to shoot anybody."

"Little you know!" said Rosaleen. She had a series of visions of Richards laying a finger on her and herself shooting him dead in his tracks. "Whatever would I do without ye, Dennis?" she asked him that night, as they sat on the steps in a soft dark-ness full of fireflies and the sound of crickets. "When I think of all the kinds of men there are in the world. That Richards!"

"When a man is young he likes his fun," said Dennis, ami-ably, beginning to yawn.

"Young, is it?" said Rosaleen, warm with anger. "The old crow! Fit to have children grown he is, the same as myself, and I'm a settled woman over her nonsense!"

Dennis almost said, "I'll never call you old," but all at once he was irritable too. "Will you stop your gossiping?" he asked censoriously.

Rosaleen sat silent, without rancor, but there was no denying the old man was getting old, old. He got up as if he gathered his bones in his arms, and carried himself in the house. Some-where inside of him there must be Dennis, but where? "The world is a wilderness," she informed the crickets and frogs and fireflies.

Richards never had offered to lay a finger on Rosaleen, but

now and again he pulled up at the gate when he was not quite drunk, and sat with them afternoons on the doorstep, and there were signs in him of a nice-behaved man before the drink got him down. He would tell them stories of his life, and what a desperate wild fellow he had been, all in all. Not when he was a boy, though. As long as his mother lived he had never done a thing to hurt her feelings. She wasn't what you might call a rugged woman, the least thing made her sick, and she was so religious she prayed all day long under her breath at her work, and even while she ate. He had belonged to a society called The Sons of Temperance, with all the boys in the countryside banded together under a vow never to touch strong drink in any form: "Not even for medicinal purposes," he would quote, raising his right arm and staring solemnly before him. Quite often he would burst into a rousing march tune which he remembered from the weekly singings they had held: "With flags of temperance flying, With banners white as snow," and he could still repeat almost word for word the favorite poem he had been called upon to recite at every meeting: "At midnight, in his guarded tent, The Turk lay dreaming of the hour—"

Rosaleen wanted to interrupt sometimes and tell him that had been no sort of life, he should have been young in Ireland. But she wouldn't say it. She sat stiffly beside Dennis and looked at Richards severely out of the corner of her eye, wondering if he remembered that time he had yelled "Hey, Rosie!" at her. It was enough to make a woman wild not to find a word in her mouth for such boldness. The cheek of him, pretending nothing had happened. One day she was racking her mind for some saying that would put him in his place, while he was telling about the clambakes his gang was always having down by the creek behind the rock pile, with a keg of home-brew beer; and the dances the Railroad Street outfit gave every Saturday night in Winston. "We're always up to some devilment," he said, looking straight at Rosaleen, and before she could say scat, the hellion had winked his near eye at her. She turned away with her mouth down at the corners; after a long minute, she said, "Good day to ye, Mr. Richards," cold as ice, and went in the house. She took down the looking-glass to see what

kind of look she had on her, but the wavy place made her eyes
broad and blurred as the palm of her hands, and she couldn't
tell her nose from her mouth in the cracked seam. . . .

The pipe salesman came back next month and brought a
patent cooking pot that cooked vegetables perfectly without
any water in them. "It's a lot healthier way of cooking, Miz
O'Toole," Dennis heard his mouthy voice going thirteen to
the dozen. "I'm telling you as a friend because you're a good
customer of mine."

"Is it so?" thought Dennis, and his gall stirred within him.

"You'll find it's going to be a perfect godsend for your husband's health. Old folks need to be mighty careful what they
eat, and you know better than I do, Miz O'Toole, that health
begins or ends right in the kitchen. Now your husband don't
look as stout as he might. It's because, tasty as your cooking
is, you've been pouring all the good vitamins, the sunlit life-
giving elements, right down the sink. . . . Right down the
sink, Miz O'Toole, is where you're pouring your husband's
health and your own. And I say it's a shame, a good-looking
woman like you wasting your time and strength standing over
a cook-stove when all you've got to do from now on is just fill
this scientific little contrivance with whatever you've planned
for dinner and then go away and read a good book in your parlor while it's cooking—or curl your hair."

"My hair curls by nature," said Rosaleen. Dennis almost
groaned aloud from his hiding-place.

"For the love of—why, Miz O'Toole, you don't mean to tell
me that! When I first saw that hair, I said to myself, why, it's so
perfect it looks to be artificial! I was just getting ready to ask
you how you did it so I could tell my wife. Well, if your hair
curls like that, without any vitamins at all, I want to come back
and have a look at it after you've been cooking in this little pot
for two weeks."

Rosaleen said, "Well, it's not my looks I'm thinking about.
But my husband isn't up to himself, and that's the truth, Mr.
Pendleton. Ah, it would have done your heart good to see that
man in his younger days! Strong as an ox he was, the way no
man dared to rouse his anger. I've seen my husband, many's
the time, swing on a man with his fist and send him sprawling

twenty feet, and that for the least thing, mind you! But Dennis could never hold his grudge for long, and the next instant you'd see him picking the man up and dusting him off like a brother and saying, 'Now think no more of that.' He was too forgiving always. It was his great fault."

"And look at him now," said Mr. Pendleton, sadly.

Dennis felt pretty hot around the ears. He stood forward at the corner of the house, listening. He had never weighed more than one hundred thirty pounds at his most, a tall thin man he had been always, a little proud of his elegant shape, and not since he left school in Bristol had he lifted his hand in anger against a creature, brute or human. "He was a fine man a woman could rely on, Mr. Pendleton," said Rosaleen, "and quick as a tiger with his fists."

"I might be dead and moldering away to dust the way she talks," thought Dennis, "and there she is throwing away the money as if she was already a gay widow woman." He tottered out bent on speaking his mind and putting a stop to such foolishness. The salesman turned a floppy smile and shrewd little eyes upon him. "Hello, Mr. O'Toole," he said, with the manly cordiality he used for husbands. "I'm just leaving you a little birthday present with the Missis here."

"It's not my birthday," said Dennis, sour as a lemon.

"That's just a manner of speaking!" interrupted Rosaleen, merrily. "And now many thanks to ye, Mr. Pendleton."

"Many thanks to *you*, Miz O'Toole," answered the salesman, folding away nine dollars of good green money. No more was said except good day, and Rosaleen stood shading her eyes to watch the Ford walloping off down the hummocky lane. "That's a nice, decent family man," she told Dennis, as if rebuking his evil thoughts. "He travels out of New York, and he always has the latest thing and the best. He's full of admiration for ye, too, Dennis. He said he couldn't call to mind another man of your age as sound as you are."

"I heard him," said Dennis. "I know all he said."

"Well, then," said Rosaleen, serenely, "there's no good saying it over." She hurried to wash potatoes to cook in the pot that made the hair curl.

*

The winter piled in upon them, and the snow was shot through with blizzards. Dennis couldn't bear a breath of cold, and all but sat in the oven, rheumy and grunty, with his muffler on. Rosaleen began to feel as if she couldn't bear her clothes on her in the hot kitchen, and when she did the barn work she had one chill after another. She complained that her hands were gnawed to the bone with the cold. Did Dennis realize that now, or was he going to sit like a log all winter, and where was the lad he had promised her to help with the outside work?

Dennis sat wordless under her unreasonableness, thinking she had very little work for a strong-bodied woman, and the truth was she was blaming him for something he couldn't help. Still she said nothing he could take hold of, only nipping his head off when the kettle dried up or the fire went low. There would come a day when she would say outright, "It's no life here, I won't stay here any longer," and she would drag him back to a flat in New York, or even leave him, maybe. Would she? Would she do such a thing? Such a thought had never occurred to him before. He peered at her as if he watched her through a keyhole. He tried to think of something to ease her mind, but no plan came. She would look at some harmless thing around the house, say—the calendar, and suddenly tear it off the wall and stuff it in the fire. "I hate the very sight of it," she would explain, and she was always hating the very sight of one thing or another, even the cow; almost, but not quite, the cats.

One morning she sat up very tired and forlorn, and began almost before Dennis could get an eye open: "I had a dream in the night that my sister Honora was sick and dying in her bed, and was calling for me." She bowed her head on her hands and breathed brokenly to her very toes, and said, "It's only natural I must go to Boston to find out for myself how it is, isn't it?"

Dennis, pulling on his chest protector she had knitted him for Christmas, said, "I suppose so. It looks that way."

Over the coffee pot she began making her plans. "I could go if only I had a coat. It should be a fur one against this weather. A coat is what I've needed all these years. If I had a coat I'd go this very day."

"You've a greatcoat with fur on it," said Dennis.

"A rag of a coat!" cried Rosaleen. "And I won't have Honora see me in it. She was jealous always, Dennis, she'd be glad to see me without a coat."

"If she's sick and dying maybe she won't notice," said Dennis.

Rosaleen agreed. "And maybe it will be better to buy one there, or in New York—something in the new style."

"It's long out of your way by New York," said Dennis. "There's shorter ways to Boston than that."

"It's by New York I'm going, because the trains are better," said Rosaleen, "and I want to go that way." There was a look on her face as if you could put her on the rack and she wouldn't yield. Dennis kept silence.

When the postman passed she asked him to leave word with the native family up the hill to send their lad down for a few days to help with the chores, at the same pay as before. And tomorrow morning, if it was all the same to him, she'd be driving in with him to the train. All day long, with her hair in curl papers, she worked getting her things together in the lazy old canvas bag. She put a ham on to bake and set bread and filled the closet off the kitchen with firewood. "Maybe there'll come a message saying Honora's better and I sha'n't have to go," she said several times, but her eyes were excited and she walked about so briskly the floor shook.

Late in the afternoon Guy Richards knocked, and floundered in stamping his big boots. He was almost sober, but he wasn't going to be for long. Rosaleen said, "I've sad news about my sister, she's on her deathbed maybe and I'm going to Boston."

"I hope it's nothing serious, Missis O'Toole," said Richards. "Let's drink her health in this," and he took out a bottle half full of desperate-looking drink. Dennis said he didn't mind. Richards said, "Will the lady join us?" and his eyes had the devil in them if Rosaleen had ever seen it.

"I will not," she said. "I've something better to do."

While they drank she sat fixing the hem of her dress, and began to tell again about the persons without number she'd known who came back from the dead to bring word about themselves, and Dennis himself would back her up in it. She told again the story of the Billy-cat, her voice warm and broken with the threat of tears.

Dennis swallowed his drink, leaned over and began to fumble with his shoelace, his face sunken to a handful of wrinkles, and thought right out plainly to himself: "There's not a word of truth in it, not a word. And she'll go on telling it to the world's end for God's truth." He felt helpless, as if he were involved in some disgraceful fraud. He wanted to speak up once for all and say, "It's a lie, Rosaleen, it's something you've made up, and now let's hear no more about it." But Richards, sitting there with his ears lengthened, stopped the words in Dennis's throat. The moment passed. Rosaleen said solemnly, "My dreams never renege on me, Mr. Richards. They're all I have to go by." "It never happened at all," said Dennis inside himself, stubbornly. "Only the Billy-cat got caught in a trap and I buried him." Could this really have been all? He had a nightmarish feeling that somewhere just out of his reach lay the truth about it, he couldn't swear for certain, yet he was *almost* willing to swear that this had been all. Richards got up saying he had to be getting on to a shindig at Winston. "I'll take you to the train tomorrow, Missis O'Toole," he said. "I love doing a good turn for the ladies."

Rosaleen said very stiffly, "I'll be going in with the letter-carrier, and many thanks just the same."

She tucked Dennis into bed with great tenderness and sat by him a few minutes, putting cold cream on her face. "It won't be for long," she told him, "and you're well taken care of the whole time. Maybe by the grace of God I'll find her recovered."

"Maybe she's not sick at all," Dennis wanted to say, and said instead, "I hope so." It was nothing to him. Everything else aside, it seemed a great fuss to be making over Honora, who might die when she liked for all Dennis would turn a hair.

Dennis hoped until the last minute that Rosaleen would come to her senses and give up the trip, but at the last minute there she was with her hat and the rag of a coat, a streak of pink powder on her chin, pulling on her tan gloves that smelt of naphtha, flourishing a handkerchief that smelt of Azurea, and going every minute to the window, looking for the postman. "In this snow maybe he'll be late," she said in a trembling voice. "What if he didn't come at all?" She took a last glimpse at herself in the mirror. "One thing I must remember, Dennis," she said in another tone. "And that is, to bring back a looking-glass that won't make my face look like a monster's."

"It's a good enough glass," said Dennis, "without throwing away money."

The postman came only a few minutes late. Dennis kissed Rosaleen good-by and shut the kitchen door so he could not see her climbing into the car, but he heard her laughing.

"It's just a born liar she is," Dennis said to himself, sitting by the stove, and at once he felt he had leaped head-first into a very dark pit. His better self tried to argue it out with him. "Have you no shame," said Dennis's better self, "thinking such thoughts about your own wife?" The baser Dennis persisted. "It's not half she deserves," he answered sternly, "leaving me here by my lone, and for what?" That was the great question. Certainly not to run after Honora, living or dying or dead. Where then? For what on earth? Here he stopped thinking altogether. There wasn't a spark in his mind. He had a lump on his chest that could surely be pneumonia if he had a cold, which he hadn't, specially. His feet ached until you'd swear it was rheumatism, only he never had it. Still, he wasn't thinking. He stayed in this condition for two days, and the under-witted lad from the native farm above did all the work, even to washing the dishes. Dennis ate pretty well, considering the grief he was under.

Rosaleen settled back in the plush seat and thought how she had always been a great traveler. A train was like home to her, with all the other people sitting near, and the smell of newspapers and some kind of nice-smelling furniture polish and the perfume from fur collars, and the train dust and something over and above she couldn't place, but it was the smell of travel: fruit, maybe, or was it machinery? She bought chocolate bars, though she wasn't hungry, and a magazine of love stories, though she was never one for reading. She only wished to prove to herself she was once more on a train going somewhere.

She watched the people coming on or leaving at the stations, greeting, or kissing good-by, and it seemed a lucky sign she did not see a sad face anywhere. There was a cold sweet

sunshine on the snow, and the city people didn't look all
frozen and bundled up. Their faces looked smooth after the
gnarled raw frost-bitten country faces. The Grand Central
hadn't changed at all, with all the crowds whirling in every
direction, and a noise that almost had a tune in it, it was so
steady. She held on to her bag the colored men were trying to
get away from her, and stood on the sidewalk trying to remember which direction was Broadway where the moving pictures were. She hadn't seen one for five years, it was high time
now! She wished she had an hour to visit her old flat in 164th
Street—just a turn around the block would be enough, but
there wasn't time. An old resentment rose against Honora,
who was a born spoil-sport and would spoil this trip for her if
she could. She walked on, getting her directions, brooding a
little because she had been such a city girl once, thinking only
of dress and a good time, and now she hardly knew one street
from another. She went into the first moving-picture theater
she saw because she liked the name of it. "The Prince of Love,"
she said to herself. It was about two beautiful young things, a
boy with black wavy hair and a girl with curly golden hair, who
loved each other and had great troubles, but it all came well in
the end, and all the time it was just one fine ballroom or garden after another, and such beautiful clothes! She sniffled a
little in the Azurea-smelling handkerchief, and ate her choco-
lates, and reminded herself these two were really alive and
looked just like that, but it was hard to believe living beings
could be so beautiful.

After the dancing warm lights of the screen the street was
cold and dark and ugly, with the slush and the roar and the
millions of people all going somewhere in a great rush, but not
one face she knew. She decided to go to Boston by boat the way
she used in the old days when she visited Honora. She gazed
into the shop windows thinking how the styles in underthings
had changed till she could hardly believe her eyes, wondering
what Dennis would say if she bought the green glove silk slip
with the tea-colored lace. Ah, was he eating his ham now as she
told him, and did the boy come to help as he had promised?

She ate ice cream with strawberry preserves on it, and bought
a powder puff and decided there was time for another moving
picture. It was called "The Lover King," and it was about a king

in a disguise, a lovely young man with black wavy hair and eyes would melt in his head, who married a poor country girl who was more beautiful than all the princesses and ladies in the land. Music came out of the screen, and voices talking, and Rosaleen cried, for the love songs went to her heart like a dagger.

Afterward there was just time to ride in a taxi to Christopher Street and catch the boat. She felt happier the minute she set foot on board, how she always loved a ship! She ate her supper thinking, "That boy didn't have much style to his waiting. Dennis would never have kept him on in the hotel"; and afterward sat in the lounge and listened to the radio until she almost fell asleep there before everybody. She stretched out in her narrow bunk and felt the engine pounding under her, and the grand steady beat shook the very marrow of her bones. The fog horn howled and bellowed through the darkness over the rush of water, and Rosaleen turned on her side. "Howl for me, that's the way I could cry in the nighttime in that lost heathen place," for Connecticut seemed a thousand miles and a hundred years away by now. She fell asleep and had no dreams at all.

In the morning she felt this was a lucky sign. At Providence she took the train again, and as the meeting with Honora came nearer, she grew sunken and tired. "Always Honora making trouble," she thought, standing outside the station holding her bag and thinking it strange she hadn't remembered what a dreary ugly place Boston was; she couldn't remember any good times there. Taxicab drivers were yelling in her face. Maybe it would be a good thing to go to a church and light a candle for Honora. The taxi scampered through winding streets to the nearest church, with Rosaleen thinking, what she wouldn't give to be able to ride around all day, and never walk at all!

She knelt near the high altar, and something surged up in her heart and pushed the tears out of her eyes. Prayers began to tumble over each other on her lips. How long it had been since she had seen the church as it should be, dressed for a feast with candles and flowers, smelling of incense and wax. The little doleful church in Winston, now who could really pray in it? "Have mercy on us," said Rosaleen, calling on fifty saints at once; "I confess . . ." she struck her breast three times, then got up suddenly, carrying her bag, and peered into

the confessionals hoping she might find a priest in one of
them. "It's too early, or it's not the day, but I'll come back,"
she promised herself with tenderness. She lit the candle for
Honora and went away feeling warm and quiet. She was blind
and confused, too, and could not make up her mind what to
do next. Where ever should she turn? It was a burning sin to
spend money on taxicabs when there was always the hungry
poor in the world, but she hailed one anyhow, and gave Honora's house number. Yes, there it was, just like in old times.

She read all the names pasted on slips above the bells, all the
floors front and back, but Honora's name was not among
them. The janitor had never heard of Mrs. Terence Gogarty,
nor Mrs. Honora Gogarty, neither. Maybe it would be in the
telephone book. There were many Gogartys but no Terence
nor Honora. Rosaleen smothered down the impulse to tell the
janitor, a good Irishman, how her dream had gone back on her.
"Thank ye kindly, it's no great matter," she said, and stepped
out into the street again. The wind hacked at her shoulders
through the rag of a coat, the bag was too heavy altogether.
Now what kind of nature was in Honora not to drop a line and
say she had moved?

Walking about with her mind in a whirl, she came to a small
dingy square with iron benches and some naked trees in it. Sitting, she began to shed tears again. When one handkerchief
was wet she took out another, and the fresh perfume put new
heart in her. She glanced around when a shadow fell on the
corner of her eye, and there hunched on the other end of the
bench was a scrap of a lad with freckles, his collar turned about
his ears, his red hair wilted on his forehead under his bulging
cap. He slanted his gooseberry eyes at her and said, "We've all
something to cry for in this world, isn't it so?"

Rosaleen said, "I'm crying because I've come a long way for
nothing."

The boy said, "I knew you was a County Sligo woman the
minute I clapped eyes on ye."

"God bless ye for that," said Rosaleen, "for I am."

"I'm County Sligo myself, long ago, and curse the day I
ever thought of leaving it," said the boy, with such anger Rosaleen dried her eyes once for all and turned to have a good
look at him.

"Whatever makes ye say that now?" she asked him. "It's a good country, this. There's opportunity for all here."

"So I've heard tell many's the countless times," said the boy. "There's all the opportunity in the wide world to shrivel with the hunger and walk the soles off your boots hunting the work, and there's a great chance of dying in the gutter at last. God forgive me the first thought I had of coming here."

"Ye haven't been out long?" asked Rosaleen.

"Eleven months and five days the day," said the boy. He plunged his hands into his pockets and stared at the freezing mud clotted around his luckless shoes.

"And what might ye do by way of a living?" asked Rosaleen.

"I'm an hostler," he said. "I used to work at the Dublin race tracks, even. No man can tell me about horses," he said proudly. "And it's good work if it's to be found."

Rosaleen looked attentively at his sharp red nose, frozen it was, and the stung look around his eyes, and the sharp bones sticking out at his wrists, and was surprised at herself for thinking, in the first glance, that he had the look of Kevin. She saw different now, but think if it had been Kevin! Better off to be dead and gone. "I'm perishing of hunger and cold," she told him, "and if I knew where there was a place to eat, we'd have some lunch, for it's late."

His eyes looked like he was drowning. "Would ye? I know a place!" and he leaped up as if he meant to run. They did almost run to the edge of the square and the far corner. It was a Coffee Pot and full of the smell of hot cakes. "We'll get our fill here," said Rosaleen, taking off her gloves, "though I'd never call it a grand place."

The boy ate one thing after another as if he could never stop: roast beef and potatoes and spaghetti and custard pie and coffee, and Rosaleen ordered a package of cigarettes. It was like this with her, she was fond of the smell of tobacco, her husband was a famous smoker, never without his pipe. "It's no use keeping it in," said the boy. "I haven't a penny, yesterday and today I didn't eat till now, and I've been fit to hang my-self, or go to jail for a place to lay my head."

Rosaleen said, "I'm a woman doesn't have to think of money, I have all my heart desires, and a boy like yourself has a right to think nothing of a little loan will never be missed."

She fumbled in her purse and brought out a ten-dollar bill, crumpled it and pushed it under the rim of his saucer so the man behind the counter wouldn't notice. "That's for luck in the new world," she said, smiling at him. "You might be Kevin or my own brother, or my own little lad alone in the world, and it'll surely come back to me if ever I need it."

The boy said, "I never thought to see this day," and put the money in his pocket.

Rosaleen said, "I don't even know your name, think of that!"

"I'm a blight on the name of Sullivan," said he. "Hugh it is —Hugh Sullivan."

"That's a good enough name," said Rosaleen. "I've cousins named Sullivan in Dublin, but I never saw one of them. There was a man named Sullivan married my mother's sister, my aunt Brigid she was, and she went to live in Dublin. You're not related to the Dublin Sullivans, are ye?"

"I never heard of it, but maybe I am."

"Ye have the look of a Sullivan to me," said Rosaleen, "and they're cousins of mine, some of them." She ordered more coffee and he lit another cigarette, and she told him how she had come out more than twenty-five years past, a greenhorn like himself, and everything had turned out well for her and all her family here. Then she told about her husband, how he had been head waiter and a moneyed man, but he was old now; about the farm, if there was someone to help her, they could make a good thing of it; and about Kevin and the way he had gone away and died and sent her news of it in a dream; and this led to the dream about Honora, and here she was, the first time ever a dream had gone back on her. She went on to say there was always room for a strong willing boy in the country if he knew about horses, and how it was a shame for him to be tramping the streets with an empty stomach when there was everything to be had if he only knew which way to look for it. She leaned over and took him by the arm very urgently.

"You've a right to live in a good Irish house," she told him. "Why don't ye come home with me and live there like one of the family in peace and comfort?"

Hugh Sullivan stared at her out of his glazed green eyes down the edge of his sharp nose and a crafty look came over him. "'Twould be dangerous," he said. "I'd hate to try it."

"Dangerous, is it?" asked Rosaleen. "What danger is there in the peaceful countryside?"

"It's not safe at all," said Hugh. "I was caught at it once in Dublin, and there was a holy row! A fine woman like yourself she was, and her husband peeking through a crack in the wall the whole time. Man, that was a scrape for ye!"

Rosaleen understood in her bones before her mind grasped it. "Whatever—" she began, and the blood boiled up in her face until it was like looking through a red veil. "Ye little whelp," she said, trying to get her breath, "so it's that kind ye are, is it? I might know you're from Dublin! Never in my whole life—" Her rage rose like a bonfire in her, and she stopped. "If I was looking for a man," she said, "I'd choose a *man* and not a half-baked little . . ." She took a deep breath and started again. "The *cheek* of ye," she said, "insulting a woman could be your mother. God keep me from it! It's plain you're just an ignorant greenhorn, doesn't know the ways of decent people, and now be off—" She stood up and motioned to the man behind the counter. "Out of that door now—"

He stood up too, glancing around fearfully with his narrow green eyes, and put out a hand as if he would try to make it up with her. "Not so loud now, woman alive, it's what any man might think the way ye're—"

Rosaleen said, "Hold your tongue or I'll tear it out of your head!" and her right arm went back in a business-like way.

He ducked and shot past her, then collected himself and lounged out of reach. "Farewell to ye, County Sligo woman," he said tauntingly. "I'm from County Cork myself!" and darted through the door.

Rosaleen shook so she could hardly find the money for the bill, and she couldn't see her way before her, but when the cold air struck her, her head cleared, and she could have almost put a curse on Honora for making all this trouble for her. . . .

She took a train the short way home, for the taste of travel had soured on her altogether. She wanted to be home and nowhere else. That shameless boy, whatever was he thinking of? "Boys do be known for having evil minds in them," she told herself, and the blood fairly crinkled in her veins. But he had said, "A fine woman like yourself," and maybe he'd met too many bold ones, and thought they were all alike; maybe she had been too free in her ways because he was Irish and looked so sad and poor. But there it was, he was a mean sort, and he would have made love to her if she hadn't stopped him, maybe. It flashed over her and she saw it clear as day—Kevin had loved her all the time, and she had sent him away to that cheap girl who wasn't half good enough for him! And Kevin a sweet decent boy would have cut off his right hand rather than give her an improper word. Kevin had loved her and she had loved Kevin and, oh, she hadn't known it in time! She bowed herself back into the corner with her elbow on the window-sill, her old fur collar pulled up around her face, and wept long and bitterly for Kevin, who would have stayed if she had said the word—and now he was gone and lost and dead. She would hide herself from the world and never speak to a soul again.

"Safe and sound she is, Dennis," Rosaleen told him. "She's been dangerous, but it's past. I left her in health."

"That's good enough," said Dennis, without enthusiasm. He took off his cap with the ear flaps and ran his fingers through his downy white hair and put the cap on again and stood waiting to hear the wonders of the trip; but Rosaleen had no tales to tell and was full of home-coming.

"This kitchen is a disgrace," she said, putting things to rights. "But not for all the world would I live in the city, Dennis. It's a wild heartless place, full of criminals in every direction as far as the eye can reach. I was scared for my life the whole time. Light the lamp, will you?"

The native boy sat warming his great feet in the oven, and his teeth were chattering with something more than cold. He burst out: "I seed sumpin' comin' up the road whiles ago. Black. Fust it went on all fours like a dawg and then it riz and walked longside of me on its hind legs. I was scairt, I was. I said Shoo! at it, and it went out, like a lamp."

"Maybe it was a dog," said Dennis.

"'Twarn't a dawg, neither," said the boy.

"Maybe 'twas a cat rising up to climb a fence," said Rosaleen.

"'Twarn't a cat, neither," said the boy. "'Twarn't nothin' I ever seed afore, nor *you*, neither."

"Never you mind about that," said Rosaleen. "I have seen it
and many times, when I was a girl in Ireland. It's famous
there, the way it comes in a black lump and rolls along the
path before you, but if you call on the Holy Name and make
the sign of the Cross, it flees away. Eat your supper now, and
sleep here the night; ye can't go out by your lone and the Evil
waiting for ye."

She bedded him down in Kevin's room, and kept Dennis
awake all hours telling him about the ghosts she'd seen in
Sligo. The trip to Boston seemed to have gone out of her
mind entirely.

In the morning, the boy's starveling black dog rose up at
the opened kitchen door and stared sorrowfully at his master.
The cats streamed out in a body, and silently, intently they
chased him far up the road. The boy stood on the doorstep
and began to tremble again. "The old woman told me to git
back fer supper," he said blankly. "Howma *ever* gointa git back
fer supper *now*? The ole man'll skin me alive."

Rosaleen wrapped her green wool shawl around her head
and shoulders. "I'll go along with ye and tell what happened,"
she said. "They'll never harm ye when they know the straight
of it." For he was shaking with fright until his knees buckled
under him. "He's away in his mind," she thought, with pity.
"Why can't they see it and let him be in peace?"

The steady slope of the lane ran on for nearly a mile, then
turned into a bumpy trail leading to a forlorn house with
broken-down steps and a litter of rubbish around them. The
boy hung back more and more, and stopped short when the
haggard, long-toothed woman in the gray dress came out carrying a stick of stove wood. The woman stopped short too
when she recognized Rosaleen, and a sly cold look came on
her face.

"Good day," said Rosaleen. "Your boy saw a ghost last night,
and I didn't have the heart to send him out in the darkness.
He slept safe in my house."

The woman gave a sharp dry bark, like a fox. "Ghosts!" she
said. "From all I hear, there's more than ghosts around your
house nights, Missis O'Toole." She wagged her head and her
faded tan hair flew in strings. "A pretty specimen you are,

Missis O'Toole, with your old husband and the young boys in
your house and the traveling salesmen and the drunkards
lolling on your doorstep all hours—"

"Hold your tongue before your lad here," said Rosaleen, the
back of her neck beginning to crinkle. She was so taken by surprise she couldn't find a ready answer, but stood in her tracks
listening.

"A pretty sight you are, Missis O'Toole," said the woman,
raising her thin voice somewhat, but speaking with deadly cold
slowness. "With your trips away from your husband and your
loud-colored dresses and your dyed hair—"

"May God strike you dead," said Rosaleen, raising her own
voice suddenly, "if you say that of my hair! And for the rest
may your evil tongue rot in your head with your teeth! I'll not
waste words on ye! Here's your poor lad and may God pity
him in your house, a blight on it! And if my own house is
burnt over my head I'll know who did it!" She turned away
and whirled back to call out, "May ye be ten years dying!"

"You can curse and swear, Missis O'Toole, but the whole
countryside knows about you!" cried the other, brandishing
her stick like a spear.

"Much good they'll get of it!" shouted Rosaleen, striding
away in a roaring fury. "Dyed, is it?" She raised her clenched
fist and shook it at the world. "Oh, the liar!" and her rage was
like a drum beating time for her marching legs. What was happening these days that everybody she met had dirty minds and
dirty tongues in their heads? Oh, why wasn't she strong enough
to strangle them all at once? Her eyes were so hot she couldn't
close her lids over them. She went on staring and walking,
until almost before she knew it she came in sight of her own
house, sitting like a hen quietly in a nest of snow. She slowed
down, her thumping heart eased a little, and she sat on a stone
by the roadside to catch her breath and gather her wits before
she must see Dennis. As she sat, it came to her that the Evil
walking the roads at night in this place was the bitter lies
people had been telling about her, who had been a good
woman all this time when many another would have gone
astray. It was no comfort now to remember all the times she
might have done wrong and hadn't. What was the good if she
was being scandalized all the same? That lad in Boston now—

the little whelp. She spat on the frozen earth and wiped her mouth. Then she put her elbows on her knees and her head in her hands, and thought, "So that's the way it is here, is it? That's what my life has come to, I'm a woman of bad fame with the neighbors."

Dwelling on this strange thought, little by little she began to feel better. Jealousy, of course, that was it. "Ah, what wouldn't that poor thing give to have my hair?" and she patted it tenderly. From the beginning it had been so, the women were jealous, because the men were everywhere after her, as if it was her fault! Well, let them talk. Let them. She knew in her heart what she was, and Dennis knew, and that was enough.

"Life is a dream," she said aloud, in a soft easy melancholy. "It's a mere dream." The thought and the words pleased her, and she gazed with pleasure at the loosened stones of the wall across the road, dark brown, with the thin shining coat of ice on them, in a comfortable daze until her feet began to feel chilled.

"Let me not sit here and take my death at my early time of life," she cautioned herself, getting up and wrapping her shawl carefully around her. She was thinking how this sad countryside needed some young hearts in it, and how she wished Kevin would come back to laugh with her at that woman up the hill; with him, she could just laugh in their faces! That dream about Honora now, it hadn't come true at all. Maybe the dream about Kevin wasn't true either. If one dream failed on you it would be foolish to think another mightn't fail you too: wouldn't it, wouldn't it? She smiled at Dennis sitting by the stove.

"What did the native people have to say this morning?" he asked, trying to pretend it was nothing much to him what they said.

"Oh, we exchanged the compliments of the season," said Rosaleen. "There was no call for more." She went about singing; her heart felt light as a leaf and she couldn't have told why if she died for it. But she was a good woman and she'd show them she was going to be one to her last day. Ah, she'd show them, the low-minded things.

In the evening they settled down by the stove, Dennis cleaning and greasing his boots, Rosaleen with the long tablecloth she'd been working on for fifteen years. Dennis kept wondering what had happened in Boston, or where ever she had been. He knew he would never hear the straight of it, but he wanted Rosaleen's story about it. And there she sat mum, putting a lot of useless stitches in something she would never use, even if she ever finished it, which she would not.

"Dennis," she said after a while, "I don't put the respect on dreams I once did."

"That's maybe a good thing," said Dennis, cautiously. "And why don't you?"

"All day long I've been thinking Kevin isn't dead at all, and we shall see him in this very house before long."

Dennis growled in his throat a little. "That's no sign at all," he said. And to show that he had a grudge against her he laid down his meerschaum pipe, stuffed his old briar and lit it instead. Rosaleen took no notice at all. Her embroidery had fallen on her knees and she was listening to the rattle and clatter of a buggy coming down the road, with Richards's voice roaring a song, "I've been working on the *railroad*, ALL the live-long day!" She stood up, taking hairpins out and putting them back, her hands trembling. Then she ran to the looking-glass and saw her face there, leaping into shapes fit to scare you. "Oh, Dennis," she cried out as if it was that thought had driven her out of her chair. "I forgot to buy a looking-glass, I forgot it altogether!"

"It's a good enough glass," repeated Dennis.

The buggy clattered at the gate, the song halted. Ah, he was coming in, surely! It flashed through her mind a woman would have a ruined life with such a man, it was courting death and danger to let him set foot over the threshold.

She stopped herself from running to the door, hand on the knob even before his knock should sound. Then the wheels creaked and ground again, the song started up; if he thought of stopping he changed his mind and went on, off on his career to the Saturday night dance in Winston, with his rapscallion cronies.

Rosaleen didn't know what to expect, then, and then: surely he couldn't be stopping? Ah, surely he *couldn't* be going on? She sat down again with her heart just nowhere, and took up the tablecloth, but for a long time she couldn't see the stitches.

She was wondering what had become of her life; every day she had thought something great was going to happen, and it was all just straying from one terrible disappointment to another. Here in the lamplight sat Dennis and the cats, beyond in the darkness and snow lay Winston and New York and Boston, and beyond that were far off places full of life and gayety she'd never seen nor even heard of, and beyond everything like a green field with morning sun on it lay youth and Ireland as if they were something she had dreamed, or made up in a story. Ah, what was there to remember, or to look forward to now? Without thinking at all, she leaned over and put her head on Dennis's knee. "Whyever," she asked him, in an ordinary voice, "did ye marry a woman like me?"

"Mind you don't tip over in that chair now," said Dennis. "I knew well I could never do better." His bosom began to thaw and simmer. It was going to be all right with everything, he could see that.

She sat up and felt his sleeves carefully. "I want you to wrap up warm this bitter weather, Dennis," she told him. "With two pairs of socks and the chest protector, for if anything happened to you, whatever would become of me in this world?"

"Let's not think of it," said Dennis, shuffling his feet.

"Let's not, then," said Rosaleen. "For I could cry if you crooked a finger at me."

Mexico City–Berlin, 1931

Hacienda

IT was worth the price of a ticket to see Kennerly take possession of the railway train among a dark inferior people. Andreyev and I trailed without plan in the wake of his gigantic progress (he was a man of ordinary height merely, physically taller by a head, perhaps, than the nearest Indian; but his moral stature in this moment was beyond calculation) through the second-class coach into which we had climbed, in our haste, by mistake. . . . Now that the true revolution of blessed memory has come and gone in Mexico, the names of many things are changed, nearly always with the view to an appearance of heightened well-being for all creatures. So you cannot ride third-class no matter how poor or humble-spirited or miserly you may be. You may go second in cheerful disorder and sociability, or first in sober ease; or, if you like, you may at great price install yourself in the stately plush of the Pullman, isolated and envied as any successful General from the north. "Ah, it is beautiful as a *pulman*!" says the middle-class Mexican when he wishes truly to praise anything. . . . There was no Pullman with this train or we should most unavoidably have been in it. Kennerly traveled like that. He strode mightily through, waving his free arm, lunging his portfolio and leather bag, stiffening his nostrils as conspicuously as he could against the smell that "poured," he said, "simply poured like mildewed pea soup!" from the teeming clutter of wet infants and draggled turkeys and indignant baby pigs and food baskets and bundles of vegetables and bales and hampers of domestic goods, each little mountain of confusion yet drawn into a unit, from the midst of which its owners glanced up casually from dark pleased faces at the passing strangers. Their pleasure had nothing to do with us. They were pleased because, sitting still, without even the effort of beating a burro, they were on the point of being carried where they wished to go, accomplishing in an hour what would otherwise have been a day's hard journey, with all their households on their backs. . . . Almost nothing can disturb their quiet ecstasy when they are finally settled among their plunder, and the engine, mysteriously and powerfully animated, draws them lightly over the miles they have so often counted step by step. And they are not troubled by the noisy white man because, by now, they are accustomed to him. White men look all much alike to the Indians, and they had seen this maddened fellow with light eyes and leather-colored hair battling his way desperately through their coach many times before. There is always one of him on every train. They watch his performance with as much attention as they can spare from their own always absorbing business; he is a part of the scene of travel.

He turned in the door and motioned wildly at us when we showed signs of stopping where we were. "No, no!" he bellowed. "NO! Not here. This will never do for you," he said, giving me a great look, protecting me, a lady. I followed on, trying to reassure him by noddings and hand-wavings. Andreyev came after, stepping tenderly over large objects and small beings, exchanging quick glances with many pairs of calm, lively dark eyes.

The first-class coach was nicely swept, there were no natives about to speak of, and most of the windows were open. Kennerly hurled bags at the racks, jerked seat-backs about rudely, and spread down topcoats and scarves until, with great clamor, he had built us a nest in which we might curl up facing each other, temporarily secure from the appalling situation of being three quite superior persons of the intellectual caste of the ruling race at large and practically defenseless in what a country! Kennerly almost choked when he tried to talk about it. It was for himself he built the nest, really: he was certain of what he was. Andreyev and I were included by courtesy: Andreyev was a Communist, and I was a writer, or so Kennerly had been told. He had never heard of me until a week before, he had never known anyone who had, and it was really up to Andreyev, who had invited me on this trip, to look out for me. But Andreyev took everything calmly, was not suspicious, never asked questions, and had no sense of social responsibility whatever— not, at least, what Kennerly would ever call by such a name; so it was hopeless to expect anything from him.

I had already proved that I lacked something by arriving at the station first and buying my own ticket, having been warned by Kennerly to meet them at the first-class window, as they were arriving straight from another town. When he discovered this, he managed to fill me with shame and confusion. "You were to have been our guest," he told me bitterly, taking my ticket and handing it to the conductor as if I had appropriated it to my own use from his pocket, stripping me publicly of guesthood once for all, it seemed. Andreyev also rebuked me: "We none of us should throw away our money when Kennerly is so rich and charitable." Kennerly, tucking away his leather billfold, paused, glared blindly at Andreyev for a moment, jumped as if he had discovered that he was stabbed clean through, said, "Rich? Me, rich? What do you mean, rich?" and blustered for a moment, hoping that somehow the proper retort would emerge; but it would not. So he sulked for a moment, got up and shifted his bags, sat down, felt in all his pockets again to make certain of something, sat back and wanted to know if I had noticed that he carried his own bags. It was because he was tired of being gypped by these people. Every time he let a fellow carry his bags, he had a fight to the death in simple self-defense. Literally, in his whole life he had never run into such a set of bandits as these train porters. Besides, think of the risk of infection from their filthy paws on your luggage handles. It was just damned dangerous, if you asked him.

I was thinking that foreigners anywhere traveling were three or four kinds of phonograph records, and of them all I liked Kennerly's kind the least. Andreyev hardly ever looked at him out of his clear, square gray eyes, in which so many different kinds of feeling against Kennerly were mingled, the total expression had become a sort of exasperated patience. Settling back, he drew out a folder of photographs, scenes from the film they had been making all over the country, balanced them on his knees and began where he left off to talk about Russia. . . . Kennerly moved into his corner away from us and turned to the window as if he wished to avoid overhearing a private conversation. The sun was shining when we left Mexico City, but mile by mile through the solemn valley of the pyramids we climbed through the maguey fields towards the thunderous blue cloud banked solidly in the east, until it dissolved and received us gently in a pallid, silent rain. We hung our heads out of the window every time the train paused, raising false hopes in the hearts of the Indian women who ran along beside us, faces thrown back and arms stretching upward even after the train was moving away.

"Fresh pulque!" they urged mournfully, holding up their clay jars filled with thick gray-white liquor. "Fresh maguey worms!" they cried in despair above the clamor of the turning wheels, waving like nosegays the leaf bags, slimy and lumpy with the worms they had gathered one at a time from the cactus whose heart bleeds the honey water for the pulque. They ran along still hoping, their brown fingers holding the bags lightly by the very tips, ready to toss them if the travelers should change their minds and buy, even then, until the engine outran them, their voices floated away and they were left clustered together, a little knot of faded blue skirts and shawls, in the indifferent rain.

Kennerly opened three bottles of luke-warm bitter beer. "The water is filthy!" he said earnestly, taking a ponderous, gargling swig from his bottle. "Isn't it horrible, the things they eat and drink?" he asked, as if, no matter what we might in our madness (for he did not trust either of us) say, he already knew the one possible answer. He shuddered and for a moment could not swallow his lump of sweet American chocolate: "I have just come back," he told me, trying to account for his extreme sensitiveness in these matters, "from God's country," meaning to say California. He ripped open an orange trademarked in purple ink. "I'll simply have to get used to all this all over again. What a relief to eat fruit that isn't full of germs. I brought them all the way back with me." (I could fairly see him legging across the Sonora desert with a knapsack full of oranges.) "Have one. Anyhow it's clean."

Kennerly was very clean, too, a walking reproach to untidiness: washed, shaven, clipped, pressed, polished, smelling of soap, brisk and firm-looking in his hay-colored tweeds. So far as that goes, a fine figure of a man, with the proper thriftiness of a healthy animal. There was no fault to find with him in this. Some day I shall make a poem to kittens washing themselves in the mornings; to Indians scrubbing their clothes to rags and their bodies to sleekness, with great slabs of sweet-smelling strong soap and wisps of henequen fiber, in the shade of trees, along river banks at midday; to horses rolling sprawling

snorting rubbing themselves against the grass to cleanse their
healthy hides; to naked children shouting in pools; to hens
singing in their dust baths; to sober fathers of families forgetting themselves in song under the discreet flood of tap-
water; to birds on the boughs ruffling and oiling their feathers
in delight; to girls and boys arranging themselves like baskets
of fruit for each other: to all thriving creatures making themselves cleanly and comely to the greater glory of life. But Kennerly had gone astray somewhere: he had overdone it; he wore
the harried air of a man on the edge of bankruptcy, keeping up
an expensive establishment because he dared not retrench. His
nerves were bundles of dried twigs, they jabbed his insides
every time a thought stirred in his head, they kept his blank
blue eyes fixed in a white stare. The muscles of his jaw jerked
in continual helpless rage. Eight months spent as business
manager for three Russian moving-picture men in Mexico had
about finished him off, he told me, quite as though Andreyev,
one of the three, were not present.

"Ah, he should have business-managed us through China
and Mongolia," said Andreyev, to me, as if speaking of an absent Kennerly. "After that, Mexico could never disturb him."

"The altitude!" said Kennerly. "My heart skips every other
beat. I can't sleep a wink!"

"There was no altitude at all in Tehuantepec," said Andreyev, with stubborn gayety, "and you should have been
there to see him."

Kennerly spewed up his afflictions like a child being sick.

"It's these Mexicans," he said as if it were an outrage to find
them in Mexico. "They would drive any man crazy in no time.
In Tehuantepec it was frightful." It would take him a week to
tell the whole story; and, besides, he was keeping notes and
was going to write a book about it some day; but "Just for example, they don't know the meaning of time and they have absolutely no regard for their word." They had to bribe every
step of the way. Graft, bribe, graft, bribe it was from morning
to night, anything from fifty pesos to the Wise Boys in the municipal councils to a bag of candy for a provincial mayor before
they were even allowed to set up their cameras. The mosquitoes ate him alive. And with the bugs and cockroaches and the

food and the heat and the water, everybody got sick: Stepanov, the camera-man, was sick; Andreyev was sick . . .

"Not seriously," said Andreyev.

The immortal Uspensky even got sick; and as for himself, Kennerly, he thought more than once he'd never live through it. Amoebic dysentery. You couldn't tell him. Why, it was a miracle they hadn't all died or had their throats cut. Why, it was worse than Africa. . . .

"Were you in Africa, too?" asked Andreyev. "Why do you always choose these inconvenient countries?"

Well, no, he had not been there, but he had friends who made a film among the pygmies and you wouldn't believe what they had gone through. As for him, Kennerly, give him pygmies or headhunters or cannibals outright, every time. At least you knew where you stood with them. Now take for example: they had lost ten thousand dollars flat by obeying the laws of the country—something nobody else does!—by passing their film of the Oaxaca earthquake before the board of censorship in Mexico City. Meanwhile, some unscrupulous native scoundrels who knew the ropes had beaten them to it and sent a complete newsreel to New York. It doesn't pay to have a conscience, but if you've got one what can you do about it? Just throw away your time and your money, that's all. He had written and protested to the censors, charging them with letting the Mexican film company get away with murder, accusing them of favoritism and deliberate malice in holding up the Russian film—everything, in a five-page typewritten letter. They hadn't even answered it. Now what can you do with people like that? Graft, bribe, bribe, graft, that's the way it went. Well, he had been learning, too. "Whatever they ask for, I give 'em half the amount, straight across the board," he said. "I tell 'em, 'Look here, I'll give you just half that amount, and anything more than that is bribery and corruption, d'you understand?' Do they take it? Like a shot. Ha!"

His overwhelming unmodulated voice brayed on agonizingly, his staring eyes accused everything they looked upon. Crickle crackle went the dried twigs of his nerve ends at every slightest jog of memory, every present touch, every cold wing from the future. He talked on. . . . He was afraid of his

brother-in-law, a violent prohibitionist who would be furious
if he ever heard that Kennerly had gone back to drinking beer
openly the minute he got out of California. In a way, his job
was at stake, for his brother-in-law had raised most of the
money among his friends for this expedition and might just
fire him out, though how the fellow expected to get along
without him Kennerly could not imagine. He was the best
friend his brother-in-law had in the world. If the man could
only realize it. Moreover, the friends would be soon, if they
were not already, shouting to have some money back on their
investment. Nobody but himself ever gave a thought to that
side of the business! . . . He glared outright at Andreyev at
this point.

Andreyev said: "I did not ask them to invest!"

Beer was the only thing Kennerly could trust—it was food
and medicine and a thirst-quencher all in one, and everything
else around him, fruit, meat, air, water, bread, were poisoned. . . . The picture was to have been finished in three
months and now they'd been there eight months and God
knew how much longer they'd have to go. He was afraid the
picture would be a failure, now it hadn't been finished on time.

"What time?" asked Andreyev, as if he had made this answer
many times before. "When it is finished it is finished."

"Yes, but it isn't merely enough to finish a job just when you
please. The public must be prepared for it on the dot." He
went on to explain that making good involves all sorts of mysterious interlocking schedules: it must be done by a certain
date, it must be art, of course, that's taken for granted, and it
must be a hit. Half the chance of making a hit depends upon
having your stuff ready to go at the psychological moment.
There are thousands of things to be thought of, and if they
miss one point, bang goes everything! . . . He sighted along
an imaginary rifle, pulled the trigger, and fell back exhausted.
His whole life of effort and despair flickered like a film across
his relaxed face, a life of putting things over in spite of hell, of
keeping up a good front, of lying awake nights fuming with
schemes and frothing with beer, rising of mornings gray-faced,
stupefied, pushing himself under cold showers and filling himself up on hot coffee and slamming himself into a fight in
which there are no rules and no referee and the antagonist is

everywhere. "God," he said to me, "you don't know. But I'm going to write a book about it. . . ."

As he sat there, talking about his book, eating American chocolate bars and drinking his third bottle of beer, sleep took him suddenly, upright as he was, in the midst of a sentence. Assertion failed, sleep took him mercifully by the nape and quelled him. His body cradled itself in the tweed, the collar rose above his neck, his closed eyes and limp mouth looked ready to cry.

Andreyev went on showing me pictures from that part of the film they were making at the pulque hacienda. . . . They had chosen it carefully, he said; it was really an old-fashioned feudal estate with the right kind of architecture, no modern improvements to speak of, and with the purest type of peons. Naturally a pulque hacienda would be just such a place. Pulque-making had not changed from the beginning, since the time the first Indian set up a rawhide vat to ferment the liquor and pierced and hollowed the first gourd to draw with his mouth the juice from the heart of the maguey. Nothing had happened since, nothing could happen. Apparently there was no better way to make pulque. The whole thing, he said, was almost too good to be true. An old Spanish gentleman had revisited the hacienda after an absence of fifty years, and had gone about looking at everything with delight. "Nothing has changed," he said, "nothing at all!"

The camera had seen this unchanged world as a landscape with figures, but figures under a doom imposed by the landscape. The closed dark faces were full of instinctive suffering, without individual memory, or only the kind of memory animals may have, who when they feel the whip know they suffer but do not know why and cannot imagine a remedy. . . . Death in these pictures was a procession with lighted candles, love a matter of vague gravity, of clasped hands and two sculptured figures inclining towards each other. Even the figure of the Indian in his ragged loose white clothing, weathered and molded to his flat-hipped, narrow-waisted body, leaning between the horns of the maguey, his mouth to the gourd, his burro with the casks on either side waiting with hanging head for his load, had this formal traditional tragedy, beautiful and hollow. There were rows of girls, like dark statues walking, their mantles streaming from their smooth brows, water jars on their shoulders; women kneeling at washing stones, their blouses slipping from their shoulders—"so picturesque, all this," said Andreyev, "we shall be accused of dressing them up." The camera had caught and fixed in moments of violence and senseless excitement, of cruel living and tortured death, the almost ecstatic death-expectancy which is in the air of Mexico. The Mexican may know when the danger is real, or may not care whether the thrill is false or true, but strangers feel the acid of death in their bones whether or not any real danger is near them. It was this terror that Kennerly had translated into fear of food, water, and air around him. In the Indian the love of death had become a habit of the spirit. It had smoothed out and polished the faces to a repose so absolute it seemed studied, though studied for so long it was now held without effort; and in them all was a common memory of defeat. The pride of their bodily posture was the mere outward shade of passive, profound resistance; the lifted, arrogant features were a mockery of the servants who lived within.

We looked at many scenes from the life of the master's house, with the characters dressed in the fashion of 1898. They were quite perfect. One girl was especially clever. She was the typical Mexican mixed-blood beauty, her mask-like face powdered white, with a round hard full mouth, and hard slanting dark eyes. Her black waved hair was combed back from a low forehead, and she wore her balloon sleeves and small stiff sailor hat with marvelous elegance.

"But this must be an actress," I said.

"Oh, yes," said Andreyev, "the only one. For that rôle we needed an actress. That is Lolita. We found her at the Jewel Theater."

The story of Lolita and doña Julia was very gay. It had begun by being a very usual story about Lolita and don Genaro, the master of the pulque hacienda. Doña Julia, his wife, was furious with him for bringing a fancy woman into the house. She herself was modern, she said, very modern, she had no old-fashioned ideas at all, but she still considered that she was being insulted. On the contrary, don Genaro was very old-fashioned in his taste for ladies of the theater. He had thought he was being discreet, besides, and was truly apologetic when he was found out. But little doña Julia was fearfully jealous. She screamed and wept and made scenes at night, first. Then she began making don Genaro jealous with other men. So that the men grew very frightened of doña Julia and almost ran when they saw her. Imagine all the things that might happen! There was the picture to think of, after all. . . . And then doña Julia threatened to kill Lolita—to cut her throat, to stab her, to poison her. . . . Don Genaro simply ran away at this, and left everything in the air. He went up to the capital and stayed two days.

When he came back, the first sight that greeted his eyes was his wife and his mistress strolling, arms about each other's waists, on the upper terrace, while a whole scene was being delayed because Lolita would not leave doña Julia and get to work.

Don Genaro, who prided himself on his speed, was thunderstruck by the suddenness of this change. He had borne with his wife's scenes because he really respected her rights and privileges as a wife. A wife's first right is to be jealous and threaten to kill her husband's mistress. Lolita also had her definite prerogatives. Everything, until he left, had gone with automatic precision exactly as it should have. This was thoroughly outrageous. He could not get them separated, either. They continued to walk and talk on the terrace under the trees all morning, affectionately entwined, heads together, one a cinema Chinese—doña Julia loved Chinese dress made by a Hollywood costumer—the other in the stiff elegance of 1898. They remained oblivious to the summons from the embattled males: Uspensky calling for Lolita to get into the scene at once, don Genaro sending messages by an Indian boy that the master had returned and wished to see doña Julia on a matter of the utmost importance. . . .

The women still strolled, or sat on the edge of the fountain, whispering together, arms lying at ease about each other's waists, for all the world to see. When Lolita finally came down the steps and took her place in the scene, doña Julia sat nearby, making up her face by her round mirror in the blinding

sunlight, getting in the way, smiling at Lolita whenever their
eyes met. When they asked her to sit somewhere else, a little
out of camera range, she pouted, moved three feet away, and
said, "I want to be in this scene too, with Lolita."

Lolita's deep throaty voice cooed at doña Julia. She tossed
strange glances at her from under her heavy eyelids, and when
she mounted her horse, she forgot her rôle, and swung her leg
over the saddle in a gesture unknown to ladies of 1898. . . .
Doña Julia greeted her husband with soft affection, and don
Genaro, who had no precedent whatever for a husband's conduct in such a situation, made a terrible scene, and pretended
he was jealous of Betancourt, one of the Mexican advisers to
Uspensky.

We turned over the pictures again, looked at some of them
twice. In the fields, among the maguey, the Indian in his hopeless rags; in the hacienda house, theatrically luxurious persons,
posed usually with a large chromo portrait of Porfirio Díaz
looming from a gaudy frame on the walls. "That is to show,"
said Andreyev, "that all this really happened in the time of
Díaz, and that all this," he tapped the pictures of the Indians,
"has been swept away by the revolution. It was the first re-
quirement of our agreement here." This without cracking a
smile or meeting my eye. "We have, in spite of everything, arrived at the third part of our picture."

I wondered how they had managed it. They had arrived
from California under a cloud as politically subversive characters. Wild rumor ran before them. It was said they had been
invited by the government to make a picture. It was said they
had not been so invited, but were being sponsored by Communists and various other shady organizations. The Mexican
government was paying them heavily; Moscow was paying
Mexico for the privilege of making the film: Uspensky was the
most dangerous agent Moscow had ever sent on a mission;
Moscow was on the point of repudiating him altogether, it was
doubtful he would be allowed to return to Russia. He was not
really a Communist at all, but a German spy. American Communists were paying for the film; the Mexican anti-government
party was at heart in sympathy with Russia and had paid

secretly an enormous sum to the Russians for a picture that would disgrace the present régime. The government officials themselves did not seem to know what was going on. They took all sides at once. A delegation of officials met the Russians at the boat and escorted them to jail. The jail was hot and uncomfortable. Uspensky, Andreyev, and Stepanov worried about their equipment, which was being turned over very thoroughly at the customs: and Kennerly worried about his reputation. Accustomed as he was to the clean, four-square business methods of God's own Hollywood, he trembled to think what he might be getting into. He had, so far as he had been able to see, helped to make all the arrangments before they left California. But he was no longer certain of anything. It was he who started the rumor that Uspensky was not a Party Member, and that one of the three was not even a Russian. He hoped this made the whole business sound more respectable. After a night of confusion another set of officials, more important than the first, arrived, all smiles, explanations and apologies, and set them free. Someone then started a rumor that the whole episode was invented for the sake of publicity.

The government officials still took no chance. They wanted to improve this opportunity to film a glorious history of Mexico, her wrongs and sufferings and her final triumph through the latest revolution; and the Russians found themselves surrounded and insulated from their material by the entire staff of professional propagandists, which had been put at their disposal for the duration of their visit. Dozens of helpful observers, art experts, photographers, literary talents, and travel guides swarmed about them to lead them aright, and to show them all the most beautiful, significant, and characteristic things in the national life and soul: if by chance anything not beautiful got in the way of the camera, there was a very instructed and sharp-eyed committee of censors whose duty it was to see that the scandal went no further than the cutting room.

"It has been astonishing," said Andreyev, "to see how devoted all of them are to art."

Kennerly stirred and muttered; he opened his eyes, closed them again. His head rolled uneasily.

"Wait. He is going to wake up," I whispered.

We sat still watching him.

"Maybe not yet," said Andreyev. "Everything," he added, "is pretty mixed up, and it's going to be worse."

We sat a few moments in silence, Andreyev still watching Kennerly impersonally.

"He would be something nice in a zoo," he said, with no particular malice, "but it is terrible to carry him around this way, all the time, without a cage." After a pause, he went on telling about Russia.

At the last station before we reached the hacienda, the Indian boy who was playing the leading rôle in the film came in looking for us. He entered as if on the stage, followed by several of his hero-worshipers, underfed, shabby youths, living happily in reflected glory. To be an actor in the cinema was enough for him to capture them utterly; but he was already famous in his village, being a pugilist and a good one. Bull-fighting is a little out of fashion; pugilism is the newest and smartest thing, and a really ambitious young man of the sporting set will, if God sends him the strength, take to boxing rather than to bulls. Fame added to fame had given this boy a brilliant air of self-confidence and he approached us, brows drawn together, with the easy self-possession of a man of the world accustomed to boarding trains and meeting his friends.

But the pose would not hold. His face, from high cheek-bones to square chin, from the full wide-lipped mouth to the low forehead, which had ordinarily the expression of professional-boxer histrionic ferocity, now broke up into a charming open look of simple, smiling excitement. He was happy to see Andreyev again, but there was something more: he had news worth hearing, and would be the first to tell us.

What a to-do there had been at the hacienda that morning! . . . Even while we were shaking hands all around, he broke out with it. "Justino—you remember Justino?—killed his sister. He shot her and ran to the mountains. Vicente—you know which one Vicente is?—chased him on horseback and brought him back." And now they had Justino in jail there in the village we were just leaving.

We were all as astounded and full of curiosity as he had hoped we would be. Yes, it had happened that very morning, at about ten o'clock. . . . No, nothing had gone wrong before that anyone knew about. No, Justino had not quarreled with anybody. No one had seen him do it. He had been in good humor all morning, working, making part of a scene on the set.

Neither Andreyev nor Kennerly spoke Spanish. The boy's words were in a jargon hard for me to understand, but I snatched key words and translated quickly as I could. Kennerly leaped up, white-eyed. . . .

"On the set? My God! We are ruined!"

"But why ruined? Why?"

"Her family will have a damage suit against us!"

The boy wanted to know what this meant.

"The law! the law!" groaned Kennerly. "They can collect money from us for the loss of their daughter. It can be blamed on us."

The boy was fairly baffled by this.

"He says he doesn't understand," I told Kennerly. "He says nobody ever heard of such a thing. He says Justino was in his own house when it happened, and nobody, not even Justino, was to blame."

"Oh," said Kennerly. "Oh, I see. Well, let's hear the rest of it. If he wasn't on the set, it doesn't matter."

He collected himself at once and sat down.

"Yes, do sit down," said Andreyev softly, with a venomous look at Kennerly. The Indian boy seized upon the look, visibly turned it over in his mind, obviously suspected it to refer to him, and stood glancing from one to another, deep frowning eyes instantly on guard.

"Do sit down," said Andreyev, "and don't be giving them all sorts of strange notions not necessary to anybody's peace of mind."

He reached out a free hand and pulled the boy down to sit on the arm of the seat. The other lads had collected near the door.

"Tell us the rest," said Andreyev.

After a small pause, the boy melted and talked. Justino had gone to his hut for the noon meal. His sister was grinding corn for the tortillas, while he stood by waiting, throwing the pistol into the air and catching it. The pistol fired; shot her through here. . . . He touched his ribs level with his heart. . . . She

fell forward on her face, over the grinding stone, dead. In no
time at all a crowd came running from everywhere. Seeing
what he had done, Justino ran, leaping like a crazy man,
throwing away the pistol as he went, and struck through the
maguey fields toward the mountains. His friend Vicente went
after him on horseback, waving a gun and yelling: "Stop or I'll
shoot!" and Justino yelled back: "Shoot! I don't care! . . ."
But of course Vicente did not: he just galloped up and bashed
Justino over the head with the gun butt, threw him across the
saddle, and brought him back. Now he was in jail, but don
Genaro was already in the village getting him out. Justino did
not do it on purpose.

"This is going to hold up everything," said Kennerly.
"Everything! It just means more time wasted."

"And that isn't all," said the boy. He smiled ambiguously,
lowered his voice a little, put on an air of conspiracy and discretion, and said: "The actress is gone too. She has gone back
to the capital. Three days ago."

"A quarrel with doña Julia?" asked Andreyev.

"No," said the boy, "it was with don Genaro she quarreled,
after all."

The three of them laughed mightily together, and Andreyev
said to me:

"You know that wild girl from the Jewel Theater."

The boy said: "It was because don Genaro was away on
other business at a bad moment." He was being more discreet
than ever.

Kennerly sat with his chin drawn in severely, almost making
faces at Andreyev and the boy in his efforts to hush them. Andreyev stared back at him in hardy innocence. The boy saw the
look, again lapsed into perfect silence, and sat very haughtily
on the seat arm, clenched fist posed on his thigh, his face
turned partly away. As the train slowed down, he rose suddenly and dashed ahead of us.

When we swung down the high narrow steps he was already
standing beside the mule car, greeting the two Indians who
had come to meet us. His young hangers-on, waving their hats
to us, set out to walk a shortcut across the maguey fields.

Kennerly was blustering about, handing bags to the Indians
to store away in the small shabby mule car, arranging the

party, settling all properly, myself between him and Andreyev, tucking my skirts around my knees with officious hands, to keep a thread of my garments from touching the no doubt infectious foreign things facing us.

The little mule dug its sharp hoof points into the stones and grass of the track, got a tolerable purchase at last on a cross tie, and set off at a finicking steady trot, the bells on its collar jingling like a tambourine.

We jogged away, crowded together facing each other three in a row, with bags under the seats, and the straw falling out of the cushions. The driver, craning around toward the mule now and then, and snapping the reins on its back, added his comments: An unlucky family. This was the second child to be killed by a brother. The mother was half dead with grief and Justino, a good boy, was in jail.

The big man sitting by him in striped riding trousers, his hat bound under his chin with red-tasseled cord, added that Justino was in for it now, God help him. But where did he get the pistol? He borrowed it from the firearms being used in the picture. It was true he was not supposed to touch the pistols, and there was his first mistake. He meant to put it back at once, but you know how a boy of sixteen loves to play with a pistol. Nobody would blame him. . . . The girl was nineteen years old. Her body had been sent already to the village to be buried. There was too much excitement over her; nothing was done so long as she was on the place. Don Genaro had gone, according to custom, to cross her hands, close her eyes, and light a candle beside her. Everything was done in order, they said piously, their eyes dancing with rich, enjoyable feelings. It is always regrettable and exciting when somebody you know gets into such dramatic trouble. Ah, we were alive under that deepening sky, jingling away through the yellow fields of blooming mustard with the pattern of spiked maguey shuttling as we passed, from straight lines to angles, to diamond shapes, and back again, miles and miles of it spreading away to the looming mountains.

"Surely they would not have had loaded pistols among those being used in the picture?" I asked, rather suddenly, of the big man with the red-tasseled cord on his hat.

He opened his mouth to say something and snapped it shut

again. There was a pause. Nobody spoke. It was my turn to be uncomfortable under a quick exchange of glances between the others.

There was again the guarded watchful expression on the Indian faces. An awful silence settled over us.

Andreyev, who had been trying his Spanish boldly, said, "If I cannot talk, I can sing," and began in his big gay Russian voice: "Ay, Sandunga, Sandunga, Mamá, por Diós!" All the Indians shouted with joy and delight at the new thing his strange tongue made of the words. Andreyev laughed, too. This laughter was an invitation to their confidence. With a burst of song in Russian, the young pugilist threw himself in turn on the laughter of Andreyev. Everybody then seized the opportunity to laugh madly in fellowship, even Kennerly. Eyes met eyes through the guard of crinkled lids, and the little mule went without urging into a stiff-legged gallop.

A big rabbit leaped across the track, chased by lean hungry dogs. It was cracking the strings of its heart in flight; its eyes started from its head like crystal bubbles. "Run, rabbit, run!" I cried. "Run, dogs!" shouted the big Indian with the red cords on his hat, his love of a contest instantly aroused. He turned to me with his eyes blazing: "What will you bet, señorita?"

The hacienda lay before us, a monastery, a walled fortress, towered in terra cotta and coral, sheltered against the mountains. An old woman in a shawl opened the heavy double gate and we slid into the main corral. The upper windows in the near end were all alight. Stepanov stood on one balcony; Betancourt, on the next; and for a moment the celebrated Uspensky appeared with waving arms at a third. They called to us, even before they recognized us, glad to see anyone of their party returning from town to relieve the long monotony of the day which had been shattered by the accident and could not be gathered together again. Thin-boned horses with round sleek haunches, long rippling manes and tails were standing under saddle in the patio. Big polite dogs of expensive breeds came out to meet us and walked with dignity beside us up the broad shallow steps.

The room was cold. The round-shaded hanging lamp hardly disturbed the shadows. The doorways, of the style called Porfirian Gothic, in honor of the Díaz period of domestic architecture, soared towards the roof in a cloud of gilded stamped wallpaper, from an undergrowth of purple and red and orange plush armchairs fringed and tassled, set on bases with springs. Such spots as this, fitted up for casual visits, interrupted the chill gloom of the rooms marching by tens along the cloisters, now and again casting themselves around patios, gardens, pens for animals. A naked player-piano in light wood occupied one corner. Standing together here, we spoke again of the death of the girl, and Justino's troubles, and all our voices were vague with the vast incurable boredom which hung in the air of the place and settled around our heads clustered together.

Kennerly worried about the possible lawsuit.

"They know nothing about such things," Betancourt assured him. "Besides, it is not our fault."

The Russians were thinking about tomorrow. It was not only a great pity about the poor girl, but both she and her brother were working in the picture; the boy's rôle was important and everything must be halted until he should come back, or if he should never come back everything must be done all over again.

Betancourt, Mexican by birth, French-Spanish by blood, French by education, was completely at the mercy of an ideal of elegance and detachment perpetually at war with a kind of Mexican nationalism which afflicted him like an inherited weakness of the nervous system. Being trustworthy and of cultured taste it was his official duty to see that nothing hurtful to the national dignity got in the way of the foreign cameras. His ambiguous situation seemed to trouble him not at all. He was plainly happy and fulfilled for the first time in years. Beggars, the poor, the deformed, the old and ugly, trust Betancourt to wave them away. "I am sorry for everything," he said, lifting a narrow, pontifical hand, waving away vulgar human pity which always threatened, buzzing like a fly at the edges of his mind. "But when you consider"—he made an almost imperceptible inclination of his entire person in the general direction of the social point of view supposed to be represented by the Russians —"what her life would have been like in this place, it is much better that she is dead. . . ."

He had burning fanatic eyes and a small tremulous mouth. His bones were like reeds.

"It is a tragedy, but it happens too often," he said.

With his easy words the girl was dead indeed, anonymously entombed. . . .

Doña Julia came in silently, walking softly on her tiny feet in embroidered shoes like a Chinese woman's. She was probably twenty years old. Her black hair was sleeked to her round skull, eyes painted, apparently, in the waxed semblance of her face.

"We never really live here," she said, in a gentle smooth voice, glancing vaguely about her strange setting, in which she appeared to be an exotic speaking doll. "It's very ugly, but you must not mind that. It is hopeless to try keeping the place up. The Indians destroy everything with neglect. We stay here now for the excitement about the film. It is thrilling." Then she added, "It is sad about the poor girl. It makes every kind of trouble. It is sad about the poor brother. . . ." As we went towards the dining-room, she murmured along beside me, "It is sad . . . very sad . . . sad. . . ."

Don Genaro's grandfather, who had been described to me as a gentleman of the very oldest school, was absent on a prolonged visit. In no way did he approve of his granddaughter-in-law, who got herself up in a fashion unknown to the ladies of his day, a fashion very upsetting to a man of the world who had always known how to judge, grade, and separate women into their proper categories at a glance. A temporary association with such a young female as this he considered a part of every gentleman's education. Marriage was an altogether different matter. In his day, she would have had at best a career in the theater. He had been silenced but in no wise changed in his conviction by the sudden, astonishing marriage of his grandson, the sole inevitable heir, who was already acting as head of the house, accountable to no one. He did not understand the boy and he did not waste time trying. He had moved his furniture and his keepsakes and his person away, to the very farthest patio in the old garden, above the terraces to the south, where he lived in bleak dignity and loneliness, without hope and without philosophy, perhaps contemptuous of both, joining his family only at mealtimes. His place at the foot of the table was empty, the weekend crowds of sightseers were gone and our party barely occupied part of the upper end.

Uspensky sat in his monkey-suit of striped overalls, his face like a superhumanly enlightened monkey's now well over-grown with a simian beard.

He had a monkey attitude towards life, which amounted almost to a personal philosophy. It saved explanation, and threw off the kind of bores he could least bear with. He amused himself at the low theaters in the capital, flattering the Mexicans by declaring they really were the most obscene he had found in the whole world. He liked staging old Russian country comedies, all the players wearing Mexican dress, on the open roads in the afternoon. He would then shout his lines broadly and be in his best humor, prodding the rear of a patient burro, accustomed to grief and indignity, with a phallus-shaped gourd. "Ah, yes, I remember," he said gallantly, on meeting some southern women, "you are the ladies who are always being raped by those dreadful negroes!" But now he was fevered, restless, altogether silent, and his bawdy humor, which served as cover and disguise for all other moods, was gone.

Stepanov, a champion at tennis and polo, wore flannel tennis slacks and polo shirt. Betancourt wore well-cut riding trousers and puttees, not because he ever mounted a horse if he could avoid it, but he had learned in California, in 1921, that this was the correct costume for a moving-picture director: true, he was not yet a director, but he was assisting somewhat at the making of a film, and when in action, he always added a green-lined cork helmet, which completed some sort of precious illusion he cherished about himself. Andreyev's no-colored wool shirt was elbow to elbow with Kennerly's brash tweeds. I wore a knitted garment of the kind which always appears suitable for any other than the occasion on which it is being worn. Altogether, we provided a staggering contrast for doña Julia at the head of the table, a figure from a Hollywood comedy, in black satin pajamas adorned with rainbow-colored bands of silk, loose sleeves falling over her babyish hands with pointed scarlet finger ends.

"We mustn't wait for my husband," said doña Julia; "he is always so busy and always late."

"Always going at top speed," said Betancourt, pleasantly, "70 kilometers an hour at least, and never on time anywhere." He prided himself on his punctuality, and had theories about speed, its use and abuse. He loved to explain that man, if he

had concentrated on his spiritual development, as he should
have done, would never have needed to rely on mechanical
aids to conquer time and space. In the meantime, he admitted
that he himself, who could communicate telepathically with
anyone he chose, and who had once levitated himself three
feet from the ground by a simple act of the will, found a great
deal of pleasurable stimulation in the control of machinery. I
knew something about his pleasure in driving an automobile.
He had for one thing a habit of stepping on the accelerator
and bounding across tracks before approaching trains. Speed,
he said, was "modern" and it was everyone's duty to be as
modern as one's means allowed. I surmised from Betancourt's
talk that don Genaro's wealth allowed him to be at least twice
as modern as Betancourt. He could afford high-powered automobiles that simply frightened other drivers off the road before
him; he was thinking of an airplane to cut distance between
the hacienda and the capital; speed and lightness at great expense was his ideal. Nothing could move too fast for don
Genaro, said Betancourt, whether a horse, a dog, a woman or
something with metal machinery in it. Doña Julia smiled ap-
provingly at what she considered praise of her husband and, by
pleasant inference, of herself.

   There came a violent commotion along the hall, at the door,
in the room. The servants separated, fell back, rushed forward,
scurried to draw out a chair, and don Genaro entered, wearing
Mexican country riding dress, a gray buckskin jacket and tight
gray trousers strapped under the boot. He was a tall, hard-
bitten, blue-eyed young Spaniard, stringy-muscled, thin-lipped,
graceful, and he was in fury. This fury he expected us to sympathize with; he dismissed it long enough to greet everybody
all around, then dropped into his chair beside his wife and
burst forth, beating his fist on the table.

   It seemed that the imbecile village judge refused to let him
have Justino. It seemed there was some crazy law about criminal negligence. The law, the judge said, does not recognize
accidents in the vulgar sense. There must always be careful
inquiry based on suspicion of bad faith in those nearest the
victim. Don Genaro gave an imitation of the imbecile judge
showing off his legal knowledge. Floods, volcanic eruptions,
revolutions, runaway horses, smallpox, train wrecks, street

fights, all such things, the judge said, were acts of God. Personal shootings, no. A personal shooting must always be inquired into severely. "All that has nothing to do with this case, I told him," said don Genaro. "I told him, Justino is my peon, his family have lived for three hundred years on our hacienda, this is MY business. I know what happened and all about it, and you don't know anything and all you have to do with this is to let me have Justino back at once. I mean today, tomorrow will not do, I told him." It was no good. The judge wanted two thousand pesos to let Justino go. "Two thousand pesos!" shouted don Genaro, thumping on the table; "try to imagine that!"

"How ridiculous!" said his wife with comradely sympathy and a glittering smile. He glared at her for a second as if he did not recognize her. She gazed back, her eyes flickering, a tiny uncertain smile in the corners of her mouth where the rouge was beginning to melt. Furiously he ignored her, shook the pause off his shoulders and hurried on, turning as he talked, hot and blinded and baffled, to one and another of his audience. It was not the two thousand pesos, it was that he was sick of paying here, paying there, for the most absurd things; every time he turned around there at his elbow was some thievish politician holding out his paw. "Well, there's one thing to do. If I pay this judge there'll be no end to it. He'll go on arresting my peons every time one of them shows his face in the village. I'll go to Mexico and see Velarde. . . ."

Everybody agreed with him that Velarde was the man to see. He was the most powerful and successful revolutionist in Mexico. He owned two pulque haciendas which had fallen to his share when the great repartition of land had taken place. He operated also the largest dairy farm in the country, furnishing milk and butter and cheese to every charitable institution, orphans' home, insane asylum, reform school and workhouse in the country, and getting just twice the prices for them that any other dairy farm would have asked. He also owned a great aguacate hacienda; he controlled the army; he controlled a powerful bank; the president of the Republic made no appointments to any office without his advice. He fought counter-revolution and political corruption, daily upon the front pages of twenty newspapers he had bought for that very purpose. He employed thousands of peons. As an employer, he would understand what don Genaro was contending with. As an honest revolutionist, he would know how to handle that dirty, bribe-taking little judge. "I'll go to see Velarde," said don Genaro in a voice gone suddenly flat, as if he despaired or was too bored with the topic to keep it up any longer. He sat back and looked at his guests bleakly. Everyone said something, it did not matter what. The episode of the morning now seemed very far away and not worth thinking about.

Uspensky sneezed with his hands over his face. He had spent two early morning hours standing up to his middle in the cold water of the horse fountain, with Stepanov and the camera balanced on the small stone ledge, directing a scene which he was convinced could be made from no other angle. He had taken cold; he now swallowed a mouthful of fried beans, drank half a glass of beer at one gulp, and slid off the long bench. His too-large striped overalls disappeared in two jumps through the nearest door. He went as if he were seeking another climate.

"He has a fever," said Andreyev. "If he does not feel better tonight we must send for Doctor Volk."

A large lumpish person in faded blue overalls and a flannel shirt inserted himself into a space near the foot of the table. He nodded to nobody in particular, and Betancourt punctiliously acknowledged the salute.

"You do not even recognize him?" Betancourt asked me in a low voice. "That is Carlos Montaña. You find him changed?"

He seemed anxious that I should find Carlos much changed. I said I supposed we had all changed somewhat after ten years. Besides, Carlos had grown a fine set of whiskers. Betancourt's glance at me plainly admitted that I, like Carlos, had changed and for the worse, but he resisted the notion of change in himself. "Maybe," he said, unwillingly, "but most of us, I think, for the better. It's poor Carlos. It's not only the whiskers, and the fat. He has, you know, become a failure."

"A Puss Moth," said don Genaro to Stepanov. "I flew it half an hour yesterday; awfully *chic*. I may buy it. I need something really fast. Something light, too, it must be fast. It must be something I can depend upon at any minute." Stepanov was an expert pilot. He excelled in every activity that don Genaro respected. Don Genaro listened attentively while Stepanov gave him some clear sensible advice about airplanes: what kind to buy, how to keep them in order, and what one might expect of airplanes as a usual thing.

"Airplanes!" said Kennerly, listening in. "I wouldn't go up with a Mexican pilot for all the money in—"

"Airplane! At last!" cried doña Julia, like a gently enraptured child. She leaned over the table and called in Spanish softly as if waking someone, "Carlos! Do you hear? Genarito is going to buy me an airplane, after all!"

Don Genaro talked on with Stepanov as if he had not heard.

"And what will you do with it?" asked Carlos, eyes round and amiable from under his bushy brows. Without lifting his head from his hand, he went on eating his fried beans and green chili sauce with a spoon, good Mexican country fashion, and enjoying them.

"I shall turn somersaults in it," said doña Julia.

"A Failure," Betancourt went on, in English, which Carlos could not understand, "though I must say he looks worse to-day than usual. He slipped and hurt himself in the bathtub this morning." It was as if this accident were another point against Carlos, symbolic proof of the fatal downward tendency in his character.

"I thought he had composed half the popular songs in Mexico," I said. "I heard nothing but his songs here, ten years ago. What happened?"

"Ah, that was ten years ago, don't forget. He does almost nothing now. He hasn't been director of the Jewel for, oh, ages!"

I observed the Failure. He seemed cheerful enough. He was beating time with the handle of his spoon and humming a song to Andreyev, who listened, nodding his head. "Like that, for two measures," said Carlos in French, "then like this," and he beat time, humming. "Then this for the dance. . . ." Andreyev hummed the tune and tapped on the table with his left forefinger, his right hand waving slightly. Betancourt watched them for a moment. "He feels better just now, poor fellow," he said, "now I have got him this job. It may be a new beginning for him. But he is sometimes tired, he drinks too much, he cannot always do his best."

Carlos had slumped back in his chair, his round shoulders

drooped, his swollen lids covered his eyes, he poked fretfully at
his plate of enchiladas with sour cream. "You'll see," he said to
Andreyev in French, "how Betancourt will not like this idea
either. There will be something wrong with it. . . ." He said
it not angrily, not timidly, but with an unhappy certainty.
"Either it will not be modern enough, or not enough in the
old style, or just not Mexican enough. . . . You'll see."

  Betancourt had spent his youth unlocking the stubborn secrets of Universal Harmony by means of numerology, astronomy, astrology, a formula of thought-transference and deep
breathing, the practice of will-to-power combined with the
latest American theories of personality development; certain
complicated magical ceremonies; and a careful choice of doctrines from the several schools of Oriental philosophies which
are, from time to time, so successfully introduced into California. From this material he had constructed a Way of Life which
could be taught to anyone, and once learned led the initiate
quietly and surely toward Success: success without pain, almost
without effort except of a pleasurable kind, success accompanied by moral and esthetic beauty, as well as the most desirable
material reward. Wealth, naturally, could not be an end in itself: alone, it was not Success. But it was the unobtrusive companion of all true Success. . . . From this point of view he
was cheerfully explicit about Carlos. Carlos had always been
contemptuous of the Eternal Laws. He had always simply written his tunes without giving a thought to the profounder in-
ferences of music, based as it is upon the harmonic system of
the spheres. . . . He, Betancourt, had many times warned
Carlos. It had done no good at all. Carlos had gone on inviting his own doom.

  "I have warned you, too," he said to me kindly. "I have
asked myself many times why you will not or cannot accept
the Mysteries which would open a whole treasure house for
you. . . . All," he said, "is possible through scientific intu-
ition. If you depend on mere intellect, you must fail."

  "You must fail," he had been saying all this time to poor
simple Carlos. "He has failed," he said of him to others. He
now looked almost fondly upon his handiwork, who sat there,
somewhat grubby and gloomy, a man who had done a good
day's work in his time, and was not altogether finished yet.

The neat light figure beside me posed gracefully upon its slender spine, the too-beautiful slender hands waved rhythmically upon insubstantial wrists. I remembered all that Carlos had done for Betancourt in other days; he had, in his thoughtless hopelessly human way, piled upon these thin shoulders a greater burden of gratitude than they could support. Betancourt had set in motion all the machinery of the laws of Universal Harmony he could command to help him revenge himself on Carlos. It was slow work, but he never tired.

"I don't, of course, understand just what you mean by failure, or by success either," I told him at last. "You know, I never could understand."

"It is true, you could not," he said, "that was the great trouble."

"As for Carlos," I said, "you should forgive him. . . ."

Betancourt said with perfect sincerity, "You know I never blame anyone for anything at all."

Carlos came round and shook hands with me as everybody pushed back his chair and began drifting out by the several doorways. He was full of humanity and good humor about Justino and his troubles. "These family love affairs," he said, "what can you expect?"

"Oh, no, now," said Betancourt, uneasily. He laughed his twanging tremulous little laugh.

"Oh, yes, now," said Carlos, walking beside me. "I shall make a *corrido* about Justino and his sister." He began to sing almost in a whisper, imitating the voice and gestures of a singer peddling broadsides in the market. . . .

> *Ah, poor little Rosalita*
> *Took herself a new lover,*
> *Thus betraying the heart's core*
> *Of her impassioned brother . . .*
>
> *Now she lies dead, poor Rosalita,*
> *With two bullets in her heart. . . .*
> *Take warning, my young sisters,*
> *Who would from your brothers part.*

"One bullet," said Betancourt, wagging a long finger at Carlos. "One bullet!"

Carlos laughed. "Very well, one bullet! Such a precisionist! Good night," he said.

Kennerly and Carlos disappeared early. Don Genaro spent the evening playing billiards with Stepanov, who won always. Don Genaro was very good at billiards, but Stepanov was a champion, with all sorts of trophies to show, so it was no humiliation to be defeated by him.

In the drafty upper-hall room fitted up as a parlor, Andreyev turned off the mechanical attachment of the piano and sang Russian songs, running his hands over the keys while he waited to remember yet other songs. Doña Julia and I sat listening. He sang for us, but for himself mostly, in the same kind of voluntary forgetfulness of his surroundings, the same self-induced absence of mind that had kept him talking about Russia in the afternoon.

We sat until very late. Doña Julia smiled steadily every time she caught the glance of Andreyev or myself, yawning now and then under her hand, her Pekinese sprawling and snoring on her lap. "You're not tired?" I asked her. "You wouldn't let us stay up too late?"

"Oh, no, let's go on with the music. I love sitting up all night. I never go to bed if I can possibly sit up. Don't go yet."

At half-past one Uspensky sent for Andreyev, for Stepanov. He was restless, in a fever, he wished to talk. Andreyev said, "I have already sent for Doctor Volk. It is better not to delay."

Doña Julia and I looked on in the billiard room downstairs, where Stepanov and don Genaro were settling the score. Several Indians leaned in at the windows, their vast straw hats tilted forward, watching in silence. Doña Julia asked her husband, "Then you're not going to Mexico tonight?"

"Why should I?" he inquired suddenly without looking at her.

"I thought you might," said doña Julia. "Good night, Stepanov," she said, her black eyes shining under her long lids painted silver blue.

"Good night, Julita," said Stepanov, his frank Northern smile meaning anything or nothing at all. When he was not smiling, his face was severe, expressive, and intensely alive. His smile was misleadingly simple, like a very young boy's. He was anything but simple; he smiled now like a merry open book

upon the absurd little figure strayed out of a marionette theater. Turning away, Doña Julia slanted at him the glittering eye
of a femme fatale in any Hollywood film. He examined the
end of his cue as if he looked through a microscope. Don
Genaro said violently, "Good night!" and disappeared violently through the door leading to the corral.

Doña Julia and I passed through her apartment, a long shallow room between the billiard and the vat-room. It was puffy
with silk and down, glossy with bright new polished wood and
wide mirrors, restless with small ornaments, boxes of sweets,
French dolls in ruffled skirts and white wigs. The air was thick
with perfume which fought with another heavier smell. From
the vat-room came a continual muffled shouting, the rumble
of barrels as they rolled down the wooden trestles to the flat
mule-car standing on the tracks running past the wide doorway. The smell had not been out of my nostrils since I came,
but here it rose in a thick vapor through the heavy drone of
flies, sour, stale, like rotting milk and blood; this sound and
this smell belonged together, and both belonged to the intermittent rumble of barrels and the long chanting cry of the Indians. On the narrow stairs I glanced back at doña Julia. She
was looking up, wrinkling her little nose, her Pekinese with his
wrinkled nose of perpetual disgust held close to her face.
"Pulque!" she said. "Isn't it horrid? But I hope the noise will
not keep you awake."

On my balcony there was no longer any perfume to disturb
the keen fine wind from the mountains, or the smell from the
vat-room. "Twenty-one!" sang the Indians in a long, melodious chorus of weariness and excitement, and the twenty-first
barrel of fresh pulque rolled down the slide, was seized by two
men and loaded on the flat-car under my window.

From the window next to mine, the three Russian voices
murmured along quietly. Pigs grunted and rooted in the soft
wallow near the washing fountain, where the women were still
kneeling in the darkness, thumping wet cloth on the stones,
chattering, laughing. All the women seemed to be laughing
that night: long after midnight, the high bright sound sparkled
again and again from the long row of peon quarters along the
corral. Burros sobbed and mourned to each other, there was
everywhere the drowsy wakefulness of creatures, stamping

hoofs, breathing and snorting. Below in the vat-room a single
voice sang suddenly a dozen notes of some rowdy song; and
the women at the washing fountain were silenced for a moment, then tittered among themselves. There occurred a light
flurry at the arch of the gate leading into the inner patio: one
of the polite, expensive dogs had lost his dignity and was
chasing, with snarls of real annoyance, a little fat-bottomed
soldier back to his proper place, the barracks by the wall opposite the Indian huts. The soldier scrambled and stumbled
silently away, without resistance, his dim lantern agitated violently. At a certain point, as if here was the invisible boundary
line, the dog stopped, watched while the soldier ran on, then
returned to his post under the archway. The soldiers, sent by
the government as a guard against the Agrarians, sprawled in
idleness eating their beans at don Genaro's expense. He toler-
ated and resented them, and so did the dogs.

I fell asleep to the long chanting of the Indians, counting their
barrels in the vat-room, and woke again at sunrise, summer
sunrise, to their long doleful morning song, the clatter of metal
and hard leather, and the stamping of mules as they were being
harnessed to the flat-cars. . . . The drivers swung their whips
and shouted, the loaded cars creaked and slid away in a procession, off to meet the pulque train for Mexico City. The field
workers were leaving for the maguey fields, driving their donkeys. They shouted, too, and whacked the donkeys with sticks,
but no one was really hurrying, nor really excited. It was just
another day's work, another day's weariness. A three-year-old
man-child ran beside his father; he drove a weanling donkey
carrying two miniature casks on its furry back. The two small
creatures imitated each in his own kind perfectly the gestures
of their elders. The baby whacked and shouted, the donkey
trudged and flapped his ears at each blow.

"My God!" said Kennerly over coffee an hour later. "Do
you remember—" he beat off a cloud of flies and filled his cup
with a wobbling hand—"I thought of it all night and couldn't
sleep—*don't* you remember," he implored Stepanov, who held
one palm over his coffee cup while he finished a cigarette,
"those scenes we shot only two weeks ago, when Justino
played the part of a boy who killed a girl by accident, tried to

escape, and Vicente was one of the men who ran him down on horseback? Well, the same thing has happened to the same people in *reality!* And—" he turned to me, "the strangest thing is, we have to make that scene again, it didn't turn out so well, and look, my God, we had it happening really, and nobody thought of it then! Then was the time. We could have got a close-up of the girl, really dead, and real blood running down Justino's face where Vicente hit him, and my God! we never even thought of it. That kind of thing," he said, bitterly, "has been happening ever since we got here. Just happens over and over. . . . Now, what was the matter, I wonder?"

He stared at Stepanov full of accusation. Stepanov lifted his palm from his cup, and beating off flies, drank. "Light no good, probably," he said. His eyes flickered open, clicked shut in Kennerly's direction, as if they had taken a snapshot of something and that episode was finished.

"If you want to look at it that way," said Kennerly, with resentment, "but after all, there it was, it had happened, it wasn't our fault, and we might as well have had it."

"We can always do it again," said Stepanov. "When Justino comes back, and the light is better. The light," he said to me, "it is always our enemy. Here we have one good day in five, or less."

"Imagine," said Kennerly, pouncing, "just try to imagine that—when that poor boy comes back he'll have to go through the same scene he has gone through twice before, once in play and once in reality. *Reality!*" He licked his chops. "Think how he'll feel. Why, it ought to drive him crazy."

"If he comes back," said Stepanov, "we must think of that."

In the patio half a dozen Indian boys, their ragged white clothes exposing their tawny smooth skin, were flinging over the sleek-backed horses great saddles of deerskin encrusted with silver embroidery and mother-of-pearl. The women were returning to the washing fountain. The pigs were out rooting in their favorite wallows, and in the vat-room, silently, the day-workers were already filling the bullhide vats with freshly drawn pulque juice. Carlos Montaña was out early too, enjoying himself in the fresh morning air, watching three dogs chase a long-legged pig from wallow to barn. The pig, screaming steadily, galloped like a rocking horse towards the known safety of his pen, the dogs nipping at his heels just enough to keep him up to his best speed. Carlos roared with joy, holding his ribs, and the Indian boys laughed with him.

The Spanish overseer, who had been cast for the rôle of villain—one of them—in the film, came out wearing a new pair of tight riding trousers, of deerskin and silver embroidery, like the saddles, and sat slouched on the long bench near the arch, facing the great corral where the Indians and soldiers were. There he sat nearly all day, as he had sat for years and might sit for years more. His long wry North-Spanish face was dead with boredom. He slouched, with his English cap pulled over his close-set eyes, and did not even glance to see what Carlos was laughing at. Andreyev and I waved to Carlos and he came over at once. He was still laughing. It seemed he had forgotten the pig and was laughing at the overseer, who had already forty pairs of fancy charro trousers, but had thought none of them quite good enough for the film and had caused to be made, at great expense, the pair he was now wearing, which were entirely too tight. He hoped by wearing them every day to stretch them. He was miserable, entirely, for his trousers were all he had to live for, anyhow. "All he can do with his life," said Andreyev, "is to put on a different pair of fancy trousers every day, and sit on that bench hoping that something, anything, may happen."

I said I should have thought there had been enough happening for the past few weeks . . . or at any rate the past few days.

"Oh, no," said Carlos, "nothing that lasts long enough. I mean real excitement like the last Agrarian raid. . . . There were machine guns on the towers, and every man on the place had a rifle and a pistol. They had the time of their lives. They drove the raiders off, and then they fired the rest of their ammunition in the air by way of celebration; and the next day they were bored. They wanted to have the whole show over again. It was very hard to explain to them that the fiesta was ended."

"They do really hate the Agrarians, then?" I asked.

"No, they love excitement," said Carlos.

We walked through the vat-room, picking our way through the puddles of sap sinking into the mud floor, idly stopping to watch, without comment, the flies drowning in the stinking liquor which seeped over the hairy bullhides sagging between the wooden frames. María Santísima stood primly in her blue painted niche in a frame of fly-blown paper flowers, with a perpetual light at her feet. The walls were covered with a faded fresco relating the legend of pulque; how a young Indian girl discovered this divine liquor, and brought it to the emperor, who rewarded her well; and after her death she became a half-goddess. An old legend: maybe the oldest: something to do with man's confused veneration for, and terror of, the fertility of women and vegetation. . . .

Betancourt stood in the door sniffing the air bravely. He glanced around the walls with the eye of an expert. "This is a very good example," he said, smiling at the fresco, "the perfect example, really. . . . The older ones are always the best, of course. It is a fact," he said, "that the Spaniards found wall paintings in the pre-Conquest pulquerías . . . always telling this legend. So it goes on. Nothing ever ends," he waved his long beautiful hand, "it goes on being and becomes little by little something else."

"I'd call that an end, of a kind," said Carlos.

"Oh, well, *you*," said Betancourt, smiling with immense indulgence upon his old friend, who was becoming gradually something else.

At ten o'clock don Genaro emerged on his way to visit the village judge once more. Doña Julia, Andreyev, Stepanov, Carlos, and I were walking on the roofs in the intermittent sun-and-cloud light, looking out over the immense landscape of patterned field and mountain. Stepanov carried his small camera and took snapshots of us, with the dogs. We had already had our pictures taken on the steps with a nursling burro, with Indian babies; at the fountain on the long upper terrace to the south, where the grandfather lived; before the closed chapel door (with Carlos being a fat pious priest); in the patio still farther back with the ruins of the old monastery stone bath; and in the pulquería.

So we were tired of snapshots, and leaned in a row over the roof to watch don Genaro take his leave. . . . He leaped down the shallow steps with half a dozen Indian boys standing back for him to pass, hurled himself at the saddle of his Arab mare, his man let go the bridle instantly and leaped to his own horse, and don Genaro rode hell-for-leather out of the corral with his mounted man pounding twenty feet behind him. Dogs, pigs, burros, women, babies, boys, chickens, scattered and fled before him, little soldiers hurled back the great outer gates at his approach, and the two went through at a dead run, disappearing into the hollow of the road. . . .

"That judge will never let Justino go without the money, I know that, and everybody knows it. Genaro knows it. Yet he will still go and fight and fight," said doña Julia in her toneless soft voice, without rebuke.

"Oh, it is barely possible he may," said Carlos. "If Velarde sends word, you'll see—Justino will pop out! like that!" He shot an imaginary pea between forefinger and thumb.

"Yes, but think how Genaro will have to pay Velarde!" said doña Julia. "It's too tiresome, just when the film was going so well." She looked at Stepanov.

He said, "Stay just that way one little second," raised his camera and pressed the lever; then turned, gazed through the lens at a figure standing in the lower patio. Foreshortened, dirty gray-white against dirty yellow-gray wall, hat pulled down over his eyes, arms folded, Vicente stood without moving. He had been standing there for some time, staring. At last he did move; walked away suddenly with some decision, almost to the gate; then stood again staring, framed in the archway. Stepanov took another picture of him.

I said, to Andreyev, walking a little apart, "I wonder why he did not let his friend Justino escape, or at least give him his chance to try. . . . Why did he go after him, I wonder?"

"Revenge," said Andreyev. "Imagine a man's friend betraying him so, and with a woman, and a sister! He was furious. He did not know what he was doing, maybe. . . . Now I imagine he is regretting it."

In two hours don Genaro and his servant were back; they approached the hacienda at a reasonable pace, but once fairly in sight they whipped up their horses and charged into the corral in the same style as when they left it. The servants, suddenly awake, ran back and forth, up and down steps, round and round; the animals scurried for refuge as before. Three Indian boys flew to the mare's bridle, but Vicente was first. He leaped and danced as the mare plunged and fought for her head, his eyes fixed on don Genaro, who flung himself to the ground, landed lightly as an acrobat, and strode away with a perfectly expressionless face.

Nothing had happened. The judge still wanted two thousand pesos to let Justino go. This may have been the answer Vicente expected. He sat against the wall all afternoon, knees drawn up to his chin, hat over his eyes, his feet in their ragged sandals fallen limp on their sides. In half an hour the evil news was known even to the farthest man in the maguey fields. At the table, don Genaro ate and drank in silent haste, like a man who must catch the last train for a journey on which his life depends. "No, I won't have this," he broke out, hammering the table beside his plate. "Do you know what that imbecile judge said to me? He asked me why I worried so much over one peon. I told him it was my business what I chose to worry about. He said he had heard we were making a picture over here with men shooting each other in it. He said he had a jailful of men waiting to be shot, and he'd be glad to send them over for us to shoot in the picture. He couldn't see why, he said, we were pretending to kill people when we could have all we needed to kill really. He thinks Justino should be shot, too. Let him try it! But never in this world will I give him two thousand pesos!"

At sunset the men driving the burros came in from the maguey fields. The workers in the vat-room began to empty the fermented pulque into barrels, and to pour the fresh maguey water into the reeking bullhide vats. The chanting and counting and the rolling of barrels down the incline began again for the night. The white flood of pulque flowed without pause; all over Mexico the Indians would drink the corpse-white liquor, swallow forgetfulness and ease by the riverful, and the money would flow silver-white into the government treasury; don Genaro and his fellow-hacendados would fret and curse, the Agrarians would raid, and ambitious politicians in the capital would be stealing right and left enough to buy such haciendas for themselves. It was all arranged.

We spent the evening in the billiard room. Doctor Volk had

arrived, had passed an hour with Uspensky, who had a simple
sore throat and a threat of tonsilitis. Doctor Volk would cure
him. Meantime he played a round of billiards with Stepanov
and don Genaro. He was a splendid, conscientious, hard-
working doctor, a Russian, and he could not conceal his delight at being once more with Russians, having a little holiday
with a patient who was not very sick, after all, and a chance to
play billiards, which he loved. When it was his turn, he climbed,
smiling, on the edge of the table, leaned halfway down the
green baize, closed one eye, balanced his cue and sighted and
balanced again. Without taking his shot, he rolled off the table,
smiling, placed himself at another angle, sighted again, leaned
over almost flat, sighted, took his shot, and missed, smiling.
Then it was Stepanov's turn. "I simply cannot understand it,"
said Doctor Volk, shaking his head, watching Stepanov with
such an intensity of admiration that his eyes watered.

Andreyev sat on a low stool playing the guitar and singing
Russian songs in a continuous murmur. Doña Julia curled up
on the divan near him, in her black pajamas, with her Pekinese
slung around her neck like a scarf. The beast snuffled and
groaned and rolled his eyes in a swoon of flabby enjoyment.
The big dogs sniffed around him with pained knotted foreheads. He yammered and snapped and whimpered at them.
"They cannot believe he is really a dog," said doña Julia in
delight. Carlos and Betancourt sat at a small table with music
and costume designs spread before them. They were talking as
if they were going over again a subject which wearied them
both. . . .

I was learning a new card game with a thin dark youth who
was some sort of assistant to Betancourt. He was very sleek
and slim-waisted and devoted, he said, to fresco painting, "only
modern," he told me, "like Rivera's, the method, but not old-
fashioned style like his. I am decorating a house in Cuernavaca, come and look at it. You will see what I mean. You
should not have played the dagger," he added; "now I shall
play the crown, and there you are, defeated." He gathered up
the cards and shuffled them. "When Justino was here," he said,
"the director was always having trouble with him in the serious
scenes, because Justino thought everything was a joke. In the

death scenes, he smiled all over his face and ruined a great deal of film. Now they are saying that when Justino comes back no one will ever have to say again to him, 'Don't laugh, Justino, this is death, this is not funny.'"

Doña Julia turned her Pekinese over and rolled him back and forth on her lap. "He will forget everything, the minute it is over . . . his sister, everything," she said, gently, looking at me with soft empty eyes. "They are animals. Nothing means anything to them. And," she added, "it is quite possible he may not come back."

A silence like a light trance fell over the whole room in which all these chance-gathered people who had nothing to say to each other were for the moment imprisoned. Action was their defense against the predicament they were in, all together, and for the moment nothing was happening. The suspense in the air seemed ready to explode when Kennerly came in almost on tiptoe, like a man entering church. Everybody turned toward him as if he were in himself a whole rescue party. He announced his bad news loudly: "I've got to go back to Mexico City tonight. There's all sorts of trouble there. About the film. I better get back there and have it out with the censors. I just talked over the telephone there and he says there is some talk about cutting out a whole reel . . . you know, that scene with the beggars at the fiesta."

Don Genaro laid down his cue. "I'm going back tonight," he said; "you can go with me."

"Tonight?" doña Julia turned her face towards him, her eyes down. "What for?"

"Lolita," he said briefly and angrily. "She must come back. They have to make three or four scenes over again."

"Ah, that's lovely!" said doña Julia. She buried her face in the fur of her little dog. "Ah, lovely! Lolita back again! Do go for her—I can't wait!"

Stepanov spoke over his shoulder to Kennerly with no attempt to conceal his impatience—"I shouldn't worry about the censors—let them have their way."

Kennerly's jaw jerked and his voice trembled: "My God! I've *got* to worry and *somebody* has got to think of the future around here!"

Ten minutes later don Genaro's powerful car roared past the billiard room and fled down the wild dark road towards the capital.

In the morning there began a gradual drift back to town, by train, by automobile. "Stay here," each said to me in turn, "we are coming back tomorrow, Uspensky will be feeling better, the work will begin again." Doña Julia was stopping in bed. I said good-by to her in the afternoon. She was sleepy and downy, curled up with her Pekinese on her shoulder. "Tomorrow," she said, "Lolita will be here, and there will be great excitement. They are going to do some of the best scenes over again." I could not wait for tomorrow in this deathly air. "If you should come back in about ten days," said the Indian driver, "you would see a different place. It is very sad here now. But then the green corn will be ready, and ah, there will be enough to eat again!"

PALE HORSE, PALE RIDER

Three Short Novels

Old Mortality

PART I: 1885–1902

SHE was a spirited-looking young woman, with dark curly hair cropped and parted on the side, a short oval face with straight eyebrows, and a large curved mouth. A round white collar rose from the neck of her tightly buttoned black basque, and round white cuffs set off lazy hands with dimples in them, lying at ease in the folds of her flounced skirt which gathered around to a bustle. She sat thus, forever in the pose of being photographed, a motionless image in her dark walnut frame with silver oak leaves in the corners, her smiling gray eyes following one about the room. It was a reckless indifferent smile, rather disturbing to her nieces Maria and Miranda. Quite often they wondered why every older person who looked at the picture said, "How lovely"; and why everyone who had known her thought her so beautiful and charming.

There was a kind of faded merriment in the background, with its vase of flowers and draped velvet curtains, the kind of vase and the kind of curtains no one would have any more. The clothes were not even romantic looking, but merely most terribly out of fashion, and the whole affair was associated, in the minds of the little girls, with dead things: the smell of Grandmother's medicated cigarettes and her furniture that smelled of beeswax, and her old-fashioned perfume, Orange Flower. The woman in the picture had been Aunt Amy, but she was only a ghost in a frame, and a sad, pretty story from old times. She had been beautiful, much loved, unhappy, and she had died young.

Maria and Miranda, aged twelve and eight years, knew they were young, though they felt they had lived a long time. They had lived not only their own years; but their memories, it seemed to them, began years before they were born, in the lives of the grownups around them, old people above forty, most of them, who had a way of insisting that they too had been young once. It was hard to believe.

Their father was Aunt Amy's brother Harry. She had been

his favorite sister. He sometimes glanced at the photograph and said, "It's not very good. Her hair and her smile were her chief beauties, and they aren't shown at all. She was much slimmer than that, too. There were never any fat women in the family, thank God."

When they heard their father say things like that, Maria and Miranda simply wondered, without criticism, what he meant. Their grandmother was thin as a match; the pictures of their mother, long since dead, proved her to have been a candle-wick, almost. Dashing young ladies, who turned out to be, to Miranda's astonishment, merely more of Grandmother's grand-children, like herself, came visiting from school for the holi-days, boasting of their eighteen-inch waists. But how did their father account for great-aunt Eliza, who quite squeezed herself through doors, and who, when seated, was one solid pyrami-dal monument from floor to neck? What about great-aunt Keziah, in Kentucky? Her husband, great-uncle John Jacob, had refused to allow her to ride his good horses after she had achieved two hundred and twenty pounds. "No," said great-uncle John Jacob, "my sentiments of chivalry are not dead in my bosom; but neither is my common sense, to say nothing of charity to our faithful dumb friends. And the greatest of these is charity." It was suggested to great-uncle John Jacob that charity should forbid him to wound great-aunt Keziah's female vanity by such a comment on her figure. "Female vanity will recover," said great-uncle John Jacob, callously, "but what about my horses' backs? And if she had the proper female van-ity in the first place, she would never have got into such shape." Well, great-aunt Keziah was famous for her heft, and wasn't she in the family? But something seemed to happen to their father's memory when he thought of the girls he had known in the family of his youth, and he declared steadfastly they had all been, in every generation without exception, as slim as reeds and graceful as sylphs.

This loyalty of their father's in the face of evidence contrary to his ideal had its springs in family feeling, and a love of leg-end that he shared with the others. They loved to tell stories, romantic and poetic, or comic with a romantic humor; they did not gild the outward circumstance, it was the feeling that mattered. Their hearts and imaginations were captivated by their past, a past in which worldly considerations had played a very minor role. Their stories were almost always love stories against a bright blank heavenly blue sky.

Photographs, portraits by inept painters who meant earnestly to flatter, and the festival garments folded away in dried herbs and camphor were disappointing when the little girls tried to fit them to the living beings created in their minds by the breathing words of their elders. Grandmother, twice a year compelled in her blood by the change of seasons, would sit nearly all of one day beside old trunks and boxes in the lumber room, unfolding layers of garments and small keepsakes; she spread them out on sheets on the floor around her, crying over certain things, nearly always the same things, looking again at pictures in velvet cases, unwrapping locks of hair and dried flowers, crying gently and easily as if tears were the only pleasure she had left.

If Maria and Miranda were very quiet, and touched nothing until it was offered, they might sit by her at these times, or come and go. There was a tacit understanding that her grief was strictly her own, and must not be noticed or mentioned. The little girls examined the objects, one by one, and did not find them, in themselves, impressive. Such dowdy little wreaths and necklaces, some of them made of pearly shells; such moth-eaten bunches of pink ostrich feathers for the hair; such clumsy big breast pins and bracelets of gold and colored enamel; such silly-looking combs, standing up on tall teeth capped with seed pearls and French paste. Miranda, without knowing why, felt melancholy. It seemed such a pity that these faded things, these yellowed long gloves and misshapen satin slippers, these broad ribbons cracking where they were folded, should have been all those vanished girls had to decorate themselves with. And where were they now, those girls, and the boys in the odd-looking collars? The young men seemed even more unreal than the girls, with their high-buttoned coats, their puffy neckties, their waxed mustaches, their waving thick hair combed carefully over their foreheads. Who could have taken them seriously, looking like that?

No, Maria and Miranda found it impossible to sympathize with those young persons, sitting rather stiffly before the camera, hopelessly out of fashion; but they were drawn and held by the mysterious love of the living, who remembered and cherished these dead. The visible remains were nothing; they were dust, perishable as the flesh; the features stamped on paper and metal were nothing, but their living memory enchanted the little girls. They listened, all ears and eager minds, picking here and there among the floating ends of narrative, patching together as well as they could fragments of tales that were like bits of poetry or music, indeed were associated with the poetry they had heard or read, with music, with the theater.

"Tell me again how Aunt Amy went away when she was married." "She ran into the gray cold and stepped into the carriage and turned and smiled with her face as pale as death, and called out 'Good-by, good-by,' and refused her cloak, and said, 'Give me a glass of wine.' And none of us saw her alive again." "Why wouldn't she wear her cloak, Cousin Cora?" "Because she was not in love, my dear." Ruin hath taught me thus to ruminate, that time will come and take my love away. "Was she really beautiful, Uncle Bill?" "As an angel, my child." There were golden-haired angels with long blue pleated skirts dancing around the throne of the Blessed Virgin. None of them resembled Aunt Amy in the least, nor the kind of beauty they had been brought up to admire. There were points of beauty by which one was judged severely. First, a beauty must be tall; whatever color the eyes, the hair must be dark, the darker the better; the skin must be pale and smooth. Lightness and swiftness of movement were important points. A beauty must be a good dancer, superb on horseback, with a serene manner, an amiable gaiety tempered with dignity at all hours. Beautiful teeth and hands, of course, and over and above all this, some mysterious crown of enchantment that attracted and held the heart. It was all very exciting and discouraging.

Miranda persisted through her childhood in believing, in spite of her smallness, thinness, her little snubby nose saddled with freckles, her speckled gray eyes and habitual tantrums, that by some miracle she would grow into a tall, cream-colored brunette, like cousin Isabel; she decided always to wear a trailing white satin gown. Maria, born sensible, had no such illusions. "We are going to take after Mamma's family," she said. "It's no use, we are. We'll never be beautiful, we'll always have freckles. And *you*," she told Miranda, "haven't even a good disposition."

Miranda admitted both truth and justice in this unkindness, but still secretly believed that she would one day suddenly receive beauty, as by inheritance, riches laid suddenly in her hands through no deserts of her own. She believed for quite a while that she would one day be like Aunt Amy, not as she appeared in the photograph, but as she was remembered by those who had seen her.

When Cousin Isabel came out in her tight black riding habit, surrounded by young men, and mounted gracefully, drawing her horse up and around so that he pranced learnedly on one spot while the other riders sprang to their saddles in the same sedate flurry, Miranda's heart would close with such a keen dart of admiration, envy, vicarious pride it was almost painful; but there would always be an elder present to lay a cooling hand upon her emotions. "She rides almost as well as Amy, doesn't she? But Amy had the pure Spanish style, she could bring out paces in a horse no one else knew he had." Young namesake Amy, on her way to a dance, would swish through the hall in ruffled white taffeta, glimmering like a moth in the lamplight, carrying her elbows pointed backward stiffly as wings, sliding along as if she were on rollers, in the fashionable walk of her day. She was considered the best dancer at any party, and Maria, sniffing the wave of perfume that followed Amy, would clasp her hands and say, "Oh, I can't *wait* to be grown up." But the elders would agree that the first Amy had been lighter, more smooth and delicate in her waltzing; young Amy would never equal her. Cousin Molly Parrington, far past her youth, indeed she belonged to the generation before Aunt Amy, was a noted charmer. Men who had known her all her life still gathered about her; now that she was happily widowed for the second time there was no doubt that she would yet marry again. But Amy, said the elders, had the same high spirits and wit without boldness, and you really could not say that Molly had ever been discreet. She dyed her hair, and made jokes about it. She had a way of collecting the men around her in a corner, where she told them stories. She was an unnatural mother to her ugly daughter Eva, an old maid past forty while

her mother was still the belle of the ball. "Born when I was fifteen, you remember," Molly would say shamelessly, looking an
old beau straight in the eye, both of them remembering that
he had been best man at her first wedding when she was past
twenty-one. "Everyone said I was like a little girl with her
doll."

Eva, shy and chinless, straining her upper lip over two enormous teeth, would sit in corners watching her mother. She
looked hungry, her eyes were strained and tired. She wore her
mother's old clothes, made over, and taught Latin in a Female
Seminary. She believed in votes for women, and had traveled
about, making speeches. When her mother was not present,
Eva bloomed out a little, danced prettily, smiled, showing all
her teeth, and was like a dry little plant set out in a gentle rain.
Molly was merry about her ugly duckling. "It's lucky for me
my daughter is an old maid. She's not so apt," said Molly
naughtily, "to make a grandmother of me." Eva would blush
as if she had been slapped.

Eva was a blot, no doubt about it, but the little girls felt she
belonged to their everyday world of dull lessons to be learned,
stiff shoes to be limbered up, scratchy flannels to be endured
in cold weather, measles and disappointed expectations. Their
Aunt Amy belonged to the world of poetry. The romance of
Uncle Gabriel's long, unrewarded love for her, her early death,
was such a story as one found in old books: unworldly books,
but true, such as the Vita Nuova, the Sonnets of Shakespeare
and the Wedding Song of Spenser; and poems by Edgar Allan
Poe. "Her tantalized spirit now blandly reposes, Forgetting or
never regretting its roses. . . ." Their father read that to
them, and said, "He was our greatest poet," and they knew
that "our" meant he was Southern. Aunt Amy was real as the
pictures in the old Holbein and Dürer books were real. The
little girls lay flat on their stomachs and peered into a world of
wonder, turning the shabby leaves that fell apart easily, not
surprised at the sight of the Mother of God sitting on a hollow
log nursing her Child; not doubting either Death or the Devil
riding at the stirrups of the grim knight; not questioning the
propriety of the stiffly dressed ladies of Sir Thomas More's
household, seated in dignity on the floor, or seeming to be.
They missed all the dog and pony shows, and lantern-slide en-

tertainments, but their father took them to see "Hamlet," and "The Taming of the Shrew," and "Richard the Third," and a long sad play with Mary, Queen of Scots, in it. Miranda thought the magnificent lady in black velvet was truly the Queen of Scots, and was pained to learn that the real Queen had died long ago, and not at all on the night she, Miranda, had been present.

The little girls loved the theater, that world of personages taller than human beings, who swept upon the scene and invested it with their presences, their more than human voices, their gestures of gods and goddesses ruling a universe. But there was always a voice recalling other and greater occasions. Grandmother in her youth had heard Jenny Lind, and thought that Nellie Melba was much overrated. Father had seen Bernhardt, and Madame Modjeska was no sort of rival. When Paderewski played for the first time in their city, cousins came from all over the state and went from the grandmother's house to hear him. The little girls were left out of this great occasion. They shared the excitement of the going away, and shared the beautiful moment of return, when cousins stood about in groups, with coffee cups and glasses in their hands, talking in low voices, awed and happy. The little girls, struck with the sense of a great event, hung about in their nightgowns and listened, until someone noticed and hustled them away from the sweet nimbus of all that glory. One old gentleman, however, had heard Rubinstein frequently. He could not but feel that Rubinstein had reached the final height of musical interpretation, and, for him, Paderewski had been something of an anticlimax. The little girls heard him muttering on, holding up one hand, patting the air as if he were calling for silence. The others looked at him, and listened, without any disturbance of their grave tender mood. They had never heard Rubinstein; they had, one hour since, heard Paderewski, and why should anyone need to recall the past? Miranda, dragged away, half understanding the old gentleman, hated him. She felt that she too had heard Paderewski.

There was then a life beyond a life in this world, as well as in the next; such episodes confirmed for the little girls the nobility of human feeling, the divinity of man's vision of the unseen, the importance of life and death, the depths of the

human heart, the romantic value of tragedy. Cousin Eva, on a
certain visit, trying to interest them in the study of Latin, told
them the story of John Wilkes Booth, who, handsomely garbed
in a long black cloak, had leaped to the stage after assassinating
President Lincoln. "Sic semper tyrannis," he had shouted su-
perbly, in spite of his broken leg. The little girls never doubted
that it had happened in just that way, and the moral seemed to
be that one should always have Latin, or at least a good classical poetry quotation, to depend upon in great or desperate
moments. Cousin Eva reminded them that no one, not even
a good Southerner, could possibly approve of John Wilkes
Booth's deed. It was murder, after all. They were to remember
that. But Miranda, used to tragedy in books and in family
legends—two great-uncles had committed suicide and a remote ancestress had gone mad for love—decided that, without
the murder, there would have been no point to dressing up
and leaping to the stage shouting in Latin. So how could she
disapprove of the deed? It was a fine story. She knew a distantly
related old gentleman who had been devoted to the art of
Booth, had seen him in a great many plays, but not, alas, at his
greatest moment. Miranda regretted this; it would have been
so pleasant to have the assassination of Lincoln in the family.

Uncle Gabriel, who had loved Aunt Amy so desperately, still
lived somewhere, though Miranda and Maria had never seen
him. He had gone away, far away, after her death. He still
owned racehorses, and ran them at famous tracks all over the
country, and Miranda believed there could not possibly be a
more brilliant career. He had married again, quite soon, and
had written to Grandmother, asking her to accept his new wife
as a daughter in place of Amy. Grandmother had written coldly,
accepting, inviting them for a visit, but Uncle Gabriel had
somehow never brought his bride home. Harry had visited
them in New Orleans, and reported that the second wife was
a very good-looking well-bred blonde girl who would undoubtedly be a good wife for Gabriel. Still, Uncle Gabriel's
heart was broken. Faithfully once a year he wrote a letter to
someone of the family, sending money for a wreath for Amy's
grave. He had written a poem for her gravestone, and had
come home, leaving his second wife in Atlanta, to see that it

was carved properly. He could never account for having written this poem; he had certainly never tried to write a single rhyme since leaving school. Yet one day when he had been thinking about Amy, the verse occurred to him, out of the air. Maria and Miranda had seen it, printed in gold on a mourning card. Uncle Gabriel had sent a great number of them to be handed around among the family.

> *"She lives again who suffered life,*
> *Then suffered death, and now set free*
> *A singing angel, she forgets*
> *The griefs of old mortality."*

"Did she really sing?" Maria asked her father.

"Now what has that to do with it?" he asked. "It's a poem."

"I think it's very pretty," said Miranda, impressed. Uncle Gabriel was second cousin to her father and Aunt Amy. It brought poetry very near.

"Not so bad for tombstone poetry," said their father, "but it should be better."

Uncle Gabriel had waited five years to marry Aunt Amy. She had been ill, her chest was weak; she was engaged twice to other young men and broke her engagements for no reason; and she laughed at the advice of older and kinder-hearted persons who thought it very capricious of her not to return the devotion of such a handsome and romantic young man as Gabriel, her second cousin, too; it was not as if she would be marrying a stranger. Her coldness was said to have driven Gabriel to a wild life and even to drinking. His grandfather was rich and Gabriel was his favorite; they had quarreled over the race horses, and Gabriel had shouted, "By God, I must have *something*." As if he had not everything already: youth, health, good looks, the prospect of riches, and a devoted family circle. His grandfather pointed out to him that he was little better than an ingrate, and showed signs of being a wastrel as well. Gabriel said, "You had racehorses, and made a good thing of them." "I never depended upon them for a livelihood, sir," said his grandfather.

Gabriel wrote letters about this and many other things to Amy from Saratoga and from Kentucky and from New Orleans, sending her presents, and flowers packed in ice, and telegrams. The presents were amusing, such as a huge cage full of small green lovebirds; or, as an ornament for her hair, a full-petaled enameled rose with paste dewdrops, with an enameled butterfly in brilliant colors suspended quivering on a gold wire above it; but the telegrams always frightened her mother, and the flowers, after a journey by train and then by stage into the country, were much the worse for wear. He would send roses when the rose garden at home was in full bloom. Amy could not help smiling over it, though her mother insisted it was touching and sweet of Gabriel. It must prove to Amy that she was always in his thoughts.

"That's no place for me," said Amy, but she had a way of speaking, a tone of voice, which made it impossible to discover what she meant by what she said. It was possible always that she might be serious. And she would not answer questions.

"Amy's wedding dress," said the grandmother, unfurling an immense cloak of dove-colored cut velvet, spreading beside it a silvery-gray watered-silk frock, and a small gray velvet toque with a dark red breast of feathers. Cousin Isabel, the beauty, sat with her. They talked to each other, and Miranda could listen if she chose.

"She would not wear white, nor a veil," said Grandmother. "I couldn't oppose her, for I had said my daughters should each have exactly the wedding dress they wanted. But Amy surprised me. 'Now what would I look like in white satin?' she asked. It's true she was pale, but she would have been angelic in it, and all of us told her so. 'I shall wear mourning if I like,' she said, 'it is *my* funeral, you know.' I reminded her that Lou and your mother had worn white with veils and it would please me to have my daughters all alike in that. Amy said, 'Lou and Isabel are not like me,' but I could not persuade her to explain what she meant. One day when she was ill she said, 'Mammy, I'm not long for this world,' but not as if she meant it. I told her, 'You might live as long as anyone, if only you will be sensible.' 'That's the whole trouble,' said Amy. 'I feel sorry for Gabriel,' she told me. 'He doesn't know what he's asking for.'

"I tried to tell her once more," said the grandmother, "that marriage and children would cure her of everything. 'All women of our family are delicate when they are young,' I said. 'Why, when I was your age no one expected me to live a year.

It was called greensickness, and everybody knew there was
only one cure.' 'If I live for a hundred years and turn green as
grass,' said Amy, 'I still shan't want to marry Gabriel.' So I
told her very seriously that if she truly felt that way she must
never do it, and Gabriel must be told once for all, and sent
away. He would get over it. 'I have told him, and I have sent
him away,' said Amy. 'He just doesn't listen.' We both laughed
at that, and I told her young girls found a hundred ways to
deny they wished to be married, and a thousand more to test
their power over men, but that she had more than enough of
that, and now it was time for her to be entirely sincere and
make her decision. As for me," said the grandmother, "I wished
with all my heart to marry your grandfather, and if he had not
asked me, I should have asked him most certainly. Amy insisted that she could not imagine wanting to marry anybody.
She would be, she said, a nice old maid like Eva Parrington.
For even then it was pretty plain that Eva was an old maid,
born. Harry said, 'Oh, Eva—Eva has no chin, that's her trouble. If you had no chin, Amy, you'd be in the same fix as Eva,
no doubt.' Your Uncle Bill would say, 'When women haven't
anything else, they'll take a vote for consolation. A pretty thin
bed-fellow,' said your Uncle Bill. 'What I really need is a good
dancing partner to guide me through life,' said Amy, 'that's
the match I'm looking for.' It was no good trying to talk to
her."

Her brothers remembered her tenderly as a sensible girl.
After listening to their comments on her character and ways,
Maria decided that they considered her sensible because she
asked their advice about her appearance when she was going
out to dance. If they found fault in any way, she would change
her dress or her hair until they were pleased, and say, "You are
an angel not to let your poor sister go out looking like a
freak." But she would not listen to her father, nor to Gabriel.
If Gabriel praised the frock she was wearing, she was apt to disappear and come back in another. He loved her long black
hair, and once, lifting it up from her pillow when she was ill,
said, "I love your hair, Amy, the most beautiful hair in the
world." When he returned on his next visit, he found her with
her hair cropped and curled close to her head. He was horrified, as if she had willfully mutilated herself. She would not let

it grow again, not even to please her brothers. The photograph hanging on the wall was one she had made at that time to send to Gabriel, who sent it back without a word. This pleased her, and she framed the photograph. There was a thin inky scrawl low in one corner, "To dear brother Harry, who likes my hair cut."

This was a mischievous reference to a very grave scandal. The little girls used to look at their father, and wonder what would have happened if he had really hit the young man he shot at. The young man was believed to have kissed Aunt Amy, when she was not in the least engaged to him. Uncle Gabriel was supposed to have had a duel with the young man, but Father had got there first. He was a pleasant, everyday sort of father, who held his daughters on his knee if they were prettily dressed and well behaved, and pushed them away if they had not freshly combed hair and nicely scrubbed fingernails. "Go away, you're disgusting," he would say, in a matter-of-fact voice. He noticed if their stocking seams were crooked. He caused them to brush their teeth with a revolting mixture of prepared chalk, powdered charcoal and salt. When they behaved stupidly he could not endure the sight of them. They understood dimly that all this was for their own future good; and when they were snively with colds, he prescribed delicious hot toddy for them, and saw that it was given them. He was always hoping they might not grow up to be so silly as they seemed to him at any given moment, and he had a disconcerting way of inquiring, "How do you *know*?" when they forgot and made dogmatic statements in his presence. It always came out embarrassingly that they did not know at all, but were repeating something they had heard. This made conversation with him difficult, for he laid traps and they fell into them, but it became important to them that their father should not believe them to be fools. Well, this very father had gone to Mexico once and stayed there for nearly a year, because he had shot at a man with whom Aunt Amy had flirted at a dance. It had been very wrong of him, because he should have challenged the man to a duel, as Uncle Gabriel had done. Instead, he just took a shot at him, and this was the lowest sort of manners. It had caused great disturbance in the whole community and had almost broken up the affair between Aunt Amy and

Uncle Gabriel for good. Uncle Gabriel insisted that the young
man had kissed Aunt Amy, and Aunt Amy insisted that the
young man had merely paid her a compliment on her hair.

During the Mardi Gras holidays there was to be a big gay
fancy-dress ball. Harry was going as a bull-fighter because his
sweetheart, Mariana, had a new black lace mantilla and high
comb from Mexico. Maria and Miranda had seen a photograph of their mother in this dress, her lovely face without a
trace of coquetry looking gravely out from under a tremendous fall of lace from the peak of the comb, a rose tucked
firmly over her ear. Amy copied her costume from a small
Dresden-china shepherdess which stood on the mantelpiece in
the parlor; a careful copy with ribboned hat, gilded crook, very
low-laced bodice, short basket skirts, green slippers and all.
She wore it with a black half-mask, but it was no disguise.
"You would have known it was Amy at any distance," said
Father. Gabriel, six feet three in height as he was, had got himself up to match, and a spectacle he provided in pale blue satin
knee breeches and a blond curled wig with a hair ribbon. "He
felt a fool, and he looked like one," said Uncle Bill, "and he
behaved like one before the evening was over."

Everything went beautifully until the party gathered downstairs to leave for the ball. Amy's father—he must have been
born a grandfather, thought Miranda—gave one glance at his
daughter, her white ankles shining, bosom deeply exposed,
two round spots of paint on her cheeks, and fell into a frenzy
of outraged propriety. "It's disgraceful," he pronounced,
loudly. "No daughter of mine is going go show herself in such
a rig-out. It's bawdy," he thundered. "Bawdy!"

Amy had taken off her mask to smile at him. "Why, Papa,"
she said very sweetly, "what's wrong with it? Look on the
mantelpiece. She's been there all along, and you were never
shocked before."

"There's all the difference in the world," said her father, "all
the difference, young lady, and you know it. You go upstairs
this minute and pin up that waist in front and let down those
skirts to a decent length before you leave this house. *And wash
your face!*"

"I see nothing wrong with it," said Amy's mother, firmly,
"and you shouldn't use such language before innocent young

girls." She and Amy sat down with several females of the household to help, and they made short work of the business. In ten minutes Amy returned, face clean, bodice filled in with lace, shepherdess skirt modestly sweeping the carpet behind her.

When Amy appeared from the dressing room for her first dance with Gabriel, the lace was gone from her bodice, her skirts were tucked up more daringly than before, and the spots on her cheeks were like pomegranates. "Now Gabriel, tell me truly, wouldn't it have been a pity to spoil my costume?" Gabriel, delighted that she had asked his opinion, declared it was perfect. They agreed with kindly tolerance that old people were often tiresome, but one need not upset them by open disobedience: their youth was gone, what had they to live for?

Harry, dancing with Mariana who swung a heavy train around her expertly at every turn of the waltz, began to be uneasy about his sister Amy. She was entirely too popular. He saw young men make beelines across the floor, eyes fixed on those white silk ankles. Some of the young men he did not know at all, others he knew too well and could not approve of for his sister Amy. Gabriel, unhappy in his lyric satin and wig, stood about holding his ribboned crook as though it had sprouted thorns. He hardly danced at all with Amy, he did not enjoy dancing with anyone else, and he was having a thoroughly wretched time of it.

There appeared late, alone, got up as Jean Lafitte, a young Creole gentleman who had, two years before, been for a time engaged to Amy. He came straight to her, with the manner of a happy lover, and said, clearly enough for everyone near by to hear him, "I only came because I knew you were to be here. I only want to dance with you and I shall go again." Amy, with a face of delight, cried out, "Raymond!" as if to a lover. She had danced with him four times, and had then disappeared from the floor on his arm.

Harry and Mariana, in conventional disguise of romance, irreproachably betrothed, safe in their happiness, were waltzing slowly to their favorite song, the melancholy farewell of the Moorish King on leaving Granada. They sang in whispers to each other, in their uncertain Spanish, a song of love and parting and that sword's point of grief that makes the heart

tender towards all other lost and disinherited creatures: Oh,
mansion of love, my earthly paradise . . . that I shall see no
more . . . whither flies the poor swallow, weary and homeless,
seeking for shelter where no shelter is? I too am far from home
without the power to fly. . . . Come to my heart, sweet bird,
beloved pilgrim, build your nest near my bed, let me listen to
your song, and weep for my lost land of joy. . . .

Into this bliss broke Gabriel. He had thrown away his shepherd's crook and he was carrying his wig. He wanted to speak
to Harry at once, and before Mariana knew what was happening she was sitting beside her mother and the two excited
young men were gone. Waiting, disturbed and displeased, she
smiled at Amy who waltzed past with a young man in Devil
costume, including ill-fitting scarlet cloven hoofs. Almost at
once, Harry and Gabriel came back, with serious faces, and
Harry darted on the dance floor, returning with Amy. The girls
and the chaperones were asked to come at once, they must be
taken home. It was all mysterious and sudden, and Harry said
to Mariana, "I will tell you what is happening, but not now—"

The grandmother remembered of this disgraceful affair only
that Gabriel brought Amy home alone and that Harry came in
somewhat later. The other members of the party straggled in
at various hours, and the story came out piecemeal. Amy was
silent and, her mother discovered later, burning with fever. "I
saw at once that something was very wrong. 'What has happened, Amy?' 'Oh, Harry goes about shooting at people at a
party,' she said, sitting down as if she were exhausted. 'It was
on your account, Amy,' said Gabriel. 'Oh, no, it was not,' said
Amy. 'Don't believe him, Mammy.' So I said, 'Now enough of
this. Tell me what happened, Amy.' And Amy said, 'Mammy,
this is it. Raymond came in, and you know I like Raymond,
and he is a good dancer. So we danced together, too much,
maybe. We went on the gallery for a breath of air, and stood
there. He said, "How well your hair looks. I like this new shingled style."' She glanced at Gabriel. 'And then another young
man came out and said, "I've been looking everywhere. This is
our dance, isn't it?" And I went in to dance. And now it seems
that Gabriel went out at once and challenged Raymond to
a duel about something or other, but Harry doesn't wait for
that. Raymond had already gone out to have his horse brought,

I suppose one doesn't duel in fancy dress,' she said, looking at Gabriel, who fairly shriveled in his blue satin shepherd's costume, 'and Harry simply went out and shot at him. I don't think that was fair,' said Amy."

Her mother agreed that indeed it was not fair; it was not even decent, and she could not imagine what her son Harry thought he was doing. "It isn't much of a way to defend your sister's honor," she said to him afterward. "I didn't want Gabriel to go fighting duels," said Harry. "That wouldn't have helped much, either."

Gabriel had stood before Amy, leaning over, asking once more the question he had apparently been asking her all the way home. "Did he kiss you, Amy?"

Amy took off her shepherdess hat and pushed her hair back. "Maybe he did," she answered, "and maybe I wished him to."

"Amy, you must not say such things," said her mother. "Answer Gabriel's question."

"He hasn't the right to ask it," said Amy, but without anger.

"Do you love him, Amy?" asked Gabriel, the sweat standing out on his forehead.

"It doesn't matter," answered Amy, leaning back in her chair.

"Oh, it does matter; it matters terribly," said Gabriel. "You must answer me now." He took both of her hands and tried to hold them. She drew her hands away firmly and steadily so that he had to let go.

"Let her alone, Gabriel," said Amy's mother. "You'd better go now. We are all tired. Let's talk about it tomorrow."

She helped Amy to undress, noticing the changed bodice and the shortened skirt. "You shouldn't have done that, Amy. That was not wise of you. It was better the other way."

Amy said, "Mammy, I'm sick of this world. I don't like anything in it. It's so *dull*," she said, and for a moment she looked as if she might weep. She had never been tearful, even as a child, and her mother was alarmed. It was then she discovered that Amy had fever.

"Gabriel is dull, Mother—he sulks," she said. "I could see him sulking every time I passed. It spoils things," she said. "Oh, I want to go to sleep."

Her mother sat looking at her and wondering how it had

happened she had brought such a beautiful child into the world. "Her face," said her mother, "was angelic in sleep."

Some time during that fevered night, the projected duel between Gabriel and Raymond was halted by the offices of friends on both sides. There remained the open question of Harry's impulsive shot, which was not so easily settled. Raymond seemed vindictive about that, it was possible he might choose to make trouble. Harry, taking the advice of Gabriel, his brothers and friends, decided that the best way to avoid further scandal was for him to disappear for a while. This being decided upon, the young men returned about daybreak, saddled Harry's best horse and helped him pack a few things; accompanied by Gabriel and Bill, Harry set out for the border, feeling rather gay and adventurous.

Amy, being wakened by the stirring in the house, found out the plan. Five minutes after they were gone, she came down in her riding dress, had her own horse saddled, and struck out after them. She rode almost every morning; before her parents had time to be uneasy over her prolonged absence, they found her note.

What had threatened to be a tragedy became a rowdy lark. Amy rode to the border, kissed her brother Harry good-by, and rode back again with Bill and Gabriel. It was a three days' journey, and when they arrived Amy had to be lifted from the saddle. She was really ill by now, but in the gayest of humors. Her mother and father had been prepared to be severe with her, but, at sight of her, their feelings changed. They turned on Bill and Gabriel. "Why did you let her do this?" they asked.

"You know we could not stop her," said Gabriel helplessly, "and she did enjoy herself so much!"

Amy laughed. "Mammy, it was splendid, the most delightful trip I ever had. And if I am to be the heroine of this novel, why shouldn't I make the most of it?"

The scandal, Maria and Miranda gathered, had been pretty terrible. Amy simply took to bed and stayed there, and Harry had skipped out blithely to wait until the little affair blew over. The rest of the family had to receive visitors, write letters, go to church, return calls, and bear the whole brunt, as they expressed it. They sat in the twilight of scandal in their little world, holding themselves very rigidly, in a shared tension as if all their nerves began at a common center. This center had received a blow, and family nerves shuddered, even into the farthest reaches of Kentucky. From whence in due time great-great-aunt Sally Rhea addressed a letter to *Mifs Amy Rhea*. In deep brown ink like dried blood, in a spidery hand adept at archaic symbols and abbreviations, great-great-aunt Sally informed Amy that she was fairly convinced that this calamity was only the forerunner of a series shortly to be visited by the Almighty God upon a race already condemned through its own wickedness, a warning that man's time was short, and that they must all prepare for the end of the world. For herself, she had long expected it, she was entirely resigned to the prospect of meeting her Maker; and Amy, no less than her wicked brother Harry, must likewise place herself in God's hands and prepare for the worst. "*Oh, my dear unfortunate young relative,*" twittered great-great-aunt Sally, "*we must in our Extremty join hands and appr before ye Dread Throne of Jdgmnt a United Fmly, if One is Mssg from ye Flock, what will Jesus say?*"

Great-great-aunt Sally's religious career had become comic legend. She had forsaken her Catholic rearing for a young man whose family were Cumberland Presbyterians. Unable to accept their opinions, however, she was converted to the Hard-Shell Baptists, a sect as loathsome to her husband's family as the Catholic could possibly be. She had spent a life of vicious self-indulgent martyrdom to her faith; as Harry commented: "Religion put claws on Aunt Sally and gave her a post to whet them on." She had out-argued, out-fought, and out-lived her entire generation, but she did not miss them. She bedeviled the second generation without ceasing, and was beginning hungrily on the third.

Amy, reading this letter, broke into her gay full laugh that always caused everyone around her to laugh too, even before they knew why, and her small green lovebirds in their cage turned and eyed her solemnly. "Imagine drawing a pew in heaven beside Aunt Sally," she said. "What a prospect."

"Don't laugh too soon," said her father. "Heaven was made to order for Aunt Sally. She'll be on her own territory there."

"For my sins," said Amy, "I must go to heaven with Aunt Sally."

During the uncomfortable time of Harry's absence, Amy went on refusing to marry Gabriel. Her mother could hear their voices going on in their endless colloquy, during many long days. One afternoon Gabriel came out, looking very sober and discouraged. He stood looking down at Amy's mother as she sat sewing, and said, "I think it is all over, I believe now that Amy will never have me." The grandmother always said afterward, "Never have I pitied anyone as I did poor Gabriel at that moment. But I told him, very firmly, 'Let her alone, then, she is ill.'" So Gabriel left, and Amy had no word from him for more than a month.

The day after Gabriel was gone, Amy rose looking extremely well, went hunting with her brothers Bill and Stephen, bought a velvet wrap, had her hair shingled and curled again, and wrote long letters to Harry, who was having a most enjoyable exile in Mexico City.

After dancing all night three times in one week, she woke one morning in a hemorrhage. She seemed frightened and asked for the doctor, promising to do whatever he advised. She was quiet for a few days, reading. She asked for Gabriel. No one knew where he was. "You should write him a letter; his mother will send it on." "Oh, no," she said. "I miss him coming in with his sour face. Letters are no good."

Gabriel did come in, only a few days later, with a very sour face and unpleasant news. His grandfather had died, after a day's illness. On his death bed, in the name of God, being of a sound and disposing mind, he had cut off his favorite grand-child Gabriel with one dollar. "In the name of God, Amy," said Gabriel, "the old devil has ruined me in one sentence."

It was the conduct of his immediate family in the matter that had embittered him, he said. They could hardly conceal their satisfaction. They had known and envied Gabriel's quite just, well-founded expectations. Not one of them offered to make any private settlement. No one even thought of repairing this last-minute act of senile vengeance. Privately they blessed their luck. "I have been cut off with a dollar," said Gabriel, "and they are all glad of it. I think they feel somehow that this justifies every criticism they ever made against me. They were right about me all along. I am a worthless poor relation," said Gabriel. "My God, I wish you could see them."

Amy said, "I wonder how you will ever support a wife, now."

Gabriel said, "Oh, it isn't so bad as that. If you would, Amy—"

Amy said, "Gabriel, if we get married now there'll be just time to be in New Orleans for Mardi Gras. If we wait until after Lent, it may be too late."

"Why, Amy," said Gabriel, "how could it ever be too late?"

"You might change your mind," said Amy. "You know how fickle you are."

There were two letters in the grandmother's many packets of letters that Maria and Miranda read after they were grown. One of them was from Amy. It was dated ten days after her marriage.

"Dear Mammy, New Orleans hasn't changed as much as I have since we saw each other last. I am now a staid old married woman, and Gabriel is very devoted and kind. Footlights won a race for us yesterday, she was the favorite, and it was wonderful. I go to the races every day, and our horses are doing splendidly; I had my choice of Erin Go Bragh or Miss Lucy, and I chose Miss Lucy. She is mine now, she runs like a streak. Gabriel says I made a mistake, Erin Go Bragh will stay better. I think Miss Lucy will stay my time.

"We are having a lovely visit. I'm going to put on a domino and take to the streets with Gabriel sometime during Mardi Gras. I'm tired of watching the show from a balcony. Gabriel says it isn't safe. He says he'll take me if I insist, but I doubt it. Mammy, he's very nice. Don't worry about me. I have a beautiful black-and-rose-colored velvet gown for the Proteus Ball. Madame, my new mother-in-law, wanted to know if it wasn't a little dashing. I told her I hoped so or I had been cheated. It is fitted perfectly smooth in the bodice, very low in the shoulders —Papa would not approve—and the skirt is looped with wide silver ribbons between the waist and knees in front, and then it surges around and is looped enormously in the back, with a train just one yard long. I now have an eighteen-inch waist, thanks to Madame Duré. I expect to be so dashing that my mother-in-law will have an attack. She has them quite often. Gabriel sends love. Please take good care of Graylie and Fiddler. I want to ride them again when I come home. We're going to Saratoga, I don't know just when. Give everybody my dear dear love. It rains all the time here, of course. . . .

"P.S. Mammy, as soon as I get a minute to myself, I'm going to be terribly homesick. Good-by, my darling Mammy."

The other was from Amy's nurse, dated six weeks after Amy's marriage.

"I cut off the lock of hair because I was sure you would like to have it. And I do not want you to think I was careless, leaving her medicine where she could get it, the doctor has written and explained. It would not have done her any harm except that her heart was weak. She did not know how much she was taking, often she said to me, one more of those little capsules wouldn't do any harm, and so I told her to be careful and not take anything except what I gave her. She begged me for them sometimes but I would not give her more than the doctor said. I slept during the night because she did not seem to be so sick as all that and the doctor did not order me to sit up with her. Please accept my regrets for your great loss and please do not think that anybody was careless with your dear daughter. She suffered a great deal and now she is at rest. She could not get well but she might have lived longer. Yours respectfully. . . ."

The letters and all the strange keepsakes were packed away and forgotten for a great many years. They seemed to have no place in the world.

PART II: 1904

During vacation on their grandmother's farm, Maria and Miranda, who read as naturally and constantly as ponies crop grass, and with much the same kind of pleasure, had by some happy chance laid hold of some forbidden reading matter, brought in and left there with missionary intent, no doubt, by some Protestant cousin. It fell into the right hands if enjoyment had

been its end. The reading matter was printed in poor type on
spongy paper, and was ornamented with smudgy illustrations
all the more exciting to the little girls because they could not
make head or tail of them. The stories were about beautiful
but unlucky maidens, who for mysterious reasons had been
trapped by nuns and priests in dire collusion; they were then
"immured" in convents, where they were forced to take the
veil—an appalling rite during which the victims shrieked
dreadfully—and condemned forever after to most uncomfortable and disorderly existences. They seemed to divide their
time between lying chained in dark cells and assisting other
nuns to bury throttled infants under stones in moldering rat-
infested dungeons.

Immured! It was the word Maria and Miranda had been
needing all along to describe their condition at the Convent of
the Child Jesus, in New Orleans, where they spent the long
winters trying to avoid an education. There were no dungeons
at the Child Jesus, and this was only one of numerous marked
differences between convent life as Maria and Miranda knew it
and the thrilling paperbacked version. It was no good at all
trying to fit the stories to life, and they did not even try. They
had long since learned to draw the lines between life, which
was real and earnest, and the grave was not its goal; poetry,
which was true but not real; and stories, or forbidden reading
matter, in which things happened as nowhere else, with the
most sublime irrelevance and unlikelihood, and one need not
turn a hair, because there was not a word of truth in them.

It was true the little girls were hedged and confined, but in
a large garden with trees and a grotto; they were locked at
night into a long cold dormitory, with all the windows open,
and a sister sleeping at either end. Their beds were curtained
with muslin, and small night-lamps were so arranged that the
sisters could see through the curtains, but the children could
not see the sisters. Miranda wondered if they ever slept, or did
they sit there all night quietly watching the sleepers through
the muslin? She tried to work up a little sinister thrill about this,
but she found it impossible to care much what either of the
sisters did. They were very dull good-natured women who
managed to make the whole dormitory seem dull. All days and

all things in the Convent of the Child Jesus were dull, in fact, and Maria and Miranda lived for Saturdays.

No one had even hinted that they should become nuns. On the contrary Miranda felt that the discouraging attitude of Sister Claude and Sister Austin and Sister Ursula towards her expressed ambition to be a nun barely veiled a deeply critical knowledge of her spiritual deficiencies. Still Maria and Miranda had got a fine new word out of their summer reading, and they referred to themselves as "immured." It gave a romantic glint to what was otherwise a very dull life for them, except for blessed Saturday afternoons during the racing season.

If the nuns were able to assure the family that the deportment and scholastic achievements of Maria and Miranda were at least passable, some cousin or other always showed up smiling, in holiday mood, to take them to the races, where they were given a dollar each to bet on any horse they chose. There were black Saturdays now and then, when Maria and Miranda sat ready, hats in hand, curly hair plastered down and slicked behind their ears, their stiffly pleated navy-blue skirts spread out around them, waiting with their hearts going down slowly into their high-topped laced-up black shoes. They never put on their hats until the last minute, for somehow it would have been too horrible to have their hats on, when, after all, Cousin Henry and Cousin Isabel, or Uncle George and Aunt Polly, were not coming to take them to the races. When no one appeared, and Saturday came and went a sickening waste, they were then given to understand that it was a punishment for bad marks during the week. They never knew until it was too late to avoid the disappointment. It was very wearing.

One Saturday they were sent down to wait in the visitors' parlor, and there was their father. He had come all the way from Texas to see them. They leaped at sight of him, and then stopped short, suspiciously. Was he going to take them to the races? If so, they were happy to see him.

"Hello," said father, kissing their cheeks. "Have you been good girls? Your Uncle Gabriel is running a mare at the Crescent City today, so we'll all go and bet on her. Would you like that?"

Maria put on her hat without a word, but Miranda stood

and addressed her father sternly. She had suffered many doubts about this day. "*Why* didn't you send word yesterday? I could have been looking forward all this time."

"We didn't know," said father, in his easiest paternal manner, "that you were going to deserve it. Remember Saturday before last?"

Miranda hung her head and put on her hat, with the round elastic under the chin. She remembered too well. She had, in midweek, given way to despair over her arithmetic and had fallen flat on her face on the classroom floor, refusing to rise until she was carried out. The rest of the week had been a series of novel deprivations, and Saturday a day of mourning; secret mourning, for if one mourned too noisily, it simply meant another bad mark against deportment.

"Never mind," said father, as if it were the smallest possible matter, "today you're going. Come along now. We've barely time."

These expeditions were all joy, every time, from the moment they stepped into a closed one-horse cab, a treat in itself with its dark, thick upholstery, soaked with strange perfumes and tobacco smoke, until the thrilling moment when they walked into a restaurant under big lights and were given dinner with things to eat they never had at home, much less at the convent. They felt worldly and grown up, each with her glass of water colored pink with claret.

The great crowd was always exciting as if they had never seen it before, with the beautiful, incredibly dressed ladies, all plumes and flowers and paint, and the elegant gentlemen with yellow gloves. The bands played in turn with thundering drums and brasses, and now and then a wild beautiful horse would career around the track with a tiny, monkey-shaped boy on his back, limbering up for his race.

Miranda had a secret personal interest in all this which she knew better than to confide to anyone, even Maria. Least of all to Maria. In ten minutes the whole family would have known. She had lately decided to be a jockey when she grew up. Her father had said one day that she was going to be a little thing all her life, she would never be tall; and this meant, of course, that she would never be a beauty like Aunt Amy, or Cousin Isabel. Her hope of being a beauty died hard, until the notion of being a jockey came suddenly and filled all her thoughts. Quietly, blissfully, at night before she slept, and too often in the daytime when she should have been studying, she planned her career as a jockey. It was dim in detail, but brilliant at the right distance. It seemed too silly to be worried about arithmetic at all, when what she needed for her future was to ride better—much better. "You ought to be ashamed of yourself," said father, after watching her gallop full tilt down the lane at the farm, on Trixie, the mustang mare. "I can see the sun, moon and stars between you and the saddle every jump." Spanish style meant that one sat close to the saddle, and did all kinds of things with the knees and reins. Jockeys bounced lightly, their knees almost level with the horse's back, rising and falling like a rubber ball. Miranda felt she could do that easily. Yes, she would be a jockey, like Tod Sloan, winning every other race at least. Meantime, while she was training, she would keep it a secret, and one day she would ride out, bouncing lightly, with the other jockeys, and win a great race, and surprise everybody, her family most of all.

On that particular Saturday, her idol, the great Tod Sloan, was riding, and he won two races. Miranda longed to bet her dollar on Tod Sloan, but father said, "Not now, honey. Today you must bet on Uncle Gabriel's horse. Save your dollar for the fourth race, and put it on Miss Lucy. You've got a hundred to one shot. Think if she wins."

Miranda knew well enough that a hundred to one shot was no bet at all. She sulked, the crumpled dollar in her hand grew damp and warm. She could have won three dollars already on Tod Sloan. Maria said virtuously, "It wouldn't be nice not to bet on Uncle Gabriel. That way, we keep the money in the family." Miranda put out her under lip at her sister. Maria was too prissy for words. She wrinkled her nose back at Miranda.

They had just turned their dollar over to the bookmaker for the fourth race when a vast bulging man with a red face and immense tan ragged mustaches fading into gray hailed them from a lower level of the grandstand, over the heads of the crowd, "Hey, there, Harry?" Father said, "Bless my soul, there's Gabriel." He motioned to the man, who came pushing his way heavily up the shallow steps. Maria and Miranda stared, first at him, then at each other. "Can that be our Uncle Gabriel?" their eyes asked. "Is that Aunt Amy's handsome romantic beau? Is that the man who wrote the poem about our Aunt Amy?" Oh, what did grown-up people *mean* when they talked, anyway?

He was a shabby fat man with bloodshot blue eyes, sad beaten eyes, and a big melancholy laugh, like a groan. He towered over them shouting to their father, "Well, for God's sake, Harry, it's been a coon's age. You ought to come out and look 'em over. You look just like yourself, Harry, how are you?"

The band struck up "Over the River" and Uncle Gabriel shouted louder. "Come on, let's get out of this. What are you doing up here with the pikers?"

"Can't," shouted Father. "Brought my little girls. Here they are."

Uncle Gabriel's bleared eyes beamed blindly upon them. "Fine looking set, Harry," he bellowed, "pretty as pictures, how old are they?"

"Ten and fourteen now," said Father; "awkward ages. Nest of vipers," he boasted, "perfect batch of serpent's teeth. Can't do a thing with 'em." He fluffed up Miranda's hair, pretending to tousle it.

"Pretty as pictures," bawled Uncle Gabriel, "but rolled into one they don't come up to Amy, do they?"

"No, they don't," admitted their father at the top of his voice, "but they're only half-baked." *Over the river, over the river*, moaned the band, *my sweetheart's waiting for me.*

"I've got to get back now," yelled Uncle Gabriel. The little girls felt quite deaf and confused. "Got the God-damnedest jockey in the world, Harry, just my luck. Ought to tie him on. Fell off Fiddler yesterday, just plain fell off on his tail— Remember Amy's mare, Miss Lucy? Well, this is her namesake, Miss Lucy IV. None of 'em ever came up to the first one, though. Stay right where you are, I'll be back."

Maria spoke up boldly. "Uncle Gabriel, tell Miss Lucy we're betting on her." Uncle Gabriel bent down and it looked as if there were tears in his swollen eyes. "God bless your sweet heart," he bellowed, "I'll tell her." He plunged down through the crowd again, his fat back bowed slightly in his loose clothes, his thick neck rolling over his collar.

Miranda and Maria, disheartened by the odds, by their first sight of their romantic Uncle Gabriel, whose language was so coarse, sat listlessly without watching, their chances missed, their dollars gone, their hearts sore. They didn't even move until their father leaned over and hauled them up. "Watch your horse," he said, in a quick warning voice, "watch Miss Lucy come home."

They stood up, scrambled to their feet on the bench, every vein in them suddenly beating so violently they could hardly focus their eyes, and saw a thin little mahogany-colored streak flash by the judges' stand, only a neck ahead, but their Miss Lucy, oh, their darling, their lovely—oh, Miss Lucy, their Uncle Gabriel's Miss Lucy, had won, had won. They leaped up and down screaming and clapping their hands, their hats falling back on their shoulders, their hair flying wild. *Whoa, you heifer*, squalled the band with snorting brasses, and the crowd broke into a long roar like the falling of the walls of Jericho.

The little girls sat down, feeling quite dizzy, while their father tried to pull their hats straight, and taking out his handkerchief held it to Miranda's face, saying very gently, "Here, blow your nose," and he dried her eyes while he was about it. He stood up then and shook them out of their daze. He was smiling with deep laughing wrinkles around his eyes, and spoke to them as if they were grown young ladies he was squiring around.

"Let's go out and pay our respects to Miss Lucy," he said. "She's the star of the day."

The horses were coming in, looking as if their hides had been drenched and rubbed with soap, their ribs heaving, their nostrils flaring and closing. The jockeys sat bowed and relaxed, their faces calm, moving a little at the waist with the movement of their horses. Miranda noted this for future use; that was the way you came in from a race, easy and quiet, whether you had won or lost. Miss Lucy came last, and a little handful of winners applauded her and cheered the jockey. He smiled and lifted his whip, his eyes and shriveled brown face perfectly serene. Miss Lucy was bleeding at the nose, two thick red rivulets were stiffening her tender mouth and chin, the round velvet chin that Miranda thought the nicest kind of chin in the world. Her eyes were wild and her knees were trembling, and she snored when she drew her breath.

Miranda stood staring. That was winning, too. Her heart clinched tight; that was winning, for Miss Lucy. So instantly and completely did her heart reject that victory, she did not know when it happened, but she hated it, and was ashamed that she had screamed and shed tears for joy when Miss Lucy, with her bloodied nose and bursting heart had gone past the judges' stand a neck ahead. She felt empty and sick and held to her father's hand so hard that he shook her off a little impatiently and said, "What is the matter with you? Don't be so fidgety."

Uncle Gabriel was standing there waiting, and he was completely drunk. He watched the mare go in, then leaned against the fence with its white-washed posts and sobbed openly. "She's got the nosebleed, Harry," he said. "Had it since yesterday. We thought we had her all fixed up. But she did it, all right. She's got a heart like a lion. I'm going to breed her, Harry. Her heart's worth a million dollars, by itself, God bless her." Tears ran over his brick-colored face and into his straggling mustaches. "If anything happens to her now I'll blow my brains out. She's my last hope. She saved my life. I've had a run," he said, groaning into a large handkerchief and mopping his face all over, "I've had a run of luck that would break a brass billy goat. God, Harry, let's go somewhere and have a drink."

"I must get the children back to school first, Gabriel," said their father, taking each by a hand.

"No, no, don't go yet," said Uncle Gabriel desperately. "Wait here a minute, I want to see the vet and take a look at Miss Lucy, and I'll be right back. Don't go, Harry, for God's sake. I want to talk to you a few minutes."

Maria and Miranda, watching Uncle Gabriel's lumbering, unsteady back, were thinking that this was the first time they had ever seen a man that they knew to be drunk. They had seen pictures and read descriptions, and had heard descriptions, so they recognized the symptoms at once. Miranda felt it was an important moment in a great many ways.

"Uncle Gabriel's a drunkard, isn't he?" she asked her father, rather proudly.

"Hush, don't say such things," said father, with a heavy frown, "or I'll never bring you here again." He looked worried and unhappy, and, above all, undecided. The little girls stood stiff with resentment against such obvious injustice. They loosed their hands from his and moved away coldly, standing together in silence. Their father did not notice, watching the place where Uncle Gabriel had disappeared. In a few minutes he came back, still wiping his face, as if there were cobwebs on it, carrying his big black hat. He waved at them from a short distance, calling out in a cheerful way, "She's going to be all right, Harry. It's stopped now. Lord, this will be good news for Miss Honey. Come on, Harry, let's all go home and tell Miss Honey. She deserves some good news."

Father said, "I'd better take the children back to school first, then we'll go."

"No, no," said Uncle Gabriel, fondly. "I want her to see the girls. She'll be tickled pink to see them, Harry. Bring 'em along."

"Is it another race horse we're going to see?" whispered Miranda in her sister's ear.

"Don't be silly," said Maria. "It's Uncle Gabriel's second wife."

"Let's find a cab, Harry," said Uncle Gabriel, "and take your little girls out to cheer up Miss Honey. Both of 'em rolled into one look a lot like Amy, I swear they do. I want Miss Honey to see them. She's always liked our family, Harry, though of course she's not what you'd call an expansive kind of woman."

Maria and Miranda sat facing the driver, and Uncle Gabriel squeezed himself in facing them beside their father. The air became at once bitter and sour with his breathing. He looked sad and poor. His necktie was on crooked and his shirt was rumpled. Father said, "You're going to see Uncle Gabriel's second wife, children," exactly as if they had not heard everything; and to Gabriel, "How *is* your wife nowadays? It must be twenty years since I saw her last."

"She's pretty gloomy, and that's a fact," said Uncle Gabriel. "She's been pretty gloomy for years now, and nothing seems to shake her out of it. She never did care for horses, Harry, if you remember; she hasn't been near the track three times since we were married. When I think how Amy wouldn't have missed a race for anything . . . She's very different from Amy, Harry, a very different kind of woman. As fine a woman as ever lived in her own way, but she hates change and moving around, and she just lives in the boy."

"Where is Gabe now?" asked father.

"Finishing college," said Uncle Gabriel; "a smart boy, but awfully like his mother. Awfully like," he said, in a melancholy way. "She hates being away from him. Just wants to sit down in the same town and wait for him to get through with his education. Well, I'm sorry it can't be done if that's what she wants, but God Almighty— And this last run of luck has about got her down. I hope you'll be able to cheer her up a little, Harry, she needs it."

The little girls sat watching the streets grow duller and dingier and narrower, and at last the shabbier and shabbier white people gave way to dressed-up Negroes, and then to shabby Negroes, and after a long way the cab stopped before a desolate-looking little hotel in Elysian Fields. Their father helped Maria and Miranda out, told the cabman to wait, and they followed Uncle Gabriel through a dirty damp-smelling patio, down a long gas-lighted hall full of a terrible smell, Miranda couldn't decide what it was made of but it had a bitter taste even, and up a long staircase with a ragged carpet. Uncle Gabriel pushed open a door without warning, saying, "Come in, here we are."

A tall pale-faced woman with faded straw-colored hair and pink-rimmed eyelids rose suddenly from a squeaking rocking chair. She wore a stiff blue-and-white-striped shirtwaist and a stiff black skirt of some hard shiny material. Her large knuckled hands rose to her round, neat pompadour at sight of her visitors.

"Honey," said Uncle Gabriel, with large false heartiness, "you'll never guess who's come to see you." He gave her a clumsy hug. Her face did not change and her eyes rested steadily on the three strangers. "Amy's brother Harry, Honey, you remember, don't you?"

"Of course," said Miss Honey, putting out her hand straight

as a paddle, "of course I remember you, Harry." She did not smile.

"And Amy's two little nieces," went on Uncle Gabriel, bringing them forward. They put out their hands limply, and Miss Honey gave each one a slight flip and dropped it. "And we've got good news for you," went on Uncle Gabriel, trying to bolster up the painful situation. "Miss Lucy stepped out and showed 'em today, Honey. We're rich again, old girl, cheer up."

Miss Honey turned her long, despairing face towards her visitors. "Sit down," she said with a heavy sigh, seating herself and motioning towards various rickety chairs. There was a big lumpy bed, with a grayish-white counterpane on it, a marble-topped washstand, grayish coarse lace curtains on strings at the two small windows, a small closed fireplace with a hole in it for a stovepipe, and two trunks, standing at odds as if somebody were just moving in, or just moving out. Everything was dingy and soiled and neat and bare; not a pin out of place.

"We'll move to the St. Charles tomorrow," said Uncle Gabriel, as much to Harry as to his wife. "Get your best dresses together, Honey, the long dry spell is over."

Miss Honey's nostrils pinched together and she rocked slightly, with her arms folded. "I've lived in the St. Charles before, and I've lived here before," she said, in a tight deliberate voice, "and this time I'll just stay where I am, thank you. I prefer it to moving back here in three months. I'm settled now, I feel at home here," she told him, glancing at Harry, her pale eyes kindling with blue fire, a stiff white line around her mouth.

The little girls sat trying not to stare, miserably ill at ease. Their grandmother had pronounced Harry's children to be the most unteachable she had ever seen in her long experience with the young; but they had learned by indirection one thing well—nice people did not carry on quarrels before outsiders. Family quarrels were sacred, to be waged privately in fierce hissing whispers, low choked mutters and growls. If they did yell and stamp, it must be behind closed doors and windows. Uncle Gabriel's second wife was hopping mad and she looked ready to fly out at Uncle Gabriel any second, with him sitting there like a hound when someone shakes a whip at him.

"She loathes and despises everybody in this room," thought

Miranda, coolly, "and she's afraid we won't know it. She needn't worry, we knew it when we came in." With all her heart she wanted to go, but her father, though his face was a study, made no move. He seemed to be trying to think of something pleasant to say. Maria, feeling guilty, though she couldn't think why, was calculating rapidly, "Why, she's only Uncle Gabriel's second wife, and Uncle Gabriel was only married before to Aunt Amy, why, she's no kin at all, and I'm glad of it." Sitting back easily, she let her hands fall open in her lap; they would be going in a few minutes, undoubtedly, and they need never come back.

Then father said, "We mustn't be keeping you, we just dropped in for a few minutes. We wanted to see how you are."

Miss Honey said nothing, but she made a little gesture with her hands, from the wrist, as if to say, "Well, you see how I am, and now what next?"

"I must take these young ones back to school," said father, and Uncle Gabriel said stupidly, "Look, Honey, don't you think they resemble Amy a little? Especially around the eyes, especially Maria, don't you think, Harry?"

Their father glanced at them in turn. "I really couldn't say," he decided, and the little girls saw he was more monstrously embarrassed than ever. He turned to Miss Honey, "I hadn't seen Gabriel for so many years," he said, "we thought of getting out for a talk about old times together. You know how it is."

"Yes, I know," said Miss Honey, rocking a little, and all that she knew gleamed forth in a pallid, unquenchable hatred and bitterness that seemed enough to bring her long body straight up out of the chair in a fury, "I know," and she sat staring at the floor. Her mouth shook and straightened. There was a terrible silence, which was broken when the little girls saw their father rise. They got up, too, and it was all they could do to keep from making a dash for the door.

"I must get the young ones back," said their father. "They've had enough excitement for one day. They each won a hundred dollars on Miss Lucy. It was a good race," he said, in complete wretchedness, as if he simply could not extricate himself from the situation. "Wasn't it, Gabriel?"

"It was a grand race," said Gabriel, brokenly, "a grand race."

Miss Honey stood up and moved a step towards the door. "Do you take them to the races, actually?" she asked, and her lids flickered towards them as if they were loathsome insects, Maria felt.

"If I feel they deserve a little treat, yes," said their father, in an easy tone but with wrinkled brow.

"I had rather, much rather," said Miss Honey clearly, "see my son dead at my feet than hanging around a race track."

The next few moments were rather a blank, but at last they were out of it, going down the stairs, across the patio, with Uncle Gabriel seeing them back into the cab. His face was sagging, the features had fallen as if the flesh had slipped from the bones, and his eyelids were puffed and blue. "Good-by, Harry," he said soberly. "How long you expect to be here?"

"Starting back tomorrow," said Harry. "Just dropped in on a little business and to see how the girls were getting along."

"Well," said Uncle Gabriel, "I may be dropping into your part of the country one of these days. Good-by, children," he said, taking their hands one after the other in his big warm paws. "They're nice children, Harry. I'm glad you won on Miss Lucy," he said to the little girls, tenderly. "Don't spend your money foolishly, now. Well, so long, Harry." As the cab jolted away he stood there fat and sagging, holding up his arm and wagging his hand at them.

"Goodness," said Maria, in her most grown-up manner, taking her hat off and hanging it over her knee, "I'm glad that's over."

"What I want to know is," said Miranda, "*is* Uncle Gabriel a real drunkard?"

"Oh, hush," said their father, sharply, "I've got the heartburn."

There was a respectful pause, as before a public monument. When their father had the heartburn it was time to lay low. The cab rumbled on, back to clean gay streets, with the lights coming on in the early February darkness, past shimmering shop windows, smooth pavements on and on, past beautiful old houses set in deep gardens, on, on back to the dark walls with the heavy-topped trees hanging over them. Miranda sat thinking so hard she forgot and spoke out in her thoughtless way: "I've decided I'm not going to be a jockey, after all." She could as usual have bitten her tongue, but as usual it was too late.

Father cheered up and twinkled at her knowingly, as if that didn't surprise him in the least. "Well, well," said he, "so you aren't going to be a jockey! That's very sensible of you. I think she ought to be a lion-tamer, don't you, Maria? That's a nice, womanly profession."

Miranda, seeing Maria from the height of her fourteen years suddenly joining with their father to laugh at her, made an instant decision and laughed with them at herself. That was better. Everybody laughed and it was such a relief.

"Where's my hundred dollars?" asked Maria, anxiously.

"It's going in the bank," said their father, "and yours too," he told Miranda. "That is your nest-egg."

"Just so they don't buy my stockings with it," said Miranda, who had long resented the use of her Christmas money by their grandmother. "I've got enough stockings to last me a year."

"I'd like to buy a racehorse," said Maria, "but I know it's not enough." The limitations of wealth oppressed her. "*What* could you buy with a hundred dollars?" she asked fretfully.

"Nothing, nothing at all," said their father, "a hundred dollars is just something you put in the bank."

Maria and Miranda lost interest. They had won a hundred dollars on a horse race once. It was already in the far past. They began to chatter about something else.

The lay sister opened the door on a long cord, from behind the grille; Maria and Miranda walked in silently to their familiar world of shining bare floors and insipid wholesome food and cold-water washing and regular prayers; their world of poverty, chastity and obedience, of early to bed and early to rise, of sharp little rules and tittle-tattle. Resignation was in their childish faces as they held them up to be kissed.

"Be good girls," said their father, in the strange serious, rather helpless way he always had when he told them good-by. "Write to your daddy, now, nice long letters," he said, holding their arms firmly for a moment before letting go for good. Then he disappeared, and the sister swung the door closed after him.

Maria and Miranda went upstairs to the dormitory to wash their faces and hands and slick down their hair again before supper.

Miranda was hungry. "We didn't have a thing to eat, after all," she grumbled. "Not even a chocolate nut bar. I think that's mean. We didn't even get a quarter to spend," she said.

"Not a living bite," said Maria. "Not a nickel." She poured out cold water into the bowl and rolled up her sleeves.

Another girl about her own age came in and went to a washbowl near another bed. "Where have you been?" she asked. "Did you have a good time?"

"We went to the races, with our father," said Maria, soaping her hands.

"Our uncle's horse won," said Miranda.

"My goodness," said the other girl, vaguely, "that must have been grand."

Maria looked at Miranda, who was rolling up her own sleeves. She tried to feel martyred, but it wouldn't go. "Immured for another week," she said, her eyes sparkling over the edge of her towel.

PART III: 1912

Miranda followed the porter down the stuffy aisle of the sleeping-car, where the berths were nearly all made down and the dusty green curtains buttoned, to a seat at the further end. "Now yo' berth's ready any time, Miss," said the porter.

"But I want to sit up a while," said Miranda. A very thin old lady raised choleric black eyes and fixed upon her a regard of unmixed disapproval. She had two immense front teeth and a receding chin, but she did not lack character. She had piled her luggage around her like a barricade, and she glared at the porter when he picked some of it up to make room for his new passenger. Miranda sat, saying mechanically, "May I?"

"You may, indeed," said the old lady, for she seemed old in spite of a certain brisk, rustling energy. Her taffeta petticoats creaked like hinges every time she stirred. With ferocious sarcasm, after a half second's pause, she added, "You may be so good as to get off my hat!"

Miranda rose instantly in horror, and handed to the old lady a wilted contrivance of black horsehair braid and shattered white poppies. "I'm dreadfully sorry," she stammered, for she had been brought up to treat ferocious old ladies respectfully, and this one seemed capable of spanking her, then and there. "I didn't dream it was your hat."

"And whose hat did you dream it might be?" inquired the old lady, baring her teeth and twirling the hat on a forefinger to restore it.

"I didn't think it was a hat at all," said Miranda with a touch of hysteria.

"Oh, you didn't think it was a hat? Where on earth are your eyes, child?" and she proved the nature and function of the object by placing it on her head at a somewhat tipsy angle, though still it did not much resemble a hat. "Now can you see what it is?"

"Yes, oh, yes," said Miranda, with a meekness she hoped was disarming. She ventured to sit again after a careful inspection of the narrow space she was to occupy.

"Well, well," said the old lady, "let's have the porter remove some of these encumbrances," and she stabbed the bell with a lean sharp forefinger. There followed a flurry of rearrangements, during which they both stood in the aisle, the old lady giving a series of impossible directions to the Negro which he bore philosophically while he disposed of the luggage exactly as he had meant to do. Seated again, the old lady asked in a kindly, authoritative tone, "And what might your name be, child?"

At Miranda's answer, she blinked somewhat, unfolded her spectacles, straddled them across her high nose competently, and took a good long look at the face beside her.

"If I'd had my spectacles on," she said, in an astonishingly changed voice, "I might have known. I'm Cousin Eva Parrington," she said, "Cousin Molly Parrington's daughter, remember? I knew you when you were a little girl. You were a lively little girl," she added as if to console her, "and very opinionated. The last thing I heard about you, you were planning to be a tight-rope walker. You were going to play the violin and walk the tight rope at the same time."

"I must have seen it at the vaudeville show," said Miranda. "I couldn't have invented it. Now I'd like to be an air pilot!"

"I used to go to dances with your father," said Cousin Eva, busy with her own thoughts, "and to big holiday parties at your grandmother's house, long before you were born. Oh, indeed, yes, a long time before."

Miranda remembered several things at once. Aunt Amy had threatened to be an old maid like Eva. Oh, Eva, the trouble with her is she has no chin. Eva has given up, and is teaching Latin in a Female Seminary. Eva's gone out for votes for women, God help her. The nice thing about an ugly daughter is, she's not apt to make me a grandmother. . . . "They didn't do you much good, those parties, dear Cousin Eva," thought Miranda.

"They didn't do me much good, those parties," said Cousin Eva aloud as if she were a mind-reader, and Miranda's head swam for a moment with fear that she had herself spoken aloud. "Or at least, they didn't serve their purpose, for I never got married; but I enjoyed them, just the same. I had a good time at those parties, even if I wasn't a belle. And so you are Harry's child, and here I was quarreling with you. You do remember me, don't you?"

"Yes," said Miranda, and thinking that even if Cousin Eva had been really an old maid ten years before, still she couldn't be much past fifty now, and she looked so withered and tired, so famished and sunken in the cheeks, so *old*, somehow. Across the abyss separating Cousin Eva from her own youth, Miranda looked with painful premonition. "Oh, must I ever be like that?" She said aloud, "Yes, you used to read Latin to me, and tell me not to bother about the sense, to get the sound in my mind, and it would come easier later."

"Ah, so I did," said Cousin Eva, delighted. "So I did. You don't happen to remember that I once had a beautiful sapphire velvet dress with a train on it?"

"No, I don't remember that dress," said Miranda.

"It was an old dress of my mother's made over and cut down to fit," said Eva, "and it wasn't in the least becoming to me, but it was the only really good dress I ever had, and I remember it as if it were yesterday. Blue was never my color."

She sighed with a humorous bitterness. The humor seemed momentary, but the bitterness was a constant state of mind.

Miranda, trying to offer the sympathy of fellow suffering, said, "I know. I've had Maria's dresses made over for me, and they were never right. It was dreadful."

"Well," said Cousin Eva, in the tone of one who did not wish to share her unique disappointments. "How is your father? I always liked him. He was one of the finest-looking young men I ever saw. Vain, too, like all his family. He wouldn't ride any but the best horses he could buy, and I used to say be made them prance and then watched his own shadow. I used to tell this on him at dinner parties, and he hated me for it. I feel pretty certain he hated me." An overtone of complacency in Cousin Eva's voice explained better than words that she had her own method of commanding attention and arousing emotion. "How *is* your father, I asked you, my dear?"

"I haven't seen him for nearly a year," answered Miranda, quickly, before Cousin Eva could get ahead again. "I'm going home now to Uncle Gabriel's funeral; you know, Uncle Gabriel died in Lexington and they have brought him back to be buried beside Aunt Amy."

"So that's how we meet," said Cousin Eva. "Yes, Gabriel drank himself to death at last. I'm going to the funeral, too. I haven't been home since I went to Mother's funeral, it must be, let's see, yes, it will be nine years next July. I'm going to Gabriel's funeral, though. I wouldn't miss that. Poor fellow, what a life he had. Pretty soon, they'll all be gone."

Miranda said, "We're left, Cousin Eva," meaning those of her own generation, the young, and Cousin Eva said, "Pshaw, you'll live forever, and you won't bother to come to our funerals." She didn't seem to think this was a misfortune, but flung the remark from her like a woman accustomed to saying what she thought.

Miranda sat thinking, "Still, I suppose it would be pleasant if I could say something to make her believe that she and all of them would be lamented, but—but—" With a smile which she hoped would be her denial of Cousin Eva's cynicism about the younger generation, she said, "You were right about the Latin, Cousin Eva, your reading did help when I began with it. I still study," she said. "Latin, too."

"And why shouldn't you?" asked Cousin Eva, sharply, adding at once mildly, "I'm glad you are going to use your mind a little, child. Don't let yourself rust away. Your mind outwears all sorts of things you may set your heart upon; you can enjoy it when all other things are taken away." Miranda was chilled by her melancholy. Cousin Eva went on: "In our part of the country, in my time, we were so provincial—a woman didn't dare to think or act for herself. The whole world was a little that way," she said, "but we were the worst, I believe. I suppose you must know how I fought for votes for women when it almost made a pariah of me—I was turned out of my chair at the Seminary, but I'm glad I did it and I would do it again. You young things don't realize. You'll live in a better world because we worked for it."

Miranda knew something of Cousin Eva's career. She said sincerely, "I think it was brave of you, and I'm glad you did it, too. I loved your courage."

"It wasn't just showing off, mind you," said Cousin Eva, rejecting praise, fretfully. "Any fool can be brave. We were working for something we knew was right, and it turned out that we needed a lot of courage for it. That was all. I didn't expect to go to jail, but I went three times, and I'd go three times three more if it were necessary. We aren't voting yet," she said, "but we will be."

Miranda did not venture any answer, but she felt convinced that indeed women would be voting soon if nothing fatal happened to Cousin Eva. There was something in her manner which said such things could be left safely to her. Miranda was dimly fired for the cause herself; it seemed heroic and worth suffering for, but discouraging, too, to those who came after: Cousin Eva so plainly had swept the field clear of opportunity.

They were silent for a few minutes, while Cousin Eva rummaged in her handbag, bringing up odds and ends: peppermint drops, eye drops, a packet of needles, three handkerchiefs, a little bottle of violet perfume, a book of addresses, two buttons, one black, one white, and, finally, a packet of headache powders.

"Bring me a glass of water, will you, my dear?" she asked Miranda. She poured the headache powder on her tongue, swallowed the water, and put two peppermints in her mouth.

"So now they're going to bury Gabriel near Amy," she said after a while, as if her eased headache had started her on a new train of thought. "Miss Honey would like that, poor dear, if she could know. After listening to stories about Amy for twenty-five years, she must lie alone in her grave in Lexington while Gabriel sneaks off to Texas to make his bed with Amy again. It was a kind of lifelong infidelity, Miranda, and now an eternal infidelity on top of that. He ought to be ashamed of himself."

"It was Aunt Amy he loved," said Miranda, wondering what Miss Honey could have been like before her long troubles with Uncle Gabriel. "First, anyway."

"Oh, that Amy," said Cousin Eva, her eyes glittering. "Your Aunt Amy was a devil and a mischief-maker, but I loved her dearly. I used to stand up for Amy when her reputation wasn't worth that." Her fingers snapped like castanets. "She used to say to me, in that gay soft way she had, 'Now, Eva, don't go talking votes for women when the lads ask you to dance. Don't recite Latin poems to 'em,' she would say, 'they got sick of that in school. Dance and say nothing, Eva,' she would say, her eyes perfectly devilish, 'and hold your chin up, Eva.' My chin was my weak point, you see. 'You'll never catch a husband if you don't look out,' she would say. Then she would laugh and fly away, and where did she fly to?" demanded Cousin Eva, her sharp eyes pinning Miranda down to the bitter facts of the case. "To scandal and to death, nowhere else."

"She was joking, Cousin Eva," said Miranda, innocently, "and everybody loved her."

"Not everybody, by a long shot," said Cousin Eva in triumph. "She had enemies. If she knew, she pretended she didn't. If she cared, she never said. You couldn't make her quarrel. She was sweet as a honeycomb to everybody. *Everybody*," she added, "that was the trouble. She went through life like a spoiled darling, doing as she pleased and letting other people suffer for it, and pick up the pieces after her. I never believed for one moment," said Cousin Eva, putting her mouth close to Miranda's ear and breathing peppermint hotly into it, "that Amy was an impure woman. Never! But let me tell you, there were plenty who did believe it. There were plenty to pity poor Gabriel for being so completely blinded by her. A great many persons were not surprised when they heard that Gabriel was perfectly miserable all the time, on their honeymoon, in New Orleans. Jealousy. And why not? But I used to say to such persons that, no matter what the appearances were, I had faith in Amy's virtue. Wild, I said, indiscreet, I said, heartless, I said, but *virtuous*, I feel certain. But you could hardly blame anyone for being mystified. The way she rose up suddenly from death's door to marry Gabriel Breaux, after refusing him and treating him like a dog for years, looked odd, to say the least. To say the very least," she added, after a moment, "odd is a mild word for it. And there was something very mysterious about her death, only six weeks after marriage."

Miranda roused herself. She felt she knew this part of the story and could set Cousin Eva right about one thing. "She died of a hemorrhage from the lungs," said Miranda. "She had been ill for five years, don't you remember?"

Cousin Eva was ready for that. "Ha, that was the story, indeed. The official account, you might say. Oh, yes, I heard that often enough. But did you ever hear about that fellow Raymond somebody-or-other from Calcasieu Parish, almost a stranger, who persuaded Amy to elope with him from a dance one night, and she just ran out into the darkness without even stopping for her cloak, and your poor dear nice father Harry— you weren't even thought of then—had to run him down to earth and shoot him?"

Miranda leaned back from the advancing flood of speech. "Cousin Eva, my father shot *at* him, don't you remember? He didn't hit him. . . ."

"Well, that's a pity."

". . . and they had only gone out for a breath of air between dances. It was Uncle Gabriel's jealousy. And my father shot at the man because he thought that was better than letting Uncle Gabriel fight a duel about Aunt Amy. There was *nothing* in the whole affair except Uncle Gabriel's jealousy."

"You poor baby," said Cousin Eva, and pity gave a light like daggers to her eyes, "you dear innocent, you—do you believe that? How old are you, anyway?"

"Just past eighteen," said Miranda.

"If you don't understand what I tell you," said Cousin Eva portentously, "you will later. Knowledge can't hurt you. You mustn't live in a romantic haze about life. You'll understand when you're married, at any rate."

"I'm married now, Cousin Eva," said Miranda, feeling for almost the first time that it might be an advantage, "nearly a year. I eloped from school." It seemed very unreal even as she said it, and seemed to have nothing at all to do with the future; still, it was important, it must be declared, it was a situation in life which people seemed to be most exacting about, and the only feeling she could rouse in herself about it was an immense weariness as if it were an illness that she might one day hope to recover from.

"Shameful, shameful," cried Cousin Eva, genuinely re-pelled. "If you had been my child I should have brought you home and spanked you."

Miranda laughed out. Cousin Eva seemed to believe things could be arranged like that. She was so solemn and fierce, so comic and baffled.

"And you must know I should have just gone straight out again, through the nearest window," she taunted her. "If I went the first time, why not the second?"

"Yes, I suppose so," said Cousin Eva. "I hope you married rich."

"Not so very," said Miranda. "Enough." As if anyone could have stopped to think of such a thing!

Cousin Eva adjusted her spectacles and sized up Miranda's dress, her luggage, examined her engagement ring and wed-ding ring, with her nostrils fairly quivering as if she might smell out wealth on her.

"Well, that's better than nothing," said Cousin Eva. "I thank God every day of my life that I have a small income. It's a Rock of Ages. What would have become of me if I hadn't a cent of my own? Well, you'll be able now to do something for your family."

Miranda remembered what she had always heard about the Parringtons. They were money-hungry, they loved money and nothing else, and when they had got some they kept it. Blood was thinner than water between the Parringtons where money was concerned.

"We're pretty poor," said Miranda, stubbornly allying herself with her father's family instead of her husband's, "but a rich marriage is no way out," she said, with the snobbishness of poverty. She was thinking, "You don't know my branch of the family, dear Cousin Eva, if you think it is."

"Your branch of the family," said Cousin Eva, with that terrifying habit she had of lifting phrases out of one's mind, "has no more practical sense than so many children. Everything for love," she said, with a face of positive nausea, "that was it. Gabriel would have been rich if his grandfather had not disinherited him, but would Amy be sensible and marry him and make him settle down so the old man would have been pleased with him? No. And what could Gabriel do without money? I wish you could have seen the life he led Miss Honey, one day buying her Paris gowns and the next day pawning her earrings. It just depended on how the horses ran, and they ran worse and worse, and Gabriel drank more and more."

Miranda did not say, "I saw a little of it." She was trying to imagine Miss Honey in a Paris gown. She said, "But Uncle Gabriel was so mad about Aunt Amy, there was no question of her not marrying him at last, money or no money."

Cousin Eva strained her lips tightly over her teeth, let them fly again and leaned over, gripping Miranda's arm. "What I ask myself, what I ask myself over and over again," she whispered, "is, what connection did this man Raymond from Calcasieu have with Amy's sudden marriage to Gabriel, and *what* did Amy do to make away with herself so soon afterward? For mark my words, child, Amy wasn't so ill as all that. She'd been flying around for years after the doctors said her lungs were weak. Amy did away with herself to escape some disgrace, some exposure that she faced."

The beady black eyes glinted; Cousin Eva's face was quite frightening, so near and so intent. Miranda wanted to say, "Stop. Let her rest. What harm did she ever do you?" but she was timid and unnerved, and deep in her was a horrid fascination with the terrors and the darkness Cousin Eva had conjured up. What was the end of this story?

"She was a bad, wild girl, but I was fond of her to the last," said Cousin Eva. "She got into trouble somehow, and she couldn't get out again, and I have every reason to believe she

killed herself with the drug they gave her to keep her quiet
after a hemorrhage. If she didn't, what happened, what happened?"

"I don't know," said Miranda. "How should I know? She
was very beautiful," she said, as if this explained everything.
"Everybody said she was very beautiful."

"Not everybody," said Cousin Eva, firmly, shaking her head.
"I for one never thought so. They made entirely too much fuss
over her. She was good-looking enough, but why did they
think she was beautiful? I cannot understand it. She was too
thin when she was young, and later I always thought she was
too fat, and again in her last year she was altogether too thin.
She always got herself up to be looked at, and so people
looked, of course. She rode too hard, and she danced too
freely, and she talked too much, and you'd have to be blind,
deaf and dumb not to notice her. I don't mean she was loud or
vulgar, she wasn't, but she was *too free*," said Cousin Eva. She
stopped for breath and put a peppermint in her mouth. Miranda could see Cousin Eva on the platform, making her
speeches, stopping to take a peppermint. But why did she hate
Aunt Amy so, when Aunt Amy was dead and she alive? Wasn't
being alive enough?

"And her illness wasn't romantic either," said Cousin Eva,
"though to hear them tell it she faded like a lily. Well, she
coughed blood, if that's romantic. If they had made her take
proper care of herself, if she had been nursed sensibly, she might
have been alive today. But no, nothing of the kind. She lay
wrapped in beautiful shawls on a sofa with flowers around her,
eating as she liked or not eating, getting up after a hemorrhage
and going out to ride or dance, sleeping with the windows
closed; with crowds coming in and out laughing and talking at
all hours, and Amy sitting up so her hair wouldn't get out of
curl. And why wouldn't that sort of thing kill a well person in
time? I have almost died twice in my life," said Cousin Eva,
"and both times I was sent to a hospital where I belonged and
left there until I came out. And I came out," she said, her
voice deepening to a bugle note, "and I went to work again."

"Beauty goes, character stays," said the small voice of ax-
iomatic morality in Miranda's ear. It was a dreary prospect;
why was a strong character so deforming? Miranda felt she

truly wanted to be strong, but how could she face it, seeing what it did to one?

"She had a lovely complexion," said Cousin Eva, "perfectly transparent with a flush on each cheekbone. But it was tuberculosis, and is disease beautiful? And she brought it on herself by drinking lemon and salt to stop her periods when she wanted to go to dances. There was a superstition among young girls about that. They fancied that young men could tell what ailed them by touching their hands, or even by looking at them. As if it mattered? But they were terribly self-conscious and they had immense respect for man's worldly wisdom in those days. My own notion is that a man couldn't—but anyway, the whole thing was stupid."

"I should have thought they'd have stayed at home if they couldn't manage better than that," said Miranda, feeling very knowledgeable and modern.

"They didn't dare. Those parties and dances were their market, a girl couldn't afford to miss out, there were always rivals waiting to cut the ground from under her. The rivalry—" said Cousin Eva, and her head lifted, she arched like a cavalry horse getting a whiff of the battlefield—"you can't imagine what the rivalry was like. The way those girls treated each other —nothing was too mean, nothing too false—"

Cousin Eva wrung her hands. "It was just sex," she said in despair; "their minds dwelt on nothing else. They didn't call it that, it was all smothered under pretty names, but that's all it was, sex." She looked out of the window into the darkness, her sunken cheek near Miranda flushed deeply. She turned back. "I took to the soap box and the platform when I was called upon," she said proudly, "and I went to jail when it was necessary, and my condition didn't make any difference. I was booed and jeered and shoved around just as if I had been in perfect health. But it was part of our philosophy not to let our physical handicaps make any difference to our work. You know what I mean," she said, as if until now it was all mystery. "Well, Amy carried herself with more spirit than the others, and she didn't seem to be making any sort of fight, but she was simply sex-ridden, like the rest. She behaved as if she hadn't a rival on earth, and she pretended not to know what marriage was about, but I know better. None of them had, and they didn't want to have, anything else to think about, and they didn't really know anything about that, so they simply festered inside —they festered—"

Miranda found herself deliberately watching a long procession of living corpses, festering women stepping gaily towards the charnel house, their corruption concealed under laces and flowers, their dead faces lifted smiling, and thought quite coldly, "Of course it was not like that. This is no more true than what I was told before, it's every bit as romantic," and she realized that she was tired of her intense Cousin Eva, she wanted to go to sleep, she wanted to be at home, she wished it were tomorrow and she could see her father and her sister, who were so alive and solid; who would mention her freckles and ask her if she wanted something to eat.

"My mother was not like that," she said, childishly. "My mother was a perfectly natural woman who liked to cook. I have seen some of her sewing," she said. "I have read her diary."

"Your mother was a saint," said Cousin Eva, automatically.

Miranda sat silent, outraged. "My mother was nothing of the sort," she wanted to fling in Cousin Eva's big front teeth. But Cousin Eva had been gathering bitterness until more speech came of it.

"'Hold your chin up, Eva,' Amy used to tell me," she began, doubling up both her fists and shaking them a little. "All my life the whole family bedeviled me about my chin. My entire girlhood was spoiled by it. Can you imagine," she asked, with a ferocity that seemed much too deep for this one cause, "people who call themselves civilized spoiling life for a young girl because she had one unlucky feature? Of course, you understand perfectly it was all in the very best humor, everybody was very amusing about it, no harm meant—oh, no, no harm at all. That is the hellish thing about it. It is that I can't forgive," she cried out, and she twisted her hands together as if they were rags. "Ah, the family," she said, releasing her breath and sitting back quietly, "the whole hideous institution should be wiped from the face of the earth. It is the root of all human wrongs," she ended, and relaxed, and her face became calm. She was trembling. Miranda reached out and took Cousin Eva's hand and held it. The hand fluttered and lay still, and Cousin Eva said, "You've not the faintest idea what some of us went through, but I wanted you to hear the other side of the story. And I'm keeping you up when you need your beauty sleep," she said grimly, stirring herself with an immense rustle of petticoats.

Miranda pulled herself together, feeling limp, and stood up. Cousin Eva put out her hand again, and drew Miranda down to her. "Good night, you dear child," she said, "to think you're grown up." Miranda hesitated, then quite suddenly kissed her Cousin Eva on the cheek. The black eyes shone brightly through water for an instant, and Cousin Eva said with a warm note in her sharp clear orator's voice, "Tomorrow we'll be at home again. I'm looking forward to it, aren't you? Good night."

Miranda fell asleep while she was getting off her clothes. Instantly it was morning again. She was still trying to close her suitcase when the train pulled into the small station, and there on the platform she saw her father, looking tired and anxious, his hat pulled over his eyes. She rapped on the window to catch his attention, then ran out and threw herself upon him. He said, "Well, here's my big girl," as if she were still seven, but his hands on her arms held her off, the tone was forced. There was no welcome for her, and there had not been since she had run away. She could not persuade herself to remember how it would be; between one home-coming and the next her mind refused to accept its own knowledge. Her father looked over her head and said, without surprise, "Why, hello, Eva, I'm glad somebody sent you a telegram." Miranda, rebuffed again, let her arms fall away again, with the same painful dull jerk of the heart.

"No one in my family," said Eva, her face framed in the thin black veil she reserved, evidently, for family funerals, "ever sent me a telegram in my life. I had the news from young Keziah who had it from young Gabriel. I suppose Gabe is here?"

"Everybody seems to be here," said Father. "The house is getting full."

"I'll go to the hotel if you like," said Cousin Eva.

"Damnation, no," said Father. "I didn't mean that. You'll come with us where you belong."

Skid, the handy man, grabbed the suitcases and started down the rocky village street. "We've got the car," said Father.

He took Miranda by the hand, then dropped it again, and reached for Cousin Eva's elbow.

"I'm perfectly able, thank you," said Cousin Eva, shying away.

"If you're so independent now," said Father, "God help us when you get that vote."

Cousin Eva pushed back her veil. She was smiling merrily. She liked Harry, she always had liked him, he could tease as much as he liked. She slipped her arm through his. "So it's all over with poor Gabriel, isn't it?"

"Oh, yes," said Father, "it's all over, all right. They're pegging out pretty regularly now. It will be our turn next, Eva?"

"I don't know, and I don't care," said Eva, recklessly. "It's good to be back now and then, Harry, even if it is only for funerals. I feel sinfully cheerful."

"Oh, Gabriel wouldn't mind, he'd like seeing you cheerful. Gabriel was the cheerfullest cuss I ever saw, when we were young. Life for Gabriel," said Father, "was just one perpetual picnic."

"Poor fellow," said Cousin Eva.

"Poor old Gabriel," said Father, heavily.

Miranda walked along beside her father, feeling homeless, but not sorry for it. He had not forgiven her, she knew that. When would he? She could not guess, but she felt it would come of itself, without words and without acknowledgment on either side, for by the time it arrived neither of them would need to remember what had caused their division, nor why it had seemed so important. Surely old people cannot hold their grudges forever because the young want to live, too, she thought, in her arrogance, her pride. I will make my own mistakes, not yours; I cannot depend upon you beyond a certain point, why depend at all? There was something more beyond, but this was a first step to take, and she took it, walking in silence beside her elders who were no longer Cousin Eva and Father, since they had forgotten her presence, but had become Eva and Harry, who knew each other well, who were comfortable with each other, being contemporaries on equal terms, who occupied by right their place in this world, at the time of life to which they had arrived by paths familiar to them both. They need not play their roles of daughter, of son, to aged per-

sons who did not understand them; nor of father and elderly
female cousin to young persons whom they did not understand. They were precisely themselves; their eyes cleared, their
voices relaxed into perfect naturalness, they need not weigh
their words or calculate the effect of their manner. "It is I who
have no place," thought Miranda. "Where are my own people
and my own time?" She resented, slowly and deeply and in
profound silence, the presence of these aliens who lectured
and admonished her, who loved her with bitterness and denied
her the right to look at the world with her own eyes, who demanded that she accept their version of life and yet could not
tell her the truth, not in the smallest thing. "I hate them
both," her most inner and secret mind said plainly, "*I will be
free of them, I shall not even remember them.*"

She sat in the front seat with Skid, the Negro boy. "Come
back with us, Miranda," said Cousin Eva, with the sharp little
note of elderly command, "there is plenty of room."

"No, thank you," said Miranda, in a firm cold voice. "I'm
quite comfortable. Don't disturb yourself."

Neither of them noticed her voice or her manner. They sat
back and went on talking steadily in their friendly family
voices, talking about their dead, their living, their affairs, their
prospects, their common memories, interrupting each other,
catching each other up on small points of dispute, with a gaiety
and freshness which Miranda had not known they were capable of, going over old memories and finding new points of
interest in them.

Miranda could not hear the stories above the noisy motor,
but she felt she knew them well, or stories like them. She knew
too many stories like them, she wanted something new of her
own. The language was familiar to them, but not to her, not
any more. The house, her father had said, was full. It would be
full of cousins, many of them strangers. Would there be any
young cousins there, to whom she could talk about things they
both knew? She felt a vague distaste for seeing cousins. There
were too many of them and her blood rebelled against the ties
of blood. She was sick to death of cousins. She did not want
any more ties with this house, she was going to leave it, and
she was not going back to her husband's family either. She
would have no more bonds that smothered her in love and

hatred. She knew now why she had run away to marriage, and
she knew that she was going to run away from marriage, and
she was not going to stay in any place, with anyone, that
threatened to forbid her making her own discoveries, that said
"No" to her. She hoped no one had taken her old room, she
would like to sleep there once more, she would say good-by
there where she had loved sleeping once, sleeping and waking
and waiting to be grown, to begin to live. Oh, what is life, she
asked herself in desperate seriousness, in those childish unanswerable words, and what shall I do with it? It is something of
my own, she thought in a fury of jealous possessiveness, what
shall I make of it? She did not know that she asked herself this
because all her earliest training had argued that life was a substance, a material to be used, it took shape and direction and
meaning only as the possessor guided and worked it; living was
a progress of continuous and varied acts of the will directed
towards a definite end. She had been assured that there were
good and evil ends, one must make a choice. But what was
good, and what was evil? I hate love, she thought, as if this
were the answer, I hate loving and being loved, I hate it. And
her disturbed and seething mind received a shock of comfort
from this sudden collapse of an old painful structure of distorted images and misconceptions. "You don't know anything
about it," said Miranda to herself, with extraordinary clearness
as if she were an elder admonishing some younger misguided
creature. "You have to find out about it." But nothing in her
prompted her to decide, "I will now do this, I will be that, I
will go yonder, I will take a certain road to a certain end."
There are questions to be asked first, she thought, but who
will answer them? No one, or there will be too many answers,
none of them right. What is the truth, she asked herself as intently as if the question had never been asked, the truth, even
about the smallest, the least important of all the things I must
find out? and where shall I begin to look for it? Her mind
closed stubbornly against remembering, not the past but the
legend of the past, other people's memory of the past, at
which she had spent her life peering in wonder like a child at a
magic-lantern show. Ah, but there is my own life to come yet,
she thought, my own life now and beyond. I don't want any
promises, I won't have false hopes, I won't be romantic about

myself. I can't live in their world any longer, she told herself, listening to the voices back of her. Let them tell their stories to each other. Let them go on explaining how things happened. I don't care. At least I can know the truth about what happens to me, she assured herself silently, making a promise to herself, in her hopefulness, her ignorance.

Noon Wine

TIME: *1896–1905*
PLACE: *Small South Texas Farm*

THE two grubby small boys with tow-colored hair who were digging among the ragweed in the front yard sat back on their heels and said, "Hello," when the tall bony man with straw-colored hair turned in at their gate. He did not pause at the gate; it had swung back, conveniently half open, long ago, and was now sunk so firmly on its broken hinges no one thought of trying to close it. He did not even glance at the small boys, much less give them good-day. He just clumped down his big square dusty shoes one after the other steadily, like a man following a plow, as if he knew the place well and knew where he was going and what he would find there. Rounding the right-hand corner of the house under the row of chinaberry trees, he walked up to the side porch where Mr. Thompson was pushing a big swing churn back and forth.

Mr. Thompson was a tough weather-beaten man with stiff black hair and a week's growth of black whiskers. He was a noisy proud man who held his neck so straight his whole face stood level with his Adam's apple, and the whiskers continued down his neck and disappeared into a black thatch under his open collar. The churn rumbled and swished like the belly of a trotting horse, and Mr. Thompson seemed somehow to be driving a horse with one hand, reining it in and urging it forward; and every now and then he turned halfway around and squirted a tremendous spit of tobacco juice out over the steps. The door stones were brown and gleaming with fresh tobacco juice. Mr. Thompson had been churning quite a while and he was tired of it. He was just fetching a mouthful of juice to squirt again when the stranger came around the corner and stopped. Mr. Thompson saw a narrow-chested man with blue eyes so pale they were almost white, looking and not looking at him from a long gaunt face, under white eyebrows. Mr. Thompson judged him to be another of these Irishmen, by his long upper lip.

232

"Howdy do, sir," said Mr. Thompson politely, swinging his churn.

"I need work," said the man, clearly enough but with some kind of foreign accent Mr. Thompson couldn't place. It wasn't Cajun and it wasn't Nigger and it wasn't Dutch, so it had him stumped. "You need a man here?"

Mr. Thompson gave the churn a great shove and it swung back and forth several times on its own momentum. He sat on the steps, shot his quid into the grass, and said, "Set down. Maybe we can make a deal. I been kinda lookin' round for somebody. I had two niggers but they got into a cutting scrape up the creek last week, one of 'em dead now and the other in the hoosegow at Cold Springs. Neither one of 'em worth killing, come right down to it. So it looks like I'd better get somebody. Where'd you work last?"

"North Dakota," said the man, folding himself down on the other end of the steps, but not as if he were tired. He folded up and settled down as if it would be a long time before he got up again. He never had looked at Mr. Thompson, but there wasn't anything sneaking in his eye, either. He didn't seem to be looking anywhere else. His eyes sat in his head and let things pass by them. They didn't seem to be expecting to see anything worth looking at. Mr. Thompson waited a long time for the man to say something more, but he had gone into a brown study.

"North Dakota," said Mr. Thompson, trying to remember where that was. "That's a right smart distance off, seems to me."

"I can do everything on farm," said the man; "cheap. I need work."

Mr. Thompson settled himself to get down to business. "My name's Thompson, Mr. Royal Earle Thompson," he said.

"I'm Mr. Helton," said the man, "Mr. Olaf Helton." He did not move.

"Well, now," said Mr. Thompson in his most carrying voice, "I guess we'd better talk turkey."

When Mr. Thompson expected to drive a bargain he always grew very hearty and jovial. There was nothing wrong with him except that he hated like the devil to pay wages. He said so himself. "You furnish grub and a shack," he said, "and then you got to pay 'em besides. It ain't right. Besides the wear and tear on your implements," he said, "they just let everything go to rack and ruin." So he began to laugh and shout his way through the deal.

"Now, what I want to know is, how much you fixing to gouge outa me?" he brayed, slapping his knee. After he had kept it up as long as he could, he quieted down, feeling a little sheepish, and cut himself a chew. Mr. Helton was staring out somewhere between the barn and the orchard, and seemed to be sleeping with his eyes open.

"I'm good worker," said Mr. Helton as from the tomb. "I get dollar a day."

Mr. Thompson was so shocked he forgot to start laughing again at the top of his voice until it was nearly too late to do any good. "Haw, haw," he bawled. "Why, for a dollar a day I'd hire out myself. What kinda work is it where they pay you a dollar a day?"

"Wheatfields, North Dakota," said Mr. Helton, not even smiling.

Mr. Thompson stopped laughing. "Well, this ain't any wheatfield by a long shot. This is more of a dairy farm," he said, feeling apologetic. "My wife, she was set on a dairy, she seemed to like working around with cows and calves, so I humored her. But it was a mistake," he said. "I got nearly everything to do, anyhow. My wife ain't very strong. She's sick today, that's a fact. She's been porely for the last few days. We plant a little feed, and a corn patch, and there's the orchard, and a few pigs and chickens, but our main hold is the cows. Now just speakin' as one man to another, there ain't any money in it. Now I can't give you no dollar a day because ackshally I don't make that much out of it. No, sir, we get along on a lot less than a dollar a day, I'd say, if we figger up everything in the long run. Now, I paid seven dollars a month to the two niggers, three-fifty each, and grub, but what I say is, one middlin'-good white man ekals a whole passel of niggers any day in the week, so I'll give you seven dollars and you eat at the table with us, and you'll be treated like a white man, as the feller says—"

"That's all right," said Mr. Helton. "I take it."

"Well, now I guess we'll call it a deal, hey?" Mr. Thompson jumped up as if he had remembered important business. "Now, you just take hold of that churn and give it a few swings, will you, while I ride to town on a coupla little errands. I ain't been able to leave the place all week. I guess you know what to do with butter after you get it, don't you?"

"I know," said Mr. Helton without turning his head. "I know butter business." He had a strange drawling voice, and even when he spoke only two words his voice waved slowly up and down and the emphasis was in the wrong place. Mr. Thompson wondered what kind of foreigner Mr. Helton could be.

"Now just where did you say you worked last?" he asked, as if he expected Mr. Helton to contradict himself.

"North Dakota," said Mr. Helton.

"Well, one place is good as another once you get used to it," said Mr. Thompson, amply. "You're a forriner, ain't you?"

"I'm a Swede," said Mr. Helton, beginning to swing the churn.

Mr. Thompson let forth a booming laugh, as if this was the best joke on somebody he'd ever heard. "Well, I'll be damned," he said at the top of his voice. "A Swede: well, now, I'm afraid you'll get pretty lonesome around here. I never seen any Swedes in this neck of the woods."

"That's all right," said Mr. Helton. He went on swinging the churn as if he had been working on the place for years.

"In fact, I might as well tell you, you're practically the first Swede I ever laid eyes on."

"That's all right," said Mr. Helton.

Mr. Thompson went into the front room where Mrs. Thompson was lying down, with the green shades drawn. She had a bowl of water by her on the table and a wet cloth over her eyes. She took the cloth off at the sound of Mr. Thompson's boots and said, "What's all the noise out there? Who is it?"

"Got a feller out there says he's a Swede, Ellie," said Mr. Thompson; "says he knows how to make butter."

"I hope it turns out to be the truth," said Mrs. Thompson. "Looks like my head never will get any better."

"Don't you worry," said Mr. Thompson. "You fret too much. Now I'm gointa ride into town and get a little order of groceries."

"Don't you linger, now, Mr. Thompson," said Mrs. Thompson. "Don't go to the hotel." She meant the saloon; the proprietor also had rooms for rent upstairs.

"Just a coupla little toddies," said Mr. Thompson, laughing loudly, "never hurt anybody."

"I never took a dram in my life," said Mrs. Thompson, "and what's more I never will."

"I wasn't talking about the womenfolks," said Mr. Thompson.

The sound of the swinging churn rocked Mrs. Thompson first into a gentle doze, then a deep drowse from which she waked suddenly knowing that the swinging had stopped a good while ago. She sat up shading her weak eyes from the flat strips of late summer sunlight between the sill and the lowered shades. There she was, thank God, still alive, with supper to cook but no churning on hand, and her head still bewildered, but easy. Slowly she realized she had been hearing a new sound even in her sleep. Somebody was playing a tune on the harmonica, not merely shrilling up and down making a sickening noise, but really playing a pretty tune, merry and sad.

She went out through the kitchen, stepped off the porch, and stood facing the east, shading her eyes. When her vision cleared and settled, she saw a long, pale-haired man in blue jeans sitting in the doorway of the hired man's shack, tilted back in a kitchen chair, blowing away at the harmonica with his eyes shut. Mrs. Thompson's heart fluttered and sank. Heavens, he looked lazy and worthless, he did, now. First a lot of no-count fiddling darkies and then a no-count white man. It was just like Mr. Thompson to take on that kind. She did wish he would be more considerate, and take a little trouble with his business. She wanted to believe in her husband, and there were too many times when she couldn't. She wanted to believe that tomorrow, or at least the day after, life, such a battle at best, was going to be better.

She walked past the shack without glancing aside, stepping carefully, bent at the waist because of the nagging pain in her

side, and went to the springhouse, trying to harden her mind
to speak very plainly to that new hired man if he had not done
his work.

The milk house was only another shack of weather-beaten
boards nailed together hastily years before because they needed
a milk house; it was meant to be temporary, and it was; already
shapeless, leaning this way and that over a perpetual cool
trickle of water that fell from a little grot, almost choked with
pallid ferns. No one else in the whole countryside had such a
spring on his land. Mr. and Mrs. Thompson felt they had a fortune in that spring, if ever they get around to doing anything
with it.

Rickety wooden shelves clung at hazard in the square
around the small pool where the larger pails of milk and butter
stood, fresh and sweet in the cold water. One hand supporting
her flat, pained side, the other shading her eyes, Mrs. Thompson leaned over and peered into the pails. The cream had been
skimmed and set aside, there was a rich roll of butter, the
wooden molds and shallow pans had been scrubbed and
scalded for the first time in who knows when, the barrel was
full of buttermilk ready for the pigs and the weanling calves,
the hard packed-dirt floor had been swept smooth. Mrs.
Thompson straightened up again, smiling tenderly. She had
been ready to scold him, a poor man who needed a job, who
had just come there and who might not have been expected to
do things properly at first. There was nothing she could do to
make up for the injustice she had done him in her thoughts
but to tell him how she appreciated his good clean work, finished already, in no time at all. She ventured near the door of
the shack with her careful steps; Mr. Helton opened his eyes,
stopped playing, and brought his chair down straight, but did
not look at her, or get up. She was a little frail woman with
long thick brown hair in a braid, a suffering patient mouth and
diseased eyes which cried easily. She wove her fingers into an
eyeshade, thumbs on temples, and, winking her tearful lids, said
with a polite little manner, "Howdy do, sir. I'm Miz Thompson, and I wanted to tell you I think you did real well in the
milk house. It's always been a hard place to keep."

He said, "That's all right," in a slow voice, without moving.

Mrs. Thompson waited a moment. "That's a pretty tune

you're playing. Most folks don't seem to get much music out of a harmonica."

Mr. Helton sat humped over, long legs sprawling, his spine in a bow, running his thumb over the square mouth-stops; except for his moving hand he might have been asleep. The harmonica was a big shiny new one, and Mrs. Thompson, her gaze wandering about, counted five others, all good and expensive, standing in a row on the shelf beside his cot. "He must carry them around in his jumper pocket," she thought, and noted there was not a sign of any other possession lying about. "I see you're mighty fond of music," she said. "We used to have an old accordion, and Mr. Thompson could play it right smart, but the little boys broke it up."

Mr. Helton stood up rather suddenly, the chair clattered under him, his knees straightened though his shoulders did not, and he looked at the floor as if he were listening carefully. "You know how little boys are," said Mrs. Thompson. "You'd better set them harmonicas on a high shelf or they'll be after them. They're great hands for getting into things. I try to learn 'em, but it don't do much good."

Mr. Helton, in one wide gesture of his long arms, swept his harmonicas up against his chest, and from there transferred them in a row to the ledge where the roof joined to the wall. He pushed them back almost out of sight.

"That'll do, maybe," said Mrs. Thompson. "Now I wonder," she said, turning and closing her eyes helplessly against the stronger western light, "I wonder what became of them little tads. I can't keep up with them." She had a way of speaking about her children as if they were rather troublesome nephews on a prolonged visit.

"Down by the creek," said Mr. Helton, in his hollow voice. Mrs. Thompson, pausing confusedly, decided he had answered her question. He stood in silent patience, not exactly waiting for her to go, perhaps, but pretty plainly not waiting for anything else. Mrs. Thompson was perfectly accustomed to all kinds of men full of all kinds of cranky ways. The point was, to find out just how Mr. Helton's crankiness was different from any other man's, and then get used to it, and let him feel at home. Her father had been cranky, her brothers and uncles had all been set in their ways and none of them alike; and every hired man she'd ever seen had quirks and crotchets of his own. Now here was Mr. Helton, who was a Swede, who wouldn't talk, and who played the harmonica besides.

"They'll be needing something to eat," said Mrs. Thompson in a vague friendly way, "pretty soon. Now I wonder what I ought to be thinking about for supper? Now what do you like to eat, Mr. Helton? We always have plenty of good butter and milk and cream, that's a blessing. Mr. Thompson says we ought to sell all of it, but I say my family comes first." Her little face went all out of shape in a pained blind smile.

"I eat anything," said Mr. Helton, his words wandering up and down.

He *can't* talk, for one thing, thought Mrs. Thompson; it's a shame to keep at him when he don't know the language good. She took a slow step away from the shack, looking back over her shoulder. "We usually have cornbread except on Sundays," she told him. "I suppose in your part of the country you don't get much good cornbread."

Not a word from Mr. Helton. She saw from her eye-corner that he had sat down again, looking at his harmonica, chair tilted. She hoped he would remember it was getting near milking time. As she moved away, he started playing again, the same tune.

Milking time came and went. Mrs. Thompson saw Mr. Helton going back and forth between the cow barn and the milk house. He swung along in an easy lope, shoulders bent, head hanging, the big buckets balancing like a pair of scales at the ends of his bony arms. Mr. Thompson rode in from town sitting straighter than usual, chin in, a towsack full of supplies swung behind the saddle. After a trip to the barn, he came into the kitchen full of good will, and gave Mrs. Thompson a hearty smack on the cheek after dusting her face off with his tough whiskers. He had been to the hotel, that was plain. "Took a look around the premises, Ellie," he shouted. "That Swede sure is grinding out the labor. But he is the closest mouthed feller I ever met up with in all my days. Looks like he's scared he'll crack his jaw if he opens his front teeth."

Mrs. Thompson was stirring up a big bowl of buttermilk cornbread. "You smell like a toper, Mr. Thompson," she said with perfect dignity. "I wish you'd get one of the little boys to bring me in an extra load of firewood. I'm thinking about baking a batch of cookies tomorrow."

Mr. Thompson, all at once smelling the liquor on his own breath, sneaked out, justly rebuked, and brought in the firewood himself. Arthur and Herbert, grubby from thatched head to toes, from skin to shirt, came stamping in yelling for supper. "Go wash your faces and comb your hair," said Mrs. Thompson, automatically. They retired to the porch. Each one put his hand under the pump and wet his forelock, combed it down with his fingers, and returned at once to the kitchen, where all the fair prospects of life were centered. Mrs. Thompson set an extra plate and commanded Arthur, the eldest, eight years old, to call Mr. Helton for supper.

Arthur, without moving from the spot, bawled like a bull calf, "Saaaaaay, Helllllllton, suuuuuupper's ready!" and added in a lower voice, "You big Swede!"

"Listen to me," said Mrs. Thompson, "that's no way to act. Now you go out there and ask him decent, or I'll get your daddy to give you a good licking."

Mr. Helton loomed, long and gloomy, in the doorway. "Sit right there," boomed Mr. Thompson, waving his arm. Mr. Helton swung his square shoes across the kitchen in two steps, slumped onto the bench and sat. Mr. Thompson occupied his chair at the head of the table, the two boys scrambled into place opposite Mr. Helton, and Mrs. Thompson sat at the end nearest the stove. Mrs. Thompson clasped her hands, bowed her head and said aloud hastily, "Lord, for all these and Thy other blessings we thank Thee in Jesus' name, amen," trying to finish before Herbert's rusty little paw reached the nearest dish. Otherwise she would be duty-bound to send him way from the table, and growing children need their meals. Mr. Thompson and Arthur always waited, but Herbert, aged six, was too young to take training yet.

Mr. and Mrs. Thompson tried to engage Mr. Helton in conversation, but it was a failure. They tried first the weather, and then the crops, and then the cows, but Mr. Helton simply did not reply. Mr. Thompson then told something funny he had seen in town. It was about some of the other old grangers at the hotel, friends of his, giving beer to a goat, and the goat's subsequent behavior. Mr. Helton did not seem to hear. Mrs. Thompson laughed dutifully, but she didn't think it was very funny. She had heard it often before, though Mr. Thompson, each time he told it, pretended it had happened that self-same day. It must have happened years ago if it ever happened at all, and it had never been a story that Mrs. Thompson thought suitable for mixed company. The whole thing came of Mr. Thompson's weakness for a dram too much now and then, though he voted for local option at every election. She passed the food to Mr. Helton, who took a helping of everything, but not much, not enough to keep him up to his full powers if he expected to go on working the way he had started.

At last, he took a fair-sized piece of cornbread, wiped his plate up as clean as if it had been licked by a hound dog, stuffed his mouth full, and, still chewing, slid off the bench and started for the door.

"Good night, Mr. Helton," said Mrs. Thompson, and the other Thompsons took it up in a scattered chorus. "Good night, Mr. Helton!"

"Good night," said Mr. Helton's wavering voice grudgingly from the darkness.

"Gude not," said Arthur, imitating Mr. Helton.

"Gude not," said Herbert, the copy-cat.

"You don't do it right," said Arthur. "Now listen to me. Guuuuuude naht," and he ran a hollow scale in a luxury of successful impersonation. Herbert almost went into a fit with joy.

"Now you *stop* that," said Mrs. Thompson. "He can't help the way he talks. You ought to be ashamed of yourselves, both of you, making fun of a poor stranger like that. How'd you like to be a stranger in a strange land?"

"I'd like it," said Arthur. "I think it would be fun."

"They're both regular heathens, Ellie," said Mr. Thompson. "Just plain ignoramuses." He turned the face of awful fatherhood upon his young. "You're both going to get sent to school next year, and that'll knock some sense into you."

"I'm going to git sent to the 'formatory when I'm old enough," piped up Herbert. "That's where I'm goin'."

"Oh, you are, are you?" asked Mr. Thompson. "Who says so?"

"The Sunday School Supintendant," said Herbert, a bright boy showing off.

"You see?" said Mr. Thompson, staring at his wife. "What did I tell you?" He became a hurricane of wrath. "Get to bed, you two," he roared until his Adam's apple shuddered. "Get now before I take the hide off you!" They got, and shortly from their attic bedroom the sounds of scuffling and snorting and giggling and growling filled the house and shook the kitchen ceiling.

Mrs. Thompson held her head and said in a small uncertain voice, "It's no use picking on them when they're so young and tender. I can't stand it."

"My goodness, Ellie," said Mr. Thompson, "we've got to raise 'em. We can't just let 'em grow up hog wild."

She went on in another tone. "That Mr. Helton seems all right, even if he can't be made to talk. Wonder how he comes to be so far from home."

"Like I said, he isn't no whamper-jaw," said Mr. Thompson, "but he sure knows how to lay out the work. I guess that's the main thing around here. Country's full of fellers trampin' round looking for work."

Mrs. Thompson was gathering up the dishes. She now gathered up Mr. Thompson's plate from under his chin. "To tell you the honest truth," she remarked, "I think it's a mighty good change to have a man round the place who knows how to work and keep his mouth shut. Means he'll keep out of our business. Not that we've got anything to hide, but it's convenient."

"That's a fact," said Mr. Thompson. "Haw, haw," he shouted suddenly. "Means you can do all the talking, huh?"

"The only thing," went on Mrs. Thompson, "is this: he don't eat hearty enough to suit me. I like to see a man set down and relish a good meal. My granma used to say it was no use putting dependence on a man who won't set down and make out his dinner. I hope it won't be that way this time."

"Tell *you* the truth, Ellie," said Mr. Thompson, picking his teeth with a fork and leaning back in the best of good humors, "I always thought your granma was a ter'ble ole fool. She'd

just say the first thing that popped into her head and call it
God's wisdom."

"My granma wasn't anybody's fool. Nine times out of ten
she knew what she was talking about. I always say, the first
thing you think is the best thing you can say."

"Well," said Mr. Thompson, going into another shout,
"you're so *ree*fined about that goat story, you just try speaking
out in mixed comp'ny sometime! You just try it. S'pose you
happened to be thinking about a hen and a rooster, hey? I
reckon you'd shock the Babtist preacher!" He gave her a good
pinch on her thin little rump. "No more meat on you than a
rabbit," he said, fondly. "Now I like 'em cornfed."

Mrs. Thompson looked at him open-eyed and blushed. She
could see better by lamplight. "Why, Mr. Thompson, sometimes I think you're the evilest-minded man that ever lived."
She took a handful of hair on the crown of his head and gave it
a good, slow pull. "That's to show you how it feels, pinching
so hard when you're supposed to be playing," she said, gently.

In spite of his situation in life, Mr. Thompson had never been
able to outgrow his deep conviction that running a dairy and
chasing after chickens was woman's work. He was fond of
saying that he could plow a furrow, cut sorghum, shuck corn,
handle a team, build a corn crib, as well as any man. Buying
and selling, too, were man's work. Twice a week he drove the
spring wagon to market with the fresh butter, a few eggs, fruits
in their proper season, sold them, pocketed the change, and
spent it as seemed best, being careful not to dig into Mrs.
Thompson's pin money.

But from the first the cows worried him, coming up regularly twice a day to be milked, standing there reproaching him
with their smug female faces. Calves worried him, fighting the
rope and strangling themselves until their eyes bulged, trying
to get at the teat. Wrestling with a calf unmanned him, like
having to change a baby's diaper. Milk worried him, coming
bitter sometimes, drying up, turning sour. Hens worried him,
cackling, clucking, hatching out when you least expected it
and leading their broods into the barnyard where the horses
could step on them; dying of roup and wryneck and getting

plagues of chicken lice; laying eggs all over God's creation so
that half of them were spoiled before a man could find them,
in spite of a rack of nests Mrs. Thompson had set out for them
in the feed room. Hens were a blasted nuisance.

Slopping hogs was hired man's work, in Mr. Thompson's
opinion. Killing hogs was a job for the boss, but scraping them
and cutting them up was for the hired man again; and again
woman's proper work was dressing meat, smoking, pickling,
and making lard and sausage. All his carefully limited fields of
activity were related somehow to Mr. Thompson's feeling for
the appearance of things, his own appearance in the sight of
God and man. "It don't *look* right," was his final reason for not
doing anything he did not wish to do.

It was his dignity and his reputation that he cared about,
and there were only a few kinds of work manly enough for Mr.
Thompson to undertake with his own hands. Mrs. Thompson,
to whom so many forms of work would have been becoming,
had simply gone down on him early. He saw, after a while, how
short-sighted it had been of him to expect much from Mrs.
Thompson; he had fallen in love with her delicate waist and
lace-trimmed petticoats and big blue eyes, and, though all those
charms had disappeared, she had in the meantime become Ellie
to him, not at all the same person as Miss Ellen Bridges, popular Sunday School teacher in the Mountain City First Baptist
Church, but his dear wife, Ellie, who was not strong. Deprived
as he was, however, of the main support in life which a man
might expect in marriage, he had almost without knowing it
resigned himself to failure. Head erect, a prompt payer of
taxes, yearly subscriber to the preacher's salary, land owner and
father of a family, employer, a hearty good fellow among men,
Mr. Thompson knew, without putting it into words, that he
had been going steadily down hill. God amighty, it did look
like somebody around the place might take a rake in hand now
and then and clear up the clutter around the barn and the
kitchen steps. The wagon shed was so full of broken-down machinery and ragged harness and old wagon wheels and battered milk pails and rotting lumber you could hardly drive in
there any more. Not a soul on the place would raise a hand to
it, and as for him, he had all he could do with his regular work.
He would sometimes in the slack season sit for hours worrying

about it, squirting tobacco on the ragweeds growing in a
thicket against the wood pile, wondering what a fellow could
do, handicapped as he was. He looked forward to the boys
growing up soon; he was going to put them through the mill
just as his own father had done with him when he was a boy;
they were going to learn how to take hold and run the place
right. He wasn't going to overdo it, but those two boys were
going to earn their salt, or he'd know why. Great big lubbers
sitting around whittling! Mr. Thompson sometimes grew
quite enraged with them, when imagining their possible future, big lubbers sitting around whittling or thinking about
fishing trips. Well, he'd put a stop to that, mighty damn quick.

As the seasons passed, and Mr. Helton took hold more and
more, Mr. Thompson began to relax in his mind a little. There
seemed to be nothing the fellow couldn't do, all in the day's
work and as a matter of course. He got up at five o'clock in the
morning, boiled his own coffee and fried his own bacon and
was out in the cow lot before Mr. Thompson had even begun
to yawn, stretch, groan, roar and thump around looking for
his jeans. He milked the cows, kept the milk house, and
churned the butter; rounded the hens up and somehow persuaded them to lay in the nests, not under the house and
behind the haystacks; he fed them regularly and they hatched
out until you couldn't set a foot down for them. Little by little
the piles of trash around the barns and house disappeared. He
carried buttermilk and corn to the hogs, and curried cockle-
burs out of the horses' manes. He was gentle with the calves, if
a little grim with the cows and hens; judging by his conduct,
Mr. Helton had never heard of the difference between man's
and woman's work on a farm.

In the second year, he showed Mr. Thompson the picture of
a cheese press in a mail order catalogue, and said, "This is a
good thing. You buy this, I make cheese." The press was
bought and Mr. Helton did make cheese, and it was sold,
along with the increased butter and the crates of eggs. Sometimes Mr. Thompson felt a little contemptuous of Mr. Helton's ways. It did seem kind of picayune for a man to go around
picking up half a dozen ears of corn that had fallen off the
wagon on the way from the field, gathering up fallen fruit to
feed to the pigs, storing up old nails and stray parts of

machinery, spending good time stamping a fancy pattern on the butter before it went to market. Mr. Thompson, sitting up high on the spring-wagon seat, with the decorated butter in a five-gallon lard can wrapped in wet towsack, driving to town, chirruping to the horses and snapping the reins over their backs, sometimes thought that Mr. Helton was a pretty meeching sort of fellow; but he never gave way to these feelings, he knew a good thing when he had it. It was a fact the hogs were in better shape and sold for more money. It was a fact that Mr. Thompson stopped buying feed, Mr. Helton managed the crops so well. When beef- and hog-slaughtering time came, Mr. Helton knew how to save the scraps that Mr. Thompson had thrown away, and wasn't above scraping guts and filling them with sausages that he made by his own methods. In all, Mr. Thompson had no grounds for complaint. In the third year, he raised Mr. Helton's wages, though Mr. Helton had not asked for a raise. The fourth year, when Mr. Thompson was not only out of debt but had a little cash in the bank, he raised Mr. Helton's wages again, two dollars and a half a month each time.

"The man's worth it, Ellie," said Mr. Thompson, in a glow of self-justification for his extravagance. "He's made this place pay, and I want him to know I appreciate it."

Mr. Helton's silence, the pallor of his eyebrows and hair, his long, glum jaw and eyes that refused to see anything, even the work under his hands, had grown perfectly familiar to the Thompsons. At first, Mrs. Thompson complained a little. "It's like sitting down at the table with a disembodied spirit," she said. "You'd think he'd find something to say, sooner or later."

"Let him alone," said Mr. Thompson. "When he gets ready to talk, he'll talk."

The years passed, and Mr. Helton never got ready to talk. After his work was finished for the day, he would come up from the barn or the milk house or the chicken house, swinging his lantern, his big shoes clumping like pony hoofs on the hard path. They, sitting in the kitchen in the winter, or on the back porch in summer, would hear him drag out his wooden chair, hear the creak of it tilted back, and then for a little while he would play his single tune on one or another of his harmonicas. The harmonicas were in different keys, some lower and sweeter than the others, but the same changeless tune went on, a strange tune, with sudden turns in it, night after night, and sometimes even in the afternoons when Mr. Helton sat down to catch his breath. At first the Thompsons liked it very much, and always stopped to listen. Later there came a time when they were fairly sick of it, and began to wish to each other that he would learn a new one. At last they did not hear it any more, it was as natural as the sound of the wind rising in the evenings, or the cows lowing, or their own voices.

Mrs. Thompson pondered now and then over Mr. Helton's soul. He didn't seem to be a church-goer, and worked straight through Sunday as if it were any common day of the week. "I think we ought to invite him to go to hear Dr. Martin," she told Mr. Thompson. "It isn't very Christian of us not to ask him. He's not a forward kind of man. He'd wait to be asked."

"Let him alone," said Mr. Thompson. "The way I look at it, his religion is every man's own business. Besides, he ain't got any Sunday clothes. He wouldn't want to go to church in them jeans and jumpers of his. I don't know what he does with his money. He certainly don't spend it foolishly."

Still, once the notion got into her head, Mrs. Thompson could not rest until she invited Mr. Helton to go to church with the family next Sunday. He was pitching hay into neat little piles in the field back of the orchard. Mrs. Thompson put on smoked glasses and a sunbonnet and walked all the way down there to speak to him. He stopped and leaned on his pitchfork, listening, and for a moment Mrs. Thompson was almost frightened at his face. The pale eyes seemed to glare past her, the eyebrows frowned, the long jaw hardened. "I got work," he said bluntly, and lifting his pitchfork he turned from her and began to toss the hay. Mrs. Thompson, her feelings hurt, walked back thinking that by now she should be used to Mr. Helton's ways, but it did seem like a man, even a foreigner, could be just a little polite when you gave him a Christian invitation. "He's not polite, that's the only thing I've got against him," she said to Mr. Thompson. "He just can't seem to behave like other people. You'd think he had a grudge against the world," she said, "I sometimes don't know what to make of it."

In the second year something had happened that made Mrs.

Thompson uneasy, the kind of thing she could not put into words, hardly into thoughts, and if she had tried to explain to Mr. Thompson it would have sounded worse than it was, or not bad enough. It was that kind of queer thing that seems to be giving a warning, and yet, nearly always nothing comes of it. It was on a hot, still spring day, and Mrs. Thompson had been down to the garden patch to pull some new carrots and green onions and string beans for dinner. As she worked, sun-bonnet low over her eyes, putting each kind of vegetable in a pile by itself in her basket, she noticed how neatly Mr. Helton weeded, and how rich the soil was. He had spread it all over with manure from the barns, and worked it in, in the fall, and the vegetables were coming up fine and full. She walked back under the nubbly little fig trees where the unpruned branches leaned almost to the ground, and the thick leaves made a cool screen. Mrs. Thompson was always looking for shade to save her eyes. So she, looking idly about, saw through the screen a sight that struck her as very strange. If it had been a noisy spectacle, it would have been quite natural. It was the silence that struck her. Mr. Helton was shaking Arthur by the shoulders, ferociously, his face most terribly fixed and pale. Arthur's head snapped back and forth and he had not stiffened in resistance, as he did when Mrs. Thompson tried to shake him. His eyes were rather frightened, but surprised, too, probably more surprised than anything else. Herbert stood by meekly, watching. Mr. Helton dropped Arthur, and seized Herbert, and shook him with the same methodical ferocity, the same face of hatred. Herbert's mouth crumpled as if he would cry, but he made no sound. Mr. Helton let him go, turned and strode into the shack, and the little boys ran, as if for their lives, without a word. They disappeared around the corner to the front of the house.

Mrs. Thompson took time to set her basket on the kitchen table, to push her sunbonnet back on her head and draw it forward again, to look in the stove and make certain the fire was going, before she followed the boys. They were sitting huddled together under a clump of chinaberry trees in plain sight of her bedroom window, as if it were a safe place they had discovered.

"What are you doing?" asked Mrs. Thompson.

They looked hang-dog from under their foreheads and Arthur mumbled, "Nothin'."

"Nothing *now*, you mean," said Mrs. Thompson, severely. "Well, I have plenty for you to do. Come right in here this minute and help me fix vegetables. This minute."

They scrambled up very eagerly and followed her close. Mrs. Thompson tried to imagine what they had been up to; she did not like the notion of Mr. Helton taking it on himself to correct her little boys, but she was afraid to ask them for reasons. They might tell her a lie, and she would have to overtake them in it, and whip them. Or she would have to pretend to believe them, and they would get in the habit of lying. Or they might tell her the truth, and it would be something she would have to whip them for. The very thought of it gave her a headache. She supposed she might ask Mr. Helton, but it was not her place to ask. She would wait and tell Mr. Thompson, and let him get at the bottom of it. While her mind ran on, she kept the little boys hopping. "Cut those carrot tops closer, Herbert, you're just being careless. Arthur, stop breaking up the beans so little. They're little enough already. Herbert, you go get an armload of wood. Arthur, you take these onions and wash them under the pump. Herbert, as soon as you're done here, you get a broom and sweep out this kitchen. Arthur, you get a shovel and take up the ashes. Stop picking your nose, Herbert. How often must I tell you? Arthur, you go look in the top drawer of my bureau, left-hand side, and bring me the vaseline for Herbert's nose. Herbert, come here to me. . . ."

They galloped through their chores, their animal spirits rose with activity, and shortly they were out in the front yard again, engaged in a wrestling match. They sprawled and fought, scrambled, clutched, rose and fell shouting, as aimlessly, noisily, monotonously as two puppies. They imitated various animals, not a human sound from them, and their dirty faces were streaked with sweat. Mrs. Thompson, sitting at her window, watched them with baffled pride and tenderness, they were so sturdy and healthy and growing so fast; but uneasily, too, with her pained little smile and the tears rolling from her eyelids that clinched themselves against the sunlight. They were so idle and careless, as if they had no future in this world, and no immortal souls to save, and oh, what had they been up to that Mr. Helton had shaken them, with his face positively dangerous?

In the evening before supper, without a word to Mr. Thompson of the curious fear the sight had caused her, she told him that Mr. Helton had shaken the little boys for some reason. He stepped out to the shack and spoke to Mr. Helton. In five minutes he was back, glaring at his young. "He says them brats been fooling with his harmonicas, Ellie, blowing in them and getting them all dirty and full of spit and they don't play good."

"Did he say all that?" asked Mrs. Thompson. "It doesn't seem possible."

"Well, that's what he meant, anyhow," said Mr. Thompson. "He didn't say it just that way. But he acted pretty worked up about it."

"That's a shame," said Mrs. Thompson, "a perfect shame. Now we've got to do something so they'll remember they mustn't go into Mr. Helton's things."

"I'll tan their hides for them," said Mr. Thompson. "I'll take a calf rope to them if they don't look out."

"Maybe you'd better leave the whipping to me," said Mrs. Thompson. "You haven't got a light enough hand for children."

"That's just what's the matter with them now," shouted Mr. Thompson, "rotten spoiled and they'll wind up in the penitentiary. You don't half whip 'em. Just little love taps. My pa used to knock me down with a stick of stove wood or anything else that came handy."

"Well, that's not saying it's right," said Mrs. Thompson. "I don't hold with that way of raising children. It makes them run away from home. I've seen too much of it."

"I'll break every bone in 'em," said Mr. Thompson, simmering down, "if they don't mind you better and stop being so bullheaded."

"Leave the table and wash your face and hands," Mrs. Thompson commanded the boys, suddenly. They slunk out and dabbled at the pump and slunk in again, trying to make themselves small. They had learned long ago that their mother always made them wash when there was trouble ahead. They looked at their plates. Mr. Thompson opened up on them.

"Well, now, what you got to say for yourselves about going into Mr. Helton's shack and ruining his harmonicas?"

The two little boys wilted, their faces drooped into the grieved hopeless lines of children's faces when they are brought to the terrible bar of blind adult justice; their eyes telegraphed each other in panic, "Now we're really going to catch a licking"; in despair, they dropped their buttered cornbread on their plates, their hands lagged on the edge of the table.

"I ought to break your ribs," said Mr. Thompson, "and I'm a good mind to do it."

"Yes, sir," whispered Arthur, faintly.

"Yes, sir," said Herbert, his lip trembling.

"Now, papa," said Mrs. Thompson in a warning tone. The children did not glance at her. They had no faith in her good will. She had betrayed them in the first place. There was no trusting her. Now she might save them and she might not. No use depending on her.

"Well, you ought to get a good thrashing. You deserve it, don't you, Arthur?"

Arthur hung his head. "Yes, sir."

"And the next time I catch either of you hanging around Mr. Helton's shack, I'm going to take the hide off *both* of you, you hear me, Herbert?"

Herbert mumbled and choked, scattering his cornbread. "Yes, sir."

"Well, now sit up and eat your supper and not another word out of you," said Mr. Thompson, beginning on his own food. The little boys perked up somewhat and started chewing, but every time they looked around they met their parents' eyes, regarding them steadily. There was no telling when they would think of something new. The boys ate warily, trying not to be seen or heard, the cornbread sticking, the buttermilk gurgling, as it went down their gullets.

"And something else, Mr. Thompson," said Mrs. Thompson after a pause. "Tell Mr. Helton he's to come straight to us when they bother him, and not to trouble shaking them himself. Tell him we'll look after that."

"They're so mean," answered Mr. Thompson, staring at them. "It's a wonder he don't just kill 'em off and be done with it." But there was something in the tone that told Arthur and Herbert that nothing more worth worrying about was going to happen this time. Heaving deep sighs, they sat up, reaching for the food nearest them.

"Listen," said Mrs. Thompson, suddenly. The little boys stopped eating. "Mr. Helton hasn't come for his supper. Arthur, go and tell Mr. Helton he's late for supper. Tell him nice, now."

Arthur, miserably depressed, slid out of his place and made for the door, without a word.

There were no miracles of fortune to be brought to pass on a small dairy farm. The Thompsons did not grow rich, but they kept out of the poor house, as Mr. Thompson was fond of saying, meaning he had got a little foothold in spite of Ellie's poor health, and unexpected weather, and strange declines in market prices, and his own mysterious handicaps which weighed him down. Mr. Helton was the hope and the prop of the family, and all the Thompsons became fond of him, or at any rate they ceased to regard him as in any way peculiar, and looked upon him, from a distance they did not know how to bridge, as a good man and a good friend. Mr. Helton went his way, worked, played his tune. Nine years passed. The boys grew up and learned to work. They could not remember the time when Ole Helton hadn't been there: a grouchy cuss, Brother Bones; Mr. Helton, the dairymaid; that Big Swede. If he had heard them, he might have been annoyed at some of the names they called him. But he did not hear them, and besides they meant no harm—or at least such harm as existed was all there, in the names; the boys referred to their father as the Old Man, or the Old Geezer, but not to his face. They lived through by main strength all the grimy, secret, oblique phases of growing up and got past the crisis safely if anyone does. Their parents could see they were good solid boys with hearts of gold in spite of their rough ways. Mr. Thompson was relieved to find that, without knowing how he had done it, he had succeeded in raising a set of boys who were not trifling whittlers. They were such good boys Mr. Thompson began to believe they were born that way, and that he had never spoken a harsh word to them in their lives, much less thrashed them. Herbert and Arthur never disputed his word.

*

Mr. Helton, his hair wet with sweat, plastered to his dripping forehead, his jumper streaked dark and light blue and clinging to his ribs, was chopping a little firewood. He chopped slowly, struck the ax into the end of the chopping log, and piled the wood up neatly. He then disappeared round the house into his shack, which shared with the wood pile a good shade from a row of mulberry trees. Mr. Thompson was lolling in a swing chair on the front porch, a place he had never liked. The chair was new, and Mrs. Thompson had wanted it on the front porch, though the side porch was the place for it, being cooler; and Mr. Thompson wanted to sit in the chair, so there he was. As soon as the new wore off of it, and Ellie's pride in it was exhausted, he would move it round to the side porch. Meantime the August heat was almost unbearable, the air so thick you could poke a hole in it. The dust was inches thick on everything, though Mr. Helton sprinkled the whole yard regularly every night. He even shot the hose upward and washed the tree tops and the roof of the house. They had laid waterpipes to the kitchen and an outside faucet. Mr. Thompson must have dozed, for he opened his eyes and shut his mouth just in time to save his face before a stranger who had driven up to the front gate. Mr. Thompson stood up, put on his hat, pulled up his jeans, and watched while the stranger tied his team, attached to a light spring wagon, to the hitching post. Mr. Thompson recognized the team and wagon. They were from a livery stable in Buda. While the stranger was opening the gate, a strong gate that Mr. Helton had built and set firmly on its hinges several years back, Mr. Thompson strolled down the path to greet him and find out what in God's world a man's business might be that would bring him out at this time of day, in all this dust and welter.

He wasn't exactly a fat man. He was more like a man who had been fat recently. His skin was baggy and his clothes were too big for him, and he somehow looked like a man who should be fat, ordinarily, but who might have just got over a spell of sickness. Mr. Thompson didn't take to his looks at all, he couldn't say why.

The stranger took off his hat. He said in a loud hearty voice, "Is this Mr. Thompson, Mr. Royal Earle Thompson?"

"That's my name," said Mr. Thompson, almost quietly, he was so taken aback by the free manner of the stranger.

"My name is Hatch," said the stranger, "Mr. Homer T. Hatch, and I've come to see you about buying a horse."

"I expect you've been misdirected," said Mr. Thompson. "I haven't got a horse for sale. Usually if I've got anything like that to sell," he said, "I tell the neighbors and tack up a little sign on the gate."

The fat man opened his mouth and roared with joy, showing rabbit teeth brown as shoeleather. Mr. Thompson saw nothing to laugh at, for once. The stranger shouted, "That's just an old joke of mine." He caught one of his hands in the other and shook hands with himself heartily. "I always say something like that when I'm calling on a stranger, because I've noticed that when a feller says he's come to buy something nobody takes him for a suspicious character. You see? Haw, haw, haw."

His joviality made Mr. Thompson nervous, because the expression in the man's eyes didn't match the sounds he was making. "Haw, haw," laughed Mr. Thompson obligingly, still not seeing the joke. "Well, that's all wasted on me because I never take any man for a suspicious character 'til he shows hisself to be one. Says or does something," he explained. "Until that happens, one man's as good as another, so far's *I'm* concerned."

"Well," said the stranger, suddenly very sober and sensible, "I ain't come neither to buy nor sell. Fact is, I want to see you about something that's of interest to us both. Yes, sir, I'd like to have a little talk with you, and it won't cost you a cent."

"I guess that's fair enough," said Mr. Thompson, reluctantly. "Come on around the house where there's a little shade."

They went round and seated themselves on two stumps under a chinaberry tree.

"Yes, sir, Homer T. Hatch is my name and America is my nation," said the stranger. "I reckon you must know the name? I used to have a cousin named Jameson Hatch lived up the country a ways."

"Don't think I know the name," said Mr. Thompson. "There's some Hatchers settled somewhere around Mountain City."

"Don't know the old Hatch family," cried the man in deep concern. He seemed to be pitying Mr. Thompson's ignorance. "Why, we came over from Georgia fifty years ago. Been here long yourself?"

"Just all my whole life," said Mr. Thompson, beginning to feel peevish. "And my pa and my grampap before me. Yes, sir, we've been right here all along. Anybody wants to find a Thompson knows where to look for him. My grampap immigrated in 1836."

"From Ireland, I reckon?" said the stranger.

"From Pennsylvania," said Mr. Thompson. "Now what makes you think we came from Ireland?"

The stranger opened his mouth and began to shout with merriment, and he shook hands with himself as if he hadn't met himself for a long time. "Well, what I always says is, a feller's got to come from *somewhere*, ain't he?"

While they were talking, Mr. Thompson kept glancing at the face near him. He certainly did remind Mr. Thompson of somebody, or maybe he really had seen the man himself somewhere. He couldn't just place the features. Mr. Thompson finally decided it was just that all rabbit-teethed men looked alike.

"That's right," acknowledged Mr. Thompson, rather sourly, "but what I always say is, Thompsons have been settled here for so long it don't make much difference any more *where* they come from. Now a course, this is the slack season, and we're all just laying round a little, but nevertheless we've all got our chores to do, and I don't want to hurry you, and so if you've come to see me on business maybe we'd better get down to it."

"As I said, it's not in a way, and again in a way it is," said the fat man. "Now I'm looking for a man named Helton, Mr. Olaf Eric Helton, from North Dakota, and I was told up around the country a ways that I might find him here, and I wouldn't mind having a little talk with him. No, siree, I sure wouldn't mind, if it's all the same to you."

"I never knew his middle name," said Mr. Thompson, "but Mr. Helton is right here, and been here now for going on nine years. He's a mighty steady man, and you can tell anybody I said so."

"I'm glad to hear that," said Mr. Homer T. Hatch. "I like to hear of a feller mending his ways and settling down. Now when I knew Mr. Helton he was pretty wild, yes, sir, wild is what he was, he didn't know his own mind atall. Well, now, it's going to be a great pleasure to me to meet up with an old friend and find him all settled down and doing well by hisself."

"We've all got to be young once," said Mr. Thompson. "It's like the measles, it breaks out all over you, and you're a nuisance to yourself and everybody else, but it don't last, and it usually don't leave no ill effects." He was so pleased with this notion he forgot and broke into a guffaw. The stranger folded his arms over his stomach and went into a kind of fit, roaring until he had tears in his eyes. Mr. Thompson stopped shouting and eyed the stranger uneasily. Now he liked a good laugh as well as any man, but there ought to be a little moderation. Now this feller laughed like a perfect lunatic, that was a fact. And he wasn't laughing because he really thought things were funny, either. He was laughing for reasons of his own. Mr. Thompson fell into a moody silence, and waited until Mr. Hatch settled down a little.

Mr. Hatch got out a very dirty blue cotton bandanna and wiped his eyes. "That joke just about caught me where I live," he said, almost apologetically. "Now I wish I could think up things as funny as that to say. It's a gift. It's . . ."

"If you want to speak to Mr. Helton, I'll go and round him up," said Mr. Thompson, making motions as if he might get up. "He may be in the milk house and he may be setting in his shack this time of day." It was drawing towards five o'clock. "It's right around the corner," he said.

"Oh, well, there ain't no special hurry," said Mr. Hatch. "I've been wanting to speak to him for a good long spell now and I guess a few minutes more won't make no difference. I just more wanted to locate him, like. That's all."

Mr. Thompson stopped beginning to stand up, and unbuttoned one more button of his shirt, and said, "Well, he's here, and he's this kind of man, that if he had any business with you he'd like to get it over. He don't dawdle, that's one thing you can say for him."

Mr. Hatch appeared to sulk a little at these words. He wiped his face with the bandanna and opened his mouth to speak, when round the house there came the music of Mr. Helton's harmonica. Mr. Thompson raised a finger. "There he is," said Mr. Thompson. "Now's your time."

Mr. Hatch cocked an ear towards the east side of the house and listened for a few seconds, a very strange expression on his face.

"I know that tune like I know the palm of my own hand," said Mr. Thompson, "but I never heard Mr. Helton say what it was."

"That's a kind of Scandahoovian song," said Mr. Hatch. "Where I come from they sing it a lot. In North Dakota, they sing it. It says something about starting out in the morning feeling so good you can't hardly stand it, so you drink up all your likker before noon. All the likker, y' understand, that you was saving for the noon lay-off. The words ain't much, but it's a pretty tune. It's a kind of drinking song." He sat there drooping a little, and Mr. Thompson didn't like his expression. It was a satisfied expression, but it was more like the cat that et the canary.

"So far as I know," said Mr. Thompson, "he ain't touched a drop since he's been on the place, and that's nine years this coming September. Yes, sir, nine years, so far as I know, he ain't wetted his whistle once. And that's more than I can say for myself," he said, meekly proud.

"Yes, that's a drinking song," said Mr. Hatch. "I used to play 'Little Brown Jug' on the fiddle when I was younger than I am now," he went on, "but this Helton, he just keeps it up. He just sits and plays it by himself."

"He's been playing it off and on for nine years right here on the place," said Mr. Thompson, feeling a little proprietary.

"And he was certainly singing it as well, fifteen years before that, in North Dakota," said Mr. Hatch. "He used to sit up in a straitjacket, practically, when he was in the asylum—"

"What's that you say?" said Mr. Thompson. "What's that?"

"Shucks, I didn't mean to tell you," said Mr. Hatch, a faint leer of regret in his drooping eyelids. "Shucks, that just slipped out. Funny, now I'd made up my mind I wouldn' say a word, because it would just make a lot of excitement, and what I say is, if a man has lived harmless and quiet for nine years it don't matter if he *is* loony, does it? So long's he keeps quiet and don't do nobody harm."

"You mean they had him in a straitjacket?" asked Mr. Thompson, uneasily. "In a lunatic asylum?"

"They sure did," said Mr. Hatch. "That's right where they had him, from time to time."

"They put my Aunt Ida in one of them things in the State asylum," said Mr. Thompson. "She got vi'lent, and they put her in one of these jackets with long sleeves and tied her to an iron ring in the wall and Aunt Ida got so wild she broke a blood vessel and when they went to look after her she was dead. I'd think one of them things was dangerous."

"Mr. Helton used to sing his drinking song when he was in a straitjacket," said Mr. Hatch. "Nothing ever bothered him, except if you tried to make him talk. That bothered him, and he'd get vi'lent, like your Aunt Ida. He'd get vi'lent and then they'd put him in the jacket and go off and leave him, and he'd lay there perfickly contented, so fars you could see, singing his song. Then one night he just disappeared. Left, you might say, just went, and nobody ever saw hide or hair of him again. And then I come along and find him here," said Mr. Hatch, "all settled down and playing the same song."

"He never acted crazy to me," said Mr. Thompson. "He always acted like a sensible man, to me. He never got married, for one thing, and he works like a horse, and I bet he's got the first cent I paid him when he landed here, and he don't drink, and he never says a word, much less swear, and he don't waste time runnin' around Saturday nights, and if he's crazy," said Mr. Thompson, "why, I think I'll go crazy myself for a change."

"Haw, ha," said Mr. Hatch, "heh, he, that's good! Ha, ha, ha, I hadn't thought of it jes like that. Yeah, that's right! Let's all go crazy and get rid of our wives and save our money, hey?" He smiled unpleasantly, showing his little rabbit teeth.

Mr. Thompson felt he was being misunderstood. He turned around and motioned toward the open window back of the honeysuckle trellis. "Let's move off down here a little," he said. "I oughta thought of that before." His visitor bothered Mr. Thompson. He had a way of taking the words out of Mr.

Thompson's mouth, turning them around and mixing them up until Mr. Thompson didn't know himself what he had said. "My wife's not very strong," said Mr. Thompson. "She's been kind of invalid now goin' on fourteen years. It's mighty tough on a poor man, havin' sickness in the family. She had four operations," he said proudly, "one right after the other, but they didn't do any good. For five years hand-runnin', I just turned every nickel I made over to the doctors. Upshot is, she's a mighty delicate woman."

"My old woman," said Mr. Homer T. Hatch, "had a back like a mule, yes, sir. That woman could have moved the barn with her bare hands if she'd ever took the notion. I used to say, it was a good thing she didn't know her own stren'th. She's dead now, though. That kind wear out quicker than the puny ones. I never had much use for a woman always complainin'. I'd get rid of her mighty quick, yes, sir, mighty quick. It's just as you say: a dead loss, keepin' one of 'em up."

This was not at all what Mr. Thompson had heard himself say; he had been trying to explain that a wife as expensive as his was a credit to a man. "She's a mighty reasonable woman," said Mr. Thompson, feeling baffled, "but I wouldn't answer for what she'd say or do if she found out we'd had a lunatic on the place all this time." They had moved away from the window; Mr. Thompson took Mr. Hatch the front way, because if he went the back way they would have to pass Mr. Helton's shack. For some reason he didn't want the stranger to see or talk to Mr. Helton. It was strange, but that was the way Mr. Thompson felt.

Mr. Thompson sat down again, on the chopping log, offering his guest another tree stump. "Now, I mighta got upset myself at such a thing, once," said Mr. Thompson, "but now I *deefy* anything to get me lathered up." He cut himself an enormous plug of tobacco with his horn-handled pocketknife, and offered it to Mr. Hatch, who then produced his own plug and, opening a huge bowie knife with a long blade sharply whetted, cut off a large wad and put it in his mouth. They then compared plugs and both of them were astonished to see how different men's ideas of good chewing tobacco were.

"Now, for instance," said Mr. Hatch, "mine is lighter colored. That's because, for one thing, there ain't any sweetenin' in this plug. I like it dry, natural leaf, medium strong."

"A little sweetenin' don't do no harm so far as I'm concerned," said Mr. Thompson, "but it's got to be mighty little. But with me, now, I want a strong leaf, I want it heavy-cured, as the feller says. There's a man near here, named Williams, Mr. John Morgan Williams, who chews a plug—well, sir, it's black as your hat and soft as melted tar. It fairly drips with molasses, jus' plain molasses, and it chews like licorice. Now, I don't call that a good chew."

"One man's meat," said Mr. Hatch, "is another man's poison. Now, such a chew would simply gag me. I couldn't begin to put it in my mouth."

"Well," said Mr. Thompson, a tinge of apology in his voice, "I jus' barely tasted it myself, you might say. Just took a little piece in my mouth and spit it out again."

"I'm dead sure I couldn't even get that far," said Mr. Hatch. "I like a dry natural chew without any artificial flavorin' of any kind."

Mr. Thompson began to feel that Mr. Hatch was trying to make out he had the best judgment in tobacco, and was going to keep up the argument until he proved it. He began to feel seriously annoyed with the fat man. After all, who was he and where did he come from? Who was he to go around telling other people what kind of tobacco to chew?

"Artificial flavorin'," Mr. Hatch went on, doggedly, "is jes put in to cover up a cheap leaf and make a man think he's gettin' somethin' more than he *is* gettin'. Even a little sweetenin' is a sign of a cheap leaf, you can mark my words."

"I've always paid a fair price for my plug," said Mr. Thompson, stiffly. "I'm not a rich man and I don't go round settin' myself up for one, but I'll say this, when it comes to such things as tobacco, I buy the best on the market."

"Sweetenin', even a little," began Mr. Hatch, shifting his plug and squirting tobacco juice at a dry-looking little rose bush that was having a hard enough time as it was, standing all day in the blazing sun, its roots clenched in the baked earth, "is the sign of—"

"About this Mr. Helton, now," said Mr. Thompson, determinedly, "I don't see no reason to hold it against a man because he went loony once or twice in his lifetime and so I don't expect to take no steps about it. Not a step. I've got nothin' against the man, he's always treated me fair. They's things and people," he went on, "'nough to drive any man loony. The wonder to me is, more men don't wind up in straitjackets, the way things are going these days and times."

"That's right," said Mr. Hatch, promptly, entirely too promptly, as if he were turning Mr. Thompson's meaning back on him. "You took the words right out of my mouth. There ain't every man in a straitjacket that ought to be there. Ha, ha, you're right all right. You got the idea."

Mr. Thompson sat silent and chewed steadily and stared at a spot on the ground about six feet away and felt a slow muffled resentment climbing from somewhere deep down in him, climbing and spreading all through him. What was this fellow driving at? What was he trying to say? It wasn't so much his words, but his looks and his way of talking: that droopy look in the eye, that tone of voice, as if he was trying to mortify Mr. Thompson about something. Mr. Thompson didn't like it, but he couldn't get hold of it either. He wanted to turn around and shove the fellow off the stump, but it wouldn't look reasonable. Suppose something happened to the fellow when he fell off the stump, just for instance, if he fell on the ax and cut himself, and then someone should ask Mr. Thompson why he shoved him, and what could a man say? It would look mighty funny, it would sound mighty strange to say, Well him and me fell out over a plug of tobacco. He might just shove him anyhow and then tell people he was a fat man not used to the heat and while he was talking he got dizzy and fell off by himself, or something like that, and it wouldn't be the truth either, because it wasn't the heat and it wasn't the tobacco. Mr. Thompson made up his mind to get the fellow off the place pretty quick, without seeming to be anxious, and watch him sharp till he was out of sight. It doesn't pay to be friendly with strangers from another part of the country. They're always up to something, or they'd stay at home where they belong.

"And they's some people," said Mr. Hatch, "would jus' as soon have a loonatic around their house as not, they can't see no difference between them and anybody else. I always say, if that's the way a man feels, don't care who he associates with, why, why, that's his business, not mine. I don't wanta have a thing to do with it. Now back home in North Dakota, we don't feel that way. I'd like to a seen anybody hiring a loonatic there, aspecially after what he done."

"I didn't understand your home was North Dakota," said Mr. Thompson. "I thought you said Georgia."

"I've got a married sister in North Dakota," said Mr. Hatch, "married a Swede, but a white man if ever I saw one. So I say *we* because we got into a little business together out that way. And it seems like home, kind of."

"What did he do?" asked Mr. Thompson, feeling very uneasy again.

"Oh, nothin' to speak of," said Mr. Hatch, jovially, "jus' went loony one day in the hayfield and shoved a pitchfork right square through his brother, when they was makin' hay. They was goin' to execute him, but they found out he had went crazy with the heat, as the feller says, and so they put him in the asylum. That's all he done. Nothin' to get lathered up about, ha, ha, ha!" he said, and taking out his sharp knife he began to slice off a chew as carefully as if he were cutting cake.

"Well," said Mr. Thompson, "I don't deny that's news. Yes, sir, news. But I still say somethin' must have drove him to it. Some men make you feel like giving 'em a good killing just by lookin' at you. His brother may a been a mean ornery cuss."

"Brother was going to get married," said Mr. Hatch; "used to go courtin' his girl nights. Borrowed Mr. Helton's harmonica to give her a serenade one evenin', and lost it. Brand new harmonica."

"He thinks a heap of his harmonicas," said Mr. Thompson. "Only money he ever spends, now and then he buys hisself a new one. Must have a dozen in that shack, all kinds and sizes."

"Brother wouldn't buy him a new one," said Mr. Hatch, "so Mr. Helton just ups, as I says, and runs his pitchfork through his brother. Now you know he musta been crazy to get all worked up over a little thing like that."

"Sounds like it," said Mr. Thompson, reluctant to agree in anything with this intrusive and disagreeable fellow. He kept thinking he couldn't remember when he had taken such a dislike to a man on first sight.

"Seems to me you'd get pretty sick of hearin' the same tune year in, year out," said Mr. Hatch.

"Well, sometimes I think it wouldn't do no harm if he learned a new one," said Mr. Thompson, "but he don't, so there's nothin' to be done about it. It's a pretty good tune, though."

"One of the Scandahoovians told me what it meant, that's how I come to know," said Mr. Hatch. "Especially that part about getting so gay you jus' go ahead and drink up all the likker you got on hand before noon. It seems like up in them Swede countries a man carries a bottle of wine around with him as a matter of course, at least that's the way I understood it. Those fellers will tell you anything, though—" He broke off and spat.

The idea of drinking any kind of liquor in this heat made Mr. Thompson dizzy. The idea of anybody feeling good on a day like this, for instance, made him tired. He felt he was really suffering from the heat. The fat man looked as if he had grown to the stump; he slumped there in his damp, dark clothes too big for him, his belly slack in his pants, his wide black felt hat pushed off his narrow forehead red with prickly heat. A bottle of good cold beer, now, would be a help, thought Mr. Thompson, remembering the four bottles sitting deep in the pool at the springhouse, and his dry tongue squirmed in his mouth. He wasn't going to offer this man anything, though, not even a drop of water. He wasn't even going to chew any more tobacco with him. He shot out his quid suddenly, and wiped his mouth on the back of his hand, and studied the head near him attentively. The man was no good, and he was there for no good, but what was he up to? Mr. Thompson made up his mind he'd give him a little more time to get his business, whatever it was, with Mr. Helton over, and then if he didn't get off the place he'd kick him off.

Mr. Hatch, as if he suspected Mr. Thompson's thoughts, turned his eyes, wicked and pig-like, on Mr. Thompson. "Fact is," he said, as if he had made up his mind about something, "I might need your help in the little matter I've got on hand, but it won't cost you any trouble. Now, this Mr. Helton here, like I tell you, he's a dangerous escaped loonatic, you might say. Now fact is, in the last twelve years or so I musta rounded up

twenty-odd escaped loonatics, besides a couple of escaped con-
victs that I just run into by accident, like. I don't make a business of it, but if there's a reward, and there usually is a reward,
of course, I get it. It amounts to a tidy little sum in the long
run, but that ain't the main question. Fact is, I'm for law and
order, I don't like to see lawbreakers and loonatics at large. It
ain't the place for them. Now I reckon you're bound to agree
with me on that, aren't you?"

Mr. Thompson said, "Well, circumstances alters cases, as the
feller says. Now, what I know of Mr. Helton, he ain't dangerous, as I told you." Something serious was going to happen,
Mr. Thompson could see that. He stopped thinking about it.
He'd just let this fellow shoot off his head and then see what
could be done about it. Without thinking he got out his knife
and plug and started to cut a chew, then remembered himself
and put them back in his pocket.

"The law," said Mr. Hatch, "is solidly behind me. Now this
Mr. Helton, he's been one of my toughest cases. He's kept my
record from being practically one hundred per cent. I knew
him before he went loony, and I know the fam'ly, so I under-
took to help out rounding him up. Well, sir, he was gone slick
as a whistle, for all we knew the man was as good as dead long
while ago. Now we never might have caught up with him, but
do you know what he did? Well, sir, about two weeks ago his
old mother gets a letter from him, and in that letter, what do
you reckon she found? Well, it was a check on that little bank
in town for eight hundred and fifty dollars, just like that; the
letter wasn't nothing much, just said he was sending her a few
little savings, she might need something, but there it was,
name, postmark, date, everything. The old woman practically
lost her mind with joy. She's gettin' childish, and it looked like
she kinda forgot that her only living son killed his brother and
went loony. Mr. Helton said he was getting along all right, and
for her not to tell nobody. Well, natchally, she couldn't keep it
to herself, with that check to cash and everything. So that's
how I come to know." His feelings got the better of him. "You
coulda knocked me down with a feather." He shook hands
with himself and rocked, wagging his head, going "Heh, heh,"
in his throat. Mr. Thompson felt the corners of his mouth
turning down. Why, the dirty low-down hound, sneaking

around spying into other people's business like that. Collecting blood money, that's what it was! Let him talk!

"Yea, well, that musta been a surprise all right," he said, trying to hold his voice even. "I'd say a surprise."

"Well, siree," said Mr. Hatch, "the more I got to thinking about it, the more I just come to the conclusion that I'd better look into the matter a little, and so I talked to the old woman. She's pretty decrepid, now, half blind and all, but she was all for taking the first train out and going to see her son. I put it up to her square—how she was too feeble for the trip, and all. So, just as a favor to her, I told her for my expenses I'd come down and see Mr. Helton and bring her back all the news about him. She gave me a new shirt she made herself by hand, and a big Swedish kind of cake to bring to him, but I musta mislaid them along the road somewhere. It don't reely matter, though, he prob'ly ain't in any state of mind to appreciate 'em."

Mr. Thompson sat up and turning round on the log looked at Mr. Hatch and asked as quietly as be could, "And now what are you aiming to do? That's the question."

Mr. Hatch slouched up to his feet and shook himself. "Well, I come all prepared for a little scuffle," he said. "I got the handcuffs," he said, "but I don't want no violence if I can help it. I didn't want to say nothing around the countryside, making an uproar. I figured the two of us could overpower him." He reached into his big inside pocket and pulled them out. Handcuffs, for God's sake, thought Mr. Thompson. Coming round on a peaceable afternoon worrying a man, and making trouble, and fishing handcuffs out of his pocket on a decent family homestead, as if it was all in the day's work.

Mr. Thompson, his head buzzing, got up too. "Well," he said, roundly, "I want to tell you I think you've got a mighty sorry job on hand, you sure must be hard up for something to do, and now I want to give you a good piece of advice. You just drop the idea that you're going to come here and make trouble for Mr. Helton, and the quicker you drive that hired rig away from my front gate the better I'll be satisfied."

Mr. Hatch put one handcuff in his outside pocket, the other dangling down. He pulled his hat down over his eyes, and reminded Mr. Thompson of a sheriff, somehow. He didn't seem in the least nervous, and didn't take up Mr. Thompson's words. He said, "Now listen just a minute, it ain't reasonable to suppose that a man like yourself is going to stand in the way of getting an escaped loonatic back to the asylum where he belongs. Now I know it's enough to throw you off, coming sudden like this, but fact is I counted on your being a respectable man and helping me out to see that justice is done. Now a course, if you won't help, I'll have to look around for help somewheres else. It won't look very good to your neighbors that you was harbring an escaped loonatic who killed his own brother, and then you refused to give him up. It will look mighty funny."

Mr. Thompson knew almost before he heard the words that it would look funny. It would put him in a mighty awkward position. He said, "But I've been trying to tell you all along that the man ain't loony now. He's been perfectly harmless for nine years. He's—he's—"

Mr. Thompson couldn't think how to describe how it was with Mr. Helton. "Why, he's been like one of the family," he said, "the best standby a man ever had." Mr. Thompson tried to see his way out. It was a fact Mr. Helton might go loony again any minute, and now this fellow talking around the country would put Mr. Thompson in a fix. It was a terrible position. He couldn't think of any way out. "You're crazy," Mr. Thompson roared suddenly, "you're the crazy one around here, you're crazier than he ever was! You get off this place or I'll handcuff you and turn you over to the law. You're trespassing," shouted Mr. Thompson. "Get out of here before I knock you down!"

He took a step towards the fat man, who backed off, shrinking, "Try it, try it, go ahead!" and then something happened that Mr. Thompson tried hard afterwards to piece together in his mind, and in fact it never did come straight. He saw the fat man with his long bowie knife in his hand, he saw Mr. Helton come round the corner on the run, his long jaw dropped, his arms swinging, his eyes wild. Mr. Helton came in between them, fists doubled up, then stopped short, glaring at the fat man, his big frame seemed to collapse, he trembled like a shied horse; and then the fat man drove at him, knife in one hand, handcuffs in the other. Mr. Thompson saw it coming, he saw the blade going into Mr. Helton's stomach, he knew he had the ax out of the log in his own hands, felt his arms go up over his head and bring the ax down on Mr. Hatch's head as if he were stunning a beef.

Mrs. Thompson had been listening uneasily for some time to the voices going on, one of them strange to her, but she was too tired at first to get up and come out to see what was going on. The confused shouting that rose so suddenly brought her up to her feet and out across the front porch without her slippers, hair half-braided. Shading her eyes, she saw first Mr. Helton, running all stooped over through the orchard, running like a man with dogs after him; and Mr. Thompson supporting himself on the ax handle was leaning over shaking by the shoulder a man Mrs. Thompson had never seen, who lay doubled up with the top of his head smashed and the blood running away in a greasy-looking puddle. Mr. Thompson without taking his hand from the man's shoulder, said in a thick voice, "He killed Mr. Helton, he killed him, I saw him do it. I had to knock him out," he called loudly, "but he won't come to."

Mrs. Thompson said in a faint scream, "Why, yonder goes Mr. Helton," and she pointed. Mr. Thompson pulled himself up and looked where she pointed. Mrs. Thompson sat down slowly against the side of the house and began to slide forward on her face; she felt as if she were drowning, she couldn't rise to the top somehow, and her only thought was she was glad the boys were not there, they were out, fishing at Halifax, oh, God, she was glad the boys were not there.

Mr. and Mrs. Thompson drove up to their barn about sunset. Mr. Thompson handed the reins to his wife, got out to open the big door, and Mrs. Thompson guided old Jim in under the roof. The buggy was gray with dust and age, Mrs. Thompson's face was gray with dust and weariness, and Mr. Thompson's face, as he stood at the horse's head and began unhitching, was gray except for the dark blue of his freshly shaven jaws and chin, gray and blue and caved in, but patient, like a dead man's face.

Mrs. Thompson stepped down to the hard packed manure of the barn floor, and shook out her light flower-sprigged dress. She wore her smoked glasses, and her wide shady leghorn hat with the wreath of exhausted pink and blue forget-me-nots hid her forehead, fixed in a knot of distress.

The horse hung his head, raised a huge sigh and flexed his stiffened legs. Mr. Thompson's words came up muffled and hollow. "Poor ole Jim," he said, clearing his throat, "he looks pretty sunk in the ribs. I guess he's had a hard week." He lifted the harness up in one piece, slid it off and Jim walked out of the shafts halting a little. "Well, this is the last time," Mr. Thompson said, still talking to Jim. "Now you can get a good rest."

Mrs. Thompson closed her eyes behind her smoked glasses. The last time, and high time, and they should never have gone at all. She did not need her glasses any more, now the good darkness was coming down again, but her eyes ran full of tears steadily, though she was not crying, and she felt better with the glasses, safer, hidden away behind them. She took out her handkerchief with her hands shaking as they had been shaking ever since *that day*, and blew her nose. She said, "I see the boys have lighted the lamps. I hope they've started the stove going."

She stepped along the rough path holding her thin dress and starched petticoats around her, feeling her way between the sharp small stones, leaving the barn because she could hardly bear to be near Mr. Thompson, advancing slowly towards the house because she dreaded going there. Life was all one dread, the faces of her neighbors, of her boys, of her husband, the face of the whole world, the shape of her own house in the darkness, the very smell of the grass and the trees were horrible to her. There was no place to go, only one thing to do, bear it somehow—but how? She asked herself that question often. How was she going to keep on living now? Why had she lived at all? She wished now she had died one of those times when she had been so sick, instead of living on for this.

The boys were in the kitchen; Herbert was looking at the funny pictures from last Sunday's newspapers, the Katzenjammer Kids and Happy Hooligan. His chin was in his hands and his elbows on the table, and he was really reading and looking at the pictures, but his face was unhappy. Arthur was building the fire, adding kindling a stick at a time, watching it catch and blaze. His face was heavier and darker than Herbert's, but he was a little sullen by nature; Mrs. Thompson thought, he takes things harder, too. Arthur said, "Hello, Momma," and went on with his work. Herbert swept the papers together and moved over on the bench. They were big boys—fifteen and seventeen, and Arthur as tall as his father. Mrs. Thompson sat down beside Herbert, taking off her hat. She said, "I guess you're hungry. We were late today. We went the Log Hollow road, it's rougher than ever." Her pale mouth drooped with a sad fold on either side.

"I guess you saw the Mannings, then," said Herbert.

"Yes, and the Fergusons, and the Allbrights, and that new family McClellan."

"Anybody say anything?" asked Herbert.

"Nothing much, you know how it's been all along, some of them keeps saying, yes, they know it was a clear case and a fair trial and they say how glad they are your papa came out so well, and all that, some of 'em do, anyhow, but it looks like they don't really take sides with him. I'm about wore out," she said, the tears rolling again from under her dark glasses. "I don't know what good it does, but your papa can't seem to rest unless he's telling how it happened. I don't know."

"I don't think it does any good, not a speck," said Arthur, moving away from the stove. "It just keeps the whole question stirred up in people's minds. Everybody will go round telling what he heard, and the whole thing is going to get worse mixed up than ever. It just makes matters worse. I wish you could get Papa to stop driving round the country talking like that."

"Your papa knows best," said Mrs. Thompson. "You oughtn't to criticize him. He's got enough to put up with without that."

Arthur said nothing, his jaw stubborn. Mr. Thompson came in, his eyes hollowed out and dead-looking, his thick hands gray white and seamed from washing them clean every day before he started out to see the neighbors to tell them his side of the story. He was wearing his Sunday clothes, a thick pepper-and-salt-colored suit with a black string tie.

Mrs. Thompson stood up, her head swimming. "Now you-all

get out of the kitchen, it's too hot in here and I need room. I'll get us a little bite of supper, if you'll just get out and give me some room."

They went as if they were glad to go, the boys outside, Mr. Thompson into his bedroom. She heard him groaning to himself as he took off his shoes, and heard the bed creak as he lay down. Mrs. Thompson opened the icebox and felt the sweet coldness flow out of it; she had never expected to have an icebox, much less did she hope to afford to keep it filled with ice. It still seemed like a miracle, after two or three years. There was the food, cold and clean, all ready to be warmed over. She would never have had that icebox if Mr. Helton hadn't happened along one day, just by the strangest luck; so saving, and so managing, so good, thought Mrs. Thompson, her heart swelling until she feared she would faint again, standing there with the door open and leaning her head upon it. She simply could not bear to remember Mr. Helton, with his long sad face and silent ways, who had always been so quiet and harmless, who had worked so hard and helped Mr. Thompson so much, running through the hot fields and woods, being hunted like a mad dog, everybody turning out with ropes and guns and sticks to catch and tie him. Oh, God, said Mrs. Thompson in a long dry moan, kneeling before the icebox and fumbling inside for the dishes, even if they did pile mattresses all over the jail floor and against the walls, and five men there to hold him to keep him from hurting himself any more, he was already hurt too badly, he couldn't have lived anyway. Mr. Barbee, the sheriff, told her about it. He said, well, they didn't aim to harm him but they had to catch him, he was crazy as a loon; he picked up rocks and tried to brain every man that got near him. He had two harmonicas in his jumper pocket, said the sheriff, but they fell out in the scuffle, and Mr. Helton tried to pick 'em up again, and that's when they finally got him. "They *had* to be rough, Miz Thompson, he fought like a wildcat." Yes, thought Mrs. Thompson again with the same bitterness, of course, they had to be rough. They always have to be rough. Mr. Thompson can't argue with a man and get him off the place peaceably; no, she thought, standing up and shutting the icebox, he has to kill somebody, he has to be a murderer and ruin his boys' lives and cause Mr. Helton to be killed like a mad dog.

Her thoughts stopped with a little soundless explosion, cleared and began again. The rest of Mr. Helton's harmonicas were still in the shack, his tune ran in Mrs. Thompson's head at certain times of the day. She missed it in the evenings. It seemed so strange she had never known the name of that song, nor what it meant, until after Mr. Helton was gone. Mrs. Thompson, trembling in the knees, took a drink of water at the sink and poured the red beans into the baking dish, and began to roll the pieces of chicken in flour to fry them. There was a time, she said to herself, when I thought I had neighbors and friends, there was a time when we could hold up our heads, there was a time when my husband hadn't killed a man and I could tell the truth to anybody about anything.

Mr. Thompson, turning on his bed, figured that he had done all he could, he'd just try to let the matter rest from now on. His lawyer, Mr. Burleigh, had told him right at the beginning, "Now you keep calm and collected. You've got a fine case, even if you haven't got witnesses. Your wife must sit in court, she'll be a powerful argument with the jury. You just plead not guilty and I'll do the rest. The trial is going to be a mere formality, you haven't got a thing to worry about. You'll be clean out of this before you know it." And to make talk Mr. Burleigh had got to telling about all the men he knew around the country who for one reason or another had been forced to kill somebody, always in self-defense, and there just wasn't anything to it at all. He even told about how his own father in the old days had shot and killed a man just for setting foot inside his gate when he told him not to. "Sure, I shot the scoundrel," said Mr. Burleigh's father, "in self-defense; I *told* him I'd shoot him if he set his foot in my yard, and he did, and I did." There had been bad blood between them for years, Mr. Burleigh said, and his father had waited a long time to catch the other fellow in the wrong, and when he did he certainly made the most of his opportunity.

"But Mr. Hatch, as I told you," Mr. Thompson had said, "made a pass at Mr. Helton with his bowie knife. That's why I took a hand."

"All the better," said Mr. Burleigh. "That stranger hadn't any right coming to your house on such an errand. Why, hell," said Mr. Burleigh, "that wasn't even manslaughter you committed. So now you just hold your horses and keep your shirt on. And don't say one word without I tell you."

Wasn't even manslaughter. Mr. Thompson had to cover Mr. Hatch with a piece of wagon canvas and ride to town to tell the sheriff. It had been hard on Ellie. When they got back, the sheriff and the coroner and two deputies, they found her sitting beside the road, on a low bridge over a gulley, about half a mile from the place. He had taken her up behind his saddle and got her back to the house. He had already told the sheriff that his wife had witnessed the whole business, and now he had time, getting her to her room and in bed, to tell her what to say if they asked anything. He had left out the part about Mr. Helton being crazy all along, but it came out at the trial. By Mr. Burleigh's advice Mr. Thompson had pretended to be perfectly ignorant; Mr. Hatch hadn't said a word about that. Mr. Thompson pretended to believe that Mr. Hatch had just come looking for Mr. Helton to settle old scores, and the two members of Mr. Hatch's family who had come down to try to get Mr. Thompson convicted didn't get anywhere at all. It hadn't been much of a trial, Mr. Burleigh saw to that. He had charged a reasonable fee, and Mr. Thompson had paid him and felt grateful, but after it was over Mr. Burleigh didn't seem pleased to see him when he got to dropping into the office to talk it over, telling him things that had slipped his mind at first: trying to explain what an ornery low hound Mr. Hatch had been, anyhow. Mr. Burleigh seemed to have lost his interest; he looked sour and upset when he saw Mr. Thompson at the door. Mr. Thompson kept saying to himself that he'd got off, all right, just as Mr. Burleigh had predicted, but, but—and it was right there that Mr. Thompson's mind stuck, squirming like an angleworm on a fishhook: he had killed Mr. Hatch, and he was a murderer. That was the truth about himself that Mr. Thompson couldn't grasp, even when he said the word to himself. Why, he had not even once *thought* of killing anybody, much less Mr. Hatch, and if Mr. Helton hadn't come out so unexpectedly, hearing the row, why, then—but then, Mr. Helton had come on the run that way to help him. What he couldn't understand was what happened next. He had seen

Mr. Hatch go after Mr. Helton with the knife, he had seen the point, blade up, go into Mr. Helton's stomach and slice up like you slice a hog, but when they finally caught Mr. Helton there wasn't a knife scratch on him. Mr. Thompson knew he had the ax in his own hands and felt himself lifting it, but he couldn't remember hitting Mr. Hatch. He couldn't remember it. He couldn't. He remembered only that he had been determined to stop Mr. Hatch from cutting Mr. Helton. If he was given a chance he could explain the whole matter. At the trial they hadn't let him talk. They just asked questions and he answered yes or no, and they never did get to the core of the matter. Since the trial, now, every day for a week he had washed and shaved and put on his best clothes and had taken Ellie with him to tell every neighbor he had that he never killed Mr. Hatch on purpose, and what good did it do? Nobody believed him. Even when he turned to Ellie and said, "You was there, you saw it, didn't you?" and Ellie spoke up, saying, "Yes, that's the truth. Mr. Thompson was trying to save Mr. Helton's life," and he added, "If you don't believe me, you can believe my wife. She won't lie," Mr. Thompson saw something in all their faces that disheartened him, made him feel empty and tired out. They didn't believe he was not a murderer.

Even Ellie never said anything to comfort him. He hoped she would say finally, "I remember now, Mr. Thompson, I really did come round the corner in time to see everything. It's not a lie, Mr. Thompson. Don't you worry." But as they drove together in silence, with the days still hot and dry, shortening for fall, day after day, the buggy jolting in the ruts, she said nothing; they grew to dread the sight of another house, and the people in it: all houses looked alike now, and the people—old neighbors or new—had the same expression when Mr. Thompson told them why he had come and began his story. Their eyes looked as if someone had pinched the eyeball at the back; they shriveled and the light went out of them. Some of them sat with fixed tight smiles trying to be friendly. "Yes, Mr. Thompson, we know how you must feel. It must be terrible for you, Mrs. Thompson. Yes, you know, I've about come to the point where I believe in such a thing as killing in self-defense.

Why, certainly, we believe you, Mr. Thompson, why shouldn't we believe you? Didn't you have a perfectly fair and above-board trial? Well, now, natchally, Mr. Thompson, we think you done right."

Mr. Thompson was satisfied they didn't think so. Sometimes the air around him was so thick with their blame he fought and pushed with his fists, and the sweat broke out all over him, he shouted his story in a dust-choked voice, he would fairly bellow at last: "My wife, here, you know her, she was there, she saw and heard it all, if you don't believe me, ask her, she won't lie!" and Mrs. Thompson, with her hands knotted together, aching, her chin trembling, would never fail to say: "Yes, that's right, that's the truth—"

The last straw had been laid on today, Mr. Thompson decided. Tom Allbright, an old beau of Ellie's, why, he had squired Ellie around a whole summer, had come out to meet them when they drove up, and standing there bareheaded had stopped them from getting out. He had looked past them with an embarrassed frown on his face, telling them his wife's sister was there with a raft of young ones, and the house was pretty full and everything upset, or he'd ask them to come in. "We've been thinking of trying to get up to your place one of these days," said Mr. Allbright, moving away trying to look busy, "we've been mighty occupied up here of late." So they had to say, "Well, we just happened to be driving this way," and go on. "The Allbrights," said Mrs. Thompson, "always was fair-weather friends." "They look out for number one, that's a fact," said Mr. Thompson. But it was cold comfort to them both.

Finally Mrs. Thompson had given up. "Let's go home," she said. "Old Jim's tired and thirsty, and we've gone far enough."

Mr. Thompson said, "Well, while we're out this way, we might as well stop at the McClellans'." They drove in, and asked a little cotton-haired boy if his mamma and papa were at home. Mr. Thompson wanted to see them. The little boy stood gazing with his mouth open, then galloped into the house shouting, "Mommer, Popper, come out hyah. That man that kilt Mr. Hatch has come ter see yer!"

The man came out in his sock feet, with one gallus up, the

other broken and dangling, and said, "Light down, Mr. Thompson, and come in. The ole woman's washing, but she'll git here." Mrs. Thompson, feeling her way, stepped down and sat in a broken rocking-chair on the porch that sagged under her feet. The woman of the house, barefooted, in a calico wrapper, sat on the edge of the porch, her fat sallow face full of curiosity. Mr. Thompson began, "Well, as I reckon you happen to know, I've had some strange troubles lately, and, as the feller says, it's not the kind of trouble that happens to a man every day in the year, and there's some things I don't want no misunderstanding about in the neighbors' minds, so—" He halted and stumbled forward, and the two listening faces took on a mean look, a greedy, despising look, a look that said plain as day, "My, you must be a purty sorry feller to come round worrying about what *we* think, *we* know you wouldn't be here if you had anybody else to turn to—my, I wouldn't lower myself that much, myself." Mr. Thompson was ashamed of himself, he was suddenly in a rage, he'd like to knock their dirty skunk heads together, the low-down white trash—but he held himself down and went on to the end. "My wife will tell you," he said, and this was the hardest place, because Ellie always without moving a muscle seemed to stiffen as if somebody had threatened to hit her; "ask my wife, she won't lie."

"It's true, I saw it—"

"Well, now," said the man, drily, scratching his ribs inside his shirt, "that sholy is too bad. Well, now, I kaint see what we've got to do with all this here, however. I kaint see no good reason for us to git mixed up in these murder matters, I shore kaint. Whichever way you look at it, it ain't none of my business. However, it's mighty nice of you-all to come around and give us the straight of it, fur we've heerd some mighty queer yarns about it, mighty queer, I golly you couldn't hardly make head ner tail of it."

"Evvybody goin' round shootin' they heads off," said the woman. "Now we don't hold with killin'; the Bible says—"

"Shet yer trap," said the man, "and keep it shet 'r I'll shet it fer yer. Now it shore looks like to me—"

"We mustn't linger," said Mrs. Thompson, unclasping her hands. "We've lingered too long now. It's getting late, and we've far to go." Mr. Thompson took the hint and followed her. The man and the woman lolled against their rickety porch poles and watched them go.

Now lying on his bed, Mr. Thompson knew the end had come. Now, this minute, lying in the bed where he had slept with Ellie for eighteen years; under this roof where he had laid the shingles when he was waiting to get married; there as he was with his whiskers already sprouting since his shave that morning; with his fingers feeling his bony chin, Mr. Thompson felt he was a dead man. He was dead to his other life, he had got to the end of something without knowing why, and he had to make a fresh start, he did not know how. Something different was going to begin, he didn't know what. It was in some way not his business. He didn't feel he was going to have much to do with it. He got up, aching, hollow, and went out to the kitchen where Mrs. Thompson was just taking up the supper.

"Call the boys," said Mrs. Thompson. They had been down to the barn, and Arthur put out the lantern before hanging it on a nail near the door. Mr. Thompson didn't like their silence. They had hardly said a word about anything to him since that day. They seemed to avoid him, they ran the place together as if he wasn't there, and attended to everything without asking him for any advice. "What you boys been up to?" he asked, trying to be hearty. "Finishing your chores?"

"No, sir," said Arthur, "there ain't much to do. Just greasing some axles." Herbert said nothing. Mrs. Thompson bowed her head: "For these and all Thy blessings. . . . Amen," she whispered weakly, and the Thompsons sat there with their eyes down and their faces sorrowful, as if they were at a funeral.

Every time he shut his eyes, trying to sleep, Mr. Thompson's mind started up and began to run like a rabbit, it jumped from one thing to another, trying to pick up a trail here or there that would straighten out what had happened that day he killed Mr. Hatch. Try as he might, Mr. Thompson's mind would not go anywhere that it had not already been, he could not see anything but what he had seen once, and he knew that was not right. If he had not seen straight that first time, then everything about his killing Mr. Hatch was wrong from start to finish, and there was nothing more to be done about it, he might just as well give up. It still seemed to him that he had done, maybe not the right thing, but the only thing he could do, that day, but had he? *Did he have to kill Mr. Hatch?* He had never seen a man he hated more, the minute he laid eyes on him. He knew in his bones the fellow was there for trouble. What seemed so funny now was this: Why hadn't he just told Mr. Hatch to get out before he ever even got in?

Mrs. Thompson, her arms crossed on her breast, was lying beside him, perfectly still, but she seemed awake, somehow. "Asleep, Ellie?"

After all, he might have got rid of him peaceably, or maybe he might have had to overpower him and put those handcuffs on him and turn him over to the sheriff for disturbing the peace. The most they could have done was to lock Mr. Hatch up while he cooled off for a few days, or fine him a little something. He would try to think of things he might have said to Mr. Hatch. Why, let's see, I could just have said, Now look here, Mr. Hatch, I want to talk to you as man to man. But his brain would go empty. What could he have said or done? But if he *could* have done anything else almost except kill Mr. Hatch, then nothing would have happened to Mr. Helton. Mr. Thompson hardly ever thought of Mr. Helton. His mind just skipped over him and went on. If he stopped to think about Mr. Helton he'd never in God's world get anywhere. He tried to imagine how it might all have been, this very night even, if Mr. Helton were still safe and sound out in his shack playing his tune about feeling so good in the morning, drinking up all the wine so you'd feel even better; and Mr. Hatch safe in jail somewhere, mad as hops, maybe, but out of harm's way and ready to listen to reason and to repent of his meanness, the dirty, yellow-livered hound coming around persecuting an innocent man and ruining a whole family that never harmed him! Mr. Thompson felt the veins of his forehead start up, his fists clutched as if they seized an ax handle, the sweat broke out on him, he bounded up from the bed with a yell smothered in his throat, and Ellie started up after him, crying out, "Oh, oh, don't! Don't! Don't!" as if she were having a nightmare. He stood shaking until his bones rattled in him, crying hoarsely, "Light the lamp, light the lamp, Ellie."

Instead, Mrs. Thompson gave a shrill weak scream, almost the same scream he had heard on that day she came around the house when he was standing there with the ax in his hand. He could not see her in the dark, but she was on the bed, rolling violently. He felt for her in horror, and his groping hands found her arms, up, and her own hands pulling her hair straight out from her head, her neck strained back, and the tight screams strangling her. He shouted out for Arthur, for Herbert. "Your mother!" he bawled, his voice cracking. As he held Mrs. Thompson's arms, the boys came tumbling in, Arthur with the lamp above his head. By this light Mr. Thompson saw Mrs. Thompson's eyes, wide open, staring dreadfully at him, the tears pouring. She sat up at sight of the boys, and held out one arm towards them, the hand wagging in a crazy circle, then dropped on her back again, and suddenly went limp. Arthur set the lamp on the table and turned on Mr. Thompson. "She's scared," he said, "she's scared to death." His face was in a knot of rage, his fists were doubled up, he faced his father as if he meant to strike him. Mr. Thompson's jaw fell, he was so surprised he stepped back from the bed. Herbert went to the other side. They stood on each side of Mrs. Thompson and watched Mr. Thompson as if he were a dangerous wild beast. "What did you do to her?" shouted Arthur, in a grown man's voice. "You touch her again and I'll blow your heart out!" Herbert was pale and his cheek twitched, but he was on Arthur's side; he would do what he could to help Arthur.

Mr. Thompson had no fight left in him. His knees bent as he stood, his chest collapsed. "Why, Arthur," he said, his words crumbling and his breath coming short. "She's fainted again. Get the ammonia." Arthur did not move. Herbert brought the bottle, and handed it, shrinking, to his father.

Mr. Thompson held it under Mrs. Thompson's nose. He poured a little in the palm of his hand and rubbed it on her forehead. She gasped and opened her eyes and turned her head away from him. Herbert began a doleful hopeless sniffling. "Mamma," he kept saying, "Mamma, don't die."

"I'm all right," Mrs. Thompson said. "Now don't you worry around. Now Herbert, you mustn't do that. I'm all right." She closed her eyes. Mr. Thompson began pulling on his best pants; he put on his socks and shoes. The boys sat on each side of the bed, watching Mrs. Thompson's face. Mr. Thompson put on his shirt and coat. He said, "I reckon I'll ride over and get the doctor. Don't look like all this fainting is a good sign. Now you just keep watch until I get back." They listened, but said nothing. He said, "Don't you get any notions in your head. I never did your mother any harm in my life, on purpose." He went out, and, looking back, saw Herbert staring at him from under his brows, like a stranger. "You'll know how to look after her," said Mr. Thompson.

Mr. Thompson went through the kitchen. There he lighted the lantern, took a thin pad of scratch paper and a stub pencil from the shelf where the boys kept their schoolbooks. He swung the lantern on his arm and reached into the cupboard where he kept the guns. The shotgun was there to his hand, primed and ready, a man never knows when he may need a shotgun. He went out of the house without looking around, or looking back when he had left it, passed his barn without seeing it, and struck out to the farthest end of his fields, which ran for half a mile to the east. So many blows had been struck at Mr. Thompson and from so many directions he couldn't stop any more to find out where he was hit. He walked on, over plowed ground and over meadow, going through barbed wire fences cautiously, putting his gun through first; he could almost see in the dark, now his eyes were used to it. Finally he came to the last fence; here he sat down, back against a post, lantern at his side, and, with the pad on his knee, moistened the stub pencil and began to write:

"Before Almighty God, the great judge of all before who I am about to appear, I do hereby solemnly swear that I did not take the life of Mr. Homer T. Hatch on purpose. It was done in defense of Mr. Helton. I did not aim to hit him with the ax but only to keep him off Mr. Helton. He aimed a blow at Mr. Helton who was not looking for it. It was my belief at the time that Mr. Hatch would of taken the life of Mr. Helton if I did not interfere. I have told all this to the judge and the jury and they let me off but nobody believes it. This is the only way I can prove I am not a cold blooded murderer like everybody seems to think. If I had been in Mr. Helton's place he would of done the same for me. I still think I done the only thing there was to do. My wife—"

Mr. Thompson stopped here to think a while. He wet the pencil point with the tip of his tongue and marked out the last two words. He sat a while blacking out the words until he had made a neat oblong patch where they had been, and started again:

"It was Mr. Homer T. Hatch who came to do wrong to a harmless man. He caused all this trouble and he deserved to die but I am sorry it was me who had to kill him."

He licked the point of his pencil again, and signed his full name carefully, folded the paper and put it in his outside pocket. Taking off his right shoe and sock, he set the butt of the shotgun along the ground with the twin barrels pointed towards his head. It was very awkward. He thought about this a little, leaning his head against the gun mouth. He was trembling and his head was drumming until he was deaf and blind, but he lay down flat on the earth on his side, drew the barrel under his chin and fumbled for the trigger with his great toe. That way he could work it.

Pale Horse, Pale Rider

IN sleep she knew she was in her bed, but not the bed she had lain down in a few hours since, and the room was not the same but it was a room she had known somewhere. Her heart was a stone lying upon her breast outside of her; her pulses lagged and paused, and she knew that something strange was going to happen, even as the early morning winds were cool through the lattice, the streaks of light were dark blue and the whole house was snoring in its sleep.

Now I must get up and go while they are all quiet. Where are my things? Things have a will of their own in this place and hide where they like. Daylight will strike a sudden blow on the roof startling them all up to their feet; faces will beam asking, Where are you going, What are you doing, What are you thinking, How do you feel, Why do you say such things, What do you mean? No more sleep. Where are my boots and what horse shall I ride? Fiddler or Graylie or Miss Lucy with the long nose and the wicked eye? How I have loved this house in the morning before we are all awake and tangled together like badly cast fishing lines. Too many people have been born here, and have wept too much here, and have laughed too much, and have been too angry and outrageous with each other here. Too many have died in this bed already, there are far too many ancestral bones propped up on the mantelpieces, there have been too damned many antimacassars in this house, she said loudly, and oh, what accumulation of storied dust never allowed to settle in peace for one moment.

And the stranger? Where is that lank greenish stranger I remember hanging about the place, welcomed by my grandfather, my great-aunt, my five times removed cousin, my decrepit hound and my silver kitten? Why did they take to him, I wonder? And where are they now? Yet I saw him pass the window in the evening. What else besides them did I have in the world? Nothing. Nothing is mine, I have only nothing but it is enough, it is beautiful and it is all mine. Do I even walk about in my own skin or is it something I have borrowed to spare my modesty? Now what horse shall I borrow for this journey I do not mean to take, Graylie or Miss Lucy or Fiddler who can jump ditches in the dark and knows how to get the bit between his teeth? Early morning is best for me because trees are trees in one stroke, stones are stones set in shades known to be grass, there are no false shapes or surmises, the road is still asleep with the crust of dew unbroken. I'll take Graylie because he is not afraid of bridges.

Come now, Graylie, she said, taking his bridle, we must out-run Death and the Devil. You are no good for it, she told the other horses standing saddled before the stable gate, among them the horse of the stranger, gray also, with tarnished nose and ears. The stranger swung into his saddle beside her, leaned far towards her and regarded her without meaning, the blank still stare of mindless malice that makes no threats and can bide its time. She drew Graylie around sharply, urged him to run. He leaped the low rose hedge and the narrow ditch beyond, and the dust of the lane flew heavily under his beating hoofs. The stranger rode beside her, easily, lightly, his reins loose in his half-closed hand, straight and elegant in dark shabby garments that flapped upon his bones; his pale face smiled in an evil trance, he did not glance at her. Ah, I have seen this fellow before, I know this man if I could place him. He is no stranger to me.

She pulled Graylie up, rose in her stirrups and shouted, I'm not going with you this time—ride on! Without pausing or turning his head the stranger rode on. Graylie's ribs heaved under her, her own ribs rose and fell, Oh, why am I so tired, I must wake up. "But let me get a fine yawn first," she said, opening her eyes and stretching, "a slap of cold water in my face, for I've been talking in my sleep again, I heard myself but what was I saying?"

Slowly, unwillingly, Miranda drew herself up inch by inch out of the pit of sleep, waited in a daze for life to begin again. A single word struck in her mind, a gong of warning, reminding her for the day long what she forgot happily in sleep, and only in sleep. The war, said the gong, and she shook her head. Dangling her feet idly with their slippers hanging, she was reminded of the way all sorts of persons sat upon her desk at the newspaper office. Every day she found someone there, sitting upon her desk instead of the chair provided, dangling his legs, eyes roving, full of his important affairs, waiting to pounce about something or other. "*Why* won't they sit in the chair? Should I put a sign on it, saying, 'For God's sake, sit here'?"

Far from putting up a sign, she did not even frown at her visitors. Usually she did not notice them at all until their determination to be seen was greater than her determination not to see them. Saturday, she thought, lying comfortably in her tub of hot water, will be pay day, as always. Or I hope always. Her thoughts roved hazily in a continual effort to bring together and unite firmly the disturbing oppositions in her day-to-day existence, where survival, she could see clearly, had become a series of feats of sleight of hand. I owe—let me see, I wish I had pencil and paper—well, suppose I *did* pay five dollars now on a Liberty Bond, I couldn't possibly keep it up. Or maybe. Eighteen dollars a week. So much for rent, so much for food, and I mean to have a few things besides. About five dollars' worth. Will leave me twenty-seven cents. I suppose I can make it. I suppose I should be worried. I am worried. Very well, now I am worried and what next? Twenty-seven cents. That's not so bad. Pure profit, really. Imagine if they should suddenly raise me to twenty I should then have two dollars and twenty-seven cents left over. But they aren't going to raise me to twenty. They are in fact going to throw me out if I don't buy a Liberty Bond. I hardly believe that. I'll ask Bill. (Bill was the city editor.) I wonder if a threat like that isn't a kind of blackmail. I don't believe even a Lusk Committeeman can get away with that.

Yesterday there had been two pairs of legs dangling, on either side of her typewriter, both pairs stuffed thickly into funnels of dark expensive-looking material. She noticed at a distance that one of them was oldish and one was youngish, and they both of them had a stale air of borrowed importance which apparently they had got from the same source. They were both much too well nourished and the younger one wore a square little mustache. Being what they were, no matter what their business was it would be something unpleasant. Miranda had nodded at them, pulled out her chair and without removing her cap or gloves had reached into a pile of letters and sheets from the copy desk as if she had not a moment to spare. They did not move, or take off their hats. At last she had said "Good morning" to them, and asked if they were, perhaps, waiting for her?

The two men slid off the desk, leaving some of her papers rumpled, and the oldish man had inquired why she had not bought a Liberty Bond. Miranda had looked at him then, and got a poor impression. He was a pursy-faced man, gross-mouthed, with little lightless eyes, and Miranda wondered why nearly all of those selected to do the war work at home were of his sort. He might be anything at all, she thought; advance agent for a road show, promoter of a wildcat oil company, a former saloon keeper announcing the opening of a new cabaret, an automobile salesman—any follower of any one of the crafty, haphazard callings. But he was now all Patriot, working for the government. "Look here," he asked her, "do you know there's a war, or don't you?"

Did he expect an answer to that? Be quiet, Miranda told herself, this was bound to happen. Sooner or later it happens. Keep your head. The man wagged his finger at her, "Do you?" he persisted, as if he were prompting an obstinate child.

"Oh, the war," Miranda had echoed on a rising note and she almost smiled at him. It was habitual, automatic, to give that solemn, mystically uplifted grin when you spoke the words or heard them spoken. "*C'est la guerre*," whether you could pronounce it or not, was even better, and always, always, you shrugged.

"Yeah," said the younger man in a nasty way, "the war." Miranda, startled by the tone, met his eye; his stare was really stony, really viciously cold, the kind of thing you might expect to meet behind a pistol on a deserted corner. This expression gave temporary meaning to a set of features otherwise nondescript, the face of those men who have no business of their own. "We're having a war, and some people are buying Liberty Bonds and others just don't seem to get around to it," he said. "That's what we mean."

Miranda frowned with nervousness, the sharp beginnings of fear. "Are you selling them?" she asked, taking the cover off her typewriter and putting it back again.

"No, we're not selling them," said the older man. "We're

just asking you why you haven't bought one." The voice was persuasive and ominous.

Miranda began to explain that she had no money, and did not know where to find any, when the older man interrupted: "That's no excuse, no excuse at all, and you know it, with the Huns overrunning martyred Belgium."

"With our American boys fighting and dying in Belleau Wood," said the younger man, "anybody can raise fifty dollars to help beat the Boche."

Miranda said hastily, "I have eighteen dollars a week and not another cent in the world. I simply cannot buy anything."

"You can pay for it five dollars a week," said the older man (they had stood-there cawing back and forth over her head), "like a lot of other people in this office, and a lot of other offices besides are doing."

Miranda, desperately silent, had thought, "Suppose I were not a coward, but said what I really thought? Suppose I said to hell with this filthy war? Suppose I asked that little thug, What's the matter with you, why aren't you rotting in Belleau Wood? I wish you were . . ."

She began to arrange her letters and notes, her fingers refusing to pick up things properly. The older man went on making his little set speech. It was hard, of course. Everybody was suffering, naturally. Everybody had to do his share. But as to that, a Liberty Bond was the safest investment you could make. It was just like having the money in the bank. Of course. The government was back of it and where better could you invest?

"I agree with you about that," said Miranda, "but I haven't any money to invest."

And of course, the man had gone on, it wasn't so much her fifty dollars that was going to make any difference. It was just a pledge of good faith on her part. A pledge of good faith that she was a loyal American doing her duty. And the thing was safe as a church. Why, if he had a million dollars he'd be glad to put every last cent of it in these Bonds. . . . "You can't lose by it," he said, almost benevolently, "and you can lose a lot if you don't. Think it over. You're the only one in this whole newspaper office that hasn't come in. And every firm in this city has come in one hundred per cent. Over at the *Daily Clarion* nobody had to be asked twice."

"They pay better over there," said Miranda. "But next week, if I can. Not now, next week."

"See that you do," said the younger man. "This ain't any laughing matter."

They lolled away, past the Society Editor's desk, past Bill the City Editor's desk, past the long copy desk where old man Gibbons sat all night shouting at intervals, "Jarge! Jarge!" and the copy boy would come flying. "Never say *people* when you mean *persons*," old man Gibbons had instructed Miranda, "and never say *practically*, say *virtually*, and don't for God's sake ever so long as I am at this desk use the barbarism *inasmuch* under any circumstances whatsoever. Now you're educated, you may go." At the head of the stairs her inquisitors had stopped in their fussy pride and vainglory, lighting cigars and wedging their hats more firmly over their eyes.

Miranda turned over in the soothing water, and wished she might fall asleep there, to wake up only when it was time to sleep again. She had a burning slow headache, and noticed it now, remembering she had waked up with it and it had in fact begun the evening before. While she dressed she tried to trace the insidious career of her headache, and it seemed reasonable to suppose it had started with the war. "It's been a headache, all right, but not quite like this." After the Committeemen had left, yesterday, she had gone to the cloakroom and had found Mary Townsend, the Society Editor, quietly hysterical about something. She was perched on the edge of the shabby wicker couch with ridges down the center, knitting on something rose-colored. Now and then she would put down her knitting, seize her head with both hands and rock, saying, "My *God*," in a surprised, inquiring voice. Her column was called Ye Towne Gossyp, so of course everybody called her Towney. Miranda and Towney had a great deal in common, and liked each other. They had both been real reporters once, and had been sent to-gether to "cover" a scandalous elopement, in which no mar-riage had taken place, after all, and the recaptured girl, her face swollen, had sat with her mother, who was moaning steadily under a mound of blankets. They had both wept painfully and implored the young reporters to suppress the worst of the story. They had suppressed it, and the rival newspaper printed it all the next day. Miranda and Towney had then taken their punishment together, and had been degraded publicly to routine female jobs, one to the theaters, the other to society. They had this in common, that neither of them could see what else they could possibly have done, and they knew they were considered fools by the rest of the staff—nice girls, but fools. At sight of Miranda, Towney had broken out in a rage: "I can't do it, I'll never be able to raise the money, I told them, I can't, I can't, but they wouldn't listen."

Miranda said, "I knew I wasn't the only person in this office who couldn't raise five dollars. I told them I couldn't, too, and I can't."

"My *God*," said Towney, in the same voice, "they told me I'd lose my job—"

"I'm going to ask Bill," Miranda said; "I don't believe Bill would do that."

"It's not up to Bill," said Towney. "He'd have to if they got after him. Do you suppose they could put us in jail?"

"I don't know," said Miranda. "If they do, we won't be lonesome." She sat down beside Towney and held her own head. "What kind of soldier are you knitting that for? It's a sprightly color, it ought to cheer him up."

"Like hell," said Towney, her needles going again. "I'm making this for myself. That's that."

"Well," said Miranda, "we won't be lonesome and we'll catch up on our sleep." She washed her face and put on fresh make-up. Taking clean gray gloves out of her pocket she went out to join a group of young women fresh from the country club dances, the morning bridge, the charity bazaar, the Red Cross workrooms, who were wallowing in good works. They gave tea dances and raised money, and with the money they bought quantities of sweets, fruit, cigarettes, and magazines for the men in the cantonment hospitals. With this loot they were now setting out, a gay procession of high-powered cars and brightly tinted faces to cheer the brave boys who already, you might very well say, had fallen in defense of their country. It must be frightfully hard on them, the dears, to be floored like this when they're all crazy to get overseas and into the trenches as quickly as possible. Yes, and some of them are the cutest things you ever saw, I didn't know there were so many good-looking men in this country, good heavens, I said, where do they come from? Well, my dear, you may ask yourself that question, who knows where they did come from? You're quite right, the way I feel about it is this, we must do everything we can to make them contented, but I draw the line at talking to them. I told the chaperons at those dances for enlisted men, I'll dance with them, every dumbbell who asks me, but I will NOT talk to them, I said, even if there is a war. So I danced hundreds of miles without opening my mouth except to say, Please keep your knees to yourself. I'm glad we gave those dances up. Yes, and the men stopped coming, anyway. But listen, I've heard that a great many of the enlisted men come from very good families; I'm not good at catching names, and those I did catch I'd never heard before, so I don't know . . . but it seems to me if they were from good families, you'd know it, wouldn't you? I mean, if a man is well bred he doesn't step on your feet, does he? At least not that. I used to have a pair of sandals ruined at every one of those dances. Well, I think any kind of social life is in very poor taste just now, I think we should all put on our Red Cross head dresses and wear them for the duration of the war—

Miranda, carrying her basket and her flowers, moved in among the young women, who scattered out and rushed upon the ward uttering girlish laughter meant to be refreshingly gay, but there was a grim determined clang in it calculated to freeze the blood. Miserably embarrassed at the idiocy of her errand, she walked rapidly between the long rows of high beds, set foot to foot with a narrow aisle between. The men, a selected presentable lot, sheets drawn up to their chins, not seriously ill, were bored and restless, most of them willing to be amused at anything. They were for the most part picturesquely bandaged as to arm or head, and those who were not visibly wounded invariably replied "Rheumatism" if some tactless girl, who had been solemnly warned never to ask this question, still forgot and asked a man what his illness was. The good-natured, eager ones, laughing and calling out from their hard narrow beds, were soon surrounded. Miranda, with her wilting bouquet and her basket of sweets and cigarettes, looking

about, caught the unfriendly bitter eye of a young fellow lying
on his back, his right leg in a cast and pulley. She stopped at
the foot of his bed and continued to look at him, and he
looked back with an unchanged, hostile face. Not having any,
thank you and be damned to the whole business, his eyes said
plainly to her, and will you be so good as to take your trash off
my bed? For Miranda had set it down, leaning over to place it
where he might be able to reach it if he would. Having set it
down, she was incapable of taking it up again, but hurried
away, her face burning, down the long aisle and out into the
cool October sunshine, where the dreary raw barracks swarmed
and worked with an aimless life of scurrying, dun-colored insects; and going around to a window near where he lay, she
looked in, spying upon her soldier. He was lying with his eyes
closed, his eyebrows in a sad bitter frown. She could not place
him at all, she could not imagine where he came from nor
what sort of being he might have been "in life," she said to
herself. His face was young and the features sharp and plain,
the hands were not laborer's hands but not well-cared-for
hands either. They were good useful properly shaped hands,
lying there on the coverlet. It occurred to her that it would be
her luck to find him, instead of a jolly hungry puppy glad of a
bite to eat and a little chatter. It is like turning a corner absorbed in your painful thoughts and meeting your state of
mind embodied, face to face, she said. "My own feelings about
this whole thing, made flesh. Never again will I come here, this
is no sort of thing to be doing. This is disgusting," she told
herself plainly. "Of course I would pick him out," she thought,
getting into the back seat of the car she came in, "serves me
right, I know better."

Another girl came out looking very tired and climbed in
beside her. After a short silence, the girl said in a puzzled way,
"I don't know what good it does, really. Some of them
wouldn't take anything at all. I don't like this, do you?"

"I hate it," said Miranda.

"I suppose it's all right, though," said the girl, cautiously.

"Perhaps," said Miranda, turning cautious also.

That was for yesterday. At this point Miranda decided there
was no good in thinking of yesterday, except for the hour after
midnight she had spent dancing with Adam. He was in her

mind so much, she hardly knew when she was thinking about him directly. His image was simply always present in more or less degree, he was sometimes nearer the surface of her thoughts, the pleasantest, the only really pleasant thought she had. She examined her face in the mirror between the windows and decided that her uneasiness was not all imagination. For three days at least she had felt odd and her expression was unfamiliar. She would have to raise that fifty dollars somehow, she supposed, or who knows what can happen? She was hardened to stories of personal disaster, of outrageous accusations and extraordinarily bitter penalties that had grown monstrously out of incidents very little more important than her failure—her refusal—to buy a Bond. No, she did not find herself a pleasing sight, flushed and shiny, and even her hair felt as if it had decided to grow in the other direction. I must do something about this, I can't let Adam see me like this, she told herself, knowing that even now at that moment he was listening for the turn of her door knob, and he would be in the hallway, or on the porch when she came out, as if by sheerest coincidence. The noon sunlight cast cold slanting shadows in the room where, she said, I suppose I live, and this day is beginning badly, but they all do now, for one reason or another. In a drowse, she sprayed perfume on her hair, put on her moleskin cap and jacket, now in their second winter, but still good, still nice to wear, again being glad she had paid a frightening price for them. She had enjoyed them all this time, and in no case would she have had the money now. Maybe she could manage for that Bond. She could not find the lock without leaning to search for it, then stood undecided a moment possessed by the notion that she had forgotten something she would miss seriously later on.

Adam was in the hallway, a step outside his own door; he swung about as if quite startled to see her, and said, "Hello. I don't have to go back to camp today after all—isn't that luck?"

Miranda smiled at him gaily because she was always delighted at the sight of him. He was wearing his new uniform, and he was all olive and tan and tawny, hay colored and sand colored from hair to boots. She half noticed again that he always began by smiling at her; that his smile faded gradually;

that his eyes became fixed and thoughtful as if he were reading in a poor light.

They walked out together into the fine fall day, scuffling bright ragged leaves under their feet, turning their faces up to a generous sky really blue and spotless. At the first corner they waited for a funeral to pass, the mourners seated straight and firm as if proud in their sorrow.

"I imagine I'm late," said Miranda, "as usual. What time is it?"

"Nearly half past one," he said, slipping back his sleeve with an exaggerated thrust of his arm upward. The young soldiers were still self-conscious about their wrist watches. Such of them as Miranda knew were boys from southern and southwestern towns, far off the Atlantic seaboard, and they had always believed that only sissies wore wrist watches. "I'll slap you on the wrist watch," one vaudeville comedian would simper to another, and it was always a good joke, never stale.

"I think it's a most sensible way to carry a watch," said Miranda. "You needn't blush."

"I'm nearly used to it," said Adam, who was from Texas. "We've been told time and again how all the he-manly regular army men wear them. It's the horrors of war," he said; "are we downhearted? I'll say we are."

It was the kind of patter going the rounds. "You look it," said Miranda.

He was tall and heavily muscled in the shoulders, narrow in the waist and flanks, and he was infinitely buttoned, strapped, harnessed into a uniform as tough and unyielding in cut as a straitjacket, though the cloth was fine and supple. He had his uniforms made by the best tailor he could find, he confided to Miranda one day when she told him how squish he was looking in his new soldier suit. "Hard enough to make anything of the outfit, anyhow," he told her. "It's the least I can do for my beloved country, not to go around looking like a tramp." He was twenty-four years old and a Second Lieutenant in an Engineers Corps, on leave because his outfit expected to be sent over shortly. "Came in to make my will," he told Miranda, "and get a supply of toothbrushes and razor blades. By what gorgeous luck do you suppose," he asked her,

"I happened to pick on your rooming house? How did I know you were there?"

Strolling, keeping step, his stout polished well-made boots setting themselves down firmly beside her thin-soled black suede, they put off as long as they could the end of their moment together, and kept up as well as they could their small talk that flew back and forth over little grooves worn in the thin upper surface of the brain, things you could say and hear clink reassuringly at once without disturbing the radiance which played and darted about the simple and lovely miracle of being two persons named Adam and Miranda, twenty-four years old each, alive and on the earth at the same moment: "Are you in the mood for dancing, Miranda?" and "I'm always in the mood for dancing, Adam!" but there were things in the way, the day that ended with dancing was a long way to go.

He really did look, Miranda thought, like a fine healthy apple this morning. One time or another in their talking, he had boasted that he had never had a pain in his life that he could remember. Instead of being horrified at this monster, she approved his monstrous uniqueness. As for herself, she had had too many pains to mention, so she did not mention them. After working for three years on a morning newspaper she had an illusion of maturity and experience; but it was fatigue merely, she decided, from keeping what she had been brought up to believe were unnatural hours, eating casually at dirty little restaurants, drinking bad coffee all night, and smoking too much. When she said something of her way of living to Adam, he studied her face a few seconds as if he had never seen it before, and said in a forthright way, "Why, it hasn't hurt you a bit, I think you're beautiful," and left her dangling there, wondering if he had thought she wished to be praised. She did wish to be praised, but not at that moment. Adam kept unwholesome hours too, or had in the ten days they had known each other, staying awake until one o'clock to take her out for supper; he smoked also continually, though if she did not stop him he was apt to explain to her exactly what smoking did to the lungs. "But," he said, "does it matter so much if you're going to war, anyway?"

"No," said Miranda, "and it matters even less if you're staying at home knitting socks. Give me a cigarette, will you?"

They paused at another corner, under a half-foliaged maple, and hardly glanced at a funeral procession approaching. His eyes were pale tan with orange flecks in them, and his hair was the color of a haystack when you turn the weathered top back to the clear straw beneath. He fished out his cigarette case and snapped his silver lighter at her, snapped it several times in his own face, and they moved on, smoking.

"I can see you knitting socks," he said. "That would be just your speed. You know perfectly well you can't knit."

"I do worse," she said, soberly; "I write pieces advising other young women to knit and roll bandages and do without sugar and help win the war."

"Oh, well," said Adam, with the easy masculine morals in such questions, "that's merely your job, that doesn't count."

"I wonder," said Miranda. "How did you manage to get an extension of leave?"

"They just gave it," said Adam, "for no reason. The men are dying like flies out there, anyway. This funny new disease. Simply knocks you into a cocked hat."

"It seems to be a plague," said Miranda, "something out of the Middle Ages. Did you ever see so many funerals, ever?"

"Never did. Well, let's be strong minded and not have any of it. I've got four days more straight from the blue and not a blade of grass must grow under our feet. What about tonight?"

"Same thing," she told him, "but make it about half past one. I've got a special job beside my usual run of the mill."

"What a job you've got," said Adam, "nothing to do but run from one dizzy amusement to another and then write a piece about it."

"Yes, it's too dizzy for words," said Miranda. They stood while a funeral passed, and this time they watched it in silence. Miranda pulled her cap to an angle and winked in the sunlight, her head swimming slowly "like goldfish," she told Adam, "my head swims. I'm only half awake, I must have some coffee."

They lounged on their elbows over the counter of a drug store. "No more cream for the stay-at-homes," she said, "and only one lump of sugar. I'll have two or none; that's the kind of martyr I'm being. I mean to live on boiled cabbage and wear shoddy from now on and get in good shape for the next round. No war is going to sneak up on me again."

"Oh, there won't be any more wars, don't you read the newspapers?" asked Adam. "We're going to mop 'em up this time, and they're going to stay mopped, and this is going to be all."

"So they told me," said Miranda, tasting her bitter luke-warm brew and making a rueful face. Their smiles approved of each other, they felt they had got the right tone, they were taking the war properly. Above all, thought Miranda, no tooth-gnashing, no hair-tearing, it's noisy and unbecoming and it doesn't get you anywhere.

"Swill," said Adam rudely, pushing back his cup. "Is that all you're having for breakfast?"

"It's more than I want," said Miranda.

"I had buckwheat cakes, with sausage and maple syrup, and two bananas, and two cups of coffee, at eight o'clock, and right now, again, I feel like a famished orphan left in the ashcan. I'm all set," said Adam, "for broiled steak and fried potatoes and—"

"Don't go on with it," said Miranda, "it sounds delirious to me. Do all that after I'm gone." She slipped from the high seat, leaned against it slightly, glanced at her face in her round mirror, rubbed rouge on her lips and decided that she was past praying for.

"There's something terribly wrong," she told Adam. "I feel too rotten. It can't just be the weather, and the war."

"The weather is perfect," said Adam, "and the war is simply too good to be true. But since when? You were all right yesterday."

"I don't know," she said slowly, her voice sounding small and thin. They stopped as always at the open door before the flight of littered steps leading up to the newspaper loft. Miranda listened for a moment to the rattle of typewriters above, the steady rumble of presses below. "I wish we were going to spend the whole afternoon on a park bench," she said, "or drive to the mountains."

"I do too," he said; "let's do that tomorrow."

"Yes, tomorrow, unless something else happens. I'd like to run away," she told him; "let's both."

"Me?" said Adam. "Where I'm going there's no running to speak of. You mostly crawl about on your stomach here and there among the debris. You know, barbed wire and such stuff.

It's going to be the kind of thing that happens once in a life-time." He reflected a moment, and went on, "I don't know a darned thing about it, really, but they make it sound awfully messy. I've heard so much about it I feel as if I had been there and back. It's going to be an anticlimax," he said, "like seeing the pictures of a place so often you can't see it at all when you actually get there. Seems to me I've been in the army all my life."

Six months, he meant. Eternity. He looked so clear and fresh, and he had never had a pain in his life. She had seen them when they had been there and back and they never looked like this again. "Already the returned hero," she said, "and don't I wish you were."

"When I learned the use of the bayonet in my first training camp," said Adam, "I gouged the vitals out of more sandbags and sacks of hay than I could keep track of. They kept bawling at us, 'Get him, get that Boche, stick him before he sticks you' —and we'd go for those sandbags like wildfire, and honestly, sometimes I felt a perfect fool for getting so worked up when I saw the sand trickling out. I used to wake up in the night sometimes feeling silly about it."

"I can imagine," said Miranda. "It's perfect nonsense." They lingered, unwilling to say good-by. After a little pause, Adam, as if keeping up the conversation, asked, "Do you know what the average life expectation of a sapping party is after it hits the job?"

"Something speedy, I suppose."

"Just nine minutes," said Adam; "I read that in your own newspaper not a week ago."

"Make it ten and I'll come along," said Miranda.

"Not another second," said Adam, "exactly nine minutes, take it or leave it."

"Stop bragging," said Miranda. "Who figured that out?"

"A noncombatant," said Adam, "a fellow with rickets."

This seemed very comic, they laughed and leaned towards each other and Miranda heard herself being a little shrill. She wiped the tears from her eyes. "My, it's a funny war," she said; "isn't it? I laugh every time I think about it."

Adam took her hand in both of his and pulled a little at the tips of her gloves and sniffed them. "What nice perfume you have," he said, "and such a lot of it, too. I like a lot of perfume on gloves and hair," he said, sniffing again.

"I've got probably too much," she said. "I can't smell or see or hear today. I must have a fearful cold."

"Don't catch cold," said Adam; "my leave is nearly up and it will be the last, the very last." She moved her fingers in her gloves as he pulled at the fingers and turned her hands as if they were something new and curious and of great value, and she turned shy and quiet. She liked him, she liked him, and there was more than this but it was no good even imagining, because he was not for her nor for any woman, being beyond experience already, committed without any knowledge or act of his own to death. She took back her hands. "Good-by," she said finally, "until tonight."

She ran upstairs and looked back from the top. He was still watching her, and raised his hand without smiling. Miranda hardly ever saw anyone look back after he had said good-by. She could not help turning sometimes for one glimpse more of the person she had been talking with, as if that would save too rude and too sudden a snapping of even the lightest bond. But people hurried away, their faces already changed, fixed, in their straining towards their next stopping place, already absorbed in planning their next act or encounter. Adam was waiting as if he expected her to turn, and under his brows fixed in a strained frown, his eyes were very black.

At her desk she sat without taking off jacket or cap, slitting envelopes and pretending to read the letters. Only Chuck Rouncivale, the sports reporter, and Ye Towne Gossyp were sitting on her desk today, and them she liked having there. She sat on theirs when she pleased. Towney and Chuck were talking and they went on with it.

"They say," said Towney, "that it is really caused by germs brought by a German ship to Boston, a camouflaged ship, naturally, it didn't come in under its own colors. Isn't that ridiculous?"

"Maybe it was a submarine," said Chuck, "sneaking in from the bottom of the sea in the dead of night. Now that sounds better."

"Yes, it does," said Towney; "they always slip up somewhere

in these details . . . and they think the germs were sprayed
over the city—it started in Boston, you know—and somebody
reported seeing a strange, thick, greasy-looking cloud float up
out of Boston Harbor and spread slowly all over that end of
town. I think it was an old woman who saw it."

"Should have been," said Chuck.

"I read it in a New York newspaper," said Towney; "so it's
bound to be true."

Chuck and Miranda laughed so loudly at this that Bill stood
up and glared at them. "Towney still reads the newspapers,"
explained Chuck.

"Well, what's funny about that?" asked Bill, sitting down
again and frowning into the clutter before him.

"It was a noncombatant saw that cloud," said Miranda.

"Naturally," said Towney.

"Member of the Lusk Committee, maybe," said Miranda.

"The Angel of Mons," said Chuck, "or a dollar-a-year man."

Miranda wished to stop hearing, and talking, she wished to
think for just five minutes of her own about Adam, really to
think about him, but there was no time. She had seen him first
ten days ago, and since then they had been crossing streets together, darting between trucks and limousines and pushcarts
and farm wagons; he had waited for her in doorways and in
little restaurants that smelled of stale frying fat; they had eaten
and danced to the urgent whine and bray of jazz orchestras,
they had sat in dull theaters because Miranda was there to
write a piece about the play. Once they had gone to the mountains and, leaving the car, had climbed a stony trail, and had
come out on a ledge upon a flat stone, where they sat and
watched the lights change on a valley landscape that was, no
doubt, Miranda said, quite apocryphal—"We need not believe
it, but it is fine poetry," she told him; they had leaned their
shoulders together there, and had sat quite still, watching. On
two Sundays they had gone to the geological museum, and
had pored in shared fascination over bits of meteors, rock for-
mations, fossilized tusks and trees, Indian arrows, grottoes
from the silver and gold lodes. "Think of those old miners
washing out their fortunes in little pans beside the streams,"
said Adam, "and inside the earth there was this—" and he had
told her he liked better those things that took long to make;

he loved airplanes too, all sorts of machinery, things carved out of wood or stone. He knew nothing much about them, but he recognized them when he saw them. He had confessed that he simply could not get through a book, any kind of book except textbooks on engineering; reading bored him to crumbs; he regretted now he hadn't brought his roadster, but he hadn't thought he would need a car; he loved driving, he wouldn't expect her to believe how many hundreds of miles he could get over in a day . . . he had showed her snapshots of himself at the wheel of his roadster; of himself sailing a boat, looking very free and windblown, all angles, hauling on the ropes; he would have joined the air force, but his mother had hysterics every time he mentioned it. She didn't seem to realize that dog fighting in the air was a good deal safer than sapping parties on the ground at night. But he hadn't argued, because of course she did not realize about sapping parties. And here he was, stuck, on a plateau a mile high with no water for a boat and his car at home, otherwise they could really have had a good time. Miranda knew he was trying to tell her what kind of person he was when he had his machinery with him. She felt she knew pretty well what kind of person he was, and would have liked to tell him that if he thought he had left himself at home in a boat or an automobile, he was much mistaken. The telephones were ringing, Bill was shouting at somebody who kept saying, "Well, but listen, well, but listen—" but nobody was going to listen, of course, nobody. Old man Gibbons bellowed in despair, "Jarge, Jarge—"

"Just the same," Towney was saying in her most complacent patriotic voice. "Hut Service is a fine idea, and we should all volunteer even if they don't want us." Towney does well at this, thought Miranda, look at her; remembering the rose-colored sweater and the tight rebellious face in the cloakroom. Towney was now all open-faced glory and goodness, willing to sacrifice herself for her country. "After all," said Towney, "I *can* sing and dance well enough for the Little Theater, and I could write their letters for them, and at a pinch I might drive an ambulance. I have driven a Ford for years."

Miranda joined in: "Well, I can sing and dance too, but who's going to do the bed-making and the scrubbing up? Those huts are hard to keep, and it would be a dirty job and we'd be perfectly miserable; and as I've got a hard dirty job and am perfectly miserable, I'm going to stay at home."

"I think the women should keep out of it," said Chuck Rouncivale. "They just add skirts to the horrors of war." Chuck had bad lungs and fretted a good deal about missing the show. "I could have been there and back with a leg off by now; it would have served the old man right. Then he'd either have to buy his own hooch or sober up."

Miranda had seen Chuck on pay day giving the old man money for hooch. He was a good-humored ingratiating old scoundrel, too, that was the worst of him. He slapped his son on the back and beamed upon him with the bleared eye of paternal affection while he took his last nickel.

"It was Florence Nightingale ruined wars," Chuck went on. "What's the idea of petting soldiers and binding up their wounds and soothing their fevered brows? That's not war. Let 'em perish where they fall. That's what they're there for."

"You can talk," said Towney, with a slantwise glint at him.

"What's the idea?" asked Chuck, flushing and hunching his shoulders. "You know I've got this lung, or maybe half of it anyway by now."

"You're much too sensitive," said Towney. "I didn't mean a thing."

Bill had been raging about, chewing his half-smoked cigar, his hair standing up in a brush, his eyes soft and lambent but wild, like a stag's. He would never, thought Miranda, be more than fourteen years old if he lived for a century, which he would not, at the rate he was going. He behaved exactly like city editors in the moving pictures, even to the chewed cigar. Had he formed his style on the films, or had scenario writers seized once for all on the type Bill in its inarguable purity? Bill was shouting to Chuck: "*And* if he comes back here take him up the alley and saw his head off *by hand!*"

Chuck said, "He'll be back, don't worry." Bill said mildly, already off on another track, "Well, saw him off." Towney went to her own desk, but Chuck sat waiting amiably to be taken to the new vaudeville show. Miranda, with two tickets, always invited one of the reporters to go with her on Monday. Chuck was lavishly hardboiled and professional in his sports writing, but he had told Miranda that he didn't give a damn about sports, really; the job kept him out in the open, and paid him enough to buy the old man's hooch. He preferred shows and didn't see why women always had the job.

"Who does Bill want sawed today?" asked Miranda.

"That hoofer you panned in this morning's," said Chuck. "He was up here bright and early asking for the guy that writes up show business. He said he was going to take the goof who wrote that piece up the alley and bop him in the nose. He said . . ."

"I hope he's gone," said Miranda; "I do hope he had to catch a train."

Chuck stood up and arranged his maroon-colored turtle-necked sweater, glanced down at the peasoup tweed plus fours and the hobnailed tan boots which he hoped would help to disguise the fact that he had a bad lung and didn't care for sports, and said, "He's long gone by now, don't worry. Let's get going; you're late as usual."

Miranda, facing about, almost stepped on the toes of a little drab man in a derby hat. He might have been a pretty fellow once, but now his mouth drooped where he had lost his side teeth, and his sad red-rimmed eyes had given up coquetry. A thin brown wave of hair was combed out with brilliantine and curled against the rim of the derby. He didn't move his feet, but stood planted with a kind of inert resistance, and asked Miranda: "Are you the so-called dramatic critic on this hick newspaper?"

"I'm afraid I am," said Miranda.

"Well," said the little man, "I'm just asking for one minute of your valuable time." His underlip shot out, he began with shaking hands to fish about in his waistcoat pocket. "I just hate to let you get away with it, that's all." He riffled through a collection of shabby newspaper clippings. "Just give these the once-over, will you? And then let me ask you if you think I'm gonna stand for being knocked by a tanktown critic," he said, in a toneless voice; "look here, here's Buffalo, Chicago, Saint Looey, Philadelphia, Frisco, besides New York. Here's the best publications in the business, *Variety*, the *Billboard*, they all broke down and admitted that Danny Dickerson knows his stuff. So you don't think so, hey? That's all I wanta ask you."

"No, I don't," said Miranda, as bluntly as she could, "and I can't stop to talk about it."

The little man leaned nearer, his voice shook as if he had been nervous for a long time. "Look here, what was there you didn't like about me? Tell me that."

Miranda said, "You shouldn't pay any attention at all. What does it matter what I think?"

"I don't care what you think, it ain't that," said the little man, "but these things get round and booking agencies back East don't know how it is out here. We get panned in the sticks and they think it's the same as getting panned in Chicago, see? They don't know the difference. They don't know that the more high class an act is the more the hick critics pan it. But I've been called the best in the business by the best in the business and I wanta know what you think is wrong with me."

Chuck said, "Come on, Miranda, curtain's going up." Miranda handed the little man his clippings, they were mostly ten years old, and tried to edge past him. He stepped before her again and said without much conviction, "If you was a man I'd knock your block off." Chuck got up at that and lounged over, taking his hands out of his pockets, and said, "Now you've done your song and dance you'd better get out. Get the hell out now before I throw you downstairs."

The little man pulled at the top of his tie, a small blue tie with red polka dots, slightly frayed at the knot. He pulled it straight and repeated as if he had rehearsed it, "Come out in the alley." The tears filled his thickened red lids. Chuck said, "Ah, shut up," and followed Miranda, who was running towards the stairs. He overtook her on the sidewalk. "I left him sniveling and shuffling his publicity trying to find the joker," said Chuck, "the poor old heel."

Miranda said, "There's too much of everything in this world just now. I'd like to sit down here on the curb, Chuck, and die, and never again see—I wish I could lose my memory and forget my own name . . . I wish—"

Chuck said, "Tough up, Miranda. This is no time to cave in. Forget that fellow. For every hundred people in show business, there are ninety-nine like him. But you don't manage right, anyway. You bring it on yourself. All you have to do is play up the headliners, and you needn't even mention the also-rans. Try to keep in mind that Rypinsky has got show business cornered in this town; please Rypinsky and you'll please the advertising department, please them and you'll get a raise. Hand-in-glove, my poor dumb child, will you never learn?"

"I seem to keep learning all the wrong things," said Miranda, hopelessly.

"You do for a fact," Chuck told her cheerfully. "You are as good at it as I ever saw. Now do you feel better?"

"This is a rotten show you've invited me to," said Chuck. "Now what are you going to do about it? If I were writing it up, I'd—"

"Do write it up," said Miranda. "You write it up this time. I'm getting ready to leave, anyway, but don't tell anybody yet."

"You mean it? All my life," said Chuck, "I've yearned to be a so-called dramatic critic on a hick newspaper, and this is positively my first chance."

"Better take it," Miranda told him. "It may be your last." She thought, This is the beginning of the end of something. Something terrible is going to happen to me. I shan't need bread and butter where I'm going. I'll will it to Chuck, he has a venerable father to buy hooch for. I hope they let him have it. Oh, Adam, I hope I see you once more before I go under with whatever is the matter with me. "I wish the war were over," she said to Chuck, as if they had been talking about that. "I wish it were over and I wish it had never begun."

Chuck had got out his pad and pencil and was already writing his review. What she had said seemed safe enough but how would he take it? "I don't care how it started or when it ends," said Chuck, scribbling away, "I'm not going to be there."

All the rejected men talked like that, thought Miranda. War was the one thing they wanted, now they couldn't have it. Maybe they had wanted badly to go, some of them. All of them had a sidelong eye for the women they talked with about it, a guarded resentment which said, "Don't pin a white feather on me, you bloodthirsty female. I've offered my meat to the crows and they won't have it." The worst thing about war for the stay-at-homes is there isn't anyone to talk to any more. The Lusk Committee will get you if you don't watch out. Bread will win the war. Work will win, sugar will win, peach pits will win the war. Nonsense. *Not* nonsense, I tell you, there's some kind of valuable high explosive to be got out of peach pits. So all the happy housewives hurry during the canning season to lay their baskets of peach pits on the altar of their country. It keeps them busy and makes them feel useful, and all these women running wild with the men away are dangerous, if they aren't given something to keep their little minds out of mischief. So rows of young girls, the intact cradles of the future, with their pure serious faces framed becomingly in Red Cross wimples, roll cock-eyed bandages that will never reach a base hospital, and knit sweaters that will never warm a manly chest, their minds dwelling lovingly on all the blood and mud and the next dance at the Acanthus Club for the officers of the flying corps. Keeping still and quiet will win the war.

"I'm simply not going to be there," said Chuck, absorbed in his review. No, Adam will be there, thought Miranda. She slipped down in the chair and leaned her head against the dusty plush, closed her eyes and faced for one instant that was a lifetime the certain, the overwhelming and awful knowledge that there was nothing at all ahead for Adam and for her. Nothing. She opened her eyes and held her hands together palms up, gazing at them and trying to understand oblivion.

"Now look at this," said Chuck, for the lights had come on and the audience was rustling and talking again. "I've got it all done, even before the headliner comes on. It's old Stella Mayhew, and she's always good, she's been good for forty years, and she's going to sing 'O the blues ain't nothin' but the easygoing heart disease.' That's all you need to know about her. Now just glance over this. Would you be willing to sign it?"

Miranda took the pages and stared at them conscientiously, turning them over, she hoped, at the right moment, and gave them back. "Yes, Chuck, yes, I'd sign that. But I won't. We must tell Bill you wrote it, because it's your start, maybe."

"You don't half appreciate it," said Chuck. "You read it too fast. Here, listen to this—" and he began to mutter excitedly. While he was reading she watched his face. It was a pleasant face with some kind of spark of life in it, and a good severity in the modeling of the brow above the nose. For the first time since she had known him she wondered what Chuck was thinking about. He looked preoccupied and unhappy, he wasn't so frivolous as he sounded. The people were crowding into the aisle, bringing out their cigarette cases ready to strike a match the instant they reached the lobby; women with waved hair clutched at their wraps, men stretched their chins to ease them of their stiff collars, and Chuck said, "We might as well go now." Miranda, buttoning her jacket, stepped into the moving crowd, thinking, What did I ever know about them? There must be a great many of them here who think as I do, and we dare not say a word to each other of our desperation, we are speechless animals letting ourselves be destroyed, and why? Does anybody here believe the things we say to each other?

Stretched in unease on the ridge of the wicker couch in the cloakroom, Miranda waited for time to pass and leave Adam with her. Time seemed to proceed with more than usual eccentricity, leaving twilight gaps in her mind for thirty minutes which seemed like a second, and then hard flashes of light that shone clearly on her watch proving that three minutes is an intolerable stretch of waiting, as if she were hanging by her thumbs. At last it was reasonable to imagine Adam stepping out of the house in the early darkness into the blue mist that might soon be rain, he would be on the way, and there was nothing to think about him, after all. There was only the wish to see him and the fear, the present threat, of not seeing him again; for every step they took towards each other seemed perilous, drawing them apart instead of together, as a swimmer in spite of his most determined strokes is yet drawn slowly backward by the tide. "I don't want to love," she would think in spite of herself, "not Adam, there is no time and we are not ready for it and yet this is all we have—"

And there he was on the sidewalk, with his foot on the first step, and Miranda almost ran down to meet him. Adam, holding her hands, asked, "Do you feel well now? Are you hungry? Are you tired? Will you feel like dancing after the show?"

"Yes to everything," said Miranda, "yes, yes. . . ." Her head was like a feather, and she steadied herself on his arm. The mist was still mist that might be rain later, and though the air was sharp and clean in her mouth, it did not, she decided, make breathing any easier. "I hope the show is good, or at least funny," she told him, "but I promise nothing."

It was a long, dreary play, but Adam and Miranda sat very quietly together waiting patiently for it to be over. Adam carefully and seriously pulled off her glove and held her hand as if he were accustomed to holding her hand in theaters. Once they turned and their eyes met, but only once, and the two pairs of eyes were equally steady and noncommittal. A deep tremor set up in Miranda, and she set about resisting herself methodically as if she were closing windows and doors and fastening down curtains against a rising storm. Adam sat watching the monotonous play with a strange shining excitement, his face quite fixed and still.

When the curtain rose for the third act, the third act did not take place at once. There was instead disclosed a backdrop almost covered with an American flag improperly and disrespectfully exposed, nailed at each upper corner, gathered in the middle and nailed again, sagging dustily. Before it posed a local dollar-a-year man, now doing his bit as a Liberty Bond salesman. He was an ordinary man past middle life, with a neat little melon buttoned into his trousers and waistcoat, an opinionated tight mouth, a face and figure in which nothing could be read save the inept sensual record of fifty years. But for once in his life he was an important fellow in an impressive situation, and he reveled, rolling his words in an actorish tone.

"Looks like a penguin," said Adam. They moved, smiled at each other, Miranda reclaimed her hand, Adam folded his together and they prepared to wear their way again through the same old moldy speech with the same old dusty backdrop. Miranda tried not to listen, but she heard. These vile Huns— glorious Belleau Wood—our keyword is Sacrifice—Martyred Belgium—give till it hurts—our noble boys Over There—Big Berthas—the death of civilization—the Boche—

"My head aches," whispered Miranda. "Oh, why won't he hush?"

"He won't," whispered Adam. "I'll get you some aspirin."

"In Flanders Field the poppies grow, Between the crosses row on row"—"He's getting into the home stretch," whispered Adam—atrocities, innocent babes hoisted on Boche bayonets

—your child and my child—if our children are spared these
things, then let us say with all reverence that these dead have
not died in vain—the war, the *war*, the WAR to end WAR, war
for Democracy, for humanity, a safe world forever and ever—
and to prove our faith in Democracy to each other, and to the
world, let everybody get together and buy Liberty Bonds and
do without sugar and wool socks—was that it? Miranda asked
herself, Say that over, I didn't catch the last line. Did you mention Adam? If you didn't I'm not interested. What about
Adam, you little pig? And what are we going to sing this time,
"Tipperary" or "There's a Long, Long Trail"? Oh, please do
let the show go on and get over with. I must write a piece
about it before I can go dancing with Adam and we have no
time. Coal, oil, iron, gold, international finance, why don't
you tell us about them, you little liar?

The audience rose and sang, "There's a Long, Long Trail
A-winding," their opened mouths black and faces pallid in the
reflected footlights; some of the faces grimaced and wept and
had shining streaks like snail's tracks on them. Adam and Miranda joined in at the tops of their voices, grinning shamefacedly at each other once or twice.

In the street, they lit their cigarettes and walked slowly as
always. "Just another nasty old man who would like to see the
young ones killed," said Miranda in a low voice; "the tom-cats
try to eat the little tom-kittens, you know. They don't fool you
really, do they, Adam?"

The young people were talking like that about the business
by then. They felt they were seeing pretty clearly through that
game. She went on, "I hate these potbellied baldheads, too fat,
too old, too cowardly, to go to war themselves, they know
they're safe; it's you they are sending instead—"

Adam turned eyes of genuine surprise upon her. "Oh, *that*
one," he said. "Now what could the poor sap do if they did
take him? It's not his fault," he explained "he can't do anything but talk." His pride in his youth, his forbearance and tolerance and contempt for that unlucky being breathed out of
his very pores as he strolled, straight and relaxed in his strength.
"What *could* you expect of him, Miranda?"

She spoke his name often, and he spoke hers rarely. The
little shock of pleasure the sound of her name in his mouth

gave her stopped her answer. For a moment she hesitated, and began at another point of attack. "Adam," she said, "the worst of war is the fear and suspicion and the awful expression in all the eyes you meet . . . as if they had pulled down the shutters over their minds and their hearts and were peering out at you, ready to leap if you make one gesture or say one word they do not understand instantly. It frightens me; I live in fear too, and no one should have to live in fear. It's the skulking about, and the lying. It's what war does to the mind and the heart, Adam, and you can't separate these two—what it does to them is worse than what it can do to the body."

Adam said soberly, after a moment, "Oh, yes, but suppose one comes back whole? The mind and the heart sometimes get another chance, but if anything happens to the poor old human frame, why, it's just out of luck, that's all."

"Oh, yes," mimicked Miranda. "It's just out of luck, that's all."

"If I didn't go," said Adam, in a matter-of-fact voice, "I couldn't look myself in the face."

So that's all settled. With her fingers flattened on his arm, Miranda was silent, thinking about Adam. No, there was no resentment or revolt in him. Pure, she thought, all the way through, flawless, complete, as the sacrificial lamb must be. The sacrificial lamb strode along casually, accommodating his long pace to hers, keeping her on the inside of the walk in the good American style, helping her across street corners as if she were a cripple—"I hope we don't come to a mud puddle, he'll carry me over it"—giving off whiffs of tobacco smoke, a manly smell of scentless soap, freshly cleaned leather and freshly washed skin, breathing through his nose and carrying his chest easily. He threw back his head and smiled into the sky which still misted, promising rain. "Oh, boy," he said, "what a night. Can't you hurry that review of yours so we can get started?"

He waited for her before a cup of coffee in the restaurant next to the pressroom, nicknamed The Greasy Spoon. When she came down at last, freshly washed and combed and powdered, she saw Adam first, sitting near the dingy big window, face turned to the street, but looking down. It was an extraordinary face, smooth and fine and golden in the shabby light, but now set in a blind melancholy, a look of pained suspense and disillusion. For just one split second she got a glimpse of Adam when he would have been older, the face of the man he would not live to be. He saw her then, rose, and the bright glow was there.

Adam pulled their chairs together at their table; they drank hot tea and listened to the orchestra jazzing "Pack Up Your Troubles."

"In an old kit bag, and smoil, smoil, smoil," shouted half a dozen boys under the draft age, gathered around a table near the orchestra. They yelled incoherently, laughed in great hysterical bursts of something that appeared to be merriment, and passed around under the tablecloth flat bottles containing a clear liquid—for in this western city founded and built by roaring drunken miners, no one was allowed to take his alcohol openly—splashed it into their tumblers of ginger ale, and went on singing, "It's a Long Way to Tipperary." When the tune changed to "Madelon," Adam said, "Let's dance." It was a tawdry little place, crowded and hot and full of smoke, but there was nothing better. The music was gay; and life is completely crazy anyway, thought Miranda, so what does it matter? This is what we have, Adam and I, this is all we're going to get, this is the way it is with us. She wanted to say, "Adam, come out of your dream and listen to me. I have pains in my chest and my head and my heart and they're real. I am in pain all over, and you are in such danger as I can't bear to think about, and why can we not save each other?" When her hand tightened on his shoulder his arm tightened about her waist instantly, and stayed there, holding firmly. They said nothing but smiled continually at each other, odd changing smiles as though they had found a new language. Miranda, her face near Adam's shoulder, noticed a dark young pair sitting at a corner table, each with an arm around the waist of the other, their heads together, their eyes staring at the same thing, whatever it was, that hovered in space before them. Her right hand lay on the table, his hand over it, and her face was a blur with weeping. Now and then he raised her hand and kissed it, and set it down and held it, and her eyes would fill again. They were not shameless, they had merely forgotten where they were, or they had no other place to go, perhaps. They said not a word, and the small pantomime repeated itself, like a melancholy short film running monotonously over and over again. Miranda envied them. She envied that girl. At least she can weep if that helps, and he does not even have to ask, What is the matter? Tell me. They had cups of coffee before them, and after a long while—Miranda and Adam had danced and sat down again twice—when the coffee was quite cold, they drank it suddenly, then embraced as before, without a word and scarcely a glance at each other. Something was done and settled between them, at least; it was enviable, enviable, that they could sit quietly together and have the same expression on their faces while they looked into the hell they shared, no matter what kind of hell, it was theirs, they were together.

At the table nearest Adam and Miranda a young woman was leaning on her elbow, telling her young man a story. "And I don't like him because he's too fresh. He kept on asking me to take a drink and I kept telling him, I don't drink and he said, Now look here, I want a drink the worst way and I think it's mean of you not to drink with me, I can't sit up here and drink by myself, he said. I told him, You're not by yourself in the first place; I like that, I said, and if you want a drink go ahead and have it, I told him, why drag *me* in? So he called the waiter and ordered ginger ale and two glasses and I drank straight ginger ale like I always do but he poured a shot of hooch in his. He was awfully proud of that hooch, said he made it himself out of potatoes. Nice homemade likker, warm from the pipe, he told me, three drops of this and your ginger ale will taste like Mumm's Extry. But I said, No, and I mean no, can't you get that through your bean? He took another drink and said, Ah, come on, honey, don't be so stubborn, this'll make your shimmy shake. So I just got tired of the argument, and I said, I don't need to drink, to shake my shimmy, I can strut my stuff on tea, I said. Well, why don't you then, he wanted to know, and I just told him—"

She knew she had been asleep for a long time when all at once without even a warning footstep or creak of the door hinge, Adam was in the room turning on the light, and she knew it was he, though at first she was blinded and turned her head away. He came over at once and sat on the side of the bed and began to talk as if he were going on with something they had been talking about before. He crumpled a square of paper and tossed it in the fireplace.

"You didn't get my note," he said. "I left it under the door. I was called back suddenly to camp for a lot of inoculations. They kept me longer than I expected, I was late. I called the office and they told me you were not coming in today. I called Miss Hobbe here and she said you were in bed and couldn't come to the telephone. Did she give you my message?"

"No," said Miranda drowsily, "but I think I have been asleep all day. Oh, I do remember. There was a doctor here. Bill sent him. I was at the telephone once, for Bill told me he would send an ambulance and have me taken to the hospital. The doctor tapped my chest and left a prescription and said he would be back, but he hasn't come."

"Where is it, the prescription?" asked Adam.

"I don't know. He left it, though, I saw him."

Adam moved about searching the tables and the mantelpiece. "Here it is," he said. "I'll be back in a few minutes. I must look for an all-night drug store. It's after one o'clock. Good-by."

Good-by, good-by. Miranda watched the door where he had disappeared for quite a while, then closed her eyes, and thought, When I am not here I cannot remember anything about this room where I have lived for nearly a year, except that the curtains are too thin and there was never any way of shutting out the morning light. Miss Hobbe had promised heavier curtains, but they had never appeared. When Miranda in her dressing gown had been at the telephone that morning, Miss Hobbe had passed through, carrying a tray. She was a little red-haired nervously friendly creature, and her manner said all too plainly that the place was not paying and she was on the ragged edge.

"My dear *child*," she said sharply, with a glance at Miranda's attire, "what is the matter?"

Miranda, with the receiver to her ear, said, "Influenza, I think."

"*Horrors*," said Miss Hobbe, in a whisper, and the tray wavered in her hands. "Go back to bed at once . . . go at *once!*"

"I must talk to Bill first," Miranda had told her, and Miss

Hobbe had hurried on and had not returned. Bill had shouted directions at her, promising everything, doctor, nurse, ambulance, hospital, her check every week as usual, everything, but she was to get back to bed and stay there. She dropped into bed, thinking that Bill was the only person she had ever seen who actually tore his own hair when he was excited enough . . . I suppose I should ask to be sent home, she thought, it's a respectable old custom to inflict your death on the family if you can manage it. No, I'll stay here, this is my business, but not in this room, I hope . . . I wish I were in the cold mountains in the snow, that's what I should like best; and all about her rose the measured ranges of the Rockies wearing their perpetual snow, their majestic blue laurels of cloud, chilling her to the bone with their sharp breath. Oh, no, I must have warmth —and her memory turned and roved after another place she had known first and loved best, that now she could see only in drifting fragments of palm and cedar, dark shadows and a sky that warmed without dazzling, as this strange sky had dazzled without warming her; there was the long slow wavering of gray moss in the drowsy oak shade, the spacious hovering of buzzards overhead, the smell of crushed water herbs along a bank, and without warning a broad tranquil river into which flowed all the rivers she had known. The walls shelved away in one deliberate silent movement on either side, and a tall sailing ship was moored near by, with a gangplank weathered to blackness touching the foot of her bed. Back of the ship was jungle, and even as it appeared before her, she knew it was all she had ever read or had been told or felt or thought about jungles; a writhing terribly alive and secret place of death, creeping with tangles of spotted serpents, rainbow-colored birds with malign eyes, leopards with humanly wise faces and extravagantly crested lions; screaming long-armed monkeys tumbling among broad fleshy leaves that glowed with sulphur-colored light and exuded the ichor of death, and rotting trunks of unfamiliar trees sprawled in crawling slime. Without surprise, watching from her pillow, she saw herself run swiftly down this gangplank to the slanting deck, and standing there, she leaned on the rail and waved gaily to herself in bed, and the slender ship spread its wings and sailed away into the jungle. The air trembled with the shattering scream and the hoarse bellow of voices all crying together, rolling and colliding above her like ragged storm-clouds, and the words became two words only rising and falling and clamoring about her head. Danger, danger, danger, the voices said, and War, war, war. There was her door half open, Adam standing with his hand on the knob, and Miss Hobbe with her face all out of shape with terror was crying shrilly, "I tell you, they must come for her *now*, or I'll put her on the sidewalk . . . I tell you, this is a plague, a plague, my God, and I've got a houseful of people to think about!"

Adam said, "I know that. They'll come for her tomorrow morning."

"Tomorrow morning, my God, they'd better come now!"

"They can't get an ambulance," said Adam, "and there aren't any beds. And we can't find a doctor or a nurse. They're all busy. That's all there is to it. You stay out of the room, and I'll look after her."

"Yes, you'll look after her, I can see that," said Miss Hobbe, in a particularly unpleasant tone.

"Yes, that's what I said," answered Adam, drily, "and you keep out."

He closed the door carefully. He was carrying an assortment of misshapen packages, and his face was astonishingly impassive.

"Did you hear that?" be asked, leaning over and speaking very quietly.

"Most of it," said Miranda, "it's a nice prospect, isn't it?"

"I've got your medicine," said Adam, "and you're to begin with it this minute. She can't put you out."

"So it's really as bad as that," said Miranda.

"It's as bad as anything can be," said Adam, "all the theaters and nearly all the shops and restaurants are closed, and the streets have been full of funerals all day and ambulances all night—"

"But not one for me," said Miranda, feeling hilarious and lightheaded. She sat up and beat her pillow into shape and reached for her robe. "I'm glad you're here, I've been having a nightmare. Give me a cigarette, will you, and light one for yourself and open all the windows and sit near one of them. You're running a risk," she told him, "don't you know that? Why do you do it?"

"Never mind," said Adam, "take your medicine," and offered her two large cherry-colored pills. She swallowed them promptly and instantly vomited them up. "*Do* excuse me," she said, beginning to laugh. "I'm so sorry." Adam without a word and with a very concerned expression washed her face with a wet towel, gave her some cracked ice from one of the packages, and firmly offered her two more pills. "That's what they always did at home," she explained to him, "and it worked." Crushed with humiliation, she put her hands over her face and laughed again, painfully.

"There are two more kinds yet," said Adam, pulling her hands from her face and lifting her chin. "You've hardly begun. And I've got other things, like orange juice and ice cream—they told me to feed you ice cream—and coffee in a thermos bottle, and a thermometer. You have to work through the whole lot so you'd better take it easy."

"This time last night we were dancing," said Miranda, and drank something from a spoon. Her eyes followed him about the room, as he did things for her with an absent-minded face, like a man alone; now and again he would come back, and slipping his hand under her head, would hold a cup or a tumbler to her mouth, and she drank, and followed him with her eyes again, without a clear notion of what was happening.

"Adam," she said, "I've just thought of something. Maybe they forgot St. Luke's Hospital. Call the sisters there and ask them not to be so selfish with their silly old rooms. Tell them I only want a very small dark ugly one for three days, or less. Do try them, Adam."

He believed, apparently, that she was still more or less in her right mind, for she heard him at the telephone explaining in his deliberate voice. He was back again almost at once, saying, "This seems to be my day for getting mixed up with peevish old maids. The sister said that even if they had a room you couldn't have it without doctor's orders. But they didn't have one, anyway. She was pretty sour about it."

"Well," said Miranda in a thick voice, "I think that's abominably rude and mean, don't you?" She sat up with a wild gesture of both arms, and began to retch again, violently.

"Hold it, as you were," called Adam, fetching the basin. He held her head, washed her face and hands with ice water, put her head straight on the pillow, and went over and looked out of the window. "Well," he said at last, sitting beside her again, "they haven't got a room. They haven't got a bed. They haven't even got a baby crib, the way she talked. So I think that's straight enough, and we may as well dig in."

"Isn't the ambulance coming?"

"Tomorrow, maybe."

He took off his tunic and hung it on the back of a chair. Kneeling before the fireplace, he began carefully to set kindling sticks in the shape of an Indian tepee, with a little paper in the center for them to lean upon. He lighted this and placed other sticks upon them, and larger bits of wood. When they were going nicely he added still heavier wood, and coal a few lumps at a time, until there was a good blaze, and a fire that would not need rekindling. He rose and dusted his hands together, the fire illuminated him from the back and his hair shone.

"Adam," said Miranda, "I think you're very beautiful." He laughed out at this, and shook his head at her. "What a hell of a word," he said, "for me." "It was the first that occurred to me," she said, drawing up on her elbow to catch the warmth of the blaze. "That's a good job, that fire."

He sat on the bed again, dragging up a chair and putting his feet on the rungs. They smiled at each other for the first time since he had come in that night. "How do you feel now?" he asked.

"Better, much better," she told him. "Let's talk. Let's tell each other what we meant to do."

"You tell me first," said Adam. "I want to know about you."

"You'd get the notion I had a very sad life," she said, "and perhaps it was, but I'd be glad enough to have it now. If I could have it back, it would be easy to be happy about almost anything at all. That's not true, but that's the way I feel now." After a pause, she said, "There's nothing to tell, after all, if it ends now, for all this time I was getting ready for something that was going to happen later, when the time came. So now it's nothing much."

"But it must have been worth having until now, wasn't it?" he asked seriously as if it were something important to know.

"Not if this is all," she repeated obstinately.

"Weren't you ever—happy?" asked Adam, and he was plainly

afraid of the word; he was shy of it as he was of the word *love*, he seemed never to have spoken it before, and was uncertain of its sound or meaning.

"I don't know," she said, "I just lived and never thought about it. I remember things I liked, though, and things I hoped for."

"I was going to be an electrical engineer," said Adam. He stopped short. "And I shall finish up when I get back," he added, after a moment.

"Don't you love being alive?" asked Miranda. "Don't you love weather and the colors at different times of the day, and all the sounds and noises like children screaming in the next lot, and automobile horns and little bands playing in the street and the smell of food cooking?"

"I love to swim, too," said Adam.

"So do I," said Miranda; "we never did swim together."

"Do you remember any prayers?" she asked him suddenly. "Did you ever learn anything at Sunday School?"

"Not much," confessed Adam without contrition. "Well, the Lord's Prayer."

"Yes, and there's Hail Mary," she said, "and the really useful one beginning, I confess to Almighty God and to blessed Mary ever virgin and to the holy Apostles Peter and Paul—"

"Catholic," he commented.

"Prayers just the same, you big Methodist. I'll bet you *are* a Methodist."

"No, Presbyterian."

"Well, what others do you remember?"

"Now I lay me down to sleep—" said Adam.

"Yes, that one, and Blessed Jesus meek and mild—you see that my religious education wasn't neglected either. I even know a prayer beginning O Apollo. Want to hear it?"

"No," said Adam, "you're making fun."

"I'm not," said Miranda, "I'm trying to keep from going to sleep. I'm afraid to go to sleep, I may not wake up. Don't let me go to sleep, Adam. Do you know Matthew, Mark, Luke and John? Bless the bed I lie upon?"

"If I should die before I wake, I pray the Lord my soul to take. Is that it?" asked Adam. "It doesn't sound right, somehow."

"Light me a cigarette, please, and move over and sit near the window. We keep forgetting about fresh air. You must have it." He lighted the cigarette and held it to her lips. She took it between her fingers and dropped it under the edge of her pillow. He found it and crushed it out in the saucer under the water tumbler. Her head swam in darkness for an instant, cleared, and she sat up in panic, throwing off the covers and breaking into a sweat. Adam leaped up with an alarmed face, and almost at once was holding a cup of hot coffee to her mouth.

"You must have some too," she told him, quiet again, and they sat huddled together on the edge of the bed, drinking coffee in silence.

Adam said, "You must lie down again. You're awake now."

"Let's sing," said Miranda. "I know an old spiritual, I can remember some of the words." She spoke in a natural voice. "I'm fine now." She began in a hoarse whisper, "'Pale horse, pale rider, done taken my lover away . . .' Do you know that song?"

"Yes," said Adam, "I heard Negroes in Texas sing it, in an oil field."

"I heard them sing it in a cotton field," she said; "it's a good song."

They sang that line together. "But I can't remember what comes next," said Adam. "'Pale horse, pale rider,'" said Miranda, "(We really need a good banjo) 'done taken my lover away—'" Her voice cleared and she said, "But we ought to get on with it. What's the next line?"

"There's a lot more to it than that," said Adam, "about forty verses, the rider done taken away mammy, pappy, brother, sister, the whole family besides the lover—"

"But not the singer, not yet," said Miranda. "Death always leaves one singer to mourn. 'Death,'" she sang, "'oh, leave one singer to mourn—'"

"'Pale horse, pale rider,'" chanted Adam, coming in on the beat, "'done taken my lover away!' (I think we're good, I think we ought to get up an act—)"

"Go in Hut Service," said Miranda, "entertain the poor defenseless heroes Over There."

"We'll play banjos," said Adam; "I always wanted to play the banjo."

Miranda sighed, and lay back on the pillow and thought, I must give up, I can't hold out any longer. There was only that pain, only that room, and only Adam. There were no longer any multiple planes of living, no tough filaments of memory and hope pulling taut backwards and forwards holding her upright between them. There was only this one moment and it was a dream of time, and Adam's face, very near hers, eyes still and intent, was a shadow, and there was to be nothing more. . . .

"Adam," she said out of the heavy soft darkness that drew her down, down, "I love you, and I was hoping you would say that to me, too."

He lay down beside her with his arm under her shoulder, and pressed his smooth face against hers, his mouth moved towards her mouth and stopped. "Can you hear what I am saying? . . . What do you think I have been trying to tell you all this time?"

She turned towards him, the cloud cleared and she saw his face for an instant. He pulled the covers about her and held her, and said, "Go to sleep, darling, darling, if you will go to sleep now for one hour I will wake you up and bring you hot coffee and tomorrow we will find somebody to help. I love you, go to sleep—"

Almost with no warning at all, she floated into the darkness, holding his hand, in sleep that was not sleep but clear evening light in a small green wood, an angry dangerous wood full of inhuman concealed voices singing sharply like the whine of arrows and she saw Adam transfixed by a flight of these singing arrows that struck him in the heart and passed shrilly cutting their path through the leaves. Adam fell straight back before her eyes, and rose again unwounded and alive; another flight of arrows loosed from the invisible bow struck him again and he fell, and yet he was there before her untouched in a perpetual death and resurrection. She herself before him, angrily and selfishly she interposed between him and the track of the arrow, crying, No, no, like a child cheated in a game, It's my turn now, why must you always be the one to die? and the

arrows struck her cleanly through the heart and through his
body and he lay dead, and she still lived, and the wood whis-
tled and sang and shouted, every branch and leaf and blade of
grass had its own terrible accusing voice. She ran then, and
Adam caught her in the middle of the room, running, and
said, "Darling, I must have been asleep too. What happened,
you screamed terribly?"

After he had helped her to settle again, she sat with her
knees drawn up under her chin, resting her head on her folded
arms and began carefully searching for her words because it
was important to explain clearly. "It was a very odd sort of
dream, I don't know why it could have frightened me. There
was something about an old-fashioned valentine. There were
two hearts carved on a tree, pierced by the same arrow—you
know, Adam—"

"Yes, I know, honey," he said in the gentlest sort of way, and
sat kissing her on the cheek and forehead with a kind of accus-
tomedness, as if he had been kissing her for years, "one of
those lace paper things."

"Yes, and yet they were alive, and were us, you understand
—this doesn't seem to be quite the way it was, but it was
something like that. It was in a wood—"

"Yes," said Adam. He got up and put on his tunic and gathered up the thermos bottle. "I'm going back to that little
stand and get us some ice cream and hot coffee," he told her,
"and I'll be back in five minutes, and you keep quiet. Good-by
for five minutes," he said, holding her chin in the palm of his
hand and trying to catch her eye, "and you be very quiet."

"Good-by," she said. "I'm awake again." But she was not,
and the two alert young internes from the County hospital
who had arrived, after frantic urgings from the noisy city editor of the Blue Mountain *News*, to carry her away in a police
ambulance, decided that they had better go down and get the
stretcher. Their voices roused her, she sat up, got out of bed
at once and stood glancing about brightly. "Why, you're all
right," said the darker and stouter of the two young men, both
extremely fit and competent-looking in their white clothes,
each with a flower in his buttonhole. "I'll just carry you." He
unfolded a white blanket and wrapped it around her. She gathered up the folds and asked, "But where is Adam?" taking hold

of the doctor's arm. He laid a hand on her drenched forehead, shook his head, and gave her a shrewd look. "Adam?"

"Yes," Miranda told him, lowering her voice confidentially, "he was here and now he is gone."

"Oh, he'll be back," the interne told her easily, "he's just gone round the block to get cigarettes. Don't worry about Adam. He's the least of your troubles."

"Will he know where to find me?" she asked, still holding back.

"We'll leave him a note," said the interne. "Come now, it's time we got out of here."

He lifted and swung her up to his shoulder. "I feel very badly," she told him; "I don't know why."

"I'll bet you do," said he, stepping out carefully, the other doctor going before them, and feeling for the first step of the stairs. "Put your arms around my neck," he instructed her. "It won't do you any harm and it's a great help to me."

"What's your name?" Miranda asked as the other doctor opened the front door and they stepped out into the frosty sweet air.

"Hildesheim," he said, in the tone of one humoring a child.

"Well, Dr. Hildesheim, aren't we in a pretty mess?"

"We certainly are," said Dr. Hildesheim.

The second young interne, still quite fresh and dapper in his white coat, though his carnation was withering at the edges, was leaning over listening to her breathing through a stethoscope, whistling thinly, "There's a Long, Long Trail—" From time to time he tapped her ribs smartly with two fingers, whistling. Miranda observed him for a few moments until she fixed his bright busy hazel eye not four inches from hers. "I'm not unconscious," she explained, "I know what I want to say." Then to her horror she heard herself babbling nonsense, knowing it was nonsense though she could not hear what she was saying. The flicker of attention in the eye near her vanished, the second interne went on tapping and listening, hissing softly under his breath.

"I wish you'd stop whistling," she said clearly. The sound stopped. "It's a beastly tune," she added. Anything, anything at all to keep her small hold on the life of human beings, a clear line of communication, no matter what, between her and the receding world. "Please let me see Dr. Hildesheim," she said, "I have something important to say to him. I must say it now." The second interne vanished. He did not walk away, he fled into the air without a sound, and Dr. Hildesheim's face appeared in his stead.

"Dr. Hildesheim, I want to ask you about Adam."

"That young man? He's been here, and left you a note, and has gone again," said Dr. Hildesheim, "and he'll be back to-morrow and the day after." His tone was altogether too merry and flippant.

"I don't believe you," said Miranda, bitterly, closing her lips and eyes and hoping she might not weep.

"Miss Tanner," called the doctor, "have you got that note?"

Miss Tanner appeared beside her, handed her an unsealed envelope, took it back, unfolded the note and gave it to her.

"I can't see it," said Miranda, after a pained search of the page full of hasty scratches in black ink.

"Here, I'll read it," said Miss Tanner. "It says, 'They came and took you while I was away and now they will not let me see you. Maybe tomorrow they will, with my love, Adam,'" read Miss Tanner in a firm dry voice, pronouncing the words distinctly. "Now, do you see?" she asked soothingly.

Miranda, hearing the words one by one, forgot them one by one. "Oh, read it again, what does it say?" she called out over the silence that pressed upon her, reaching towards the dancing words that just escaped as she almost touched them. "That will do," said Dr. Hildesheim, calmly authoritarian. "Where is that bed?"

"There is no bed yet," said Miss Tanner, as if she said, We are short of oranges. Dr. Hildesheim said, "Well, we'll manage something," and Miss Tanner drew the narrow trestle with bright crossed metal supports and small rubbery wheels into a deep jut of the corridor, out of the way of the swift white figures darting about, whirling and skimming like water flies all in silence. The white walls rose sheer as cliffs, a dozen frosted moons followed each other in perfect self-possession down a white lane and dropped mutely one by one into a snowy abyss.

What is this whiteness and silence but the absence of pain?

Miranda lay lifting the nap of her white blanket softly between eased fingers, watching a dance of tall deliberate shadows moving behind a wide screen of sheets spread upon a frame. It was there, near her, on her side of the wall where she could see it clearly and enjoy it, and it was so beautiful she had no curiosity as to its meaning. Two dark figures nodded, bent, curtsied to each other, retreated and bowed again, lifted long arms and spread great hands against the white shadow of the screen; then with a single round movement, the sheets were folded back, disclosing two speechless men in white, standing, and another speechless man in white, lying on the bare springs of a white iron bed. The man on the springs was swathed smoothly from head to foot in white, with folded bands across the face, and a large stiff bow like merry rabbit ears dangled at the crown of his head.

The two living men lifted a mattress standing hunched against the wall, spread it tenderly and exactly over the dead man. Wordless and white they vanished down the corridor, pushing the wheeled bed before them. It had been an entrancing and leisurely spectacle but now it was over. A pallid white fog rose in their wake insinuatingly and floated before Miranda's eyes, a fog in which was concealed all terror and all weariness, all the wrung faces and twisted backs and broken feet of abused, outraged living things, all the shapes of their confused pain and their estranged hearts; the fog might part at any moment and loose the horde of human torments. She put up her hands and said, Not yet, not yet, but it was too late. The fog parted and two executioners, white clad, moved towards her pushing between them with marvelously deft and practiced hands the misshapen figure of an old man in filthy rags whose scanty beard waggled under his opened mouth as he bowed his back and braced his feet to resist and delay the fate they had prepared for him. In a high weeping voice he was trying to explain to them that the crime of which he was accused did not merit the punishment he was about to receive; and except for this whining cry there was silence as they advanced. The soiled cracked bowls of the old man's hands were held before him beseechingly as a beggar's as he said, "Before God I am not guilty," but they held his arms and drew him onward, passed, and were gone.

The road to death is a long march beset with all evils, and the heart fails little by little at each new terror, the bones rebel at each step, the mind sets up its own bitter resistance and to what end? The barriers sink one by one, and no covering of the eyes shuts out the landscape of disaster, nor the sight of crimes committed there. Across the field came Dr. Hildesheim, his face a skull beneath his German helmet, carrying a naked infant writhing on the point of his bayonet, and a huge stone pot marked Poison in Gothic letters. He stopped before the well that Miranda remembered in a pasture on her father's farm, a well once dry but now bubbling with living water, and into its pure depths he threw the child and the poison, and the violated water sank back soundlessly into the earth. Miranda, screaming, ran with her arms above her head; her voice echoed and came back to her like a wolf's howl, Hildesheim is a Boche, a spy, a Hun, kill him, kill him before he kills you. . . . She woke howling, she heard the foul words accusing Dr. Hildesheim tumbling from her mouth; opened her eyes and knew she was in a bed in a small white room, with Dr. Hildesheim sitting beside her, two firm fingers on her pulse. His hair was brushed sleekly and his buttonhole flower was fresh. Stars gleamed through the window, and Dr. Hildesheim seemed to be gazing at them with no particular expression, his stethoscope dangling around his neck. Miss Tanner stood at the foot of the bed writing something on a chart.

"Hello," said Dr. Hildesheim, "at least you take it out in shouting. You don't try to get out of bed and go running around." Miranda held her eyes open with a terrible effort, saw his rather heavy, patient face clearly even as her mind tottered and slithered again, broke from its foundation and spun like a cast wheel in a ditch. "I didn't mean it, I never believed it, Dr. Hildesheim, you musn't remember it—" and was gone again, not being able to wait for an answer.

The wrong she had done followed her and haunted her dream: this wrong took vague shapes of horror she could not recognize or name, though her heart cringed at sight of them. Her mind, split in two, acknowledged and denied what she saw in the one instant, for across an abyss of complaining darkness her reasoning coherent self watched the strange frenzy of the other coldly, reluctant to admit the truth of its visions, its tenacious remorses and despairs.

"I know those are your hands," she told Miss Tanner, "I know it, but to me they are white tarantulas, don't touch me."

"Shut your eyes," said Miss Tanner.

"Oh, no," said Miranda, "for then I see worse things," but her eyes closed in spite of her will, and the midnight of her internal torment closed about her.

Oblivion, thought Miranda, her mind feeling among her memories of words she had been taught to describe the unseen, the unknowable, is a whirlpool of gray water turning upon itself for all eternity . . . eternity is perhaps more than the distance to the farthest star. She lay on a narrow ledge over a pit that she knew to be bottomless, though she could not comprehend it; the ledge was her childhood dream of danger, and she strained back against a reassuring wall of granite at her shoulders, staring into the pit, thinking, There it is, there it is at last, it is very simple; and soft carefully shaped words like oblivion and eternity are curtains hung before nothing at all. I shall not know when it happens, I shall not feel or remember, why can't I consent now, I am lost, there is no hope for me. Look, she told herself, there it is, that is death and there is nothing to fear. But she could not consent, still shrinking stiffly against the granite wall that was her childhood dream of safety, breathing slowly for fear of squandering breath, saying desperately, Look, don't be afraid, it is nothing, it is only eternity.

Granite walls, whirlpools, stars are things. None of them is death, nor the image of it. Death is death, said Miranda, and for the dead it has no attributes. Silenced she sank easily through deeps under deeps of darkness until she lay like a stone at the farthest bottom of life, knowing herself to be blind, deaf, speechless, no longer aware of the members of her own body, entirely withdrawn from all human concerns, yet alive with a peculiar lucidity and coherence; all notions of the mind, the reasonable inquiries of doubt, all ties of blood and the desires of the heart, dissolved and fell away from her, and there remained of her only a minute fiercely burning particle of being that knew itself alone, that relied upon nothing beyond itself for its strength; not susceptible to any appeal or

inducement, being itself composed entirely of one single motive, the stubborn will to live. This fiery motionless particle set
itself unaided to resist destruction, to survive and to be in its
own madness of being, motiveless and planless beyond that
one essential end. Trust me, the hard unwinking angry point
of light said. Trust me. I stay.

At once it grew, flattened, thinned to a fine radiance, spread
like a great fan and curved out into a rainbow through which
Miranda, enchanted, altogether believing, looked upon a deep
clear landscape of sea and sand, of soft meadow and sky, freshly
washed and glistening with transparencies of blue. Why, of
course, of course, said Miranda, without surprise but with
serene rapture as if some promise made to her had been kept
long after she had ceased to hope for it. She rose from her narrow ledge and ran lightly through the tall portals of the great
bow that arched in its splendor over the burning blue of the
sea and the cool green of the meadow on either hand.

The small waves rolled in and over unhurriedly, lapped upon
the sand in silence and retreated; the grasses flurried before a
breeze that made no sound. Moving towards her leisurely as
clouds through the shimmering air came a great company of
human beings, and Miranda saw in an amazement of joy that
they were all the living she had known. Their faces were trans-
figured, each in its own beauty, beyond what she remembered
of them, their eyes were clear and untroubled as good weather,
and they cast no shadows. They were pure identities and she
knew them every one without calling their names or remembering what relation she bore to them. They surrounded her
smoothly on silent feet, then turned their entranced faces again
towards the sea, and she moved among them easily as a wave
among waves. The drifting circle widened, separated, and each
figure was alone but not solitary; Miranda, alone too, questioning nothing, desiring nothing, in the quietude of her ecstasy, stayed where she was, eyes fixed on the overwhelming
deep sky where it was always morning.

Lying at ease, arms under her head, in the prodigal warmth
which flowed evenly from sea and sky and meadow, within
touch but not touching the serenely smiling familiar beings
about her, Miranda felt without warning a vague tremor of apprehension, some small flick of distrust in her joy; a thin frost

touched the edges of this confident tranquillity; something, somebody, was missing, she had lost something, she had left something valuable in another country, oh, what could it be? There are no trees, no trees here, she said in fright, I have left something unfinished. A thought struggled at the back of her mind, came clearly as a voice in her ear. Where are the dead? We have forgotten the dead, oh, the dead, where are they? At once as a curtain had fallen, the bright landscape faded, she was alone in a strange stony place of bitter cold, picking her way along a steep path of slippery snow, calling out, Oh, I must go back! But in what direction? Pain returned, a terrible compelling pain running through her veins like heavy fire, the stench of corruption filled her nostrils, the sweetish sickening smell of rotting flesh and pus; she opened her eyes and saw pale light through a coarse white cloth over her face, knew that the smell of death was in her own body, and struggled to lift her hand. The cloth was drawn away; she saw Miss Tanner filling a hypodermic needle in her methodical expert way, and heard Dr. Hildesheim saying, "I think that will do the trick. Try another." Miss Tanner plucked firmly at Miranda's arm near the shoulder, and the unbelievable current of agony ran burning through her veins again. She struggled to cry out, saying, Let me go, let me go; but heard only incoherent sounds of animal suffering. She saw doctor and nurse glance at each other with the glance of initiates at a mystery, nodding in silence, their eyes alive with knowledgeable pride. They looked briefly at their handiwork and hurried away.

Bells screamed all off key, wrangling together as they collided in mid air, horns and whistles mingled shrilly with cries of human distress; sulphur colored light exploded through the black window pane and flashed away in darkness. Miranda waking from a dreamless sleep asked without expecting an answer, "What is happening?" for there was a bustle of voices and footsteps in the corridor, and a sharpness in the air; the far clamor went on, a furious exasperated shrieking like a mob in revolt.

The light came on, and Miss Tanner said in a furry voice, "Hear that? They're celebrating. It's the Armistice. The war is over, my dear." Her hands trembled. She rattled a spoon in a cup, stopped to listen, held the cup out to Miranda. From

the ward for old bedridden women down the hall floated a
ragged chorus of cracked voices singing, "My country, 'tis of
thee . . ."

Sweet land . . . oh, terrible land of this bitter world where
the sound of rejoicing was a clamor of pain, where ragged
tuneless old women, sitting up waiting for their evening bowl
of cocoa, were singing, "Sweet land of Liberty—"

"Oh, say, can you see?" their hopeless voices were asking
next, the hammer strokes of metal tongues drowning them
out. "The war is over," said Miss Tanner, her underlip held
firmly, her eyes blurred. Miranda said, "Please open the
window, please, I smell death in here."

Now if real daylight such as I remember having seen in this
world would only come again, but it is always twilight or just
before morning, a promise of day that is never kept. What has
become of the sun? That was the longest and loneliest night
and yet it will not end and let the day come. Shall I ever see
light again?

Sitting in a long chair, near a window, it was in itself a
melancholy wonder to see the colorless sunlight slanting on
the snow, under a sky drained of its blue. "Can this be my face?"
Miranda asked her mirror. "Are these my own hands?" she
asked Miss Tanner, holding them up to show the yellow tint
like melted wax glimmering between the closed fingers. The
body is a curious monster, no place to live in, how could anyone feel at home there? Is it possible I can ever accustom myself to this place? she asked herself. The human faces around
her seemed dulled and tired, with no radiance of skin and eyes
as Miranda remembered radiance; the once white walls of her
room were now a soiled gray. Breathing slowly, falling asleep
and waking again, feeling the splash of water on her flesh, taking
food, talking in bare phrases with Dr. Hildesheim and Miss
Tanner, Miranda looked about her with the covertly hostile
eyes of an alien who does not like the country in which he finds
himself, does not understand the language nor wish to learn it,
does not mean to live there and yet is helpless, unable to leave
it at his will.

"It is morning," Miss Tanner would say, with a sigh, for she
had grown old and weary once for all in the past month,

"morning again, my dear," showing Miranda the same monotonous landscape of dulled evergreens and leaden snow. She would rustle about in her starched skirts, her face bravely powdered, her spirit unbreakable as good steel, saying, "Look, my dear, what a heavenly morning, like a crystal," for she had an affection for the salvaged creature before her, the silent ungrateful human being whom she, Cornelia Tanner, a nurse who knew her business, had snatched back from death with her own hands. "Nursing is nine-tenths, just the same," Miss Tanner would tell the other nurses; "keep that in mind." Even the sunshine was Miss Tanner's own prescription for the further recovery of Miranda, this patient the doctors had given up for lost, and who yet sat here, visible proof of Miss Tanner's theory. She said, "Look at the sunshine, now," as she might be saying, "I ordered this for you, my dear, do sit up and take it."

"It's beautiful," Miranda would answer, even turning her head to look, thanking Miss Tanner for her goodness, most of all her goodness about the weather, "beautiful, I always loved it." And I might love it again if I saw it, she thought, but truth was, she could not see it. There was no light, there might never be light again, compared as it must always be with the light she had seen beside the blue sea that lay so tranquilly along the shore of her paradise. That was a child's dream of the heavenly meadow, the vision of repose that comes to a tired body in sleep, she thought, but I have seen it when I did not know it was a dream. Closing her eyes she would rest for a moment remembering that bliss which had repaid all the pain of the journey to reach it; opening them again she saw with a new anguish the dull world to which she was condemned, where the light seemed filmed over with cobwebs, all the bright surfaces corroded, the sharp planes melted and formless, all objects and beings meaningless, ah, dead and withered things that believed themselves alive!

At night, after the long effort of lying in her chair, in her extremity of grief for what she had so briefly won, she folded her painful body together and wept silently, shamelessly, in pity for herself and her lost rapture. There was no escape. Dr. Hildesheim, Miss Tanner, the nurses in the diet kitchen, the chemist, the surgeon, the precise machine of the hospital, the whole humane conviction and custom of society, conspired to pull her inseparable rack of bones and wasted flesh to its feet, to put in order her disordered mind, and to set her once more safely in the road that would lead her again to death.

Chuck Rouncivale and Mary Townsend came to see her, bringing her a bundle of letters they had guarded for her. They brought a basket of delicate small hothouse flowers, lilies of the valley with sweet peas and feathery fern, and above these blooms their faces were merry and haggard.

Mary said, "You *have* had a tussle, haven't you?" and Chuck said, "Well, you made it back, didn't you?" Then after an uneasy pause, they told her that everybody was waiting to see her again at her desk. "They've put me back on sports already, Miranda," said Chuck. For ten minutes Miranda smiled and told them how gay and what a pleasant surprise it was to find herself alive. For it will not do to betray the conspiracy and tamper with the courage of the living; there is nothing better than to be alive, everyone has agreed on that; it is past argument, and who attempts to deny it is justly outlawed. "I'll be back in no time at all," she said; "this is almost over."

Her letters lay in a heap in her lap and beside her chair. Now and then she turned one over to read the inscription, recognized this handwriting or that, examined the blotted stamps and the postmarks, and let them drop again. For two or three days they lay upon the table beside her, and she continued to shrink from them. "They will all be telling me again how good it is to be alive, they will say again they love me, they are glad I am living too, and what can I answer to that?" and her hardened, indifferent heart shuddered in despair at itself, because before it had been tender and capable of love.

Dr. Hildesheim said, "What, all these letters not opened yet?" and Miss Tanner said, "Read your letters, my dear, I'll open them for you." Standing beside the bed, she slit them cleanly with a paper knife. Miranda, cornered, picked and chose until she found a thin one in an unfamiliar handwriting. "Oh, no, now," said Miss Tanner, "take them as they come. Here, I'll hand them to you." She sat down, prepared to be helpful to the end.

What a victory, what triumph, what happiness to be alive, sang the letters in a chorus. The names were signed with flour-

ishes like the circles in air of bugle notes, and they were the
names of those she had loved best; some of those she had
known well and pleasantly; and a few who meant nothing to
her, then or now. The thin letter in the unfamiliar handwriting
was from a strange man at the camp where Adam had been,
telling her that Adam had died of influenza in the camp hospital. Adam had asked him, in case anything happened, to be
sure to let her know.

If anything happened. To be sure to let her know. If anything happened. "Your friend, Adam Barclay," wrote the
strange man. It had happened—she looked at the date—more
than a month ago.

"I've been here a long time, haven't I?" she asked Miss Tanner, who was folding letters and putting them back in their
proper envelopes.

"Oh, quite a while," said Miss Tanner, "but you'll be ready
to go soon now. But you must be careful of yourself and not
overdo, and you should come back now and then and let us
look at you, because sometimes the aftereffects are very—"

Miranda, sitting up before the mirror, wrote carefully: "One
lipstick, medium, one ounce flask Bois d'Hiver perfume, one
pair of gray suède gauntlets without straps, two pairs gray
sheer stockings without clocks—"

Towney, reading after her, said, "Everything without something so that it will be almost impossible to get?"

"Try it, though," said Miranda, "they're nicer without. One
walking stick of silvery wood with a silver knob."

"That's going to be expensive," warned Towney. "Walking
is hardly worth it."

"You're right," said Miranda, and wrote in the margin, "a
nice one to match my other things. Ask Chuck to look for this,
Mary. Good looking and not too heavy." Lazarus, come forth.
Not unless you bring me my top hat and stick. Stay where you
are then, you snob. Not at all. I'm coming forth. "A jar of cold
cream," wrote Miranda, "a box of apricot powder—and,
Mary, I don't need eye shadow, do I?" She glanced at her face
in the mirror and away again. "Still, no one need pity this corpse
if we look properly to the art of the thing."

Mary Townsend said, "You won't recognize yourself in a
week."

"Do you suppose, Mary," asked Miranda, "I could have my old room back again?"

"That should be easy," said Mary. "We stored away all your things there with Miss Hobbe." Miranda wondered again at the time and trouble the living took to be helpful to the dead. But not quite dead now, she reassured herself, one foot in either world now; soon I shall cross back and be at home again. The light will seem real and I shall be glad when I hear that someone I know has escaped from death. I shall visit the escaped ones and help them dress and tell them how lucky they are, and how lucky I am still to have them. Mary will be back soon with my gloves and my walking stick, I must go now, I must begin saying good-by to Miss Tanner and Dr. Hildesheim. Adam, she said, now you need not die again, but still I wish you were here; I wish you had come back, what do you think I came back for, Adam, to be deceived like this?

At once he was there beside her, invisible but urgently present, a ghost but more alive than she was, the last intolerable cheat of her heart; for knowing it was false she still clung to the lie, the unpardonable lie of her bitter desire. She said, "I love you," and stood up trembling, trying by the mere act of her will to bring him to sight before her. If I could call you up from the grave I would, she said, if I could see your ghost I would say, I believe . . . "I believe," she said aloud. "Oh, let me see you once more." The room was silent, empty, the shade was gone from it, struck away by the sudden violence of her rising and speaking aloud. She came to herself as if out of sleep. Oh, no, that is not the way, I must never do that, she warned herself. Miss Tanner said, "Your taxicab is waiting, my dear," and there was Mary. Ready to go.

No more war, no more plague, only the dazed silence that follows the ceasing of the heavy guns; noiseless houses with the shades drawn, empty streets, the dead cold light of tomorrow. Now there would be time for everything.

THE LEANING TOWER
AND OTHER STORIES

The Old Order

THE SOURCE

ONCE a year, in early summer, after school was closed and the children were to be sent to the farm, the Grandmother began to long for the country. With an air of tenderness, as if she enquired after a favorite child, she would ask questions about the crops, wonder what kind of gardens the Negroes were making, how the animals were faring. She would remark now and then, "I begin to feel the need of a little change and relaxation, too," in a vague tone of reassurance, as if to say this did not mean that she intended for a moment really to relax her firm hold on family affairs. It was her favorite theory that change of occupation was one way, probably the best way, of resting. The three grandchildren would begin to feel the faint sure stirrings of departure in the house; her son, their father, would assume the air of careful patience which imperfectly masked his annoyance at the coming upsets and inconveniences to be endured at the farm. "Now, Harry, now, Harry!" his mother would warn him, for she was never deceived by his manner; indeed, he never meant her to be; and she would begin trying to placate him by wondering falsely if she could possibly get away, after all, with so much yet to be done where she was. She looked forward with pleasure to a breath of country air. She always imagined herself as walking at leisure in the shade of the orchards watching the peaches ripen; she spoke with longing of clipping the rosebushes, or of tying up the trellised honeysuckle with her own hands. She would pack up her summer-weight black skirts, her thin black-and-white basques, and would get out a broad-brimmed, rather battered straw shepherdess hat she had woven for herself just after the war. Trying it on, turning her head critically this way and that before the mirror, she would decide that it might do nicely for the sun and she always took it along, but never wore it. She wore instead a stiffly starched white chambray bonnet,

with a round crown buttoned on a narrow brim; it sat pertly
on the top of her head with a fly-away look, the long strings
hanging stiffly. Underneath this headdress, her pale, tightly
drawn, very old face looked out with stately calm.

In the early spring, when the Indian cling peach-tree against
the wall of the town house began to bloom, she would say, "I
have planted five orchards in three States, and now I see only
one tree in bloom." A soft, enjoyable melancholy would come
over her; she would stand quite still for a moment looking at the
single tree, representing all her beloved trees still blooming,
flourishing, and preparing to bring forth fruit in their separate
places.

Leaving Aunt Nannie, who had been nurse to her children,
in charge of the town house, she set out on her journey.

If departure was a delightful adventure for the children, arriving
at the farm was an event for Grandmother. Hinry came running
to open the gate, his coal-black face burst into a grin, his voice
flying before him: "Howdy-do, Miss Sophia Jane!", simply not
noticing that the carry-all was spilling over with other members
of the family. The horses jogged in, their bellies jolting and
churning, and Grandmother, calling out greetings in her feast-
day voice, alighted, surrounded by her people, with the same
flurry of travel that marked her journeys by train; but now with
an indefinable sense of homecoming, not to the house but to
the black, rich soft land and the human beings living on it.
Without removing her long veiled widow's bonnet, she would
walk straight through the house, observing instantly that everything was out of order; pass out into the yards and gardens,
silently glancing, making instant plans for changes; down the
narrow path past the barns, with a glance into and around
them as she went, a glance of firm and purposeful censure; and
on past the canebrake to the left, the hayfields to the right,
until she arrived at the row of Negro huts that ran along the
bois d'arc hedge.

Stepping up with a pleasant greeting to all, which in no way
promised exemption from the wrath to come, she went into
their kitchens, glanced into their meal barrels, their ovens, their
cupboard shelves, into every smallest crevice and corner, with
Littie and Dicey and Hinry and Bumper and Keg following,

trying to explain that things was just a little out of shape right
now because they'd had so much outside work they hadn't just
been able to straighten out the way they meant to; but they
were going to get at it right away.

Indeed they were, as Grandmother well knew. Within an
hour someone would have driven away in the buckboard with
an order for such lime for whitewash, so many gallons of kerosene oil, and so much carbolic acid and insect powder. Home-
made lye soap would be produced from the washhouse, and
the frenzy would begin. Every mattress cover was emptied of
its corn husks and boiled, every little Negro on the place was
set to work picking a fresh supply of husks, every hut was
thickly whitewashed, bins and cupboards were scrubbed, every
chair and bedstead was varnished, every filthy quilt was brought
to light, boiled in a great iron washpot and stretched in the
sun; and the uproar had all the special character of any annual
occasion. The Negro women were put at making a fresh supply of shirts for the men and children, cotton dresses and aprons
for themselves. Whoever wished to complain now seized his
opportunity. Mister Harry had clean forgot to buy shoes for
Hinry, look at Hinry: Hinry had been just like that, barefooted
the live-long winter. Mister Miller (a red-whiskered man who
occupied a dubious situation somewhere between overseer
when Mister Harry was absent, and plain hired hand when he
was present) had skimped them last winter on everything you
could think of—not enough cornmeal, not half enough bacon,
not enough wood, not enough of anything. Littie had needed
a little sugar for her cawfy and do you think Mister Miller
would let her have it? No. Mister Miller had said nobody
needed sugar in their cawfy. Hinry said Mister Miller didn't
even take sugar in his own cawfy because he was just too
stingy. Boosker, the three-year-old baby, had earache in January and Miz Carleton had come down and put lodnum in it
and Boosker was acting like she was deef ever since. The black
horse Mister Harry bought last fall had gone clean wild and
jumped a barbed wire fence and tore his chest almost off and
hadn't been any good from that time on.

All these annoyances and dozens like them had to be
soothed at once, then Grandmother's attention was turned to
the main house, which must be overhauled completely. The

big secretaries were opened and shabby old sets of Dickens, Scott, Thackeray, Dr. Johnson's dictionary, the volumes of Pope and Milton and Dante and Shakespeare were dusted off and closed up carefully again. Curtains came down in dingy heaps and went up again stiff and sweet-smelling; rugs were heaved forth in dusty confusion and returned flat and gay with flowers once more; the kitchen was no longer dingy and desolate but a place of heavenly order where it was tempting to linger.

Next the barns and smokehouses and the potato cellar, the gardens and every tree or vine or bush must have that restoring touch upon it. For two weeks this would go on, with the Grandmother a tireless, just and efficient slave driver of every creature on the place. The children ran wild outside, but not as they did when she was not there. The hour came in each day when they were rounded up, captured, washed, dressed properly, made to eat what was set before them without giving battle, put to bed when the time came and no nonsense . . . They loved their Grandmother; she was the only reality to them in a world that seemed otherwise without fixed authority or refuge, since their mother had died so early that only the eldest girl remembered her vaguely: just the same they felt that Grandmother was tyrant, and they wished to be free of her; so they were always pleased when, on a certain day, as a sign that her visit was drawing to an end, she would go out to the pasture and call her old saddle horse, Fiddler.

He had been a fine, thorough-paced horse once, but he was now a weary, disheartened old hero, gray-haired on his jaw and chin, who spent his life nuzzling with pendulous lips for tender bits of grass or accepting sugar cautiously between his shaken teeth. He paid no attention to anyone but the Grandmother. Every summer when she went to his field and called him, he came doddering up with almost a gleam in his filmy eyes. The two old creatures would greet each other fondly. The Grandmother always treated her animal friends as if they were human beings temporarily metamorphosed, but not by this accident dispensed from those duties suitable to their condition. She would have Fiddler brought around under her old sidesaddle—her little granddaughters rode astride and she saw no harm in it, for them—and mount with her foot in Uncle Jimbilly's curved hand. Fiddler would remember his youth and break into a stiff-legged gallop, and off she would go with her crepe bands and her old-fashioned riding skirt flying. They always returned at a walk, the Grandmother sitting straight as a sword, smiling, triumphant. Dismounting at the horse-block by herself, she would stroke Fiddler on the neck before turning him over to Uncle Jimbilly, and walk away carrying her train grandly over her arm.

This yearly gallop with Fiddler was important to her; it proved her strength, her unabated energy. Any time now Fiddler might drop in his tracks, but she would not. She would say, "He's getting stiff in the knees," or "He's pretty short-winded this year," but she herself walked lightly and breathed as easily as ever, or so she chose to believe.

That same afternoon or the next day, she would take her long-promised easy stroll in the orchards with nothing to do, her grandchildren running before her and running back to her side: with nothing at all to do, her hands folded, her skirts trailing and picking up twigs, turning over little stones, sweeping a faint path behind her, her white bonnet askew over one eye, an absorbed fixed smile on her lips, her eyes missing nothing. This walk would usually end with Hinry or Jimbilly being dispatched to the orchards at once to make some trifling but indispensable improvement.

It would then come over her powerfully that she was staying on idling when there was so much to be done at home . . . There would be a last look at everything, instructions, advices, good-bys, blessings. She would set out with that strange look of leaving forever, and arrive at the place in town with the same air of homecoming she had worn on her arrival in the country, in a gentle flurry of greeting and felicitations, as if she had been gone for half a year. At once she set to work restoring to order the place which no doubt had gone somewhat astray in her absence.

THE JOURNEY

In their later years, the Grandmother and old Nannie used to sit together for some hours every day over their sewing. They

shared a passion for cutting scraps of the family finery, hoarded
for fifty years, into strips and triangles, and fitting them together again in a carefully disordered patchwork, outlining
each bit of velvet or satin or taffeta with a running briar stitch
in clear lemon-colored silk floss. They had contrived enough
bed and couch covers, table spreads, dressing table scarfs, to
have furnished forth several households. Each piece as it was
finished was lined with yellow silk, folded, and laid away in a
chest, never again to see the light of day. The Grandmother
was the great-granddaughter of Kentucky's most famous pioneer: he had, while he was surveying Kentucky, hewed out
rather competently a rolling pin for his wife. This rolling pin
was the Grandmother's irreplaceable treasure. She covered it
with an extraordinarily complicated bit of patchwork, added
golden tassels to the handles, and hung it in a conspicuous
place in her room. She was the daughter of a notably heroic
captain in the War of 1812. She had his razors in a shagreen case
and a particularly severe-looking daguerreotype taken in his
old age, with his chin in a tall stock and his black satin waistcoat smoothed over a still-handsome military chest. So she
fitted a patchwork case over the shagreen and made a sort of
envelope of cut velvet and violet satin, held together with briar
stitching, to contain the portrait. The rest of her handiwork
she put away, to the relief of her grandchildren, who had arrived at the awkward age when Grandmother's quaint old-
fashioned ways caused them acute discomfort.

In the summer the women sat under the mingled trees of
the side garden, which commanded a view of the east wing,
the front and back porches, a good part of the front garden
and a corner of the small fig grove. Their choice of this loca-
tion was a part of their domestic strategy. Very little escaped
them: a glance now and then would serve to keep them fairly
well informed as to what was going on in the whole place. It is
true they had not seen Miranda the day she pulled up the
whole mint bed to give to a pleasant strange young woman
who stopped and asked her for a sprig of fresh mint. They had
never found out who stole the giant pomegranates growing
too near the fence: they had not been in time to stop Paul
from setting himself on fire while experimenting with a miniature blowtorch, but they had been on the scene to extinguish

him with rugs, to pour oil on him, and lecture him. They never saw Maria climbing trees, a mania she had to indulge or pine away, for she chose tall ones on the opposite side of the house. But such casualties were so minor a part of the perpetual round of events that they did not feel defeated nor that their strategy was a failure. Summer, in many ways so desirable a season, had its drawbacks. The children were everywhere at once and the Negroes loved lying under the hackberry grove back of the barns playing seven-up, and eating watermelons. The summer house was in a small town a few miles from the farm, a compromise between the rigorously ordered house in the city and the sprawling old farmhouse which Grandmother had built with such pride and pains. It had, she often said, none of the advantages of either country or city, and all the discomforts of both. But the children loved it.

During the winters in the city, they sat in Grandmother's room, a large squarish place with a small coal grate. All the sounds of life in the household seemed to converge there, echo, retreat, and return. Grandmother and Aunt Nannie knew the whole complicated code of sounds, could interpret and comment on them by an exchange of glances, a lifted eyebrow, or a tiny pause in their talk.

They talked about the past, really—always about the past. Even the future seemed like something gone and done with when they spoke of it. It did not seem an extension of their past, but a repetition of it. They would agree that nothing remained of life as they had known it, the world was changing swiftly, but by the mysterious logic of hope they insisted that each change was probably the last; or if not, a series of changes might bring them, blessedly, back full-circle to the old ways they had known. Who knows why they loved their past? It had been bitter for them both, they had questioned the burdensome rule they lived by every day of their lives, but without rebellion and without expecting an answer. This unbroken thread of inquiry in their minds contained no doubt as to the utter rightness and justice of the basic laws of human existence, founded as they were on God's plan; but they wondered perpetually, with only a hint now and then to each other of the uneasiness of their hearts, how so much suffering and confusion could have been built up and maintained on such a foundation.

The Grandmother's rôle was authority, she knew that; it was her duty to portion out activities, to urge or restrain where necessary, to teach morals, manners, and religion, to punish and reward her own household according to a fixed code. Her own doubts and hesitations she concealed, also, she reminded herself, as a matter of duty. Old Nannie had no ideas at all as to her place in the world. It had been assigned to her before birth, and for her daily rule she had all her life obeyed the authority nearest to her.

So they talked about God, about heaven, about planting a new hedge of rose bushes, about the new ways of preserving fruit and vegetables, about eternity and their mutual hope that they might pass it happily together, and often a scrap of silk under their hands would start them on long trains of family reminiscences. They were always amused to notice again how the working of their memories differed in such important ways. Nannie could recall names to perfection; she could always say what the weather had been like on all important occasions, what certain ladies had worn, how handsome certain gentlemen had been, what there had been to eat and drink. Grandmother had masses of dates in her mind, and no memories attached to them: her memories of events seemed detached and floating beyond time. For example, the 26th of August, 1871, had been some sort of red-letter day for her. She had said to herself then that never would she forget that date; and indeed, she remembered it well, but she no longer had the faintest notion what had happened to stamp it on her memory. Nannie was no help in the matter; she had nothing to do with dates. She did not know the year of her birth, and would never have had a birthday to celebrate if Grandmother had not, when she was still Miss Sophia Jane, aged ten, opened a calendar at random, closed her eyes, and marked a date unseen with a pen. So it turned out that Nannie's birthday thereafter fell on June 11, and the year, Miss Sophia Jane decided, should be 1827, her own birth-year, making Nannie just three months younger than her mistress. Sophia Jane then made an entry of Nannie's birth-date in the family Bible, inserting it just below her own. "Nannie Gay," she wrote, in stiff careful letters, "(black)," and though there was some uproar when this was discovered, the ink was long since sunk deeply into the paper, and besides no one was really upset enough to have it scratched out. There it remained, one of their pleasantest points of reference.

They talked about religion, and the slack way the world was going nowadays, the decay of behavior, and about the younger children, whom these topics always brought at once to mind. On these subjects they were firm, critical, and unbewildered. They had received educations which furnished them an assured habit of mind about all the important appearances of life, and especially about the rearing of young. They relied with perfect acquiescence on the dogma that children were conceived in sin and brought forth in iniquity. Childhood was a long state of instruction and probation for adult life, which was in turn a long, severe, undeviating devotion to duty; the largest part of which consisted in bringing up children. The young were difficult, disobedient, and tireless in wrongdoing, apt to turn unkind and undutiful when they grew up, in spite of all one had done for them, or had tried to do: for small painful doubts rose in them now and again when they looked at their completed works. Nannie couldn't abide her new-fangled grandchildren. "Wuthless, shiftless lot, jes plain scum, Miss Sophia Jane; I cain't undahstand it aftah all the raisin' dey had."

The Grandmother defended them, and dispraised her own second generation—heartily, too, for she sincerely found grave faults in them—which Nannie defended in turn. "When they are little, they trample on your feet, and when they grow up they trample on your heart." This was about all there was to say about children in any generation, but the fascination of the theme was endless. They said it thoroughly over and over with thousands of small variations, with always an example among their own friends or family connections to prove it. They had enough material of their own. Grandmother had borne eleven children, Nannie thirteen. They boasted of it. Grandmother would say, "I am the mother of eleven children," in a faintly amazed tone, as if she hardly expected to be believed, or could even quite believe it herself. But she could still point to nine of them. Nannie had lost ten of hers. They were all buried in Kentucky. Nannie never doubted or expected anyone else to doubt she had children. Her boasting was of another order. "Thirteen of 'em," she would say, in an appalled voice, "yas, my Lawd and my Redeemah, thirteen!"

The friendship between the two old women had begun in early childhood, and was based on what seemed even to them almost mythical events. Miss Sophia Jane, a prissy, spoiled five-year-old, with tight black ringlets which were curled every day on a stick, with her stiffly pleated lawn pantalettes and tight bodice, had run to meet her returning father, who had been away buying horses and Negroes. Sitting on his arm, clasping him around the neck, she had watched the wagons filing past on the way to the barns and quarters. On the floor of the first wagon sat two blacks, male and female, holding between them a scrawny, half-naked black child, with a round nubbly head and fixed bright monkey eyes. The baby Negro had a potbelly and her arms were like sticks from wrist to shoulder. She clung with narrow, withered, black leather fingers to her parents, a hand on each.

"I want the little monkey," said Sophia Jane to her father, nuzzling his cheek and pointing. "I want that one to play with."

Behind each wagon came two horses in lead, but in the second wagon there was a small shaggy pony with a thatch of mane over his eyes, a long tail like a brush, a round, hard barrel of a body. He was standing in straw to the knees, braced firmly in a padded stall with a Negro holding his bridle. "Do you see that?" asked her father. "That's for you. High time you learned to ride."

Sophia Jane almost leaped from his arm for joy. She hardly recognized her pony or her monkey the next day, the one clipped and sleek, the other clean in new blue cotton. For a while she could not decide which she loved more, Nannie or Fiddler. But Fiddler did not wear well. She outgrew him in a year, saw him pass without regret to a small brother, though she refused to allow him to be called Fiddler any longer. That name she reserved for a long series of saddle horses. She had named the first in honor of Fiddler Gay, an old Negro who made the music for dances and parties. There was only one Nannie and she outwore Sophia Jane. During all their lives together it was not so much a question of affection between them as a simple matter of being unable to imagine getting on without each other.

Nannie remembered well being on a shallow platform out in front of a great building in a large busy place, the first town she had ever seen. Her father and mother were with her, and there was a thick crowd around them. There were several other small groups of Negroes huddled together with white men bustling them about now and then. She had never seen any of these faces before, and she never saw but one of them again. She remembered it must have been summer, because she was not shivering with cold in her cotton shift. For one thing, her bottom was still burning from a spanking someone (it might have been her mother) had given her just before they got on the platform, to remind her to keep still. Her mother and father were field hands, and had never lived in white folks' houses. A tall gentleman with a long narrow face and very high curved nose, wearing a great-collared blue coat and immensely long light-colored trousers (Nannie could close her eyes and see him again, clearly, as he looked that day) stepped up near them suddenly, while a great hubbub rose. The red-faced man standing on a stump beside them shouted and droned, waving his arms and pointing at Nannie's father and mother. Now and then the tall gentleman raised a finger, without looking at the black people on the platform. Suddenly the shouting died down, the tall gentleman walked over and said to Nannie's father and mother, "Well, Eph! Well, Steeny! Mister Jimmerson comin' to get you in a minute." He poked Nannie in the stomach with a thickly gloved forefinger. "Regular crowbait," he said to the auctioneer. "I should have had lagniappe with this one."

"A pretty worthless article right now, sir, I agree with you," said the auctioneer, "but it'll grow out of it. As for the team, you won't find a better, I swear."

"I've had an eye on 'em for years," said the tall gentleman, and walked away, motioning as he went to a fat man sitting on a wagon tongue, spitting quantities of tobacco juice. The fat man rose and came over to Nannie and her parents.

Nannie had been sold for twenty dollars: a gift, you might say, hardly sold at all. She learned that a really choice slave sometimes cost more than a thousand dollars. She lived to hear slaves brag about how much they had cost. She had not known how little she fetched on the block until her own mother taunted her with it. This was after Nannie had gone to live for good at the big house, and her mother and father were still in the fields. They lived and worked and died there. A good worming had cured Nannie's potbelly, she thrived on plentiful food and a species of kindness not so indulgent, maybe, as that given to the puppies; still it more than fulfilled her notions of good fortune.

The old women often talked about how strangely things come out in this life. The first owner of Nannie and her parents had gone, Sophia Jane's father said, hog-wild about Texas. It was a new Land of Promise, in 1832. He had sold out his farm and four slaves in Kentucky to raise the money to take a great twenty-mile stretch of land in southwest Texas. He had taken his wife and two young children and set out, and there had been no more news of him for many years. When Grandmother arrived in Texas forty years later, she found him a prosperous ranchman and district judge. Much later, her youngest son met his granddaughter, fell in love with her, and married her— all in three months.

The judge, by then eighty-five years old, was uproarious and festive at the wedding. He reeked of corn liquor, swore by God every other breath, and was rearing to talk about the good old times in Kentucky. The Grandmother showed Nannie to him. "Would you recognize her?" "For God Almighty's sake!" bawled the judge, "is that the strip of crowbait I sold to your father for twenty dollars? Twenty dollars seemed like a fortune to me in those days!"

While they were jolting home down the steep rocky road on the long journey from San Marcos to Austin, Nannie finally spoke out about her grievance. "Look lak a jedge might had better raisin'," she said, gloomily, "look lak he didn't keer how much he hurt a body's feelins."

The Grandmother, muffled down in the back seat in the corner of the old carryall, in her worn sealskin pelisse, showing coffee-brown at the edges, her eyes closed, her hands wrung together, had been occupied once more in reconciling herself to losing a son, and, as ever, to a girl and a family of which she could not altogether approve. It was not that there was anything seriously damaging to be said against any of them; only —well, she wondered at her sons' tastes. What had each of them in turn found in the wife he had chosen? The Grandmother had always had in mind the kind of wife each of her sons needed; she had tried to bring about better marriages for them than they had made for themselves. They had merely resented her interference in what they considered strictly their personal affairs. She did not realize that she had spoiled and pampered her youngest son until he was in all probability unfit to be any kind of a husband, much less a good one. And there was something about her new daughter-in-law, a tall, handsome, firm-looking young woman, with a direct way of speaking, walking, talking, that seemed to promise that the spoiled Baby's days of clover were ended. The Grandmother was annoyed deeply at seeing how self-possessed the bride had been, how she had had her way about the wedding arrangements down to the last detail, how she glanced now and then at her new husband with calm, humorous, level eyes, as if she had already got him sized up. She had even suggested at the wedding dinner that her idea of a honeymoon would be to follow the chuck-wagon on the round-up, and help in the cattle-branding on her father's ranch. Of course she may have been joking. But she was altogether too Western, too modern, something like the "new" woman who was beginning to run wild, asking for the vote, leaving her home and going out in the world to earn her own living . . .

The Grandmother's narrow body shuddered to the bone at the thought of women so unsexing themselves; she emerged with a start from the dark reverie of foreboding thoughts which left a bitter taste in her throat. "Never mind, Nannie. The judge just wasn't thinking. He's very fond of his good cheer."

Nannie had slept in a bed and had been playmate and work-fellow with her mistress; they fought on almost equal terms, Sophia Jane defending Nannie fiercely against any discipline but her own. When they were both seventeen years old, Miss Sophia Jane was married off in a very gay wedding. The house was jammed to the roof and everybody present was at least fourth cousin to everybody else. There were forty carriages and more than two hundred horses to look after for two days. When the last wheel disappeared down the lane (a number of the guests lingered on for two weeks), the larders and bins were half empty and the place looked as if a troop of cavalry had been over it. A few days later Nannie was married off to a boy she had known ever since she came to the family, and they were given as a wedding present to Miss Sophia Jane.

Miss Sophia Jane and Nannie had then started their grim and terrible race of procreation, a child every sixteen months or so, with Nannie nursing both, and Sophia Jane, in dreadful discomfort, suppressing her milk with bandages and spirits of wine. When they each had produced their fourth child, Nannie almost died of puerperal fever. Sophia Jane nursed both children. She named the black baby Charlie, and her own child Stephen, and she fed them justly turn about, not favoring the white over the black, as Nannie felt obliged to do. Her husband was shocked, tried to forbid her; her mother came to see her and reasoned with her. They found her very difficult and quite stubborn. She had already begun to develop her implicit character, which was altogether just, humane, proud, and simple. She had many small vanities and weaknesses on the surface: a love of luxury and a tendency to resent criticism. This tendency was based on her feeling of superiority in judgment and sensibility to almost everyone around her. It made her very hard to manage. She had a quiet way of holding her ground which convinced her antagonist that she would really die, not just threaten to, rather than give way. She had learned now that she was badly cheated in giving her children to another woman to feed; she resolved never again to be cheated in just that way. She sat nursing her child and her foster child, with a sensual warm pleasure she had not dreamed of, translating her natural physical relief into something holy, God-sent, amends from heaven for what she had suffered in childbed. Yes, and for what she missed in the marriage bed, for there also something had failed. She said to Nannie quite calmly, "From now on, you will nurse your children and I will nurse mine," and it was so. Charlie remained her special favorite among the Negro children. "I understand now," she said to her older sister Keziah, "why the black mammies love their foster children. I love mine." So Charlie was brought up in the house as playmate for her son Stephen, and exempted from hard work all his life.

Sophia Jane had been wooed at arm's length by a mysteriously attractive young man whom she remembered well as rather a snubby little boy with curls like her own, but shorter, a frilled white blouse and kilts of the Macdonald tartan. He was her second cousin and resembled her so closely they had been mistaken for brother and sister. Their grandparents had been first cousins, and sometimes Sophia Jane saw in him, years after they were married, all the faults she had most abhorred in her elder brother: lack of aim, failure to act at crises, a philosophic detachment from practical affairs, a tendency to set projects on foot and then leave them to perish or to be finished by someone else; and a profound conviction that everyone around him should be happy to wait upon him hand and foot. She had fought these fatal tendencies in her brother, within the bounds of wifely prudence she fought them in her husband, she was long after to fight them again in two of her sons and in several of her grandchildren. She gained no victory in any case, the selfish, careless, unloving creatures lived and ended as they had begun. But the Grandmother developed a character truly portentous under the discipline of trying to change the characters of others. Her husband shared with her the family sharpness of eye. He disliked and feared her deadly willfulness, her certainty that her ways were not only right but beyond criticism, that her feelings were important, even in the lightest matter, and must not be tampered with or treated casually. He had disappeared at the critical moment when they were growing up, had gone to college and then for travel; she forgot him for a long time, and when she saw him again forgot him as he had been once for all. She was gay and sweet and decorous, full of vanity and incredibly exalted daydreams which threatened now and again to cast her over the edge of some mysterious forbidden frenzy. She dreamed recurrently that she had lost her virginity (her virtue, she called it), her sole claim to regard, consideration, even to existence, and after frightful moral suffering which masked altogether her physical experience she would wake in a cold sweat, disordered and terrified. She had heard that her cousin Stephen was a little "wild," but that was to be expected. He was leading, no doubt, a dashing life full of manly indulgences, the sweet dark life of the knowledge of evil which caused her hair to crinkle on her scalp when she thought of it. Ah, the delicious, the free, the wonderful, the mysterious and terrible life of men! She thought about it a great deal. "Little daydreamer," her mother or father would say to her, surprising her in a brown study, eyes moist, lips smiling

vaguely over her embroidery or her book, or with hands fallen
on her lap, her face turned away to a blank wall. She memo-
rized and saved for these moments scraps of high-minded
poetry, which she instantly quoted at them when they offered
her a penny for her thoughts; or she broke into a melancholy
little song of some kind, a song she knew they liked. She
would run to the piano and tinkle the tune out with one hand,
saying, "I love this part best," leaving no doubt in their minds
as to what her own had been occupied with. She lived her whole
youth so, without once giving herself away; not until she was
in middle age, her husband dead, her property dispersed, and
she found herself with a houseful of children, making a new
life for them in another place, with all the responsibilities of a
man but with none of the privileges, did she finally emerge
into something like an honest life: and yet, she was passionately honest. She had never been anything else.

Sitting under the trees with Nannie, both of them old and
their long battle with life almost finished, she said, fingering a
scrap of satin, "It was not fair that Sister Keziah should have
had this ivory brocade for her wedding dress, and I had only
dotted swiss . . ."

"Times was harder when you got married, Missy," said
Nannie. "Dat was de yeah all de crops failed."

"And they failed ever afterward, it seems to me," said
Grandmother.

"Seems to me like," said Nannie, "dotted swiss was all the
style when you got married."

"I never cared for it," said Grandmother.

Nannie, born in slavery, was pleased to think she would not
die in it. She was wounded not so much by her state of being
as by the word describing it. Emancipation was a sweet word
to her. It had not changed her way of living in a single particular, but she was proud of having been able to say to her mistress, "I aim to stay wid you as long as you'll have me." Still,
Emancipation had seemed to set right a wrong that stuck in
her heart like a thorn. She could not understand why God,
Whom she loved, had seen fit to be so hard on a whole race
because they had got a certain kind of skin. She talked it over
with Miss Sophia Jane. Many times. Miss Sophia Jane was

always brisk and opinionated about it: "Nonsense! I tell you, God does not know whether a skin is black or white. He sees only souls. Don't be getting notions, Nannie—of course you're going to Heaven."

Nannie showed the rudiments of logic in a mind altogether untutored. She wondered, simply and without resentment, whether God, Who had been so cruel to black people on earth, might not continue His severity in the next world. Miss Sophia Jane took pleasure in reassuring her; as if she, who had been responsible for Nannie, body and soul in this life, might also be her sponsor before the judgment seat.

Miss Sophia Jane had taken upon herself all the responsibilities of her tangled world, half white, half black, mingling steadily and the confusion growing ever deeper. There were so many young men about the place, always, younger brothers-in-law, first cousins, second cousins, nephews. They came visiting and they stayed, and there was no accounting for them nor any way of controlling their quietly headstrong habits. She learned early to keep silent and give no sign of uneasiness, but whenever a child was born in the Negro quarters, pink, worm-like, she held her breath for three days, she told her eldest granddaughter, years later, to see whether the newly born would turn black after the proper interval . . . It was a strain that told on her, and ended by giving her a deeply grounded contempt for men. She could not help it, she despised men. She despised them and was ruled by them. Her husband threw away her dowry and her property in wild investments in strange territories: Louisiana, Texas; and without protest she watched him play away her substance like a gambler. She felt that she could have managed her affairs profitably. But her natural activities lay elsewhere, it was the business of a man to make all decisions and dispose of all financial matters. Yet when she got the reins in her hands, her sons could persuade her to this and that enterprise or investment; against her will and judgment she accepted their advice, and among them they managed to break up once more the stronghold she had built for the future of her family. They got from her their own start in life, came back for fresh help when they needed it, and were divided against each other. She saw it as her natural duty to provide for her household, after her husband had fought

stubbornly through the War, along with every other man of
military age in the connection; had been wounded, had lingered helpless, and had died of his wound long after the great
fervor and excitement had faded in hopeless defeat, when to
be a man wounded and ruined in the War was merely to have
proved oneself, perhaps, more heroic than wise. Left so, she
drew her family together and set out for Louisiana, where her
husband, with her money, had bought a sugar refinery. There
was going to be a fortune in sugar, he said; not in raising the
raw material, but in manufacturing it. He had schemes in his
head for operating cotton gins, flour mills, refineries. Had he
lived . . . but he did not live, and Sophia Jane had hardly repaired the house she bought and got the orchard planted when
she saw that, in her hands, the sugar refinery was going to be a
failure.

She sold out at a loss, and went on to Texas, where her husband had bought cheaply, some years before, a large tract of
fertile black land in an almost unsettled part of the country.
She had with her nine children, the youngest about two, the
eldest about seventeen years old; Nannie and her three sons,
Uncle Jimbilly, and two other Negroes, all in good health, full
of hope and greatly desiring to live. Her husband's ghost persisted in her, she was bitterly outraged by his death almost as if
he had willfully deserted her. She mourned for him at first with
dry eyes, angrily. Twenty years later, seeing after a long absence the eldest son of her favorite daughter, who had died
early, she recognized the very features and look of the husband
of her youth, and she wept.

During the terrible second year in Texas, two of her younger
sons, Harry and Robert, suddenly ran away. They chose good
weather for it, in mid-May, and they were almost seven miles
from home when a neighboring farmer saw them, wondered
and asked questions, and ended by persuading them into his
gig, and so brought them back.

Miss Sophia Jane went through the dreary ritual of discipline she thought appropriate to the occasion. She whipped
them with her riding whip. Then she made them kneel down
with her while she prayed for them, asking God to help them
mend their ways and not be undutiful to their mother; her
duty performed, she broke down and wept with her arms

around them. They had endured their punishment stoically, because it would have been disgraceful to cry when a woman hit them, and besides, she did not hit very hard; they had knelt with her in a shamefaced gloom, because religious feeling was a female mystery which embarrassed them, but when they saw her tears they burst into loud bellows of repentance. They were only nine and eleven years old. She said in a voice of mourning, so despairing it frightened them: "Why did you run away from me? What do you think I brought you here for?" as if they were grown men who could realize how terrible the situation was. All the answer they could make, as they wept too, was that they had wanted to go back to Louisiana to eat sugar cane. They had been thinking about sugar cane all winter . . . Their mother was stunned. She had built a house large enough to shelter them all, of hand-sawed lumber dragged by ox-cart for forty miles, she had got the fields fenced in and the crops planted, she had, she believed, fed and clothed her children; and now she realized they were hungry. These two had worked like men; she felt their growing bones through their thin flesh, and remembered how mercilessly she had driven them, as she had driven herself, as she had driven the Negroes and the horses, because there was no choice in the matter. They must labor beyond their strength or perish. Sitting there with her arms around them, she felt her heart break in her breast. She had thought it was a silly phrase. It happened to her. It was not that she was incapable of feeling afterward, for in a way she was more emotional, more quick, but griefs never again lasted with her so long as they had before. This day was the beginning of her spoiling her children and being afraid of them. She said to them after a long dazed silence, when they began to grow restless under her arms: "We'll grow fine ribbon cane here. The soil is perfect for it. We'll have all the sugar we want. But we must be patient."

By the time her children began to marry, she was able to give them each a good strip of land and a little money, she was able to help them buy more land in places they preferred by selling her own, tract by tract, and she saw them all begin well, though not all of them ended so. They went about their own affairs, scattering out and seeming to lose all that sense of family unity

so precious to the Grandmother. They bore with her infrequent visits and her advice and her tremendous rightness, and
they were impatient of her tenderness. When Harry's wife died
—she had never approved of Harry's wife, who was delicate
and hopelessly inadequate at housekeeping, and who could
not even bear children successfully, since she died when her
third was born—the Grandmother took the children and began
life again, with almost the same zest, and with more indulgence. She had just got them brought up to the point where
she felt she could begin to work the faults out of them—faults
inherited, she admitted fairly, from both sides of the house—
when she died. It happened quite suddenly one afternoon in
early October, after a day spent in helping the Mexican gardener of her third daughter-in-law to put the garden to rights.
She was on a visit in far western Texas and enjoying it. The
daughter-in-law was exasperated but apparently so docile, the
Grandmother, who looked upon her as a child, did not notice
her little moods at all. The son had long ago learned not to
oppose his mother. She wore him down with patient, just, and
reasonable argument. She was careful never to venture to command him in anything. He consoled his wife by saying that
everything Mother was doing could be changed back after she
was gone. As this change included moving a fifty-foot adobe
wall, the wife was not much consoled. The Grandmother came
into the house quite flushed and exhilarated, saying how well
she felt in the bracing mountain air—and dropped dead over
the doorsill.

THE WITNESS

Uncle Jimbilly was so old and had spent so many years bowed
over things, putting them together and taking them apart,
making them over and making them do, he was bent almost
double. His hands were closed and stiff from gripping objects
tightly, while he worked at them, and they could not open
altogether even if a child took the thick black fingers and tried
to turn them back. He hobbled on a stick; his purplish skull
showed through patches in his wool, which had turned greenish gray and looked as if the moths had got at it.

He mended harness and put half soles on the other Negroes' shoes, he built fences and chicken coops and barn doors; he stretched wires and put in new window panes and fixed sagging hinges and patched up roofs; he repaired carriage tops and cranky plows. Also he had a gift for carving miniature tombstones out of blocks of wood; give him almost any kind of piece of wood and he could turn out a tombstone, shaped very like the real ones, with carving, and a name and date on it if they were needed. They were often needed, for some small beast or bird was always dying and having to be buried with proper ceremonies: the cart draped as a hearse, a shoe-box coffin with a pall over it, a profuse floral outlay, and, of course, a tombstone. As he worked, turning the long blade of his bowie knife deftly in circles to cut a flower, whittling and smoothing the back and sides, stopping now and then to hold it at arm's length and examine it with one eye closed, Uncle Jimbilly would talk in a low, broken, abstracted murmur, as if to himself; but he was really saying something he meant one to hear. Sometimes it would be an incomprehensible ghost story; listen ever so carefully, at the end it was impossible to decide whether Uncle Jimbilly himself had seen the ghost, whether it was a real ghost at all, or only another man dressed like one; and he dwelt much on the horrors of slave times.

"Dey used to take 'em out and tie 'em down and whup 'em," he muttered, "wid gret big leather strops inch thick long as yo' ahm, wid round holes bored in 'em so's evey time dey hit 'em de hide and de meat done come off dey bones in little round chunks. And wen dey had whupped 'em wid de strop till dey backs was all raw and bloody, dey spread dry cawnshucks on dey backs and set 'em afire and pahched 'em, and den dey poured vinega all ovah 'em . . . Yassuh. And den, the ve'y nex day dey'd got to git back to work in the fiels or dey'd do the same thing right ovah agin. Yassah. Dat was it. If dey didn't git back to work dey got it all right ovah agin."

The children—three of them: a serious, prissy older girl of ten, a thoughtful sad looking boy of eight, and a quick flighty little girl of six—sat disposed around Uncle Jimbilly and listened with faint tinglings of embarrassment. They knew, of course, that once upon a time Negroes had been slaves; but they had all been freed long ago and were now only servants.

It was hard to realize that Uncle Jimbilly had been born in slavery, as the Negroes were always saying. The children thought that Uncle Jimbilly had got over his slavery very well. Since they had known him, he had never done a single thing that anyone told him to do. He did his work just as he pleased and when he pleased. If you wanted a tombstone, you had to be very careful about the way you asked for it. Nothing could have been more impersonal and faraway than his tone and manner of talking about slavery, but they wriggled a little and felt guilty. Paul would have changed the subject, but Miranda, the little quick one, wanted to know the worst. "Did they act like that to you, Uncle Jimbilly?" she asked.

"No, *mam*," said Uncle Jimbilly. "Now whut name you want on dis one? Dey nevah did. Dey done 'em dat way in the rice swamps. I always worked right here close to the house or in town with Miss Sophia. Down in the swamps . . ."

"Didn't they ever die, Uncle Jimbilly?" asked Paul.

"Cose dey died," said Uncle Jimbilly, "cose dey died—dey died," he went on, pursing his mouth gloomily, "by de thousands and tens upon thousands."

"Can you carve 'Safe in Heaven' on that, Uncle Jimbilly?" asked Maria in her pleasant, mincing voice.

"To put over a tame jackrabbit, Missy?" asked Uncle Jimbilly indignantly. He was very religious. "A heathen like dat? No, *mam*. In de swamps dey used to stake 'em out all day and all night, and all day and all night and all day wid dey hans and feet tied so dey couldn't scretch and let de muskeeters eat 'em alive. De muskeeters 'ud bite 'em tell dey was all swole up like a balloon all over, and you could heah 'em howlin and prayin all ovah the swamp. Yassuh. Dat was it. And nary a drop of watah noh a moufful of braid . . . Yassuh, dat's it. Lawd, dey done it. Hosanna! Now take dis yere tombstone and don' bother me no more . . . or I'll . . ."

Uncle Jimbilly was apt to be suddenly annoyed and you never knew why. He was easily put out about things, but his threats were always so exorbitant that not even the most credulous child could be terrified by them. He was always going to do something quite horrible to somebody and then he was going to dispose of the remains in a revolting manner. He was going to skin somebody alive and nail the hide on the barn

door, or he was just getting ready to cut off somebody's ears
with a hatchet and pin them on Bongo, the crop-eared brindle
dog. He was often all prepared in his mind to pull somebody's
teeth and make a set of false teeth for Ole Man Ronk . . .
Ole Man Ronk was a tramp who had been living all summer in
the little cabin behind the smokehouse. He got his rations
along with the Negroes and sat all day mumbling his naked
gums. He had skimpy black whiskers which appeared to be set
in wax, and angry red eyelids. He took morphine, it was said;
but what morphine might be, or how he took it, or why, no
one seemed to know . . . Nothing could have been more unpleasant than the notion that one's teeth might be given to
Ole Man Ronk.

The reason why Uncle Jimbilly never did any of these things
he threatened was, he said, because he never could get round
to them. He always had so much other work on hand he never
seemed to get caught up on it. But some day, somebody was
going to get a mighty big surprise, and meanwhile everybody
had better look out.

THE CIRCUS

The long planks set on trestles rose one above the other to a
monstrous height and stretched dizzyingly in a wide oval ring.
They were packed with people—"lak fleas on a dog's ear," said
Dicey, holding Miranda's hand firmly and looking about her
with disapproval. The white billows of enormous canvas
sagged overhead, held up by three poles set evenly apart down
the center. The family, when seated, occupied almost a whole
section on one level.

On one side of them in a long row sat Father, sister Maria,
brother Paul, Grandmother; great-aunt Keziah, cousin Keziah,
and second-cousin Keziah, who had just come down from
Kentucky on a visit; uncle Charles Breaux, cousin Charles
Breaux, and aunt Marie-Anne Breaux. On the other side sat
small-cousin Lucie Breaux, big cousin Paul Gay, great-aunt
Sally Gay (who took snuff and was therefore a disgrace to the
family); two strange, extremely handsome young men who
might be cousins but who were certainly in love with cousin

Miranda Gay; and cousin Miranda Gay herself, a most dashing young lady with crisp silk skirts, a half dozen of them at once, a lovely perfume and wonderful black curly hair above enormous wild gray eyes, "like a colt's," Father said. Miranda hoped to be exactly like her when she grew up. Hanging to Dicey's arm she leaned out and waved to cousin Miranda, who waved back smiling, and the strange young men waved to her also. Miranda was most fearfully excited. It was her first circus; it might also be her last because the whole family had combined to persuade Grandmother to allow her to come with them. "Very well, this once," Grandmother said, "since it's a family reunion."

This once! This once! She could not look hard enough at everything. She even peeped down between the wide crevices of the piled-up plank seats, where she was astonished to see odd-looking, roughly dressed little boys peeping up from the dust below. They were squatted in little heaps, staring up quietly. She looked squarely into the eyes of one, who returned her a look so peculiar she gazed and gazed, trying to understand it. It was a bold grinning stare without any kind of friendliness in it. He was a thin, dirty little boy with a floppy old checkerboard cap pulled over crumpled red ears and dust-colored hair. As she gazed he nudged the little boy next to him, whispered, and the second little boy caught her eye. This was too much. Miranda pulled Dicey's sleeve. "Dicey, what are those little boys doing down there?" "Down where?" asked Dicey, but she seemed to know already, for she bent over and looked through the crevice, drew her knees together and her skirts around her, and said severely: "You jus mind yo' own business and stop throwin' yo' legs around that way. Don't you pay any mind. Plenty o' monkeys right here in the show widout you studyin dat kind."

An enormous brass band seemed to explode right at Miranda's ear. She jumped, quivered, thrilled blindly and almost forgot to breathe as sound and color and smell rushed together and poured through her skin and hair and beat in her head and hands and feet and pit of her stomach. "Oh," she called out in her panic, closing her eyes and seizing Dicey's hand hard. The flaring lights burned through her lids, a roar of laughter like rage drowned out the steady raging of the drums and horns.

She opened her eyes . . . A creature in a blousy white overall
with ruffles at the neck and ankles, with bone-white skull and
chalk-white face, with tufted eyebrows far apart in the middle
of his forehead, the lids in a black sharp angle, a long scarlet
mouth stretching back into sunken cheeks, turned up at the
corners in a perpetual bitter grimace of pain, astonishment,
not smiling, pranced along a wire stretched down the center of
the ring, balancing a long thin pole with little wheels at either
end. Miranda thought at first he was walking on air, or flying,
and this did not surprise her; but when she saw the wire, she
was terrified. High above their heads the inhuman figure
pranced, spinning the little wheels. He paused, slipped, the
flapping white leg waved in space; he staggered, wobbled,
slipped sidewise, plunged, and caught the wire with frantic
knee, hanging there upside down, the other leg waving like a
feeler above his head; slipped once more, caught by one fren-
zied heel, and swung back and forth like a scarf . . . The
crowd roared with savage delight, shrieks of dreadful laughter
like devils in delicious torment . . . Miranda shrieked too,
with real pain, clutching at her stomach with her knees drawn
up . . . The man on the wire, hanging by his foot, turned his
head like a seal from side to side and blew sneering kisses from
his cruel mouth. Then Miranda covered her eyes and screamed,
the tears pouring over her cheeks and chin.

"Take her home," said her father, "get her out of here at
once," but the laughter was not wiped from his face. He merely
glanced at her and back to the ring. "Take her away, Dicey,"
called the Grandmother, from under her half-raised crepe veil.
Dicey, rebelliously, very slowly, without taking her gaze from
the white figure swaying on the wire, rose, seized the limp,
suffering bundle, prodded and lumped her way over knees and
feet, through the crowd, down the levels of the scaffolding,
across a space of sandy tanbark, out through a flap in the tent.
Miranda was crying steadily with an occasional hiccough. A
dwarf was standing in the entrance, wearing a little woolly
beard, a pointed cap, tight red breeches, long shoes with
turned-up toes. He carried a thin white wand. Miranda almost
touched him before she saw him, her distorted face with its
open mouth and glistening tears almost level with his. He
leaned forward and peered at her with kind, not-human golden

eyes, like a near-sighted dog: then made a horrid grimace at her, imitating her own face. Miranda struck at him in sheer ill temper, screaming. Dicey drew her away quickly, but not before Miranda had seen in his face, suddenly, a look of haughty, remote displeasure, a true grown-up look. She knew it well. It chilled her with a new kind of fear: she had not believed he was really human.

"Raincheck, get your raincheck!" said a very disagreeable looking fellow as they passed. Dicey turned toward him almost in tears herself. "Mister, caint you see I won't be able to git back? I got this young un to see to . . . What good dat lil piece of paper goin to do *me*?" All the way home she was cross, and grumbled under her breath: little ole meany . . . little ole scare-cat . . . gret big baby . . . never go nowhere . . . never see nothin . . . come on here now, hurry up—always ruinin everything for othah folks . . . won't let anybody rest a minute, won't let anybody have any good times . . . come on here now, you wanted to go home and you're going there . . . snatching Miranda along, vicious but cautious, careful not to cross the line where Miranda could say outright: "Dicey did this or said this to me . . ." Dicey was allowed a certain freedom up to a point.

The family trooped into the house just before dark and scattered out all over it. From every room came the sound of chatter and laughter. The other children told Miranda what she had missed: wonderful little ponies with plumes and bells on their bridles, ridden by darling little monkeys in velvet jackets and peaked hats . . . trained white goats that danced . . . a baby elephant that crossed his front feet and leaned against his cage and opened his mouth to be fed, *such* a baby! . . . more clowns, funnier than the first one even . . . beautiful ladies with bright yellow hair, wearing white silk tights with red satin sashes had performed on white trapezes; they also had hung by their toes, but how gracefully, like flying birds! Huge white horses had lolloped around and round the ring with men and women dancing on their backs! One man had swung by his teeth from the top of the tent and another had put his head in a lion's mouth. Ah, what she had not missed! Everybody had been enjoying themselves while she was missing her first big circus and spoiling the day for Dicey. Poor Dicey. Poor dear

Dicey. The other children who hadn't thought of Dicey until that moment, mourned over her with sad mouths, their malicious eyes watching Miranda squirm. Dicey had been looking forward for weeks to this day! And then Miranda must get scared—"Can you *imagine* being afraid of that funny old clown?" each one asked the other, and then they smiled pityingly on Miranda . . .

Then too, it had been a very important occasion in another way: it was the first time Grandmother had ever allowed herself to be persuaded to go to the circus. One could not gather, from her rather generalized opinions, whether there had been no circuses when she was young, or there had been and it was not proper to see them. At any rate for her usual sound reasons, Grandmother had never approved of circuses, and though she would not deny she had been amused somewhat, still there had been sights and sounds in this one which she maintained were, to say the least, not particularly edifying to the young. Her son Harry, who came in while the children made an early supper, looked at their illuminated faces, all the brothers and sisters and visiting cousins, and said, "This basket of young doesn't seem to be much damaged." His mother said, "The fruits of their present are in a future so far off, neither of us may live to know whether harm has been done or not. That is the trouble," and she went on ladling out hot milk to pour over their buttered toast. Miranda was sitting silent, her underlip drooping. Her father smiled at her. "You missed it, Baby," he said softly, "and what good did that do you?"

Miranda burst again into tears: had to be taken away at last, and her supper was brought up to her. Dicey was exasperated and silent. Miranda could not eat. She tried, as if she were really remembering them, to think of the beautiful wild beings in white satin and spangles and red sashes who danced and frolicked on the trapezes; of the sweet little furry ponies and the lovely pet monkeys in their comical clothes. She fell asleep, and her invented memories gave way before her real ones, the bitter terrified face of the man in blowsy white falling to his death—ah, the cruel joke!—and the terrible grimace of the unsmiling dwarf. She screamed in her sleep and sat up crying for deliverance from her torments.

Dicey came, her cross, sleepy eyes half-closed, her big dark mouth pouted, thumping the floor with her thick bare feet. "I *swear*," she said, in a violent hoarse whisper. "What the matter with you? You need a good spankin, I *swear!* Wakin everybody up like this . . ."

Miranda was completely subjugated by her fears. She had a way of answering Dicey back. She would say, "Oh, hush up, Dicey." Or she would say, "I don't have to mind *you*. I don't have to mind anybody but my grandmother," which was provokingly true. And she would say, "You don't know what you're talking about." The day just past had changed that. Miranda sincerely did not want anybody, not even Dicey, to be cross with her. Ordinarily she did not care how cross she made the harassed adults around her. Now if Dicey must be cross, she still did not really care, if only Dicey might not turn out the lights and leave her to the fathomless terrors of the darkness where sleep could overtake her once more.

She hugged Dicey with both arms, crying, "Don't, don't leave me. *Don't* be so angry! I c-c-can't b-bear it!"

Dicey lay down beside her with a long moaning sigh, which meant that she was collecting her patience and making up her mind to remember that she was a Christian and must bear her cross. "Now you go to sleep," she said, in her usual warm being-good voice. "Now you jes shut yo eyes and go to sleep. I ain't going to leave you. Dicey ain't mad at nobody . . . *no*body in the whole worl' . . ."

THE LAST LEAF

Old Nannie sat hunched upon herself expecting her own death momentarily. The Grandmother had said to her at parting, with the easy prophecy of the aged, that this might be their last farewell on earth; they embraced and kissed each other on the cheeks, and once more promised to meet each other in heaven. Nannie was prepared to start her journey at once. The children gathered around her: "Aunt Nannie, never you mind! We love you!" She paid no attention; she did not care whether they loved her or not. Years afterward, Maria, the elder girl, thought with a pang, they had not really been so very nice to Aunt Nannie. They went on depending upon her as they always had, letting her assume more burdens and more, allowing her to work harder than she should have. The old woman grew silent, hunched over more deeply—she was thin and tall also, with a nobly modeled Negro face, worn to the bone and a thick fine sooty black, no mixed blood in Nannie—and her spine seemed suddenly to have given way. They could hear her groaning at night on her knees beside her bed, asking God to let her rest.

When a black family moved out of a little cabin across the narrow creek, the first cabin empty for years, Nannie went down to look at it. She came back and asked Mister Harry, "Whut you aim to do wid dat cabin?" Mister Harry said, "Nothing," he supposed; and Nannie asked for it. She wanted a house of her own, she said; in her whole life she never had a place of her very own. Mister Harry said, of course she could have it. But the whole family was surprised, a little wounded. "Lemme go there and pass my last days in peace, chil'ren," she said. They had the place scrubbed and whitewashed, shelves put in and the chimney cleaned, they fixed Nannie up with a good bed and a fairly good carpet and allowed her to take all sorts of odds and ends from the house. It was astonishing to discover that Nannie had always liked and hoped to own certain things, she had seemed so contented and wantless. She moved away, and as the children said afterwards to each other, it was almost funny and certainly very sweet to see how she tried not to be too happy the day she left, but they felt rather put upon, just the same.

Thereafter she sat in the serene idleness of making patchwork and braiding woolen rugs. Her grandchildren and her white family visited her, and all kinds of white persons who had never owned a soul related to Nannie, went to see her, to buy her rugs or leave little presents with her.

She had always worn black wool dresses, or black and white figured calico with starchy white aprons and a white ruffled mobcap, or a black taffety cap for Sundays. She had been finicking precise and neat in her ways, and she still was. But she was no more the faithful old servant Nannie, a freed slave: she was an aged Bantu woman of independent means, sitting on the steps, breathing the free air. She began wearing a blue bandanna wrapped around her head, and at the age of eighty-five she took to smoking a corncob pipe. The black iris of the deep, withdrawn old eyes turned a chocolate brown and seemed to spread over the whole surface of the eyeball. As her sight failed, the eyelids crinkled and drew in, so that her face was like an eyeless mask.

The children, brought up in an out-of-date sentimental way of thinking, had always complacently believed that Nannie was a real member of the family, perfectly happy with them, and this rebuke, so quietly and firmly administered, chastened them somewhat. The lesson sank in as the years went on and Nannie continued to sit on the doorstep of her cabin. They were growing up, times were changing, the old world was sliding from under their feet, they had not yet laid hold of the new one. They missed Nannie every day. As their fortunes went down, and they had very few servants, they needed her terribly. They realized how much the old woman had done for them, simply by seeing how, almost immediately after she went, everything slackened, lost tone, went off edge. Work did not accomplish itself as it once had. They had not learned how to work for themselves, they were all lazy and incapable of sustained effort or planning. They had not been taught and they had not yet educated themselves. Now and then Nannie would come back up the hill for a visit. She worked then almost as she had before, with a kind of satisfaction in proving to them that she had been almost indispensable. They would miss her more than ever when she went away. To show their gratitude, and their hope that she would come again, they would heap upon her baskets and bales of the precious rubbish she loved, and one of her great grandsons Skid or Hasty would push them away beside her on a wheelbarrow. She would again for a moment be the amiable, dependent, like-one-of-the-family old servant: "I know my chil'ren won't let me go away empty-handed."

Uncle Jimbilly still pottered around, mending harness, currying horses, patching fences, now and then setting out a few plants or loosening the earth around shrubs in the spring. He muttered perpetually to himself, his blue mouth always moving in an endless disjointed comment on things past and present, and even to come, no doubt, though there was nothing about him that suggested any connection with even the nearest future . . . Maria had not realized until after her grandmother's death that Uncle Jimbilly and Aunt Nannie were husband and wife . . . That marriage of convenience, in which they had been mated with truly royal policy, with an eye to the blood and family stability, had dissolved of itself between them when the reasons for its being had likewise dissolved . . . They took no notice whatever of each other's existence, they seemed to forget they had children together (each spoke of "my children"), they had stored up no common memories that either wished to keep. Aunt Nannie moved away into her own house without even a glance or thought for Uncle Jimbilly, and he did not seem to notice that she was gone . . . He slept in a little attic over the smoke-house, and ate in the kitchen at odd hours, and did as he pleased, lonely as a wandering spirit and almost as invisible . . . But one day he passed by the little house and saw Aunt Nannie sitting on her steps with her pipe. He sat down awhile, groaning a little as he bent himself into angles, and sunned himself like a weary old dog. He would have stayed on from that minute, but Nannie would not have him. "Whut you doin with all this big house to yoself?" he wanted to know. "'Tain't no more than just enough fo' me," she told him pointedly; "I don' aim to pass my las' days waitin on no man," she added, "I've served my time, I've done my do, and dat's all." So Uncle Jimbilly crept back up the hill and into his smoke-house attic, and never went near her again . . .

On summer evenings she sat by herself long after dark, smoking to keep away the mosquitoes, until she was ready to sleep. She said she wasn't afraid of anything: never had been, never expected to be. She had long ago got in the way of thinking that night was a blessing, it brought the time when she didn't have to work any more until tomorrow. Even after she stopped working for good and all, she still looked forward with longing to the night, as if all the accumulated fatigues of her life, lying now embedded in her bones, still begged for easement. But when night came, she remembered that she didn't have to get up in the morning until she was ready. So she would sit in the luxury of having at her disposal all of God's good time there was in this world.

*

When Mister Harry, in the old days, had stood out against her word in some petty dispute, she could always get the better of him by slapping her slatty old chest with the flat of her long hand and crying out: "Why, Mister Harry, you, ain't you shamed to talk lak dat to me? I nuhsed you at dis bosom!"

Harry knew this was not literally true. She had nursed three of his elder brothers; but he always said at once, "All right, Mammy, all right, for God's sake!"—precisely as he said it to his own mother, exploding in his natural irascibility as if he hoped to clear the air somewhat of the smothering matriarchal tyranny to which he had been delivered by the death of his father. Still he submitted, being of that latest generation of sons who acknowledged, however reluctantly, however bitterly, their mystical never to be forgiven debt to the womb that bore them, and the breast that suckled them.

THE FIG TREE

Old Aunt Nannie had a habit of gripping with her knees to hold Miranda while she brushed her hair or buttoned her dress down the back. When Miranda wriggled, Aunt Nannie squeezed still harder, and Miranda wriggled more, but never enough to get away. Aunt Nannie gathered up Miranda's scalp lock firmly, snapped a rubber band around it, jammed a freshly starched white chambray bonnet over her ears and forehead, fastened the crown to the lock with a large safety pin, and said: "Got to hold you still someways. Here now, don't you take this off your head till the sun go down."

"I didn't want a bonnet, it's too hot, I wanted a hat," said Miranda.

"You not goin' to get a hat, you goin' to get just what you got," said Aunt Nannie in the bossy voice she used for washing and dressing time, "and mo'over some of these days I'm goin' to *sew* this bonnet to your topknot. Your daddy says if you get freckles he blame me. Now, you're all ready to set out."

"Where are we going, Aunty?" Miranda could never find out about anything until the last minute. She was always being surprised. Once she went to sleep in her bed with her kitten curled on the pillow purring, and woke up in a stuffy tight bed in a train, hugging a hot-water bottle; and there was Grandmother stretched out beside her in her McLeod tartan dressing-gown, her eyes wide open. Miranda thought something wonderful had happened. "My goodness, Grandmother, where are we going?" And it was only for another trip to El Paso to see Uncle Bill.

Now Tom and Dick were hitched to the carry-all standing outside the gate with boxes and baskets tied on everywhere. Grandmother was walking alone through the house very slowly, taking a last look at everything. Now and then she put something else in the big leather portmoney on her arm until it was pretty bulgy. She carried a long black mohair skirt on her other arm, the one she put on over her other skirt when she rode horseback. Her son Harry, Miranda's father, followed her saying: "I can't see the sense in rushing off to Halifax on five minutes' notice."

Grandmother said, walking on: "It's five hours exactly." Halifax wasn't the name of Grandmother's farm at all, it was Cedar Grove, but Father always called it Halifax. "Hot as Halifax," he would say when he wanted to describe something very hot. Cedar Grove was very hot, but they went there every summer because Grandmother loved it. "I went to Cedar Grove for fifty summers before you were born," she told Miranda, who remembered last summer very well, and the summer before a little. Miranda liked it for watermelons and grasshoppers and the long rows of blooming chinaberry trees where the hounds flattened themselves out and slept. They whined and winked their eyelids and worked their feet and barked faintly in their sleep, and Uncle Jimbilly said it was because dogs always dreamed they were chasing something. In the middle of the day when Miranda looked down over the thick green fields towards the spring she could simply see it being hot: everything blue and sleepy and the mourning doves calling.

"Are we going to Halifax, Aunty?"

"Now just ask your dad if you wanta know so much."

"Are we going to Halifax, Dad?"

Her father twitched her bonnet straight and pulled her hair forward so it would show. "You mustn't get sunburned. No, let it alone. Show the pretty curls. You'll be wading in Whirly-pool before supper this evening."

Grandmother said, "Don't say Halifax, child, say Cedar Grove. Call things by their right names."

"Yes, ma'am," said Miranda. Grandmother said again, to her son, "It's five hours, exactly, and your Aunt Eliza has had plenty of time to pack up her telescope, and take my saddle horse. She's been there three hours by now. I imagine she's got the telescope already set up on the hen-house roof. I hope nothing happens."

"You worry too much, Mammy," said her son, trying to conceal his impatience.

"I am not worrying," said Grandmother, shifting her riding skirt to the arm carrying the portmoney. "It will scarcely be any good taking this," she said; "I might in fact as well throw it away for this summer."

"Never mind, Mammy, we'll send to the Black Farm for Pompey, he's a good easy saddler."

"You may ride him yourself," said Grandmother. "I'll never mount Pompey while Fiddler is alive. Fiddler is my horse, and I hate having his mouth spoiled by a careless rider. Eliza never could ride, and she never will. . . ."

Miranda gave a little skip and ran away. So they were going to Cedar Grove. Miranda never got over being surprised at the way grown-up people simply did not seem able to give anyone a straight answer to any question, unless the answer was "No." Then it popped out with no trouble at all. At a little distance, she heard her grandmother say, "Harry, have you seen my riding crop lately?" and her father answered, at least maybe he thought it was an answer, "Now, Mammy, for God's sake let's get this thing over with." That was it, exactly.

Another strange way her father had of talking was calling Grandmother "Mammy." Aunt Jane was Mammy. Sometimes he called Grandmother "Mama," but she wasn't Mama either, she was really Grandmother. Mama was dead. Dead meant gone away forever. Dying was something that happened all the time, to people and everything else. Somebody died, and there was a long string of carriages going at a slow walk over the rocky ridge of the hill towards the river while the bell tolled and tolled, and that person was never seen again by anybody. Kittens and chickens and specially little turkeys died much oftener, and sometimes calves, but hardly ever cows or horses. Lizards on rocks turned into shells, with no lizard inside at all. If caterpillars all curled up and furry didn't move when you poked them with a stick, that meant they were dead—it was a sure sign.

When Miranda found any creature that didn't move or make a noise, or looked somehow different from the live ones, she always buried it in a little grave with flowers on top and a smooth stone at the head. Even grasshoppers. Everything dead had to be treated this way. "This way and no other!" Grandmother always said when she was laying down the law about all kinds of things. "It must be done *this* way, and no other!"

Miranda went down the crooked flat-stone walk hopping zigzag between the grass tufts. First there were pomegranate and cape jessamine bushes mixed together; then it got very dark and shady and that was the fig grove. She went to her favorite fig tree where the deep branches bowed down level with her chin, and she could gather figs without having to climb and skin her knees. Grandmother hadn't remembered to take any figs to the country the last time, she said there were plenty of them at Cedar Grove. But the ones at Cedar Grove were big soft greenish white ones, and these at home were black and sugary. It was strange that Grandmother did not seem to notice the difference. The air was sweet among the fig trees, and chickens were always getting out of the run and rushing there to eat the figs off the ground. One mother hen was scurrying around scratching and clucking. She would scratch around a fig lying there in plain sight and cluck to her children as if it was a worm and she had dug it up for them.

"Old smarty," said Miranda, "you're just pretending."

When the little chickens all ran to their mother under Miranda's fig tree, one little chicken did not move. He was spread out on his side with his eyes shut and his mouth open. He was yellow fur in spots and pinfeathers in spots, and the rest of him was naked and sunburned. "Lazy," said Miranda, poking him with her toe. Then she saw that he was dead.

Oh, and in no time at all they'd be setting out for Halifax. Grandmother never went away, she always set out for somewhere. She'd have to hurry like anything to get him buried properly. Back into the house she went on tiptoe hoping not to be seen, for Grandmother always asked: "Where are you going, child? What are you doing? What is that you're carrying? Where did you get it? Who gave you permission?" and after Miranda had explained all that, even if there turned out not to be anything wrong in it, nothing ever seemed so nice any more. Besides it took forever to get away.

Miranda slid open her bureau drawer, third down, left-hand side where her new shoes were still wrapped in tissue paper in a nice white box the right size for a chicken with pinfeathers. She pushed the rustling white folded things and the lavender bags out of the way and trembled a little. Down in front the carry-all wheels screeched and crunched on the gravel, with Old Uncle Jimbilly yelling like a foghorn, "Hiyi, thar, back up, you steeds! Back up thar, you!" and of course, that meant he was turning Tom and Dick around so they would be pointing towards Halifax. They'd be after her, calling and hurrying her, and she wouldn't have time for anything and they wouldn't listen to a word.

It wasn't hard work digging a hole with her little spade in the loose dry soil. Miranda wrapped the slimpsy chicken in tissue paper, trying to make it look pretty, laid it in the box carefully, and covered it up with a nice mound, just like people's. She had hardly got it piled up grave shape, kneeling and leaning to smooth it over, when a strange sound came from somewhere, a very sad little crying sound. It said Weep, weep, weep, three times like that slowly, and it seemed to come from the mound of dirt. "My goodness," Miranda asked herself aloud, "what's that?" She pushed her bonnet off her ears and listened hard. "Weep, weep," said the tiny sad voice. And People began calling and urging her, their voices coming nearer. She began to clamor, too.

"Yes, Aunty, wait a minute, Aunty!"

"You come right on here this minute, we're goin'!"

"You *have* to wait, Aunty!"

Her father was coming along the edge of the fig trees. "Hurry up, Baby, you'll get left!"

Miranda felt she couldn't bear to be left. She ran all shaking with fright. Her father gave her the annoyed look he always gave her when he said something to upset her and then saw that she was upset. His words were kind but his voice scolded: "Stop getting so excited, Baby, you know we wouldn't leave you for anything." Miranda wanted to talk back: "Then why did you say so?" but she was still listening for that tiny sound: "Weep, weep." She lagged and pulled backward, looking over her shoulder, but her father hurried her towards the carry-all. But things didn't make sounds if they were dead. They couldn't. That was one of the signs. Oh, but she had heard it.

Her father sat in front and drove, and old Uncle Jimbilly didn't do anything but get down and open gates. Grandmother and Aunt Nannie sat in the back seat, with Miranda between them. She loved setting out somewhere, with everybody smiling and settling down and looking up at the weather, with the horses bouncing and pulling on the reins, the springs jolting and swaying with a creaky noise that made you feel sure you were traveling. That evening she would go wading with Maria and Paul and Uncle Jimbilly, and that very night she would lie out on the grass in her nightgown to cool off, and they would all drink lemonade before going to bed. Sister Maria and Brother Paul would already be burned like muffins because they were sent on ahead the minute school was out. Sister Maria had got freckled and Father was furious. "Keep your bonnet on," he said to Miranda, sternly. "Now remember. I'm not going to have that face ruined, too." But oh, what had made that funny sound? Miranda's ears buzzed and she had a dull round pain in her just under her front ribs. She had to go back and let him out. He'd never get out by himself, all tangled up in tissue paper and that shoebox. He'd never get out without her.

"Grandmother, I've got to go back. Oh, I've *got* to go back!"

Grandmother turned Miranda's face around by the chin and looked at her closely, the way grown folks did. Grandmother's eyes were always the same. They never looked kind or sad or angry or tired or anything. They just looked, blue and still. "What is the matter with you, Miranda, what happened?"

"Oh, I've got to go back—I forg-got something important."

"Stop that silly crying and tell me what you want."

Miranda couldn't stop. Her father looked very anxious. "Mammy, maybe the Baby's sick." He reached out his handkerchief to her face. "What's the matter with my honey? Did you eat something?"

Miranda had to stand up to cry as hard as she wanted to. The wheels went grinding round in the road, the carry-all wobbled so that Grandmother had to take her by one arm, and her father by the other. They stared at each other over Miranda's head with a moveless gaze that Miranda had seen often, and their eyes looked exactly alike. Miranda blinked up at them, waiting to see who would win. Then Grandmother's hand fell away, and Miranda was handed over to her father. He gave the reins to Uncle Jimbilly, and lifted her over the top of the seat. She sprawled against his chest and knees as if he were an armchair and stopped crying at once. "We can't go back just for notions," he told her in the reasoning tone he always talked in when Grandmother scolded, and held the muffly handkerchief for her. "Now, blow hard. What did you forget, honey? We'll find another. Was it your doll?"

Miranda hated dolls. She never played with them. She always pulled the wigs off and tied them on the kittens, like hats. The kittens pulled them off instantly. It was fun. She put the doll clothes on the kittens and it took any one of them just half a minute to get them all off again. Kittens had sense. Miranda wailed suddenly, "Oh, I want my doll!" and cried again, trying to drown out the strange little sound, "Weep, weep"—

"Well now, if that's all," said her father comfortably, "there's a raft of dolls at Cedar Grove, and about forty fresh kittens. How'd you like that?"

"Forty?" asked Miranda.

"About," said Father.

Old Aunt Nannie leaned and held out her hand. "Look, honey, I toted you some nice black figs."

Her face was wrinkled and black and it looked like a fig upside down with a white ruffled cap. Miranda clenched her eyes tight and shook her head.

"Is that a pretty way to behave when Aunt Nannie offers you something nice?" asked Grandmother in her gentle reminding tone of voice.

"No, ma'am," said Miranda meekly. "Thank you, Aunt Nannie." But she did not accept the figs.

Great-Aunt Eliza, half way up a stepladder pitched against the flat-roofed chicken house, was telling Hinry just how to set up her telescope. "For a fellow who never saw or heard of a telescope," Great-Aunt Eliza said to Grandmother, who was really her sister Sophia Jane, "he doesn't do so badly so long as I tell him."

"I do wish you'd stop clambering up stepladders, Eliza," said Grandmother, "at your time of life."

"You're nothing but a nervous wreck, Sophia, I declare. When did you ever know me to get hurt?"

"Even so," said Grandmother tartly, "there is such a thing as appropriate behavior at your time of . . ."

Great-Aunt Eliza seized a fold of her heavy brown pleated skirt with one hand, with the other she grasped the ladder one rung higher and ascended another step. "Now Hinry," she called, "just swing it around facing west and leave it level. I'll fix it the way I want when I'm ready. You can come on down now." She came down then herself, and said to her sister: "So long as you can go bouncing off on that horse of yours, Sophia Jane, I s'pose I can climb ladders. I'm three years younger than you, and *at your time of life* that makes all the difference!"

Grandmother turned pink as the inside of a seashell, the one on her sewing table that had the sound of the sea in it; Miranda knew that she had always been the pretty one, and she was pretty still, but Great-Aunt Eliza was not pretty now and never had been. Miranda, watching and listening—for everything in the world was strange to her and something she had to know about—saw two old women, who were proud of being grandmothers, who spoke to children always as if they knew best about everything and children knew nothing, and they told children all day long to come here, go there, do this, do not do that, and they were always right and children never were except when they did anything they were told right away without a word. And here they were bickering like two little girls at school, or even the way Miranda and her sister Maria bickered and nagged and picked on each other and said things

on purpose to hurt each other's feelings. Miranda felt sad and
strange and a little frightened. She began edging away.

"Where are you going, Miranda?" asked Grandmother in
her everyday voice.

"Just to the house," said Miranda, her heart sinking.

"Wait and walk with us," said Grandmother. She was very
thin and pale and had white hair. Beside her, Great-Aunt Eliza
loomed like a mountain with her grizzled iron-colored hair
like a curly wig, her steel-rimmed spectacles over her snuff-
colored eyes, and snuff-colored woollen skirts billowing about
her, and her smell of snuff. When she came through the door
she quite filled it up. When she sat down the chair disappeared
under her, and she seemed to be sitting solidly on herself from
her waistband to the floor.

Now with Grandmother sitting across the room rummaging
in her work basket and pretending not to see anything, Great-
Aunt Eliza took a small brown bottle out of her pocket, opened
it, took a pinch of snuff in each nostril, sneezed loudly, wiped
her nose with a big white starchy-looking handkerchief, pushed
her spectacles up on her forehead, took a little twig chewed into
a brush at one end, dipped and twisted it around in the little
bottle, and placed it firmly between her teeth. Miranda had
heard of this shameful habit in women of the lower classes, but
no lady had been known to "dip snuff," and surely not in the
family. Yet here was Great-Aunt Eliza, a lady even if not a very
pretty one, dipping snuff. Miranda knew how her grandmother
felt about it; she stared fascinated at Great-Aunt Eliza until her
eyes watered. Great-Aunt Eliza stared back in turn.

"Look here, young one, d'ye s'pose if I gave you a gumdrop
you'd get out from underfoot?"

She reached in the other pocket and took out a roundish,
rather crushed-looking pink gumdrop with the sugar coating
pretty badly crackled. "Now take this, and don't let me lay
eyes on you any more today."

Miranda hurried away, clenching the gumdrop in her palm.
When she reached the kitchen it was oozing through her fingers. She went to the tap and held her hand under the water
and tried to wash off the snuffy smell. After this crime she did
not really dare go near Great-Aunt Eliza again soon. "What

did you do with that gumdrop so quickly, child?" she could almost hear her asking.

Yet Miranda almost forgot her usual interests, such as kittens and other little animals on the place, pigs, chickens, rabbits, anything at all so it was a baby and would let her pet and feed it, for Great-Aunt Eliza's ways and habits kept Miranda following her about, gazing, or sitting across the dining-table, gazing, for when Great-Aunt Eliza was not on the roof before her telescope, always just before daylight or just after dark, she was walking about with a microscope and a burning glass, peering closely at something she saw on a tree trunk, something she found in the grass; now and then she collected fragments that looked like dried leaves or bits of bark, brought them in the house, spread them out on a sheet of white paper, and sat there, poring, as still as if she were saying her prayers. At table she would dissect a scrap of potato peeling or anything else she might be eating, and sit there, bowed over, saying, "Hum," from time to time. Grandmother, who did not allow the children to bring anything to the table to play with and who forbade them to do anything but eat while they were there, ignored her sister's manners as long as she could, then remarked one day, when Great-Aunt Eliza was humming like a bee to herself over what her microscope had found in a raisin, "Eliza, if it is interesting save it for me to look at after dinner. Or tell me what it is."

"You wouldn't know if I told you," said Great-Aunt Eliza, coolly, putting her microscope away and finishing off her pudding.

When at last, just before they were all going back to town again, Great-Aunt Eliza invited the children to climb the ladder with her and see the stars through her telescope, they were so awed they looked at each other like strangers, and did not exchange a word. Miranda saw only a great pale flaring disk of cold light, but she knew it was the moon and called out in pure rapture, "Oh, it's like another world!"

"Why, of course, child," said Great-Aunt Eliza, in her growling voice, but kindly, "other worlds, a million other worlds."

"Like this one?" asked Miranda, timidly.

"Nobody knows, child. . . ."

"Nobody knows, nobody knows," Miranda sang to a tune in her head, and when the others walked on, she was so dazzled with joy she fell back by herself, walking a little distance behind Great-Aunt Eliza's swinging lantern and her wide-swinging skirts. They took the dewy path through the fig grove, much like the one in town, with the early dew bringing out the sweet smell of the milky leaves. They passed a fig tree with low hanging branches, and Miranda reached up by habit and touched it with her fingers for luck. From the earth beneath her feet came a terrible, faint troubled sound. "Weep weep, weep weep . . ." murmured a little crying voice from the smothering earth, the grave.

Miranda bounded like a startled pony against the back of Great-Aunt Eliza's knees, crying out, "Oh, oh, oh, wait . . ."

"What on earth's the matter, child?"

Miranda seized the warm snuffy hand held out to her and hung on hard. "Oh, there's something saying 'weep weep' out of the ground!"

Great-Aunt Eliza stooped, put her arm around Miranda and listened carefully, for a moment. "Hear them?" she said. "They're not in the ground at all. They are the first tree frogs, means it's going to rain," she said, "weep weep—hear them?"

Miranda took a deep trembling breath and heard them. They were in the trees. They walked on again, Miranda holding Great-Aunt Eliza's hand.

"Just think," said Great-Aunt Eliza, in her most scientific voice, "when tree frogs shed their skins, they pull them off over their heads like little shirts, and they eat them. Can you imagine? They have the prettiest little shapes you ever saw— I'll show you one some time under the microscope."

"Thank you, ma'am," Miranda remembered finally to say through her fog of bliss at hearing the tree frogs sing, "Weep weep . . ."

THE GRAVE

The grandfather, dead for more than thirty years, had been twice disturbed in his long repose by the constancy and possessiveness of his widow. She removed his bones first to Louisiana and then to Texas as if she had set out to find her own burial place, knowing well she would never return to the places she had left. In Texas she set up a small cemetery in a corner of her first farm, and as the family connection grew, and oddments of relations came over from Kentucky to settle, it contained at last about twenty graves. After the grandmother's death, part of her land was to be sold for the benefit of certain of her children, and the cemetery happened to lie in the part set aside for sale. It was necessary to take up the bodies and bury them again in the family plot in the big new public cemetery, where the grandmother had been buried. At last her husband was to lie beside her for eternity, as she had planned.

The family cemetery had been a pleasant small neglected garden of tangled rose bushes and ragged cedar trees and cypress, the simple flat stones rising out of uncropped sweet-smelling wild grass. The graves were lying open and empty one burning day when Miranda and her brother Paul, who often went together to hunt rabbits and doves, propped their twenty-two Winchester rifles carefully against the rail fence, climbed over and explored among the graves. She was nine years old and he was twelve.

They peered into the pits all shaped alike with such purposeful accuracy, and looking at each other with pleased adventurous eyes, they said in solemn tones: "These were graves!" trying by words to shape a special, suitable emotion in their minds, but they felt nothing except an agreeable thrill of wonder: they were seeing a new sight, doing something they had not done before. In them both there was also a small disappointment at the entire commonplaceness of the actual spectacle. Even if it had once contained a coffin for years upon years, when the coffin was gone a grave was just a hole in the ground. Miranda leaped into the pit that had held her grandfather's bones. Scratching around aimlessly and pleasurably as any young animal, she scooped up a lump of earth and weighed it in her palm. It had a pleasantly sweet, corrupt smell, being mixed with cedar needles and small leaves, and as the crumbs fell apart, she saw a silver dove no larger than a hazel nut, with spread wings and a neat fan-shaped tail. The breast had a deep round hollow in it. Turning it up to the fierce sunlight, she saw that the inside of the hollow was cut in little whorls. She scrambled out, over the pile of loose earth that had fallen back into one end of the grave, calling to Paul that she had found something, he must guess what . . . His head appeared smiling over the rim of another grave. He waved a closed hand at her. "I've got something too!" They ran to compare treasures, making a game of it, so many guesses each, all wrong, and a final showdown with opened palms. Paul had found a thin wide gold ring carved with intricate flowers and leaves. Miranda was smitten at sight of the ring and wished to have it. Paul seemed more impressed by the dove. They made a trade, with some little bickering. After he had got the dove in his hand, Paul said, "Don't you know what this is? This is a screw head for a *coffin!* . . . I'll bet nobody else in the world has one like this!"

Miranda glanced at it without covetousness. She had the gold ring on her thumb; it fitted perfectly. "Maybe we ought to go now," she said, "maybe one of the niggers 'll see us and tell somebody." They knew the land had been sold, the cemetery was no longer theirs, and they felt like trespassers. They climbed back over the fence, slung their rifles loosely under their arms —they had been shooting at targets with various kinds of firearms since they were seven years old—and set out to look for the rabbits and doves or whatever small game might happen along. On these expeditions Miranda always followed at Paul's heels along the path, obeying instructions about handling her gun when going through fences; learning how to stand it up properly so it would not slip and fire unexpectedly; how to wait her time for a shot and not just bang away in the air without looking, spoiling shots for Paul, who really could hit things if given a chance. Now and then, in her excitement at seeing birds whizz up suddenly before her face, or a rabbit leap across her very toes, she lost her head, and almost without sighting she flung her rifle up and pulled the trigger. She hardly ever hit any sort of mark. She had no proper sense of hunting at all. Her brother would be often completely disgusted with her. "You don't care whether you get your bird or not," he said. "That's no way to hunt." Miranda could not understand his indignation. She had seen him smash his hat and yell with fury when he had missed his aim. "What I like about shooting," said Miranda, with exasperating inconsequence, "is pulling the trigger and hearing the noise."

"Then, by golly," said Paul, "whyn't you go back to the range and shoot at bulls-eyes?"

"I'd just as soon," said Miranda, "only like this, we walk around more."

"Well, you just stay behind and stop spoiling my shots," said Paul, who, when he made a kill, wanted to be certain he had made it. Miranda, who alone brought down a bird once in twenty rounds, always claimed as her own any game they got when they fired at the same moment. It was tiresome and unfair and her brother was sick of it.

"Now, the first dove we see, or the first rabbit, is mine," he told her. "And the next will be yours. Remember that and don't get smarty."

"What about snakes?" asked Miranda idly. "Can I have the first snake?"

Waving her thumb gently and watching her gold ring glitter, Miranda lost interest in shooting. She was wearing her summer roughing outfit: dark blue overalls, a light blue shirt, a hired-man's straw hat, and thick brown sandals. Her brother had the same outfit except his was a sober hickory-nut color. Ordinarily Miranda preferred her overalls to any other dress, though it was making rather a scandal in the countryside, for the year was 1903, and in the back country the law of female decorum had teeth in it. Her father had been criticized for letting his girls dress like boys and go careering around astride barebacked horses. Big sister Maria, the really independent and fearless one, in spite of her rather affected ways, rode at a dead run with only a rope knotted around her horse's nose. It was said the motherless family was running down, with the Grandmother no longer there to hold it together. It was known that she had discriminated against her son Harry in her will, and that he was in straits about money. Some of his old neighbors reflected with vicious satisfaction that now he would probably not be so stiffnecked, nor have any more high-stepping horses either. Miranda knew this, though she could not say how. She had met along the road old women of the kind who smoked corn-cob pipes, who had treated her grandmother with most sincere respect. They slanted their gummy old eyes side-ways at the granddaughter and said, "Ain't you ashamed of yoself, Missy? It's aginst the Scriptures to dress like that. Whut yo Pappy thinkin about?" Miranda, with her powerful social sense, which was like a fine set of antennae radiating from every pore of her skin, would feel ashamed because she knew well it was rude and ill-bred to shock anybody, even bad-tempered old crones, though she had faith in her father's judgment and was perfectly comfortable in the clothes. Her father had said, "They're just what you need, and they'll save your dresses for school . . ." This sounded quite simple and natural to her. She had been brought up in rigorous economy. Wastefulness was vulgar. It was also a sin. These were truths; she had heard them repeated many times and never once disputed.

Now the ring, shining with the serene purity of fine gold on her rather grubby thumb, turned her feelings against her over-alls and sockless feet, toes sticking through the thick brown leather straps. She wanted to go back to the farmhouse, take a good cold bath, dust herself with plenty of Maria's violet tal-cum powder—provided Maria was not present to object, of course—put on the thinnest, most becoming dress she owned, with a big sash, and sit in a wicker chair under the trees . . . These things were not all she wanted, of course; she had vague stirrings of desire for luxury and a grand way of living which could not take precise form in her imagination but were founded on family legend of past wealth and leisure. These im-mediate comforts were what she could have, and she wanted them at once. She lagged rather far behind Paul, and once she thought of just turning back without a word and going home. She stopped, thinking that Paul would never do that to her, and so she would have to tell him. When a rabbit leaped, she let Paul have it without dispute. He killed it with one shot.

When she came up with him, he was already kneeling, ex-amining the wound, the rabbit trailing from his hands. "Right through the head," he said complacently, as if he had aimed for it. He took out his sharp, competent bowie knife and started to skin the body. He did it very cleanly and quickly.

Uncle Jimbilly knew how to prepare the skins so that Miranda always had fur coats for her dolls, for though she never cared much for her dolls she liked seeing them in fur coats. The children knelt facing each other over the dead animal. Miranda watched admiringly while her brother stripped the skin away as if he were taking off a glove. The flayed flesh emerged dark scarlet, sleek, firm; Miranda with thumb and finger felt the long fine muscles with the silvery flat strips binding them to the joints. Brother lifted the oddly bloated belly. "Look," he said, in a low amazed voice. "It was going to have young ones."

Very carefully he slit the thin flesh from the center ribs to the flanks, and a scarlet bag appeared. He slit again and pulled the bag open, and there lay a bundle of tiny rabbits, each wrapped in a thin scarlet veil. The brother pulled these off and there they were, dark gray, their sleek wet down lying in minute even ripples, like a baby's head just washed, their unbelievably small delicate ears folded close, their little blind faces almost featureless.

Miranda said, "Oh, I want to *see*," under her breath. She looked and looked—excited but not frightened, for she was accustomed to the sight of animals killed in hunting—filled with pity and astonishment and a kind of shocked delight in the wonderful little creatures for their own sakes, they were so pretty. She touched one of them ever so carefully, "Ah, there's blood running over them," she said and began to tremble without knowing why. Yet she wanted most deeply to see and to know. Having seen, she felt at once as if she had known all along. The very memory of her former ignorance faded, she had always known just this. No one had ever told her anything outright, she had been rather unobservant of the animal life around her because she was so accustomed to animals. They seemed simply disorderly and unaccountably rude in their habits, but altogether natural and not very interesting. Her brother had spoken as if he had known about everything all along. He may have seen all this before. He had never said a word to her, but she knew now a part at least of what he knew. She understood a little of the secret, formless intuitions in her own mind and body, which had been clearing up, taking form, so gradually and so steadily she had not realized that she was learning what she had to know. Paul said cautiously, as if he were talking about something forbidden: "They were just about ready to be born." His voice dropped on the last word. "I know," said Miranda, "like kittens. I know, like babies." She was quietly and terribly agitated, standing again with her rifle under her arm, looking down at the bloody heap. "I don't want the skin," she said, "I won't have it." Paul buried the young rabbits again in their mother's body, wrapped the skin around her, carried her to a clump of sage bushes, and hid her away. He came out again at once and said to Miranda, with an eager friendliness, a confidential tone quite unusual in him, as if he were taking her into an important secret on equal terms: "Listen now. Now you listen to me, and don't ever forget. Don't you ever tell a living soul that you saw this. Don't tell a soul. Don't tell Dad because I'll get into trouble. He'll say I'm leading you into things you ought not to do. He's always saying that. So now don't you go and forget and blab out sometime the way you're always doing . . . Now, that's a secret. Don't you tell."

Miranda never told, she did not even wish to tell anybody. She thought about the whole worrisome affair with confused unhappiness for a few days. Then it sank quietly into her mind and was heaped over by accumulated thousands of impressions, for nearly twenty years. One day she was picking her path among the puddles and crushed refuse of a market street in a strange city of a strange country, when without warning, plain and clear in its true colors as if she looked through a frame upon a scene that had not stirred nor changed since the moment it happened, the episode of that far-off day leaped from its burial place before her mind's eye. She was so reasonlessly horrified she halted suddenly staring, the scene before her eyes dimmed by the vision back of them. An Indian vendor had held up before her a tray of dyed sugar sweets, in the shapes of all kinds of small creatures: birds, baby chicks, baby rabbits, lambs, baby pigs. They were in gay colors and smelled of vanilla, maybe. . . . It was a very hot day and the smell in the market, with its piles of raw flesh and wilting flowers, was like the mingled sweetness and corruption she had smelled that other day in the empty cemetery at home: the day she had remembered always until now vaguely as the time she and her brother had found treasure in the opened graves. Instantly upon this thought the dreadful vision faded, and she saw clearly her brother, whose childhood face she had forgotten, standing again in the blazing sunshine, again twelve years old, a pleased sober smile in his eyes, turning the silver dove over and over in his hands.

The Downward Path to Wisdom

In the square bedroom with the big window Mama and Papa were lolling back on their pillows handing each other things from the wide black tray on the small table with crossed legs. They were smiling and they smiled even more when the little boy, with the feeling of sleep still in his skin and hair, came in and walked up to the bed. Leaning against it, his bare toes wriggling in the white fur rug, he went on eating peanuts which he took from his pajama pocket. He was four years old.

"Here's my baby," said Mama. "Lift him up, will you?"

He went limp as a rag for Papa to take him under the arms and swing him up over a broad, tough chest. He sank between his parents like a bear cub in a warm litter, and lay there comfortably. He took another peanut between his teeth, cracked the shell, picked out the nut whole and ate it.

"Running around without his slippers again," said Mama. "His feet are like icicles."

"He crunches like a horse," said Papa. "Eating peanuts before breakfast will ruin his stomach. Where did he get them?"

"You brought them yesterday," said Mama, with exact memory, "in a grisly little cellophane sack. I have asked you dozens of times not to bring him things to eat. Put him out, will you? He's spilling shells all over me."

Almost at once the little boy found himself on the floor again. He moved around to Mama's side of the bed and leaned confidingly near her and began another peanut. As he chewed he gazed solemnly in her eyes.

"Bright-looking specimen, isn't he?" asked Papa, stretching his long legs and reaching for his bathrobe. "I suppose you'll say it's my fault he's dumb as an ox."

"He's my little baby, my only baby," said Mama richly, hugging him, "and he's a dear lamb." His neck and shoulders were quite boneless in her firm embrace. He stopped chewing long enough to receive a kiss on his crumby chin. "He's sweet as clover," said Mama. The baby went on chewing.

"Look at him staring like an owl," said Papa.

Mama said, "He's an angel and I'll never get used to having him."

"We'd be better off if we never *had* had him," said Papa. He was walking about the room and his back was turned when he said that. There was silence for a moment. The little boy stopped eating, and stared deeply at his Mama. She was looking at the back of Papa's head, and her eyes were almost black. "You're going to say that just once too often," she told him in a low voice. "I hate you when you say that."

Papa said, "You spoil him to death. You never correct him for anything. And you don't take care of him. You let him run around eating peanuts before breakfast."

"You gave him the peanuts, remember that," said Mama. She sat up and hugged her only baby once more. He nuzzled softly in the pit of her arm. "Run along, my darling," she told him in her gentlest voice, smiling at him straight in the eyes. "Run along," she said, her arms falling away from him. "Get your breakfast."

The little boy had to pass his father on the way to the door. He shrank into himself when he saw the big hand raised above him. "Yes, get out of here and stay out," said Papa, giving him a little shove toward the door. It was not a hard shove, but it hurt the little boy. He slunk out, and trotted down the hall trying not to look back. He was afraid something was coming after him, he could not imagine what. Something hurt him all over, he did not know why.

He did not want his breakfast; he would not have it. He sat and stirred it round in the yellow bowl, letting it stream off the spoon and spill on the table, on his front, on the chair. He liked seeing it spill. It was hateful stuff, but it looked funny running in white rivulets down his pajamas.

"Now look what you're doing, dirty boy," said Marjory. "You dirty little old boy."

The little boy opened his mouth to speak for the first time. "You're dirty yourself," he told her.

"That's right," said Marjory, leaning over him and speaking so her voice would not carry. "That's right, just like your papa. Mean," she whispered, "mean."

The little boy took up his yellow bowl full of cream and

oatmeal and sugar with both hands and brought it down with a crash on the table. It burst and some of the wreck lay in chunks and some of it ran all over everything. He felt better.

"You see?" said Marjory, dragging him out of the chair and scrubbing him with a napkin. She scrubbed him as roughly as she dared until he cried out. "That's just what I said. That's exactly it." Through his tears he saw her face terribly near, red and frowning under a stiff white band, looking like the face of somebody who came at night and stood over him and scolded him when he could not move or get away. "Just like your papa, *mean*."

The little boy went out into the garden and sat on a green bench dangling his legs. He was clean. His hair was wet and his blue woolly pull-over made his nose itch. His face felt stiff from the soap. He saw Marjory going past a window with the black tray. The curtains were still closed at the window he knew opened into Mama's room. Papa's room. Mommanpoppas-room, the word was pleasant, it made a mumbling snapping noise between his lips; it ran in his mind while his eyes wandered about looking for something to do, something to play with.

Mommanpoppas' voices kept attracting his attention. Mama was being cross with Papa again. He could tell by the sound. That was what Marjory always said when their voices rose and fell and shot up to a point and crashed and rolled like the two tomcats who fought at night. Papa was being cross, too, much crosser than Mama this time. He grew cold and disturbed and sat very still, wanting to go to the bathroom, but it was just next to Mommanpoppasroom; he didn't dare think of it. As the voices grew louder he could hardly hear them any more, he wanted so badly to go to the bathroom. The kitchen door opened suddenly and Marjory ran out, making the motion with her hand that meant he was to come to her. He didn't move. She came to him, her face still red and frowning, but she was not angry; she was scared just as he was. She said, "Come on, honey, we've got to go to your gran'ma's again." She took his hand and pulled him. "Come on quick, your gran'ma is waiting for you." He slid off the bench. His mother's voice rose in a terrible scream, screaming something he could not understand, but she was furious; he had seen her clenching her fists and stamping in one spot, screaming with her eyes shut; he knew how she looked. She was screaming in a tantrum, just as he remembered having heard himself. He stood still, doubled over, and all his body seemed to dissolve, sickly, from the pit of his stomach.

"Oh, my God," said Marjory. "Oh, my God. Now look at you. Oh, my God. I can't stop to clean you up."

He did not know how he got to his grandma's house, but he was there at last, wet and soiled, being handled with disgust in the big bathtub. His grandma was there in long black skirts saying, "Maybe he's sick; maybe we should send for the doctor."

"I don't think so, m'am," said Marjory. "He hasn't et anything; he's just scared."

The little boy couldn't raise his eyes, he was so heavy with shame. "Take this note to his mother," said Grandma.

She sat in a wide chair and ran her hands over his head, combing his hair with her fingers; she lifted his chin and kissed him. "Poor little fellow," she said. "Never you mind. You always have a good time at your grandma's, don't you? You're going to have a nice little visit, just like the last time."

The little boy leaned against the stiff, dry-smelling clothes and felt horribly grieved about something. He began to whimper and said, "I'm hungry. I want something to eat." This reminded him. He began to bellow at the top of his voice; he threw himself upon the carpet and rubbed his nose in a dusty woolly bouquet of roses. "I want my peanuts," he howled. "Somebody took my peanuts."

His grandma knelt beside him and gathered him up so tightly he could hardly move. She called in a calm voice above his howls to Old Janet in the doorway, "Bring me some bread and butter with strawberry jam."

"I want peanuts," yelled the little boy desperately.

"No, you don't, darling," said his grandma. "You don't want horrid old peanuts to make you sick. You're going to have some of grandma's nice fresh bread with good strawberries on it. That's what you're going to have." He sat afterward very quietly and ate and ate. His grandma sat near him and Old Janet stood by, near a tray with a loaf and a glass bowl of jam upon the table at the window. Outside there was a trellis with tube-shaped red flowers clinging all over it, and brown bees singing.

"I hardly know what to do," said Grandma, "it's very . . ."

"Yes, m'am," said Old Janet, "it certainly is . . ."

Grandma said, "I can't possibly see the end of it. It's a terrible . . ."

"It certainly is bad," said Old Janet, "all this upset all the time and him such a baby."

Their voices ran on soothingly. The little boy ate and forgot to listen. He did not know these women, except by name. He could not understand what they were talking about; their hands and their clothes and their voices were dry and far away; they examined him with crinkled eyes without any expression that he could see. He sat there waiting for whatever they would do next with him. He hoped they would let him go out and play in the yard. The room was full of flowers and dark red curtains and big soft chairs, and the windows were open, but it was still dark in there somehow; dark, and a place he did not know, or trust.

"Now drink your milk," said Old Janet, holding out a silver cup.

"I don't want any milk," he said, turning his head away.

"Very well, Janet, he doesn't have to drink it," said Grandma quickly. "Now run out in the garden and play, darling. Janet, get his hoop."

A big strange man came home in the evenings who treated the little boy very confusingly. "Say 'please,' and 'thank you,' young man," he would roar, terrifyingly, when he gave any smallest object to the little boy. "Well, fellow, are you ready for a fight?" he would say, again, doubling up huge, hairy fists and making passes at him. "Come on now, you must learn to box." After the first few times this was fun.

"Don't teach him to be rough," said Grandma. "Time enough for all that."

"Now, Mother, we don't want him to be a sissy," said the big man. "He's got to toughen up early. Come on now, fellow, put up your mitts." The little boy liked this new word for hands. He learned to throw himself upon the strange big man, whose name was Uncle David, and hit him on the chest as hard as he could; the big man would laugh and hit him back with his huge, loose fists. Sometimes, but not often, Uncle David came home in the middle of the day. The little boy missed him on the other days, and would hang on the gate looking down the street for him. One evening he brought a large square package under his arm.

"Come over here, fellow, and see what I've got," he said, pulling off quantities of green paper and string from the box which was full of flat, folded colors. He put something in the little boy's hand. It was limp and silky and bright green with a tube on the end. "Thank you," said the little boy nicely, but not knowing what to do with it.

"Balloons," said Uncle David in triumph. "Now just put your mouth here and blow hard." The little boy blew hard and the green thing began to grow round and thin and silvery.

"Good for your chest," said Uncle David. "Blow some more." The little boy went on blowing and the balloon swelled steadily.

"Stop," said Uncle David, "that's enough." He twisted the tube to keep the air in. "That's the way," he said. "Now I'll blow one, and you blow one, and let's see who can blow up a big balloon the fastest."

They blew and blew, especially Uncle David. He puffed and panted and blew with all his might, but the little boy won. His balloon was perfectly round before Uncle David could even get started. The little boy was so proud he began to dance and shout, "I beat, I beat," and blew in his balloon again. It burst in his face and frightened him so he felt sick. "Ha ha, ho ho ho," whooped Uncle David. "That's the boy. I bet I can't do that. Now let's see." He blew until the beautiful bubble grew and wavered and burst into thin air, and there was only a small colored rag in his hand. This was a fine game. They went on with it until Grandma came in and said, "Time for supper now. No, you can't blow balloons at the table. Tomorrow maybe." And it was all over.

The next day, instead of being given balloons, he was hustled out of bed early, bathed in warm soapy water and given a big breakfast of soft-boiled eggs with toast and jam and milk. His grandma came in to kiss him good morning. "And I hope you'll be a good boy and obey your teacher," she told him.

"What's teacher?" asked the little boy.

"Teacher is at school," said Grandma. "She'll tell you all sorts of things and you must do as she says."

Mama and Papa had talked a great deal about School, and how they must send him there. They had told him it was a fine place with all kinds of toys and other children to play with. He felt he knew about School. "I didn't know it was time, Grandma," he said. "Is it today?"

"It's this very minute," said Grandma. "I told you a week ago."

Old Janet came in with her bonnet on. It was a prickly looking bundle held with a black rubber band under her back hair. "Come on," she said. "This is my busy day." She wore a dead cat slung around her neck, its sharp ears bent over under her baggy chin.

The little boy was excited and wanted to run ahead. "Hold to my hand like I told you," said Old Janet. "Don't go running off like that and get yourself killed."

"I'm going to get killed, I'm going to get killed," sang the little boy, making a tune of his own.

"Don't say that, you give me the creeps," said Old Janet. "Hold to my hand now." She bent over and looked at him, not at his face but at something on his clothes. His eyes followed hers.

"I declare," said Old Janet, "I did forget. I was going to sew it up. I might have known. I *told* your grandma it would be that way from now on."

"What?" asked the little boy.

"Just look at yourself," said Old Janet crossly. He looked at himself. There was a little end of him showing through the slit in his short blue flannel trousers. The trousers came halfway to his knees above, and his socks came halfway to his knees below, and all winter long his knees were cold. He remembered now how cold his knees were in cold weather. And how sometimes he would have to put the part of him that came through the slit back again, because he was cold there too. He saw at once what was wrong, and tried to arrange himself, but his mittens got in the way. Janet said, "Stop that, you bad boy," and with a firm thumb she set him in order, at the same time reaching under his belt to pull down and fold his knit undershirt over his front.

"There now," she said, "try not to disgrace yourself today." He felt guilty and red all over, because he had something that showed when he was dressed that was not supposed to show then. The different women who bathed him always wrapped him quickly in towels and hurried him into his clothes, because they saw something about him he could not see for himself. They hurried him so he never had a chance to see whatever it was they saw, and though he looked at himself when his clothes were off, he could not find out what was wrong with him. Outside, in his clothes, he knew he looked like everybody else, but inside his clothes there was something bad the matter with him. It worried him and confused him and he wondered about it. The only people who never seemed to notice there was something wrong with him were Mommanpoppa. They never called him a bad boy, and all summer long they had taken all his clothes off and let him run in the sand beside a big ocean.

"Look at him, isn't he a love?" Mama would say and Papa would look, and say, "He's got a back like a prize fighter." Uncle David was a prize fighter when he doubled up his mitts and said, "Come on, fellow."

Old Janet held him firmly and took long steps under her big rustling skirts. He did not like Old Janet's smell. It made him a little quivery in the stomach; it was just like wet chicken feathers.

School was easy. Teacher was a square-shaped woman with square short hair and short skirts. She got in the way sometimes, but not often. The people around him were his size; he didn't have always to be stretching his neck up to faces bent over him, and he could sit on the chairs without having to climb. All the children had names, like Frances and Evelyn and Agatha and Edward and Martin, and his own name was Stephen. He was not Mama's "Baby," nor Papa's "Old Man"; he was not Uncle David's "Fellow," or Grandma's "Darling," or even Old Janet's "Bad Boy." He was Stephen. He was learning to read, and to sing a tune to some strange-looking letters or marks written in chalk on a blackboard. You talked one kind of lettering, and you sang another. All the children talked and sang in turn, and then all together. Stephen thought it a fine game. He felt awake and happy. They had soft clay and paper and wires and squares of colors in tin boxes to play with, colored blocks to build houses with. Afterward they all danced in a big ring, and then they danced in pairs, boys with girls. Stephen danced with Frances, and Frances kept saying, "Now you just follow me." She was a little taller than he was, and her hair stood up in short, shiny curls, the color of an ash tray on Papa's desk. She would say, "You can't dance." "I can dance too," said Stephen, jumping around holding her hands, "I can, too, dance." He was certain of it. "*You* can't dance," he told Frances, "you can't dance at all."

Then they had to change partners, and when they came round again, Frances said, "I don't *like* the way you dance." This was different. He felt uneasy about it. He didn't jump quite so high when the phonograph record started going dum-diddy dumdiddy again. "Go ahead, Stephen, you're doing fine," said Teacher, waving her hands together very fast. The dance ended, and they all played "relaxing" for five minutes. They relaxed by swinging their arms back and forth, then rolling their heads round and round. When Old Janet came for him he didn't want to go home. At lunch his grandma told him twice to keep his face out of his plate. "Is that what they teach you at school?" she asked. Uncle David was at home. "Here you are, fellow," he said and gave Stephen two balloons. "Thank you," said Stephen. He put the balloons in his pocket and forgot about them. "I told you that boy could learn something," said Uncle David to Grandma. "Hear him say 'thank you'?"

In the afternoon at school Teacher handed out big wads of clay and told the children to make something out of it. Anything they liked. Stephen decided to make a cat, like Mama's Meeow at home. He did not like Meeow, but he thought it would be easy to make a cat. He could not get the clay to work at all. It simply fell into one lump after another. So he stopped, wiped his hands on his pull-over, remembered his balloons and began blowing one.

"Look at Stephen's horse," said Frances. "Just look at it."

"It's not a horse, it's a cat," said Stephen. The other children gathered around. "It looks like a horse, a little," said Martin.

"It is a cat," said Stephen, stamping his foot, feeling his face turning hot. The other children all laughed and exclaimed over Stephen's cat that looked like a horse. Teacher came down among them. She sat usually at the top of the room before a big table covered with papers and playthings. She picked up Stephen's lump of clay and turned it round and examined it with her kind eyes. "Now, children," she said, "everybody has the right to make anything the way he pleases. If Stephen says this is a cat, it *is* a cat. Maybe you were thinking about a horse, Stephen?"

"It's a *cat*," said Stephen. He was aching all over. He knew then he should have said at first, "Yes, it's a horse." Then they would have let him alone. They would never have known he was trying to make a cat. "It's Meeow," he said in a trembling voice, "but I forgot how she looks."

His balloon was perfectly flat. He started blowing it up again, trying not to cry. Then it was time to go home, and Old Janet came looking for him. While Teacher was talking to other grown-up people who came to take other children home, Frances said, "Give me your balloon; I haven't got a balloon." Stephen handed it to her. He was happy to give it. He reached in his pocket and took out the other. Happily, he gave her that one too. Frances took it, then handed it back. "Now you blow up one and I'll blow up the other, and let's have a race," she said. When their balloons were only half filled Old Janet took Stephen by the arm and said, "Come on here, this is my busy day."

Frances ran after them, calling, "Stephen, you give me back my balloon," and snatched it away. Stephen did not know whether he was surprised to find himself going away with Frances' balloon, or whether he was surprised to see her snatching it as if it really belonged to her. He was badly mixed up in his mind, and Old Janet was hauling him along. One thing he knew, he liked Frances, he was going to see her again tomorrow, and he was going to bring her more balloons.

That evening Stephen boxed awhile with his uncle David, and Uncle David gave him a beautiful orange. "Eat that," he said, "it's good for your health."

"Uncle David, may I have some more balloons?" asked Stephen.

"Well, what do you say first?" asked Uncle David, reaching for the box on the top bookshelf.

"Please," said Stephen.

"That's the word," said Uncle David. He brought out two balloons, a red and a yellow one. Stephen noticed for the first time they had letters on them, very small letters that grew taller and wider as the balloon grew rounder. "Now that's all, fellow," said Uncle David. "Don't ask for any more because that's all." He put the box back on the bookshelf, but not before Stephen had seen that the box was almost full of balloons. He didn't say a word, but went on blowing, and Uncle David blew also. Stephen thought it was the nicest game he had ever known.

He had only one left, the next day, but he took it to school and gave it to Frances. "There are a lot," he said, feeling very proud and warm; "I'll bring you a lot of them."

Frances blew it up until it made a beautiful bubble, and said, "Look, I want to show you something." She took a sharp-pointed stick they used in working the clay; she poked the balloon, and it exploded. "Look at that," she said.

"That's nothing," said Stephen, "I'll bring you some more."

After school, before Uncle David came home, while Grandma was resting, when Old Janet had given him his milk and told him to run away and not bother her, Stephen dragged a chair to the bookshelf, stood upon it and reached into the box. He did not take three or four as he believed he intended; once his hands were upon them he seized what they could hold and jumped off the chair, hugging them to him. He stuffed them into his reefer pocket where they folded down and hardly made a lump.

He gave them all to Frances. There were so many, Frances gave most of them away to the other children. Stephen, flushed with his new joy, the lavish pleasure of giving presents, found almost at once still another happiness. Suddenly he was popular among the children; they invited him specially to join whatever games were up; they fell in at once with his own notions for play, and asked him what he would like to do next. They had festivals of blowing up the beautiful globes, fuller and rounder and thinner, changing as they went from deep color to lighter, paler tones, growing glassy thin, bubbly thin, then bursting with a thrilling loud noise like a toy pistol.

For the first time in his life Stephen had almost too much of something he wanted, and his head was so turned he forgot how this fullness came about, and no longer thought of it as a secret. The next day was Saturday, and Frances came to visit him with her nurse. The nurse and Old Janet sat in Old Janet's room drinking coffee and gossiping, and the children sat on the side porch blowing balloons. Stephen chose an apple-colored one and Frances a pale green one. Between them on the bench lay a tumbled heap of delights still to come.

"I once had a silver balloon," said Frances, "a beyootiful silver one, not round like these; it was a long one. But these are even nicer, I think," she added quickly, for she did want to be polite.

"When you get through with that one," said Stephen, gazing at her with the pure bliss of giving added to loving, "you can blow up a blue one and then a pink one and a yellow one and a purple one." He pushed the heap of limp objects toward her. Her clear-looking eyes, with fine little rays of brown in them like the spokes of a wheel, were full of approval for Stephen. "I wouldn't want to be greedy, though, and blow up all your balloons."

"There'll be plenty more left," said Stephen, and his heart rose under his thin ribs. He felt his ribs with his fingers and discovered with some surprise that they stopped somewhere in front, while Frances sat blowing balloons rather halfheartedly. The truth was, she was tired of balloons. After you blow six or seven your chest gets hollow and your lips feel puckery. She had been blowing balloons steadily for three days now. She had begun to hope they were giving out. "There's boxes and boxes more of them, Frances," said Stephen happily. "Millions more. I guess they'd last and last if we didn't blow too many every day."

Frances said somewhat timidly, "I tell you what. Let's rest awhile and fix some liquish water. Do you like liquish?"

"Yes, I do," said Stephen, "but I haven't got any."

"Couldn't we buy some?" asked Frances. "It's only a cent a stick, the nice rubbery, twisty kind. We can put it in a bottle with some water, and shake it and shake it, and it makes foam on top like soda pop and we can drink it. I'm kind of thirsty," she said in a small, weak voice. "Blowing balloons all the time makes you thirsty, I think."

Stephen, in silence, realized a dreadful truth and a numb feeling crept over him. He did not have a cent to buy licorice for Frances and she was tired of his balloons. This was the first real dismay of his whole life, and he aged at least a year in the next minute, huddled, with his deep, serious blue eyes focused down his nose in intense speculation. What could he do to please Frances that would not cost money? Only yesterday Uncle David had given him a nickel, and he had thrown it away on gumdrops. He regretted that nickel so bitterly his neck and forehead were damp. He was thirsty too.

"I tell you what," he said, brightening with a splendid idea, lamely trailing off on second thought, "I know something we can do, I'll—I . . ."

"I *am* thirsty," said Frances with gentle persistence. "I think I'm so thirsty maybe I'll have to go home." She did not leave the bench, though, but sat, turning her grieved mouth toward Stephen.

Stephen quivered with the terrors of the adventure before him, but he said boldly, "I'll make some lemonade. I'll get sugar and lemon and some ice and we'll have lemonade."

"Oh, I love lemonade," cried Frances. "I'd rather have lemonade than liquish."

"You stay right here," said Stephen, "and I'll get everything."

He ran around the house, and under Old Janet's window he heard the dry, chattering voices of the two old women whom he must outwit. He sneaked on tiptoe to the pantry, took a lemon lying there by itself, a handful of lump sugar and a china teapot, smooth, round, with flowers and leaves all over it. These he left on the kitchen table while he broke a piece of ice with a sharp metal pick he had been forbidden to touch. He put the ice in the pot, cut the lemon and squeezed it as well as he could—a lemon was tougher and more slippery than he had thought—and mixed sugar and water. He decided there was not enough sugar so he sneaked back and took another handful. He was back on the porch in an astonishingly short time, his face tight, his knees trembling, carrying iced lemonade to thirsty Frances with both his devoted hands.

A pace distant from her he stopped, literally stabbed through with a thought. Here he stood in broad daylight carrying a teapot with lemonade in it, and his grandma or Old Janet might walk through the door at any moment.

"Come on, Frances," he whispered loudly. "Let's go round to the back behind the rose bushes where it's shady." Frances leaped up and ran like a deer beside him, her face wise with knowledge of why they ran; Stephen ran stiffly, cherishing his teapot with clenched hands.

It was shady behind the rose bushes, and much safer. They sat side by side on the dampish ground, legs doubled under, drinking in turn from the slender spout. Stephen took his just share in large, cool, delicious swallows. When Frances drank she set her round pink mouth daintily to the spout and her throat beat steadily as a heart. Stephen was thinking he had really done something pretty nice for Frances. He did not know where his own happiness was; it was mixed with the sweet-sour taste in his mouth and a cool feeling in his bosom because Frances was there drinking his lemonade which he had got for her with great danger.

Frances said, "My, what big swallows you take," when his turn came next.

"No bigger than yours," he told her downrightly. "You take awfully big swallows."

"Well," said Frances, turning this criticism into an argument for her rightness about things, "that's the way to drink lemonade anyway." She peered into the teapot. There was quite a lot of lemonade left and she was beginning to feel she had enough. "Let's make up a game and see who can take the biggest swallows."

This was such a wonderful notion they grew reckless, tipping the spout into their opened mouths above their heads until lemonade welled up and ran over their chins in rills down their fronts. When they tired of this there was still lemonade left in the pot. They played first at giving the rosebush a drink and ended by baptizing it. "Name father son holygoat," shouted Stephen, pouring. At this sound Old Janet's face appeared over the low hedge, with the tan, disgusted-looking face of Frances' nurse hanging over her shoulder.

"Well, just as I thought," said Old Janet. "Just as I expected." The bag under her chin waggled.

"We were thirsty," he said; "we were awfully thirsty." Frances said nothing, but she gazed steadily at the toes of her shoes.

"Give me that teapot," said Old Janet, taking it with a rude snatch. "Just because you're thirsty is no reason," said Old Janet. "You can ask for things. You don't have to steal."

"We didn't steal," cried Frances suddenly. "We didn't. We didn't!"

"That's enough from you, missy," said her nurse. "Come straight out of there. You have nothing to do with this."

"Oh, I don't know," said Old Janet with a hard stare at Frances' nurse. "*He* never did such a thing before, by himself."

"Come on," said the nurse to Frances, "this is no place for you." She held Frances by the wrist and started walking away so fast Frances had to run to keep up. "Nobody can call *us* thieves and get away with it."

"You don't have to steal, even if others do," said Old Janet to Stephen, in a high carrying voice. "If you so much as pick up a lemon in somebody else's house you're a little thief." She lowered her voice then and said, "Now I'm going to tell your grandma and you'll see what you get."

"He went in the icebox and left it open," Janet told Grandma, "and he got into the lump sugar and spilt it all over the floor. Lumps everywhere underfoot. He dribbled water all over the clean kitchen floor, and he baptized the rose bush, blaspheming. And he took your Spode teapot."

"I didn't either," said Stephen loudly, trying to free his hand from Old Janet's big hard fist.

"Don't tell fibs," said Old Janet; "that's the last straw."

"Oh, dear," said Grandma. "He's not a baby any more." She shut the book she was reading and pulled the wet front of his pullover toward her. "What's this sticky stuff on him?" she asked and straightened her glasses.

"Lemonade," said Old Janet. "He took the last lemon."

They were in the big dark room with the red curtains. Uncle David walked in from the room with the bookcases, holding a box in his uplifted hand. "Look here," he said to Stephen. "What's become of all my balloons?"

Stephen knew well that Uncle David was not really asking a question.

Stephen, sitting on a footstool at his grandma's knee, felt sleepy. He leaned heavily and wished he could put his head on her lap, but he might go to sleep, and it would be wrong to go to sleep while Uncle David was still talking. Uncle David walked about the room with his hands in his pockets, talking to Grandma. Now and then he would walk over to a lamp and, leaning, peer into the top of the shade, winking in the light, as if he expected to find something there.

"It's simply in the blood, I told her," said Uncle David. "I told her she would simply have to come and get him, and keep him. She asked me if I meant to call him a thief and I said if she could think of a more exact word I'd be glad to hear it."

"You shouldn't have said that," commented Grandma calmly.

"Why not? She might as well know the facts. . . . I suppose he can't help it," said Uncle David, stopping now in front of Stephen and dropping his chin into his collar, "I shouldn't expect too much of him, but you can't begin too early—"

"The trouble is," said Grandma, and while she spoke she took Stephen by the chin and held it up so that he had to meet her eye; she talked steadily in a mournful tone, but Stephen could not understand. She ended, "It's not just about the balloons, of course."

"It *is* about the balloons," said Uncle David angrily, "because balloons now mean something worse later. But what can you expect? His father—well, it's in the blood. He—"

"That's your sister's husband you're talking about," said Grandma, "and there is no use making things worse. Besides, you don't really *know*."

"I *do* know," said Uncle David. And he talked again very fast, walking up and down. Stephen tried to understand, but the sounds were strange and floating just over his head. They were talking about his father, and they did not like him. Uncle

David came over and stood above Stephen and Grandma. He hunched over them with a frowning face, a long, crooked shadow from him falling across them to the wall. To Stephen he looked like his father, and he shrank against his grandma's skirts.

"The question is, what to do with him now?" asked Uncle David. "If we keep him here, he'd just be a—I won't be bothered with him. Why can't they take care of their own child? That house is crazy. Too far gone already, I'm afraid. No training. No example."

"You're right, they must take him and keep him," said Grandma. She ran her hands over Stephen's head; tenderly she pinched the nape of his neck between thumb and forefinger. "You're your Grandma's darling," she told him, "and you've had a nice long visit, and now you're going home. Mama is coming for you in a few minutes. Won't that be nice?"

"I want my mama," said Stephen, whimpering, for his grandma's face frightened him. There was something wrong with her smile.

Uncle David sat down. "Come over here, fellow," he said, wagging a forefinger at Stephen. Stephen went over slowly, and Uncle David drew him between his wide knees in their loose, rough clothes. "You ought to be ashamed of yourself," he said, "stealing Uncle David's balloons when he had already given you so many."

"It wasn't that," said Grandma quickly. "Don't say that. It will make an impression—"

"I hope it does," said Uncle David in a louder voice; "I hope he remembers it all his life. If he belonged to me I'd give him a good thrashing."

Stephen felt his mouth, his chin, his whole face jerking. He opened his mouth to take a breath, and tears and noise burst from him. "Stop that, fellow, stop that," said Uncle David, shaking him gently by the shoulders, but Stephen could not stop. He drew his breath again and it came back in a howl. Old Janet came to the door.

"Bring me some cold water," called Grandma. There was a flurry, a commotion, a breath of cool air from the hall, the door slammed, and Stephen heard his mother's voice. His howl died away, his breath sobbed and fluttered, he turned his dimmed eyes and saw her standing there. His heart turned over within him and he bleated like a lamb, "Maaaaama," running toward her. Uncle David stood back as Mama swooped in and fell on her knees beside Stephen. She gathered him to her and stood up with him in her arms.

"What are you doing to my baby?" she asked Uncle David in a thickened voice. "I should never have let him come here. I should have known better—"

"You always should know better," said Uncle David, "and you never do. And you never will. You haven't got it here," he told her, tapping his forehead.

"David," said Grandma, "that's your—"

"Yes, I know, she's my sister," said Uncle David. "I know it. But if she must run away and marry a—"

"Shut up," said Mama.

"And bring more like him into the world, let her keep them at home. I say let her keep—"

Mama set Stephen on the floor and, holding him by the hand, she said to Grandma all in a rush as if she were reading something, "Good-by, Mother. This is the last time, really the last. I can't bear it any longer. Say good-by to Stephen; you'll never see him again. You let this happen. It's your fault. You know David was a coward and a bully and a self-righteous little beast all his life and you never crossed him in anything. You let him bully me all my life and you let him slander my husband and call my baby a thief, and now this is the end. . . . He calls my baby a thief over a few horrible little balloons because he doesn't like my husband. . . ."

She was panting and staring about from one to the other. They were all standing. Now Grandma said, "Go home, daughter. Go away, David. I'm sick of your quarreling. I've never had a day's peace or comfort from either of you. I'm sick of you both. Now let me alone and stop this noise. Go away," said Grandma in a wavering voice. She took out her handkerchief and wiped first one eye and then the other and said, "All this hate, hate—what is it for? . . . So this is the way it turns out. Well, let me alone."

"You and your little advertising balloons," said Mama to

Uncle David. "The big honest businessman advertises with balloons and if he loses one he'll be ruined. And your beastly little moral notions . . ."

Grandma went to the door to meet Old Janet, who handed her a glass of water. Grandma drank it all, standing there.

"Is your husband coming for you, or are you going home by yourself?" she asked Mama.

"I'm driving myself," said Mama in a far-away voice as if her mind had wandered. "You know he wouldn't set foot in this house."

"I should think not," said Uncle David.

"Come on, Stephen darling," said Mama. "It's far past his bedtime," she said, to no one in particular. "Imagine keeping a baby up to torture him about a few miserable little bits of colored rubber." She smiled at Uncle David with both rows of teeth as she passed him on the way to the door, keeping between him and Stephen. "Ah, where would we be without high moral standards," she said, and then to Grandma, "Good night, Mother," in quite her usual voice. "I'll see you in a day or so."

"Yes, indeed," said Grandma cheerfully, coming out into the hall with Stephen and Mama. "Let me hear from you. Ring me up tomorrow. I hope you'll be feeling better."

"I feel very well now," said Mama brightly, laughing. She bent down and kissed Stephen. "Sleepy, darling? Papa's waiting to see you. Don't go to sleep until you've kissed your papa good night."

Stephen woke with a sharp jerk. He raised his head and put out his chin a little. "I don't want to go home," he said; "I want to go to school. I don't want to see Papa, I don't like him."

Mama laid her palm over his mouth softly. "Darling, don't."

Uncle David put his head out with a kind of snort. "There you are," he said. "There you've got a statement from headquarters."

Mama opened the door and ran, almost carrying Stephen. She ran across the sidewalk, jerking open the car door and dragging Stephen in after her. She spun the car around and dashed forward so sharply Stephen was almost flung out of the seat. He sat braced then with all his might, hands digging into the cushions. The car speeded up and the trees and houses whizzed by all flattened out. Stephen began suddenly to sing to himself, a quiet, inside song so Mama would not hear. He sang his new secret; it was a comfortable, sleepy song: "I hate Papa, I hate Mama, I hate Grandma, I hate Uncle David, I hate Old Janet, I hate Marjory, I hate Papa, I hate Mama . . ."

His head bobbed, leaned, came to rest on Mama's knee, eyes closed. Mama drew him closer and slowed down, driving with one hand.

A Day's Work

THE dull scrambling like a giant rat in the wall meant the dumb-waiter was on its way up, the janitress below hauling on the cable. Mrs. Halloran paused, thumped her iron on the board, and said, "There it is. Late. You could have put on your shoes and gone around the corner and brought the things an hour ago. I can't do everything."

Mr. Halloran pulled himself out of the chair, clutching the arms and heaving to his feet slowly, looking around as if he hoped to find crutches standing near. "Wearing out your socks, too," added Mrs. Halloran. "You ought either go barefoot outright or wear your shoes over your socks as God intended," she said. "Sock feet. What's the good of it, I'd like to know? Neither one thing nor the other."

She unrolled a salmon-colored chiffon nightgown with cream-colored lace and broad ribbons on it, gave it a light flirt in the air, and spread it on the board. "God's mercy, look at that indecent thing," she said. She thumped the iron again and pushed it back and forth over the rumpled cloth. "You might just set the things in the cupboard," she said, "and not leave them around on the floor. You might just."

Mr. Halloran took a sack of potatoes from the dumb-waiter and started for the cupboard in the corner next the icebox. "You might as well take a load," said Mrs. Halloran. "There's no need on earth making a half-dozen trips back and forth. I'd think the poorest sort of man could well carry more than five pounds of potatoes at one time. But maybe not."

Her voice tapped on Mr. Halloran's ears like wood on wood. "Mind your business, will you?" he asked, not speaking to her directly. He carried on the argument with himself. "Oh, I couldn't do that, Mister Honey," he answered in a dull falsetto. "Don't ever ask me to think of such a thing, even. It wouldn't be right," he said, standing still with his knees bent, glaring bitterly over the potato sack at the scrawny strange woman he had never liked, that one standing there ironing clothes with a dirty look on her whole face like a suffering saint. "I may not be much good any more," he told her in his

402

own voice, "but I still have got wits enough to take groceries off a dumb-waiter, mind you."

"That's a miracle," said Mrs. Halloran. "I'm thankful for that much."

"There's the telephone," said Mr. Halloran, sitting in the armchair again and taking his pipe out of his shirt pocket.

"I heard it as well," said Mrs. Halloran, sliding the iron up and down over the salmon-colored chiffon.

"It's for you, I've no further business in this world," said Mr. Halloran. His little greenish eyes glittered; he exposed his two sharp dogteeth in a grin.

"You could answer it. It could be the wrong number again or for somebody downstairs," said Mrs. Halloran, her flat voice going flatter, even.

"Let it go in any case," decided Mr. Halloran, "for my own part, that is." He struck a match on the arm of his chair, touched off his pipe, and drew in his first puff while the telephone went on with its nagging.

"It might be Maggie again," said Mrs. Halloran.

"Let her ring, then," said Mr. Halloran, settling back and crossing his legs.

"God help a man who won't answer the telephone when his own daughter calls up for a word," commented Mrs. Halloran to the ceiling. "And she in deep trouble, too, with her husband treating her like a dog about the money, and sitting out late nights in saloons with that crowd from the Little Tammany Association. He's getting into politics now with the McCorkery gang. No good will come of it, and I told her as much."

"She's no troubles at all, her man's a sharp fellow who will get ahead if she'll let him alone," said Mr. Halloran. "She's nothing to complain of, I could tell her. But what's a father?" Mr. Halloran cocked his head toward the window that opened on the brick-paved areaway and crowed like a rooster, "What's a father these days and who would heed his advice?"

"You needn't tell the neighbors, there's disgrace enough already," said Mrs. Halloran. She set the iron back on the gas ring and stepped out to the telephone on the first stair landing. Mr. Halloran leaned forward, his thin, red-haired hands hanging loosely between his knees, his warm pipe sending up

its good decent smell right into his nose. The woman hated
the pipe and the smell; she was a woman born to make any
man miserable. Before the depression, while he still had a good
job and prospects of a raise, before he went on relief, before
she took in fancy washing and ironing, in the Good Days
Before, God's pity, she didn't exactly keep her mouth shut,
there wasn't a word known to man she couldn't find an answer
for, but she knew which side her bread was buttered on, and
put up with it. Now she was, you might say, buttering her own
bread and she never forgot it for a minute. And it's her
own fault we're not riding round today in a limousine with ash
trays and a speaking tube and a cut-glass vase for flowers in it.
It's what a man gets for marrying one of these holy women.
Gerald McCorkery had told him as much, in the beginning.

"There's a girl will spend her time holding you down," Gerald had told him. "You're putting your head in a noose will
strangle the life out of you. Heed the advice of one who wishes
you well," said Gerald McCorkery. This was after he had barely
set eyes on Lacey Mahaffy one Sunday morning in Coney
Island. It was like McCorkery to see that in a flash, born judge
of human nature that he was. He could look a man over, size
him up, and there was an end to it. And if the man didn't pass
muster, McCorkery could ease him out in a way that man
would never know how it happened. It was the secret of
McCorkery's success in the world.

"This is Rosie, herself," said Gerald that Sunday in Coney
Island. "Meet the future Mrs. Gerald J. McCorkery." Lacey
Mahaffy's narrow face had gone sour as whey under her big
straw hat. She barely nodded to Rosie, who gave Mr. Halloran
a look that fairly undressed him right there. Mr. Halloran had
thought, too, that McCorkery was picking a strange one; she
was good-looking all right, but she had the smell of a regular
little Fourteenth Street hustler if Halloran knew anything
about women. "Come on," said McCorkery, his arm around
Rosie's waist, "let's all go on the roller coaster." But Lacey
would not. She said, "No, thank you. We didn't plan to stay,
and we must go now." On the way home Mr. Halloran said,
"Lacey, you judge too harshly. Maybe that's a nice girl at heart;
hasn't had your opportunities." Lacey had turned upon him a
face ugly as an angry cat's, and said, "She's a loose, low woman,

and 'twas an insult to introduce her to me." It was a good while before the pretty fresh face that Mr. Halloran had fallen in love with returned to her.

Next day in Billy's Place, after three drinks each, McCorkery said, "Watch your step, Halloran; think of your future. There's a straight good girl I don't doubt, but she's no sort of mixer. A man getting into politics needs a wife who can meet all kinds. A man needs a woman knows how to loosen her corsets and sit easy."

Mrs. Halloran's voice was going on in the hall, a steady dry rattle like old newspapers blowing on a park bench. "I told you before it's no good coming to me with your troubles now. I warned you in time but you wouldn't listen. . . . I told you just how it would be, I tried my best. . . . No, you couldn't listen, you always knew better than your mother. . . . So now all you've got to do is stand by your married vows and make the best of it. . . . Now listen to me, if you want himself to do right you have to do right first. The woman has to do right first, and then if the man won't do right in turn it's no fault of hers. You do right whether he does wrong or no, just because he does wrong is no excuse for you."

"Ah, will you hear that?" Mr. Halloran asked the areaway in an awed voice. "There's a holy terror of a saint for you."

". . . the woman has to do right first, I'm telling you," said Mrs. Halloran into the telephone, "and then if he's a devil in spite of it, why she has to do right without any help from him." Her voice rose so the neighbors could get an earful if they wanted. "I know you from old, you're just like your father. You must be doing something wrong yourself or you wouldn't be in this fix. You're doing wrong this minute, calling over the telephone when you ought to be getting your work done. I've got an iron on, working over the dirty nightgowns of a kind of woman I wouldn't soil my foot on if I'd had a man to take care of me. So now you do up your housework and dress yourself and take a walk in the fresh air. . . ."

"A little fresh air never hurt anybody," commented Mr. Halloran loudly through the open window. "It's the gas gets a man down."

"Now listen to me, Maggie, that's not the way to talk over the public wires. Now you stop that crying and go and do your duty and don't be worrying me any more. And stop saying you're going to leave your husband, because where will you go, for one thing? Do you want to walk the streets or set up a laundry in your kitchen? You can't come back here, you'll stay with your husband where you belong. Don't be a fool, Maggie. You've got your living, and that's more than many a woman better than you has got. Yes, your father's all right. No, he's just sitting here, the same. God knows what's to become of us. But you know how he is, little he cares. . . . Now remember this, Maggie, if anything goes wrong with your married life it's your own fault and you needn't come here for sympathy. . . . I can't waste any more time on it. Goodby."

Mr. Halloran, his ears standing up for fear of missing a word, thought how Gerald J. McCorkery had gone straight on up the ladder with Rosie; and for every step the McCorkerys took upward, he, Michael Halloran, had taken a step downward with Lacey Mahaffy. They had started as greenhorns with the same chances at the same time and the same friends, but McCorkery had seized all his opportunities as they came, getting in steadily with the Big Shots in ward politics, one good thing leading to another. Rosie had known how to back him up and push him onward. The McCorkerys for years had invited him and Lacey to come over to the house and be sociable with the crowd, but Lacey would not.

"You can't run with that fast set and drink and stay out nights and hold your job," said Lacey, "and you should know better than to ask your wife to associate with that woman." Mr. Halloran had got into the habit of dropping around by himself, now and again, for McCorkery still liked him, was still willing to give him a foothold in the right places, still asked him for favors at election time. There was always a good lively crowd at the McCorkerys, wherever they were; for they moved ever so often to a better place, with more furniture. Rosie helped hand around the drinks, taking a few herself with a good word for everybody. The player piano or the victrola would be going full blast, with everybody dancing, all looking like ready money and a bright future. He would get home late these evenings, back to the same little cold-water walk-up flat, because Lacey would not spend a dollar for show. It must all go into savings against old age, she said. He would be full of good food and drink, and find Lacey, in a bungalow apron, warming up the fried potatoes once more, cross and bitterly silent, hanging her head and frowning at the smell of liquor on his breath. "You might at least eat the potatoes when I've fried them and waited all this time," she would say. "Ah, eat them yourself, they're none of mine," he would snarl in his disappointment with her, and with the life she was leading him.

He had believed with all his heart for years that he would one day be manager of one of the G. and I. chain grocery stores he worked for, and when that hope gave out there was still his pension when they retired him. But two years before it was due they fired him, on account of the depression, they said. Overnight he was on the sidewalk, with no place to go with the news but home. "Jesus," said Mr. Halloran, still remembering that day after nearly seven years of idleness.

The depression hadn't touched McCorkery. He went on and on up the ladder, giving beefsteaks and beanfests and beer parties for the boys in Billy's Place, standing in with the right men and never missing a trick. At last the Gerald J. McCorkery Club chartered a whole boat for a big excursion up the river. It was a great day, with Lacey sitting at home sulking. After election Rosie had her picture in the papers, smiling at McCorkery; not fat exactly, just a fine figure of a woman with flowers pinned on her spotted fur coat, her teeth as good as ever. Oh, God, there was a girl for any man's money. Mr. Halloran saw out of his eye-corner the bony stooped back of Lacey Mahaffy, standing on one foot to rest the other like a tired old horse, leaning on her hands waiting for the iron to heat.

"That was Maggie, with her woes," she said.

"I hope you gave her some good advice," said Mr. Halloran. "I hope you told her to take up her hat and walk out on him."

Mrs. Halloran suspended the iron over a pair of pink satin panties. "I told her to do right and leave wrong-doing to the men," she said, in her voice like a phonograph record running down. "I told her to bear with the trouble God sends as her mother did before her."

Mr. Halloran gave a loud groan and knocked out his pipe on the chair arm. "You would ruin the world, woman, if you could, with your wicked soul, treating a new-married girl as if she had

no home and no parents to come to. But she's no daughter of
mine if she sits there peeling potatoes, letting a man run over
her. No daughter of mine and I'll tell her so if she—"

"You know well she's your daughter, so hold your tongue,"
said Mrs. Halloran, "and if she heeded you she'd be walking
the streets this minute. I brought her up an honest girl, and an
honest woman she's going to be or I'll take her over my knee
as I did when she was little. So there you are, Halloran."

Mr. Halloran leaned far back in his chair and felt along the
shelf above his head until his fingers touched a half-dollar he
had noticed there. His hand closed over it, he got up instantly
and looked about for his hat.

"Keep your daughter, Lacey Mahaffy," he said, "she's none
of mine but the fruits of your long sinning with the Holy Ghost.
And now I'm off for a little round and a couple of beers to
keep my mind from dissolving entirely."

"You can't have that dollar you just now sneaked off the
shelf," said Mrs. Halloran. "So you think I'm blind besides?
Put it back where you found it. That's for our daily bread."

"I'm sick of bread daily," said Mr. Halloran, "I need beer. It
was not a dollar, but a half-dollar as you know well."

"Whatever it was," said Mrs. Halloran, "it stands instead of
a dollar to me. So just drop it."

"You've got tomorrow's potatoes sewed up in your pocket
this minute, and God knows what sums in that black box
wherever you hide it, besides the life savings," said Mr. Halloran. "I earned this half-dollar on relief, and it's going to be
spent properly. And I'll not be back for supper, so you'll save
on that, too. So long, Lacey Mahaffy, I'm off."

"If you never come back, it will be all the same," said Mrs.
Halloran, not looking up.

"If I came back with a pocket full of money, you'd be glad
to see me," said Mr. Halloran.

"It would want to be a great sum," said Mrs. Halloran.

Mr. Halloran shut the door behind him with a fine slam.

He strolled out into the clear fall weather, a late afternoon
sun warming his neck and brightening the old red-brick, high-
stooped houses of Perry Street. He would go after all these
years to Billy's Place, he might find some luck there. He took
his time, though, speaking to the neighbors as he went.

"Good afternoon, Mr. Halloran." "Good afternoon to you, Missis Caffery." . . . "It's fine weather for the time of year, Mr. Gogarty." "It is indeed, Mr. Halloran." Mr. Halloran thrived on these civilities, he loved to flourish his hat and give a hearty good day like a man who has nothing on his mind. Ah, there was the young man from the G. and I. store around the corner. He knew what kind of job Mr. Halloran once held there. "Good day, Mr. Halloran." "Good day to you, Mr. McInerny, how's business holding up with you?" "Good for the times, Mr. Halloran, that's the best I can say." "Things are not getting any better, Mr. McInerny." "It's the truth we are all hanging on by the teeth now, Mr. Halloran."

Soothed by this acknowledgment of man's common misfortune Mr. Halloran greeted the young cop at the corner. The cop, with his quick eyesight, was snatching a read from a newspaper on the stand across the sidewalk. "How do you do, Young O'Fallon," asked Mr. Halloran, "is your business lively these days?"

"Quiet as the tomb itself on this block," said Young O'Fallon. "But that's a sad thing about Connolly, now." His eyes motioned toward the newspaper.

"Is he dead?" asked Mr. Halloran; "I haven't been out until now, I didn't see the papers."

"Ah, not yet," said Young O'Fallon, "but the G-men are after him, it looks they'll get him surely this time."

"Connolly in bad with the G-men? Holy Jesus," said Mr. Halloran, "who will they go after next? The meddlers."

"It's that numbers racket," said the cop. "What's the harm, I'd like to know? A man must get his money from somewhere when he's in politics. They oughta give him a chance."

"Connolly's a great fellow, God bless him, I hope he gives them the slip," said Mr. Halloran, "I hope he goes right through their hands like a greased pig."

"He's smart," said the cop. "That Connolly's a smooth one. He'll come out of it."

Ah, will he though? Mr. Halloran asked himself. Who is safe if Connolly goes under? Wait till I give Lacey Mahaffy the news about Connolly, I'll like seeing her face the first time in twenty years. Lacey kept saying, "A man is a downright fool must be a crook to get rich. Plenty of the best people get rich and do no

harm by it. Look at the Connollys now, good practical
Catholics with nine children and more to come if God sends
them, and Mass every day, and they're rolling in wealth richer
than your McCorkerys with all their wickedness." So there you
are, Lacey Mahaffy, wrong again, and welcome to your pious
Connollys. Still and all it was Connolly who had given Gerald
McCorkery his start in the world; McCorkery had been publicity man and then campaign manager for Connolly, in the
days when Connolly had Tammany in the palm of his hand
and the sky was the limit. And McCorkery had begun at the
beginning, God knows. He was running a little basement
place first, rent almost nothing, where the boys of the Connolly Club and the Little Tammany Association, just the mere
fringe of the district, you might say, could drop in for quiet
evenings for a game and a drink along with the talk. Nothing
low, nothing but what was customary, with the house taking a
cut on the winnings and a fine profit on the liquor, and holding the crowd together. Many was the big plan hatched there
came out well for everybody. For everybody but myself, and
why was that? And when McCorkery says to me, "You can take
over now and run the place for the McCorkery Club," ah,
there was my chance and Lacey Mahaffy wouldn't hear of it,
and with Maggie coming on just then it wouldn't do to excite
her.

Mr. Halloran went on, following his feet that knew the way
to Billy's Place, head down, not speaking to passersby any
more, but talking it out with himself again, again. What a track
to go over seeing clearly one by one the crossroads where he
might have taken a different turn that would have changed all
his fortunes; but no, he had gone the other way and now it
was too late. She wouldn't say a thing but "It's not right and
you know it, Halloran," so what could a man do in all? Ah, you
could have gone on with your rightful affairs like any other
man, Halloran, it's not the woman's place to decide such
things; she'd have come round once she saw the money, or a
good whack on the backsides would have put her in her place.
Never had mortal woman needed a good walloping worse
than Lacey Mahaffy, but he could never find it in his heart to
give it to her for her own good. That was just another of your
many mistakes, Halloran. But there was always the lifelong job

with the G. and I. and peace in the house more or less. Many a man envied me in those days I remember, and I was resting easy on the savings and knowing with that and the pension I could finish out my life with some little business of my own. "What came of that?" Mr. Halloran inquired in a low voice, looking around him. Nobody answered. You know well what came of it, Halloran. You were fired out like a delivery boy, two years before your time was out. Why did you sit there watching the trick being played on others before you, knowing well it could happen to you and never quite believing what you saw with your own eyes? G. and I. gave me my start, when I was green in this country, and they were my own kind or I thought so. Well, it's done now. Yes, it's done now, but there was all the years you could have cashed in on the numbers game with the best of them, helping collect the protection money and taking your cut. You could have had a fortune by now in Lacey's name, safe in the bank. It was good quiet profit and none the wiser. But they're wiser now, Halloran, don't forget; still it's a lump of grief and disappointment to swallow all the same. The game's up with Connolly, maybe; Lacey Mahaffy had said, "Numbers is just another way of stealing from the poor, and you weren't born to be a thief like that McCorkery." Ah, God, no, Halloran, you were born to rot on relief and maybe that's honest enough for her. That Lacey!— A fortune in her name would have been no good to me whatever. She's got all the savings tied up, such as they are, she'll pinch and she'll starve, she'll wash dirty clothes first, she won't give up a penny to live on. She has stood in my way, McCorkery, like a skeleton rattling its bones, and you were right about her, she has been my ruin. "Ah, it's not too late yet, Halloran," said McCorkery, appearing plain as day inside Mr. Halloran's head with the same old face and way with him. "Never say die, Halloran. Elections are coming on again, it's a busy time for all, there's work to be done and you're the very man I'm looking for. Why didn't you come to me sooner, you know I never forget an old friend. You don't deserve your ill fortune, Halloran," McCorkery told him; "I said so to others and I say it now to your face, never did man deserve more of the world than you, Halloran, but the truth is, there's not always enough good luck to go round; but it's your turn now, and I've got a

job for you up to your abilities at last. For a man like you,
there's nothing to it at all, you can toss it off with one hand
tied, Halloran, and good money in it. Organization work, just
among your own neighbors, where you're known and respected for a man of your word and an old friend of Gerald
McCorkery. Now look, Halloran," said Gerald McCorkery,
tipping him the wink, "do I need to say more? It's voters in
large numbers we're after, Halloran, and you're to bring them
in, alive or dead. Keep your eye on the situation at all times
and get in touch with me when necessary. And name your figure in the way of money. And come up to the house sometimes, Halloran, why don't you? Rosie has asked me a hundred
times, 'Whatever went with Halloran, the life of the party?'
That's the way you stand with Rosie, Halloran. We're in a two-
story flat now with green velvet curtains and carpets you can
sink to your shoe-tops in, and there's no reason at all why you
shouldn't have the same kind of place if you want it. With your
gifts, you were never meant to be a poor man."

Ah, but Lacey Mahaffy wouldn't have it, maybe. "Then get
yourself another sort of woman, Halloran, you're a good man
still, find yourself a woman like Rosie to snuggle down with at
night." Yes, but McCorkery, you forget that Lacey Mahaffy
had legs and hair and eyes and a complexion fit for a chorus
girl. But would she do anything with them? Never. Would you
believe there was a woman wouldn't take off all her clothes at
once even to bathe herself? What a hateful thing she was with
her evil mind thinking everything was a sin, and never giving a
man a chance to show himself a man in any way. But she's
faded away now, her mean soul shows out all over her, she's
ugly as sin itself now, McCorkery. "It's what I told you would
happen," said McCorkery, "but now with the job and the
money you can go your ways and let Lacey Mahaffy go hers."
I'll do it, McCorkery. "And forget about Connolly. Just remember I'm my own man and always was. Connolly's finished, but I'm not. Stronger than ever, Halloran, with Connolly
out of the way. I saw this coming long ever ago, Halloran, I got
clear of it. They don't catch McCorkery with his pants down,
Halloran. And I almost forgot . . . Here's something for the
running expenses to start. Take this for the present, and
there's more to come. . . ."

Mr. Halloran stopped short, a familiar smell floated under his nose: the warm beer-and-beefsteak smell of Billy's Place, sawdust and onions, like any other bar maybe, but with something of its own besides. The talk within him stopped also as if a hand had been laid on his mind. He drew his fist out of his pocket almost expecting to find green money in it. The half dollar was in his palm. "I'll stay while it lasts and hope McCorkery will come in."

The moment he stepped inside his eye lighted on McCorkery standing at the bar pouring his own drink from the bottle before him. Billy was mopping the bar before him idly, and his eye, swimming toward Halloran, looked like an oyster in its own juice. McCorkery saw him too. "Well, blow me down," he said, in a voice that had almost lost its old County Mayo ring, "if it ain't my old sidekick from the G. and I. Step right up, Halloran," he said, his poker-face as good as ever, no man ever saw Gerald McCorkery surprised at anything. "Step up and name your choice."

Mr. Halloran glowed suddenly with the warmth around the heart he always had at the sight of McCorkery, he couldn't put a name on it, but there was something about the man. Ah, it was Gerald all right, the same, who never forgot a friend and never seemed to care whether a man was rich or poor, with his face of granite and his eyes like blue agates in his head, a rock of a man surely. There he was, saying "Step right up," as if they had parted only yesterday; portly and solid in his expensive-looking clothes, as always; his hat a darker gray than his suit, with a devil-may-care roll to the brim, but nothing sporting, mind you. All first-rate, well made, and the right thing for him, more power to him. Mr. Halloran said, "Ah, McCorkery, you're the one man on this round earth I hoped to see today, but I says to myself, maybe he doesn't come round to Billy's Place so much nowadays."

"And why not?" asked McCorkery, "I've been coming around to Billy's Place for twenty-five years now, it's still head-quarters for the old guard of the McCorkery Club, Halloran." He took in Mr. Halloran from head to foot in a flash of a glance and turned toward the bottle.

"I was going to have a beer," said Mr. Halloran, "but the smell of that whiskey changes my mind for me." McCorkery poured a second glass, they lifted the drinks with an identical crook of the elbow, a flick of the wrist at each other.

"Here's to crime," said McCorkery, and "Here's looking at you," said Mr. Halloran, merrily. Ah, to hell with it, he was back where he belonged, in good company. He put his foot on the rail and snapped down his whiskey, and no sooner was his glass on the bar than McCorkery was filling it again. "Just time for a few quick ones," he said, "before the boys get here." Mr. Halloran downed that one, too, before he noticed that McCorkery hadn't filled his own glass. "I'm ahead of you," said McCorkery, "I'll skip this one."

There was a short pause, a silence fell around them that seemed to ooze like a fog from somewhere deep in McCorkery, it was suddenly as if he had not really been there at all, or hadn't uttered a word. Then he said outright: "Well, Halloran, let's have it. What's on your mind?" And he poured two more drinks. That was McCorkery all over, reading your thoughts and coming straight to the point.

Mr. Halloran closed his hand round his glass and peered into the little pool of whiskey. "Maybe we could sit down," he said, feeling weak-kneed all at once. McCorkery took the bottle and moved over to the nearest table. He sat facing the door, his look straying there now and then, but he had a set, listening face as if he was ready to hear anything.

"You know what I've had at home all these years," began Mr. Halloran, solemnly, and paused.

"Oh, God, yes," said McCorkery with simple good-fellowship. "How is herself these days?"

"Worse than ever," said Mr. Halloran, "but that's not it."

"What is it, then, Halloran?" asked McCorkery, pouring drinks. "You know well you can speak out your mind to me. Is it a loan?"

"No," said Mr. Halloran. "It's a job."

"Now that's a different matter," said McCorkery. "What kind of a job?"

Mr. Halloran, his head sunk between his shoulders, saw McCorkery wave a hand and nod at half a dozen men who came in and ranged themselves along the bar. "Some of the boys," said McCorkery. "Go on." His face was tougher, and quieter, as if the drink gave him a firm hold on himself. Mr.

Halloran said what he had planned to say, had said already on
the way down, and it still sounded reasonable and right to
him. McCorkery waited until he had finished, and got up, putting a hand on Mr. Halloran's shoulder. "Stay where you are,
and help yourself," he said, giving the bottle a little push, "and
anything else you want, Halloran, order it on me. I'll be back
in a few minutes, and you know I'll help you out if I can."

Halloran understood everything but it was through a soft
warm fog, and he hardly noticed when McCorkery passed him
again with the men, all in that creepy quiet way like footpads on
a dark street. They went into the back room, the door opened
on a bright light and closed again, and Mr. Halloran reached
for the bottle to help himself wait until McCorkery should
come again bringing the good word. He felt comfortable and
easy as if he hadn't a bone or muscle in him, but his elbow
slipped off the table once or twice and he upset his drink on
his sleeve. Ah, McCorkery, is it the whole family you're taking
on with the jobs? For my Maggie's husband is in now with the
Little Tammany Association. "There's a bright lad will go far
and I've got my eye on him, Halloran," said the friendly voice
of McCorkery in his mind, and the brown face, softer than he
remembered it, came up clearly behind his closed eyes.

"Ah, well, it's like myself beginning all over again in him,"
said Mr. Halloran, aloud, "besides my own job that I might
have had all this time if I'd just come to see you sooner."

"True for you," said McCorkery in a merry County Mayo
voice, inside Mr. Halloran's head, "and now let's drink to the
gay future for old times' sake and be damned to Lacey Mahaffy." Mr. Halloran reached for the bottle but it skipped sideways, rolled out of reach like a creature, and exploded at his
feet. When he stood up the chair fell backward from under
him. He leaned on the table and it folded up under his hands
like cardboard.

"Wait now, take it easy," said McCorkery, and there he was,
real enough, holding Mr. Halloran braced on the one side,
motioning with his hand to the boys in the back room, who
came out quietly and took hold of Mr. Halloran, some of
them, on the other side. Their faces were all Irish, but not an
Irishman Mr. Halloran knew in the lot, and he did not like any
face he saw. "Let me be," he said with dignity, "I came here to

see Gerald J. McCorkery, a friend of mine from old times, and let not a thug among you lay a finger upon me."

"Come on, Big Shot," said one of the younger men, in a voice like a file grating, "come on now, it's time to go."

"That's a fine low lot you've picked to run with, McCorkery," said Mr. Halloran, bracing his heels against the slow weight they put upon him toward the door, "I wouldn't trust one of them far as I could throw him by the tail."

"All right, all right, Halloran," said McCorkery. "Come on with me. Lay off him, Finnegan." He was leaning over Mr. Halloran and pressing something into his right hand. It was money, a neat little roll of it, good smooth thick money, no other feel like it in the world, you couldn't mistake it. Ah, he'd have an argument to show Lacey Mahaffy would knock her off her feet. Honest money with a job to back it up. "You'll stand by your given word, McCorkery, as ever?" he asked, peering into the rock-colored face above him, his feet weaving a dance under him, his heart ready to break with gratitude.

"Ah, sure, sure," said McCorkery in a loud hearty voice with a kind of curse in it. "Crisakes, get on with him, do." Mr. Halloran found himself eased into a taxicab at the curb, with McCorkery speaking to the driver and giving him money. "So long, Big Shot," said one of the thug faces, and the taxicab door thumped to. Mr. Halloran bobbed about on the seat for a while, trying to think. He leaned forward and spoke to the driver. "Take me to my friend Gerald I. McCorkery's house," he said, "I've got important business. Don't pay any attention to what he said. Take me to his house."

"Yeah?" said the driver, without turning his head. "Well, here's where you get out, see? Right here." He reached back and opened the door. And sure enough, Mr. Halloran was standing on the sidewalk in front of the flat in Perry Street, alone except for the rows of garbage cans, the taxicab hooting its way around the corner, and a cop coming toward him, plainly to be seen under the street light.

"You should cast your vote for McCorkery, the poor man's friend," Mr. Halloran told the cop, "McCorkery's the man who will get us all off the spot. Stands by his old friends like a maniac. Got a wife named Rosie. Vote for McCorkery," said

Mr. Halloran, working hard at his job, "and you'll be Chief of the Force when Halloran says the word."

"To hell with McCorkery, that stooge," said the cop, his mouth square and sour with the things he said and the things he saw and did every night on that beat. "There you are drunk again, Halloran, shame to you, with Lacey Mahaffy working her heart out over the washboard to buy your beer."

"It wasn't beer and she didn't buy it, mind you," said Mr. Halloran, "and what do you know about Lacey Mahaffy?"

"I knew her from old when I used to run errands for St. Veronica's Altar Society," said the cop, "and she was a great one, even then. Nothing good enough."

"It's the same today," said Mr. Halloran, almost sober for a moment.

"Well, go on up now and stay up till you're fit to be seen," said the cop, censoriously.

"You're Johnny Maginnis," said Mr. Halloran, "I know you well."

"You should know me by now," said the cop.

Mr. Halloran worked his way upstairs partly on his hands and knees, but once at his own door he stood up, gave a great blow on the panel with his fist, turned the knob and surged in like a wave after the door itself, holding out the money toward Mrs. Halloran, who had finished ironing and was at her mending.

She got up very slowly, her bony hand over her mouth, her eyes starting out at what she saw. "Ah, did you steal it?" she asked. "Did you kill somebody for that?" the words grated up from her throat in a dark whisper. Mr. Halloran glared back at her in fear.

"Suffering Saints, Lacey Mahaffy," he shouted until the whole houseful could hear him, "haven't ye any mind at all that you can't see your husband has had a turn of fortune and a job and times are changed from tonight? Stealing, is it? That's for your great friends the Connollys with their religion. Connolly steals, but Halloran is an honest man with a job in the McCorkery Club, and money in pocket."

"McCorkery, is it?" said Mrs. Halloran, loudly too. "Ah, so there's the whole family, young and old, wicked and innocent, taking their bread from McCorkery, at last. Well, it's no bread of mine, I'll earn my own as I have, you can keep your dirty money to yourself, Halloran, mind you I mean it."

"Great God, woman," moaned Mr. Halloran, and he tottered from the door to the table, to the ironing board, and stood there, ready to weep with rage, "haven't you a soul even that you won't come along with your husband when he's riding to riches and glory on the Tiger's back itself, with everything for the taking and no questions asked?"

"Yes, I have a soul," cried Mrs. Halloran, clenching her fists, her hair flying. "Surely I have a soul and I'll save it yet in spite of you. . . ."

She was standing there before him in a kind of faded gingham winding sheet, with her dead hands upraised, her dead eyes blind but fixed upon him, her voice coming up hollow from the deep tomb, her throat thick with grave damp. The ghost of Lacey Mahaffy was threatening him, it came nearer, growing taller as it came, the face changing to a demon's face with a fixed glassy grin. "It's all that drink on an empty stomach," said the ghost, in a hoarse growl. Mr. Halloran fetched a yell of horror right out of his very boots, and seized the flatiron from the board. "Ah, God damn you, Lacey Mahaffy, you devil, keep away, keep away," he howled, but she advanced on air, grinning and growling. He raised the flatiron and hurled it without aiming, and the specter, whoever it was, whatever it was, sank and was gone. He did not look, but broke out of the room and was back on the sidewalk before he knew he had meant to go there. Maginnis came up at once. "Hey there now, Halloran," he said, "I mean business this time. You get back upstairs or I'll run you in. Come along now, I'll help you get there this time, and that's the last of it. On relief the way you are, and drinking your head off."

Mr. Halloran suddenly felt calm, collected; he would take Maginnis up and show him just what had happened. "I'm not on relief any more, and if you want any trouble, just call on my friend, McCorkery. He'll tell you who I am."

"McCorkery can't tell me anything about you I don't know already," said Maginnis. "Stand up there now." For Halloran wanted to go up again on his hands and knees.

"Let a man be," said Mr. Halloran, trying to sit on the cop's feet. "I killed Lacey Mahaffy at last, you'll be pleased to hear," he said, looking up into the cop's face. "It was high time and past. But I did not steal the money."

"Well, ain't that just too bad," said the cop, hauling him up under the arms. "Chees, why'n't you make a good job while you had the chance? Stand up now. Ah, hell with it, stand up or I'll sock you one."

Mr. Halloran said, "Well, you don't believe it so wait and see."

At that moment they both glanced upward and saw Mrs. Halloran coming downstairs. She was holding to the rail, and even in the speckled hall-light they could see a great lumpy clout of flesh standing out on her forehead, all colors. She stopped, and seemed not at all surprised.

"So there you are, Officer Maginnis," she said. "Bring him up."

"That's a fine welt you've got over your eye this time, Mrs. Halloran," commented Officer Maginnis, politely.

"I fell and hit my head on the ironing board," said Mrs. Halloran. "It comes of overwork and worry, day and night. A dead faint, Officer Maginnis. Watch your big feet there, you thriving, natural fool," she added to Mr. Halloran. "He's got a job now, you mightn't believe it, Officer Maginnis, but it's true. Bring him on up, and thank you."

She went ahead of them, opened the door, and led the way to the bedroom through the kitchen, turned back the covers, and Officer Maginnis dumped Mr. Halloran among the quilts and pillows. Mr. Halloran rolled over with a deep groan and shut his eyes.

"Many thanks to you, Officer Maginnis," said Mrs Halloran.

"Don't mention it, Mrs. Halloran," said Officer Maginnis.

When the door was shut and locked, Mrs. Halloran went and dipped a large bath towel under the kitchen tap. She wrung it out and tied several good hard knots in one end and tried it out with a whack on the edge of the table. She walked in and stood over the bed and brought the knotted towel down in Mr. Halloran's face with all her might. He stirred and muttered, ill at ease. "That's for the flatiron, Halloran," she told him, in a cautious voice as if she were talking to herself, and whack, down came the towel again. "That's for the half-dollar," she said, and whack, "that's for your drunkenness—" Her arm swung around regularly, ending with a heavy thud on the face that was beginning to squirm, gasp, lift itself from the pillow and fall back again, in a puzzled kind of torment. "For your sock feet," Mrs. Halloran told him, whack, "and your laziness, and this is for missing Mass and"—here she swung half a dozen times— "that is for your daughter and your part in her. . . ."

She stood back breathless, the lump on her forehead burning in its furious colors. When Mr. Halloran attempted to rise, shielding his head with his arms, she gave him a push and he fell back again. "Stay there and don't give me a word," said Mrs. Halloran. He pulled the pillow over his face and subsided again, this time for good.

Mrs. Halloran moved about very deliberately. She tied the wet towel around her head, the knotted end hanging over her shoulder. Her hand ran into her apron pocket and came out again with the money. There was a five-dollar bill with three one-dollar bills rolled in it, and the half-dollar she had thought spent long since. "A poor start, but something," she said, and opened the cupboard door with a long key. Reaching in, she pulled a loosely fitted board out of the wall, and removed a black-painted metal box. She unlocked this, took out one five-cent piece from a welter of notes and coins. She then placed the new money in the box, locked it, put it away, replaced the board, shut the cupboard door and locked that. She went out to the telephone, dropped the nickel in the slot, asked for a number, and waited.

"Is that you, Maggie? Well, are things any better with you now? I'm glad to hear it. It's late to be calling, but there's news about your father. No, no, nothing of that kind, he's got a job. I said a *job*. Yes, at last, after all my urging him onward. . . . I've got him bedded down to sleep it off so he'll be ready for work tomorrow. . . . Yes, it's political work, toward the election time, with Gerald McCorkery. But that's no harm, getting votes and all, he'll be in the open air and it doesn't mean I'll have to associate with low people, now or ever. It's clean enough work, with good pay; if it's not just what I prayed for, still it beats nothing, Maggie. After all my trying . . . it's like a miracle. You see what can be done with patience and doing your duty, Maggie. Now mind you do as well by your own husband."

Holiday

AT that time I was too young for some of the troubles I was having, and I had not yet learned what to do with them. It no longer can matter what kind of troubles they were, or what finally became of them. It seemed to me then there was nothing to do but run away from them, though all my tradition, background, and training had taught me unanswerably that no one except a coward ever runs away from anything. What nonsense! They should have taught me the difference between courage and foolhardiness, instead of leaving me to find it out for myself. I learned finally that if I still had the sense I was born with, I would take off like a deer at the first warning of certain dangers. But this story I am about to tell you happened before this great truth impressed itself upon me—that we do not run from the troubles and dangers that are truly ours, and it is better to learn what they are earlier than later, and if we don't run from the others, we are fools.

I confided to my friend Louise, a former schoolmate about my own age, not my troubles but my little problem: I wanted to go somewhere for a spring holiday, by myself, to the country, and it should be very simple and nice and, of course, not expensive, and she was not to tell anyone where I had gone; but if she liked, I would send her word now and then, if anything interesting was happening. She said she loved getting letters but hated answering them; and she knew the very place for me, and she would not tell anybody anything. Louise had then—she has it still—something near to genius for making improbable persons, places, and situations sound attractive. She told amusing stories that did not turn grim on you until a little while later, when by chance you saw and heard for yourself. So with this story. Everything was just as Louise had said, if you like, and everything was, at the same time, quite different.

"I know the very place," said Louise, "a family of real old-fashioned German peasants, in the deep blackland Texas farm country, a household in real patriarchal style—the kind of thing you'd hate to live with but is very nice to visit. Old father, God Almighty himself, with whiskers and all; old mother, matriarch in men's shoes; endless daughters and sons and sons-in-law and fat babies falling about the place; and fat puppies —my favourite was a darling little black thing named Kuno— cows, calves, and sheep and lambs and goats and turkeys and guineas roaming up and down the shallow green hills, ducks and geese on the ponds. I was there in the summer when the peaches and watermelons were in——"

"This is the end of March," I said, doubtfully.

"Spring comes early there," said Louise. "I'll write to the Müllers about you, you just get ready to go."

"Just where is this paradise?"

"Not far from the Louisiana line," said Louise. "I'll ask them to give you my attic—oh, that was a sweet place! It's a big room, with the roof sloping to the floor on each side, and the roof leaks a little when it rains, so the shingles are all stained in beautiful streaks, all black and grey and mossy green, and in one corner there used to be a stack of dime novels, *The Duchess*, Ouida, Mrs. E.D.E.N. Southworth, Ella Wheeler Wilcox's poems—one summer they had a lady boarder who was a great reader, and she went off and left her library. I loved it! And everybody was so healthy and good-hearted, and the weather was perfect. . . . How long do you want to stay?"

I hadn't thought of this, so I said at random, "About a month."

A few days later I found myself tossed off like an express package from a dirty little crawling train onto the sodden platform of a country station, where the stationmaster emerged and locked up the waiting room before the train had got round the bend. As he clumped by me he shifted his wad of tobacco to his cheek and asked, "Where you goin'?"

"To the Müller farm," I said, standing beside my small trunk and suitcase with the bitter wind cutting through my thin coat.

"Anybody meet you?" he asked, not pausing.

"They *said* so."

"All right," he said, and got into his little ragged buckboard with a sway-backed horse and drove away.

I turned my trunk on its side and sat on it facing the wind and the desolate mud-colored shapeless scene and began making up my first letter to Louise. First I was going to tell her that unless she was to be a novelist, there was no excuse for her having so much imagination. In daily life, I was going to tell her, there are also such useful things as the plain facts that should be stuck to, through thick and thin. Anything else led to confusion like this. I was beginning to enjoy my letter to Louise when a sturdy boy about twelve years old crossed the platform. As he neared me, he took off his rough cap and bunched it in his thick hand, dirt-stained at the knuckles. His round cheeks, his round nose, his round chin were a cool, healthy red. In the globe of his face, as neatly circular as if drawn in bright crayon, his narrow, long, tip-tilted eyes, clear as pale-blue water, seemed out of place, as if two incompatible strains had collided in making him. They were beautiful eyes, and the rest of the face was not to be taken seriously. A blue woollen blouse buttoned up to his chin ended abruptly at his waist as if he would outgrow it in another half hour, and his blue drill breeches flapped about his ankles. His old clod-hopper shoes were several sizes too big for him. Altogether, it was plain he was not the first one to wear his clothes. He was a cheerful, detached, self-possessed apparition against the tumbled brown earth and ragged dark sky, and I smiled at him as well as I could with a face that felt like wet clay.

He smiled back slightly without meeting my eye, motioning for me to take up my suitcase. He swung my trunk to his head and tottered across the uneven platform, down the steps slippery with mud where I expected to see him crushed beneath his burden like an ant under a stone. He heaved the trunk into the back of his wagon with a fine smash, took my suitcase and tossed it after, then climbed up over one front wheel while I scrambled my way up over the other.

The pony, shaggy as a wintering bear, eased himself into a grudging trot, while the boy, bowed over with his cap pulled down over his ears and eyebrows, held the reins slack and fell into a brown study. I studied the harness, a real mystery. It met and clung in all sorts of unexpected places; it parted company in what appeared to be strategic seats of jointure. It was mended sketchily in risky places with bits of hairy rope. Other seemingly unimportant parts were bound together irrevocably with wire. The bridle was too long for the pony's stocky head, so he had shaken the bit out of his mouth at the start, apparently, and went his own way at his own pace.

Our vehicle was an exhausted specimen of something called a spring wagon, who knows why? There were no springs, and the shallow enclosed platform at the back, suitable for carrying various plunder, was worn away until it barely reached midway of the back wheels, one side of it steadily scraping the iron tire. The wheels themselves spun not dully around and around in the way of common wheels, but elliptically, being loosened at the hubs, so that we proceeded with a drunken, hilarious swagger, like the rolling motion of a small boat on a choppy sea.

The soaked brown fields fell away on either side of the lane, all rough with winter-worn stubble ready to sink and become earth again. The scanty leafless woods ran along an edge of the field nearby. There was nothing beautiful in those woods now except the promise of spring, for I detested bleakness, but it gave me pleasure to think that beyond this there might be something else beautiful in its own being, a river shaped and contained by its banks, or a field stripped down to its true meaning, ploughed and ready for the seed. The road turned abruptly and was almost hidden for a moment, and we were going through the woods. Closer sight of the crooked branches assured me that spring was beginning, if sparely, reluctantly: the leaves were budding in tiny cones of watery green besprinkling all the new shoots; a thin sedate rain began again to fall, not so opaque as a fog, but a mist that merely deepened overhead, and lowered, until the clouds became rain in one swathing, delicate grey.

As we emerged from the woods, the boy roused himself and pointed forward, in silence. We were approaching the farm along the skirts of a fine peach orchard, now faintly colored with young bud, but there was nothing to disguise the gaunt and aching ugliness of the farmhouse itself. In this Texas valley, so gently modulated with small crests and shallows, "rolling country" as the farmers say, the house was set on the peak of the barest rise of ground, as if the most infertile spot had been thriftily chosen for building a shelter. It stood there staring and naked, an intruding stranger, strange even beside the

barns ranged generously along the back, low-eaved and weathered to the color of stone.

The narrow windows and the steeply sloping roof oppressed
me; I wished to turn away and go back. I had come a long way
to be so disappointed, I thought, and yet I must go on, for
there could be nothing here for me more painful than what I
had left. But as we drew near the house, now hardly visible
except for the yellow lamplight in the back, perhaps in the
kitchen, my feelings changed again toward warmth and tenderness, or perhaps just an apprehension that I could feel so,
maybe, again.

The wagon drew up before the porch, and I started climbing
down. No sooner had my foot touched ground than an enormous black dog of the detestable German shepherd breed
leaped silently at me, and as silently I covered my face with my
arms and leaped back. "Kuno, down!" shouted the boy,
lunging at him. The front door flew open and a young girl
with yellow hair ran down the steps and seized the ugly beast
by the scruff. "He does not mean anything," she said seriously
in English. "He is only a dog."

Just Louise's darling little puppy Kuno, I thought, a year or
so older. Kuno whined, apologized by bowing and scraping
one front paw on the ground, and the girl holding his scruff
said, shyly and proudly, "I teach him that. He has always such
bad manners, but I teach him!"

I had arrived, it seemed, at the moment when the evening
chores were about to begin. The entire Müller household
streamed out of the door, each man and woman going about
the affairs of the moment. The young girl walked with me up
the porch and said, "This is my brother Hans," and a young
man paused to shake hands and passed by. "This is my brother
Fritz," she said, and Fritz took my hand and dropped it as he
went. "My sister Annetje," said the young girl, and a quiet
young woman with a baby draped loosely like a scarf over her
shoulder smiled and held out her hand. Hand after hand went
by, their palms variously younger or older, broad or small,
male or female, but all thick hard decent peasant hands, warm
and strong. And in every face I saw again the pale, tilted eyes,
on every head that taffy-colored hair, as though they might all
be brothers and sisters, though Annetje's husband and still

another daughter's husband had gone by after greeting me. In the wide hall with a door at front and back, full of cloudy light and the smell of soap, the old mother, also on her way out, stopped to offer her hand. She was a tall strong-looking woman wearing a three-cornered black wool shawl on her head, her skirts looped up over a brown flannel petticoat. Not from her did the young ones get those water-clear eyes. Hers were black and shrewd and searching, a band of hair showed black streaked with grey, her seamed dry face was brown as seasoned bark, and she walked in her rubber boots with the stride of a man. She shook my hand briefly and said in German English that I was welcome, smiling and showing her blackened teeth.

"This is my girl Hatsy," she told me, "and she will show you to your room." Hatsy took my hand as if I were a child needing a guide. I followed her up a flight of steps steep as a ladder, and there we were, in Louise's attic room, with the sloping roof. Yes, the shingles were stained all the colors she had said. There were the dime novels heaped in the corner. For once, Louise had got it straight, and it was homely and familiar, as if I had seen it before. "My mother says we could give you a better place on the downstairs," said Hatsy, in her soft blurred English, "but *she* said in her letter you would like it so." I told her indeed I did like it so. She went down the steep stairs then, and her brother came up as if he were climbing a tree, with the trunk on his head and the suitcase in his right hand, and I could not see what kept the trunk from crashing back to the bottom, as he used the left hand to climb with. I wished to offer help but feared to insult him, having noted well the tremendous ease and style with which he had hurled the luggage around before, a strong man doing his turn before a weakling audience. He put his burden down and straightened up, wriggling his shoulders and panting only a little. I thanked him and he pushed his cap back and pulled it forward again, which I took for some sort of polite response, and clattered out hugely. Looking out of my window a few minutes later, I saw him setting off across the fields carrying a lighted lantern and a large steel trap.

I began changing my first letter to Louise. "I'm going to like it here. I don't quite know why, but it's going to be all right. Maybe I can tell you later——"

The sound of the German speech in the household below was part of the pleasantness, for they were not talking to me and did not expect me to answer. All the German I understood then was contained in five small deadly sentimental songs of Heine's, learned by heart; and this was a very different tongue, Low German corrupted by three generations in a foreign country. A dozen miles away, where Texas and Louisiana melted together in a rotting swamp whose sluggish under-tow of decay nourished the roots of pine and cedar, a colony of French emigrants had lived out two hundred years of exile, not wholly incorruptible, but mystically faithful to the marrow of their bones, obstinately speaking their old French by then as strange to the French as it was to the English. I had known many of these families during a certain long summer happily remembered, and here again, listening to another language nobody could understand except those of this small farming community, I knew that I was again in a house of perpetual exile. These were solid, practical, hard-bitten, land-holding German peasants, who struck their mattocks into the earth deep and held fast wherever they were, because to them life and the land were one indivisible thing; but never in any wise did they confuse nationality with habitation.

I liked the thick warm voices, and it was good not to have to understand what they were saying. I loved that silence which means freedom from the constant pressure of other minds and other opinions and other feelings, that freedom to fold up in quiet and go back to my own center, to find out again, for it is always a rediscovery, what kind of creature it is that rules me finally, makes all the decisions no matter who thinks they make them, even I; who little by little takes everything away except the one thing I cannot live without, and who will one day say, "Now I am all you have left—take me." I paused there a good while listening to this muted unknown language which was si-lence with music in it; I could be moved and touched but not troubled by it, as by the crying of frogs or the wind in the trees.

The catalpa tree at my window would, I noticed, when it came into leaf, shut off my view of the barns and the fields beyond. When in bloom the branches would almost reach through the window. But now they were a thin screen through

which the calves, splotchy red and white, moved prettily
against the weathered darkness of the sheds. The brown fields
would soon be green again; the sheep washed by the rains and
become clean grey. All the beauty of the landscape now was in
the harmony of the valley rolling fluently away to the wood's
edge. It was an inland country, with the forlorn look of all
unloved things; winter in this part of the south is a moribund
coma, not the northern death sleep with the sure promise of
resurrection. But in my south, my loved and never-forgotten
country, after her long sickness, with only a slight stirring, an
opening of the eyes between one breath and the next, between
night and day, the earth revives and bursts into the plenty of
spring with fruit and flowers together, spring and summer at
once under the hot shimmering blue sky.

The freshening wind promised another light sedate rain to
come at evening. The voices below stairs dispersed, rose again,
separately calling from the yards and barns. The old woman
strode down the path toward the cow sheds, Hatsy running
behind her. The woman wore her wooden yoke, with the
milking pails covered and closed with iron hasps, slung easily
across her shoulders, but her daughter carried two tin milking
pails on her arm. When they pushed back the bars of cedar
which opened onto the fields, the cows came through lowing
and crowding, and the calves scampered each to his own dam
with reaching, opened mouths. Then there was the battle of
separating the hungry children from their mothers when they
had taken their scanty share. The old woman slapped their
little haunches with her open palm, Hatsy dragged at their halters, her feet slipping wide in the mud, the cows bellowed and
brandished their horns, the calves bawled like rebellious babies.
Hatsy's long yellow braids whisked around her shoulders, her
laughter was a shrill streak of gaiety above the angry cow
voices and the raucous shouting of the old woman.

From the kitchen porch below came the sound of splashing
water, the creaking of the pump handle, and the stamping
boots of men. I sat in the window watching the darkness come
on slowly, while all the lamps were being lighted. My own
small lamp had a handle on the oil bowl, like a cup's. There
was also a lantern with a frosted chimney hanging by a nail on
the wall. A voice called to me from the foot of my stairs and I

looked down into the face of a dark-skinned, flaxen-haired young woman, far advanced in pregnancy, and carrying a prosperous year-old boy on her hip, one arm clutching him to her, the other raised above her head so that her lantern shone upon their heads. "The supper is now ready," she said, and waited for me to come down before turning away.

In the large square room the whole family was gathering at a long table covered with a red checkered cotton cloth, with heaped-up platters of steaming food at either end. A crippled and badly deformed servant girl was setting down pitchers of milk. Her face was so bowed over it was almost hidden, and her whole body was maimed in some painful, mysterious way, probably congenital, I supposed, though she seemed wiry and tough. Her knotted hands shook continually, her wagging head kept pace with her restless elbows. She ran unsteadily around the table scattering plates, dodging whoever stood in her way; no one moved aside for her, or spoke to her, or even glanced after her when she vanished into the kitchen.

The men then moved forward to their chairs. Father Müller took his patriarch's place at the head of the table, Mother Müller looming behind him like a dark boulder. The younger men ranged themselves about on one side, the married ones with their wives standing back of their chairs to serve them, for three generations in this country had not made them self-conscious or disturbed their ancient customs. The two sons-in-law and three sons rolled down their shirt sleeves before beginning to eat. Their faces were polished with recent scrubbing and their open collars were damp.

Mother Müller pointed to me, then waved her hand at her household, telling off their names rapidly. I was a stranger and a guest, so was seated on the men's side of the table, and Hatsy, whose real name turned out to be Huldah, the maiden of the family, was seated on the children's side of the board, attending to them and keeping them in order. These infants ranged from two years to ten, five in number—not counting the one still straddling his mother's hip behind his father's chair—divided between the two married daughters. The children ravened and gorged and reached their hands into the sugar bowl to sprinkle sugar on everything they ate, solemnly elated over their food and paying no attention to Hatsy, who struggled with them only a little less energetically than she did with the calves, and ate almost nothing. She was about seventeen years old, pale-lipped and too thin, and her sleek fine butter-yellow hair, streaked light and dark, real German peasant hair, gave her an air of fragility. But she shared the big-boned structure and the enormous energy and animal force that was like a bodily presence itself in the room; and seeing Father Müller's pale-grey deep-set choleric eyes and high cheekbones, it was easy to trace the family resemblance around the table: it was plain that poor Mother Müller had never had a child of her own—black-eyed, black-haired South Germany people. True, she had borne them, but that was all; they belonged to their father. Even the tawny Gretchen, expecting another baby, obviously the pet of the family, with the sly smiling manner of a spoiled child, who wore the contented air of a lazy, healthy young animal, seeming always about to yawn, had hair like pulled taffy and those slanted clear eyes. She stood now easing the weight of her little boy on her husband's chair back, reaching with her left arm over his shoulder to refill his plate from time to time.

Annetje, the eldest daughter, carried her newly born baby over her shoulder, where he drooled comfortably down her back, while she spooned things from platters and bowls for her husband. Whenever their eyes met, they smiled with a gentle, reserved warmth in their eyes, the smile of long and sure friendship.

Father Müller did not in the least believe in his children's marrying and leaving home. Marry, yes, of course; but must that take a son or daughter from him? He always could provide work and a place in the household for his daughters' husbands, and in time he would do the same for his sons' wives. A new room had lately been built on, to the northeast, Annetje explained to me, leaning above her husband's head and talking across the table, for Hatsy to live in when she should be married. Hatsy turned very beautifully pink and ducked her head almost into her plate, then looked up boldly and said, "Jah, jah, I am marrit now soon!" Everybody laughed except Mother Müller, who said in German that girls at home never knew when they were well off—no, they must go bringing in husbands. This remark did not seem to hurt anybody's feelings, and Gretchen said it was nice that I was going to be here for the wedding. This reminded Annetje of something, and she spoke in English to the table at large, saying that the Lutheran pastor had advised her to attend church oftener and put her young ones in Sunday school, so that God would give her a blessing with her fifth child. I counted around again, and sure enough, with Gretchen's unborn, there were eight children at that table under the age of ten; somebody was going to need a blessing in all that crowd, no doubt. Father Müller delivered a short speech to his daughter in German, then turned to me and said, "What I say iss, it iss all craziness to go to church and pay a preacher goot money to talk his nonsense. Say rather that he pay me to come and lissen, then I vill go!" His eyes glared with sudden fierceness above his square speckled grey and yellow beard that sprouted directly out from the high cheekbones. "He thinks, so, that my time maybe costs nothing? That iss goot! Let him pay me!"

Mother Müller snorted and shuffled her feet. "Ach, you talk, you talk. Now you vill make the pastor goot and mad if he hears. Vot ve do, if he vill not chrissen the babies?"

"You give him goot money, he vill chrissen," shouted Father Müller. "You vait und see!"

"Ah sure, dot iss so," agreed Mother Müller. "Only do not let him hear!"

There was a gust of excited talk in German, with much rapping of knife handles on the table. I gave up trying to understand, but watched their faces. It sounded like a pitched battle, but they were agreeing about something. They were united in their tribal scepticisms, as in everything else. I got a powerful impression that they were all, even the sons-in-law, one human being divided into several separate appearances. The crippled servant girl brought in more food and gathered up plates and went away in her limping run, and she seemed to me the only individual in the house. Even I felt divided into many fragments, having left or lost a part of myself in every place I had travelled, in every life mine had touched, above all, in every death of someone near to me that had carried into the grave some part of my living cells. But the servant, she was whole, and belonged nowhere.

*

I settled easily enough into the marginal life of the household ways and habits. Day began early at the Müllers', and we ate breakfast by yellow lamplight, with the grey damp winds blowing with spring softness through the open windows. The men swallowed their last cups of steaming coffee standing, with their hats on, and went out to harness the horses to the ploughs at sunrise. Annetje, with her fat baby slung over her shoulder, could sweep a room or make a bed with one hand, all finished before the day was well begun; and she spent the rest of the day outdoors, caring for the chickens and the pigs. Now and then she came in with a shallow boxful of newly hatched chickens, abject dabs of wet fluff, and put them on a table in her bedroom where she might tend them carefully on their first day. Mother Müller strode about hugely, giving orders right and left, while Father Müller, smoothing his whiskers and lighting his pipe, drove away to town with Mother Müller calling out after him final directions and instructions about household needs. He never spoke a word to her and appeared not to be listening, but he always returned in a few hours with every commission and errand performed exactly. After I had made my own bed and set my attic in order, there was nothing at all for me to do, and I walked out of this enthusiastic bustle into the lane, feeling extremely useless. But the repose, the almost mystical inertia of their minds in the midst of this muscular life, communicated itself to me little by little, and I absorbed it gratefully in silence and felt all the hidden knotted painful places in my own mind beginning to loosen. It was easier to breathe, and I might even weep, if I pleased. In a very few days I no longer felt like weeping.

One morning I saw Hatsy spading up the kitchen garden plot, and my offer to help, to spread the seeds and cover them, was accepted. We worked at this for several hours each morning, until the warmth of the sun and the stooping posture induced in me a comfortable vertigo. I forgot to count the days, they were one like the other except as the colors of the air changed, deepening and warming to keep step with the advancing season, and the earth grew firmer underfoot with the swelling tangle of crowding roots.

The children, so hungry and noisy at the table, were peaceable little folk who played silent engrossed games in the front yard. They were always kneading mud into loaves and pies and carrying their battered dolls and cotton rag animals through the operations of domestic life. They fed them, put them to bed; they got them up and fed them again, set them to their chores making more mud loaves; or they would harness themselves to their carts and gallop away to a great shady chestnut tree on the opposite side of the house. Here the tree became the *Turnverein*, and they themselves were again human beings, solemnly ambling about in a dance and going through the motions of drinking beer. Miraculously changed once more into horses, they harnessed themselves and galloped home. They came at call to be fed and put to sleep with the docility of their own toys or animal playmates. Their mothers handled them with instinctive, constant gentleness; they never seemed to be troubled by them. They were as devoted and caretaking as a cat with her kittens.

Sometimes I took Annetje's next to youngest child, a baby of two years, in her little wagon, and we would go down through the orchard, where the branches were beginning to sprout in cones of watery green, and into the lane for a short distance. I would turn again into a smaller lane, smoother because less travelled, and we would go slowly between the aisle of mulberry trees where the fruit was beginning to hang and curl like green furry worms. The baby would sit in a compact mound of flannel and calico, her pale-blue eyes tilted and shining under her cap, her two lower teeth showing in a rapt smile. Sometimes several of the other children would follow along quietly. When I turned, they all turned without question, and we would proceed back to the house as sedately as we had set out.

The narrow lane, I discovered, led to the river, and it became my favorite walk. Almost every day I went along the edge of the naked wood, passionately occupied with looking for signs of spring. The changes there were so subtle and gradual I found one day that branches of willows and sprays of blackberry vine alike were covered with fine points of green; the color had changed overnight, or so it seemed, and I knew that tomorrow the whole valley and wood and edge of the river would be quick and feathery with golden green blowing in the winds.

And it was so. On that day I did not leave the river until after dark and came home through the marsh with the owls and night jars crying over my head, calling in a strange and broken chorus in the woods until the farthest answering cry was a ghostly echo. When I went through the orchard the trees were all abloom with fireflies. I stopped and looked at it for a long time, then walked slowly, amazed, for I had never seen anything that was more beautiful to me. The trees were freshly budded out with pale bloom, the branches were immobile in the thin darkness, but the flower clusters shivered in a soundless dance of delicately woven light, whirling as airily as leaves in a breeze, as rhythmically as water in a fountain. Every tree was budded out with this living, pulsing fire as fragile and cool as bubbles. When I opened the gate their light shone on my hands like fox fire. When I looked back, the shimmer of golden light was there, it was no dream.

Hatsy was on her knees in the dining room, washing the floor with heavy dark rags. She always did this work at night, so the men with their heavy boots would not be tracking it up again and it would be immaculate in the morning. She turned her young face to me in a stupor of fatigue. "Ottilie! Ottilie!" she called, loudly, and before I could speak, she said, "Ottilie will give you supper. It is waiting, all ready." I tried to tell her that I was not hungry, but she wished to reassure me. "Look, we all must eat. Now or then, it's no trouble." She sat back on her heels, and raising her head, looked over the window sill at the orchard. She smiled and paused for a moment and said happily, "Now it is come spring. Every spring we have that." She bent again over the great pail of water with her mops.

The crippled servant came in, stumbling perilously on the slippery floor, and set a dish before me, lentils with sausage and red chopped cabbage. It was hot and savory and I was truly grateful, for I found I was hungry, after all. I looked at her—so her name was Ottilie?—and said, "Thank you." "She can't talk," said Hatsy, simply stating a fact that need not be emphasized. The blurred, dark face was neither young nor old, but crumpled into criss cross wrinkles, irrelevant either to age or suffering; simply wrinkles, patternless blackened seams as if the perishable flesh had been wrung in a hard cruel fist. Yet in that mutilated face I saw high cheekbones, slanted water-blue eyes, the pupils very large and strained with the anxiety of one peering into a darkness full of danger. She jarred heavily against the table as she turned, her bowed back trembling with the perpetual working of her withered arms, and ran away in aimless, driven haste.

Hatsy sat on her heels again for a moment, tossed her braids back over her shoulder and said, "That is Ottilie. She is not sick now. She is only like that since she was sick when she was a baby. But she can work so well as I can. She cooks. But she cannot talk so you can understand." She went up on her knees, bowed over, and began to scrub again, with new energy. She was really a network of thin taut ligaments and long muscles elastic as woven steel. She would always work too hard, and be tired all her life, and never know that this was anything but perfectly natural; everybody worked all the time, because there was always more work waiting when they had finished what they were doing then. I ate my supper and took my plate to the kitchen and set it on the table. Ottilie was sitting in a kitchen chair with her feet in the open oven, her arms folded and her head waggling a little. She did not see or hear me.

At home, Hatsy wore an old brown corduroy dress and galoshes without stockings. Her skirts were short enough to show her thin legs, slightly crooked below the knees, as if she had walked too early. "Hatsy, she's a good, quick girl," said Mother Müller, to whom praising anybody or anything did not come easily. On Saturdays, Hatsy took a voluminous bath in a big tub in the closet back of the kitchen, where also were stored the extra chamber pots, slop jars, and water jugs. She then unplaited her yellow hair and bound up the crinkled floss with a wreath of pink cotton rosebuds, put on her pale-blue China silk dress, and went to the *Turnverein* to dance and drink a seidel of dark-brown beer with her suitor, who resembled her brothers enough to be her brother, though I think nobody ever noticed this except myself, and I said nothing because it would have been the remark of a stranger and hopeless outsider. On Sundays, the entire family went to the *Turnverein* after copious washings, getting into starched dresses and shirts, and getting the baskets of food stored in the wagons. The servant, Ottilie, would rush out to see them off, standing with both shaking arms folded over her forehead, shading her troubled eyes to watch them to the turn of the lane. Her muteness seemed nearly absolute; she had no coherent language of signs. Yet three times a day she spread that enormous table with solid food, freshly baked bread, huge platters of vegetables, immoderate roasts of meat, extravagant tarts, strudels, pies—enough for twenty people. If neighbors came in for an afternoon on some holiday, Ottilie would stumble into the big north room, the parlor, with its golden oak melodeon, a harsh-green Brussels carpet, Nottingham lace curtains, crocheted lace antimacassars on the chair backs, to serve them coffee with cream and sugar and thick slices of yellow cake.

Mother Müller sat but seldom in her parlor, and always with an air of formal unease, her knotted big fingers cramped in a cluster. But Father Müller often sat there in the evenings, where no one ventured to follow him unless commanded; he sometimes played chess with his elder son-in-law, who had learned a good while ago that Father Müller was a good player who abhorred an easy victory, and he dared not do less than put up the best fight he was able, but even so, if Father Müller felt himself winning too often, he would roar, "No, you are not trying! You are not doing your best. Now we stop this nonsense!" and son-in-law would find himself dismissed in temporary disgrace.

Most evenings, however, Father Müller sat by himself and read *Das Kapital.* He would settle deeply into the red plush base rocker and spread the volume upon a low table before him. It was an early edition in blotty black German type, stained and ragged in its leather cover, the pages falling apart, a very bible. He knew whole chapters almost by heart, and added nothing to, took nothing from, the canonical, once-delivered text. I cannot say at that time of my life I had never heard of *Das Kapital,* but I had certainly never known anyone who had read it, though if anyone mentioned it, it was always with profound disapproval. It was not a book one had to read in order to reject it. And here was this respectable old farmer who accepted its dogma as a religion—that is to say, its legendary inapplicable precepts were just, right, proper, one must believe in them, of course, but life, everyday living, was another and unrelated thing. Father Müller was the richest man in his community; almost every neighboring farmer rented land from him, and some of them worked it on the share system. He explained this to me one evening after he had given up trying to teach me chess. He was not surprised that I could not learn, at least not in one lesson, and he was not surprised either that I knew nothing about *Das Kapital*. He explained his own arrangements to me thus: "These men, they cannot buy their land. The land must be bought, for Kapital owns it, and Kapital will not give back to the worker the land that is his. Well, somehow, I can always buy land. Why? I do not know. I only know that with my first land here I made good crops to buy more land, and so I rent it cheap, more than anybody else I rent it cheap, I lend money so my neighbors do not fall into the hands of the bank, and so I am not Kapital. Someday these workers, they can buy land from me, for less than they can get it anywhere else. Well, that is what I can do, that is all." He turned over a page, and his angry grey eyes looked out at me under his shaggy brows. "I buy my land with my hard work, all my life, and I rent it cheap to my neighbors, and then they say they will not elect my son-in-law, my Annetje's husband, to be sheriff because I am atheist. So then I say, all right, but next year you pay more for your land or more shares of your crops. If I am atheist I will act like one. So, my Annetje's husband is sheriff, that is all."

He had put a stubby forefinger on a line to mark his place, and now he sank himself into his book, and I left quietly without saying good night.

The *Turnverein* was an octagonal pavilion set in a cleared space in a patch of woods belonging to Father Müller. The German colony came here to sit about in the cool shade, while a small brass band played cloppity country dances. The girls danced with energy and direction, their starched petticoats rustling like dry leaves. The boys were more awkward, but willing; they clutched their partners' waists and left crumpled sweaty spots where they clutched. Here Mother Müller took her ease after a hard week. Her gaunt limbs would relax, her knees spread squarely apart, and she would gossip over her beer with the women of her own generation. They would cast an occasional caretaking glance at the children playing nearby, allowing the younger mothers freedom to dance or sit in peace with their own friends.

On the other side of the pavilion, Father Müller would sit with the sober grandfathers, their long curved pipes wagging on their chests as they discussed local politics with profound gravity, their hard peasant fatalism tempered only a little by a shrewd worldly distrust of all officeholders not personally known to them, all political plans except their own immediate ones. When Father Müller talked, they listened respectfully, with faith in him as a strong man, head of his own house and his community. They nodded slowly whenever he took his pipe from his mouth and gestured, holding it by the bowl as if it were a stone he was getting ready to throw. On our way back from the *Turnverein* one evening, Mother Müller said to me, "Well, now, by the grace of Gott it is all settled between Hatsy and her man. It is next Sunday by this time they will be marrit."

All the folk who usually went to the *Turnverein* on Sundays came instead to the Müller house for the wedding. They brought useful presents, mostly bed linen, pillow covers, a white counterpane, with a few ornaments for the bridal chamber—a home-braided round rug in many colors, a brass-bottomed lamp with a round pink chimney decorated with red roses, a stone china washbowl and pitcher also covered with red roses; and the bridegroom's gift to the bride was a neck-lace, a double string of red coral twigs. Just before the short ceremony began, he slipped the necklace over her head with trembling hands. She smiled up at him shakily and helped him disentangle her short veil from the coral, then they joined hands and turned their faces to the pastor, not letting go until time for the exchange of rings—the widest, thickest, reddest gold bands to be found, no doubt—and at that moment they both stopped smiling and turned a little pale. The groom re-covered first, and bent over—he was considerably taller than she—and kissed her on the forehead. His eyes were a deep blue, and his hair not really Müller taffy color, but a light chestnut; a good-looking, gentle-tempered boy, I decided, and he looked at Hatsy as if he liked what he saw. They knelt and clasped hands again for the final prayer, then stood together and ex-changed the bridal kiss, a very chaste reserved one, still not on the lips. Then everybody came to shake hands and the men all kissed the bride and the women all kissed the groom. Some of the women whispered in Hatsy's ear, and all burst out laughing except Hatsy, who turned red from her forehead to her throat. She whispered in turn to her husband, who nodded in agreement. She then tried to slip away quietly, but the watchful young girls were after her, and shortly we saw her running through the blossoming orchard, holding up her white ruffled skirts, with all the girls in pursuit, shrieking and calling like excited hunters, for the first to overtake and touch her would be the next bride. They returned, breathless, dragging the lucky one with them, and held her against her ecstatic resistance, while all the young boys kissed her.

The guests stayed on for a huge supper, and Ottilie came in, wearing a fresh blue apron, sweat beaded in the wrinkles of her forehead and around her formless mouth, and passed the food around the table. The men ate first and then Hatsy came in with the women for the first time, still wearing her square little veil of white cotton net bound on her hair with peach blossoms shattered in the bride's race. After supper, one of the girls played waltzes and polkas on the melodeon, and everyone danced. The bridegroom drew gallons of beer from a keg set up in the hall, and at midnight everybody went away, warmly emotional and happy. I went down to the kitchen for a pitcher of hot water. The servant was still setting things to rights, hobbling between table and cupboard. Her face was a brown smudge of anxiety, her eyes were wide and dazed. Her uncertain hands rattled among the pans, but nothing could make her seem real, or in any way connected with the life around her. Yet when I set my pitcher on the stove, she lifted the heavy kettle and poured the scalding water into it without spilling a drop.

The clear honey green of the early morning sky was a mirror of the bright earth. At the edge of the woods there had sprung a reticent blooming of small white and pale-colored flowers. The peach trees were now each a separate nosegay of shell rose and white. I left the house, meaning to take the short path across to the lane of mulberries. The women were deep in the house, the men were away to the fields, the animals were

turned into the pastures, and only Ottilie was visible, sitting on
the steps of the back porch peeling potatoes. She gazed in my
direction with eyes that fell short of me, and seemed to focus
on a point midway between us, and gave no sign. Then she
dropped her knife and rose, her mouth opened and closed several times, she strained toward me, motioning with her right
hand. I went to her, her hands came out and clutched my
sleeve, and for a moment I feared to hear her voice. There was
no sound from her, but she drew me along after her, full of
some mysterious purpose of her own. She opened the door of
a dingy bitter-smelling room, windowless, which opened off
the kitchen, beside the closet where Hatsy took her baths. A
lumpy narrow cot and chest of drawers supporting a blistered
looking-glass almost filled the space. Ottilie's lips moved,
struggling for speech, as she pulled and tumbled over a heap of
rubbish in the top drawer. She took out a photograph and put
it in my hands. It was in the old style, faded to a dirty yellow,
mounted on cardboard elaborately clipped and gilded at the
edges.

I saw a girl child about five years old, a pretty smiling German
baby, looking curiously like a slightly elder sister of Annetje's
two-year-old, wearing a frilled frock and a prodigious curl of
blonde hair, called a roach, on the crown of her head. The
strong legs, round as sausages, were encased in long white
ribbed stockings, and the square firm feet were laced into old-
fashioned soft-soled black boots. Ottilie peered over the picture, twisted her neck, and looked up into my face. I saw the
slanted water-blue eyes and the high cheekbones of the Müllers
again, mutilated, almost destroyed, but unmistakable. This
child was what she had been, and she was without doubt the
elder sister of Annetje and Gretchen and Hatsy; in urgent pantomime she insisted that this was so—she patted the picture
and her own face, and strove terribly to speak. She pointed to
the name written carefully on the back, Ottilie, and touched
her mouth with her bent knuckles. Her head wagged in her
perpetual nod; her shaking hand seemed to flap the photograph at me in a roguish humor. The bit of cardboard connected her at once somehow to the world of human beings I
knew; for an instant some filament lighter than cobweb spun
itself out between that living center in her and in me, a fila-

ment from some center that held us all bound to our un-
escapable common source, so that her life and mine were kin,
even a part of each other, and the painfulness and strangeness
of her vanished. She knew well that she had been Ottilie, with
those steady legs and watching eyes, and she was Ottilie still
within herself. For a moment, being alive, she knew she suffered, for she stood and shook with silent crying, smearing
away her tears with the open palm of her hand. Even while her
cheeks were wet, her face changed. Her eyes cleared and fixed
themselves upon that point in space which seemed for her to
contain her unaccountable and terrible troubles. She turned
her head as if she had heard a voice and disappeared in her
staggering run into the kitchen, leaving the drawer open and
the photograph face downward on the chest.

At midday meal she came hurrying and splashing coffee on
the white floor, restored to her own secret existence of perpetual amazement, and again I had been a stranger to her like all
the rest but she was no stranger to me, and could not be again.

The youngest brother came in, holding up an opossum he
had caught in his trap. He swung the furry body from side to
side, his eyes fairly narrowed with pride as he showed us the
mangled creature. "No, it is cruel, even for the wild animals,"
said gentle Annetje to me, "but boys love to kill, they love to
hurt things. I am always afraid he will trap poor Kuno." I
thought privately that Kuno, a wolfish, ungracious beast, might
well prove a match for any trap. Annetje was full of silent, tender solicitudes. The kittens, the puppies, the chicks, the lambs
and calves were her special care. She was the only one of the
women who caressed the weanling calves when she set the
pans of milk before them. Her child seemed as much a part of
her as if it were not yet born. Still, she seemed to have forgotten that Ottilie was her sister. So had all the others. I remembered how Hatsy had spoken her name but had not said she
was her sister. Their silence about her was, I realized, exactly
that—simple forgetfulness. She moved among them as invisible to their imaginations as a ghost. Ottilie their sister was
something painful that had happened long ago and now was
past and done for; they could not live with that memory or its
visible reminder—they forgot her in pure self-defense. But I
could not forget her. She drifted into my mind like a bit of

weed carried in a current and caught there, floating but fixed, refusing to be carried away. I reasoned it out. The Müllers, what else could they have done with Ottilie? By a physical accident in her childhood she had been stripped of everything but her mere existence. It was not a society or a class that pampered its invalids and the unfit. So long as one lived, one did one's share. This was her place, in this family she had been born and must die; did she suffer? No one asked, no one looked to see. Suffering went with life, suffering and labor. While one lived one worked, that was all, and without complaints, for no one had time to listen, and everybody had his own troubles. So, what else could they have done with Ottilie? As for me, I could do nothing but promise myself that I would forget her, too; and to remember her for the rest of my life.

Sitting at the long table, I would watch Ottilie clattering about in her tormented haste, bringing in that endless food that represented all her life's labors. My mind would follow her into the kitchen where I could see her peering into the great simmering kettles, the crowded oven, her whole body a mere machine of torture. Straight up to the surface of my mind the thought would come urgently, clearly, as if driving time toward the desired event: Let it be now, let it be *now*. Not even tomorrow, no, today. Let her sit down quietly in her rickety chair by the stove and fold those arms, and let us find her there like that, with her head fallen forward on her knees. She will rest then. I would wait, hoping she might not come again, ever again, through that door I gazed at with wincing eyes, as if I might see something unendurable enter through it. Then she would come, and it was only Ottilie, after all, in the bosom of her family, and one of its most useful and competent members; and they with a deep right instinct had learned to live with her disaster on its own terms, and hers; they had accepted and then made use of what was for them only one more painful event in a world full of troubles, many of them much worse than this. So, a step at a time, I followed the Müllers as nearly as I could in their acceptance of Ottilie, and the use they made of her life, for in some way that I could not quite explain to myself, I found great virtue and courage in their steadiness and refusal to feel sorry for anybody, least of all for themselves.

*

Gretchen bore her child, a son, conveniently between the hours of supper and bedtime, one evening of friendly and domestic-sounding rain. The next day brought neighboring women from miles around, and the child was bandied about among them as if he were a new kind of medicine ball. Sedate and shy at dances, emotional at weddings, they were ribald and jocose at births. Over coffee and beer the talk grew broad, the hearty gutturals were swallowed in the belly of laughter; those honest hard-working wives and mothers saw life for a few hours as a hearty low joke, and it did them good. The baby bawled and suckled like a young calf, and the men of the family came in for a look and added their joyful improprieties.

Cloudy weather drove them home earlier than they had meant to go. The whole sky was lined with smoky black and grey vapor hanging in ragged wisps like soot in a chimney. The edges of the woods turned dull purple as the horizon reddened slowly, then faded, and all across the sky ran a deep shuddering mumble of thunder. All the Müllers hurried about getting into rubber boots and oilcloth overalls, shouting to each other, making their plan of action. The youngest boy came over the ridge of the hill with Kuno helping him to drive the sheep down into the fold. Kuno was barking, the sheep were baaing and bleating, the horses freed from the ploughs were excited; they whinnied and trotted at the lengths of their halters, their ears laid back. The cows were bawling in distress and the calves cried back to them. All the men went out among the animals to round them up and quiet them and get them enclosed safely. Even as Mother Müller, her half-dozen petticoats looped about her thighs and tucked into her hip boots, was striding to join them in the barns, the cloud rack was split end to end by a shattering blow of lightning, and the cloudburst struck the house with the impact of a wave against a ship. The wind broke the windowpanes and the floods poured through. The roof beams strained and the walls bent inward, but the house stood to its foundations. The children were huddled into the inner bedroom with Gretchen. "Come and sit on the bed with me now," she told them calmly, "and be still." She sat up with a shawl around her, suckling the baby. Annetje came then and left her baby with Gretchen, too; and standing at the doorsteps with one arm caught over the porch rail, reached down into the furious waters which were rising to the very threshold and dragged in a half-drowned lamb. I followed her. We could not make ourselves heard above the cannonade of thunder, but together we carried the creature into the hall under the stairs, where we rubbed the drowned fleece with rags and pressed his stomach to free him from the water and finally got him sitting up with his feet tucked under him. Annetje was merry with triumph and kept saying in delight, "Alive, alive! look!"

We left him there when we heard the men shouting and beating at the kitchen door and ran to open it for them. They came in, Mother Müller among them, wearing her yoke and milk pails. She stood there with the water pouring from her skirts, the three-cornered piece of black oilcloth on her head dripping, her rubber boots wrinkled down with the weight of her petticoats stuffed into them. She and Father Müller stood near each other, looking like two gnarled lightning-struck old trees, his beard and oilcloth garments streaming, both their faces suddenly dark and old and tired, tired once for all; they would never be rested again in their lives. Father Müller suddenly roared at her, "Go get yourself dry clothes. Do you want to make yourself sick?"

"Ho," she said, taking off her milk yoke and setting the pails on the floor. "Go change yourself. I bring you dry socks." One of the boys told me she had carried a day-old calf on her back up a ladder against the inside wall of the barn and had put it safely in the hayloft behind a barricade of bales. Then she had lined up the cows in the stable, and, sitting on her milking stool in the rising water, she had milked them all. She seemed to think nothing of it.

"Hatsy!" she called, "come help with this milk!" Little pale Hatsy came flying barefoot because she had been called in the midst of taking off her wet shoes, her thick yellow and silver braids thumping on her shoulders as she ran. Her new husband followed her, rather shy of his mother-in-law.

"Let me," he said, wishing to spare his dear bride such heavy work, and started to lift the great pails. "No!" shouted Mother Müller, so the poor young man nearly jumped out of his shirt, "not you. The milk is not business for a man." He fell back and stood there with dark rivulets of mud seeping from his boots, watching Hatsy pour the milk into pans. Mother Müller started to follow her husband to attend him, but said at the door, turning back, "Where is Ottilie?", and no one knew, no one had seen her. "Find her," said Mother Müller, going. "Tell her we want supper now."

Hatsy motioned to her husband, and together they tiptoed to the door of Ottilie's room and opened it silently. The light from the kitchen showed them Ottilie, sitting by herself, folded up on the edge of the bed. Hatsy threw the door wide open for more light and called in a high penetrating voice as if to a deaf person or one at a great distance, "Ottilie! Suppertime. We are hungry!", and the young pair left the kitchen to look under the stairway to see how Annetje's lamb was getting on. Then Annetje, Hatsy, and I got brooms and began sweeping the dirty water and broken glass from the floors of the hall and dining room.

The storm lightened gradually, but the flooding rain continued. At supper there was talk about the loss of animals and their replacement. All the crops must be replanted, the season's labor was for nothing. They were all tired and wet, but they ate heartily and calmly, to strengthen themselves against all the labor of repairing and restoring which must begin early tomorrow morning.

By morning the drumming on the roof had almost ceased; from my window I looked upon a sepia-colored plain of water moving slowly to the valley. The roofs of the barns sagged like the ridge poles of a tent, and a number of drowned animals floated or were caught against the fences. At breakfast Mother Müller sat groaning over her coffee cup. "Ach," she said, "what it is to have such a pain in the head. Here too," she thumped her chest. "All over. Ach, Gott, I'm sick." She got up sighing hoarsely, her cheeks flushed, calling Hatsy and Annetje to help her in the barn.

They all came back very soon, their skirts draggled to the knees, and the two sisters were supporting their mother, who was speechless and could hardly stand. They put her to bed, where she lay without moving, her face scarlet. Everybody was confused, no one knew what to do. They tucked the quilts about her, and she threw them off. They offered her coffee, cold water, beer, but she turned her head away. The sons came in and stood beside her, and joined the cry: "*Mutterchen, Mutti, Mutti*, what can we do? Tell us, what do you need?" But she could not tell them. It was impossible to ride the twelve miles to town for a doctor; fences and bridges were down, the roads were washed out. The family crowded into the room, unnerved in panic, lost unless the sick woman should come to herself and tell them what to do for her. Father Müller came in and, kneeling beside her, he took hold of her hands and spoke to her most lovingly, and when she did not answer him he broke out crying openly in a loud voice, the great tears rolling, "Ach, Gott, Gott. A hundert tousand tollars in the bank"—he glared around at his family and spoke broken English to them, as if he were a stranger to himself and had forgotten his own language—"and tell me, tell, what goot does it do?"

This frightened them, and all at once, together, they screamed and called and implored her in a tumult utterly beyond control. The noise of their grief and terror filled the place. In the midst of this, Mother Müller died.

In the midafternoon the rain passed, and the sun was a disc of brass in a cruelly bright sky. The waters flowed thickly down to the river, leaving the hill bald and brown, with the fences lying in a flattened tangle, the young peach trees stripped of bloom and sagging at the roots. In the woods had occurred a violent eruption of ripe foliage of a jungle thickness, glossy and burning, a massing of hot peacock green with cobalt shadows.

The household was in such silence, I had to listen carefully to know that anyone lived there. Everyone, even the younger children, moved on tiptoe and spoke in whispers. All afternoon the thud of hammers and the whine of a saw went on monotonously in the barn loft. At dark, the men brought in a shiny coffin of new yellow pine with rope handles and set it in the hall. It lay there on the floor for an hour or so, where anyone passing had to step over it. Then Annetje and Hatsy, who had been washing and dressing the body, appeared in the doorway and motioned: "You may bring it in now."

Mother Müller lay in state in the parlor throughout the night, in her black silk dress with a scrap of white lace at the collar and a small lace cap on her hair. Her husband sat in the plush chair near her, looking at her face, which was very contemplative, gentle, and remote. He wept at intervals, silently, wiping his face and head with a big handkerchief. His daughters brought him coffee from time to time. He fell asleep there toward morning.

The light burned in the kitchen nearly all night, too, and the sound of Ottilie's heavy boots thumping about unsteadily was accompanied by the locust whirring of the coffee mill and the smell of baking bread. Hatsy came to my room. "There's coffee and cake," she said, "you'd better have some," and turned away crying, crumbling her slice in her hand. We stood about and ate in silence. Ottilie brought in a fresh pot of coffee, her eyes bleared and fixed, her gait as aimless-looking and hurried as ever, and when she spilled some on her own hand, she did not seem to feel it.

For a day longer they waited; then the youngest boy went to fetch the Lutheran pastor, and a few neighbors came back with them. By noon many more had arrived, spattered with mud, the horses heaving and sweating. At every greeting the family gave way and wept afresh, as naturally and openly as children. Their faces were drenched and soft with their tears; there was a comfortable relaxed look in the muscles of their faces. It was good to let go, to have something to weep for that nobody need excuse or explain. Their tears were at once a luxury and a cure of souls. They wept away the hard core of secret trouble that is in the heart of each separate man, secure in a communal grief; in sharing it, they consoled each other. For a while they would visit the grave and remember, and then life would arrange itself again in another order, yet it would be the same. Already the thoughts of the living were turning to tomorrow, when they would be at the work of rebuilding and replanting and repairing—even now, today, they would hurry back from the burial to milk the cows and feed the chickens, and they might weep again and again for several days, until their tears could heal them at last.

On that day I realized, for the first time, not death, but the terror of dying. When they took the coffin out to the little country hearse and I saw that the procession was about to form, I went to my room and lay down. Staring at the ceiling, I heard and felt the ominous order and purpose in the movements and sounds below—the creaking harness and hoofbeats and grating wheels, the muted grave voices—and it was as if my blood fainted and receded with fright, while my mind stayed wide awake to receive the awful impress. Yet when I knew they were leaving the yard, the terror began to leave me. As the sounds receded, I lay there not thinking, not feeling, in a mere drowse of relief and weariness.

Through my half-sleep I heard the howling of a dog. It seemed to be a dream, and I was troubled to awaken. I dreamed that Kuno was caught in the trap; then I thought he was really caught, it was no dream and I must wake, because there was no one but me to let him out. I came broad awake, the cry rushed upon me like a wind, and it was not the howl of a dog. I ran downstairs and looked into Gretchen's room. She was curled up around her baby, and they were both asleep. I ran to the kitchen.

Ottilie was sitting in her broken chair with her feet on the edge of the open oven, where the heat had died away. Her hands hung at her sides, the fingers crooked into the palm; her head lay back on her shoulders, and she howled with a great wrench of her body, an upward reach of the neck, without tears. At sight of me she got up and came over to me and laid her head on my breast, and her hands dangled forward a moment. Shuddering, she babbled and howled and waved her arms in a frenzy through the open window over the stripped branches of the orchard toward the lane where the procession had straightened out into formal order. I took hold of her arms where the unnaturally corded muscles clenched and strained under her coarse sleeves; I led her out to the steps and left her sitting there, her head wagging.

In the barnyard there remained only the broken-down spring wagon and the shaggy pony that had brought me to the farm on the first day. The harness was still a mystery, but somehow I managed to join pony, harness, and wagon not too insecurely, or so I could only hope; and I pushed and hauled and tugged at Ottilie and lifted her until she was in the seat and I had the reins in hand. We careened down the road at a grudging trot, the pony jolting like a churn, the wheels spinning elliptically in a truly broad comedy swagger. I watched the jovial antics of those wheels with attention, hoping for the best. We slithered into round pits of green mud, and jogged perilously into culverts where small bridges had been. Once, in what was left of the main road, I stood up to see if I might overtake the funeral train; yes, there it was, going inch-meal up the road over the little hill, a bumbling train of black beetles crawling helter-skelter over clods.

Ottilie, now silent, was doubled upon herself, slipping loosely on the edge of the seat. I caught hold of her stout belt with my free hand, and my fingers slipped between her clothes and bare flesh, ribbed and gaunt and dry against my knuckles. My sense of her realness, her humanity, this shattered being that was a woman, was so shocking to me that a howl as dog-like and despairing as her own rose in me unuttered and died again, to be a perpetual ghost. Ottilie slanted her eyes and peered at me, and I gazed back. The knotted wrinkles of her face were grotesquely changed, she gave a choked little whimper, and suddenly she laughed out, a kind of yelp but unmistakably laughter, and clapped her hands for joy, the grinning mouth and suffering eyes turned to the sky. Her head nodded and wagged with the clownish humor of our trundling lurching progress. The feel of the hot sun on her back, the bright air, the jolly senseless staggering of the wheels, the peacock green of the heavens: something of these had reached her. She was happy and gay, and she gurgled and rocked in her seat, leaning upon me and waving loosely around her as if to show me what wonders she saw.

Drawing the pony to a standstill, I studied her face for a while and pondered my ironical mistake. There was nothing I could do for Ottilie, selfishly as I wished to ease my heart of her; she was beyond my reach as well as any other human reach, and yet, had I not come nearer to her than I had to anyone else in my attempt to deny and bridge the distance between us, or rather, her distance from me? Well, we were both equally the fools of life, equally fellow fugitives from death. We had escaped for one day more at least. We would celebrate our good luck, we would have a little stolen holiday, a breath of spring air and freedom on this lovely, festive afternoon.

Ottilie fidgeted, uneasy at our stopping. I flapped the reins, the pony moved on, we turned across the shallow ditch where the small road divided from the main travelled one. I measured the sun westering gently; there would be time enough to drive to the river down the lane of mulberries and to get back to the house before the mourners returned. There would be plenty of time for Ottilie to have a fine supper ready for them. They need not even know she had been gone.

The Leaning Tower

ARLY one morning on his sixth day in Berlin, on the
twenty-seventh of December, 1931, Charles Upton left his
dull little hotel in Hedemanstrasse and escaped to the café
across the street. The air of the hotel was mysteriously oppressive to him; a yellow-faced woman and an ill-tempered looking
fat man were the proprietors, and they seemed to be in perpetual conspiracy of some sort before open linen closets, in a corner of the dining room, along the halls, or over the account
books behind a varnished desk in the lobby. His room was
dark, airless, cold, and once when he had supper there, small
white worms had come squirming out of the liver sausage on
his plate. It was too expensive for him, besides, and he had decided to change. The café was dull, too, but with a look of
thrifty cheerfulness, and Charles had pleasant associations with
it. He had spent his first Christmas Eve in Europe there, among
a small company of amiable noisy people who all seemed, by
their conversation, to work in the same factory. No one but
the old waiter had spoken to him, but the others talked heartily
among themselves in what Charles recognized already as the
Berlin accent, blunt, full of a wooden kind of clucking and
quacking and explosive hissing. During his voyage on a German boat, the German passengers had taken occasion to praise
each his own province in the matter of speech, but not one of
them said a good word for Berlin in the matter, not even the
Berliners themselves. Charles, who had learned his German
partly from textbooks, partly from phonograph records, a little
from listening to the Germans in his native town, heard with
pleasure the tough speech, drank his beer slowly, the good
dark beer that already had spoiled his taste for any other, and
rather determinedly began to persuade himself that he had not
made a mistake. Yes, Germany was the right place for him,
Berlin was the city, Kuno had been right and would be glad if
he could know his friend was here at last.

He had thought, fitfully, of Kuno all that Christmas Eve, instead of his parents, who wrote long letters timed to reach him
at the holiday saying how gloomy they would be without him.

451

He had sent them a cable and had meant to think of them constantly, but he had not. Again, sitting in the café in the morning, with a map of the city and a pamphlet for tourists containing a list of pensions with prices, he found himself remembering Kuno in rather sudden, unexpected pictures, even seeing himself as he was then, and these flashes of memory came against still other flashes, and back somewhere in the dark of his mind was the whole story, whatever it was. He and Kuno did not remember when they had not known each other. Their first recollection was of standing next each other in a row of children like themselves, singing, or some such nonsense—it must have been kindergarten. They had lived and had gone to school together in an old small city in Texas settled early by the Spaniards. Mexicans, Spaniards, Germans, and Americans mostly from Kentucky had mingled there more or less comfortably for several generations, and though they were all equally citizens, the Spaniards, who were mainly rich and showy, went back to visit Spain from time to time. The Germans went back to Germany and the Mexicans, who lived mostly by themselves in the old quarter, went back to Mexico when they could afford it. Only the Kentuckians stayed where they were, rarely did any of them even go back to Kentucky, and though Charles heard them talk about the place often and lovingly, it seemed farther away and less desirable than Germany, because Kuno went there with his parents.

Though Kuno's mother was said to be a Baroness in Germany, in Texas she was the wife of a prosperous merchant, a furniture dealer. The Kentuckians, who were gradually starving on the land, thought the land the only honorable means to a living, unless one entered a profession; and Charles, whose family made their living, such as it was, from a blackland farm, wondered at the pride with which Kuno would lead him past his father's shop windows to show him the latest display of fashionable, highly polished and stuffed furniture. Looking through the broad clear window into the depths of the shop, Mr. Hillentafel, Kuno's father, could be seen dimly, pencil behind his ear, in his black alpaca coat, his head inclined attentively before a customer. Charles, used to seeing his father on horseback, or standing about the barns with the Negroes, looking at the animals, or walking the fields in his big boots, or riding on the cast iron seat of a plow or harrow, felt he would have been ashamed to see his father in a store, following someone about trying to sell him something. The only time he had ever felt like fighting with Kuno was after Kuno had returned from the second visit to Germany, when they were both about eight years old. Kuno one day spoke contemptuously of farmers, calling them a name in German which Charles did not understand. "They're as good as storekeepers," Charles said in a fury. "Your papa's just a storekeeper." Kuno had shouted back, "My mother is a Baroness, and we were all born in Germany, so we would be Germans. In Germany only low-down people work on farms."

"Well, if you are German, why don't you go and live there?" Charles had shouted back, and Kuno had said very proudly, "There is a big war there, and they wanted to keep my mama and my papa and all of us there, but we had to come back." Kuno then began to explain in a mystified way how they almost hadn't got back; they had almost got locked up in a prison somewhere, but some big important people came and got them out, and in the exciting but confused tale which followed, Charles forgot his quarrel with Kuno. "It was because my mother is a Baroness," Kuno said. "That is why we got away."

But after the war, Mr. Hillentafel took his family back to Germany for a few months every two years, and Kuno's postcards, with their foreign stamps, coming from far-off places like Bremen and Wiesbaden and Mannheim and Heidelberg and Berlin, had brought the great world across the sea, the blue silent deep world of Europe, straight to Charles' door. When he returned, Kuno always had new, odd but serious-looking clothes. He brought fascinating mechanical toys; and later, neckties of strange rich material, coats with stitched pockets, and blunt-toed thick shoes of light brown leather, all made by hand, he said. Kuno would say in the little accent he always brought back and which took several weeks to wear off, "No, but if you don't go to Berlin, you miss everything. We waste time always in those horrid little places, Mannheim and so on, we have to visit with our dull relatives, of course, they are stuck to the necks there, but in Berlin . . ." and he would talk for hours about Berlin until Charles in his imagination saw it as a

great shimmering city of castles towering in misty light. How
had he got such an image? Kuno had said only, "The streets
are polished like a table top and they are as wide as—" he would
measure with his eye the street they were walking in, a very
narrow crooked dirty little street in an old colonial Spanish
city—"oh, five times as wide as this. And the buildings—" he
would glance up, disgust in his face for the flat roofs lowering
over them—"they are all of stone and marble and are carved,
carved all over, with pillars and statues everywhere and staircases wider than a house, winding . . ."

"My father says," Charles said once, trying to keep abreast
of all this knowledge of grandeur, "in Mexico the horses have
silver bridles."

"I don't believe it," said Kuno, "and if they do, it's nonsense. Who would be so silly as to bridle a horse with silver?
But in Berlin, there are marble houses carved all over with
roses, loops of roses . . ."

"That sounds silly too," said Charles, but feebly, because it
did not sound silly at all, any more than did the silver bridles
on the horses of Mexico. Those things were what he would
like, what he most longed to see, and he said, easily, "I'll go
there too, some day."

Kuno played the violin, and went twice a week to a stern old
German teacher who cracked him over the head with a bow
when he made mistakes; and his parents forced him to practice
three hours every day. Charles wanted to paint and draw, but
his parents thought he wasted time at it when he could have
been doing something useful, like studying, so he merely
scratched around with charcoal on odd sheets of paper, or dabbled for hours in some retired spot with brushes that shed
hairs in his poorly equipped paint boxes. On the fourth or fifth
voyage to Germany, when Kuno was about fifteen, he died
there and was buried in Wiesbaden. His parents, bringing
back, beside the elder brother and sister, a new baby, the second within Charles' memory, were very silent on the subject.
They were all fair, tall, lightboned, rather lifeless people, and
Charles, who had no friendship with any of them but Kuno,
hardly saw them or thought of them any more.

Charles, sitting in the café, trying to put his mind on the necessity for beginning a search for a cheaper room, thought, If

it hadn't been for Kuno I should never have come here. I would have gone to Paris, or to Madrid. Maybe I should have gone to Mexico. That's a good place for painters. . . . This is not right. There is something wrong with the shapes, or the light, or something. . . .

His father had been to Mexico when he was young and had told Charles long stories, but Charles had never listened to him as he had to Kuno. So here he was, trying to be a painter, even believing by now that he was really going to be a good one, and he had come, as he believed, on a reasoned decision strictly his own. In his new, vague, almost shapeless misgivings, his half-acknowledged disappointment in the place—what was it?—he began to understand that he had come to Berlin because Kuno had made it seem the one desirable place to be. He hardly ever thought of Kuno any more, or had not for a long time, except simply as dead, though that went on being hard to believe; still it was just those colored postcards of Kuno's and those stories, and the way Kuno had felt then, and had made him feel, that had brought him here. Soberly facing facts, he decided that wasn't enough reason, not half enough. But still he decided also to stay, if he possibly could.

It would be four days until New Year's, and Charles began to think seriously about money. The next boat would bring him a check from his father, who had decided, in a kind of mixed despair and pride in his son's talent, to help him. Charles, keeping accounts in a book, had resolved it should all be repaid. The editor of a small art magazine was publishing a series of his drawings, and was going to pay for them. If these failed, he saw clearly that even beer for his New Year's celebration would be out of the question. Still, at one time or another, the sooner the better, there would be a boat coming from America, and it would bring him money, not much, but enough to keep him going. Meantime, he thought of his expensive camera, which a Kentucky aunt had given him, and decided instantly to pawn it. He also had his grandfather's big gold watch. Why, he was rich. This settled, the question went out of his mind, except for a faint uneasiness as to where his money had gone. In the days before Christmas he had dropped, rather carelessly, without counting, small change into the hats and outspread handkerchiefs of the men along the streets, who

were making the most of their holiday licenses to beg. Some of
them begged in orderly groups, singing carols familiar to him
from the days when his parents took him to the German
Singing Society at home: "Heilige Nacht," "O Tannenbaum,"
Martin Luther's "Cradle Song," in the familiar singing society
voices, even, full, melodious. They had stood there with their
ragged shoes sunk in the slushy snow, starving and blue-nosed,
singing in their mourning voices, accepting coins with grave
nods, keeping their eyes fixed on each other as they beat time
softly with their hands.

Others stood alone, and these the most miserable, each man
isolated in his incurable misfortune. Those blinded or otherwise mutilated in the war wore a certain band on their sleeves
to prove that they had more than any others earned the right
to beg, and merited special charity. Charles, with his almost
empty pockets, nothing in them except the future, which he
felt he owned, saw a tall young man so emaciated his teeth
stood out in ridges under the mottled tight skin of his cheeks,
standing at the curb with a placard around his neck which
read: "I will take any work you can offer." Almost furtively,
Charles slipped a mark into the limp hollowed palm, then
stepped into the doorway near by, and sheltered by fir trees
piled before a shop, their sweet odor in his nostrils, with cold
fingers he sketched hastily the stiff figure in its abject garments, surmounted by that skull of famine.

He walked on thinking it would be a relief when the necessity for appearing to celebrate something was over, remembering with the present smell of freshly cut fir the smell of
apples along the curbs of New York streets, while he was
roaming about the picture galleries waiting for his boat. Men
stood shivering by the fruit, or patrolled the sidewalks, saying,
"Brother, can you spare a dime?" The saying had become famous, a catchword, at once. Then almost overnight the whole
thing had become simply a picturesque aspect of the times, a
piece of local color, a current fad. Even if the plight of the men
was real, it was not going to last; the breadlines were only temporary, the newspapers insisted, and gave strange wonderful
far-fetched reasons for the situation, as if it had been a phenomenon of nature, like an earthquake, or a cloudburst.

Here, Charles could see, the misery was acknowledged as

real and the sufferers seemed to know they had no reason for hope. There was none of the raffish manner of the apple-sellers, but just complete hopelessness and utter endurance. . . . Yet back of them the windows along Kurfürstendamm and Unter den Linden were filled with fine wools and furs and overcoats and great shining motor cars. Charles, walking and gazing, compared them with the New York windows back of the apple sellers and the beggars. They were by no means so fine, but where were the buyers? In New York the buyers streamed gaily in and out of shops, dropping dimes into extended hands. Here, a few dully dressed persons stood and stared, but when he glanced in, the shops were almost empty. The streets were full of young people, lean and tough, boys and girls alike dressed in leather jackets or a kind of uniform blue ski suit, who whizzed about the streets on bicycles without a glance at the windows. Charles saw them carrying skis on their shoulders, shouting and laughing in groups, getting away to the mountains over the weekend. He watched them enviously; maybe if he stayed on long enough he would know some of them, he would be riding a bicycle and going away for the skiing, too. It seemed unlikely, though.

He would wander on, and the thicker the crowd in which he found himself, the more alien he felt himself to be. He had watched a group of middle-aged men and women who were gathered in silence before two adjoining windows, gazing silently at displays of toy pigs and sugar pigs. These persons were all strangely of a kind, and strangely the most prevalent type. The streets were full of them—enormous waddling women with short legs and ill-humored faces and round-headed men with great rolls of fat across the backs of their necks, who seemed to support their swollen bellies with an effort that drew their shoulders forward. Nearly all of them were leading their slender, overbred, short-legged dogs in pairs on fancy leashes. The dogs wore their winter clothes: wool sweaters, fur ruffs, and fleece-lined rubber boots. The creatures whined and complained and shivered, and their owners lifted them up tenderly to show them the pigs.

In one window there were sausages, hams, bacon, small pink chops; all pig, real pig, fresh, smoked, salted, baked, roasted, pickled, spiced, and jellied. In the other were dainty artificial pigs, almond paste pigs, pink sugar chops, chocolate sausages, tiny hams and bacons of melting cream streaked and colored to the very life. Among the tinsel and lace paper, at the back were still other kinds of pigs: plush pigs, black velvet pigs, spotted cotton pigs, metal and wooden mechanical pigs, all with frolicsome curled tails and appealing infant faces.

With their nervous dogs wailing in their arms, the people, shameless mounds of fat, stood in a trance of pig worship, gazing with eyes damp with admiration and appetite. They resembled the most unkind caricatures of themselves, but they were the very kind of people that Holbein and Dürer and Urs Graf had drawn, too: not vaguely, but positively like, their late-medieval faces full of hallucinated malice and a kind of sluggish but intense cruelty that worked its way up from their depths slowly through the layers of helpless gluttonous fat.

The thin snow continued to fall and whiten rounded shoulders and lumpy hat brims. Charles, feeling the flakes inside his collar, had walked on with intention to get away from the spectacle which struck him as revolting. He had walked on into Friedrichstrasse, where, in the early evening, the thin streetwalkers came out and moved rather swiftly in the middle of the pavement, and though they all appeared to be going somewhere, they never left each one her own certain fixed station. They seemed quite unapproachable to Charles in their black lace skirts and high gilded heels, their feathered hats and grease paint. On his first evening in Berlin a young unsmiling one had spoken to him, inviting him without enthusiasm to come with her. He had stammered a phrase which he hoped meant, "I haven't time now," fearing that she would insist. She had given him a serious, appraising glance, saw, to his shame, that the market was no good, and had turned away with an indifferent, "Well, good evening." At home, his adventures had all been with girls he knew, and the element of chance had always been present. Any given occasion might go off very well, and it might not; he felt he had learned a lot from what he described to himself as the block and tackle, balance and check, trial and error method. These reserved-looking professional women, almost as regimented as soldiers in uniform, roused in him uneasy curiosity and distrust. He hoped quite constantly he was going to meet some gay young girls, students perhaps; there seemed to be plenty of them about, but not one had given him the eye yet. He had stopped in a doorway and hastily jotted a few broad-bottomed figures, sagging faces, and dressed pigs, in his notebook. He sketched a specially haggard and frustrated looking streetwalker with a preposterous tilt to her feathered hat. He tried at first not to be seen at his occupation, but discovered soon that he need not worry, for, in fact, nobody noticed him.

These rather scattered impressions were in his mind and he was very dissatisfied with all of them as he folded up his map and pamphlet and set out walking to find a room in Berlin. In the first dozen squares he counted five more of those rather sick-looking young men with fresh wounds in their cheeks, long heavy slashes badly mended with tape and cotton, and thought again that nobody had told him to expect that.

Two days later he was still tramping the snowy streets, ringing doorbells and crawling back to the little hotel in the evenings pretty well dead on his feet. On the morning of the third day, when his search brought him finally to the third floor of a solid looking apartment house in Bambergerstrasse, he took pains to observe very attentively the face of the woman who opened the door. In such a short time he had learned a wholesome terror of landladies in that city. They were smiling foxes, famished wolves, slovenly house cats, mere tigers, hyenas, furies, harpies: and sometimes worst of all they were sodden melancholy human beings who carried the history of their disasters in their faces, who all but wept when they saw him escape, as if he carried their last hope with him. Except for four winters in a minor southern university, Charles had lived at home. He had never looked for a lodging before, and he felt guilty, as if he had been peeping through cracks and keyholes, spying upon human inadequacy, its kitchen smells and airless bedrooms, the staleness of its poverty and the stuffiness of its prosperity. He had been shown spare cubbyholes back of kitchens where the baby's wash was drying on a string while the desolate room waited for a tenant. He had been ushered into regions of gilded carving and worn plush, full of the smell of yesterday's cabbage. He had ventured into bare expanses of glass brick and chrome-steel sparsely set out with white leather couches and mirror-topped tables, where, it always turned out, he would be expected to stay for a year at least, at frightening expense. He peered into a sodden little den fit, he felt, only for the scene of a murder; and into another where a sullen young woman was packing up, and the whole room reeked of some nasty perfume from her underwear piled upon the bed. She had given him a deliberately dirty smile, and the landlady had said something in a very brutal tone to her. But mostly, there was a stuffy tidiness, a depressing air of constant and unremitting housewifery, a kind of repellent gentility in room after room after room, varying only in the depth of feather bed and lavishness of draperies, and out of them all in turn he fled back to the street and the comparative freedom of the air.

The woman who opened the door presently, he saw, was a fairly agreeable looking person of perhaps fifty years or more—above a certain age they all looked alike to Charles—with a pinkish face, white hair and very lively light blue eyes. She gave the impression of being dressed up, she had a little high-faluting manner which seemed harmless and she was evidently very pleased to see him. He noticed that the hall was almost empty but highly polished, perhaps here was the perfect compromise between overstuffed plush and a rat trap.

The landlady showed him her best room, the only one unoccupied, she explained. He might be glad to know she had only young gentlemen in the house, three in fact, she hoped he might make a fourth. "I have here," she said with pride, "a young student from the University of Berlin, a young pianist, and a young student from Heidelberg on leave, so you see the company will not be so bad. May I ask your profession?"

"I am a kind of painter," said Charles, hopefully.

"Charming," said the landlady. "We lacked only an artist."

"I hope you will excuse my poor German," said Charles, a little overwhelmed by all the high manner.

"You will learn," said the landlady, smiling graciously as a mother, and added, "I am Viennese, which accounts perhaps for any little difference you may notice between my speech and that which you hear ordinarily in Berlin. I may say, the Viennese way of talking is not the worst in the world, if you really wish to learn German while you are here."

The room. Well, the room. He had seen it several times

before in his search. It was not what he would choose if he had
a choice, but it was the least tiresome example of what he recognized now as a fixed style, with its sober rich oriental carpet,
the lace curtains under looped-back velvet hangings, the large
round table covered with another silky oriental rug in sweet,
refined colors. One corner was occupied by deep couches
heaped with silk and velvet cushions, the wall above it adorned
with a glass-doored cabinet filled with minute curiosities mostly
in silver filigree and fine porcelain, and upon the table stood a
huge lamp with an ornate pink silk shade, fluted and fringed and
draped with silken tassels. The bed was massive with feather
quilt and shot-silk cover, the giant wardrobe of dark polished
wood was carved all out of shape.

A hell of a place, really, but he would take it. The landlady
looked human, and the price was no higher than he would be
asked anywhere else for such a monstrosity. She agreed at once
that he would need a plain work table and a student lamp, and
added, "I hope you expect to stay for six months."

"I'm sorry," said Charles, who had been waiting for this.
"Only three months."

The landlady concealed her disappointment unsuccessfully
in a sweet little smile. "It is usual to agree for six months," she
told him.

"But I am going to another country in three months," said
Charles.

"Oh, really? Where are you going?" she asked, and her
whole face lighted as if the prospect of travel were her own.

"To Italy, perhaps," said Charles. "First to Rome and then
to Florence. And then all over Europe," he added recklessly,
feeling certain for the first time that this was really true, it was
bound to happen.

"Oh, Italy," cried the landlady. "I spent the three happiest
months of my life there, I have dreamed of going back."

Charles was standing near the table. On the silk rug, near
the lamp, there stood a small plaster replica, about five inches
high, of the Leaning Tower of Pisa. As they talked, his hand
wandered towards it, he picked it up lightly by the middle with
his finger tips, and the delicate plaster ribs caved in. They simply crumbled at his touch, and the fragments dropped around
the weighted base as he snatched back his hand. He saw in

horror that the landlady had gone very pale, her blue eyes instantly suffused.

Charles' self-possession crumbled with the tower. He stammered, "Oh, I'm so sorry," seeing that to the landlady the accident was serious and feeling himself shamefully exposed before her in his proved and demonstrated clumsiness, the aimless wandering curiosity of his mind, his bad habit of pawing things. Why couldn't he have kept his hands to himself? "Please allow me to replace it."

"It cannot be replaced," said the landlady, with a severe, stricken dignity. "It was a souvenir of the Italian journey. My husband and I brought it back as a pleasantry from our honeymoon. My husband has been dead for many years. No, the little tower is not a thing that can be replaced."

Charles, wishing to escape with his humiliation into the open air, said, "Perhaps I had better go for my luggage. I will be back in an hour."

"Yes," she said, absently, gathering up the ruins bit by bit on a sheet of paper. "My only hope is, it may be repaired."

"Do please let me pay for that, at least," said Charles. "I am so very sorry."

"It is not your fault, but mine," said the landlady, "I should never have left it here for—" She stopped short, and walked away carrying the paper in her two cupped hands. For barbarians, for outlandish crude persons who have no respect for precious things, her face and voice said all too clearly.

Charles, red and frowning, moved warily around the furniture towards the windows. A bad start, a very bad start indeed. The double panes were closed tightly, the radiator cast an even warmth through the whole room. He drew the lace curtains and saw, in the refracted pallor of the midmorning, winter light, a dozen infant-sized pottery cupids, gross, squat limbed, wanton in posture and vulgarly pink, with scarlet feet and cheeks and backsides, engaged in what appeared to be a perpetual scramble to avoid falling off the steep roof of a house across the street. Charles observed grimly their realistic toe holds among the slate, their clutching fat hands, their imbecile grins. In pouring rain, he thought, they must keep up their senseless play. In snow, their noses would be completely buried. Their behinds were natural victims to the winter winds. And to think that whoever had put them there had meant them to be oh, so whimsical and so amusing, year in, year out. He clutched his hat and overcoat with a wild impulse to slip out quietly and disappear. Maybe he wouldn't come back at all. He hadn't signed or paid anything yet. Oh, yes, but he would, though. For the landlady appeared at once, again smiling and composed, carrying a card, a slip of paper with printing on it, pen, ink, and her receipt blanks, all on a silver tray. He did not escape without leaving on that tray a full report of himself for the benefit of the police, a signed agreement to keep the room for three months, and a month's rent in marks, instead of dollars. "What a pity you have no dollars," she said brightly, and tilted her head at him in a brave gesture of acceptance. On her left hand she wore a rather inordinate diamond, square and blue, obviously a very fine one, set elaborately at great height. He had not noticed it before.

The sallow wornout looking hotel proprietess greeted him with an almost pleasant expression when he approached her desk. He was surprised at the violent change in her face when he explained that he had found another room and would be leaving at once. Instantly she seemed ready to weep with anger and disappointment.

"But I do not understand," she told him stiffly, her lids reddening. "You agree to stay for a month, I give you very special rates, and now in eight days you are saying you must go. Do you find us disagreeable, perhaps? Isn't your room cared for properly? What has happened?"

"It is simply true that I must find something less expensive still," he told her, carefully. "That is all."

"But our charges here are most reasonable," she said, her dry mouth working over her long teeth. "Why will you not stay?"

"They are reasonable," he admitted, feeling cornered, and as if he were making a humiliating confession, "but I cannot afford them."

The woman opened her account book and began copying from it rapidly, her face stiff with indignation as if she had caught him snatching her purse. "That is your own business," she told him, in a low voice, "but naturally you must expect to pay by the day, in this case."

"Naturally," he agreed.

"You will find you cannot change your mind for nothing," said the woman, in a severe, lecturing tone. "Indecision is a very expensive luxury."

"I suppose so," said Charles, uneasily watching the notations on the sheet of paper lengthening rapidly.

She glanced up and over his shoulder, and Charles saw her face change again to a hard boldness, she raised her voice sharply and said with insolence, "You will pay your bill as I present it or I shall call the police."

Charles, who had his money in hand ready to pay what she asked, believed for an instant he had not understood properly. Turning in the direction of her glance, he saw standing a few feet away the middle-aged podgy partner. His head was like a soft block, covered with scanty gray bristles. Hands in pockets he was eyeing Charles with a peculiarly malignant smile on his wide lipless mouth. Charles, amazed at the sum written at the foot of the page, counted out the money to the last pfennig, suddenly afraid that if he gave her a round sum she would not give him back the change. She swept it away from him, together with the bill, without speaking.

"Will you please give me the receipt?" asked Charles.

She did not answer, but moved away a little, and the man approached silently and said in a voice of edged, false courtesy, "I must require you, before you go, to let me see your papers."

Charles said, "I showed them when I came here," and picked up his suitcases.

"But not to me," said the man, and his pale little eyes behind their puffy lids were piggish with malice. "Not to me, I am sorry to say, and that will be necessary before you are allowed to go, let me assure you."

He seemed struggling with some hidden excitement. His neck swelled and flushed, he closed his mouth until it was a mere slit across his face, and rocked slightly on his toes. Charles had been well prepared for the nuisance of being under constant observation, experienced travelers had told him he would feel like a criminal on parole in Europe, especially in Germany, at first, but that he would soon grow accustomed to it, and he was to be certain to hand his papers over at once to anyone who asked for them. He set his suitcases down and felt in his pockets, then remembered he had tucked the flat leather case containing his papers in one of his suitcases. Which one?

He opened the larger of the two, exposing a huddle of untidy clothing. The man and the woman leaned forward to gaze at his belongings, and the woman said, "So," in a contemptuous voice. Charles, in outraged silence, closed the suitcase and opened the other. He handed the leather case to the man, who drew out the passports and other papers one by one with maddening slowness, regarded them with a skeptical eye, puffing his cheeks and clicking his tongue by turns. With deliberation he handed them back and said, "Very good. You may go now," with the insulting condescension of a petty official dismissing a subordinate.

They continued to look at him in a hateful silence, with their faces almost comically distorted in an effort to convey the full depths of their malice. It was as if they doubted, from his manner, that he had understood the extent to which they were insulting and cheating him, or as if, being safe in their advantage, they wished to goad him to protest so they might do him further damage. Awkwardly under their fixed stare, Charles returned his papers to the suitcase, closed it with difficulty after some trouble with the fastenings. As the door closed behind him he heard them laughing together like a pair of hyenas, with deliberate loudness, to make certain he should hear them.

He felt all at once rather too poor to afford a taxicab, so he walked, lugging his rather battered possessions, and as their weight increased and the distance stretched before him, he meditated rather shapelessly on the treatment he had just received. He was a tall, personable young man, there was nothing wrong with his looks or his intentions, though at that moment, a trifle beetle-browed, hat over eyes, he seemed sullen and rather ugly. His first furious impulse to hit the fat man in the teeth with his fist had been overcome instantly by the clear cold spot in his mind which knew that this situation was hopeless, there was no chance for any sort of reparation, he could either keep quiet and escape from the two thugs or quite simply he would be in worse trouble. His anger remained and settled, took root and became a new part of him.

His landlady opened the door for him again. He observed there seemed to be no servant about the place. After a few

more formalities of greeting, restlessly he took to the street
again, telling himself he needed a haircut. Consulting his map,
he bore towards Kurfürstendamm. The sun had disappeared,
it was colder suddenly, the snow began to fall again on the
smooth dark streets gleaming in the light like polished metal.
The weighty laborious city was torpid in the early darkness.

The barber shop was small and clean, wrapped in white
towels, shining with mirrors and full of warm soapy steam. A
weakly shaped, bloodless little man took him in hand and
began to tuck cloths around his neck. He had scanty discouraged hair the color of tow, and a sickly, unpleasant breath. He
wanted to cut Charles' hair long on top, clip it to the skin
around the back of his head in a wide swath over the ears. His
own was cut that way, the streets were full of such heads, and a
photograph, clipped from a newspaper and stuck in the corner
of the mirror, showed a little shouting politician, top lock on
end, wide-stretched mouth adorned by a square mustache, who
had, apparently, made the style popular. It required a great
deal of head shaking, rather desperately assembled German,
some pointing to other photographs in a barber's journal of
fashion, to persuade the man to a more reasonable point of
view.

The barber, sad enough at his gayest, drooped rather more as
he tapered Charles' hair almost imperceptibly towards the neck;
and to change the whole topic he spoke of the weather. The last
day or two had been mild, even milder than anyone thought,
for it had deceived the storks. The papers that morning had
mentioned that storks had been seen flying over the city, certain signs of good weather and an early spring. Had the young
gentleman noticed a dispatch from New York that said the
trees in Central Park were putting out green buds—imagine,
at this time of year.

"There is nothing in the Tiergarten at this time," said the
little barber, sighing. "This is a dark place in winter. I lived in
Malaga once, I worked there in a barber shop for a whole
year—nearly thirteen months, in fact. The barber shops there
are not like ours, they are very dirty, but there, flowers were in
bloom outside, in December. There, they use real almond oil
for their hair lotions—real. And they have such an extract of
rosemary as you cannot find anywhere else. Olive oil the

poorer people use for their hair, as well as for cookery. Olive oil, imagine, here so expensive, there they pour it out on their heads. Olive oil, they told me, inside and out, that is what makes hair grow. Well, maybe. Here, everyone wants his hair dry, and mostly," he returned to the hateful subject, "they like it close above the ears and full on top. Say it is only our poor German taste," he said sourly, and then, "In Malaga, I never wore my topcoat all winter. Ah, I hardly knew it was winter." His fingers were clammy and his front teeth looked weak, as if they had never got a proper start. "It was strange there in many ways, naturally, considering the kind of people they are, but then they did not have to worry so much about living. Sometimes, there, I put my hand in my pocket and felt my last peseta, but I was not alarmed as I would have been here. I thought that when that was gone I could get more. I should have saved something there," he said, with a guilty look, "but I did not, and here I save and save, but there is nothing." He coughed, turning his head away. "In Malaga," he said, and he was like a man talking about a homeland he had lost, "I never had a cough, though here I cough all the time."

"Flu?" asked Charles, through the towels.

"No, gas," said the little barber, modestly. "The war."

After a dismal pause, Charles said, "I noticed the other day that Malaga froze stiff too, this winter."

"Well, yes, once perhaps, but only for a few days," admitted the barber, shaking his head slowly. "Once, perhaps—"

When Charles felt carefully in his pocket for the smallest coin he could give, uneasy because he knew it was not enough, but all at once unnerved by caution, not daring to reduce his cash store by a single pfennig more than necessary, the barber held out his bluish narrow hand, glanced discreetly into the palm, smiled and said with genuine feeling, "Thank you, thank you very much." Charles nodded his head, in shame, and hurried away.

The knob turned from within and the door flew open as Charles was bending, key in hand, and the landlady fluted at him sweetly. She had been expecting him, she had wondered what was keeping him, she had happened to be in the hall and had heard his step on the stair. She believed she had him nicely settled now, and at what hour would he have his afternoon coffee? Charles said he supposed five o'clock would be all right. "So," she said, smiling and tilting her head at him with what struck Charles as a slightly too intimate, possessive gleam. Still smiling, she hurried away to the farther end of the hall and rapped sharply at a closed door.

It was opened at once, and Charles got a full glimpse of a drooping heavy-set dark young man with a big cropped head and blunt features. The landlady went straight past him, talking in a rapid authoritative tone as if she were giving orders. Charles closed his own door with some relief and looked around for his luggage. It had disappeared. He glanced into the big wardrobe and saw with a peculiar sense of invasion that his things were unpacked—he had long since lost the keys and had never got into the habit of locking things, anyway—and arranged with an orderliness that exposed all their weaknesses of quality and condition. His shoes, needing minor repairs and a coat of polish, were set in wooden supports. His other two suits, the tweed with its buttons hanging, were on silk padded frames. His meager toilet articles, his frayed hair brushes and his flabby leather cases were in array on the middle shelf. Conspicuous among them, looking somehow disreputable, was his quart bottle of brandy, a third empty, and he realized that he had in effect taken to secret drinking during his search for a room. He peered into the lumpy laundry bag hanging on a hook, and shuddered with masculine shame. Its snowy sweet-smelling whiteness concealed his socks that needed darning, his soiled shirts worn too long for economy's sake, and his stringy underwear. On the pillow of his bed, half concealing the long effeminate lace pillow ruffles, lay a pair of neatly folded clean pajamas.

Last effrontery of all, the woman had unpacked his papers and his drawing material and his cardboard folders of unfinished work. Had she looked into them? He hoped she had a good time. A great many of his sketches were not meant for publication. Everything was laid out carefully stacked with a prime regard for neatness and a symmetrical appearance. He had noticed before the strange antagonism of domesticated females for papers. They seemed to look upon papers as an enemy of order, mere dust-catching nuisances. At home he had waged perpetual silent warfare with his mother and the servants about his papers. They wanted to straighten them out, or better, hide them away in the deepest shelves of a closet. Why in God's name couldn't they let his work alone? But they could not, under their curious compulsion; and neither could this woman, that was clear. Consulting his little phrase book, he began constructing and memorizing a polite sentence beginning, "Please don't trouble yourself about my table . . ."

The table was large, though not plain, the lamp was good enough, but the straight-backed chair was a delicate affair with curved spindle legs and old mended tapestry in seat and back: a museum piece beyond doubt, Charles decided, and sat upon it experimentally. It held up. He proposed to overlook and forget the whole damned situation, put his stuff in order and get to work. First he emptied his pockets of accumulated bits of notes, sketches, receipts, scribbled addresses of restaurants, postcard reproductions of paintings he had bought at museums, and the agreement he had signed to stay in this house for three months. He noticed that the landlady's name was Rosa Reichl, written in a tall, looping, affectedly elegant hand. He could not see the end of those three months. He felt a blind resentment all the more deep because it could have no particular object, and helpless as if he had let himself be misled by bad advice. Vaguely but in the most ghastly sort of way, he felt that someone he trusted had left him in the lurch, and of course, that was nonsense, as Kuno used to say. "Nonsense" was one of Kuno's favorite words, especially just after his returns from abroad.

The voices in the next room were going on, rising and tightening somewhat with an excitement that might be anger. Charles listened carefully with no sense of eavesdropping, as always surprised that he understood German so well and spoke it so poorly.

"Herr Bussen, Herr Bussen," Frau Reichl was crying, in a flighty, impassioned voice, her light Viennese accent slightly blurred, "you treat my good chairs like this, my beautiful old chairs I have had for so long—in spite of my other troubles you must add this? How can you, when you know I shall never have chairs like these again?"

Charles, who had begun testing crayons and sharpening pencils, stopped to light a cigarette, leaning back in his own chair. He balanced on the back legs for a split second and came down with a thump, his heart seeming to turn over as the thin joints complained in a human voice.

Herr Bussen, who began by defending himself half-heartedly, gave in and took his scolding dutifully as if Frau Reichl were his mother or his conscience. Yes, he knew better, Charles heard him saying in heavy Low-German, he had been brought up properly even if she did not think so. His mother had such chairs too, he would not let it happen again. Herr Bussen's speech sounded to Charles like some ungainly English dialect, but in no language would he have been a match for Frau Reichl. Charles found himself feeling very sorry for that poor devil as he blundered on apologizing; she was to excuse him this time if she could.

"Yes, this time," rejoined Frau Reichl, exasperated to a point beyond all grace, "this time," she said sarcastically in her sweetest tones, "and how many others, past and to come?"

Herr Bussen found no answer for this. After a silent moment of triumph, Frau Reichl emerged and swished past Charles' door while he waited uneasily for her to stop before it, and knocked on the door just next his at the right.

"*Jawohl!*" shouted the young man inside in the drowning voice of one dredged too suddenly out of sleep. "Yes, yes, come in." Then a gay and youthful voice cleared and added, "Oh, it's you, Rosa dear. Well, I thought there must be a fire."

Rosa, is it? thought Charles, hearing their voices running on together, quick and friendly, in lowered tones, with now and again a small duet of good-humored laughter. Rosa seemed very cheerful indeed, moving about the room as she talked, crossing the hall to her own apartment and back several times. At last she said, "Now then, please tell me when you need anything. Only, no more ice. There is no more."

"Who cares?" called the young man, and Rosa laughed again. Charles began to think of her as Rosa, and a nuisance, if affairs went on at this rate all day in the house.

Daylight had failed. Charles settled himself firmly to his drawing under the lamp which was better than he expected. He began with many small anxieties. Suppose that editor changed his mind? Suppose his drawings were not published and paid for, after all? How long could his father continue to send him money? How long, and this was the real question, this was what worried him most, how long should he go on taking money from his father? Should he have come to Europe at all? A lot of good painters had never been in Europe. He tried to think of one. Well, he was here, horribly disturbed and miserable really, he might as well face it, he had got a much harder blow than he expected from the place. At least he must try to find what he came for, if it wasn't to be just a wild goose chase. He refused to listen any further to the sounds in the house, but focused his eyes upon a certain spot on the paper, remembered what he meant to do, and went to work. All his energy seemed to flow and balance in his right hand, he felt steadied and at ease, he belonged to himself and knew what he was doing. Then he forgot himself altogether. Some time later he sat back and looked at what he had done. It wouldn't do, it was absolutely all wrong.

A light rap on the door saved him. He had an excuse to stop, to turn the page over and let it cool off before he looked at it again. Hardly waiting for his word, Rosa came in. She glanced sharply first at the light and then at the table, already in disorder.

"Ah, you need light early, I see," she commented, with an uncertain smile, a deprecating tilt of the head. "As for Herr Bussen, he does not work in the evenings until after supper. And Herr Mey, the Polish gentleman, quite often plays in the dark because he wishes. Our young student from Heidelberg doesn't have anything to think about but his face at this moment, and the less light on that, the better. Ah me, it is a sight. But," she said, fondly and mysteriously, "he is young, it is his first, he will know what to expect the next time. But the wound is infected, you know, he is here for treatment. Ah, the young one," she said, tenderly, clasping her hands over her breast, "he is very brave all day, but when the dark comes, it is very hard for him. He is so young and tender," she told Charles, almost tearful in her pride and pity, "but he did well, you can see. The wound—well, it is a beauty!"

She moved about the room while she talked, straightening the chairs ever so little, giving a flick at the cushions here, a whisk at the curtains there. Standing beside Charles at the table, she even reached round him to take a light turn among his papers, setting up a small commotion by moving his ash tray and the India ink a few inches out of their places. "After all, there is no more daylight," she admitted, finally, "and if you draw, you need light, isn't it true? Now I shall bring your coffee at once," she promised, brightly, and went away with that extraordinarily busy air of hers.

No more daylight. Charles, feeling helpless, as if he were taking part in a play, and had forgotten his lines if he ever knew them, watched the street as he waited, silent under the falling snow, empty in the frosty shimmer of the corner lamps. Lights were coming on one by one in the many windows of the houses opposite.

In the past few days he had watched each morning by lamplight the feeble sun crawl later and later barely to the level of the housetops, slide slowly around in a shallow arc and drop away in midafternoon. The long nights oppressed him with unreasonable premonitions of danger. The darkness closed over the strange city like the great fist of an enemy who had survived in full strength, a voiceless monster from a prehuman, older and colder and grimmer time of the world. "It is just because I was born in a sunny place and took the summer for granted," he told himself, but that did not explain why he could not endure with patience, even enjoy, even look upon as something new and memorable to see, unfamiliar weather in a foreign climate. Of course it was not the weather. No one paid attention to weather if he had the proper clothes for it; he remembered a teacher of his saying once that all great cities are built in uninhabitable places. He knew that people love even the worst of the climate in the place they know, and can wonder at the feelings of strangers about it. At home in Texas he had seen northern travelers turn upon the southern weather with the ferocity of exhaustion; it gave them the excuse they needed to hate everything else they hated in the place, too. It would be so easy and simple, it would put such an end to the argument to be able to say, "I can't settle down in this place because the sun doesn't rise until ten o'clock in December," but that was not his trouble here.

There were the faces. Faces with no eyes. And these no-eyes, pale, lightless, were set in faces shriveled as if they were gnawed hollow; or worse, faces sodden in fat with swollen eyelids in which the little no-eyes peered blindly as if all the food, the plates of boiled potatoes and pig's knuckles and cabbage fed to the wallowing body, had weighed it down and had done it no good. The no-eyes in the faces of the women were too ready to shed tears. Charles had not understood in the least the first thing that had happened to him in Berlin. He had bought some cheap socks in a little shop. At the hotel he saw they were too small, and had gone back at once to exchange them for a larger size. The woman who had sold them to him saw him coming in with the package in his hand, had remembered him and instantly stood transfixed, the tears welling up in her eyes. While he was trying to explain in awful embarrassment that he merely wished larger socks in place of those she had given him, the tears rolled over her cheeks and she said, "I have no larger size."

"Could you get them for me?" he asked, and she said, "Oh, yes," in such pain that Charles said awkwardly, "Don't bother, I'll keep these," and ran out, annoyed and mystified. A day or two later it was all clear to him and seemed quite natural. She needed badly to sell the stock she had. She could not afford to order just a few pairs of larger socks. She was frightened at seeing the goods she had on hand, unsold, and she had deliberately given him the socks she had already, hoping he could not, a stranger, a traveler, find his way back to complain.

Men who sold wine and fruit in tiny corners did not seem to prosper in their rich and warming commodities, they got no nourishment of their company and obviously they could not afford to enjoy them. These men were silent, usually middle-aged, deeply sullen, and if Charles asked them a question, hearing the foreign voice they would shout out their answer as if in a burst of fury, though the words were harmless. Among themselves they talked in a dead tone of disheartenment that seemed an old habit. With his limited money, he was frightened to go to any place where things were for sale. Because he was poor, he went to poor places, and felt trapped, for they could not let him go until he had bought something. They tried desperately to sell him things he did not want or need, could not use, or could not afford. It was no good trying to explain this to them. They could not hear him.

No more daylight. No more ice. No more chairs with

tapestry on them and legs that broke if you leaned back in them. No more of those table rugs with their nasty sweet colors. If the corner whatnot should be knocked over, just once, there would be no more of that silly bric-a-brac and a good thing too, thought Charles, hardening his heart.

"Coffee at last," said Rosa, coming in without knocking this time, carrying a very dressed up tray. No more coffee at five o'clock, unless you were a foreigner, and—it followed naturally —rich. Charles felt he was living under false pretenses of the kind his early training had taught him to despise. "I am poorer than she is," he thought, watching Rosa arrange the fine porcelain cup with butterfly handle, and spread out thin napery. "But of course not. A boat is coming from America for me, but there is no boat for her. For nobody in this house but me is a boat coming from America, with money. I can get along here, I can leave when I like, I can always go home—"

He felt young, ignorant, awkward, he had so much to learn he hardly knew where to begin. He could always go home, but that was not the point. It was a long way home from where he stood, he could see that. No more Leaning Tower of Pisa, he remembered with guilt, when Rosa, with a last little fussy pat as if she could not quite give up her coffee table, stood back and said, "Now, if you will sit, I will pour your coffee. Pity it is we are not in Vienna," she told him, with a gay little air, "then I could give you real coffee. But this is not the worst in the world, either." Then she ran away, and the flurry of her wake did not settle until some seconds after she was gone.

The coffee was indeed as good as Charles had ever tasted, more than good enough, and he had just taken the first swallow when he heard Herr Bussen's voice in the hall. "Ha," he pronounced in his loud Low-German, "how that coffee stinks."

"Don't tell me you wouldn't like it just the same," said Rosa cruelly. "Just because you drink milk like a big baby and leave the dirty bottles under the bed. Shame on you, Herr Bussen."

They were silenced in the sound of a piano, struck firmly and softly at first, and then without pause there followed a long rippling continuous music. Charles loved music without knowing how or why, and he listened carefully. That would be the Polish student, and it seemed to Charles he was doing pretty well. He sat back in a pleasant daze, hypnotized by the steady rhythm and delighted with the running melody that he could follow easily. Rosa tapped and came in on tiptoe, finger on lip, eyebrows raised, eyes shining. She approached the table and with careful lightness gathered up the napery and silver. "Herr Mey," she whispered, and then, reverently, "Chopin—" and before Charles could think of any response, she had the tray up and had tiptoed out again.

Charles, lightly asleep, dreamed the house was burning down, silently alive and pulsing with flame in every part. With no fear or hesitation at all, he walked safely through the fiery walls and out into the wide bright street, carrying a suitcase which knocked against his knees and weighed him down, but he could not leave it because it contained all the drawings he meant to do in his whole life. He walked a safe distance and watched the dark skeleton of the house tall as a tower standing in a fountain of fire. Seeing that he was alone, he said in wonder, "They all escaped, too," when a loud and ghostly groan was uttered in his ear. He spun about and saw no one. The groan sounded again over his shoulder and woke him sharply. He found he was wallowing in the airless deeps of the feather quilt, hot and half smothered. He fought his way out and sat up to listen, turning this way and that to locate the sound.

"Ah,—ahoooooooo," sighed a voice hopelessly from the room to the right, falling and dying away in a heavily expelled breath of weariness. Without deciding to do anything, Charles found himself at the right hand door tapping with the extreme tips of his fingers.

"Well, what is it?" came a drowsed but soberly indignant voice.

"Is there anything I can do for you?" asked Charles.

"No, no," said the voice in despair. "No, thank you, no no . . ."

"I'm sorry," said Charles, thinking he had been saying this to somebody or other, or thinking it, or feeling it, all day and every day since he had been in that city. The soles of his feet were tingling on the bare floor.

"But come in, please," said the voice, changing to a shade of affability.

The young man sitting on the side of the tumbled bed was

of the extreme pale blondness such as Charles had often noticed among the young people in the streets. His hair, eyebrows and eyelashes were pale taffy color, the skin taffy blond,
the eyes a flat grayish blue almost expressionless except for a
certain modeling of the outer lids that gave him the look of
a young, intelligent fox. He had a long, narrow head, with
smooth, sharply cut features of the kind Charles vaguely regarded as aristocratic. So far, a good-looking fellow, perhaps
twenty-one years old; he stood up slowly and was eye level
with Charles' six feet of height. There was only one thing
wrong with him: the left side of his face was swollen badly, the
eye was almost closed from beneath, and glued along his cheek
from ear to mouth was an inch-wide strip of court plaster, the
flesh at its edges stained in dirty blues and greens and purples.
He was the Heidelberg student, all right. He stood cupping
his hand lightly over his cheek without touching.

"Well," he said, keeping his mouth stiff and looking from
under his downy light brows at Charles. "You can see for yourself. Nothing to speak of, but it gives me the devil. Like a
toothache, you know. I heard myself roaring in my sleep," he
said, and his eyes quietly dared Charles to doubt his word. "I
woke myself up at it. When you knocked, to tell you the truth,
I thought it was Rosa with an ice cap. I don't want any more
ice caps. Sit down, please."

Charles said, "I've got some brandy, maybe that would do
something."

The boy said, "God, yes," and sighed again in spite of himself. He moved around the room aimlessly, holding his spread
hand just beside his face as if he expected his head to drop and
hoped to catch it as it fell. His pale gray cotton pajamas gave
him the look of being about to fade away in the yellowish light
of the bed lamp.

Charles, in his old blanket robe and felt slippers, brought
two glasses and the brandy bottle. As he poured, the young
man watched the liquid filling the glass as if he would spring
upon it, but he held his hands until the glass was offered,
smelled the brim, they touched glasses and drank.

"Ah," said the young man, swallowing carefully, head back
and tipped to the right. He curled up the right side of his

mouth at Charles and his right eye glimmered at him gratefully. "What a relief." He added suddenly, "Hans von Gehring,
at your service."

Charles spoke his own name, the other nodded, there was a
pause while the glasses were filled again.

"And how do you like it, here in Berlin?" Hans asked politely, warming the brandy between his palms.

"So far, very well," said Charles; "of course, I'm not settled
yet." He observed Hans' face in the hope that language was
not going to get in the way of their talk. Hans seemed to
understand perfectly. He nodded, and drank.

"I've walked nearly all over, and have been to a lot of museums, cafés, all the first things, of course. It is a great city. The
Berliners are not proud of it, though, or pretend not to be."

"They know it's no good compared with any other city at
all," said Hans, forthrightly. "I was wondering why you came
here. Why this city, of all places? You may go where you please,
isn't that so?"

"I suppose so," said Charles. "Yes, that's true."

Hans said, "My father sent me here to see a doctor who is an
old friend of his, but in ten days I shall be back in Heidelberg.
The Polish fellow is a pianist so he came here because pianists
seem to think old Schwartzkopf is the only Master. Herr
Bussen, down the hall, he is Platt Deutsch to begin with and
he lives in Dalmatia, so anything would perhaps be a change
for the better to him. He thinks he is getting an education
here and maybe he is. But look at you. A free man and you
come to Berlin." He smiled on one side of his face, then shuddered bitterly. "Are you staying on, then?"

"Three months," said Charles, rather gloomily. "I don't
know why I came, except that I had a good friend who was
German. He used to come here with his family—that was years
ago—and he would say, Go to Berlin. I always thought it was
the place to be, and if you haven't seen anything else much, this
looks pretty good. Of course, there is New York. I stayed there
only about a week, but I liked it, I think I could live there."

"Of course, New York," said Hans, indifferently. "But here,
there are Vienna, and Prague, and Munich and Budapest, and
Nice and Rome and Florence, and, ah, Paris, Paris, Paris," said

Hans, suddenly almost gay. Imitating a German actor imitating a Frenchman, he kissed his fingers and wiggled them lightly towards the west.

"I am going to Paris later," said Charles. "Were you ever there?"

"No, but I am going," said Hans. "My plans are all made." He got up as if his words excited him, wrapped his robe around his knees, felt his cheek tenderly and sat down again.

"I hope to stay there a year, I'm going to some atelier and get some painting done. Maybe you will be there before I leave."

"Oh, I have another year in Heidelberg," said Hans, "and my grandfather, who is old, is giving me the money, so I must stop with him for at least a few months first. But then I may go, I shall be free then for a while, perhaps for two years."

"It is strange to have everything mapped out so," said Charles. "I haven't a notion where I'll be two years from now. Something might even happen to keep me from Paris."

"Oh, it is necessary to plan everything," said Hans, soberly, "or how should we know where we were? Besides, the family has it arranged. I even know the girl I am to marry," he said, "and I know how much money she has. She is an extremely fine girl," he said, without enthusiasm. "Paris will be my own, though, my holiday. I shall do as I please."

"Well," said Charles, seriously, "I am glad to be here. All Americans want to come to Europe one time or another, you know. They think there is something here." He sat back and crossed his legs, feeling comfortable with Hans.

"There is something in Europe," said Hans, "but not in Berlin. You are wasting your time here. Go to Paris if you can." He kicked off his slippers and slid into bed, piling up his pillows and letting his head down very carefully.

"I hope you are feeling better," said Charles. "Perhaps you could sleep now."

Hans frowned slightly, retreated. "There is nothing wrong with me," he declared, "and I was asleep before. This is perfectly normal, it happens quite often."

"Well, good night," said Charles, getting up.

"Oh, no, don't go yet," said Hans, starting to sit up and thinking better of it. "I tell you—knock on Tadeusz' door and

get him up, too. He sleeps too much. It's just there, next door.
If you please, dear fellow. He'll like it."

A moment of complete silence followed Charles' knock, and
in silence the door opened on darkness. A thin, tallish young
man, his small sharp head thrust forward like a bird's, appeared
in the hall. He wore a thin plum-colored silk dressing gown
and his long yellowed hands were flattened one above the other
over his chest, the fingers lying together. He seemed entirely
awake, and his keen little dark eyes were smiling and good
tempered. "What's up now?" he asked in an English accent
lying over a Polish accent. "Is the damnation dueler raising
hell again?"

"Not exactly," said Charles, pleased at hearing English and
astonished at the speech, "but he isn't resting easy, either. We
were having some brandy. I'm Charles Upton."

"Tadeusz Mey," said the Pole, sliding out and closing the
door noiselessly. He spoke just above a whisper in an easy voice.
"Polish in spite of the misleading name. Indiscreet grandmother married an Austrian. The rest of my family have names
like Zamoisky, lucky devils."

They entered Hans' room and Tadeusz said instantly in
German, "Yes, yes, you are going to have a real beauty," and
leaned over to examine the wound with a knowing eye. "It's
doing very well."

"It will last," said Hans. Over his face spread an expression
very puzzling to Charles. It was there like a change of light,
slow and deep, with no perceptible movement of eyelids or
face muscles. It rose from within in the mysterious place where
Hans really lived, and it was amazing arrogance, pleasure, in-
expressible vanity and self-satisfaction. He lay entirely motionless and this look came, grew, faded and disappeared on the
tidal movement of his true character. Charles thought, Why, if
I drew him without that look I should never have him at all.
Tadeusz was talking along in his low voice, amiably in a mixture of French and German. The easy use of languages was a
mystery to Charles. He listened acutely, but Tadeusz, ges-
turing neatly with his brandy glass, did not seem to be saying
anything in particular, though Hans was also listening attentively.

Charles, feeling free not to talk, was trying to see Hans in Paris, with that scar. Trying to see him in America, in a small American town like San Antonio, for example, with that scar. In Paris perhaps they would understand, but how would it look in San Antonio, Texas? The people there would think he had got into a disgraceful cutting scrape, probably with a Mexican, or that he had been in an automobile accident. They would think it a pity that such a nice fellow should be so disfigured, they would be tactful and not mention it and try to keep their eyes off it. Even in Paris, Charles imagined, those who understood would also disapprove. Hans would simply be another of those Germans with a dueling scar carefully made livid and jagged to last him a lifetime. It occurred to him that nowhere but in this one small country could Hans boast of his scar and his way of getting it. In any other place at all, it would seem strange, a misfortune, or discreditable. Listening to Tadeusz chattering along, Charles watched Hans and thought hard in a series of unsatisfactory circles, trying to get out of them. It was just a custom of the country, that was all. That was the way to look at it, of course. But Charles didn't know, had never known, very likely never would know, a friend in the world who, if he saw Hans, wouldn't ask privately afterwards, "Where did he get that scar?" Except Kuno, perhaps. But Kuno had never said a word about this. Kuno had said, that if you didn't get off the sidewalk when army officers came along, you would be pushed off, and when his mother and he were walking together, she would always step into the street and let them by. Kuno had not minded this, he had rather admired the tall officers with their greatcoats and helmets, but his mother had not liked it at all. Charles remembered this for years; it was nothing related to anything he knew in his own life, yet remained in his memory as unquestioned truth, that part of Kuno's life lived in absence and strangeness which seemed to him more real than any life they had shared.

Prize fighters got cauliflower ears, but not purposely. It was a hazard of the game. Waiters got something called kidney feet. Glass blowers blow their cheeks all out of shape, so they hang like bags. Violinists sometimes get abscesses on their jaws where they hold the violin. Soldiers now and then have their faces blown off and have to get them put back by surgery. All kinds of things happen to men in the course of their jobs, accidents or just deformities that come on so gradually they are hardly noticed until it is too late to do much about it. Dueling had been a respectable old custom almost everywhere, but there had to be a quarrel first. He had seen his great-grandfather's dueling pistols, the family pride in a velvet-lined case. But what *kind* of man would stand up in cold blood and let another man split his face to the teeth just for the hell of it? And then ever after to wear the wound with that look of self-satisfaction, with everybody knowing how he had got it? And you were supposed to admire him for that. Charles had liked Hans on sight, but there was something he wouldn't know about him if they both lived for a thousand years; it was something you were, or were not, and Charles rejected that wound, the reason why it existed, and everything that made it possible, then and there, simply because there were no conditions for acceptance in his mind.

Still he liked Hans, and wished the wound were not there. But it was there, an improbable and blood-chilling sight, as if at broad noon he should meet in Kurfürstendamm a knight in armor, or the very skeleton from the Dance of Death.

"You don't speak French?" Tadeusz asked at last, turning to Charles.

"A little," said Charles, but fearing to begin.

"You are lucky," said Tadeusz. "You have a language everyone tries to learn. So have the French. But for me, I have to learn every pest of language there is, because no one but a Pole speaks Polish."

He was a narrow, green-faced young man and in the light his eyes were liver colored. He looked bilious, somehow, and he continually twisted a scorched looking lock of hair on the crown of his head as he talked, a tight clever little smile in the corners of his mouth. "I can even speak Platt Deutsch, but Herr Bussen pretends not to understand me."

"That is the fellow our landlady was scolding today," said Charles, and felt instantly that he had been tactless.

"Today?" asked Tadeusz. "She scolds him every day for one thing or another. He's very stupid. All the Platt Deutsch are stupid beyond hope. Let Rosa take it all out on him. She won't annoy the rest of us so much. She is a terror, that woman."

"Well," said Hans fretfully, pouting under his lip, "what do you expect? This is a *pension*."

"On the recommended list, too," said Tadeusz, amiably, smoking, holding his cigarette at the base of his third and fourth finger, lighted end towards the palm. "I don't expect anything."

"It would be all right if only she would let my papers alone," said Charles.

"You're the rich American who pays the rent for all of us," said Tadeusz, smiling. "You've got the real lace curtains and the best feather bed. But if you do anything tactless, remember, Herr Bussen will catch it."

Charles shook his head at this, thinking it was too near the truth to be funny for him, at least. He poured more brandy, and they lighted fresh cigarettes all around. The visitors sat back comfortably and Hans turned on his side. They all felt well disposed and at peace and as if they were beginning to get acquainted with each other. Three sharp little raps upon the door were followed by Rosa's voice. With sweet severity she reminded them in a set speech that it was three o'clock and others in the house might like some sleep. They glanced at each other with conspiratorial smiles.

"Rosa, dear," said Hans, putting a good deal of patient persuasion in his tone, "I was feeling frightfully and they came to sit up with me."

"You do not need anyone to sit up with you," said Rosa, briskly. "You need sleep."

Tadeusz, rising in silence, opened the door suddenly and Rosa fled with small squeaks, an apparition in dressing gown and hair net. He called after her soothingly, "We are going at once," and turned back with a monkeyish gleam in his near-sighted little eyes. "I thought that would rout her," he said, "that woman is vain as if she were twenty. You'd think we were living in a damnation jail," he went on, taking his glass again, "but all Berlin is just that. Let me tell you," he said to Charles, "I can hardly wait to get back to London. You should go there by all means. Believe me, I have seen nearly all the cities— except your fabulous New York, and those photographs made from the air terrorize me—and London is the only place for a civilized man."

Hans shook his head cautiously and repeated, "No, Paris, Paris."

"All right," said Tadeusz in English. "Okay. I learned that from one of your Americans: typical 100 per cent specimen, he told me. He was a cowboy from Arizona with a five gallon hat. He was a Holy Roller and a vegetarian and he drank a tumblerful of whiskey every morning before breakfast. He was in love with a snake charmer who also did a fan dance. When I knew him he was running a little *boîte* on the Left Bank; the walls were covered with steers' horns and lariats. When he quarreled with the snake charmer, he dragged her all around the floor by one of the lariats. She left him at once, but not before putting a venomous serpent in his bed. However, no harm was done. As he said, it was all okay by him."

Hans said, "What are you saying, please? Remember I don't know English."

Tadeusz said in German, "I was explaining where I learned to say Okay."

Hans nodded. "Ah, yes, I understand that very well, okay. That is the only English I know."

By way of proving they were still men, masters of themselves, they lingered somewhat and took their sweet time about saying good night and separating.

Charles, emerging from the bathroom in the morning, met Herr Bussen in the hall. Herr Bussen was wearing a short cotton bathrobe and carrying a rather draggled towel. His fat round face wore a grieved and bewildered look, like a child who had been so sternly treated at home it did not expect better from the rest of the world. Charles had been wakened by the sound of Rosa scolding Herr Bussen about something or other. Presently she came in with coffee and rolls and butter, looking very well combed and dressed so early in the morning, but with a light sparkle of roused temper in her eyes. She opened the curtains and turned out the light, leaving the winter day like dirty water in the room. She spun away and knocked at the bathroom door, saying in a prissy voice of authority, "It is fifteen minutes, your time is up, Herr Bussen." Returning, she stripped the bed with one gesture, creating a small breeze over Charles' head as he sat at the table. Standing

close beside him she sighed suddenly: "Oh, how hard it is to
have an orderly and peaceful life, a correct life of the kind I was
accustomed to. And the bathroom. Always shaving soap, toothpaste and water, water on the linoleum, the mirrors themselves
splashed, everything so unclean, oh, Herr Upton, I do not
know why gentlemen will never wash the bathtub. And oh, the
Herr Bussen. Every day his bed is full of cheese and bread
crumbs, there are often tins of sardines open in the chest
among his clothes, he eats walnuts and hides the shells in the
closet. It is no excuse to say he is going to be a professor. And
every month late, late with the rent. How does he think I shall
exist if I cannot have the rent promptly?"

Charles, positively blushing all over, got up and said, "If you
will wait a few minutes, I am going out and won't trouble
you."

"Ah, you don't trouble me. I am going about my work, you
about yours. No, it is not that." She smiled brightly upon him,
her despair seemed to pass. "Let me tell you, before the war I
had five servants besides a gardener and a chauffeur, my frocks
came from Paris and my furniture from England; I had three
diamond necklaces, Herr Upton, three—so now, is it strange
that sometimes I wonder what is to become of me? I make up
beds like a servant," she said, "and I wash dirty floors. . . ."

Charles, feeling cornered, got his hat and coat, stammered a
sentence in German unintelligible to himself even, and rushed
away, appalled at Rosa's lack of decency in her confidences,
and her shameful knowledge of his own untidy bathroom
habits.

He pawned his camera, expecting to get almost nothing for
it, but the quiet little man in the shop took his thin nose out of
a book, examined the handsome contrivance with professional
approval, and gave him a hundred marks without question.
Feeling unreasonably rich and cheered up, Charles rushed
back to the apartment hoping to work for a while. A few steps
from his own door, he saw Herr Bussen going in, clutching a
small brown paper parcel—bread and liver sausage, perhaps—
and without an overcoat in the wolfish cold. Charles overtook
him on the stairway, for Herr Bussen was moving slowly, his
shoulders bent. From the back he appeared to be a middle-
aged man, but the face he turned to Charles seemed even

younger than it should have been, with an underlying half-spent childhood still lingering in it. His nose was red and wet, his eyes were full of tears, his bare hand holding the parcel was cracked at the knuckles.

"Good morning," said Herr Bussen, and his lumpy face lightened, just for a moment, as if he expected something pleasant to happen. Charles slowed down, they exchanged names, and went on together in silence. Rosa opened the door for them.

"Ah," she remarked, glancing from one to the other suspiciously, "so you are acquainted already?"

"Yes," they said in one voice, and strong in solidarity, they moved past her without another word. Rosa disappeared into her own part of the house, talking to herself.

"Does she insult you every time she speaks to you?" asked Herr Bussen, with resigned patience.

"Not yet," said Charles, who was beginning to find his immunity a disadvantage. He felt he was on the wrong side, he would not if he could help it be a pet of Rosa's. Herr Bussen said, "Every day she insults me for at least half an hour, then she goes and insults Herr Mey, but in a different way, for he is very sharp and answers her in little ways she does not understand, but he really insults her in turn. She makes a house cat of Herr von Gehring because he fought a *mensur*, but it won't last, and she is polite to you because you are a foreigner and pay more rent than we do. But you wait. Your turn will come."

"Well, when it does," said Charles, easily, "I'll just get out."

"And pay your whole three months' rent or have her report you to the police?" asked Herr Bussen in wonder. "My God, you *must* be rich."

Charles shook his head, feeling that it was all pretty much no use. A look of envy so deep it was almost hatred spread over Herr Bussen's face, he paused and his eye wandered over Charles from head to foot as if he were some improbable faintly repellent creature of another species. "Ah, well," he said, "seriously, I advise you to observe our curious customs, and do nothing, not the smallest thing, to attract the attention of the police. I tell you this because you are unfamiliar with the country—they are not fond of outlanders here."

"Thank you," said Charles stuffily, feeling deeply offended.

This melancholy conversation first depressed him, then it put him in a temper. He sat down in a dull but pleasant fury and began to draw hastily, without plan. Now and then he raised his elbows, drew his lungs full of air. The walls seemed to be closing in upon him, he imagined he could hear the breathing of those people in the other rooms, he smelt the iodoform on Hans' bandage, the spoiled sardines on Herr Bussen's breath, Rosa's sweetish female hysteria made him ill. He drew the people at the hotel, the woman a sick fox, the man half pig, half tiger. He drew Herr Bussen's unenlightened face, several times, growing more tender with each version. There was something about the fellow. With concentrated malice he drew Rosa, first as kitchen sloven, then as a withered old whore, finally without any clothes on. Studying these, he decided he had paid off a large installment of his irritation with her, and tore them all into minute bits. Instantly he regretted it, but there was no place to hide them from her. Then quite calmly he began to draw Hans' face from the memory of that strange expression of pride in his wound, and this absorbed him so that he grew calm, was ashamed of his anger, wondered what had got into him. They were all good people, they were in terrible trouble, jammed up together in this little flat with not enough air or space or money, not enough of anything, no place to go, nothing to do but gnaw each other. I can always go home, he told himself, but why did I come here in the first place?

The sound of Tadeusz' piano stopped him. He listened with pleasure, sitting back at ease. That fellow really could play. Charles had heard a great many famous pianists, by radio, who didn't, it seemed to him, sound so much better than that. Tadeusz knew what he was doing. He drew Tadeusz sitting over the piano, bird head, little stiff wrinkles at the corners of his mouth, fingers like bird claws. "Hell, maybe I'm a caricaturist," he thought, but he did not really worry about it. He settled down again and forgot to listen.

A scurrying about in the hall and Rosa's voice raised in a shrill whimpering got through to him slowly, he did not wake up altogether until she was beating at his door, crying aloud in real terror, "Oh, God, oh, God, Herr Upton, come and help me. Come help. Herr Bussen—" Charles opened the door.

Tadeusz and Hans were already at Herr Bussen's door. Rosa's face was streaming with tears, her hair was draggled. "Herr Bussen has poisoned himself."

Charles shuddered with a mortal chill of fear. He came straight out and joined the others and they went in to Herr Bussen's room together.

Herr Bussen was kneeling beside his bed, clutching a large bedroom jar in his arms, vomiting and retching, speechless except for a gasp between convulsions. Yet he could still raise his hand in a violent waving motion, gurgling, "Go away, go away. . . ."

"Get him to the bathroom," cried Rosa, "fetch a doctor, bring water, for God's sake look out for the rug," and while Charles seized Herr Bussen under the arms to lift him up, Tadeusz came with wet towels and Hans, holding his face, ran to the telephone.

"No, no, God damn it," shouted Herr Bussen, fiercely. "No doctor, no." Freeing himself partially from Charles, he doubled up over the footboard of his bed, holding his stomach, apparently in agony, his face a terrifying purple green, a shower of sweat pouring over his eyebrows and nose.

"Oh, why did you do it?" cried Rosa, weeping. "To poison yourself, here among your friends, how could you?"

Herr Bussen collected himself for protest. "I tell you, I did not poison myself," he shouted in a good strong baritone, "I told you, I ate something and it poisoned me." He collapsed again over the jar, and the upheavals recommenced.

"Get him to the bathroom," cried Rosa, wringing her hands. "I know," she said, turning on Herr Bussen, indignant again. "That sausage. All those sardines. That liver paste. I warned you, but no, you would not listen. No, you knew best. How many times did I tell you . . ."

"Let me alone," cried Herr Bussen, desperately. "Leave me."

Charles and Tadeusz joined forces. "Come on," said Tadeusz, in Platt Deutsch, with a conversational tone, "come on, we'll help you."

They took hold of him around the middle so that he hung down rather like a sack, and began hauling him as well as they could. "Oh, Almighty God," groaned Herr Bussen in sincere despair, "let me alone." But they got him in the bathroom, with no more regard for his feelings than if he were already dead, closed the door and locked it. At once Charles came out again, and left the apartment at a run, without his hat. He was back in a very few minutes with a large package, purchases from a pharmacy, and again closing the bathroom door, ignoring Rosa's questions, he and Tadeusz got to work on Herr Bussen seriously.

Rosa turned on Hans, her face quite sodden by then, and still weeping, ordered him back to bed. Hans said, "No, don't trouble yourself. I am better, I am going out to the clinic now."

"You will make yourself worse," wept Rosa.

"No, you may be surprised, I shall be quite all right," said Hans, coolly, leaving.

Herr Bussen, eased, soothed, cleansed, safe in bed with an ice cap on his brow, the object of all attention from his three new friends, lay in bitter, ungrateful silence. He does not seem to be very pleased with us, thought Charles, and we did a roaring good job, too. Herr Bussen—why did they call him that? He wasn't more than twenty-four years old—seemed sunken and shame-faced, he kept his eyes closed or turned to the wall, and when Tadeusz came in with hot soup from a restaurant, he shook his head and seemed about to shed tears. Rosa was injured by the sight of the soup, also.

"You must let me prepare his food," she said to Tadeusz, "I do not want him poisoned again." She took away the soup and brought it again freshly hot on an elegant tray. She seemed very subdued and Herr Bussen was melancholy and without appetite.

Charles, noticing the piles of papers on Herr Bussen's desk, saw written upon them only endless mathematical calculations which he could recognize but not read. Rosa fidgeted among them, trying to straighten them out. In the hall she said to Charles, "You may not know it, but Herr Bussen is considered, at the University, to be a very brilliant mathematician. He promises to become a very learned man." She spoke with pride and possessiveness. "If I am annoyed with him at times, it is because he needs someone to teach him good habits. He eats—ah, it is no better than offal. And now he is ashamed because you know—you have found him out in his misery. It is a terrible thing to be poor," she said, and the tears seemed to come not only from her eyes but from her skin, the tears and the sweat mingled in a stream and covered her face. "What shall we do? What is to become of us?"

Tadeusz came out and took her by the arm. "Enough of that, Rosa," he said, shaking her gently. "Now what happened, really? Herr Bussen eats a sardine and makes a nuisance of himself. Go and lie down, we will look after him and not disturb anything."

"I am very nervous," said Rosa, smiling at him gratefully.

They looked in upon Herr Bussen. He was lying with his arm thrown over his face, quietly, as if the sleeping powders were taking effect. "Come along with me," said Tadeusz to Charles, "I have an odd spot of brandy, too."

Hans came in with his face done up in fresh lint and court plaster, much improved. He refused brandy and said, "Do you suppose we ought to watch him? Do you suppose?"

"No, I don't believe it for a minute," said Tadeusz, after a small pause. "Do you?" he asked Charles.

"I think he told the truth," said Charles.

"Good," said Hans. "Have one for me," he said, and closed his door.

Tadeusz' narrow room was crowded with an upright piano, and a small silent keyboard which Charles examined, touching stiffly. "I work on that seven hours a day," said Tadeusz, spreading his hands and turning them about, "and you'd better be grateful. Now the damnation suicide is asleep, I shan't be able to play any more today. We may as well get drunk," he said, showing four inches of brandy in a bottle. "Seriously, I don't drink. But if I stayed too long in this place I would."

Charles said, "It's getting me down, too, and I wish I knew why. Compared to really poor people, people I have seen, here and at home, even Herr Bussen is almost rich. Compared to even well-off people, I suppose I'm almost a pauper. But I never felt poor, I never was afraid of it. I always thought that if I really wanted money more than anything else, I could get it. But here—I don't know . . . everybody seems so *crowded*, somehow, so worried, and they can't get their minds off of money for a second."

"They lost that war, please don't forget," said Tadeusz,

running his fingers over the silent keyboard that gave forth an
even wooden clatter. "That damages a nation's personality no
end, you know. But I have no sympathy for them, none. And
as for feeling crowded, ha, you would have to be a Pole to
know what that means. These big fat ugly people," he said,
and he crossed his knees and began torturing his scalp lock.
"By God they should be Poles for a while to know what it is to
be hungry."

"They aren't all ugly," said Charles. "Not by a long shot."

"Okay," said Tadeusz, indifferently and his little eyes closed.
Charles thought, Well, what should I say? Am I supposed to
go into an impassioned defense of the Poles? Or a denunciation of the Germans? He was thinking really of his fleece-lined
coat, wondering if it would be good enough to offer to Herr
Bussen and how to go about it. Could he just knock at his
door and say, "Here is a coat I don't happen to need?" Or (no,
this wouldn't do), "If you don't have a coat with you, why not
use this one for a while?" There should be some way of doing
it decently. He explained to Tadeusz and asked for advice.

"Oh, never," said Tadeusz. "You can't do that. He is very
proud and he would be furious as hell. And besides," Tadeusz
swung a foot, "we have to realize that a man's sufferings are
his own, quite often he chooses them to some ends of his own
—how do we know? We pity people too often for the wrong
reasons. They may not need it or want it at all, you know. Poor
Old Bussen, we are able to say, and it makes us feel better,
more secure, in our own fortune. Sometimes there are worse
things than cold and hunger. Had you thought of that? Do
you know him at all, his feelings, or his plan for himself? I
think until you do, don't interfere."

"If we hadn't interfered today, he might be dead by now,"
said Charles.

"We may have made a mistake even so," said Tadeusz,
calmly. "Now we must wait and see. Of course if we could give
him money or food without letting him know why we did it,
that would be another thing. But we can't. If you go now after
all that has happened and offer him a coat, just like that, why,
what can you expect? He would feel like throwing it back at
you. A man might accept charity if he did not fear the contempt of the giver. But only good friends can accept or ex-

change favors. Otherwise it doesn't do." Tadeusz stood up and walked about quickly, bent at the waist and peering at Charles. "Dear fellow, don't mind if I say, you Americns have some very odd notions. Why all this benevolence? What do you expect to gain by it?"

Charles said, "I wouldn't gain anything by it, and I would expect to lose a coat. But I don't need the coat," he said, "and so far as I am concerned that would be the end of it."

"You sound morally indignant," said Tadeusz. He paused before Charles and smiled. "Don't get mad, you hear how well I speak American? You would gain from it the pride in being able to give a coat. And Herr Bussen would be warm, but he would owe his coat to the charity of a stranger, and it might spoil his whole career. Try to understand. I know more about this than you do. If ever I come to your country I will take your advice about Americans."

"I don't believe Americans are so different from other people as all that," said Charles.

"Believe me," said Tadeusz, "you are like beings from another planet to us. Don't offer a coat to Herr Bussen. He will hate you for it."

Charles said, "I can't believe it really."

"If you set yourself up as a benefactor," said Tadeusz, "you must expect to be hated. Let me tell you something. A very rich man I know wished to give good sums of money to help young musicians. But he went to his lawyer and insisted that the gift must be anonymous; under no circumstances must the giver be known. Well, the lawyer said of course it would be arranged, but it would make work, mystery, why did his client want that? And this very wise man said, 'I am superstitious and I do not want them to be able to curse me by name.'"

"Good God," said Charles, sincerely horrified.

"Ah, yes, good God," said Tadeusz, amiably.

Charles left the coat in his closet, and brought milk and oranges instead to Herr Bussen. Hans was there already, sitting beside the bed offering Herr Bussen more soup.

The invalid accepted, and swallowed the nourishment as if it were bitter medicine. Charles thought, Yes, it's true, he isn't getting any good out of it; and he saw plainly that Herr Bussen felt himself being engulfed slowly in a debt he had no hope of paying. Charles, at the foot of the bed, had a curious scene flash through his mind: Herr Bussen, the object of charity, fleeing like a stag across the snowy waste, with Hans and Tadeusz and Rosa and he, Charles, after him in full cry, bringing him down, by the throat if necessary, to give him aid and comfort. Charles heard the deep mournful voices of his father's liver-spotted hounds.

When Rosa brought the coffee tray, one end of it was occupied by an ordinary looking black japanned metal box. She stood, without pouring the coffee, her hands on the table, and said in a low voice, "This hasn't been a very good day for anybody, I suppose. But I have on my conscience my sharpness to Herr Bussen. I have told him so, and he answered—he answered kindly," she said. "But I know that you, a stranger, and from a rich country—"

"The country may be rich," said Charles, "but most of the people in it are not—"

"Couldn't be expected to understand," Rosa went on, waving his speech away without listening. "Look, I want to show you something, then maybe you will see a little of what has happened to us. Outlanders, all the world, come here with their money—"

"I tell you I am not rich, for one," said Charles, hopelessly. She gave him a stare very much like contempt for his lying speech; she knew better. He was the worst kind of rich American, the kind who pretended to be poor. "With their money," she said, angrily, raising her voice, "and then they think we are cheap because we worry about how we shall live. You despise us because we are ruined and why are we ruined, tell me that? It is because your country deserted and betrayed us in the war, you should have helped us and you did not." Her voice dropped and became bitter and quiet.

Charles said in a matter-of-fact, reasoning tone: "All the way over on the boat, the Germans kept telling me that. The truth is, I've heard talk about that war all my life, but I hardly remember it. I have to confess I hadn't thought much about it. If I had, maybe I would never have come here."

"You didn't have to think about it," said Rosa, "but here, we have nothing else to think about." She opened the black box. It was full of paper money, thick bales of it in rubber bands, such an amount of printed money as Charles had seen only in glimpses at the elbow of a clerk behind the barred windows of a great bank. Rosa lifted one of the bundles.

"These are nothing," she said with affected airiness, "these are only a hundred thousand marks each. . . . Wait." She lifted another and flirted the edges through her fingers. "These are five hundred thousand marks each—look," she said, her voice wavering. "One million marks each, these." She dropped each bundle as she spoke upon the table beside them without glancing up. Terror and awe were in her face, as if again for just a moment, she believed in the value of this paper as she had once believed. "Did you ever see a note for five million marks? Here are a hundred of them, you will never see this again—and oh," she cried suddenly, in a frenzy of grief, clutching the treacherous stuff with both hands, "try now to buy a loaf of bread with all this, try it, try it!"

Her voice rose and she wept shamelessly without hiding her face, her arms hanging loosely, the worthless money dropping to the floor.

Charles looked about as if he expected help, rescue, to come by miracle. He backed away from her thinking only of escape, saying as well as he could, "I know it is all a horrible business —but, what can I do?"

This dull question had a remarkable effect. Rosa's tears dried almost instantly, her voice deepened a note, she spoke with intense anger. "You can do nothing," she said vehemently, "nothing, you know nothing at all, you cannot even imagine—"

Charles picked up the money from the carpet, and Rosa began placing the stiff pale colored bundles again in the box, carefully, arranging them first one way and another, stopping now and then to squeeze the end of her nose with her thin little handkerchief. "Nothing to say, nothing to be done," she repeated, giving him a resentful look as if he had failed her, a look as personal and angry as if she were a member of his family, or at least a familiar friend, or—what on earth was Rosa to him? A middle-aged stranger who had rented him a room, someone he had expected to see and speak to perhaps once a week, and here she was, swarming all over him, weeping on his

neck, telling her troubles, putting the blame for the troubles of
the world on him, driving him nuts, and no way that he could
see of getting out of it. She closed the box and leaned her
hands on the table. "When you are so poor," she said, "you are
frightened of the poor and unfortunate. I was frightened of
Herr Bussen—no, I almost hated him. I thought every day,
'My God, such a man will bring bad luck on us all, he will drag
us all down with him.'" She spoke in a very low tone. "But today, it came to me that Herr Bussen will live through everything, he is strong, he is not really afraid. And that is a comfort
to me, because I am afraid of everything."

She poured the coffee, took up the japanned box and went
out.

The household settled down that night for a good sleep.
What a relief, thought Charles, to put a long quiet stretch of
darkness between you and the thing that happened. Suppose
Old Bussen had popped off? He felt warmly towards Old
Bussen, who was still breathing—snoring, in fact, in long rich
groans, as if he couldn't breathe hard enough.

When Charles put his head in to look at Herr Bussen the
next morning, two rawboned solemn youths with identical
leather-colored forelocks were sitting with him, one on the
bed, one on the spindling chair. They turned and gazed at the
stranger with profound blue eyes exactly alike, and Herr
Bussen, looking very well and merry, introduced them. Twin
brothers, he said, school friends of his, who were at that moment on the point of fulfilling a life's ambition. On New Year's
Eve they were going to open a small cabaret of their own, a
snug little half-cellar with the best beer, a supper table and
pretty girls who could sing and dance. Nothing big, but a
good place, and Herr Bussen hoped Charles would go with
him to celebrate the first evening. Charles said it sounded a
fine idea to him, and thought perhaps Hans and Tadeusz
would like to go, too. The brothers eyed him without a flicker
of expression.

Herr Bussen sat up as if he had new life in him. "Oh, yes, we
will all go together." The brothers stood up to giant heights,
and one of them said, "It will not be expensive, either." As if
being able to give this piece of good news was pleasant to him,
he grinned broadly and reassuringly at Charles, who grinned

in turn. He said to Herr Bussen, "I'm going out. Could I bring you anything?"

"Oh, no," said Herr Bussen, firmly, shaking his head with a small glitter of resentment in his eye. "Thank you, nothing at all. I'm getting up now."

At the foot of the shallow flight of steps leading to the new cabaret, a dish of food scraps had been set out for the hungry small animals. A black cat was there, eating very fast, glancing nervously over his shoulder as he swallowed. One of the twins put his head out, invited his four visitors in festively, noticed the cat and said ritually, "May it do him good." He threw open the door to disclose a small, freshly painted, well-lighted little place, full of tables covered with red checkerboard cloths, a modest bar, and at the farther end, a long table set out with cold supper. It could all be seen at a glance. There was a home-made air about the colored paper decorations, the feathery tinsel draped above the bar mirror, the rack full of steins and the small cuckoo clock.

It was hardly Charles' notion of a Berlin cabaret; he had heard about Berlin night life and expected something more sophisticated. He remarked as much to Tadeusz.

"Oh, no," said Tadeusz, "this is another kind of thing altogether. This is going to be nice-stuffy-middle-class-German full of rosy emotions and beer. You could bring your most innocent child here if you had an innocent child." He seemed pleased, and so did Hans and Herr Bussen: they walked about and praised everything the brothers had done. All of them were pleasantly excited because none of them had ever known anyone who ran a cabaret, and they enjoyed a cozy feeling of being on the inside of things for once. Almost immediately they began calling Herr Bussen by his first name. Tadeusz began it.

"Otto, dear fellow, could you give me a light?" he asked, and Otto, who did not smoke, blushed with pleasure and felt in his pockets as if he expected to find matches.

They were the first comers. As the brothers went on about their last-minute business, rushing back and forth through the swinging door leading to the kitchen, Otto led the way to the supper table, where they helped themselves comfortably

but carefully, for at close range there was an air of thrift about
the food, as if the cheese and sausages had been counted and
the bread weighed, perhaps. A boy in a white jacket brought
them tall steins of beer; they lifted them to each other, waved
them at the brothers, and drank long and deeply.

"In Munich," said Tadeusz, "I used to drink with a crowd
of music students, all Germans. We drank and drank, and the
man who had to leave the table first paid for all. I always paid.
It was a bore, really."

"A dull custom at best," commented Hans, "and of course
the kind of thing foreigners would notice and tell about, as if it
were typical." His face was quietly annoyed, he looked past
Tadeusz, who refused to be snubbed.

"I have already agreed with you it was a bore," he said, "and
after all, only an incident of life in Munich." His tone was
soothing, indulgent, a little insolent. Charles, observing,
thought with some slight surprise that these fellows did not
like each other, after all. And almost instantly he felt indifference tinged with dislike for them both, and an uneasy feeling
that he was in the wrong company; he wished pretty thoroughly he had not come to that place with them.

One of the brothers leaned over them with his open, single-
minded expression, calling their attention to newcomers. A
stupidly handsome young man with a careful thatch of curls
above a self-consciously god-like brow was helping an olive-
skinned, yellow-haired young woman with her wraps. "A star
in the moving pictures," whispered the brother, excitedly,
"and that girl is his mistress and his leading lady." He dived
towards his celebrities awkwardly, saw them settled and was
back in a moment. "There comes Lutte, a model, one of the
most beautiful girls in Berlin," he said, his voice throbbing.
"She is going to dance a rumba when the time comes."

They all turned in natural curiosity and saw indeed a very
beautiful slender girl, her head shining like a silver yellow pe-
ony above her rather skimpy black dress. She smiled and waved
her hand at them, they stood up and bowed, but she did not
approach them as they had hoped. Leaning on the bar, she
talked to the boy in the white jacket. The room filled then
rather rapidly, there was a rush for the long table and the
brothers, flushed with success, beamed and scurried with trays

and steins. A small orchestra moved into the space beside the bar.

Almost every guest, Charles noticed, had brought a musical instrument, a violin or flute or white piano accordion, a clarinet; and one man lumbered in under the burden of a violoncello in a green baize-covered case. A young woman with huge haunches and thick legs, a knot of sleek brown hair slipping upon her unpowdered neck, came in by herself, looked around with a vague smile which no one returned, and went behind the bar, where she began competently to set up trays of beer.

"There you see her," said Hans, looking at Lutte possessively, "the truest type of German beauty—tell me, have you seen anything better anywhere?"

"Oh, come now," said Tadeusz, mildly, "there aren't a half dozen like her in this town. The legs and feet, surely they aren't typical? She might have French blood, or even a little Polish," he said. "Only she is perhaps a little flat-bosomed for that."

"What you seem never to understand," said Hans, in a slightly edged voice, "is that when I say German I don't mean peasants or these fat Berliners."

"Perhaps we should always mean peasants when we speak of a race," said Tadeusz. "The nobility and the royalty are always mixed bloods, the complete mongrel, really, they have no nationality at all. Even the middle classes marry everywhere, but the peasant stays in his own region and marries his own kind, generation after generation, and creates the race, quite simply, as I see it."

"The trouble with that notion," said Hans, "is that the peasantry of almost any country looks quite like the peasantry of any other."

"Oh, superficially," said Otto. "Their heads are very different, if you will study them." He leaned forward earnestly. "No matter how it came about," he told them, "the true great old Germanic type is lean and tall and fair as gods." His forehead formed a deep wrinkle which sank to a meaty cleft between his brows. His small puffy eyes swam tenderly, the roll of fat across his collar flushed with emotion. "We are not by any means all the pig type," he said humbly, spreading his thick hands, "though I know the foreign caricaturists make us all appear so. Those were perhaps the old Wendish people, and after all, they were a single tribe, they are not of the old true great Germanic—"

"Type," finished Tadeusz, mildly rude. "Let's agree then, the Germans are all of the highest type of beauty and they have preposterously fine manners. Look at all the heel-clicking and bowing from the waist and elegant high-toned voices. And how polite and smiling a seven-foot policeman can be when he is getting ready to crack your skull open. I have seen it. No, Hans, you have a great culture here, no doubt, but I think no civilization. You will be the last race on earth to be civilized, but does it matter?"

"On the other hand," said Hans with extreme politeness, smiling, a cold gleam in his eye, "the Poles, if you like that high-cheeked, low-browed Tartar style, have also great physical beauty, and though they have contributed exactly nothing to world-culture, they are civilized in a medieval sort of way, I suppose."

"Thanks," said Tadeusz, turning towards Hans as if to show his flat cheeks and narrow high forehead. "One of my grandmothers was a Tartar, and you can see how typical I am."

"One of your grandfathers was an Austrian, too," said Otto; "I'd never think of you as a Pole. You seem to me an Austrian."

"Oh, by God, I can't have that," said Tadeusz, decidedly, and he laughed with his lips tightly closed. "No, no, I'll be a Tartar first. But I am a Pole just the same."

Charles had never seen any Poles except a few short-legged broad-faced men laying railroad ties somewhere in the South, and he would not have known they were Poles unless someone had told him, and the man called them Polacks, besides. He could make nothing of Tadeusz, but Hans and Otto both seemed persons he had known before; Texas was full of boys like Otto, and Hans reminded him of Kuno. It seemed to him that the discussion was getting nowhere, and it reminded him of quarrels during his schooldays between the German boys and Mexican boys and the Kentucky boys; the Irish boys fought everybody, and Charles, who was partly Irish, remembered that he had done a good deal of fighting in which all sight of the original dispute had been lost in the simple love of violence. He said, "All the way over on the boat the Germans kept telling me I was not a typical American. How could they know? Of course I am perfectly typical."

"Oh, not at all," said Tadeusz, and this time his good humor was real. "We know all about you. Americans are all cowboys or very rich, and when they are rich they get drunk in poor countries and paste thousand-franc notes on their suitcases, or light cigarettes with them—"

"Oh, God," said Charles simply. "Who started that story?" Even American tourists went about repeating it with complacent horror, as if to prove they were not that sort of tourist.

"You know what is the trouble?" asked Tadeusz, amiably. "The Americans we know are all so filthy rich. There is nothing Europeans love and crave and covet more than wealth. If we didn't believe your country has all the money, there would be nothing wrong with you, particularly."

"We're punch drunk, anyhow," said Charles. "We don't give a damn any more."

"Europeans hate each other for everything and for nothing; they've been trying to destroy each other for two thousand years, why do you Americans expect us to like you?" asked Tadeusz.

"We don't expect it," said Charles. "Who said we did? We, naturally, like just everybody. We are sentimental. Just like the Germans. You want to be loved for yourselves alone and you are always right and you can never see why other people can't see you in the same rosy light you see yourselves. Look what a glorious people you are and yet nobody loves you. Well, that's a great pity."

Otto gazed earnestly at Charles from under his deep brows, wagged his head and said, "I do not think you really like anybody, you Americans. You are indifferent to everybody and so it is easy for you to be gay, to be careless, to seem friendly. You are really a coldhearted indifferent people. You have no troubles. You have no troubles because you do not know how to have them. Even if you get troubles, you think it is just a package meant for the people next door, delivered to you by mistake. That is what I really believe."

Charles, embittered, said, "I can't talk about whole countries because I never knew one, not even my own. I only know a few persons here and there and some I like and some I don't like and I never thought it anything but a personal matter. . . ."

Tadeusz said, "Oh, dear fellow, that is being much too modest. The whole art of self-importance is to raise your personal likes and dislikes to the plane of moral or esthetic principle, and to apply on an international scale your smallest personal experience. . . . If someone steps on your foot, you should not rest until you have raised an army to avenge you. . . . And as for us, what are we doing with our evening? At this rate I shall have indigestion. . . ."

"What about our friends the French?" asked Hans, suddenly. "Can anyone find fault with them? Their food, their wine, their dress, their manners—" he lifted his stein and drank without enjoyment, and added—"a race of monkeys."

"They have very bad manners," said Tadeusz, "and they would cut you into ribbons with a dull pair of scissors for five francs in hand. A shortsighted and selfish people, and how I love them. But not as I do the English. Take the English—"

"Take the Italians," said Charles, "all of them."

"Nothing worth mentioning since Dante," said Tadeusz. "I detest their lumpy Renaissance."

"Now that's settled," said Charles, "let's take the pigmies, or the Icelanders, or the head hunters of Borneo—"

"I love them all," cried Tadeusz, "especially the Irish. I like the Irish because they are nearly as damnation patriotic as the Poles."

"I was brought up on Irish patriotism," said Charles. "My mother's name was O'Hara, and I was supposed to be proud of it, but you have a tough time being proud if you are called Harp and Potato Mouth at school where the others are all Scotch Presbyterians or of English descent."

Tadeusz said, "What nonsense," and he began to talk pleasantly and quietly about the great ancient Celtic race, slyly too, aiming at Hans; praising their ancient culture of which traces were found in all parts of Europe. "Yes, even the Germans have been improved by it," he said. Hans and Otto shook their heads, but their anger seemed to have disappeared, their faces smoothed and their eyes met openly once more. Charles was soothed and flattered to find Irish greatness acknowledged at

last by somebody other than his immediate family. He said to
Tadeusz, "My father used to tell me, 'Ah, the Irish, my boy.
God knows they went down early in time, but don't forget
this, they had a great national culture when the British were
still painting themselves blue, and the old French used to exchange scholars with them!'"

Tadeusz translated this to Hans and Otto, and Hans
laughed so suddenly he put his hand to his cheek with a grimace. "Be careful," said Tadeusz, looking at the wound as he
always did, with an air of clinical interest, which he knew Hans
liked. Charles went on to say he had never seen such a statement in any history books, which seemed very vague about the
Irish until they began fighting with the British. By that time,
the books said in effect, they were just a lot of wild bog-
jumpers. He had felt sorry for his father, trying to wring a drop
of comfort out of the myth of his splendid past, but the usual
run of histories on the subject hadn't borne him out. He was
pleased to think he had simply got hold of the wrong books.

"They are very like the Poles," said Tadeusz, "those Irish,
living on the glory of their past, on their poetry and the jeweled Book of Kells and the great cups and crowns of ancient
Ireland, the memories of victories and defeats godlike in intensity, the hope of rising again to glory: and in the meantime,"
he added, "always fighting quite a lot and very unsuccessfully."

Hans leaned forward and spoke with importance, as if he
were a professor addressing his class: "The fate of Ireland (and
of Poland, too, Tadeusz, don't forget) is an example, a most
terrible example, of what can happen to a country when it di-
vides against itself and lets the enemy in . . . the Irish, so nationalistic at this late day, are yet divided. What do they expect?
They could have saved themselves in early time by uniting and
attacking the enemy, instead of waiting to be attacked."

Tadeusz reminded him, "Hans, that does not always work
either," but Hans ignored the little gibe.

Charles, ill-informed as he was, floundering in the quick-
sands of popular history, could not answer, yet the whole notion was offensive to him. "But why jump on a man unless he
jumps first?"

Hans, the youthful oracle, was ready. "Why, because he
always attacks when you are not looking, or when you have

put down your arms for an instant. So you are punished for carelessness really, for not troubling to learn the intentions of your enemy. You are beaten, and that is the end of you, unless you can gather strength and fight again."

"The Celts aren't ended," said Tadeusz; "they exist in great numbers and are scattered all over and still have influence everywhere they touch."

"Influence?" asked Hans. "A purely oblique, feminine, worthless thing, influence. Power, pure power is what counts to a nation or a race. You must be able to tell other peoples what to do, and above all what they may not do, you must be able to enforce every order you give against no matter what opposition, and when you demand anything at all, it must be given you without question. That is the only power, and power is the only thing of any value or importance in this world."

"It doesn't last, though, any better than some other things," said Tadeusz. "It doesn't always work as well as long ruse and intelligent strategy. It goes down in the long run."

"Maybe it goes down because powerful people get tired of power," said Otto, leaning his head on his hand and looking discouraged; "maybe they wear themselves out beating other people and spying on them and ordering them about and robbing them. Maybe they exhaust themselves."

"And maybe one day they overstep themselves, or a new young power rises to put an end to them," said Tadeusz; "that happens."

"Maybe they find out it doesn't pay," said Charles.

"It always pays," said Hans; "that is the point. It pays, and nothing else does. Everything else is childish beside it. Otto, you surprise me. That is a strange point of view for you."

Otto sagged, guilty and uncomfortable. "I am not a soldier," he said. "I love study and quiet."

Hans sat very stiffly, an alienated hostile glitter in his eyes. He turned halfway to Charles and said, "We Germans were beaten in the last war, thanks partly to your great country, but we shall win in the next."

A chill ran down Charles' spine, he shrugged his shoulders. They were all a little drunk, there might be a row if they didn't pull themselves together. He did not want to quarrel with anybody, nor to fight the war over again. "We were all in short pants when that war was ended," he said. Hans answered instantly, "Ah, yes, but we will all be in uniforms for the next."

Tadeusz said, "Oh, come now, dear Hans, I never felt less bloodthirsty in my life. I only want to play the piano."

"I want to paint," said Charles.

"I want to teach mathematics," said Otto.

"Neither am I bloodthirsty," said Hans, "but I know what will happen." His cheek, under its band of court plaster, was slightly more swollen than earlier in the evening. The fingers of his left hand explored tenderly along the line of angry blue flesh. He said, in a bright impersonal tone, "Look, it is most interesting to remember one thing. We should have won that war, and we lost it in the first three days, though we did not know it, or could not believe it, for four years. What was the cause? One single delayed order, one sole failure of a body of troops to move at a given moment, on that first advance through Belgium. A delay of three days lost us that war. Well, it won't happen the next time."

"No," said Tadeusz, gently, "the next time, there will be another kind of mistake, something else quite different will go wrong, who knows how or why? It is always like that. Wars are not won by intelligence, Hans. Can't you see that? All the fine planning in the world can't insure an army against that one fellow who will, when the moment comes, delay, or give the wrong order, or be in the wrong place. Why, the other side did nothing but blunder all the way through, and yet they won, that time."

"Sea power," said Charles, "good old sea power. I bet on that. It wins in the long run."

"Carthage was a sea power, but she didn't beat Rome," said Otto.

"The next time," said Hans, with cool stubbornness, "they won't win. You'll see. The next time, there will be no mistakes on our side."

"I can wait," said Tadeusz, "I am in no hurry."

"I can wait, all right," said Charles, "and meantime, let me get the beer."

The orchestra, increased by the efforts of guests with their fiddles, flutes and the violoncello, had been making a fine din, so that the four voices had been rising gradually. "Let's give it up for the present," said Tadeusz; "it can't be settled this evening."

The actor and his mistress were gone, and Lutte remained the only beauty in the room. She was sitting with several young men and another girl at a table near by, all drinking beer heartily, laughing constantly and falling into each other's arms at intervals for embraces and smacks on the cheek, the boys kissing boys or girls alike with indiscriminate warmth. Lutte caught Charles' glance and waved her beer glass at him. He waved back and smiled excitedly. She was a knockout and he hoped quite violently to know her better. And even at that moment, like the first symptoms of some fatal sickness, there stirred in him a most awful premonition of disaster, and his thoughts, blurred with drink and strangeness and the sound of half-understood tongues and the climate of remembered wrongs and hatreds, revolved dimly around vague remembered tales of Napoleon and Genghis Khan and Attila the Hun and all the Caesars and Alexander the Great and Darius and the dim Pharaohs and lost Babylon. He felt helpless, undefended, looked at the three strange faces near him and decided not to drink any more, for he must not be drunker than they; he trusted none of them.

Otto, leaving his beer, wandered away, and one of the brothers handed him a white piano accordion as he passed. The change in Otto was miraculous. From soggy gloom his face turned to a great mask of simple enjoyment, he took up the tune the orchestra was playing and roamed among the tables, the instrument folding and unfolding in his arms, his blunt fingers flying over the keys. In a fine roaring voice he began to sing:

> *"Ich armes welsches Teufelein*
> *Ich kann nicht mehr marschieren—"*

"MARSCHIEREN!" roared every voice in the place, joyously. "Ich kann nicht mehr marschier'n."

Otto sang:

> *"Ich hab' verlor'n mein Pfeiflein*
> *Aus meinen Mantelsack—"*

" 'SACK!" yelled the chorus, "Aus meinen Mantelsack."

Hans stood up and sang in a clear light voice: "Ich hab', ich hab' gefunden, was du verloren hast—"

"HAST!" bawled the chorus, and everybody was standing now, their laughing faces innocent and pure as lambs at play, "was du verloren hast."

There was a great wave of laughter after this, and the orchestra suddenly changed to "The Peanut Vendor." Lutte, with a serious face as if she were fulfilling her duty, stood up and began to dance alone, something supposed no doubt to be a rumba, but to Charles, it seemed rather a combination of the black bottom and the hoochy-coochy such as he had seen, sneaking off furtively with other boys, in carnival sideshows during his innocent boyhood in Texas. He had danced the rumba to the tune of "The Peanut Vendor" all the way from his home town, across the Atlantic and straight into Bremen harbor, and it occurred to him that here was something he could really do. He took the gourds from the quiet little fellow who was clacking them rather feebly, and began to do his version of the rumba, shaking the gourds and cracking them together with great authority.

He could hear hands clapping in rhythm all over the room, and Lutte, abandoning her solo, began to dance with him. He handed back the gourds at once and took Lutte firmly around her warm, agitated waist, very thinly covered. She held her face back from him stiffly, smiled with a fair imitation of a cinematic *femme fatale*, and rather clumsily but with great meaning bumped her hip against him. He gathered her in, folded her up to him as close as he could, but she stiffened again and bumped him, this time full in the stomach. "What say we give up the technique and let nature take its course," said Charles, with a straight face.

"What is that?" she asked, unexpectedly in English. "I do not understand."

"Well," said Charles, kissing her on the cheek, "it speaks English too." She did not kiss back, but went limp and began to dance naturally.

"Am I as beautiful as that moving picture actress who was here this evening?" asked Lutte, wistfully.

"At least," said Charles.

"Would I do for the moving pictures in America, in your Hollywood?" she asked, leaning upon him.

"Don't bump," said Charles. "Yes, you would do fine in Hollywood."

"Do I dance well enough?" asked Lutte.

"Yes, darling, you do. You are a whizz."

"What is that?"

"Something wonderful," said Charles. "Come to me, angel."

"Do you know anybody in Hollywood?" asked Lutte, sticking firmly to her one interest.

"No, but you might," said Charles; "all Germany and Central Europe are there already; you'd be bound to run into friends. Anyway you won't be lonesome long."

Lutte put her mouth like a ripe peach to his ear and blowing warmly upon it whispered, "Take me to America with you."

"Let's go," said Charles, and seizing her more firmly he ran a few steps towards the door. She held back. "No, I am serious, I want to go to America."

"So do I," said Charles, recklessly, "so does everybody."

"That is not true," said Lutte, severely, almost stopping in her tracks. At this moment Hans cut in. Charles sat down feeling cheated. Lutte's manner changed completely. She melted towards Hans, they danced slowly and as they danced, she kissed him softly and continually and gently on his right cheek, her mouth meek and sweet, her eyes nearly closed. Over Hans' disfigured face came that same look of full-fed pride, of composed self-approval—of arrogance, that was the word. Charles felt a flicker of sharp hatred for Hans. Then it passed. "Hell," he said, aloud, yet to no one, "what of it?"

"I think so too," said Tadeusz, "I think, hell, what of it?"

"Let's have some brandy," said Charles. Otto was sitting quietly, he roused and smiled.

"What a fine evening!" he said. "We are all friends, are we not?"

"Completely," said Tadeusz, "we are all friends to you, Otto." He had grown quieter and softer in his gestures, his eyes peered vaguely between his wrinkled lids, his little tight smile was constant. "I am getting damnation drunk, and my conscience will begin hurting soon," he said, contentedly. Then the others, listening dimly, heard him telling some story about his childhood in Cracow. ". . . in the old house where my family have lived since the twelfth century . . ." he said. "At Easter we ate only pork in contempt of the Jews, and after the long fasting of Lent naturally we gorged ourselves shamelessly. . . . On Easter morning after High Mass I would eat until I was perfectly round, and in pain. Then I would lie down and cry, and when they asked me what troubled me, I would say, out of shame, that my conscience was hurting me. They would be very respectful and comfort me, but sometimes I thought I saw a gleam in an eye, or just a flash of a look on a face—not my mother's, but my sister's, perhaps—she was a horrid, knowing little thing—and my nurse's. One day my nurse gave me some soothing syrup and rubbed my stomach with that insulting false sympathy and said, 'There now, your conscience feels better, doesn't it?' I went howling and told my mother that my nurse had kicked me in the stomach. Then I upchucked all my Easter pork, so the Jews had their revenge for once. My nurse said, 'What a little monster it is'; then she and my mother talked in the next room, and when they came back smiling I knew the game was up. I never mentioned my conscience again to them. But once after I was grown up, or nearly, I was very drunk and came home at four in the morning, and I crawled upstairs because it seemed unreasonable, this business of people walking about on their hind legs all the time. The red stair carpet gave me a sense of great security and ease, and I remember feeling that I was a kind of prophet of good for mankind, restoring an old way of locomotion which would probably revolutionize all society once I had proved its pleasures and possibilities. The first obstacle I encountered was my mother. She stood at the head of the stairs holding a lighted candle, waiting without a word. I waved one paw at her but she did not respond. And when I put my head above the last step she kicked me under the chin and almost knocked me out. She never mentioned this incident and I could hardly believe it myself except for my sore tongue the next day. Well, such was my upbringing in that old city, but I remember it dearly now, something between a cemetery and a Lost Paradise, with an immense sound of bells. . . ."

Otto said, "Maybe we should have some beer," and with a sad mouth he talked a little about his own childhood. His mother had beaten him quite hard one day, without warning, when he was cracking walnuts and eating them. With tears he had asked her why, and she said, "Don't ask me any questions. What is good enough for Martin Luther is good enough for you." And later in a child's book he had read how Luther's mother had beaten him until the blood came because he annoyed her with the sound of cracking nuts. "Until then I had thought of Luther as a great, forbidding cruel man who loved bloodshed, but after that I felt sorry for him. He was once a poor helpless child like me, beaten for nothing," Otto said, "and yet he became great." His face was full of humble apology. "That was child's nonsense, but it helped me to live," he said.

The drifting smoke and the lights and the voices and the music were all mingled and swimming together around their heads. The big young woman who had been helping at the bar came then, her knot of hair slipping still further down her neck, and seemed to be pulling chairs and tables towards the wall. Her fine haunches jiggled under her tight skirt, her great breasts were stretching and falling as she raised and lowered her arms, her heavy legs were braced far apart as she pushed at a table. The men sitting about watched her without moving or offering help. Charles observed another change in Otto. He was watching the girl intently, his mouth moistening. He seemed lost in a pleasant daze, his nose twitched, his eyes grew round and took on the calculating ferocity of a tomcat's. The girl leaned over and the hollows of her knees showed; she straightened up and the muscles of her back and shoulders writhed. Slowly, feeling Otto's gaze upon her, she began to blush. Her neck turned red, her cheeks, her forehead, the whole face stiffened and darkened as if she were resisting pain, or a surge of anger. But the corners of her soft formless mouth were smiling, and she did not raise her eyes again after her first quick glance. Quite suddenly she gave a last plunge at a chair, set it in place with a thump, and ran away, her body full of awkward, contradictory motions. Otto turned to Charles, and showered upon him the remains of his impassioned gaze at the girl.

"There is a fine armful for you," he said; "I like big strong girls." Charles nodded as if he agreed, and looked again at Lutte, still dancing with Hans and kissing him.

A wooden cuckoo about the size of a humming bird leaped from his little door above the clockface and began his warning note. Instantly everybody rose and each one embraced the person nearest him, shouting, "Happy New Year, health, good luck, happy New Year, God bless you." Glasses and stems danced aloft in half circles, spilling foam on uplifted faces. A disordered circle formed, arms interlocked, and a ragged singing began which smoothed out almost at once into a deep chorus, the fine voices swinging along together in frolicsome tunes Charles did not know. He swayed with the circle, woven into it, he opened his mouth and sang tunelessly without words. Real joy, warm and careless, swept him away; this was a place to be, these were wonderful people, he liked absolutely everybody there. The circle broke up, ran together, whirled, loosened, fell apart.

Hans came over smiling on one side of his face, Lutte beside him. They put their arms around Charles together and wished him a happy New Year. He stood there swaying with an arm around each, all jealousy gone. Lutte kissed him sweetly on the mouth, and he kissed back but like a child. Then they all saw Tadeusz leaning over Otto, who was sprawled at the little table, head pillowed on his arms.

"He's gone completely, he has deserted us," said Tadeusz. "Now we must drag him about with us wherever we go for the rest of the evening."

"We aren't going anywhere else, are we," asked Charles, "for God's sake?"

Otto was indeed gone, altogether. They got him up by the arms, and in a busy sort of scramble they found themselves on the sidewalk, with a tall policeman watching mildly, getting into a taxicab, where their feet were tangled hopelessly and they all seemed to hang at once dangerously far out of the windows. Lutte was saying, to all of them alike, "Good night, happy New Year," her face shining but sober looking.

On the staircase, Otto collapsed once for all. The three pulled him along slowly, pausing at every step. At moments the whole structure tottered, they would stagger and lose hold of each other and step on Otto, who groaned and howled, but without resentment. They would heave themselves together more firmly and start again, making wild sounds of laughter, nodding at each other as if agreed on some inexplicable but gloriously comic truth. "Let's crawl," shouted Charles to Tadeusz; "maybe it will work this time." Hans disapproved of this instantly.

"No crawling," he said, taking command at once. "Every man goes up on his own feet, except perhaps Otto." They assembled themselves once more for a last effort, and arrived at the door known to be theirs.

Rosa's door was ajar slightly, a streak of light shining into the hall. They regarded it with sobering gloom, expecting the door to fly open and Rosa to rush forth scolding. Nothing happened. They changed their tactics, and dragging Otto, they rushed her door, beating on it in tattoo and shouting recklessly, "Happy New Year, Roslein, Roslein, happy New Year."

There was a small flurry inside, the door opened a few inches more, and Rosa put out a sleek, orderly head. Her eyes were a little pink and sleepy looking, but she was smiling a gay, foxy smile. Her pensioners were most lordly drunk, she saw at a glance, none the worse for it, thank God. Hans' cheek was discolored somewhat more, but he was laughing, Charles and Tadeusz were quieter, trying to appear sober and responsible, but their eyelids drooped, they leered drolly. The three were supporting Herr Bussen between them, and Herr Bussen, hanging at random, his knees bent, had a blissful innocent confidence in his sleeping face.

"Happy New Year, you owls," said Rosa, proud of her household who knew how to celebrate an occasion. "I had champagne too, with friends, and New Year's punch. I am a little merry too," she told them, boasting. "Go to sleep now, look, this is the New Year. You must start it well tomorrow. Good night."

Charles sat on the feather bed and wriggled out of his clothes, pushing them off any old way and leaving them where they fell. As he fumbled with his pajamas, his eyes swam about in his head, seeing first one thing and then another, but none of it familiar, nothing that was his. He did notice at last that the

Leaning Tower seemed to be back, sitting now safely behind the glass of the corner cabinet. By a roundabout way he brought himself across the room to the Tower. It was there, all right, and it was mended pretty obviously, it would never be the same. But for Rosa, poor old woman, he supposed it was better than nothing. It stood for something she had, or thought she had, once. Even all patched up as it was, and worthless to begin with, it meant something to her, and he was still ashamed of having broken it; it made him feel like a heel. It stood there in its bold little frailness, as if daring him to come on; how well he knew that a thumb and forefinger would smash the thin ribs, the mended spots would fall at a breath. Leaning, suspended, perpetually ready to fall but never falling quite, the venturesome little object—a mistake in the first place, a whimsical pain in the neck, really, towers shouldn't lean in the first place; a curiosity, like those cupids falling off the roof —yet had some kind of meaning in Charles' mind. Well, what? He tousled his hair and rubbed his eyes and then his whole head and yawned himself almost inside out. What had the silly little thing reminded him of before? There was an answer if he could think what it was, but this was not the time. But just the same, there was something terribly urgent at work, in him or around him, he could not tell which. There was something perishable but threatening, uneasy, hanging over his head or stirring angrily, dangerously, at his back. If he couldn't find out now what it was that troubled him so in this place, maybe he would never know. He stood there feeling his drunkenness as a pain and a weight on him, unable to think clearly but feeling what he had never known before, an infernal desolation of the spirit, the chill and the knowledge of death in him. He wrapped his arms across his chest and expelled his breath, and a cold sweat broke out all over him. He went towards the bed and fell upon it and rolled himself into a knot, being rather unpleasant with himself. "All you need is a crying jag to make it complete," he said. But he didn't feel sorry for himself, and no crying jag or any other kind of jag would ever, in this world, do anything at all for him.

Berlin 1931

ESSAYS, REVIEWS,
AND OTHER WRITINGS

"I needed both . . ."

From the foreword to
The Days Before, by Katherine Anne Porter.
New York: Harcourt, Brace & Co., 1952.

IT is my hope that the reader will find in this collection of papers written throughout my thirty years as published writer, the shape, direction, and connective tissue of a continuous, central interest and preoccupation of a lifetime.

They represent the exact opposite of my fiction, in that they were written nearly all by request, with limitations of space, a date fixed for finishing, on a chosen subject or theme, as well as with the certainty that they would be published. I wrote as well as I could at any given moment under a variety of pressures, and said what I meant as nearly as I could come to it: so as they stand, the pieces are really parts of a journal of my thinking and feeling. Then too, they served to get me a living, such as it was, so that I might be able to write my stories in their own time and way. My stories had to be accepted and published exactly as they were written: that rule has never once been broken. There was no one, whose advice I respected, whose help I would not have been glad to get, and many times did get, on almost any of these articles. I have written, re-written, and revised them. My stories, on the other hand, are written in one draft, and if short enough, at one sitting. In fact, this book would seem to represent the other half of a double life: but not in truth. It is all one thing. The two ways of working helped and supported each other: I needed both.

K.A.P.

Rue Jacob, Paris
25 July 1952

Contents

CRITICAL

The Days Before

Really, universally, relations stop nowhere, and the exquisite problem of the artist is eternally but to draw, by a geometry of his own, the circle within which they shall happily *appear* to do so.

H.J.: Preface to *Roderick Hudson.*

WE have, it would seem, at last reluctantly decided to claim Henry James as our own, in spite of his having renounced, two years before his death, so serious an obligation as his citizenship, but with a disturbing tendency among his critics and admirers of certain schools to go a step further and claim him for the New England, or Puritan, tradition.

This is merely the revival and extension of an old error first made by Carlyle in regard to Henry James the elder: "Mr. James, your New-England friend," wrote Carlyle in a letter, "I saw him several times and liked him." This baseless remark set up, years later, a train of reverberations in the mind of Mr. James's son Henry, who took pains to correct the "odd legend" that the James family were a New England product, mentioning that Carlyle's mistake was a common one among the English, who seemed to have no faintest care or notion about our regional differences. With his intense feeling for place and family relations and family history, Henry James the younger could not allow this important error to pass uncorrected. With his very special eyes, whose threads were tangled in every vital center of his being, he looked long through "a thin golden haze" into his past, and recreated for our charmed view an almost numberless family connection, all pure Scotch-Irish so far back as the records run, unaltered to the third generation in his branch of the family; and except for the potent name-grandfather himself—a Presbyterian of rather the blue-nosed caste, who brought up his eleven or was it thirteen children of three happy marriages in the fear of a quite improbable God—almost nothing could be less Puritanic, less New England, than their careers, even if they were all of Protestant descent. The earliest branch came late to this country (1764) according to Virginia or New England standards, and they settled in the comparatively newly opened country of upstate

New York—new for the English and Scotch-Irish, that is, for the Dutch and the French had been there a good while before, and they married like with like among the substantial families settled along the Hudson River. Thus the whole connection in its earlier days was spared the touch of the specifically New England spirit, which even then was spreading like a slow blight into every part of the country.

(But the young Henry James feared it from the first, distrusted it in his bones. Even though his introduction to New England was by way of "the proud episcopal heart of Newport," when he was about fifteen years old, and though he knew there at least one artist, and one young boy of European connection and experience, still, Boston was not far away, and he felt a tang of wintry privation in the air, a threat of "assault and death." By way of stores against the hovering famine and siege, he collected a whole closet full of the beloved *Revue des Deux Mondes*, in its reassuring salmon-pink cover.)

Henry James's grandfather, the first William James, arrived in America from Ireland, County Cavan, an emigrant boy of seventeen, and settled in Albany in 1789. He was of good solid middle-class stock, he possessed that active imagination and boundless energy of the practical sort so useful in ancestors; in about forty years of the most blameless, respected use of every opportunity to turn an honest penny, on a very handsome scale of operations, he accumulated a fortune of three million dollars, in a style that was to become the very pattern of American enterprise. The city of Albany was credited to him, it was the work of his hands, it prospered with him. His industries and projects kept hundreds of worthy folk gainfully employed the year round, in the grateful language of contemporary eulogy; in his time only John Jacob Astor gathered a larger fortune in New York state. We may as well note here an obvious irony, and dismiss it: James's grandfather's career was a perfect example of the sort of thing that was to become "typically American," and still is, it happens regularly even now; and Henry James the younger had great good of it, yet it did create the very atmosphere which later on he found so hard to breathe that he deserted it altogether for years, for life.

The three millions were divided at last among the widow

and eleven surviving children, the first Henry James, then a young man, being one of them. These twelve heirs none of them inherited the Midas touch, and all had a taste for the higher things of life enjoyed in easy, ample surroundings. Henry the younger lived to wonder, with a touch of charming though acute dismay, just what had become of all that delightful money. Henry the elder, whose youth had been gilded to the ears, considered money a topic beneath civilized discussion, business a grimy affair they all agreed to know nothing about, and neglected completely to mention what he had done with his share. He fostered a legend among his children that he had been "wild" and appeared, according to his fascinating stories, to have been almost the only young man of his generation who had not come to a bad end. His son Henry almost in infancy had got the notion that the words "wild" and "dissipated" were synonymous with "tipsy." Be that as it may, Henry the first in his wild days had a serious if temporary falling out with his father, whom he described as the tenderest and most sympathetic of parents; but he also wrote in his fragment of autobiography, "I should think indeed that our domestic intercourse had been on the whole most innocent as well as happy, were it not for a certain lack of oxygen which is indeed incidental to the family atmosphere and which I may characterize as the lack of any ideal of action except that of self-preservation." Indeed, yes. Seeking fresh air, he fled into the foreign land of Massachusetts: Boston, precisely: until better days should come. "It was an age," wrote his son Henry, "in which a flight from Albany to Boston . . . counted as a far flight." It still does. The point of this episode for our purposes was, that Henry the first mildewed in exile for three long months, left Boston and did not again set foot there until he was past thirty-five. His wife never went there at all until her two elder sons were in Harvard, a seat of learning chosen *faute de mieux*, for Europe, Europe was where they fain all would be; except that a strange, uneasy, even artificially induced nationalism, due to the gathering war between the states, had laid cold doubts on their minds—just where did they belong, where was their native land? The two young brothers, William and Henry, especially then began, after their shuttlings to and from Europe, to make unending efforts to "find America" and to place themselves once for all either in it or out of it. But this was later.

It is true that the elder Jameses settled in Boston, so far as a James of that branch could ever be said to settle, for the good reason that they wished to be near their sons; but they never became, by any stretch of the word, New Englanders, any more than did their son William, after all those years at Harvard; any more than did their son Henry become an Englishman, after all those years in England. He realized this himself, even after he became a British subject in 1914; and the British agree with him to this day. He was to the end an amiable, distinguished stranger living among them. Yet two generations born in this country did not make them Americans, either, and in the whole great branching family connection, with its "habits of ease" founded on the diminishing backlog of the new fortune, the restless blood of the emigrant grandparents ran high. Europe was not so far away as it is now, and though Albany and "the small, warm dusky homogeneous New York world of the mid-century" were dear to them, they could not deny, indeed no one even thought of denying, that all things desirable in the arts, architecture, education, ways of living, history, the future, the very shape of the landscape and the color of the air, lay like an inheritance they had abandoned, in Europe.

"This question of Europe" which never ceased to agitate his parents from his earliest memory was paradoxically the only permanent element in the Jameses' family life. All their movements, plans, interests were based, you might say, on that perpetually unresolved problem. It was kept simmering by letters from friends and relatives traveling or living there; cousins living handsomely at Geneva, enjoying the widest possible range of desirable social amenities; other cousins living agreeably at Tours, or Trouville; the handsomest of the Albany aunts married advantageously and living all over Europe, urging the Henry Jameses to come with their young and do likewise for the greater good of all. There was an older cousin who even lived in China, came back to fill a flat in Gramercy Square with "dim Chinoiseries" and went on to old age in Surrey and her last days in Versailles. There was besides the constant delicious flurry of younger cousins and aunts with strange wonderful clothes and luggage who had always just been there, or who were just going there, "there" meaning always Europe, and oddly enough, specifically Paris, instead of London. The infant Henry, at the age of five, received his "positive initiation into History" when Uncle Gus returned bringing the news of the flight of Louis Philippe to England. To the child, *flight* had been a word with a certain meaning; *king* another. "Flight of kings" was a new, portentous, almost poetic image of strange disasters, it early gave to political questions across the sea a sense of magnificence they altogether lacked at home, where society outside the enthralling family circle and the shimmering co-rona of friends seemed altogether to consist of "the busy, the tipsy, and Daniel Webster."

Within that circle, however, nothing could exceed the free-dom and ease with which artists of all sorts, some of them for-gotten now, seemed to make the James fireside, wherever it happened to be, their own. The known and acclaimed were also household guests and dear friends.

Mr. Emerson, "the divinely pompous rose of the philosoph-ical garden," as Henry James the elder described him, or, in other lights and views, the "man without a handle"—one sim-ply couldn't get hold of him at all—had been taken upstairs in the fashionable Astor Hotel to admire the newly born William; and in later times, seated in the firelit dusk of the back parlor in the James house, had dazzled the young Henry, who knew he was great. General Winfield Scott in military splendor had borne down upon him and his father at a street corner for a greeting; and on a boat between Fort Hamilton and New York Mr. Washington Irving had apprised Mr. James of the ship-wreck of Margaret Fuller, off Fire Island, only a day or so before. Edgar Allan Poe was one of the "acclaimed," the idol-ized, most read and recited of poets; his works were on every drawing room or library table that Henry James knew, and he never outgrew his wonder at the legend that Poe was neg-lected in his own time.

Still it was Dickens who ruled and pervaded the literary world from afar; the books in the house, except for a few French novels, were nearly all English; the favorite bookstore was English, where the James children went to browse, sniffing the pages for the strong smell of paper and printer's ink, which they called "the English smell." The rule of the admired, revered *Revue des Deux Mondes* was to set in shortly; France and French for Henry James, Germany and German for William James, were to have their great day, and stamp their images to such a degree that ever after the English of the one, and of the other, were to be "larded" and tagged and stuffed with French and German. In the days before, however, the general deliciousness and desirability of all things English was in the domestic air Henry James breathed; his mother and father talked about it so much at the breakfast table that, re-membering, he asked himself if he had ever heard anything else talked about over the morning coffee cups. They could not relive enough their happy summer in England with their two babies, and he traveled again and again with them, by way of "Windsor and Sudbrook and Ham Common"; an earthly Paradise, they believed, and he believed with them. A young aunt, his mother's sister, shared these memories and added her own: an incurable homesickness for England possessed her. Henry, asking for stories, listened and "took in" everything: taking in was to be his life's main occupation: as if, he said, his "infant divination proceeded by the light of nature," and he had learned already the importance of knowing in advance of any experience of his own, just what life in England might be like. A small yellow-covered English magazine called *Charm* also "shed on the question the softest lustre" and caused deep pangs of disappointment when it failed to show up regularly at the bookstore.

Henry James refers to all these early impressions as an "in-fection," as a sip of "poison," as a "twist"—perhaps of some psychological thumbscrew—but the twinges and pangs were all exciting, joyful, mysterious, thrilling, sensations he enjoyed and sought eagerly, half their force at least consisting of his imaginative projection of his own future in the most brilliant possible of great worlds. He saw his parents and his aunt per-petually homesick for something infinitely lovable and splendid they had known, and he longed to know it too. "Homesick-ness was a luxury I remember craving from the tenderest age," he confessed, because he had at once perhaps too many homes and therefore no home at all. If his parents did not feel at home anywhere, he could not possibly, either. He did not know what to be homesick for, unless it were England, which he had seen but could not remember.

This was, then, vicarious, a mere sharing at second-hand; he needed something of his own. When it came, it was rather dismaying; but it was an important episode and confirmed in him the deep feeling that England had something formidable in its desirability, something to be lived up to: in contrast to France as he discovered later, where one "got life," as he expressed it; or Germany, where the very trees of the great solemn forests murmured in his charmed ear of their mystical "culture." What happened was this: the celebrated Mr. Thackeray, fresh from England, seated as an honored much-at-ease guest in the James library, committed an act which somehow explains everything that is wrong with his novels.

"Come here, little boy," he said to Henry, "and show me your extraordinary jacket." With privileged bad manners he placed his hand on the child's shoulder and asked him if his garments were the uniform of his "age and class," adding with brilliant humor that if he should wear it in England he would be addressed as "Buttons." No matter what Mr. Thackeray thought he was saying—very likely he was not thinking at all— he conveyed to the overwhelmed admirer of England that the English, as so authoritatively represented by Mr. Thackeray, thought Americans "queer." It was a disabling blow, recalled in every circumstance fifty years later, with a photograph, of all things, to illustrate and prove its immediate effect.

Henry was wearing that jacket, buttoned to the chin with a small white collar, on the hot dusty summer day when his companionable father, who never went anywhere without one or the other of his two elder sons, brought him up from Staten Island, where the family were summering, to New York, and as a gay surprise for everybody, took him to Mr. Brady's for their photograph together. A heavy surprise indeed for Henry, who forever remembered the weather, the smells and sights of the wharf, the blowzy summer lassitude of the streets, and his own dismay that by his father's merry whim he was to be immortalized by Mr. Brady in his native costume which would appear so absurd in England. Mr. Brady that day made one of the most expressive child pictures I know. The small straight figure has a good deal of grace and dignity in its unworthy (as he feared) clothes; the long hands are holding with what composure they can to things they know; his father's shoulder, his large and, according to the fashion plates of the day, stylish straw hat. All the life of the child is in the eyes, rueful, disturbed, contemplative, with enormous intelligence and perception, much older than the face, much deeper and graver than his father's. His father and mother bore a certain family resemblance to each other, such as closely interbred peoples of any nation are apt to develop; Henry resembled them both, but his father more neatly, and judging by later photographs, the resemblance became almost identical, except for the expression of the eyes —the unmistakable look of one who was to live intuitively and naturally a long life in "the air of the passions of the intelligence."

In Mr. Brady's daguerreotype, he is still a child, a stranger everywhere, and he is unutterably conscious of the bright untimeliness of the whole thing, the lack of proper ceremony, ignored as ever by the father; the slack, unflattering pose. His father is benevolent and cheerful and self-possessed and altogether pleased for them both. He had won his right to gaiety of heart in his love; after many a victorious engagement with the powers of darkness, he had Swedenborg and all his angels round about, bearing him up, which his son was never to have; and he had not been lately ridiculed by Mr. Thackeray, at least not to his face. Really it was not just the jacket that troubled him—that idle remark upon it was only one of the smallest of the innumerable flashes which lighted for him, blindingly, whole territories of mystery in which a long lifetime could not suffice to make him feel at home. "I lose myself in wonder," he wrote in his later years, "at the loose ways, the strange process of waste, through which nature and fortune may deal on occasion with those whose faculty for application is all and only in their imagination and sensibility."

By then he must have known that in his special case, nothing at all had been wasted. He was in fact a most glorious example in proof of his father's favorite theories of the uses and virtues of waste as education, and at the end felt he had "mastered the particular history of just that waste." His father was not considered a good Swedenborgian by those followers of Sweden-

borg who had, against his expressed principles, organized
themselves into a church. Mr. James could not be organized in
the faintest degree by anyone or anything. His daughter Alice
wrote of him years later: ". . . Father, the delicious infant,
couldn't submit even to the thralldom of his own whim." That
smothering air of his childhood family life had given him a permanent longing for freedom and fresh air; the atmosphere he
generated crackled with oxygen; his children lived in such a
state of mental and emotional stimulation that no society ever
again could overstimulate them. Life, as he saw it—was nobly
resolved to see it, and to teach his beloved young ones to see
it—was so much a matter of living happily and freely by spiritual, ethical, and intellectual values, based soundly on sensuous richness, and inexhaustible faith in the goodness of God; a
firm belief in the divinity in human nature, God's self in it; a
boundlessly energetic aspiration toward the higher life, the
purest humanities, the most spontaneous expression of feeling
and thought.

Despair was for the elder James a word of contempt. He declared "that never for a moment had he known a skeptical
state." Yet, "having learned the nature of evil, and admitted its
power, he turned towards the sun of goodness." He believed
that "true worship is always spontaneous, the offspring of delight, not duty." Thus his son Henry: "The case was really of
his feeling so vast a rightness close at hand or lurking immediately behind actual arrangements that a single turn of the inward wheel, one real response to the pressure of the spiritual
spring, would bridge the chasms, straighten the distortions,
rectify the relations, and in a word redeem and vivify the whole
mass." With all his considerable powers of devotion translated
into immediate action, the father demonstrated his faith in the
family circle; the children responded to the love, but were
mystified and respectful before the theory: they perceived it
was something very subtle, as were most of "father's ideas."
But they also knew early that their father did not live in a fool's
paradise. "It was of course the old story that we had only to *be*
with more intelligence and faith—an immense deal more, certainly, in order to work off, in the happiest manner, the many-
sided ugliness of life; which was a process that might go on,
blessedly, in the quietest of all quiet ways. *That* wouldn't be

blood and fire and tears, or would be none of these things stupidly precipitated; it would simply take place by *enjoyed* communication and contact, enjoyed concussion or convulsion
even—since pangs and agitations, the very agitations of perception itself, are the highest privilege of the soul, and there is
always, thank goodness, a saving sharpness of play or complexity of consequence in the intelligence completely alive."

   Blood and fire and tears each in his own time and way each
of them suffered, sooner or later. Alice, whose life was a mysterious long willful dying, tragic and ironic, once asked her
father's permission to kill herself. He gave it, and she understood his love in it, and refrained: he wrote to Henry that he
did not much fear any further thoughts of suicide on her part.
William took the search for truth as hard as his father had, but
by way of philosophy, not religion; the brave psychologist and
philosopher was very sick in his soul for many years. Henry
was maimed for life in an accident, as his father had been
before him, but he of them all never broke, never gave way,
sought for truth not in philosophy nor in religion, but in art,
and found his own; showed just what the others had learned
and taught, and spoke for them better than they could for
themselves, thus very simply and grandly fulfilling his destiny
as artist; for it was destiny and he knew it and never resisted a
moment, but went with it as unskeptically as his father had
gone with religion.

The James family, as we have seen, were materially in quite
comfortable circumstances. True the fine fortune had misted
away somewhat, but they had enough. If people are superior
to begin with, as they were, the freedom of money is an added
freedom of grace and the power of choice in many desirable
ways. This accounts somewhat then for the extraordinary ability, ease of manners, and artless, innocent unselfconsciousness
of the whole family in which Henry James was brought up,
which he has analyzed so acutely, though with such hovering
tenderness. It was merely a fact that they could afford to be
beyond material considerations because in that way they were
well provided. Their personal virtues, no matter on what
grounds, were real, their kindness and frankness were un-
feigned. "The cousinship," he wrote, "all unalarmed and un-

suspecting and unembarrassed, lived by pure serenity, sociability, and loquacity." Then with the edge of severity his own
sense of truth drew finally upon any subject, he added: "The
special shade of its identity was thus that it was not conscious
—really not conscious of anything in the world; or was conscious of so few possibilities at least, and these so immediate,
and so a matter of course, that it came to the same thing."
There he summed up a whole society, limited in number but
of acute importance in its place; and having summed up, he
cannot help returning to the exceptions, those he loved and
remembered best.

There were enough intellectual interests and consciousness
of every kind in his father's house to furnish forth the whole
connection, and it was the center. Education, all unregulated,
to be drawn in with the breath, and absorbed like food, proceeded at top speed day and night. Though William, of all the
children, seemed to be the only one who managed to acquire a
real, formal university training of the kind recognized by acade-
micians, Henry got his, in spite of the dozen schools in three
countries, in his own time and his own way; in the streets, in
theaters (how early grew in him that long, unrequited passion
for the theater!), at picture galleries, at parties, on boats, in
hotels, beaches, at family reunions; by listening, by gazing,
dawdling, gaping, wondering, and soaking in impressions and
sensations at every pore, through every hair. Though at moments he longed to be an orphan when he saw the exciting life
of change and improvisation led by his cheerful orphaned
cousins, "so little sunk in the short range," it is clear that his
own life, from minute to minute, was as much as he could endure; he had the only family he could have done with at all,
and the only education he was capable of receiving. His intuitions were very keen and pure from the beginning, and fore-
knowledge of his ineducability in any practical sense caused
him very rightly to kick and shriek as they hauled him however
fondly to his first day of school. There he found, as he was to
find in every situation for years and years, elder brother William,
the vivid, the hardy, the quick-learning, the outlooking one,
seated already: accustomed, master of his environment, lord of
his playfellows. For so Henry saw him; William was a tremendous part of his education. William was beyond either envy or

imitation: the younger brother could only follow and adore at the right distance.

So was his mother his education. Her children so possessed her they did not like her even to praise them or be proud of them because that seemed to imply that she was separate from them. After her death, the younger Henry wrote of her out of depths hardly to be stirred again in him, "she was our life, she was the house, she was the keystone of the arch"—suddenly his language took on symbols of the oldest poetry. Her husband, who found he could not live without her, wrote in effect to a friend that very early in their marriage she had awakened his torpid heart, and helped him to become a man.

The father desired many things for the childen, but two things first: spiritual decency, as Henry James says it, and "a sensuous education." If Henry remembered his share in the civilizing atmosphere of Mr. Jenks's school as "merely contemplative," totally detached from any fact of learning, at home things were more positive. Their father taught them a horror of piggishness, and of conscious virtue; guarded them, by precept and example, from that vulgarity he described as "flagrant morality"; and quite preached, if his boundless and changing conversation could be called that, against success in its tangible popular meaning. "We were to convert and convert, success—in the sense that was in the general air—or no success; and simply everything that happened to us, every contact, every impression and every experience we should know, were to form our soluble stuff; with only ourselves to thank should we remain unaware, by the time our perceptions were decently developed, of the substance finally projected and most desirable. That substance might be just consummately Virtue, as a social grace and value . . . the moral of all of which was that we need never fear not to be good enough if only we were social enough. . . ."

Again he told them that the truth—the one truth as distinguished from the multiple fact—"was never ugly and dreadful, and (we) might therefore depend upon it for due abundance, even of meat and drink and raiment, even of wisdom and wit and honor."

No child ever "took in" his father's precepts more exactly and more literally than did Henry James, nor worked them more subtly and profoundly to his own needs. He was at last, looking back, "struck . . . with the rare fashion after which, in any small victim of life, the inward perversity may work. It works by converting to its uses things vain and unintended, to the great discomposure of their prepared opposites, which it by the same stroke so often reduces to naught; with the result indeed that one may most of all see it—so at least have I quite exclusively seen it, the little life out for its chance—as proceeding by the inveterate process of conversion."

The little life out for its chance was oh how deeply intent on the chance it *chose* to take; and all this affected and helped to form a most important phase of his interests: money, exactly, and success, both of which he desired most deeply, but with the saving justifying clause that he was able only to imagine working for and earning them honestly—and though money was only just that, once earned, his notion of success was really his father's, and on nothing less than the highest ground did it deserve that name. In the meantime, as children, they were never to be preoccupied with money. But how to live? "The effect of his attitude, so little thought out as shrewd or vulgarly providential, but . . . so socially and affectionately founded, could only be to make life interesting to us at worst, in default of making it extraordinarily paying." His father wanted all sorts of things for them without quite knowing what they needed, but Henry the younger began peering through, and around the corners of, the doctrine. "With subtle indirectness," the children, perhaps most of all Henry, got the idea that the inward and higher life, well rounded, *must* somehow be lived in good company, with good manners and surroundings fitting to virtue and sociability, good, you might say, attracting good on all planes: of course. But one of the goods, a main good, without which the others might wear a little thin, was material ease. Henry James understood and anatomized thoroughly and acutely the sinister role of money in society, the force of its corrosive powers on the individual; the main concern of nearly all his chief characters is that life shall be, one way or another, and by whatever means, a paying affair . . . and the theme is the consequences of their choice of means, and their notion of what shall pay them.

This worldly knowledge, then, was the end-product of that

unworldly education which began with the inward life, the
early inculcated love of virtue for its own sake, a belief in
human affections and natural goodness, a childhood of extraordinary freedom and privilege, passed in a small warm world
of fostering love. This world for him was never a landscape
with figures, but a succession of rather small groups of persons
intensely near to him, for whom the landscape was a setting,
the houses they lived in the appropriate background. The
whole scene of his childhood existed in his memory in terms of
the lives lived in it, with his own growing mind working away
at it, storing it, transmuting it, reclaiming it. Through his extreme sense of the appearance of things, manners, dress, social
customs, the lightest gesture, he could convey mysterious but
deep impressions of individual character. In crises of personal
events, he could still note the look of tree-shaded streets, family gardens, the flash of a grandmother's scissors cutting grapes
or flowers, fan-shaped lights, pink marble steps; the taste of
peaches, baked apples, custards, ice creams, melons, food indeed by the bushel and the barrel; the colors and shapes of
garments, the headdresses of ladies, their voices, the way they
lifted their hands. If these were all, they would have been next
to nothing, but the breathing lives are somewhere in them.

The many schools he attended, if that is the word, the children he knew there, are perfectly shown in terms of their looks
and habits. He was terrorized by the superior talents of those
boys who could learn arithmetic, apparently without effort, a
branch of learning forever closed to him, as by decree of nature. A boy of his own age, who lived in Geneva, "opened
vistas" to him by pronouncing Ohio and Iowa in the French
manner: an act of courage as well as correctness which was impressive, surrounded as he was by tough little glaring New
Yorkers with stout boots and fists, who were not prepared to
be patronized in any such way. Was there anybody he ever
thought stupid, he asked himself, if only they displayed some
trick of information, some worldly sleight of hand of which he
had hitherto been ignorant? On a sightseeing tour at Sing Sing
he envied a famous criminal his self-possession, inhabiting as he
did a world so perilous and so removed from daily experience.
His sense of social distinctions was early in the bud: he recognized a Dowager on sight, at a very tender age. An elegant im-

age of a "great Greek Temple shining over blue waters"—
which seems to have been a hotel at New Brighton called the
Pavilion—filled him with joy when he was still in his nurse's
arms. He had thought it a finer thing than he discovered it to
be, and this habit of thought was to lead him far afield for a
good number of years.

For his freedoms were so many, his instructions so splendid,
and yet his father's admirable, even blessed teachings failed
to cover so many daily crises of the visible world. The visible
world was the one he would have, all his being strained and
struggled outward to meet it, to absorb it, to understand it, to
be a part of it. The other children asked him to what church he
belonged, and he had no answer; for the even more important
question, "What does your father *do*?" or "What business is he
in?" no reply had been furnished him for the terrible occasion.
His father was no help there, though he tried to be. How
could a son explain to his father that it did no good to reply
that one had the freedom of all religion, being God's child;
or that one's father was an author of books and a truth-seeker?

So his education went forward in all directions and on all
surfaces and depths. He longed "to be somewhere—almost
anywhere would do—and somehow to receive an impression or
an accession, feel a relation or a vibration"; while all the time a
performance of *Uncle Tom's Cabin*, which gave him his first
lesson in ironic appreciation of the dowdy, the overwrought
and underdone; or Mrs. Cannon's mystifyingly polite establishment full of scarfs, handkerchiefs, and colognes for gentlemen, with an impalpable something in the air which hinted at
mysteries, and which turned out to be only that gentlemen,
some of them cousins, from out of town took rooms there; or
the gloomy show of Italian Primitives, all frauds, which was to
give him a bad start with painting—such events were sinking
into him as pure sensation to emerge from a thousand points
in his memory as knowledge.

Knowledge—knowledge at the price of finally, utterly
"seeing through" everything—even the fortunate, happy childhood; yet there remained to him, to the very end, a belief in
that good which had been shown to him as good in his infancy, embodied in his father and mother. There was a great
deal of physical beauty in his family, and it remained the kind

that meant beauty to him: the memory of his cousin Minnie Temple, the face of his sister Alice in her last photograph, these were the living images of his best-loved heroines; the love he early understood as love never betrayed him and was love at the latest day; the extraordinarily sensitive, imaginative excitements of first admirations and friendships turned out to be not perhaps so much irreplaceable as incomparable. What I am trying to say is that so far as we are able to learn, nothing came to supplant or dislocate in any way those early affections and attachments and admirations.

This is not to say he never grew up with them, for they expanded with his growth, and as he grew his understanding gave fresh life to them; nor that he did not live to question them acutely, to inquire as to their nature and their meaning, for he did; but surely no one ever projected more lovingly and exactly the climate of youth, of budding imagination, the growth of the tender, perceptive mind, the particular freshness and keenness of feeling, the unconscious generosity and warmth of heart of the young brought up in the innocence which is their due, and the sweet illusion of safety, dangerous because it must be broken at great risk. He survived all, and made it his own, and used it with that fullness and boldness and tenderness and intent reverence which is the sum of his human qualities, indivisible from his sum as artist. For though no writer ever "grew up" more completely than Henry James, and "saw through" his own illusions with more sobriety and pure intelligence, still there lay in the depths of his being the memory of a lost paradise; it was in the long run the standard by which he measured the world he learned so thoroughly, accepted in certain ways—the ways of a civilized man with his own work to do—after such infinite pains: or pangs, as he would have called them, that delight in deep experience which at a certain point is excruciating, and by the uninstructed might be taken for pain itself. But the origin is different, it is not inflicted, not even invited, it comes under its own power and the end is different; and the pang is *not* suffering, it is delight.

Henry James knew about this, almost from the beginning. Here is his testimony: "I foresee moreover how little I shall be able to resist, throughout these notes, the force of persuasion expressed in the individual *vivid* image of the past wherever encountered, these images having always such terms of their own, such subtle secrets and insidious arts for keeping us in relation with them, for bribing us by the beauty, the authority, the wonder of their saved intensity. They have saved it, they seem to say to us, from such a welter of death and darkness and ruin that this alone makes a value and a light and a dignity for them. . . . Not to be denied also, over and above this, is the downright pleasure of the illusion yet again created, the *apparent* transfer from the past to the present of the particular combination of things that did at its hour ever so directly operate and that isn't after all then drained of virtue, wholly wasted and lost, for sensation, for participation in the act of life, in the attesting sights, sounds, smells, the illusion, as I say, of the recording senses."

Brother William remained Big Brother to the end, though Henry learned to stand up to him manfully when the philosopher invaded the artist's territory. But William could not help being impatient with all this reminiscence, and tried to discourage Henry when he began rummaging through his precious scrapbags of bright fragments, patching them into the patterns before his mind's eye. William James was fond of a phrase of his philosopher friend Benjamin Paul Blood: "There is no conclusion. What has concluded, that we might conclude in regard to it?"

That is all very well for philosophy, and it has within finite limits the sound of truth as well as simple fact—no man has ever seen any relations concluded. Maybe that is why art is so endlessly satisfactory: the artist can choose his relations, and "draw, by a geometry of his own, the circle within which they shall happily *appear* to do so." While accomplishing this, one has the illusion that destiny is not absolute, it can be arranged, temporized with, persuaded, a little here and there. And once the circle is truly drawn around its contents, it too becomes truth.

First version: July, 1943
Revised: 27 February 1952

Reflections on Willa Cather

I NEVER knew her at all, nor anyone who did know her; do not to this day. When I was a young writer in New York I knew she was there, and sometimes wished that by some charming chance I might meet up with her; but I never did, and it did not occur to me to seek her out. I had never felt that my condition of beginning authorship gave me a natural claim on the attention of writers I admired, such as Henry James and W. B. Yeats. Some proper instinct told me that all of any importance they had to say to me was in their printed pages, mine to use as I could. Still it would have been nice to have seen them, just to remember how they looked. There are three or four great ones, gone now, that I feel, too late, I should not have missed. Willa Cather was one of them.

There exist large numbers of critical estimates of her work, appreciations; perhaps even a memoir or two, giving glimpses of her personal history—I have never read one. She was not, in the popular crutch-word to describe almost any kind of sensation, "exciting"; so far as I know, nobody, not even one of the Freudian school of critics, ever sat up nights with a textbook in one hand and her works in the other, reading between the lines to discover how much sexual autobiography could be mined out of her stories. I remember only one photograph— Steichen's—made in middle life, showing a plain smiling woman, hers arms crossed easily over a girl scout sort of white blouse, with a ragged part in her hair. She seemed, as the French say, "well seated" and not very outgoing. Even the earnestly amiable, finely shaped eyes, the left one faintly askew, were in some mysterious way not expressive, lacking as they did altogether that look of strangeness which a strange vision is supposed to give to the eye of any real artist, and very often does. One doesn't have to be a genius absolutely to get this look, it is often quite enough merely to believe one is a genius; and to have had the wild vision only once is enough—the afterlight stays, even if, in such case, it is phosphorescence instead of living fire.

Well, Miss Cather looks awfully like somebody's big sister, or maiden aunt, both of which she was. No genius ever looked less like one, according to the romantic popular view, unless it was her idol, Flaubert, whose photographs could pass easily for those of any paunchy country squire indifferent to his appearance. Like him, none of her genius was in her looks, only in her works. Flaubert was a good son, adoring uncle of a niece, devoted to his friends, contemptuous of the mediocre, obstinate in his preferences, fiercely jealous of his privacy, unyielding to the death in his literary principles and not in the slightest concerned with what was fashionable. No wonder she loved him. She had been rebuffed a little at first, not by his astronomical standards in art—none could be too high for her—but by a certain coldness of heart in him. She soon got over that; it became for her only another facet of his nobility of mind.

Very early she had learned to reverence that indispensable faculty of aspiration of the human mind toward perfection called, in morals and the arts, nobility. She was born to the idea and brought up in it: first in a comfortable farmhouse in Virginia, and later, the eldest of seven children, in a little crowded ranch house in Nebraska. She had, as many American country people did have in those times and places, literate parents and grandparents, soundly educated and deeply read, educated, if not always at schools, always at their own firesides. Two such, her grandmothers, taught her from her infancy. Her sister, Mrs. Auld, in Palo Alto, California, told it like this:

"She mothered us all, took care of us, and there was a lot to do in such a big family. She learned Greek and Latin from our grandmothers before she ever got to go to school. She used to go, after we lived in Red Cloud, to read Latin and Greek with a little old man who kept a general store down the road. In the evenings for entertainment—there was nowhere to go, you know, almost nothing to see or hear—she entertained us, it was good as a theater for us! She told us long stories, some she made up herself, and some were her versions of legends and fairy tales she had read; she taught us Greek mythology this way, Homer, and tales from the Old Testament. We were all story tellers," said her sister, "all of us wanted to be the one to tell the stories, but she was the one who told them. And we loved to listen all of us to her, when maybe we would not have listened to each other."

She was not the first nor the last American writer to be formed in this system of home education; at one time it was the customary education for daughters, many of them never got to school at all or expected to; but they were capable of educating their grandchildren, as this little history shows. To her last day Willa Cather was the true child of her plain-living, provincial farming people, with their aristocratic ways of feeling and thinking; poor, but not poverty-stricken for a moment; rock-based in character, a character shaped in an old school of good manners, good morals, and the unchallenged assumption that classic culture was their birthright; the belief that knowledge of great art and great thought was a good in itself not to be missed for anything; she subscribed to it all with her whole heart, and in herself there was the vein of iron she had inherited from a long line of people who had helped to break wildernesses and to found a new nation in such faiths. When you think of the whole unbelievable history, how did anything like this survive? Yet it did, and this life is one of the proofs.

I have not much interest in anyone's personal history after the tenth year, not even my own. Whatever one was going to be was all prepared for before that. The rest is merely confirmation, extension, development. Childhood is the fiery furnace in which we are melted down to essentials and that essential shaped for good. While I have been reading again Willa Cather's essays and occasional papers, and thinking about her, I remembered a sentence from the diaries of Anne Frank, who died in the concentration camp in Bergen-Belsen just before she was sixteen years old. At less than fifteen, she wrote: "I have had a lot of sorrow, but who hasn't, at my age?"

In Miss Cather's superb little essay on Katherine Mansfield, she speaks of childhood and family life: "I doubt whether any contemporary writer has made one feel more keenly the many kinds of personal relations which exist in an everyday 'happy family' who are merely going on with their daily lives, with no crises or shocks or bewildering complications. . . . Yet every individual in that household (even the children) is clinging passionately to his individual soul, is in terror of losing it in the general family flavor . . . the mere struggle to have anything of one's own, to be oneself at all, creates an element of strain which keeps everybody almost at breaking point.

". . . Even in harmonious families there is this double life . . . the one we can observe in our neighbor's household, and, underneath, another—secret and passionate and intense —which is the real life that stamps the faces and gives character to the voices of our friends. Always in his mind each member is escaping, running away, trying to break the net which circumstances and his own affections have woven about him. One realizes that human relationships are the tragic necessity of human life; that they can never be wholly satisfactory, that every ego is half the time greedily seeking them, and half the time pulling away from them."

This is masterly and water-clear and autobiography enough for me: my mind goes with tenderness to the lonely slow-moving girl who happened to be an artist coming back from reading Latin and Greek with the old storekeeper, helping with the housework, then sitting by the fireplace to talk down an assertive brood of brothers and sisters, practicing her art on them, refusing to be lost among them—the longest-winged one who would fly free at last.

I am not much given to reading about authors, or not until I have read what they have to say for themselves. I found Willa Cather's books for myself, early, and felt no need for intermediaries between me and them. My reading went on for a good many years, one by one as they appeared: *O Pioneers!*; *The Song of the Lark*; *My Ántonia*; *Youth and the Bright Medusa*; *Death Comes for the Archbishop*; *Obscure Destinies*; just these, and no others, I do not know why, and never anything since, until I read her notebooks about two years ago. Those early readings began in Texas, just before World War I, before ever I left home; they ended in Paris, twenty years later, after the longest kind of journey.

With her first book I was reading also Henry James, W. B. Yeats, Joseph Conrad, my introduction to "modern" literature, for I was brought up on solid reading, too, well aged. About the same time I read Gertrude Stein's *Tender Buttons*, for sale at a little bookshop with a shoeshine stand outside;

inside you could find magazines, books, newspapers in half-a-dozen languages, avant-garde and radical and experimental; this in a Texas coast town of less than ten thousand population but very polyglot and full of world travelers. I could make little headway with Miss Stein beyond the title. It was plain that she meant "tender buds" and I wondered why she did not say so. It was the beginning of my quarrel with a certain school of "modern" writing in which poverty of feeling and idea were disguised, but not well enough, in tricky techniques and disordered syntax. A year or two after *Tender Buttons* I was reading Joyce's *Dubliners*, and maybe only a young beginning writer of that time, with some preparation of mind by the great literature of the past, could know what a revelation that small collection of matchless stories could be. It was not a shock, but a revelation, a further unfolding of the deep world of the imagination. I had never heard of Joyce. By the pure chance of my roving curiosity, I picked up a copy of the book at that little shoeshine bookstore. It was a great day.

By the time I reached Paris, I had done my long apprenticeship, published a small book of my own, and had gone like a house afire through everything "new"—that word meant something peculiar to the times—absolutely everything "new" that was being published; also in music; also painting. I considered almost any painting with the varnish still wet, the artist standing by, so to speak, as more interesting than anything done even the year before. But some of the painters were Klee, Juan Gris, Modigliani. . . . I couldn't listen to music happily if it wasn't hot from the composer's brain, preferably conducted or played by himself. Still, some of the music was Stravinsky's and Béla Bartók's and Poulenc's. I was converted to the harpsichord by the first New York recital of Wanda Landowska. In the theater I preferred dress rehearsals, or even just rehearsals, to the finished performance; I was mad about the ballet and took lessons off and on with a Russian for two years; I even wrote a ballet libretto way back in 1920 for a young Mexican painter and scene designer who gave the whole thing to Pavlova, who danced it in many countries but not in New York, because the scenery was done on paper, was inflammable and she was not allowed to use it in New York. I saw photographs, however, and I must say they did not look in the least like anything I had provided for in the libretto. It was most unsatisfactory.

What has this to do with Willa Cather? A great deal. I had had time to grow up, to consider, to look again, to begin finding my way a little through the inordinate clutter and noise of my immediate day, in which very literally everything in the world was being pulled apart, torn up, turned wrong side out and upside down; almost no frontiers left unattacked, governments and currencies falling; even the very sexes seemed to be changing back and forth and multiplying weird, unclassifiable genders. And every day, in the arts, as in schemes of government and organized crime, there was, there had to be, something New.

Alas, or thank God, depending on the way you feel about it, there comes that day when today's New begins to look a little like yesterday's New, and then more and more so; you begin to suffer slightly from a sense of sameness or repetition: that painting, that statue, that music, that kind of writing, that way of thinking and feeling, that revolution, that political doctrine —is it really New? The answer is simply no, and if you are really in a perverse belligerent mood, you may add a half-truth—no, and it never was. Looking around at the debris, you ask has newness merely for its own sake any virtue? And you find that all along you had held and wound in your hand through the maze an unbreakable cord on which one by one, hardly knowing it, you had strung your life's treasures; it was as if they had come of themselves, while you were seeking and choosing and picking up and tossing away again, down all sorts of by-paths and up strange stairs and into queer corners; and there they were, things old and new, the things you loved first and those you loved last, all together and yours, and no longer old or new, but outside of time and beyond the reach of change, even your own; for that part of your life they belong to was in some sense made by them; if they went, all that part of your life would be mutilated, unrecognizable. While you hold and wind that cord with its slowly accumulating, weightless, unaccountable riches, the maze seems a straight road; you look back through all the fury you have come through, when it seemed so much, and so dismayingly, destruction, and so much just the pervasively trivial, stupid, or malignant-dwarfish tricks:

fur-lined cups as sculpture, symphonies written for kitchen batteries, experiments on language very similar to the later Nazi surgical experiments of cutting and uniting human nerve ends never meant to touch each other: so many perversities crowding in so close you could hardly see beyond them. Yet look, you shared it, you were part of it, you even added to the confusion, so busy being new yourself. The fury and waste and clamor was, after all, just what you had thought it was in the first place, even if you had lost sight of it later—life, in a word, and great glory came of it, and splendid things that will go on living cleared of all the rubbish thrown up around their creation. Things you would have once thought incompatible to eternity take their right places in peace, in proper scale and order, in your mind—in your blood. They become that marrow in your bones where the blood is renewed.

I had liked best of all Willa Cather's two collections of short stories. They live still with morning freshness in my memory, their clearness, warmth of feeling, calmness of intelligence, an ample human view of things; in short the sense of an artist at work in whom one could have complete confidence: not even the prose attracted my attention from what the writer was saying—really saying, and not just in the words. Also I remember well my deeper impression of reserve—a reserve that was personal because it was a matter of temperament, the grain of the mind; yet conscious too, and practiced deliberately: almost a method, a technique, but not assumed. It was instead a manifesting, proceeding from the moral nature of the artist, morality extended to aesthetics—not aesthetics as morality but simply a development of both faculties along with all the others until the whole being was indivisibly one, the imagination and its expression fused and fixed.

A magnificent state, no doubt, at which to arrive; but it should be the final one, and Miss Cather seemed to be there almost from the first. What was it? For I began to have an image of her as a kind of lighthouse, or even a promontory, some changeless phenomenon of art or nature or both. I have a peculiar antipathy to thinking of anyone I know in symbols or mythical characters and this finally quietly alienated me from

her, from her very fine books, from any feeling that she was a
living, working artist in our time. It is hard to explain, for it
was a question of tone, of implication, and what else? Finally,
after a great while, I decided that Miss Cather's reserve
amounted to a deliberate withholding of some vital part of
herself as artist; not as if she had hidden herself at the center of
her mystery but was still there to be disclosed at last; no, she
had absented herself willfully.

I was quite wrong of course. She is exactly at the center of
her own mystery, where she belongs. My immoderate reading
of our two or three invaluably afflicted giants of contemporary
literature, and their abject army of camp followers and imitators, had blurred temporarily my perception of that thin line
separating self-revealment from self-exhibition. Miss Cather
had never any intention of using fiction or any other form of
writing as a device for showing herself off. She was not Paul in
travesty, nor the opera singer in "The Diamond Mine," nor that
girl with the clear eyes who became an actress: above all, not
the Lost Lady. Of course she was all of them. How not? She
made all of them out of herself, where else could they have
taken on life?

Her natural lack of picturesqueness was also a good protec-
tive coloring: it saved her from the invasive prying of hangers-
on: and no "school" formed in her name. The young writers
did not swarm over her with flattery, manuscripts in hand,
meaning to use her for all she was worth; publishers did not
waylay her with seductions the instant her first little book appeared; all S. S. McClure could think of to do for her, after he
published *The Troll Garden*, was to offer her a job as one of his
editors on *McClure's Magazine*, where she worked hard for six
mortal years before it seems to have occurred to her that she
was not being a writer, after all, which was what she had
started out for. So she quit her job, and the next year, more or
less, published *Alexander's Bridge*, of which she afterward re-
pented, for reasons that were to last her a lifetime. The scene,
London, was strange and delightful to her; she was trying to
make a novel out of some interesting people in what seemed to
her exotic situations, instead of out of something she really
knew about with more than the top of her mind. "London

is supposed to be more engaging than, let us say, Gopher Prairie," she remarks, "even if the writer knows Gopher Prairie very well and London very casually."

She realized at once that *Alexander's Bridge* was a mistake, her wrong turning, which could not be retraced too instantly and entirely. It was a very pretty success, and could have been her finish, except that she happened to be Willa Cather. For years she still found people who liked that book, but they couldn't fool her. She knew what she had done. So she left New York and went to Arizona for six months, not for repentance but for refreshment, and found there a source that was to refresh her for years to come. Let her tell of her private apocalypse in her own words: "I did no writing down there, but I recovered from the conventional editorial point of view."

She then began to write a book for herself—*O Pioneers!*— and it was "a different process altogether. Here there was no arranging or 'inventing'; everything was spontaneous and took its own place, right or wrong. This was like taking a ride through a familiar country on a horse that knew the way, on a fine morning when you felt like riding. The other was like riding in a park, with someone not altogether congenial, to whom you had to be talking all the time."

What are we to think? For certainly here is a genius who simply will not cater to our tastes for drama, who refuses to play the role in any way we have been accustomed to seeing it played. She wrote with immense sympathy about Stephen Crane: "There is every evidence that he was a reticent and unhelpful man, with no warmhearted love of giving out opinions." If she had said "personal confidences" she could as well have been writing about herself. But she was really writing about Stephen Crane and stuck to her subject. Herself, she gave out quite a lot of opinions, not all of them warmhearted, in the course of two short little books, the second a partial reprint of the first. You hardly realize how many and how firm and how cogent while reading her fine pure direct prose, hearing through it a level, well-tempered voice saying very good, sensible right things with complete authority—things not in fashion but close to here and now and always, not like a teacher or a mother—like an artist—until, after you have closed the book, her point of view begins to accumulate and take shape in your mind.

Freud had happened: but Miss Cather continued to cite the old Hebrew prophets, the Greek dramatists, Goethe, Shakespeare, Dante, Tolstoy, Flaubert, and such for the deeper truths of human nature, both good and evil. She loved Shelley, Wordsworth, Walter Pater, without any reference to their public standing at the time. In her essay, "The Novel Demeublé," she had the inspired notion to bring together for purposes of comparison Balzac and Prosper Merimée; she preferred Merimée on the ground quite simply that he was the better artist: you have to sort out Balzac's meanings from a great dusty warehouse of misplaced vain matter—furniture, in a word. Once got at, they are as vital as ever. But Merimée is as vital, and you cannot cut one sentence without loss from his stories. The perfect answer to the gross power of the one, the too-finished delicacy of the other was, of course, Flaubert.

Stravinsky had happened; but she went on being dead in love with Wagner, Beethoven, Schubert, Gluck, especially *Orpheus*, and almost any opera. She was music-mad, and even Ravel's *La Valse* enchanted her; perhaps also even certain later music, but she has not mentioned it in these papers.

The Nude had Descended the Staircase with an epoch-shaking tread but she remained faithful to Puvis de Chavannes, whose wall paintings in the Panthéon of the legend of St. Genevieve inspired the form and tone of *Death Comes for the Archbishop*. She longed to tell old stories as simply as that, as deeply centered in the core of experience without extraneous detail as in the lives of the saints in *The Golden Legend*. She loved Courbet, Rembrandt, Millet and the sixteenth-century Dutch and Flemish painters, with their "warmly furnished interiors" but always with a square window open to the wide gray sea, where the masts of the great Dutch fleets were setting out to "ply quietly on all the waters of the globe. . . ."

Joyce had happened: or perhaps we should say, *Ulysses*, for the work has now fairly absorbed the man we knew. I believe that this is true of all artists of the first order. They are not magnified in their work, they disappear in it, consumed by it. That subterranean upheaval of language caused not even the barest tremor in Miss Cather's firm, lucid sentences. There is good internal evidence that she read a great deal of contemporary literature, contemporary over a stretch of fifty years, and think what contemporaries they were—from Tolstoy and Hardy and James and Chekhov to Gide and Proust and Joyce and Lawrence and Virginia Woolf, to Sherwood Anderson and Theodore Dreiser: the first names that come to mind. There was a regiment of them; it was as rich and fruitfully disturbing a period as literature has to show for several centuries. And it did make an enormous change. Miss Cather held firmly to what she had found for herself, did her own work in her own way as all the others were doing each in his unique way, and did help greatly to save and reassert and illustrate the validity of certain great and dangerously threatened principles of art. Without too much fuss, too—and is quietly disappearing into her work altogether, as we might expect.

Mr. Maxwell Geismar wrote a book about her and some others, called *The Last of the Provincials.* Not having read it I do not know his argument; but he has a case: she is a provincial; and I hope not the last. She was a good artist, and all true art is provincial in the most realistic sense: of the very time and place of its making, out of human beings who are so particularly limited by their situation, whose faces and names are real and whose lives begin each one at an individual unique center. Indeed, Willa Cather was as provincial as Hawthorne or Flaubert or Turgenev, as little concerned with aesthetics and as much with morals as Tolstoy, as obstinately reserved as Melville. In fact she always reminds me of very good literary company, of the particularly admirable masters who formed her youthful tastes, her thinking and feeling.

She is a curiously immovable shape, monumental, virtue itself in her art and a symbol of virtue—like certain churches, in fact, or exemplary women, revered and neglected. Yet like these again, she has her faithful friends and true believers, even so to speak her lovers, and they last a lifetime, and after: the only kind of bond she would recognize or require or respect.

1952

A NOTE ON "THE TROLL GARDEN"

Afterword to
The Troll Garden, by Willa Cather.
New York: Signet/New American Library, 1961.

Willa Cather called her first collection of seven short stories, published in 1905 when she was thirty-two, *The Troll Garden*. It sets its theme on page ii with a verse from Christina Rossetti's "The Goblin Market":

> We must not look at Goblin men,
>   We must not buy their fruits;
> Who knows upon what soil they fed
>   Their thirsty, hungry roots?

Mr. E. K. Brown in his critical biography, *Willa Cather*, explains that the trolls are of course the dedicated working artists, and the goblins the savage, famished noncreators, the corruptors and prisoners of the mind and spirit.

Willa Cather was the first writer to express a horror of middle- and lower-class poverty and to give an appalling picture of life in the provinces of this country for the gifted or even just romantic, self-indulgent dreamer like Paul in "Paul's Case." The story of a strange boy who simply wanted luxury, a pathological liar, a real "case" in the clinical sense of the word, this is in one way the most contemporary of Miss Cather's stories: the number of boys like Paul has increased. In the incredible romanticism of "A Death In the Desert," a young singer has returned to her native Wyoming to die of tuberculosis. Wyoming is for her not only an earthly desert but one of the heart, the mind, the spirit.

Willa Cather did everything by emotional, instinctive choice; she was carried here and there, from country to country, from discovery to discovery, so she believed, and so she did, at very rich levels; but it was like mining gold and precious stones out of rocks, for she had a wonderful balance of mind, a true severity and steadfastness of character, and a discipline that came of will and character formed by intelligence and reason. Without her grand perfectly natural capacity to love, to love her own chosen few, deeply, narrowly, entirely, and to the end; and her power to attract and hold the love of those near her, she can be easily imagined as heading for the bitterest of ends. But the day she died had been a happy day for her and her friends and it ended serenely. And we have her books that should last as long as we are able to know what our treasures of literature are.

Gertrude Stein: Three Views

"EVERYBODY IS A REAL ONE"

The Making of Americans: Being a History of a Family's Progress,
Written by Gertrude Stein 1906–1908.
Paris: Contact Editions/Three Mountains Press, 1925.

ALL I know about Gertrude Stein is what I find in her first two books, *Three Lives* and *The Making of Americans.* Many persons know her, they tell amusing stories about her and festoon her with legends. Next to James Joyce she is the great influence on the younger literary generation, who see in her the combination of tribal wise woman and arch-priestess of aesthetic.

This is all very well; but I can go only by what I find in these pages. They form not so much a history of Americans as a full description and analysis of many human beings, including Gertrude Stein and the reader and all the reader's friends; they make a psychological source book and the diary of an aesthetic problem worked out momently under your eyes.

One of the many interesting things about *The Making of Americans* is its date. It was written twenty years ago (1906–1908), when Gertrude Stein was young. It precedes the war and cubism; it precedes *Ulysses* and *Remembrance of Things Past.* I doubt if all the people who should read it will read it for a great while yet, for it is in such a limited edition, and reading it is anyhow a sort of permanent occupation. Yet to shorten it would be to mutilate its vitals, and it is a very necessary book. In spite of all there is in it Gertrude Stein promises all the way through it to write another even longer and put in it all the things she left unfinished in this. She has not done it yet; at least it has not been published.

Twenty years ago, when she had been living in Paris only a few years, Gertrude Stein's memory of her American life was fresh, and I think both painful and happy in her. "The old people in a new world, the new people made out of the old, that is the story that I mean to tell, for that is what really is and what I really know." This is a deeply American book, and without "movies" or automobiles or radio or prohibition or any of the mechanical properties for making local color, it is a very up-to-date book. We feel in it the vitality and hope of the first generation, the hearty materialism of the second, the vagueness of the third. It is all realized and projected in these hundreds of portraits, the deathlike monotony in action, the blind diffusion of effort, "the spare American emotion," "the feeling of rich American living"—rich meaning money, of course—the billion times repeated effort of being born and breathing and eating and sleeping and working and feeling and dying to no particular end that makes American middle-class life. We have almost no other class as yet. "I say vital singularity is as yet an unknown product with us." So she observes the lack of it and concerns herself with the endless repetition of pattern in us only a little changed each time, but changed enough to make an endless mystery of each individual man and woman.

In beginning this book you walk into what seems to be a great spiral, a slow, ever-widening, unmeasured spiral unrolling itself horizontally. The people in this world appear to be motionless at every stage of their progress, each one is simultaneously being born, arriving at all ages and dying. You perceive that it is a world without mobility, everything takes place, has taken place, will take place; therefore nothing takes place, all at once. Yet the illusion of movement persists, the spiral unrolls, you follow; a closed spinning circle is even more hopeless than a universe that will not move. Then you discover it is not a circle, not machinelike repetition, the spiral does open and widen, it is repetition only in the sense that one wave follows upon another. The emotion progresses with the effort of a giant parturition. Gertrude Stein describes her function in terms of digestion, of childbirth: all these people, these fragments of digested knowledge, are in her, they must come out.

The progress of her family, then, this making of Americans, she has labored to record in a catalogue of human attributes, acts and emotions. Episodes are nothing, narrative is by the way, her interest lies in what she calls the bottom natures of men and women, all men, all women. "It is important to me, very important indeed to me, that I sometimes understand every one. . . . I am hoping some time to be right about every one, about everything."

In this intensity of preoccupation there is the microscopic observation of the near-sighted who must get so close to their object they depend not alone on vision but on touch and smell and the very warmth of bodies to give them the knowledge they seek. This nearness, this immediacy, she communicates also, there is no escaping into the future nor into the past. All time is in the present, these people are "being living," she makes you no gift of comfortable ripened events past and gone. "I am writing everything as I am learning everything," and so we have lists of qualities and defects, portraits of persons in scraps, with bits and pieces added again and again in every round of the spiral: they repeat and repeat themselves to you endlessly as living persons do, and always you feel you know them, and always they present a new bit of themselves.

Gertrude Stein reminds me of Jacob Boehme in the way she sees essentials in human beings. He knew them as salt, as mercury; as moist, as dry, as burning; as bitter, sweet or sour. She perceives them as attacking, as resisting, as dependent independent, as having a core of wood, of mud, as murky, engulfing; Boehme's chemical formulas are too abstract, she knows the substances of man are mixed with clay. Materials interest her, the moral content of man can often be nicely compared to homely workable stuff. Sometimes her examination is almost housewifely, she rolls a fabric under her fingers, tests it. It is thus and so. I find this very good, very interesting. "It will repay good using."

"In writing a word must be for me really an existing thing." Her efforts to get at the roots of existing life, to create fresh life from them, give her words a dark liquid flowingness, like the murmur of the blood. She does not strain words or invent them. Many words have retained their original meaning for her, she uses them simply. Good means good and bad means bad—next to the Jews the Americans are the most moralistic people, and Gertrude Stein is American Jew, a combination which by no means lessens the like quality in both. Good and bad are attributes to her, strength and weakness are real things that live inside people, she looks for these things, notes them in their likenesses and differences. She loves the difficult virtues, she is tender toward good people, she has faith in them.

An odd thing happens somewhere in the middle of this book. You will come upon it suddenly and it will surprise you. All along you have had a feeling of submergence in the hidden lives of a great many people, and unaccountably you will find yourself rolling up to the surface, on the outer edge of the curve. A disconcerting break into narrative full of phrases that might have come out of any careless sentimental novel, alternates with scraps of the natural style. It is astounding, you read on out of chagrin. Again without warning you submerge, and later Miss Stein explains she was copying an old piece of writing of which she is now ashamed, the words mean nothing: "I commence again with words that have meaning," she says, and we leave this limp, dead spot in the middle of the book.

Gertrude Stein wrote once of Juan Gris that he was, somehow, saved. She is saved, too; she is free of pride and humility, she confesses to superhuman aspirations simply, she was badly frightened once and has recovered, she is honest in her uncertainties. There are only a few bits of absolute knowledge in the world, people can learn only one or two fundamental facts about each other, the rest is decoration and prejudice. She is very free from decoration and prejudice.

SECOND WIND

Useful Knowledge, by Gertrude Stein.
New York: Payson & Clarke, 1928.

Spirals and corkscrews are whirlwinds if we spin a big top and not stop. Not stop nor drag a herring. She confused them all, yet called every day offering new feather pillows. If you wish to amuse yourself you may have your palm read, or do you drink gin? There is also the flea circus, and there is a Congressman. Romance is useful knowledge; America is romance, but you must first live in Paris. Theaters and ticker tape and the states to escape. Ticker tape and ticker tacker, tick tack toe.

> Now you know.
> This is so.
> This sounds silly.
> As you please.
> Now I will explain.

She mentioned a little of everything reasonable in order not to tell the secret. When the photographs came she said there had been a mistake. Dead things when they go dead go dead and do not come alive. They go dead. They said yes it is pretty but we miss the color. This was ended then.

This was not all. This was another one a younger one a sadder one a wiser one a smaller one a darker one with gray skin being reading the Making of Americans three times all summer. It was ended then. But you say she is wiser then why is she sadder then it is not sadder to be wiser then. Oh, yes, but when things go dead it is different.

You don't understand. Let me tell you then.

We were saying it is different now it was different then it is finished now it was finished then you may go up close and look if you like. This is an American habit with romance.

In *Useful Knowledge* you will look for sex to vex. There is no sex to vex. Look visibly. Stimulation is one and irritation is another. Another to smother Americans, who wear glasses and read if a hat is dropped suddenly. They send white wedding cake too in painted boxes. We are told this is being American, but it is not pleasant. She says it is pleasant. I doubt doubt it. If this is being American I doubt it. If this is being making romance I doubt it. If this is owning the earth I doubt it. If I doubt it it is sometimes necessary to let this be all. Iowa is not Maine Maine is not Iowa Louisiana is not either there are many states.

> In Spain there is no rain.
> Mr. Lewis.
> Mr. Lewis.

Page Mr. Wyndham Lewis on this page. Page on page. Why does he rage and when. Not American being human Mr. Lewis calls her Gerty and says she stammers. Who will be enemies because his name is not Gerty and he stammers. Being

stammering is being Mr. Lewis in one way and being stammering is being Gerty in another way and it's all in the day.
This way today. Being stammering together is a chorus and a
chorus being stammering together is thinking. Thinking being
stammering. Many rivers but only two rivers. There will be
only a few two rivers with furry edges. The cost is nothing.
The cost is nothing much. Much. Much is what you pay for.
Only a few. Two by two and one by one. Two is too few.

Now all together.
Repetition makes subways.
I know what I am saying and if you flatter me I am insulted.

THE WOODEN UMBRELLA

. . . I want to say that just today I met Miss Hennessy and she was carrying, she did not have it with her, but she usually carried a wooden umbrella. This wooden umbrella is carved out of wood and looks like a real
one even to the little button and the rubber string that holds it together.
It is all right except when it rains. When it rains it does not open and Miss
Hennessy looks a little foolish but she does not mind because it is after all
the only wooden umbrella in Paris. And even if there were lots of others
it would not make any difference.

Gertrude Stein: *Everybody's Autobiography*

When Kahnweiler the picture dealer told Miss Stein that Picasso had stopped painting and had taken to writing poetry,
she confessed that she had "a funny feeling" because "things
belonged to you and writing belonged to me. I know writing
belongs to me, I am quite certain," but still it was a blow.
". . . No matter how certain you are about anything belonging to you if you hear that somebody says it belongs to them it
gives you a funny feeling."

Later she buttonholed Picasso at Kahnweiler's gallery,
shook him, kissed him, lectured him, told him that his poetry
was worse than bad, it was offensive as a Cocteau drawing and
in much the same way, it was unbecoming. He defended himself by reminding her that she had said he was an extraordinary
person, and he believed an extraordinary person should be

able to do anything. She said that to her it was a repellent sight when a person who could do one thing well dropped it for something else he could not do at all. Convinced, or defeated, he promised to give back writing to its natural owner.

Writing was no doubt the dearest of Miss Stein's possessions, but it was not the only one. The pavilion atelier in rue de Fleurus was a catch-all of beings and created objects, and everything she looked upon was hers in more than the usual sense. Her weighty numerous divans and armchairs covered with dark, new-looking horsehair; her dogs, Basket and Pépé, conspicuous, special, afflicted as neurotic children; her clutter of small tables each with its own clutter of perhaps valuable but certainly treasured objects; her Alice B. Toklas; her visitors; and finally, ranging the walls from floor to ceiling, giving the impression that they were hung three deep, elbowing each other, canceling each other's best effects in the jealous way of pictures, was her celebrated collection of paintings by her collection of celebrated painters. These were everybody of her time whom Miss Stein elected for her own, from her idol Picasso (kidnapped bodily from brother Leo, who saw him first) to minuscule Sir Francis Rose, who seems to have appealed to the pixy in her.

Yet the vaguely lighted room where things accumulated, where they appeared to have moved in under a compulsion to be possessed once for all by someone who knew how to take hold firmly, gave no impression of disorder. On the contrary, an air of solid comfort, of inordinate sobriety and permanence, of unadventurous middle-class domesticity—respectability is the word, at last—settled around the shoulders of the guest like a Paisley shawl, a borrowed shawl of course, something to be worn and admired for a moment and handed back to the owner. Miss Stein herself sat there in full possession of herself, the scene, the spectators, wearing thick no-colored shapeless woolen clothes and honest woolen stockings knitted for her by Miss Toklas, looking extremely like a handsome old Jewish patriarch who had backslid and shaved off his beard.

Surrounded by her listeners, she talked in a slow circle in her fine deep voice, the word "perception" occurring again and again and yet again like the brass ring the children snatch for as their hobby horses whirl by. She was in fact at one period

surrounded by snatching children, the literary young, a good
many of them American, between two wars in a falling world.
Roughly they were divided into two parties: those who were
full of an active, pragmatic unbelief, and those who searched
their own vitals and fished up strange horrors in the style of
transition. The first had discovered that honor is only a word,
and an embarrassing one, because it was supposed to mean
something wonderful and was now exposed as meaning
nothing at all. For them, nothing worked except sex and alcohol and pulling apart their lamentable Midwestern upbringings
and scattering the pieces. Some of these announced that they
wished their writings to be as free from literature as if they had
never read a book, as indeed too many of them had not up to
the time. The *transition* tone was even more sinister, for
though it was supposed to be the vanguard of international
experimental thought, its real voice was hoarse, anxious, corrupted mysticism speaking in a thick German accent. The editor, Eugene Jolas, had been born in the eternally disputed land
of Alsace, bilingual in irreconcilable tongues, French and German, and he spoke both and English besides with a foreign accent. He had no mother tongue, nor even a country, and so he
fought the idea of both, but his deepest self was German: he
issued frantic manifestoes demanding that language be reduced to something he could master, crying aloud in "defense
of the hallucinative forces," the exploding of the verb, the "occult hypnosis of language," "chthonian grammar"; reason he
hated, and defended the voice of the blood, the disintegration
of syntax—with a special grudge against English—preaching
like an American Methodist evangelist in the wilderness for
"the use of a language which is a mantic instrument, and which
does not hesitate to adopt a revolutionary attitude toward
word syntax, going even so far as to invent a hermetic language, if necessary." The final aim was "the illumination of a
collective reality and a totalistic universe." Meanwhile Joyce, a
man with a mother tongue if ever there was one, and a master
of languages, was mixing them in strange new forms to the delight and enrichment of language for good and all.

    Miss Stein had no problems: she simply exploded a verb as if
it were a soap bubble, used chthonian grammar long before
she heard it named (and she would have scorned to name it),

was a born adept in occult hypnosis of language without even trying. Serious young men who were having a hard time learning to write realized with relief that there was nothing at all to it if you just relaxed and put down the first thing that came into your head. She gave them a romantic name, the Lost Generation, and a remarkable number of them tried earnestly if unsuccessfully to live up to it. A few of them were really lost, and disappeared, but others had just painted themselves into a very crowded corner. She laid a cooling hand upon their agitated brows and asked with variations, What did it matter? There were only a few geniuses, after all, among which she was one, only the things a genius said made any difference, the rest was "just there," and so she disposed of all the dark questions of life, art, human relations, and death, even eternity, even God, with perfect Stein logic, bringing the scene again into its proper focus, upon herself.

Some of the young men went away, read a book, began thinking things over, and became the best writers of their time. Humanly, shamefacedly, they then jeered at their former admiration, and a few even made the tactical error of quarreling with her. She enjoyed their discipleship while it lasted, and dismissed them from existence when it ended. It is easy to see what tremendous vitality and direction there was in the arts all over the world; for not everything was happening only in France; life was generated in many a noisy seething confusion in many countries. Little by little the legitimate line of succession appeared, the survivors emerged each with his own shape and meaning, the young vanguard became the Old Masters and even old hat.

In the meantime our heroine went on talking, vocally or on paper, and in that slow swarm of words, out of the long drone and mutter and stammer of her lifetime monologue, often there emerged a phrase of ancient native independent wisdom, for she had a shrewd deep knowledge of the commoner human motives. Her judgments were neither moral nor intellectual, and least of all aesthetic, indeed they were not even judgments, but simply her description from observation of acts, words, appearances giving her view; limited, personal in the extreme, prejudiced without qualification, based on assumptions founded in the void of pure unreason. For example,

French notaries' sons have always something strange about
them—look at Jean Cocteau. The Spaniard has a natural center of ignorance, all except Juan Gris. On the other hand, Dali
had not only the natural Spanish center of ignorance, but still
another variety, quite malignant, of his own. Preachers' sons
do not turn out like other people—E. E. Cummings, just for
one. Painters are always little short round men—Picasso and a
crowd of them. And then she puts her finger lightly on an
American peculiarity of our time: ". . . so perhaps they are
right the Americans in being more interested in you than in
the work you have done, although they would not be interested in you if you had not done the work you had done." And
she remarked once to her publisher that she was famous in
America not for her work that people understood but for that
which they did not understand. That was the kind of thing she
could see through at a glance.

It was not that she was opposed to ideas, but that she was
not interested in anybody's ideas but her own, except as material to put down on her endless flood of pages. Like writing,
opinion also belonged to Miss Stein, and nothing annoyed her
more—she was easily angered about all sorts of things—than
for anyone not a genius or who had no reputation that she respected, to appear to be thinking in her presence. Of all those
GI's who swarmed about her in her last days, if anyone showed
any fight at all, any tendency to question her pronouncements,
she smacked him down like a careful grandmother, for his own
good. Her GI heroes Brewsie and Willie are surely as near to
talking zombies as anything ever seen in a book, and she loved,
not them, but their essential zombiness.

Like all talkers, she thought other people talked too much,
and there is recorded only one instance of someone getting
the drop on her—who else but Alfred Stieglitz? She sat through
a whole session at their first meeting without uttering one
word, a feat which he mentioned with surprised approval. If
we knew nothing more of Stieglitz than this we would know
he was a great talker. She thought that the most distressing
sound was that of the human voice, other people's voices, "as
the hoot owl is almost the best sound," but in spite of this she
listened quite a lot. When she was out walking the dogs, if
workmen were tearing up the streets she would ask them what

they were doing and what they would be doing next. She only stopped to break the monotony of walking, but she remembered their answers. When a man passed making up a bitter little song against her dog and his conduct vis-à-vis lamp posts and house walls, she put it all down, and it is wonderfully good reporting. Wise or silly or nothing at all, down everything goes on the page with the air of everything being equal, unimportant in itself, important because it happened to her and she was writing about it.

She had not always been exactly there, exactly that. There had been many phases, all in consistent character, each giving way in turn for the next, of her portentous being. Ford Madox Ford described her, in earlier Paris days, as trundling through the streets in her high-wheeled American car, being a spectacle and being herself at the same time. And this may have been near the time of Man Ray's photograph of her, wearing a kind of monk's robe, her poll clipped, her granite front and fine eyes displayed at their best period.

Before that, she was a youngish stout woman, not ever really young, with a heavy shrewd face between a hard round pompadour and a round lace collar, looking more or less like Picasso's earliest portrait of her. What saved her then from a good honest husband, probably a stockbroker, and a houseful of children? The answer must be that her envelope was a tricky disguise of Nature, that she was of the company of Amazons which nineteenth-century America produced among its many prodigies: not-men, not-women, answerable to no function in either sex, whose careers were carried on, and how successfully, in whatever field they chose: they were educators, writers, editors, politicians, artists, world travelers, and international hostesses, who lived in public and by the public and played out their self-assumed, self-created roles in such masterly freedom as only a few early medieval queens had equaled. Freedom to them meant precisely freedom from men and their stuffy rules for women. They usurped with a high hand the traditional masculine privileges of movement, choice, and the use of direct, personal power. They were few in number and they were not only to be found in America, and Miss Stein belonged with them, no doubt of it, in spite of a certain temperamental passivity which was Oriental, not feminine. With the top of her brain she was a modern girl, a New Woman, interested in scientific experiment, historical research, the rational view; for a time she was even a medical student, but she could not deceive herself for long. Even during her four years at Radcliffe, where the crisp theories of higher education battle with the womb-shaped female mind (and "they always afterward seemed foolish" to her at Radcliffe, she said, meaning perhaps the promoters of these theories) she worried and worried, for worrying and thinking were synonyms to her, about the meaning of the universe, the riddle of human life, about time and its terrible habit of passing, God, death, eternity, and she felt very lonely in the awful singularity of her confusions. Added to this, history taught her that whole civilizations die and disappear utterly, "and now it happens again," and it gave her a great fright. She was sometimes frightened afterward, "but now well being frightened is something less frightening than it was," but her ambiguous mind faced away from speculation. Having discovered with relief that all knowledge was not her province, she accepted rightly, she said, every superstition. To be in the hands of fate, of magic, of the daemonic forces, what freedom it gave her not to decide, not to act, not to accept any responsibility for anything—one held the pen and let the mind wander. One sat down and somebody did everything for one.

Still earlier she was a plump solemn little girl abundantly upholstered in good clothes, who spent her allowance on the work of Shelley, Thackeray, and George Eliot in fancy bindings, for she loved reading and *Clarissa Harlowe* was once her favorite novel. These early passions exhausted her; in later life she swam in the relaxing bath of detective and murder mysteries, because she liked somebody being dead in a story, and of them all Dashiell Hammett killed them off most to her taste. Her first experience of the real death of somebody had taught her that it could be pleasant for her too. "One morning we could not wake our father." This was in East Oakland, California. "Leo climbed in by the window and called out that he was dead in his bed and he was." It seems to have been the first thing he ever did of which his children, all five of them, approved. Miss Stein declared plainly they none of them liked him at all: "As I say, fathers are depressing but our family had one," she confessed, and conveys the notion that he was a bore of the nagging, petty sort, the kind that worries himself and others into the grave.

Considering her tepid, sluggish nature, really sluggish like something eating its way through a leaf, Miss Stein could grow quite animated on the subject of her early family life, and some of her stories are as pretty and innocent as lizards running over tombstones on a hot day in Maryland. It was a solid, getting-on sort of middle-class Jewish family of Austrian origin, Keyser on one side, Stein on the other: and the Keysers came to Baltimore about 1820. All branches of the family produced their individual eccentrics—there was even an uncle who believed in the Single Tax—but they were united in their solid understanding of the value of money as the basis of a firm stance in this world. There were incomes, governesses, spending money, guardians appointed when parents died, and Miss Stein was fascinated from childhood with stories about how people earned their first dollar. When, rather late, she actually earned some dollars herself by writing, it changed her entire viewpoint about the value of her work and of her own personality. It came to her as revelation that the only difference between men and four-footed animals is that men can count, and when they count, they like best to count money. In her first satisfaction at finding she had a commercial value, she went on a brief binge of spending money just for the fun of it. But she really knew better. Among the five or six of the seven deadly sins which she practiced with increasing facility and advocated as virtues, avarice became her favorite. Americans in general she found to be rather childish about money: they spent it or gave it away and enjoyed it wastefully with no sense of its fierce latent power. "It is hard to be a miser, a real miser, they are as rare as geniuses it takes the same kind of thing to make one, that is time must not exist for them. . . . There must be a reality that has nothing to do with the passing of time. I have it and so had Hetty Green . . ." and she found only one of the younger generation in America, a young man named Jay Laughlin, who had, she wrote, praising him, avarice to that point of genius which makes the true miser. She made a very true distinction between avarice, the love of getting and keeping, and love of money, the love of making and spending. There is a third love, the love of turning a penny by ruse, and this was illustrated by brother Michael, who once grew a beard to make himself look old enough to pass for a G.A.R. veteran, and so disguised he got a cut-rate railway fare for a visit home during a G.A.R. rally, though all the men of his family fought on the Confederate side.

The question of money and of genius rose simultaneously with the cheerful state of complete orphanhood. Her mother disappeared early after a long illness, leaving her little nest of vipers probably without regret, for vipers Miss Stein shows them to have been in the most Biblical sense. They missed their mother chiefly because she had acted as a buffer between them and their father, and also served to keep them out of each other's hair. Sister Bertha and Brother Simon were simple-minded by family standards, whatever they were, Brother Leo had already started being a genius without any regard for the true situation, and after the death of their father, Brother Michael was quite simply elected to be the Goat. He had inherited the family hatred of responsibility—from their mother, Miss Stein believed, but not quite enough to save him. He became guardian, caretaker, business manager, handy-man, who finally wangled incomes for all of them, and set them free from money and from each other. It is pleasant to know he was a very thorny martyr who did a great deal of resentful lecturing about economy, stamping and shouting about the house with threats to throw the whole business over and let them fend for themselves if they could not treat him with more consideration. With flattery and persuasion they would cluster around and get him back on the rails, for his destiny was to be useful to genius, that is, to Miss Stein.

She had been much attached to her brother Leo, in childhood they were twin souls. He was two years older and a boy, and she had learned from Clarissa Harlowe's uncle's letter that older brothers are superior to younger sisters, or any boy to any girl in fact. Though she bowed to this doctrine as long as it was convenient, she never allowed it to get in her way. She followed her brother's advice more or less, and in turn he waited on her and humored and defended her when she was a selfish lazy little girl. Later he made a charming traveling companion who naturally, being older and a man, looked after all the boring details of life and smoothed his sister's path every-where. Still, she could not remember his face when he was ab-sent, and once was very nervous when she went to meet him on a journey, for fear she might not recognize him. The one thing wrong all this time was their recurring quarrel about who was the genius of the two, for each had assumed the title and neither believed for a moment there was room for more than one in the family. By way of proving himself, brother Leo took the pavilion and atelier in the rue de Fleurus, installed himself well, and began trying hard to paint. Miss Stein, seeing all so cozy, moved in on him and sat down and began to write —no question of trying. "To try is to die" became one of her several hundred rhyming aphorisms designed to settle all con-ceivable arguments; after a time, no doubt overwhelmed by the solid negative force of that massive will and presence, her brother moved out and took the atelier next door, and went on being useful to his sister, and trying to paint.

But he also went on insisting tactlessly that he, and not she, was the born genius; and this was one of the real differences between them, that he attacked on the subject and was uneasy, and could not rest, while his sister reasoned with him, pa-tiently at first, defending her title, regretting she could not share it. Insist, argue, upset himself and her as much as he liked, she simply, quietly knew with a Messianic revelation that she was not only a genius, but *the* genius, and sometimes, she was certain, one of not more than half a dozen real ones in the world. During all her life, whenever Miss Stein got low in her mind about anything, she could always find consolation in this beautiful knowledge of being a born genius, and her brother's contentiousness finally began to look like treason to her. She could not forgive him for disputing her indivisible right to her natural property, genius, on which all her other rights of pos-session were founded. It shook her—she worried about her work. She had begun her long career of describing "how every one who ever lived eats and drinks and loves and sleeps and talks and walks and wakes and forgets and quarrels and likes and dislikes and works and sits"—everybody's autobiography, in fact, for she had taken upon herself the immense task of ex-plaining everybody to himself, of telling him all he needed to know about life, and she simply could not have brother Leo hanging around the edges of this grandiose scheme pinching off bits and holding them up to the light. By and by, too, she had Alice B. Toklas to do everything for her. So she and her brother drifted apart, but gradually, like one of Miss Stein's paragraphs. The separation became so complete that once, on meeting her brother unexpectedly, she was so taken by surprise she bowed to him, and afterward wrote a long poem about it in which her total confusion of mind and feeling were expressed with total incoherence: for once, form, matter and style stuttering and stammering and wallowing along together with the agitated harmony of roiling entrails.

There are the tones of sloth, of that boredom which is a low-pressure despair, of monotony, of obsession, in this portrait; she went walking out of boredom, she could drive a car, talk, write, but anything else made her nervous. People who were doing anything annoyed her: to be doing nothing, she thought, was more interesting than to be doing something. The air of deathly solitude surrounded her; yet the parade of names in her book would easily fill several printed pages, all with faces attached which she could see were quite different from each other, all talking, each taking his own name and person for granted—a thing she could never understand. Yet she could see what they were doing and could remember what they said. She only listened attentively to Picasso—for whose sake she would crack almost any head in sight—so she half-agreed when he said Picabia was the worst painter of all; but still, found herself drawn to Picabia because his name was Francis. She had discovered that men named Francis were always elegant, and though they might not know anything else, they always knew about themselves. This would remind her that she had never found out who she was. Again and again she would doubt her own identity, and that of everyone else. When she worried about this aloud to Alice B. Toklas, saying she believed it impossible for anyone ever to be certain who he was, Alice B. Toklas made, in context, the most inspired remark in the whole book. "It depends on who you are," she said, and you might think that would have ended the business. Not at all.

These deep-set, chronic fears led her to a good deal of quarreling, for when she quarreled she seems to have felt more real.

She mentions quarrels with Max Jacob, Francis Rose, with Dali, with Picabia, with Picasso, with Virgil Thomson, with Braque, with Breton, and how many others, though she rarely says just why they quarrelled or how they made it up. Almost nobody went away and stayed, and the awful inertia of habit in friendships oppressed her. She was sometimes discouraged at the prospect of having to go on seeing certain persons to the end, merely because she had once seen them. The world seemed smaller every day, swarming with people perpetually in movement, full of restless notions which, once examined by her, were inevitably proved to be fallacious, or at least entirely useless. She found that she could best get rid of them by putting them in a book. "That is very funny if you write about any one they do not exist any more, for you, so why see them again. Anyway, that is the way I am."

But as she wrote a book and disposed of one horde, another came on, and worried her afresh, discussing their ludicrous solemn topics, trying to understand things, and being unhappy about it. When Picasso was fretful because she argued with Dali and not with him, she explained that "one discusses things with stupid people but not with sensible ones." Her true grudge against intelligent people was that they talked "as if they were getting ready to change something." Change belonged to Miss Stein, and the duty of the world was to stand still so that she could move about in it comfortably. Her top flight of reasoning on the subject of intelligence ran as follows: "The most actively war-like nations could always convince the pacifists to become pro-German. That is because pacifists were such intelligent beings they could follow what any one is saying. If you follow what any one is saying then you are a pacifist you are a pro-German . . . therefore understanding is a very dull occupation."

Intellectuals, she said, always wanted to change things because they had an unhappy childhood. "Well, I never had an unhappy childhood, what is the use of having an unhappy anything?" Léon Blum, then Premier of France, had had an unhappy childhood, and she inclined to the theory that the political uneasiness of France could be traced to this fact.

There was not, of course, going to be another war (this was in 1937!), but if there was, there *would* be, naturally; and she

never tired of repeating that dancing and war are the same
thing "because both are forward and back," while revolution,
on the contrary, is up and down, which is why it gets nowhere.
Sovietism was even then going rapidly out of fashion in her circles, because they had discovered that it is very conservative,
even if the Communists do not think so. Anarchists, being rarities, did not go out of fashion so easily. The most interesting
thing that ever happened to America was the Civil War; but
General Lee was severely to be blamed for leading his country
into that war, just the same, because he must have known they
could not win; and to her, it was absurd that anyone should
join battle in defense of a principle in face of certain defeat. For
practical purposes, honor was not even a word. Still it was an
exciting war and gave an interest to America which that country would never have had without it. "If you win you do not
lose and if you lose you do not win." Even as she was writing
these winged words, the Spanish Civil War, the Republicans
against the Franco-Fascists, kept obtruding itself. And why?
"Not because it is a revolution, but because I know so well the
places they are mentioning and the things there they are destroying." When she was little in Oakland, California, she loved
the big, nice American fires that had "so many horses and fire-
men to attend them," and when she was older, she found that
floods, for one thing, always read worse in the papers than they
really are; besides how can you care much about what is going
on if you don't see it or know the people? For this reason she
had Santa Teresa being indifferent to faraway Chinese while
she was founding convents in Spain. William Seabrook came
to see her to find out if she was as interesting as her books.
She told him she was, and he discovered black magic in the
paintings of Sir Francis Rose. And when she asked Dashiell
Hammett why so many young men authors were writing novels about tender young male heroines instead of the traditional
female ones, he explained that it was because as women grew
more and more self-confident, men lost confidence in themselves, and turned to each other, or became their own subjects
for fiction. This, or something else, reminded her several times
that she could not write a novel, therefore no one could any
more, and no one should waste time trying.

Somehow by such roundabouts we arrive at the important,

the critical event in all this eventful history. Success. Success in this world, here and now, was what Miss Stein wanted. She knew just what it was, how it should look and feel, how much it should weigh and what it was worth over the counter. It was not enough to be a genius if you had to go on supporting your art on a private income. To be the center of a recondite literary cult, to be surrounded by listeners and imitators and seekers, to be mentioned in the same breath with James Joyce, and to have turned out bales of titles by merely writing a half-hour each day: she had all that, and what did it amount to? There was a great deal more and she must have it. As to her history of the human race, she confessed: "I have always been bothered . . . but mostly . . . because after all I do as simply as it can, as commonplacely as it can say, what everybody can and does do; I never know what they can do, I really do not know what they are, I do not think that any one can think because if they do, then who is who?"

It was high time for a change, and yet it occurred at hazard. If there had not been a beautiful season in October and part of November, 1932, permitting Miss Stein to spend that season quietly in her country house, the *Autobiography of Alice B. Toklas* might never have been written. But it was written, and Miss Stein became a best-seller in America; she made real money. With Miss Toklas, she had a thrilling tour of the United States and found crowds of people eager to see her and listen to her. And at last she got what she had really wanted all along: to be published in the *Atlantic Monthly* and the *Saturday Evening Post.*

Now she had everything, or nearly. For a while she was afraid to write any more, for fear her latest efforts would not please her public. She had never learned who she was, and yet suddenly she had become somebody else. "You are you because your little dog knows you, but when your public knows you and does not want to pay you, and when your public knows you and does want to pay you, you are not the same you."

This would be of course the proper moment to take leave, as our heroine adds at last a golden flick of light to her self-portrait. "Anyway, I was a celebrity." The practical result was that she could no longer live on her income. But she and Alice B. Toklas moved into an apartment once occupied by Queen

Christina of Sweden, and they began going out more, and seeing even more people, and talking, and Miss Stein settled every question as it came up, more and more. But who wants to read about success? It is the early struggle which makes a good story.

She and Alice B. Toklas enjoyed both the wars. The first one especially being a lark with almost no one getting killed where you could see, and it ended so nicely too, without changing anything. The second was rather more serious. She lived safely enough in Bilignin throughout the German occupation, and there is a pretty story that the whole village conspired to keep her presence secret. She had been a citizen of the world in the best European tradition; for though America was her native land, she had to live in Europe because she felt at home there. In the old days people paid little attention to wars, fought as they were out of sight by professional soldiers. She had always liked the notion, too, of the gradual Orientalization of the West, the peaceful penetration of the East into European culture. It had been going on a great while, and all Western geniuses worth mentioning were Orientals: look at Picasso, look at Einstein. Russians are Tartars, Spaniards are Saracens—had not all great twentieth-century painting been Spanish? And her cheerful conclusion was, that "Einstein was the creative philosophic mind of the century, and I have been the creative literary mind of the century also, with the Oriental mixing with the European." She added, as a casual afterthought, "Perhaps Europe is finished."

That was in 1938, and she could not be expected to know that war was near. They had only been sounding practice *alertes* in Paris against expected German bombers since 1935. She spoke out of her natural frivolity and did not mean it. She liked to prophesy, but warned her hearers that her prophecies never came out right, usually the very opposite, and no matter what happened, she was always surprised. She was surprised again: as the nations of Europe fell, and the Germans came again over the frontiers of France for the third time in three generations, the earth shook under her own feet, and not somebody else's. It made an astonishing difference. Something mysterious touched her in her old age. She got a fright, and this time not for ancient vanished civilizations, but for this civilization, this moment; and she was quite thrilled with relief and gay when the American army finally came in, and the Germans were gone. She did not in the least know why the Germans had come, but they were gone, and so far as she could see, the American army had chased them out. She remembered with positive spread-eagle patriotism that America was her native land. At last America itself belonged to Miss Stein, and she claimed it, in a formal published address to other Americans. Anxiously she urged them to stay rich, to be powerful and learn how to use power, not to waste themselves; for the first time she used the word "spiritual." Ours was a spiritual as well as a material fight; Lincoln's great lucid words about government of the people by the people for the people suddenly sounded like a trumpet through her stammering confession of faith, she wanted nothing now to stand between her and her newly discovered country. By great good luck she was born on the winning side and she was going to stay there. And we were not to forget about money as the source of power; "Remember the depression, don't be afraid to look it in the face and find out the reason why, if you don't find out the reason why you'll go poor and my God, how I would hate to have my native land go poor."

The mind so long shapeless and undisciplined could not now express any knowledge out of its long willful ignorance. But the heart spoke its crude urgent language. She had liked the doughboys in the other war well enough, but this time she fell in love with the whole American army below the rank of lieutenant. She "breathed, ate, drank, lived GI's," she told them, and inscribed numberless photographs for them, and asked them all to come back again. After her flight over Germany in an American bomber, she wrote about how, so often, she would stand staring into the sky watching American war planes going over, longing to be up there again with her new loves, in the safe, solid air. She murmured, "bless them, bless them." She had been impatient with many of them who had still been naïve enough to believe they were fighting against an evil idea that threatened everybody; some of them actually were simple enough to say they had been—or believed they had been—fighting for democratic government. "What difference does it make what kind of government you have?" she would ask. "All governments are alike. Just remember you won the war." But still, at the end, she warned them to have courage and not be just yes or no men. And she said, "Bless them, bless them."

It was the strangest thing, as if the wooden umbrella feeling the rain had tried to forsake its substance and take on the nature of its form; and was struggling slowly, slowly, much too late, to unfold.

1947

"It Is Hard to Stand in the Middle"

E. P.: CANTO XIII (*Kung*)

The Letters of Ezra Pound: 1907–1941, edited by D. D. Paige,
with a preface by Mark Van Doren.
New York: Harcourt, Brace & Co., 1950.

IN Mexico, many years ago, Hart Crane and I were reading
again *Pavannes and Divisions,* and at some dogmatic statement in the text Crane suddenly burst out: "I'm tired of Ezra
Pound!" And I asked him: "Well, who else is there?" He
thought a few seconds and said: "It's true there's nobody like
him, nobody to take his place." This was the truth for us then,
and it is still the truth for many of us who came up, were educated, you might say, in contemporary literature, not at schools
at all but by five writers: Henry James, James Joyce, W. B.
Yeats, T. S. Eliot, and Ezra Pound. The beginning artist is educated by whoever helps him to learn how to work his own
vein, who helps him to fix his standards, and who gives him
courage. I believe I can speak for a whole generation of writers
who acknowledge that these five men were in just this way, the
great educators of their time.

The temptation in writing about *The Letters of Ezra Pound:
1907–1941* is to get down to individual letters, to quote endlessly, to lapse into gossip, to go into long dissertations on the
state of society; the strange confusions of the human mind;
music, sculpture, painting, war, economics; the menace of the
American university; the weakness of having a private life; and
finally the hell on earth it is to be at once a poet and a man of
perfect judgment in all matters relating to art in a world of the
deaf, dumb, and blind, of nitwits, numbskulls, and outright
villains. One might go on for hours and pages citing instances,
comparing letters, tracing change and development from year
to year, noting enthusiasms turning into abhorrence, admirations into contempt, splendid altruistic plans to foster the arts
falling into ruin because almost nobody would help, and following the frantic pattern of the poet's relations with his assortment of friends, for such I suppose they must be called.

Friendship with Pound seems to have been a very uncertain state.

It would all be false, and misleading from the main road. These letters are the most revealing documents I have read since those of Boswell or Jane Carlyle, but how differently revealing. For where nearly all letters we know are attempts to express personal feeling, to give private news, to entertain; or set-pieces on a subject, but still meant for one reader; these letters as published contain hardly one paragraph which does not relate in one way or another to one sole theme—the arts. Almost nothing about the weather, or how the writer is feeling that day; and a magnificent disregard for how the reader is feeling, except now and then: to William Carlos Williams, 1909, "I hope to God you have no feelings. If you have, burn this *before* reading." He then launches into a scarifying analysis of his dear friend's latest poetry.

There are very few landscapes; very little about health. The poet is married, a marriage that now has lasted nearly thirty-five years, so there must have been some sort of family life, but the reader would hardly guess it. Now and then he remarks on the difficulty of paying rent, but you understand at once that the difficulties of paying rent and being an artist are closely connected. He mentions once or twice that he is aging a trifle, or feels tired, but he is tired of fighting people who fight art, or he feels too old to take on a certain job of work. Once he mentions kittens in a letter to William Carlos Williams, but I feel sure he meant something else; it must have been a code.* To his father he writes literary gossip, and remarks that he is playing tennis that afternoon. To his mother he mentions the marriage of Hilda Doolittle and Richard Aldington, and later writes to her, "I am profoundly pained to hear that you prefer Marie Corelli to Stendhal, but I cannot help it." He remembers Yeats's father on an elephant at Coney Island; but that was Jack Yeats, after all, a painter—otherwise one knows he might have sat on an elephant all day without a glance from Pound.

---

*W. B. Yeats told how Ezra Pound carried food scraps in his pockets for the hungry street cats who had so many enemies. Yeats doubted he really liked cats, though. "He never nurses the café cat," he observed. Of course not. The café cat was safe and comfortable.

No, this was not the point. Ezra Pound detested the "private life," denied that he ever had one, and despised those who were weak enough to need one. He was a warrior who lived on the battlefield, a place of contention and confusion, where a man shows all sides of himself without taking much thought for appearances. His own individual being is all the time tucked safely away within him, guiding his thoughts and feelings, as well as, at a long remove, his acts and words.

How right he was in so many things. The ferocious urge of his energy, his belief in himself with all his fears, his longing to be part of the world and his time, his curious lack of judgment of things outside his real interest now appear in these letters, and it is the truest document I have seen of that falling world between 1850 and 1950. We have been falling for a century or more, and Ezra Pound came along just at the right time to see what was happening.

He was a man concerned with public questions: specifically at first the question of the arts, the place of the artist in society, and he had a fanatical desire to force entire populations to respect art even if they could not understand it. (Indeed, he demanded reverence without understanding, for he sincerely did not believe that art was for the multitude. Whatever was too much praised he distrusted—even to the works of Sophocles. This is the inconsistency of his attitude all the way through: the attempt to force poetry upon people whom he believed not fitted to understand it.)

He believed himself to be the most patient soul alive, but he was not patient, he was tenacious, quite another thing. He was blowing up in wrath regularly from the very start, but he did not give up. He did not give up because he was incapable of abandoning a faith so furious it had the quality of religious fanaticism.

Witness his running fight, beginning in 1912, with Harriet Monroe, who controlled *Poetry*, *Poetry* was Pound's one hope in this country for a good number of years, so, some of the time, and at great cost to his nervous system, he controlled Miss Monroe. His exasperation with that innocent, unteachable, hard-trying woman came to the point where he was all the same as beating her over the head with a baseball bat. I should like to see the other side of this correspondence: her patience, or whatever it was, and her ability to absorb punishment, were equal to her inability to change her ways.

When Miss Monroe got really frightened at some of the things he sent her, he wrote: "Don't print anything of mine you think will kill the review, but . . . the public can go to the devil. It is the public's function to prevent the artist's expression by hook or by crook. . . . Given my head I'd stop any periodical in a week, only we are bound to run five years anyhow, we're in such a beautiful position to save the public's soul by punching its face that it seems a crime not to do so."

So it went for twenty-four long years, one of the most sustained literary wars on record, and yet it is hard to see what they would have done without each other. Harriet Monroe was his one instrument in this country, and continually she broke in his hands. She had some very genteel notions about language, and a schoolgirl taste for pretty verses that rhymed nicely and expressed delicate feelings, preferably about nature. ("No, most emphatically I will not ask Eliot to write down to any audience whatever," Pound wrote her in 1914. "I daresay my instinct was sound enough when I volunteered to quit the magazine a year ago. Neither will I send you Eliot's address in order that he may be insulted.") Bloody, Harriet's head undoubtedly was, but she would not let him go, and he would have been outraged if she had.

When after long years and in her old age, she tried at last to give up *Poetry*, to escape into private life with her family, he wrote: "The intelligence of the nation more important than the comfort or life of any one individual or the bodily life of a whole generation." That is truly the public spirit, the Roman senator speaking. Why did he take the trouble? For he adds, in contempt: "It is difficult enough to give the god damn amoeba a nervous system." Still, she had done her bit and could go, but she had no right to allow *Poetry* to die "merely because you have a sister in Cheefoo. . . ."

Pound was one of the most opinionated and unselfish men who ever lived, and he made friends and enemies everywhere by the simple exercise of the classic American constitutional right of free speech. His speech was free to outrageous license.

He was completely reckless about making enemies. His so-called anti-Semitism was, hardly anyone has noted, only equaled by his anti-Christianism. It is true he hated most in the Catholic faith the elements of Judaism. It comes down squarely to anti-monotheism, which I have always believed was the real root of the difficulty between Judaism and the West. Pound felt himself to be in the direct line of Mediterranean civilization, rooted in Greece. Monotheism is simply not natural to the thought of such people and there are more of them than one might think without having looked into the question a little. Pound believed, rightly or wrongly, that Christianity was a debased cult composed of too many irreconcilable elements, and as the central power of this cult, he hated Catholicism worse than he did Judaism, and for many more reasons.

He was not a historian, and apparently did not know that religion flows from a single source, and that all are by now mingled and interrelated. Yet he did quote some things from ancient Chinese thought that are purely Christian in the sense that Christianity teaches the same ethics and morality, and so do the Jews, no matter from what earlier religion either of them derived it. So he was reckless and bitter and badly informed, but said what he thought, and in religious matters, in this period perhaps the most irreligious the world has ever known, it is still dangerous enough to be frank on that subject. "Anti-Semite" is a stupid, reprehensible word in that it does not mean what it says, for not only Semitic peoples have taught the doctrine of the One God, and Anti-Semite is used now largely for purposes of moral blackmail by irresponsible people.

Pound's lapses, his mistakes—and this would include his politics—occur when he deals with things outside his real interest, which was always art, literature, poetry. He was a lover of the sublime, and a seeker after perfection, a true poet, of the kind born in a hair shirt—a God-sent disturber of the peace in the arts, the one department of human life where peace is fatal. There was no peace in that urgent, overstimulated mind, where everything was jumbled together at once, a storehouse of treasure too rich ever to be sorted out by one man in one lifetime. And it was treasure.

It held exasperation, too; and related to the exasperation, but going deeper, are the cursing, and the backwoods spelling, and the deliberate illiteracy—at first humorous, high animal spirits, youthfully charming. They become obsessional, exaggerated, the tone of near-panic, the voice of Pound's deep fears. His fears were well founded; he was hard beset in a world of real and powerful enemies. I heard a stowaway on a boat once, cursing and shouting threats in that same monotonous, strained, desperate voice; in the end his captors only put him in the brig for the voyage. The artist Pound knew had become a kind of stowaway in society.

With the same kind of energy and obsessional faith Pound collided with the Douglas theory of social credit. He himself appears to have a basic principle of thought about economics: "Debt is slavery." Ernestine Evans said she heard it on a gramophone record that got stuck, and Pound's voice repeated steadily at least fifty times: "Debt is slavery." She said the more often she heard it the more sense it made. This technique of repetition, in this case accidental, is known to the spreaders of lies. Maybe, though, it would be useful to repeat now and again a simple basic fact like that. "Debt is slavery." But for Pound even the Douglas plan was immediately drawn into the service of the arts.

Often in these letters there is in Pound a kind of socks-down, shirttail-out gracelessness which many will take delightedly for his true Americanism. In these moments he was a lout, and that is international. But he wore his loutishness with a difference. It is in his judgments, and his earlier judgments were much better than his later: though his pronouncements even on those he most admires run up and down like a panicky stock market. It is always praise or dispraise precisely according to what they have done in that present moment, and he is indignant when they do not always sit down quietly under it. He thundered not with just the voice of Jove, he *was* Jove. His judgments were indeed fallible, but his faith in them was not. "It isn't as if I were set in a groove. I read any number of masters, and recognize any number of kinds of excellence. But I'm sick to loathing of people who don't care for the masterwork, who set out as artists with no intention of producing it, who make no effort toward the best, who are content with publicity and the praise of reviewers." He loathed rightly in this case, if ever a man did, yet so often simply in arrogant temper.

His perfect assurance that he knew a work of art when he saw one, and his bent toward all kinds of excellence, led him into some lamentable errors which time little by little may correct.

As critic he was at his very best in the teacher-pupil relationship, when he had a manuscript under his eye to pull apart and put together again, or in simply stating the deep changeless principles of the highest art, relating them to each other and to their time and society. As one of the great poets of his time, his advice was unfathomably good and right in these things, and they are not outdated, and they cannot be unless the standard is simply thrown out.

Pound understood the nature of greatness: not that it voluntarily separates itself from the mass but that by its very being it is separate because it is higher. Greatness in art is like any other greatness: in religious experience, in love, it is great because it is beyond the reach of the ordinary, and cannot be judged by the ordinary, nor be accountable to it. The instant it is diluted, popularized, and misunderstood by the fashionable mind, it is no longer greatness, but window dressing, interior decorating, another way of cutting a sleeve. . . . Ezra Pound understood this simple law of natural being perfectly, and it is what redeems every fault and mitigates every failure and softens to the outraged ear of the mind and heart all that shouting and bullying and senseless obscenity—makes one respect all those wild hopeful choices of hopeless talents.

There is a doctrine that we should be patient in times of darkness and decline: but darkness and decline are the very things to fight, they are man-made, and can be unmade by man also. I am glad Pound was not patient in that sense, but obstinate and tenacious and obsessed and enraged. When you read these letters you will see what good sound reasons he had to be, if he was to make any headway against the obsessed tenacious inertia of his particular time. Most of the things and the kind of people he fought are still sitting about running things, fat and smug. That is true. And a great many of the talents he tried to foster came to nothing. Fighting the dark is a very unfashionable occupation now; but it is not altogether dead, and will survive and live again largely because of his life and example.

Eudora Welty and
"A Curtain of Green"

FRIENDS of us both first brought Eudora Welty to visit me two and a half years ago in Louisiana. It was hot midsummer, they had driven over from Mississippi, her home state, and we spent a pleasant evening together talking in the cool old house with all the windows open. Miss Welty sat listening, as she must have done a great deal of listening on many such occasions. She was and is a quiet, tranquil-looking, modest girl, and unlike the young Englishman of the story, she has something to be modest about, as *A Curtain of Green* proves.

She considers her personal history as hardly worth mentioning, a fact in itself surprising enough, since a vivid personal career of fabulous ups and downs, hardships and strokes of luck, travels in far countries, spiritual and intellectual exile, defensive flight, homesick return with a determined groping for native roots, and a confusion of contradictory jobs have long been the mere conventions of an American author's life. Miss Welty was born and brought up in Jackson, Mississippi, where her father, now dead, was president of a Southern insurance company. Family life was cheerful and thriving; she seems to have got on excellently with both her parents and her two brothers. Education, in the Southern manner with daughters, was continuous, indulgent, and precisely as serious as she chose to make it. She went from school in Mississippi to the University of Wisconsin, thence to Columbia, New York, and so home again where she lives with her mother, among her lifelong friends and acquaintances, quite simply and amiably. She tried a job or two because that seemed the next thing, and did some publicity and newspaper work; but as she had no real need of a job, she gave up the notion and settled down to writing.

She loves music, listens to a great deal of it, all kinds; grows flowers very successfully, and remarks that she is "underfoot locally," meaning that she has a normal amount of social life.

Normal social life in a medium-sized Southern town can become a pretty absorbing occupation, and the only comment her friends make when a new story appears is, "Why, Eudora, when did you write that?" Not how, or even why, just when. They see her about so much, what time has she for writing? Yet she spends an immense amount of time at it. "I haven't a literary life at all," she wrote once, "not much of a confession, maybe. But I do feel that the people and things I love are of a true and human world, and there is no clutter about them. . . . I would not understand a literary life."

We can do no less than dismiss that topic as casually as she does. Being the child of her place and time, profiting perhaps without being aware of it by the cluttered experiences, foreign travels, and disorders of the generation immediately preceding her, she will never have to go away and live among the Eskimos, or Mexican Indians; she need not follow a war and smell death to feel herself alive: she knows about death already. She shall not need even to live in New York in order to feel that she is having the kind of experience, the sense of "life" proper to a serious author. She gets her right nourishment from the source natural to her—her experience so far has been quite enough for her and of precisely the right kind. She began writing spontaneously when she was a child, being a born writer; she continued without any plan for a profession, without any particular encouragement, and, as it proved, not needing any. For a good number of years she believed she was going to be a painter, and painted quite earnestly while she wrote without much effort.

Nearly all the Southern writers I know were early, omnivorous, insatiable readers, and Miss Welty runs reassuringly true to this pattern. She had at arm's reach the typical collection of books which existed as a matter of course in a certain kind of Southern family, so that she had read the ancient Greek and Roman poetry, history and fable, Shakespeare, Milton, Dante, the eighteenth-century English and the nineteenth-century French novelists, with a dash of Tolstoy and Dostoievsky, before she realized what she was reading. When she first discovered contemporary literature, she was just the right age to find first W. B. Yeats and Virginia Woolf in the air around her;

but always, from the beginning until now, she loved folk tales, fairy tales, old legends, and she likes to listen to the songs and stories of people who live in old communities whose culture is recollected and bequeathed orally.

She has never studied the writing craft in any college. She has never belonged to a literary group, and until after her first collection was ready to be published she had never discussed with any colleague or older artist any problem of her craft. Nothing else that I know about her could be more satisfactory to me than this; it seems to me immensely right, the very way a young artist should grow, with pride and independence and the courage really to face out the individual struggle; to make and correct mistakes and take the consequences of them, to stand firmly on his own feet in the end. I believe in the rightness of Miss Welty's instinctive knowledge that writing cannot be taught, but only learned, and learned by the individual in his own way, at his own pace and in his own time, for the process of mastering the medium is part of a cellular growth in a most complex organism; it is a way of life and a mode of being which cannot be divided from the kind of human creature you were the day you were born, and only in obeying the law of this singular being can the artist know his true directions and the right ends for him.

Miss Welty escaped, by miracle, the whole corrupting and destructive influence of the contemporary, organized tampering with young and promising talents by professional teachers who are rather monotonously divided into two major sorts: those theorists who are incapable of producing one passable specimen of the art they profess to teach; or good, sometimes first-rate, artists who are humanly unable to resist forming disciples and imitators among their students. It is all well enough to say that, of this second class, the able talent will throw off the master's influence and strike out for himself. Such influence has merely added new obstacles to an already difficult road. Miss Welty escaped also a militant social consciousness, in the current radical-intellectual sense, she never professed communism, and she has not expressed, except implicitly, any attitude at all on the state of politics or the condition of society. But there is an ancient system of ethics, an unanswerable, indispensable moral law, on which she is grounded firmly, and this, it would seem to me, is ample domain enough; these laws have never been the peculiar property of any party or creed or nation, they relate to that true and human world of which the artist is a living part; and when he dissociates himself from it in favor of a set of political, which is to say, inhuman, rules, he cuts himself away from his proper society—living men.

There exist documents of political and social theory which belong, if not to poetry, certainly to the department of humane letters. They are reassuring statements of the great hopes and dearest faiths of mankind and they are acts of high imagination. But all working, practical political systems, even those professing to originate in moral grandeur, are based upon and operate by contempt of human life and the individual fate; in accepting any one of them and shaping his mind and work to that mold, the artist dehumanizes himself, unfits himself for the practice of any art.

Not being in a hurry, Miss Welty was past twenty-six years when she offered her first story, "The Death of a Traveling Salesman," to the editor of a little magazine unable to pay, for she could not believe that anyone would buy a story from her; the magazine was *Manuscript*, the editor John Rood, and he accepted it gladly. Rather surprised, Miss Welty next tried the *Southern Review*, where she met with a great welcome and the enduring partisanship of Albert Erskine, who regarded her as his personal discovery. The story was "A Piece of News" and it was followed by others published in the *Southern Review*, the *Atlantic Monthly*, and *Harper's Bazaar*.

She has, then, never been neglected, never unappreciated, and she feels simply lucky about it. She wrote to a friend: "When I think of Ford Madox Ford! You remember how you gave him my name and how he tried his best to find a publisher for my book of stories all that last year of his life; and he wrote me so many charming notes, all of his time going to his little brood of promising writers, the kind of thing that could have gone on forever. Once I read in the *Saturday Review* an article of his on the species and the way they were neglected by publishers, and he used me as the example chosen at random. He ended his cry with 'What is to become of both branches of Anglo-Saxondom if this state of things continues?' Wasn't that wonderful, really, and typical? I may have been more impressed by that than would other readers who knew him. I did not know him, but I knew it was typical. And here I myself have turned out to be not at all the martyred promising writer, but have had all the good luck and all the good things Ford chided the world for withholding from me and my kind."

But there is a trap lying just ahead, and all short-story writers know what it is—The Novel. That novel which every publisher hopes to obtain from every short-story writer of any gifts at all, and who finally does obtain it, nine times out of ten. Already publishers have told her, "Give us first a novel, and then we will publish your short stories." It is a special sort of trap for poets, too, though quite often a good poet can and does write a good novel. Miss Welty has tried her hand at novels, laboriously, dutifully, youthfully thinking herself perhaps in the wrong to refuse, since so many authoritarians have told her that was the next step. It is by no means the next step. She can very well become a master of the short story, there are almost perfect stories in *A Curtain of Green*. The short story is a special and difficult medium, and contrary to a widely spread popular superstition it has no formula that can be taught by correspondence school. There is nothing to hinder her from writing novels if she wishes or believes she can. I only say that her good gift, just as it is now, alive and flourishing, should not be retarded by a perfectly artificial demand upon her to do the conventional thing. It is a fact that the public for short stories is smaller than the public for novels; this seems to me no good reason for depriving that minority. I remember a reader writing to an editor, complaining that he did not like collections of short stories because, just as he had got himself worked into one mood or frame of mind, he was called upon to change to another. If that is an important objection, we might also apply it to music. We might compare the novel to a symphony, and a collection of short stories to a good concert recital. In any case, this complainant is not our reader, yet our reader does exist, and there would be more of him if more and better short stories were offered.

The stories in *A Curtain of Green* offer an extraordinary range of mood, pace, tone, and variety of material. The scene is limited to a town the author knows well; the farthest reaches of that scene never go beyond the boundaries of her own state, and many of the characters are of the sort that caused a Bostonian to remark that he would not care to meet them socially. Lily Daw is a half-witted girl in the grip of social forces represented by a group of earnest ladies bent on doing the best thing for her, no matter what the consequences. Keela, the Outcast Indian Maid, is a crippled little Negro who represents a type of man considered most unfortunate by W. B. Yeats: one whose experience was more important than he, and completely beyond his powers of absorption. But the really unfortunate man in this story is the ignorant young white boy, who had innocently assisted at a wrong done the little Negro, and for a most complex reason, finds that no reparation is possible, or even desirable to the victim. . . . The heroine of "Why I Live at the P.O." is a terrifying family poltergeist, when one reconsiders it. While reading, it is gorgeously funny. In this first group—for the stories may be loosely classified on three separate levels—the spirit is satire and the key grim comedy. Of these, "The Petrified Man" offers a fine clinical study of vulgarity—vulgarity absolute, chemically pure, exposed mercilessly to its final subhuman depths. Dullness, bitterness, rancor, self-pity, baseness of all kinds, can be most interesting material for a story provided these are not also the main elements in the mind of the author. There is nothing in the least vulgar or frustrated in Miss Welty's mind. She has simply an eye and an ear sharp, shrewd, and true as a tuning fork. She has given to this little story all her wit and observation, her blistering humor and her just cruelty; for she has none of that slack tolerance or sentimental tenderness toward symptomatic evils that amounts to criminal collusion between author and character. Her use of this material raises the quite awfully sordid little tale to a level above its natural habitat, and its realism seems almost to have the quality of caricature, as complete realism so often does. Yet, as painters of the grotesque make only detailed reports of actual living types observed more keenly than the average eye is capable of observing, so Miss Welty's little human monsters are not really caricatures at all, but individuals exactly and clearly presented: which is perhaps a case against realism, if we cared to go into it.

She does better on another level—for the important reason that the themes are richer—in such beautiful stories as "Death of a Traveling Salesman," "A Memory," "A Worn Path." Let me admit a deeply personal preference for this particular kind of story, where external act and the internal voiceless life of the human imagination almost meet and mingle on the mysterious threshold between dream and waking, one reality refusing to admit or confirm the existence of the other, yet both conspiring toward the same end. This is not easy to accomplish, but it is always worth trying, and Miss Welty is so successful at it, it would seem her most familiar territory. There is no blurring at the edges, but evidences of an active and disciplined imagination working firmly in a strong line of continuity, the waking faculty of daylight reason recollecting and recording the crazy logic of the dream. There is in none of these stories any trace of autobiography in the prime sense, except as the author is omnipresent, and knows each character she writes about as only the artist knows the thing he has made, by first experiencing it in imagination. But perhaps in "A Memory," one of the best stories, there might be something of early personal history in the story of the child on the beach, estranged from the world of adult knowledge by her state of childhood, who hoped to learn the secrets of life by looking at everything, squaring her hands before her eyes to bring the observed thing into a frame —the gesture of one born to select, to arrange, to bring apparently disparate elements into harmony within deliberately fixed boundaries. But the author is freed already in her youth from self-love, self-pity, self-preoccupation, that triple damnation of too many of the young and gifted, and has reached an admirable objectivity. In such stories as "Old Mr. Marblehall," "Powerhouse," "The Hitch-Hikers," she combines an objective reporting with great perception of mental or emotional states, and in "Clytie" the very shape of madness takes place before your eyes in a straight account of actions and speech, the personal appearance and habits of dress of the main character and her family.

In all of these stories, varying as they do in excellence, I find nothing false or labored, no diffusion of interest, no wavering of mood—the approach is direct and simple in method, though the themes and moods are anything but simple, and there is even in the smallest story a sense of power in reserve which makes me believe firmly that, splendid beginning that this is, it is only the beginning.

1941

The Wingèd Skull

This is Lorence:
A Narrative of the Reverend Laurence Sterne, by Lodwick Hartley.
Chapel Hill: University of North Carolina Press, 1943.

DID the chaise break down under the broiling sun in a treeless waste near Toulouse, as Sterne wrote in a letter to his banker, or was it much earlier and more amusing, near Lyons, as he says in *Tristram Shandy*, or were there two accidents? And why did he say in that book he decided to dash to France so suddenly it never entered his mind that England and France were at war, when plainly he had planned it long before, and had to get leave from his Bishop and ask for a safe conduct from Mr. Pitt? To say nothing of a twenty-pound loan from Mr. David Garrick. Did he really get into bed with that long procession of shadowy ladies, from Catherine Fourmentelle early to Eliza Draper late, or did he just think and talk and write about it and make a great display of sentiment and then back out more or less gracefully at the right, or wrong, moment? Exactly how diabolic were those nightlong frolics at Skelton Castle with his old friend Hall-Stevenson and the other demoniacs, squires and parsons as they mostly were? Were they imitating feebly the goings-on of the Medmenham Monks, from which now and then John Wilkes strayed over to Skelton? Did he actually leave his mother to die in the workhouse (Byron thought so, and many before him and since), or did he care for her last days? Was his wife's belief, for a time, that she was the Queen of Bohemia due to his neglect and infidelities, or was it a strain of paranoia in that ill-starred mind? Was his mother really low Irish as he said, or member of a respectable Lancashire family? Just how deeply in love is a man who writes, through the years, substantially the same letters to a series of women, sometimes keeping copies for himself? Just where does truth end and fiction begin in Sterne's account of himself in *Tristram Shandy* and *The Sentimental Journey*?

Mr. Hartley wrestles manfully with these and a hundred other trivial or dubious or off-color questions of Laurence

Sterne's career with a discretion and strait regard for the records that might surprise his subject, who, being a novelist, was hampered by no such scruples. An immense amount of devoted study and trained research appears to have gone into this fairly short book, which handles with ease a baffling complexity of detail and carries the story along swiftly and with concentration on several planes at once. It is only the tone I find a little troublesome at times; such a balancing of the evidence for and against, such a leveling down of both the good and the evil in the history of Sterne, almost succeeds in smoothing the man away. There is a smack of prudishness at times, small biased hints of moral disapproval dragged in by the ears as if under some compulsion not the author's own. Mr. Hartley confesses that one of his aims was to make the book palatable to the lay, or general, reader in the hope that this mysterious being may be encouraged to seek out *Tristram Shandy* and read it for himself. I never saw a general reader, but I am convinced he exists, so many books are written for him. It is a mistake, just the same; general reader should not be pampered in any such way; Laurence Sterne should not be arranged to advantage or disadvantage for his view; he should be made to take his chances along with the rest of us, not only with the available truths of life but also with the very best work the author can do. For this book, in spite of its placating foreword, will be a stiff introduction indeed to a reader who does not already know something of the period.

For one who knows *Tristram Shandy*, *This Is Lorence* may bring to mind again how melancholy a cloud lies over all the recorded life of Laurence Sterne, even his triumphs and frolics, and how clear and merry the light shed by *Tristram Shandy*. That book contains more living, breathing people you can see and hear, whose garments have texture between your finger and thumb, whose flesh is knit firmly to their bones, who walk about their affairs with audible footsteps, than any other one novel in the world, I do believe. Uncle Toby, Corporal Trim, Yorick and Mrs. Yorick, the Widow Wadman, Bridget, Dr. Slop, Susannah, Obadiah, the infant Tristram hovering between breeches and tunics, all live in one house with floorboards under their boot soles, a roof over their heads, the fires burning and giving off real smoke, cooking smells coming from the kitchen, real weather outside and air blowing through the windows. When Dr. Slop cuts his thumb real blood issues from it, and everybody has a navel and his proper distribution of vital organs. One hangs around the place like an enchanted ghost, all eyes and ears for fear of missing something. The story roams apparently at random all over creation, following the living thoughts of these human beings in their infinitely varied experiences, memories, points of view. Sparks of association flash in showers at the slightest collision of temperaments. Every word spoken gets its instant response in the hearer; they are all intensely interested in each other and everything else under heaven all the time. Little clashes of wills lead to the most complicated roundabouts of personal history, anecdotes, opinion; a mere gesture is enough to set up a whole new train of thought and deed in these people, who live and go about their affairs every instant, not just at moments chosen by the author when it suits his convenience. Meanwhile, steadily, like time passing visibly before your eyes, Uncle Toby's unbroken devoted occupation with his campaigns, and the building of his fortified town, go on, accompanied by the most remarkable theories of military strategy and a running comment on the science of warfare, full of deep and sly satire. The celebrated comic improprieties go on too, a running fire of double talk punctuated by episodes such as that of the hot chestnut, the Abbess and the Novice who divided the sinful words which move a balky mule, the courtship of the Widow Wadman, the accidental circumcision of the newly born Tristram. It all has the most illusive air of having been dropped upon the paper by a flying pen which never stopped long enough for the author to read what he had written. Sterne drew on a page a few little graphs of his progress in *Tristram Shandy*; they are amusing but also accurate. That lightness was achieved with the intensity and painstakingness of a spider spinning its web, during those twenty obscure years as parson, along with the farming, and the philandering, and the wife driven distracted with jealousy, and the breaking blood vessels in his lungs, and the rows among his large family connection, and the local politics and the jollifications at Skelton Hall and the hunting and the August racing season at York.

Then his life work was published, a book or so at a time, and he went up modestly to London in the wake of Squire Crofts, a local worthy who paid the expenses of the trip, and there found scandalous fashionable success and enjoyed it enormously. Dr. Johnson thought his sermons "froth," Oliver Goldsmith found him dull, the Bishop of Gloucester called him "an irrecoverable scoundrel," but Sir Joshua Reynolds painted his portrait, David Garrick carried him into the orbit of the theater, the extremely mixed society around the Duke of York found him fascinating, for there was nothing they liked better than the cloven hoof peeping from beneath a cassock; he was in the dear tradition of the worldly abbé, and could write it all down, besides. Religion in any formal sense, and I greatly doubt any sense at all, he had not, and with some relief he ceased to feign it. He took some pains to be cultivated by respectable society, but what he loved best among even that was the fringe of wealthy young rakehells and their desperate sports. The rest is flight from death and pursuit of fame and pleasure: he "met" most of the great of his time, but his happiest days seem to have been a few weeks (when he had already the look of a dancing skeleton) of rioting around Paris with John Wilkes, interrupted, alas, by another blood vessel breaking at the height of the fun. As for women, to whom he gave so much attention, and who responded infallibly in their various ways, there is no fathoming his feelings or his motives. He appears to have squandered his whole available fund of human love upon his daughter Lydia, a headless, flighty creature ruled by her mother; judged by her story, she was the fine flower of all the weaknesses of every branch of all his families, a notably faulty lot. Even the highfalutin affair with Eliza Draper died, as all his fancies died, of his own weariness with his own role in them.

Mr. Hartley makes all the ladies rather duller than they may have been, even, but his wife must be admitted as a total loss. She was a homely woman whose husband made cruel caricatures of her, and wrote to a friend that he grew more sick and tired of her every day. She loved pleasure too, and had had a dull dog's life of it for years. She was delighted to get to France, and her ruses, and stratagems to be allowed to stay on there, with her daughter and without her husband, would have been pitiable if they had not succeeded. But they did.

Sterne died in lodgings in London with the nurse and landlady present, and a footman sent to inquire after him by John Crauford of Errol, who was giving a dinner to Garrick, Lord Ossory, David Hume, the Earl of March, Lord Roxburgh, the Duke of Grafton, and Mr. James, husband of Anne—the gay and good-hearted, who visited Sterne almost constantly in his last days. The footman reported to the waiting guests: "He was just a-dying . . . he said: now it is come. He put up his hand as if to stop a blow, and died in a minute."

His friends were saddened, but went on with their dinner. His wife and daughter and Eliza Draper were severally bitterly inconvenienced by his death. This and much more is in the book, but where is the real Laurence Sterne, the one who wrote *Tristram Shandy*? That wingèd skull seems to have made his getaway again, taking his main secret with him.

On a Criticism of Thomas Hardy

THE Bishop of Wakefield, after reading Thomas Hardy's latest (and as it proved, his last) novel, *Jude the Obscure*, threw it in the fire, or said he did. It was a warm midsummer, and Hardy suggested that the bishop may have been speaking figuratively, heresy and bonfires being traditionally associated in his mind, or that he may have gone to the kitchen stove. The bishop wrote to the papers that he had burned the book, in any case, and he wrote also to a local M.P. who caused the horrid work to be withdrawn from the public library, promising besides to examine any other novels by Mr. Hardy carefully before allowing them to circulate among the bishop's flock. It was a good day's work, added to the protests of the reviewers for the press, and twenty-five years of snubbing and nagging from the professional moralists of his time; Thomas Hardy resigned as novelist for good. As in the case of the criticism presently to be noted, the attack on his book included also an attack on his personal character, and the bishop's action wounded Thomas Hardy. He seems to have remarked in effect "that if the bishop could have known him as he was, he would have found a man whose personal conduct, views of morality, and of vital facts of religion, hardly differed from his own."

This is an indirect quotation by his second wife, devoted apologist and biographer, and it exposes almost to the point of pathos the basic, unteachable charity of Hardy's mind. Of all evil emotions generated in the snake-pit of human nature, theological hatred is perhaps the most savage, being based on intellectual concepts and disguised in the highest spiritual motives. And what could rouse this hatred in a theologian like the sight of a moral, virtuous, well-conducted man who presumed to agree with him in the "vital facts of religion," at the same time refusing to sign the articles of faith? It was long ago agreed among the Inquisitors that these are the dangerous men.

The bishop threw the book in the fire in 1896. In 1928, Mrs. Hardy was happy to record that another "eminent clergyman of the church" had advised any priest preparing to become a village rector to make first a good retreat and then a careful study of Thomas Hardy's novels. "From Thomas Hardy," concluded this amiable man, "he would learn the essential dignity of country people and what deep and passionate interest belongs to every individual life. You cannot treat them in the mass: each single soul is to be the object of your special and peculiar prayer."

Aside from the marginal note on the social point of view which made it necessary thus to warn prospective rectors that country people were also human entities, each possessed of a soul important, however rural, to God, and the extraordinary fact that an agnostic novelist could teach them what the church and their own hearts could not, it is worth noting again that churchmen differ even as the laymen on questions of morality, and can preach opposing doctrine from the same text. The history of these differences, indeed, is largely the calamitous history of institutional religion. In 1934, a layman turned preacher almost like a character in a Hardy novel, runs true to his later form by siding with the bishop. Since his spectacular conversion to the theology and politics of the Church of England, Mr. T. S. Eliot's great gifts as a critic have been deflected into channels where they do not flow with their old splendor and depth. More and more his literary judgments have assumed the tone of lay sermons by a parochial visitor, and his newer style is perhaps at its most typical in his criticism of Thomas Hardy:

The work of the late Thomas Hardy represents an interesting example of a powerful personality uncurbed by any institutional attachment or by submission to any objective beliefs; unhampered by any ideas, or even by what sometimes acts as a partial restraint upon inferior writers, the desire to please a large public. He seems to me to have written as nearly for the sake of "self-expression" as a man well can, and the self which he had to express does not strike me as a particularly wholesome or edifying matter of communication. He was indifferent even to the prescripts of good writing: he wrote sometimes overpoweringly well, but always very carelessly; at times his style touches sublimity without ever having passed through the stage of being good. In consequence of his self-absorption, he makes a great deal of landscape; for landscape is a passive creature which lends itself to an author's mood. Landscape is fitted, too, for the purpose of an author who is interested not at all in men's minds, but only in their emotions, and perhaps only in men as vehicles for emotions.

After some useful general reflections on the moral undesirability of extreme emotionalism, meant as a rebuke to Hardy and to which we shall return briefly later, Mr. Eliot proceeds:

I was [in a previous lecture] . . . concerned with illustrating the limiting and crippling effect of a separation from tradition and orthodoxy upon certain writers whom I nevertheless hold up for admiration for what they have attempted against great obstacles. Here I am concerned with the intrusion of the *diabolic* into modern literature in consequence of the same lamentable state of affairs. . . . I am afraid that even if you can entertain the notion of a positive power for evil working through human agency, you may still have a very inaccurate notion of what Evil is, and will find it difficult to believe that it may operate through men of genius of the most excellent character. I doubt whether what I am saying can convey very much to anyone for whom the doctrine of Original Sin is not a very real and tremendous thing.

Granting the premises with extreme reservations, Thomas Hardy was a visible proof of the validity of this disturbing doctrine. He had received early religious training in the Established Church, and by precept and example in a household of the most sincere piety, and of the most aggressive respectability. He remarked once, that of all the names he had been called, such as agnostic (which tag he adopted later, ruefully), atheist, immoralist, pessimist, and so on, a properly fitting one had been overlooked altogether: "churchy." He had once meant to be a parson. His relations with the church of his childhood had been of the homely, intimate, almost filial sort. His grandfather, his father, his uncle, all apt in music, had been for forty years the mainstay of the village choir. He felt at home in the place, as to its customs, feasts, services. He had a great love for the ancient churches, and as a young architect his aesthetic sense was outraged by the fashionable and silly "restorations" amounting to systematic destruction which overtook some of the loveliest examples of medieval church architecture in England during the nineteenth century. His devotion to the past, and to the history and character of his native Wessex, became at times a kind of antiquarian fustiness.

His personal morals were irreproachable, he had an almost queasy sense of the awful and permanent effects of wrong-doing on the human soul and destiny. Most of his novels deal with these consequences; his most stupendous tragedies are the result of one false step on the part of his hero or heroine. Genius aside, he had all the makings of a good, honest, church-going country squire; but the worm of original sin was settled in his mind, of all fatal places; and his mind led him out of the tradition of orthodoxy into another tradition of equal antiq-uity, equal importance, equal seriousness, a body of opinion running parallel throughout history to the body of law in church and state: the great tradition of dissent. He went, per-haps not so much by choice as by compulsion of *belief*, with the Inquirers rather than the Believers. His mind, not the greatest, certainly not the most flexible, but a good, candid, strong mind, asked simply the oldest, most terrifying ques-tions, and the traditional, orthodox answers of the church did not satisfy it. It is easy to see how this, from the churchly point of view, is diabolic. But the yawning abyss between question and answer remains the same, and until this abyss is closed, the dissent will remain, persistent, obdurate, a kind of church it-self, with its leaders, teachers, saints, martyrs, heroes; a thorn in the flesh of orthodoxy, but I think not necessarily of the Devil on that account, unless the intellect and all its questions are really from the Devil, as the Eden myth states explicitly, as the church seems to teach, and Mr. Eliot tends to confirm.

There is a great deal to examine in the paragraphs quoted above, but two words in their context illustrate perfectly the unbridgeable abyss between Hardy's question and Mr. Eliot's answer. One is, of course, the word *diabolic*. The other is *edi-fying*. That struck and held my eye in a maze, for a moment. With no disrespect I hope to conventional piety, may I venture that in the regions of art, as of religion, edification is not the highest form of intellectual or spiritual experience. It is a happy truth that Hardy's novels are really not edifying. The mental and emotional states roused and maintained in the reader of *The Mayor of Casterbridge* or *The Return of the Native* are con-siderably richer, invoked out of deeper sources in the whole human consciousness, more substantially nourishing, than this lukewarm word can express. A novel by Thomas Hardy can be a chastening experience, an appalling one, there is great and sober pleasure to be got out of those novels, the mind can be disturbed and the heart made extremely uneasy, but the complacency of edification is absent, as it is apt to be from any true tragedy.

Mr. Eliot includes Lawrence and Joyce in his list of literary men of "diabolic" tendencies. Deploring Lawrence's "untrained" mind, he adds: "A trained mind like that of Mr. Joyce is always aware of what master it is serving. . . ."

Untrained minds have always been a nuisance to the military police of orthodoxy. God-intoxicated mystics and untidy saints with only a white blaze of divine love where their minds should have been, are perpetually creating almost as much disorder within the law as outside it. To have a trained mind is no guarantee at all that the possessor is going to walk infallibly in the path of virtue, though he hardly fails in the letter of the law. St. Joan of Arc and St. Francis in their own ways have had something to say about that. The combination of a trained mind and incorruptible virtue is ideal, and therefore rare: St. Thomas More is the first name that occurs to me as example. Hardy's mind, which had rejected the conclusions though not the ethical discipline of organized religion (and he knew that its ethical system in essentials is older than Christianity), was not altogether an untrained one, and like all true Dissenters, he knew the master he was serving: his conscience. He had the mathematical certainties of music and architecture, and the daily, hourly training of a serious artist laboring at his problems over a period of more than half a century. That he was unhampered by ideas is therefore highly improbable. He wrote a few fine poems among a large number of poor ones. He wrote fifteen novels, of which a round half-dozen are well the equal of any novel in the English language; even if this is not to say he is the equal of Flaubert or of Dostoievsky. His notebooks testify to a constant preoccupation with ideas, not all of them his own, naturally, for he inherited them from a very respectable race of thinkers, sound in heterodoxy.

He had got out of the very air of the nineteenth century something from Lucian, something from Leonardo, something from Erasmus, from Montaigne, from Voltaire, from the Encyclopaedists, and there were some powerful nineteenth century Inquirers, too, of whom we need only mention Darwin, perhaps. Scientific experiment leads first to skepticism; but we have seen in our time, how, pursued to the verge of the infinite, it sometimes leads back again to a form of mysticism. There is at the heart of the universe a riddle no man can solve, and in the end, God may be the answer. But this is fetching up at a great distance still from orthodoxy, and still must be suspect in that quarter. Grant that the idea of God is the most splendid single act of the creative human imagination, and that all his multiple faces and attributes correspond to some need and satisfy some deep desire in mankind; still, for the Inquirers, it is impossible not to conclude that this mystical concept has been harnessed rudely to machinery of the most mundane sort, and has been made to serve the ends of an organization which, ruling under divine guidance, has ruled very little better, and in some respects, worse, than certain rather mediocre but frankly manmade systems of government. And it has often lent its support to the worst evils in secular government, fighting consistently on the side of the heavy artillery. And it has seemed at times not to know the difference between Good and Evil, but to get them hopelessly confused with legalistic right and wrong; justifying the most cynical expedients of worldly government by a high morality; and committing the most savage crimes against human life for the love of God. When you consider the political career of the church in the light of its professed origins and purposes, perhaps Original Sin *is* the answer. But Hardy preferred to remove the argument simply to another ground. As to himself, in his personal life, he had a Franciscan tenderness in regard to children, animals, laborers, the poor, the mad, the insulted and injured. He suffered horror and indignation at human injustice, more especially at the kind committed by entrenched authority and power upon the helpless. In middle age he remembered and recorded an early shock he received on hearing that, in his neighborhood, a young boy, a farm laborer, was found dead of sheer starvation in the fruitful field he had worked to cultivate. When he was planning *The Dynasts*, he wrote in his notebook: "The human race is to be shown as one great net-work or tissue which quivers in every part when one point is shaken, like a spider's web if touched." For Hardy, the death of that boy was a blow that set the whole great web trembling; and all mankind received a lasting wound. Here was a human fate for which human acts were responsible, and it would not serve Hardy at all to put the blame on Original Sin, or the inscrutable decrees of Divine Providence, or any other of the manifold devices for not letting oneself be too uncomfortable at the spectacle of merely human suffering. He was painfully uncomfortable all his life, and his discomfort was not for himself—he was an extraordinarily selfless sort of man—but the pervasiveness of what he considered senseless and unnecessary human misery. Out of the strange simplicity of his own unworldliness he could write at the age of 78: "As to pessimism, my motto is, first correctly diagnose the complaint—in this case human ills—and ascertain the cause: then set about finding a remedy if one exists. The motto or practise of the optimists is: Blind the eyes to the real malady, and use empirical panaceas to suppress the symptoms." Reasonableness: the use of the human intelligence directed toward the best human solution of human ills; such, if you please, was the unedifying proposal of this diabolic soul.

He himself in his few remarks on public and practical affairs had always been very reasonable. War, he believed, was an abomination, but it recurred again and again, apparently an incurable ill. He had no theories to advance, but wished merely that those who made wars would admit the real motives; aside from the waste and destruction, which he viewed with purely humane feelings, he objected to the immoralities of statecraft and religion in the matter. He was opposed to capital punishment on the simple grounds that no man has the right to take away the life of another. But he believed it acted as a material deterrent to crime, and if the judges would admit that it was social expediency, with no foundation in true morality, that was another matter. On the Irish question he was acute and explicit in expressing his view in this direction. "Though he did not enter it here [in his notebook] Hardy . . . said of Home Rule that it was a staring dilemma, of which good policy and good philanthropy were the huge horns. Policy for England required that it should not be granted; humanity to Ireland that it should. Neither Liberals nor Conservatives would honestly own up to this opposition between two moralities, but speciously insisted that humanity and policy were

both on one side—of course their own." At another time he
complained that most of the philosophers began on the theory
that the earth had been designed as a comfortable place for
man. He could no more accept this theory than he could the
theological notion that the world was a testing ground for the
soul of man in preparation for eternity, and that his sufferings
were part of a "divine" plan, or indeed, so far as the personal
fate of mankind was concerned, of any plan at all. He did
believe with a great deal of common sense that man could
make the earth a more endurable place for himself if he would,
but he also realized that human nature is not grounded in
common sense, that there is a deep place in it where the mind
does not go, where the blind monsters sleep and wake, war
among themselves, and feed upon death.

He did believe that there is "a power that rules the world,"
though he did not name it, nor could he accept the names that
had been given it, or any explanation of its motives. He could
only watch its operations, and to me it seems he concluded
that both malevolence and benevolence originated in the mind
of man, and the warring forces were within him alone; such
plan as existed in regard to him he had created for himself, his
Good and his Evil were alike the mysterious inventions of his
own mind; and why this was so, Hardy could not pretend to
say. He knew there was an element in human nature not subject to mathematical equation or the water-tight theories of
dogma, and this intransigent, measureless force, divided against
itself, in conflict alike with its own system of laws and the unknown laws of the universe, was the real theme of Hardy's
novels; a genuinely tragic theme in the grand manner, of sufficient weight and shapelessness to try the powers of any artist.
Generally so reluctant to admit any influence, Hardy admits to
a study of the Greek dramatists, and with his curious sense of
proportion, he decided that the Wessex countryside was also
the dwelling place of the spirit of tragedy; that the histories of
certain obscure persons in that limited locality bore a strong
family resemblance to those of the great, the ancient, and the
legendary. Mr. Eliot finds Hardy's beloved Wessex a "stage
setting," such as the Anglo-Saxon heart loves, and Hardy's
Wessex farmers "period peasants pleasing to the metropolitan
imagination." Hardy was Anglo-Saxon and Norman; that land-

scape was in his blood. Those period peasants were people he had known all his life, and I think that in this passage Mr. Eliot simply speaks as a man of the town, like those young rectors who need to be reminded of the individual dignity and importance of the country people. Further, taking all the Hardy characters in a lump, he finds in them only blind animal emotionalism, and remarks: ". . . strong passion is only interesting or significant in strong men; those who abandon themselves without resistance to excitements which tend to deprive them of reason become merely instruments of feeling and lose their humanity; and unless there is moral resistance and conflict there is no meaning." True in part: and to disagree in detail would lead to an endless discussion of *what* exactly constitutes interest in the work of a writer; *what* gives importance to his characters, their intrinsic value as human beings, or the value their creator is able to give them by his own imaginative view of them.

Hardy seems almost to agree with Mr. Eliot for once: "The best tragedy—highest tragedy in short—is that of the WORTHY encompassed by the INEVITABLE. The tragedies of immoral and worthless people are not of the best." My own judgment is that Hardy's characters are in every way superior to those of Mr. Eliot, and for precisely the reason the two writers are agreed upon. Hardy's people suffer the tragedy of being, Mr. Eliot's of not-being. The strange creatures inhabiting the wasteland of Mr. Eliot's particular scene are for the most part immoral and worthless, the apeneck Sweeneys, the Grishkins, and all. . . . They have for us precisely the fascination the poet has endowed them with, and they also have great significance: they are the sinister chorus of the poet's own tragedy, they represent the sum of the poet's vision of human beings without God and without faith, a world of horror surrounding this soul thirsting for faith in God. E. M. Forster has remarked that *The Waste Land* is a poem of real horror, the tragedy of the rains that came too late—or perhaps, never came at all. For how else can one explain the self-absorbed despair of Eliot's point of view, even in religion? That uncontrolled emotion of loathing for his fellow pilgrims in this mortal life? Was there not one soul worth tender treatment, not one good man interesting enough to the poet to inhabit his tragic scene? It is a curious paradox. Hardy feels no contempt for his characters at all; he writes of them as objectively as if they existed by themselves, they are never the background, the chorus, for the drama of his own experience. Beside Eliot's wasteland, with its inhuman beings, Hardy's Wessex seems an airy, familiar place, his characters at least have living blood in them, and though Mr. Eliot complains that Hardy was not interested in the minds of men, still their headpieces are not deliberately stuffed with straw by their creator.

Hardy's characters are full of moral conflicts and of decisions arrived at by mental processes, certainly. Jude, Gabriel Oak, Clym Yeobright, above all, Henchard, are men who have decisions to make, and if they do not make them entirely on the plane of reason, it is because Hardy was interested most in that hairline dividing the rational from the instinctive, the opposition, we might call it, between nature, and second nature; that is, between instinct and the habits of thought fixed upon the individual by his education and his environment. Such characters of his as are led by their emotions come to tragedy; he seems to say that following the emotions blindly leads to disaster. Romantic miscalculation of the possibilities of life, of love, of the situation; of refusing to reason their way out of their predicament; these are the causes of disaster in Hardy's novels. Angel Clare is a man of the highest principles, trained in belief, religion, observance of moral law. His failure to understand the real nature of Christianity makes a monster of him at the great crisis of his life. The Mayor of Casterbridge spends the balance of his life in atonement and reparation for a brutal wrong committed in drunkenness and anger; his past overtakes and destroys him. Hardy had an observing eye, a remembering mind; he did not need the Greeks to teach him that the Furies do arrive punctually, and that neither act, nor will, nor intention will serve to deflect a man's destiny from him, once he has taken the step which decides it.

A word about that style which Mr. Eliot condemns as touching "sublimity without ever having passed through the stage of being good." Hardy has often been called by critics who love him, the good simple man of no ideas, the careless workman of

genius who never learned to write, who cared nothing for the
way of saying a thing.

His own testimony is that he cared a great deal for *what* he
said: "My art is to intensify the expression of things, as is done
by Crivelli, Bellini, etc., so that the heart and inner meaning is
made vividly visible." Again: "The Realities to be the true realities of life, hitherto called abstractions. The old material realities to be placed behind the former, as shadowy accessories."
His notebooks are dry, reluctant, unmethodical; he seems to
have spent his time and energies in actual labor at his task rather
than theorizing about it, but he remarks once: "Looking
around on a well-selected shelf of fiction, how few stories of
any length does one recognize as well told from beginning to
end! The first half of this story, the last half of that, the middle
of another . . . the modern art of narration is yet in its infancy." He made few notes on technical procedure, but one or
two are valuable as a clue to his directions: "A story must be
exceptional enough to justify its telling. We tale tellers are all
Ancient Mariners, and none of us is warranted in stopping
Wedding Guests . . . unless he has something more unusual
to relate than the ordinary experiences of every average man
and woman." Again: "The whole secret of fiction and drama—
in the constructional part—lies in the adjustment of things
unusual to things eternal and universal. The writer who knows
exactly how exceptional, and how non-exceptional, his events
should be made, possesses the key to the art."

So much for theory. Not much about the importance of
style, the care for the word, the just and perfect construction
of a paragraph. But Hardy was not a careless writer. The difference between his first and last editions proves this, in matters
of style aside from his painful reconstruction of his manuscripts mutilated for serial publication. He wrote and wrote
again, and he never found it easy. He lacked elegance, he never
learned the trick of the whip-lash phrase, the complicated lar-
iat twirling of the professed stylists. His prose lumbers along, it
jogs, it creaks, it hesitates, it is as dull as certain long passages
in the Tolstoy of *War and Peace*, for example. That celebrated
first scene on Egdon Heath, in *The Return of the Native*. Who
does not remember it? And in actual rereading, what could be

duller? What could be more labored than his introduction of the widow Yeobright at the heath fire among the dancers, or more unconvincing than the fears of the timid boy that the assembly are literally raising the Devil? Except for this in my memory of that episode, as in dozens of others in many of Hardy's novels, I have seen it, I was there. When I read it, it almost disappears from view, and afterward comes back, phraseless, living in its somber clearness, as Hardy meant it to do, I feel certain. This to my view is the chief quality of good prose as distinguished from poetry. By his own testimony, he limited his territory by choice, set boundaries to his material, focused his point of view like a burning glass down on a definite aspect of things. He practiced a stringent discipline, severely excised and eliminated all that seemed to him not useful or appropriate to his plan. In the end his work was the sum of his experience, he arrived at his particular true testimony; along the way, sometimes, many times, he wrote sublimely.

1940

E. M. Forster

Two Cheers for Democracy, by E. M. Forster.
New York: Harcourt, Brace & Co., 1951.

Dates memorable to me escape my mind, so I write them down on bits of paper. Bits of paper escape me, too; they love to hide themselves at the bottoms of large baskets of other papers marked "Miscellany." But E. M. Forster's volume of essays, called *Abinger Harvest*, until now my favorite book of his except *A Passage to India*, is never far from my reach, so by turning to a certain page in it, I am able to name exactly the time, the first and last time, that I ever saw Mr. Forster.

Mr. Forster sees so clearly the damage that Olympic Games, or any other form of commercialized, politicalized sport, does to everybody concerned I cannot help but hope that he sees through all those Cultural Fronts by now, too. We were nearly all of us taken in at least once. So it was one crowded, dusty evening, June 21, 1935, in Paris, that Mr. Forster appeared before a meeting of the International Congress of Writers. You can read about it in *Abinger Harvest*. I distrusted the whole thing for good reasons and attended only on the one evening when Mr. Forster was to speak. At that time, the Communists were busy dividing the whole world into two kinds of people: Fascist and Communist. They said you could tell Fascists by their abhorrence of culture, their racial prejudices, and their general inhumanity. This was true. But they said also that Communists were animated solely by a love of culture and the general good of their fellow man. Alas, this was not true.

But for great numbers of well-disposed persons, especially in France, England, and some of the Americas, it was dear, familiar talk and we fell for it like a ton of scrap iron. When I say, then, that the evening Mr. Forster spoke in Paris was dusty and crowded, it was literally true: but it also is a way of saying that Communists in numbers running a show anywhere always gave me this sense of suffocation; and heaven knows they were there, with their usual solidarity of effrontery, efficiency and dullness, all over the place making muddlement, as ubiquitous and inescapable as a plague of June bugs in Texas.

Yet there were on the program as window-dressing a convincing number of artists not Communists, others just political geldings by Communist standards, and a few honest but uncommitted sympathizers. Among these last I suppose they counted Mr. Forster, and he did manage to get in a kind word for communism on the ground that its intentions were good; a high compliment, all considered. He also defended a mediocre book in the defense of free speech and the right to publish; restated his humane, liberal political views, and predicted that he and all his kind, including Aldous Huxley, should expect to be swept away by the next war.

I heard nothing of this at the time. I had to wait and read it in *Abinger Harvest*. I think it was just after André Malraux—then as dogmatic in communism as he is now in some other faith—had leaped to the microphone barking like a fox to halt the applause for Julien Benda's speech, that a little slender man with a large forehead and a shy chin rose, was introduced and began to read his paper carefully prepared for this occasion. He paid no attention to the microphone, but wove back and forth, and from side to side, gently, and every time his face passed the mouthpiece I caught a high-voiced syllable or two, never a whole word, only a thin recurring sound like the wind down a chimney as Mr. Forster's pleasant good countenance advanced and retreated and returned. Then, surprisingly, once he came to a moment's pause before the instrument and there sounded into the hall clearly but wistfully a complete sentence: "I DO believe in liberty!"

The applause at the end was barely polite, but it covered the antics of that part of the audience near me; a whole pantomime of malignant ridicule, meaning that Mr. Forster and all his kind were already as extinct as the dodo. It was a discouraging moment.

Well, sixteen unbelievably long, painful years have passed, and it is very reassuring to observe that, far from having been swept away, Mr. Forster has been thriving in an admirable style—that is to say, his own style, spare, unportentous but serious, saying his say on any subject he chooses, as good a say as any we are likely to have for a long time; fearless but not aggressive; candid without cruelty; and with that beautiful, purely secular common sense which can hardly be distinguished in its more inspired moments from a saintly idealism.

Indeed, Mr. Forster is an artist who lives in that constant state of grace which comes of knowing who he is, where he lives, what he feels and thinks about his world. Virginia Woolf once wrote: "One advantage of having a settled code of morals is that you know exactly what to laugh at." She knew, and so does Mr. Forster. He pokes fun at things in themselves fatally without humor, things oppressive and fatal to human happiness: megalomania, solemn-godliness, pretentiousness, self-love, the meddlesome impulse which leads to the invasion and destruction of human rights. He disclaims a belief in Belief, meaning one can only suppose the kind of dogmatism promoted by meddlesomeness and the rest; come right down to it, I hardly know a writer with more beliefs than Mr. Forster; and all on the side of the angels.

Two Cheers for Democracy, a collection of his short writings on a tremendous range of subjects, is his first book since *Abinger Harvest*. It is an extension and enlargement of his thought, a record of the life and feelings of an artist who has been in himself an example of all he has defended from the first: the arts as a civilizing force, civilization itself as the true right aim of the human spirit, no matter what its failures may have been, above all, his unalterable belief in the first importance of the individual relationships between human beings founded on the reality of love—not in the mass, not between nations, nonsense!—but between one person and another. This is of course much more difficult than loving just everybody and everything, for each one must really do something about it, and show his faith in works. He manages to raise two mild cheers for poor old misprized, blasphemed, abused Democracy, who took an awful thrashing lately, but may recover; and he hopes to be able honestly some day to give three. He has long since earned his three cheers, and a tiger.

Virginia Woolf

The Captain's Death Bed and Other Essays, by Virginia Woolf,
edited, with a foreword, by Leonard Woolf.
New York: Harcourt, Brace & Co., 1950.

LEONARD WOOLF, in selecting and publishing the shorter
writings of his wife, Virginia Woolf, has taken occasion to
emphasize, again and again, her long painstaking ways of
working, her habit of many revisions and rewritings, and her
refusal to publish anything until she had brought it to its final
state. The four volumes to appear in the nine years since her
death will probably be the lot, Mr. Woolf tells us. There seems
to remain a certain amount of unfinished manuscripts—
unfinished in the sense that she had intended still to reconsider
them and would not herself have published them in their present versions. One cannot respect enough the devoted care and
love and superb literary judgment of the executor of this precious estate.

"In the previous volumes," Mr. Woolf writes in his foreword
to the latest collection, *The Captain's Death Bed*, "I made no
attempt to select essays in accordance with what I thought to
be their merit or importance; I aimed at including in each volume some of all the various kinds of essay."

It is easy to agree with him when he finds "The essays in this
volume are . . . no different in merit and achievement from
those previously published." Indeed, I found old favorites and
new wonders in each of the earlier collections, finding still
others again in this: the celebrated "Mr. Bennett and Mrs.
Brown"; "Memories of a Working Woman's Guild"; "The
Novels of Turgenev"; "Oliver Goldsmith." She speaks a convincing good word for Ruskin, such was her independence of
taste, for surely this word is the first Ruskin has received in
many a long year. She does a really expert taxidermy job on Sir
Walter Raleigh, poor man, though he certainly deserved it; does
another on reviewing, so severe her husband feels he must
modify it a little with a footnote.

The Captain's Death Bed contains in fact the same delicious things to read as always; apparently her second or third draft was as good as her ninth or fifteenth; her last would be a little different, but surely not much better writing, that is clear. Only she, the good artist, without self-indulgence, would have known how much nearer with each change she was getting to the heart of her thought. For an example of how near she could come to it, read the three and one-half pages called "Gas." It is about having a tooth out, in the same sense, as E. M. Forster once remarked, that *Moby Dick* is a novel about catching a whale.

Now it is to be supposed that with this final gathering up of her life's work the critics will begin their formal summings-up, analyses, exegeses; the various schools will attack or defend her; she will be "placed" here and there; Freud will be involved, if he has not been already; elegies will be written: Cyril Connolly has already shed a few morning tears, and advised us not to read her novels for at least another decade: she is too painfully near to our most disastrous memories.

It turns out merely that Mr. Connolly wishes us to neglect her because she reminds him of the thirties, which he, personally, cannot endure. A great many of us who have no grudges against either the twenties or the thirties will find this advice mystifying. And there is a whole generation springing up, ready to read what is offered, who know and care nothing for either of those decades. My advice must be exactly the opposite: read everything of Virginia Woolf's now, for she has something of enormous importance to say at this time, here, today; let her future take care of itself.

I cannot pretend to be coldly detached about her work, nor, even if I were able, would I be willing to write a purely literary criticism of it. It is thirty-five years since I read her first novel, *The Voyage Out*. She was one of the writers who touched the real life of my mind and feeling very deeply; I had from that book the same sense of some mysterious revelation of truth I had got in earliest youth from Laurence Sterne ("of all people!" jeers a Shandy-hating friend of mine), from Jane Austen, from Emily Brontë, from Henry James. I had grown up with these, and I went on growing with W. B. Yeats, the first short stories of James Joyce, the earliest novels of Virginia Woolf.

In the most personal way, all of these seemed and do seem

to be my contemporaries; their various visions of reality, their worlds, merged for me into one vision, one world view that revealed to me little by little my familiar place. Living as I did in a world of readers devoted to solid, tried and true literature, in which unimpeachable moral grandeur and inarguable doctrine were set forth in balanced paragraphs, these writers were my own private discoveries. Reading as I did almost no contemporary criticism, talking to no one, still it did not occur to me that these were not great artists, who if only people could be persuaded to read them (even if by the light of Dr. Johnson or Dean Swift) they would be accepted as simply and joyously as I accepted them.

In some instances I was to have rude surprises. I could never understand the "revival" of Henry James; I had not heard that he was dead. Rather suddenly Jane Austen came back into fashionable favor; I had not dreamed she had ever been out of it.

In much the same way I have been amazed at the career of Virginia Woolf among the critics. To begin with, there has been very little notice except of the weekly review variety. Compared to the libraries of criticism published about Joyce, Lawrence, Eliot and all her other fellow artists of comparable stature, she has had little consideration. In 1925 she puzzled E. M. Forster, whose fountain pen disappeared when he was all prepared in his mind to write about her early novels.

Almost everything has been said, over and over, about Virginia Woolf's dazzling style, her brilliant humor, her extraordinary sensibility. She has been called neurotic, and hypersensitive. Her style has been compared to cobwebs with dew drops, rainbows, landscapes seen by moonlight, and other unsubstantial but showy stuff. She has been called a Phoenix, Muse, a Sybil, a Prophetess, in praise, or a Feminist, in dispraise. Her beauty and remarkable personality, her short way with fools and that glance of hers, which chilled many a young literary man with its expression of seeing casually through a millstone—all of this got in the way. It disturbed the judgment and drew the attention from the true point of interest.

Virginia Woolf was a great artist, one of the glories of our time, and she never published a line that was not worth reading. The least of her novels would have made the reputation of a lesser

writer, the least of her critical writings compare more than favorably with the best criticism of the past half-century. In a
long, sad period of fear, a world broken by wars, in which the
artists have in the most lamentable way been the children of
their time, knees knocking, teeth chattering, looking for personal salvation in the midst of world calamity, there appeared
this artist, Virginia Woolf.

She was full of secular intelligence primed with the profane
virtues, with her love not only of the world of all the arts created by the human imagination, but a love of life itself and of
daily living, a spirit at once gay and severe, exacting and generous, a born artist and a sober craftsman; and she had no plan
whatever for her personal salvation; or the personal salvation
even of someone else; brought no doctrine; no dogma. Life,
the life of this world, here and now, was a great mystery, no
one could fathom it; and death was the end. In short, she was
what the true believers always have called a heretic.

What she did, then, in the way of breaking up one of the
oldest beliefs of mankind, is more important than the changes
she made in the form of the novel. She wasn't even a heretic—
she simply lived outside of dogmatic belief. She lived in the
naturalness of her vocation. The world of the arts was her native territory; she ranged freely under her own sky, speaking
her mother tongue fearlessly. She was at home in that place as
much as anyone ever was.

D. H. Lawrence

QUETZALCOATL

The Plumed Serpent, by D. H. Lawrence.
New York: Alfred A. Knopf, 1926.

The Plumed Serpent is a confession of faith, a summing up of the mystical philosophy of D. H. Lawrence. Mexico, the Indians, the cult of the Aztec god Quetzalcoatl—the Plumed Serpent—all these are pretexts, symbols made to the measure of his preoccupations. It seems only incidentally a novel, in spite of the perfection of its form; it is a record of a pilgrimage that was, that must have been, a devastating experience. Lawrence went to Mexico in the hope of finding there, among alien people and their mysterious cult, what he had failed to find in his own race or within himself: a center and a meaning to life. He went to the Indians with the hope of clinching once for all his argument that blood-nodality is the source of communion between man and man, and between man and the implacable gods. He desired to share this nodality, to wring from it the secret of the "second strength" which gives magic powers to a man. But blood itself stood between him and his desire.

"She had noticed that usually, when an Indian looked at a white man, both stood back from actual contact, from actual meeting of each other's eyes. They left a wide space of neutral territory between them. . . ." This acute flash of insight he gives to Kate Leslie, the Irish woman, the only white person among his chief characters. She carries all the burden of doubt and fear for the author, and is the most valid human being in the book. With all his will, his psychoanalytic equipment, and his curiosity, which is like a steel probe, Lawrence could not cross this neutral territory. These, and his poetic imagination touched to wonder, drive him resistlessly within touching distance. His mind sniffs out delicately, the filaments of his thought are like living nerve-ends, they shudder and are repelled at the nearness of a secret steeped, for him, in cosmic possibilities. He remains a stranger gazing at a mystery he cannot share, but still hopes to ravish, and his fancy dilates it to monstrous proportions.

He has confessed somewhere that he was in a raging temper from the moment he passed over the line from the United States to Mexico. He blames this on the vibrations of cruelty and bloodshed in the country, the dark hopelessness that rises from the Indians and the very soil in an almost palpable vapor. He felt that the Mexican motive of existence is hatred. Lawrence is a good hater; he should know hate when he sees it. But it was not altogether an occult effluvium from the earth. His terror came halfway to meet it. A serpent lies coiled in the Indian vitals; their eyes are centerless. He cannot acknowledge blood-kin with them. He gives them a soul and takes it away again; they are dragon worshipers, only half-created; he surmises reptilian ichor in their veins. Yet he loves their beauty, and with all his soul he adores their phallic god; and so he remain a stranger, but makes his obeisance.

The genius of Lawrence lies in his power to create out of his own inner experience, his own sensitized fibers, a personal world which is also our world, peopled with human beings recognizably of our own time and place. His world is a place of complex despair, his tragedies are of the individual temperament in double conflict, against the inner nightmare and the outer unendurable fact. Terror of death and nausea of life, sexual egotism and fear, a bitter will-to-power and an aspiration after mystical apartness, an impotent desire for the act of faith, combine into a senseless widdershins; they spin dizzily on their own centers of sensation, with a sick void at the core.

Lawrence has turned away from this world, these persons, exhausted by their futility, unable to admit that their despairs and futilities are also his own. "Give me the mystery and let the world live again for me," Kate cried in her own soul. "And deliver me from man's automatism!" This woman is a perfect study of that last upsurge of romantic sex-hunger, disguised as a quest of the spirit, that comes with the grand climacteric. Lawrence identifies her purpose with his own, she represents his effort to touch the darkly burning Indian mystery. It could not happen: he is too involved in preconceptions and simple human prejudice. His artificial Western mysticism came in

collision with the truly occult mind of the Indian, and he suffered an extraordinary shock. He turned soothsayer, and began
to interpret by a formula: the result is a fresh myth of the
Indian, a deeply emotional conception, but a myth none the
less, and a debased one.

For sheer magnificence of writing, Lawrence has surpassed
himself. His style has ripened, softened, there is a melancholy
hint of the overrichness of autumn. Who looks for mere phrases
from him? He writes by the passage, by the chapter, a prose flexible as a whiplash, uneven and harmonious as breakers rolling
upon a beach, and the sound is music. His language rises from
the page not in words but in a series of images before the eye:
human beings move in vivid landscapes, wrapped in a physical
remoteness, yet speaking with a ghostly intimacy, as if you were
listening to the secret pulse of their veins.

All of Mexico that can be *seen* is here, evoked clearly with
the fervor of things remembered out of impressions that filled
the mind to bursting. There is no laborious building up of
local color, but an immense and prodigal feeling for the background, for every minute detail seen with the eyes of a poet.
He makes you a radiant gift of the place. It is no Rousseau-like
jungle of patterned leaves and fruits half concealing impersonally savage beasts. The skies change, the lights and colors, the
smells and feel of the air change with the time of day; the
masses of the Indians move with purpose against this shifting
landscape; the five chief characters live out a romantic drama
of emotions, accompanied by all the commonplaces of every
day, of dress, of food, of weather. A nationwide political and
religious movement provides the framework for a picture that
does not omit a leaf, a hanging fruit, an animal, a cloud, a
mood, of the visible Mexico. Lawrence puts in besides all his
own accumulated protest against the things he hates: his grudge
against women as opposed to his concept of woman, his
loathing of the machine. His contempt for revolution and the
poor is arrogant, not aristocratic: but he is plainly proud of his
attitude. It is a part of his curiously squeamish disgust of
human contact.

The triumph of this book as a work of art lies in this: that
out of his confusions, the divisions of his mind, he has gained

by sheer poetic power to a fine order, a mystical truth above his obsessions and debased occult dogma.

Mexico pulls you down, the people pull you down like a great weight! But it may be they pull you down as the earth pull of gravitation does, that you can balance on your feet. Maybe they draw you down as the earth draws down the roots of the tree so that it may be clenched deep in the soil. . . . Loose leaves and aeroplanes blow away on the wind, in what they call freedom. . . . All that matters to me are the roots that reach down beyond all destruction.

Thus Ramon, the Spanish-Indian scholar who has taken upon himself the role of the living Quetzalcoatl. "God must come to the Mexicans in a blanket and huaraches, else he is no god of the Mexican. . . . We live by manifestations." A full-blooded Indian joins him in the role of Huitzilopochtli, the god of war. Kate Leslie goes with them as Malintzi, wife of the war-god. They set about to restore the old phallic cult, based on an ancient religious tenet of the human race: that the male element is godhead, that man carries the unique secret of creation in his loins, that divinity originates in the potent germ. "I look . . . for my own manhood," says the living Quetzalcoatl. "It comes from the middle from God. . . . I have nothing but my manhood. The God gives it to me, and leaves me to do further." And again: "The universe is a nest of dragons, with a perfectly unfathomable life mystery at the center of it. . . . If I call the mystery the Morning Star, what does it matter? . . . And man is a creature who wins his own creation inch by inch from the nest of cosmic dragons." "Man is a column of blood, woman is a valley of blood." And man must be saved again by blood. Blood touches blood in the Morning Star, and thus the otherwise incommunicable secret will be shared.

And what, in fact, is the conclusion after all this grandiose preparation? The Indians must still be saved by a superior expert tribal Messiah and by means of the same worn-out devices. The living Quetzalcoatl works through the cumbrous machinery of drums, erotic-mystic ritual, ceremonial bloodshed. He is a marvelous study of the priestly pedagogue fired with a fanatic vision of a world saved and standing at his right hand praising his name forever. This is the answer we are given to a great quest for the meaning of life: man is not a god, and he must die. But he may hypnotize himself into momentary forgetfulness by means of ceremonial robes and a chorus of mystic mumblings, accompanied by synthesized gesture in praise of his own virility, that most variable and treacherous of all his powers.

The hymns of Quetzalcoatl form a broken cycle through the story, curious interruptions to the muscular power of the prose. There are many beautiful lines: "And say to thy sorrow, 'Ax, thou art cutting me down. Yet did a spark fly out of thy edge and my wound.'" Mostly they are booming, hollow phrases, involved as the high-sounding nonsense of a sixteenth-century Spanish mystic; their ecstasy follows the pattern of artificial raptures, self-conscious as a group of Gurdjieff's American disciples revolving in a dervish dance.

Altogether Lawrence cannot be freed from the charge of pretentiousness in having invaded a mystery that remained a mystery to him, and in having set down his own personal reactions to a whole race as if they were the inspired truth. His Indians are merely what the Indians might be if they were all D. H. Lawrences. The three characters who act as his mouthpieces are simply good Europeans at bottom—further variations of Lawrence's arch-type, the flayed and suffering human being in full flight from the horrors of a realistic mechanical society, and from the frustrations of sex.

When you have read this book read *Sons and Lovers* again. You will realize the catastrophe that has overtaken Lawrence.

A WREATH FOR THE GAMEKEEPER

Lady Chatterley's Lover, by D. H. Lawrence,
with an introduction by Mark Schorer
and a preface by Archibald MacLeish.
New York: Grove Press, 1959.

The dubious Crusade is over, anybody can buy the book now in hardcover or paperback, expurgated or unexpurgated, in drugstores and railway stations as well as in the bookshops, and 'twas a famous victory for something or other, let's wait and see. Let us remark as we enter the next phase that we may hope this episode in the history of our system of literary censorship will mark the end of one of our most curious native customs—calling upon the police and the post office officials to act as literary critics in addition to all their other heavy duties. It is not right nor humane and I hope this is the end of it; it is enough to drive good men out of those services altogether.

When I first read *Lady Chatterley's Lover*, thirty years ago, I thought it a dreary, sad performance with some passages of unintentional hilarious low comedy, one scene at least simply beyond belief in a book written with such inflamed apostolic solemnity, which I shall return to later; and I wondered then at all the huzza and hullabaloo about suppressing it. I realize now there were at least two reasons for it—first, Lawrence himself, who possessed to the last degree the quality of high visibility; and second, the rise to power of a demagoguery of political and social censorship by unparalleled ignoramuses in all things, including the arts, which they regarded as the expression of peculiarly dangerous forms of immorality. These people founded organizations for the suppression of Vice, and to them nearly everything *was* Vice, and other societies for the promotion of Virtue, some of them very dubious, and their enthusiasms took some weird and dangerous directions. Prohibition was their major triumph, with its main result of helping organized crime to become big business; but the arts, and especially literature, became the object of a morbid purblind interest to those strange beings who knew nothing about any art, but knew well what they feared and hated.

It is time to take another look at this question of censorship and protest which has been debated intermittently ever since I can remember. Being a child of my time, naturally I was to be found protesting: I was all for freedom of speech, of action, of belief, of choice, in every department of human life; and for authors all this was to be comprehended in the single perfect right to express their thoughts without reserve, write anything they chose, with publishers to publish and booksellers to sell it, and the vast public gloriously at liberty to buy and read it by the tens of thousands.

It was a noble experiment, no doubt, an attempt to bring a root idea of liberty to flower; but in practice it soon showed serious defects and abuses, for the same reason that prohibition of alcohol could not be made to work: gangsters and crooks took over the business of supplying the human demand for intoxication and obscenity, which hitherto had been in the hand of respectable elements who regulated it and kept it more or less in its place; but it still is a market that never fails no matter who runs it. (I have often wondered what were the feelings of the old-line pious prohibitionists when they discovered that their most powerful allies in the fight to maintain prohibition were the bootleggers.)

Publishers were certainly as quick to take advantage of the golden moment as the gangsters, and it did not take many of them very long to discover that the one best way to sell a book with "daring" passages was to get it banned in Boston, or excluded from the United States mails. Certain authors, not far behind the publishers, discovered that if they could write books the publisher could advertise as in peril from the censor, all the better. Sure enough, the censor would rise to the bait, crack down in a way that would be front-page news, the alarm would go out to all fellow writers and assorted lovers of liberty that one of the guild was being abused in his basic human rights guaranteed by our Constitution, by those hyenas in Boston or the Post Office. The wave of publicity was on, and the sales went up. Like too many such precariously balanced schemes, it was wonderful while it lasted, but it carried the seeds of its own decay. Yet those were the days when people really turned out and paraded with flags and placards, provocative songs and slogans, openly inviting arrest and quite often succeeding in being hauled off to the police station in triumph, there to sit in a cell perfectly certain that somebody was going to show up and bail them out before night.

Writers—I was often one of them—did not always confine their aid to freedom of the word, though that was their main concern. They would sometimes find themselves in the oddest company, defending strange causes and weirdly biased viewpoints on the grounds that they most badly wanted defense. But we also championed recklessly the most awful wormy little books we none of us would have given shelf room, and more than once it came over us in mid-parade that this was no downtrodden citizen being deprived of his rights, but a low cynic cashing in on our high-minded application of democratic principles. I suppose for a good many of us, all this must just be chalked up to Experience. After some time, I found myself asking, "Why should I defend a worthless book just because it has a few dirty words in it? Let it disappear of itself and the sooner the better."

No one comes to that state of mind quickly, and it is danger-ous ground to come to at all, I suppose, but one comes at last. My change of view began with the first publication in 1928 of *Lady Chatterley's Lover*. He has become, this lover of Lady Chatterley's, as sinister in his effect on the minds of critics as that of Quint himself on the children and the governess in *The Turn of the Screw*. I do not know quite what role Lady Chat-terley should play to Quint-Mellors. She is not wicked, as Miss Jessel is; she is merely a moral imbecile. She is not intense, imaginative, and dazzled like the governess, she is stupid; and it is useless to go on with the comparison, for she is not the center of the critics' attention as the Gamekeeper is, she has not that baneful fascination for them that he has. But there is one quality both books have in common and they both suc-ceed in casting the same spell on plain reader and critic alike: the air of evil which shrouds them both, the sense of a situa-tion of foregone and destined failure, to which there can be no outcome except despair. Only, the Lawrence book is sadder, because Lawrence was a badly flawed, lesser artist than James. He did not really know what he was doing, or if he did, pre-tended to be doing something else; and his blood-chilling anatomy of the activities of the rutting season between two rather dull persons comes with all the more force because the relations are precisely not between the vengeful seeking dead and living beings, but between the living themselves who seem to me deader than any ghost.

Yet for the past several months there has been a steady flood of extremely well-managed publicity in defense of Lawrence's motives and the purity of his novel, into which not only critics, but newspaper and magazine reporters, editorial writers, min-isters of various religious beliefs, women's clubs, the police, postal authorities, and educators have been drawn, clamorously. I do not object to censorship being so loudly defeated again for the present. I merely do not approve of the way it was done. Though there were at this time no parades, I believe, we have seen such unanimity and solidarity of opinion among American critics, and many of them of our first order, as I do not remember to have seen before. What are we to think of them, falling in like this with this fraudulent crusade of raising an old tired Cause out of its tomb? For this is no longer just a book, and it never was a work of literature worth all this attention. It is no longer a Cause, if it ever was, but a publicity device and a well-worn one by now, calculated to rouse a salacious itch of curiosity in the prospective customer. This is such standard procedure by now it seems unnecessary to mention it. Yet these hard-headed, experienced literary men were trapped into it once more, and lent a strong hand to it. There is something touching, if misguided, in this fine-spirited show of manly solidarity, this full-throated chorus in defense of Lawrence's vocabulary and the nobility of his intentions. I have never questioned either; I wish only to say that I think that from start to finish he was about as wrong as can be on the whole subject of sex, and that he wrote a very laboriously bad book to prove it. The critics who have been carried away by a generous desire to promote freedom of speech, and give a black eye to prudes and nannies overlook sometimes—and in a work of literature this should not be overlooked, at least not by men whose profession it is to criticize literature—that purity, nobility of intention, and apostolic fervor are good in themselves at times, but at others they depend on context, and in this instance they are simply not enough. Whoever says they are, and tries to persuade the public to accept a book for what it is not, a work of good art, is making a grave mistake, if he means to go on writing criticism.

As for the original uproar, Lawrence began it himself, as he nearly always did, loudly and bitterly on the defensive, throwing out each book in turn as if he were an early Christian throwing himself to the lions. "Anybody who calls my novel a dirty, sexual novel is a liar." Further: "It'll infuriate mean people; but it will surely soothe decent ones." The Readers' Subscription (an

American book club) in its brochure offering the book, carries on the tone boldly: "Now, at long last, a courageous American publisher is making available the unexpurgated version of *Lady Chatterley's Lover*—exactly as the author meant it to be seen by the intelligent, sensitive reader." No, this kind of left-handed flattery won't quite do: it is the obverse of the form of blackmail used by publishers and critics to choke their ambiguous wares down our throats. They say in effect, "If you disapprove of this book, you are proved to be (1) illiterate, (2) insensitive, (3) unintelligent, (4) low-minded, (5) 'mean,' (6) a hypocrite, (7) a prude, and other unattractive things." I happen to have known quite a number of decent persons, not too unintelligent or insensitive, with some love and understanding of the arts, who were revolted by the book; and I do not propose to sit down under this kind of bullying.

Archibald MacLeish regards it as "pure" and a work of high literary merit. He has a few reservations as to the whole with which I heartily agree so far as they go; yet even Mr. MacLeish begins trailing his coat, daring us at our own risk to deny that the book is "one of the most important works of the century, or to express an opinion about the literature of our own time or about the spiritual history that literature expresses without making his peace in one way or another with D. H. Lawrence and with this work."

Without in the least making my peace with D. H. Lawrence or with this work, I wish to say why I disagree profoundly with the above judgments, and also with the following:

Harvey Breit: "The language and the incidents or scenes in question are deeply moving and very beautiful—Lawrence was concerned how love, how a relationship between a man and a woman can be most touching and beautiful, but only if it is uninhibited and total." This is wildly romantic and does credit to Mr. Breit's feelings but there can be no such thing as a total relationship between two human beings—to begin with, what is total in such a changing, uncertain, limited state? and if there could be, just how would the persons involved know when they had reached it? Judging from certain things he wrote and said on this subject, I think Lawrence would have been the first to protest at even an attempt to create such a condition.

He demanded the right to invade anybody, but he was notice-ably queasy when anyone took a similar liberty with him.

Edmund Wilson: "The most inspiring book I have seen in a long time . . . one of his best written . . . one of his most vigorous and brilliant. . . ."

This reminds me that I helped parade with banners in California in defense of Mr. Wilson's *Memoirs of Hecate County*—a misguided act of guild loyalty and personal admiration I cannot really regret, so far as friendship is concerned. But otherwise the whole episode was deplorably unnecessary. My preference has not changed for his magnificent *To the Finland Station* and for almost any of his criticisms and essays on literary and public affairs.

Jacques Barzun: "I have no hesitation in saying that I do not consider Lawrence's novel pornographic." I agree with this admirably prudent statement, and again when Mr. Barzun notes Lawrence's ruling passion for reforming everything and everybody in sight. My quarrel with the book is that it really is not pornographic—the great wild, free-wheeling Spirit of Pornography has here been hitched to a rumbling little domestic cart and trundled off to chapel, its ears pinned back and its mouth washed out with soap.

Mr. Schorer, who contributes the preface, even brings in Yeats to defend this tiresome book. Yeats, bless his memory, when he talked bawdy, knew what he was saying and why. He enjoyed the flavor of gamey words on his tongue, and never deceived himself for one moment as to the nature of that enjoyment; he never got really interestingly dirty until age had somewhat cooled the ardors of his flesh, thus doubling his pleasure in the thoughts of it in the most profane sense. Mr. Schorer reprints part of a letter from Yeats, written years ago, to Mrs. Shakespear: "These two lovers the gamekeeper and his employer's wife each separated from their class by their love and fate are poignant in their loneliness; the coarse language of the one accepted by both becomes a forlorn poetry, uniting their solitudes, something ancient and humble and terrible."

This comes as a breath of fresh air upon a fetid topic. Yeats reached acutely into the muddlement and brings up the simple facts: the real disaster for the lady and the gamekeeper is that they face perpetual exile from their own proper backgrounds and society. Stale, pointless, unhappy as both their lives were before, due to their own deficiencies of character, it would seem yet now they face, once the sexual furor is past, an utter aimlessness in life shocking to think about. Further, Yeats notes an important point I have not seen mentioned before—only one of the lovers uses the coarse language, the other merely accepts it. The gamekeeper talks his dirt and the lady listens, but never once answers in kind. If she had, the gamekeeper would no doubt have been deeply scandalized.

Yet the language needs those words, they have a definite use and value and they should not be used carelessly or imprecisely. My contention is that obscenity is real, is necessary as expression, a safety valve against the almost intolerable pressures and strains of relationship between men and women, and not only between men and women but between any human being and his unmanageable world. If we distort, warp, abuse this language which is the seamy side of the noble language of religion and love, indeed the necessary defensive expression of insult toward the sexual partner and contempt and even hatred of the insoluble stubborn mystery of sex itself which causes us such fleeting joy and such cureless suffering, what have we left for a way of expressing the luxury of obscenity which, for an enormous majority of men, by their own testimony, is half the pleasure of the sexual act?

I would not object, then, to D. H. Lawrence's obscenity if it were really that. I object to his misuse and perversions of obscenity, his wrong-headed denial of its true nature and meaning. Instead of writing straight, healthy obscenity, he makes it sickly sentimental, embarrassingly so, and I find that obscene sentimentality is as hard to bear as any other kind. I object to this pious attempt to purify and canonize obscenity, to castrate the Roaring Boy, to take the low comedy out of sex. We cannot and should not try to hallow these words because they are not hallowed and were never meant to be. The attempt to make pure, tender, sensitive, washed-in-the-blood-of-the-lamb words out of words whose whole intention, function, place in our language is meant to be exactly the opposite is sentimentality, and of a very low order. Our language is rich and full and I daresay there is a word to express every shade of meaning and feeling a human being is capable of, if we are not too lazy to look for it; or if we do not substitute one word for another, such as calling a nasty word—meant to be nasty, we need it that way—"pure," and a pure word "nasty." This is an unpardonable tampering with definitions, and, in Lawrence, I think it comes of a very deep grained fear and distrust of sex itself; he was never easy on that subject, could not come to terms with it for anything. Perhaps it was a long hangover from his Chapel piety, a violent revulsion from the inane gibberish of some of the hymns. He wrote once with deep tenderness about his early Chapel memories and said that the word "Galilee" had magic for him, and that his favorite hymn was this:

> *Each gentle dove, and sighing bough,*
> *That makes the eve so dear to me,*
> *Has something far diviner now,*
> *That takes me back to Galilee.*
> *Oh Galilee, sweet Galilee,*
> *Where Jesus loved so well to be,*
> *Oh Galilee, sweet Galilee,*
> *Come sing again thy songs to me.*

His first encounter with dirty words, as he knew them to be, must have brought a shocking sense of guilt, especially as they no doubt gave him great secret pleasure; and to the end of his life he was engaged in the hopeless attempt to wash away that sense of guilt by denying the reality of its cause. He never arrived at the sunny truth so fearlessly acknowledged by Yeats, that "Love has pitched his mansion in the place of excrement"; but Yeats had already learned, long before, in his own experience that love has many mansions and only one of them is pitched there—a very important one that should be lived in very boldly and in hot blood at its own right seasons; but to deny its nature is to vulgarize it indeed. My own belief is this, that anything at all a man and a woman wish to do or say in their sexual relations, their lovemaking, or call it what you please, is exactly their own business and nobody else's. But let them keep it to themselves unless they wish to appear ridiculous at best, at worst debased and even criminal. For sex resembles many other acts which may in themselves be harmless, yet when committed in certain circumstances may be not only a sin, but a crime against human life itself, human feelings, human rights—I do not say against ethics, morality, sense of honor (in a discussion of the motives not of the author perhaps, but of the characters in this novel, such words are nearly meaningless), but a never-ending wrong against those elements in the human imagination which were capable of such concepts in the first place. If they need the violent stimulation of obscene acrobatics, ugly words, pornographic pictures, or even low music—there is a Negro jazz trumpeter who blows, it is said, a famous aphrodisiac noise—I can think of no argument against it, unless it might be thought a pity their nervous systems are so benumbed they need to be jolted and shocked into pleasure. Sex shouldn't be that kind of hard work, nor should it, as this book promises, lead to such a dull future. For nowhere in this sad history can you see anything but a long, dull gray monotonous chain of days, lightened now and then by a sexual bout. I can't hear any music, or poetry; or the voices of friends, or children. There is no wine, no food, no sleep nor refreshment, no laughter, no rest nor quiet—no love. I remember then that this is the fevered daydream of a dying man sitting under his umbrella pines in Italy indulging his sexual fantasies. For Lawrence is a Romantic turned wrong side out, and like Swift's recently flayed woman, it does alter his appearance for the worse—and his visions are easy, dreamlike, not subject to any real interruptions, and interferences—for like children they see the Others as the Enemy—a mixture of morning dew and mingled body-secretions, a boy imagining a female partner who is nothing but one yielding, faceless, voiceless organ of consent.

An organ, and he finally bestows on those quarters his accolade of approval in the language and tone of praise he might give to a specially succulent scrap of glandular meat fresh from the butcher's. "Tha's a tasty bit of tripe, th'art," he says in effect, if not in just those words. And adds (these *are* his words), "Tha'rt real, even a bit of a bitch." Why a bitch is more real than other forms of life he does not explain. Climbing on his lap, she confirms his diagnosis by whispering, "Kiss me!"

Lawrence was a very gifted, distraught man who continually overreached himself in an effort to combine all the authorities of artist, prophet, messiah, leader, censor, and mentor, by use of an unstable and inappropriate medium, the novel. His poetry and painting aside, he should be considered first as a writer of prose, and as a novelist. If a novelist is going to be so opinionated and obstinate and crazed on so many subjects he will need to be a Tolstoy, not a Lawrence. Only Tolstoy could be so furiously and fiercely wrong. He can nearly persuade you by sheer overwhelming velocity of will to agree with him.

Tolstoy once said—as reported by Gorky in his little memoir of Tolstoy—that in effect (I have the book in the house, but cannot find it now) the truth about women was so hideous he dared not tell it, except when his grave was dug and ready for him. He would run to it—or was it to his coffin?—tell the truth about women, and then pull the lid, or was it the clods, over his head. . . .

It's a marvelous picture. Tolstoy was merely roaring in the frenzy roused in him in face of his wife's terrible, relentless adoration; her shameless fertility, her unbearable fidelity, the shocking series of jealous revenges she took upon him for his hardness of heart and wickedness to her, the whole mystery of her oppressive femaleness. He did not know the truth about women, not even about that one who was the curse of his life. He did not know the truth about himself. This is not surprising, for no one does know the truth, either about himself or about anyone else, and all recorded human acts and words are open testimony to our endless efforts to know each other, and our failure to do so. I am only saying that it takes Homer or Sophocles or Dante or Chaucer or Shakespeare, or, at rather a distance, Tolstoy, to silence us, to force us to listen and almost to believe in their version of things, lulled or exalted or outraged into a brief acceptance. Lawrence has no grandeur in wrath or arrogance in love; he buzzes and darts like a wasp, irritable and irritating, hovering and bedeviling with a kind of insectlike persistence—he nags, in a word, and that is intolerable from anyone but surely unpardonable in an artist.

This tendency to nag, to disguise poorly as fiction a political, sociological tract, leads Lawrence, especially in this book, into some scenes on the grisly comic-order; they remind me of certain passages in *The Grapes of Wrath*, and pretty much on the same level, regarded as literature. Yet Steinbeck's genius for bathos never exceeded a certain scene by Lawrence which I have never heard mentioned by anyone, in talk or in print, by any critic however admiring—certainly, I have not heard all the talk or seen all the print on this subject—but I sympathize with this omission for I hardly know where to begin with it. It is the unbelievably grotesque episode of this besotted couple weaving flowers in each other's pubic hair, hanging bouquets and wreaths in other strategic bodily spots, making feeble little dirty jokes, inventing double-meaning nicknames for their sexual organs, and altogether, though God knows it is of an imbecilic harmlessness, and is meant in all solemn God's-earnestness to illustrate true passion at lyric play, I for one feel that I have overheard talk and witnessed acts never meant for me to hear or witness. The act itself I could not regard as shocking or in any way offensive except for its lack of reserve and privacy. Lovemaking surely must be, for human beings at our present state of development, one of the more private enterprises. Who would want a witness to that entire self-abandonment and helplessness? So it is best in such a case for the intruder to tip-toe away quietly, and say nothing. I hold that this is not prudery nor hypocrisy; I still believe in the validity of simple respect and regard for the dark secret things of life—that they should be inviolable, and guarded by the two who take part, and that no other presence should be invited. Let us go on with the scene in question. The lovers are in his gamekeeper's lodge, it is raining, the impulsive woman takes off to the woods, stark naked except for a pair of rubbers, lifting her heavy breasts to the rain (she is constitutionally overweight), and doing eurythmic movements she had learned long ago in Dresden. The gamekeeper is so exalted by this spectacle he takes out after her, faunlike, trips her up, and they splash about together in the rilling rainwater. . . . It could, I suppose, be funnier, but I cannot think how. And somewhere in these ex- tended passages the gamekeeper pauses to give his lady a lec- ture on the working class and its dullness due to the industrial system. He blames everything on the mechanized life "out there," and his complaint recurs with variations: "Though it's a shame, what's been done to people these last hundred years: man turned into nothing but labour-insects, and all their man- hood taken away, and all their real life." Hadn't Lawrence got

any notion of what had been done to such people the hundred
years before the last, and the hundred before that, and so on,
back to the beginning?

Yet both the lovers did accept the standards of her world in appearances at least; over and over she observes that her gamekeeper is really quite elegant or self-possessed or looks "like a
gentleman," and is pleased to think that she could introduce
him anywhere. He observes the same thing of himself from
time to time in an oblique way—he is holding his own among
them, even now and again putting them down. Here are
glimpses of Lady Chatterley sizing up Mellors on their first
meeting: "He was a man in dark green velveteen and gaiters
. . . the old style, with a red face and red moustache and distant eyes. . . ." And later, she noted that "he breathed rather
quickly, through parted lips," while pushing his invalid employer's wheelchair uphill. "He was rather frail, really. Curiously full of vitality, but a little frail and quenched." Earlier she
has been described as "a soft, ruddy, country-looking girl, inclined to freckles, with big blue eyes, and curling hair, and a
soft voice and rather strong, female loins"; in fact, "she was
too feminine to be quite smart."

Essentially, these are fairly apt descriptions of Lawrence and
Frieda Lawrence, as one would need only to have seen photographs to recognize. This is useful only because the artist's life
is always his material and it seems pointless to look for hidden
clues when they are so obviously on the surface. Lawrence the
man and Lawrence the artist are more than usually inseparable:
he is everywhere, and everywhere the same, in his letters, his
criticism, his poetry, his painting, the uneasy, suffering, vociferous man who wanted to be All-in-All in all things, but never
discovered what the All is, or if it exists indeed. This will to
omniscience is most clearly seen in *Lady Chatterley's Lover*. In
the entire series of sexual scenes, growing in heat and intensity
quite naturally, with the language not coarsening particularly,
it could not be coarser than it began, there is only more of
it, with the man showing off his prowess as he perceives his
success—all this is exposed from the point of view of the
woman. Lawrence constantly described what the man *did*, but
tells us with great authority what the woman *felt*. Of course,

he cannot possibly know—it is like a textbook of instructions to a woman as to how she *should* feel in such a situation. That is not his territory, and he has no business there. This shameless, incessant, nosy kind of poaching on the woman's nature as if determined to leave her no place of her own is what I find peculiarly repellent. The best he can ever do is to gather at secondhand, by hearsay, from women, in these matters; and though he had the benefit no doubt of some quite valid confidences and instruction from women entirely honest with him, it still just looks pretty fraudulent; somehow he shouldn't pretend he is the woman in the affair, too, as well as the man. It shows the obsessional nature of his self-centeredness; he gives the nightmarish impression of the bisexual snail squeezed into its narrow house making love to itself—my notion of something altogether undesirable even in the lowest possible forms of life. We have seen in his writings his hatred and distrust of women—of the female principle, that is; with some of its exemplars he managed to get along passably—shown in his perpetual exasperated admonition to woman to be what he wants her to be, without any regard to what she possibly may be—to stop having any will or mind or indeed any existence of her own except what he allows her. He will dole out to her the kind of sex he thinks is good for her, and allow her just the amount of satisfaction in it he wishes her to have—not much. Even Lady Chatterley's ration seems more in the head than in the womb.

Yet, where can it end? The gamekeeper, in spite of a certain fragility of appearance, seems to be the fighting-cock sort, wiry and tough enough, and he certainly runs through a very creditable repertory of sexual styles and moods. Yet he is a man of physical limitations like any other. Lady Chatterley is the largish, slow-moving, solid sort, and we know by her deeds and her words she is not worn down by an active mind. Such a woman often wears extremely well, physically. How long will it be before that enterprising man exhausts himself trying to be everything in that affair, both man and woman too, while she has nothing to do but be passive and enjoy whatever he wants her to have in the way he wants her to have it? It seems to me a hopelessly one-sided arrangement, it places all responsibility on him, and he will be the loser. Such a woman could use up half a dozen such men, and it is plain already that she will shortly be looking for another man; I give him two years at the rate he is going, if sex is really all he has to offer her, or all she is able to accept. For if sex alone is what she must have, she will not abide with him.

Jean Cocteau has told somewhere a terrible story of a priest in a hotel, who hearing the death-rattle of a man in the next room, mistook it for animal noises of a successful intercourse and knocked censoriously on the wall. We should all be very careful not to make the same mistake.

Lawrence, who was prickly as a hedgehog where his own privacies were concerned, cannot in his mischievous curiosity allow to a woman even the privacy of her excremental functions. He has to tell her in so many words just where her private organs are located, what they are good for, and how praiseworthy he finds the whole arrangement. Nothing will do for him but to try to crawl into her skin; finding that impossible, at last he admits unwillingly a fact you would think a sensible person would have been born knowing, or would have learned very early: that we *are* separate, each a unique entity, strangers by birth, that our envelopes are meant as the perfect device for keeping us separate. We are meant to share, not to devour each other; no one can claim the privilege of two lives, his own and another's.

Mr. Schorer in his preface hails the work as "a great hymn to marriage." That, I should say, it is not, above all. No matter what the protagonists think they are up to, this is the story of an "affair," and a thoroughly disreputable one, based on the treachery of a woman to her husband who has been made impotent by wounds received in war; and by the mean trickery of a man of low origins out to prove he is as good as, or better than, the next man. Mr. Schorer also accepts and elucidates for us Lawrence's favorite, most pathetic fallacy. He writes:

The pathos of Lawrence's novel arises from the tragedy of modern society. What is tragic is that we cannot feel our tragedy. We have grown slowly into a confusion of these terms, these two forms of power, and in confusing them we have left almost no room for the free creative functions of the man or woman who, lucky souls, possess "integrity of self." The force of this novel probably lies in the degree

of intensity with which his indictment of the world and the conse-
quent solitude of his lovers suggest such larger meanings.

If Mr. Schorer means to say—he sometimes expresses himself a little cloudily—that the modern industrial world, Lawrence's pet nightmare, has destroyed, among a number of
other things, some ancient harmony once existing between the
sexes which Lawrence proposes to restore by uttering of short
words during the sexual act, I must merely remind him that all
history is against his theory. The world itself, as well as the relationship between men and women, has not "grown into
confusion." We have never had anything else, or anything much
better; all human life since recorded time has been a terrible
struggle from confusion to confusion to more confusion, and
Lawrence, aided by his small but vociferous congregation—for
there remain in his doctrine and manner the style of the parochial messiah, the Chapel preacher's threats and cajolements
—has done nothing but add his own peculiar mystifications to
the subject.

One trouble with him, always, and it shows more plainly
than ever in this book, is that he wanted to play all the roles, be
everywhere and everybody at once. He wished to be the godhead in his dreary rigamarole of primitive religion as in *The
Plumed Serpent*, but must be the passive female too. Until he
tires of it, and comes up with a fresh set of rules for everybody.
Mr. Schorer cites a passage from a letter Lawrence wrote to
someone when his feelings were changing. "The leader-cum-
follower relationship is a bore," he decided, "and the new relationship will be some sort of tenderness, sensitive, between
men and men, and between men and women." He gets a good
deal of himself into these few words. First, when he is tired of
the game he has invented and taught as a religion, everybody
must drop it. Second, he seems not to have observed that tenderness is not a new relationship between persons who love
one another. Third, he said between men and men, and men
and women. He did not say between women and women, for
his view of women is utterly baleful, and he has expressed it ferociously over and over. Women must be kept apart, for they
contaminate each other. They are to be redeemed one by one
through the sexual offices of a man, who seems to have no

other function in her life, nor she in his. One of the great en-
lightenments of Lady Chatterley after her experience of the
sentimental obscenities of her gamekeeper is to see other
women clearly, women sexually less lucky than she, and to realize that they are all horrible! She can't get away fast enough,
and back to the embraces of her fancy man—and yet—and
yet—

True marriage? Love, even? Even really good sex-as-such? It
seems a very sad, shabby sort of thing to have to settle for,
poor woman. I suppose she deserves anything she gets, really,
but her just deserts are none of our affair. The pair are so
plainly headed, not for tragedy, but just a dusty limbo, their
fate interests us as a kind of curiosity. It is true that her youth
was robbed by her husband's fate in the war. I think he was
worse robbed, even with no way out, yet nobody seems to feel
sorry for him. He is shown as having very dull ideas with conversation to match, but he is not more dull than the gamekeeper, who forgets that the lady's aristocratic husband was
not born impotent, as Lawrence insists by way of his dubious
hero, all upper class men were. At this point Lawrence's confusion of ideas and feelings, the pull and haul between his
characters who go their own dreary way in spite of him, and
the ideas he is trying to express through them, become pretty
nearly complete. It would take another book to thread out and
analyze the contradictions and blind alleys into which the
reader is led.

   Huizinga, on page 199 of his book, *The Waning of the Middle
Ages*, tells of the erotic religious visions of a late medieval
monk, and adds: "The description of his numerous visions is
characterised at the same time by an excess of sexual imagination and by the absence of all genuine emotion." Lawrence
used to preach frantically that people must get sex out of their
heads and back where it belongs; and never learned that sex
lives in all our parts, and must have the freedom of the whole
being—to run easily in the blood and nerves and cells, adding
its glow of life to everything it touches. The ineptitudes of these
awful little love-scenes seem heart-breaking—that a man of
such gifts should have lived so long and learned no more about
love than that!

"The Laughing Heat of the Sun"

The Canticle of the Rose:
Selected Poems 1917–1949, by Edith Sitwell.
New York: The Vanguard Press, 1949.

O F all fine sights in the world to me, the best is that of an artist growing great, adding to his art with his years, as his life and his art are inseparable. Henry James's and W. B. Yeats's careers occur to mind first as spectacles in which I took delight, and Edith Sitwell, with *The Canticle of the Rose*, the collected volume of her work of more than thirty years, joins them. The true sign of this growth, in all alike, is the unfailing renewal, the freshness of every latest piece of work, the gradual, steady advance from phase to phase of increased power and direction, depth of feeling, and virtuosity, that laurel leaf added to technical mastery. Decade by decade, the familiar voice adds other notes to its range, a fuller tone, more sustained breath: an organic growth of the whole being.

Miss Sitwell's early work belonged to youth—it had the challenging note of natural arrogance, it was boldly experimental, inventive from a sense of adventure, full of high spirits and curiosity as to how many liberties the language would suffer to be taken without hitting back. There was sometimes also a certain artifice, the dew upon the rose turned out to be a crystal bead on a mother-of-pearl petal. Yet it was the work of a deft artificer, and a most ornamental rose, meant to amuse and charm, never intended to be mistaken for a natural flower.

It was the shimmer, the glancing light of this wit, this gaiety, one found so refreshing, for they were qualities markedly absent from the serious poetry of that long grim generation of censorious poets who were her contemporaries or later. Hardly anyone knew how to laugh, and those who did hardly dared to; it was no time for frivolity, and laughter was frivolous in such a murderous time. Miss Sitwell dared: she laughed outright whenever she felt like it, and the reader laughed too: for plainly this laughter was not levity nor frivolity, it was the spontaneous merriment of a vital spirit, full of natural courage

635

and confidence. The idea of death, which has paralyzed the humanity of so many poets for more than a century, affected her very differently. In the old robust way, she set out to make hay while her sun still shone. One felt this quality in her then, one is reassured of it now: "My poems are hymns in praise of the glory of life," she writes without any shade of apology for such an antique point of view. This praise is as clear in the early "Trio for Two Cats and a Trombone," or "Hornpipe," as it is in "Still Falls the Rain," written during a night raid in 1940.

The glory of life—the force of the affirmative passion of love in this poet, the feeling for glory in her, are the ground-virtues of her art, twin qualities almost lost for the present in the arts as in all human existence; as in her youth it sharpened her wit and her comedy, in middle life her sensuous celebration of the noble five human senses, in age her spiritual perceptions. This is such a progression as makes life and art worth practicing.

Her early poetry was, for me, associated, for all its "modern" speed and strepitation, with the old courtly music of Lully, Rameau, Purcell, Monteverdi, that I loved and do love: festival music, meant to be played in theaters, at weddings, christenings, great crystal-lighted banquets; or in the open air, in sweet-smelling gardens and the light of the full moon, with the torches waving their banners under the trees—gay music, serious great music, one can trust one's joy in it.

So with Edith Sitwell's poetry in those days between two wars, and so it is still. I am tempted to pick out here and there a few lines from some of those early things, but they do not take well to it. They are in full flight, it would be like plucking feathers from a bird. Pretty feathers, but they do not sing. Every word, every syllable does its part toward the final effect —her country songs are fresh as country mornings; her kitchen songs are a welter of sooty pots, hard cold early light and tangle-haired sleepy girls fighting with early cook-fires that will not catch. The beggar maid is "that pink flower spike full of honey." Rain is rain in these poems, it rains on the page and you can smell it and feel it. There are "horses as fat as plums" —of course, I have seen them. When witches are on the prowl, one ". . . hears no sound but wind in trees;/One candle spills out thick gold coins,/Where quilted dark with tree shade joins." Who does not remember ". . . the navy-blue ghost of Mr. Belaker/The allegro Negro Cocktail shaker?" asking, at four in the morning, his violent, unanswerable question, "Why did the cock crow? Why am I lost?" "The gaiety of some" (of her poems) "masks darkness," writes Miss Sitwell.

Large numbers of the public felt lost, too. It all sounded horridly novel and they hated it. Miss Sitwell did not have an easy time of it. The story has been told by her brother Sir Osbert Sitwell in his memoirs, so we need not go into it here. After all these years, Time having brought it about that Miss Sitwell is now being called "classic" by the younger generation, she being famous, a Doctor of Letters, at last she has time to sit down and explain what she was doing in those days and why, and what she meant by it.

She chooses many poems, those which caused the most disturbance when they were new; line by line, syllable by syllable, sometimes letter by letter, patiently she threads out meanings and makes a design of them. It makes good sense—that good sense the artist can always make of his intentions and methods after he has done the work. It is an endearing habit artists have, and I find nothing so enthralling as to hear or read a good artist telling how he does it. For practical purposes he might as well try to communicate his breath for our use. For example, Miss Sitwell chooses words not only for their meaning, but for sound, number of syllables, color, shape, texture, speed or slowness, thickness, thinness, weight, and for the shadow they cast upon the words near them. "Said King Pompey" is built on a scheme of R's for very good reasons. It is also "a poem about materialism and the triumphant dust."

Her introduction to *The Canticle* is good reading, and you can see, by the passages she cites, that whether or not it was so deliberate a thing as she now believes, she got her effects by just the means she says she did; a good deal more than most artists can prove. Beginning poets should be warned that this is not a ready-made technique, a bridge to anywhere. The live, inborn instinct for language, for the mother-tongue, must first be present, and whoever else has it to anywhere near this degree, will not get anything from Miss Sitwell except the pleasure of reading her poetry and an incitement to get on with his own work. This is about all that one artist can do for another, and it is really quite enough.

This poet's vision: "Seeing the immense design of the world, one image of wonder mirrored by another image of wonder—the pattern of fern and feather by the frost on the window-pane, the six rays of the snowflake mirrored in the rock-crystal's six-rayed eternity—seeing the pattern on the scaly legs of birds mirrored in the pattern of knot-grass, I asked myself, were those shapes molded by blindness? Are not these the correspondences, to quote a phrase of Swedenborg, whereby we speak with the angels?" Her theme: the eternal theme of saints and poets: the destiny of Man is to learn the nature of love and to seek spiritual rebirth. Her range of variations on this theme is endless. Every poem therefore is a love poem, even those towering songs of denunciation out of her counter-passion of hatred for the infamies of life and the willful wrong man does to the image of God in himself. So many peevish and obscene little writers of late have been compared to Swift I hesitate to set his name here even where I feel it is not out of place. In "Gold Coast Customs" I find for the first time in my contemporary reading a genius for invective as ferocious as Swift's own, invective in the high-striding authoritative style, the same admirable stateliness of wrath, the savage indignation of a just mind and generous heart outraged to the far edge of endurance. The mere natural murderousness of the human kind is evil enough, but her larger rejection is of "the terrible ideal of useless Suffering" symbolized by "Lazarus, the hero of death and the mud, taking the place in men's minds of the Hero of Life who was born in a stable."

This passage is from "Gold Coast Customs":

> But Lady Bamburgher's Shrunken Head
> Slum hovel, is full of the rat-eaten bones
> Of a fashionable god that lived not
> Ever, but still has bones to rot:
> A bloodless and an unborn thing
> That cannot wake, yet cannot sleep,
> That makes no sound, that cannot weep,
> That hears all, bears all, cannot move—

> It is buried so deep
> Like a shameful thing
> In that plague-spot heart, Death's last dust-heap.

Again: "Though Death has taken/And pig-like shaken/Rooted, and tossed/the rags of me—"

"At one time," writes Miss Sitwell, "I wrote of the world reduced to the Ape as mother, teacher, protector. But too, with poor Christopher Smart, I blessed Jesus Christ with the Rose and his people, a nation of living sweetness. My time of experiment was over."

This was later, and there is still the vast middle section of the work, the rages, the revolts, the burning noon of drunkenness on sensuous sound and image, the exaltation of the pagan myth, the earth's fertility; the bold richness of the roving imagination taking every land and every sea, every far-off and legendary place, every dream and every nightmare of the blood, every response of every human sense for its own. In this part, I find my own favorites are all, one way or another, songs of mourning: "Colonel Fantock"; "Elegy on Dead Fashion"; "Three Rustic Elegies"—"O perfumed nosegay brought for noseless death!" She acknowledges his power over the suffering flesh, the betrayed heart: but he can plant only carrion which belongs to his kingdom of the dust; Christ the Golden Wheat sows Himself perpetually for our perpetual resurrection. Rarely in the poetry of our time is noseless death stared down so boldly.

"After 'Gold Coast Customs,'" writes Miss Sitwell, "I wrote no poetry for several years, with the exception of a long poem called 'Romance,' and one poem in which I was finding my way. Then after a year of war, I began to write again—of the state of the world, of the terrible rain" (of bombs). During this long pause, she made the transition from the short, violently accented line, to a long curving line, a changed tone and pace. Of the late poems, the first one begins:

> I who was once a golden woman like those who walk,
> In the dark heavens—but am now grown old
> And sit by the fire, and see the fire grow cold,
> Watch the dark fields for a rebirth of faith and of wonder.

Again, in "Tattered Serenade":

> These are the nations of the Dead, their million-year-old
> Rags about them—these, the eternally cold,
> Misery's worlds, with Hunger, their long sun
> Shut in by polar worlds of ice, known to no other,
> Without a name, without a brother,
> Though their skin shows that they yet are men.

In these later poems, without exception tragic, a treasure of distilled tragic experience, the mysterious earthly rapture is mingled with a strain of pure, Evangelical Christianity, raised to the apocalyptic vision. Here, rightly, are some of the most wonderful (wonderful, and I know the meaning of that word) love songs in the English language: "Anne Boleyn's Song"; "Green Song"; "The Poet Laments the Coming of Old Age"; "Mary Stuart to James Bothwell"; and here begins the sustained use of the fire symbols, of gold the color of fire, the sun, the sun's flame, the gold of wheat, of lions' manes, of foxes' pelts, of Judas' hair, fire of the hearth, molten gold, gold seed, the gold of corn, golden cheeks, golden eyelids; "the great gold planets, spangling the wide air," "gold-bearded thunders"—a crescendo of rapture in celebration of fire after the ice-locked years of war when fire carried only death. As every symbol has many meanings, and is corruption or purification according to its relationships, so the sun, "the first lover of the earth," has been harnessed by man to his bloody purposes, and must be restored as the lover, as the giver of life:

> And I who stood in the grave-clothes of my flesh
> Unutterably spotted with the world's woes,
> Cry, "I am Fire. See, I am the bright gold
> That shines like a flaming fire in the night—the gold-trained
>   planet,
> The laughing heat of the Sun that was born from darkness."

In "The Song of the Cold," the cold which is the symbol of poverty, death, the hardened human heart, there is the final speech of marrow-frozen grief: "I will cry to the Spring to give me the birds' and the serpents' speech,/That I may weep for those who die of the cold—" but "The Canticle of the Rose" says:

The Rose upon the wall
Cries—"I am the voice of Fire:
And in me grows
The pomegranate splendor of Death, the ruby, garnet, almandine
Dews: Christ's wounds in me shine!"

This is the true flowering branch springing fresh from the old, unkillable roots of English poetry, with the range, variety, depth, fearlessness, the passion and elegance of great art.

The Art of Katherine Mansfield

The Short Stories of Katherine Mansfield,
with an introduction by John Middleton Murry.
New York: Alfred A. Knopf, 1937.

THIS past fourteenth of October [1937] would have been Katherine Mansfield's forty-ninth birthday. This year is the fifteenth since her death. During her life she had a fabulous prestige among young writers in England and America. Her readers were not numerous but they were devoted. It must be a round dozen years since I have read any of her stories; reading them again in the collected edition, I am certain she deserved her fame, and I wonder why it was not greater.

Of late I find my interest diverted somewhat from her achievement as artist to the enigma of her personal history. Actually there is little in her work to justify this, since the work itself can stand alone without clues or notes as to its origins in her experience; a paper chase for autobiographical data in these stories may be interesting in itself, but it adds nothing to the value of the stories. They exist in their own right. Yet I find it impossible to make these few notes without a certain preoccupation with her personal life of constant flight and search with her perpetual longing for certainties and repose; her beginnings in New Zealand; going to London to find the kind of place and the kind of people she wanted; her life there first as musician and then as writer; the many influences upon her mind and emotions of her friends and enemies—who in effect seem to have been interchangeable; her prolonged struggle with tuberculosis; her insoluble religious dilemma; her mysterious loss of faith in her own gifts and faculties; the disastrous failure of her forces at thirty-three, and the slowly engulfing despair that brought her finally to die at Fontainebleau.

These things are of first importance in a study which is yet to be done of the causes of Katherine Mansfield's own sense of failure in her work and in her life, but they do little to explain the work itself, which is superb. This misplaced emphasis of my attention I owe perhaps to her literary executor,* who has edited and published her letters and journals with a kind of merciless insistence, a professional anxiety for her fame on what seems to be the wrong grounds, and from which in any case his personal relation to her might have excused him for a time. Katherine Mansfield's work is the important fact about her, and she is in danger of the worst fate that an artist can suffer— to be overwhelmed by her own legend, to have her work neglected for an interest in her "personality."

There are eighty-eight stories in the collected edition, fifteen of which, her last, were left unfinished. The matter for regret is in these fifteen stories. Some of her best work is in them. She had been developing steadily, along a straight and fairly narrow path, working faithfully toward depth and concentration. Her handling of her material was firmer, her style had reached the flexibility of high tension and control, she had all her prime virtues and was shedding her faults, but her work had improved strictly in kind and not in difference. It is the same quick, ironic, perceptive mind, the same (very sensual) emotional nature, at work here from beginning to end.

In her the homely humility of the good craftsman toward his medium deepened slowly into a fatal self-distrust, and she set up for herself a standard of impossible perfection. It seems to have been on the grounds of the morality of art and not aesthetics that she began to desire a change in her own nature, who would have had quite literally to be born again to change. But the point is, she believed (or was persuaded that she believed) she could achieve a spiritual and mental rebirth by the practice of certain disciplines and the study of esoteric doctrines. She was innately religious, but she had no point of reference, theologically speaking; she was unable to accept her traditional religion, and she did finally, by what appears to have been an act of the will against all her grain, adopt means to make her fatal experiment in purification. As her health failed, her fears grew, her religious impulse wasted itself in an anxious straining toward some unknown infinite source of strength, of energy-renewing power, from which she might at the cost of

*John Middleton Murry, her husband.

single-hearted invocation find some fulfillment of true being beyond her flawed mortal nature. Now for her help and counsel in this weighty matter she had all about her, at different periods, the advice and influence of John Middleton Murry, A. R. Orage, D. H. Lawrence, and, through Orage, Gurdjieff.

Katherine Mansfield has been called a mystic, and perhaps she was, but in the severe hierarchy of mysticism her rank cannot be very high. André Maurois only yesterday wrote of her "pure feminine mysticism." Such as it was, her mysticism was not particularly feminine, nor any purer than the mysticism of D. H. Lawrence; and that was very impure matter indeed. The secret of her powers did not lie in this domain of her mind, and that is the puzzle: that such a good artist could so have misjudged herself, her own capacities and directions. In that rather loosely defined and changing "group" of variously gifted persons with whom Katherine Mansfield was associated through nearly all her working years, Lawrence was the prophet, and the idol of John Middleton Murry. They all were nervously irritable, self-conscious, and groping, each bent on painting his own portrait (The Young Man as Genius), and Katherine Mansfield's nerves suffered too from the teaching and the preaching and the quarreling and the strange vocabulary of perverted ecstasy that threw a pall over any true joy of living.

She possessed, for it is in her work, a real gaiety and a natural sense of comedy; there were many sides to her that made her able to perceive and convey in her stories a sense of human beings living on many planes at once, with all the elements justly ordered and in right proportion. This is a great gift, and she was the only one among them who had it, or at least the only one able to express it. Lawrence, whose disciple she was not, was unjust to her as he was to no one else, and that is saying a good deal. He did his part to undermine her, and to his shame, for personal rather than other reasons. His long maudlin relationship with John Middleton Murry was the source of his malignance toward her.

Mr. Murry's words in praise of her are too characteristic of the time and the special point of view to be ignored. Even today he can write that "her art was of a peculiarly instinctive kind." I confess I cannot understand the use of this word.

That she was born with the potentialities of an artist, perhaps? I judge her work to have been to a great degree a matter of intelligent use of her faculties, a conscious practice of a hard-won craftsmanship, a triumph of discipline over the unruly circumstances and confusions of her personal life and over certain destructive elements in her own nature. She was deliberate in her choice of material and in her methods of using it, her technical resources grew continually, she cleared away all easy effects and tricky turns of phrase; and such mastership is not gained by letting the instincts have it all their own way.

Again Mr. Murry, in his preface to the stories: "She accepted life . . . she gave herself . . . to life, to love . . . she loved life, with all its beauty and pain . . . she responded to life more completely than any writer I have known except D. H. Lawrence. . . ."

Life, love, beauty, pain, acceptance, response, these are great words and they should mean something, and their meaning depends upon their exact application and reference. Whose life? What kind of love? What sort of beauty? Pain from what cause? And so on. It was this kind of explicitness that Katherine Mansfield possessed and was able to use, when she was at her best and strongest. She was magnificent in her objective view of things, her real sensitiveness to climate, mental or physical, her genuinely first-rate equipment in the matter of the five senses, and my guess, based on the evidence of her stories, is that she by no means accepted everything, either abstractly or in detail, and that whatever her vague love of something called Life may have been, there was as much to hate as to love in her individual living. Mistakenly she fought in herself those very elements that combined to form her main virtue: a certain grim, quiet ruthlessness of judgment, an unsparing and sometimes cruel eye, a natural malicious wit, an intelligent humor; and beyond all she had a burning, indignant heart that was capable of great compassion. Read "The Woman at the Store," or "A Birthday," and "The Child-Who-Was-Tired," one of the most terrible of stories; read "The Fly," and then read "Millie," or "The Life of Ma Parker." With fine objectivity she bares a moment of experience, real experience, in the life of some one human being; she states no belief, gives no motives, airs no theories, but simply presents to the reader a situation, a place, and a character, and there it is; and the emotional content is present as implicitly as the germ is in the grain of wheat.

Katherine Mansfield has a reputation for an almost finicking delicacy. She was delicate as a surgeon's scalpel is delicate. Her choice of words was sure, a matter of good judgment and a good ear. Delicate? Read, in "A Married Man's Story," the passage describing the prostitute who has been beaten, coming into the shop of the evil little chemist for his famous "pick-me-up." Or such a scene as the fat man spitting over the balcony in "Violet"; or the seduction of Miss Moss in "Pictures." "An Indiscreet Journey" is a story of a young pair of lovers, set with the delicacy of sober knowledge against the desolate and brutalized scene of, not war, but a small village where there has been fighting, and the soldiers in the place are young Frenchmen, and the inn is "really a barn, set out with dilapidated tables and chairs." There are a few stories which she fails to bring off, quite, and these because she falls dangerously near to triviality or a sentimental wistfulness, of which she had more than a streak in certain moments and which she feared and fought in herself. But these are few, and far outweighed by her best stories, which are many. Her celebrated "Prelude" and "At the Bay," "The Doll's House," "The Daughters of the Late Colonel" keep their freshness and curious timelessness. Here is not her view of life but her many views of many kinds of lives, and there is no sign of even a tacit acquiescence in these sufferings, these conflicts, these evils deep-rooted in human nature. Mr. Murry writes of her adjusting herself to life as a flower, etc.; there is an elegiac poesy in this thought, but—and remember I am judging by her pages here under my eye—I see no sign that she ever adjusted herself to anything or anybody, except at an angle where she could get exactly the slant and the light she needed for the spectacle.

She had, then, all her clues; she had won her knowledge honestly, and she turned away from what she knew to pursue some untenable theory of personal salvation under a most dubious teacher. "I fail in my personal life," she wrote in her journal, and this sense of failure infected her life as artist, which is also personal. Her decision to go to Fontainebleau was no whim, no accident. She had long been under the influence of Orage, her first publisher and her devoted friend, and he was the chief disciple of Gurdjieff in England. In her last finished story, "The Canary," a deep parable of her confusion and despair, occurs the hopeless phrase: "Perhaps it does not so much matter what one loves in this world. But love something one must." It seems to me that St. Augustine knew the real truth of the matter: "It doth make a difference whence cometh a man's joy."

"The Canary" was finished in July, 1922. "In the October following she deliberately abandoned writing for a time and went into retirement at Fontainebleau, where she died suddenly and unexpectedly on the night of January 9, 1923." And so joined that ghostly company of unfulfilled, unhappy English artists who died and are buried in strange lands.

The Hundredth Role

The Book of Catherine Wells,
with an Introduction by Her Husband, H. G. Wells.
Garden City, N.Y.: Doubleday, Doran & Co., 1928.

Probably the best that a married pair have to offer each other at the end of a long life together is a courteous mutual apology. But this should be privately spoken and the secret guarded. Husbands and wives do ill to explain each other in print, more especially if the one explained is dead.

The preface written by Mr. H. G. Wells for the collected short stories of his wife is a singularly unfortunate example of the literature of marital bereavement. Catherine Wells was a noble wife, a happy mother and the maker of a free, kind and hospitable home. She was sweet and valiant, faithful, wise and self-forgetful. Pity and habitual helpfulness were very characteristic of her. She was stoical in suffering, shy and reserved in her real emotions and briskly impatient of nonsense in any form. She died with courage and dignity after months of suffering.

All this, it seems to me, should have served fully for the enrichment of Mr. Wells's life while she lived and for the present consolation of his memories. It is rather sadly beside the point in a preface written with the stated purpose of introducing Catherine Wells, not as the wife of her distinguished husband but as a talented writer of short stories.

The literary judgment of Mr. Wells seems somewhat at fault, too, as well as his taste in other matters. The short stories in this book of Catherine Wells have qualities of delicacy, tender feeling and a restrained fancy, but the book as a whole belongs to her husband and will attract the reader because his name is conspicuous on the cover.

This is sad and the end of a story full of irony. Amy Catherine Robbins meant to become a biologist; she married H. G. Wells while she was a member of his class in practical biology. This was about 1893. They had £50 between them and small expectations of a long life, for neither of them was in good health. Mrs. Wells developed at once the hundred-sided capacity necessary for successful wifehood to a driving, ambitious, vastly confused but completely self-centered literary man. The compromises, the adjustments of temperament to the common life were mainly hers: she furnished the faith and the attention to practical details of daily life; she was the charming companion and the good housekeeper; she acted as private secretary, literary agent and shock-absorber for her busy husband, and she had the legitimate satisfaction of seeing him famous and wealthy at an early age. The role of hostess to the many friends of fame now devolved upon her. She became a talented amateur actress and the inventive entertainer of her two children. Her gardens were works of art. Her husband and his friends even took the liberty of changing her name to fit their conception of her domestic character. They called her Jane and she answered to it cheerfully.

In the classic role of woman her life was complete. Yet this indefatigable woman asked for one thing more. She asked for one fragment of her mind that might be her own to use as she liked. She resolutely set herself to write and took no one, not even her husband, into her confidence. Through agencies unconnected with her husband and under her right name of Catherine she attempted to market her stories, rejecting the easy use of her husband's influence. Most of the stories remained unpublished.

Jane had quite supplanted Catherine. When Mrs. Wells searched that part of her mind left for her own uses there remained only the heroically suppressed preoccupations with death, the terror fantasies of ghosts, of childish disappointments and griefs, the young maiden dreams of frustrated romantic love. All the adult experiences of her life since marriage refused to be transmuted into literature. She could not evoke the realities of Jane on paper.

Within less than a year after her death the stories she could not publish by herself have been collected, chosen by her husband as final critic and introduced with his praise, his name joined to hers on the cover. Death served to force her withheld confidences and shatter her last reserves. The stories offer a strange contrast to the portrait her husband gives of a vivid, tireless, beautiful woman whose endless good sense and ground loyalty to the man of her choice make her a model for all good women and prove that she was a writer of very slender talents. An act of conscious cruelty could never have been so subtle.

"She stuck to me so sturdily that in the end I stuck to myself," says Mr. H. G. Wells. That is her epitaph.

Dylan Thomas

"A DEATH OF DAYS . . ."

Dylan Thomas in America: An Intimate Journal,
by John Malcolm Brinnin, with a foreword by Caitlin Thomas.
Boston: Atlantic Monthly Press/Little, Brown & Co., 1955.

JOHN MALCOLM BRINNIN has described this personal memoir of his friend and fellow-poet, Dylan Thomas, as an act of
exorcism, and the reader will easily understand why, as he reads
on; but I take it also as a very honorable attempt to set his
share of the record straight, at a time when the events he
writes about are so near and bitter a memory to him. Dylan
Thomas died two years ago [November 9th] in a New York
hospital of brain lesions caused by alcoholism.

Certain English newspaper critics were very quick to say that
we, the Americans, had in our usual thoughtless way destroyed
a great poet by tempting him with our easy money to work
himself to death traveling about exhibiting himself. It was not
easy money, to begin with, and after he was here the poet confessed that he hated his public readings and suffered fearful
anxieties on account of them. But he needed money desperately and this was something he could do well. It is perhaps
true that he came here out of despair, in his poverty and dis-
traction. This may have been the jumping-off place, but there
was going to be one soon, anywhere at all—time was closing in
on him; he was probably as well-off here as he would have
been anywhere at that exact time, for the simple reason that he
was not going to be well-off anywhere ever again.

But obviously he did not know this, and Mr. Brinnin's idea
of bringing him to this country, to arrange for him a transcon-
tinental poetry-reading tour, and to manage his financial affairs for the time being, resulted in one of those fateful events
which leaves moral and emotional wreckage, an almost incurable sense of wrong and bitterness and frustration in all those
concerned in it. Yet as so often happens, the thing began for
such good reasons, in such charming high hopes on Brinnin's

part, at least good faith, good motives, and splendid practical prospects all around.

There was quite simply nothing visibly wrong with the plan; Thomas confessed he had been longing for years to come to America, but nothing had happened to put him in the way of it. Brinnin, himself a fine poet, was in a position as director of programs for the Poetry Center to be positively helpful. Dylan Thomas was at the top of his fame, he had achieved what turned out to be his life work, and though his first youthful poetic fervor had passed, he appeared to be in a cycle of change for further development; yet, as all artists do at that time, he feared a waning of his powers. He needed a radical change by way of rest and refreshment; and he would make enough money to go back to Wales to his fishing village, his wife and three extraordinarily beautiful children and go on writing poetry.

This book is the story of disgrace and disaster and death that came of all these hopes and plans. For the poet the end was death, tragic yet sordid, in a strange uproar of conflicting claims and feelings, from the most oddly assorted lot of people; with hospital discipline and medical science and the few steadfast friends keeping vigil hardly able to stem the rush of rage and hysteria and melodrama of visitors to his bedside; and all around the cloud of scandal and outrageous gossip floated like dirty smoke in anybody's ears, leaving its gritty deposit in the memory. But the dying of the silent figure at the center of this disturbance, already wrapped in darkness, has its own majesty, and Brinnin never loses sight of this reality in the clutter of mean detail.

No man can be explained by his personal history, least of all a poet. Dylan Thomas' life was formed by his temperament, his genius, in relation—in collision—with his particular human situation. As Brinnin discovered in his saddest days, a drunken poet is not more interesting than any other drunken man behaving badly and stupidly. His daily, personal life in fact was no better than that of tens of thousands of dull alcoholics who never wrote a line of poetry. His poetry made the difference, and that is all the difference in this world. All his splendor and virtue are in this poetry—the terrors and follies of his short life here below may very well be put away and forgotten. He wrote his own epitaph, as a poet should: "This was not ever-lasting death, but a death of days; this was a sleep with no heart. We bury the dead, said the voice that heard my heart, the brief, and the everlasting."

"A FEVER CHART . . ."

Leftover Life to Kill, by Caitlin Thomas.
Boston: Atlantic Monthly Press/Little, Brown & Co., 1957.

"I added that I loved him still, and perhaps later . . . so re-luctant is love to part with any part of itself. Or should I say so tenacious is a bitch of her carrion meat." This is one of the milder tones of this book which Caitlin Thomas promised to write, telling her side of the story, in her foreword to John Malcolm Brinnin's memoir, *Dylan Thomas in America*. She felt bitterly injured then, and one might have expected a counter-attack. But time has worked its changes, and, while her hatreds of others and fierce repudiation of almost every human rela-tionship is as hot as ever (except for a few chosen ones who in-dulge her moods), her rage, as W. B. Yeats once described it, is now like a knife turned against itself. Subjective, self-centered to the last degree, she tells nothing that contradicts or falsifies Mr. Brinnin's story, nor the stories of others, even the wildest rumors that flew about. This is quite simply another story, from her own valid point of view, and a more painful one than any I have known.

On one plane it is a melancholy account of her furious at-tempts to waste and spoil her life out of a mingling of revenge against, and remorse for, her dead husband. It is a memoir, an apology, an accusation against God, the devil, life and death alike; a show-off temper tantrum with a vocabulary of self-hatred and abuse of others that often goes far beyond the merely outrageous. It is a losing battle to free herself from a medieval sense of guilt in an almost medieval ferocity of lan-guage: "I sought filthily to purge the blood-thronging devils out by using the devil's own filthier still instruments." These instruments seem to have been the husbands of her neighbors

during, the first year or two of her widowhood, if I make out
the time, first in Laugharne, where Dylan Thomas' family still
live, and then on the island of Elba, with her younger son,
Colm, the witness of her disorders.

She describes her daily life and habits as "buckets of squalor
and fecklessness." And though one feels that she does pile it
on at times, I daresay by any standards things were grubby and
wretched, even sordid. She confesses, or rather boasts, that
this was so, and it was as if she were determined to trample herself into the mud. Her husband, who thought women fit only
for bed and board, betrayed her as masculine matter of course,
but demanded of her the most rigid fidelity—not even a sidelong glance permitted. She therefore had two separate affairs
on the island where she had once visited with her husband,
both of them in the very room they had occupied together.

Both men were highly ineligible—one nearly as young as
her eldest son, the other her middle-aged landlord, with a wife
in the same house. She describes the young one as enchant-
ingly beautiful and charming, the older as a paragon of manly
virtue; yet I got the impression that the one was stupid as a
pot, and the other really vicious. She lived in sloth and lethargy,
in dirt and drunkenness; she describes herself as "stinking" for
want of a bath. The old lover slaps her around for jealousy and
orders her out of the house more than once as if she were a
sluttish servant, a tramp or a beggar; and she refuses to go and
will take any amount of abuse because she has no other place
to go. She was a woman noted for her beauty in the grand
style, and even this grace and treasure she treated with the utmost disrespect, as if she could not despise and destroy herself
brutally enough.

Why? It is a true mystery, and to her as much as to any one.
One might think it came about because of her fatal collision in
love, her marriage to a poet who had a secret he could not
share with her or with anyone, whose obstinate impervious
genius exasperated her, and whose final escape into death was
taken by her as a bitter personal wrong; but all this seems to
have been only the final provocation to a spirit blindly rebellious from the beginning.

She says of her disasters: "By such devilish devices, you'd
swear there was somebody behind it with the lowest inten-

tions; my rindy fruit of bitterness, already installed since child-hood, though I can trace no evidence of suppression," had tainted everything. She has always had this rage and panic in her, though she does not plead the shabby excuse of an un-happy, mistreated childhood. She says further: "My bitterness is not an abstract substance, it is solid as a Christmas cake. I can cut it in slices and hand it around and there is still plenty left for tomorrow." Wrath can be a great healing power when put to use in some direction or other—but this seems to be going nowhere. She rages that no one loves her, no one needs her, and that all she ever needed was love: and goes on to re-late some bloodchilling incidents of what she did to several un-fortunates who mistakenly took her at her word.

One has trouble following the line of this story because it is like a wild fever chart without the guiding squares on the background. The disorderly sentences and the relentless vio-lence of the style become at times as dull as dullness itself. In her writing, as apparently in her several other diffused talents, Mrs. Thomas is untrained and wildly runaway. She has no more control over her thoughts and method than she has over her emotions and behavior. I feel that she must be a wonderful talker and she might be a splendid writer if she had not such contempt for any and all disciplines. There are many passages of power and feeling as expressive as the most knowledgeable art could make them, and they seem accidental, though they may have been done in full consciousness. It is possible, for Mrs. Thomas regrets that she is not a spontaneous person, and that this book cost her heavy labor and suffering. We may well believe it.

So far as the actual events of her life go this is not an inter-esting or a particularly unusual story. There are too many women with ambitions beyond their talents, experiences beyond their capacity, with romantic daydreams of glory and fame as the center of attention—we have many of their sad histories.

If they happen to marry men of gifts or even genius, they in-evitably stubbornly refuse to play their natural role of second fiddle. But this one, Caitlin Thomas, passes all bounds; her war was with her god, hand-to-hand, like Lucifer's; she would be damned rather than take second place, and again, would be damned on her own terms. So this pathetic and apparently pointless escapade on Elba ends as it must; she takes away again the same despair that she brought with her.

Yet this book has a good reason to be and a beauty of its own. It is not only about dingy love affairs and senseless hatreds. It is a long lament, the heart-moving lyke-wake dirge that the widow Caitlin Thomas set down and brought back from her funerary island where she went to perform the antique rituals of tearing her hair and befouling her flesh in mourning. Sometimes she screams like a banshee; she howls and curses and blasphemes like a lost soul; even, though not often, she weeps like a woman. There is something grand and legendary in this self-punishing grief, a true note of wild primitive poetry which runs through the book, a theme with numberless variations, a refrain repeated and repeated to the hundredth return, as if there could never be an end to memory and to tears.

Beginning tenderly as a lullaby over the newly dead, not yet changed beyond recognition: "The same endearing childish hair," the tone changes to raptures of rebellion, to bitter, ugly memories, to resentment, to terrible grudges and remorse, to homely, dearly treasured things, to a nightmare vision of the rotting body in the grave and her ghoulish descent into the earth to feed again upon his corruptible part. It is a curiously impressive performance, and I could wish to see it isolated from the rest of the story, for I feel that this is what she really wished to say.

Yet—strange woman—after all this; after going back to that island where she had once been with her love, and there in search of a cure she had done all that she could to degrade and humiliate herself in all the ways that would most surely put her love and her marriage to shame, and offend most deeply the ghost of her husband, she says quite suddenly and flatly: "I was not even sure I ever loved Dylan."

After a short coda, the story closes, or rather, comes to a pause, on a note of sentimental collapse into total bathos of nursery rhyme and rather tardy maternal tenderness. And yet, and yet! There is a paradox of a hopeful kind in this whole muddle; it is a true chronicle of despair, it is not shameless, but shameful, it is not irreparable, for there is almost nothing one can do to be disgraced at present. Getting this book down on

paper must have been a good, hard, steady, galling job of work
—that in itself is a good sign of returning health and the sense
of form. In spite of hell, the afflicted, unhappy woman got this
work done, an act I don't doubt of positive therapeutic value.
She says herself somewhere in this work that sooner or later
one has to take hold and do plain hard work. I have always
doubted that art could be used as a medicine for the artist's
personal unhappiness or confusions. But this is not art, it is a
huge loud clamor out of the depths, and sometimes as oppressive to read as if the raging woman was in the same room
making daylight hideous with her unreason.

"IN THE MORNING OF THE POET . . ."

Dylan Thomas: Letters to Vernon Watkins,
edited, with an introduction, by Vernon Watkins.
New York: New Directions, 1957.

This collection of letters from Dylan Thomas to his best, earliest friend and fellow-poet, Vernon Watkins, is fresh and reassuring as a spring of water—a very lively spring to be sure,
bubbling and leaping and running sometimes through muddy
flats and stones and rubbish, but a true source, just the same; a
good long look at the poet in the morning of his energies and
gifts. So many persons have looked at Dylan Thomas through
themselves, it is a change for the better to have Thomas
looking at himself through a friend, a good, faithful, gifted
friend who played it straight. Here are no perverse sexual
motives, no wifely jealousy and rivalry, no literary hangers-on
elbowing each other out of the reflected glory, no wistful
would-be's hoping that a little of the genius would rub off on
them if only they could get close enough. Oh, none of all that
dreariness!
    Besides the early gaiety in some of the letters and the hub-
bub of daily life lived quite literally from hand to mouth, and
later family life and the almost constant shifting of domestic
arrangements, the eternal grind of poverty, which oppressed
him constantly for years, these pages record the growth of a

poet into the mastery of his art, and that with the simplicity of a man with his sleeves rolled up, working. The excitement of this occupation carries all the accidents and mischances of living triumphantly up to a certain point, and then the signs of exhaustion, the hints and surmises of disaster to come, begin to oppress the reader's mind—or is it only because we know the end?

Though Watkins adds no word of his own except the most reserved introduction, the reserve of the man who does not need to explain anything to anybody, and a few very enlightening notes to some of the letters, and though he saved all of Thomas' letters, while apparently Thomas saved none of Watkins', yet the latter is the central figure in this history of a friendship, which for all we know was unique in both their lives; a long, faithful friendship in which Watkins was the touchstone. Several very important letters, he says, "disappeared" mysteriously as letters of persons who become celebrated have a way of doing.

He accuses no one, but regrets that he did not publish earlier while the collection was intact, and mentions that, rather tardily, he has made copies of those still in his possession.

The dignity and restraint of Watkins in the face of the insoluble problem of how to guard your treasures from anonymous "collectors" is very impressive, but so is his entire character in this long-drawn-out trial of friendship. Their bond was poetry, the common topic between them which did not need to be defined—poetry, or rather, the making of poetry, the daily search for the word, getting it in the phrase, making it mean what it should mean and the best way of doing this; for they were both hard-working poets, and, in the end and in spite of all, nothing else.

It is strange, for those who know only the lamentable last years, to see Dylan Thomas treating anything or anybody with respect, but Watkins plainly had him convinced from the beginning, and I believe quite simply by his profound reserves of moral force, calm generosity, acute critical sense, besides a first-rate talent and a head start as a practicing poet who could teach Thomas a number of things he badly needed to know. Who could better instruct a Welsh poet than another Welsh poet? Each one liked the work of only two poets—his own and the other's. Far from being merely an amiable weakness, or narrowness (think of the vast reaches of poetry they agreed to ignore for the time being!) this mutual admiration was a source of strength to them both, and insured their unbroken attention to each other's words and feelings.

Then, besides, Thomas was by nature melancholy, living at odds with a world he never trusted, and how rightly; and he believed that Watkins was the only really happy person he knew, and for the only good reason, because he had come through everything and was safely out on the other side of the fears and horrors of life. All these circumstances, so formed and directed and given meaning by Watkins' own personal character, make up this lucky episode in both their lives.

For Thomas was the one always in trouble, one escapade after another, always needing to borrow money on the instant, asking for advice and quite often not taking it, making engagements for all sorts of occasions from tea "with toasted things" to Watkins' own wedding, and just not making it, by hair's breadth always.

He had a gorgeous sense of the comic whenever he could get his head above his troubles. Besides the constant discussion of poetry, the unbroken thread running through all the confusions and worries, his passing account of the events of his days fall on the page as freshly as talk; yet there is a certain reserve even in his bitter-merry letter about being stuck in Cornwall with a lady who speaks no language but Freud—nothing like the utter sprawl of his shameless confidences to others who have also published some of his letters.

This record begins in April, 1936, and ends December 29, 1952: that is, from youth to manhood, his whole life as poet, through marriage, fatherhood, part of the American adventure and the beginning of the end. He was enchanted with Caitlin: just after they were married he wrote to Watkins: "I think you'll like [her] very much, she looks like the princess on the top of a Christmas tree, or like a stage Wendy; but, for God's sake, don't tell her that." His children enchanted him: several of his best poems are written to or about his first son, Llewelyn, especially "This Side of the Truth."

His attachment to his family was touching, and another great poem, "Do Not Go Gentle into That Dark Night," was

written to his father. His people were of small means, no education worth mentioning, of humble occupation, of no particular ability in any member except the poet, and full of that
pious mediocrity which is the worst enemy not only of poets,
but of all life itself. Yet it is plain they loved him dearly and did
what they could for him.*

He was continually running back to them for shelter and
comfort long after he was a famous poet and a husband and
the father of two children and a third to come, and they shared
their miseries; "I am so cold this morning I could sing an
opera, all the parts, and do the orchestra with my asthma"
(November 23, 1948). And on the 13th of December, same
year, same place, same household: "All well, but poor and
tired here."

What is left is the poetry, and his book of letters to a friend.
Here is one dated February 1, 1939, that delights me almost
more than any: "Dear Vernon: This is just to tell you that
Caitlin and I have a son aged 48 hours. Its name is Llewelyn
Thomas. It is red-faced, very angry and blue-eyed. Bit blue,
bit green. Caitlin is well, and beautiful. I'm sorry Yeats is dead.
What a loss of the great poems he would write. Aged 73, he
died in his prime. Caitlin's address—if you would like to send
her a word—is Maternity Ward, Cornelia Hospital, Poole,
Dorset. Our love to you. Dylan."

*Note. Mr. Vernon Watkins wrote me a pleasant letter about this, saying
Dylan enjoyed telling stories about the hardships of his childhood, family
ignorance, and so on. They were certainly not rich, and they were religious
enough, but *not* illiterates—educated, respectable people, and most loving
and tender parents. n.b. I sent this letter to *The New York Times* to be published. The editor did not return the letter, and published it changed to appear
that the letter had been written to *The Times* instead of to me.

A Most Lively Genius

Short Novels of Colette: Cheri, The Last of Cheri,
The Other One, Duo, The Cat, The Indulgent Husband,
with an introduction by Glenway Wescott.
New York: The Dial Press, 1951.

THE important thing to read in this collection is Glenway Wescott's introduction. It is a labor of love, affectionate but unblinded; a deserved tribute to a most lively genius, full of Mr. Wescott's wry judgments—all well seated in a long knowledge of all the works, in French—possibly the only language that can ever really contain them—and a true introduction. This long study, or meditation, on the life and writings of Colette does his dear author the justice to tell the new reader who is depending on translations that these short novels, for all their varying brilliancy, are not her best work.

He re-tells from her own autobiographical writings, and with more reserve than she, the highlights of that long, difficult, complicated life of hers, much more absorbing, much deeper and more truthful, than any of her fictions. He relates this life, headlong, willful, full of gaiety and suffering, "almost scandalous," as he says, yet strangely disciplined and austere in sum, to her work; in the end she could absorb, survive, re-see and re-make almost everything. To an astonishing degree she could use her experience as an artist and yet not lose her memory of what it cost her as a living, growing human being; so that her later writings, especially about her disastrous, perverse first marriage, have a strange daylight, morning freshness on them that her earlier work did not have.

It was hardly fair to American readers to have kept Colette from them for so long; nor fair to Colette, either, who should have been the fashion here at least twenty-five years ago— when we think how her lessers were being brought in all that time with fanfares, from every direction. In France she has been known and loved and read from the beginning, and though one always heard of her as "a light writer," that was no term of disrespect—quite the contrary. The French above all know how much strength and discipline and even sheer genius it takes to write lightly of serious things; they never called her frivolous, far from it.

Yet there was always that tone of particular indulgence, reserved for gifted women who make no pretentions and know how to keep their place in the arts: a modest second-best, no matter how good, to the next ranking male. Wescott, mentioning that both Proust and Gide wrote her letters of praise, says, flatly: "For, now that the inditers are both dead and gone, Colette is the greatest living French fiction writer."

I agree to this extent: that she is the greatest living French writer of fiction; and that she was while Gide and Proust still lived; that these two preposterously afflicted self-adoring, frankly career-geniuses certainly got in Colette's light; they certainly diminished her standing, though not her own kind of genius. She lived in the same world, more or less in the same time—without their money or their leisure. Where they could choose their occasions, she lived on a treadmill of sheer labor. Compared to their easy road of acknowledged great literary figures, her life path was a granite cliff sown with cactus and barbed wire.

But she had the immense daylight sense of reality they both lacked and, beyond that, something that Gide tried all his life to have, or to appear to have, and which he lacked to the end: a genuine moral sense founded on a genuine capacity for human feeling. She never attempts to haul God into criminal collusion with the spiritual deformities of her characters. Being a generous woman born to be exploited by men, she has for some of them the abject tenderness and indulgence which is so terribly womanly. Yet she knows this; she does not deceive herself. And her women, if possible less attractive even than the men, are still women, which Proust's never were.

The beings who people these six short novels are all of the race of the half-born, the incomplete, turning each one in his narrow space. They have no minds to speak of, they are in a limbo of physical indulgences, and they live and die their desolate lives in the longest waking dream. In the end, it is middle-classness, incapacity for tragedy—or comedy either—for faith, for any steadfastness except in delusion and obsession. It is stupidity—which the introduction once charitably tries to interpret as innocence.

The two must not be confounded, ever; innocence is a not-knowing of childhood, or inexperience. Stupidity is the inability to learn in spite of experience. Innocence can lead the innocent into evil; stupidity is itself an evil. Colette is the wisest kind of artist; the light of her quick intelligence plays over this Limbo, in her warmth of emotion she cannot reject or condemn them, and here is the strangest thing—the stories are full of light, and air, and greenery and freshness, the gayest sparkle of laughter, all in a way misleading, if you like; for there is a satire of the sharpest kind in this contrast between the sordidness, the obstinate dreariness, of human conduct and motive, and the disregarded, the ignored, the unused possibilities for human happiness.

Colette conceals her aim, her end, in her method. Without setting her up in rivalry with her great jealous, dubious male colleagues and contemporaries, let us just be glad of such a good, sound, honest artist, a hard-working one; we could really do nicely with more "light writers" like her. The really light-weight ones weigh a ton beside her.

Orpheus in Purgatory

Rilke and Benvenuta: A Book of Thanks, by Magda von Hattingberg, translated from the German by Cyrus Brooks. New York: W. W. Norton & Co., 1949.

O N his fiftieth birthday, "What a bore, what futility!" Rilke wrote to a friend about all the flowers and messages and visitors. ". . . Naturally, if one looks at it justly, there was something dear in it, but where is the love that does not make more trouble?"

It is hardly possible to exaggerate the lovelessness in which most people live, men or women: wanting love, unable to give it, or inspire it, unable to keep it if they get it, not knowing how to treat it, lacking the humility, or the very love itself that could teach them how to love: it is the painfullest thing in human life, and, since love is purely a creation of the human imagination, it is merely perhaps the most important of all the examples of how the imagination continually outruns the creature it inhabits. . . . Having imagined love, we are condemned to its perpetual disappointment; or so it seems.

"You know Rilke . . . you know how he is and how much he means to me. . . . You have never asked how it will end. . . . I . . . have not asked that question either, and perhaps that was wrong of me, I have been happy with him in the present . . . because of his noble and lofty spirit . . . because of his inexhaustible kindness. Every time I saw him was a gift of God to me. And I thought that if some day he had to withdraw, and be quite alone with his work, then I should be alone again . . . far away from him, not hearing from him any more but guarding his holy image in my heart. I should almost forbid myself to think of him."

This is Magda von Hattingberg, Rilke's Benvenuta (The Welcome One), writing to her sister when her curious association, whatever its real nature, with Rainer Maria Rilke was drawing to its close in 1914. It had been brief: two months of letters, three of living together; and strange: for by this account, the obvious conditions of such a relationship seem never to have existed. They traveled openly together for those three months, to Paris, to Berlin, Munich, Venice, besides visits to houses and castles of his friends. Yet Benvenuta says plainly (and she does wrap some plain things in the sustained fanatic rapture of her style) that when they parted forever they kissed for the first and last time. This statement comes as rather an anticlimax after the heroic if fevered effort of an apparently healthy, all-too-feminine young woman to grow wings for her god, devoted as he was to angels.

One hardly knows where to place *Rilke and Benvenuta* in the clutter of letters, memoirs, critical studies, and biographies so steadily accumulating around Rilke's name. As much hysterical nonsense has been written about him as about D. H. Lawrence, if that is possible. Like Lawrence, his personal attractiveness drew to him the parasitic kind of adorers who insist on feeding on the artist himself instead of on his work: who make mystification of the mysterious, and scandals instead of legends. But Rilke was luckier than Lawrence in this: that he also had many faithful good friends who anxiously and constantly for long years succeeded in defending and helping him, almost in spite of himself. For he demanded, and would have, and would content himself with nothing less than, the humanly impossible in all human relationships. As relatives, friends, publishers now dole out mangled fragments of his literary estate, the secret of their long enchantment with him seems lost, for a temperament rather less than enchanting is being revealed little by little. His afterlife of fame is very similar to his former life in his restless, painful flesh: the perpetual unsatisfied guest, the helpless dependent, the alienated genius seeking silence and solitude to work out his destiny—Paul Valéry was shocked at the inhumanity of an "existence so separated . . . in such an abuse of the intimacy with silence, so much license given to one's dreams . . ."—the continuing stranger who claimed the veneration due to the poet, that is to say, prophet, priest, seer, one set apart by his tremendous mission. In the meantime: "One lives so badly one always comes into the present unready, unfit, and distraught for everything . . . only the ten days after Ruth's (his daughter's) birth, I think, did I live without the smallest waste; finding reality as indescribable, even to the smallest detail, as it doubtless always is." This to his wife in 1907.

By 1914 he had not yet discovered the truths of reality, indeed, it was not his goal; but after seven years of search and flight, of homelessness and poverty, added to his double sense of failure as human being and as poet—for the two warring beings were never to be reconciled in him—he was ready, or hoped he was ready, for "a more human and natural footing in life," and Magda von Hattingberg seemed to be the one who could provide it for him. She wrote him first, as women so often did, an adoring letter; he hastened to answer it, and thirty-five long years later, she publishes some of his letters—very interesting letters, too—some of hers, passages from her diary, some very valuable transcriptions of conversations they had, and for the rest, a rhapsodical, high-flung, farfetched romance which for style is an extraordinary blend of Marianna Alcoforado and The Duchess. . . .

In the best German Romantic tradition of the 1840's, not only all nature, and all society, but heaven itself, are tender accomplices in this transcendent episode. Nature especially assists with manifestations symbolically appropriate: the rains, the snows, the fogs, the sunshine, flowers of spring, arrive punctually; the moon is always obligingly full to witness a high encounter. They travel through enchanted landscapes like spirits in a dream, they even sit up all night outdoors somewhere at a crisis, she sleeps on his shoulder and the dawn finds them there, weary, a little stiff in their bones, but with exaltation undiminished. It is absurd, no other word for it. For the heroine was a young, beautiful, professional concert pianist, and too often, especially in the castles and drawing rooms, it is as if she played out her dream-romance on a grand piano, her costume always perfect, the moment perfect, the high-born spectators always on hand and attentive, the cultural ambience of the purest edelweiss.

But the fact that she has made herself so easy a target does not mean that she can be dismissed so easily. E. M. Butler, in her *Rilke*, tells her story in a few lines, and does not mention her name but quotes a letter from Rilke about her, written shortly after he had broken with her, broken with a decision and finality which shows plainly how dangerous to his future he considered her. For he was incapable of the kind of love she gave, and humanly wished to have from him; he could not endure the burden of her adoring warmth and energy and naturalness. After admitting that for years he had tried to flatter himself that his failures in love and in friendship had been the fault of others, that each in turn had violated, injured, wronged him, he writes: "I have entirely altered my opinion now after these last months of suffering. This time I have been obliged to rec- ognize the fact that no one can help me, no one at all. And even if he (she) should come with the best and most loving of hearts, and should prove his worth to the very stars . . . keeping his regard for me pure and untroubled, however often I broke the ray of his spirit with the cloudiness and density of my submarine world I would yet (I know it now) find the means to strip him of the fulness of his ever-renewed assistance, and to enclose him in a loveless vacuum, so that his useless succor would rot and wither and die a terrible death."

It is pleasant to know that none of this happened to his ten- derly nicknamed Benvenuta; she had to a triumphant degree the womanly knack of starving gracefully on the thinnest ra- tion of love, and yet at last spreads her own feast—a strange feast, but her food—out of that famine.

Only once had he succeeded in almost frightening her off. He was admiring some fantastic doll figure, and she protested that the virtue of a toy was in its effect on a child, and she could not imagine an innocent, healthy little girl not being re- pelled by this monster. Rilke proceeded to rip to shreds her notions of childish innocence, and to explain to her at length the innate corruptness of toys—and quoted also at length from his fierce essay against dolls, published shortly afterwards. She had unknowingly touched him on the quick: his mother had dressed him as a girl, and had given him dolls to play with.

The faithful and patient Princess Marie of Thurn and Taxis witnessed not only this love affair at one point, but many others with many other women. She was disconcerted, she wrote in her journal, at the attraction women had for Rilke. Rilke was equally disconcerted many times at the attraction he had for them: it seemed to him that what a man did only for God, a woman did always for a man. For a while he could impersonate a man, imitate his functions passably—provided the woman was infatuated enough, and most often she was, for women, of all sorts, and for all sorts of reasons, are flattered by the attentions of genius—even he could deceive himself into a plausible enough feeling, or a belief that he felt, or was capable of feeling, a natural, spontaneous sexual desire. But nothing of this could last: in no time at all he was faced with the terrible alternative: to go on with a eunuchlike sniffing and fumbling, or flight—flight in almost any direction, to any goal, even into another trap of womanly tenderness and incomprehension.

He depended in all faith, and with good reason too, on the tenderness and sympathy of women: all of them high-minded, romantic, some of them very gifted, many nobly born and rich: but alas, seekers after a man-god rather than the God in man. By the simplest means, and without any method except that provided by the natural duplicity of his need to be adored and taken care of, Rilke wove his web about them for good. This web was the Word—the Word multiplied, an endless spinning of high, poetic, noble words, flowing easily as a melody carrying with it painless didactic counsel, and if they had not been so flattered, they might have read as we do now the warning between the lines: This is what I have to give, ask for nothing more.

He flattered the soul, or the intellect, or the heart, or all three at once; whatever the individual woman craved that words could supply, he gave her generously. There were more than enough words to go around. Not one of them had any real right to complain, for he was faithful to them all, and he paid them the highest compliment of never confusing one of them with another. . . . And he asked of them all the same thing—that they would save him for himself and from them.

In Memoriam

FORD MADOX FORD
(1873–1939)

SEVERAL years ago Ford Madox Ford remarked to me, at Olivet—and to how many others? I don't know—with a real pride and satisfaction, that he had a book to show for every year of his life. Now he knew as well as anyone that no man can write sixty *good* books, he said himself there were books on that list he was willing to have out of print forever. But at the time of writing them, he had believed firmly each book was going to be good; in any case, each book was as good as he was capable of making it at that moment, that given circumstance; and in any case he could not have stopped himself from the enterprise, because he was a man of letters, born and bred. His life work and his vocation happened to be one and the same thing. A lucky man, in spite of what seems, sometimes, to the onlooker, as unlucky a life as was ever lived.

His labors were constant, his complicated seeking mind was never for one moment diverted from its speculations on the enduring topic of literature, the problems of creation, the fascinating pitfalls of technique, the moral, psychic, aesthetic aspects of art, all art, any one of the arts. He loved to live the life of the artist, he loved to discover, foster, encourage young beginners in what another admirer of his, Glenway Wescott, has described as "this severe and fantastic way of life." Toward the end, when he was at Olivet, Ford described himself as "an old man mad about writing." He was not really an old man— think of Hardy, think of Tolstoy, think of Yeats—and his madness was an illuminated sanity; but he had, when he wrote this, intimations of mortality in him, and he had always practiced, tongue in cheek, that "pride which apes humility." It pleased him to think of himself in that way; and indeed, when you consider his history, the tragic mischances of his life, his times of glory and success alternating with painful bouts with poverty and neglect, you might think, unless you were an artist, that he was a little mad to have run all the risks and to have taken all the punishment he did take at the hands of fortune—and for what? I don't think he ever asked himself that question. I doubt greatly he ever seriously considered for one moment any other mode of life than the life he lived. I knew him for twelve years, in a great many places and situations, and I can testify that he led an existence of marvelous discomfort, of insecurity, of deep and pressing anxiety as to his daily bread; but no matter where he was, what his sufferings were, he sat down daily and wrote, in his crabbed fine hand, with pen, the book he was working on at the moment; and I never knew him when he was not working on a book. It is not the moment to estimate those books, time may reverse his own severe judgment on some of them, but any of you who have read the Tietjens cycle, or *The Good Soldier*, must have taken a long step forward in your knowledge of craftsmanship, or just what it takes to write a fine novel. His influence is deeper than we are able to measure, for he has influenced writers who never read his books, which is the fate of all masters.

There was in all something so typical, so classical in his way of life, his history, some phases of his career, so grand in the old manner of English men of letters, I think a reading of his books and a little meditation on his life and death might serve at once as guiding sign and a finger of warning to all eager people who thoughtlessly, perhaps, "want to write." You will learn from him what the effort really is; what the pains, and what the rewards, of a real writer; and if that is not enough to frighten you off, you may proceed with new confidence in yourself.

1942

JAMES JOYCE
(1882–1941)

From the Notebooks

Boulder, Colorado. July, 1942. The death of James Joyce distressed me more than any other since the death of Yeats. How the tall old towers are falling: these were the men I most ad-

mired in my youth: I discovered Yeats for myself; he was the
first contemporary poet I read, and the first poem was in a
magazine in 1915:

> There is a Queen in China, or maybe 'tis in Spain
> And birthdays and holidays such praises can be heard
> Of her unblemished loveliness, a whiteness without stain
> You might think her that sprightly girl
> Was trodden by a bird.*

If this is not quite exact, it is the way I remembered it for years
and years before I saw it again in a collection. But beginning
there, and with his *Celtic Twilight*, a book which seems to have
disappeared, I followed Yeats with the most faithful adoring
love, and discovered a new shining world. Joyce came a little
later, but not much. I read *Dubliners* in 1917, and that was another revelation, this time of what a short story might be, even
though I had believed that *Chekov* had written the last one
worth reading, until then.

As between these two great artists, I should say that Yeats
was the greater imagination; Joyce did not have greatness in
the grand manner, as Yeats did: Joyce had a dryness of heart,
and very limited perceptions of human nature. Yeats *grew*
great, the only kind of greatness, really: as if all his life he was
fulfilling some promise to himself to use every cell of his genius to its fullest power. Yesterday's newspaper was just sent
over to me with an account of Joyce which reminded me of
the day I first heard of his death. He died in his second war
exile, two variations of his perpetual exile. He was a homeless
man, the most life-alienated artist of our time. Yet more than
anybody, he gave fresh breath and meaning to language, and
new heart, new courage, new hope to all serious writers who
came after him. Rest his soul in peace.

I saw him only once. When I first went to Paris, in February,
1932, he was already world-famous, half-blind, surrounded by

*"His Phoenix." It was later collected in the volume *The Wild Swans at
Coole* (1919) and appears as follows:

> There is a Queen in China, or maybe it's in Spain,
> And birthdays and holidays such praises can be heard
> Of her unblemished lineaments, a whiteness with no stain,
> That she might be that sprightly girl trodden by a bird.

friends all faithful to him, apparently, but jealous of each other, watching him for signs of favor, each claiming to be first, trying to prevent anyone new from coming near him: and on the outer rim of this group was a massed ring of eager followers trying to get into the sacred circle: it was pretty grim to witness even from a safe distance: but he had reached that point of near defenselessness against the peculiar race of people who live in reflected glory: I did not wish to see him, or speak to him—what was there to say? And it was no doubt true that no new acquaintance could do more than disturb or bore him. But I never went near him, and this idea of him was presented to me as the true state of affairs by Sylvia Beach, Eugene and Maria Jolas, by Ford Madox Ford, by all of the many persons I knew there who had known Joyce, and befriended him for years. I think, too, that most of them had quarreled more or less among themselves about Joyce, and in a way, with Joyce himself. Sylvia most certainly had good cause for her belated resentment of his callous use of her life; but no one I knew was really easy in regard to him: he seems to have been a preposterously difficult man to get along with. His blindness was like the physical sign of his mind turning inward to its own darkness: after all, if the accounts now given are true, it seems not to have been the optic nerves but his teeth: and at last his intestines killed him.

One evening a crowd gathered in Sylvia's bookshop to hear T. S. Eliot read some of his own poems. Joyce sat near Eliot, his eyes concealed under his dark glasses, silent, motionless, head bowed a little, eyes closed most of the time, as I could plainly see from my chair a few feet away in the same row, as far removed from human reach as if he were already dead. Eliot, in a dry but strong voice, read some of his early poems, turning the pages now and again with a look very near to distaste, as if he did not like the sound of what he was reading. I had been misled by that too-often published photograph showing him as the young Harvard undergraduate, hair sleekly parted in the middle over a juvenile, harmless face. The poet before us had a face as severe as Dante's, the eyes fiercely defensive, the mouth bitter, the nose grander and much higher bridged than his photographs then showed; the whole profile looked like a bird of prey of some sort. He might have been alone, reading to himself aloud, not once did he glance at his listeners.

Joyce sat as still as if he were asleep, except for his attentive expression. His head was fine and handsome, the beard and hair very becoming to the bony thrust of his skull and face, the face of "a too pained whitelwit," as he said it, in the bodily affliction and prolonged cureless suffering of the mind. . . .

To those of my own generation and after, I can only say, what would we have done without him? He had courage for all of us, and patience beyond belief, and the total intensity of absorption in his gift, and the will to live in it and for it in spite of hell: and more often than not, it was hell: but as bad and worse things have happened to many quite good men who suffered quite as much, who had no gift, no toy, no special mystery of their own, to console them.

1965

SYLVIA BEACH
(1887–1962)

A Little Incident in the Rue de l'Odéon

Last summer in Paris I went back to the place where Sylvia Beach had lived, to the empty bookshop, Shakespeare and Company, and the flat above, where she brought together for sociable evenings the most miscellaneous lot of people I saw; persons you were surprised to find on the same planet together, much less under the same roof.

The bookshop at 12 rue de l'Odéon has been closed ever since the German occupation, but her rooms have been kept piously intact by a faithful friend, more or less as she left them, except for a filmlike cobweb on the objects, a grayness in the air, for Sylvia is gone, and has taken her ghost with her. All sorts of things were there, her walls of books in every room, the bushels of papers, hundreds of photographs, portraits, odd bits of funny toys, even her flimsy scraps of underwear and stockings left to dry near the kitchen window; a coffee cup and a small coffeepot as she left them on the table; in her bedroom, her looking glass, her modest entirely incidental vanities, face powder, beauty cream, lipstick. . . .

Oh, no. She was not there. And someone had taken away the tiger skin from her bed—narrow as an army cot. If it was not a tiger, then some large savage cat with good markings; real fur.

I remember, spotted or streaked, a wild woodland touch shining out in the midst of the pure, spontaneous, persevering austerity of Sylvia's life; maybe a humorous hint of some hidden streak in Sylvia, this preacher's daughter of a Baltimore family, brought up in unexampled high-mindedness, gentle company and polite learning; this nervous, witty girl whose only expressed ambition in life was to have a bookshop of her own. Anywhere would do, but Paris for choice. God knows modesty could hardly take denser cover, and this she did at incredible expense of hard work and spare living and yet with the help of quite dozens of devoted souls one after the other; the financial and personal help of her two delightful sisters and the lifetime savings of her mother, a phoenix of a mother who consumed herself to ashes time and again in aid of her wild daughter.

For she was wild—a wild, free spirit if ever I saw one, fearless, untamed to the last, which is not the same as being reckless or prodigal, or wicked, or suicidal. She was not really afraid of anything human, a most awe-inspiring form of courage. She trusted her own tastes and instincts and went her own way; and almost everyone who came near her trusted her too. She laid her hands gently, irresistibly on hundreds of lives, and changed them for the better; she had second sight about what each person really needed.

James Joyce, his wife, his children, his fortunes, his diet, his eyesight, and his book *Ulysses* turned out to be the major project of her life; he was her unique darling, all his concerns were hers. One could want a rest cure after merely reading an account of her labors to get that book written in the first place, then printed and paid for and distributed even partially. Yet it was only one, if the most laborious and exhausting, of all her pastimes, concerned as she was solely with bringing artists together—writers preferred, any person with a degree of talent practicing or connected with the art of Literature, and in getting their work published and set before the eyes of the world. Painters and composers were a marginal interest. There was nothing diffused or shapeless in Sylvia's purpose; that bizarre assortment of creatures shared a common center—they were artists or were trying to be. Otherwise many of them had only Sylvia in common. She had introduced many of them to each other.

We know now from many published memoirs what Ford Madox Ford thought of Hemingway, what Hemingway thought of Ford and F. Scott Fitzgerald, how William Carlos Williams felt about Paris Literary Life, how Bryher felt herself a stranger to everyone but Sylvia. They seemed to be agreed about her, she was a touchstone.

She was a thin, twiggy sort of woman, quick-tongued, quick-minded and light on her feet. Her nerves were as tight as a tuned-up fiddle string and she had now and then attacks of migraine that stopped her in her tracks before she spun herself to death, just in the usual run of her days.

When I first saw her, in the early spring of 1932, her hair was still the color of roasted chestnut shells, her light golden brown eyes with greenish glints in them were marvelously benign, acutely attentive, and they sparkled upon one rather than beamed, as gentle eyes are supposed to do. She was not pretty, never had been, never had tried to be; she was attractive, a center of interest, a delightful presence not accountable to any of the familiar attributes of charm. Her power was in the unconscious, natural radiation of her intense energy and concentration upon those beings and arts she loved.

Sylvia loved her hundreds of friends, and they all loved her —many of whom loved almost no one else except perhaps himself—apparently without jealousy, each one sure of his special cell in the vast honeycomb of her heart; sure of his welcome in her shop with its exhilarating air of something pretty wonderful going on at top speed. Her genius was for friendship; her besetting virtue, generosity, an all-covering charity in its true sense; and courage that reassured even Hemingway, the distrustful, the wary, the unloving, who sized people up on sight, who couldn't be easy until he had somehow got the upper hand. Half an hour after he was first in her shop, Hemingway was sitting there with a sock and shoe laid aside, showing Sylvia the still-painful scars of his war wounds got in Italy. He told her the doctors thought he would die and he was baptized there in the hospital. Sylvia wrote in her memoirs, "Baptized or not—and I am going to say this whether Hemingway shoots me or not—l have always felt he was a deeply religious man."

Hemingway tried to educate her in boxing, wrestling, any kind of manly sport, but it seemed to remain to Sylvia mere reeling and writhing and fainting in coils; but Hemingway and Hadley his wife, and Bumby the Baby, and Sylvia and Adrienne Monnier, her good friend, all together at a boxing match must have been one of the sights of Paris. Sylvia tells it with her special sense of comedy, very acute, and with tenderness. Hemingway rather turns out to be the hero of her book, helping to bootleg copies of *Ulysses* into the United States, shooting German snipers off her roof on the day the American army entered Paris; being shown in fact as the man he wished and tried to be. . . .

As I say, Sylvia's friends did not always love each other even for her sake, nor could anyone but Sylvia expect them to, yet it is plain that she did. At parties especially, or in her shop, she had a way, figuratively, of taking two of her friends, strangers to each other, by the napes of their necks and cracking their heads together, saying in effect always, and at times in so many words, "My dears, you *must* love one another," and she could cite the best of reasons for this hope, compounding her error by describing them in turn as being of the highest rank and quality each in his own field.

Usually the strangers would give each other a straight, skeptical stare, exchange a few mumbling words under her expectant, fostering eyes; and the instant she went on to other greetings and exchanges, they faced about from each other and drifted away. There may have been some later friendships growing from this method, but I don't know of any; it never made one for me, nor, I may say, the other way about.

It was in Sylvia's shop that I saw Ernest Hemingway for the first and last time. If this sounds portentous now, it is only because of all that has happened since to make of him a tragic figure. Then he was still the *beau garçon* who loved blood sports, the dark-haired, sunburned muscle boy of American literature; the war hero with scars to show for it; the unalloyed male who had licked Style to a standstill. He had exactly the right attitude toward words like "glory" and so on. It was not particularly impressive: I preferred Joyce and Yeats and Henry James, and I had seen all the bullfights and done all the hunting I wanted in Mexico before I ever came to Paris. He seemed to me then to be the walking exemplar of the stylish literary attitudes of his time; he may have been, but I see now how very good he was; he paid heavily, as such men do, for their right to live on beyond the fashion they helped to make, to play out to the end not the role wished on them by their public, but the destiny they cannot escape because there was a moment in their lives when they chose that destiny.

It was such a little incident, and so random and rather comic at the time, and Sylvia and I laughed over it again years later, the last time I saw her in New York.

I had dropped into Sylvia's shop looking for something to read, just at early dark on a cold, rainy winter evening, maybe in 1934, I am not sure. We were standing under the light at the big round table piled up with books, talking; and I was just saying good-bye when the door burst open, and Hemingway unmistakably Ernest stood before us, looking just like the snapshots of him then being everywhere published—tall, bulky, broadfaced (his season of boyish slenderness was short), cropped black moustache, watchful eyes, all reassuringly there.

He wore a streaming old raincoat and a drenched floppy rain hat pulled over his eyebrows. Sylvia ran to him calling like a bird, both arms out; they embraced in a manly sort of way (quite a feat, sizes and sexes considered), then Sylvia turned to me with that ominous apostolic sweetness in her eyes.

Still holding one of Hemingway's hands, she reached at arm's length for mine. "Katherine Anne Porter," she said, pronouncing the names in full, "this is Ernest Hemingway . . . Ernest, this is Katherine Anne, and I want the two best modern American writers to know each other!"

Our hands were not joined.

"Modern" was a talismanic word then, but this time the magic failed. At that instant the telephone rang in the back room, Sylvia flew to answer, calling back to us merrily, merrily, "Now you two just get acquainted, and I'll be right back."

Hemingway and I stood and gazed unwinkingly at each other with poker faces for all of ten seconds, in silence. Hemingway then turned in one wide swing and hurled himself into the rainy darkness as he had hurled himself out of it, and that was all. I am sorry if you are disappointed. All personal lack of sympathy and attraction aside, and they were real in us both, it must have been galling to this most famous young man to have his name pronounced in the same breath as writer with someone he had never heard of, and a woman at that. I nearly felt sorry for him.

Sylvia seemed mystified that her hero had vanished. "Where did he go?" "I don't know." "What did he say?" she asked, still wondering, I had to tell her: "Nothing, not a word. Not even good-bye." She continued to think this very strange; I didn't, and don't.

1964

FLANNERY O'CONNOR
(1925–1964)

I saw our lovely and gifted Flannery O'Connor only three times over a period, I think, of three years or more, but each meeting was spontaneously an occasion and I want to write about her just as she impressed me.

I want to tell what she looked like and how she carried herself and how she sounded standing balanced lightly on her aluminum crutches, whistling to her peacocks who came floating and rustling to her, calling in their rusty voices.

I do not want to speak of her work because we all know what it was and we don't need to say what we think about it but to read and understand what she was trying to tell us.

Now and again there hovers on the margin of the future a presence that one feels as imminent—if I may use stylish vocabulary. She came up among us like a presence, a carrier of a gift not to be disputed but welcomed. She lived among us like a presence and went away early, leaving her harvest perhaps not yet all together gathered, though, like so many geniuses who have small time in this world, I think she had her warning and accepted it and did her work even if we all would like to have had her stay on forever and do more.

It is all very well for those who are left to console themselves. She said what she had to say. I'm pretty certain that her work was finished. We shouldn't mourn for her but for ourselves and our loves.

After all, I saw her just twice—memory has counted it three —for the second time was a day-long affair at a Conference and a party given by Flannery's mother in the evening. And I want to tell you something I think is amusing because Flannery lived in such an old-fashioned Southern village very celebrated in Southern history on account of what took place during the War. But in the lovely, old, aerie, tall country house and the life of a young girl living with her mother in a country town so that there was almost no way for her knowing the difficulties of human beings and her general knowledge of this was really very impressive because she was so very young and you wondered where—how—she had learned all that. But this is a question that everybody always asks himself about genius. I want to just tell something to illustrate the Southern custom.

Ladies in Society there—in that particular society, I mean— were nearly always known, no matter if they were married once or twice, they were known to their dying day by their maiden names. They were called "Miss Mary" or whoever it was. And so, Flannery's mother, too; her maiden name was Regina Cline and so she was still known as "Miss Regina Cline" and one evening at a party when I was there after the Conference, someone mentioned Flannery's name and another—a neighbor, mind you, who had probaby been around there all her life— said, "Who is Flannery O'Connor? I keep hearing about her." The other one said, "Oh, you know! Why, that's Regina Cline's daughter: that little girl who writes." And that was the atmosphere in which her genius developed and her life was lived and her work was done. I myself think it was a very healthy, good atmosphere because nobody got in her way, nobody tried to interfere with her or direct her and she lived easily and simply and in her own atmosphere and her own way of thinking. I believe this is the best possible way for a genius to live. I think that they're too often tortured by this world and when people discover that someone has a gift, they all come with their claws out, trying to snatch something of it, trying to share something they have no right even to touch. And she was safe from that: she had a mother who really took care of her. And I just think that's something we ought to mention, ought to speak of.

She managed to mix, somehow, two very different kinds of chickens and produced a bird hitherto unseen in this world. I asked her if she were going to send it to the County Fair. "I might, but first I must find a name for it. You name it!" she said. I thought of it many times but no fitting name for that creature ever occurred to me. And no fitting word now occurs to me to describe her stories, her particular style, her view of life, but I know its greatness and I see it—and see that it was one of the great gifts of our times.

I want to speak a little of her religious life though it was very sacred and quiet. She was as reserved about it as any saint. When I first met her, she and her mother were about to go for a seventeen-day trip to Lourdes. I said, "Oh, I wish I could go with you!" She said, "I wish you could. But I'll write you a letter." She never wrote that letter. She just sent a post card and she wrote: "The sight of Faith and affliction joined in prayer—very impressive." That was all.*

In some newspaper notice of her death, mention of her self-portrait with her favorite peacock was made. It spoke of her plain features. She had unusual features but they were anything but plain. I saw that portrait in her home and she had not flattered herself. The portrait does have her features, in a way, but here's something else. She had a young softness and gentleness of face and expression. The look—something in the depth of the eyes and the fixed mouth; the whole pose fiercely intent gives an uncompromising glimpse of her character. Something you might not see on first or even second glance in that tenderly fresh-colored, young, smiling face; something she saw in herself, knew about herself, that she was trying to tell us in a way less personal, yet more vivid than words.

That portrait, I'm trying to say, looked like the girl who wrote those blood-curdling stories about human evil—NOT

*She *did* write that letter, which was misplaced for a number of years—a very good letter, which I found when going over my papers for the University of Maryland. The line I remembered was this marvel of composure in the face of Death itself and her own death.

the living Flannery, whistling to her peacocks, showing off her delightfully freakish breed of chickens.

I want to thank you for giving me the opportunity to tell you about the Flannery O'Connor I know. I loved and valued her dearly, her work and her strange unworldly radiance of spirit in a human being so intelligent and undeceived by the appearance of things. I would feel too badly if I did not honor myself by saying a word in her honor: it is a great loss.

1964

Personal and Particular

On Writing

MY FIRST SPEECH*

I HAVE always had a fixed notion that a writer should lead a private life and keep silent in so far as writing is concerned and let published works speak for themselves, so, in trying to tell you something of what I think and believe about certain aspects of writing, I speak strictly as an individual and not as the spokesman for one school or the enemy of another.

Legend and memory is the title of the first section of a long novel I am now working on, and I called it that because it is from these two sources I am attempting to recreate a history of my family, which begins almost with the beginnings of the settlement of America. I have for this only legend, those things I have been told or that I read as a child; and I may say here that I consider most of our published history available to children quite as legendary as the siege of Troy: and my own memory of events taking place around me at the same time. And there is a third facet: my present memory and explanation to myself of my then personal life, the life of a child, which is in itself a mystery, while being living and legendary to that same child grown up. All this is working at once in my mind, in a confusion of dimensions. This may not sound so simple, and I believe it is less simple even than it sounds. But I feel that to give a true testimony it is necessary to know and remember what I was, what I felt, and what I knew then, and not confuse it with what I know or think I know now. So, I shall try to tell the truth, but the result will be fiction. I shall not be at all surprised at this result: it is what I mean to do; it is, to my way of thinking, the way fiction is made.

It is a curious long process, roundabout to the last degree, like a slow chemical change, and I believe it holds true as much when one is not recreating one's own life and past but the

*These are short hand notes taken of a lecture I made before the American Women's Club in Paris, 1934.—K.A.P.

life-history of another person. I think there are very few living characters in fiction who were not founded on a real living original. I think of Anna Karenina, Madame Bovary, and the tragic characters in *The Possessed*. Thackeray, so far as I know, never admitted that there had ever lived an Englishwoman like Becky Sharp. He was far too chivalrous for that. But that he did know, disapprove of, and admire such a person seems to me by the internal evidence fairly certain. I believe she could not have had so much vitality, if nature had not first created her for Thackeray to transmute into a work of art.

I should dare to say that none of these characters so living in fiction would have recognized their own portraits, for if the transformation is successful the character becomes something else in its own right, as alive as the person who posed for the portrait.

This is not a particularly easy thing to do, and I think of late a great many writers have found what they consider a way out, which leads really to an impasse. I mean the very thinly disguised autobiographical novel. It is an old saying that every human being possesses in his own life and experience the material for one novel. This may be true. It is one of those generalities hard to prove or disprove. It has been accepted a shade too literally, I think, by a great group of recent writers. This tendency is to make one's self the hero or heroine of one's own adventure, in literature as in life. It is only, I think, when the writer is adult enough to face the rather disheartening truth that he is not by any means always the hero of his own little history, much less the center of the universe, that we can begin to get near a human chronicle that could be worth reading. If writers, and not always professional writers, but anyone who really has a story to tell, could only tell the facts in such matters: the plain facts, it would be worth hearing. The novel is not really the vehicle for autobiography. It grows even more confusing when literary people live in such close-knitted groups that all of them have only one experience in common, and each one sits down to give his version of it, with himself as the hero and the others either pallid, minor figures, fools, or outright villains. For in the anxiety of each one to justify himself, he hardly takes care to disguise his characters other than in a kind of distortion.

Most certainly the artist is present in all he creates. He is his own work; and, if he were not, then there could be, I think, no true creation. But it is a confession of failure of what I shall call imaginative honesty to make one's self always the shining protagonist of one's own novels. It is true there do exist, I can't name one off hand, heroes who are the wishfulfillment of the author. Everyone knows that Stendhal (Henri Beyle) was a short, lumpy, timid fellow, unattractive, and unlucky in love. He had a kind of minor official post under Napoleon, a dull job that he detested—we know from internal evidence that Stendhal was brilliant, witty, a great sober artist. He dreamed of himself and created to his heart's desire a hero whom I consider one of the most detestable in all fiction: Julien Sorel. But Julien Sorel is nonetheless a superb creation, a work of art beyond a doubt. Still, as I follow the adventures of Julien Sorel, the workings of his pretentious, disorderly, shallow mind and heart, I am beset by the uneasy feeling that Stendhal meant him to be an admirable, complicated, unusually sensitive young man: portrait of Stendhal, the handsome French mask of little Henri Beyle—in a word. Too many quite promising young writers have been misled by the same vanity, but with less adroitness, along this same path; and how many little books do I know written by rather drab young men whose experience has not been unusual but who make themselves always the golden hero, and how many young women of ordinary charm cannot resist being either the spangle-eyed heroine or much the brightest girl in the class.

In America there is a great deal of excitement about the importance of being American. Even the writers have taken it up. When I was in America, all my writing friends were here,* sending me word that Paris, or some city in Europe, was to be their final choice of a dwelling place; when I finally came here, it was only to begin receiving letters from them all, now back in America, telling me that I was wrong to expatriate myself. The discussion runs on and on about "typical" and "not typical" American writers. So far as I am able to remember, for such classifications mean little to me, Bret Harte, Mark Twain, Sara Orne Jewett, Ralph Waldo Emerson, and other such

*In France.

diverse personalities are mentioned most frequently as American; while such strangely different writers as Hemingway and Hergesheimer, let us say, are called "not typical."

This may seem a digression, yet it belongs to what I am trying to say.

What is a typical American? In any profession? or state of life? I believe that different periods produce a certain typical mode of thought, or habit of mind, and the causes for this habit of mind are so complicated, so much a matter of the converging of a thousand influences to a given point, that I, for one, could never attempt to account for them. I think that artists are quite often not prophets, and there is very little reason why they should be. They have a way of being formed by their epoch, as other people are. Their code of morals, their religions, their mode of dress, even their styles in writing, can usually be dated and placed without much trouble. Now there was a time, or so legend insists, when there was a stable, settled world of society, when everybody thought, felt, and believed the same thing. This was never true, but it has become the fashion to say so; and in America we also had our golden age, which seems to have ended around 1910. Now, to a great many of us, and this includes the larger number of our so-called modern writers, there have been varieties of experience, historical changes. For some of them, life dates from the great war.* Their independent life, if that after-war life could be said to have had any independence (it had revolt, and disillusion, and hardship, and the privilege of sinking or swimming); but that is hardly independence, and above all there is nothing solid or comfortable about it. Also, with the new mixture of races, the breaking up of caste to some extent, economic upheavals, is it not possible that the author is merely again being the child of his time and is running to variety instead of to type? But we have always had variety.

We have always had variety, and an American writer who, thirsting for change, imitates Joyce is at least stating a point of view and a preference not likely to make his fortune; but he had better do that than to write slick fiction for a slick weekly or attempt to return to an America and an American mode of

*1914–1918.

thought which no longer exists except possibly in a past which is too recent to be appropriately revived. What we look upon now as typical may simply have been, once, one thing among many but was chosen as a type. You might say that Buffalo Bill was a typical American, or that Mark Twain was typical, or that Charles Francis Adams is, or that Nathan Hale was, or Jesse James. I believe that these men were not typical at all. They were individuals, who by the mysterious workings of environment and education in blood and tradition became the finished products of a certain sort of society; more than that, a certain section or region of America. They became typical in two ways, by being distinguished enough to be imitated and by being so admired or hated that their lives became symbols: but there was really, let us remember, only one of each of these men; and, different as they are, they were all Americans. Our blood has become pretty well mixed by now, and it was fairly well mixed before we came here. It is European or Oriental blood, transplanted to a new Continent, our roots are here; and our types are as varied. I dare say there is no man living who can with certainty name *all* the bloods that flow in his veins.

Lately the mixing process has speeded up and is now going through a new phase. The changes that are taking place will end by giving us a new set of features, so that I, for one, would be puzzled to say just what is a typical American. Think of our American writers. Let me name a few of them at random. They come on all levels of talent and achievement, from several periods, and from all parts of that tremendous country. Herman Melville, Sherwood Anderson, Edgar Allan Poe, Henry Adams, Stephen Crane, Sinclair Lewis, Ralph Waldo Emerson, Henry James, Walt Whitman, John Dos Passos, Ernest Hemingway, Washington Irving. Think of these last two together. But how can we say that they are not all Americans, and each one typically, oh quite typically, exactly himself and nobody else. They are typical as Chekhov, Dostoievsky, and Tolstoy are typical Russians, and each one a unique creature. I should think, one might very well say that Joyce is not a typical Irishman. No, but now that he has done it it is hard to imagine any other than an Irishman reacting in just such a way against his particular country, time, and society. It is fairly easy to say that now, because it just happens that no one but this one Irishman has ever behaved in just that way. Whether you like him or not, I fancy he is here to stay for some time. He will be there in the road: you may walk around him, climb over him, or dig under; but he will be there. I admire him immensely, but one of him is enough. Indeed, that is all there *can* be of him. I know better than to try to imitate him, and I wouldn't be influenced by him for the world; but I think he is going to begin a tradition, indeed has already. Now when one speaks of tradition, even American tradition, which we are in the habit of speaking of as new, it is better to remember that there are already a great many different traditions and most of them quite feasible. The artist, after having served his apprenticeship, may discover in what tradition he belongs. But the artist is usually too busy and too preoccupied with his own undertaking to worry much about whether he has got into the right tradition, or, indeed, into any at all. There have been more of them lately worrying about how they were going to get out of the beaten track. I think they were mistaken. An artist does better to leave all such classifications to the critics. He had better follow the bent of his own mind, whether it is for the moment fashionable or not; and it isn't for him to worry about whether he is really great or a true genius: that throws him off most frightfully, and his audience too. I should say that a major work of art occurs in any medium when a first-rate creative intelligence gets hold of a great theme and does something hitherto unexampled with it. And if this happens in our time we had better bless our luck and not worry about whether this marks the beginning or the end of a tradition. The other day a young writing friend of mine burst out suddenly: "I am going to write like Racine!" Now this is an American boy, an Irish-American boy with a very good talent. He added, in a moment: "I am Racine." Well, of course, the only possible answer to that was: "You're nothing of the sort." And then he explained, and it wasn't so foolish as all that: he meant he admired the qualities of clearness and directness in the style of Racine, what he called Racine's coldness. He meant, after all, that he feels a sympathy in his mind for that kind of writing; and if he goes on writing and his mind goes on working that way he may develop a good measured spare style. But I feel pretty certain no one will even be reminded of Racine by it; above all, not if our American boy does a really good job.

It is my belief that the less typical a writer is the less you are able to catalogue him, the more apt he is to be a writer worth your attention. We don't need any more types. We need individuals. We always did need them. The value of a writer can be measured best, probably, by his capacity to express what he feels, knows, is, has been, has seen, and experienced, by means of this paraphrase which is art, this process of taking his own material and making what he wants to make of it. He cannot do this, indeed he is not an artist, if he allows himself to be hampered by any set of conventions outside of the severe laws and limitations of his own medium. No one else can tell him what life is like to him, in what colors he sees the world. He cannot sit down and say, Go to, I will be a writer because it's an interesting career! Even less can he say, I must be an American writer; or French, or whatever. He has already been born one kind of person or another, and taking thought about it cannot change much. He cannot even worry about whether the publishers are going to accept his work or not; if he does, he is as good as done for: he may as well never have begun. He may be interpreter, critic, rebel, prophet, conformist, devil, or angel, or he may be all these things in turn, or all of them a little at once; but he can be none of these things to order: nobody's order, not even his own.

Simply stated, maybe too simply, it is the writer's business first to have something of his own to say; second, to say it in his own language and style. You must have heard this many times before; but I think it is one of the primary rules to keep in mind. The great thing is to convey to you, in this saying, a sense of the reality and the truth of what he tells you, with some new light thrown upon it that gives you a glimpse into some wider world not built with hands. It is like the dizzying blue in the upper right-hand corner of some of Brueghel's paintings. I remember especially the two versions of the fall of Icarus. The lower left-hand corner is real, no doubt about it: we have all seen such fields, such figures of men, such furrows and animals; but the upper right-hand corner is true too, though it is this vast transfiguration of blue such as we may never have seen in the sky over us, but it exists for us because

Brueghel has made it. Artists create monsters and many different sorts of landscapes; and they are true, if the artists are great
enough to show you what they have seen. Matisse has said: the
painter should paint the thing he knows. So far as it goes, this is
good advice. The question is, how much more does any artist
know imaginatively than factually? That is his test; for Dante
knew both heaven and hell without ever having seen them;
and described them for us so that we know them too: and
Shakespeare, taking legends and his own great fertility, created
for us countries which did not exist until then: but they exist
now, and we may travel in them when we please. Only yesterday, I was looking again at some of Dürer's scenes representing St. John's revelations, and I am glad Dürer chose not
to stick by the thing he knew with the eye of the flesh even
though that was an exceptionally clear and magical eye too.
But I have his view of the Apocalypse, and it is mine: I was
there.

So the reader, whether with pleasure, pain, or even disgust
(it is not necessary for you always to be pleased), must still find
himself in the atmosphere created for him by the artists, and
the artists do not always create a pleasant world, because that is
not their business. If they do that, you will be right not to trust
them in anything. We must leave all that to people whose affair
it is, to smooth our daily existence a little. Great art is hardly
ever agreeable; the artist should remind you that, for some, experience is a horror in this world, and that the human imagination also knows horror. He should direct you to points of
view you have not examined before, or cause you to comprehend, even if you do not sympathize with predicaments not
your own, ways of life, manners of speech, even of dress, above
all of the unique human heart, outside of your normal experience. And this can better be done by presentation than by argument. This presentation must be real, with a truth beyond
the artist's own prejudices, loves, hates; I mean his personal
ones. The outright propagandist sets up in me such a fury of
opposition I am not apt to care much whether he has got his
facts straight or not. He is like someone standing on your toes,
between you and an open window, describing the view to you.
All I ask of him to do is to open the window, stand out of the
way, and let me look at the view for myself. Now truth is a very

tall word, and we are rather apt to tag our pet theories and beliefs with this abused word. Let me reconsider a moment and
say, the writer must have honesty, he should not wilfully distort and obscure. Now I have said always that honesty in any
case is not enough, but it is an indispensable element in the arts.
No legend is ever true, but I believe all of them are founded
on some germ of truth; and even these truths appear in different lights to every mind they are presented to, and the legend
is that work of art which goes on in the human mind, adding
to and arranging, harmonizing and rounding out, making
larger or smaller than life, and holding the entire finished product in a good light and asking you to believe it. And it is true.
No memory is really faithful. It has too far to go, too many
changing landscapes of the human mind and heart, to bear any
sort of really trustworthy witness, except in part. So the truth
in art is got by change. In the work of art, nothing can be accidental: the sprawling, chaotic sense of that word as we use it
in everyday life, where so many things happen to us that we by
no means plan, it takes craftsmanship quite often beyond our
powers to manage by plan even a short day for ourselves. The
craftsmanship of the artist can make what he wishes of anything that excites his imagination. Craftsmanship is a homely,
workaday thing. It is a little like making shoes, or weaving
cloth. A writer may be inspired occasionally: that's his good
luck; but he doesn't learn to write by inspiration: he works at
it. In that sense the writer is a worker, a workingman, a working-
woman. Writing is not an elegant pastime, it is a sober and
hardworked trade, which gives great joy to the worker. The
artist is first a worker. He must roll up his sleeves and get to
work like a bricklayer. The romantic notion of the artist—
persons who live their romances, those who depend on the
gestures, the dress, the habits, of what they hope is genius—
hoping by presenting the appearance of genius, genius would
be added to them.

It is not a career, it is a vocation; it is not a means to fame
and glory—it is a discipline of living—and unless you think
this, it is better not to take it up. It is not the sort of thing one
"takes up" as one might take up knitting and put it down
again.

All this you can learn about the mechanics, the technique,

and it is all to the good for your education. It cannot make you
an artist. But it will make of you a better reader, a cleverer
critic, it will make of you some one the artist must look out
for, and it will make for him an audience that he can't trifle
with even if he would.

1934

"I MUST WRITE FROM MEMORY . . ."

From the Notebooks

Paris, Fall, 1936

Perhaps in time I shall learn to live more deeply and consistently in that undistracted center of being where the will does
not intrude, and the sense of time passing is lost, or has no
power over the imagination. Of the three dimensions of time,
only the past is "real" in the absolute sense that it has occurred, the future is only a concept, and the present is that
fateful split second in which all action takes place. One of the
most disturbing habits of the human mind is its willful and destructive forgetting of whatever in its past does not flatter or
confirm its present point of view. I must very often refer far
back in time to seek the meaning or explanation of today's
smallest event, and I have long since lost the power to be astonished at what I find there. This constant exercise of memory seems to be the chief occupation of my mind, and all my
experience seems to be simply memory, with continuity, marginal notes, constant revision and comparison of one thing with
another. Now and again thousands of memories converge,
harmonize, arrange themselves around a central idea in a coherent form, and I write a story. I keep notes and journals only
because I write a great deal, and the habit of writing helps me
to arrange, annotate, stow away conveniently the references I
may need later. Yet when I begin a story, I can never work in
any of those promising paragraphs, those apt phrases, those
small turns of anecdote I had believed would be so valuable. I
must know a story "by heart" and I must write from memory.
Certain writing friends whose judgments I admire, have told

me I lack detail, exact observation of the physical world, my people hardly ever have features, or not enough—that they live in empty houses, et cetera. At one time, I was so impressed by this criticism, I used to sit on a camp stool before a landscape and note down literally every object, every color, form, stick and stone before my eyes. But when I remembered that landscape, it was quite simply not in those terms that I remembered it, and it was no good pretending I did, and no good attempting to describe it because it got in the way of what I was really trying to tell. I was brought up with horses, I have harnessed, saddled, driven and ridden many a horse, but to this day I do not know the names for the different parts of a harness. I have often thought I would learn them and write them down in a note book. But to what end? I have two large cabinets full of notes already.

1940

NO PLOT, MY DEAR, NO STORY

This is a fable, children, of our times. There was a great big little magazine with four and one half million subscribers, or readers, I forget which; and the editors sat up nights thinking of new ways to entertain these people who bought their magazine and made a magnificent argument to convince advertisers that $3,794.36 an inch space-rates was a mere gift at the price. Look at all the buying-power represented. Look at all the money these subscribers must have if they can afford to throw it away on a magazine like the one we are talking about. So the subscribers subscribed and the readers read and the advertisers bought space and everything went on ring-around-the-rosy like that for God knows how long. In fact, it is going on right now.

So the editors thought up something beautiful and sent out alarms to celebrated authors and the agents of celebrated authors, asking everybody to think hard and remember the best story he had ever read, anywhere, anytime, and tell it over again in his own words, and he would be paid a simply appalling price for this harmless pastime.

By some mistake a penniless and only semi-celebrated author got on this list, and as it happened, that was the day the government had threatened to move in and sell the author's typewriter for taxes overdue, and a dentist had threatened to sue for a false tooth in the very front of the author's face; and there was also a grocery bill. So this looked as if Providence had decided to take a hand in the author's business, and he or she, it doesn't matter, sat down at once and remembered at least one of the most beautiful stories he or she had ever read anywhere.* It was all about three little country women finding a wounded man in a ditch, giving him cold water to drink out of his own cap, piling him into their cart and taking him off to a hospital, where the doctors said they might have saved their trouble for the man was as good as dead.

The little women were just silly enough to be happy anyway that they had found him, and he wasn't going to die by himself in a ditch, at any rate. So they went on to market.

A month later they went back to the hospital, each carrying a wreath to put on the grave of the man they had rescued and found him there still alive in a wheelchair; and they were so overcome with joy they couldn't think, but just dropped on their knees in gratitude that his life was saved; this in spite of the fact that he probably was not going to be of any use to himself or anybody else for a long time if ever. . . . It was a story about instinctive charity and selfless love. The style was fresh and clear as the living water of their tenderness.

You may say that's not much of a story, but I hope you don't for it would pain me to hear you agree with the editors of that magazine. They sent it back to the author's agent with a merry little note: "No plot, my dear—no *story*. Sorry."

So it looks as if the tax collector will get the author's typewriter, and the dentist the front tooth, and the crows may have the rest; and all because the poor creature was stupid enough to think that a short story needed *first* a *theme*, and then a point of view, a certain knowledge of human nature and strong feeling about it, and style—that is to say, his own special way of telling a thing that makes it precisely his own and no one

*"Living Water" by S. Sergeev-Tzensky, *The Dial*, July, 1929.

else's. . . . The greater the theme and the better the style, the better the story, you might say.

You might say, and it would be nice to think you would. Especially if you are an author and write short stories. Now listen carefully: except in emergencies, when you are trying to manufacture a quick trick and make some easy money, you don't really need a plot. If you have one, all well and good, if you know what it means and what to do with it. If you are aiming to take up the writing *trade*, you need very different equipment from that which you will need for the *art*, or even just the *profession* of writing. There are all sorts of schools that can teach you exactly how to handle the 197 variations on any one of the 37 basic plots; how to take a parcel of characters you never saw before and muddle them up in some difficulty and get the hero or heroine out again, and dispose of the bad uns; they can teach you the O. Henry twist; the trick of "slanting" your stuff toward this market and that; you will learn what goes over big, what not so big, what doesn't get by at all; and you will learn for yourself, if you stick to the job, *why* all this happens. Then you are all set, maybe. After that you have only to buy a pack of "Add-a-Plot" cards (free ad.) and go ahead. Frankly, I wish you the luck you deserve. You have richly earned it.

But there are other and surer and much more honest ways of making money, and Mama advises you to look about and investigate them before leaping into such a gamble as mercenary authorhood. Any plan to make money is a gamble, but grinding out "slanted" stuff takes a certain knack, a certain willingness to lose all, including honor; you will need a cold heart and a very thick skin and an allowance from your parents while you are getting started toward the big money. You stand to lose your youth, your eyesight, your self-respect, and whatever potentialities you may have had in other directions, and if the worst comes to the worst, remember, nobody promised you anything. . . . Well, if you are going to throw all that, except the self-respect, into the ash can, you may as well, if you wish to write, be as good a writer as you can, say what you think and feel, add a little something, even if it is the merest fraction of an atom, to the sum of human achievement.

First, have faith in your theme, then get so well acquainted with your characters that they live and grow in your imagination exactly as if you saw them in the flesh; and finally, tell their story with all the truth and tenderness and severity you are capable of, and if you have any character of your own, you will have a style of your own; it grows, as your ideas grow, and as your knowledge of your craft increases.

You will discover after a great while that you are probably a writer. You may even make some money at it.

One word more: I have heard it said, boldly and with complete sincerity by persons who should know better, that the only authors who do not write for the high-paying magazines are those who have not been able to make the grade; that any author who professes to despise or even disapprove of such writing and such magazines is a hypocrite; that he would be too happy to appear in those pages if only he were invited.

To such effrontery I have only one answer, based on experience and certain knowledge. It is simply not true.

1942

"WRITING CANNOT BE TAUGHT . . ."

(recorded on tape)

In full summer, eighteen years ago, during a short return from Paris, where I was then living, I stood up before my first group of student writers at a Writers' Conference in a small midwestern college, Olivet College, Olivet, Michigan, 1936. The students, a mixed audience of all ages and sorts of persons, gazed at me with what I took to be challenging if not hostile expectancy; I gazed back, stricken. The full rather awful meaning of our gathering there, confronting each other, had just dawned upon me for I confess I had not taken the invitation to speak there to beginning writers very seriously. I still took it for granted that any writer worth taking seriously would naturally be at home where he belonged doing his work by himself under his own power. Why in this world should he be asking advice from me or any other writer, and what could he get from talk that he could not better find in the published books of those he wished to study? Yet, I told myself, it cannot possibly harm anyone to spend two weeks in a year reading and talking about great literature, even trying his hand at putting words and phrases together to discover what the work really is; at least it will help to do away with careless reading, as the study of music makes for good listening; whoever tries to paint never just glances carelessly at a canvas or a statue again. Or so I wish to believe. Lightheartedly I had come there, happy at the chance to see some of my old friends who were writers, to enjoy the human sociability, and to talk a little about writing, which I then liked to do. I don't anymore, and it is the Writers' Conferences which have cured me.

So I stood there frozen under the weight of a responsibility I had assumed so easily it seems now, remembering, almost to have been frivolity on my part. These people sitting there were expecting something from me that I had been engaged to deliver without knowing what I had promised. They had come, many of them, from teaching jobs, from offices, from work of all kinds, using their vacation time and their savings and their few days of freedom for the whole year; and for this price and the price of their attention and hard trying, they expected to be taught how to write.

Whatever my carefully prepared opening line was to be, it disappeared. I said: "If you came here hoping for a miracle, there can be none. If you believe that you have paid to receive here a magic formula, a secret you may use at will, you have done no such thing. Writing, in any sense that matters, cannot be taught. It can only be learned, and learned by each separate one of us in his own way, by the use of his own powers of imagination and perception, the ability to learn the lessons he has set for himself. That is, if your intention is to try yourself out, to find whether or not you have the makings of an artist. If you have come to make this test on yourself, then this place might be a very good trial field for you—or better, a workshop, like a silversmith's or a cabinetmaker's. I mention these two because they are two of many fine crafts in which trickiness, dishonesty or just poor sense of form cannot be disguised, any more than they can be in writing; and you may properly expect here professional instruction in the working of what Henry James calls your 'soluble stuff.' The good artist is first a good workman, and yet you may become a very good workman without ever becoming a master. Nothing else is worth aspiring to, and we all run the risk of never arriving at it. If you have the vocation, it is very well worth spending a lifetime at it by living in the love of your work, you cannot be wasted. After all it is a lovely thing to live in the light and the presence of the great arts, and by this light and this presence to practice your own to the farthest reach of your own gift. So I am here to read your manuscripts and talk to you about them, so that in talking to me you may perhaps be able better to clear up your own doubts and difficulties. A working artist myself trying hopefully to do better someday, I shall show you as well as I can such technical devices as may have worked for me— eventually you must find your own. It is a good thing to know all the rules, but remember they are not the wings of Pegasus, but mere step-ladders, stilts, or even crutches, if you rely on them as such. The great works of literature come first, remember, and all rules, devices, techniques, forms, are founded on them, made out of their tissues, and every true genius creates new ones, or gives us imaginative (and workable) variations on the old. The familiar knowledge of this continuous, changing, bountiful life of the human imagination is something not to be missed, should be valued for its own sake, even if no one in this room ever writes another line."

Since then, the Writers' Conference has become a thriving domestic industry: sure enough, there have been no miracles. The effect has been to increase by the thousand the number of those who write, and there is almost no writer so bad (or so good!) that he cannot find a publisher. What the family magazines, regular publishers, literary reviews, cannot absorb, the paperback books and the anthologies can, and do. Processions of publishers' scouts visit the "creative writing" courses in hundreds of universities and colleges. Strolling bands of older critics, poets, novelists yearly ride circuit on writers' conferences in dozens of colleges and universities. I dare say prizes, grants, fellowships for every kind of writing there is number yearly into the hundreds. A brilliant young writer, William Styron, recently remarked in effect that this is not the Lost Generation, but the subsidized one. (There never was a lost generation of artists—that is only a cheerful myth, by the way.)

I am happy to see four hundred and ninety-nine promising young writers comfortably provided for while they reach their level, for the sake of that one indispensable first-rater, even maybe a genius, we all look for and hope for. And don't worry, he will come, he always does. Usually only one or two in a century, now and then in a cluster or galaxy, in a well spring of richness, but he does not fail. In the present fevered rush to publish just anything and anybody, and all the critics hailing all writing on his own level of understanding as great, with books and poets of the year, of the month, of the hour, of the minute, we can get a little confused. Be calm. The real poet, the real novelist, will emerge out of the uproar. He will be here, he is even now on his way.

1954

The Situation of the Writer

THE SITUATION IN AMERICAN WRITING

Responses to questions asked by *Partisan Review*

1. *Are you conscious, in your own writing, of the existence of a "usable past"? Is this mostly American? What figures would you designate as elements in it? Would you say, for example, that Henry James's work is more relevant to the present and future of American writing than Walt Whitman's?*

All my past is "usable," in the sense that my material consists of memory, legend, personal experience, and acquired knowledge. They combine in a constant process of re-creation. I am quite unable to separate the influence of literature or the history of literary figures from influences of background, upbringing, ancestry; or to say just what is American and what is not. On one level of experience and a very important one, I could write an autobiography based on my reading until I was twenty-five.

Henry James and Walt Whitman are relevant to the past and present of American literature or of any other literature. They are world figures, they are both artists, it is better not to mortgage the future by excluding either. Be certain that if the present forces and influences bury either of them, the future will dig him up again. The James-minded and the Whitman-minded people have both the right to their own kind of nourishment.

For myself I choose James, holding as I do with the conscious, disciplined artist, the serious expert against the expansive, indiscriminately "cosmic" sort. James, I believe, was the better workman, the more advanced craftsman, a better thinker, a man with a heavier load to carry than Whitman. His feelings are deeper and more complex than Whitman's; he had more confusing choices to make, he faced and labored over harder problems. I am always thrown off by arm-waving and shouting, I am never convinced by breast-beating or huge shapeless statements of generalized emotion. In particular, I think the influence of Whitman on certain American writers has been disastrous, for he encourages them in the vices or self-love (often disguised as love of humanity, or the working classes, or God), the assumption of prophetic powers, of romantic superiority to the limitations of craftsmanship, inflated feeling and slovenly expression.

Neither James nor Whitman is more relevant to the present and future of American literature than, say, Hawthorne or Melville, Stephen Crane or Emily Dickinson; or for that matter, any other first-rank poet or novelist or critic of any time or country. James or Whitman? The young writer will only confuse himself, neglect the natural sources of his education as artist, cramp the growth of his sympathies, by lining up in such a scrimmage. American literature belongs to the great body of world literature, it should be varied and free to flow into what channels the future shall open; all attempts to limit and exclude at this early day would be stupid, and I sincerely hope, futile. If a young artist must choose a master to admire and emulate, that choice should be made according to his own needs from the widest possible field and after a varied experience of study. By then perhaps he shall have seen the folly of choosing a master. One suggestion: artists are not political candidates; and art is not an arena for gladiatorial contests.

2. *Do you think of yourself as writing for a definite audience? If so, how would you describe this audience? Would you say that the audience for serious American writing has grown or contracted in the last ten years?*

In the beginning I was not writing for any audience, but spent a great while secretly and with great absorption trying to master a craft, to find a medium; my respect for this medium and the masters of it—no two of them alike—is very great. My search was all for the clearest and most arresting way to tell the things I wished to tell. I still do not write for any definite audience, though perhaps I have in mind a kind of composite reader.

It appears to me that the audience for serious American writing has grown in the past ten years. This opinion is based on my own observation of an extended reputation, a widening sphere of influence, an increasing number of readers, among poets, novelists, and critics of our first rank.

It is true that I place great value on certain kinds of perceptive criticism but neither praise nor blame affects my actual work, for I am under a compulsion to write as I do; when I am working I forget who approved and who dispraised, and why. The worker in an art is dyed in his own color, it is useless to ask him to change his faults or his virtues; he must, rather more literally than most men, work out his own salvation. No novelist or poet could possibly ask himself, while working: "What will a certain critic think of this? Will this be acceptable to my publisher? Will this do for a certain magazine? Will my family and friends approve of this?" Imagine what that would lead to. . . . And how much worse, if he must be thinking, "What will my political cell or block think of this? Am I hewing to the party line? Do I stand to lose my job, or head, on this?" This is really the road by which the artist perishes.

3. *Do you place much value on the criticism your work has received? Would you agree that the corruption of the literary supplements by advertising—in the case of the newspapers—and political pressures—in the case of the liberal weeklies—has made serious literary criticism an isolated cult?*

As to criticism being an isolated cult, for the causes you suggest or any other, serious literary criticism was never a crowded field; it cannot be produced by a formula or in bulk any more than can good poetry or fiction. It is not, any more than it ever was, the impassioned concern of a huge public. Proportionately to number, both of readers and publishers, there are as many good critics who have a normal audience as ever. We are discussing the art of literature and the art of criticism, and this has nothing to do with the vast industry of copious publishing, and hasty reviewing, under pressure from the advertising departments, or political pressure. It is a pernicious system: but I surmise the same kind of threat to freedom in a recently organized group of revolutionary artists who are out to fight and suppress if they can, all "reactionary" artists—that is, all artists who do not subscribe to their particular political faith.

4. *Have you found it possible to make a living by writing the sort of thing you want to, and without the aid of such crutches as*

*teaching and editorial work? Do you think there is any place in
our present economic system for literature as a profession?*

No, there has not been a living in it, so far. The history of
literature, musical composition, painting shows there has never
been a living in art, except by flukes of fortune; by weight of
long, cumulative reputation, or generosity of a patron; a prize,
a subsidy, a commission of some kind; or (in the American
style) anonymous and shamefaced hackwork; in the English
style, a tradition of hackwork, openly acknowledged if de-
plored. The grand old English hack is a melancholy spectacle
perhaps, but a figure not without dignity. He is a man who
sticks by his trade, does the best he can with it on its own
terms, and abides by the consequences of his choice, with a
kind of confidence in his way of life that has some merit,
certainly.

Literature as a profession? It *is* a profession, and the professional literary man is on his own as any other professional
man is.

If you mean, is there any place in our present economic system for the practice of literature as a source of steady income
and economic security, I should say, no. There never has been,
in any system, any guarantee of economic security for the artist,
unless he took a job and worked under orders as other men do
for a steady living. In the arts, you simply cannot secure your
bread and your freedom of action too. You cannot be a hostile
critic of society and expect society to feed you regularly. The
artist of the present day is demanding (I think childishly) that
he be given, free, a great many irreconcilable rights and privileges. He wants as a right freedoms which the great spirits of
all time have had to fight and often to die for. If he wants freedom, let him fight and die for it too, if he must, and not expect
it to be handed to him on a silver plate.

5. *Do you find, in retrospect, that your writing reveals any alle-
giance to any group, class, organization, region, religion, or system of thought, or do you conceive of it as mainly the expression of
yourself as an individual?*

I find my writing reveals all sorts of sympathies and interests
which I had not formulated exactly to myself; "the expression

of myself as an individual" has never been my aim. My whole attempt has been to discover and understand human motives, human feelings, to make a distillation of what human relations and experiences my mind has been able to absorb. I have never known an uninteresting human being, and I have never known two alike; there are broad classifications and deep similarities, but I am interested in the thumbprint. I am passionately involved with these individuals who populate all these enormous migrations, calamities; who fight wars and furnish life for the future; these beings without which, one by one, all the "broad movements of history" could never take place. One by one—as they were born.

6. *How would you describe the political tendency of American writing as a whole since 1930? How do you feel about it yourself? Are you sympathetic to the current tendency toward what may be called "literary nationalism"—a renewed emphasis, largely uncritical, on the specifically "American" elements in our culture?*

Political tendency since 1930 has been to the last degree a confused, struggling, drowning-man-and-straw sort of thing, stampede of panicked crowd, each man trying to save himself —one at a time trying to work out his horrible confusions. How do I feel about it? I suffer from it, and I try to work my way out to some firm ground of personal belief, as the others do. I have times of terror and doubt and indecision, I am confused in all the uproar of shouting maddened voices and the flourishing of death-giving weapons. . . . I should like to save myself, but I have no assurance that I can, for if the victory goes as it threatens, I am not on that side.* The third clause of this question I find biased. Let me not be led away by your phrase "largely uncritical" in regard to the "emphasis on specifically American" elements in our culture. If we become completely uncritical and nationalistic, it will be the most European state of mind we could have. I hope we may not. I hope we shall have balance enough to see ourselves plainly, and choose what we shall keep and what discard according to

---

*At the time this was written it was clear enough that I was opposed to every form of authoritarian, totalitarian government or religion, under whatever name in whatever country. I still am.

our own needs; not be rushed into fanatic self-love and self-praise as a defensive measure against assaults from abroad. I think the "specifically American" things might not be the worst things for us to cultivate, since this is America, and we are Americans, and our history is not altogether disgraceful. The parent stock is European, but this climate has its own way with transplantations, and I see no cause for grievance in that.

7. *Have you considered the question of your attitude toward the possible entry of the United States into the next world war? What do you think the responsibilities of writers in general are when and if war comes?*

I am a pacifist. I should like to say now, while there is still time and place to speak, without inviting immediate disaster (for I love life), to my mind the responsibility of the artist toward society is the plain and simple responsibility of any other human being, for I refuse to separate the artist from the human race: his prime responsibility "when and if war comes" is not to go mad. Madness takes many subtle forms, it is the old deceiver. I would say, don't be betrayed into all the old outdated mistakes. If you are promised something new and blissful at the mere price of present violence under a new master, first examine these terms carefully. New ideas call for new methods, the old flaying, drawing, and quartering for the love of God and the King will not do. If the method is the same, trust yourself, the idea is old, too. If you are required to kill someone today, on the promise of a political leader that someone else shall live in peace tomorrow, believe me, you are not only a double murderer, you are a suicide, too.

1939

TRANSPLANTED WRITERS

Response to a question asked by *Books Abroad*

*One of the most disquieting by-products of the world disorders of
the past few years has been the displacement of the most influ-
ential writers. The ablest German authors and journalists, for
example, are no longer in Berlin and Leipzig, but in London
and New York. The most articulate of the Spanish intelligentsia
are not in Madrid but in Mexico City and Buenos Aires. This
paradoxical situation must have far-reaching consequences, not
only for the intellectuals themselves but for Germany, England
and the United States, Spain, Mexico, and the Argentine. What,
in your opinion, may these consequences be, immediate and remote, desirable and unfortunate?*

The deepest harm in forced flight lies in the incurable
wound to human pride and self-respect, the complete dislocation of the spiritual center of gravity. To be beaten and driven
out of one's own place is the gravest disaster that can occur
to a human being, for in such an act he finds his very humanity denied, his person dismissed with contempt, and this is a
shock very few natures can bear and recover any measure of
equilibrium.

Artists and writers, I think, do not suffer more than other
people under such treatment, but they are apt to be more
aware of the causes of their sufferings, they are better able to
perceive what is happening, not only to them, but to all their
fellow beings. I would not attempt to prophesy what the consequences of all this world displacement by violence of so
many people might be; but I can only hope they will have
learned something by it, and will leave in the grave of Europe
their old quarrels and the old prejudices that have brought this
catastrophe upon all of us. We have here enough of those things
to fight without that added weight.

Americans are not going anywhere, and I am glad of it.
Here we stay, for good or ill, for life or death; and my hope is
that all those articulate intelligences who have been driven
here will consent to stand with us, and help us put an end to
this stampede of human beings driven like sheep over one
frontier after another; I hope they will make an effort to understand what this place means in terms of the final battlefield.

For the present, they must live here or nowhere, and they must share the responsibility for helping to make this a place where man can live as man and not as victim, pawn, a lower order of animal driven out to die beside the road or to survive in stealth and cunning.

The force at work in the world now is the oldest evil with a new name and new mechanisms and more complicated strategies; if the intelligent do not help to clarify the issues, maintain at least internal order, understand themselves and help others to understand the nature of what is happening, they hardly deserve the name. I agree with Mr. E. M. Forster that there are only two possibilities for any real order: in art and in religion. All political history is a vile mess, varying only in degrees of vileness from one epoch to another, and only the work of saints and artists gives us any reason to believe that the human race is worth belonging to.

Let these scattered, uprooted men remember this, and remember that their one function is to labor at preserving the humanities and the dignity of the human spirit. Otherwise they are lost and we are lost with them and whether they stay here or go yonder will not much matter.

1940

THE INTERNATIONAL
EXCHANGE OF WRITERS

Remarks on the Agenda of the Institute of International Education's
Conference on Arts and Exchange of Persons, New York City

1. *Is foreign experience valuable for the writer, or does it deprive him of his "roots"? Why not just send his written works?*
A human being carries his "roots" in his blood, his nervous system, the brain cells; no man can get rid of them. Even his attempts to disguise them will betray his origins and true nature. I think foreign travel and experience are good for everybody—not just writers, but for writers they are an invaluable, irreplaceable education in life. Yes, I know; Dante never left Italy and Shakespeare never left England. We call to mind a few

house-bound women—geniuses too—Jane Austen, Emily Brontë, Emily Dickinson—but we are not talking now about geniuses, but writers. One thing fourteen years of travel and living in six foreign countries did for me besides giving me a wonderful time is, I am delighted to stay at home!

It is an absurd but rather touching little human weakness, but any number of people would rather see and hear a live author than read his works.

2. *Are more opportunities for exchange of writers needed?*

Yes, I do think nations should exchange writers and all artists more than they do; but not officially, not with any political affiliations. Several years ago when I was in Washington there was some vague talk of sending me as "cultural attaché" to a Spanish-speaking American country. Our Ambassador or Minister to that country turned the entire idea down saying: "I don't want any culture mixed with my politics." This delighted me, and I sent him a message through the proper channels: "And I don't want any politics mixed with my culture!" And I still don't like the mixture.

3. *Should an attempt be made to lift the "iron curtain" through the exchange of writers?*

This is a bear trap of a question. Within my memory, before World War I, we had in effect an open world; no passports needed anywhere in Europe, or in the Americas. Russia, then as now, was closed. It was considered a barbarous government (and it was barbarous in other ways too) because passports were required, and Russian subjects could not leave the country without permission; and the Tsar's secret police and Siberian prison camps were the scandals of the world. (The world itself had quite a few horrors in every country, but Russia was then as now considered the worst.) Writers and artists came and went, even to Russia; they were free as birds at other international frontiers; their books were translated into all languages, and so far as peace, understanding, freedom, between nations is concerned, they might all as well never have left their own back yards. I daresay there is not at this moment a single government in this world which really trusts another government, and we know too well that last year's enemy can be this year's friend, and the other way around; but we can't blame this state of affairs on the writers, and we can't quite expect them to remedy it, either.

4. *What role can or should the U.S. government play in sending writers abroad and bringing writers here?*

The U.S. government might appoint good, well-proved poets and novelists to consular or other foreign posts as the French do, and certain Latin American countries: or appoint first-rate writers for a certain length of time—one, two, three years—as cultural attachés at a salary commensurate with the dignity of the place, to be awarded as an honor. Even the Consular or other foreign service jobs would not be any harder work or take more time than teaching, which is what so many of our best writers do to make a living.

But any political strings attached to any of this would quite simply be fatal, and no honest artist could survive in such a situation.

5. *What are the writer's personal objectives in going abroad? Do these differ from the objectives of most sponsoring organizations?*

I think most writers probably have the same motives as other people—for going abroad. They love to see the world, hear and maybe learn other languages; unfamiliar habits and customs, other peoples' lives and ways of feeling, are so fascinating and exciting and, if one lives there long enough, as I did in Mexico and France, one loves the place and the people; I may never see them again, but I shall never outlive my tenderness and sympathy for those glorious beautiful countries. I suppose the "objective" of a writer is just to live and do his work as well as he can, in his own way and time—his lifetime—and most sponsoring organizations want "production" right now!

6. *What kinds of writers should be selected to go abroad? (Criteria) Who should do the selecting? (Mechanisms)*

a) Good ones. The standard cannot be too high. The Library of Congress has a Chair of Poetry, and I don't know exactly what method they have of choosing but they haven't had a bad poet there yet! The National Institute of Arts and Letters has a pretty good system of choosing their Gold Medalists,

and their speakers at the annual wing-ding in May: I have seen
an impressive row of talent sitting there waiting to be handed
that thousand-dollar grant.

b) For judges, I should look over the committee lists of such
organizations. Second-rate judges will not know how to pick
first-rate writers.

7. *What should a writer do, if anything, to prepare for a sojourn
abroad? Does the writer need assistance or can he do it for
himself?*

The only assistance any writer worth his salt needs is enough
money to take him where he wants to go and keep him there
for as long as he needs to stay. Sometimes he can save up
money—if he teaches, for example—and go on a sabbatical
year; sometimes he can support himself with free-lance writing,
but it is very risky; almost the only hope is a grant or fellowship
of some sort, though at this time there are very few that give
enough for anyone to live on. Also the grants to what I believe
are called "creative" writers, which I suppose means poets,
novelists, as distinct from critics, essayists, and journalists, have
been cut down to a mere token number in nearly all the foundations; yet I feel that our best poets and novelists are the
ones we should send if we are going to send anybody to other
countries.

8. *How can the sojourns of visiting writers be made more
profitable to themselves and to their sponsors? What obligations
does the writer have to a sponsor?*

a) If they are going to a country for the first time, they
should have entirely practical advice and information about
housing, cost of living, and local conditions. It is better if he
knows the language, even slightly. If not he should set himself
to speak at once.

b) As to the obligation of the writer to the sponsor, let me
again cite my personal experience with the Guggenheim Foundation; their grant took me to Europe for a year, and I managed to stay for five in all. I was worried because the change
was a tremendous one for me, full of violent reactions and
intense feelings—not unhappy ones, simply unsettling to the
last degree. It took me better than a year to settle to work,

though I kept enormous notebooks. I wrote to Mr. Henry Allen Moe full of contrition that I hadn't turned out a book in that year. And Mr. Moe wrote that nobody had expected me to! That the grant was not just for the work of that year, but was meant to help me go on for all my life. And this has been true—without that grant, I might have just stayed in Mexico, or here at home; I should certainly not have gone to Europe when I did; and so in the most absolute sense, that Guggenheim Foundation Fellowship has helped to nourish my life as a writer to this day; I am today unable to imagine even faintly what I should have done without my wonderful years in Europe.

The writer owes to his sponsor to write, as well as he is able, in his own time and his own way, exactly what he wishes to write insofar as anyone has ever done that! In fact, he owes to his sponsor exactly what he owes to himself, no more, no less, except thanks!

9. *What can the writer do, if anything, to maintain contact with the country visited after his return home?*

One finds friends anywhere; my way of keeping up is to subscribe to a magazine or newspaper in the languages I can read—French, German, Spanish—and writing and getting letters from friends in those countries I have visited. Isn't this enough, and very pleasant, too? One wouldn't want to make *work* of it!

1956

The Author on Her Work

NO MASTERS OR TEACHERS

Response to the question "How does talent grow?"
asked by Don M. Wolfe, editor,
New Voices 2: American Writing Today.
New York: Hendricks House, 1955.

To begin with, I did not know I had talent. My little stories and drawings to go with them were regarded by the grownups and the other children around me as another pastime to keep me busy and contented. All of us danced, sang, drew, modelled in clay: were taught to recite poetry when asked and no nonsense. Our elders liked bright children, but not showoffs. So nobody tampered with my talent, if I had any: this kept me from being self-conscious, and I think now it slowed down a great deal of my own realization of just what I was headed for. I began reading very early, and as the house was full of good books gathered for several generations, by people who really liked good reading, I had read an almost unbelievable amount of great literature before I knew what I was reading.

I was a very bad writer to begin with, and I knew it, because I knew what the standard was—and is, so far as I have been able to learn. But write I would, it was a passion and a compulsion and a long ordeal, but I had no choice. Many times I gave up, and tried very hard to turn to something else. It was no good. Besides my reading, I had no masters or teachers. I never even read a book on how to write, I'm not sure there were any, when I was sixteen. And I got no encouragement from my environment; on the contrary, a bitter and furious opposition from family and the society around me; entirely irrational and personal, it was deep enough to lead to the breakup and shattering of the life I felt hardening around me. I got out of that place as if I were leaving a falling house in an earthquake. And then I faced my little private destiny and took on my work: wrote three novels and burned them; wrote dozens

714

of stories and destroyed them. Worked at various jobs to support myself—not very good at it, but I lived. Finally, one day—I was just back from Mexico, when I was about twenty-eight years old, I sat down in a room in an old house in Washington Square South, now disappeared, and decided that I would finish a certain short story, no matter what. It took seventeen days and nights, quite literally: I kept no hours, but ate when I could, and slept a little when I was exhausted. But I finished it, and that battle was fought for good: writing will never be anything but hard work, but I crossed my deepest river then and there. The story was *María Concepción*, and it was published almost at once by the old Century magazine, and they paid me six hundred dollars for it.

(I mention this because it was of the greatest importance. I was, as the saying is, by that time "on starvation.") You might think this was a great how-do-you-do for just a little story, but it was exhilarating, illuminating, one of the profoundly happy moments of my life. I've had some tussles since, and I have loved them. The great good I have had from writing has been just exactly the writing itself. Nobody promised me anything for it; I never expected to have a "career." I never showed a manuscript to anybody in my life except to the editor I sent it to when it was finished, with one exception. I had written a story in one evening, but I did not trust it. It threw around among my papers for about a year, then I asked a friend whose judgement I trusted to read it. She advised me to send it away at once. It was *The Jilting of Granny Weatherall*. I am still not really capable of judging my own stories. I write them, and I have to trust myself without question; if by now I cannot rely upon my power, such as it is whatever it is, why then, what was my life for?

Of course now I feel my work was not enough, not as good as I hoped it would be, and it is only half-finished, if that. Once I lived as if I had a thousand years to squander, now, I pray for time. I've got four books to do yet.

ON "FLOWERING JUDAS"

Introduction to a contribution to
This Is My Best, edited by Clifton Fadiman.
New York: The Dial Press, 1943.

"Flowering Judas" was written between seven o'clock and midnight of a very cold December, 1929, in Brooklyn. The experiences from which it was made occurred several years before, in Mexico, just after the Obregon revolution.

All the characters and episodes are based on real persons and events, but naturally, as my memory worked upon them and time passed, all assumed different shapes and colors, formed gradually around a central idea, that of self-delusion, the order and meaning of the episodes changed, and became in a word fiction.

The idea first came to me one evening when going to visit the girl I call Laura in the story, I passed the open window of her living room on my way to the door, through the small patio which is one of the scenes in the story. I had a brief glimpse of her sitting with an open book in her lap, but not reading, with a fixed look of pained melancholy and confusion in her face. The fat man I call Braggioni was playing the guitar and singing to her.

In that glimpse, no more than a flash, I thought I understood, or perceived, for the first time, the desperate complications of her mind and feelings, and I knew a story; perhaps not her true story, not even the real story of the whole situation, but all the same a story that seemed symbolic truth to me. If I had not seen her face at that very moment, I should never have written just this story because I should not have known it to write.

The editor has asked for my favorite story. I have no favorites though there is perhaps one, a short novel, for which now and then I do feel a preference, for extremely personal reasons. I offer this story which falls within the stipulated length because it comes very near to being what I meant for it to be, and I suppose an author's choice of his own work must always be decided by such private knowledge of the margin between intention and the accomplished fact.

Boulder, Colo.
July 13, 1942

"THE ONLY REALITY . . ."

Introduction to
Flowering Judas and Other Stories,
by Katherine Anne Porter.
New York: The Modern Library, 1940.*

It is just ten years since this collection of short stories first appeared. They are literally first fruits, for they were written and published in order of their present arrangement in this volume, which contains the first story I ever finished. Looking at them again, it is possible still to say that I do not repent of them; if they were not yet written, I should have to write them still. They were done with intention and in firm faith, though I had no plan for their future and no notion of what their meaning might be to such readers as they would find. To any speculations from interested sources as to why there were not more of them, I can answer simply and truthfully that I was not one of those who could flourish in the conditions of the past two decades. They are fragments of a much larger plan which I am still engaged in carrying out, and they are what I was then able to achieve in the way of order and form and statement in a period of grotesque dislocations in a whole society when the world was heaving in the sickness of a millennial change. They were first published by what seems still merely a lucky accident, and their survival through this crowded and slowly darkening decade is the sort of fate no one, least of all myself, could be expected to predict or even to hope for.

We none of us flourished in those times, artists or not, for art, like the human life of which it is the truest voice, thrives

---

*This was written on June 21, 1940, seven days after the fall of France.

best by daylight in a green and growing world. For myself, and I was not alone, all the conscious and recollected years of my life have been lived to this day under the heavy threat of world catastrophe, and most of the energies of my mind and spirit have been spent in the effort to grasp the meaning of those threats, to trace them to their sources and to understand the logic of this majestic and terrible failure of the life of man in the Western world. In the face of such shape and weight of present misfortune, the voice of the individual artist may seem perhaps of no more consequence than the whirring of a cricket in the grass; but the arts do live continuously, and they live literally by faith; their names and their shapes and their uses and their basic meanings survive unchanged in all that matters through times of interruption, diminishment, neglect; they outlive governments and creeds and the societies, even the very civilizations that produced them. They cannot be destroyed altogether because they represent the substance of faith and the only reality. They are what we find again when the ruins are cleared away. And even the smallest and most incomplete offering at this time can be a proud act in defense of that faith.

"NOON WINE": THE SOURCES

By the time a writer has reached the end of a story, he has lived it at least three times over—first in the series of actual events that, directly or indirectly, have combined to set up that commotion in his mind and senses that causes him to write the story; second, in memory; and third, in recreation of this chaotic stuff. One might think this is enough; but no, the writer now finds himself challenged to trace his clues to their sources and to expose the roots of his work in his own most secret and private life; and is asked to live again this sometimes exhausting experience for the fourth time! There was a time when critics of literature seemed quite happy to try digging out the author's meanings without help; or, failing to find any, to invent meanings of their own, often just as satisfactory to everybody—except perhaps to the author, whose feelings or opinion traditionally do not count much, anyway.

The private reader too has always been welcome to his own notions of what he is reading, free to remark upon it to his heart's content, with no cramping obligation to be "right" in his conclusions, such as weighs upon the professionals or paid critics; it is enough for him to be moved and stimulated to speak his thoughts freely; the author will not mind even harshness, if only he can be sure he is being read! But it is, I think, a relatively late thing for authors to be asked to explain themselves, though some have done it in self-defense against their hardier critics. Flaubert occurs to me as, if not the earliest, one of the most lucid and painstaking; Henry James as the most prodigally, triumphantly eloquent, and thorough. Yet they held closely to the work as a finished piece of literature, and made almost no attempt—perhaps they knew better—to trace its history to its sources in their blood and bones, the subterranean labyrinths of infancy and childhood, family histories, memories, visions, daydreams, and nightmares—or to connect these gauzy fantasies to the solid tissues of their adult professional lives.

Truth is, it is quite an impossible undertaking, or so I have found it; a little like attempting to tap one's spinal fluid—and if that is a gruesome and painful comparison, be sure that I meant it to be. For this incomplete account has cost me more work and trouble and presented me with more insoluble problems and unanswerable questions than the story itself ever did, in any phase of its growth. Indeed perhaps I have not succeeded in explaining anything at all, and this is a meditation rather than an exposition; for there are still, intact if somewhat disturbed by my agitating hand, all those same ancient areas of mystery and darkness in which all beginnings are hidden: I have confronted them before, and again, and again, only to return each time not altogether defeated, but with only a few tattered fragments of the human secret in my hand. Such as these mysteries are, or such as they reveal themselves in fragments to me, I love them, I do not fear them but I treat them with the respect I know they well deserve.

I chose to write about "Noon Wine" because among my stories it is at once the most remote and the most familiar, the most obscure in origin and the most clearly visible in meanings to me; or indeed, these are my reasons, but I do not know exactly why I chose it any more than I really know why I wrote it in the first place.

This short novel, "Noon Wine," exists so fully and wholly in its own right in my mind, that when I attempt to trace its growth from the beginning, to follow all the clues to their sources in my memory, I am dismayed; because I am confronted with my own life, the whole society in which I was born and brought up, and the facts of it. My aim is to find the truth in it, and to this end my imagination works and reworks its recollections in a constant search for meanings. Yet in this endless remembering which surely must be the main occupation of the writer, events are changed, reshaped, interpreted again and again in different ways, and this is right and natural because it is the intention of the writer to write fiction, after all—real fiction, not a *roman à clef*, or a thinly disguised personal confession which better belongs to the psychoanalyst's séance. By the time I wrote "Noon Wine" it had become "real" to me almost in the sense that I felt not as if I had made that story out of my own memory and real events and imagined consequences, but as if I were quite simply reporting events I had heard or witnessed. This is not in the least true: the story is fiction; but it is made up of thousands of things that did happen to living human beings in a certain part of the country, at a certain time of my life, things that are still remembered by others as single incidents; not as I remembered them, floating and moving with their separate life and reality, meeting and parting and mingling in my thoughts until they established their relationship and meaning to me. I could see and feel very clearly that all these events, episodes—hardly that, sometimes, but just mere glimpses and flashes here and there of lives strange or moving or astonishing to me—were forming a story, almost of themselves, it seemed; out of their apparent incoherence, unrelatedness, they grouped and clung in my mind in a form that gave a meaning to the whole that the individual parts had lacked. So I feel that this story is "true" in the way that a work of fiction should be true, created out of all the scattered particles of life I was able to absorb and combine and to shape into a living new being.

But why did this particular set of memories and early impressions combine in just this way to make this particular story?

I do not in the least know. And though it is quite true that I intended to write fiction, this story wove itself in my mind for years before I ever intended to write it; there were many other stories going on in my head at once; some of them evolved and were written, more were not. Why? This to me is the most interesting question, because I am sure there is an answer, but nobody knows it yet.

When the moment came to write this story, I knew it; and I had to make quite a number of practical arrangements to get the time free for it, without fear of interruptions. I wrote it as it stands except for a few pen corrections, in just seven days of trancelike absorption in a small room in an inn in rural Pennsylvania, from the early evening of November 7 to November 14, 1936. Yet I had written the central part, the scene between Mr. Hatch and Mr. Thompson, which leads up to the murder in Basel, Switzerland, in the summer of 1932.

I had returned from Europe only fifteen days before I went to the inn in Pennsylvania: this was the end, as it turned out of my living abroad, except for short visits back to Paris, Brittany, Rome, Belgium: but meantime I had, at a time of great awareness and active energy, spent nearly fourteen years of my life out of this country: in Mexico, Bermuda, Spain, Germany, Switzerland, but, happiest and best, nearly five years in Paris. Of my life in these places I felt then, and feel now, that it was all entirely right, timely, appropriate, exactly where I should have been and what doing at that very time. I did not feel exactly at home; I knew where home was; but the time had come for me to see the world for myself, and so I did, almost as naturally as a bird taking off on his new wing-feathers. In Europe, things were not so strange; sometimes I had a pleasant sense of having here and there touched home base; if I was not at home, I was sometimes with friends. And all the time, I was making notes on stories—stories of my own place, my South—for my part of Texas was peopled almost entirely by Southerners from Virginia, Tennessee, the Carolinas, Kentucky, where different branches of my own family were settled, and I was almost instinctively living in a sustained state of mind and feeling, quietly and secretly, comparing one thing with another, always remembering; and all sorts of things were falling into their proper places, taking on their natural shapes and sizes, and going back and back clearly into right perspective—right for me as artist, I simply mean to say; and it was like breathing—I did not have consciously to urge myself to think about it. So my time in Mexico and Europe served me in a way I had not dreamed of, even, besides its own charm and goodness: it gave me back my past and my own house and my own people—the native land of my heart.

This summer country of my childhood, this place of memory, is filled with landscapes shimmering in light and color, moving with sounds and shapes I hardly ever describe, or put in my stories in so many words; they form only the living background of what I am trying to tell, so familiar to my characters they would hardly notice them; the sound of mourning doves in the live oaks, the childish voices of parrots chattering on every back porch in the little towns, the hoverings of buzzards in the high blue air—all the life of that soft blackland farming country, full of fruits and flowers and birds, with good hunting and good fishing; with plenty of water, many little and big rivers. I shall name just a few of the rivers I remember—the San Antonio, the San Marcos, the Trinity, the Nueces, the Rio Grande, the Colorado, and the small clear branch of the Río Blanco, full of colored pebbles, Indian Creek, the place where I was born. The colors and tastes all had their smells, as the sounds have now their echoes: the bitter whiff of air over a sprawl of animal skeleton after the buzzards were gone; the smells and flavors of roses and melons, and peach bloom and ripe peaches, of cape jessamine in hedges blooming like popcorn, and the sickly sweetness of chinaberry florets; of honeysuckle in great swags on a trellised gallery; heavy tomatoes dead ripe and warm with the midday sun, eaten there, at the vine; the delicious milky green corn, savory hot corn bread eaten with still-warm sweet milk; and the clinging brackish smell of the muddy little ponds where we caught and boiled crawfish—in a discarded lard can—and ate them, then and there, we children, in the company of an old Negro who had once been my grandparent's slave, as I have told in another story. He was by our time only a servant, and a cantankerous old cuss very sure of his place in the household.

Uncle Jimbilly, for that was his name, was not the only one who knew exactly where he stood, and just about how far he could go in maintaining the rights, privileges, exemptions of his status so long as he performed its duties. At this point, I want to give a rather generalized view of the society of that time and place as I remember it, and as talks with my elders since confirm it. (Not long ago I planned to visit a very wonderful old lady who was a girlhood friend of my mother. I wrote to my sister that I could not think of being a burden to Miss Cora, and would therefore stop at the little hotel in town and call on her. And my sister wrote back air mail on the very day saying: "For God's sake, don't mention the word hotel to Miss Cora—she'll think you've lost your raising!") The elders all talked and behaved as if the final word had gone out long ago on manners, morality, religion, even politics: nothing was ever to change, they said, and even as they spoke, everything was changing, shifting, disappearing. This had been happening in fact ever since they were born; the greatest change, the fatal dividing change in this country, the War between the States, was taking place even as most of my father's generation were coming into the world. But it was the grandparents who still ruled in daily life; and they showed plainly in acts, words, and even looks (an enormously handsome generation they seemed to have been I remember—all those wonderful high noses with diamond-shaped bony structure in the bridge!) the presence of good society, very well based on traditional Christian beliefs. These beliefs were mainly Protestant but not yet petty middle-class puritanism: there remained still an element fairly high stepping and wide gestured in its personal conduct. The petty middle class of fundamentalists who saw no difference between wine-drinking, dancing, card-playing, and adultery, had not yet got altogether the upper hand in that part of the country—in fact, never did except in certain limited areas; but it was making a brave try. It was not really a democratic society; if everybody had his place, sometimes very narrowly defined, at least he knew where it was, and so did everybody else. So too, the higher laws of morality and religion were defined; if a man offended against the one, or sinned against the other, he knew it, and so did his neighbors, and they called everything by its right name.

This firm view applied also to social standing. A man who had humble ancestors had a hard time getting away from them and rising in the world. If he prospered and took to leisurely ways of living, he was merely "getting above his raising." If he managed to marry into one of the good old families, he had simply "outmarried himself." If he went away and made a success somewhere else, when he returned for a visit he was still only "that Jimmerson boy who went No'th." There is—was, perhaps I should say—a whole level of society of the South where it was common knowledge that the mother's family outranked the father's by half, at least. This might be based on nothing more tangible than that the mother's family came from Richmond or Charleston, while the father's may have started out somewhere from Pennsylvania, or have got bogged down one time or another in Arkansas. If they turned out well, the children of these matches were allowed their mother's status, for good family must never be denied, but father remained a member of the Plain People to the end. Yet there was nothing against anyone hinting at better lineage and a family past more dignified than the present, no matter how humble his present circumstances, nor how little proof he could offer for his claim. Aspiration to higher and better things was natural to all men, and a sign of proper respect for true blood and birth. Pride and hope may be denied to no one.

In this society of my childhood there were all sorts of tender ways of feeling and thinking, subtle understanding between people in matters of ritual and ceremony; I think in the main a civilized society, and yet, with the underlying, perpetual ominous presence of violence; violence potential that broke through the smooth surface almost without warning, or maybe just without warning to children, who learned later to know the signs. There were old cruel customs, the feud, for one, gradually dying out among the good families, never in fact prevalent among them—the men of that class fought duels, and abided, in theory at least, on the outcome; and country life, ranch life, was rough in Texas, at least. I remember tall bearded booted men striding about with clanking spurs, and carrying loaded pistols inside their shirts next to their ribs, even to church. It was quite matter of course that you opened a closet door in a bedroom and stared down into the cold eyes of shotguns and rifles, stacked there because there was no more room in the gun closet. In the summer, in that sweet-smelling flowery country, we children with our father or some grown-up in charge, spent long afternoons on a range, shooting at fixed targets or clay pigeons with the ordinary domestic fire arms, pistols, rifles of several calibers, shotguns to be fired single and double. I never fired a shotgun, but I knew the sounds and could name any round of fire I heard, even at great distances.

Someone asked me once where I had ever heard that conversation in "Noon Wine" between two men about chewing tobacco—that apparently aimless talk between Mr. Hatch and Mr. Thompson which barely masks hatred and is leading toward a murder. It seems that I *must* have heard something of the sort somewhere, sometime or another; I do not in the least remember it. But that whole countryside was full of tobacco-chewing men, whittling men, hard-working farming men perched on fences with their high heels caught on a rail, or squatting on their toes, gossiping idly and comfortably for hours at a time. I often wondered what they found to say to each other, day in day out year after year; but I should never have dared go near enough to listen profitably; yet I surely picked up something that came back whole and free as air that summer in Basel, Switzerland, when I thought I was studying only the life of Erasmus and the Reformation. And I have seen them many a time take out their razor-sharp long-bladed knives and slice a "chew" as delicately and precisely as if they were cutting a cake. These knives were so keen, often I have watched my father, shelling pecans for me, cut off the ends of the hard shells in a slow circular single gesture; then split them down the sides in four strips and bring out the nut meat whole. This fascinated me, but it did not occur to me to come near the knife, or offer to touch it. In our country life, in summers, we were surrounded by sharpened blades—hatchets, axes, plowshares, carving knives, Bowie knives, straight razors. We were taught so early to avoid all these, I do not remember ever being tempted to take one in my hand. Living as we did all our summers among loaded guns and dangerous cutting edges, four wild, adventurous children, always getting hurt in odd ways, we none of us were ever injured seriously. The worst thing that happened was, my elder sister got a broken collar bone from a fall, not as you might expect from a horse, for we almost lived on horseback, but from a three-foot fall off a fence where she had climbed to get a better view of a battle between two bulls. But these sharp blades slicing tobacco—did I remember it because it was an unusual sight? I think not. I must have seen it, as I remember it, dozens of times—but one day I really *saw* it: and it became part of Mr. Thompson's hallucinated vision when he killed Mr. Hatch, and afterward could not live without justifying himself.

There is an early memory, not the first, but certainly before my third year, always connected with this story, "Noon Wine"; it is the source, if there could be only one. I was a very small child. I know this by the remembered vastness of the world around me, the giant heights of grown-up people; a chair something to be scaled like a mountain; a table top to be peered over on tiptoe. It was late summer and near sunset, for the sky was a clear green-blue with long streaks of burning rose in it, and the air was full of the mournful sound of swooping bats. I was all alone in a wide grassy plain—it was the lawn on the east side of the house—and I was in that state of instinctive bliss which children only know, when there came like a blow of thunder echoing and rolling in that green sky, the explosion of a shotgun, not very far away, for it shook the air. There followed at once a high, thin, long-drawn scream, a sound I had never heard, but I knew what it was—it was the sound of death in the voice of a man. How did I know it was a shotgun? How should I not have known? How did I know it was death? We are born knowing death.

Let me examine this memory a little, which, though it is of an actual event, is like a remembered dream; but then all my childhood is that; and if in parts of this story I am trying to tell you, I use poetic terms, it is because in such terms do I remember many things and the feeling is valid, it cannot be left out, or denied.

In the first place, could I have been alone when this happened? It is most unlikely. I was one of four children, brought up in a houseful of adults of ripening age; a grandmother, a father, several Negro servants, among them two aged, former slaves; visiting relatives, uncles, aunts, cousins; grandmother's other grandchildren older than we, with always an ill-identified old soul or two, male or female, who seemed to be guests but helped out with stray chores. The house, which seemed so huge to me, was probably barely adequate to the population it accommodated; but of one thing I am certain—nobody was ever alone except for the most necessary privacies, and certainly no child at any time. Children had no necessary privacies. We were watched and herded and monitored and followed and spied upon and corrected and lectured and scolded (and kissed, let's be just, loved tenderly, and prayed over!) all day, every day, through the endless years of childhood—endless, but where did they go? So the evidence all points to the fact that I was not, could not have been, bodily speaking, alone in that few seconds when for the first time I heard the sound of murder. Who was with me? What did she say—for it was certainly one of the caretaking women around the house. Could I have known by instinct, of which I am so certain now, or did some- one speak words I cannot remember which nonetheless told me what had happened? There is nothing more to tell, all speculations are useless; this memory is a spot of clear light and color and sound, of immense, mysterious illumination of feeling against a horizon of total darkness.

Yet, was it the next day? next summer? In that same place, that grassy shady yard, in broad daylight I watched a poor little funeral procession creeping over the stony ridge of the near horizon, the dusty road out of town which led also to the cemetery. The hearse was just a spring wagon decently roofed and curtained with black oil cloth, poverty indeed, and some members of our household gathered on the front gallery to watch it pass, said, "Poor Pink Hodges—old man A— got him just like he said he would." Had it been Pink Hodges then, I had heard screaming death in the blissful sunset? And who was old man A—, whose name I do not remember, and what became of him, I wonder? I'll never know. I remember only that the air of our house was full of pity for Pink Hodges, for his harmlessness, his helplessness, "so pitiful, poor thing," they said; and, "It's just not right," they said. But what did they do to bring old man A— to justice, or at least to a sense of his evil? Nothing, I am afraid. I began to ask all sorts of questions and was silenced invariably by some elder who told me I was too young to understand such things.

Yet here I am coming to something quite clear, of which I am entirely certain. It happened in my ninth year, and again in that summer house in the little town near the farm, with the yard full of roses and irises and honeysuckle and hackberry trees, and the vegetable garden and the cow barn in back. It was already beginning to seem not so spacious to me; it went on dwindling year by year to the measure of my growing up.

One hot moist day after a great thunderstorm and heavy long rain, I saw a strange horse and buggy standing at the front gate. Neighbors and kin in the whole countryside knew each other's equipages as well as they did their own, and this outfit was not only strange, but not right; don't ask me why. It was not a good horse, and the buggy was not good, either. There was something wrong in the whole thing, and I went full of curiosity to see why such strangers as would drive such a horse and buggy would be calling on my grandmother. (At this point say anything you please about the snobbism of children and dogs. It is real. As real as the snobbism of their parents and owners, and much more keen and direct.)

I stood just outside the living-room door, unnoticed for a moment by my grandmother, who was sitting rather stiffly, with an odd expression on her face; a doubtful smiling mouth, brows knitted in painful inquiry. She was a woman called upon for decisions, many decisions every day, wielding justice among her unruly family. Once she struck, justly or unjustly, she dared not retract—the whole pack would have torn her to pieces. They did not want justice in any case, but revenge, each in his own favor. But this situation had nothing to do with her family, and there she sat, worried, undecided. I had never seen her so, and it dismayed me.

Then I saw first a poor sad pale beaten-looking woman in a faded cotton print dress and a wretched little straw hat with a wreath of wilted forgetmenots. She looked as if she had never eaten a good dinner, or slept in a comfortable bed, or felt a gentle touch; the mark of life-starvation was all over her. Her hands were twisted right in her lap and she was looking down at them in shame. Her eyes were covered with dark glasses. While I stared at her, I heard the man sitting near her almost shouting in a coarse, roughened voice: "I swear, it was in self-defense! His life or mine! If you don't believe me, ask my wife here. She saw it. My wife won't lie!" Every time he repeated these words, without lifting her head or moving, she would say in a low voice, "Yes, that's right. I saw it."

In that moment, or in another moment later as this memory sank in and worked my feelings and understanding, it was quite clear to me, and seems now to have been clear from the first, that he expected her to lie, was indeed forcing her to tell a lie; that she did it unwillingly and unlovingly in bitter resignation to the double disgrace of her husband's crime and her own sin; and that he, stupid, dishonest, soiled as he was, was imploring her as his only hope, somehow to make his lie a truth.

I used this scene in "Noon Wine," but the man in real life was not lean and gaunt and blindly, foolishly proud like Mr. Thompson; no, he was just a great loose-faced, blabbing man full of guilt and fear, and he was bawling at my grandmother, his eyes bloodshot with drink and tears, "Lady, if you don't believe me, ask my wife! She won't lie!" At this point my grandmother noticed my presence and sent me away with a look we children knew well and never dreamed of disobeying. But I heard part of the story later, when my grandmother said to my father, with an unfamiliar coldness in her voice, for she had made her decision about this affair, too: "I was never asked to condone a murder before. Something new." My father said, "Yes, and a coldblooded murder too if there ever was one."

So, there was the dreary tale of violence again, this time with the killer out on bail, going the rounds of the countryside with his wretched wife, telling his side of it—whatever it was; I never knew the end. In the meantime, in one summer or another, certainly before my eleventh year, for that year we left that country for good, I had two memorable glimpses. My father and I were driving from the farm to town, when we met with a tall black-whiskered man on horseback, sitting so straight his chin was level with his Adam's apple, dressed in clean mended blue denims, shirt open at the throat, a big devil-may-care black felt hat on the side of his head. He gave us a lordly gesture of greeting, caused his fine black horse to curvet and prance a little, and rode on, grandly. I asked my father who that could be, and he said, "That's Ralph Thomas, the proudest man in seven counties." I said, "What's he proud of?" And my father said, "I suppose the horse. It's a very fine horse," in a good-humored, joking tone, which made the poor man quite ridiculous, and yet not funny, but sad in some way I could not quite understand.

On another of these journeys I saw a bony, awkward, tired-looking man, tilted in a kitchen chair against the wall of his comfortless shack, set back from the road under the thin shade of hackberry trees, a thatch of bleached-looking hair between his eyebrows, blowing away at a doleful tune on his harmonica, in the hot dull cricket-whirring summer day; the very living image of loneliness. I was struck with pity for this stranger, his eyes closed against the alien scene, consoling himself with such poor music. I was told he was someone's Swedish hired man.

In time—when? how?—Pink Hodges, whom I never knew except in the sound of his death-cry, merged with my glimpse of the Swedish hired man to become the eternal Victim; the fat bullying whining man in my grandmother's living room became the Killer. But nothing can remain so simple as that, this was only a beginning. Helton too, the Victim in my story, is also a murderer, with the dubious innocence of the madman; but no less a shedder of blood. Everyone in this story contributes, one way or another directly or indirectly, to murder, or death by violence; even the two young sons of Mr. Thompson who turn on him in their fright and ignorance and side with their mother, who does not need them; they are guiltless, for they meant no harm, and they do not know what they have contributed to; indeed in their innocence they believe they are doing, not only right, but the only thing they could possibly do in the situation as they understand it: they must defend their mother. . . .

Let me give you a glimpse of Mr. and Mrs. Thompson, not as they were in their real lives, for I never knew them, but as they have become in my story. Mr. Thompson is a member of the plain people who has, by a hair's breadth, outmarried himself. Mrs. Thompson's superiority is shown in her better speech, her care for the proprieties, her social sense; even her physical fragility has some quality of the "genteel" in it; but in the long run, her strength is in the unyielding chastity of her morals, at once her yoke and her crown, and the prime condition of her right to the respect of her society. Her great power is that, while both she and her husband believe that the moral law, once broken, is irreparable, she will still stand by her principles no matter what; and in the end he stands by too. They are both doomed by this belief in their own way: Mr. Thompson from the moment he swung the ax on Mr. Hatch; Mrs. Thompson from the moment she acted the lie which meant criminal collusion. That both law and society expect this collusion of women with their husbands, so that safeguards for and against it are provided both by custom and statute, means nothing to Mrs. Thompson. When Mr. Burleigh planned for her to sit in court, he was not being cynical, but only showing himself a lawyer who knew his business.

This Mrs. Thompson of "Noon Wine" I understand much better, of course, than I do that woman I saw once for five minutes when I was nine years old. She is a benign, tender, ignorant woman, in whom the desire for truthfulness is a habit of her whole being; she is the dupe of her misunderstanding of what virtue really is; a woman not meant for large emergencies. Confronted with pure disaster she responds with pure suffering, and yet will not consent to be merely the passive Victim, or as she thinks, the criminal instrument of her husband's self-justification. Mr. Thompson, of course, has not been able to explain anything to himself, nor to justify himself in the least. By his own standards of morality, he is a murderer, a fact he cannot face: he needs someone to tell him this is not so, not so by some law of higher truth he is incapable of grasping. Alas, his wife, whose judgment he respects out of his mystical faith in the potency of her virtue, agrees with him—he is indeed a murderer. He has been acquitted, in a way he is saved; but in making a liar of her he has in effect committed a double murder—one of the flesh, one of the spirit.

Mr. Thompson, having invented his account of the event out of his own hallucinations, would now like to believe in it: he cannot. The next best thing would be for his wife to believe it: she does not believe, and he knows it. As they drive about the countryside in that series of agonizing visits, she tells her lie again and again, steadfastly. But privately she withholds the last lie that would redeem him, or so he feels. He wants her to turn to him when they are alone sometime, maybe just driving along together, and say, "Of course, Mr. Thompson, it's as clear as day. I remember it now. It was all just as you said!"

This she will never say, and so he must accept his final self-condemnation. There is of course a good deal more to it than

this, but this must do for the present—it is only meant to show
how that unknown woman, sitting in my grandmother's parlor
twisting her hands in shame all those years ago, got up one day
from her chair and started her long journey through my remembering and transmuting mind, and brought her world
with her.

And here I am brought to a pause, for almost without
knowing it, I have begun to write about these characters in a
story of mine as though they were real persons exactly as I
have shown them. And these fragments of memory on which
the story is based now seem to have a random look; they
nowhere contain in themselves, together or separately, the
story I finally wrote out of them; a story of the most painful
moral and emotional confusions, in which everyone concerned,
yes, in his crooked way, even Mr. Hatch, is trying to do right.

It is only in the varying levels of quality in the individual nature that we are able finally more or less to measure the degree
of virtue in each man. Mr. Thompson's motives are most certainly mixed, yet not ignoble; not the highest but the highest
he is capable of, he helps someone who helps him in turn;
while acting in defense of what he sees as the good in his own
life, the thing worth trying to save at almost any cost, he is trying
at the same time to defend another life—and the life of Mr.
Helton, who has proved himself the bringer of good, the present help, the true friend. Mr. Helton would have done as
much for me, Mr. Thompson says, and he is right. Yet he
hated Mr. Hatch on sight, wished to injure him before he had
a reason: could it not be a sign of virtue in Mr. Thompson that
he surmised and resisted at first glance the evil in Mr. Hatch?
The whole countryside, let us remember (for this is most important, the relations of a man to his society), agrees with Mr.
Burleigh the lawyer, and the jury and the judge, that Mr.
Thompson's deed was justifiable homicide: but this did not, as
his neighbors confirmed, make it any less a murder. Mr. Thompson was not an evil man, he was only a poor sinner doing his
best according to his lights, lights somewhat dimmed by his
natural aptitude for Pride and Sloth. He still had his virtues,
even if he did not quite know what they were, and so gave
himself credit for some few that he had not.

But Hatch was the doomed man, evil by nature, a lover and

doer of evil, who did no good thing for anyone, not even, in the long run, for himself. He was evil in the most dangerous irremediable way: one who works safely within the law, and has reasoned himself into believing his motives, if not good, are at least no worse than anyone else's: for he believes quite simply and naturally that the motives of others are no better than his own; and putting aside all nonsense about good, he will always be found on the side of custom and common sense and the letter of the law. When challenged he has his defense pat and ready, and there is nothing much wrong with it—it only lacks human decency, of which he has no conception beyond a faint hearsay. Mr. Helton is, by his madness, beyond good and evil, his own victim as well as the victim of others. Mrs. Thompson is a woman of the sort produced in numbers in that time, that class, that place, that code: so trained to the practice of her prescribed womanly vocation of virtue as such—manifest, un-relenting, sacrificial, stupefying—she has almost lost her human qualities, and her spiritual courage and insight, to boot. She commits the, to her, dreadful unforgivable sin of lying; more-over, lying to shield a criminal, even if that criminal is her own husband. Having done this, to the infinite damage, as she sees it, of her own soul (as well as her self-respect which is founded on her feeling of irreproachability), she lacks the courage and the love to see her sin through to its final good purpose; to commit it with her whole heart and with perfect acceptance of her guilt to say to her husband the words that might have saved them both, soul and body—might have, I say only. I do not know and shall never know. Mrs. Thompson was not that robust a character, and his story, given all, must end as it does end. . . . There is nothing in any of these beings tough enough to work the miracle of redemption in them.

Suppose I imagine now that I really saw all of these persons in the flesh at one time or another? I saw what I have told you, a few mere flashes of a glimpse here and there, one time or an-other; but I do know why I remembered them, and why in my memory they slowly took on their separate lives in a story. It is because there radiated from each one of those glimpses of strangers some element, some quality that arrested my atten-tion at a vital moment of my own growth, and caused me, a child, to stop short and look outward, away from myself; to look at another human being with that attention and wonder and speculation which ordinarily, and very naturally, I think, a child lavishes only on himself. Is it not almost the sole end of civilized education of all sorts to teach us to be more and more highly, sensitively conscious of the reality of the existence, the essential being, of others, those around us so very like us and yet so bafflingly, so mysteriously different? I do not know whether my impressions were on the instant, as I now believe, or did they draw to their magnet gradually with time and confirming experience? That man on the fine horse, with his straight back, straight neck, shabby and unshaven, riding like a cavalry officer, "the proudest man in seven counties"—I saw him no doubt as my father saw him, absurd, fatuous, but with some final undeniable human claim on respect and not to be laughed at, except in passing, for all his simple vanity.

The woman I have called Mrs. Thompson—I never knew her name—showed me for the first time, I am certain, the face of pure shame; humiliation so nearly absolute it could not have been more frightening if she had groveled on the floor; and I knew that whatever the cause, it was mortal and beyond help. In that bawling sweating man with the loose mouth and staring eyes, I saw the fear that is moral cowardice and I knew he was lying. In that yellow-haired, long-legged man playing his harmonica I felt almost the first glimmer of understanding and sympathy for any suffering not physical. Most certainly I had already done my share of weeping over lost or dying pets, or beside someone I loved who was very sick, or my own pains and accidents; but *this* was a spiritual enlightenment, some tenderness, some first awakening of charity in my self-centered heart. I am using here some very old-fashioned noble words in their prime sense. They have perfect freshness and reality to me, they are the irreplaceable names of Realities. I know well what they mean, and I need them here to describe as well as I am able what happens to a child when the bodily senses and the moral sense and the sense of charity are unfolding, and are touched once for all in that first time when the soul is prepared for them; and I know that the all-important things in that way have all taken place long and long before we know the words for them.

1956

Notes on the Texas I Remember

NOT long ago there appeared in a weekly news magazine the snapshot of a lady in advanced years, of solid weight and vitality, and a smiling face full of comic humor. She wore large blue jeans, a country-style shirt, and a floppy straw hat much like the ten-cent peanut straw hat I wore on the farm every summer from more or less 1893 to 1901. The lady was armed with a rake, and was raking up the leaves and trash from the courthouse square of a small town of which she is the mayor. The town is Kyle, Texas, and our lady is Mayor Mary Kyle, the daughter of Old Captain Fergus Kyle, who founded and named the place, and lived out his life admired, respected, and loved by the five hundred citizens who lived there with him rather as contented guests. Everybody knew the town belonged to him, and now it belongs to Miss Mary by divine right, and though her working outfit—jeans and shirts or turtlenecks—has been the high fashion among all classes and kinds for some time, yet other things are changed in an important way. In my time of childhood there, Miss Mary would have had a squad of boys eager to rake the square just for the fun of it. Now she could not find, not for money nor thought of love, any lad in the place so underprivileged he would rake that lawn at any price.

My grandmother lived on a corner of the stony, crooked little road called Main Street, in a six-room house of a style known as Queen Anne, who knows why? It had no features at all except for two long galleries, front and back galleries—mind you, *not* porches or verandas, and I shall stick without further translation to whatever other word of my native dialect occurs here—and these galleries were shuttered in green lattice and then covered again with honeysuckle and roses, adding two delightful long summer rooms to the house, the front a dining room, the back furnished with swings and chairs for conversation and repose, iced tea, limeade, sangaree—well, have it your way: sangria—and always, tall frosted beakers of mint julep, for the gentlemen, of course.

Stories I see in newspapers now remind me constantly

of things as they were then, in my childhood, in my little town.

Let me quote from the Washington *Post* of Monday, October 28, 1974, a report of a certain incident: "A U.S. Army Private, Felix Longoria, was buried in Arlington National Cemetery in 1949. Only his family, a representative of President Truman and some Texas Congressmen attended the ceremony. Among the Congressmen was Senator Lyndon B. Johnson, who had arranged for the re-interment of Pvt. Longoria who had died while fighting in the Philippines but who was refused burial in his Texas home town of Three Trees because of his heritage." He was a Mexican-Indian peon. The *Post* published this story because it had what I suppose we may regard as a happy ending—after twenty-five years and a good deal of agitation on the subject from several equality-loving sources, our hero's remains were recently accepted for burial in his native town in the white cemetery in Three Trees, Texas.

I remember one of the annual religious "Revivals" in the Methodist church in Kyle. The Mexicans of the Spanish-Indian peon class lived in a colony just outside town; they subsisted by rudimentary farming, selling chickens and eggs and vegetables. They were poor, most humble, never employed in any regularly paid work, such as gardening for the town people; or, for the women, housework of any kind. These jobs were for Negroes strictly, who also occupied a servant place, but privileged. The prejudices against the Mexicans were simple: they were foreigners, they spoke Spanish, they ate strange stuff, they were Catholic in an iron-bound Protestant region. There was no Catholic church nearer than San Marcos, a good two hours' trip away by family surrey.

Everybody of whatever denomination, all white, of course, attended these Revivals. It was a social occasion, with visiting preachers renowned for dramatic orations. Little by little, the Mexican people began to show up at the meetings, which started in the morning and went on until late in the evening, all singing and shouting and praying, tears and sacred joy. But there was uneasiness among the white congregation as the number of Mexicans increased in attendance. They sat in the back benches, in silence. They knelt or stood or sat as the others did, and their faces were eager and pleasant and very attentive.

So one morning (I was there, seven years old) an old deacon named Schwartz rose and made a stern talk which I could not understand, but he turned and gestured in the direction of the Mexicans and poured out hard-voiced words. I remember only the last line: "We must do something in self-defense." At this point the preacher rose and said, "Let us pray for guidance." Everybody bowed his head and the prayer ended with a chorus of Amens. The preacher moved near the Mexicans and very politely asked them to leave, saying that the revival was a private occasion, only for church members (a lie, incidentally), he regretted not being able to invite them, and he wished them well. They rose in silence, some of them trying to smile, and they went out in a bowed little huddle, with tears in their eyes—even the old men wept. One old woman whimpered, "Dios, Dios . . ." as if trying to invoke the return of her vanished God.

You can see how bitterly I remember this. I was mystified and unhappy, but I knew something was badly wrong when my father motioned to us. He and my grandmother, Aunt Jane, grandmother's former slave, my sister and brother rose also in a group and walked out just behind the Mexicans. And I heard what my family thought of the event for a good while. (My grandmother, when she heard that Mr. Lincoln had abolished slavery and the Negroes were free, was heard to say "I hope it works both ways," and lived to realize that it did not.) We were a mixed company of Catholics, Episcopalians, Methodists, and Presbyterians, and all were equally outraged. It fixed my point of view on that subject unchangeably for life. I had not imagined it still happened, now, at this time.

An earlier memory I have is when I was about two-and-a-half years old. I was still wearing soft shoes, and a white wool crochet cap with a bunch of crochet grapes on top and a large ribbon bow under my chin. I know this because I was on a train, being held up on the lap of my nurse, a smiling Negro girl I was to know for a good number of years. I was romping on my nurse's lap, and gazing in the looking glass, fascinated by my cap with the soft woolly grapes. My father was facing us, and now and then he would reach over, pull the cap off my head, and fluff up my short, black, curly hair with gentle fingers, and he would try to persuade me to leave it off—"Let's show the pretty hair," he would say—but I would hold on to the cap, and put it on again and gaze at myself in the looking glass, something new and exciting. The cap was the magic, not my face.

I remember driving through Texas a good many years ago with my father. We passed through Round Rock and my father remembered that it was here Sam Bass, the train robber, and his Right Bower companion were shot, and I said, "Those poor lugs were big popular heroes, weren't they?" and my father said, "No, not with my generation. We knew exactly who and what they were. It's the movies have made them out heroes." Later, he pointed out in another part of the state a clump of live oak on a small hill and remembered Sam Bass again. He was supposed to have hidden there at one time or another. But the really important memory to my father was that he and his older brother had once been riding together there and had taken refuge in this knoll of trees to let a herd of buffalo go by. They sheltered within on their horses and the buffalo herd divided and went around them. "There were several hundred of them," my father said.

I remember the fruits of my childhood, the orchards, red grape-fruit, oranges, peaches, watermelon, cantaloupes, figs, pecans, wild grapes. I remember the barrels of grape juice under the trees on the farm, with long tubes from the vent bubbling into great pails of water, red foam running down the sides, the chickens sitting on the barrels or clustering under them, staggering, flopping, wobbling drunk, and glad of it. They were seen leaning against tree trunks, or seated in open space as if on nests, but there were no fatalities or terminal alcoholics among them. Hens, as with all domestic creatures and most human females in that region, led fairly laborious, monotonous country lives. As I grew up a little, I began to see this melancholy state of affairs, and thought it only just and right that they should have an occasional spree. But it was really only the chickens who enjoyed the wine-making. The roosters went fairly mad and spent their time trying to seduce any hen in sight, who for once ignored their advances. We, the children, thought we knew exactly what the wild flurry among the chicken flock meant: a rooster chasing a hen meant they were making eggs, which we took pleasure in looking for all over the place, because no number of carefully prepared nests ever lured the hens into settling down to leaving their eggs where we could pick them up tidily. It seems curious to me now that all this nonchalant, casual knowledge of what went on in the chicken society never taught us anything about sex generally speaking. Their antics had no relation to the way calves, pigs, ponies (colts), or children came into the world.

From earliest days I remember a dollop of wine in my glass of water making it a pleasantly perfumed pink tint, and I remember Governor Hogg and my grandmother in her parlor in the little house in Kyle, Texas, drinking a stirrup cup of cold buttermilk. They were good friends. I remember the doctors, the ministers, the professors, gentlemen of her generation who visited her in all seasons, dressed always in the vestments of their callings and condition of life: black broadcloth, long-tailed coat known as Prince Albert, waistcoat white in summer, black in winter, stiff starched while shirt, a collar like white cardboard, a black silk or satin or white lawn tie. The doctors and professors wore wide-brimmed black hats, very becoming and rather gallant in style; the ministers and politicians wore solemn top hats. These were not articles of formal dress: just everyday uniform of the calling. For some reason I remember best Governor Hogg and Dr. White; Governor Hogg because it was said his children were named Harry Hogg, Ura Hogg, and Ima Hogg, which seemed to me carrying a joke too far; but his daughter, Miss Ima Hogg, lived to a great age in dignity, and in the joyful pastime of turning bare acres into a fine wood filled with flowers. Dr. White was handsome, a real beau, much in request as family physician. He drove a fine matched pair of Kentucky thoroughbreds—a reassuring sight, admirable in every respect.

I remember a train trip with my grandmother. It was the slowest train; they had no streamliners, just little rickety trains, and it was a long trip. We went two days and a night to get to Marfa, a little town in the Pecos country. Here was the famous and beautiful Pecos Bridge, then supposed to be, I don't know the figures, the highest and one of the longest bridges in the world. I don't know its history, when it was built, who built it, or what. I only know that in my time it had been condemned for quite a while, but when my grandmother and I went from San Antonio to Marfa and then to El Paso to visit Uncle Asbury and Uncle Bill, we crossed this bridge. It was much this way: the train stopped at the edge of the bridge and we looked down into this great chasm and wondered at the long slender spidery legs that held up this bridge that we were going to cross. Everybody got out except the engineer and fireman. All of us, carrying our light luggage and our suitcases, walked across the bridge. All of us arrived on the other side and waited as the train came after us and we stood watching—I don't remember any particular wonder or excitement at all, but I remember watching this train cross this shambling bridge; you could see it shaking and the train wobbling from side to side. Nothing happened. The train arrived, and after the last wheel was on firm ground, we all climbed back and proceeded with our journey. Grandmother and I did this three times. I wonder what became of that bridge. I never heard of it being torn down or another being put up in its place. I haven't kept up with the history of my part of this country as I should have.

Just across the Pecos Bridge on the other side was the famous man who set himself up as Law west of the Pecos. His name was Roy Bean and he used to chase bandits in that part of the country. He took it upon himself to judge and actually to have desperadoes hanged. He was going full tilt when I was there. I don't know how long he lasted, either. These are memories of my childhood and I left Texas and the South almost for good and forever when I was nineteen years old. I haven't gone back except once for fifty-five years.

Near the railroad track there was in those days a little clear circle that had no particular marking; except that it was a circle; it had no fence, no row of stones. There was a painted stick in the middle and it was known that here was Roy Bean, Law west of the Pecos. The circle with the painted stick marked where Lily Langtry had stood while Roy Bean drew a ring around her as a memento of her unbelievable Presence.

Lily Langtry, the famous English actress and beauty, was not much of an actress but she was a great beauty, and her fame rested mostly on the fact that she was the mistress of the Prince of Wales who later became King of England, Edward VII. She was making a tour of the United States and in those days all of the stars traveled in special trains or at least special cars gaily decorated, painted with their names on them. They traveled all over the country and they stopped at the smaller towns. I remember in my childhood I saw all the greatest actors and actresses, heard all the great pianists and violinists and singers in the world who came to the United States, because sooner or later they landed in San Antonio and El Paso and other small cities and they took them in, every season. There was no reason why all of us shouldn't hear or see them, and we did; that is something that has changed greatly.

My nephews and nieces who are now in young middle age (past fifty years) were twenty and twenty-one years old before they had ever ridden in a train or heard a live orchestra or seen a living actress because they had it on radio and later on television. They didn't travel in anything but their own automobiles, they had never seen a live ballet, and I will tell you it was a strange thing. I was horrified at the terrible lack in their education; I can't exaggerate their excitement when they did first see living people and heard voices coming from living chests. It was like a new life and new world opened up to them; they found it hard to believe that I managed to hear Paderewski when I was eight or nine years old. But he came to Texas as all the rest did. I heard him in San Antonio, because he had a special car and his accompanist, his chef, and waiters, and make-up man—everything. His wife and he traveled with their entire family in this one big car. He went all over the United States and people used to go to those big, splendid, Wide-Worldly shows. You can't make the young understand how much music and theater we saw and knew because you go to Texas now and people of middling means don't know anything except what they learn from TV. Since the oil came, of course, there are the ones who ramble, who go everywhere and see everything, but I am talking about the people anywhere you go, most of them just see TV—they hear and see quite a lot but it isn't as good. You have nobody to say what he thinks and feels about what he sees and hears. In those days you went

to the theater with hundreds of others and sat together and
had this experience together and it meant something to you.
This has disappeared. They used to travel, even the families
of the very poor who would come in the same wagons they
took the cotton to the gin in; they would travel in all kinds of
weather to see a great actor or hear a great pianist or singer. It
is hard for people to understand now, but it is true.

When I'm asked if I remember bandits and cowboy songs, I
confess I don't know any bandit ballads except "Sam Bass"
and "Jesse James." But I miss "There was blood on the saddle,
and blood on the ground" from the collections I have seen;
and I am wondering if "My Love is a Rider," the dashing
romantic ditty, should really be ascribed to Belle Starr, the
woman outlaw of the slashing, shooting 1880s. For those who
remember another era, it is instructive to compare this delicate, rosy view of a cowboy with Mae West's song, so hot it
had to be muted down and mumbled in her picture, *Diamond
Lil*—"Oh tell me, where is my easy rider gone?" At least that is
the way my eager ears snagged it at the time, and it wasn't
easy. Miss West was a highly conventional type of fancy lady
with a real respect for the law, and when the Hollywood censors said "mumble that line," she mumbled it and let her shape
and her eyebrows do the work instead.

   Belle Starr had no such problems. She just sang it right
out—

> The first time I met him was early one spring,
> He was riding a bronco, a high-headed thing.
> He tipped me a wink as he gaily did go,
> For he wished me to look at his bucking bronco.

How blushing and guileless can a lady bandit be? She goes on:
"The next time I saw him . . ."—but it doesn't matter. That
occasion was as innocuous as the first, and so it went on, with
the traditional warning at last to maidens to beware of
sprightly young cowboys who will court you and leave you and
finally "go up the trail in the spring on his bucking bronco."
The knight on horseback playing fast and loose with the shepherdess as they did in the twelfth century, judging by their

songs. Isn't there anything new to be said on this subject, even by a lady bandit in late nineteenth-century Texas? Or was she just the Nut-Brown Maid in another dress? The only differences are she did have a six-shooter and ride a horse. Her photograph shows a face that would scare a crow; it also scared quite a few of her colleagues.

The bandits themselves didn't seem to do much singing, and their admirers were not much on the musical side, either. The really grand and horrible outlaws were not at all those poor shock-headed Wild West cutups, but the Natchez Trace, Mississippi and Louisiana and Tennessee ones—their stories can make your blood run cold even now. They were not much given to song, either.

I am now speaking of the old-timers in the days of Audubon and the Mississippi River gamblers and pirates.

Not long ago, I saw a photograph of a whole row of dead bandits of that era, all laid out orderly in their working clothes, looking very helpless and unkempt and homeless in a barn or kind of shed and with a touchingly indifferent stare in their open eyes; this is what I remember from just a quick glimpse, turning the page in a hurry, but the impression has stayed by me of something pitiable, mysteriously innocent, somehow wronged and wasted—all the soft-headed western Christian sentiments I was brought up on, in short. And seeing what this sort of thing can lead to, I fight it furiously in myself. For I have seen how insidiously our natures will work almost unconsciously in defense of the killer rather than his victim. How at last we can persuade ourselves that the victim, not the killer, was really in the deepest sense the guilty one. I suppose there are those who really believe this, or can gradually persuade themselves, but I am not one of them . . . I can always rule my misguided sympathies by remembering how the men they murdered looked—much the same, no doubt—and how their families and friends looked, and just what it was like for them; and I am still able to draw that fine hairline between justice and revenge. They are two quite opposite procedures that may sometimes have a surface resemblance; they are both real, and they mean what they say, and both serve their ends perfectly.

Ah dear—space is up. I must stop, and I have hardly begun.

Memory for me is a tidal wave. I have lived for so long and so many lives, I hardly dare to begin with even the smallest, most trivial-seeming recollection. Nothing is trivial, not for a moment, if you really delve into the past. It can stop your heart for a beat or two.

1975

Portrait: Old South

I AM the grandchild of a lost War, and I have blood-knowledge of what life can be in a defeated country on the bare bones of privation. The older people in my family used to tell such amusing little stories about it. One time, several years after the War ended, two small brothers (one of them was my father) set out by themselves on foot from their new home in south Texas, and when neighbors picked them up three miles from home, hundreds of miles from their goal, and asked them where they thought they were going, they answered confidently, "To Louisiana, to eat sugar cane," for they hadn't tasted sugar for months and remembered the happy times in my grandmother's cane fields there.

Does anyone remember the excitement when for a few months we had rationed coffee? In my grandmother's day, in Texas, everybody seemed to remember that man who had a way of showing up with a dozen grains of real coffee in his hand, which he exchanged for a month's supply of corn meal. My grandmother parched a mixture of sweet potato and dried corn until it was black, ground it up and boiled it, because her family couldn't get over its yearning for a dark hot drink in the mornings. But she would never allow them to call it coffee. It was known as That Brew. Bread was a question, too. Wheat flour, during the period euphemistically described as Reconstruction, ran about $100 a barrel. Naturally my family ate corn bread, day in, day out, for years. Finally Hard Times eased up a little, and they had hot biscuits, nearly all they could eat, once a week for Sunday breakfast. My father never forgot the taste of those biscuits, the big, crusty tender kind made with buttermilk and soda, with melted butter and honey, every blessed Sunday that came. "They almost made a Christian of me," he said.

My grandfather, a soldier, toward the end of the War was riding along one very cold morning, and he saw, out of all reason, a fine big thick slice of raw bacon rind lying beside the road. He dismounted, picked it up, dusted it off and made a hearty breakfast of it. "The best piece of bacon rind I ever ate in my life," said my grandfather. These little yarns are the first that come to mind out of hundreds; they were the merest surface ripples over limitless deeps of bitter memory. My elders all remained nobly unreconstructed to their last moments, and my feet rest firmly on this rock of their strength to this day.

The woman who made That Brew and the soldier who ate the bacon rind had been bride and groom in a Kentucky wedding somewhere around 1850. Only a few years ago a cousin of mine showed me a letter from a lady then rising ninety-five who remembered that wedding as if it had been only yesterday. She was one of the flower girls, carrying a gilded basket of white roses and ferns, tied with white watered-silk ribbon. She couldn't remember whether the bride's skirt had been twenty-five feet or twenty-five yards around, but she inclined to the latter figure; it was of white satin brocade with slippers to match.

The flower girl was allowed a glimpse of the table set for the bridal banquet. There were silver branched candlesticks everywhere, each holding seven white candles, and a crystal chandelier holding fifty white candles, all lighted. There was a white lace tablecloth reaching to the floor all around, over white satin. The wedding cake was tall as the flower girl and of astonishing circumference, festooned all over with white sugar roses and green leaves, actual live rose leaves. The room, she wrote, was a perfect bower of southern smilax and white dogwood. And there was butter. This is a bizarre note, but there was an enormous silver butter dish, *with feet* (italics mine), containing at least ten pounds of butter. The dish had cupids and some sort of fruit around the rim, and the butter was molded or carved, to resemble a set-piece of roses and lilies, every petal and leaf standing out sharply, natural as life. The flower girl, after the lapse of nearly a century, remembered no more than this, but I think it does well for a glimpse.

That butter. She couldn't get over it, and neither can I. It seems as late-Roman and decadent as anything ever thought up in Hollywood. Her memory came back with a rush when she thought of the food. All the children had their own table in a small parlor, and ate just what the grownups had: Kentucky ham, roast turkey, partridges in wine jelly, fried chicken, dove pie, half a dozen sweet and hot sauces, peach pickle, watermelon pickle and spiced mangoes. A dozen different fruits, four kinds of cake and at last a chilled custard in tall glasses with whipped cream capped by a brandied cherry. She lived to boast of it, and she lived along with other guests of that feast to eat corn pone and bacon fat, and yes, to be proud of that also. Why not? She was in the best of company, and quite a large gathering too.

In my childhood we ate, my father remarked, "as if there were no God." By then my grandmother, her brocaded wedding gown cut up and made over to the last scrap for a dozen later brides in the connection, had become such a famous cook it was mentioned in her funeral eulogies. There was nobody like her for getting up a party, for the idea of food was inseparably connected in her mind with social occasions of a delightful nature, and though she loved to celebrate birthdays and holidays, still any day was quite good enough to her. Several venerable old gentlemen, lifelong friends of my grandmother, sat down, pen in hand, after her death and out of their grateful recollection of her bountiful hospitality—their very words—wrote long accounts of her life and works for the local newspapers of their several communities, and each declared that at one time or another he had eaten the best dinner of his life at her table. The furnishings of her table were just what were left over from times past, good and bad; a mixture of thin old silver and bone-handled knives, delicate porcelain, treasured but not hoarded, and such crockery as she had been able to replace with; fine old linen worn thin and mended, and stout cotton napery with fringed borders; no silver candlesticks at all, and a pound of sweet butter with a bouquet of roses stamped upon it, in a plain dish—plain for the times; it was really a large opal-glass hen seated on a woven nest, rearing aloft her scarlet comb and beady eye.

Grandmother was by nature lavish, she loved leisure and calm, she loved luxury, she loved dress and adornment, she loved to sit and talk with friends or listen to music; she did not in the least like pinching or saving and mending and making things do, and she had no patience with the kind of slackness that tried to say second-best was best, or half good enough. But the evil turn of fortune in her life tapped the bottomless reserves of her character, and her life was truly heroic. She had no such romantic notion of herself. The long difficulties of her life she regarded as temporary, an unnatural interruption to her normal fate, which required simply firmness, a good deal of will-power and energy and the proper aims to re-establish finally once more. That no such change took place during her long life did not in the least disturb her theory. Though we had no money and no prospects of any, and were land-poor in the most typical way, we never really faced this fact as long as our grandmother lived because she would not hear of such a thing. We had been a good old family of solid wealth and property in Kentucky, Louisiana and Virginia, and we remained that in Texas, even though due to a temporary decline for the most honorable reasons, appearances were entirely to the contrary. This accounted for our fragmentary, but strangely useless and ornamental education, appropriate to our history and our station in life, neither of which could be in the least altered by the accident of straitened circumstances.

Grandmother had been an unusually attractive young woman, and she carried herself with the graceful confidence of a natural charmer to her last day. Her mirror did not deceive her, she saw that she was old. Her youthful confidence became matriarchal authority, a little way of knowing best about almost everything, of relying upon her own experience for sole guide, and I think now she had earned her power fairly. Her bountiful hospitality represented only one of her victories of intelligence and feeling over the stubborn difficulties of life. Her mind and her instinct ran in flashes of perception, and she sometimes had an airy, sharp, impatient way of speaking to those who didn't keep up with her. She believed it was her duty to be a stern methodical disciplinarian, and made a point of training us as she had been trained even to forbidding us to cross our knees, or to touch the back of our chair when we sat, or to speak until we were spoken to: love's labors lost utterly, for she had brought up a houseful of the worst spoiled children in seven counties, and started in again hopefully with a long series of motherless grandchildren—for the daughters of that afterwar generation did not survive so well as their mothers, they died young in great numbers, leaving young husbands and children—who were to be the worst spoiled of any. She never punished anyone until she was exasperated beyond all endurance, when she was apt to let fly with a lightning, long-armed slap at the most unexpected moments, usually quite unjustly and ineffectually.

Truth was, when she had brought her eleven children into the world, she had had a natural expectation of at least as many servants to help her bring them up; her gifts were social, and she should never have had the care of children except in leisure, for then she was delightful, and communicated some of her graces to them, and gave them beautiful memories. We loved the smell of her face powder and the light orange-flower perfume she wore, the crinkled waves of her hair, the knot speared through with a small pointed Spanish comb. We leaned upon her knee, and sniffed in the sweetness of her essential being, we nuzzled her face and the little bit of lace at her collar, enchanted with her sweetness.

Her hands were long since ruined, but she was proud of her narrow feet with their high insteps, and liked to dress them in smooth black kid boots with small spool-shaped heels. When she went "abroad"—that is, shopping, calling, or to church—she wore her original mourning gowns, of stiff, dull, corded silks, made over and refurbished from time to time, and a sweeping crape veil that fell from a peaked cap over her face and to the hem of her skirt in the back. This mourning had begun for her husband, dead only twenty-five years, but it went on for him, and for her daughters and for grandchildren, and cousins, and then brothers and sisters, and, I suspect, for an old friend or so. In this garb, holding up her skirt in front with one black-gloved hand, she would walk with such flying lightness her grandchild would maintain a heated trot to keep pace with her.

She loved to have us say our prayers before bedtime in a cluster around her knees, and in our jealousy to be nearest, and to be first, we often fell fighting like a den of bear cubs, instead of christened children, and she would have to come in among us like an animal trainer, the holy hour having gone quite literally to hell. "Birds in their little nests agree, and 'tis a shameful sight," she would remark on these occasions, but she never finished the rhyme, and for years I wondered why it was a shameful sight for little birds to agree, when Grandmother was rather severe with us about our quarreling. It was "vulgar," she said, and for her, that word connoted a peculiarly detestable form of immorality, that is to say, bad manners. Inappropriate conduct was bad manners, bad manners were bad morals, and bad morals led to bad manners, and there you were, ringed with fire, and no way out.

She was an individual being if ever I knew one, and yet she never did or said anything to make herself conspicuous; there are no strange stories to tell, no fantastic gestures. She rode horseback at a gallop until the year of her death, but it seemed only natural. Her sons had to restrain her from an engineering project, which seemed very simple to her and perhaps was really simple: she had wished to deflect the course of a small river which was encroaching on her land in Louisiana; she knew exactly how it should be done, and it would have made all the difference, she felt. She smoked cubeb cigarettes, for her throat, she would say, and add that she had always imagined she would enjoy the taste of tobacco. She and my father would sit down for a noggin of hot toddy together on cold evenings, or just a drop of good Bourbon before dinner because they enjoyed it. She could not endure to see a horse with its head strung up in a checkrein, and used to walk down a line of conveyances drawn up around the church, saying amiably to the dozing Negro drivers, "Good morning, Jerry; good morning, Uncle Squire," reaching up deftly and loosing the checkrein. The horses hung their heads and so did the drivers, and the reins stayed unfastened for that time, at any rate.

In a family full of willful eccentrics and headstrong characters and unpredictable histories, her presence was singularly free from peaks and edges and the kind of color that leaves a trail of family anecdotes. She left the lingering perfume and the airy shimmer of grace about her memory.

1944

A Christmas Story

W HEN she was five years old, my niece asked me again why we celebrated Christmas. She had asked when she was three and when she was four, and each time had listened with a shining, believing face, learning the songs and gazing enchanted at the pictures which I displayed as proof of my stories. Nothing could have been more successful, so I began once more confidently to recite in effect the following:

The feast in the beginning was meant to celebrate with joy the birth of a Child, an event of such importance to this world that angels sang from the skies in human language to announce it and even, if we may believe the old painters, came down with garlands in their hands and danced on the broken roof of the cattle shed where He was born.

"Poor baby," she said, disregarding the angels, "didn't His papa and mama have a house?"

They weren't quite so poor as all that, I went on, slightly dashed, for last year the angels had been the center of interest. His papa and mama were able to pay taxes at least, but they had to leave home and go to Bethlehem to pay them, and they could have afforded a room at the inn, but the town was crowded because everybody came to pay taxes at the same time. They were quite lucky to find a manger full of clean straw to sleep in. When the baby was born, a goodhearted servant girl named Bertha came to help the mother. Bertha had no arms, but in that moment she unexpectedly grew a fine new pair of arms and hands, and the first thing she did with them was to wrap the baby in swaddling clothes. We then sang together the song about Bertha the armless servant. Thinking I saw a practical question dawning in a pure blue eye, I hurried on to the part about how all the animals—cows, calves, donkeys, sheep——

"And pigs?"

Pigs perhaps even had knelt in a ring around the baby and breathed upon Him to keep Him warm through His first hours in this world. A new star appeared and moved in a straight course toward Bethlehem for many nights to guide three kings who came from far countries to place important gifts in the straw beside Him: gold, frankincense and myrrh.

"What beautiful clothes," said the little girl, looking at the picture of Charles the Seventh of France kneeling before a meek blond girl and a charming baby.

It was the way some people used to dress. The Child's mother, Mary, and His father, Joseph, a carpenter, were such unworldly simple souls they never once thought of taking any honor to themselves nor of turning the gifts to their own benefit.

"What became of the gifts?" asked the little girl.

Nobody knows, nobody seems to have paid much attention to them, they were never heard of again after that night. So far as we know, those were the only presents anyone ever gave to the Child while He lived. But He was not unhappy. Once he caused a cherry tree in full fruit to bend down one of its branches so His mother could more easily pick cherries. We then sang about the cherry tree until we came to the words *Then up spake old Joseph, so rude and unkind.*

"Why was he unkind?"

I thought perhaps he was just in a cross mood.

"What was he cross about?"

Dear me, what should I say now? After all, this was not *my* daughter, whatever would her mother answer to this? I asked her in turn what she was cross about when she was cross? She couldn't remember ever having been cross but was willing to let the subject pass. We moved on to *The Withy Tree*, which tells how the Child once cast a bridge of sunbeams over a stream and crossed upon it, and played a trick on little John the Baptist, who followed Him, by removing the beams and letting John fall in the water. The Child's mother switched Him smartly for this with a branch of withy, and the Child shed loud tears and wished bad luck upon the whole race of withies for ever.

"What's a withy?" asked the little girl. I looked it up in the dictionary and discovered it meant osiers, or willows.

"Just a willow like ours?" she asked, rejecting this intrusion of the commonplace. Yes, but once, when His father was struggling with a heavy piece of timber almost beyond his strength, the Child ran and touched it with one finger and the timber rose and fell properly into place. At night His mother cradled Him and sang long slow songs about a lonely tree waiting for Him in a far place; and the Child, moved by her tears, spoke long before it was time for Him to speak and His first words were, "Don't be sad, for you shall be Queen of Heaven." And there she was in an old picture, with the airy jeweled crown being set upon her golden hair.

I thought how nearly all of these tender medieval songs and legends about this Child were concerned with trees, wood, timbers, beams, cross-pieces; and even the pagan north transformed its great druidic tree festooned with human entrails into a blithe festival tree hung with gifts for the Child, and some savage old man of the woods became a rollicking saint with a big belly. But I had never talked about Santa Claus, because myself I had not liked him from the first, and did not even then approve of the boisterous way he had almost crowded out the Child from His own birthday feast.

"I like the part about the sunbeam bridge the best," said the little girl, and then she told me she had a dollar of her own and would I take her to buy a Christmas present for her mother.

We wandered from shop to shop, and I admired the way the little girl, surrounded by tons of seductive, specially manufactured holiday merchandise for children, kept her attention fixed resolutely on objects appropriate to the grown-up world. She considered seriously in turn a silver tea service, one thousand dollars; an embroidered handkerchief with lace on it, five dollars; a dressing-table mirror framed in porcelain flowers, eighty-five dollars; a preposterously showy crystal flask of perfume, one hundred twenty dollars; a gadget for curling the eyelashes, seventy-five cents; a large plaque of colored glass jewelry, thirty dollars; a cigarette case of some fraudulent material, two dollars and fifty cents. She weakened, but only for a moment, before a mechanical monkey with real fur who did calisthenics on a crossbar if you wound him up, one dollar and ninety-eight cents.

The prices of these objects did not influence their relative value to her and bore no connection whatever to the dollar she carried in her hand. Our shopping had also no connection with the birthday of the Child or the legends and pictures. Her air of reserve toward the long series of blear-eyed, shapeless old men wearing red flannel blouses and false, white-wool whiskers said all too plainly that they in no way fulfilled her notions of Christmas merriment. She shook hands with all of them politely, could not be persuaded to ask for anything from them and seemed not to question the obvious spectacle of thousands of persons everywhere buying presents instead of waiting for one of the army of Santa Clauses to bring them, as they all so profusely promised.

Christmas is what we make it and this is what we have so cynically made of it: not the feast of the Child in the straw-filled crib, nor even the homely winter bounty of the old pagan with the reindeer, but a great glittering commercial fair, gay enough with music and food and extravagance of feeling and behavior and expense, more and more on the order of the ancient Saturnalia. I have nothing against Saturnalia, it belongs to this season of the year: but how do we get so confused about the true meaning of even our simplest-appearing pastimes?

Meanwhile, for our money we found a present for the little girl's mother. It turned out to be a small green pottery shell with a colored bird perched on the rim which the little girl took for an ash tray, which it may as well have been.

"We'll wrap it up and hang it on the tree and *say* it came from Santa Claus," she said, trustfully making of me a fellow conspirator.

"You don't believe in Santa Claus any more?" I asked carefully, for we had taken her infant credulity for granted. I had already seen in her face that morning a skeptical view of my sentimental legends, she was plainly trying to sort out one thing from another in them; and I was turning over in my mind the notion of beginning again with her on other grounds, of making an attempt to draw, however faintly, some boundary lines between fact and fancy, which is not so difficult; but also further to show where truth and poetry were, if not the same being, at least twins who could wear each other's clothes. But that couldn't be done in a day nor with pedantic intention. I was perfectly prepared for the first half of her answer, but the second took me by surprise.

"No, I don't," she said, with the freedom of her natural candor, "but please don't tell my mother, for she still does."

For herself, then, she rejected the gigantic hoax which a whole powerful society had organized and was sustaining at the vastest pains and expense, and she was yet to find the grain of truth lying lost in the gaudy debris around her, but there remained her immediate human situation, and that she could deal with, or so she believed: her mother believed in Santa Claus, or she would not have said so. The little girl did not believe in what her mother had told her, she did not want her mother to know she did not believe, yet her mother's illusions must not be disturbed. In that moment of decision her infancy was gone forever, it had vanished there before my eyes.

Very thoughtfully I took the hand of my budding little diplomat, whom we had so lovingly, unconsciously prepared for her career, which no doubt would be quite a successful one; and we walked along in the bright sweet-smelling Christmas dusk, myself for once completely silenced.

1946

Audubon's Happy Land

THE center of St. Francisville is ugly as only small towns trying frantically to provide gasoline and sandwiches to passing motorists can be, but its lanelike streets unfold almost at once into grace and goodness. On the day of our visit, the only sign of special festivity was a splendid old Negro, in top hat, frock coat with nosegay in buttonhole, a black cotton umbrella shading his venerable head, seated before the casually contrived small office where we bought our tickets for the Audubon pilgrimage and were joined by our guide. The old Negro rose, bowed, raised his hat at arm's length to an angle of forty-five degrees more or less, playing his role in the ceremonies not only as a detail of the scene, but as part also of its history. Our guide appeared in a few minutes, tying a flowered kerchief under her chin, *babushka* fashion, as she came. She was dark and thin and soft-voiced, so typically Louisiana French that we thought she must be from New Orleans, or the Bayou Teche country. It turned out that she was from Idaho, lately married to a cousin of the Percys at "Greenwood." No matter; she belonged also, by virtue of love and attachment, as well as appearance, to the scene and its history.

Saint Francis, who preached to the birds, and Audubon, who painted them as no one before or since, are both commemorated in this place. In 1779, the monks of Saint Francis founded the town and christened it. Spain ruled the territory then, though the brothers Le Moyne—Iberville and Bienville —had claimed it three quarters of a century before for France. The Spanish government made a classical error with the classical result. It invited wealthy foreign investors to help settle the country, and the foreign investors ended by taking final possession. These particular foreigners bore such names as Ratliff, Barrow, Wade, Hamilton, Percy; they were all men of substance and of worldly mind, mostly from Virginia and the Carolinas, who obtained by Spanish grant splendid parcels of land of about twelve thousand acres each. These acres formed a subtropical jungle to the very banks of the Mississippi. A man could not, said an old woodsman, sink his hunting knife to the hilt in it anywhere.

The newcomers had on their side the strong arm of slave labor, and definite views on caste, property, morals, and manners. They pushed back the Louisiana jungle mile by mile, uncovered rich lands, and raised splendid crops. They built charming houses and filled them with furniture from France and England. Their silver and porcelain and linen were such as befitted their pride, which was high, and their tastes, which were delicate and expensive. Their daughters sang, danced, and played the harpsichord; their sons played the flute and fought duels; they collected libraries, they hunted and played chess, and spent the winter season in New Orleans. They traveled much in Europe, and brought back always more and more Old World plunder. Everywhere, with ceaseless, intensely personal concern, they thought, talked, and played politics.

In a few short years, these wealthy, nostalgic Americans were, in the phrase of the day, "groaning under the galling yoke of Spain." They forgathered evening after evening in one or another of their mansions and groaned; that is to say, discussed the matter with shrewdness, realism, and a keen eye to the possibilities. They called upon President Madison to lend a hand in taking this territory from Spain, which continued to hold it for some reason long after the Louisiana Purchase. "President Madison," says a local historian of that day, "remained deaf to their cries." The Feliciana planters then stopped crying, organized a small army, and marched on the Spanish capital, Baton Rouge. Harsh as it sounds in such a gentlemanly sort of argument, they caused the Spanish Commandant to be killed as proof of the seriousness of their intentions. They then declared for themselves the Independent Republic of West Florida, with St. Francisville as its capital. A certain Mr. Fulwar Skipwith was elected President. All was done in form, with a Constitution, a Body of Laws, and a flag designed for the occasion. The strategy was a brilliant success. President Madison sent friendly troops to annex the infant republic to the United States of America. This Graustarkian event took place in 1810.

The next year, a Roosevelt (Nicholas), partner in an Eastern steamship company, sent the first steamboat into the Mississippi, straight past St. Francisville and her sister town, Bayou Sara. The days of opulence and glory began in earnest, based solidly on land, money crops, and transportation, to flourish for just half a century.

It is quite finished as to opulence, and the glory is now a gentle aura, radiating not so much from the past as from the present, for St. Francisville lives with graceful competence on stored wealth that is not merely tangible. The legend has, in fact, magnified the opulence into something more than it really was, to the infinite damage of a particular truth: that wealth in the pre-War South was very modest by present standards, and it was not ostentatious, even then. The important thing to know about St. Francisville, as perhaps a typical survivor of that culture, is this: no one there tells you about steamboat wealth, or wears the air of poverty living on its memories, or (and this is the constant, rather tiresome accusation of busy, hasty observers) "yearns for the good old days."

The town's most treasured inhabitant was Audubon, and its happiest memory. This is no afterthought, based on his later reputation. And it is the more interesting when we consider what kind of reputation Audubon's was, almost to the end; nothing at all that a really materialistic society would take seriously. He was an artist, but not a fashionable one, never successful by any worldly standards; but the people of St. Francisville loved him, recognized him, took him to themselves when he was unknown and almost in despair. And now in every house, they will show you some small memento of him, some record that he was once a guest there. The Pirries, of New Orleans and Oakley, near St. Francisville, captured him in New Orleans at the moment when he was heading East, disheartened, and brought him to Oakley for the pleasant employment of teaching their young daughter, Miss Eliza, to dance and draw, of mornings. His afternoons, and some of his evenings, he spent in the Feliciana woods, and we know what he found there.

The Feliciana country is not a jungle now, nor has it been for a great while. The modest, occasional rises of earth, called hills, are covered with civilized little woods, fenced grazing-fields for fine cattle, thatches of sugar cane, of corn, and or-

chards. Both Felicianas, east and west, are so handsome and
amiable you might mistake them for one, instead of twins. For
fear they will be confounded in the stranger's eye, the boundaries are marked plainly along the highway. The difference was
to me that West Feliciana was holding a spring festival in
honor of Audubon, and I, a returned Southerner, in effect a
tourist, went straight through East Feliciana, which had not
invited visitors, to West Feliciana, which had.

You are to think of this landscape as an April garden, flowering with trees and shrubs of the elegant, difficult kind that live
so securely in this climate: camellias, gardenias, crêpe myrtle,
fine old-fashioned roses; with simpler things, honeysuckle, dogwood, wisteria, magnolia, bridal-wreath, oleander, redbud,
leaving no fence or corner bare. The birds of Saint Francis and
of Audubon fill the air with their light singing and their un-
disturbed flight. The great, dark oaks spread their immense
branches fronded with moss; the camphor and cedar trees add
their graceful shapes and their dry, spicy odors; and yes, just as
you have been told, perhaps too often, there are the white,
pillared houses seated in dignity, glimpsed first at a distance
through their parklike gardens.

The celebrated oak *allées* are there at "Live Oak," at
"Waverly," at "Rosedown," perhaps the finest grove of all at
"Highland"—the wide, shaded driveways from the gate to the
great door, all so appropriately designed for the ritual events of
life, a wedding or a funeral procession, the christening party,
the evening walks of betrothed lovers. W. B. Yeats causes one
of his characters to reflect, in face of a grove of ancient trees,
"that a man who planted trees, knowing that no descendant
nearer than his great-grandson could stand under their shade,
had a noble and generous confidence." That kind of confidence created this landscape, now as famous, as banal, if you
like, as the horse-chestnuts along the Champs Elysées, as the
perfume gardens of Grasse, as the canals of Venice, as the lilies-
of-the-valley in the forest of Saint-Cloud. It possesses, too, the
appeal of those much-visited scenes, and shares their nature,
which is to demand nothing by way of arranged tribute; each
newcomer may discover it for himself; but this landscape shares
its peculiar treasure only with such as know there is something
more here than mere hungry human pride in mahogany

staircases and silver doorknobs. The real spirit of the place planted those oaks, and keeps them standing.

The first thing that might strike you is the simplicity, the comparative smallness of even the largest houses (in plain figures, "Greenwood" is one hundred feet square; there is a veranda one hundred and ten feet long at "The Myrtles," a long, narrow house), compared not only to the grandeur of their legend, but to anything of corresponding fame you may have seen, such as the princely houses of Florence or the Spanish palaces in Mexico, or, as a last resort, the Fifth Avenue museums of the fantastically rich of two or three generations ago. Their importance is of another kind—that of the oldest New York houses, or the Patrizieren houses in Basel; with a quality nearly akin to the Amalienburg in the forest near Munich, quite the loveliest house I ever saw, or expect to see. These St. Francisville houses are examples of pure domestic architecture, somehow urban in style, graceful, and differing from city houses in this particular, that they sit in landscapes designed to show them off; they are meant to be observed from every point of view. No two of them are alike, but they were all built to be lived in, by people who had a completely aristocratic sense of the house as a dwelling-place.

They are ample and their subtle proportions give them stateliness not accounted for in terms of actual size. They are placed in relation to the south wind and the morning sun. Their ceilings are high, because high ceilings are right for this kind of architecture, and this kind of architecture is right for a hot climate. Their fireplaces are beautiful, well placed, in harmony with the rooms, and meant for fine log fires in the brief winters. Their windows are many, tall and rightly spaced for light and air, as well as for the view outward. All of them, from "Live Oak," built in 1779, to "The Myrtles," built in the 1840's, have in common the beauty and stability of cypress, blue poplar, apparently indestructible brick made especially for the chimneys and foundations, old methods of mortising and pinning, hand-forged nails.

"Live Oak" stands on a green knoll, and, from the front door, one looks straight through the central room to the rolling meadow bordered with iris in profuse bloom. This house is really tired, worn down to the bare grain, the furniture just what might have been left from some remote disaster, but it is beautiful, a place to live in, with its wide, double porches and outside staircase in the early style of the Spanish in Louisiana, its dark paneling, and its air of gentle remoteness.

"Waverly" is another sort of thing altogether, a bright place full of color, where the old furniture is set off with gaily flowered rugs, and the heavy old Louisiana four-poster beds—of a kind to be found nowhere else—are dressed sprucely in fresh curtains. The white pillars of "Waverly" are flat and slender, and the graceful fan-lights of the front door are repeated on the second floor, with an especially airy effect. The vestiges of the old boxwood maze are being coaxed back to life there, and gardenias grow in hedges, as they should.

At "The Myrtles," the flowery iron grille of the long veranda sets the Victorian tone; the long dining-room still wears, between the thin moldings, its French wallpaper from 1840—sepia-colored panels from floor to ceiling of game birds and flowers. The cypress floor is honey-colored, the Italian marble mantelpiece was that day banked with branches of white dogwood. All the rooms are long, full of the softest light lying upon the smooth surfaces of old fruitwood and mahogany. From the back veranda, an old-fashioned back yard, full of country living, lay in the solid shade of grape arbors and trees rounded like baskets of flowers. Chickens roamed and picked there; there was a wood-pile with a great iron wash-pot up-ended against it, near the charred spot where the fire is still built to heat the water.

At "Virginia," we saw George Washington's account-book, made, I believe, at Valley Forge, with all the detailed outlay of that troublesome episode. "Virginia" is by way of being an inn now—that is to say, if travelers happen along they will be put up in tall, canopied beds under fine old quilted coverlets. The large silver spoons in the dining-room came from an ancestor of the Fisher family—Baron de Würmser, who had them as a gift from Frederick the Great. Generous-sized ladles they are, too, paper-thin and flexible. Like so many old coin silver spoons, they appear to have been chewed, and they have been.

A thin silver spoon was once considered the ideal object for an infant to cut his teeth upon. But there were dents in a de Würmser soup ladle which testified that some Fisher infant must have been a saber-toothed tiger. "Surely no teething child did that," I remarked. "No," said the hostess, a fleeting shade of severity on her brow. "It was thrown out with the dishwater once, and the pigs got it." Here is the French passport for a Fisher grandfather, dated 1836. It was then he brought back the splendid flowered wallpaper, even now fresh in its discreet colors, the hand-painted mauve linen window-shades on rollers, then so fashionable, replacing the outmoded Venetian blinds; the ornate, almost morbidly feminine drawing-room chairs and sofas.

At "Greenwood," the host was engaged with a group of oil prospectors, for, beneath their charming, fruitful surfaces, the Felicianas are suspected of containing the dark, the sinister new treasure more powerful than gold. If so, what will become of the oaks and the flourishing fields and the gentle cattle? What will become of these lovely houses? "They make syrup and breed cattle here," said our guide; "that keeps 'Greenwood' going very well. Some people [she named them] wanted Mr. Percy to make a dude ranch of this place, but he wouldn't hear of it."

We mentioned our premonitions about St. Francisville if oil should be discovered. Our guide spoke up with the quiet recklessness of faith. "It wouldn't do any harm," she said. "The Feliciana people have had what money can buy, and they have something money can't buy, and they know it. They have nothing to sell. Tourists come here from all over and offer them thousands of dollars for their little things, just little things they don't need and hardly ever look at, but they won't sell them."

"Greenwood" is the typical Southern mansion of too many songs, too many stories—with the extravagant height of massive, round pillar, the too-high ceiling, the gleaming sweep of central hall, all in the 1830 Greek, gilded somewhat, but lightly. There is bareness; space dwarfing the human stature and breathing a faint bleakness. Yet the gentle groves and small hills are framed with overwhelming effect between those columns;

effect grandiose beyond what the measuring eye knows is actually there.

It seems now that the builders should have known that this
house was the end, never the beginning. It is quite improbable
that anyone should again build a house like "Greenwood" to
live in. But there it is, with the huge beams of the gallery being
replaced, oil prospectors roaming about, and the hostess sitting in her drawing-room with the green-and-gold chairs, the
lace curtains fine as bride veils drifting a little; the young girls in
jodhpurs are going out to ride. Here, as everywhere else, there
were no radios or gramophones going, no telephones visible
or ringing; and it seemed to me suddenly that this silence, the
silence of a house in order, of people at home, the silence of
leisure, is the most desirable of all things we have lost.

At "Highland," descendants in the fourth generation stand
in the shade of the oaks planted, as the old House Book records, in January, 1832. The house is older. It has its share of
drum tables, fiddle-backed chairs, carved door-frames and wain-
scoting, but its real beauty lies in the fall of light into the ample,
square rooms, the rise of the stair tread, the energy and firmness of its structure. The paneled doors swing on their hand-
forged hinges as they did the day they were hung there; the
edge of the first doorstep—an immense log of cypress square-
hewn—is as sharp as though feet had not stepped back and
forth over it for one hundred and forty years.

"Rosedown" is more formal, with its fish pool and eighteenth-century statuary set along the *allée*, and in a semicircle
before the conventionally planted garden. The office still stands
there, and the "slave bell" in its low wooden frame. The "slave
bell" was the dinner-bell for the whole plantation. Above all,
at "Rosedown," the Ancestors still rule, still lend their unquenchable life to a little world of fabulous old ladies and a
strange overgrowth of knickknacks sprouting like small, harmless fungi on a tree-trunk. Their portraits—Sully seems to have
been the preferred painter—smile at you, or turn their attentive heads toward one another; as handsome and as gallant and
elegantly dressed a set of young men and women as you would
be apt to find blood-kin under one roof. "My great-great-
grandfather," said the old, old lady, smiling back again at
the high-headed, smooth-cheeked young beau in the frilled

shirt-bosom and deep blue, sloping-shouldered coat. His eyes are the same bright hazel as her own. This was the only house in which the past lay like a fine dust in the air.

Steamboats brought wealth and change to St. Francisville once, and oil may do it again. In that case, we are to suppose that new grand pianos would replace the old, square, black Steinways of 1840, as they had in turn replaced the harpsichords. There would be a great deal of shoring up, replacement, planting, pruning, and adding. There would be travel again, and humanistic education. The young people who went away cannot, alas, come back young, but the young there now would not have to go away.

And what else would happen to this place, so occupied, so self-sufficient, so reassuringly solid and breathing? St. Francisville is not a monument, nor a decor, nor a wailing-wall for mourners for the past. It is a living town, moving at its own pace in a familiar world. But it was comforting to take a last glance backward as we turned into the main highway, at Audubon's Happy Land, reflecting that, for the present, in the whole place, if you except the fruits of the earth and the picture postcards at "Rosedown," there was nothing, really nothing, for sale.

1939

The Flower of Flowers

Rose, O pure contradiction, bliss
To be the sleep of no one under so many eyelids.
RAINER MARIA RILKE: *Epitaph*

ITS beginnings were obscure, like that of the human race whose history it was destined to adorn. The first rose was small as the palm of a small child's hand, with five flat petals in full bloom, curling in a little at the tips, the color red or white, perhaps even pink, and maybe sometimes streaked. It was a simple disk or wheel around a cup of perfume, a most intoxicating perfume, like that of no other flower. This perfume has been compared to that of many fruits: apricot, peach, melon; to animal substance: musk, ambergris; to honey (which has also many perfumes), to other flowers, to crushed leaves of the tea plant—this from China, naturally—and perhaps this is the secret of its appeal: it offers to the individual sense of smell whatever delights it most. For me, a rose smells like a rose, no one exactly like another, but still a rose and it reminds me of nothing else.

This rose grew everywhere in Africa and Asia, and it may have had many names, but they are lost.

This shall be a mere glimpse at some aspects of the life of the rose; it keeps the best company in the world, and the worst, and also the utterly mediocre: all with the same serenity, knowing one from the other; and all by name, but making, in the natural world, no difference between individuals, like any saint: which perhaps is a sign of its true greatness. In working miracles, as we shall see, it exercises the most scrupulous discrimination between one thing and another.

It was, and is, thorny by nature, for it detests the proximity of any other kind of plant, and serious botanists have deduced seriously that the rose was given its thorns as a weapon against other crowding vegetation. With such a perfume as it has, it needs more than thorns for its protection. It has no honey, yet even the bees and wasps who rob its generous pollen for food, get silly-drunk on the perfume, and may sometimes be seen swooping hilariously away at random, buzzing wildly and

765

colliding with each other in air. For the sake of this perfume other great follies of extravagance have been committed. The Romans with their genius for gluttony devoured the roses of Egypt by the shipload, covering their beds and floors and banquet tables with petals; rose leaves dropped in their wine helped to prevent, or at least delay, drunkenness; heroes were crowned with them; and they were at last forced to bloom out of season by being grown in a network of hot water pipes.

The debasement of the rose may be said to have begun with this Roman invention of the hot house. After a long period in Europe when the rose fell into neglect, there came a gradual slow return in its popularity; and for the past century or so, in Europe and America, the rose has been cultivated extravagantly, crossbred almost out of recognition, growing all the time larger, showier. The American Beauty Rose—in the 1900's the rose of courtship, an expensive florist's item, hardly ever grown in good private gardens—in its hugeness, its coarse texture and vulgar color, its inordinate length of cane, still stands I believe as the dreariest example of what botanical experiment without wisdom or taste can do even to the rose. In other varieties it has been deprived of its thorns, one of its great beauties, and—surely this can never have been intended—its very perfume, the true meaning of the rose, has almost vanished. Yet they are all children of that precious first five-petaled rose which we call the Damask, the first recorded name of a rose.

It has been popularly supposed that the Crusaders brought the rose and the name back with them to Europe from Damascus, where they saw it for the first time. Rosarians argue back and forth, saying, *not* so, the Damask Rose was known in France and by that name many centuries before the Crusades. It is very likely, for the Christian penitential pilgrimages to Rome, to the tombs and shrines of saints, and to the Holy Sepulchre, had begun certainly as early as the eighth century. The most difficult and dangerous and meritorious of these pilgrimages was, of course, to the Holy Land, and the rose may very well have been among the dear loot in the returning pilgrim's scrip, along with water from the Jordan, bits of stone from the Sepulchre, fragments of the True Cross, Sacred Nails, and a few Thorns; and, judging by medieval European music, he had got a strange tune or two fixed in his head, also. We know that more than this came into Europe through long traffic and negotiation with the East, the great threatening power which encroached steadily upon the New World and above all, upon the new religion.

By the time of the troubadours, the rose was a familiar delight. In Richard Lion-heart's day, Raoul, Sire de Coucy, a famous poet, singer, soldier, nobleman, was writing poems full of nightingales, morning dew, roses, lilies, and love to his lady, the Dame de Fayel. He went with Richard on the Third Crusade, and was killed by the Saracens at the battle of St. Jean d'Acres, in 1191. The whole tone of his glittering little songs, their offhand ease of reference, makes it clear that roses and all those other charming things had long been the peculiar property of European poets. De Coucy names no species. "When the rose and lily are born," he sings blithely, knowing and caring nothing about Rosa Indica, Rosa Gallica, Rosa Centifolia, Eglantina; no, for the troubadour a rose was a rose. It was beautiful to look at, especially with morning dew on it, a lily nearby and a nightingale lurking in the shrubbery, all ready to impale his bosom on the thorn; it smelled sweet and reminded him of his lady, as well as of the Blessed Virgin, though never, of course, at the same moment. That would have been sacrilege, and the knight was nothing if not pious. Sacred and profane love in the Western World had by then taken their places at opposite poles, where they have remained to this day; the rose was the favorite symbol of them both.

Woman has been symbolized almost out of existence. To man, the myth maker, her true nature appears unfathomable, a dubious mystery at best. It was thought proper to becloud the riddle still further by referring to her in terms of something else vaguely, monstrously, or attractively resembling her, or at least her more important and obvious features. Therefore she was the earth, the moon, the sea, the planet Venus, certain stars, wells, lakes, mines, caves; besides such other works of nature as the fig, the pear, the pomegranate, the shell, the lily, wheat or any grain, Night or any kind of darkness, any seed pod at all; above all, once for all, the Rose.

The Rose. What could be more flattering? But wait. It was the flower of Venus, of Aurora, a talisman against witchcraft, and the emblem, when white, and suspended over a banquet table, of friendly confidence: one spoke and acted freely under the rose, for all present were bound to silence afterward. It was the flower of the Blessed Virgin, herself the Mystical Rose; symbol of the female genitals, and the Gothic disk of celestial color set in the brows of great cathedrals. For Christian mystics the five red petals stood for the five wounds of Christ; for the pagans, the blood of Venus who stepped on a thorn while hurrying to the aid of Narcissus. It is the most subtle and aristocratic of flowers, yet the most varied of all within its breed, most easily corruptible in form, most susceptible to the changes of soil and climate. It is the badge of kings, and the wreath to crown every year the French girl chosen by her village as the most virtuous: *La Rosière. Le Spectre de la Rose*: a perverted image. No young girl ever dreamed of her lover in the form of a rose. She is herself the rose. . . .

The rose gives its name to the prayer-beads themselves slipped millions of times a day all over the world between prayerful fingers: these beads are still sometimes made of the dried hardened paste of rose petals. The simple flower is beloved of kings and peasants, children, saints, artists, and prisoners, and then all those numberless devoted beings who grow them so faithfully in little plots of gardens everywhere. It is a fragile flower that can survive for seventy-five years draped over a rail fence in a deserted farm otherwise gone to jungle; it blooms by the natural exaltation of pure being in a tin, with its roots strangling it to death; yet it is by nature the grossest feeder among flowers. With very few exceptions among wild roses, they thrive best, any good gardener will tell you, in deep trenches bedded with aged cow manure. One famous grower of Old Roses (Francis E. Lester, *My Friend the Rose*, 1942) advises one to bury a big beef bone, cooked or raw, deep under the new plant, so that its growing roots may in time descend, embrace and feed slowly upon this decayed animal stuff in the private darkness. Above, meanwhile, it brings to light its young pure buds, opening shyly as the breasts of virgins. (See: Lyric Poetry: Through the Ages.) Aside from the bloom, out of this tranced absorption with the rot and heat and moisture of the earth, there is distilled the perfume of perfumes from this flower of flowers.

(The nose is surely one of the most impressionable, if not

positively erotic, of all our unruly members. I remember a kind
old nun, rebuking me for my delight in the spectacle of this
world saying, "Beware of the concupiscence of the eye!" I had
never heard the word, but I knew what she meant. Then what
about the ear? The pores of the skin, the tips of the fingers? We
are getting on quicksand. Back, back to the rose, that tempts
every mortal sense except the ear, lends itself to every pleasure,
and helps by its presence or even its memory, to assuage every
mortal grief.)

The rose: its perfume. It is—ten to one—the odor of sanctity
that rises from the corpses of holy women, and the oil with
which Laïs the Corinthian anoints herself after her bath. Saint
Thérèse of Lisieux is shown holding a sheaf of roses, promising
her faithful to shower them with roses—that is to say, blessings.
The women in Minsky's old Burlesque Theater on the Bowery
pinned large red cotton velvet roses over their abused breasts
and public thighs, forming a triangle. They then waggled themselves as obscenely as they knew how; they did know how, and
it was obscene; and the helpless caricatures of roses would
waggle too: the symbol being brought to the final depths of
aesthetic and moral imbecility.

"A rose said, 'I am the marvel of the universe. Can it be that a
perfume maker shall have the courage to cause me suffering?'"
Yes, it is possible. "A nightingale answered, 'One day of joy
prepares a year of tears.'" (Note: My translation of a stanza of
Omar Khayyam's from the French version.)

This divine perfume from the bone-devouring rose is sometimes got by distilling, a process of purification. The petals are
mixed with the proper amount of water, put in the alembic,
and the sweetness is sweated out, drop by drop, with death
and resurrection for the rose in every drop. Or, and this must
be a very old way of doing, one takes the sweet petals, picked
tenderly in the morning unbruised, with the dew on them, and
lays them gently on a thick bed of fat, beef fat, pork fat, or perhaps oil, just so it is pure, and fat. The perfume seeps from the
veins of the rose into the fat, which in turn is mingled with
alcohol which takes the fragrance to itself, and there you
are. . . . Thinking it over, I am certain there is a great deal
more to the art of extracting perfume from petals than this. I
got my information from a small French household book,

published in 1830, which gives receipts for making all sorts of
fascinating messes: liqueurs, bleaching pastes for the complexion, waters of beauty—invariably based on rosewater or rose
oil, hair dyes, lip salves, infusions of herbs and flowers, perfumes, heaven knows what. They look plausible on the page,
while reading I trust them implicitly, and have never dared to
try one of them. One important point the perfume receipt
omitted: it did not say you must begin with Damask Roses. In
India, in the Balkans, in the south of France, wherever the art
of making rosewater and attar of rose is still practiced, as in ancient Cyrenaica whose rose perfume was "the sweetest in the
world," there is one only rose used: Rosa Damascena, five-
petaled in the Balkans and in India, thirty-petaled in Grasse,
and called the Provence Rose. In this Rose of Provence there is
perhaps a mixture with Rosa Centifolia, native of the Caucasus
—Cabbage Rose to us, to those of us who ever saw it, and
smelled it—next to the Damask, the most deeply, warmly
perfumed. Once in California, in a nursery, lost in a jungle of
strange roses, I asked an old gardener, no doubt a shade too
wistfully, "Haven't you a Cabbage Rose, or a Damask, or a
Moss Rose?" He straightened up and looked at me won-
deringly and said, "Why, my God, I haven't even heard those
names for thirty years! Do you actually know those roses?" I
told him yes, I did, I had been brought up with them. Slowly,
slowly, slowly like moisture being squeezed out of an oak, his
eyes filled with tears. "So was I," he said, and the tears dried
back to their source without falling. We walked then among
the roses, some of them very fine, very beautiful, of honorable
breed and proved courage, but the roses which for me are the
very heart of the rose were not there, nor had ever been.

They have as many pests as sheep, or bees, two notoriously
afflicted races. Aphis, mildew, rust, caterpillars, saw-flies, leaf-
cutting bees, thrips, canker worms, beetles, and so on. Spraying
has become the bane of rose growers, for the new sorts of
roses seem to be more susceptible than the old. I remember
my grandmother occasionally out among her roses with a little
bowl of soapy water and a small rag. She would wash the backs
of a few leaves and dry them tenderly as if they were children's

fingers. That was all I ever saw her do in that way, and her roses were celebrated.

Mankind early learned that the rose, except for its thorns, is a benevolent useful flower. It was good to eat, to drink, to smell, to wear, to cure many ailments, to wash and perfume with, to look at, to meditate upon, to offer in homage, piety, or love; in religion it has always been a practical assistant in the working of miracles. It was good to write poetry about, to paint, to draw, to carve in wood, stone, marble; to work in tapestry, plaster, clay, jewels, and precious metals. Besides roseleaf jam, still made in England, one may enjoy candied rose leaves, rose honey, rose oil—good for the bath *or* for flavoring cakes and pastries; infusion of roses, a delicious tea once prescribed for many ills; above all, rose-hip syrup, an old valuable remedy in medieval pharmacies, manufactured by monks and housewives. The Spanish Mission fathers brought the Damask Rose—which they called the Rose of Castile—to America and planted it in their dispensary gardens. Rose-hip syrup was one of their great remedies. It was known to cure aches and pains, collywobbles in the midriff, a pallid condition, general distemper, or ill-assortedness. And why not? Modern medical science has in this instance proved once more that ancient herbalists were not just old grannies out pulling weeds and pronouncing charms over them. Rose-hip syrup, say British medical men, contains something like four hundred times more of vitamin C, measure for measure, than oranges or black currants, and whoever drinks freely of it will be largely benefited, if he needs vitamin C, as most of us do, no doubt. They needed it in medieval times, too, and it is pleasant to think that quite large numbers of them got it.

Bear's grease mixed with pounded rose petals made a hopeful hair restorer. The ancient Persians made a rose wine so powerful yet so benign it softened the hardest heart, and put the most miserable wretch to sleep. In Elizabethan England they made a rose liqueur warranted to "wash the mulligrubs out of a moody brain." Mulligrubs is a good word yet in my part of the country, the South, to describe that state of lowered resistance to life now known generally as the "blues." In turn, "blues," in its exact present sense, was a good word in seventeenth-century England, and was brought to America by the early Virginia settlers. Whether they brought roses at first I do not know, nor whether they found any here; but there is a most beautiful rose, single, large-petaled, streaked red and white, called the Cherokee Rose, of a heavenly perfume, which is perfectly at home here. It came from Asia by way of England, however, a long time ago, and has not a drop of Indian blood in it. Maybe the Virginians did bring it—it flourishes best in the Southern states.

The celebrated botanists, rose growers, collectors, hybridizers, perfume makers, as well as the scientific or commercial exploiters of the rose, have all been men; so far as I know, not a woman among them. And naturally in such a large company we find a few who labor restlessly to grow a rose with a six-foot stem; with a thousand petals, and a face broad as a plate; to color them blue, or black, or violet. The rose being by nature a shrub they could not rest until they made a tree of it. In the same spirit, there are those who embalm them in wax, dip them in dye-stuffs, manufacture them in colored paper, and sprinkle them with synthetic perfume. This is not real wickedness but something worse, sheer poverty of feeling and misdirected energy with effrontery, a combination found in all vulgarizers. The "arrangers" of great music, the "editors" of literary masterpieces, the re-painters of great pictures, the falsifiers of noble ideas—that whole race of the monkey-minded and monkey-fingered "adapters"; the rose too has been their victim. Remy de Gourmont cursed all women in the name of the rose, with the ferocity of perverted love; and aesthetic hypersensibility turned not to hatred but to something even more painful, disgust, nausea, at the weight of false symbol, the hypocritical associations, the sickly sentiment which appeared to have overwhelmed it. With the wild logic of bitterness and disillusion, he cursed the rose, that is, woman, and through it, all those things which had degraded it in his eyes, concluding that the rose itself is vile by nature, and attracts vileness. Only a disappointed lover behaves so unreasonably. He got a brilliant poem out of it, however (*Litanies de la Rose*).

Women have been the treasurers of seedlings and cuttings; they are the ones who will root a single slip in a bottle of water in the corner of a closet; or set out, as the pioneer American women did, on their bitter journeys to the Carolinas, to Kentucky, to Texas, to California, the Middle West, the Indian territories, guarding who knows how their priceless little store of seeds and roots of apples, plums, pears, grapes, and roses—always roses. China Rose, Bengal Rose, Musk Rose, Moss Rose, Briar Rose, Damask Rose—in how many places those very same pioneer rose bushes are blooming yet. But where did all those hedges of wild roses spring from? Were they always there? Gloire de Dijon, Cup of Hebe, Old Blush, Roger Lambelin, Cherokee, Maréchal Niel, Cramoisy—these are some names I remember from gardens I knew; and Noisette, a small perfect rose, result of the first crossbreeding in this country, a century and a quarter ago. . . . Where did I see that little story about someone advertising a place for sale as an earthly paradise, "the only drawbacks being the litter of rose petals and the noise of nightingales"?

The rose is sacred to religion, to human love, and to the arts. It is associated with the longing for earthly joy, and for eternal life. There is a noticeable absence of them, or flowers of any kind, in the textbooks of magic, witchcraft, the Black Arts by any name. The world of evil is mechanistic, furnished with alembics, retorts, ovens, grinding stones; herbs, mainly poisonous; the wheel, but not the rose; hollow circles, zones of safety for the conjuror. The alchemist with his madness for gold—for what did they devote all that hermetic wisdom, that moral grandeur, that spiritual purity they professed but to the dream of making gold? Or of turning pebbles into jewels, as St. John was said to have done? A slander, I do believe, unless taken symbolically. But the evidence is against this: the alchemists meant to make real gold. It is the most grotesquely materialistic of all ends. The witch, with her blood vows and her grave robbing and her animal rites and transformations, how stupid and poor her activities and aims! Where can pictures more coarse and gross and debased be found than in books of magic: they cannot even rouse horror except in the offended eye.

Evil is dull, that is the worst of it, and black magic is the dullest of all evils. . . . Only when the poor metamorphosed Ass can find and eat of good Venus's roses may he be restored again to his right form, and to the reassuring, purely human world of love and music and poetry, reclaimed by the benign sweetness of its petals and leaves from the subhuman mechanistic domain of evil.

And then, the rose of fire: that core of eternal radiance in which Dante beheld the Beatific Vision; this rose still illuminates the heart of Poets:

> ". . . From my little span
> I cry of Christ, Who is the ultimate Fire
> Who will burn away the cold in the heart of Man. . . ."
> Springs come, springs go. . . .
> "I was reddere on Rode than the Rose in the rayne."
> "This smel is Crist, clepid the plantynge of the Rose in Jerico."
> (Edith Sitwell, "The Canticle of the Rose")

And:

> All shall be well and
> All manner of thing shall be well
> When the tongues of flame are in-folded
> Into the crowned knot of fire
> And the fire and the rose are one.
> (T. S. Eliot, "Little Gidding")

1950

A Note on Pierre-Joseph Redouté
(1750–1840)

For the reproductions of his water colors, he invented a process of printing in colors which he never consented to perfect to the point where it
would be completely mechanical. Each one of these prints had further to
be retouched by hand. They owe to these light but indispensable re-
touchings the capricious illusion and movement of life—a life prolonged
beyond its term. In effect, the greater part of the roses who posed for
Redouté no longer exist today, in nature. Rosarians are not conservators.
They have come to create a race of roses, they do not care whether they
shall endure, but only that they, the creators, shall give shape to a new
race. So the old species disappear little by little; or if they survive, it is not
in famous rosaries, which disdain them, but in old gardens, scattered, forgotten, where there is no concern for fashions in flowers.

Jean-Louis Vaudoyer: *Les Roses de Bagatelle*

HERE is an eye-witness description of Pierre-Joseph Redouté: "A short thick body, with the members of an elephant, a face heavy and flat as a Holland cheese, thick lips, a
dull voice, crooked fat fingers, a repellent aspect altogether;
and under this rind, an extreme fineness of tact, exquisite taste,
a profound sense of the arts, great delicacy of feeling, with the
elevation of character and constancy in his work necessary to
develop his genius: such was Redouté, the painter of flowers,
who had as his students all the pretty women in Paris." This is
by Joseph-François Grillé, a lively gossip in his time.

A writer of our own time, looking at Redouté's portraits, by
Gérard and others, concludes: "In spite of the solid redingote,
the ample cravat and the standing collar of the bourgeois, his
portraits make one think of some old gardener weathered and
wrinkled like a winter apple."

Dear me: I have seen only the engraving after a painting by
Gérard, and can find nothing at all strange, much less monstrous, in it. He seems a man of moderate build, in the becoming
dress of his age, though plainer than most; with a very good
face indeed with rather blunt features, and pleasant, candid, attentive eyes. Perhaps Gérard loved the man who lived inside

that unpromising but useful rind, and showed him as he really was.

He was born in Saint-Hubert, Belgium, the son and grandson of artisan-painters, decorators of churches and municipal buildings. His two brothers became also painter-decorators. In the hardy fashion of the times, after a solid apprenticeship to his father, at the age of thirteen he was turned out in the world to make his own way. Dreaming of fame, riches, glory, he roamed all Belgium and Flanders looking for jobs and starving by the way. He took a year of hard work at Liège in the ateliers of famous painters and was sent to Luxembourg to paint portraits of his first royalties, the Princess de Tornaco and others. The Princess was so pleased with his work she gave him letters to present to certain persons of quality residing in Versailles.

In Flanders he studied deeply the painters of the ancient Flemish school. After ten years of this laborious apprenticeship, he joined his elder brother Antoine-Ferdinand in Paris; Antoine-Ferdinand had all that time been unadventurously earning a good living as painter-decorator. Pierre-Joseph helped his brother decorate the Italian Theater, and painted flowers wherever he was allowed. He learned the art of engraving, and he managed to get into the King's Garden, a botanical wonder, in that time, of royal and noble gardens, in order to study, draw and paint plants and flowers. There he met Charles-Louis L'Héritier of Belgium, a man of great wealth, an impassioned botanist and adherent of the classical methods of Linnaeus.

From this time Redouté's history is the straight road to fame, fortune, and the happy life of a man capable of total constancy to his own gifts, who had the great good fortune to be born at the right hour in time, in the right place, and with the pure instinct which led him infallibly to the place where he could flourish and the people who needed and wanted precisely the thing that he could do. The rage for botanical gardening which had been growing for nearly two centuries had reached its climax. Only the royal, the noble, only the newly rich could afford these extravagant collections of rare shrubs, trees, flowers. There were no more simple adorers of flowers, but collectors of rarities and amateur botanists. It was an age of nature lovers, whose true god was science. Redouté was a botanist and a scientist, a decorator with a superior talent for painting. He stepped into the whole company of such combination scientists and decorator-artisans which surrounded and lived by the bounty of rich amateurs. Armed with brush, pencil, microscope, copper plates, stains, colors and acids, they adhered mightily and single-mindedly to their sources of benefits—intellectual bees, they were. Nothing could have been more touching than their indifference to social significance: they hadn't got the faintest notion where the times were driving them, or why; theirs only to pursue their personal passions and pleasures with scientific concentration, theirs to invent new processes of engraving, coloring, more exact representations of the subject in hand. The gardeners were concerned only to invent new roses, the botanists to botanize them, the artist-artisans to anatomize and engrave them. They were good workmen to whom the employment and not the employer was important.

It is astonishing how a world may turn over, and a whole society fall into ruin, and yet there is always a large population which survives, and hardly knows what has happened; indeed, can with all good faith write as a student in Paris did to his anxious father in Bordeaux, at the very height of the troubles of 1792: "All is quiet here," he declared, mentioning casually an execution or so. Later, he gave most painful descriptions of seeing, at every step in the street, the hideous bleeding rags of corpses piled up, uncovered; once he saw seven tumbrils of them being hauled away, the wheels leaving long tracks of blood. Yet there was dancing in the streets (he did not like to dance), bonfires at the slightest pretext (he hated bonfires), and all public places of entertainment were going at full speed. A craze for a new game called Coblentz, later Yo-yo, came to the point that everybody played it no matter where, all the time. When the King was beheaded, in January, 1793, Mercier tells how people rushed to dip handkerchiefs, feathers, bits of paper in his blood, like human hyenas: one man dipped his finger in it, tasted it, and said: "It's beastly salty!" (*Il est bougrement salé!*) Yet no doubt there were whole streets and sections where no terror came. Our student, an ardent Republican and stern moralist, got his four years of tutoring and college, exactly as planned. The Collège de France opened its doors promptly every autumn the whole time he was there.

Redouté, in the center of the royal family, as private painting teacher to the Queen, later appointed as "Designer of the Royal Academy of Sciences," designer in Marie Antoinette's own Cabinet, seemed destined to go almost as untouched by political disasters as the student writing to his father. On the very eve of the revolution, he was called before the royal family in the Temple, to watch the unfolding of a particularly ephemeral cactus bloom, and to paint it at its several stages.

When the Queen was put to death in October, 1793, it was David, patriot-painter, who made the terrible little sketch of her in the cart on her way to the scaffold: a sunken-faced old woman with chopped-off hair, the dress of a fishwife, hands bound behind her, eyes closed: but her head carried as high, her spine as straight, as if she were on her throne. We see for the first time clearly the long curved masculine-looking nose, the brutal Hapsburg jaw. But something else that perhaps David did not mean to show comes through his sparse strokes: as if all the elements of her character in life had been transmuted in the hour of her death—stubbornness to strength, arrogance to dignity, recklessness to courage, frivolity to tragedy. It is wonderful what strange amends David, moved by hatred, made to his victim.*

Her friendly, but preoccupied, painter-decorator happened to be in England with L'Héritier, who had done some very fancy work indeed getting away with a treasure of botanical specimens against a capricious government order. The two sat poring over their precious loot in perfect peace while France was being put together again. They returned, and went on with their work under the National Convention, which took great pride in the embellishment of the King's Garden, renamed the Garden of Natural History. (By 1823, after four overturns of the French government, this garden settled down

---

*In 1790, the Queen's lover, Count Fersen, wrote to his sister: "She is an angel of courage, of conduct, of sensibility: no one ever knew how to love as she does." He had known her since they were both eighteen years old, and had been her lover for more than five years. He had himself all the qualities he found in her, and more.

for a good while under the name of the Museum of Natural History of the King's Garden.)

Josephine Bonaparte of course had the most lavish, extravagant collection of rare plants, trees, and flowers at Malmaison, and Redouté became her faithful right hand as painter, decorator, straight through her career as Empress, and until her death. In the meantime he was teacher of painting to Empress Marie-Louise; went on to receive a gold medal from the hand of Louis XVIII for his invention of color printing from a single plate; the ribbon of the Legion of Honor was bestowed upon him by Charles X, in 1825; he painted the portrait of the rose named for Queen Marie Amélie; and lived to see his adored pupil Princess Marie-Louise, elder daughter of Louis-Philippe, become Queen of the Belgians.

During one upset or another, his beautiful house and garden at Fleury-sous-Meudon, were almost destroyed; he seems to have invested all the handsome fortune he had made in this place. Yet he simply moved into Paris with his family and went on working. In 1830 again there were the crowds milling savagely in the gardens of the Royal Palace, this time roaring: "Long live the Charter. Down with Charles X! Down with the Bourbons!" Charles went down and Louis-Philippe came in, the last king Redouté was to see. While royal figures came and went in the Tuileries, "that inn for crowned transients," as Béranger remarked, the painters Gérard, Isabey, and Redouté remained a part of the furniture of the Crown, no matter who wore it.

Such a charmed life! Only one of that huge company of men living in the tranced reality of science and art, was for a moment in danger. L'Héritier almost got his head cut off during the first revolution; in 1805 he was killed in the street near his own door—I have seen no account which says why. Did even those who murdered him know why they did it? Did L'Héritier himself know?

The story of Redouté's labors, his teaching, painting, engraving, his valuable discoveries in methods of engraving, coloring plates, and printing, is overwhelming. He worked as he breathed, with such facility, fertility of resources, and abundant energy, he was the wonder of his colleagues, themselves good masters of the long hard day's work. Redouté is said to have painted more than one thousand pictures of roses alone, many of them now vanished; it is on these strange, beautiful portrait-anatomies that his popular fame endures. He loved fame, and was honestly eager for praise, like a good child; but he took no short cuts to gain them, nor any unworthy method. When he invented a certain process of printing in colors, he saw its danger, and stopped short of perfecting it; he did not want any work to become altogether mechanical. All his prints made by this process required to be retouched by hand, for as a good artist he understood, indeed had learned from nature itself, the divine law of uniqueness: that no two leaves on the same tree are ever exactly alike.

His life had classical shape and symmetry. It began with sound gifts in poverty, labor and high human aspirations, rose to honestly won fame and wealth, with much love, too, and admiration without envy from his fellow artists and his students. It went on to very old age in losses and poverty again, with several friends and a royalty or two making ineffectual gestures toward his relief. But then, his friends, both artist and royal, were seeing hard times too. On the day of his death he received a student for a lesson. The student brought him a lily, and he died holding it.

1950

A House of My Own

NOT long ago, my sister returned to me a bundle of my letters to her, dated from my nineteenth year. My life has been, to say the least, varied: I have lived in five countries and traveled in several more. But at recurring intervals I wrote, in all seriousness: "Next year I shall find a little house in the country and settle there." Meantime I was looking at little houses in the country, all sorts of houses in all sorts of countries.

I shopped with friends in Bucks County long before that place became the fashion. I chose a perfect old stone house and barn sitting on a hill there, renovated it splendidly, and left it forever, all in one fine June morning. In this snapshot style, I have also possessed beautiful old Texas ranch houses; a lovely little Georgian house in Alexandria, Virginia; an eighteenth-century Spanish-French house in Louisiana.

I have stood in a long daydream over an empty, roofless shell of white coral in Bermuda; in several parts of my native South, I admired and would have been glad to live in one of those little, sloping-roofed, chimneyed houses the Negroes live in, houses quite perfectly proportioned and with such dignity in their desolation. In Mexico, I have walked through empty, red-tiled houses, in their patios, and under their narrow, arched cloisters, living a lifetime there in a few hours. In Switzerland, my house was tall, steep-roofed, the very one I chose was built in 1390. It was still occupied, however, with lace curtains at the window and a cat asleep on the window sill. In France, it was a pleasant house, standing flush to the village street, with a garden in back. Indeed, I have lived for a few hours in any number of the most lovely houses in the world.

There was never, of course, much money, never quite enough; there was never time, either; there was never permanency of any sort, except the permanency of hope.

This hope had led me to collect an unreasonable amount of furniture and books, unreasonable for one who had no house to keep them in. I lugged them all with me from Mexico to Paris to New York to Louisiana and back to New York, then stored them, and accepted an invitation to Yaddo, in Saratoga

Springs. Yaddo invites artists with jobs to finish to come, and work quietly in peace and great comfort, during summers. My invitation was for two months. That was a year ago, and I am still here, seemingly having taken root at North Farm on the estate. Several times I went away for a few weeks, and when I returned, as the train left Albany, I began to have a sense of homecoming. One day, hardly knowing when it happened, I knew I was going to live here, for good and all, and I was going to have a house in the country. I began to move my personal equivalent of heaven and earth to make it possible. As travelers in Europe make it a point of good taste to drink the wine of the country, so I had always chosen the house of the country. Here, the house of the country is plain, somewhat prim, not large, late Colonial; perhaps modified Georgian would be a useful enough description.

Some friends recommended to me an honest man who knew every farm within miles around. "You can believe every word he says," they assured me. On the first of January, in zero weather and deep snow, I explained to him what I was looking for, and we started touring the countryside. My house must be near Saratoga Springs, my favorite small town of all America that I had seen.* It must be handsomely located in a good, but domestic landscape, with generous acres, well-watered and wooded, and it must not cost above a certain modest sum.

Nodding his head understandingly, he drove me at once sixty miles away into Vermont and showed me a nineteen-room house on a rock-bound spot. He showed me, within the next eighteen days, every sort of house from pink brick mansions on a quarter acre to shingle camp bungalows in wild places far from human habitation. We slogged through snow to our knees to inspect Victorian Gothic edifices big enough to house a boarding school. We crept into desolate little shacks where snow and leaves were piled in the corners of the living-room.

Between each wild goose chase, I repeated, patiently and monotonously as a trained crow, my simple wants, my unalterable wishes. At last I reminded him that our friends had told me I could believe every word he said, but until he believed

*That was *then!*

every word I said, too, we could make no progress whatever. And I said good-bye, which seemed to make no impression. Two days later he called again and said perhaps he had a house for me, after all.

That was January 21, 1941. As our car turned into the road, a hen pheasant flew up and struck lightly against the radiator-cap and lost a few breast-feathers. With desperate superstition I got out and picked them up and put them in my handbag, saying they might bring me luck.

We drove for a few miles around Saratoga Lake, turned into an inclined road between a great preserve of spruce and pine, turned again to the right on a small rise, and my honest man pointed into the valley before us. I looked at an old Colonial house, rather small, modified Georgian, with a red roof and several cluttery small porches and sheds clinging to its sides. It sat there in a modest state, surrounded by tall, bare trees, against a small hill of evergreen.

"But that is my house," I told him. "That's mine."

We struggled around it again knee-deep in snowdrifts, peering through windows.

"Let's not bother," I said. "I'll take it."

"But you must see inside first," he insisted.

"I know what's inside," I said. "Let's go to see the owner."

The owner, a woman of perhaps fifty who looked incapable of surprise, had to be told several times, in different phrases, that her house was sold at last, really sold. My honest man had had it on his list for seven long years. Her hopes were about exhausted. I gave him a look meant to be terrible, but he missed it, somehow.

She wanted to tell the history of her house. It was one of the first built in this part of the country, by first settlers, related to Benedict Arnold. It had been lived in since the day it was finished; her own family had been there for eighty-five years. She was the last of her immediate family. With a difficult tear, she said that she had buried all her nearest and dearest from that house; and living there alone as she had been, there were times in the winter evenings when it seemed they were all in the same room with her.

*

In no time at all, it seems now, the transaction was complete, and I was well seized of my property. I had always thought that was a mere picturesque phrase. It is simply a statement of fact. I am seized of my property, and my property is well seized of me. It is described as having one hundred and five acres of meadow and woodland, with two brooks, a spring, and an inexhaustible well. Besides all this, there are forty acres of molding sand, of which eighteen are under contract to a sand dealer. However, I should not mind this, as the land to be mined for sand lay far away; the operations would be conducted safely out of sight. Of this more later.

I remembered a remark of Mr. E. M. Forster on taking possession of his woods: the first thing he noticed was that his land made him feel heavy. I had become almost overnight a ton weight of moral, social, and financial responsibility, subject to state and county tax, school tax, and an astonishing variety of insurance. Besides the moral, legal, and financial aspects peculiar to myself, the affair had become a community interest. My new-found friends gave me any amount of advice, all seriously good. They were anxious about me. They told me how pleased they were I was going to live there. Other friends drove out to visit, inspect, and approve. My house was solid as a church, in foundation, beams, walls, and roof, and the cellar was an example to all cellars.

Friends came up in the spring from New York, strolled in the meadows, picked flowers, and advised me to practice virtue and circumspection in every act of my new life. There began arriving presents, such as five incredibly elegant very early Victorian chairs and settles, Bohemian mirror glass lamps with crystal-beaded shades, cranberry glass bowls.

My life began to shape itself to fit a neighborhood, and that neighborhood included everybody who came near my house or knew that I had got it. All this is strange new pleasure.

And almost at once I encountered some strange new troubles, oh, a sea of them, some of them surprising, yet once encountered, nothing that does not seem more or less in the natural order of being. For example, the inexhaustible well. It was that for a family who drew water by the pailful, but not enough for two little baths and a new kitchen. I went out the other day to look again at my lovely landscape and my beloved house, indeed I can hardly bear to stay away from them, and there were three strange men pulling up the pump, dropping plumb-lines into the well, and sinking points in the earth here and there. They had also with them a rosy-colored, forked, hazel wand, and they almost blushed their heads off when I knew what it was and asked them if it worked.

"Naw, it's all just a lot of nonsense," said the one who was trying to make it work. They all agreed there was nothing in it, but each of them knew several well-diggers who had seen it work or who could even work it themselves. "There are actually men," said one of them, "who just walk around holding it like this, and when he comes to where there is water, it turns and twists itself right out of his hands." But there wasn't anything to it, just the same, and just the same they never go to look for water without taking one along. They haven't found a well yet, but I do not let my mind dwell on this.

The sand man, thinking that the place was vacated and nobody would know or care, came and leveled over the entire slope of my east meadow within a few steps of the house, before I got into action and persuaded him he was, to say it mildly, not within his rights. There is a great and dreadful scar four feet deep and seventy-five feet long, where I had meant to plant the rose hedge, which must be filled in with tons of soil.

I have a tenant house, which a Southern friend described as something transplanted from *Tobacco Road*. Be that as it may. There are broad plans afoot for it, and I am looking for a tenant farmer. With this in view, I bought, of the best and sturdiest, the following implements: one metal rake, one wooden rake, one hoe, one ax (of the kind used by champion wood-cutters in contests), one handsaw, one spading fork, one mattock, one spade, one brush hook, one snath and blade (medium), one wheelbarrow, one long, dangerous-looking scythe blade, one hammer, one ten-inch file, one grindstone, one four-gallon water-pail, and this is the merest beginning. But I have no tenant farmer.

There is a half-ton of old lumber thrown down on a bed of flowers whose name I do not know, but who were just getting ready to bloom. The sand men hacked a road through my pine woods, taking off great branches of fine trees. Contractors came and went in series. Through the years I have collected a small library of architectural magazines, photographs of old houses before and after, plans for remodeling, and a definite point of view of my own. The first man on the ground looked everything over, listened patiently to my plans and hopes, asked me, "Why take all that trouble for an old house?" and disappeared, never to be seen again. The second was magnificently sympathetic and competent, but he was used to building houses for the Whitneys and Vanderbilts and other racing people in Saratoga, and it was impossible to scale down his ideas.

Others went out, pried up the old random-width floors, tore chunks out of the plaster, knocked bricks out of the chimney, pumped out the well, tested beams, ripped slates off the roof, pulled down sheds and porches, and one by one disappeared. . . . I have a contractor, though. He is Swedish, he has been in this country seventeen years, he is an authority on American Colonial houses, and I decided he should do the work when he went through my house, looked around once, nodded his head, and remarked gently, "Ah, yes, I know just what is here." The house and the furniture are only about ten miles apart now. There remains nothing except to draw them together.

It seems a very long ten miles, perhaps the longest I shall ever travel. I am saving the pheasant feathers to burn, for luck, on the first fire I light in the fine old fireplace with its bake oven and graceful mantelpiece. It will be high time for fires again, no doubt, when I get there.

NOTE. July, 1952: I lived there just thirteen months.

1941

The Necessary Enemy

SHE is a frank, charming, fresh-hearted young woman who married for love. She and her husband are one of those gay, good-looking young pairs who ornament this modern scene rather more in profusion perhaps than ever before in our history. They are handsome, with a talent for finding their way in their world, they work at things that interest them, their tastes agree and their hopes. They intend in all good faith to spend their lives together, to have children and do well by them and each other—to be happy, in fact, which for them is the whole point of their marriage. And all in stride, keeping their wits about them. Nothing romantic, mind you; their feet are on the ground.

Unless they were this sort of person, there would be not much point to what I wish to say; for they would seem to be an example of the high-spirited, right-minded young whom the critics are always invoking to come forth and do their duty and practice all those sterling old-fashioned virtues which in every generation seem to be falling into disrepair. As for virtues, these young people are more or less on their own, like most of their kind; they get very little moral or other aid from their society; but after three years of marriage this very contemporary young woman finds herself facing the oldest and ugliest dilemma of marriage.

She is dismayed, horrified, full of guilt and forebodings because she is finding out little by little that she is capable of hating her husband, whom she loves faithfully. She can hate him at times as fiercely and mysteriously, indeed in terribly much the same way, as often she hated her parents, her brothers and sisters, whom she loves, when she was a child. Even then it had seemed to her a kind of black treacherousness in her, her private wickedness that, just the same, gave her her only private life. That was one thing her parents never knew about her, never seemed to suspect. For it was never given a name. They did and said hateful things to her and to each other as if by right, as if in them it was a kind of virtue. But when they said to her, "Control your feelings," it was never when she was amiable and obedient, only in the black times of her hate. So it was her secret, a shameful one. When they punished her, sometimes for the strangest reasons, it was, they said, only because they loved her—it was for her good. She did not believe this, but she thought herself guilty of something worse than ever they had punished her for. None of this really frightened her: the real fright came when she discovered that at times her father and mother hated each other; this was like standing on the doorsill of a familiar room and seeing in a lightning flash that the floor was gone, you were on the edge of a bottomless pit. Sometimes she felt that both of them hated her, but that passed, it was simply not a thing to be thought of, much less believed. She thought she had outgrown all this, but here it was again, an element in her own nature she could not control, or feared she could not. She would have to hide from her husband, if she could, the same spot in her feelings she had hidden from her parents, and for the same no doubt disreputable, selfish reason: she wants to keep his love.

Above all, she wants him to be absolutely confident that she loves him, for that is the real truth, no matter how unreasonable it sounds, and no matter how her own feelings betray them both at times. She depends recklessly on his love; yet while she is hating him, he might very well be hating her as much or even more, and it would serve her right. But she does not want to be served right, she wants to be loved and forgiven—that is, to be sure he would forgive her anything, if he had any notion of what she had done. But best of all she would like not to have anything in her love that should ask for forgiveness. She doesn't mean about their quarrels—they are not so bad. Her feelings are out of proportion, perhaps. She knows it is perfectly natural for people to disagree, have fits of temper, fight it out; they learn quite a lot about each other that way, and not all of it disappointing either. When it passes, her hatred seems quite unreal. It always did.

Love. We are early taught to say it. I love you. We are trained to the thought of it as if there were nothing else, or nothing else worth having without it, or nothing worth having which it could not bring with it. Love is taught, always by precept, sometimes by example. Then hate, which no one meant to teach us, comes of itself. It is true that if we say I love you, it may be received with doubt, for there are times when it is hard to believe. Say I hate you, and the one spoken to believes it instantly, once for all.

Say I love you a thousand times to that person afterward and mean it every time, and still it does not change the fact that once we said I hate you, and meant that too. It leaves a mark on that surface love had worn so smooth with its eternal caresses. Love must be learned, and learned again and again; there is no end to it. Hate needs no instruction, but waits only to be provoked . . . hate, the unspoken word, the unacknowledged presence in the house, that faint smell of brimstone among the roses, that invisible tongue-tripper, that unkempt finger in every pie, that sudden oh-so-curiously *chilling* look —could it be boredom?—on your dear one's features, making them quite ugly. Be careful: love, perfect love, is in danger.

If it is not perfect, it is not love, and if it is not love, it is bound to be hate sooner or later. This is perhaps a not too exaggerated statement of the extreme position of Romantic Love, more especially in America, where we are all brought up on it, whether we know it or not. Romantic Love is changeless, faithful, passionate, and its sole end is to render the two lovers happy. It has no obstacles save those provided by the hazards of fate (that is to say, society), and such sufferings as the lovers may cause each other are only another word for delight: exciting jealousies, thrilling uncertainties, the ritual dance of courtship within the charmed closed circle of their secret alliance; all *real* troubles come from without, they face them unitedly in perfect confidence. Marriage is not the end but only the beginning of true happiness, cloudless, changeless to the end. That the candidates for this blissful condition have never seen an example of it, nor ever knew anyone who had, makes no difference. That is the ideal and they will achieve it.

How did Romantic Love manage to get into marriage at last, where it was most certainly never intended to be? At its highest it was tragic: the love of Héloïse and Abélard. At its most graceful, it was the homage of the trouvère for his lady. In its most popular form, the adulterous strayings of solidly married couples who meant to stray for their own good reasons, but at the same time do nothing to upset the property settle-ments or the line of legitimacy; at its most trivial, the pretty tri-fling of shepherd and shepherdess.

This was generally condemned by church and state and a word of fear to honest wives whose mortal enemy it was. Love within the sober, sacred realities of marriage was a matter of personal luck, but in any case, private feelings were strictly a private affair having, at least in theory, no bearing whatever on the fixed practice of the rules of an institution never intended as a recreation ground for either sex. If the couple discharged their religious and social obligations, furnished forth a copious progeny, kept their troubles to themselves, maintained public civility and died under the same roof, even if not always on speaking terms, it was rightly regarded as a successful mar-riage. Apparently this testing ground was too severe for all but the stoutest spirits; it too was based on an ideal, as impossible in its way as the ideal Romantic Love. One good thing to be said for it is that society took responsibility for the conditions of marriage, and the sufferers within its bonds could always blame the system, not themselves. But Romantic Love crept into the marriage bed, very stealthily, by centuries, bringing its absurd notions about love as eternal springtime and marriage as a personal adventure meant to provide personal happiness. To a Western romantic such as I, though my views have been much modified by painful experience, it still seems to me a charming work of the human imagination, and it is a pity its central notion has been taken too literally and has hardened into a convention as cramping and enslaving as the older one. The refusal to acknowledge the evils in ourselves which there-fore are implicit in any human situation is as extreme and un-workable a proposition as the doctrine of total depravity; but somewhere between them, or maybe beyond them, there does exist a possibility for reconciliation between our desires for im-possible satisfactions and the simple unalterable fact that we also desire to be unhappy and that we create our own suffer-ings; and out of these sufferings we salvage our fragments of happiness.

Our young woman who has been taught that an important part of her human nature is not real because it makes trouble and interferes with her peace of mind and shakes her self-love, has been very badly taught; but she has arrived at a most important stage of her re-education. She is afraid her marriage is going to fail because she has not love enough to face its difficulties; and this because at times she feels a painful hostility toward her husband, and cannot admit its reality because such an admission would damage in her own eyes her view of what love should be, an absurd view, based on her vanity of power. Her hatred is real as her love is real, but her hatred has the advantage at present because it works on a blind instinctual level, it is lawless; and her love is subjected to a code of ideal conditions, impossible by their very nature of fulfillment, which prevents its free growth and deprives it of its right to recognize its human limitations and come to grips with them. Hatred is natural in a sense that love, as she conceives it, a young person brought up in the tradition of Romantic Love, is not natural at all. Yet it did not come by hazard, it is the very imperfect expression of the need of the human imagination to create beauty and harmony out of chaos, no matter how mistaken its notion of these things may be, nor how clumsy its methods. It has conjured love out of the air, and seeks to preserve it by incantations; when she spoke a vow to love and honor her husband until death, she did a very reckless thing, for it is not possible by an act of the will to fulfill such an engagement. But it was the necessary act of faith performed in defense of a mode of feeling, the statement of honorable intention to practice as well as she is able the noble, acquired faculty of love, that very mysterious overtone to sex which is the best thing in it. Her hatred is part of it, the necessary enemy and ally.

1948

"Marriage Is Belonging"

HAVING never written a word about marriage, so far as I remember,* and being now at the point where I have learned better than to have any theories about it, if I ever had; and believing as I do that most of the stuff written and talked about it is more or less nonsense; and having little hope that I shall add luster to the topic, it is only logical and natural that I should venture to write a few words on the subject.

My theme is marriage as the art of belonging—which should not be confused with possessing—all too often the art, or perhaps only the strategy, and a risky one, of surrendering gracefully with an air of pure disinterestedness as much of your living self as you can spare without incurring total extinction; in return for which you will, at least in theory, receive a more than compensatory share of another life, the life in fact presumably dearest to you, equally whittled down in your favor to the barest margin of survival. This arrangement with variations to suit the circumstances is of course the basis of many contracts besides that of marriage; but nowhere more than in marriage does the real good of the relationship depend on intangibles not named in the bond.

The trouble with me is—always was—that if you say "marriage" to me, instantly the word translates itself into "love," for only in such terms can I grasp the idea at all, or make any sense of it. The two are hopelessly associated, or rather identified, in my mind; that is to say, love is the only excuse for marriage, if any excuse is necessary. I often feel one should be offered. Love without marriage can sometimes be very awkward for all concerned; but marriage without love simply removes that institution from the territory of the humanly admissible, to my mind. Love is a state in which one lives who loves, and whoever loves has given himself away; love then, and not marriage, is belonging. Marriage is the public declaration of a man and a woman that they have formed a secret alliance, with the intention to belong to, and share with each

*See preceding. So much for memory.

other, a mystical estate; mystical exactly in the sense that the real experience cannot be communicated to others, nor explained even to oneself on rational grounds.

By love let me make it clear, I do not refer only to that ecstatic reciprocal cannibalism which goes popularly under the name, and which is indeed commonly one of the earliest biological symptoms (Boy Eats Girl and vice versa), for, like all truly mystical things, love is rooted deeply and rightly in this world and this flesh. This phase is natural, dangerous but not necessarily fatal; so remarkably educational it would be a great pity to miss it; further, of great importance, for the flesh in real love is one of the many bridges to the spirit; still, a phase only, which being passed is too often mistaken for the whole thing, and the end of it. This is an error based on lack of imagination, or the simple incapacity for further and deeper exploration of life, there being always on hand great numbers of people who are unwilling or unable to grow up, no matter what happens to them. It leads to early divorce, or worse. Like that young man whose downward career began with mere murder, this error can lead to infidelity, lying, eavesdropping, gambling, drinking, and finally to procrastination and incivility. These two last can easily have destroyed more marriages than any amount of murder, or even lying.

Let us recall a few generalities about marriage in its practical aspects which are common knowledge, such as: it is one of the most prevalent conditions of the human adult, heading the list of vital statistics, I believe. It has been made very easy to assume, and fairly easy in the legal sense, at least, to abandon; and it is famous for its random assortment of surprises of every kind—leaf-covered booby traps, spiders lurking in cups, pots of gold under rainbows, triplets, poltergeists in the stair closet, and flights of cupids lolling on the breakfast table—anything can happen. Every young married pair believes their marriage is going to be quite different from the others, and they are right—it always is. The task of regulating its unruly impulses is a thorn in the souls of theologians, its social needs and uses the insoluble riddle of law-makers. Through all ages known to man almost everybody, even those who wouldn't be seen dead wearing a wedding ring, having agreed that somehow, in some way, at some time or another, marriage has simply got to be made to work better than it does, or ever has, for that matter. Yet on the whole, my guess is that it works about as well as any other human institution, and rather better than a great many. The drawback is, it is the merciless revealer, the great white searchlight turned on the darkest places of human nature; it demands of all who enter it the two most difficult achievements possible: that each must be honest with himself, and faithful to another. I am speaking here only of the internal reality of marriage not its legal or even its social aspects.

In its present form it is comparatively modern. As an idea, it must have begun fairly soon after the human male discovered his highly important role in the bringing forth of young. For countless aeons, we are told by those who pretend to know, it was believed that the powers of generation were vested in women alone, people having never been very bright about sex, right from the start. When men at last discovered, who knows how? that they were fathers, their pride in their discovery must have been equaled only by their indignation at having worshiped women as vessels of the Great Mystery when all along they should have been worshiping themselves. Pride and wrath and no doubt the awful new problem of what to do with the children, which had never bothered them before, drove them on to an infinite number of complicated and contradictory steps toward getting human affairs on a sounder basis. And, after all this time (skipping lightly over the first few hundred thousand years of total confusion), in our fine big new busy Western world, we have succeeded in establishing not only as the ideal, but in religious and legal fact (if not altogether in practice), as the very crown and glory of human ties, a one-man-one-woman-until-death sort of marriage, rivaling the swans for purity, with a ritual oath exchanged not only to stick to each other through thick and thin, to practice perfect fidelity, flawless forbearance, a modified bodily servitude, but to love each other dearly and kindly to the end.

All this is to be accomplished in a physical situation of the direst intimacy, in which all claims to the most ordinary privacy may be disregarded by either, or both. I shall not attempt to catalogue the daily accounting for acts, words, states of feeling and even thoughts, the perpetual balance and check between individual wills and points of view, the unbelievable amount of tact, intelligence, flexibility, generosity, and God knows what, it requires for two people to go on growing together and in the same directions instead of cracking up and falling apart.

Take the single point of fidelity: It is very hard to be entirely faithful, even to things, ideas, above all, persons one loves. There is no such thing as perfect faithfulness any more than there is perfect love or perfect beauty. But it is fun trying. And if I say faithfulness consists of a great many things beside the physical, never let it be dreamed that I hold with the shabby nonsense that physical infidelity is a mere peccadillo beneath the notice of enlightened minds. Physical infidelity is the signal, the notice given, that all the fidelities are undermined. It is complete betrayal of the very principle on which love and marriage are based, and besides, a vulgar handing over of one's partner to public shame. It is exactly as stupid as that, to say nothing more.

Yet every day quite by the thousands delightfully honest young couples, promising, capable, sometimes gifted, but in no way superhuman, leap gaily into marriage—a condition which, for even reasonable success and happiness (both words seem rather trivial in this connection), would tax the virtues and resources and staying powers of a regiment of angels. But what else would you suggest that they do?

Then there come the children. Gladly, willingly (if you do not think so, I refer you to the birth records of this country for the past ten years. There haven't been so many young wives having so many babies so fast for at least four generations!) these pairs proceed to populate their houses, or flats—often very small flats, and mother with a job she means to keep, too —with perfect strangers, often hostile, whose habits even to the most adoring gaze are often messy and unattractive. They lie flat on their noses at first in what appears to be a drunken slumber, then flat on their backs kicking and screaming, demanding impossibilities in a foreign language. They are human nature in essence, without conscience, without pity, without love, without a trace of consideration for others, just one seething cauldron of primitive appetites and needs; and what do they really need? We are back where we started. They need love, first; without it everything worth saving is lost or damaged in them; and they have to be taught love, pity, conscience, courage—everything. And what becomes of them? If they are lucky, among all the million possibilities of their fates, along with the innumerable employments, careers, talents, ways of life, they will learn the nature of love, and they will marry and have children.

If this all sounds a little monotonous, and gregarious, well, sometimes it is, and most people like that sort of thing. They always have. It is hardly possible to exaggerate the need of a human being, not a madman, or a saint, or a beast, or a self-alienated genius who is all of these in one, and therefore the scapegoat for all the rest, to live at peace—and by peace I mean in reconciliation, not easy contentment—with another human being, and with that one in a group or society where he feels he belongs. The best, the very best, of all these relationships is that one in marriage between a man and a woman who are good lovers, good friends, and good parents; who belong to each other, and to their children, and whose children belong to them: that is the meaning of the blood tie that binds them, and may bind them sometimes to the bone. Children cut their teeth on their parents and their parents cut their wisdom teeth on each other: that is what they are there for. It is never really dull, and can sometimes be very memorably exciting for everybody. In any case, the blood-bond, however painful, is the condition of human life in this world, the absolute point of all departure and return. The ancient biological laws are still in force, the difference being merely in the way human beings regard them, and though I am not one to say all change is progress, in this one thing, a kind of freedom and ease of mind between men and women in marriage—or at least the possibility of it, change has been all for the better. At least they are able now to fight out their differences on something nearer equal terms.

We have the bad habit, some of us, of looking back to a time—almost any time will do—when society was stable and orderly, family ties stronger and deeper, love more lasting and faithful, and so on. Let me be your Cassandra prophesying after the fact, and a long study of the documents in the case: it was never true, that is, no truer than it is now. Above all, it was not true of domestic life in the nineteenth century. Then, as now, it was just as good in individual instances as the married pairs involved were able to make it, privately, between themselves. The less attention they paid to what they were expected to think and feel about marriage, and the more attention to each other as loved and loving, the better they did, for themselves and for everybody. The laws of public decorum were easy to observe, for they had another and better understanding. The Victorian marriage feather bed was in fact set upon the shaky foundation of the wavering human heart, the inconsistent human mind, and was the roiling hotbed of every dislocation and disorder not only in marriage but all society, which we of the past two generations have lived through. Yet in love—this is what I have been talking about all the time—a certain number of well-endowed spirits, and there are surprisingly quite a lot of them in every generation, have always been able to take their world in stride, to live and die together, and to keep all their strange marriage vows not because they spoke them, but because like centuries of lovers before them, they were prepared to live them in the first place.

Example: A certain woman was apparently a prisoner for life in several ways: already thirty-five or -six years old, supposed to be an incurable invalid, whose father had forbidden any of his children to marry; and above all, a poet at a time when literary women were regarded as monsters, almost. Yet she was able to write, in the first flush of a bride's joy: "He preferred . . . of free and deliberate choice, to be allowed to sit only an hour a day by my side, to the fulfillment of the brightest dream which should exclude me in any possible world."

This could be illusion, but the proof of reality came fifteen years later. Just after her death her husband wrote to a friend: "Then came what my heart will keep till I see her again and longer—the most perfect expression of her love to me within my whole knowledge of her. Always smilingly, and happily, and with a face like a girl's; and in a few minutes she died in my arms, her head on my cheek."

If you exclaim that this is not fair, for, after all, these two were, of course, the Robert Brownings, I can only reply that it is because I sincerely believe they were not so very special that I cite them. Don't be thrown off by that lyrical nineteenth-century speech, nor their fearless confidence not only in their own feelings, but the sympathy of their friends; it is the kind of love that makes real marriage, and there is more of it in the world than you might think, though the ways of expressing it follow the fashions of the times; and we certainly do not find much trace of it in our contemporary literature. It is *very* old-style, and it was, long before the Brownings. It is new, too, it is the very newest thing, every day renewed in an endless series of those fortunate people who may not have one point in common with the Brownings except that they know, or are capable of learning, the nature of love, and of living by it.

1951

A Defense of Circe

S HE was one of the immortals, a daughter of Helios; on her mother's side, granddaughter to the Almighty Ancient of Days, Oceanus. Of sunlight and sea water was her divine nature made, and her unique power as goddess was that she could reveal to men the truth about themselves by showing to each man himself in his true shape according to his inmost nature. For this she was rightly dreaded and feared; her very name was a word of terror.

She was a beautiful, sunny-tempered, merry-hearted young enchantress, living on her own island in a dappled forest glade, in her great high open hall of polished stone, with her four handmaidens, nymphs "born of the wells and of the woods and of the holy rivers, that flow forward into the salt sea." Tall, golden haired, serene, she walked up and down before her high loom, weaving her imperishable web of shining, airy splendid stuff such as goddesses weave. As she walked she sang in such a high clear sweet voice the sound carried through the halls and into the forest to the suspicious ears of the fearful men, that half of Odysseus' companions chosen by lot for the dangerous task of approaching and entering if possible the enchanted lair.

The proud and lofty-souled Eurylochus, near kinsman of Odysseus, was by his bad luck at the head of this foray or was supposed to be. He had not liked anything about his mission. Far from leading, he held back. But peril was everywhere—there roamed about the place savage mountain-bred lions and wolves, which gave our heroes a fresh turn. These boisterous veterans of the ten years' war over Helen (I follow Homer strictly) had gone through more than enough disaster lately, and almost anything could upset them. These frightful animals behaved in a way to confirm their worst fears: far from attacking the company, they came romping and fawning with a human

AUTHOR'S NOTE: In this retelling of the Circe episode I have followed the old Butcher-Arnold translation, the first I ever knew, and it still has for me the wonder of early love and true poetry. I believe I have every translation into English of the Odyssey but I preferred this for my Defense.

gaze of entreaty in their eyes; unnerved at last, the heroes rushed upon the palace, shouting in voices tuned between fear and anger; when Circe instantly opened the great door and gently bade her uninvited guests welcome, they surged in heedlessly—except Eurylochus. He, guessing treason to lurk within, deserted promptly and ran back to the safety of Odysseus and the rest of the company on the shore near the long black ship, bawling like a calf all the way, of course; this dastardly act—dastardly even by ancient Greek heroic standards—has not been so generally condemned as it merits. But, he brought the terrible news they had been half-expecting. Odysseus, against the clamor and tears and lamentations of Eurylochus, who refused to show him the way back, cast upon his shoulder his silver-studded sword, and slung his bow about him and set out by himself to the rescue.

Odysseus was Pallas Athene's darling, she never failed him in battle or any manly exploit. She loved to swoop down like an eagle at the side of her hero in times of hurly-burly and uproar. There was nobody like her for putting on whatever shape was suitable to the occasion and appearing beside him upon the disordered scene with her powers in full play. He was, she told him, the only mortal who could almost match her for guile and subtle trickery—for that she loved him. But she took no interest in his erotic entanglements and at such times abandoned him to his troubles. Such trivialities were not her province— she left that sort of thing to Hermes, whose business and delight it was to interfere in the love between men and women and to sever and to separate; he was the messenger of the high gods in this matter; for, as the goddesses had cause to complain, the gods who made so free with mortal women were jealous of goddesses who loved mortal men; Calypso complained bitterly of this, and even Aphrodite, the very goddess of love herself, was not free from the reproaches of Zeus or the tamperings of Hermes.

So there was Hermes, the ambiguous and beautiful, a youth with the first down on his lip; in his golden sandals, carrying his wand, lurking in the forest to waylay Odysseus, to give him advice about Circe and to offer him the curious herb moly, more easily gathered by gods than by men, the one sure countermagic for men against the enchantments of women. Now all the gods were crafty, but they kept their word with their favored ones. Not Hermes—he was on all sides at once, stealing from anybody—Admetus' oxen, you remember, and the girdle of Aphrodite right off of her, that time he begot the monster on her; and other incidents besides. A thoroughly untidy if fascinating character, he was, in this instance, thoroughly reliable; his heart was in his work. Odysseus accepted the herb and the advice, and there was a wonderful fairness in him being thus armed, for Odysseus, often called divine, was not so; he was of the seed of Zeus but not a half-god; and it was not justice that he should encounter with merely mortal weapons the half-goddess Circe with her fearful power. Circe, said Hermes, once outmagicked by the herb, will invite Odysseus to become her lover. She will be very likely to amuse herself by making him "a dastard and unmanned" once she has got him stripped and in bed.

Odysseus, therefore, to avoid this fate worse than death, must force her to "swear a mighty oath by the blessed gods" that she will do no such thing, nor any other harm to him or his companions.

This gives us an oblique glimmer of truth about Circe; for these two methodically unreliable beings, strangely enough, never doubt for a moment that Circe can be trusted to honor her oath. It might reasonably be expected that she could not be relied upon any more than any of the other gods once they were set against one; but she could be trusted, it seems; they both knew it and set out cheerfully to take advantage of their knowledge.

Not even a god, having once formed a man, can make a swine of him. That is for him to choose. Circe's honeyed food with the lulling drug in it caused them to reveal themselves. The delicate-minded goddess touched them then with her wand, the wand of the transforming truth, and penned the groaning, grunting, weeping, bewildered creatures in the sty back of the hall. In the whole episode she showed one touch of witty malice, when she tossed them a handful of acorns and other victuals suitable to their new condition. No doubt she did it smilingly with her natural grace; what else should she have offered them at that moment? I think it was very good of her to go on feeding them at all. But then I am only human.

Then Odysseus with a darkly troubled heart called aloud at the great shining door, and the goddess like a rainbow made of sunlight and sea water welcomed him gently, and the drama was played out again, up to that point where she tapped him with her wand and said, "Go thy way now to the sty, couch thee there with the rest of thy company." The gods know each other on first sight but they do not always fathom each other's magic. Was Circe so blinded by Hermes' ambiguous herb she could not see she was dealing with a fox?

Hermes had advised Odysseus instantly to draw his sword upon her and threaten her with death. She was deathless, as Hermes must have known and Odysseus might have guessed; but he seems to have forgot this, so convincing was her manner and look of a mortal woman. She did then, instantly and flatteringly, exactly what Hermes had said she would do—she slipped down and clasped his knees and bewailed her fate in perfect form, and said the one thing most calculated to win his heart; she guessed that he was Odysseus and that he had a mind within him that could not be enchanted, and ended: "Nay come, put thy sword into the sheath, and thereafter let us go up into my bed, that meeting in love and sleep we may trust each other." Her tender, appropriate, womanly intentions were entirely misunderstood by Odysseus, experienced as he was in the ways of goddesses and women. He was irresistible to them all alike, except to Helen; he was the fate of women as Helen was the fate of men. He had married his dear mortal Penelope as a long second choice after half-goddess Helen, who refused him along with a phalanx of other suitors. Penelope had no rivals but goddesses ever after. In a way, he was tender to weakness with women, as men who really need them are apt to be; he wept upon them and pleaded and touched their hearts when he was getting ready to go. . . .

He showed unexpected firmness and severity with Circe, defended as he was by the moly; he accused her of all the evil Hermes had spoken against her, and required of her the mighty oath, which she swore at once; and kept.

And then—but this is all pure magic, this poem, the most

enchanting thing ever dreamed of in the human imagination, how have I dared to touch it? And what is this passage that stops my heart with joy, as do so many others—the description of Calypso's island; the scene of recognition between Odysseus and Penelope; Argive Helen in tears before Telemachus, remembering Troy and wondering at herself, so shameless, so blinded by Aphrodite; and all the rest? It is a description of women casting purple and white linen coverlets on silverstudded chairs, with golden baskets and golden wine goblets and silver wine bowls on silver tables; and "a great fire beneath a mighty cauldron" to warm the water; and of the goddess herself bathing away weariness of the loved mortal body under her hands; and it celebrates the smoothness of olive oil on the skin, and of fine linen next the flesh, and of good cheer and comfort and sweet smells and savors . . . a song of praise and delight in the pure senses, fresh as the pearl rosy morning of that morning world. . . .

But Odysseus still grieved, could not eat, could not be at rest until she had restored his dear companions. So she took her wand and went out and drove them back into the hall, a herd of great pigs shedding human tears. Circe, compelled by countermagic to give them back their belying human shapes, was still a goddess, and in this moment she showed an easy, godlike magnanimity. While she anointed the unhappy beasts, they went on weeping; ancient Greek heroes spent a good part of their time lamenting, howling in anguish, bewailing their fates. They wept alike for joy or grief, tears like spring rain; for they lived in a world of mystery and they were its children— what is the strength and the skill of even the bravest and wisest man when matched against the gods, their inscrutable wills, their incomprehensible purposes? As they wept, first in pain and then in happiness, Circe restored them not merely to what they had been but taller, younger, more beautiful than they were born to be—the act of a creatrix, the pure aesthetic genius at play; and we must not be tempted to think of it drearily in our sad terms as an act of divine mercy and reparation, full of profound moral and theological meanings, such as: that the regenerated soul, after punishment and purification, rises in a perfection it could never know except through suffering. No. In this sunny high comedy there are profound meanings, some lovely truth almost lost to us but that still hovers glimmering at the farthest edge of consciousness, a nearly remembered dream of glory; and it is our fault and our utter loss if we tarnish the bright vision with our guilt-laden breath, our nightmare phantasies. . . .

The transformed warrior and the whole company, joined by still reluctant Eurylochus, stayed on cheerfully for a year as the guests of Circe. Odysseus shared her beautiful bed, in gentleness and candor, with that meeting in love and sleep and trust she had promised him. No one was in the least changed, no one learned anything by his experiences. They were not intent on building their characters or improving themselves; they were what they were and their concern was to fulfill their destinies.

Meantime they were in the earthly Elysian fields, feasting themselves on the abundant roast flesh and sweet red wine, lolling in perfumed baths and rolling in perfumed oil, sleeping soft and waking easy to another rosy-fingered dawn. The goddess sat among them taking her own nectar and ambrosia, or walked singing back and forth before her endless shining web. This life was suitable to her; but the men became bored, then satiated, then sickened with all this abundance and generosity, this light and grace, tenderness, freedom from care, godlike splendor—they could endure it no longer. They complained to Odysseus when she was not present, or so Odysseus told her, and it could very well be true, but the warriors spoke his secret thought too. Circe had borne him a son, the quarter-godling Telegonus; Odysseus remembered with longing Telemachus and Penelope and Ithaca his kingdom. He longed to be again in the hollow black ship breasting the wild sea; the time had come for him to go. So, by her fair bed at her knees, he wept and told her all his longing, and reminded her of her promise that she would send him and his companions safely on their way toward home. Search Homer as you may, it is clear that she made no such promise at any time—no hint of it in any of her flowing honeyed words.

Now one may ask, since she knew that the ambiguous Hermes had outcharmed her, why did she not, as some women or even some goddesses might have done, steal the herb and destroy it or cast a counterspell to annul it? Why did she not, as Calypso did later, make a towering scene, remind Odysseus that she had promised him nothing and then, with a smart tap of her wand, turn him into a fox to run his life away with those other wild creatures outside her walls?

The only answer I can give is, this is Circe, and this is Odysseus; when he says to her, "Now is my spirit eager to be gone," she replies at once, with gentle remoteness, "Odysseus of many devices, tarry ye now no longer in my house against your will," and breaks to him the dreadful news that he must at once perform another journey, to Hades, to seek out The-ban Teiresias, the blind soothsayer, who will give him direc-tions how to reach home. This broke his heart and he went and groveled and implored her to tell him who would guide him on his way—"no man ever yet sailed to hell in a black ship."

"Set up the mast and spread abroad the white sails and sit thee down," she told him, and promised to send the North Wind to waft his ship on its way. And she told him the cere-monies proper to one entering the place of the dead, the sacri-fice of the black ram and the black ewe and the guarding of the blood from the voracious ghosts until Teiresias had spoken. Then things moved very swiftly and with great beauty and dig-nity. In the dawn Odysseus went through the hall waking his men; Circe gave him a mantle and doublet and "clad herself in a great shining robe . . . and put a veil upon her head." But the youngest lad, Elpenor, heavy with wine, was sleeping on the roof, and roused too suddenly, fell, and his neck was bro-ken. The men, who had arrived mourning and in tears, now departed the same way, tearing their hair. The goddess made herself invisible and went ahead of them and fastened a black ram and a black ewe by the dark ship: "lightly passing us by," said Odysseus in wonder, "who may behold a god against his will, whether going to or fro?"

When they returned to the island to give Elpenor burial and quiet his uneasy spirit, while they were mourning and per-forming the rites, Circe came with her handmaids bringing "flesh and bread in plenty and dark red wine." She made them a noble speech of salutation: "Men overbold, who have gone alive into the house of Hades, to know death twice, while all men else die once for all. Nay come, eat ye meat and drink wine here all day long; and with the breaking of the day ye shall set sail, and myself I will show you the path and declare each thing, that ye may not suffer pain or hurt through any grievous ill-contrivance by sea or on the land."

As if she could! As if her divine amiability and fostering care could save these headstrong creatures from their ordained sufferings. But Odysseus was wise in his mortal wisdom: He knew that man cannot live as the gods do. His universal fate: birth, death, and the larger disasters, are from the gods; but within that circle he must work out his personal fate with or without their help. He saw his own inevitable end in the swarming, angry, uneasy, grieving shades of the dark underworld of death; but when later the lonely goddess Calypso offered him immortality he was not shaken. When she spoke jealously and contemptuously of Penelope's beauty he answered her in a speech that is the key to all his history, a mortal bent on mortality: "Myself I know it well, how wise Penelope is meaner to look upon than thou, in comeliness and stature. *But she is mortal and thou knowest not age or death.* [Note: my italics.] Yet even so, I wish and long day by day to see the day of my returning. Yes, and if some god shall wreck me in the wine-dark deep, even so I will endure, with a heart within me patient of affliction. For already I have suffered full much, and much have I toiled in perils of waves and war; let this be added to the tales of these."

And there it is. But earlier, on the island of Circe, at the very last moment there was a memorable scene. After the ship and the men were supplied and ready, "then she took me by the hand," Odysseus remembered long afterward, "and led me apart from my dear company, and made me sit down and laid herself at my feet, and asked all my tale." He told everything about the journey to Hades, and she warned him again against the dangers to come, trying one last time to guide her wayward lover safely home. . . .

After this long night of good counsel and loving kindness, "anon came the golden-throned Dawn. Then the fair goddess took her way up the island. . . ."

This should be the end. But someone is certain to ask:

"What about the unpleasant episode of Circe turning Scylla into a monster?" Ah, well—without troubling to deny, or even mention, that hideous rumor, Circe told Odysseus plainly that Scylla was born a monster. In view of what we know about Circe, I am entirely happy to believe her.

1954

St. Augustine and the Bullfight

ADVENTURE. The word has become a little stale to me, because it has been applied too often to the dull physical exploits of professional "adventurers" who write books about it, if they know how to write; if not, they hire ghosts who quite often can't write either.

I don't read them, but rumors of them echo, and re-echo. The book business at least is full of heroes who spend their time, money and energy worrying other animals, manifestly their betters such as lions and tigers, to death in trackless jungles and deserts only to be crossed by the stoutest motorcar; or another feeds hooks to an inedible fish like the tarpon; another crosses the ocean on a raft, living on plankton and seaweed, why ever, I wonder? And always always, somebody is out climbing mountains, and writing books about it, which are read by quite millions of persons who feel, apparently, that the next best thing to going there yourself is to hear from somebody who went. And I have heard more than one young woman remark that, though she did not want to get married, still, she would like to have a baby, for the adventure: not lately though. That was a pose of the 1920s and very early '30s. Several of them did it, too, but I do not know of any who wrote a book about it—good for them.

W. B. Yeats remarked—I cannot find the passage now, so must say it in other words—that the unhappy man (unfortunate?) was one whose adventures outran his capacity for experience, capacity for experience being, I should say, roughly equal to the faculty for understanding what has happened to one. The difference then between mere adventure and a real experience might be this? That adventure is something you seek for pleasure, or even for profit, like a gold rush or invading a country; for the illusion of being more alive than ordinarily, the thing you will to occur; but experience is what really happens to you in the long run; the truth that finally overtakes you.

Adventure is sometimes fun, but not too often. Not if you can remember what really happened; all of it. It passes, seems to lead nowhere much, is something to tell friends to amuse them, maybe. "Once upon a time," I can hear myself saying, for I once said it, "I scaled a cliff in Boulder, Colorado, with my bare hands, and in Indian moccasins, barelegged. And at nearly the top, after six hours of feeling for toe- and finger-holds, and the gayest feeling in the world that when I got to the top I should see something wonderful, something that sounded awfully like a bear growled out of a cave, and I scut-tled down out of there in a hurry." This is a fact. I had never climbed a mountain in my life, never had the least wish to climb one. But there I was, for perfectly good reasons, in a hut on a mountainside in heavenly sunny though sometimes stormy weather, so I went out one morning and scaled a very minor cliff; alone, unsuitably clad, in the season when rattlesnakes are casting their skins; and if it was not a bear in that cave, it was some kind of unfriendly animal who growls at people; and this ridiculous escapade, which was nearly six hours of the hardest work I ever did in my life, toeholds and fingerholds on a cliff, put me to bed for just nine days with a complaint the local people called "muscle poisoning." I don't know exactly what they meant, but I do remember clearly that I could not turn over in bed without help and in great agony. And did it teach me anything? I think not, for three years later I was climbing a volcano in Mexico, that celebrated unpronounceably named volcano, Popocatepetl, which everybody who comes near it climbs sooner or later; but was that any reason for me to climb it? No. And I was knocked out for weeks, and that finally did teach me: I am not supposed to go climbing things. Why did I not know in the first place? For me, this sort of thing must come under the head of Adventure.

I think it is pastime of rather an inferior sort; yet I have heard men tell yarns like this only a very little better: their mountains were higher, or their sea was wider, or their bear was bigger and noisier, or their cliff was steeper and taller, yet there was no point whatever to any of it except that it had hap-pened. This is not enough. May it not be, perhaps, that expe-rience, that is, the thing that happens to a person living from day to day, is anything at all that sinks in? is, without making any claims, a part of your growing and changing life? what it is that happens in your mind, your heart?

Adventure hardly ever seems to be that at the time it is

happening: not under that name, at least. Adventure may be an afterthought, something that happens in the memory with imaginative trimmings if not downright lying, so that one should suppress it entirely, or go the whole way and make honest fiction of it. My own habit of writing fiction has provided a wholesome exercise to my natural, incurable tendency to try to wangle the sprawling mess of our existence in this bloody world into some kind of shape: almost any shape will do, just so it is recognizably made with human hands, one small proof the more of the validity and reality of the human imagination. But even within the most limited frame what utter confusion shall prevail if you cannot take hold firmly, and draw the exact line between what really happened, and what you have since imagined about it. Perhaps my soul will be saved after all in spite of myself because now and then I take some unmanageable, indigestible fact and turn it into fiction; cause things to happen with some kind of logic—my own logic, of course—and everything ends as I think it should end and no back talk, or very little, from anybody about it. Otherwise, and except for this safety device, I should be the greatest liar unhung. (When was the last time anybody was hanged for lying?) What is Truth? I often ask myself. Who knows?

A publisher asked me a great while ago to write a kind of autobiography, and I was delighted to begin; it sounded very easy when he said, "Just start, and tell everything you remember until now!" I wrote about a hundred pages before I realized, or admitted, the hideous booby trap into which I had fallen. First place, I remember quite a lot of stupid and boring things: there were other times when my life seemed merely an endurance test, or a quite mysterious but not very interesting and often monotonous effort at survival on the most primitive terms. There are dozens of things that might be entertaining but I have no intention of telling them, because they are nobody's business; and endless little gossipy incidents that might entertain indulgent friends for a minute, but in print they look as silly as they really are. Then, there are the tremendous, unmistakable, life-and-death crises, the scalding, the bone-breaking events, the lightnings that shatter the landscape of the soul—who would write that by request? No, that is for a secretly written manuscript to be left with your papers, and if your executor is a good friend, who has probably been brought up on St. Augustine's *Confessions*, he will read it with love and attention and gently burn it to ashes for your sake.

Yet I intend to write something about my life, here and now, and so far as I am able without one touch of fiction, and I hope to keep it as shapeless and unforeseen as the events of life itself from day to day. Yet, look! I have already betrayed my occupation, and dropped a clue in what would be the right place if this were fiction, by mentioning St. Augustine when I hadn't meant to until it came in its right place in life, not in art. Literary art, at least, is the business of setting human events to rights and giving them meanings that, in fact, they do not possess, or not obviously, or not the meanings the artist feels they should have—we do understand so little of what is really happening to us in any given moment. Only by remembering, comparing, waiting to know the consequences can we sometimes, in a flash of light, see what a certain event really meant, what it was trying to tell us. So this will be notes on a fateful thing that happened to me when I was young and did not know much about the world or about myself. I had been reading St. Augustine's *Confessions* since I was able to read at all, and I thought I had read every word, perhaps because I did know certain favorite passages by heart. But then, it was something like having read the Adventures of Gargantua by Rabelais when I was twelve and enjoying it; when I read it again at thirty-odd, I was astounded at how much I had overlooked in the earlier reading, and wondered what I thought I had seen there.

So it was with St. Augustine and my first bullfight. Looking back nearly thirty-five years on my earliest days in Mexico, it strikes me that, for a fairly serious young woman who was in the country for the express purpose of attending a Revolution, and studying Mayan people art, I fell in with a most lordly gang of fashionable international hoodlums. Of course I had Revolutionist friends and artist friends, and they were gay and easy and poor as I was. This other mob was different: they were French, Spanish, Italian, Polish, and they all had titles and good names: a duke, a count, a marquess, a baron, and they all were in some flashy money-getting enterprise like importing cognac wholesale, or selling sports cars to newly rich politicians; and they all drank like fish and played fast games like polo or tennis or jai alai; they haunted the wings of theaters, drove slick cars like maniacs, but expert maniacs, never missed a bull-fight or a boxing match; all were reasonably young and they had ladies to match, mostly imported and all speaking French. These persons stalked pleasure as if it were big game—they took their fun exactly where they found it, and the way they liked it, and they worked themselves to exhaustion at it. A fast, tough, expensive, elegant, high lowlife they led, for the ladies and gentlemen each in turn had other friends you would have had to see to believe; and from time to time, without being in any way involved or engaged, I ran with this crowd of shady characters and liked their company and ways very much. I don't like gloomy sinners, but the merry ones charm me. And one of them introduced me to Shelley. And Shelley, whom I knew in the most superficial way, who remained essentially a stranger to me to the very end, led me, without in the least ever knowing what he had done, into one of the most impor-tant and lasting experiences of my life.

He was British, a member of the poet's family; said to be au-thentic great-great-nephew; he was rich and willful, and had come to Mexico young and wild, and mad about horses, of course. Coldly mad—he bred them and raced them and sold them with the stony detachment and merciless appraisal of the true horse lover—they call it love, and it could be that: but he did not like them. "What is there to like about a horse but his good points? If he has a vice, shoot him or send him to the bullring; that is the only way to work a vice out of the breed!"

Once, during a riding trip while visiting a ranch, my host gave me a stallion to ride, who instantly took the bit in his teeth and bolted down a steep mountain trail. I managed to stick on, held an easy rein, and he finally ran himself to a stand-still in an open field. My disgrace with Shelley was nearly com-plete. Why? Because the stallion was not a good horse. I should have refused to mount him. I said it was a question how to re-fuse the horse your host offered you—Shelley thought it no question at all. "A lady," he reminded me, "can always excuse herself gracefully from anything she doesn't wish to do." I said, "I wish that were really true," for the argument about the bullfight was already well started. But the peak of his disap-proval of me, my motives, my temperament, my ideas, my ways, was reached when, to provide a diversion and end a dull discussion, I told him the truth: that I had liked being run away with, it had been fun and the kind of thing that had to happen unexpectedly, you couldn't arrange for it. I tried to convey to him my exhilaration, my pure joy when this half-broken, crazy beast took off down that trail with just a hoof-hold between a cliff on one side and a thousand-foot drop on the other. He said merely that such utter frivolity surprised him in someone whom he had mistaken for a well-balanced, intelligent girl; and I remember thinking how revoltingly fatherly he sounded, exactly like my own father in his stuffier moments.

He was a stocky, red-faced, muscular man with broad shoulders, hard-jowled, with bright blue eyes glinting from puffy lids; his hair was a grizzled tan, and I guessed him about fifty years old, which seemed a great age to me then. But he mentioned that his Mexican wife had "died young" about three years before, and that his eldest son was only eleven years old. His whole appearance was so remarkably like the typical horsy, landed-gentry sort of Englishman one meets in books by Frenchmen or Americans, if this were fiction I should feel obliged to change his looks altogether, thus falling into one stereotype to avoid falling into another. However, so Shelley did look, and his clothes were magnificent and right beyond words, and never new-looking and never noticeable at all except one could not help observing sooner or later that he was beyond argument the best-dressed man in America, North or South; it was that kind of typical British inconspicuous good taste: he had it, superlatively. He was evidently leading a fairly rakish life, or trying to, but he was of a cast-iron conventionality even in that. We did not fall in love—far from it. We struck up a hands-off, quaint, farfetched, tetchy kind of friendship which consisted largely of good advice about worldly things from him, mingled with critical marginal notes on my character —a character of which I could not recognize a single trait; and if I said, helplessly, "But I am not in the least like that," he would answer, "Well, you should be!" or "Yes, you are, but you don't know it."

This man took me to my first bullfight. I'll tell you later how St. Augustine comes into it. It was the first bullfight of that season; Covadonga Day; April; clear, hot blue sky; and a long procession of women in flower-covered carriages; wearing their finest lace veils and highest combs and gauziest fans; but I shan't describe a bullfight. By now surely there is no excuse for anyone who can read or even hear or see not to know pretty well what goes on in a bullring. I shall say only that Sánchez Mejías and Rudolfo Gaona each killed a bull that day; but before the Grand March of the toreros, Hattie Welton rode her thoroughbred High School gelding into the ring to thunders of shouts and brassy music.

She was Shelley's idol. "Look at that girl, for God's sake," and his voice thickened with feeling, "the finest rider in the world," he said in his dogmatic way, and it is true I have not seen better since.

She was a fine buxom figure of a woman, a highly colored blonde with a sweet, childish face; probably forty years old, and perfectly rounded in all directions; a big round bust, and that is the word, there was nothing plural about it, just a fine, warm-looking bolster straight across her front from armpit to armpit, fine firm round hips—again, why the plural? It was an ample seat born to a sidesaddle, as solid and undivided as the bust, only more of it. She was tightly laced and her waist was small. She wore a hard-brimmed dark gray Spanish sailor hat, sitting straight and shallow over her large golden knot of hair; a light gray bolero and a darker gray riding skirt—not a Spanish woman's riding dress, nor yet a man's, but something tight and fit and formal and appropriate. And there she went, the most elegant woman in the saddle I have ever seen, graceful and composed in her perfect style, with her wonderful, lightly dancing, learned horse, black and glossy as shoe polish, perfectly under control—no, not under control at all, you might have thought, but just dancing and showing off his paces by himself for his own pleasure.

"She makes the bullfight seem like an anticlimax," said Shelley, tenderly.

I had not wanted to come to this bullfight. I had never intended to see a bullfight at all. I do not like the slaughtering of animals as sport. I am carnivorous, I love all the red juicy meats and all the fishes. Seeing animals killed for food on the farm in summers shocked and grieved me sincerely, but it did not cure my taste for flesh. My family for as far back as I know anything about them, only about 450 years, were the huntin', shootin', fishin' sort: their houses were arsenals and their dominion over the animal kingdom was complete and unchallenged. When I was older, my father remarked on my tiresome timidity, or was I just pretending to finer feelings than those of the society around me? He hardly knew which was the more tiresome. But that was perhaps only a personal matter. Morally, if I wished to eat meat I should be able to kill the animal—otherwise it appeared that I was willing to nourish myself on other people's sins? For he supposed I considered it a sin. Otherwise why bother about it? Or was it just something unpleasant I wished to avoid? Maintaining my own purity—and a very doubtful kind of purity he found it, too—at the expense of the guilt of others? Altogether, my father managed to make a very sticky question of it, and for some years at intervals I made it a matter of conscience to kill an animal or bird, something I intended to eat. I gave myself and the beasts some horrible times, through fright and awkwardness, and to my shame, nothing cured me of my taste for flesh. All forms of cruelty offend me bitterly, and this repugnance is inborn, absolutely impervious to any arguments, or even insults, at which the red-blooded lovers of blood sports are very expert; they don't admire me at all, any more than I admire them. . . . Ah, me, the contradictions, the paradoxes! I was once perfectly capable of keeping a calf for a pet until he outgrew the yard in the country and had to be sent to the pastures. His subsequent fate I leave you to guess. Yes, it is all revoltingly sentimental and, worse than that, confused. My defense is that no matter whatever else this world seemed to promise me, never once did it promise to be simple.

So, for a great tangle of emotional reasons I had no intention of going to a bullfight. But Shelley was so persistently unpleasant about my cowardice, as he called it flatly, I just wasn't able to take the thrashing any longer. Partly, too, it was his natural snobbery: smart people of the world did not have such feelings; it was to him a peculiarly provincial if not downright Quakerish attitude. "I have some Quaker ancestors," I told him. "How absurd of you!" he said, and really meant it.

The bullfight question kept popping up and had a way of

spoiling other occasions that should have been delightful. Shelley was one of those men, of whose company I feel sometimes that I have had more than my fair share, who simply do not know how to drop a subject, or abandon a position once they have declared it. Constitutionally incapable of admitting defeat, or even its possibility, even when he had not the faintest shadow of right to expect a victory—for why should he make a contest of my refusal to go to a bullfight?—he would start an argument during the theater intermissions, at the fronton, at a street fair, on a stroll in the Alameda, at a good restaurant over coffee and brandy; there was no occasion so pleasant that he could not shatter it with his favorite gambit: "If you would only see one, you'd get over this nonsense."

So there I was, at the bullfight, with cold hands, trembling innerly, with painful tinglings in the wrists and collarbone: yet my excitement was not altogether painful; and in my happiness at Hattie Welton's performance I was calmed and off guard when the heavy barred gate to the corral burst open and the first bull charged through. The bulls were from the Duke of Veragua's* ranch, as enormous and brave and handsome as any I ever saw afterward. (This is not a short story, so I don't have to maintain any suspense.) This first bull was a beautiful monster of brute courage: his hide was a fine pattern of black and white, much enhanced by the goad with fluttering green ribbons stabbed into his shoulder as he entered the ring; this in turn furnished an interesting design in thin rivulets of blood, the enlivening touch of scarlet in his sober color scheme, with highly aesthetic effect.

He rushed at the waiting horse, blindfolded in one eye and standing at the proper angle for the convenience of his horns, the picador making only the smallest pretense of staving him off, and disemboweled the horse with one sweep of his head. The horse trod in his own guts. It happens at least once every bullfight. I could not pretend not to have expected it; but I had not been able to imagine it. I sat back and covered my eyes. Shelley, very deliberately and as inconspicuously as he could, took both my wrists and held my hands down on my knees. I shut my eyes and turned my face away, away from the

*Lineal descendant of Christopher Columbus.

arena, away from him, but not before I had seen in his eyes a look of real, acute concern and almost loving anxiety for me— he really believed that my feelings were the sign of a grave flaw of character, or at least an unbecoming, unworthy weakness that he was determined to overcome in me. He couldn't shoot me, alas, or turn me over to the bullring; he had to deal with me in human terms, and he did it according to his lights. His voice was hoarse and fierce: "Don't you dare come here and then do this! You must face it!"

Part of his fury was shame, no doubt, at being seen with a girl who would behave in such a pawky way. But at this point he was, of course, right. Only he had been wrong before to nag me into this, and I was altogether wrong to have let him persuade me. Or so I felt then. "You have got to face this!" By then he was right; and I did look and I did face it, though not for years and years.

During those years I saw perhaps a hundred bullfights, all in Mexico City, with the finest bulls from Spain and the greatest bullfighters—but not with Shelley—never again with Shelley, for we were not comfortable together after that day. Our odd, mismatched sort of friendship declined and neither made any effort to revive it. There was bloodguilt between us, we shared an evil secret, a hateful revelation. He hated what he had revealed in me to himself, and I hated what he had revealed to me about myself, and each of us for entirely opposite reasons; but there was nothing more to say or do, and we stopped seeing each other.

I took to the bullfights with my Mexican and Indian friends. I sat with them in the cafés where the bullfighters appeared; more than once went at two o'clock in the morning with a crowd to see the bulls brought into the city; I visited the corral back of the ring where they could be seen before the corrida. Always, of course, I was in the company of impassioned adorers of the sport, with their special vocabulary and manner- isms and contempt for all others who did not belong to their charmed and chosen cult. Quite literally there were those among them I never heard speak of anything else; and I heard then all that can be said—the topic is limited, after all, like any other— in love and praise of bullfighting. But it can be tiresome, too. And I did not really live in that world, so narrow and so trivial, so cruel and so unconscious; I was a mere visitor. There was something deeply, irreparably wrong with my being there at all, something against the grain of my life; except for this (and here was the falseness I had finally to uncover): I loved the spectacle of the bullfights, I was drunk on it, I was in a strange, wild dream from which I did not want to be awakened. I was now drawn irresistibly to the bullring as before I had been drawn to the race tracks and the polo fields at home. But this had death in it, and it was the death in it that I loved. . . . And I was bitterly ashamed of this evil in me, and believed it to be in me only—no one had fallen so far into cruelty as this! These bullfight buffs I truly believed did not know what they were doing—but I did, and I knew better because I had once known better; so that spiritual pride got in and did its deadly work, too. How could I face the cold fact that at heart I was just a killer, like any other, that some deep corner of my soul consented not just willingly but with rapture? I still clung obstinately to my flattering view of myself as a unique case, as a humane, blood-avoiding civilized being, somehow a fallen angel, perhaps? Just the same, what was I doing there? And why was I beginning secretly to abhor Shelley as if he had done me a great injury, when in fact he had done me the terrible and dangerous favor of helping me to find myself out?

In the meantime I was reading St. Augustine; and if Shelley had helped me find myself out, St. Augustine helped me find myself again. I read for the first time then his story of a friend of his, a young man from the provinces who came to Rome and was taken up by the gang of clever, wellborn young hoodlums Augustine then ran with; and this young man, also wellborn but severely brought up, refused to go with the crowd to the gladiatorial combat; he was opposed to them on the simple grounds that they were cruel and criminal. His friends naturally ridiculed such dowdy sentiments; they nagged him slyly, bedeviled him openly, and, of course, finally some part of him consented—but only to a degree. He would go with them, he said, but he would not watch the games. And he did not; until the time for the first slaughter, when the howling of the crowd brought him to his feet, staring: and afterward he was more bloodthirsty than any.

Why, of course: oh, it might be a commonplace of human

nature, it might be it could happen to anyone! I longed to be free of my uniqueness, to be a fellow-sinner at least with some-one: I could not bear my guilt alone—and here was this stu-dent, this boy at Rome in the fourth century, somebody I felt I knew well on sight, who had been weak enough to be led into adventure but strong enough to turn it into experience. For no matter how we both attempted to deceive ourselves, our acts had all the earmarks of adventure: violence of motive, events taking place at top speed, at sustained intensity, under powerful stimulus and a willful seeking for pure sensation; willful, I say, because I was not kidnapped and forced, after all, nor was that young friend of St. Augustine's. We both pro-ceeded under the power of our own weakness. When the time came to kill the splendid black and white bull, I who had pitied him when he first came into the ring stood straining on tiptoe to see everything, yet almost blinded with excitement, and crying out when the crowd roared, and kissing Shelley on the cheekbone when he shook my elbow and shouted in the voice of one justified: "Didn't I tell you? Didn't I?"

1955

Act of Faith: 4 July 1942

S INCE this war began I have felt sometimes that all our good words had been rather frayed out with constant repetition, as if they were talismans that needed only to be spoken against the evil and the evil would vanish; or they have been debased by the enemy, part of whose business is to disguise fascism in the language of democracy. And I have noticed that the people who are doing the work and the fighting and the dying, and those who are doing the talking, are not at all the same people.*

By natural sympathy I belong with those who are not talking much at present, except in the simplest and straightest of terms, like the young Norwegian boy who escaped from Norway and joined the Canadian forces. When asked how he felt about Norway's fate, he could say only, "It is hard to explain how a man feels who has lost his country." I think he meant it was impossible; but he had a choice, to accept defeat or fight, and he made the choice, and that was his way of talking. There was the American boy going into the navy, who answered the same foolish question: "It's too serious a thing to be emotional about." And the young American wife who was one of the last civilians to escape, by very dangerous and exhausting ways, from a bombarded island where her husband was on active duty. She was expecting her first baby. "Oh yes, I had the baby," she said, matter-of-factly, "a fine healthy boy." And another girl, twenty-one years old, has a six-month-old girl baby and a husband who will be off to the army any day now. She wrote: "I'm glad I have that job. Her Daddy won't have to worry about us."

While the talkers have been lecturing us, saying the American people have been spoiled by too much prosperity and made slack of fiber by too much peace and freedom, and gloating rather over the painful times we are about to endure for our own good, I keep my mind firmly on these four young ones, not because they are exceptional but precisely because they are not. They come literally in regiments these days, though not

*Note and read again, December Second, 1969—K. A. P. in Memoriam.

all of them are in uniform, nor should be. They are the typical millions of young people in this country, and they have not been particularly softened by prosperity; they were brought up on the depression. They have not been carefully sheltered: most of them have worked for a living when they could find work, and an astonishing number of them have helped support their families. They do their jobs and pay their taxes and buy War Savings Stamps and contribute to the Red Cross and China Relief and Bundles for Britain and all the rest. They do the work in factories and offices and on farms. The girls knit and nurse and cook and are learning to replace the boys in skilled work in war production. The boys by the thousand are getting off to camp, carrying their little two-by-four suitcases or bundles. I think of this war in terms of these people, who are my kind of people; the war they are fighting is my war, and yes, it is hard to find exactly the right word to say to them. I wait to hear what they will have to say to the world when this war is won and over and they must begin their lives again in the country they have helped to save for democracy.

I wait for that with the most immense and deep longing and hope and belief in them.

In the meantime let us glance at that theory, always revived in the heat and excitement of war, that peace makes spirits slothful and bodies flabby. In this season, when Americans are celebrating the birthday of our Republic, its most important birthday since that first day of our hard-won beginnings, we might remember that the men who wrote the Constitution and compiled the Body of Liberties were agreed on the revolutionary theory that peace was a blessing to a country—one of the greatest blessings—and they were careful to leave recorded their opinions on this subject. And they were right. Peace is good, and the arts of peace, and its fruits. The freedom we may have only in peace is good. It was never true there was too much of either; the truth is, there was never enough, never rightly exercised, never deeply enough understood. But we have been making a fairly steady headway this century and a half in face of strong and determined opposition from enemies within as well as from without. We have had poverty in a country able to support in plenty more than twice its present population, yet by long effort we were arriving at an increasing standard of good living for greater and greater numbers of people. One of the prime aims of the democratic form of government was to create an economy in which all the people were to be allowed access to the means and materials of life, and to share fairly in the abundance of the earth. This has been the hardest fight of all, the bitterest, but the battle is by no means lost, and it is not ended, and it will be won in time.

Truth is, the value of peace to us was that it gave us time, and the right to fight for our liberties as a people, against our internal enemies, using those weapons provided for us within our own system of government; and the first result of war with an external enemy is that this right is suspended, and there is the danger that, even if the foreign war is won, the gains at home may be lost, and must be fought for all over again.

It has been the habit and the principle of this people to think in terms of peace, and perhaps to live in rather a too-optimistic faith that peace could be maintained when all the plainest signs pointed in the opposite direction; but they have fought their wars very well, and they will fight this one well, too. And it is no time to be losing our heads and saying, or thinking, that in the disciplines and the restrictions and the heavy taxes and the restraint on action necessary to concerted effort, we have already lost the freedoms we are supposed to be fighting for. If we lose the war, there will be nothing left to talk about; the blessed and sometimes abused American freedom of speech will have vanished with the rest. But we are not going to lose this war, and the people of this country are going to have the enormous privilege of another chance to make of their Republic what those men who won and founded it for us meant for it to be. We aren't going anywhere, that is one great thing. Every single soul of us is involved personally in this war; this is the last stand, and this is our territory. Here is the place and now is the time to put a stop, once and for all, to the stampede of the human race like terrorized cattle over one world frontier after another. We stay here.

And during this period of suspension of the humanities, in the midst of the outrage and the world horror staggering to the imagination, we might find it profitable to examine the true nature of our threatened liberties, and their political, legal, and social origins and meanings, and decide exactly what their value is, and where we should be without them. They were not accidental by any means; they are implicit in our theory of government, which was in turn based on humanistic concepts of the importance of the individual man and his rights in society. They are not mere ornaments on the façade, but are laid in the foundation stone of the structure, and they will last so long as the structure itself but no longer. They are not inalienable: the house was built with great labor and it is made with human hands; human hands can tear it down again, and will, if it is not well loved and defended. The first rule for any effective defense is: Know your enemies. Blind, fanatical patriotism which shouts and weeps is no good for this war. This is another kind of war altogether. I trust the quiet coldness of the experienced fighters, I like their knowing that words are wasted in this business.

1942

The Future Is Now

NOT so long ago I was reading in a magazine with an enormous circulation some instructions as to how to behave
if and when we see that flash brighter than the sun which means
that the atom bomb has arrived. I read of course with the intense interest of one who has everything to learn on this subject; but at the end, the advice dwindled to this: the only real
safety seems to lie in simply being somewhere else at the time,
the farther away the better; the next best, failing access to deep
shelters, bombproof cellars and all, is to get under a stout table
—that is, just what you might do if someone were throwing
bricks through your window and you were too nervous to
throw them back.

This comic anticlimax to what I had been taking as a serious
educational piece surprised me into real laughter, hearty and
carefree. It is such a relief to be told the truth, or even just the
facts, so pleasant not to be coddled with unreasonable hopes.
That very evening I was drawn away from my work table to my
fifth-story window by one of those shrill terror-screaming
sirens which our excitement-loving city government used then
to affect for so many occasions: A fire? Police chasing a gang-
ster? Somebody being got to the hospital in a hurry? Some distinguished public guest being transferred from one point to
another? Strange aircraft coming over, maybe? Under the lights
of the corner crossing of the great avenue, a huge closed vehicle whizzed past, screaming. I never knew what it was, had not
in fact expected to know; no one I could possibly ask would
know. Now that we have bells clamoring away instead for such
events, we all have one doubt less, if perhaps one expectancy
more. The single siren's voice means to tell us only one thing.

But at that doubtful moment, framed in a lighted window
level with mine in the apartment house across the street, I saw
a young man in a white T-shirt and white shorts at work polishing a long, beautiful dark table top. It was obviously his own
table in his own flat, and he was enjoying his occupation. He
was bent over in perfect concentration, rubbing, sandpapering,
running the flat of his palm over the surface, standing back

now and then to get the sheen of light on the fine wood. I am sure he had not even raised his head at the noise of the siren, much less had he come to the window. I stood there admiring his workmanlike devotion to a good job worth doing, and there flashed through me one of those pure fallacies of feeling which suddenly overleap reason: surely all that effort and energy so irreproachably employed were not going to be wasted on a table that was to be used merely for crawling under at some unspecified date. Then why take all those pains to make it beautiful? Any sort of old board would do.

I was so shocked at this treachery of the lurking Foul Fiend (despair *is* a foul fiend, and this was despair) I stood a moment longer, looking out and around, trying to collect my feelings, trying to think a little. Two windows away and a floor down in the house across the street, a young woman was lolling in a deep chair, reading and eating fruit from a little basket. On the sidewalk, a boy and a girl dressed alike in checkerboard cotton shirts and skin-tight blue denims, a costume which displayed acutely the structural differences of their shapes, strolled along with their arms around each other. I believe this custom of lovers walking enwreathed in public was imported by our soldiers of the First World War from France, from Paris indeed. "You didn't see that sort of thing here before," certain members of the older generation were heard to remark quite often, in a tone of voice. Well, one sees quite a lot of it now, and it is a very pretty, reassuring sight. Other citizens of all sizes and kinds and ages were crossing back and forth; lights flashed red and green, punctually. Motors zoomed by, and over the great city—but where am I going? I never read other peoples' descriptions of great cities, more particularly if it is a great city I know. It doesn't belong here anyway, except that I had again that quieting sense of the continuity of human experience on this earth, its perpetual aspirations, set-backs, failures and re-beginnings in eternal hope; and that, with some appreciable differences of dress, customs and means of conveyance, so people have lived and moved in the cities they have built for more millennia than we are yet able to account for, and will no doubt build and live for as many more.

Why did this console me? I cannot say; my mind is of the sort that can often be soothed with large generalities of that

nature. The silence of the spaces between the stars does not af-
fright me, as it did Pascal, because I am unable to imagine it
except poetically; and my awe is not for the silence and space
of the endless universe but for the inspired imagination of
man, who can think and feel so, and turn a phrase like that to
communicate it to us. Then too, I like the kind of honesty and
directness of the young soldier who lately answered someone
who asked him if he knew what he was fighting for. "I sure
do," he said, "I am fighting to live." And as for the future, I
was once reading the first writings of a young girl, an apprentice author, who was quite impatient to get on with the business and find her way into print. There is very little one can say
of use in such matters, but I advised her against haste—she
could so easily regret it. "Give yourself time," I said, "the future will take care of itself." This opinionated young person
looked down her little nose at me and said, "The future is
now." She may have heard the phrase somewhere and liked it,
or she may just have naturally belonged to that school of
metaphysics; I am sure she was too young to have investigated
the thought deeply. But maybe she was right and the future
does arrive every day and it is all we have, from one second to
the next.

So I glanced again at the young man at work, a proper-
looking candidate for the armed services, and realized the
plain, homely fact: he was not preparing a possible shelter,
something to cower under trembling; he was restoring a beautiful surface to put his books and papers on, to serve his plates
from, to hold his cocktail tray and his lamp. He was full of the
deep, right, instinctive, human belief that he and the table
were going to be around together for a long time. Even if he is
off to the army next week, it will be there when he gets back.
At the very least, he is doing something he feels is worth doing
now, and that is no small thing.

At once the difficulty, and the hope, of our special time in this
world of Western Europe and America is that we have been
brought up for many generations in the belief, however tacit,
that all humanity was almost unanimously engaged in going
forward, naturally to better things and to higher reaches. Since
the eighteenth century at least when the Encyclopedists seized

upon the Platonic theory that the highest pleasure of mankind was pursuit of the good, the true, and the beautiful, progress, in precisely the sense of perpetual, gradual amelioration of the hard human lot, has been taught popularly not just as theory of possibility but as an article of faith and the groundwork of a whole political doctrine. Mr. Toynbee has even simplified this view for us with picture diagrams of various sections of humanity, each in its own cycle rising to its own height, struggling beautifully on from craggy level to level, but always upward. Whole peoples are arrested at certain points, and perish there, but others go on. There is also the school of thought, Oriental and very ancient, which gives to life the spiral shape, and the spiral moves by nature upward. Even adherents of the circular or recurring-cycle school, also ancient and honorable, somehow do finally allow that the circle is a thread that spins itself out one layer above another, so that even though it is perpetually at every moment passing over a place it has been before, yet by its own width it will have risen just so much higher.

These are admirable attempts to get a little meaning and order into our view of our destiny, in that same spirit which moves the artist to labor with his little handful of chaos, bringing it to coherency within a frame; but on the visible evidence we must admit that in human nature the spirit of contradiction more than holds its own. Mankind has always built a little more than he has hitherto been able or willing to destroy; got more children than he has been able to kill; invented more laws and customs than he had any intention of observing; founded more religions than he was able to practice or even to believe in; made in general many more promises than he could keep; and has been known more than once to commit suicide through mere fear of death. Now in our time, in his pride to explore his universe to its unimaginable limits and to exceed his possible powers, he has at last produced an embarrassing series of engines too powerful for their containers and too tricky for their mechanicians; millions of labor-saving gadgets which can be rendered totally useless by the mere failure of the public power plants, and has reduced himself to such helplessness that a dozen or less of the enemy could disable a whole city by throwing a few switches. This paradoxical creature has committed all these extravagances and created all these dangers and sufferings in a quest—we are told—for peace and security.

How much of this are we to believe, when with the pride of Lucifer, the recklessness of Icarus, the boldness of Prometheus and the intellectual curiosity of Adam and Eve (yes, intellectual; the serpent promised them wisdom if . . .) man has obviously outreached himself, to the point where he cannot understand his own science or control his own inventions. Indeed he has become as the gods, who have over and over again suffered defeat and downfall at the hands of their creatures. Having devised the most exquisite and instantaneous means of communication to all corners of the earth, for years upon years friends were unable even to get a postcard message to each other across national frontiers.* The newspapers assure us that from the kitchen tap there flows a chemical, cheap and available, to make a bomb more disturbing to the imagination even than the one we so appallingly have; yet no machine has been invented to purify that water so that it will not spoil even the best tea or coffee. Or at any rate, it is not in use. We are the proud possessors of rocket bombs that go higher and farther and faster than any ever before, and there is some talk of a rocket ship shortly to take off for the moon. (My plan is to stow away.) We may indeed reach the moon some day, and I dare predict that will happen before we have devised a decent system of city garbage disposal.

This lunatic atom bomb has succeeded in rousing the people of all nations to the highest point of unanimous moral dudgeon; great numbers of persons are frightened who never really had much cause to be frightened before. This world has always been a desperately dangerous place to live for the greater part of the earth's inhabitants; it was, however reluctantly, endured as the natural state of affairs. Yet the invention of every new weapon of war has always been greeted with horror and righteous indignation, especially by those who failed to invent it, or who were threatened with it first . . . bows and arrows, stone cannon balls, gunpowder, flintlocks, pistols, the dumdum bullet, the Maxim silencer, the machine gun,

*Fall, 1952. The hydrogen bomb has just been exploded, very successfully, to the satisfaction of the criminals who caused it to be made.

poison gas, armored tanks, and on and on to the grand climax—if it should prove to be—of the experiment on Hiroshima. Nagasaki was bombed too, remember? Or were we already growing accustomed to the idea? And as for Hiroshima, surely it could not have been the notion of sudden death of others that shocked us? How could it be, when in two great wars within one generation we have become familiar with millions of shocking deaths, by sudden violence of most cruel devices, and by agonies prolonged for years in prisons and hospitals and concentration camps. We take with apparent calmness the news of the deaths of millions by flood, famine, plague—no, all the frontiers of danger are down now, no one is safe, no one, and that, alas, really means all of us. It is our own deaths we fear, and so let's out with it and give up our fine debauch of moralistic frenzy over Hiroshima. I fail entirely to see why it is more criminal to kill a few thousand persons in one instant than it is to kill the same number slowly over a given stretch of time. If I have a choice, I'd as lief be killed by an atom bomb as by a hand grenade or a flame thrower. If dropping the atom bomb is an immoral act, then the making of it was too; and writing of the formula was a crime, since those who wrote it must have known what such a contrivance was good for. So, morally speaking, the bomb is only a magnified hand grenade, and the crime, if crime it is, is still murder. It was never anything else. Our protocriminal then was the man who first struck fire from flint, for from that moment we have been coming steadily to this day and this weapon and this use of it. What would you have advised instead? That the human race should have gone on sitting in caves gnawing raw meat and beating each other over the head with the bones?

And yet it may be that what we have is a world not on the verge of flying apart, but an uncreated one—still in shapeless fragments waiting to be put together properly. I imagine that when we want something better, we may have it: at perhaps no greater price than we have already paid for the worse.

1950

The Never-Ending Wrong

For several years in the early 1920s when I was living part of the time in Mexico, on each return to New York, I would follow again the strange history of the Italian emigrants Nicola Sacco a shoemaker, and Bartolomeo Vanzetti a fishmonger, who were accused of a most brutal holdup of a payroll truck, with murder, in South Braintree, Massachusetts, in the early afternoon of April 15, 1920. They were tried before a Massachusetts court and condemned to death about eighteen months later.

In appearance it was a commonplace crime by quite ordinary, average, awkward gangsters, the only unusual feature being that these men were tried, convicted, and put to death; for gangsters in those days, at any rate those who operated boldly enough on a large scale, while not so powerful or so securely entrenched as the Mafia today, enjoyed a curious immunity in society and under the law. We have only to remember the completely public career of Al Capone, who, as chief of the bloodiest gang ever known until that time in this country, lived as if a magic circle had been drawn around him: he could at last be convicted only of not paying his income tax—that "income" he had got by methodical wholesale crime, murder, drug traffic, bootleg liquor, prostitution, and a preposterous mode of blackmail called "protection," a cash payment on demand instead of a gunpoint visit, the vampire bat of small businesses such as family delicatessens, Chinese laundries, et cetera. After serving his time on Alcatraz, he retired to Florida to live in peace and respectable luxury while his syphilitic brain softened into imbecility. When he died, there was a three-day sentimental wallow on the radio, a hysterical orgy of nostalgia for the good old times when a guy could really get away with it. I remember the tone of drooling bathos in which one of them said, "Ah, just the same, in spite of all, he was a great guy. They just don't make 'em like that anymore." Of course, time has proved since how wrong the announcer was—it is obvious they do make 'em like that nearly every day . . . like that but even more indescribably monstrous—and world radio told us day by day that this was not just local stuff, it was pandemic.

That of course was in a time later than this episode, this case of Sacco and Vanzetti which began so obscurely and ended as one of the important turning points in the history of this country; not the cause, but the symptom of a change so deep and so sinister in the whole point of view and direction of this people as a nation that I for one am not competent to analyze it. I only know what happened by what has happened to us since, by remembering what we were, or what many of us believed we were, before. We were most certainly then of a different cast of mind and feeling than we are now, or such a thing as the Sacco–Vanzetti protest could never have been brought about by any means; and I much doubt such a commotion could be roused again for any merciful cause at all among us.

Four incidents a good many years apart are somehow sharply related in my mind. Long ago a British judge was quoted as saying he refused clemency at popular demand to uphold the principle of capital punishment and to prove he was not to be intimidated by public protest. During Hitler's time, Himmler remarked that for the good of the state, popular complaints should be ignored, and if they persisted, the complainers should be punished. Judge Webster Thayer, during the Sacco–Vanzetti episode, was heard to boast while playing golf, "Did you see what I did to those anarchistic bastards?" and the grim little person named Rosa Baron (she shall come later) who was head of my particular group during the Sacco–Vanzetti demonstrations in Boston snapped at me when I expressed the wish that we might save the lives of Sacco and Vanzetti: "Alive—what for? They are no earthly good to us alive." These painful incidents illustrate at least four common perils in the legal handling that anyone faces when accused of a capital crime of which he is not guilty, especially if he has a dubious place in society, an unpopular nationality, erroneous political beliefs, the wrong religion socially, poverty, low social standing—the list could go on but this is enough. Both of these unfortunate men, Sacco and Vanzetti, suffered nearly all of these disadvantages.

A fearful word had been used to cover the whole list of prejudices and misinformation, and in some deeply mysterious way, their names had been associated with it—Anarchy.

If there really was a South Braintree gang as it is claimed, to which two Anarchists belonged, it seems to have been a small affair operating under rather clumsy leadership; its real crime seems not to have been exactly robbery and murder, but political heresy: they were Anarchists it was said who robbed and murdered to get funds for their organization—in this case, Anarchy—another variation on the Robin Hood myth.

Anarchy had been a word of fear in many countries for a long time, nowhere more so than in this one; nothing in that time, not even the word "Communism," struck such terror, anger, and hatred into the popular mind; and nobody seemed to understand exactly what Anarchy as a political idea meant any more than they understood Communism, which has muddied the water to the point that it sometimes calls itself Socialism, at other times Democracy, or even in its present condition, the Republic. Fascism, Nazism, new names for very ancient evil forms of government—tyranny and dictatorship—came into fashion almost at the same time with Communism; at least the aims of those two were clear enough; at least their leaders made no attempt to deceive anyone as to their intentions. But Anarchy had been here all the nineteenth century, with its sinister offspring Nihilism, and it is a simple truth that the human mind can face better the most oppressive government, the most rigid restrictions, than the awful prospect of a lawless, frontierless world. Freedom is a dangerous intoxicant and very few people can tolerate it in any quantity; it brings out the old raiding, oppressing, murderous instincts; the rage for revenge, for power, the lust for bloodshed. The longing for freedom takes the form of crushing the enemy—there is always the enemy!—into the earth; and where and who is the enemy if there is no visible establishment to attack, to destroy with blood and fire? Remember all that oratory when freedom is threatened again. Freedom, remember, is not the same as liberty.

On May 15, 1927, Nicola Sacco wrote from the prison in Charlestown, where he had been in and out of the death cell since July 1921, to his faithful friend Leon Henderson: "I frankly tell you, dear friend, that if he [Governor Fuller of Massachusetts] have a chance he'll hang us, and it is too bad to see you and all the other good friends this optimism while to-day we are facing the electric chair."

Bartolomeo Vanzetti, his fellow prisoner, wrote as early as 1924, after four years in prison under sentence of death, with a reprieve: "I am tired, tired, tired: I ask if to live like now, for love of life, is not rather than wisdom or heroism mere cowardness." He did consent to live on: he wished so dearly to live that he let his life be taken from him rather than take it himself. Yet near the end, he arrived apparently without help at a profound, painful understanding: "When one has reason to despair and he despairs not, he may be more abnormal than if he would despair."

They were put to death in the electric chair at Charlestown Prison at midnight on the 23rd of August, 1927, a desolate dark midnight, a night for perpetual remembrance and mourning. I was one of the many hundreds who stood in anxious vigil watching the light in the prison tower, which we had been told would fail at the moment of death; it was a moment of strange heartbreak.

The trial of Jesus of Nazareth, the trial and rehabilitation of Joan of Arc, any one of the witchcraft trials in Salem during 1691, the Moscow trials of 1937 during which Stalin destroyed all of the founders of the 1924 Soviet Revolution, the Sacco–Vanzetti trial of 1920 through 1927—there are many trials such as these in which the victim was already condemned to death before the trial took place, and it *took* place only to cover up the real meaning: the accused was to be put to death. These are trials in which the judge, the counsel, the jury, and the witnesses are the criminals, not the accused. For any believer in capital punishment, the fear of an honest mistake on the part of all concerned is cited as the main argument against the final terrible decision to carry out the death sentence. There is the frightful possibility in all such trials as these that the judgment has already been pronounced and the trial is just a mask for murder.

*

Both of them knew English very well—not so much in grammar and syntax but for the music, the true meaning of the words they used. They were Italian peasants, emigrants, laborers, self-educated men with an exalted sense of language as an incantation. *Read those letters!* They also had in common a distrust in general of the powers of this world, well founded in their knowledge of life as it is lived by people who work with their hands in humble trades for wages. Vanzetti had raised himself to the precarious independence of fish peddler, Sacco had learned the skilled trade of shoemaker; his small son was named Dante, and a last letter to this child is full of high-minded hopes and good counsel. At the very door of death, Sacco turned back to recall a glimpse of his wife's beauty and their happiness together. Their minds, each one in its very different way, were ragbags of faded Anarchic doctrine, of "class consciousness," of "proletarian snobbism," yet their warmth of feeling gave breath and fresh meaning to such words as Sacco wrote to Mrs. Leon Henderson: "Pardon me, Mrs. Henderson, it is not to discredit and ignore you, Mrs. Evans and other generosity work, which I sincerely believe is a noble one and I am respectful: But it is the warm sincere voice of an unrest heart and a free soul that lived and loved among the workers class all his life."

This was a state of mind, or point of view, which many of the anxious friends from another class of society found very hard to deal with, not to be met on their own bright, generous terms in this crisis of life and death; to be saying, in effect, we are all brothers and equal citizens; to receive, in effect, the reserved answer: No, not yet. It is clear now that the condemned men understood and realized their predicament much better than any individual working with any organization devoted to their rescue. Their friends from a more fortunate destiny had confidence in their own power to get what they asked of their society, their government; courts were not sacrosanct, they could be mistaken; it was a civic duty now and then to protest their judgments, persuade them by one means or another to reverse their sentences. The two laboring men, who had managed to survive and scramble up a few steps from nearly the bottom level of life, knew well from the beginning that they had every reason to despair, they did not really trust these strangers from the upper world who furnished the judges and lawyers to the courts, the politicians to the offices, the faculties to the universities, who had all the money and the influence— why should they be turning against their own class to befriend two laborers? Sacco wrote to Gardner Jackson, member of an upper-middle-class family, rich enough and ardent enough to devote his means and his time to the Sacco–Vanzetti Defense Committee: "Although we are one heart, unfortunately we represent two opposite class." What they may not have known —we can only hope they did not know—was that some of the groups apparently working for them, people of their own class in many cases, were using the occasion for Communist propaganda, and hoping only for their deaths as a political argument. I know this because I heard and saw. By chance and nothing else I was with a committee from the Communist line of defense. The exact title is of no importance. It was a mere splinter group from the national and world organization. It was quiet, discreet, at times the action seemed to be moving rather in circles; most of the volunteers, for we were all that, were no more Communists than I was. A young man who did a lot of running about, on what errands I never tried to discover, expressed what most of us thought when we learned that we were working under Communist direction: "Well, what of it? If he's fighting on my side, I'll go with the Devil!"*

It was the popular way of talking and a point of view fatal to any moral force or any clear view of issues; it was only a kind of catchphrase, but a symptom of the confusion of the times, the loss and denial of standards, the scumbling of boundary lines, and the whole evil trend toward reducing everything human to the mud of the lowest common demoninator.

A certain hotel near the Boston Common had been quite taken over by several separate and often rather hostile organizers of the demonstrations and I was prepared to fall eagerly and with a light heart into the atmosphere I found established there—even though it held a menace I could not instantly define—of monastic discipline, obedience, the community spirit,

---

*I heard this again years later from Germans in Berlin when Hitler was beginning to infect the local mind like a medieval plague.

everybody working toward a common end, with faith in their cause and in each other. In this last, I was somewhat mistaken, as I was very soon to find out. The air was stiff with the cold, mindless, irrational compliance with orders from "higher up." The whole atmosphere was rank with intrigue and deceit and the chilling realization that any one of them would have sold another to please superiors and to move himself up the ladder.

Politically I was mistaken in my hopes, also. For I see now that they were only that, based on early training in ethics and government, courses which I have not seen lately in any curriculum. Based on these teachings, I never believed that this country would alienate China in the Boxer Rebellion of 1900; or that we would not help France chase Hitler out of the Ruhr, as Mussolini had chased him single-handedly out of the Polish Corridor (and Mussolini himself was receiving heavy financial and political support from very powerful people in this country); or that we would let the Communists dupe us into deserting Republican Spain; or that we would aid and abet Franco; or let Czechoslovakia, a republic we had helped to found, fall to Soviet Russia. It is quite obvious by now that my political thinking was the lamentable "political illiteracy" of a liberal idealist—we might say, a species of Jeffersonian.

In the reckless phrase of the confirmed joiner in the fight for whatever relief oppressed humanity was fighting for, I had volunteered "to be useful wherever and however I could best serve," and was drafted into a Communist outfit all unknowing; this is no doubt because my name was on the list of contributors to funds in aid of Sacco and Vanzetti for several years. Even from Mexico, I sent what bits of money I could, when I could, to whatever group solicited at the moment: I never inquired as to the shades of political belief because that was not what was important to me in that cause, which concerned common humanity. In the same way, I went with the first organization that invited me, and at the Boston boat at the foot of Christopher Street was pleasantly surprised to see several quite good friends there, none of whom had any more definite political opinions than I had. I was then, as now, a registered voting member of the Democratic Party, a convinced liberal— not then a word of contempt—and a sympathizer with the new (to me) doctrines brought out of Russia from 1919 to 1920 onward by enthusiastic, sentimental, misguided men and women who were looking for a New Religion of Humanity, as one of them expressed it, and were carrying the gospel that the New Jerusalem could be expected to rise any minute in Moscow or thereabouts.

It is hard to explain, harder no doubt for a new generation to understand, how the "intellectuals" and "artists" in our country leaped with such abandoned, fanatic credulity into the Russian hell-on-earth of 1920. They quoted the stale catch-phrases and slogans. They were lifted to starry patriotism by the fraudulent Communist organization called the Lincoln Brigade. The holy name was a charm which insured safety and victory. The bullet struck your Bible instead of your heart. Not all of them merit being enclosed in the pejorative quotation marks; they were quite simply the most conventionally brought-up, middle-class people of no intellectual or other pretensions. There was a Bessie Beatty who was all for the Revolution, capital "R," but who meanwhile did nicely in New York as editor of a popular magazine for women; Albert Rhys Williams, a minister's son, very religious himself, whose main recognition was based on the amusing story of how he had spent the first three days of the fall of the Russian Empire in complete formal attire—white tie, wing collar, tails—and was somewhat the worse for wear when the third day appeared. (Nobody ever explained to me how anyone, no matter how sympathetic, could have survived a true Communist revolt in that dress belonging to the most criminal of the classes of society, or how Mr. Williams, a dedicated fellow traveler, should have had occasion to appear in that outfit.) But let us go on. There was Frank Tannenbaum, Jewish by birth, a good journalist, really trying to help build a New Jerusalem anywhere and everywhere and believing firmly that the foundation stone had at last been laid in Moscow.

"For me and others like me, the Kremlin meant the Third International, and this meant the organization of the 'workers of the world' to vindicate their human rights against everything we hated in contemporary society."* Edmund Wilson

*Edmund Wilson, *The American Earthquake*, page 573, chapter called "Postscript of 1957."

wrote that, as well and clearly expressed as it has been until now.

"I have seen the future and it works." Lincoln Steffens is reported to have said this, though it has been much denied. It is claimed that he did not ever say such a reckless thing. He was there, on the spot, admiring everything in Russia at the time of William Bullitt's 1919 visit to Russia, carrying on a delightful social life, although no one says quite how it was done in that particular atmosphere. I can say, once for all, that he may not have said this in Russia, but I heard him say it in Mexico in 1922 at a victorious desert celebration where the President, the Cabinet, "Congress," and all the radical politicians in the government were holding a great fiesta on a wonderful hot dusty day, where there were dozens of mariachi bands playing— drums and trumpets going—and all of us were sitting on the ground in a joyous picnic spirit eating *mole*, the national dish. I was with a party with which Mr. Steffens had come to see what a true revolution could do for people who needed a revolution. He was frightfully unhappy and uncomfortable. He did not like sitting on the ground and he did not see the beauty and the picturesqueness of the Indians' figures and clothing, and he referred to them as "uncivilized." He could not endure the sight, the taste, the smell, or even the presence of the *mole*; it was very peppery. The rest of the party were eating and scraping up the sauce with savory folded tortillas. His eyes behind their thick glasses swiveled around once at us and he said, "I wish you could see your mouths—you would rub your faces in the sand to clean them up."

It was some time later that afternoon when we were discussing world events, and all of us wanted to know how in the world Russian people could survive the latest disaster to their government, and he said: "All progress takes its toll in human life. Russia is the coming power of the world. I have seen the future and it works." So much for that. No matter how sad it may seem now, Mr. Steffens said it then, jovially, but in earnest. I wrote it down word for word, then and there, in my notebook.

My group was headed by Rosa Baron, a dry, fanatical little woman who wore thick-lensed spectacles over her blue, accusing eyes—a born whip hand, who talked an almost impenetrable jargon of party dogma. Her "approach" to every "question" (and everything *was* a question) was "purely dialectical." Phrases such as "capitalistic imperialism," "bourgeois morality," "slave mentality," "the dictatorship of the proletariat," "the historical imperative" (meaning more or less, I gathered, that history makes man and not the other way around), "the triumph of the workers," "social consciousness," and "political illiteracy" flew from her dry lips all day long. She viewed a "political illiterate" as a conventional mind might a person of those long-ago days born out of wedlock: an unfortunate condition, but reprehensible and without remedy even for its victim. Conservative was only a slightly less pejorative term than Reactionary, and as for Liberal, it was a dirty word, quite often linked in speech with other vaguely descriptive words, even dirtier, if possible. There were many such groups, for this demonstration had been agitated for and prepared for many years by the Communists. They had not originated the protest, I believe, but had joined in and tried to take over, as their policy was, and is. Their presence created the same confusion, beclouding the issue and discrediting the cause as it always had done and as they intended it to do. It appeared in its true form and on its most disastrous scale in Spain later. They were well organized to promote disorder and to prevent any question ever being settled—but I had not then discovered this; I remarked to our Communist leader that even then, at that late time, I still hoped the lives of Sacco and Vanzetti might be saved and that they would be granted another trial. "Saved," she said, ringing a change on her favorite answer to political illiteracy, "who wants them saved? What earthly good would they do us alive?"

I was another of those bourgeois liberals who got in the way of serious business, yet we were needed, by the thousands if possible, for this great agitation must be made to appear to be a spontaneous uprising of the American people, and for practical reasons, the more non-Communists, the better. They were all sentimental bleeders, easily impressed.

Rosa Baron's young brother once presumed to argue with her on some point of doctrine when I was present. "I'll report you to the Committee," she said, "if you talk about Party business before outsiders." This was the first time I had ever come face to face, here and now personally, with the Inquisitorial spirit hard at work.

"From each according to his capacity, to each according to his need."

Lenin was known to think little of people who let their human feelings for decency get in the way of the revolution which was to save mankind; he spoke contemptuously of the "saints" who kept getting underfoot; he had only harsh words for those "weak sisters" who flew off the "locomotive of history" every time it rounded a sharp curve. History was whatever was happening in Russia, and the weak sisters, who sometimes called themselves "fellow travelers," were perhaps, many of them, jolted by the collision with what appeared to be a dream of the ideal society come true, dazzled by the bright colors of a false dawn.

I flew off Lenin's locomotive and his vision of history in a wide arc in Boston, Massachusetts, on August 21, 1927; it was two days before the putting to death of Sacco and Vanzetti, to the great ideological satisfaction of the Communist-headed group with which I had gone up to Boston. It was exactly what they had hoped for and predicted from the first: another injustice of the iniquitous capitalistic system against the working class.

Toasts were drunk at parties "To the Red Dawn"—a very pretty image indeed. "See you on the barricades!" friends would say at the end of an evening of dancing in Harlem. Nobody thought any of this strange; in those days the confusion on this subject by true believers, though not great, was not quite so bad and certainly not so sinister as it is now. It was not then subversive to associate with Communists, nor even treasonable to belong to the Communist Party. It is true that Communists, or a lot of people who thought themselves Communists—and it is astonishing how many of them have right-about-faced since they got a look at the real thing in action—held loud meetings in Union Square, and they often managed to get a few heads cracked by the police—all the better! Just the proof they needed of the brutalities of the American Gestapo. On the other hand, they could gather thousands of "sympathizers" of every shade of political and religious belief and every known nationality and carry off great May Day parades peaceably under police protection. The innocent fellow travelers of this country were kept in a state of excited philanthropy by carefully planted stories of the struggle that the great Russian reformers were having against local rebellious peasants, blasted crops, and plagues of various kinds, bringing the government almost to starvation. Our fellow travelers picketed, rebuking our government for failure to send food and other necessaries to aid the great cause in that courageous country. I do not dare say that our government responded to these childish appeals, but tons upon tons of good winter wheat and other supplies were sent in fabulous quantities. It turned out that the threatened famine took place there—it was real—under orders from Lenin, who directed a great famine or an occasional massacre by way of bringing dissidence under the yoke, and I remember one blood-curdling sentence from a letter of his to a subordinate, directing him to conduct a certain massacre as "a model of mercilessness."

What struck me later was that I had already met and talked to refugees from Russia in Mexico who had got out with their lives and never ceased to be amazed at it. In New York I saw picketing in Times Square and Wall Street, solemn placard-carrying processions of second-generation descendants of those desolate, ragged, hopeful people who had landed on Ellis Island from almost every country in the West, escaping from the dreadful fates now being suffered by their blood kin in Russia and other parts of the world. Not one of them apparently could see that the starvation and disease and utter misery were brought on methodically and most successfully for the best of political and economic reasons without any help from us, while the Party was being fed richly with our wheat.

Then there was AMTORG, headquartered in New York, managed by a Russian Jewish businessman of the cold steel variety, advertised as a perfectly legal business organization for honest, aboveboard trade with the Soviets.

There was ROSTA (later TASS), the official Russian news agency and propaganda center in America, run by an American citizen, Kenneth Durant, who enjoyed perfect immunity in every Red scare of the period when dozens of suspects were

arrested—not he. I assisted the editor of ROSTA for a short
time and I know the subsidy was small, although the agency
was accused of enjoying floods of "Moscow gold." If this was
so, I don't know where it went. The editor claimed that Moscow gold was passed out at the rate of $75.00 a week for salaries
(he took $50.00 and gave me $25.00). A perennial candidate
for President of the United States popped up every four years
regularly on the Communist ticket—an honest man. I knew
nothing of his private politics, but his public life was admirable
and his doctrine was pure Christian theory.

Once on the picket line, I took a good look at the crowd
moving slowly forward. I wouldn't have expected to see some
of them on the same street, much less the same picket line and
in the same jail. I knew very few people in that first picket line,
but I remember Lola Ridge, John Dos Passos, Paxton Hibben,
Michael Gold, Helen O'Lochlainn Crowe, James Rorty, Edna
St. Vincent Millay, Willie Gropper, Grace Lumpkin, all very
well known then and mostly favorably—most of them have
vanished, and I wonder who but me is alive to remember them
now? I have a strangely tender memory of them all, as well as
the faces of strangers who were being led away by the police.
  We were as miscellaneous, improbable, almost entirely unas-
sorted a gathering of people to one place in one cause as ever
happened in this country. I say almost because among the
pickets I did not see anyone identifiably a workingman, or "proletarian," as our Marxist "dialecticians" insisted on calling
everybody who worked for his living in a factory, or as they
said, "sweatshop," or "slave mill," or "salt mine." It is true
that these were workdays and maybe all the workingmen were
at their jobs. Suppose one of them said to his boss, "I want a
day off, with pay, to picket for Sacco and Vanzetti." He would
be free to picket at his leisure from then on, no doubt. There
were plenty of people of the working class there, but they had
risen in the world and had become professional paid proletari-
ans, recruits to the intelligentsia, dabbling in ideas as editors,
lawyers, agitators, writers who dressed and behaved and looked
quite a lot like the bourgeoisie they were out to annihilate. What
a vocabulary—proletarian, intelligentsia, bourgeoisie, dialectic
—pure exotics transplanted from the never-never-land of the

theoretically classless society which could not take root and finally withered on the stalk. Yet, they had three classes of their own and were drawing the lines shrewdly. During that time I went to a meeting of radicals of all kinds and shades, most of them workers, but not all by any means; and Michael Gold made a speech and kept repeating: "Stick to your class, *damn it, stick* to your *class.*" It struck me as being such good advice that I decided to take it and tiptoed out the way one leaves church before the end.

Each morning I left the hotel, walked into the blazing August sun, and dropped into the picket line before the State House; the police would allow us to march around once or twice, then close in and make the arrests we invited; indeed, what else were we there for? My elbow was always taken quietly by the same mild little blond officer, day after day; he was very Irish, very patient, very damned bored with the whole incomprehensible show. We always greeted each other politely. It was generally understood that the Pink Tea Squad, white cotton gloves and all, had been assigned to this job, well instructed that in no circumstance were they to forget themselves and whack a lady with their truncheons, no matter how far she forgot herself in rudeness and contrariety. In fact, I never saw a lady—or a gentleman either—being rude to a policeman in that picket line, nor any act of rudeness from a single policeman. That sort of thing was to come later, from officers on different duty. The first time I was arrested, my policeman and I walked along stealing perplexed, questioning glances at each other; the gulf between us was fixed, but not impassable; neither of us wished to deny that the other was a human being; there was no natural hostility between us. I had been brought up in the fixed social belief that the whole police system existed to protect and befriend me and all my kind. Without giving this theory any attention, I had found no reason to doubt it.

Here are some notes of my conversations with my policeman during our several journeys under the August sun, down the rocky road to the Joy Street Station:

He: "What good do you think you're doing?"

I: "I hope a *little* . . . I don't believe they had a fair trial. That is all I want for them, a fair trial."

He: "This is no way to go about getting it. You ought to know you'll *never* get anywhere with this stuff."

I: "Why not?"

He: "It makes people mad. They take you for a lot of tramps."

I: "We did everything else we could think of first, for years and years, and nothing worked."

He: "I don't believe in showing contempt for the courts this way."

I: "Neither do I, in principle. But this time the court is wrong."

He: "I trust the courts of the land more than I do all these sapheads making public riot."

I: "We aren't rioting. Look at us, how calm we are."

He (still mildly): "What I think is, you all ought to be put in jail and kept there till it's over."

I: "They don't want us in jail. There isn't enough room there."

Second day:

He (taking my elbow and drawing me out of the line; I go like a lamb): "Well, what have you been doing since yesterday?"

I: "Mostly copying Sacco's and Vanzetti's letters. I wish you could read them. You'd believe in them if you could read the letters."

He: "Well, I don't have much time for reading."

Third day:

The picket line was crowded, anxious, and slow-moving. I reached the rounding point before I saw my policeman taking his place. I moved out and reached for his arm before we spoke. "You're late," I said, not in the least meaning to be funny. He astonished me by nearly smiling. "What have we got to hurry for?" he inquired, and my scalp shuddered—we moved on in silence.

This was the 23rd of August, the day set for the execution, and the crowds of onlookers that had gathered every morning were becoming rather noisy and abusive. My officer and I ran into a light shower of stones, a sprinkling of flowers, confetti, and a flurry of boos, catcalls, and cheers as we rounded the corner into Joy Street. We ducked our heads and I looked back and saw other prisoners and other policemen put up their hands and turn away their faces.

I: "Can you make out which is for which of us? I can't."

He: "No, I can't, and I don't care."

Silence.

He: "How many times have you been down this street today?"

I: "Only once. I was only sent out once today. How many times for you?"

It was now late afternoon, and as it turned out, this was the last picket line to form. The battle was lost and all of us knew it by then.

He (in mortal weariness): "God alone knows."

As we stood waiting in line at the desk, I said, "I expect this will be the last time you'll have to arrest me. You've been very kind and patient and I thank you."

I remember the blinded exhaustion of his face, its gray pallor with greenish shadows in it. He said "Thank *you*," and stood beside me at the desk while my name was written into the record once more. We did not speak or look at each other again, but as I followed the matron to a cell I saw him working his way slowly outward through the crowd.

The same plain, middle-aged, rather officious woman with a gold front tooth always came and put me in a cell and locked the door. Sometimes I was alone in the foggy light and stale air, being forbidden to smoke and wishing for something to read. Sometimes there would be other women, though never once a soul I knew, and we would begin at once to talk, to exchange our gossip and rumors and ideas, for, being in the dead center of this disturbance, it was quite hard to find out what was really happening. After a time, usually two or three hours, the matron would come with her keys, open the door, and say, "Come on out." Out we would come, knowing that Mr. Edward James, Henry James's nephew, was there again, putting up our bail, getting us set free for the next round. Helen O'Lochlainn Crowe, who had trained with Jim Larkin as his disciple and mistress in the Irish Trouble, tried to refuse bail, insisted on staying in prison, and was finally hauled out and set on the sidewalk. Not roughly, just firmly and finally. She was, her jailers told her, bailed out whether she liked it or not, and this was very ungrateful behavior to Mr. James who was only trying to help.

Mr. James was a thin, stiff, parchment roll of a man, maybe sixty years old, immaculately turned out in tones of expensive-looking gray from head to foot, to match his gray pointed beard and his severe pale gray eyes with irritable points of light in them. He left the hall once with several of my group, and the dark young Portuguese boy who always came with him walked beside me. He was a picture of exuberance, with his oily, swarthy skin, his thick, glistening black hair, the soft corners of his full red mouth always a little moist; his young, lazy fat heaving and walloping at every step. I asked him what organization they were working with, for by now I knew too well that this whole protest was the work of a complicated machine or a set of machines working together, even if not always intentionally or with the same motives, and we were all of us being put rather expertly through set paces by distant operators, unknown manipulators whose motives and designs were far different from ours. "Oh, Mr. James and I," said the smiling, eupeptic being trundling along at my side, his red silk scarf necktie flapping, "we have our own little organization. I'm Mr. James's secretary," he said in his childish voice, "and we are perfectly independent!" He gave a coy little bounce and wiggle. He was as contented and unconcerned as a piglet in clover.

"That's charming," I said in a breath of relief from the distrust and fright growing in my mind as if I had breathed an infection from the air, "it's nice to know someone is acting on his own!"

"Mr. James and me, we've been working on this for *years!*"

I have only to sort out and copy these notes down here to realize how long fifty years are, not only in the life of an individual, but of a nation, a world—to realize again, not for the first time, how one sets out for a certain goal and ends at another, different, unforeseen, and too often dismaying. We need restored to us of course that blinded obscured third eye said once to exist in the top of the brain for our guidance. Lacking it we go skew-gee in great numbers, especially those of us brought up so believingly on Judeo-Greek-Christian ethics, prone to trust the good faith of our fellows, and therefore vulnerable to betrayal because of our virtues, such as they are; that is to say, our human weaknesses. There are many notes, saved almost at random these long past years, many by mere chance; they were scrambled together in a battered yellow envelope marked Sacco–Vanzetti, and had worked their way to the bottom of many a basket of papers in many a change of houses, cities, and even a change of country. They are my personal experiences of the whirlwinds of change that brought Lenin, Stalin, Mussolini, Franco, and Hitler crowded into one half a century or less; and my understanding of this event in Boston as one of the most portentous in the long death of the civilization made by Europeans in the Western world, in the millennial upheaval which brings always every possible change but one—the two nearly matched forces of human nature, the will to give life and the will to destroy it. So, at that time and after what I have learned since, it seems strange that I was not better informed at Boston about my committee until I arrived there and was seated at a typewriter copying the Sacco and Vanzetti letters to the world. However, I was not informed and I did not ask, and this is a story of what happened, not what should have been.

After more than half a long lifetime, I find that any recollection, however vivid and lasting, must unavoidably be mixed with many afterthoughts. It is hard to remember anything perfectly straight, accurate, no matter whether it was painful or pleasant at that time. I find that I remember best just what I felt and thought about this event in its own time, in its inalterable setting; my impressions of this occasion remain fast, no matter how many reviews or recollections or how many afterthoughts have added themselves with the years. It is fifty years, very long ones, since Sacco and Vanzetti were put to death in Boston, accused and convicted of a bitter crime, of which, it is still claimed, they may or may not have been guilty. I did not know then and I still do not know whether they were guilty (in spite of reading at this late day the learned, stupendous, dearly human work of attorney Herbert B. Ehrmann), but still I had my reasons for being there to protest the terrible penalty they were condemned to suffer; these reasons were of the heart, which I believe appears in these pages with emphasis. The core of this account of that fearful episode was written nearly a half-century ago, during the time in Boston and later; for years I refused to read, to talk or listen, because I couldn't endure the memory—I wanted to escape from it. Some of the account was written at the scene of the tragedy itself and, except for a word or two here and there in those early notes, where I have added a line in the hope of a clearer statement, it is unchanged in feeling and point of view. The evils prophesied by that crisis have all come true and are enormous in weight and variety.

Books have been written by many illustrious persons who took part in that strange event—a lawyer who was to be an Associate Justice of the Supreme Court, Felix Frankfurter, and others; a lady who was to be American Minister to Norway, Mrs. J. Borden ("Daisy") Harriman, was attending meetings there; celebrated faculty members from universities, such as Paxton Hibben; novelists such as John Dos Passos; poets such as Edna St. Vincent Millay; all of whom the public knew well, at least by name. There were many politicians in full career, some of them risking their careers by their appearances in Boston—useless to name names, there were too many, all reputable and with good influence—all of them streamed sooner or later through that large but crowded room where I sat, among other members of my special committee, at the typewriter, doing what was called "kitchen police," that is, all the dull, dusty little jobs that the more important committee members couldn't be burdened with. This was my good luck. My work was not only the melancholy pleasure of copying Sacco's and Vanzetti's letters to their friends working for them on the outside, or even of composing propaganda in the form of news items which I doubt ever got printed. I did not see a newspaper the whole time. Now and then the pioneer lady Minister, pleasant Daisy Harriman, floated in all white, horse-haired lace garden hats and pink or maybe blue chiffon frocks, on her way to or from some social afternoon festivity. She sat beside my desk one day when I had just returned from my daily picketing and said, "One needs a little recreation, even in these terrible times. You should just go out and get a little breath of fresh air—a quiet walk by yourself."

I said, "My idea of recreation would be a nice long night's sleep," for the evenings, six of them, usually were spent at some fevered mass meeting or sitting about talking with the rather random groups that formed in one stifling hot hotel room or another. I said to her, "I sometimes wonder what we are doing really. The whole thing is losing shape in my mind, but I can only hope we may learn something we need to know—that something good will come of this."

She said very gently, "What good?—Oh, they'll forget all about it. Most of them are just here for the excitement. They don't really know what is going on; and they want to forget anything unpleasant." Her broad, healthy face smiled reassuringly from under its flowering shade. Intoxicating perfume waved from her spread handkerchief when she dried her forehead. I repeated what John Dos Passos once remarked on the "imbecile" (or was the word "idiot"?) lack of memory of the human race, generally speaking.

There was the charming good woman of great riches and even greater charity and sweetness of mind—Mrs. Leon Henderson —who had been a champion of Sacco's and Vanzetti's from the first. I trusted her delicate, intuitional mind. She had been prodigal of all her resources, money and energy and imaginative stratagems and loving kindness. Now, at the end, when she rightly feared the worst, she was writing them letters to persuade them to break their fast, to save their strength for the new trial she was sure they would be given. She was a vegetarian and advised them to drink milk and fruit juice by way of easing themselves back into a regular diet.

She invited me to lunch. I did not then know she was a vegetarian and when she asked me what I would like, I asked for broiled lamb chops. She shuddered a little, the pupils of her eyes dilated, and she gave me a little lecture on cruelty to animals, just the same.

"I could not eat any food that had the taint of suffering and death in it; imagine my dear! Eating blood?"

I retracted at once, in painful embarrassment, and ate a savory lunch of scrambled eggs and spinach with her, and things went on very nicely. Still, I could not avoid seeing her very handsome leather handbag, her suede shoes and belt, and a light summer fur of some species I was unable to identify lying across her shoulders. My mind would wander from our topic while, bewildered once more by the confusions in human feelings, above all my own, I gazed into the glass eyes of the small, unknown, peaked-faced animal.

"We should be very wrong to despair," she said as we were getting ready to go, "even if their lives are taken away from them; nothing can take away the truth of our wish to help them, the fact of their courage in the face of death; they have never despaired or become bitter."

I said, "Yes, and if they are innocent, it must be almost unbearable not to have had the chance to prove it . . ."

She was shocked at this. "Do you mean you have a *doubt* of their innocence?" she asked.

"I simply don't know," I told her. "I thought one of the questions in this whole uproar is just precisely that—that they have not had a fair trial."

"Fair trial or not," she said—by now we were standing on the corner ready to separate—"that is not the point at all, my dear. They are innocent and their death will be a legal crime."

I have described that scene and the conversation from the notes I took when I got back to my desk at the hotel that day.

Several of the more enterprising young reporters, who were swarming over the scene like crows to a freshly planted cornfield, had put out a few invitations to some of the girls in the various groups to something they called "a little party." Rosa Baron, the head of my committee, went into action with the authority and prudence of a boarding school chaperone. "Just don't go, that's all," she told her two or three eligibles, "just don't be seen with them. That is the one thing we can't afford—a scandal of that kind!" So we didn't accept any invitations, and heard nothing more about them.

I remember small, slender Mrs. Sacco with her fine copper-colored hair and dark brown, soft, dazed eyes moving from face to face but still smiling uncertainly, surrounded in our offices by women pitying and cuddling her, sympathetic with her as if she were a pretty little girl; they spoke to her as if she were five years old or did not understand—this Italian peasant wife who, for seven long years, had shown moral stamina and emotional stability enough to furnish half a dozen women amply. I was humiliated for them, for their apparent insensibility. But I was mistaken in my anxiety—their wish to help, to show her their concern, was real, their feelings were true and lasting, no matter how awkwardly expressed; their love and tenderness and wish to help were from the heart. All through those last days in Boston, those strangely innocent women enlisted their altar societies, their card clubs, their literary round tables, their music circles, and their various charities in the campaign to save Sacco and Vanzetti. On their rounds, they came now and then to the office of my outfit in their smart thin frocks, stylish hats, and their indefinable air of eager sweetness and light, bringing money they had collected in the endless, wittily devious ways of women's organizations. They would talk among themselves and to her about how they felt, with tears in their eyes, promising to come again soon with more help. They were known as "sob sisters" by the cynics and the hangers-on of the committee I belonged to who took their money and described their activities as "sentimental orgies," of course with sexual overtones, and they jeered at "bourgeois morality." "Morality" was a word along with "charitable" and "humanitarian" and "liberal," all, at one time, in the odor of sanctity but now despoiled and rotting in the gutter where suddenly it seemed they belonged. I found myself on the side of the women; I resented the nasty things said about them by these self-appointed world reformers and I thought again, as I had more than once in Mexico, that yes, the world was a frightening enough place as it was, but think what a hell it would be if such people really got the power to do the things they planned.*

A last, huge rally took place the night before the execution, with Rosa Sacco and Luigia Vanzetti, Vanzetti's sister, on the platform. Luigia had been brought from Italy and taken through Paris, where she had been photographed as she was marched through the streets at the head of an enormous crowd —the gaunt, striding figure of a middle-aged, plain woman who looked more like a prisoner herself than the leader of a

*They seem to have it and are getting on with it—1976.

public protest. Now they brought her forward with Mrs. Sacco and the two timid women faced the raging crowd, mostly Italians, who rose at them in savage sympathy, shouting, tears pouring down their faces, shaking their fists and calling childish phrases, their promises of revenge for their wrongs. "Never you mind, Rosina! You wait, Luigia! They'll pay, they'll pay! Don't be afraid . . . !" Rosa Sacco spread her hands over her face, but Luigia Vanzetti stared stonily down into their distorted faces with a pure horror in her own. They screamed their violence at her in her own language, trying to hearten her, but she was not consoled. She was led away like a corpse walking. The crowd roared and cursed and wept and threatened. It was the most awesome, the most bitter scene I had ever witnessed.

As we crowded out to the street, a great mass of police all around us, one of the enterprising young reporters who had helped to get up the "little party" for the girls seized my wrist, calling out, "Was this a swell show, I ask you? Did it come off like a house afire? It was all my idea; I got the whole thing up!" *His* face was savage too, wild with his triumph. "I got Luigia out of bed to come here. She said she was too sick, but I got her up! I said, 'Don't you want to help your brother?'"

"She speaks English?" I asked in wonder at him. "What did she say?" I had rather liked him before. I have forgotten his name.

"Hell no!" he said. "She's got an interpreter. She didn't say anything; she just got up and came along."

The most terrible irony of this incident of Luigia Vanzetti I learned later: that Mussolini wrote a personal letter to Governor Fuller of Massachusetts asking for mercy for the two Italians. I had known and talked with a number of the earlier refugees from Mussolini's Italy of 1922 and onward in Mexico, and I knew well what his mercy was like toward anyone unlucky enough to displease him. But at that time, Mussolini had many admirers and defenders in this country—he was more than respectable; he was getting enormous flattering publicity. There was a group of Mussolini enthusiasts in Boston, picketing and working and going to jail and being let out, then putting their heads together in the evening to sing "Giovinezza." No harm done. The Communists thought them beneath contempt, and the liberals, the true democrats as they believed themselves to be, were then in the heyday of practicing what they preached, and were ready to fight and die for anybody's right to his own beliefs, no matter what—religious, social, or political. I thought wryly of Voltaire's impassioned defense of an individual's right to say what he believed, but all I could salvage at that time was that *I* disagreed with most of what some of these "liberals" were saying and *I* would defend to the death my right to disagree. "Ha," said my little publicity inventor, listening a split second to the sweating, howling, cheering crowd—"Talk about free speech! How's that? Their heads will be the first to roll." This phrase was one of the Communist crowd's favorites, and the very thought of rolling heads would bring a mean, relishing smile to even the dourest face.

After Mr. James had bailed us out for the last time, we returned to the hotel and got ready to go to the Charlestown Prison where the execution was to take place at midnight. It seems odd, perhaps, but I joined with a group of persons to go in a taxi to the prison and I cannot remember a name or a face among them. It is possible that they were all strangers to me. There were several hundred of us who had been picketing in relays all day, every day from the 21st and for four days, and their faces and names, perhaps known at that moment, have vanished; and yet, when the thing was done, I remember returning with persons well known to me and several incidents which happened later. The driver of our cab did not want us to go to the Charlestown Prison. Neither did the police stationed at regular distances along the whole route. They stopped our cab and turned us back half a dozen times. We would direct the driver to go a roundabout way, or to take a less traveled street. But at last, he refused to drive farther. We left him then, after making up the fare among ourselves. I was nearly penniless and I know now that a good many others among us were too. We walked on toward the prison, coming as near as we could, for the crowd was enormous and in the dim light silent, almost motionless, like crowds seen in a dream. I was never in that place but once, but I seem to remember it was a great open square with the crowd massed back from a center the police worked constantly to keep clear. They were all mounted on fine horses and loaded with pistols and hand grenades and tear gas bombs. They galloped about, bearing down upon anybody who ventured out beyond the edge of the crowd, charging and then pulling their horses up short violently so that they reared and their forehoofs beat in the air over a human head, but always swerving sharply and coming down on one side. They were trained, probably, to this spectacular, dangerous-looking performance, but still, I know it is very hard to force a good horse to step on any living thing. I have seen them in their stalls at home shudder all over at stepping on a stray, newly hatched chicken. I do not believe the police meant for the hoofs to strike and crush heads—it possibly was just a very showy technique for intimidating and controlling a mob.

This was not a mob, however. It was a silent, intent assembly of citizens—of anxious people come to bear witness and to protest against the terrible wrong about to be committed, not only against the two men about to die, but against all of us, against our common humanity and our shared will to avert what we believed to be not merely a failure in the use of the instrument of the law, an injustice committed through mere human weakness and misunderstanding, but a blindly arrogant, self-righteous determination not to be moved by any arguments, the obstinate assumption of the infallibility of a handful of men intoxicated with the vanity of power and gone mad with wounded self-importance.

A few foolish persons played a kind of game with the police, waiting until they had turned to charge in the other direction, stepping out defiantly into the center, rushing with raucous yells of glee back to safety when the police turned their horses and came on again. But these were only the lunatic fringe that follows excitement—anything will do. Most of the people moved back passively before the police, almost as if they ignored their presence; yet there were faces fixed in agonized disbelief, their eyes followed the rushing horses as if this was not a sight they had expected to see in their lives. One tall, thin figure of a woman stepped out alone, a good distance into the empty square, and when the police came down at her and the horse's hoofs beat over her head, she did not move, but stood with her shoulders slightly bowed, entirely still. The charge was repeated again and again, but she was not to be driven away. A man near me said in horror, suddenly recognizing her, "That's Lola Ridge!" and dashed into the empty space toward her. Without any words or a moment's pause, he simply seized her by the shoulders and walked her in front of him back to the edge of the crowd, where she stood as if she were half-conscious. I came near her and said, "Oh no, don't let them hurt you! They've done enough damage already." And she said, "This is the beginning of the end—we have lost something we shan't find again." I remember her bitter hot breath and her deathlike face. She had not long to live.

For an endless dreary time we had stood there, massed in a measureless darkness, waiting, watching the light in the tower of the prison. At midnight, this light winked off, winked on and off again, and my blood chills remembering it even now— I do not remember how often, but we were told that the extinction of this light corresponded to the number of charges of electricity sent through the bodies of Sacco and Vanzetti. This was not true, as the newspapers informed us in the morning. It was only one of many senseless rumors and inventions added to the smothering air. It was reported later that Sacco was harder to kill than Vanzetti—two or three shocks for that tough body. Almost at once, in small groups, the orderly, subdued people began to scatter, in a sound of voices that was deep, mournful, vast, and wavering. They walked slowly toward the center of Boston. Life felt very grubby and mean, as if we were all of us soiled and disgraced and would never in this world live it down. I said something like this to the man walking near me, whose name or face I never knew, but I remember his words—"What are you talking about?" he asked bitterly, and answered himself: "There's no such thing as disgrace anymore."

I don't remember where we left Lola Ridge, nor how it came about that a certain number of us gathered in one of the hotel rooms, among them, Grace Lumpkin, Willie Gropper the cartoonist, Helen O'Lochlainn Crowe, Michael Gold, a man or two whose names I never knew—yet I recall that one of them said, "Damn it, I'm through. I'd like to leave this country!" Someone asked bitterly, "Well, where would you go?" and half a dozen voices called as one, "Russia!" in their infatuated ignorance, but it was touching because of its sincerity; there was a fervor like an old-fashioned American revival meeting in them and there was a bond between them. Some of them were the children of the oldest governing families and founders of this nation, and an astonishing number were children of country preachers or teachers or doctors—the "salt of the earth"—besides the first-born generation of emigrants who had braved the escape, the steerages, the awful exile, to reach this land where the streets, they had heard, were paved with gold. I felt somewhat alien from this company because of my experience with would-be Communists in Mexico and because of my recent exposure to the view of a genuine Party official; yet in those days, I was still illusioned to the extent that I half accepted the entirely immoral doctrine that one *should* go along with the Devil if he worked on your side; but my few days in the same office with Rosa Baron and her crowd had shaken this theory too, as it proved, to the foundation. Two truisms: The end does *not* justify the means and one I discovered for myself then and there, The Devil is *never* on your side except for his own purposes.

Does all of this sound very old-fashioned, like the Communist vocabulary or the early Freudian theories? Well, it was fifty years ago and I am not trying to bring anything up-to-date. I am trying to sink back into the past and recreate a certain series of events recorded in scraps at the time which have haunted me painfully for life.

Somebody suggested that he would like a drink. Michael Gold said he knew where to find it and went out and bought a bottle of bootleg gin; and then, nobody wanted to drink after all except one girl I have not named—an Irish Catholic girl I had never known to be anything but tender and gentle, now strode up and down the room in pure hysteria, swinging the open bottle of gin and singing in a loud flat voice a comic old song about an Irish wake: "They took the ice from off the corpse and put it in the beer—your feyther was a grand old man—give us a drink!" and she would upend the bottle and take a swig with a terrible tragic face and try to hand it around. Somebody shouted the first line of the Internationale; someone else began "*Giovinezza, giovinezza! Primavera di bellezza!*" drowning each other out and the hysterical striding girl too—I was ashamed of it, for it was no moment for a low sense of humor to assert itself, or so it seemed to me, but I thought, "Suppose I started singing 'The Star-Spangled Banner'? I bet I'd get thrown out of a window!" I felt a chill of distrust or estrangement—I was far from home, a stranger in a strange land indeed, for the first time in my life.

"No, don't, darling," said one of the men to the girl as she went on crying her tuneless chorus aloud, pouring the raw gin down her throat as she changed her tune to the gibberish of "The Battle Hymn of the Republic." "In the beauty of the lilies, Christ was born across the sea," she sang the silly words to the claptrap tune in march time, striding back and forth. The Communist sympathizers and the Jews alike flinched, offended, and all the faces turned sour, frowning.

"Jesus," said Mike Gold, "leave Christ out of this!"

"With a glory in His bosom that transfigures you and me," sang the girl, swinging the bottle and marching, her eyes blinded, her face as white as a frosted lantern.

"We've got to *stop* her," said a young woman—I don't remember who but I remember the words—"This is dangerous!" and she must have heard them too, for she turned instantly and broke from the room and ran down the hall toward the window at the end. Several of us ran after her and two of the men seized her from the open window. She broke into submissive tears and gave way at once. They brought her back and we put her to bed, fully dressed, then and there; she slept almost at once. The rest of us sat up nearly all night, with nothing to say, nothing to do, brought to a blank pause, keeping a vigil with the dead in the first lonely long night of death. It was no consolation to say their long ordeal was ended. It was not ended for us—and perhaps I should speak for myself—their memory was already turning to stone in my mind. In my whole life I have never felt such a weight of pure bitterness, helpless anger in utter defeat, outraged love and hope, as hung over us all in that room—or did we breathe it out of ourselves? A darkness of shame, too, settled down with us, a most deplorable kind of shame. It was in every pair of eyes that met other eyes in furtive roving. Shame at our useless, now self-indulgent emotions, our disarmed state, our absurd lack of spirit. At last we broke up and parted—I remember nothing more of this incident. It dissolves and disappears like salt poured into water—but the salt taste is there.

In the morning when we began straggling out in small parties on our way to the trial, several of us went down in the elevator with three entirely correct old gentlemen looking much alike in their sleekness, pinkness, baldness, glossiness of grooming, such stereotypes as no proletarian novelist of the time would have dared to use as the example of a capitalist monster in his novel. We were pale and tight-faced; our eyelids were swollen; no doubt in spite of hot coffee and cold baths, we looked rumpled, unkempt, disreputable, discredited, vaguely guilty, pretty well frayed out by then. The gentlemen regarded us glossily, then turned to each other. As we descended the many floors in silence, one of them said to the others in a cream-cheese voice, "It is very pleasant to know we may expect things to settle down properly again," and the others nodded with wise, smug, complacent faces.

To this day, I can feel again my violent desire just to slap his whole slick face all over at once, hard, with the flat of my hand, or better, some kind of washing bat or any useful domestic appliance being applied where it would really make an impression —a butter paddle—something he would feel through that smug layer of too-well-fed fat. For a long time after, I felt that I had sprained my very soul in the effort I had to make resisting that impulse to let fly. I shut my eyes and clenched my hands behind me and saw, in lightning flashes, myself doing ferocious things, like pushing him down an endless flight of stairs, or dropping him without warning into a bottomless well, or stringing him up to a stout beam and leaving him to dangle, or—or other things of the sort; no guns, no knives, no baseball bats, nothing to cause outright bloodshed, just silent, grim, sudden murder by hand was my intention. All this was far beyond my bodily powers of course, and I like to believe beyond my criminal powers too. For I woke when we struck the searing hot light of the August morning as if I had come out of a nightmare, horrified at my own thoughts and feeling as if I had got some incurable wound to my very humanity—as indeed I had. However inflicted, a wound there was, with painful scar tissue, left upon my living self by that appalling event. My conscience stirs as if, in my impulse to do violence to my enemy, I had assisted at his crime.

In the huge, bare, dusty room where the court sat, it was instantly clear that the Pink Tea Squad had been taken off duty for this round. We were all huddled in together—I don't remember any chairs—and stood around, or sat on the grimy floor or on a shallow flight of steps leading I forget where; the place was as dismal and breathless as a tenement fire escape in August. Big, overmuscled, beefy policemen with real thug faces bawled at us senselessly (we were all of us merely passive by then), crowded in among us to keep us moving and generally hustled us around, not violently, just viciously and sordidly and impudently, by way of showing what they *could* do if sufficiently provoked. We were forbidden to smoke but I tried it anyway—the whole scene struck me as just second-rate melodrama, nothing to be taken seriously anymore. John Dos Passos, sitting near me, held a spread newspaper above me while I snatched a whiff, but we were seen and yelled at. I was sorry then to have involved him in such a useless disturbance, though he did not seem in the least to mind; he always had in those days—I have hardly seen him since*—a wonderful, gentle composure of manner, and I have never forgotten his expression of amiable distance from the whole grubby scene as I put out the cigarette and he folded his newspaper, while the greasy, sweating man in the blue suit stood above us and went on glaring and bawling a little longer, just in case we had not heard him the first time.

Mrs. Stuart Chase, who had been faithfully on the picket line and was now waiting trial with the rest, also had been one of the speakers at some of the rallies; she showed me several anonymous letters she had received, of an unbelievable obscenity and threatening her with some very imaginative mutilations. It was Mrs. Chase who told me that there was a rumor afloat that we were going to be treated simply as common nuisances, the charge was to be "loitering and obstructing traffic"! Arthur Garfield Hays, the attorney for all of us, for all the various defense committees, had explained that if we were

---

*He died long after this was written.

to be tried on the real charge, God knew where it would end, there could easily be embarrassing consequences all around— more to the prosecution than to us, it seemed, and I remember wondering why, at that point, we should be troubled to spare their feelings. Naturally it turned out not to be a matter of feelings in any direction but of legal points obscure to perhaps any but the legal mind. There was then in existence—is it still, I wonder?—an infamous law called Baumes' Law, which provided that anyone who had been arrested as much as four times—or was it *more* than four times?—should be eligible to imprisonment for life. There were a good number of perennial, roving, year-round emergency picketers in that group— people whose good pleasure it was to join almost any picket line on sight, and of course they would be arrested sooner or later and these arrests could mount up to a pretty respectable number very soon. One woman said to me, "Suppose I told them I've been arrested seventeen times?" and I said, "Well, why *don't* you?" but of course she could not because for one thing she was not allowed to get within speaking distance of the court.

However, on getting this news straight, about twenty-five of us decided that under Baumes' Law (some of us couldn't believe such a monstrosity existed on our statute books; we thought someone was playing a low joke on our ignorance) we must surely be more than eligible for at least ninety-nine years each in the clink and decided to agitate for it. Our plan was to make a point of forcing them to observe that lunatic Baumes' Law and overload their jails. For a number of us, writers and artists of all kinds particularly, it might so nicely have settled the problem of where we were to eat and sleep while writing that book or doing whatever it was we had in mind. In those days it was believed that political prisoners were not treated too badly; we learned our mistake later, that it was the big gangsters who were treated well, but at that time, in our innocence, it looked to some of us like the last broad highway to the practice of the arts.

It was not to be; we should have known from the first. The prisoners who had records of more than three arrests were simply pushed back into a captive audience, while several celebrities from various walks were chosen as tokens to stand trial for all of us. I remember of them—a half-dozen—only Edna St. Vincent Millay and Paxton Hibben. It was worth going there to see our attorney, Arthur Garfield Hays, in confidential palaver with the judge, a little old gray man with pointed whiskers and the face of a smart, conspiratorial chipmunk. In a single rolling sentence the judge, not just with a straight face but portentously, as if pronouncing another death sentence, found us guilty of loitering and obstructing traffic, fined us five dollars each, and the tragic farce took its place in history.

When two or three of our number tried to raise and demand separate trials on sterner grounds, they were squelched by everybody—the judge, our attorney, the policemen, and even their own neighbors—for a lot of them were after all homekeeping persons who had come out, as you might say, on borrowed time and now were anxious to get back home again. The judge, the lawyers, the police, the whole court, the whole city of Boston, and the State of Massachusetts desired nothing in the world so much as to be rid of us, to see the last of us forever, to hear the last of this scandal (though they have never, alas, and will never!), and all the slightest signs of dissent from any direction were so adroitly and quickly suppressed that even the most enthusiastic troublemaker never quite knew how it was done. Simply our representatives were tried in a group in about five minutes.

A busy, abstracted woman wearing pinch-nose spectacles, whom I never saw before or since, pushed her way among us, pressing five dollars into every hand, instructing us one and all to pay our fines, then and there, which we did. I do not in the least remember how my note changed hands again, but no doubt I gave it to the right person as all of us did, and there we were, out on the sidewalk again, discredited once for all, it seemed, mere vagrants but in movement, no longer loitering and obstructing traffic. "Get on there," yelled our policemen, "get going there, keep moving"; and their parting advice to us was that we all go back where we came from and stay there. It was their next-best repartee, but a poor, thin substitute for one good whack at our skulls with their truncheons.

I returned to the hotel and found the temporary office already being dismantled. Another woman came up and said,

"Are you packed and ready to go?" She pressed into my hand a railroad ticket to New York and ten dollars in cash. "Go straight to the station now and take the next train," she said. I did this with no farewells and no looking back. I found several other persons, some of whom I had sat up with nearly all night more than once, also being banished from the scene of the crime. We greeted each other without surprise or pleasure and scattered out singly and separately with no desire for each other's company. I do not even remember who many of them were, if I ever knew their names at all. I only remember our silence and the dazed melancholy in all the faces.

In all this I should speak only for myself, for never in my life have I felt so isolated as I did in that host of people, all presumably moved in the same impulse, with the same or at least sympathetic motive; when one might think hearts would have opened, minds would respond with kindness we did not find it so, but precisely the contrary. I went through the time in a mist of unbelief, or the kind of unwillingness to believe what is passing before one's eyes that comes often in nightmares. But before in my sleep I could always say, "It is only a dream and you will wake and wonder at yourself for being frightened." But I was suffering, I know it now, from pure fright, from shock—I was not an inexperienced girl, I was thirty-seven years old; I knew a good deal about the evils and abuses and cruelties of the world; I had known victims of injustice, of crime. I was not ignorant of history, nor of literature; I had witnessed a revolution in Mexico, had in a way taken part in it, had seen it follow the classic trail of all revolutions. Besides all the moral force and irreproachable motives of so many, I knew the deviousness and wickedness of both sides, on all sides, and the mixed motives—plain love of making mischief, love of irresponsible power, unscrupulous ambition of many men who never stopped short of murder, if murder would advance their careers an inch. But this was something very different, unfamiliar.

Now, through all this distance of time, I remember most vividly Mrs. Harriman's horsehair lace and flower garden party hats; Lola Ridge standing in the half darkness before Charlestown Prison under the rearing horse's hoofs; the gentle young girl striding and drinking gin from the bottle and singing her wake-dirges; Luigia Vanzetti's face as she stared in horror down into the crowd howling like beasts; and Rosa Baron's little pin-points of eyes glittering through her spectacles at me and her shrill, accusing voice: "Saved? Who wants them saved? What earthly good would they do us alive?"

I cannot even now decide by my own evidence whether or not they were guilty of the crime for which they were put to death. They expressed in their letters many thoughts, if not always noble, at least elevated, exalted even. Their fervor and human feelings gave the glow of life to the weary stock phrases of those writing about them, and we do know now, all of us, that the most appalling cruelties are committed by apparently vir-tuous governments in expectation of a great good to come, never learning that the evil done now is the sure destroyer of the expected good. Yet, no matter what, it was a terrible mis-carriage of justice; it was a most reprehensible abuse of legal power, in their attempt to prove that the law is something to be inflicted—not enforced—and that it is above the judgment of the people.

AFTERWORD

I have, for my own reasons, refused to read any book or any article on the Sacco–Vanzetti trial before I had revised or arranged my notes on this trial. Since I have finished, I have read the book by Herbert B. Ehrmann, the "last surviving lawyer involved in the substance of the case on either side," who, I feel, tells the full story of the case. Also, I have read since I finished my story "The Never-Ending Wrong," the article by Francis Russell in the *National Review*, page 887 of August 17, 1973, which was discovered among my magazines early last year and which I have decided should be the epigraph to this story. Mr. Russell believes that the fact that Dante Sacco, Nicola Sacco's son, kept his superhuman or subhuman silence on the whole history of his father proves that Nicola Sacco was guilty; that he refused to confess and so implicated Vanzetti, who died innocent. Sacco, therefore, proved himself doubly, triply, a murderer, an instinctive killer. Maybe.

Another maybe—Vanzetti's speech at the electric chair was the final word of an honest man. It is proven by testimony that he was innocent of murder. He was selling eels on that day, for Christmas. The Italian tradition of eating eels on Christmas Eve occupied his time all that day. He called on all the families he knew who were his friends, to deliver their orders for eels, and during the trial these people, when questioned, told exactly the same story, even to each housewife remembering the hour he delivered the eels, and some of them even went so far as to say how they had prepared them. Their testimonies were ignored when the real trial was begun. Mr. Russell has, I think, overlooked one point in his argument. Vanzetti was comrade-in-arms and in mind and heart with Sacco. They were Anarchists foresworn, committed for life to death, for death was the known fate of all who were brought to trial for the crime, as it was considered. My point is this: Sacco was guilty if you like; some minor points make it reasonable, though *barely* reasonable, to believe it. Vanzetti knew his will and he believed in the cause which he knew contained death for him unless he was very lucky indeed. Anarchy is a strange belief to die for, but my good friend in Mexico, Felipe Carillo, the Governor of Yucatan, explained to me why the revolutionists in his country who were robbing trains, wrecking haciendas, burning houses, destroying crops and even whole villages of helpless people, were right. In their utter misery, they gathered money with violence, seized the materials built with their blood, to create their idea of a good society. It was right to destroy material evil and to take its loot for their cause.

This is the doctrine of desperation, the last murderous rage before utter despair. They were wrong, but not more wrong than the thing they themselves were trying to destroy. The powerful society they opposed gained its power and grew up on the same methods they were taking. Vanzetti kept a sacred pact, not just with his comrade Sacco but with the whole great solemn oath of his life, to the cause of freedom. He fasted, kept his silence, and went to his death with his fellow, a sacrifice to his faith. As he was being strapped into the electric chair, he said, "I wish to tell you that I am an innocent man. I never committed any crime but sometimes some sin. I wish to forgive *some* people for what they are now doing to me." They

both spoke nobly at the end, they kept faith with their vows
for each other. They left a great heritage of love, devotion,
faith, and courage—all done with the sure intention that holy
Anarchy should be glorified through their sacrifice and that
the time would come that no human being should be humiliated or be made abject. Near the end of their ordeal Vanzetti
said that if it had not been for "these thing" he might have
lived out his life talking at street corners to scorning men. He
might have died unmarked, unknown, a failure. "Now, we are
not a failure. This is our career and our triumph. Never in our
full life could we hope to do such work for tolerance, for justice, for man's understanding of man as now we do by accident. Our words—our lives—our pains—nothing! The taking
of our lives—lives of a good shoemaker and a poor fish peddler
—all! That last moment belongs to us—that agony is our
triumph."

This is not new—all the history of our world is pocked with
it. It is very grand and noble in words and grand, noble souls
have died for it—it is worth weeping for. But it doesn't work
out so well. In order to annihilate the criminal State, they have
become criminals. The State goes on without end in one form
or another, built securely on the base of destruction. Nietzsche
said: "The State is the coldest of all cold monsters," and the
revolutions which destroy or weaken at least one monster
bring to birth and growth another.

Far away and long ago, I read Emma Goldman's story of her
life, her first book in which she told the grim, deeply touching
narrative of her young life during which she worked in a
scrubby sweatshop making corsets by the bundle. At the same
time, I was reading Prince Kropotkin's memoirs, his account of
the long step he took from his early princely living to his membership in the union of the outcast, the poor, the depressed,
and it was a most marvelous thing to have two splendid, courageous, really noble human beings speaking together, telling
the same tale. It was like a duet of two great voices telling a
tragic story. I believed in both of them at once. The two of
them joined together left me no answerable argument; their
dream was a grand one but it was exactly that—a dream. They
both lived to know this and I learned it from them, but it has

not changed my love for them or my lifelong sympathy for the cause to which they devoted their lives—to ameliorate the anguish that human beings inflict on each other—the never-ending wrong, forever incurable.

In 1935 in Paris, living in that thin upper surface of comfort and joy and freedom in a limited way, I met this most touching and interesting person, Emma Goldman, sitting at a table reserved for her at the Select, where she could receive her friends and carry on her conversations and sociabilities over an occasional refreshing drink. She was half blind (although she was only sixty-six years old), wore heavy spectacles, a shawl, and carpet slippers. She lived in her past and her devotions, which seemed to her glorious and unarguably right in every purpose. She accepted the failure of that great dream as a matter of course. She finally came to admit sadly that the human race in its weakness demanded government and all government was evil because human nature was basically weak and weakness is evil. She was a wise, sweet old thing, grandmotherly, or like a great-aunt. I said to her, "It's a pity you had to spend your whole life in such unhappiness when you could have had such a nice life in a good government, with a home and children."

She turned on me and said severely: "What have I just said? There is no such thing as a good government. There never was. There can't be."

I closed my eyes and watched Nietzsche's skull nodding.

1977

Mexican

Why I Write About Mexico

A Letter to the Editor of *The Century*

I WRITE about Mexico because that is my familiar country. I was born near San Antonio, Texas. My father lived part of his youth in Mexico, and told me enchanting stories of his life there; therefore the land did not seem strange to me even at my first sight of it. During the Madero revolution I watched a street battle between Maderistas and Federal troops from the window of a cathedral; a grape-vine heavy with tiny black grapes formed a screen, and a very old Indian woman stood near me, perfectly silent, holding my sleeve. Later she said to me, when the dead were being piled for burning in the public square, "It is all a great trouble now, but it is for the sake of happiness to come." She crossed herself, and I mistook her meaning.

"In heaven?" I asked. Her scorn was splendid.

"No, on earth. Happiness for men, not for angels!"

She seemed to me then to have caught the whole meaning of revolution, and to have said it in a phrase. From that day I watched Mexico, and all the apparently unrelated events that grew out of that first struggle never seemed false or alien or aimless to me. A straight, undeviating purpose guided the working of the plan. And it permitted many fine things to grow out of the national soil, only faintly surmised during the last two or three centuries even by the Mexicans themselves. It was as if an old field had been watered, and all the long-buried seeds flourished.

About three years ago I returned to Mexico, after a long absence, to study the renascence of Mexican art—a veritable rebirth, very conscious, very powerful, of a deeply racial and personal art. I was not won to it by any artificial influence; I recognized it at once as something very natural and acceptable, a feeling for art consanguine with my own, unfolding in a revolution which returned to find its freedoms in profound and honorable sources. It would be difficult to explain in a very few words how the Mexicans have enriched their national life through the medium of their native arts. It is in everything they do and are. I cannot say, "I gathered material" for it; there was nothing so mechanical as that, but the process of absorption went on almost unconsciously, and my impressions remain not merely as of places visited and people known, but as of a moving experience in my own life that is now a part of me.

My stories are fragments, each one touching some phase of a versatile national temperament, which is a complication of simplicities: but I like best the quality of aesthetic magnificence, and, above all, the passion for individual expression without hypocrisy, which is the true genius of the race.

I have been accused by Americans of a taste for the exotic, for foreign flavors. Maybe so, for New York is the most foreign place I know, and I like it very much. But in my childhood I knew the French-Spanish people in New Orleans and the strange "Cajans" in small Louisiana towns, with their curious songs and customs and blurred patois; the German colonists in Texas and the Mexicans of the San Antonio country, until it seemed to me that all my life I had lived among people who spoke broken, laboring tongues, who put on with terrible difficulty, yet with such good faith, the ways of the dominant race about them. This is true here in New York also, I know: but I have never thought of these people as any other than American. Literally speaking, I have never been out of America; but my America has been a borderland of strange tongues and commingled races, and if they are not American, I am fearfully mistaken. The artist can do no more than deal with familiar and beloved things, from which he could not, and, above all, would not escape. So I claim that I write of things native to me, that part of America to which I belong by birth and association and temperament, which is as much the province of our native literature as Chicago or New York or San Francisco. All the things I write of I have first known, and they are real to me.

1923

Reports from Mexico City, 1920–1922

THE NEW MAN AND THE NEW ORDER

December 1920

IT would be useless to deny that a man throws dice with death when he becomes president of Mexico. "He plays blind man's buff with La Muerte" says a Mexican writer. It is a high adventure, not to be undertaken lightly. Tremendous inner compulsion forces a man into the presidency of the Mexican Republic. In the past, this official has been infallibly one of these things—an egoist without horizons, an adventurer who loves danger, an idealist with a self sacrifice complex, a steel nerved dictator sure of his butchering strength. Once or twice it has been a fantastic combination of these qualities. But in all of them, the flair for personal magnificence, has made one-half of the formula. All things considered Mexico has borne with her presidents leniently, a divine patience has marked her dealings with her chance-appointed Chiefs. Some of them were aristocrats and all of them were opportunists. There was a dreamer once, hands raised in ineffectual blessings, dictators more than once, and the beautiful gold laced seekers of glory were the most numerous of all. But they shared ineluctably one glittering assortment of qualities—a baffling self sufficiency that blinded them to the importance of pacific international relations; a racial arrogance that made them not fusible with their neighbors; a personal pride that forbade them to learn the practical problems of their country; a startling ignorance of the conditions of labor and commerce and economics and industry that are the very life fluid of a nation.

It was high time Mexico had a simple working president with his feet firmly set in his native soil. After the scintillating procession of remote and inaccessible rulers, there came up from the land a farmer, Alvaro Obregon, prosperous and well acquainted with his country in its working dress; a man of straight literal mind, with a detached legal passion for setting disorder to rights. He became a soldier when the need for an honest fighting man became all too plain. He kept himself clear of the intricacies of professional diplomacy and politics through several years as general when Carranza was Chief of the Army. Later he became minister of War with this same Carranza as president, and somehow stood straight in this post too, not once fooled or circumvented by the devious methods of the President and his group of flattering shadows.

And now it is December 1st, 1920, and here is General Obregon about to become President of Mexico, after spectacular events, and a series of stupendous tragic blunders on the part of the fleeing Carranza. At twelve o'clock at night provisional President de la Huerta is to give over his office to General Alvaro Obregon. Preparations are all very festive, for everybody shares in a fiesta in Mexico. The city is strange with the voices of foreign people—we hear the shrill American voice, the tinkling Mexican voice, the gurgling Indian vocables, a scattering volley of French, truncated British speech, Spanish spoken in twenty different accents, for the South Americans are here in force. Here are the city Mexicans, rancheros grandiose in buckskin charros and great embroidered sombreros, Indians with sandaled feet and softly woven blankets luminous with color. They are all fearfully alive, fearfully bent on getting somewhere—the narrow sidewalks will not do, everybody takes to the street center, and disputes rancorously for place with the outraged drivers of cars.

Plainly, Obregon becoming President has a definite interest for all parts of the world, each part nursing its particular interest, its personal hope. Mexico is a mine unexploited, and all the riches to be had here shout from the gray earth, speaking all tongues, heard and understood of all men. Here are soils fit to grow anything human beings can use. Here are silver and gold, coal and oil—the air is redolent with the sound of these unctuous words. Men mouth them lovingly, and stare at vague and varied horizons.

Beauty is here too—color of mountain and sky and green things rooted in earth. Beauty of copper colored human things not yet wholly corrupted by civilization. Those things are well enough in their way, but business first. And our immediate business is getting this new President inaugurated, and finding out what he means to do with all the power vested in him.

Hours before the time of taking the oath the Camara is filled. The boxes of the ambassadors blaze with gold lace and glinting ceremonious swords and the jewels around the necks of the women. Next door are the governors' boxes, not quite so impressive, but gay with the gowns of the governors' ladies. Below, the diputados come in, leisurely, one at a time, each man uniformed in black dress suit, gleaming white shirt front, imperturbable dignity of demeanor. On the right hand side the aristocrats seat themselves. You notice a great many long Bourbon faces, with hair rolled back from thin brows. They are men with several centuries of power back of them, and they love the accepted order of things. What they think of this occasion no one knows. For Alvaro Obregon's face is not in the least Bourbon. He is Mexican, and a soldier, and a farmer, and a business man. On the left wing one notes a curious assortment of folk, evidently there by right, and vastly interested in the proceedings. One of them is Soto y Gama, thorn in the side of the old government, a man of wide education and culture, who rode his native mountains for seven years with a copy of Karl Marx, and another of the Bible in his pocket. Near him sits a wiry little nervous man, with an intrepid face, eyes tilted a bit at the corners. He is trim in his magpie uniform. His fingers drum the arm of his chair. He shifts about impatiently and crosses his legs repeatedly. He is Luis Leon, educated for an agricultural engineer, who could not work with the Carranza government for his conscience's sake, and therefore became a bull fighter—one of the best in Mexico. When Obregon came in, Leon came in also, and was elected diputado. So we see him sitting there, his plain black and white a long step from the silver embroidered splendor of his torero's cloak. And a longer step still, from the time he fought nine black bulls in a pen in Vera Cruz for the benefit of Zapatista revolutionists who mistook him for a spy. He did not have a torero cloak that day. He killed bulls, one at a time until there were no more bulls to be killed, and the revolutionists were convinced of his vocation as he had declared it to them. They let him go, in order, as you see, that he might sit tonight with his wing collar chafing his chin, waiting for Obregon to come in and be made president. There is Felipe Carrillo, poet, friend of poets, champion of the Indians in Yucatan, who is also here on grave business.

There are others, on both sides of the house, who are worth watching. There is not an interest in all Mexico unrepresented by these seated men. They arrive in small groups, with the look of folk who have dined in peace and are now prepared carefully to consider the business of state. The diplomatic boxes and the governors' boxes are now rivaled by the society boxes, where ladies fling off great cloaks and sit bare shouldered in the chill spaces of the Camara. We in the Camara are growing a trifle nervous. Two minutes until midnight. One minute. Half Minute. "My God," murmurs a man sitting next, "Something must have happened!" They are so accustomed to things happening at inaugurations in Mexico, they doubt if even so civilized and dignified a procedure as this can pass without exciting and untoward events.

A blare of trumpets sounds in the streets. Nearer. A great muffled shout, a sustained mellow roar soaks through the walls of the Camara. Another and milder roar inside, as the people rise to their feet. The clock hands point straight to twelve. The main portal swings back ponderously, and two men in plain dress suits, one wearing a white and green and scarlet ribbon across his chest, enter. The man wearing the ribbon has only one arm. The other has been left by the wayside between the farm and the President's chair.

The top gallery folk shout "Viva Obregon! Viva de la Huerta!" while the others applaud. President de la Huerta walks a step ahead of General Obregon. Presently, in not more than three minutes, they go again, and this time President Obregon walks a step ahead of citizen de la Huerta. But before this Mr. de la Huerta steps forward and embraces the new President. It has every evidence of heartiness and good will. And the incident is remarkable for being only the second of its kind recorded here. The old and the new have not been distinguished for amiable relations to one another.

Once again Mexico has a duly installed constitutional government. Splendor, pomp, militarism, democracy, and internationalism have combined in one grand pageant to do honor to the new regime. It has begun with a thick surface layer of good will and gayety, a hopeful way for a new government to begin. The jubilation and applause was an indication of harmony at the moment at least—a sincere, deep down desire for a better and more livable Mexico; an obliterating psychological moment when personal desires, ambitions and private interests sink into the common weal and an unbreathed hope that this nation will take its rightful place in the commonwealth of the world.

Being part and parcel of this grand spectacle, yet removed in sort of an impersonal observant way, one is compelled to pause and wonder. What will history say of this new man? What symbolism will designate the new order upon the destiny of the nation—this conglomerate and but little understood people?

An unenviable position certainly is that of President Obregon. There are those who do envy, but surely from the point of personal ambition and aggrandizement and not from high minded service to country or as the solvent of the innumerable problems that hang over and wind about the presidential chair. He stands at the head of a nation that for a long time has been at utter discord with itself and its neighbors. Unharmonizing causes date back to the Spanish conquest and beyond. Republican form of government has never been successfully engrafted upon the Aztec and other primeval roots. There has been a steady oscillation between despotism and revolution. Constitutions have come and gone between volleys of musketry.

It has been well remarked that there never was a country for which God did more or man did less. Its very richness is its danger. Personal ambition and private self interest of those who constitute themselves the chosen few is rampant in Mexico today. It only exceeds the same virulent species of other nations in its tendency to subvert the ballot and the constitution by the rifle and the cannon, and by the richness of the prize sought. Neither does the exploitation by the arrogant few confine itself to Mexican citizenry. They are here from every point of the globe and the conflict for riches and prestige rage between race, color, and creed of every known angle and combination. There are plots for prestige, there are plots for political preference, there are plots for graft, great business interests are at stake, international problems of growing importance, an interweaving of selfish, private and governmental problems without end. Not hopeless to be true, unless the whole world is hopeless, for it may be truly said that for every problem of Mexico the rest of the world has a bigger one. Yet like the naughty boy in school, all eyes are on this turbulent one. For these great problems Destiny has handed the text book to President Obregon.

"Mexican Sovereignty must be kept inviolable." This is his answer to the first question on the first page. To this, every right thinking man of every nationality agrees. Only those who believe their own personal interest could be better served otherwise, can raise any objections to this and then only in whispered words in secret places. However the president has intimated by his public utterances that he does not consider sovereignty and provincialism as synonymous, that narrowness does not build a nation and that national rights as well as those of humans must work two ways, to the mutual best and equal division of interests and benefits—a sort of a national golden rule. If this policy is maintained as well as spoken, it will make the rest of the problems easy and many of them will disappear as corollary to the major premise.

Carrying for some years the title of General is the policy of the new man to be militaristic? Is the iron hand of Porfirio Diaz again to rule? The enormous mass of Mexican people, like all other nations, detest the tyranny of an army. The president's answer was given long ago. "I would rather teach the Mexican people the use of the tooth brush than to handle a rifle. I would rather see them in school than on battle fields. I prefer any day a good electrician, machinist, carpenter, or farmer to a soldier." A modern statement of "And their swords to plowshares beating, nations shall learn war no more." Yet this must not be taken for a high sounding platitude. President Obregon has his critics and severe ones but he is not accused of being unpractical and a dreamer of dreams for dreams' sake. He has method and is a disciplinarian—nerve if you please—as has been shown on many occasions. He hates and distrusts professional diplomacy and politics. He is a man of action primarily. He has a curious suddenness in action very disconcerting to the professional politician, accustomed to weaving situations deftly and slowly.

Granting he is right on the two great problems of sovereignty and citizenry the rest is comparatively easy. With a nation granting complete recognition of all rights legitimately acquired, it will soon be right with the other nations at issue whether to the North or more remote. With order, cleanliness, industry and labor established, Mexico with its riches would bound to the front. The capital of the world would come to its aid and capital is the one and only material need of this retarded, stunted and potential giant. With its great natural resources under development, debts would soon be paid, confidence restored, economic conditions adjusted, and bankruptcy turned to credit balances at the ports of the world. Being a farmer from the farm the land question should find easy solution at the president's hands.

To be right with his neighbors an individual must be right within himself. So it is with Nations. Possessed of brilliant mind, seasoned along the hard road of experience within his own land and broadened by travel without, President Obregon indicates by his words and actions that he has grasped the great principle of right dealing. At his first cabinet meeting he impressed most emphatically upon his collaborators the necessity of absolute morality in government. The English language employs the hard fibered word integrity, yet morality is broader and expresses the profundity of feeling of the new man for the desire to make the "Inner Chamber" of Mexico fit for the inspection of the world. Mr. Obregon knows, and the world will know, that he has enemies—many of them—strong and capable of deep hate, stopping at no thing to accomplish his downfall. Some will tell you he has done this or that discreditable thing in the past; others will say he will never stand to the end of his constitutional term. Yet strange to say none accuse him of stultifying official position to personal gain or placing personal ambition above his country's good. Close observation would lead one to the conclusion that he is the choice of a great majority of his people and that he is the strongest available man to fulfill their need and longing for peace. They want room for expansion of their business, freedom and opportunity to manage their own affairs in their own country, and in their own way. These rights they claim with a calmness of men standing on their own solid earth. The great majority, peace loving by nature, want that prosperity that comes from stable conditions and they see in their new president a man who sincerely and with only the personal interest of real service, desires that they have these rightful inheritances and their God given dominion. Others, only luke warm, wish him well for they too want peace and the other things that go with it. His antagonists, when asked to name a better man, either admit it can not be done or by a national shrug of the shoulders refuse to nominate. Some go so far as to claim that with Mr. Obregon the last card has been played. If he can not bring about and maintain order in this troubled land, Mexico does not have a son capable of the task. This however, is only heard where zealous partisanship is strong or personal interest is involved. However two supremely important and terse questions arise and will not down wherever and whenever the possibility of failure from any source of Mr. Obregon's administration is discussed. These are the questions. Who? What?

Yet perhaps the new president's greatest distinction is in his knowledge that of his own self he can do nothing. He has frankly told his people this and given them the admonition that only by their co-operation could Mexico take its rightful place. He can guide, direct and counsel; give the most useful service, stamp out evil practices, and put down incipient revolutions, yet if the public conscience is not attuned, General Alvaro Obregon must bow before defeat unavoidable though undeserved.

So in its last analysis the new order which is beginning with every evidence of permanence and stability rests with all the people of Mexico, from president to peon, each responsible according to his own degree and station in the scheme of destiny.

No better words can be found than those used by Waddy Thompson, Envoy Extraordinary and Minister Plenipotentiary to Mexico, in a book written in 1846, which were as follows: "God grant them success, both on their own account as well as for the great cause in which they have so long struggled, and under circumstances so discouraging."

THE FIESTA OF GUADALUPE

December 12, 1920

I followed the crowd of tired burdened pilgrims, bowed under their loads of potteries and food and babies and baskets, their clothes dusty and their faces a little streaked with long-borne fatigue. Indians all over Mexico had gathered at the feet of Mary Guadalupe for this greatest *fiesta* of the year, which celebrates the initiation of Mexico into the mystic company of the Church, with a saint and a miracle all her own, not transplanted from Spain. Juan Diego's long-ago vision of Mary on the bare hillside made her Queen of Mexico where before she had been Empress.

Members of all tribes were there in their distinctive costumes. Women wearing skirts of one piece of cloth wrapped around their sturdy bodies and women wearing gaily embroidered blouses with very short puffed sleeves. Women wearing their gathered skirts of green and red, with blue *rebosos* wrapped tightly around their shoulders. And men in great hats with peaked crowns, wide flat hats with almost no crown. Blankets, and *serapes*, and thonged sandals. And a strange-appearing group whose men all wore a large square of fiber cloth as a cloak, brought under one arm and knotted on the opposite shoulder exactly in the style depicted in the old drawings of Montezuma.

A clutter of babies and dolls and jars and strange-looking people lined the sidewalks, intermingled with booths, red curtained and hung with paper streamers, where sweets and food and drinks were sold and where we found their astonishing crafts—manlike potteries and jars and wooden pails bound with hard wrought clasps of iron, and gentle lacework immaculately white and unbelievably cheap of price.

I picked my way through the crowd looking for the dancers, that curious survival of the ancient Dionysian rites, which in turn were brought over from an unknown time. The dance and blood sacrifice were inextricably tangled in the worship of men, and the sight of men dancing in a religious ecstasy links one's imagination, for the moment, with all the lives that have been.

A woven, moving arch of brilliant-colored paper flowers

gleaming over the heads of the crowd drew me near the gate of the cathedral as the great bells high up began to ring— sharply, with shocking clamor, they began to sway and ring, their ancient tongues shouting notes of joy a little out of tune. The arches began to leap and flutter. I managed to draw near enough to see, over the fuzzy poll of sleeping baby on his mother's back. A group of Indians, fantastically dressed, each carrying an arch of flowers, were stepping it briskly to the smart jangle of the bells. They wore tinsel crowns over red bandanas which hung down their necks in Arab fashion. Their costumes were of varicolored bits of cloth, roughly fashioned into short skirts and blouses. Their muscular brown legs were disfigured with cerise and blue cotton stockings. They danced a short, monotonous step, facing each other, advancing, re- treating, holding the arches over their crowns, turning and bowing, in a stolid sarabande. The utter solemnity of their faces made it a moving sight. Under their bandanas, their fore- heads were knitted in the effort to keep time and watch the figures of the dance. Not a smile, and not a sound save the mad hysteria of the old bells awakened from their sleep, shrieking praise to the queen of Heaven and the Lord of Life.

Then the bells stopped, and a man with a mandolin stood near by, and began a quiet rhythmic tune. The master of cere- monies, wearing around his neck a stuffed rabbit clothed in a pink satin jacket, waved the flagging dancers in to line, helped the less agile to catch step, and the dancing went on. A jammed and breathless crowd and pilgrims inside the churchyard peered through the iron fence, while the youths and boys scrambled up, over the heads of the others, and watched from a precarious vantage. They reminded one irresistibly of a me- nagerie cage lined with young monkeys. They spraddled and sprawled, caught toeholds and fell, gathered themselves up and shinned up the railings again. They were almost as busy as the dancers themselves.

Past stalls of fruits and babies crawling underfoot away from their engrossed mothers, and the vendors of images, scapulars and rosaries, I walked to the church of the well, where is guarded the holy spring of water that gushed from beneath Mary's feet at her last appearance to Juan Diego, December twelve, in the year of grace fifteen and thirty-one.

It is a small darkened place, the well covered over with a handsomely wrought iron grating, through which the magic waters are brought up in a copper pail with a heavy handle. The people gather here and drink reverently, passing the pail from mouth to mouth, praying the while to be delivered of their infirmities and sins.

A girl weeps as she drinks, her chin quivering. A man, sweating and dusty, drinks and drinks and drinks again, with a great sigh of satisfaction, wipes his mouth and crosses himself devoutly.

My pilgrimage leads me back to the great cathedral, intent on seeing the miraculous Tilma of Juan Diego, whereon the queen of Heaven deigned to stamp her lovely image. Great is the power of that faded virgin curving like a new moon in her bright blue cloak, dim and remote and immobile in her frame above the soaring altar columns.

From above, the drone of priests' voices in endless prayers, answered by the shrill treble of boy singers. Under the overwhelming arches and the cold magnificence of the white altar, their faces lighted palely by the glimmer of candles, kneel the Indians. Some of them have walked for days for the privilege of kneeling on these flagged floors and raising their eyes to the Holy Tilma.

There is a rapt stillness, a terrible reasonless faith in their dark faces. They sigh, turn toward the picture of their beloved Lady, printed on the garment of Juan Diego only ten years after Cortes had brought the new God, with fire and sword, into Mexico. Only ten years ago, but it is probable that Juan Diego knew nothing about the fire and sword which have been so often the weapons of the faithful servants of our Lady. Maybe he had learned religion happily, from some old gentle priest, and his thoughts of the Virgin, ineffably mysterious and radiant and kind, must have haunted him by day and by night for a long time; until one day, oh, miracle of miracles, his kindled eyes beheld her, standing, softly robed in blue, her pale hands clasped, a message of devotion on her lips, on a little hill in his own country, the very spot where his childhood had been passed.

Ah well—why not? And I passed on to the steep winding ascent to the chapel of the little hill, once a Teocalli, called the

Hill of Tepeyac, and a scene of other faiths and other pilgrimages. I think, as I follow the path, of those early victims of Faith who went up (mighty slowly and mighty heavily, let the old Gods themselves tell you) to give up their beating hearts in order that the sun might rise again on their people. Now there is a great crucifix set up with the transfixed and bleeding heart of one Man nailed upon it—one magnificent Egoist who dreamed that his great heart could redeem from death all the other hearts of earth destined to be born. He has taken the old hill by storm with his mother, Mary Guadalupe, and their shrine brings the Indians climbing up, in silent groups, pursued by the prayers of the blind and the halt and the lame who have gathered to reap a little share of the blessings being rained upon the children of faith. Theirs is a doleful litany: "In the name of our Lady, Pity, a little charity for the poor—for the blind, for the little servants of God, for the humble in heart!" The cries waver to you on the winds as the slope rises, and comes in faintly to the small chapel where is the reclining potent image of Guadalupe, second in power only to the Holy Tilma itself.

It is a more recent image, copied from the original picture, but now she is lying down, hands clasped, supported by a company of saints. There is a voluptuous softness in her face and pose—a later virgin, grown accustomed to homage and from the meek maiden receiving the announcement of the Angel Gabriel on her knees, she has progressed to the role of Powerful Intercessor. Her eyes are vague and a little indifferent, and she does not glance at the devout adorer who passionately clasps her knees and bows his head upon them.

A sheet of glass protects her, or she would be literally wiped away by the touches of her devotees. They crowd up to the case, and rub their hands on it, and cross themselves, then rub the afflicted parts of their bodies, hoping for a cure. A man reached up and rubbed the glass, then gently stroked the head of his sick and pallid wife, who could not get near enough to touch for herself. He rubbed his own forehead, knees, then stroked the woman's chest. A mother brought her baby and leaned his little toes against the glass for a long time, the tears rolling down her cheeks.

Twenty brown and work-stained hands are stretched up to

touch the magic glass—they obscure the still face of the adored Lady, they blot out with their insistent supplications her remote eyes. Over that painted and carved bit of wood and plaster, I see the awful hands of faith, the credulous and worn hands of believers; the humble and beseeching hands of the millions and millions who have only the anodyne of credulity. In my dreams I shall see those groping insatiable hands reaching, reaching, reaching, the eyes turned blinded away from the good earth which should fill then, to the vast and empty sky.

Out upon the downward road again, I stop and look over the dark and brooding land, with its rim of mountains swathed in layer upon layer of filmy blue and gray and purple mists, the low empty valleys blackened with clumps of trees. The flat-topped houses of adobe drift away casting no shadows on the flooding blue, I seem to walk in a heavy, dolorous dream.

It is not Mary Guadalupe nor her son that touches me. It is Juan Diego I remember, and his people I see, kneeling in scattered ranks on the flagged floor of their church, fixing their eyes on mystic, speechless things. It is their ragged hands I see, and their wounded hearts that I feel beating under their work-stained clothes like a great volcano under the earth and I think to myself, hopefully, that men do not live in a deathly dream forever.

THE FUNERAL OF GENERAL BENJAMÍN HILL

December 16, 1920

Under a brilliant morning sky, clean-swept by chill winds straight from the mountains; with busy people thronging the streets, the vendors of sweets and fruits and toys nagging gently at one's elbow; with three "ships" circling so close above the trees of the Alameda one could see the faces of the pilots; with the air live with the calls of bugles and the rattle of drums, the Minister of War, General Hill, passed yesterday through the streets of the city on his final march, attended by his army.

Life, full and careless and busy and full of curiosity, clamored around the slow moving metallic coffin mounted on the gun carriage. Death, for the most, takes his sure victories silently and secretly. And all the cacophony of music and drum and clatter of horses' hoofs and shouts of military orders was merely a pall of sound thrown over the immobile calm of that brown box proceeding up the life-filled streets. It sounded, somehow, like a shout of defiance in the face of our sure and inevitable end. But it was only a short dying in the air. Death, being certain of Himself, can afford to be quiet.

CHILDREN OF XOCHITL

March 1921

Xochimilco is an Indian village of formidable history, most of which I learned and have happily forgotten. It is situated near the city of Mexico, and is in danger of being taken up by rich tourists. Spared that fate, no doubt it will continue as it is for a dozen generations longer. The name Xochimilco means in Aztec "the place of flowers." In a way, the village is a namesake of Xochitl herself, the goddess of flowers and fruit.

There are flat roofed houses in it that have resisted destruction since the days of Cortes. The silver blue skyline is jagged with crosses and tiled domes of churches, for these Indians have suffered the benefits of Christianity to an unreasonable degree.

Some one tells me there are seventeen churches here—or more. A hospitable patriarch leads us into a small church dedicated to San Felipe, its portals open to the roadside, elbowing a pulque shop on the one side, and shows us a fiesta in progress, honoring the patron saint. The church is merely a quadrangle of walls, the roof having been blown off, whether by accident or design, in a revolution. They are collecting money for a new roof, and in the meantime a tent of white canvas clarifies the stone walls, dappled with mold and shell-powder. The lilies on the altar glitter like tinsel.

The saints support ponderous plush robes on their flattened chests, and the patron himself leans slightly to the wall. His face is yellowed with age and fatigue. They are all untouched, the man points out carefully, by the hail of bullets which swept the holy place. The patron is rich and generous, and more-over, the church is protected by four Virgins, the Virgin of Guadalupe, Our Lady of Lourdes, Our Lady of Pity and Our Lady of Help (de Los Remedios). If one Virgin did not answer a prayer, it was always simple to turn to another—and in this way it was often quite possible to get blessings from all four of them.

Quite incidentally he added, as we left, that the great Reina Xochitl was also a patroness of this church, and was often more abundant with her favors than all the others together. . . . Xochitl is the legendary Aztec goddess of the earth, of fruit, of abundance, who discovered pulque—especially the strawberry flavored kind!—and also made known the many other uses of the maguey plant, by which the Indians can live almost entirely.

"Xochitl?" we ask, for we cannot quite place her among this assembly. The Indian makes a slow gesture about the church; his pointed finger pauses a moment before each saint—"This one gives health after sickness, this one discovers lost things, this one is powerful to intercede for the Poor Souls (in Purgatory), this one helps us bear our sorrows—"

"What about Xochitl?" we must interrupt for eagerness.

He turned and flung his arm toward the wide portal, where the smell of the clean open world defied the grey mold of centuries prisoned in damp stones. "Xochitl sends rain. Xochitl makes the crops grow—the maguey and the maize and the sweet fruits and the pumpkins. Xochitl feeds us!"

He remembers that food is not spiritual. We see the thought in his face. "She is a saint of the body," he adds, apologetically. "These are saints of the soul." We detect the inflection of piety. It is most annoying. It is a good heathen putting on a starched shirt. Unendurable!

Of all the great women deities from Mary to Diana, Dana of the Druids to Kwanyin of the Buddhists, this Xochitl has been endowed with the most cleanly, the most beneficent attributes. In a race where the women sowed and reaped, wove and span and cooked and brewed, it was natural that a goddess should be fruitful and strong. We looked with intense sympathy and interest at the decaying and alien stronghold where Xochitl had set her powerful foot, there to compete with usurping gods in caring for her strayed family. We did not contribute to the roof fund, fearing influences other than hers at work in this business.

My memory of Xochimilco is always a drowsy confusion of wet flowers on the chinampas, the taste of cold sweetened pulque flavored with strawberries, the sting of the sunshine scorching my neck, the silent Indian girl in the wide straw hat, working with her bees, lifting the tops of the hives to find me a comb of honey; an Indian baby, in shape resembling a pumpkin, wrapped in red fibre cloth, kicking up dust in the road ahead of me. . . . things of no importance whatever, except that I love them. The pumpkin shaped baby is joined by several others, all friendly as chipmunks and as alert, who will walk with you, and smile at you, but will not speak or come nearer than arm's length.

At a turn of the road a band of Indian boys clad in white cotton, wild heads crowned by prodigious straw hats, leap howling upon us. They clamor one question repeatedly. "Do you wish a canoa?" We do, but the choosing of it is the adventure of the day. It is not in our plan to be seized and propelled, with courteous finality, into just any sort of boat. A few visits to the gardens develop in one a discriminating taste in flower decoration. With smiles and dumb arm wavings and shouts above the shouting, we finally disperse all of them but one. There is a brown determined youth who lags along with us, his eyes fixed upon us hauntingly. He insists in low tones that his "canoa" is the most beautiful one in the gardens. It is also to be had for an absurdly small price.

We resign ourselves. It is written that we are to have a boat, and it will be rowed by this boy.

We are in the midst of a spare forest of straight tranquil poplars, lining the banks of the canals. The sunshine falls in long strips between these trees, and gardens grow luxuriously in the midst of them. It is March, but the foliage is lush as midsummer, the pansies and cabbages and chrysanthemums and lettuce glowing and drowsing in the benign air.

The earth is swept clean and bare before the thatched huts

that line the waterside. They are contrived of sheaves of maize stalks bound together flatly, burned golden and sweet with year long sunshine. The leaning fences are also of maguey stalks and maize, woven with henequen fibre, dry and rattling in the slight winds.

In the enclosed places are placid children, playing inconsequently, without toys or invention, as instinctively as little animals. Women on their knees sweep their thresholds with a handful of split maguey leaves. Men sit, their legs straight before them, tinkering with boats or mending their rude farming implements.

Everywhere is a leisurely industry, a primitive cleanliness and rigor.

These Xochimilco Indians are a splendid remnant of the Aztecs. They are suspicious of strange peoples, with good reason. They have maintained an almost unbroken independence of passing governments, and live their simple lives in a voluntary detachment, not hostile, from the ruling race of their country. They get all material for their needs from the earth; vegetables and flowers from the chinampas are their wares offered to the outer world. The freshest pansies in Mexico are brought from the chinampas—a word that means an island with flowers. These islands do not float, but are moored substantially, girdled with woven branches.

Our "canoa" is decorated with chrysanthemums and cedar, the flowers woven into a flat background of the sweet smelling greenery. The awning is supported by arches of poplar, bowed while the wood was full of sap. We sit in benches along the sides, looping up the curtains back of us. There is something Egyptian, we decide, about this long, narrow barge of hand sawed wood, with legends carved along the sides. There is something darkly African about it, too with the boy standing in the prow, bending slowly as he rows, the long tapering pole sweeping through the water, disturbing the loosened blossoms floating with us.

It is early, and the small boats of the Indian women are still moored to stakes before the thatched huts, while the women and their children are washing and dressing at the water's edge. They are lovely creatures, the color of polished brown stone, very demure and modest. They spread their long hair on the rocks to dry, their heads thrown back, eyes closed before the light.

A child is bathing her feet, standing on a wet stone. We pass almost near enough to touch her. Mary throws her a few pansies. Her eyes are vague and gentle, the color of brown one sees in the native pottery. She is too amazed at the sight of us to pick up the pansies. She turns her head away, and blushes— arms, legs and curved neck suffuse. She stands fixed in a trance of instinctive modesty, one foot standing over the other, toes in.

The heat of the day rises in slow waves. Singly, the women come out in their tiny narrow boats, pointed at prow and bow, so shallow the rim is only a few inches above the water. They kneel before their braseros, small furnaces for burning charcoal, and cook their complicated foods, which they serve hot to the people in the be-flowered barges. In this limited space, the woman will keep her supplies, her cooked food and dishes. She will serve any number of customers, without haste or nervousness, in competent silence. Her face will be smooth and untroubled, her voice not edged. Primitive woman cooks the greater part of her time; she has made of it, if not a fine art, then a most exact craft. There are no neurotics among them. No strained lines of sleeplessness or worry mar their faces. It is their muscles, not their nerves, that give way in old age; when the body can no longer lift and strain and tug and bear, it is worn out, and sits in the sun a while, with the taste of tobacco in the mouth. It counsels and reminisces, and develops skill in tribal witchcraft. And dies. But the nerves did not kill it.

Nearly all the women in the boats are young; many of them adolescent girls. One of these wears a gay pink reboso, and thick gold hoops quiver in her ear lobes. She sits in the midst of a great bouquet of violets, pansies, sweet peas, and delicate pale roses. Her slender oar barely touches the water. She darts forward in response to our nod, her shallop runs along the barge, her brown hand, gleaming and wet, grips the rim. Under the parted sleekness of her carbon colored hair, her round innocent eyes speculate. We are openly pleased with her. She charges us twice the usual sum. We pay it, and receive an armload of flowers, done into tight little bouquets, bound with henequen fibre, arranged in long loops whereby one may trail them in the water to keep them fresh.

The sun is blazing with noonday fervor. The canals are alive with barges and the darting shallops, swift as swallows. A ponderous boat, overflowing with cabbages and celery and onions, drifts out and floats downstream guided casually by an old man whose white cotton garments are rolled up at shoulders and knees, his hat shading him as completely as an umbrella. He drags his pole through the water with a tremendous gesture, then rests leaning upon it, staring out across the chinampas, past the valley to the mountains. His face is massive, hugely wrinkled, not happy nor unhappy. He lives as a tree lives, rightly a part of the earth.

A tall girl washes clothes in a hollow of bushes matted into a shadowed cave. She rolls the garments on a slanted stone, and scoops up fresh water with a Oaxaca bowl splashed with blue and green and orange. Her blouse, almost sleeveless, is embroidered in an Aztec pattern. Her full crimson skirts are looped over bare ankles. Her braids, tied together in front, dip in the water when she leans forward. There is a trance like quality in her motions, an unconsciousness in her sharpened profile, as if she had never awakened from the prenatal dream.

"She should live for a century," says Michael, who is tormented with neuroses. "Fancy her inner repose!"

Another girl, her shallop brimming with lettuce and celery massed in fragile shades of cream color and pale green, rows swiftly down a side canal. She sits perfectly straight, her wide hat almost obscures her face, all save the pointed chin and calm, full lipped mouth.

Her oar sends faint ripples out to lap the banks and stir the broadleafed lilies. We read, cut along the curving side of weathered wood, "No me olvide, Lupita!" (Do not forget me, Lupita.) One imagines the giver, whittling and carving before his hut, making a pretty boat for Lupe to carry her vegetables in. He offers his work and his thought, but humanly cannot forbear his one request—"Do not forget me, Lupita!"

This sentimental discovery sets us on the watch for other like mottoes. At once we read this, carved in a cumbersome craft draped with willow branches—"I was once a beautiful tree in the mountains of Cordoba, but a strong axeman cut me down, and now I live to serve his friends." A strange, ironical cry out of captivity. It is the Indian who speaks. He tells a tragic story in a few words, without complaint. "Remember lovely Elena, with the sweet mouth and the green eyes," entreats another, passing to the laughter of young voices and the muted whine of mandolin strings. A line of boats keeps the eye busy searching for inscriptions. . . . "For remembrance of dear little Pancho," says one. "For the daughter of Pepe Gonzalez," reads another. A boat about four feet long, very old, unpainted, is christened "La Fortuna de Juan Ortega." Juan himself stands in this battered shell, plying up and down the canals with a few heads of lettuce, and cabbage, seeking that fortune, but without haste or greed. Juan is small and shabby, his shirt is faded, his hat is a ruin. He smiles at us, and offers lettuce, slightly wilted. He accepts our coin with a fine air of indifference, makes a grand bow, and is away. Juan could go to town and be a servant in a rich house, but depend upon it, he will not. It is the fashion among town people to go to the country for Indian servants. Many of them are docile and hardworking. But the Xochimilco Indians do not make good servants. They are apt to return on the second day to their chinampas, and finding them again is hard work.

We face a fleet of barges coming in from the side canals. They are majestic and leisurely, grouped with charming effect, their arches as individual as human faces. One is slightly pointed and woven of yellow maize, studded with chrysanthemums and pale green stalks of corn. Another is made of purple tinted henequen with small bouquets of jasmines set at intervals. Yet another is lovely with cornflowers and cedar. Each man has decorated his boat in the manner that pleases him and one cannot choose which is the most beautiful.

Under the awnings small parties of young Mexican people, attended by their chaperones, eat fruit and throw flowers to each other; in every second barge, it seems, there is a gifted youth with a guitar or mandolin, and they all strum in the careless manner of the true amateur of music. There are many types of Mexican youth and age—young school teachers and clerks, stenographers and shop keepers, with a scattering of the more wealthy folk; there is every type of girl from the modern young person in the flannel walking skirt, to the more reactionary type who wears a fluffy dress with a pretty scarf over her shoulders. It is the Mexico of industry and work and sober family virtues, the respectable, comfortably well off people whom we see here for the most part; all of them happy, bent on a day of leisure and recreation in their incomparable playground.

We are about to pass under a low stone bridge, built before the days of Cortes in Mexico, and the fleet of boats approaching meet us here in a narrow passageway where it will be a problem for two boats to pass each other. One barge has swung in under the bridge already, and we are also in the shadow of the arch. It has the look of an imminent collision. One expects mutual recrimination, a crash of boatsides, much talk.

Nothing of the sort, each boatman makes way. Each steers carefully, running his own boat almost into the bank in his effort to make room for the other. "Have a care, comrade!" says one, when he is crowded a little too closely. "Pardon me!" says the other, and somehow in the midst of the work he finds a hand with which to doff his shaggy hat, and to make a bow. The other bows in turn, good days are exchanged, the occupants of the boat smile at us as we glide through, and the flying garden of flowers fills the air between boats once more. The waiting barges form in a line and pass under the arch in a quiet procession, the awnings casting wavering shadows deep in the clear water.

From the shadowed recesses of the pavilions along the bank the native orchestras play gay tunes. Guitar, mandolin, violin, flute make scattered harmony. A medley of airs comes mingled to us on the water. "La Adelita," "La Pajarera," "La Sandunga," "La Norteña,"—all of us hum the music we prefer, with curious tonal results. The young people are dancing in the pavilions. Children play in the swings and rope trapezes. Parties sit at long tables in the shade, having luncheon festively. It all has the look of a huge special fiesta, though it is merely the usual Sunday holiday.

Toward the end of the main canal small boys run up and down the bank, or stand holding patient small horses, saddled disproportionately in leather contrivances very elaborate and heavy. The ponies are for hire by the hour, and the boys shout the attractions of their mounts. One of them leans fondly on the neck of his steed, and says, "Muy bonito, muy fuerte caballito," (Very pretty, very strong little horse!) stroking the ragged mane, while the small creature sleeps obliviously.

"Your pony looks cynical even in his sleep," we told the boy. "As though he doubted your motives."

"What does he expect?" asks the boy. "To be loved for himself alone? It does not happen in the world."

We decide not to ride the pony. "He will have his supper anyhow," says Mary. "He will lose nothing by it."

"What about me?" the owner wants to know.

"We cannot pity you—you are a philosopher!" Michael tells him.

We stop in the shade of a wide willow tree near the bank. Our boatboy seats himself crosslegged in the prow. He has the composure of a young idol, his eyes slanted and meditative. His scarlet cotton sash is knotted twice and hangs with a definite air of smartness. His feet are bound with thonged sandals of leather. We admire him immensely as he sits, eating peanuts in a remote, lordly way, placing the shells in the upcurving brim of his hat.

A flower girl passing in a slender boat throws him a bunch of purple and yellow pansies. He smiles, makes a grandiose acknowledging gesture the full length of his arm and places the flowers in his hat brim also.

He stretches on the mat, his face to the softening afternoon sky, arms under his head. The hat is by his side. He whistles "Adelita" gently, and smiles to himself. It is a pity to disturb him, but we must be going.

THE MEXICAN TRINITY

July 1921

Uneasiness grows here daily. We are having sudden deportations of foreign agitators, street riots and parades of workers carrying red flags. Plots thicken, thin, disintegrate in the space of thirty-six hours. A general was executed today for counterrevolutionary activities. There is fevered discussion in the newspapers as to the best means of stamping out Bolshevism, which is the inclusive term for all forms of radical work. Battles occur almost daily between Catholics and Socialists in many parts of the Republic: Morelia, Yucatán, Campeche, Jalisco. In brief, a clamor of petty dissension almost drowns the complicated debate between Mexico and the United States.

It is fascinating to watch, but singularly difficult to record because events overlap, and the news of today may be stale before it reaches the border. It is impossible to write fully of the situation unless one belongs to that choice company of folk who can learn all about peoples and countries in a couple of weeks. We have had a constant procession of these strange people: they come dashing in, gather endless notes and dash out again and three weeks later their expert, definitive opinions are published. Marvelous! I have been here for seven months, and for quite six of these I have not been sure of what the excitement is all about. Indeed, I am not yet able to say whether my accumulated impression of Mexico is justly proportioned; or that if I write with profound conviction of what is going on I shall not be making a profoundly comical mistake. The true story of a people is not to be had exclusively from official documents, or from guarded talks with diplomats. Nor is it to be gathered entirely from the people themselves. The life of a great nation is too widely scattered and complex and vast; too many opposing forces are at work, each with its own intensity of self-seeking.

Has any other country besides Mexico so many types of enemy within the gates? Here they are both foreign and native, hostile to each other by tradition, but mingling their ambitions in a common cause. The Mexican capitalist joins forces with the American against his revolutionary fellow-countryman. The Catholic Church enlists the help of Protestant strangers in the subjugation of the Indian, clamoring for his land. Reactionary Mexicans work faithfully with reactionary foreigners to achieve their ends by devious means. The Spanish, a scourge of Mexico, have plans of their own and are no better loved than they ever were. The British, Americans and French seek political and financial power, oil and mines; a splendid horde of invaders, they are distrustful of each other, but unable to disentangle their interests. Then there are the native bourgeoisie, much resembling the bourgeoisie elsewhere, who are opposed to all idea of revolution. "We want peace, and more business," they chant uniformly, but how these blessings are to be obtained they do not know. "More business, and no Bolshevism!" is their cry, and they are ready to support any man or group of men who can give them what they want. The professional politicians of Mexico likewise bear a strong family likeness to gentlemen engaged in this line of business in other parts of the world. Some of them have their prejudices; it may be against the Americans, or against the Church, or against the radicals, or against the other local political party, but whatever their prejudices may be they are pathetically unanimous in their belief that big business will save the country.

The extreme radical group includes a number of idealists, somewhat tragic figures these, for their cause is so hopeless. They are nationalists of a fanatical type, recalling the early Sinn Feiners. They are furious and emotional and reasonless and determined. They want, God pity them, a free Mexico at once. Any conservative newspaper editor will tell you what a hindrance they are to the "best minds" who are now trying to make the going easy for big business. If a reasonable government is to get any work done, such misguided enthusiasts can not be disposed of too quickly. A few cooler revolutionists have been working toward civilized alleviations of present distresses pending the coming of the perfect State. Such harmless institutions as free schools for the workers, including a course in social science, have been set going. Clinics, dispensaries, birth control information for the appallingly fertile Mexican woman, playgrounds for children—it sounds almost like the routine program of any East Side social-service worker. But here in Mexico such things have become dangerous, bolshevistic. Among the revolutionists, the Communists have been a wildly disturbing element. This cult was composed mostly of discontented foreigners, lacking even the rudiments of the Russian theory, with not a working revolutionist among them. The Mexicans, when they are not good party-revolutionists, are simple syndicalists of an extreme type. By party-revolutionists I mean the followers of some leader who is not an adherent of any particular revolutionary formula, but who is bent on putting down whatever government happens to be in power and establishing his own, based on a purely nationalistic ideal of reform.

The present government of Mexico is made up of certain intensely radical people, combined with a cast-iron reactionary group which was added during the early days of the administration. In the Cabinet at the extreme left wing is Calles, the most radical public official in Mexico today, modified by de la Huerta at his elbow. At the extreme right wing is Alberto Pani, Minister of Foreign Relations, and Capmany, Minister of Labor. The other members are political gradations of these four minds. The pull-and-haul is intense and never ceases. Such a coalition government for Mexico is a great idea, and the theory is not unfamiliar to American minds: that all classes have the right to equal representation in the government. But it will not work. Quite naturally, all that any group of politicians wants is their own way in everything. They will fight to the last ditch to get it; coalition be hanged!

The revolution has not yet entered into the souls of the Mexican people. There can be no doubt of that. What is going on here is not the resistless upheaval of a great mass leavened by teaching and thinking and suffering. The Russian writers made the Russian Revolution, I verily believe, through a period of seventy-five years' preoccupation with the wrongs of the peasant, and the cruelties of life under the heel of the Tsar. Here in Mexico there is no conscience crying through the literature of the country. A small group of intellectuals still writes about romance and the stars, and roses and the shadowy eyes of ladies, touching no sorrow of the human heart other than the pain of unrequited love.

But then, the Indians cannot read. What good would a literature of revolt do them? Yet they are the very life of the country, this inert and slow-breathing mass, these lost people who move in the oblivion of sleepwalkers under their incredible burdens; these silent and reproachful figures in rags, bowed face to face with the earth; it is these who bind together all the accumulated and hostile elements of Mexican life. Leagued against the Indian are four centuries of servitude, the incoming foreigner who will take the last hectare of his land, and his own church that stands with the foreigners.

It is generally understood in Mexico that one of the conditions of recognition by the United States is that all radicals holding office in the Cabinet and in the lesser departments of government must go. That is what must be done if Mexico desires peace with the United States. This means, certainly, the dismissal of everyone who is doing constructive work in lines that ought to be far removed from the field of politics, such as education and welfare work among the Indians.

Everybody here theorizes endlessly. Each individual member of the smallest subdivision of the great triumvirate, Land, Oil, and the Church, has his own pet theory, fitting his prophecy to his desire. Everybody is in the confidence of somebody else who knows everything long before it happens. In this way one hears of revolutions to be started tomorrow or the next day or the day after that; but though the surface shifts and changes, one can readily deduce for oneself that one static combination remains, Land, Oil, and the Church. In principle these three are one. They do not take part in these petty national dissensions. Their battleground is the world. If the oil companies are to get oil, they need land. If the Church is to have wealth, it needs land. The partition of land in Mexico, therefore, menaces not only the *haciendados* (individual landholders), but foreign investors and the very foundations of the Church. Already, under the land-reform laws of Juárez, the Church cannot hold land; it evades this decree, however, by holding property in guardianship, but even this title will be destroyed by repartition.

The recent encounters between Catholics and Socialists in different parts of Mexico have been followed by a spectacular activity on the part of the Catholic clergy. They are pulling their old familiar wires, and all the bedraggled puppets are dancing with a great clatter. The clever ones indulge in skillful moves in the political game, and there are street brawls for the hot-heads. For the peons there is always the moldy, infallible device; a Virgin—this time of Guadalupe—has been seen to move, to shine miraculously in a darkened room! A poor woman in Puebla was favored by Almighty God with the sight of this miracle, just at the moment of the Church's greatest political uncertainty; and now this miraculous image is to be brought here to Mexico City. The priests are insisting on a severe investigation to be carried on by themselves, and the statue is to be placed in an *oratorio*, where it will be living proof to the faithful that the great patroness of Mexico has set her face against reform.

The peons are further assured by the priests that to accept the land given to them by the reform laws is to be guilty of simple stealing, and everyone taking such land will be excluded from holy communion—a very effective threat. The agents who come to survey the land for the purposes of partition are attacked by the very peons they have come to benefit. Priests who warn their congregations against the new land-laws have been arrested and imprisoned, and now and then a stick of dynamite has been hurled at a bishop's palace by a radical hot-head. But these things do not touch the mighty power of the Church, solidly entrenched as it is in its growing strength, and playing the intricate game of international politics with gusto and skill.

So far, I have not talked with a single member of the American colony here who does not eagerly watch for the show to begin. They want American troops in here, and want them quickly—they are apprehensive that the soldiers will not arrive soon enough, and that they will be left to the mercy of the Mexicans for several weeks, maybe. It is strange talk one hears. It is indulged in freely over café tables and on street-corners, at teas and at dances.

Meanwhile international finance goes on its own appointed way. The plans that were drawn up more than a year ago by certain individuals who manage these things in the United States, are going forward nicely, and are being hampered no more than normally by upstarts who have plans of their own. Inevitably certain things will have to be done when the time comes, with only a few necessary deviations due to the workings of the "imponderables." The whole program has been carefully worked out by Oil, Land, and the Church, the powers that hold this country securely in their grip.

WHERE PRESIDENTS
HAVE NO FRIENDS

Spring 1922

Let me first repeat to you a story about Carranza told to me by
a young Spaniard, Mexican born, who had identified his fortunes with that regime which ended with the sorry flight and
death of its chief executive in the month of May, 1920.

A civilized creature was this Spaniard, suffering with a complication of spiritual disgusts. He maintained a nicely ironic
tone of amusement in relating his adventure, wherein he had
followed the high promptings of a fealty that led him into a situation gravely dubious, false, and pitiable. Because of this, he
permitted himself an anodyne gesture of arrogance.

"Be as Anglo-Saxon, as American, as you like, madame, but
try also to understand a little."

"I do not know whether this is understanding," I told him,
"but whatever you may tell me, I promise you I shall not be
amazed."

"That is good. I ask you to regard it as a *macabre* episode
outside of all possible calculation of human events. I desire
that you may be pleasantly amused at the picture I shall make
for you. Here is a wide desert, harsh with cactus, the mountains glittering under the sun-rays like heaps of hewn brass. Hot!
O Dios! our early summer! Many trains of coaches crowding
upon one another in their gaudy and ridiculous colors, a little
resembling the building-blocks for children, miles of them, you
understand, attached to busy engines madly engaged in the ludicrous business of dragging a Government, equipped and en-
cumbered, into exile.

"As Carranza goes, driven out by one of his own generals,
he takes the *matériel* of government with him, and means to
reestablish it in Vera Cruz. There are gold bars and coins, guns
and ammunition, soldiers and women and horses, furnishings
and silver from the castle, postage-stamps, champagne, jewels,
a confusion of things seized in frantic emergency.

"His cabinet, his personal friends, were with him. I had the honor, having been recalled suddenly from Washington, to share this calamity with my chief. We numbered in all sixteen thousand people in those trains, officials, soldiers, friends— and enemies. How could a president fail to have enemies among sixteen thousand persons?

"Lupe Sánchez, general in the Federal Army, was waiting for us with his men along the way. Later there would be little Candido Aguilar, son-in-law of the chief. We were not without hope.

"If for a moment, madame, we thought escape possible, put it down, please, to that persistent naïveté of faith in the incredible which is in the heart of every Mexican. *La Suerte* will not fail forever! And still *la Suerte* betrays us, and still we are faithful to her. It is our happiest fidelity.

"Some one performed the simple feat of disconnecting the air-brakes of the first train. While we waited many hours on account of this, we smiled, for we had wondered what the first treachery would be, and it was this—trivial and potent, anonymous and certain. When we moved on slowly, revolutionary troops were stationed, waiting for us. We ran through a gantlet of bullets. We listened to the noise of firing, and drank champagne. The chief was silent, composed. We had nearly ten thousand effective soldiers. If he doubted them, no one knows to this day.

"The attacking forces were defeated, though our soldiers were disconcerted by rifle-shells refusing to explode. It was not surprising to discover that nearly half the shells were filled with sand and pepper. Who did it? It was convenient to blame it on the Japanese munition-makers.

"On the third day we met Lupe Sánchez, who had changed his mind, and had diverted his troops to the defense of the revolution. We had a battle with him all day, and in the morning he was joined by the troops of deserted little Candido, left armyless in some village to the south. Trevino came also with a fresh army. They attacked together.

"That was all. Now we were certain of failure, and we did what we could toward the destruction of the train we must leave with the enemy. We dynamited and set fire to the coaches, and all of us gathered what gold we could for flight into the

United States and Europe. My brother and I had each a satchel of gold, thirty thousand pesos, maybe; not much. Only for the moment, you see.

"All of us who had arms joined the soldiers for a while. Two little revolvers and a belt of shells do not go far. We were beaten, and the chief gave orders for each man to go for himself. He released them all from their loyalty to him. He knew how to value it, you see.

"I found a small horse, very lean, standing with his saddle on, a dead man hanging by one heel to the stirrup, head down. I rode with a group of soldiers. They were trying to desert to the enemy. I said to the leader:

"'Why do you desert the chief? I shall kill you!'

"'If you are not a fool, you will come with us,' he replied very amiably. 'This is a lost day.' I let him go. Well, it was his own affair. A man's honor is his own, no?

"The soldiers spread flat over the earth behind cactus and hillock, firing at one another, no man knowing whether the other was friend or enemy. Carranza was riding away on horseback, followed by several hundred of his men. I gave my brother place behind me in the saddle, and we set out after the party. Our bags of gold were too heavy for the little horse; so we buried them under a boulder (I could never find that place again!) and later we joined the old man.

"I remember him in this way, riding always ahead of us, without a word, his white beard blowing over his shoulder. I loathe all causes, madame, and all politics, but the man inspired admiration. At dark we stopped before a hut to buy tortillas, and mind what I say, the old man had not a centavo. One of us loaned him the few pennies needed. We made a dark camp that night, and all the next day we rode between hill and cactus.

"Men were falling away from the party. One or two at a time, they saluted and left him, or turned back with no sign at all, or pleaded fatigue and promised to overtake us. But not one came back.

"In the early evening we entered a friendly hacienda and there slept. At midnight I heard a continuous tramp of horses passing the outer wall under my window. I stood listening. I felt some one breathing beside me in the dark. One of the other men stood listening also.

" 'They are bandits hunting for the Old Man,' he whispered, 'on their way into the mountains.'

" 'We should wake the chief and tell him,' I said.

" 'Let him sleep,' said the man. 'What is the good of disturbing him now?'

"In the morning my brother and I decided to go no farther. The chief was a dead man; well, we would not be implicated in his death. So we saluted, and turned back also on our one little pony."

His eyes fixed themselves steadily upon me, a bitter regard of inquiry.

"Madame, it was a desperate little jest, played out. There are, no doubt, causes worth dying for, but that was not one of them."

"Who killed him?"

"It could have been any one of that group who went on with him. It could have been the bandits I heard passing in the night. Maybe an enemy who made this his special mission, or a friend who found himself in a situation he did not care for. He might, you see, go back to the new people in power and say: 'See, here I am, your servant. I have just escaped from the bandits of Carranza.' A poor chance, but an only one. Maybe the newest chief would believe him, maybe not. A President of Mexico can trust no one."

That final corroding phrase is the point of a cynical truth: a hundred years of revolutions have taught the President of Mexico that he can trust no one except his enemies. They may be depended upon to hate him infallibly; they will be faithful in contriving for his downfall.

In Mexican revolution the cause and the leader are interchangeable symbols. A man has his adherents, who follow him in the hope of arriving, through him, one step nearer to the thing they want, whatever that may be. Obregón is the leader, and his followers are the proletariat. The proletariat being for him, naturally the other classes and subdivisions of classes are opposed to him, acting on the curious theory that what is good for the laborer must logically be very bad for everybody else. Obregón's proletarian recalls that what was good for everybody else was very terrible for him, and he has set about evening up scores with more enthusiasm than justice, probably. Obregón has difficult work on hand. Himself a man of hardy good sense, an intellectually detached point of view, and civilized instincts, he must deal with the most conflicting welter of enmities and demands, surely, that ever harassed a holder of the executive office.

His Indians, his revolutionist mestizos, are filled with grievances and wrongs, suffering cruel exigencies; they turn the tragic, threatening eyes of their faith toward him, and wait for him to fulfill his promises to them. Those promises mean realities, immediate benefits, if they have any meaning at all: land, work, freedom. He must deal with these honestly and without delay.

As an Indian, exceedingly insular in his political views, he must deal in the subtleties of international finance and diplomacy with foreign politicians and capitalists who think in terms of continents and billions, and who are leagued powerfully with his chief enemies of his own country, the landholders, the church. These in turn may be divided again into delicate classifications: the aristocracy, the wealthy upper-class mestizo, the middle-class shopkeeping folk, and the great body of Indians who cling to their religion. For the sake of sufficient identification, they may call themselves reactionary or conservative or liberal. It does not signify. They have also a label for this present governing group. They call them bandits. It means nothing, and has a disreputable sound.

The chief complaint among the anti-Obregón factions is that the new Government is acting on the theory that the lands of Mexico belong to the Indian, and that it is to the interest of the country to care first for this prodigious majority of its population. This is true, and it is revolutionary enough, indeed. But all the men now concerned in the Government are frankly nationalists. Only three of them have ever had a glimpse of Europe or this country. They studied in text-books the forms of government in other countries. But when the time came, they went about their business with their eyes fixed on their native earth. Only afterward their international point of view, such as it is, was formed, when they had come into power.

For the first time they found themselves dealing not with the fervent episodes of battles fought out with personal minuteness of detail, where a general lay in ambush and fought beside his men, but with the gigantic and implacable facts: Mexico, a backward and menaced nation, dangerously rich in resource and weak in defenses, was in actual relation with a world of hostile, critical governments, all more powerful than Mexico herself, all more than a match for her in organized pillage, more nicely adjusted in a cynical freemasonry of finance, diplomacy, and war, the three Graces of civilization.

In selecting his cabinet Obregón announced his belief that de la Huerta, radical philosopher, would work harmoniously with Alberto Pani, friend of the American Senator Fall. That Calles, Sonora revolutionist, would somehow make his terms with Capmany, millionaire reactionary. That Vasconselos, radical minister of education, and Villarreal, revolutionary minister of agriculture, could both be counted on not to be too extreme in moments of crisis. As an act of faith, this was magnificent. Faith in what? Watching Obregón's methods of disposing of his enemies each according to his degree, I believe his faith is in himself.

With this cabinet he set about the gigantic task of bringing order to a country in which order has been the least regarded of all laws. He had against him four tremendous opposing forces, the reactionaries against the radicals, the foreign against the native, an inextricably tangled mass of conflicting claims, any one of which he cannot afford to ignore. With a treasury virtually empty, he shouldered a national debt which, though not hopelessly large, is still enough to be a weapon in the hands of his opponents. And when he set about dividing the land, as he had promised, and collecting funds from the oil products to add to the national treasury, he cited Article Twenty-seven of the Mexican Constitution as amended by Carranza in 1917, and announced that it should now be made effective.

That has caused all, or nearly all, of his trouble. It delayed recognition from the United States. It has been the peg upon which to hang many promising little counter-revolutionary schemes. It may yet prove fatal to his Government.

Briefly, Article Twenty-seven gives to the Mexican Government full title to all the lands of Mexico, both surface and subsoil. It empowers the Department of Agriculture to break up unwieldy landholdings, and to divide the acreage among the Indians. It provides for a tax on all subsoil products, and thereby diverts to the national treasury and to the common life the fruit of the nation's labor and products.

This was the ideal which Obregón as President of Mexico designed to carry out. It had the noble simplicity of a hermit's vision of beauty, and it was about as sympathetically related to practical politics.

The oil interests were unanimous in opposing this article. Oil should be Mexico's greatest asset, but the Guggenheims and Dohenys have made of it a liability almost insupportable to the country. It is the fashion now to blame all the present difficulties between Mexico and the United States on the Obregón regime; but it was Carranza who redrafted the Mexican Constitution, aside from a detail or two, to its present form. It was his administration that set the tax of ten percent on the selling price of oil, with a fifteen-percent royalty payable in produce on all oil obtained. The land partition had been one of his political plans. He did not carry it out, it is true. It is one of the reasons why he is not now President of Mexico. But Obregón inherited all his problems, dead ripe.

El Aguila petroleum, a British company, and the Guffey interests made their peace, and announced their intention of complying with the national regulation of oil export. The Doheny interests, most implacable of all Mexico's interior enemies, together with other companies, have side-stepped the payment in this way: they admit that the tax is nominal; they will pay taxes cheerfully on the price paid them for oil by the boat companies, which they allege is about forty cents a barrel. The boat companies claim they buy the oil outright, and, once loaded into the tanks, Mexico has no further claim of interest. The price they sell for in foreign markets is their own affair.

This would be quite simple if the oil-producing companies and the oil-transportation companies were separate interests. But the case being what it is, the Government says pipelines shall have meters, the oil shall be measured as it flows into the tank-boats, and the amount shall be taxed at the selling price of oil, which fluctuates with the market. And there the matter sticks.

The Doheny interests are the source of eternal unrest. They

want Obregón out, and nothing less will please them. A man of the old guard, say Esteban Cantu, is the choice of the Doheny faction. A good man, Cantu. Enormously wealthy, mixed upper-class blood, interested in oil. "Emperor of Lower California" they used to call him. When Obregón became president, Cantu was required to disband his standing army, was given to understand his vast estates would be repartitioned when the time came for it. Now, sporadically, he makes counterrevolution, designed to keep the oil and land question prominently before the eyes of the American public, or, I should say, the American politician.

That much for the subsoil controversy. The surface lands are needed for agricultural purposes. The country must be fed on its own fruits. The drain of import is too heavy. The farming lands are held almost exclusively by Spaniards who have held the grants for centuries, by oil companies, and by the church. These three are in effect one. If the Government continues to carry out its drastic plan, it means that the old haciendas will be destroyed, church lands confiscated, and every foot of earth will be subject to government control. The entire question of recognition hangs on this one sword's point.

In the meantime, so far as the oil people are concerned, they cheerfully admit it is cheaper to keep a few minor revolutions going than to pay taxes. So Pablo Gonzales and Esteban Cantu and all that restless body of Mexicans with political ambitions and no love of country can be sure of a measure of support and aid in their operations.

You see what Obregón has in the way of organized opposition. Even in the Chamber of Deputies he has a minority. In his own cabinet he can with difficulty strike a balance in his favor at moments of crisis. Yet he has held the Government together for two years, and appears to be growing steadily in strength. The currency exchange is at par; gold is the circulating medium; business is good; banks are steady. What is the source of his power?

He has, as I have said, the organized proletariat, the laborunions. They are for him exactly as long as he is for them. He encounters no obscurities of motive there. His influence has wavered precariously at moments when he was threatened from foreign sources. His followers watch him, and criticize him savagely when he decides on compromise as preferable to extermination.

The unorganized proletariat follows, as a rule, the organized. There are his federal troops, a loose body of men not given to loyalties. As soldiers they follow the leader. They followed him at a time when they were theoretically loyal to Carranza. He has them—maybe.

There are the Yaqui Indians, a fierce and evil tribe who fight like demons lately unchained from hell. Obregón is the only man who has ever succeeded in taming them to regular warfare. His humanizing mediums were land and food and decent treatment. He has them—maybe.

The socialist bandits of Morelia are his. They are the most promising of all the radical groups, a fantastic mixture of doctors and lawyers and poets and teachers who took to the high roads against Carranza, soldiers who detached themselves from the army without leave and engaged in a personal pursuit of glory, plain road-pillagers converted to the revolutionary ideal. They were the remnants of Zapata's horde, those fanatic highwaymen who used to make speeches to their victims after this manner, poking them in the ribs with revolvers to emphasize the moral points of their discourse:

"In giving up your gold to us you are honored in contributing to the cause of freedom. These funds shall be used to further the revolution, to bring to our downtrodden brothers justice and peace and liberty. Be happy, brother, that we do not blow out your capitalistic brains."

These men are now engaged in running the state of Morelia on an outright socialist program. The state is at peace except for May-day battles between Catholics and Socialists and an occasional riot on feast days.

Yucatán, also a revolutionary state, is loyal to Obregón. It is a nation by itself, removed by language, by tradition, and custom from the rest of the country. The last of the Mayas are there, a spectacular, insular people, up to the eyes in social and economic grievances, who make their state a battle-ground. Felipe Carillo, a Maya, was elected governor by sixty thousand majority, and if he lives to take the chair, we shall see revolutionary theory practised freely in Yucatán.

From high to low, this is the strength of Obregón. He

works quietly, slowly, holding his ground as he gains it with a tenacity that cannot be stampeded into action even with his mob of revolutionists growling at his heels, demanding that he ignore the claims of foreign capital and politics.

He gives personal interviews to all manner of strange persons who track him down indefatigably: reporters and magazine-writers from the United States; delegations from chambers of commerce; representatives of every type of promotion scheme under heaven, all designed to benefit Mexico; walking delegates from the labor-unions; unofficial diplomats and business-men who wish to establish some sort of trades relation with Mexico.

Take this sort of thing to illustrate: Mexico has a body of lawmakers known as the Chamber of Deputies, which functions somewhat in the manner of our House of Congress. On one occasion the conservative faction went openly to war with Carillo, then deputy from Yucatán. The disturbances became a riot. For three days the lawmakers went on a debauch of dissension. A committee of deputies appealed to the president to put an end to the disgraceful episode. Acting through the governor of the district, Obregón ordered that the riot be quelled after the ordinary procedure against disturbances of the peace. Whereupon the city fire department went down to the white-pillared Chamber of Deputies, turned on high-pressure hose through the open windows, and the disorderly deputies were drenched to the bone. The disturbances stopped.

It would be absurd, comic, if death were not in it. The role of dictator is strangely associated with a civilized perception of government. Wherever generals playing the counterrevolutionary game are captured, there they are executed, usually within twelve hours. Pablo Gonzales has escaped so far, but only one of his numerous small forays recently resulted in the execution of five men, two of them being generals in the president's army.

If the revolutionists were all Mexicans, it would be, possibly, a local business. But Mexico has been hospitable to political refugees from all parts of the world. They have come making mischief each after his own taste, arrogantly bringing their diverse doctrines to a land already overborne with doctrines. A sudden flurry of antiradical sentiment resulted in a few of the more obviously annoying of the aliens being set gently over the borders of their native lands, in accordance with Article Thirty-three of the Mexican Constitution, which provides that a too impossible guest may be thrown out.

The foreign radicals, bereft of the security of government toleration, declared the Mexican Government was betraying its highest revolutionary ideals by way of currying favor with the United States. They accused the cabinet of taking orders from the American chargés d'affaires. Maybe so. Oddly enough, it did happen that most of the deportees were received hospitably by the American jails on their return from exile. But one might believe also that the long-suffering Mexican Government had grown humanly sick of gnat-stings, and had rid itself of a few minor curses in order to concentrate on greater ones.

Every foreign opportunist with a point to make can find the support of other opportunists in Mexico. The result is a hotbed of petty plotting, cross purposes between natives and foreigners, from the diplomats down to the unwashed grumbler who sits in the Alameda and complains about the sorrows of the proletariat. In all this the men in present power are struggling toward practicable economic and political relations with the world.

Psychologically, we are as alien to them as we are to the French, and in much the same way; for the Mexican upper class social and business customs are to-day more French than Spanish.

The hope of the Labor party is to establish an interdependent union with the South American states, leading naturally to clear avenues of trade and communication with Europe. It is the logical sequence of events, and would be a tremendous source of strength to Mexico. But if the union is established, it will be an achievement of finesse which Mexico may take pride in; for the idea is rankest treason to our high financial rights in that country.

Luis Morones, present chief of munitions for the Government, is the leader of this Labor party. He is wholly Indian, a leader by temperament, executive, and powerful. His pride is in his factories and plants, where the working conditions are ideal, and the wage is the highest paid in the republic.

In the educational work Vasconcelos, minister of education and president of the National University, has begun an intensive program of school founding among the Indians, with special attention to industrial and agricultural schools, his intention being not to oppress the Indian with an education he cannot use, but to fit him for his natural work, which is on the land.

Vasconcelos is, despite what we would call radical tendencies, a believer in applied Christianity. He might be called a Tolstoyan, except that he is Mexican, and the doctrine of non-resistance does not engage his faith. He claims in his calm way that the true purpose of higher education is to lift the souls of men above this calamitous civilization. We cannot outwear it until we have fixed the aspirations of our souls on something better. He publishes a magazine of religion, philosophy, and literature in Mexico City, giving translations from the works of Tolstoy, Rolland, Anatole France, and Shaw.

Other men, in no wise connected with politics, are each in his own individual manner deeply concerned with the rebuilding of his country. Widely separated as they are in caste and political sympathies, they are strangely of one mind with the others in their will to be of service to their shattered nation. There is Manuel Gamio, archaeologist and writer, wholly Spanish, but born in Mexico, whose research work and restoration of the Teotihuacán pyramids is sponsored and financed by the present Government. Mr. Gamio is studying race sources in Mexico with the sole aim of discovering the genuine needs of the Indian, and the most natural method of supplying them.

Jorge Enciso, also Spanish, is an authority on early Aztec art and design, and is making a comparative study of motives used by the early and widely separated tribes. Adolfo Best-Maugard, a painter, has spent eight years in creating a new manner of design, using as a foundation the Aztec motives. He has done valuable work in reviving among the Indian schoolchildren the native instinct for drawing and designing. His belief is that a renascence of the older Aztec arts and handicrafts among these people will aid immeasurably in their redemption.

Redemption—it is a hopeful, responsible word one hears often among these men. Strangely assorted are the true patriots of Mexico, and few as numbers go. But what country has many faithful sons? These men are divided as only social castes can divide persons from one another in a Latin-minded country, and yet they share convictions which, separately arrived at, are almost indivisible in effect.

They all are convinced, quite simply, that twelve millions of their fifteen millions of peoples cannot live in poverty, illiteracy, a most complete spiritual and mental darkness, without constituting a disgraceful menace to the state. They have a civilized conviction that the laborer is worthy of his hire, a practical perception of the waste entailed in millions of acres of untilled lands while the working people go hungry. And with this belief goes an esthetic appreciation of the necessity of beauty in the national life, the cultivation of racial forms of art, and the creation of substantial and lasting unity in national politics.

As a nation, we love phrases. How do you like this one? "Land and liberty for all, forever!" If we needed a fine ringing phrase to fight a war on, could we possibly improve on that one? The tragic, the incredible thing about this phrase is that the men who made it, meant it. Just this: land, liberty, for all, forever!

They fought a long, dreary, expensive revolution on it. As soon as they had it fought, they began to translate the phrase into action. Their situation today is as I have described it to you.

In a Mexican Patio

S MALL sounds and smells filter up from the patio, and float vaguely through the grey net of my morning sleep. A delicate slapping together of hands, rhythmic and energetic, would be young Maria making tortillas. The splash of running water, plentiful as rain, would be Manuel washing the square brown paving stones of the driveway. The smell of roasting coffee and of carbon smoke means that Lupe the cook is fanning the charcoal blaze in the red-tiled brasero in the first balcony. The gentle conciliating whimper of a very young voice, with occasional commands in a very old rattling voice mean that Consuelo is having her hair brushed by her grandmother, Josefina the portress.

The latticed iron outer gates and the tall inner gate of carved wood are not yet opened. The enclosed garden is mottled with cold early shadows. The stagnant shallow fountain, where the tangled shrubberies weave green mats to the water's edge, has not a ripple. Lilies grow here, spreading pale leaves under a trellis weighted by an arrogant bougainvillea vine, whose fronds rise to my balcony, thrusting their purple through hospitable windows.

They give warmth to the frosty white room with the high ceilings and glass candelabras. The sunshine strikes across the bare floor thinly. In the afternoon it will be there again from the other side, thawing and yellowing the chill spaces. Now I stand in the strip of light while I dress, shivering.

I cross the inner balcony to breakfast. The red and delft blue tilings are slippery and damp from recent washings. This balcony extends around three sides of the patio, with blue plaster pots set in wrought iron containers fastened at intervals along the top of the railing. The pots nourish a miscellany of struggling vegetation, flowering in pink and scarlet. A roof bordered with a ribbon of iron cut and painted in a lace pattern protects one side of the house. Here the walls are nicely tinted in squares of rose and yellow and blue, with thin edgings of mustard colour. On the opposite side the surface is rainwashed, sunfaded, streaked in pallid pink and grey.

Near the door of the dining room, grave faced Heraclia hangs the bird cages of decorated wicker on the outer wall, where the gold coloured birds may bathe and spread their feathers in the vehement sunrays. Her long blue reboso falls back straightly almost to her feet as she stretches up her neck. The black bands of her hair bind her forehead and cheeks in a sleek curve. Her eyes are fixed with curious intensity on her simple task. A kitten sleeps on the threshold, where I step over him carefully.

A thin little boy, very brown, is already setting a plate for me at one corner of the long table. His head is thrust through a slit in his short green and yellow serape. His hair stands up all around, like the bristles of a horse brush. He has bread crumbs on his chin.

I sit and regard the light through window glass stained in orange and red and rose: greenish orange and purplish rose, done in relentless symmetry of pattern. I sniff the bitter fragrance of poppies sprawling in a blue bowl at my elbow. A mirror framed in a confusion of carved oak roses and bulbous Cupids over-sophisticated of eye and posture, reflects in its ravelled silver three dying annunciation lilies, shrivelled pale ochre at the edges.

I think calmly of death as I butter a roll and examine the lilies. Then I turn my eyes toward the pine tree with four planes of branches rising above the wall, drowned in prodigious blue distances, and feel immortal. It always pleases me to feel immortal at this hour of the day, while I drink my coffee. The muchacho brings the coffee in a pottery cup, capacious as a bowl. He holds it with extraordinary care, gripping the saucer with both hands. But he splashes it anyhow, on the cloth, on my plate, on my sleeve, and on his own thumb. He gives a strangled yelp of surprise and puts his thumb in his mouth. Thank heaven, that means the coffee is hot for once.

An Indian girl wearing huge brass hoops in her ears trots through the dining room carrying an immense tray of food on her head. Her hair is braided in a thick round coil on her crown, making a flat surface for carrying burdens. Her raised arms are curved as softly as the handles of a native jar. She disappears into the corridor leading to Doña Rosa's apartment.

Doña Rosa is the hostess, as the courteous phrase has it, of this guest house. She is large and leisurely and placid. She lives in rooms adjoining the kitchen, whence her two children, a son and a daughter, both as fat and wholesome looking as apple dumplings, emerge and disappear again at intervals. Doña Rosa herself rarely comes out. She sits inside and rings a bell which sounds in the rear hall. At the first jingle, a cook, a maid, and several of their children rush to answer it. In a moment they all rush back to the kitchen, where after some confusion and excited talk, they clatter again through the dining room, carrying a cup of chocolate and a plate of rice and a pitcher of hot water for Doña Rosa.

On rare occasions I have seen her, at the noon hour, returning from market. The cleanly brown skin of her face is unmarred by powder. Her smooth black hair is fastened with three flat jet pins. Her eyes are clear brown, her teeth strong and white. She is tall, and her ample black skirts sweep the floor, swinging handsomely over her opulent hips. A black reboso of heavy crinkled silk, fringed thickly and at great length, falls about her shoulders. She moves with extraordinary decision, turning her head slowly on her muscular neck, observing everything serenely. She is the widow of a general who was killed in a casual battle at the frayed end of some revolution, when her children were babies.

Now she wears mourning, and goes to church, and to market.

I take occasion to speak with Doña Rosa concerning the young coyote tethered to the water pipe on my roof. He is a pilgrim on his way to another fate; Heraclia's brother will take him to the country in a few days, and there, I hope, he will become the pet of an indulgent household. But in the meantime he grieves, and although I grieve with him, still I cannot devote all my time to it. Is it possible to have him removed to a far corner of the patio for the rest of his stay? He has an enormous voice for so young a creature.

With this question carefully assembled in Spanish from a

phrase book, I enter the darkened room of Doña Rosa. Against the precision of the maroon coloured wall paper design hang pictures of obscure saints, their upturned eyes glazed with highly specialized agonies. A shrine lamp is blood colour before a pallid Virgin gazing into the mysteries of a paper-flower bouquet.

Doña Rosa sits in a vast bed overflowing with puffy quilts riotous with strange blossoms. Her daughter sits at one elbow, her son at another. The three of them wear dressing gowns of the same material. The tray is on her flattened knees. They are drinking hot milk flavoured with coffee, munching great sugared buns.

Daughter feeds a grey kitten. Son feeds a yellow kitten, and with difficulty persuades him not to drink from the family milk pitcher. A pair of slightly fevered, ill-humoured eyes and a moist, black lacquered nose burrowing under Doña Rosa's arm, belong to Pipo the naked Chihuahua dog. We have met only once before, but I remember him well. He was then painted a watermelon pink, and wore a blue ribbon on his tail. He was eating beans from an orange and red Oaxaca bowl, and it occurred to me then that I had never sufficiently understood the phrase "local colour." Pipo was It. Now, he struggles out a bit from his smother of blankets, and I see that his crepe de chine surface is tinted emerald green. No wonder his eyes are fevered.

Doña Rosa offers me a cup of coffee. Daughter gives me a roll. I sit on the billowing bedside, and we straighten out the coyote question with the utmost amiability, in snatches of three languages.

This is a house of respectable age merely, not antique. It was built during Emperor Maximilian's time, and therefore clings to doubtful grandeurs of the Italian type, such as stained glass windows, steps of streaked marble, and other steps painted to resemble marble. The floors are bare and rough from much scrubbing. The furnishings must be wedding presents of several generations, for carved walnut and horse hair share the same rooms with gilt chairs and sofas upholstered in rose brocaded satin, and slab settees in that deplorable style known as Mission. Plaster casts of smiling ladies, effulgent of bust and hair, are set about in corners that would otherwise be happily empty.

Doña Rosa takes no pleasure in her house, except in that one big overfilled room where she sits, and where her children love to play. She spends part of her afternoons in the shady garden beside the fountain where friends come for long visits. They sit here, gossiping over chocolate thick as soup, sipping slowly with long handled wooden spoons from little lacquered gourds.

The natural industry of the servants is reason enough for the general air of freshness and dampness that pervades the house. They mop and sweep and dust, talking softly all the time. There is no quarrelling, no dissension. La Cocinera is maybe a trifle brittle of temper at times, but she is an overworked, distracted woman with three children at her skirts. Life is a tragic business for her.

This morning when she came to my room with ten o'clock chocolate her smallest son came with her, and sat on my bed as we talked, his round grubby face as friendly as a little dog's. His mother shrieked. Her act of seizing and flinging him out of the room was done in one curving motion. I have never seen anything so finished. Then she examined the spot where he had been. There was the complete outline of his little shape, done neatly in charcoal dust. Her gesture of despair measured calamity. And these people face real calamity with perfect stoicism.

On the walls of the servants' quarters is painted a curious landscape: a tall castle in the middle distance, abnormally rotund domestic animals in the immediate foreground, and dying trees along the water's edge. It is acutely surprising to the eye when one first walks through the gate to see this painting, so utterly removed from anything resembling either life or art, down the hundred foot vista of patio. At its base the servants' children, Consuelo, her cousins and friends, play amid a confusion of brown cooking pots and baskets and mats. They are contented little people, who rarely weep and who are never punished. I have seen Consuelo busy for an hour, trying to bend a bit of wire into a shape that pleased her. It is a pity she must be a servant when she grows up. She is very beautiful, with finely formed hands and feet. In a decade, she will be like her mother, a seventeen year old girl already haggard, who works with a baby on her arm, wound in her reboso. In two decades she will resemble her grandmother, who cannot be older than forty years. But she has the look of something agelessly old, that was born old, that could never have been young.

Why not? One may have the complete use of a human being here for eight or ten pesos a month. They carry water in huge jars to the stone washing tubs, where they kneel at their work. They toil up and down endless flights of stairs: to the roof to hang linen, down again for another load, crossing long courts on hundreds of small errands. If I go to sleep at twelve, it is to the sound of their voices on the other side of the wall, still gathering together the ends of the day's labour. If I wake at six, they are pattering about, their bare feet clumping like pony hoofs.

My poor Gatito de Oro (Golden Kitten) has passed out attended by every circumstance of tragedy.

He did not come in for breakfast this morning, nor did he appear for his noon bowl of milk. I had begun to miss him seriously this afternoon, when the small brown child from the patio came up to tell me that poor Gatito was dead, in the garden, with blood on his arms and breast, and dried blood on his mouth.

I inquired no further into particulars, but she supplied them lavishly. They had found him lying twisted, so, with his head so,—and the ants were at him. His teeth were showing, and he seemed very angry. But he was not angry—of course not, he was only dead. Pobrecito!

Pobrecito indeed. He was a gentle, childlike beast, living by his affections. He was the first cat I ever saw who required to be loved. He came to my window one morning wailing aloud, his yellow fur standing up; I thought he was sick. But no, he wished only to be petted. When I stroked his head, he purred. When I stopped, he wailed. For weeks after he came, he went back to the patio kitchen for his food, and never for one moment could I accuse him of self interest in the matter of shelter. He was fat and thriving when he took up his abode with me.

He slept on my pillow at night, and sat on the window sill

by day, washing his adolescent person carefully; or he followed me about, talking to himself, answering when I called. He understood my Spanish very well.

Pobrecito! The night before he died, the wind rattled the window latches, as though a hand was trying to unfasten them. Gatito de Oro stared at the window and listened, his eyes blackened with uneasiness. He growled in his throat forebodingly, like a little dog. Now he is not afraid of anything. It is too bad.

Five Indian men, their women and six children are on the roof of my neighbor's house this morning. They have come from Xochimilco to build her a thatched hut, which she means to use for a tea house. The men are setting up roughly hewn sapling trunks, and the women are tying the thatch together with thick strands of twisted maguey fibre. They have their food baskets, a collection of beautiful brown decorated pottery, and many blankets and mats. One of the women is building a charcoal fire on the cement paved roof. They will eat, sleep and build the hut up there for two days.

The babies roll about almost naked. One of them, a large child, is hanging at his mother's breast nursing, arms and legs clutching monkey-like, as she walks about unconcernedly with both hands free, arranging her household. The women are quite nice. Their blouses are embroidered in red and green, they wear very wide skirts wrapped about them, plain and smooth across their hips, pleated amply in front and bound with a woven girdle in many colours.

The hut is finished. It stands solemnly, the thatch droops around the edges like the brim of a dilapidated hat. It seems strangely different from those we saw in Xochimilco. But my neighbor, an American, regards it affectionately, and promises us tea in it. Her husband explains to the Indians that he means to call it the Hula Hula Hall because of the grass skirt. They smile politely.

I encounter at dinner today the young married couple. She is fat, with the fresh and blooming fatness of the happily married bride who apparently is living by the twin delights of food and love. If a thought ever ruffled that sleek brow, or darkened those full thick-lidded eyes, it left no trace. Wearing a pink silk pleated jacket, and thin green slippers on her white stockinged feet, she comes to dine with her husband, leaning on his arm. He is a portly, rather too-knowing young man, who scolds her and reproves her and slaps her resoundingly on the back, to the amazement of every one. She reacts like a devoted, slightly bewildered dog: she snaps when he scolds and fawns when he pats. Either response seems equally to amuse him.

When she dresses to go out, her hat is enormous, of fluffy black lace, strapped under her full chin. Her complexion is a chemical marvel of whiteness and smoothness, her lips a bleeding bow. Her light blue silk dress strains over her round high bosom, and she tilts forward perilously in her tight French slippers. Her husband admires her immensely at these times, and cannot take his eyes from the sight of all that magnificent femaleness.

He tells me his wife is clever, and does not wish to be idle merely because she is married. "A very modern girl," he pronounces in English. He allows her to have her voice trained. Ah, so it is she I have heard for the past four days, singing the Musetta Waltz, a half tone off key.

I will have dinner in my room this evening. It is brought to me by the sweet sentimental-eyed Dolores, who often helps in small ways, though she is cousin to Doña Rosa. The tray resembles the food-dream of a delirious person. There is a huge plate of rice, deliciously cooked with peppers and spices, very dry and rich. A dish of ground meat mingled with peppers and garlic, flooded with red sauce. Coarse spinach with onions. A croquette of frijoles. Two very red apples, a dish of zapote, the suave delicately flavoured black fruit pulp I like, and coffee. I eat heroically, because a failure to do so will bring the household about my ears, inquiring if I am sick.

Dolores seats herself with the air of one come for a visit, and sews on a dress which hung over her arm while she carried the tray. She is accompanied by Duquesa her little copper-coloured collie dog, who folds her paws and watches her mistress prayerfully.

Dolores applies the diminutive to everything. "Un momentito," she says, bringing her thumb and forefinger almost together, measuring the smallest possible fraction of time. "Pobrecita," she calls the prosperous Duquesa, everybody's pet. "Yo solita," she calls herself, her appealing black eyes floating suddenly in inexplicable tears. She sews as she talks, stitching lace on a dress that has even now too much lace. A blue reboso over her head, a black muslin dress with red ribbons showing in her embroidered chemise top, a hiatus of four inches of white cotton stockings between her skirts and her yellow topped shoes, she talks and smiles, her brown hands vague and groping among the folds of her material. When I see the sadness of her down drooping face, I know she is beginning to think of love. "Yo solita," she calls herself.

In the early evening, fragments of life quite different from those of the hurrying day drift through our street. I like to stand in my balcony and watch them. A wide hatted man drives a two wheeled cart, cumbrous and full of groans, the shafts too high for the struggling little mule, who wavers from side to side, his hoofs knocking against the wheels. An Indian boy carries a bundle of long handled feather dusters, used for sweeping the ceilings. He walks steadily, balancing the wicker poles, setting one foot exactly before the other. The feathers nod in time, and his vending cry shatters the silence. A very old woman with scanty grey hair drives a burdened burro; a tiny girl trots beside her, bent under a sack of corn. They are country Indians leaving town until another day. They all carry lighted candles set in deep cups of paper, and the pointed flames flutter delicately as birds' wings.

Others are also watching life pass by; I count the young girl heads at this moment nodding under high coiffures, discreetly visible at upper windows. There are two in my house, one on either side, and three in houses across the narrow street.

The girl in the balcony at my left hand is Dolores, only fifteen years old. Her hair is not yet pinned up, but falls in two thick braids to her knees. Darkness is here, and the heads in the windows are lost. Here and there a pale face glimmers for a moment in the framing blackness, and floats away. The girl on the right hand balcony is gone.

Dolores leans forward, her chin on the rail, and stares at a blotch, humanly shaped, defined against the fog grey of the

wall of the opposite house. The flare of a match lights the face
of a man whose eyes peer upward. His lighted cigarette moves
and traces lines before him. The spark spins gently, in long
curves, sudden down-jutting lines, circles. I read: "Yo te amo,
Cielito Lindo . . ." and then three times over, "Dolores, Dolores, Dolores!"

Observing this, I ponder the finished technique of ardency
required to form those burning words with so fragile a torch.
How practised are those fingers, turning delicately on a steady
wrist, scrivening in ash veiled flame upon a wall of air!

Dolores rises and leans over the wall. She kisses her fingers
many times toward the spot of light. Her outstretched bared
arm shudders to the shoulder with the agitation of her shaking
hand.

Tonight, hurrying through the patio, with the moon not yet
risen over the massed tree tops, I saw a man leaning against a
pillar on the narrow driveway. A wide black hat blurred his
face, a spectral black cloak swathed him. . . . In such a moment, one's conscious mind contracts, and cancels all engagements for this world. . . . But the nervous centers know
better. They gather themselves and spring for safety, remembering for your helpless mind that tomorrow also will be
sweet. From the top step I glanced back. He was gone. In the
lower hall, I collided with Heraclia, wearing a white lace veil
over her hair, and carrying a lighted candle. I leaned on her
arm, shaking, my breath gone. "Don't go in the patio," I said.
"Something is there."

Heraclia was very calm. She held the candle above her head,
so it shone on both our faces, and smiled gently. "It is probably the ghost of the house," she explained in a low whisper.
"He comes often. But he is harmless. Do not be afraid. I will
go with you up the stairway." She followed me to my door.
"Buenas noches," she said, her grave eyes shining a little. "I assure you, you need not fear ghosts."

I listened to her footsteps down the stairs, across the hall,
and from the patio her candle glimmered an instant, and was
snuffed out. There were happy, confused little noises—a whisper, a rush of skirts, smothered laughter, feet running on tip
toe. I am very much amused. She is two years older than poor
little sister Dolores, and has managed to learn a great deal, it

seems. Doña Rosa would take it out of the skin of Josefina the portera if she knew; but I am pleased that Heraclia will have her love messages by another medium than lighted cigarettes writing in cold air.

Josefina is not usually so hospitable, to ghosts or other shape of folk. Lying awake listening to noises, I hear insistently now near, now far, up and down the little Eliseo, the rat-tat-tat and thump-thump of late returning persons knocking at their barred gates. Getting into the house after ten o'clock is an achievement of no mean order.

Josefina sleeps soundly, without sympathy for those owlish ones who love the world by starlight. Two nights since a pilgrim entertained himself with rhythms for the better part of an hour, playing upon the knocker in waltz time, both slow and fast. He changed to the jota, and jingled away cheerfully. Then he experimented with the two-step, and not doing so well, he ended with a marvelous flourish, a soft shoe dance finale. At last he settled down for the night in doleful marching time, a steady processional knock-knock-knock. In the midst of this, Josefina opened the door arguing shrilly. He replied with laughter, keeping a high good humour . . . to have got in was enough.

I danced the other night with a group of young Mexican boys and girls in an old square garden, paved with tiles and lined with rose bushes and palms. Jasmine and violets were sweet in shallow bowls. Two Indians from the country made melancholy music with fiddle and flute, and our feet followed the sad, gay pattern of rhythm. Now and then someone clicked his heels ringingly on the glassy tiles. There was no light except a late-rising moon, swung between stars like a plaque of white-gold beaten thin.

A man draws his thumb lightly across all the strings of his guitar . . . a sighing breeze of sound. He sings, mournfully, with a jolly face. . . . "What does he say?"

"He is singing about love, how it is cruel, because life devours us, a day at a time, and a dream at a time, until we are ended utterly. . . ."

He wails on and on, ecstatically.

We danced until the moon went down, and by candle light

we danced until the morning. When we went home, the sky was grey and our faces were grey. . . . Sancha had drunk a little too much wine. She looked at us, as we silently stepped into motor cars and huddled silently together. She touched her own face. . . . "I am a ghost too!" she cried out in a high shocked voice. Her mouth became a turned down crescent moon. She began to cry. "I am a ghost, a ghost! I can never dance again!"

A woman in this house plays Chopin at two o'clock in the morning. I know it is a woman, because she plays very softly, with many mistakes, and for her, you understand plainly, the music takes the place of tears. Women always corrupt the music of Chopin with tears. It is like listening to one who weeps in a dream. In the sunlight one may laugh, and sniff the winds, but the night is crowded with thoughts darker than the sunless world.

Now I lean on my window ledge, wrapped in a shawl, shivering. The sky is empty, the patio is like a well. I listen to the Mexican woman who weeps Chopin through her sleepless nights. It is a group of Preludes . . . why be so stubborn, so intent on composure? I love them. I am thankful for her tears.

1921

Leaving the Petate

THE petate is a woven straw mat, in shape an oblong square, full of variations in color and texture, and very sweet smelling when it is new. In its ordinary form, natural colored, thick and loosely contrived, it is the Mexican Indian bed, an ancient sort of sleeping mat such as all Oriental peoples use. There is a proverb full of vulgar contempt which used to be much quoted here in Mexico: "Whoever was born on a *petate* will always smell of the straw." Since 1910, I shall say simply to fix a date on changes which have been so gradual it is impossible to say when the transition actually was made, this attitude has disappeared officially. The *petate*, an object full of charm for the eye, and immensely useful around any house, is no longer a symbol of racial and economic degradation from which there is no probable hope of rising. On the contrary, many of the best 1920 revolutionists insisted on smelling of the straw whether they were born on the *petate* or not. It was a mark of the true revolutionary to acknowledge Indian blood, the more the better, to profess Indian points of view, to make, in short, an Indian revolution. All the interlocking advances of the *mestizo* (mixed Spanish and Indian) revolution since Benito Juárez have been made for the Indian, and only secondarily by him—much as the recent famous renascence of Indian sculpture and painting was the work of European-trained *mestizos*. No matter: this article is not going to deal with grand generalities. I am interested in a few individual human beings I have met here lately, whose lives make me believe that the Indian, when he gets a chance, is leaving the *petate*.

And no wonder. He wraps himself in his *serape*, a pure-wool blanket woven on a hand loom and colored sometimes with vegetable dyes, and lies down to rest on his *petate*. The blankets are very beautiful, but they are always a little short, and in this table-land of Mexico at least, where the nights are always cold, one blanket is not enough. The *petate*, beautiful as it is, is also a little short, so the man curls down on his side, draws his knees up and tucks his head down in a prenatal posture, and sleeps like that. He can sleep like that anywhere: on street corners, by the roadside, in caves, in doorways, in his own hut, if he has one. Sometimes he sleeps sitting with his knees drawn up to his chin and his hat over his eyes, forming a kind of pyramid with his blanket wound about him. He makes such an attractive design as he sits thus: no wonder people go around painting pictures of him. But I think he sleeps there because he is numbed with tiredness and has no other place to go, and not in the least because he is a public decoration. Toughened as he may be to hardship, you can never convince me he is really comfortable, or likes this way of sleeping. So the first moment he gets a chance, a job, a little piece of land, he leaves his *petate* and takes as naturally as any other human or brute being to the delights of kinder living. At first he makes two wooden stands, and puts boards across them, and lays his *petate* on a platform that lifts him from the chill of the earth. From this there is only a step to thin cotton mattresses, and pillows made of lumps of rags tied up in a square of muslin, and thence. . . .

There were presently three women near me who had lately left the *petate*: Consuelo, Eufemia and Hilaria. Consuelo is the maid of a young American woman here, Eufemia was my maid, and Hilaria is her aunt. Eufemia is young, almost pure Aztec, combative, acquisitive, secretive, very bold and handsome and full of tricks. Hilaria is a born intriguer, a carrier of gossip and maker of mischief. Until recently she worked for a hot-headed Mexican man who managed his servants in the classical middle-class way: by bullying and heckling. This gentleman would come in for his dinner, and if it was not ready on the instant, he would grab his hat and stamp shouting into the street again. "My señor has an incredibly violent nature," said Hilaria, melting with pride. But she grew into the habit of sitting in my kitchen most of the time, whispering advice to Eufemia about how best to get around me; until one day the señor stamped around his house shouting he would rather live in the streets than put up with such a cook, so Hilaria has gone back to her native village near Toluca—back, for a time at least, to her *petate*. She has never really left it in spirit. She wears her *reboso*, the traditional dark-colored cotton-fringed scarf, in the old style, and her wavy black hair is braided in two short tails tied together in the back. Her niece Eufemia came to me dressed in the same way, but within a week she returned from her first day off with a fashionable haircut, parted on the side, waved and peaked extravagantly at the nape—"In the shape of a heart," she explained—and a pair of high-heeled patent-leather pumps which she confessed hurt her feet shockingly.

Hilaria came over for a look, went away, and brought back Eufemia's godmother, her cousins and a family friend, all old-fashioned women like herself, to exclaim over Eufemia's haircut. They turned her about and uttered little yips of admiration tempered with rebuke. What a girl! but look at that peak in the back! What do you think your mother will say? But see, the curls on top, my God! Look here over the ears—like a boy, Eufemia, aren't you ashamed of yourself! and so on. And then the shoes, and then Eufemia's dark-red crochet scarf which she wore in place of a *reboso*—well, well. . . .

They were really very pleased and proud of her. A few days later a very slick pale young man showed up at the house and with all formality explained that he was engaged to marry Eufemia, and would I object if now and then he stopped by to salute her? Naturally I should never object to such a thing. He explained that for years upon years he had been looking for a truly virtuous, honorable girl to make his wife, and now he had found her. Would I be so good as to watch her carefully, never allow her to go on the street after dark, nor receive other visitors? I assured him I would have done this anyhow. He offered me a limp hand, bowed, shook hands with Eufemia, who blushed alarmingly, and disappeared gently as a cat. Eufemia dashed after me to explain that her young man was not an Indian—I could see that—that he was a barber who made good money, and it was he who had given her the haircut. He had also given her a black lace veil to wear in church—lace veils were once the prerogative of the rich—and had told her to put aside her *reboso*. It was he who had advised her to buy the high-heeled shoes.

After this announcement of the engagement, Eufemia began saving her money and mine with miserly concentration. She was going to buy a sewing machine. In every department of the household I began to feel the dead weight of Eufemia's sewing machine. Food doubled in price, and there was less of it. Everything, from soap to a packet of needles, soared appallingly until I began to look about for a national economic crisis. She would not spend one penny of her wages, and whenever I left town for a few days, leaving her the ordinary allowance for food, I always returned to find the kitten gaunt and yelling with famine and Eufemia pallid and inert from a diet of tortillas and coffee. If all of us perished in the effort, she was going to have a sewing machine, and if we held out long enough, a brass bed and a victrola.

In the meantime, Consuelo came down with a mysterious and stubborn malady. Her young American woman briskly advised her to go to one of the very up-to-date public clinics for treatment. Consuelo at once "went Indian," as her employer defines that peculiar state of remoteness which is not sullenness nor melancholy, nor even hostility—simply a condition of not-thereness to all approach. So long as it lasts, a mere foreigner might as well save his breath. Consuelo is Totonac, speaks her own tongue with her friends, is puritanically severe, honest and caretaking. Her village is so far away you must travel by train for a day or so, and then by horseback for two days more, and in her sick state she turned with longing to this far-off place where she could get the kind of help she really trusted.

Somehow she was prevented from going, so she called in a *curandera* who came from this same village. A *curandera* is a cross between a witch wife and an herb doctor. She steeped Consuelo in home-made brews and incantations, and what we had feared was a tumor the *curandera* identified as a rib which had been jarred from its moorings. Whatever it was, Consuelo recovered, more or less. Consuelo has two cousins who left the *petate* and are now nurses in a famous American homeopathic sanitarium. They send her long lists of dietary rules and hygienic counsels, which her American employer follows with great effect. Consuelo prefers to stick to her own witch doctors, and lets the foreign ones alone.

Hilaria is a *curandera*, and so is Eufemia in a limited way, and both of them remind me very much of the early American housewife who kept her family medicine chest supplied with her own remedies from tried recipes. They have extensive herb knowledge, and Eufemia was always bringing me a steaming glassful of brew for every smallest discomfort imaginable. I swallowed them down, and so ran a gamut of flavors and aromas, from the staggering bitterness of something she called the "prodigious cup" to the apple-flavored freshness of manzanilla flowers. Hilaria pierces ears when the moon is waning, to prevent swelling, and ritually dabs the ear with boiling fat, which should be an excellent antiseptic. To cure headache, a bottle of hot water at the feet draws the pain from the head. This works better if the sign of the cross is made over the head and the bottle. Every benefit is doubled if given with a blessing, and Eufemia, who knows the virtues of rubbing alcohol, always began my alcohol bath with "In the name of the Father, and of the Son, and of the Holy Ghost, may this make you well," which was so gracious an approach I could hardly refuse to feel better.

She agrees with Hilaria that a small green *chile* rubbed on the outer eyelid will cure inflammation of the eye, but you must toss it over your shoulder from you, and walk hastily away without glancing back. During my illness she moistened a cloth with orange-leaf water and put it on my head as a cure for fever. In the morning I found between the folds a little picture of the Holy Face. Eufemia takes up readily with every new thing, and uses iodoform, lysol, patent toothpaste, epsom salts, bicarbonate of soda, rubbing alcohol and mustard plasters very conveniently. Hilaria sticks firmly to her native herbs, and to cure colds puts a plaster of *zapote*—a soft black fruit—heated red hot, on the chest of her patients. Both remedies are remarkably helpful. But Eufemia is leaving the *petate* and Hilaria is going back to it.

I sympathized with Eufemia's ambitions, even to her fondness for toilet articles of imported German celluloid, her adoration for Japanese cups and saucers in preference to the Mexican pottery which I so love. But I had not reckoned on providing a dowry for a young woman, and the time came for us to part. I set the day two weeks off, and she agreed amiably. Then I gave her her month's wages and two hours later she had packed up her bed and sent it away. Her young man came in and professed astonishment at the state of affairs. "She is not supposed to go for two weeks," I told him, "and at least she must stay until tomorrow." "I will see to that," said the oily Enrique, "this is very surprising." "Tomorrow she may go and welcome, in peace," I assured him.

"Ah, yes, peace, peace," said Enrique. "Peace," I echoed, and we stood there waving our hands at each other in a peculiar horizontal gesture, palms downward, crossing back and forth at our several wrists, about eye level. Between us we wore Eufemia down, and there was peace of a sort.

But in the meantime, she had no bed, so she slept that night on a large *petate* with two red blankets, and seemed very cheerful about it. After all, it was her last night on a *petate*. I discovered later that it was Enrique who had suggested to her that she leave at once, so they might be married and go to Vera Cruz. Eufemia will never go back to her village. She is going to have a brass bed, and a sewing machine and a victrola, and there is no reason why a good barber should not buy a Ford. Her children will be added to the next generation of good little conservative right-minded dull people, like Enrique, or, with Eufemia's fighting spirit, they may become *mestizo* revolutionaries, and keep up the work of saving the Indian.

My new cook is Teodora. "Think of Eufemia going away with just a barber," she says. "My cousin Nicolasa captured a chauffeur. A chauffeur is somebody. But a barber!"

"Just the same, I am glad she is married," I say.

Teodora says, "Oh, not really married, just behind the church, as we say. We marry with everybody, one here, one there, a little while with each one."

"I hope Eufemia stays married, because I have plans for her family," I tell her.

"Oh, she will have a family, never fear," says Teodora.

1931

The Charmed Life

IN 1921, he was nearly eighty years old, and he had lived in Mexico for about forty years. Every day of those years he had devoted exclusively to his one interest in life: discovering and digging up buried Indian cities all over the country. He had come there, an American, a stranger, with this one idea. I had heard of him as a fabulous, ancient eccentric completely wrapped up in his theory of the origins of the Mexican Indian. "He will talk your arm off," I was told.

His shop was on the top floor of a ramshackle old building on a side street in Mexico City, reached by an outside flight of steps, and it had the weathered, open look of a shed rather than a room. The rain came in, and the dust, and the sunlight. A few battered showcases and long rough tables were piled up carelessly with "artifacts," as the Old Man was careful to call them. There were skulls and whole skeletons, bushels of jade beads and obsidian knives and bronze bells and black clay whistles in the shape of birds.

I was immensely attracted by the air of authenticity, hard to define, but easy to breathe. He was tough and lean, and his face was burned to a good wrinkled leather. He greeted me with an air of imperfect recollection as if he must have known me somewhere. We struck up an easy acquaintance at once, and he talked with the fluency of true conviction.

Sure enough, within a quarter of an hour I had his whole theory of the origin of the ancient Mexicans. It was not new or original; it was one of the early theories since rejected by later scientists, but plainly the Old Man believed he had discovered it by himself, and perhaps he had. It was religion with him, a poetic, mystical, romantic concept. About the lost continent, and how the original Mexican tribes all came from China or Mongolia in little skiffs, dodging between hundreds of islands now sunk in the sea. He loved believing it and would listen to nothing that threatened to shake his faith.

At once he invited me to go with him on a Sunday to dig in his latest buried city, outside the capital. He explained his system to me. He had unearthed nearly a half-hundred ancient cities in all parts of Mexico. One by one, in his vague phrase, he "turned them over to the government." The government thanked him kindly and sent in a staff of expert scientists to take over, and the Old Man moved on, looking for something new.

Finally by way of reward, they had given him this small and not very important city for his own, to settle down with. He sold in his shop the objects he found in the city, and with the profits he supported the digging operations on Sunday.

He showed me photographs of himself in the early days, always surrounded by Indian guides and pack-mules against landscapes of cactus or jungle, a fine figure of a man with virile black whiskers and a level, fanatic eye. There were rifles strapped to the bales on the pack-mules, and the guards bristled with firearms. "I never carried a gun," he told me. "I never needed to. I trusted my guides, and they trusted me."

I enjoyed the company of the Old Man, his impassioned singleness of purpose, his fervid opinions on his one topic of conversation, and the curiously appealing unhumanness of his existence. He was the only person I ever saw who really seemed as independent and carefree as a bird on a bough.

He ate carelessly at odd hours, fried beans and tortillas from a basket left for him by the wife of his head digger, or he would broil a scrawny chicken on a stick, offer me half, and walk about directing his men, waving the other half. He had an outdoors sort of cleanliness and freshness; his clothes were clean, but very old and mended. Who washed and mended them I never knew. My own life was full of foolish and unnecessary complications, and I envied him his wholeness. I enjoyed my own sentimental notion of him as a dear, harmless, sweet old man of an appealing sociability, riding his hobby-horse in triumph to the grave, houseless but at home, completely free of family ties and not missing them, a happy, devoted man who had known his own mind, had got what he wanted in life, and was satisfied with it. Besides he was in perfect health and never bored.

Crowds of visitors came and bought things, and he dropped the money in a cigar-box behind a showcase. He invited almost everybody to come out and watch him dig on Sundays, and a great many came, week after week, always a new set. He received a good many letters, most of them with foreign post-marks, and after a few rapid glances he dropped them into the drawer of a long table. "I know a lot of people," he said, shuf-fling among the heap one day. "I ought to answer these. Big bugs, too, some of them."

One day, among a pile of slant-eyed clay faces, I found a dusty, dog-eared photograph of a young girl, which appeared to have been taken about fifty years before. She was elegant, fashionable, and so astonishingly beautiful I thought such per-fection could belong only to a world-famous beauty. The Old Man noticed it in my hand. "My wife," he said in his imper-sonal, brisk tone. "Just before we were married. She was about eighteen then."

"She is unbelievably beautiful," I said.

"She was the most beautiful woman I ever saw," he said, matter-of-factly. "She is beautiful still." He dropped the photo-graph in the drawer with the letters and came back talking about something else.

After that, at odd moments, while he was polishing jade beads or brushing the dust off a clay bird, he dropped little phrases about his wife and children. "She was remarkable," he said. "She had five boys in eight years. She was just too proud to have anything but boys, I used to tell her."

Again, later: "She was a perfect wife, perfect. But she wouldn't come to Mexico with me. She said it was no place to bring up children."

One day, counting his money and laying it out in small heaps, one for each workman, he remarked absently: "She's well off, you know—she has means." He poured the heaps into a small sack and left the rest in the cigar-box. "I never wanted more money than I needed from one week to the next," he said. "I don't fool with banks. People say I'll be knocked in the head and robbed some night, but I haven't been, and I won't."

One day we were talking about a plot to overthrow the Gov-ernment which had just been frustrated with a good deal of uproar. "I knew about that months ago," said the Old Man. "One of my politician friends wrote me. . . ." He motioned toward the table drawer containing the letters. "You're interested in those things," he said. "Would you like to read some of those letters? They aren't private."

Would I? I spent a long summer afternoon reading the Old Man's letters from his international big bugs, and I learned then and there that hair *can* rise and blood *can* run cold. There was enough political dynamite in those casually written letters to have blown sky-high any number of important diplomatic and financial negotiations then pending between several powerful governments. The writers were of all sorts, from the high-minded and religious to the hearty, horse-trading type to the worldly, the shrewd, the professional adventurer, down to the natural moral imbecile, but they were all written in simple language with almost boyish candor and an indiscretion so complete it seemed a kind of madness.

I asked him if he had ever shown them to anyone else. "Why, no," he said, surprised at my excitement.

I tried to tell him that if these letters fell into certain hands his life would be in danger. "Nonsense," he said vigorously. "Everybody knows what I think of that stuff. I've seen 'em come and go, making history. Bah!"

"Burn these letters," I told him. "Get rid of them. Don't even be caught dead with them."

"I need them," he said. "There's a lot about ancient Mexican culture in them you didn't notice." I gave up. Perhaps the brink of destruction was his natural habitat.

A few days later, I went up the dusty stairs and, there, in a broad square of sunlight, the Old Man was sitting in a cowhide chair with a towel around his neck, and a woman was trimming his moustache with a pair of nail scissors. She was as tall as he, attenuated, with white hair, and the beauty of an aged goddess. There was an extraordinary pinched, starved kind of sweetness in her face, and she had perfect simplicity of manner. She removed the towel, and the Old Man leaped up as if she had loosed a spring. Their son, a man in middle age, a masculine reincarnation of his mother, came in from the next room, and we talked a little, and the wife asked me with gentle pride if I did not find the shop improved.

It was indeed in order, clean, bare, with the show-windows

and cases set out properly, and tall vases of flowers set about. They were all as polite and agreeable to one another as if they were well-disposed strangers, but I thought the Old Man looked a little hunched and wary, and his wife and son gazed at him almost constantly as if they were absorbed in some fixed thought. They were all very beautiful people, and I liked them, but they filled the room and were not thinking about what they were saying, and I went away very soon.

The Old Man told me later they had stayed only a few days; they dropped in every four or five years to see how he was getting on. He never mentioned them again.

Afterward when I remembered him it was always most clearly in that moment when the tall woman and her tall son searched the face of their mysterious Wild Man with baffled, resigned eyes, trying still to understand him years after words wouldn't work any more, years after everything had been said and done, years after love had worn itself thin with anxieties, without in the least explaining what he was, why he had done what he did. But they had forgiven him, that was clear, and they loved him.

I understood then why the Old Man never carried a gun, never locked up his money, sat on political dynamite and human volcanoes, and never bothered to answer his slanderers. He bore a charmed life. Nothing would ever happen to him.

1942

Corridos

I N Mexico, most of the birds, and all of the people, sing.
They sing out freely and cheerfully, to the extent of the
voice Heaven has endowed them with, in all places, and at all
hours. The lover warbles serenades under the balcony of his
lady, the children sing on their way to school, the truck drivers
and pedlars whistle and sing, the beggars fiddle and murmur
doleful songs about love and death. High pitched, untrained
voices of girls murmur sentimental songs softly to the set waltz
accompaniment of pianos, from *patio* after *patio* the music
floats out as one passes along the bright streets. In a cafe across
from my hotel, a set of lively youngsters used to gather almost
every night in the week and sing at the top of their voices until
the very sunrise. On birthdays and feast days, the guests begin
singing at the windows of the celebrant a little after midnight,
and sing until breakfast time. These charming songs are known
as *las Mañanitas*, (morning songs) modern sister to the old
Provençal madrigal. There are marching songs, dancing, wedding and funeral songs: no possible occasion for singing has
been overlooked, and the gayest, freshest, most spirited popular music in the world can be heard in Mexico.

There is still another type of song, altogether distinct from
these popular airs; these are ruder, lustier, they have a unique
flavor. They are meant to be listened to; one could not dance
to them, the measure is too erratic, and besides, one would
miss the story. This type of song is called the *corrido*, and it is
the primitive, indigenous song of the Mexican people.

The *corrido* is, in effect, a ballad. Mexico is one of the few
countries where a genuine folk poetry still exists, a word of
mouth tradition which renews itself daily in the heroic, sensational or comic episodes of the moment, an instant record of
events, a moment caught in the quick of life. They are informal, copious, filled with irrelevant matter. The story wanders
on by itself, filled with minute details, often with meaningless
words tacked on at the end of a phrase in order to make the

rhyme. But the form is quite definitive, four lines to the verse, eight syllables to the line, and a refrain. If the perfection of this ideal is not always achieved in the stanza, the music takes care of that by deftly crowding the two or three extra syllables into a note meant for one. The effect is hilarious in the extreme, and is usually deliberate.

These *corridos* are composed and sung by the people all over Mexico. The Indians, the country people and the very humble folk of the town, all know these stories. In them are contained their legends and folk lore. Most of them are handed on by word of mouth, and only a comparatively small number have been written down. But for the past twenty-five years the publication of *corridos* has increased. They are printed on spongy, luridly dyed strips of paper and sold, two for a *centavo*, in the markets.

The composers are usually anonymous, so far as the printed sheet is concerned. Theirs is the more subtle fame of the enlightened word spoken among the elect. Popular singers vend the wares during early mornings when the citizens crowd to the narrow cobbled streets of the markets. Among the open booths hung with streamers of bright muslins and thin silks, mounds of pottery and colored glass, the heaped melting fragrance of figs, apricots, mangoes and peaches, birds in wicker cages (those sweet-throated doomed creatures whose modest colors have been disguised with brilliant lead paints, which will shortly bring them to death), withies and mats of palm fiber, fowls whose legs have been broken to keep them from wandering, intricate foods simmering over charcoal *braziers*, soft-eyed, self-possessed Indian girls with small stands of brass and silver jewelry, a huddle of beggars and dogs: there, in some accessible corner, the singers squat, strum their guitars, and sing.

They are uniformly hoarse of voice, but no matter. A certain sweated, rugged earnestness in the telling merely emphasizes the innate quality of the narrative. The *corrido* should be shouted. Shouted it is, and the presence of three or four rival vendors, each with the fixed intention of shouting down his competitor, makes a fine, exciting racket. The crowd collects, it takes sides, offers odds on its favorites. Sometimes an entire family, father, mother, and children even down to the five-year-old, sing turn and turn about, until all are hoarse as corn-crakes —and why not? But the bright colored strips of song sell instantly, everybody wishes the newest one, they go away memorising the story, humming the tune.

The homely, earthy soul of a people is in them: Gay, tragic, superstitious, devout, cruel, in love with life and a little desperate. The stories are always concerned with immediate fundamental things; death, love, acts of vengeance, the appalling malignities of Fate. They celebrate heroes. A hero is usually one who kills huge numbers of his enemies and dies bravely. He must be a bold, high stepping and regardless person, whether he gives his energies to saving his country or to robbing trains. Motives do not matter. They love deeds, concrete and measurable. They wield a truly murderous bludgeon of sarcasm, they have the gift of the grand manner in relating a love tragedy. An amazing air of realism is achieved through their habit of giving names, dates and places. The tune is composed or improvised on the spot, maybe, by the singer. Or they squeeze the lines of a new story into the measures of an old, familiar melody. Either way, they will be remembered, and sung.

A collection of these *corridos* which I have seen,* dating from about 1890, has a curious sub-historical value. Revolution after revolution has risen, broken and passed over the heads of these singers, and there is not a single revolutionary *corrido*. With the true temperament of the minor poet, the folk singer concerns himself with personalities, with intimate emotions, with deeds of heroism and crime. If many of their favorite subjects were revolutionists, it is because the men themselves possessed the admired qualities of nonchalance, bravado and quickness in action. Carranza was not loved by the *corrido* singer: Madero was loved as a saint and a hero. The difference was not one of revolutionary spirit, but of personality. Victoriano Huerta was rightly dubbed "butcher" in several *corridos—and* a poltroon. He let other men do his fighting. That is the root of the *corrido* singers' contempt for him.

Emiliano Zapata, the bandit general who made of Morelos

*Loaned me by Bertram D. Wolfe, of Mexico City.

the first genuinely socialist state of Mexico, was a popular subject of *corridos*. At the time of his assassination, hundreds of rhymed narratives appeared, reflecting every shade of provincial opinion. He was martyr, hero, bandit, a man who betrayed his friends, the savior of his state, a scoundrel who destroyed churches, all depending on the section of the country and the personal bias of the composer . . . but not one of them mentions that he revolutionized the agrarian system of Morelos, or was one of the first Mexicans to apprehend the principles of soviet government. . . . Such things are ephemerae to the maker of ballads. He is concerned with eternal verities.

The records of accident and murder are set down with a taste for explicit horror; after thirty stanzas the singer will break off by saying he cannot finish the sad tale for weeping. It is their habit to begin by asking the attention of those present, in the manner of the Irish "come-all-ye" and to finish by asking prayers for the soul of the singer, or less often, by mentioning the composer's name, adding that he is one of the most talented *corrido* makers of his time.

Within two days after the death of Pancho Villa last year, the street singers were shouting long histories of the event, with melancholy insistence on particulars. "He was dishonorably killed, his entrails were out," sang one, gayly, a literal fact proved by the photograph of the body printed at the top of the sheet. Villa was the hero of hundred *corridos*, and his exploits took on, even while he lived, that legendary character which is the very heart of romance. When going on raids he flew in aeroplanes at a speed of fifty kilometers a minute. He vanquished one hundred fifty thousand Gringos who came to capture Villa, looked about for him, did not see him, ate a great quantity of corn and beans, and so went home again . . . the subject was meat for their intensely personal kind of humor. One says that the poor Texans were so tired when they reached Mexico, the ones on horseback could not sit, and those on foot could not stand. So they all drank freely of *tequila* and lay down.

These ballads are saturated with faith in the supernatural. A very recent one tells of a man born with the head of a pig, who

grew up into an extremely disturbing demon in his community. Devils are gravely accused of aiding a man in Guanajuato
to murder a helpless female. Divine Providence in the shape
of a white angel with wings intervened when two bandits attempted to rob a priest. The apparition of the Virgin of Guadalupe takes place somewhere in Mexico, and endless *corridos*
piously give the facts of the event. Illustrations sometimes accompany them, rude cuts used many times over, of strange
devils, horned and tailed and saber-toothed, blood kin to
those of Albrecht Dürer. They urge weak mortals into crime,
usually murder or sacrilege.

Laments for the dead are often joined with the story of how
the mourner has seen and talked with the ghost. Beautiful
young ladies who died unwed are notably restless. They are
always rising and frightening their families by appearing at the
midnight hour, wan, covered with grave mold, bitterly complaining of their too-early fate.

The laments have passionate, grieved choruses: "Oh, Death,
why didst thou turn thine eyes toward my little flower, the white
rose of my heart?" sings one. "Oh, Death, thou monster, why
didst thou take my child, and leave my step-daughter?" inquires another. And one sturdy souled singer counsels a ghostly
wife to return to her tomb, and leave her husband, now happily
re-wed, in peace.

The loneliness of the men facing death far away from home
and friends is the recurring motif of many *corridos*. They turn
their eyes toward the sky, they invoke birds as messengers. A
young soldier of fortune, finding himself back to wall and the
levelled rifles at his heart, calls on a swallow to fly swiftly and
tell his mother how they are going to kill him. The swallow
takes the message, and the mother comes weeping to kiss her
child goodbye. Ah, the weeping women of the *corridos*. No
man can be so utterly brought down but there will always be
left one devoted, steadfast woman to come, weeping, bringing
what consolation her love can devise. "Pray for her who prayed
for me," sings a dying man after battle, "She who bound up
my wounds and brought me water, she who will remember my
grave when all others have forgotten!"

Corridos celebrating the executions of men taken bearing
arms against the government are curious mixtures of admira-

tion for valor come to a hard death, and cautious warning to all who revolt against the government.

This adding of a postscript, slightly moralistic in tone, is merely a gesture of good manners, a courtesy nod to convention. The story is the thing, and a deliciously terrifying ghost story will end with a warning against faith in apparitions and false miracles. The story of some glittering escapade in outlawry will conclude with a word of caution against hateful anarchy. This is done with perfect gravity, tongue in cheek, eyes beaming with charming, natural malice, all a trifle "edgy," a little impious, perfect complaisant mirror of the popular mind.

A *corrido* still popular, with the wicked mother-in-law motif, has many marks of extreme antiquity. It is called "Marbella and the Newly-born," and resembles the old English carol of Mary and the Cherry Tree, in which the unborn child speaks in defense of his mother.

Marbella, the *corrido* begins, was in the hard pains of birth that brought her to her knees. Her lord the Count was absent, and the deceitful mother-in-law advises her to return to her home, where she will be in more skillful hands. Marbella utters a moving plaint of homesick longing: "Oh, if I were once more in Castle Valledal at the side of my father the King, he would give me help and comfort. . . . But when my lord comes home, who will give him his supper?" she asks the mother-in-law.

"I will give him bread and wine. There is barley for his horse and meat for the sparrow hawk," answers the wicked woman.

After Marbella has gone her husband comes home and asks for his mirror. The mother asks whether he wants his mirror of fine silver, or the one of crystal, or of ivory? He answers that he wants none of these, but Marbella, his wife, his royal mirror.

The mother tells him that Marbella has betrayed him with a Jew, and has now returned to her father's castle to hide her guilt, and to leave her child there.

The husband, with the fatal credulity of all lovers in tragic love stories, sets off to Castle Valledal and finds Marbella there, surrounded by her maids, her newly born child at her breast. He commands her to rise and come with him. He places the mother at the pillion and the child at his breast straps. They ride for seven leagues without a word, so fast the horse's hooves strike fire from the stones. Marbella implores him, "Do not kill me in this mountain where the eagles may devour me. Leave me in the open road where some merciful soul may find me. Or take me to the hermitage yonder where I may confess, for I am at my last breath." At the hermitage she is taken down, dying, unable to speak. But by the never ending grace of God, the newly born child finds language: "I tell you truly, my mother is going at once to Paradise without a stain on her soul. And now I must go to limbo unless I am baptised, for I shall follow my mother into death. But my wicked grandmother shall suffer eternally for this work."

Over their bodies, the Count swore by the bread and wine that he would not touch food again until he had slain his wicked mother. He placed her in a barrel lined with iron skewers and cast her over a mountain side; because, the song hints, he could invent nothing worse.

A race of singing people . . . used to sorrowful beginnings and tragic endings, in love with life, fiercely independent, a little desperate, but afraid of nothing. They see life as a flash of flame against a wall of darkness. Conscious players of vivid roles, they live and die well, and as they live and die, they sing.

1924

Sor Juana: A Portrait of the Poet

JUANA DE ASBAJE, in religion Sor Juana Inés de la Cruz, was, like most great spirits, at once the glory and the victim of her age. She was born in Mexico in 1651, of aristocratic Spanish parentage, and won the respect of the most advanced scholars of her time by her achievements in mathematics, astronomy, languages, and poetry. Her austere, impassioned and mystical mind led her to the cloister, where she ended by renouncing her studies, and writing out her confession of faith in her own blood.

She was, in her beauty, her learning and her Catholicism, the perfect flowering of seventeenth century European civilization in the New World, a civilization imperfectly transplanted, imposed artificially, due to be swept away by the rising flood of revolution. But her own pure and candid legend persists and grows, a thing beloved for its unique beauty. She died in her forty-fifth year of a plague which swept Mexico City. This sonnet is almost literally translated.

TO A PORTRAIT OF THE POET

by Sor Juana Inés de la Cruz
translated from the Spanish by Katherine Anne Porter

This which you see is merely a painted shadow
Wrought by the boastful pride of art,
With falsely reasoned arguments of colours,
A wary, sweet deception of the senses.

This picture, where flattery has endeavored
To mitigate the terrors of the years,
To defeat the rigorous assaults of Time,
And triumph over oblivion and decay—

Is only a subtle careful artifice,
A fragile flower of the wind,
A useless shield against my destiny.

It is an anxious diligence to preserve
A perishable thing: and clearly seen
It is a corpse, a whirl of dust, a shadow,—
      nothing.

1924

Notes on the Life and Death of a Hero

Introduction to
The Itching Parrot (*El Periquillo Sarniento*),
by José Joachín Fernández de Lizardi (The Mexican Thinker),
translated from the Spanish by Katherine Anne Porter.
Garden City, N.Y.: Doubleday, Doran & Co., 1942.

THE author of *The Itching Parrot* was born November 15, 1776, in Mexico City, baptized the same day, in the parish church of Santa Cruz y Soledad, and christened José Joaquín Fernández de Lizardi.

His parents were Creoles (Mexican-born Spaniards), vaguely of the upper middle class, claiming relationship with several great families. They were poor, she the daughter of a bookseller in Puebla, he a rather unsuccessful physician, a profession but lately separated from the trade of barber. They made an attempt to give their son the education proper to his birth, hoping to prepare him for the practice of law.

The child, who seems to have been precocious, willful, and somewhat unteachable, spent his childhood and early youth in an immensely Catholic, reactionary, socially timid, tight-minded atmosphere of genteel poverty and desperately contriving middle-class ambitions. Though his parents' heads were among the aristocracy, their feet threatened daily to slip into the dark wallow of the lower classes, and their son witnessed and recorded their gloomy struggle to gain enough wealth to make the worldly show that would prove their claim to good breeding. There was no other way of doing it. In Spain, as in Europe, scholarship might be made to serve as a second choice, but in Mexico there was no place for scholarship. The higher churchly honors were reserved for the rich and nobly born; as for the army, it offered for a young Mexican only the most ignoble end: a father could wield as the last resort of authority the threat to send his son to be a soldier.

The outlook was pretty thin for such as our hero. But he was to prove extraordinarily a child of his time, and his subsequent career was not the result of any personal or family plan, but

943

was quite literally created by a movement of history, a true world movement, in which he was caught up and spun about and flung down again. His life story cannot be separated in any particular from the history of the Mexican Revolutionary period. He was born at the peak of the Age of Reason, in the year that the thirteen states of North America declared themselves independent of England. When he was a year old, the United States government decreed religious freedom. In Mexico the Inquisition was still in power, and the Spanish clergy in that country had fallen into a state of corruption perhaps beyond anything known before or since. The viceregal court was composed entirely of Spanish nobles who lived in perpetual luxurious exile; the Indian people were their natural serfs, the mixed Indian and Spanish were slowly forming a new intractable, unpredictable race, and all were ruled extravagantly and unscrupulously by a long succession of viceroys so similar and so unremarkable it is not worth while to recall their names.

The French Revolution occurred when Lizardi was about fourteen years old. At twenty, he was a student in the University of Mexico, College of San Ildefonso. It is not likely that any newfangledness in social or political theory had yet managed to creep in there. There was very little thinking of any kind going on in Mexico at that time, but there were small, scattered, rapidly increasing groups of restless, inquiring minds, and whoever thought at all followed eagerly the path of new doctrines that ran straight from France. The air was full of mottoes, phrases, namewords for abstractions: Democracy, the Ideal Republic, the Rights of Man, Human Perfectibility, Liberty, Equality, Fraternity, Progress, Justice, and Humanity; and the new beliefs were based firmly on the premise that the first duty of man was to exercise freedom of conscience and his faculty of reason.

In Mexico as in many other parts of the world, it was dangerous to mention these ideas openly. All over the country there sprang up secret political societies, disguised as clubs for literary discussion; these throve for a good many years before discussion became planning, and planning led to action and so to revolution.

In 1798, his twenty-second year, Lizardi left the university without taking his bachelor's degree, perhaps because of poverty, for his father died about this time, and there seems to have been nothing much by way of inheritance. Or maybe he was such a wild and careless student as he describes in *El Periquillo*. It is also possible that he was beginning to pick up an education from forbidden sources, such as Diderot, d'Alembert, Voltaire, Rousseau. At any rate, he never ceased to deplore the time he had spent at acquiring ornamental learning, a thing as useless to him, he said, as a gilded coach he could not afford to keep up. The fact seems to be, his failure was a hard blow to his pride and his hopes, and he never ceased either to bewail his ignorance. "To spout Latin is for a Spaniard the surest way to show off his learning," he commented bitterly, and himself spouted Latin all his life by way of example. In later days he professed to regret that his parents had not apprenticed him in an honest trade. However, there was no help for it, he must live by his wits or not at all.

After he left the university without the indispensable academic laurel that would have admitted him to the society of the respectably learned, he disappeared, probably penniless, for seven long years. These years of the locust afterwards were filled in suitably with legends of his personal exploits as a revolutionary. He was supposed to have known Morelos, and to have been in active service with the early insurgents. He says nothing of this in his own account of his life, written a great while afterwards: it is probable that he was a public scrivener in Acapulco. In 1805 he returned to Mexico City and married Doña Dolores Orendain, who brought him a small dowry. As late as 1811 he appears to have been a Justice of the Peace in Taxco, when Morelos took that town from the Viceroy's troops, and was said to have delivered secretly a store of royalist arms and ammunition to Morelos. For this act he was supposed to have been arrested, taken to Mexico, tried and freed, on the plea that he had acted not of his own will but under threat of death from Morelos' insurgents.

The particularly unlikely part of this story is that the royalist officers would never have taken the trouble to escort Lizardi, an obscure young traitor to the Spanish throne, all the way from Taxco to Mexico City for trial. It is still a long road, and was then a terrible journey of several days. They would have shot him then and there, without further ceremony. A more

unlikely candidate than Lizardi for gun-toting was never born.
He shared with all other humanist reformers from Erasmus
onward a hatred of war, above all, civil war, and his words on
this subject read like paraphrases from Erasmus' own writings,
as indeed many of them were. Lizardi's services to his country
were of quite another kind, and his recompense was meager to
the last degree.

Just when those agile wits of his, which he meant to live by,
first revealed themselves to him as intransigent and not for sale,
it is difficult to discover. As late as 1811 he wrote a poem in
praise of the Virgin of Guadalupe, who had protected the capital city and defeated by miracle the insurgent army led by Hidalgo. He wrote another entirely loyal and conventional poem
to celebrate the accession of Philip VII to the Spanish throne.
He belonged with the Liberal faction, that is, he opposed alike
the excesses of the extreme insurgents and the depravities of
the viceroys, he began by believing himself to be a citizen of the
world, wrote against narrow patriotism, and refused to put
himself at the service of any lesser cause than that of absolute
morality, in every department of state and church. His literary
career began so obscurely that it is difficult to trace its beginnings, but by 1811 he was writing and publishing, on various
presses in Mexico City, a copious series of pamphlets, poems,
fables, dialogues, all in the nature of moral lectures with rather
abstract political overtones, designed to teach broadly social
sanity, political purity, and Christian ethics. These were sold in
the streets, along with a swarm of broadside, loose-leaf literature by every kind of pamphleteer from the most incendiary
Mexican nationalist to the most draggle-tailed anonymous
purveyors of slander and pornography.

A series of rapid events occurred which brought Lizardi out
into the open, decided the course of his beliefs and therefore
of his acts, and started him once for all on his uncomfortable
career as perpetual dissenter. In 1810 the Council of Cádiz decreed the freedom of the press, for Spain and her colonials.
The Viceroy of Mexico, Xavier Vanegas, believed, with his overworked board of censors, that the Mexican press had already
taken entirely too much freedom for itself. He suppressed the
decree, by the simple means of refraining from publishing it.

By July, 1811, the insurgent army under Hidalgo had been

defeated, and late in that month the heads of Hidalgo and his fellow heroes, Aldama, Jimínez, and Allende, were hanging as public examples in iron cages at Guanajuato. The Empire was re-established, with Vanegas still Viceroy, and during that year and into the next, the censorship of the press became extremely severe. Every printer in Mexico was required to show a copy of every title he published, and among the items that showed up regularly were quite hundreds of flimsy little folders with such names as "The Truthful Parrot," in which a loquacious bird uttered the most subversive remarks in the popular argot of the lower classes, mixed freely with snatches of rhyme, puns in Mexican slang, and extremely daring double meanings. There were such titles as "The Dead Make No Complaints"; "The Cat's Testimony," a fable imitating La Fontaine; "It Is All Right to Cut the Hair But Don't Take the Hide Too," which in Spanish contains a sly play on words impossible to translate; "There Are Many Shepherds Who Shall Dance in Bethlehem," another punning title, meaning that many priests shall go to Belén (Bethlehem), the great prison which exists still in Mexico City; "Make Things So Clear That Even the Blind May See Them"; "Even Though Robed in Silk, a Monkey Is Still a Monkey"; "All Wool Is Hair," which has a most salty double meaning; "The Nun's Bolero," concerning scandals in convents; "The Dog in a Strange Neighborhood"; "The Devil's Penitents"—these were only a few of the provocations Lizardi showered upon the censors, the royalist party, the church, venal politicians of all parties, social and political abuses of every kind. The censors could hardly find a line that did not contain willful but oblique offense, yet nothing concrete enough to pin the author down on a criminal charge, so the Council of Safety contented itself with harrying him about somewhat, suppressing his pamphlets from time to time, forbidding various presses to publish for him, and threatening him occasionally with worse things.

But it is plain that Lizardi had discovered that he was, in particular, a Mexican, and a patriotic one, though still in general a citizen of the world. It would seem that those truly heroic heads of Father Hidalgo and the others in Guanajuato had brought him down from the airy heights of abstract morality to a solid and immediate field of battle. For, in June,

1812, three months before the new constitution took effect, Viceroy Vanegas, who seems to have been a rather weak, short-sighted man, alarmed by the continued rebelliousness of a people he had believed he had conquered, took a fateful step. He issued an edict condemning to death all churchmen of regular or secular state who might take part in the revolution. This clause dealt with those many priests who rose to take the place of Father Hidalgo. All officers from the rank of sublieutenant upwards were condemned to death. There were all over the country an immense number of captainless men who went independently into battle. These were to be decimated on the spot wherever captured. This last clause might seem to have covered the business; but the Viceroy added a final generous provision for wholesale slaughter. After such decimation, those who by chance had escaped death were, if convenient, to be sent to the Viceroy for suitable punishment. If this was not convenient, it was left to the discretion of each commandant to do with them as he saw fit.

So far, the edict was in its nature a fairly routine measure in times of emergency. But there was a further clause condemning to death all authors of incendiary gazettes, pamphlets or other printed matter. This was sensational, considering that unpublished decree granting freedom of the press. The liberal wing of the Constitutionalist (or royalist) party, together with all the forces that aimed for a peaceable settlement and some sort of compromise with the revolutionists, protested against this edict and advised the Viceroy seriously against such drastic means. The Viceroy did not cancel the edict, but as a sop to public opinion, he did publish the Cádiz decree on October 5, 1812, and the Mexican press, theoretically at least, was free.

Lizardi was ready to take advantage of this freedom. He leaped into print just four days later with the first number of his first periodical, which had for title his own pen name, *The Mexican Thinker*. For two numbers he praised the glories of a free press and the wonders of liberty, but in the third he broke out in high style against the whole Spanish nation, its pride, its despotism; against the corruptions of the viceregal court, the infamies of officials in every station. Seeing that no revenge overtook him, he dared further in a later number: "There is no civilized nation which has a worse government than ours, and the worst in America, nor any other vassal country that has suffered more harshly in its arbitrary enslavement." He turned upon the Spanish governors the very words they had used against Hidalgo. "Cursed monsters," he wrote, and printed, and sold in the streets to be read by all, "you despots and the old evil government are responsible for the present insurrection, not as you say the Cura Hidalgo. It is you together who have stripped our fields, burned our villages, sacrificed our children and made a shambles of this continent."

It is worth noticing here that among his fellow pamphleteers, Lizardi was famous for his moderate language and his courtesy in debate.

No consequences followed this wrathful page. Lizardi went on safely enough until the ninth number, published on December 2, 1812. He devoted this number to an appeal to the Viceroy Vanegas to revoke at least that clause of the edict against revolutionaries which called for the trial of insurgent priests before a military court. He also wrote a personal letter to the Viceroy, timed the publication date to coincide with the Viceroy's Saint's Day, and appeared at court with a specially printed copy. With his own hands he delivered this little bombshell into the very hands of Vanegas, and received the viceregal thanks.

It is hardly probable that Vanegas troubled to examine the papers given him, but the Council of Safety, alarmed, informed him of its contents. The following day the Viceroy and his council suspended the freedom of the press, "for reason of the unsettled conditions of the country." They sent for Lizardi's printer, manager of the Jáurigui press, who admitted that Lizardi had written the offending article.

On the fifth of December they ordered Lizardi to appear before the Court. He disappeared into ineffectual hiding in the house of a friend, Gabriel Gil, where, at three o'clock in the morning, December 7, he was seized and taken to prison. He wrote the story ten years later at great length, and he was still as indignant as he was the day it occurred, but he was proud, also, of the number of men who came to help with the arrest. There were more than seventy of the "dirty birds."

It must be remembered that, under the edict, Lizardi was in danger of death. It would appear his jailers set out methodically to terrorize him, and they succeeded. It does not appear that his judges had any intention of sentencing him to death, but the whole proceedings had the air of making a stern example of troublesome scribblers. They put him in the death cell, where he passed a hideous night, expecting a priest to come to administer the last rites, expecting to be tortured, mistaking the rattle of the jailor's keys for chains. In the morning they took him before a judge he knew, and suspected of having headed the plot to imprison him, where he had to listen patiently to a great deal of foul insult and injury.

Lizardi, in the speeches of his celebrated hero, El Periquillo, declared repeatedly that he feared physical violence more than anything else. The Periquillo is merry and shameless about it, for cowardice is possibly the most disgraceful trait known to man in Mexico, but his author did not find it amusing in himself. Later in his defense to the Viceroy he admitted quite simply that he had refused to obey the first summons to appear because he feared violence and not because he had a sense of guilt. His fears were reasonable. Worse had happened to other men for less cause, or at any rate for no more.

Still, when he gathered that harsh language was probably going to be the worst of it, and he was not going to be tortured and hanged, or at any rate, not that day, he recovered his spirits somewhat and took a rather bantering tone with his infuriated questioners. He was a tall, slender man of a naturally elegant manner, of the longheaded, well-featured Hidalgo kind; his portrait shows a mouth sensitive almost to weakness, and a fine alert picaresque eye. His judges, being also Spanish, and prone to judge a man's importance by his dress—a reflection of his financial state, which was in turn proof of his caste— were inclined to doubt he was so dangerous as they had thought, since Lizardi at that moment was "emaciated, pallid, of shabby appearance," with his "black cloak smeared and crumpled from using it as a bed" in his cell; ten years after he remembered with regret that he had no time to clean it properly before having to show himself. Lizardi told them that indeed they were right, not he but two ladies, one respectable, the other plebeian, had written the articles. They insisted humorlessly that he explain himself. He sobered down and confessed himself as the author. "The respectable lady was the constitu-

tion of Cádiz, which allowed him to write on political questions; the plebeian was his own ignorance which had misled
him into believing the Viceroy would not be angered by a request to revoke an edict distasteful to the people."

Their ferocity rose at this, they demanded an account of his
whole life, and pursued him with questions meant to trap him
until, seeing the affair still threatened to be serious, he grew
frightened again and implicated his friend Gabriel Gil as well as
Carlos María Bustamante, an active insurgent, and writer, who
had "warned him his life was in danger and advised him to
leave the city."

Probably because of these interesting bits of evidence and
not, as Lizardi boasted years afterwards, on account of his own
astuteness, for he certainly does not seem to have shown any,
the sentence of solitary confinement was lifted, he was re-
manded to the common jail among a number of his comrade
insurgent prisoners and Gil was arrested.

Feeling himself betrayed by the man whom he had befriended at so much danger to himself, Gil said that Lizardi
had come to him in distress, and that he, Gil, had done his best
to persuade him to obey the summons. Gil then went on to
make a bad matter worse by saying that Lizardi had confided
that a certain friend had told him he could escape safely with
five hundred insurgents who were about to leave the city.

In panic, Lizardi denied this and involved another friend,
Juan Olaeta, who had, Lizardi said, offered to allow him to
escape with the insurgents. Olaeta, brought before the judges,
passed on the responsibility to an unnamed priest from Toluca,
who had overheard a conversation between two persons unknown to him, concerning the plans of five hundred insurgents who were about to leave the city. Olaeta's part had been
merely an offer to Lizardi to take him to the priest. Lizardi insisted to Olaeta's face that Olaeta had "told him the Tolucan
priest would arrange for his escape with the insurgents. Olaeta
insisted that Lizardi had misunderstood him, and the two, together with Gabriel Gil, were sent back to jail." If they were in
the same cell, it must have been a frightfully embarrassing situation for Lizardi. And he was not done yet.

After nine days in prison, exhausted by repeated questioning
and anxieties, he wrote a personal appeal to the Viceroy saying

in effect and in short that he had acted innocently in handing him the protest against the edict and that before giving it he had shown it to a priest who approved of it, and by way of justifying himself further, he added with appalling lack of ethical sense that Carlos María Bustamante, and a Doctor Peredo had "written with more hostility than he against the same edict." He continued to drag names into the business, adding that of a Señor Torres, and even blaming his error on them.

The first judge advised the Viceroy to turn Lizardi's case over to the Captain General and the Military Court. Lizardi asked for bail which was his constitutional right, but it was refused. He was handed about from court to court, military and civil, for months, gradually modifying his statements, or retracting, or insisting that he had been misunderstood. Gil and Olaeta were freed, Bustamante, Torres and Peredo were never arrested at all, and Bustamante, an admirable and heroic spirit, never held any grudge against him, but wrote well of him afterwards. But Lizardi lingered on in jail, writing to the Viceroy, asking for an attorney, asking that his case be turned over to the war department, being mysteriously blocked here and there by hostile agencies, and there he might have stayed on to the end if Vanegas had not been succeeded as Viceroy on March 4, 1813, by Calleja.

Lizardi began a fresh barrage of importunities and explanations to this new, possibly more benign power. He praised him for the good he hoped for from him, and published this praise as a proclamation of the Thinker to the People of Mexico. This got him no new friends anywhere and did not get him his liberty either. He was allowed now and then to visit his family, which consisted of his wife, a newly born daughter, and four unnamed members which, dependent upon him, were almost starving. He had supported them somewhat while in prison by getting out number 10 and number 11 of *The Mexican Thinker*, in December, and number 12 and number 13 in January, but in a considerably chastened and cautious style.

One of its periodic plagues came upon Mexico City and raged as usual, and the churches were crowded with people kissing the statues and handing on the disease to each other. In one number of *The Thinker*, Lizardi advised them to clean up the streets, to burn all refuse, to wash the clothes of the sick not in the public fountains but in a separate place, not to bury the dead in the churches, and as a final absurdity, considering the time and place, he counseled them to use the large country houses of the rich as hospitals for the poor. None of these things was done, the plague raged on and raged itself out.

Lizardi also wrote a statement of his quarrel with the existing state of politics, but a very discreet one, and he could think of no better remedy, his own situation being still perilous as it was, than that both sides in the struggle should obey the counsels of Christ and love one another.

Naturally this sloppy thinking brought upon him the contempt of all sides. The royalists thought no better of him than before, and the liberals, who favored the new constitution, now distrusted him, as they had no intention of loving either an out-and-out royalist or any insurgent, and as for the insurgents themselves, they damned Lizardi freely.

All this was going on, remember, while our hero was still in prison.

In Mexico there was the celebrated "Society of Guadalupe," the most effective of such societies which, under cover of more polite interests, were at the service of Morelos and kept him well informed of events in the capital. The new Viceroy, Calleja, proved to be an even more bitter enemy of the insurgents than Vanegas had been, and Lizardi's unfortunate eulogy of Calleja had been sent to Morelos with a note by a member of the Society of Guadalupe. "This person," said the note, "is not worth your attention, because when they imprisoned him, he showed his weakness, and has written several pamphlets praising this damnable government, and has most basely harmed several men."

At last the Viceroy, finding no new things against Lizardi, wearied of the case; the last judge who took it over recommended that Lizardi be set free, and so he was, on July 1, 1813, after nearly seven months in prison. "Enough to ruin me, as I was ruined, with my family," he wrote.

This is the least handsome episode of Lizardi's life, and he behaved like a green recruit stampeded under his first fire, who may yet become as good a soldier as any man. Lizardi became a better soldier than most, and if he had been once afraid to die, he was not afraid to suffer a long, miserable existence for the sake of his beliefs. He was by no means ruined. He had scarcely been scotched. He returned to his dependents, his six-month-old daughter and the wife who had almost died at her birth, to a brazier without coals and a cupboard without food; and sat down at once to write indignantly against all the causes of misery and the effects of injustice in this maddening world.

The Holy Office of the Inquisition had recently been abolished by decree. Lizardi, with that unbelievable speed of his, wrote a history of that institution, a very bitter history, and he rejoiced over its downfall. He published it on September 30, 1813, as a number of *The Thinker*, and went on with his many projects for local reforms, not attacking the government except by indirection. He wrote against ignorant doctors; against the speculators in food who hoarded for higher prices; he wrote rebuking the Creoles, telling them they had the vices of both the Indians and the Spaniards. If he had poured boiling oil upon them he could not have offended them more bitterly. He wrote against the depravity of the lower classes, and the plague of thieves, beggars, and drunkards in the streets. In November he enjoyed a small popular triumph. A crowd gathered at sight of him and cheered him in the street, shouting that he told them the naked truth. ("La Verdad Pelada" was one of his most lively efforts.) But no royalist or liberal or insurgent or priest or anyone that mattered then was in this cheering rabble; these were the shirtless ones, the born losers no matter which side might win. They shouted his name, and worsened his reputation, but they did not follow his advice and could not if they would. They liked him because he was sharp and angry, full of their own kind of humor, and talked to them in their own language. It was the first time they had ever seen their own kind of talk in print. The flattery was great and they responded to it; for a few centavos they could buy this highly flavored reading matter which expressed all their secret wrongs and grudges and avenged them vicariously; and his words worked afterwards in their thoughts; they trusted him and believed him.

In December, 1813, three months after Lizardi's attack, the Inquisition was reestablished. The absolutist monarch Ferdinand VII after his eclipse was back on the throne of Spain, and all grudgingly granted liberties were at an end again for Spain and her colonies.

Lizardi was by then a man without a party indeed. For in that month someone of the Society of Guadalupe sent Morelos a marked copy of Lizardi's attack on the native-born Mexicans, commenting: "Merely to show you how this author abuses us. We know his weakness since the time of his imprisonment, and we wish that in the press of Oaxaca you shall give him a good shaking up [literal translation] as a mere sycophant."

And one month later, January 14, 1814, a priest called the attention of the head Inquisitor, Flores, to *The Mexican Thinker*'s denunciation of the Inquisition. More than a year later Flores sent the article to two priests for examination, and in June, 1815, they denounced it as "a mass of lies, impostures, iniquitous comparisons, scandals, seductions, offensive to pious ears, injurious to the sanctity of the sovereign Popes, and the piety of our monarch."

Once more the harassed manager of the Jáuregui press was tracked down, this time by an officer of the Inquisition. The printer said that Lizardi lived in Arco Street, number 3, tenement A, then reconsidered and said Lizardi had lived there when he wrote the article but was now living in Prieto Nuevo Street. Lizardi was always moving about from one poverty-stricken tenement in a shabby back street to another. Nothing more came of this affair just then.

The only sign Lizardi gave that he knew he had been denounced to the Inquisition was a softening in the tone of his indignation, a generally lowered quality of resistance, a methodical search for themes on which he might express himself freely without touching too dangerous topics. That year he wrote some rather sensible plans for relieving the sufferings of lepers; against gambling and gambling houses; and criticisms of the prevailing system of public education. He began a campaign for modern education, based on the ideas of Blanchard, a Jesuit priest who had modified Rousseau's theories as expressed in *Emile* "to suit the needs of Christian education."

Sometime during 1815 Lizardi tried a new series of pamphlets under a single title, "Alacena de Frioleras," meaning a cupboard of cold food, scraps, leftovers. He fell into disgrace with the censors at the second number, and was refused license to print it. He was bitterly discouraged but not without some resources still. He decided to try his hand at a novel; what censor would look for political ideas in a paltry fiction?

Lizardi's friend Dr. Beristain, a man of letters, who was writing and compiling a Library of Northern Spanish Americana, did not agree with the censors, but declared Lizardi to be "an original genius, native of New Spain." Dr. Beristain also believed that Lizardi, for his knowledge of the world and of men, and for his taste in literature, merited to be called "if not the American Quevedo, at least the Mexican Torres Villaroel . . . he has now in hand a life of Periquito Sarmiento, which judging by what I have seen of it, much resembles Guzman de Alfarache."

The censor's report for February, 1816, mentions the appearance of *El Periquillo* from the prologue to chapter 6; in July, another series of chapters; the third series was suppressed on November, 29, 1816, because it contained an attack on the system of human slavery.

This is the first mention of that book, undertaken as Lizardi's last hope of outwitting the censorship, as well as of making a living by its sales as it was being written. He finished it, but it was not published in full until after his death.

There followed a long dreary period of pamphlet writing, against bullfighting, against dandyism—his Don Catrín remains a stock character in that line until today—calendars, almanacs, stainless essays on morals and manners, hymns and little songs for children. In the meantime the insurgents, who had been growing in strength, were weakened and the Liberal-Constitutionalist party got into power. At once they suppressed both the Inquisition and the Board of Press Censorship, and at once Lizardi was ready for them. He founded a small periodical called *The Lightning Conductor* and began to tell again the naked truth.

There were to be several changes of government yet during Lizardi's lifetime, but there was never to be one he could get along with, or accept altogether. After twenty-four numbers of *The Lightning Conductor*, he could not find a printer who would risk printing his periodical for him. Lizardi by no means defended the entire Constitutionalist idea, he only defended those tendencies which led to such reforms as he had just wit-nessed in regard to the Inquisition and the censorship. But in doing this he offended again the rockbound royalist clergy, who used the whip of spiritual authority to force their parish-ioners to oppose the constitution, as it curtailed the Spanish power and automatically their own. These and all other die-hard royalists hated Lizardi; the insurgents distrusted him. He was a gadfly to the Viceroy, always addressing complaints directly to him: he was opposed to war still, civil war above all, and considered the insurgents to be almost as obnoxious to the good of the country as the royalists themselves. He con-sidered himself "as Catholic as the Pope," but the clergy hated and attacked him bitterly. A priest named Soto wrote such a vicious pamphlet against him that the censors suppressed it.

During that period, almost frantic in his hornets' nest of personal and public enemies, Lizardi found time and a little money to open a reading room, where for a small fee the pub-lic might read the current books, newspapers, pamphlets. Almost nobody came to read, he lost his money and closed the place after a few months.

The struggle between Mexico and Spain was approaching the grand climax, and with peculiar timeliness Lizardi did precisely the thing calculated to get him into trouble. In February, 1821, Augustín Iturbide and Canon Monteagudo, at the head of the Anti-constitutionalist party, boldly declared themselves ready to separate Mexico from Spain, without any further compro-mises. The Liberal party had held out for an independence to be granted by Spain, peacefully. The new constitution granted when Vanegas was Viceroy had been a makeshift affair, with no real concessions in it. Iturbide's party appeared to be only the acting head of the insurgents, for this seizing of independence for Mexico was exactly what the insurgents had been fighting for all along. Iturbide, with an ambition of his own, decided to use the strength of the insurgents and the growing nationalist spirit to his own ends. He and Monteagudo published their program as the Plan of Iguala.

In the meantime, Lizardi had been writing on this topic, too. Just four days after the Plan of Iguala was published, Lizardi printed a pamphlet which was described as a serio-comic dialogue between two popular and sharp-tongued characters called Chamorro arid Dominiquín. They discussed the possibilities of independence for Mexico, and looked forward to the day of freedom, believed it would be a good thing for both countries, but still hoped it might be granted legally by the Spanish government.

The liberal constitutionalist but still very royalist government, with its free press, saw nothing to laugh at in this work, suppressed it at once, arrested Lizardi and kept him in jail for several days. On this occasion he flattered no one, implicated no one, and retracted nothing. He was released, and wrote a halfhearted pamphlet on the beauties of reconciliation between factions. And in his next pamphlet he stated boldly a change of mind. "It is true that if we do not take our independence by force of arms, they will never concede us our liberty by force of reason and justice."

When he had been imprisoned, he was accused of being a follower of Iturbide, and a supporter of the Plan of Iguala. Lizardi replied merely that he had not known about the plan when he wrote his own suggestions; in effect no answer at all, and perhaps true in itself. But immediately after this last pamphlet boldly counseling the violent way to freedom, the next thing we know, Lizardi is showing a letter from Iturbide to a certain Spaniard, and this Spaniard is supplying him with money and equipment and a horse, and Lizardi, by urgent request of Iturbide, is riding toward Tepotzotlan to take charge of the insurgent press there. This press was devoted entirely to the doctrine of Mexican independence and the necessity of gaining it by force.

Iturbide's troops fought their way steadily through the country toward Mexico City, and Lizardi was close on their heels with his press turning out patriotic broadsides. Iturbide entered the capital in triumph on September 21, 1821. The great deed was accomplished, the eleven years of revolutionary war came to a close, and Mexico was declared an independent government. Lizardi naturally entered the city in triumph also, with his press still going at top speed. Let the censors fume. He had a whole victorious army with him.

There was still no thought in anyone's mind of establishing a Republic. Lizardi expressed the hopes of the victors clearly:

that Iturbide should be made Emperor by acclamation, at the first session of Congress. "Oh," cried our misguided hero, who had waited so long to espouse any faction, and now had taken to heart so utterly the wrong one, "may I have the joy of kissing once the hand of the Emperor of America, and then close my eyes forever in death."

How little becoming to Lizardi was this new garment of acquiescence. It was never made for him and he could not carry it off. Two months later his eyes, closed in enthusiasm, were opened violently, he gazed clearly upon the object of his infatuation, and rejected it. He saw that Iturbide had done as other ambitious men do. He had used the force of a great popular movement to seize power for himself, and meant to set himself up as head of a government more oppressive if possible than the old.

Lizardi wrote a pamphlet called "Fifty Questions to Whoever Cares to Answer Them," and the questions were very embarrassing to the new Emperor, to the church authorities leagued with him, and to all who had promised reforms in government. Iturbide had at least gone through the formality of having himself elected Emperor, and Lizardi accused the priests of controlling the election. They called Lizardi unpatriotic, hostile to religion, accused him of political ambitions. Iturbide was disconcerted by the sudden defection of a man to whom he had given money and a press and a horse to boot, and finding that Lizardi was abusing the freedom of the press, urged that a new censorship be established.

Finding himself the chief obstacle to that freedom of the press which had now become his main object in life, Lizardi proceeded to multiply his offenses. Freemasonry had been creeping in quietly from France by way of Spain. It was the nightmare of the Church everywhere and two Popes had issued bulls against it: Clement XII in 1738, Benedict XIV in 1751. The alarmed clergy in Mexico republished these bulls in 1821, and by way of response Lizardi wrote a pamphlet called plainly "A Defense of the Freemasons." He used arguments that were in the main those of a good Christian, an informed Catholic and a fairly good student of the Bible. It was also a heated, tactless and illogical performance, and the Church simply came down on him like a hammer. Nine days after the

pamphlet was published, Lizardi was publicly and formally excommunicated by the board of ecclesiastical censorship, and
the notice was posted in all the churches.

So it was done at last, and The Thinker passed a little season
in hell which made all his former difficulties seem, as he would
say, "like fruit and frosted cake." He was kept more or less a
prisoner in his own house, where by the rules no member of
his own household was supposed to speak to him, or touch
him, or help or serve him in any way.

It is improbable that this state of affairs ever existed in that
family, but the neighbors would not speak to his wife or
daughter, they had great hardships procuring food, and no
servant would stay in the house. When he ventured out certain
persons drew aside from him; at least once a small mob gathered and threatened to stone him; a group of friars also threatened to come and beat him in his own house, and he advised
them defiantly to come well prepared. They did not come,
however. He had no defenders for no one would defend an
excommunicated man. His wife went to appeal to the Vicar-
General, who would not allow her to approach or speak, but
waved her away, shouting, "In writing, in writing," since it was
forbidden to speak to any member of his family.

Lizardi, announcing that he was "as Catholic as the Pope,"
which in fact he does not seem to have been, began to defend
himself. It was a sign of the times that he could still find presses
to print his pamphlets. He appealed to Congress to have the
censure of the Church lifted within the prescribed legal period,
and asked that body to appoint a lawyer to defend him in the
secular courts, but nothing was done in either case. He continued to harry the government, giving sarcastic advice to Iturbide, and recorded with pride that after he had been cut off
from human kind by his excommunication his friends were
more faithful than ever. It is true he did enjoy some rather
furtive moral support from radical sources, but he was bold as
if he had all society on his side. He wrote a second defense of
the Freemasons, wrote a bitter defense of his entire career and
beliefs in the famous "Letter to a Papist," and dragged on his
miserable life somehow until 1823, when Iturbide was over-
thrown by General Antonio López de Santa Ana, head of a
"Federalist" party which pretended to found a Republic based

on the best elements of the American and French models. It turned out to be another dictatorship which lasted for about thirty years, with Santa Ana at its head. The Catholic Church was still the only recognized religion, a blow to Lizardi, but he took hope again. The appearance of the written Constitution deceived him momentarily, and as unofficial uninvited member of the Federalist party he began again agitating for all those reforms so dear to his heart: Freedom of the press, first, last and forever, compulsory free education, religious liberty, liberty of speech and universal franchise, and naturally, almost as a result of these things, justice, sweet justice, for everybody, regardless of race, class, creed or color.

Almost at once he found himself in jail again.

He gives his account of it as follows, tongue in cheek: "In the month of June (1823), I was imprisoned for writing an innocent little paper called 'If Congress Sits Much Longer We Shall Lose Our Shirts.' I described a dream I had in which a set of petty thieves were debating the best way of robbing us . . . they denounced me . . . on the strength of the title alone, arrested me and I was forced to labor again in my own defense." ("Letter to a Papist.")

This must have blown over, for on the 20th of that same June he was again prisoner in St. Andrés' hospital, but this was probably one of those dreary mischances which befall poor people unable to keep up with the rent: at any rate he insulted the landlady and she threw him out of the house, lock, stock, and barrel, accusing him of defamation of her character. He got out of this, too, and in revenge wrote a poem called "Epithalamium" in which he seems to have married off the judge and the landlady with appropriate ribaldry; but they could do nothing as he mentioned no names.

By then no printer would publish for him: he appears to have got hold of a press of his own, but the authorities forbade newsboys to sell his papers in the streets. At last he left the city for a while, but there was no fate for him in such a case except death in exile. He returned and late in December, 1823, he wrote a letter to the ecclesiastical board of censorship, saying he would no longer attempt to defend himself by civil law, and asked for absolution. This was granted and the documents were published in a periodical in January, 1824.

"Time will mend all things," he wrote at about this time, "in effect, today this abuse will be remedied, tomorrow, another . . . in eight or ten years everything will go as it should." He lived by, and for, this illusion, but these are the words of a mortally weary man. He had never been strong and he was already suffering from the tuberculosis of which he was to die. He had at this time an intimation of approaching death.

He began a small bi-weekly sheet called *The Yokel and the Sacristan*, and in June, 1825, a number of this was pronounced heretical. He was given eight days in which to make a reply, and asked for three months, which was not granted. He allowed himself even a little more time than he had asked for, then made an evasive and unsatisfactory reply. He was not pursued any further about this.

The reason may have been that Lizardi had quarreled successfully, even triumphantly, just five months before, with the Bishop of Sonora. This Bishop had issued a manifesto pronouncing the new Federalist Constitution of Mexico Anti-Catholic (in spite of that clause legalizing the Church alone which had so nearly broken Lizardi's spirit). The Bishop argued for the divine right of Kings, and said that God had been deprived of his rights. Lizardi replied with a defense of the republican form of government, in his usual animated style. The public response to him was so great a governmental commission waited upon the Bishop, escorted him to Acapulco and put him on board a ship which returned him to Spain for good. And Santa Ana's government suddenly gave Lizardi a pension of sixty-five pesos a month "to reward him for his services to the revolution, until something better could be found." The something better was the editorship of the official organ of the new government, called *The Gazette*, at a salary of 100 pesos a month. For the times, this was not a bad income for a man who had never had one and this short period was the only one of his life in which Lizardi was free from financial misery. He was at once pestered by his enemies who coveted no doubt the fortune he had fallen into, and though he went on with the job for a year or two, in the end he quarreled with everybody and was out of favor again. . . .

So it went, to the end. The rest of the history has to do with suits for defamation, plays about to be produced and failing, troubles with the censors, suppressions rather monotonously more of the same. "Let the judges answer whether they are fools or bought men," he wrote, when they found for his enemy in a slander trial. He maintained this spirit until the end. He wrote publicly denying that he had ever yielded to the ecclesiastical censors, or asked for absolution. The fact is clear that if he had not done so, the sentence of excommunication would never have been lifted. He boasted of his prudence in the business, and hinted at secret, important diplomatic strategy. Let it go. In the end, it was a matter of yielding, or of starving his family and himself to death.

In 1825, General Guadalupe Victoria, then President, proclaimed the end of slavery. One might have thought this would please Lizardi, and perhaps it did in a measure. But at once he discovered that the proclamation referred only to Negro slaves, and to the outright buying and selling of human flesh. It did not refer to the slavery of the Indian, which he found as bitter and hopeless under the Creole Republic as it had been under the Spanish Viceroys. . . . He pointed out this discrepancy, and insisted that it should be remedied. By that time, he had such a reputation for this kind of unreasonableness, the new government decided to ignore him as far as they were able. He was dismissed from consideration as a crack-brained enthusiast.

By the end of April, 1827, Lizardi knew that death was near. Someone reported on his state of health: he was "a mere skeleton." Lying in bed, he wrote and had printed his "Testament and Farewell of The Mexican Thinker." At some length, and with immense bitterness, he repeated for the last time his stubborn faiths, his unalterable beliefs, his endless opposition to every form of social, political, and human wrong, to every abuse of power and to every shade of dishonesty, particularly the dishonesty of those in power. He still considered himself as Catholic as the Pope, but he could not admit the infallibility of His Holiness. He still did not believe in the apparitions of saints, calling them "mere goblins." He was as good a patriot as ever, but he was still no party man, and he could not condone in the republican government those same abuses he had fought in the days of the Empire. With sad irony he willed to his country "A Republic whose constitution denies religious

freedom; a Cathedral on which the canons would at the first
opportunity replace the Spanish coat of arms; an ecclesiastical
chapter which ignores the civil law altogether; streets full of
stray dogs, beggars, idle police; thieves and assassins who flourish in criminal collusion with corrupt civil employees," and so
on as ever, in minute detail, no evil too petty or too great for
attack, as if they were all of one size and one importance. I
think this does not argue at all a lack of the sense of proportion, but is proof of his extraordinary perception of the implicit relationship between all manifestations of evil, the greater
breeding and nourishing the lesser, the lesser swarming to support and confirm the greater.

He advised the President of the Republic to get acquainted
with the common people and the workers, to study his army
and observe the actions of his ministers; and he desired that his
wife and friends should not make any loud mourning over
him; they were not to light candles around him, and they were
to bury him not in the customary friar's robe, but in the uniform of a soldier. Further, he wished that his wife would pay
only the regular burial fees of seven pesos, and not haggle with
the priest, who would try to charge her more for a select spot
in the cemetery. He wished that his epitaph might be: "Here
lies the ashes of The Mexican Thinker, who did what he could
for his country."

For long days and nights he strangled to death slowly in the
wretched little house, number 27, Fuente Quebrado (The Broken Fountain), with his wife and young daughter watching
him die, unable to relieve his sufferings with even the most
rudimentary comforts, without medical attendance, without
money, almost without food. He called two priests to hear his
final confession, wishing them to be witnesses for each other
that he had not died without the last rites; but he put off receiving Extreme Unction because he hoped the ritual might
be attended by a number of former friends who believed him
to be a heretic. The friends for some reason failed to arrive for
this occasion. Lizardi lingered on, hoping, but no one came;
and on June 27, still hoping, but refusing the ceremony until
his witnesses should arrive, he died. Almost at once it was ru-
mored abroad that he died possessed of the devil. The friends
came then, to see for themselves, and his pitiable corpse was

exposed to public view in the hovel where he died, as proof that the devil had not carried him off.

The next day a few former acquaintances, his family and a small mob of curious busybodies followed the body of Fernández de Lizardi to the cemetery of San Lázaro, and buried him with the honors of a retired Captain. Neither the epitaph that he composed for himself, nor any other, was inscribed on his gravestone, for no stone was ever raised. His wife died within four months and was buried beside him. His fifteen-year-old daughter was given in charge of a certain Doña Juliana Guevara de Ceballos, probably her godmother, or a female relation, who seems to have handed her over to the care of another family whose name is not known. This family removed to Vera Cruz shortly, and there Lizardi's daughter died of yellow fever.

So the grave closed over them all, and Mexico almost forgot its stubborn and devoted Thinker. The San Lázaro cemetery disappeared, and with it his unmarked grave. His numberless pamphlets disappeared, a few into private collections and storerooms of bookshops; a great many more into moldering heaps of wastepaper. In effect, Lizardi was forgotten.

His novel, his one novel that he had never meant to write, which had got itself suppressed in its eleventh chapter, is without dispute The Novel of the past century, not only for Mexico but for all Spanish-speaking countries. It was published in full in 1830, three years after Lizardi's death, and there were eight editions by 1884. In spite of this, in 1885 there appeared an edition, "corrected, explained with notes, and adorned with thirty fine illustrations," and announced as the second edition, though it was really the ninth.

After that, no one troubled any more to number editions correctly or not. Until the recent disaster in Spain, a big popular press in Barcelona reprinted it endlessly at the rate of more than a million copies a year, on pulp paper, in rotten type, with a gaudy paper cover illustrating some wild scene, usually that of the corpse-robbing in the crypt. In Mexico I used to see it at every smallest sidewalk book stall; in the larger shops there were always a good number of copies on hand, selling steadily. It was given to the young to read as an aid to manners and morals, and for a great while it must have been the one source of a liberal education for the great mass of people, the only ethical and moral instruction they could have, for Lizardi's ideas of modern education got no foothold in Mexico for nearly a century after him.

It is not to be supposed that anybody ever read a picaresque tale for the sake of the sugar plums of polite instruction concealed in it, but Lizardi had the knack of scattering little jokes and curious phrases all through his sermons, and he managed to smuggle all his pamphlets into the final version of *El Periquillo*. They were all there, at great length; the dog in the strange neighborhood, the dead who make no noise, the monkey dressed in silk; with all his attacks on slavery, on bullfighting, on dishonest apothecaries and incompetent doctors; his program for enlightened education, his proposals for cleaning the city in time of plague; against the vicious and mercenary clergy, the unscrupulous politicians; against gambling, against—ah well, they are all there, and the trouble for the translator is getting them out again without leaving too many gaps. For try as he might, by no art could the good Thinker make his dreary fanatic world of organized virtue anything but terrifying to the reader, it was so deadly dull. But once these wrappings are stripped from the story, there is exposed a fine, traditional Rogue's Progress, the history of a true pícaro, a younger brother of Guzman de Alfarache, as Dr. Beristain said, or of Gil Blas. He has English relations too—Peregrine Pickle, Roderick Random, Tom Jones, all of that family of lucky sinners who end well. In the best style, more things happen to El Periquillo than might reasonably happen to one man, events move at top speed, disasters pile up; but he comes through one way or another, shedding his last misadventure with a shake of his shoulders, plunging straightway into the next. Like all his kind, he is hard and casual and thickskinned and sentimental, and he shares their expedient, opportunist morality, which always serves to recall to his mind the good maxims of his early upbringing when his luck is bad, but never once when it is good.

The typical pícaro also is always the incomplete hero of his own story, for he is also a buffoon. Periquillo is afflicted with the itch, he loses his trousers during a bullfight in the presence of ladies, he is trapped into the wrong bed by the malice of his best friend, he is led again and again into humiliating situations by wits quicker than his own.

Living by his wits, such as they are, he is a true parasite, attaching himself first to one then another organism to feed upon. He is hardly ever without a "master" or "mentor" or "patron" and this person is always doing something for him, which El Periquillo accepts as his right and gives nothing, or as little as possible, in return.

Only once does he feel real gratitude. After leaving the house of the Chinese Mandarin, improbable visitor from the Island Utopia, whom Periquillo has succeeded in gulling for a while, he has been beaten and called a pimp by three girls. None of his other disgraces could equal this, so he gets drunk and goes to hang himself. He fails of course, goes to sleep instead, and wakes to find himself robbed and stripped to the shirt by wayside thieves. He is rescued by a poor old Indian woman who clothes and feeds him. In an untypical rush of tenderness, he embraces and kisses the unsightly creature. This is almost the only truly and honestly tender episode in the book, uncorrupted by any attempts to point a moral, for Lizardi's disillusionment with human nature was real, and based on experience, and most of his attempts to play upon the reader's sentiments ring false.

As El Periquillo's adventures follow the old picaresque pattern, so do those of the other characters, for they are all pretty much fairly familiar wares from the old storehouse. But the real heroes of this novel, by picaresque standards, are some of El Periquillo's comrades, such as Juan Largo, and the Eaglet. One is hanged and one dies leading a bandit raid, neither of them repents or ponders for a moment, but goes to his destined end in good form and style. Juan Largo says, "A good bullfighter dies on the horns of the bull," and El Periquillo answers that he has no wish to die a bullfighter's death. Indeed, he wants no heroics, either in living or dying. He wants to eat his cake and have it too and to die at last respectably in a comfortable bed surrounded by loving mourners. He does it, too. A thoroughly bad lot.

As in all picaresque literature, the reader has uneasy moments of wondering whether it is the hero or the author who is deficient in moral sensibility; or whether the proposed satire has not staggered and collapsed under its weight of moral connotation. When Januario is about to become a common thief, there is a long and solemn dialogue between him and Periquillo, Januario holding out firmly against Periquillo's rather cut-and-dried exhortations to honesty, or at any rate, as a last resort, plain prudence. Januario there repeats word for word the whole Catechism. Having done this, he goes out on his first escapade, and is half successful—that is he escapes from the police, but leaves his swag. On this occasion, Lizardi, by the demands of the plot, is hard beset to have Periquillo present, a witness, yet innocent. The best he can manage is to have him act as lookout, by distracting the watchman's attention and engaging him in conversation. Periquillo then believes that this act does not involve him in the least, and is most virtuously outraged when he is arrested and accused as confederate.

Again, Periquillo, in prison, and watching for a chance to cheat at cards, reflects at length and piously on the illicit, crafty methods of the trusty for turning a dishonest penny by cheating the prisoners. Thinking these thoughts, Periquillo refrains from cheating only because he realizes that he is in very fast company and will undoubtedly be caught at it. Don Antonio, a jail mate, formerly a dealer in contraband, in telling his story of how he lost his ill-gained fortune, innocently assumes and receives the complete sympathy of his hearers, not all of them mere thugs either. This Don Antonio, by the way, who is meant to shine as an example of all that is honorable, upright and unfortunate in human nature, is certainly one of the most abject and nitwitted characters in all fiction. He is smug, pious, dishonest, he feels dreadfully sorry for himself, and his ineptitude and bad management of his affairs cause much suffering to innocent persons. In fact, Lizardi was singularly uninspired in his attempts to portray virtue in action. In his hands it becomes a horrid device of boredom, a pall falls over his mind, he retreats to the dryest kind of moral saws and proverbs. He seemed to realize this, seemed to know that this kind of goodness, the only kind he dared recommend or advertise, was deadly dull. He tried to make it interesting but could not, and turned again with relief to his tough thieves and merry catchalls and horners and unrepentant bandits. Their talk is loose and lively, their behavior natural; he cheers up at once and so does his reader.

A contemporary critic complained that the book was "an uneven and extravagant work in very bad taste . . . written in an ugly style, with a badly invented plot . . . made worse by the author's treatment." He then confessed that what really annoyed him was the author's choice of characters, who were all from the lowest walks of life. They talked and behaved exactly like the vulgar people one saw in the streets, and their language was the sort heard in taverns. This left-handed praise must have pleased Lizardi, who had aimed at precisely this effect. The critic went on to say that the vices of polite society were perhaps no less shocking, but they seemed less gross because it was possible to gloss them over, decorate them, polish them up a bit, and make them less ridiculous. "When a rich man and a poor man drink together," answered Lizardi, in a little jingle, "the poor man gets drunk, but the rich man only gets merry."

Lizardi's infrequent flights into a more rarefied social atmosphere are malicious, comic, and a conventional caricature, designed to confirm in his lower-class readers all their worst suspicions regarding the rich and titled. Now and again he drags in by the ears a set speech on the obligations of nobility to be truly noble and of the poor to be truly virtuous, in the most Lizardian sense of those words, but he makes it clear that he has no real hopes that this will come to pass.

For him, the very rich and the very poor are the delinquent classes, to use a current sociological phrase. He called aloud for the pure mediocrity of morals and manners, the exact center of the road in all things. The middling well off, he insisted, were always good, because they practiced moderation, they were without exorbitant desires, ambitions, or vices. (That this was what made them middling was what Lizardi could never see, and that only those born to the middling temperament, rather than middling fortune, could practice the tepid virtues.) Every time El Periquillo falls into poverty, he falls also into the vices of the poor. When by his standards he is rich, he practices at once the classical vices of the rich. His feelings, thoughts, and conduct contract and expand automatically to the measure of his finances. He was always astounded to meet with morality in the poor, though he did meet it now and then, but never once did he find any good among the rich. His favorite virtue was generosity, and particularly that generosity practiced toward himself, though he almost never practiced it toward others. Even during a period of relative respectability, financially speaking, when El Periquillo is planning to marry, he discusses with Roque, one of his fly-by-night friends, the possibility of Periquillo's Uncle Maceta standing as security for the bridegroom's finery at the tailor's and the silversmith's, along with a plot to rid himself of his mistress, a girl whom he had seduced from a former employer. All goes smoothly for a time: the Uncle is complacent, the mistress is thrown out of the house in good time, the marriage takes place, with bad faith on both sides, El Periquillo's transitory small fortune is thrown away on fast living, and the Uncle is rooked out of his money. El Periquillo comments that it served him right for being such a stingy, unnatural relative.

So much for the Parrot as the faulty medium of Lizardi's social and moral ideas: some of his other characters were hardly less successful in this role . . . for example, his army officer, a colonel, in Manila.

This man is a brilliant example of what a military man is not, never was, could not in the nature of things be, yet Lizardi introduces him quite naturally as if he believed him to be entirely probable. The Colonel is full of the most broadly socialistic ideas, democratic manners, with agrarian notions on nationalism. He believes that rich deposits of gold and silver are a curse to a country instead of the blessings they are supposed to be, and that the lucky country was one which must depend upon its fruits, wool, meats, grain, in plenty but not enough to tempt invaders. He notes that Mexico and the Americas in general are deplorable examples of that false wealth which caused them to neglect agriculture and industry and fall prey to rapacious foreigners. . . . The Colonel, in his fantasy, is no more strange than the entire Manila episode. El Periquillo is deported there as a convict. It is hardly probable that Lizardi ever saw Manila, though there was a legend that he had visited there during the vague "lost years." It is more probable that while he lived in Acapulco he listened to stories of storm and shipwreck and life in strange ports. That he loved the sea is quite plain, with a real love, not romantic or sentimental; he expresses in simple phrases a profound feeling for the deep waters and the sweet majesty of ships. But otherwise, the Manila episode has the vague and far-fetched air of second-hand reporting.

It is not his moral disquisitions, then, nor his portrayal of character, nor his manner of telling his story, that keeps El Periquillo alive after more than a hundred years: it is simply and broadly the good show he managed to get up out of the sights and sounds and smells of his native town. His wakes, funerals, weddings, roaring drunken parties, beggars in their flop-houses, the village inns where families rumbled up in coaches, bringing servants, beds, food, exactly as they did in medieval Europe: they all exist with extraordinary vividness, and yet there is very little actual description. There are dozens of scenes which stick in the memory: Luisa standing in the door, greeting with cool scorn her former lover; the wake with the watchers playing cards through the night, and as their own candles give out, borrowing one by one the blessed candles from the dead; the robbing of the corpse, with its exaggerated piling of horror upon horror; the hospital scenes, the life in prisons; all this is eyewitness, first-hand narrative, and a worm's-eye view beside. It is a true picture of the sprawling, teeming, swarming people of Mexico, ragged, eternally cheated, crowding about the food stalls which smoke along the market side, sniffing the good smells through the dirt and confusion, insatiably and hope-lessly hungry, but indestructible. Lizardi himself was hungry nearly all his life, and his Periquillo has also an enormous, un-failing preoccupation with food. He remembers every meal, good or bad, he ever ate, he refers punctually three times a day to the fact that he was hungry, or it was now time to eat: "And my anxious stomach," says Periquillo, in one of the more painful moments of his perpetual famine, "was cheeping like a bird to gobble up a couple of plates of chile sauce and a platter of toasted tortillas." Even in exile, in Manila, when he had almost forgotten persons he had known, could hardly remem-ber the lovely face of his native city, he still remembered with longing the savory Mexican food. . . .

Lizardi was once insulted by a picayune critic, who wrote that his work was worthless and he himself a worthless charac-ter who wrote only in order to eat. This was not altogether true, for if it had been, Lizardi might easily have been much better fed than he was: but he did, having written, do what he could to sell his work to gain his bread, and though he did not choose the easy way, still he was bitterly stung by this taunt, poor man, and to save his pride, mentioned that at least he had lived by what he made, and not squandered his wife's dowry.

The Thinker's style has been admired as a model of clarity in Mexican literature by some of his later friends, but I think that must be the bias of loyalty. By the loosest standard, that style was almost intolerably wordy, cloudy, vague, the sentences of an intricate slovenliness, the paragraphs of inordinate length; indeed it was no style at all, but merely the visible shape of his harassed mind which came of his harassed life. He nearly always began his pamphlets, as he began his novel, with great dignity, deliberation and clearness, with a consciously affected pedantry, with echoes of the grand manner, a pastiche of Cervantes or Góngora, but he knew it could not last; he knew also his readers' tastes; he could do no more than promise a patchwork, and patchwork it was. There are times too when it is apparent he wrote at top speed in order to get the number finished and handed to the printer, needing desperately the few pesos the sale would bring him, padding and repeating, partly because his mind was too tired to remember what he had written, and partly because he must give his readers good weight for the money, or they would not buy.

The censors complained constantly of his obscenity and use of double meanings, and indeed he was a master in this mode. All of his writings I have seen are full of sly hints and some not so sly, curious associations of ideas one would need to be very innocent indeed to miss. The Mexicans love them with a special affection, the language is a honeycomb of them, no doubt Lizardi enjoyed writing them, and it was a certain device for catching his readers' undivided attention. He did not need to invent anything, he had only to listen to the popular talk, which was and is ripe and odorous. Some of it is very comic and witty, some of it simply nasty, humorless, and out of place in a translation where the meaning could be conveyed only by substituting a similar phrase in English, since they are often untranslatable in the technical sense. And was he—to imitate one of his own rhetorical questions—so simple as to believe that his readers would take the trouble to wade through his moral dissertations if he did not spice them with the little obscenities they loved? He was not, and he did his best by them in the matter of seasoning. At least a hundred million readers have found his novel savory, and perhaps a few of them repaid his hopes by absorbing here and there in it a little taste of manners and morals, with some liberal political theory besides. Certainly the causes for which he fought have been never altogether defeated, but they have won no victory, either: a lukewarm, halfway sort of process, the kind of thing that exasperated him most, that might well end by disheartening the best and bravest of men. Lizardi was not the best of men, nor the bravest, he was only a very good man and a very faithful one. If he did not have perfect courage or judgment, let him who has require these things of him.

December 10, 1941

A Mexican Chronicle, 1920–1943

BLASCO IBANEZ ON
"MEXICO IN REVOLUTION"

Mexico in Revolution, by Vicente Blasco Ibáñez,
translated from the Spanish by Arthur Livingston and José Padin.
New York: E. P. Dutton & Co., 1920.

NEWSPAPER notes gathered into a book make patchwork reading. Even Lafcadio Hearn's republished "Fantasies" could not survive the test. Six months after they are written, Blasco Ibanez' hurried observations on Mexico in Revolution are staler than even half year old news has any right to be. Tacit forgiveness is extended to daily potboilers in the swift forgetfulness accorded them. When the reporter seeks to revive and perpetuate his mistakes as literature, or even as propaganda, he invites the irritation of the reader.

Ordinarily, one does not review newspaper notes, even though the writer of them is "the most magnificent reporter in the world" as some sly critic dubbed the prolific Spaniard, who has discovered there is money in writing if you write fast enough and badly enough. Yet for one blazing moment when he was younger, he was an artist. He wrote "The Cabin." He was a revolutionary in those days, too, and spent eighteen months in prison for the sake of his political faith.

No doubt as one grows older things are different. Even a fellow countryman of Don Quixote tilts with no windmills at sixty or thereabout. It is better to stand solidly with editors and publishers who buy much and pay well. It is better to write racy, clever stuff: to tell quarter-truths amusingly and convincingly, than to content one's self with the obscure honor of having created "The Cabin."

I read portions of Ibanez' notes on Mexico when they were appearing serially in a New York newspaper. I read them again this week in a book decorated on both sides of the slip cover with an inconsiderately homely photograph of the late Carranza posing with Ibanez. They are evidently conversing on a subject painful to them both. Cordial intent is not visibly established. Ibanez is blinking in that strong light he claims Carranza always forced the visitor to face during interviews. Carranza's manner is nicely divided between boredom and suspicion.

The boredom was his personal affair, but he did well to be suspicious. It would have been better for many other Mexicans if they had been a little less frank in their welcome of the visiting third cousin who embraced them in order to feel of their pistol belts: who led them on to talk about themselves with humorous carelessness in order that he, the visiting third cousin, should be enabled to prove afterward in print what a very clever, knowing sort of chap he was. "See how I understand these people," you may imagine Ibanez saying. "Note the ease with which I tripped them up, and obtained their simple secrets. Really, dear friends, I was as amusing as a weasel in a Rat hole!"

I marvel again at his inverted Latin wit, his gift for stripping the personal dignity from a fellow creature, with deliberate intent so to strip him before as wide a public as he can muster. I resent his not dealing clean wounds that bleed freely. I protest against his sadistic pastime of removing an inch of skin at a time with a razor edge.

He attacks all of us insidiously at points where we are without protection. Who believes in militarism? Who does not feel for the sufferings of the poor peon? His indignation against the one, his proper sympathy for the other are sentiments beyond reproach. Who can help smiling over his sardonic account of the Mexican "soldierette," or laughing outright over the infernally amusing story of Don Jesús Carranza and the Red Cow in Hell?

That is the trouble with this affair. His malice touches the kindred spark of malice in all of us. Blasco Ibanez brought with him to Mexico—Blasco Ibanez. He carried about with him his taste for scandal—his will to believe evil of all he saw. He talked with everybody who had a shady story to tell. Over cafe tables and on street corners he gathered together the most trivial and scandalous untruths ever put between book covers as a serious account of a nation, carefully mixed with an occasional grain of fact when its exclusion would have been too glaringly obvious.

Any one like-minded could spend a short time in any capital of the world and come away with a similar collection of anecdotes.

He brought with him intellectual snobbishness—witness the "Belasco" story—and racial hatred he owns to in words between words. For six whole weeks he sat at cafe tables or stood on street corners discovering the truth about Mexico in Revolution. Then he went away and wrote a delightful, an informing, a profoundly truthful mental autobiography of Blasco Ibanez!

If the reader knew nothing of Mexico except the political propaganda published for years in American journals, it might be very easy to believe nearly all of this book.

It races along so fluently, never at a loss for a word, with a keen and poisonous little anecdote capping each incident sharply. He speaks fairly well of the dead—of Díaz, of Carranza, of Zapata; indiscriminately he scatters a few kindly, condescending words upon these harmless graves. But it is nearly always in order to point more precisely the villainy of some one now in power. Living men at work he hates, it seems.

For young de la Huerta he has a sentence of praise to stress his contention that there are no other idealists in all the government of Mexico. Reading his book, one remembers acquaintance with enough flaming and disinterested revolutionary idealists to employ the fingers of two hands in naming them, and is willing on the strength of that knowledge to admit the existence of numberless others one has never met, and will never hear of. But one feels that somewhere along the road, late or early, Ibanez has laid down his burden of faith in his kind, and groaningly cannot make shift to take it up again. He has taken masters, and serves them excellently well.

He writes always with a weather eye on these masters. Now and again he tucks in sweet pilules of flattery for the delectation of the great northern public for whom he wrote. Deftly he tickles the ear of the white man who indirectly made it worth his while to write this book.

And, ironically and caustically, with relish and innuendo, with much dropping of the eyelid and sweet turning of phrase would he delight a Spanish audience with an account of that so-amusing America he has just discovered if a Spanish publisher decided to make it worth his while.

It is not likely to happen. They have never made it worth Ibanez' while in Spain. Let him fill American platters with his spiced and vinegared scandal-mongering between nations. That is the logical place for it. But it should be devoured and forgotten by the third day.

PATERNALISM AND THE MEXICAN PROBLEM

Some Mexican Problems,
by Moisés Sáenz and Herbert I. Priestly.
Chicago: University of Chicago Press, 1926.

Aspects of Mexican Civilization,
by José Vasconcelos and Manuel Gamio.
Chicago: University of Chicago Press, 1926.

I shall not pretend that these books present unbiased opinions of conclusions on the problem of Mexican-American relations, for liberalism has a bias of its own. The main virtue of the liberal temperament is its almost pious regard for the facts, its genius for patient research: for me, the wonder of the liberal temperament is that no amount of findings can upset its preconceived theories. Earth hath no sorrows that a firm mild course of popular education cannot cure.

It is true that ill-regimented minded are inclined to be noisy, warm and argumentative, and there is something about the Mexican question that raises the hackles even on the peaceful minded. These admirable books contain all the elements of free-for-all controversy, but all is so adroitly smoothed away there is nothing in the tone to frighten the most timid liberal. Four diverse, informed and civilized minds have here collaborated in presenting quite horrifying facts in an almost painless form. In this series of lectures they tested their theories of education before the Chicago Annual Institute, and it is cheerful to think that hundreds, maybe even thousands of students went away from there happy in the thought that nations may be taught understanding of each other by gentle degrees, as children are led from one grade to another. Even oil magnates may be taught international good manners by suggestion. In this thought everybody may happily go to sleep and leave the job of teaching them to some one else.

Each of these four gentlemen is an expert in his subject, a fine flower of academic culture. They share an Olympian balance in viewing all sides of a question. If at times Mr. Saenz shows fight he controls himself quickly, remembers his rôle of mediator, and gives a superhumanly just statement of the present intolerable situation in Mexico due to foreign investments, the condition of Mexican labor and the problem of rural education. He is a nationalist, a good one, I should like to hear him speak more freely. But he remains well within the bounds of what is expected from a foreign lecturer before an institute, and ends on a note of optimism scarcely warranted by the facts he has managed to expose. I suspect him of radical tendencies. Given a chance, I believe he would be warm and noisy. The balance of his head is threatened by the insurgence of his heart.

Mr. Vasconcelos, former secretary of education in Mexico, has for some years past occupied himself with promoting peaceful relationship between the Latin countries of America. He is equally opposed to the present system of government in these countries—dictatorship or caudillism—and foreign interference. He professes faith, more especially in the Mexican Indian, and rejects alien paternalism, but preaches a vast religious native paternalism fully as debilitating to his people. Mr. Vasconcelos has an incurable, almost romantic faith in the perfectibility of human nature, and his plan roughly is this: the lion and the lamb have essential differences, it is true, but one should reason with the lion and persuade him not to eat the lamb. In the meantime, the lamb shall be given a few setting up exercises that will enable him to hold his own with the lion in case one or the other of these essential differences should crop up in their future together.

Aside from this he gives an excellent historical survey of Mexico.

Into Mr. Priestley's scholarly essay creeps now and again his sense of responsibility as big brother of Mexico. He, with the others, is pleased that the Ford and the phonograph are now commonplaces of Mexican life. He believes in sane, conservative propaganda for Mexico, such as these books represent, setting aside all the roaring of distempered radicals and frivolous reports by prosperous Chamber of Commerce gentlemen. Truth being, of course, our aim, I only wish that these honest men and good investigators could manage to be half so entertaining as the liars and hotheads. There must be some way of making facts attractive! Why do not these liberals find it?

In his first chapter Mr. Priestley is gloomy as death about sickness in Mexico. But this, he says, is being remedied. Sanitary measures are being enforced, active steps taken against contagion and infection, a study of regional diseases promises a cure of them. These things are good, who could quarrel with them? But they continually miscall this sort of thing civilization. Maybe it is, and I am thinking of something else: I am persuaded it is too tall a name for our cult of machinery and the bathtub. Still the standard of washing and eating in Mexico remains very low.

The average of washing and eating in the United States is, as you know, unnaturally high. We have our bread lines, true, and miners' strikes, and the garment workers of this superlatively clothed nation have a permanent grievance, and the silk manufacturers will tell you that if we wear silk, even at excessive prices, a certain number of workers must live in acute discomfort. In the South we persist in the aristocratic old tradition, of Negro peonage, and there is a discouraging percentage of poor whites whose insides are riddled with the hookworm. We are exceedingly rude to multitudes of our foreign population, and what with our modern efficient methods of banditry, somebody should hold a round-table discussion about us.

But this round-table is about Mexico, so let us get on. Mr. Gamio is a true scientist; I feel he has come nearer to the real life of his own country than either of his compatriots or the liberal minded Mr. Priestley. During his work as director of the Bureau of Anthropology he made a profound sympathetic study of racial origins. His findings presented him with his own special phase of the Mexican problem: that of incorporating this deep-grounded native Indian life with the modern mixed currents of Mexican culture. This incorporation would result in a recognized Indian nation instead of a three-layer, disorganized structure of white, mestizo and Indian. He knows that Mexico and the Indian belong to each other, and consistently refuses to regard him as other than the rightful owner and proprietor of his country. He recognizes the futility of imposing on the Indian customs and standards alien to him: considers the economic and geographical factors and the human one.

The appeal has not all been aimed at the altruistic spirit which may or may not function, according to the weather, in the bosom of man. Each lecturer in turn has pointed out that there would be money, good solid gold to be had out of Mexico in exchange for the same rules of commerce and diplomacy that more important nations are able to enforce from us. They recommend that the wealth now concentrated in the hands of a few vast corporations be loosed and allowed to flow through a thousand new channels, reminding us that there are other riches in Mexico besides oil.

These are books to be read for solid information. The remedies suggested are so very slow the problems they are intended to solve will have died by nature, decayed and reflowered into something else, before they could begin to take effect. Cleaning up is dirty work, this is a mere project for washing face and hands. The thundering racket you hear outside is Mexico getting her pockets picked by her foreign investors.

LA CONQUISTADORA

The Rosalie Evans Letters from Mexico,
arranged, with comment, by Daisy Caden Pettus.
Indianapolis: The Bobbs-Merrill Co., 1926.

Rosalie Caden Evans was an American woman, born in Galveston, Texas. She married a British subject, Harry Evans, who became owner of several haciendas in Mexico during the Díaz regime. They lost their property in the Madero revolution, and for several years lived in the United States and in Europe.

In 1917 Mr. Evans died while in Mexico, after an unsuccessful attempt to regain his property under the Carranza administration. Mrs. Evans returned to Mexico, and for more than six years she proved a tough enemy to the successive revolutionary governments, holding her hacienda under almost continuous fire. This contest required a great deal of attention from three governments, Mexico, Great Britain, and the United States, and furnished a ready bone of contention in the long-drawn argument between Mexico and foreign powers respecting the famous Article 27 of the new Mexican Constitution, which provides among other things that the large landholdings of Mexico shall be repartitioned among the Indians, subject to proper indemnification to the former owner.

H. A. C. Cummins, of the British legation, was expelled from Mexico for his championship of Mrs. Evans, and a fair amount of trouble ensued between Mexico and Great Britain about it. The case of Mrs. Evans was cited in the United States as an argument against our recognition of the Obregón government. An impressive volume of diplomatic correspondence was exchanged between the three governments concerning the inflexible lady, who held her ground, nevertheless, saying that she could be removed from her holdings only as a prisoner or dead.

In August, 1924, the news came that Mrs. Evans had been shot from ambush by a number of men while driving in a buckboard from the village of San Martín to her hacienda, San Pedro Coxtocan.

Reading the letters Rosalie Evans wrote her sister, Mrs. Daisy Caden Pettus, from Mexico, this adventure takes on all the colors of a lively temperament; the story is lighted for us like a torch. The aim in publishing the letters was to present Mrs. Evans to a presumably outraged Anglo-Saxon world as a martyr to the sacred principles of private ownership of property: to fix her as a symbol of devotion to a holy cause. "Some Americans," says Mrs. Pettus in a foreward to the volume, "in ignorance of Mexican conditions, have said the fight carried on by Mrs. Evans was unwise, if not unworthy, in that it is charged that she was resisting the duly established laws and principles of the Mexican people. This is very far from true."

It is true, however, that she opposed, and to her death, the

attempts of the Mexican people to establish those laws and
principles which were the foundation of their revolution, and
on which their national future depends. She cast her individual
weight against the march of an enormous social movement,
and though her fight was gallant, brilliant and wholehearted,
admirable as a mere exhibition of daring, energy and spirit, still
I cannot see how she merits the title of martyr. She was out for
blood, and she had a glorious time while the fight lasted.

Her letters are a swift-moving account of a life as full of
thrills and action as any novel of adventure you may find. They
are written at odd moments, dashed off in the midst of a dozen
things all going at once: the episodes are struck off white-hot.
The result is a collection of letters that could scarcely be equaled
for speed, for clarity, for self-revelation, for wit and charm. We
are shown the most fantastic blend of a woman: fanaticism,
physical courage, avarice, mystical exaltation and witch-wife
superstition; social poise and financial shrewdness, a timeless
feminine coquetry tempered by that curious innocence which
is the special gift of the American woman: all driven mercilessly
by a tautness of the nerves, a deep-lying hysteria that urges her
to self-hypnosis. Toward the last she had almost lost her natural
reactions. Anger, fear, delight, hope—no more of these. She
was a Will.

Mrs. Evans returned to Mexico to take up her husband's
fight when he had wearied to death of it. Belief in private
property had not yet become a religion. She was animated by
sentiment for her dead husband. All feminine, she insisted that
his shade still guarded and directed her. The demon that possessed her was by no means of so spiritual a nature as she fancied: she was ruled by a single-minded love of money and
power. She came into Mexico at harvest time, and after a short,
sharp battle she got hold of the ripened wheat on her main hacienda. This victory fired her, and was the beginning of the
end. Shortly afterward the shade of her husband left her. "I
stand alone."

No single glimmer of understanding of the causes of revolution or the rights of the people involved ever touched her
mind. She loved Spaniards, the British, the Americans of the
foreign colony. She thought the Indians made good servants,
though occasionally they betrayed her. She writes with annoy-

ance of Obregón's taking Mexico City and creating a disturbance when she was on the point of wresting from the Indians
her second crop of wheat—"gold in color, gold in reality!" She
is most lyrical, most poetic when she contemplates this gold
which shall be hers, though all Mexico go to waste around her.
Carranza's flight interested her merely because it menaced her
chances of getting the only threshing machine in the Puebla
Valley.

Of all the machinations, the crooked politics, the broken
faiths, the orders and counter orders, the plots and counterplots
that went on between literally thousands of people over this
single holding, I have not time to tell. Mrs. Evans was passed
from hand to hand, nobody wanted to be responsible for what
must eventually happen to her. She pressed everybody into her
service, from her maids to the high diplomats. Every man of
any official note in Mexico, connected with the three governments, finally got into the business, and she shows them all up
in turn.

The story of the double dealing here revealed is not pretty,
showing as it does some of our eminent diplomats engaged in
passing the buck and gossiping behind each other's backs. But
sooner or later they all advised her to listen to reason, accept
100,000 pesos for her land and give way. At least they perceived what she could not; that here was a national movement
that must be reckoned with.

At first she would not. And later, she could not. She loved
the romantic danger of her situation, she admired herself in
the role of heroine. Her appetite for excitement increased; she
confessed herself jaded, and sought greater danger.

Speaking of a safe conduct she obtained in order to go over
her hacienda and inspect the crops, she says: "You see it means
a chance of gaining 80,000 pesos besides the adventure." After
each hairbreadth encounter with sullen Indians armed with
rope and scythe, with troops bearing bared arms, she was
flushed with a tense joy. Later, when she came to open war, she
would ride into armed groups with her pistol drawn, singing
"*Nous sommes les enfants de Gasconne!*" She cracked an Indian
agrarian over the head with her riding whip during an alterca-
tion over the watercourse and patrolled the fields during harvest with a small army.

Her love of the drama was getting the upper hand of principle. If at first her cry was all for law and justice, later she refers
to herself merrily as an outlaw. "You have no idea how naturally one takes to the greenwood!" She became a female
conquistador—victory was her aim, and she was as unscrupulous in her methods as any other invader.

There is not a line in her letters to show that she had any grasp
of the true inward situation, but her keen eye and ready wit
missed no surface play of event. She maintained peaceable relations first with one, then another of the many groups of
rebels. Inexplicably the situation would shift and change, her
allies would vanish, leaving her mystified. She had all Mexico
divided into two classes: the Good, who were helping her hold
her property, and the Bad, who were trying to take it from her.
    She could be self-possessed in the grand manner, and seemed
to have second-sight in everything immediately concerning
herself. She sat for three days and fed her pigeons while serious
persons advised her to pay the 300 pesos ransom demanded for
her majordomo, kidnapped to the hills. She refused. It was too
much to pay for a majordomo, and she felt they would not
shoot him anyhow. They did not. When he returned she sent
him back with a present of $80 to the kidnappers.
    At another crisis she played chess. After a brilliant encounter
with some hint of gunfire, she came in and washed her hair. At
times she studied astronomy, other times she read Marcus
Aurelius or poetry. At all times she played the great lady. Her
love for her horses, her dogs, her servants, her workers and
allies was all of a piece, grounded in her sense of possession.
They were hers; almost by virtue of that added grace she loved
them, and she looked after them in the feudal manner.
    There was something wild and strange in her, a hint of mad-
ness that touches genius; she lived in a half-burned ranch house
with her dogs, near a haunted chapel, hourly expecting attack,
and longed to join the coyotes in their weird dances outside her
door. She foretold the manner of her own death, and related
for sober fact the most hair-raising ghost story I have ever read:

The last night I was there I had been in bed an hour perhaps and was
growing drowsy when I heard some one crying at my window. The

most gentle attenuated sobbing; the most pitiful sounds you ever heard. I never for a minute thought of the spirits, but called the girl to light the candle. She heard it too—but the strange part is, *I* said it was at the back window and *she* heard it at the front, and neither did *she* think of spirits. As she opened to see who was there, IT came in sobbing—and we looked at each other and closed the windows. Perhaps you think we were frightened or horrified? I can only answer for myself—it filled me with an intense pity. I only wanted to comfort it and I said to the girl: "If it would *only* be quiet." I then promised to have the mass said and invite the people, and it left, sobbing. And we, of course, both went to our beds to sleep dreamlessly till morning.

Revolution is not gentle, either for those who make it or those who oppose it. This story has its own value as a record of one life lived very fully and consciously. I think the life and death of Mrs. Evans were her own private adventures, most gladly sought and enviably carried through. As a personality, she is worth attention, being beautiful, daring and attractive. As a human being she was avaricious, with an extraordinary hardness of heart and ruthlessness of will; and she died in a grotesque cause.

¡AY, QUE CHAMACO!

The Prince of Wales and Other Famous Americans,
caricatures by Miguel Covarrubias.
New York: Alfred A. Knopf, 1925.

In Mexico there is a well seasoned tradition of fine caricature: almost every one of the younger painters possesses this lacerating gift. It goes with the Mexican aptitude for deadly discernment of the comic in the other person, together with each man's grave regard for his own proper dignity. In arguments, whether personal or political, they resort early to popular songs and cartoons that carry sharper fangs than any other sort of debate. They have a charming habit of disregarding the main point at issue long enough to call attention to some defect or weakness, preferably an irremediable one, in the opponent. The quick-witted public, humanly fond of a joke on someone else, laughs the loser out.

Covarrubias in this is more Mexican than the Mexicans. As a youth he moved among that group of younger insurgents who revolutionized Mexican painting almost overnight. He was the youngest, and no one was ever born so naïve as he appeared. He did no serious painting, but amused himself at the innocent pastime of making caricatures of the serious paintings of others, and thereafter it was an effort to look at those paintings with an untangled viewpoint. He had a merry little way of dropping into the cafés haunted by his set, joining the carefree group gathered there, and dashing off a few careless impressions of their faces that would spoil their evening for them.

While he was yet too young to be called to account, he brought his talents to New York, and for once the favorite success legend of this nation jibed with the pure truth. The brilliant suddenness of his popularity made the old-fashioned tales of the hardships of genius sound a trifle drab, as his caricature of our native celebrities put a crimp in the high seriousness of intellectual life as she was being led in this city.

Smart New York, under whose garment of custom tailored sophistication beats an eager barbarian heart, touched to wonder by all that is deft, off-hand and of high visibility, had found a new champion; a boy with sure-fire stuff, backed up with the invaluable social gift of malice. "Enfant du siècle" they dubbed him, among other things. He is more than a mere child of his century; more than contemporaneous. He is current—as aptly present in the public interest as this month's leading musical revue.

It is his speed, his wit, his lively accuracy that first arrest the attention. But beyond his showy technique he has the spontaneous combustion called genius. In this collection of more than sixty drawings, there is only one failure: Babe Ruth. And that merely a comparative failure. There are less than half a dozen that are not superb. The rest are beyond criticism as keen satirical comment, and I claim it is a comment considerably more than skin-deep.

Covarrubias has a wide range of symbols, a command of many styles, and he adapts his medium and his method of approach with an impish understanding of the personality of his subject. Compare the caricatures of Alfred Stieglitz, of Calvin Coolidge, of Robert Edmond Jones, of Xavier Algara. If in the case of President Coolidge he has subtly piled up the miserable details, at other times he strips his subject to the buff: literally, in the drawing of Jack Dempsey, where in a few strokes we are given three dimensions, a framework with a skeleton inside: and in all of them, something else that belongs to metaphysics: a feeling that he has exposed the very outer appearance of a sitter that is the clue to an inner quality the sitter has spent most of his life trying to hide, or disguise. If that isn't murder, what is it? And what is?

The victims in Mexico used to shake their heads, to get the blood out of their eyes, no doubt. There, let a good joke get out on you just once, and you're done for. Their civilized perception of the power of wit makes for caution. "Ay, que chamaco!" they would say. "What a brat!" They preserved the drawings he made of them on scraps of paper around café tables, and if they were published, what a book that would be! But they will never be published. New York knows a good joke on itself when it sees it: and Covarrubias is the latest, and the best one.

OLD GODS AND NEW MESSIAHS

Idols Behind Altars, by Anita Brenner,
with photographs by Tina Modotti and Edward Weston.
New York: Payson & Clarke, 1929.

This book is like an ancient chronicle, owing its existence to so many sources, so many articulate lives, that the author does not even attempt the impossible task of acknowledging all her indebtedness. The anthropologist, the explorer, the teacher, the artist, the folk-heroes, the makers of the legend and miracle have joined in pouring out their riches to make of this a communal work, like everything else that comes out of Mexico. It is true there are a few names to lend reality, and the attempt to present reality is a brave one, but there is a portentous air of legend in the style, and in spite of herself the author writes in a heightened mood of one enchanted and convinced by a miracle. Mexico is a disturbing country, and it has this effect on those who love it. The contradictions are too violent in this land of miracles, of Messiahs, of venal politicians, of dedicated scholars, of sober artists and extravagant dreams.

Miss Brenner wrote her book, the first attempt at an ordered story of art and artists in Mexico, with the official sanction and the unlimited aid of the University of Mexico. She has the equipment of a good annalist: youth and enthusiastic sympathies, the gift of close and penetrating observation, a genius for listening and remembering what she hears and an admirably energetic style. She was accompanied on her search by Tina Modotti and Edward Weston, whose photographs are more than mere illustrations: and her material has the freshness of things gathered by word of mouth and through the eye, for later Mexican history has never been written fully and survives in stories told and songs sung in pictures.

After investigating the precise nature of the Aztec idol which lies under the Catholic altars of Mexico, attended by kneeling pilgrims who still gather to worship not the appearance but the true holy substance concealed beneath the appearance, Miss Brenner ranges the present scene gathering all elements together in the grand hope of proving an inner spiritual unity between the ancient Indian of Mexico, the current revolutionary program and, above all, the perfect validity of that revolution in art once called the Mexican Renascence, though I doubt if the label still persists there.

In the course of this procedure, done in obedience to many inner and external compulsions, almost in spite of this tremendous effort to reconcile all things, Miss Brenner has written a really beautiful book. She interprets symbols in terms of human life, describes the now-famous mural paintings of the Syndicate of Painters and Sculptors in a lively intelligible painters' jargon, and devotes a series of remarkably fresh and delightful biographical chapters to individual painters who helped to make the most exciting period of art in the history of America. The chapter on the syndicate conveys the breathless commotion of those few years in Mexico when the new way of painting progressed in Mexico in a whirlwind of manifestos, public demonstrations, newspaper campaigns, with adolescent mob violence expending itself on the still unfinished murals and respectable ladies demanding that the vile pictures be covered over before they would consent to hold a meeting in the patio of the preparatory school. Art occupied no ivory tower, but rolled in the dust of conflict with local politics, religion and the agrarian question and came out victorious, for the walls are there, covered with the simple and irrefutable testimony that once, for a short time, a group of extraordinary artists collaborated in producing works of art.

The artists in Mexico followed the revolution and their activities occurred at the end of a period, not at a beginning, as most of them involved in it wished to believe. In the first part of the decade between 1910 and 1921 several good artists, now well known, were working in obscurity—floating particles lost in the confusion, as were the artists of Russia during the first years of readjustment from 1917. The artists returned to Mexico at the first promise of peace—for they were nearly all abroad— and though they took their color from the political and economic atmosphere, still they came late and their revolution was the crowning pyrotechnical display that marked the end of the long groaning process of political change.

Still they were revolutionists and in a sense above politics, for they recognized, they exhumed from under the debris of extraneous hostile life, the art of the Indian in Mexico, and they restored the Indian himself, a perpetual exile in his own land, to the status of a human problem before a world that had almost ceased to regard that race as a living force in Mexico. They fought the enemies of their idea within the walls and without. They adopted habits of thought, and adapted methods of working, and went, in the process, very consciously "primitive," imitating the Indian miracle paintings, delving among ruins, searching in the archives, attending Indian fiestas, using the native earths for their colors. They talked among themselves, compared findings, defending each his own point of view, and ended, evidently, in confirming one another's discoveries in all essentials. The Indian was the only real artist in America, they said, and they proved it by pointing to his serapes, his jugs, his ex-votos, his pulqueria decorations and his way of living. They discarded awareness for the darker, profounder current of instinct, which when followed faithfully, did not, they believed, betray. They rejected the mechanistic devices for keeping the surfaces of life in motion and plunged boldly to the depths of the "unconscious."

This led to a remarkable paradox.

Dr. Manuel Gamio, the anthropologist, who has devoted his life to the cause of Indian life in Mexico, is a Spaniard, Mexican born. Jose Vasconcelos, then Minister of Education, who fostered the work of the Syndicate of Painters and Sculptors, is Spanish-Mexican. Siqueiros, Mexican born, who furnished the theory of action for the syndicate and organized it, was sent to Europe by the Carranza government to study. Adolfo Best-Maugard, who created a method of design based on Aztec motives, is Spanish-French, educated in Europe. Jean Charlot is mostly French and Parisian. Merida is a Guatemalan, who in Europe was associated with Modigliani. Dr. Atl, one of the true pioneers, is partly German. Diego Rivera is a Mexican-born Spaniard, who spent sixteen years in Europe, following the erratic course of modern painting in many capitals. Some of these have a tinge of Jewish blood, others have Indian blood. The great renascence of Indian art was a movement of mestizos and foreigners who found in Mexico, simultaneously, a direction they could take toward extended boundaries. They respected the fruitful silence of the Indian and they shouted for this silence at the top of their lungs.

Those of us in Mexico at the time saw this happen: that not one pure-blooded Indian artist contributed his motivating force to initiate this movement. Several of them joined in, but of the active men not one but had fled out of Europe with years of training and experience, saturated with theories and methods, bent on fresh discoveries. This excepts Orozco and a prodigious child, Abraham Angel, who learned from his elders, then surpassed them in a single leap, and died at nineteen years. Xavier Guerrero, a full-blooded Indian, joined the syndicate, kept his silence and did magnificent work. When he wished to articulate a faith he edited a Communist periodical, in itself a work of art. For him his way of painting sprang from no intellectual or sentimental atavism; it was a simple continuing. He wasted no words on it.

The non-Indians made the experiments and did the explaining.

The famous Syndicate of Painters and Sculptors, with Diego Rivera as a storm center, presented a front of formidable solidarity to the hostile public and fought ferociously among themselves because communality of work and idea can be won only by endless war. The younger artists admired Diego, imitated his work without shame, and ended by convincing themselves that they had worked in that method from the cradle. They revolted against this top-heavy personality which threatened the balance of the group and drew caricatures of Diego, swathed monumentally in a Ku-Klux Klan sheet, shoving them into graves and pushing earth over them. But they held together and followed him just the same.

If the syndicate painters purified the atmosphere of the more obvious picturesqueness already exploited sickeningly by their immediate predecessors, still they found their reality ready to hand. The Indian sat, a complete design in space, ready for them. The painters learned soberly and did not corrupt the thing they found. All the symbols are preserved intact. For example, as Miss Brenner notes, ancient symbol of the hand with the flower; this appears over again, and the laboring hand is esteemed a thing of marvelous beauty; great hands of war clasped over a sword hilt; hands grasping a machete, molding a pot; weaving, digging in the mines, delving in the earth, scattering the seeds; this laboring hand became a vast basic symbol. Tina Modotti, an Italian, makes photographs of hands and has made a beautiful study of the hands of Amado Galvan, the potter, for this book, and so united were the artists, no matter what their medium, and so faithful were they to their visions, Tina Modotti's photographs from life appear at first glance to be photographs of Diego's paintings.

I wish some one as well equipped for the work might do for the United States of North America what Miss Brenner has done for Mexico. Surely this country, which exhibits such special and florid contradictions, such gargantuan appetites, such magnificence of crime, architecture and machinery, might also be discovered to have some common, unifying source. Explained in terms of creative vitality and racial intermixtures, we might find ourselves justified in being "with pleasure and talent" Americans. We practice to a degree the "vacilada" which Miss Brenner defines as the loud laughter meant to conceal, but which reveals the waverings of despair induced by the necessity to face tragedy without signs of fear. Miss Brenner says this is very Mexican, very mestizo. It would be simpler to say it is very human and excessively Western. What else is the Italian farce? What else the *Merry Wives of Windsor*? The Punch and Judy show? Our own comic strip for the sake of which large numbers of persons buy the newspapers? In Mexico, true, they are immensely vivid in everything, and in spite of her hatred for the "picturesque," for that word is rightly outlaw, Miss Brenner is more than once captured and misled by this definitely Mexican talent for high visibility. Why not? It is one of their attractions.

Miss Brenner distributes honors among the painters by a somewhat incalculable system of estimates, and I rather finished her book feeling that if one admired Orozco, then it was not quite possible to give high rank to Diego Rivera. The witty and talented Jean Charlot receives as much attention as either of these important figures, and there are other mysterious selections and exclusions. But in the end this is a book about Mexico not to be missed—a stimulating record of a vital period in the history of American art told by a contemporary eyewitness.

DIEGO RIVERA

These Pictures Must Be Seen

The Frescoes of Diego Rivera,
with an introduction by Ernestine Evans.
New York: Harcourt, Brace & Co., 1929.

For seven years, during a period of more than ordinarily ecstatic turbulence in the life of his native country, the frescoes of Diego Rivera have been spreading, with the power and persistence of an organic growth, upon the walls of public buildings in Mexico. After sixteen years of experiment and discovery in Europe he went home and proceeded to make the question of art an issue as immediate, disturbing and almost as dangerous as a Presidential election. He was a veteran of the series of campaigns which followed cubism after 1912, and his mission to Mexico was not one of peace. In politics he was a revolutionary. Painters sprang up around him by the dozen, for luckily all the good ones were also radical, at least in theory. The mediocre ones stuck by the Academy and the good old times. There was a gratifying amount of seething and ferment, during which his syndicate of painters and sculptors produced some of the best modern painting, if not sculpture, to be found in the world. Rivera, because of his phenomenal personality and his absolute mastery of the situation, was in danger of becoming a legend, a symbol, before his work was half finished. His followers have for him a warmth of adulation little short of worship. His enemies are positively worth having.

It is almost impossible to exaggerate the excitements, the disorders of the life around him when he began his frescoes, or the pressure under which he worked. The group he had gathered shattered from within and dispersed after the first year. Rivera remained alone and painted. Except for two visits to Russia, where he worked for short periods, he moved from the walls of the Ministry of Education to the National Preparatory School in Mexico City, and from thence to the National Agricultural Academy in Chapingo. The mere volume of his labors is impressive, a testimony to the singleness of his idea, and the union of his individual mind with the tradition which formed it.

Tough fibered and resistant, he is an emotional revolutionist, and when he explains his social beliefs in words it comes down pretty fairly to a simple philosophic anarchy, such as almost any Spaniard might express. Within the province of his art all is complete harmony, order, obedience. He selected a difficult, uncompromising medium and proceeded to inclose his intractable material within the confines of a formal beauty. For him the enormous confusion of the visible world can be reduced to a study in geometrical balance, sober color and cross rhythms suspended at the moment of precise harmony. The vision is grand and simple, a little too bucolic, maybe, at times a trifle inflated, but I believe he is the most important living painter.

We are indebted to Miss Ernestine Evans for this first collection of photographs of the murals and an interesting introduction to the artist. The reproductions are very fine and preserve to a degree the values of the subdued grays, brick reds, silvery greens and deep blues of the paintings. The color is secondary, for Rivera emphasizes structure and rhythm. It is a very timely and valuable book.

RIVERA'S PERSONAL REVOLUTION

Portrait of Mexico, paintings by Diego Rivera,
text by Bertram D. Wolfe.
New York: Covici-Friede, 1937.

Portrait of Mexico might well be the good, honest final job destined to end books about Mexico. Or maybe that is only cheerful wish-thinking on the part of this reviewer.

There is—or was, for friendships collapse as swiftly as other things in Mexico—a long and firm bond between the collaborators on this book: personal and esthetic sympathies, similarity of political belief, and a shared continuous loving preoccupation with Mexico. This has resulted happily in a sound book, giving for the first time in my experience an inclusive and coherent history of Mexico from preconquest days to the present, and a key to the work of Diego Rivera, not only as painter but as pictorial historian of Mexico, the land and its people.

Mr. Wolfe is the typical international Jew, born student and reformer, a man without a country save as he adopts it; even then, as we see at present in Germany, he is always in peril of finding himself homeless. Still, this capacity for choice makes for a special kind of patriotism, as for instance in Mr. Wolfe, based on love and attention and a desire to know one's chosen country really. Mr. Wolfe has the keen eye and the nose for research of a first-rate reporter, and he is in fact the only man I ever trusted to give me a straight story about political and social situations as they came in Mexico. He has his own political faith, schismatic and obdurate, and this gives to his conclusions a certain slant, of course, but in the mean time he has told a dreadful story of cross-purpose and treachery and corruption which would appall and discourage a less-seasoned campaigner.

Mr. Wolfe has sorted out his mass of material and divided it into logical sections, each admirably concise and full. He finds his way deftly through the almost inextricable knot of political and personal relationships and conflicting motives of the "revolutionists" from Madero to the present Cardenas. He proves by implication rather clearly that the first step to a stable "revolutionary" government is to kill off all the real rebels as early in the game as possible. His list of honest murdered men and living crooks is impressive.

He has incorporated into this history the history of Diego Rivera as painter in Mexico, painter of Mexico, with a key to the no-doubt thousands of square yards of murals, crowded with historical faces drawn from life, from imagination, and all too often, from bad photographs or old portraits, which cover nearly all the available wall space in Mexico's public buildings. The total effect is monstrous, as is the total energy of this big slow-moving man, half hero, half mountebank, as artists sometimes are. He has been "news" in the most literal sense of the word, from the day he first mounted his scaffoldings in the Preparatoria: broadbeamed, ox eyed, wearing the costume of the day laborer and the pistols of the mestizo, and he has been "news" ever since, on this side of the world. Amid interruptions, uproar, personal battles and political ones, he has continued imperturbably at his self-appointed task: to make the walls of Mexico his monument, as once the walls of Basel were Hans Holbein's. But there is a moral here; for Hans Holbein's wall paintings have clean vanished from Basel, and his monument is elsewhere. All the more reason, then, for this book, to keep the record when all that is left of Rivera's work will be his canvases, preserved in private collections and museums.

No single man in his time has ever had more influence on the eye and mind of the public who know his work than Diego Rivera; for he has made them see his Mexico, to accept his version of it, and often to think it better than their own. This is no small feat, and indeed, the hugeness of his accomplishment is the wonder of America, given as we are to the love of minor masterpieces and the minute perfections. For myself, and I believe I speak for great numbers, Mexico does not appear to me as it did before I saw Rivera's paintings of it. The mountains, the Indians, the horses, the flowers and children, have all subtly changed in outlines and colors. They are Rivera's Indians and flowers and all now, but I like looking at them.

The photographs are good, not too brilliantly reproduced perhaps, but not misleading, they give one a very good notion of the originals. There are in these pictures—there were always, from the beginning—some stunningly beautiful spots, whole walls of painting better, I dare say, than anything else being done today. There are also long dreary stretches of plain hack-work, overcrowded, incoherent, mechanical; a breathless jostling of anachronistic characters, and too much detail, which, when shown in the large, do not justify their presence by any special beauty or excellence.

One of the best spots has been reproduced on the jacket. Rivera, for all his completely muddled politics, his childish social theories and personal opportunism, is saying, in this painting, just this: that bullets cannot destroy the spirit you see looking out of the eyes of these three men. Wolfe, much clearer and more "literate," as the special jargon of his special wing has it, backs him up with the facts. But even he is confused as to the probable results of the encroaching machine on the Indian, agrarian, manual worker, primitive communist. He ends his valuable study on the conventional note of hope for a new dawn, and soon; a hope so rosy one would like to share it, and so vague one does not know where to begin. It seems, in this book, to be based on the expectation of an organized and expertly directed revolt of the Indian peasant and worker, and bestows upon them, for the future, a capacity for unity and steadiness of purpose they have not shown in the past. According to Mr. Wolfe's own findings, the Indian social system was decayed with class war, religious tyranny, social injustice, even when Cortés found them. There was, it would seem, revolution in Mexico, even then.

PARVENU . . .

Mexico: A Study of Two Americas, by Stuart Chase,
in collaboration with Marian Tyler.
New York: The Literary Guild of America, 1931.

Mexico is not really a place to visit any more, or to live in. The land has fallen prey to its friends, organized and unorganized; its arts and customs are in the dreadful convulsions of being saved, preserved, advertised and exploited by a horde of appreciators, amateur or professional. They swarm over the place and eat the heart out of it like a plague of locusts. Tourist busses go roaring over the beautiful mountain roads, loaded with persons carrying note books and cameras, and you may be certain that one in five of them is writing a study, or an interpretation, or a survey; hardly one of them will admit he is a simple traveller taking the air and viewing the scenery and buying harmless little knickknacks by way of proving to himself he is really travelling.

In a published letter Kay Boyle has written that Americans are the best travellers. In Spain they become entirely Carmen swinging her behind, they are each in turn Christ on the cross in Jerusalem. In Mexico, I find, they are all prophets and experts, flustered and uneasy, nosing about in a crowd of other self-appointed prophets, trying to squeeze themselves into the esoteric skin of the Indian; their ears buzz with the altitude and the cross-currents of misinformation, and besides, often they are under contract to stuff it all down in a hurry and rush back with a book while the racket is still good.

Most of these travellers fall with deadly monotony into the arms of the resident authorities on Mexico, who have placed the whole subject on production basis. They publish slipshod little magazines full of glib pieces about those native dances; they peddle Mexican painting, act as scouts for art shops, instruct the Indian craftsman how to make his stuff more acceptable to the tourist taste, and in every way help on the destruction of Mexican art and life as much as they can. Next the visitor is introduced to a picked half-dozen of "representative" Mexicans, who speak English, and who are invariably courteous, hospitable and charming. He then goes, or is taken, on a

sightseeing tour: to Xochimilco (floating gardens!), Teotihuacan (the pyramids!), the frescoes of Diego Rivera (the greatest
painter in the world!), to a show school in the country (Ac-
topan or Oaxtepec), Cuernavaca (Mr. Morrow's town), Taxco,
with the only foreign art colony in Mexico, and Acapulco,
once a great port. Back to the capital, and off again for a
glimpse of the deep hidden Mexico: through Puebla to certain
parts of Oaxaca and Michoacan, and if he is a do or die visitor,
bent on making his study complete, on to Yucatan to see those
oft-discovered Maya ruins. . . .

    Mr. Chase did it all, and in record time. His *Mexico: A Study*
is a got-up, trivial affair, concocted out of two short trips and
two other books which had covered very thoroughly all the
ground he goes over: *Tepoztlan* by Robert Redfield, and
Middletown by Helen and Robert Lynd. The knack of re-
writing other people's books, using other people's researches
as one's own, is a trick on which many a journalistic career is
based. One expects better of Mr. Chase, who has a field of his
own and credit for original findings. Brilliant as his idea may
have been of making a comparison between Middletown and
Tepoztlan, he is the victim of his own mind, and has turned out
a machine-made hymn of praise to life without machines. . . .
Or is it a cautious bread-and-butter letter to a friendly host?
For of all bad books written recently on Mexico, this is the
most peculiarly irritating mixture of glossing over, of tactful
omission, of superficial observation, of, above all, surprising
errors in simple fact. It dashes in all directions at once, with a
hasty flick at everything in sight, full of the confusions apt to
occur when a trained economist attempts in one short volume
to be historian, explorer, critic and apologist of a way of life
strange to him. With a little patience and work he might have
learned something. But he repeats at second, third, fourth
hand all the old familiar jargon about the Indians (they are un-
changeable, they have no nerves or inhibitions, they don't
want anything, they are insulted if you offer them money for
their work, and so on to eternity), takes a passing whack at
grafting politicians but is careful not really to tell anything,
praises all the things the professional propagandists have been
paid for praising all these years; in short, there is not one shred
of evidence that Mr. Chase ever set foot in this country, except

for some rather sketchy glances at the scenery. Everything else, he could, and did, I believe, read from books, and most of them very silly books recently published on Mexico. His bibliography itself is a curiosity.

Mr. Chase winds up by some extraordinary advice to the Mexicans from a parvenu cousin. I know better than to give advice to Mexicans, after living here for four years over a period of ten. But I should like to seize this opportunity for a little advice to my fellow authors who come here. You would do well to visit Mexico quite as you visit other countries, without meddling, without presuming that you are a natural candidate for official favor, and without that condescending kindness which is so infuriating to intelligent Mexicans. If you really love the way of life you find here, keep your hands off it. All this uproar of publicity helps to change, commercialize, falsify it. Do not apologize for Mexican political corruption, any more than you would for your own rotten politicians. Mexicans are quick to resent this. The Indian arts are very beautiful, but so are the folk arts of other countries, and there is no special occult value to them. Their fiestas have about the same degree of meaning as popular fiestas in other countries. The nature of the Indian is as complicated and mysterious as human nature is, and if one of you would take the time and trouble to be well acquainted with even one of them, I think you might be ashamed to talk of him always as a problem, a spectacle, a kind of picturesque social monstrosity to be approached always in this arty-scientific-sociological manner. Americans, travelling, seem to believe there is nothing so integral, so good of its kind, but can be improved by their pawing and fumbling it over a little. It is better, when you visit here, to leave your superiorities at home, and if possible to shed your ignorances here, before you write a book interpreting Mexico.

With these farewell words, I sit back and wait for the next flood of books written by this year's crop of seminarists, folk lorists, prophets, students, friends of Mexico, propagandists, art enthusiasts, and the common carriers of good will. But I shall not read them.

HISTORY ON THE WING

The Stones Awake: A Novel of Mexico, by Carleton Beals.
Philadelphia: J. B. Lippincott Co., 1936.

Shortly before my last visit to Mexico, 1930–31, Carleton Beals, with several friends of his, looked over the roof ledge of his apartment and saw several strange men coming in, as it proved, to arrest him. They took him away very quietly and popped him into jail and kept him incommunicado for an uncomfortable length of time. Mr. Beals, who rarely confuses himself with the hero of his own works, was bored and angry and nervous all at once, being uncertain whether they meant to shoot him. He persuaded himself that it seemed unlikely. In the meantime, they had interrupted several books, articles and journeys of his, all of which have been finished since, and dozens more. His arrest had been ordered by a certain politician, really a quite dangerous thug, who objected to Mr. Beals's truthful and therefore damaging account of the politician's life and works. Why he let Mr. Beals go again I do not remember, but I imagine he is regretting it. Mr. Beals has gone on his cheerful career of gathering, arranging more or less neatly and publishing great floods of damaging, disrespectful truths about Mexico's corrupt politicians ever since. Side by side with this tenacious labor of hatred, or rather, knotted and woven in with it, goes his labor of love: a patient, constant presentation of the life and fate of the Indians, the wronged, the disinherited, the endlessly exploited industrial and agricultural workers of Mexico.

He never fails, you know always where to find him. It must be nearly twenty years since he went to Mexico, and if he lives a hundred more he could never write all he has seen and heard and learned about the life in that most complicated and confused country. But no doubt he means to try, and if anyone of our time can get all the essentials on record, he can.

He might have been a fine novelist if he had had time to stop and learn. He could have been a frightfully overpaid newspaperman if a sensational career had been his aim. He is neither, as it happens; when he writes facts, he really sticks to the facts, and that capacity is beyond praise. But when he turns to the art of the novel, he does not stick to art, and that is a pity. He is still a first-rate reporter writing his memories, telling good stories, explaining the predicament of the Indian and rousing sympathy and indignation for him, kidnaping his characters whole and sound out of real life and setting them in the midst of real events, so that instead of marveling at their reality, you would think it odd if they didn't seem real. Of course they are real. That is why, in his scenes of absolutely private lives and relationships, Mr. Beals suffers from a failure of imagination. He cannot follow his characters into the locked doors of their hearts and minds because he did not create them. With one exception. He knows Esperanza, the Indian village girl born in peonage. She is one of the most natural, breathing, appealing women in American fiction. No doubt he has worked faithfully from a model, for knowing his methods any other assumption would be fantastic, but he knows, for once, more about a certain kind of woman than she could be apt to know about herself. And he presents her, carries her through, develops her character and mind and personality, shows her growing up, growing older, arriving at a logical point of experience, in the end, which is merely a point of departure for another cycle of experience, and she really does live on quite tangibly after the book is closed.

This is a feat; how it happens I do not know, in the jungle of episode, the confusion of political crime and constant revolution, the crowds of characters and changes of scene. You will learn a great deal about Mexico from any one of Mr. Beals's books, whether novel or chronicle of that country. But you can know Esperanza only by reading *The Stones Awake*. She is worth knowing.

THIRTY LONG YEARS OF REVOLUTION

The Wind That Swept Mexico:
The History of the Mexican Relvolution, 1910–1942,
by Anita Brenner, with 184 historical photographs
assembled by George R. Leighton.
New York: Harper & Brothers, 1943.

In Cuernavaca there is a pavement with the celebrated commemorative motto, "It is more honorable to die standing than to live kneeling." The great beauty of this saying, the reason no doubt why it rings with such confident reassurance in the mind, is that the Mexican revolutionists always knew it was true and acted upon it long before any one thought of making the phrase. They have not only died standing, but attacking, weapons in hand, their spiritual boots on. I say spiritual boots because many of them in fact were barefooted. Mexico is comparatively a small country, yet by conservative estimate a million men have died for this cause: that is to say, for the most primary and rudimentary things of life for a man, a scrap of land to grow his food, and official legal recognition of his mere humanity by government and society. Mexico is potentially a vastly rich country, so seven-tenths, perhaps, of her enemies have come from without; the other three-tenths, as happens in all countries, we know more clearly than ever now, are among her own people. For more than thirty long, bitter years the Mexican revolutionists have fought for the minimum of human rights against a mostly ungodly united force consisting of their own proto-Quislings, the Church, the oil and metal-mining companies of the United States and Great Britain, the trading interests of Germany and the stubborn reactionary hold of Spanish influence. There were besides the internal quarrels between the various schools of revolution, the personal rivalries, individual struggles for mere power, all the most dreary and average history of human weakness and failure. Yet for all of this the Mexican revolutionists have made a good showing; they exhibited high qualities of tenaciousness, personal courage, incorrigible love of country, a fixed determination not to live kneeling, besides a gradually developing sense of method, of political strategy, and a pretty fair understanding of just what they were up against in a world sense. The whole story of the relations of that country with the United States alone is ugly, grim, bitter beyond words, and so scandalous I suppose the whole truth, or even the greater part of the simple facts, can never be published: it might blow the roof off this continent.

Keeping these things well in mind, Miss Brenner has written a rather light sketch of the whole period, hitting the high spots only but choosing the spots so tactfully that the plot is never lost; and though I have known the story, and for many years, so well it is possible I fill in the gaps as I go, yet I like to feel that the reader who knows little can find here a clear statement, a logical exposition, that will serve safely as a starting point if he wishes to pursue this history further. The facts are straight so far as they go, the deep, underlying motives of the whole restless and aspiring period are understood and explained, but I think Miss Brenner yields again to her old temptation to give too pretty and simple a picture—for, mind you, this terrible little story she tells is a mere bedtime lullaby beside the reality —and in general, to treat individual villains, whom she really knows to be such, too gently. A few scorching lines it seems to me might have been devoted to, for example, Alberto Pani's career as Foreign Minister. I think the deeds of some of the oil companies could have been exposed with somewhat more vigor. The betrayal of Felipe Carillo-Puerto might have been clarified to the great benefit of the story. Yet, within the limitations of space—the story is only 100 pages long—the author has performed prodigies of condensation, and within the more multiple and complicated limitations of the present international political situation, she has perhaps ventured as far as she might and still have her book published at all.

The best thing is, she realizes the importance of easy relations between Mexico and the United States just now, and the dangers, too; for, as she says frankly, this being the point of the book, that as the diplomatic and other understandings between the United States and the Mexican governments grow amiable, the Mexican people grow uneasy for their own prospects of freedom; and they may well do so, for Lavals and Pétains do not grow only in France. The Mexican people have been handed over to the invaders by their own leaders before, and they are not so childish as to think it cannot happen again. Invasion takes many forms, and they have experienced most of them.

Mr. Leighton's collection of pictures is distinguished, realistic; with extracts from Miss Brenner's texts, they could stand as a book by themselves. . . . They tell the story all over again and in some ways more boldly, of a whole race disinherited in its own country and fighting against desperate odds. Besides being superior photography, chosen with a fine sense of form and progression, these pictures lack entirely the slickness, the made-to-order look, of too much of the photography in this present war, which gives the impression that the man with the camera has instructions to shoot from only certain angles and no others: "A little," wrote a friend not long ago, "as if this war were something being produced by M.G.M." Happily, these Mexican pictures were made before that period set in. They have a wonderfully casual air; the man with the camera took what he saw before him, whatever it happened to be, not thinking, apparently, whether it would be good propaganda or not. . . . It turns out that he made the most convincing, most moving kind of straight narrative; and, oh, the faces. . . . It seems to me one need not be partisan; one need only to be human in the most average way, not to see what was bound to happen, comparing, let's say, just the face of Zapata (in Tina Modotti's masterly working out of an old negative) with that of Archbishop Pascual Diaz; or of Hearst with that of Obregon, taken when his shattered arm was healing, and not to be able to know at once which side one is on, now and forever. . . .

AUTOBIOGRAPHICAL

About the Author

Autobiographical sketch for
Authors Today and Yesterday, edited by Stanley J. Kunitz
with Howard Haycraft and Wilbur C. Hadden.
New York: The H. W. Wilson Co., 1933.

I WAS born May 15, 1894, at Indian Creek, Texas, brought up in Texas and Louisiana, and educated in small southern schools for girls. I was precocious, nervous, rebellious, unteachable, and made life very uncomfortable for myself, and I suppose for those around me. In fact, simply a certain type of child. As soon as I learned to form letters on paper, at about three years, I began to write stories, and this has been the basic and absorbing occupation, the intact line of my life which directs my actions, determines my point of view, profoundly affects my character and personality, my social beliefs and economic status, and the kind of friendships I form. I did not choose this vocation, and if I had had any say in the matter, I would not have chosen it. I made no attempt to publish anything until about ten years ago, but I have written and destroyed manuscripts quite literally by the trunkful. I say trunkful because I have spent fifteen years wandering about, weighted horribly with masses of paper and little else. Yet for this vocation I was and am willing to live and die, and I consider very few other things of the slightest importance.

All my intense growing years were lived completely outside of literary centers; I knew no other writers and had no one to consult with on the single vital issue of my life. This self-imposed isolation, which seems to have been almost unconscious on my part, a natural way of living, prolonged and made more difficult my discipline as artist. But it saved me from discipleship, personal influences, and membership in groups. I began to read at about five years and have read ever since, but my reading until my twenty-fifth year was the most important, being a grand sweep of all English and translated classics from the beginning up to about 1800. And then I began with the newcomers, and found new incitements.

Within the past dozen years I have lived in New Orleans, Chicago, Denver, Mexico City, New York, Bermuda, Berlin, Basel, and now live in Paris, and in all these places I have done book-reviewing, political articles, hack writing of all kinds for newspapers, editing, re-writing other people's manuscripts, by way of earning a living, and a sorry living it was, too. Without the help of devoted friends I should have perished many times over.

My short stories have been published by *Century*, *transition*, the *New Masses*, the *Second American Caravan*, the *Gyroscope*, *Scribner's*, and the *Hound and Horn*; poems in *Measure* and *Pagany*. A small collection of short stories was published in 1930 under the title of *Flowering Judas*. In 1931 I received a Guggenheim Fellowship for writing abroad and as this is written I am still working on my novel *Many Redeemers* which I began in Mexico years ago. A book of old French songs which I translated last year will be published in Paris this summer. I have also resumed work on a study of Cotton Mather, which I began in 1927, got half way thru, and had to give up for other work.

Politically my bent is to the Left. As for esthetic bias, my one aim is to tell a straight story and to give true testimony. My personal life has been the jumbled and apparently irrelevant mass of experiences which can only happen, I think, to a woman who goes with her mind permanently absent from the place where she is. My physical eye is unnaturally far-sighted, and I have no doubt this affects my temperament in some way. I have very little time sense and almost no sense of distance. I have no sense of direction and have seen a great deal of the world by getting completely lost and simply taking in the scenery as I roamed about getting my bearings. I lack entirely a respect for money values, and for caste of any kind, social or intellectual or whatever. I have a personal and instant interest in every human being that comes within ten feet of me, and I have never seen any two alike, but I discover the most marvelous differences. It is the same with furred animals. I love best remembered landscapes two or three countries away. I should like to settle to live in a place where I might swim in the sea, sail a cat boat, and ride horseback. These are the only recreations I really care for, and they all take a good deal of elbow room. Not for nothing am I the great-great-great-grand daughter of Daniel Boone.

This spring in Paris I married Eugene Pressly, originally from Pennsylvania, and we plan to live here for several years.

Fall 1933

The Land That Is Nowhere

FINALLY, after some meditation, I have made up my mind to be a good Christian for once and forgive a certain critic with whom I have had a friendly if somewhat random acquaintance for, as the Mexicans say, "A ball of years" (*una bola de años*).

Let me begin again. This is difficult. I forgive that critic here and now, and forever, for calling me a "newspaper woman," in the public prints. I consider it actionable libel, but, as is too often the case in these incidents, he has a small patch of solid ground under him, which I am going to make a cheerful roundabout attempt to cut away. Fifty-odd years ago, for eight short months of my ever-lengthening (or shortening?) life, I did have a kind of job on a newspaper, the *Rocky Mountain News*, in Denver, Colorado. On the advice of a doctor, I had gone there as to a climate suitable for my lungs, which had been misdiagnosed as tubercular. Naturally while taking the cure and doing my apprentice writing I had also to find a job of some sort; the city editor recklessly hired me, and though he was much too good-tempered a man to say so, it is fairly certain he lived to regret it. I too regret it, if the fame of it is to stick to me for the rest of my days. It was the first of quite dozens of temporary low-salaried breathing spaces between one crisis and another. But never a second newspaper job. For though now I recollect in what, for me, is comparative tranquillity, life, on the whole, has consisted mostly of crises, never two alike, resolved by whatever means were handiest, which led inevitably to another crisis which was resolved, which led. . . .

The critic's second error is more serious. He shares, with his literary contemporaries and fellow pilgrims of that strange American migration to Europe during the 1920's, a passion for the too-early autobiography, the premature summing up, the pronouncing of verdicts and passing of sentences before the evidence is all in: the cropping of living histories to fit them into a pattern. We none of us know each other's stories well enough to venture conclusions about them. We do not even each of us know our own, because we do not know the end.

In the epilogue to his republished memoirs, first written when he was a tired Old Master of thirty-three, more or less, our critic, nevertheless, attempts to set all American writers or painters or critics who happened to travel during that ill-starred decade into a careful theory of motive: self-willed exile in search of life; flight, pursuit, return. Sometime later, as an afterthought, he accounts for my absence, hitherto unnoticed, from the crowded European scene of that hour by concluding: "Mexico City was her Paris, and Taxco her South of France."

After trying at length and in vain to chase this mad logic from its untenable conclusion back, back to the lair of its fantastic premise, I am able only to say: No. Mexico City was my well-loved Mexico City, and Taxco was my abomination. I never saw that town until my last year in Mexico; it was already neatly divided in three, among an American lady (Natalie Scott) speculating in real estate, an American gentleman (William Spratling) who ran an art silverworks factory with Indian workmen, and a few charming Mexican high-career politicians such as Moises Saenz, Minister of Public Charities, who decreed some very rococo pleasure domes in the most picturesque locations. Paris for me is the city I did not arrive at until January, 1932, because until then I had no occasion to be there, and I have yet to see the South of France, though I have heard a great deal about it, from Ford Madox Ford and Janice Biala. I was never one for viewing scenery as such, or for visiting around among friends; if I traveled extensively, it was only on lawful occasions, for I was ever under the necessity of earning, if not exactly a living, a subsistence. Descendant as I am of a vast tribe of nomads who in the course of less than a century, from 1648 to 1720, according to family records, migrated in swarms from England to America, from Virginia and Pennsylvania to the South in 1774 and on to the Southwest around 1850, the field farthest from me always looked the greenest and still does. I am sure my own temperament is in some way to blame for the curious fact that people have so often been willing to pay me to go away on an errand, or having gone, they have often paid me to come back on another. So when I bought a ticket for any place, it was for a sound reason, and I always knew where I was going, and why. The one thing never certain was how or when I should get back, the least disturbing of all

questions to me—I like going onward. Being a writer by vocation and by fate, a fate I had no chance of escaping by any sort
of strategy—I carried my breathing life with me wherever I
went, and that is an indestructible hearthstone.

Since I had to support my writing by working at other
things, my main concern was always to allow myself as much
margin of time and energy as was available between my succession of weird chores. On the day enough money had been
saved to sit down and work for a while, I dropped whatever I
was doing and disappeared. Yet the margins were narrow, the
energy unstable. All my early work up to the publishing of my
first book was done in these conditions, and a great deal of
it since. If they were sometimes dismaying, yet they seemed
inevitable, for I had not regarded writing either as career or
profession—it was the thing I did, the stipulated work of my
life. Nobody had promised me anything for it, and it is inexplicable how little, in a worldly way, I expected from it. Yet I
worked as well as I was able, in a constant, irrational, mystical
state of hope that in the end, by some grace from whatever
source, or some faculty not yet revealed in me, I might become
a good artist. That is still my hope.

The appearance of my first book in 1930 led to the grant of a
Guggenheim Fellowship in literature. In those days it was
good form on receiving this fellowship to leave wherever you
were and go somewhere else, the farther away the better. It
gave Americans specializing in many fields a modest version of
the classic Grand Tour, or a partial substitute for a year or two
in a foreign school or university—a good idea. I was in Mexico
at the time, where in several visits, from late 1920, I had spent
altogether more than five years. Happy to go, I dismembered
my lightly assembled household, sold the scraps of furniture I
had bought from the National Pawnshop, rendered up the remaining livestock (two ducks and one infant goat) as burnt
offerings in farewell feasts to friends, and left the dear country
of my predilection and childhood associations once and for all,
as it seems now, for I did not go back for thirty years, and had
no reason to believe that I should ever (I have twice since, short
visits, tours of duty, culturally speaking, for the State Department). At last I had the perfect reason for being in Europe. I
went first to Berlin, to Paris, then to Madrid, then to Basel,

then back to Paris, where I stopped short for five years; three of them were lived in "the *pavillon* or summer house, that stood in the courtyard of 70 bis rue Notre-Dame-des-Champs, near the Luxembourg Gardens," where Ezra Pound lived in 1923 when young men-of-letters eagerly went to call on him.

My husband and I were merely looking for a house; after a long search we found this delightful place, and learned only after we had moved in that it was simply stiff with literary history. Our concierge did not remember Mr. Pound, I daresay the only person who ever saw him who didn't, but she did recall an unfortunate American monsieur who had committed suicide very untidily, not to say inconsiderately, in one of the back *ateliers*; she remembered him gratefully, though, because he had left a cat who had proved to be ever since the joy of her days.

From my earliest recollection I had known that some day I should live in Paris; it was not even a daydream, merely one of the splendid things I was certain would happen when I grew up. Well, there I was, living in Paris, and it was splendid, though my definition of splendor had changed almost right about face with time. Also the 'twenties in Paris, about which everyone had read so much, were safely past, or so I believed. What a mistake that was.

E. M. Forster once wrote about Conrad: "He has no respect for adventure, unless it comes incidentally. If pursued for its own sake it leads to 'red noses and watery eyes,' and 'lays a man under no obligation of faithfulness to an idea'."

One thing is certain, I never had any notion of looking for adventure; just plain daily experience was more than I could handle. All I wanted was to live pleasantly with a good, long work table and a bright light over it. All sorts of people kept getting in the way of this plan, too simple and reasonable to carry through. And another thing I know well, wherever I went, for whatever reason, I was not looking for culture and civilization, but the life people were living now, and I wanted to live in the world, too. We had culture and civilization at home, in Texas, of all places. Our means were small, our circumstances anything but secure and comfortable, and it was all going to grow worse, not better. But we were brought up on the tallest possible standards of morals, manners, and ideals of learning—indeed to heights impossible, given the situation, to scale. Still we knew what the standards were and acknowledged them.

I was nourished almost incidentally on good literature, good music, and good art without ever being told it was great, or even good. It was what one read and heard and looked at to the exclusion of everything else. If one pulled out a battered, spine-broken, gotch-eared book, from any shelf or secretary or old cedar chest, it was inevitably an early translation of Dante's complete works, or one of half a dozen volumes of Shakespeare's plays, or the sonnets with marginal notes in twenty different handwritings, or Marlowe's plays, or Erasmus's *The Praise of Folly*, or the *Letters* of Madame de Sévigné, or the poems of Alexander Pope, or Jane Austen's *Mansfield Park*, or Boswell's *The Life of Samuel Johnson*, or *Gulliver's Travels* (not the one rewritten for children), or the *Essays* of Montaigne, or novels, such as *Tristram Shandy*. Laurence Sterne was the first author I ever read who made me feel that I, too, might some day become a real author, such is the incredible two-facedness of that man. *Wuthering Heights*, and *Anna Karenina*, for some reason, together with the letters of Heloise and Abelard, gave me my first inklings of the nature of love—mainly it was painfully disturbing and caused troubles of an extremely serious nature, and was not to be invited lightly, though it was clear that almost no one declined the gambit.

Then there was always Mark Twain, so far as I knew, the only living author of the time. Friends of the family, persons I might actually touch and speak to, had *seen* him, more than once. We did not have *Candide*, or the works of Dr. Rabelais, but a fourteen-year-old girl could hear of them and find them and be allowed to borrow them from the public library in a small, West Texas city, San Antonio; moreover, to sit around reading them in the bosom of her family without a soul even troubling to look over her shoulder. In fact I read at home everything that I was not allowed to read in school. We had beside Dr. Percy's *Reliques of Ancient English Poetry* and Arber *English Reprints* of Elizabethan poetry, the *Confessions* of St. Augustine; and Voltaire's *Philosophical Dictionary* complete with notes by Smollett, which took me nine long years to work through from A to Z. I started at eleven years and wound up, a little staggered, the complete skeptic, at twenty. We had every line of verse ever published by Edgar Allan Poe, which we used to sing to tunes of our own. When I was thirteen years old, the beautiful German-born mother of my dearest childhood friend asked me what I was reading. It happened to be Dostoyevsky—*The House of the Dead*—from the public library. "Oh, my dear child, Dostoyevsky? Of course you must read the Russians, but I will give you something beautiful you will like better." And she gave me Turgenev's *Torrents of Spring*. I read it dutifully, and went back to Dostoyevsky, whose surfaces were easier to grasp, and certainly the surface was all I could grasp at that time. I had to grow up to Turgenev; but then I had to spend a lifetime growing up to the reading I did before I was sixteen. Yet, the transition, at about that time, to Flaubert, to Thomas Hardy, to Henry James, and from thence to James Joyce (*Dubliners*), W. B. Yeats, Virginia Woolf, E. M. Forster, T. S. Eliot, and so on, on, came gradually, easily, simply, all in good time, with no sense of shock. It may have been because I had not been told there was a modern movement in literature.

I had begun to write early, at six years, and invented some fearfully bloodthirsty characters and carried them though interminable, improbable events, in deadly earnest. My family passed them around, reading the richest bits aloud, and laughing their heads off. They gave some of the "nobbles" to friends nearby, who laughed *their* heads off. Such were my beginnings in my predestined art.

I will leave out nearly everything about the music, and the wonderful famous old actors and actresses on their last legs who trouped the country in those days in their private trains, playing Shakespeare, Schiller, Alexandre Dumas, Sardou, and Henry Arthur Jones. All the celebrated singers, violinists, and pianists of the world who visited this country stopped at least once in San Antonio, Texas, and even in Austin, and always in New Orleans. They played nobly straight through the wide land in every direction out of New York; there was really no excuse for anyone almost anywhere who could raise half a dollar for a balcony seat not hearing and seeing whatever was going in the regions of the sublime.

Trainloads of audiences from all the small towns came in

when Paderewski played, or Ada Rehan did *The Taming of the Shrew*, or Madame Modjeska appeared as Mary Stuart, and who would have missed Sarah Bernhardt playing *Camille* in a tent? I saw and heard all this when I was so young it was just a dazzling troubling dream, I knew nothing of it but the wonder. The wonder was enough. I would go dazed with my head a mere hive of honey-making bees for weeks, months, years. It unfitted me for living as a simple child should, it tormented me with feelings and thoughts beyond my capacity, it urged me to strain against the bonds of childhood and the rules and the limitations, and the company of other children.

I do not believe that childhood is a happy time, it is a time of desperate cureless bitter griefs and pains, of shattering disillusionments, when everything good and evil alike is happening for the first time, and there is no answer to any question. . . . I was prematurely experienced in the mind, and yet brought up in such a way that I was not allowed even the normal advance in common experience suitable for a growing child. The whole effort of the elders around us was to keep us in total ignorance, so far as they were able, of the actual world we were to live in. But I remember best and most clearly and with love the things I am telling now; they are my true memories, and those experiences in books, in music, in the theater were the real events of my life, my recollections of them is the thin continuous line of consciousness by which I can trace myself, and recognize myself as the same being no matter how endless a series of changing situations.

Patience, please. I still know where I am and where I am going, my aim being merely to set a very minor biographical error straight, but it looks as if in doing it, I too shall write an autobiography—all because I should like you to know, though you have never asked, just why Mexico City was not my Paris, and why, though I have lived of my own happy choice more than fourteen years out of this country, I was never, for one moment, anywhere, no, not even in the place where I was born, an Exile. And I have discovered, without looking for it, "The Land that is Nowhere—That is the true home."

1974

Chronology

1890   Born Callie Russell Porter, May 15, in Indian Creek,
        Texas, the fourth child of Harrison Boone Porter (b. 1857,
        Hays County, Texas) and (Mary) Alice Jones Porter (b.
        1859, Guadalupe County, Texas). (Alice Porter, a former
        schoolteacher, was the second of three children of pros-
        perous farmer John Newton Jones, 1833–1886, and Caro-
        line Lee Frost Jones, b. 1835; she met Harrison Porter, a
        graduate of the Texas Military Institute, at a family wed-
        ding in 1880. In 1883, when Alice's mother was declared
        insane, John Jones placed her in private care and moved
        to Indian Creek, a frontier settlement in Brown County,
        North Central Texas, where he purchased a 640-acre
        farm. In 1885, he invited Alice and Harrison, married two
        years earlier, to join him and Alice's brothers at the farm,
        offering them free tenancy on a small farming tract. Har-
        rison Porter was the fourth of 11 children born to Asbury
        Duval Porter, 1814–1879, a veteran of the Confederate
        Army, and Catharine Ann Skaggs ["Cat"] Porter, b. 1827,
        a native of Warren County, Kentucky. Harrison and
        Alice's first child, Anna Gay [called "Gay"], was born in
        1885, and their second, Harry Ray, in 1887. Their third
        child, Johnnie, was born in 1889 and died shortly after his
        first birthday.)

1892   The Porters' fifth child, a daughter, born January 25; Alice
        Porter, always frail, dies March 20. To honor her memory,
        Harrison christens the infant Mary Alice, but she will
        always be known as "Baby." Harrison takes the children
        to Kyle, a town of 500 in Hays County, to live in the home
        of his widowed mother, Cat Skaggs Porter. Family divides
        time between Kyle and Cat's small farm on nearby Plum
        Creek.

1893–95 Grieving and directionless, Harrison is a distracted and
        often-absent father. Cat takes charge of the children: she
        demands obedience, excellent schoolwork, attendance at
        the local Methodist Church, and good manners. She also
        instills in Callie the pleasures and powers of storytelling,
        spinning family tales in which her Skaggs ancestors are

larger-than-life figures: her father, Abraham Moredock Skaggs, fought with distinction in the War of 1812; her mother, Rhoda Boone Smith Skaggs, was a descendant of Jonathan Boone, brother of Daniel; her grandfather James Skaggs served under General George Washington; and her great-grandfather Henry Skaggs was an intrepid explorer in the Kentucky territory. "I was fed from birth on myth and legend," Porter will recall, "and a conviction of natural superiority bestowed by birth and tradition."

1895–1900   Educated at home by live-in governesses hired by Cat. Enters Kyle public school and precociously reads everything at hand—selections from McGuffey's Readers (especially the lives of Cotton Mather and Joan of Arc), dime novels, and "trashy romances." Attempts to write stories, the earliest an illustrated "nobbel" called "The Hermit of Halifax Cave." Produces plays on grandmother's porch. Sings duets with best friend, Erna Victoria Schlemmer, the daughter of prosperous German-immigrant merchants. Taken by Cat to San Antonio to see traveling performers such as Ignace Paderewski and Helena Modjeska. Devours the 18th-century English classics, including Boswell's *Life of Johnson*, Sterne's *Sentimental Journey*, and Swift's *Gulliver's Travels*.

1901–2   Distraught by sudden death of Cat, October 2, 1901. Comforted by housekeeper Masella Daney ("Aunt Jane"), a former slave of Cat, and her husband, Squire Bunton. Completes school year in spring 1902, and spends summer at Plum Creek farm. Father disposes of Cat's estate and takes family on round of visits to Texas and Louisiana relatives. Grows closer to brother and to sister Gay, but resents sister Baby, father's favorite. Reads all of Shakespeare's plays and memorizes many of his sonnets.

1903–4   Family stays for short period with father's cousin Ellen Myers Thompson, who with her husband runs a dairy farm in Buda, Texas. Family settles in rented rooms near San Antonio, where Harrison takes a series of temporary jobs. Girls attend various Catholic day schools in San Antonio, and then board at a convent school in New Orleans. Visits Erna Schlemmer in Kyle and is introduced by her mother to works of Russian writers and European artists.

1904–5   Family moves to rented house near West End Lake in San

Antonio. Girls attend the Thomas School (Methodist) for full academic year. In September 1904, Callie asks family and classmates to call her by new name, "Katherine," adopted in honor of grandmother Cat. (Harry Ray simultaneously changes his name to "Harrison Paul" and asks that he be called "Paul.") Reads Edward Gibbon's *Decline and Fall of the Roman Empire*, William James's *Varieties of Religious Experience*, and the works of Chaucer and Voltaire. Writes school essay defending woman suffrage. Accompanies father to hear stump speech by Eugene Debs, the Socialist Party candidate for U.S. president. Takes singing lessons at Our Lady of the Lake Convent. Performs dramatic reading of "Lasca," a ballad about a Texas cowboy and his Mexican sweetheart, in Thomas School commencement program. Urged by drama teacher to consider stage career. Performs with Gay in summer-stock theater at Electric Park in San Antonio. Moves with family to Victoria, Texas, near the Gulf of Mexico, and advertises lessons in "music, dramatic reading, and physical culture" in the *Victoria Advocate*. Writes stories and sends them to Paul, now a Navy recruit. At Christmas dance, meets John Henry Koontz, the 19-year-old son of a wealthy rancher in nearby Inez.

1906   Family moves to Lufkin, in East Texas; there, in a double ceremony on June 20, Gay, age 21, marries Thomas H. Holloway, and Katherine, 16, marries John Henry Koontz. Moves to Lafayette, Louisiana, where Koontz works for Southern Pacific Railway. Begins "one long orgy of reading" including works "from the beginning until about 1800," Nietzsche and Freud, and a dozen re-readings of *Wuthering Heights*.

1907   Publicizes herself in the *Lafayette Daily Advertiser* as "Mrs. J. H. Koontz, Teacher of Elocution, Physical Culture, and English." Disillusioned in relationship with Koontz, who is tightfisted, verbally and physically abusive, often drunk. Attempts to write stories in the styles of Samuel Johnson and Laurence Sterne and sonnets in the styles of Petrarch and Shakespeare.

1908   Moves to Houston with Koontz when he is offered a position with a wholesale grocery and cotton-factoring company. Yearns for a child of her own and becomes attached to Koontz's little niece Mary Koontz.

1909   Knocked unconscious and thrown down stairs by Koontz;
        suffers broken bones. Temporarily escapes to home of
        uncle Asbury M. Porter, in Marfa, Texas.

1910   Converts to Roman Catholicism, her husband's faith, in
        effort to stabilize marriage. Reads and rereads *The Con-
        fessions of St. Augustine* and the lives of the saints, espe-
        cially Joan, Ursula, Teresa of Ávila, Anne, and Catherine
        of Siena. Distressed by unabated physical abuse by Koontz.
        Suffers a miscarriage at end of year.

1911   Moves to Corpus Christi with Koontz when he takes a
        job as a traveling salesman. Writes stories and poems
        during Koontz's absences. Discovers in a local book and
        stationery store Gertrude Stein's *Tender Buttons* and James
        Joyce's *Dubliners*.

1912   In January, poem "Texas: By the Gulf of Mexico," her
        first known publication, appears on the cover of *Gulf
        Coast Citrus Fruit Grower and Southern Nurseryman*, a
        trade magazine. Visits Gay in Dallas after Gay's daughter,
        Mary Alice, is born in December.

1913   Undergoes surgery for ovarian cyst. Recuperates at Spring
        Branch, near Houston, with family friends, the Heinrich
        von Hillendahls. Weighs the social and financial conse-
        quences of leaving Koontz; decides to stay married but
        instructs Koontz to "take his pleasures elsewhere." Spends
        long days with childhood friend Erna Schlemmer, now
        living in Corpus Christi. Depressed that she has found
        neither marital happiness nor artistic success.

1914   In February buys one-way train ticket to Chicago and
        flees marriage. Works as extra in movies *The Song in the
        Dark* and *From Out the Wreck*. Prose sketch, "How
        Brother Spoiled a Romance," published in the *Chicago
        Tribune*. Attends performance of J. M. Synge's *Playboy of
        the Western World* by the Abbey Players ("the only mem-
        orable artistic experience I had in Chicago"). Returns to
        Texas to help her widowed sister Baby after the birth of a
        son, then moves to Gibsland, Louisiana, to help Gay, tem-
        porarily abandoned by her philandering husband during a
        difficult pregnancy. Works the Lyceum circuit in a three-
        state area as a singer of ballads such as "Bonny Barbara
        Allen" and "Lord Randall." Unaware of death of mater-

nal grandmother, Caroline Lee Frost Jones, November 14, at the Southwestern Lunatic Asylum, San Antonio.

1915   Moves to boarding house at 1520 Ross Avenue, Dallas, and addresses envelopes for $2.50 a day. Divorces Koontz, June 21, and legalizes name as "Katherine Porter." Marries and soon divorces T. Otto Taskett, a business acquaintance of Koontz. Works as sales clerk at Neiman Marcus. Begins to call herself "Katherine *Anne* Porter," completing her identification with grandmother Catharine Ann Skaggs Porter. In November contracts tuberculosis and, destitute and afraid, enters a Dallas County charity hospital.

1916   With financial assistance from Paul, relocates to the J. B. McKnight sanatorium in Carlsbad, Texas. Finds friend in fellow patient Kitty Barry Crawford, society columnist for the *Fort Worth Critic*. Transfers to Woodlawn Sanatorium, Dallas, where she teaches tubercular children in exchange for medical care. After discharge from hospital, marries acquaintance Carl von Pless, whom she will divorce within the year.

1917   Children's story, "How Baby Talked to the Fairies," published in the *Dallas Morning News*. Lives briefly with Gay and her children in Dubach, Louisiana, and is enchanted with niece Mary Alice. At invitation of Kitty Crawford, moves into Fort Worth home of Kitty and her husband, Garfield, and assumes Kitty's duties as *Critic* society columnist. Does volunteer publicity work for the Red Cross Corps.

1918   With financial help from Paul, travels to Denver, Colorado, to strengthen lungs at private sanatorium The Oaks. In summer joins Kitty Crawford in Colorado Springs, where they share a cabin with Kitty's friends, the writers Jane Anderson and Gilbert Seldes. In September, hired as reporter for the *Rocky Mountain News* at $15 a week. In early October, nearly dies in hospital during the Spanish flu pandemic; claims near-death experience of euphoria, "what the Christians call the 'beatific vision,' and the Greeks called the 'happy day.'" Recovers in Dubach under Gay's care, and enjoys Christmas with five-year-old Mary Alice.

1919   Returns to work at the *News*, weak and permanently white-haired, and is promoted to drama critic and feature writer; publishes more than 80 signed pieces between February and August. Joins the Denver Players, performs in several of its productions, and is briefly engaged to company manager Park French. In July is grief-stricken at sudden death of niece Mary Alice. Arrives in New York, October 19, determined to write fiction and poetry. Rents studio apartment on Grove Street, in Greenwich Village. Joins staff of Arthur Kane Agency and writes publicity releases for movies. Meets writers Genevieve Taggard, Gertrude Emerson, Rose Wilder Lane, Edmund Wilson, and Edna St. Vincent Millay; radical journalists Kenneth Durant, Mike Gold, and Helen Black; and editors Ernestine Evans, Bessie Beatty, Floyd Dell, and Harold E. Stearns. Enjoys company of several Mexican expatriates—painter Adolfo Best-Maugard, pianist Ignacio Fernández Esperón (Tata Nacho), and poet and critic José Juan Tablada among them—who encourage her to live and work in Mexico.

1920   Publishes re-told fairy tales in *Everyland*, a magazine for children, and *Asia*, a magazine promoting world trade and global understanding. Signs contract with *Asia* to ghost-write "My Chinese Marriage," the memoirs of a young midwestern woman, Mae Franking, who in 1912 married an American-educated lawyer from Shanghai and later settled in China. In October, takes train to Mexico City with reporting assignments from the *Christian Science Monitor* and the prospective *Magazine of Mexico*. Befriended by American journalist Thorberg Haberman, editor of the English-language section of the daily *Heraldo de México*, and her husband, Robert, a labor organizer and a speechwriter for Mexican president Alvaro Obregón. Writes articles, reviews, and editorials for the left-wing *Heraldo* and soon comes under surveillance by U.S. Military Intelligence Division, Bureau of Investigation. Writes public letters and sends money in support of Italian anarchists Nicola Sacco and Bartolomeo Vanzetti, convicted of murdering two payroll clerks during a Massachusetts holdup. Becomes acquainted with President Obregón, cabinet members José Vasconcelos, Plutarco Elías Calles, and Antonio Villarreal, and labor leader Luis Morones, as well as archaeologist William Niven, artist Gerardo Murillo

(Dr. Atl), and anthropologist and archaeologist Manuel Gamio. Joins the Mexican Feminist Council. Has brief love affair with Felipe Carillo Puerto, governor of Yucatán.

1921 Meets American social worker Mary Doherty, who will become a close friend, as well as muckraking journalist Lincoln Steffens, labor leader Samuel Gompers, and Mexican revolutionary Samuel Yúdico. Has successive love affairs with Polish diplomat Jerome Retinger and Nicaraguan poet Salomón de la Selva. Has abortion after becoming pregnant by De la Selva. Reports from Mexico City appear in the *New York Call*, the *Christian Science Monitor*, *The Freeman*, and other publications. *My Chinese Marriage* published serially in *Asia*, June through September, and then as a short book by Duffield & Co., New York. Returns to Fort Worth, stays with the Crawfords, and writes articles for Garfield Crawford's *Oil Journal*. Performs in local Little Theatre productions *Poor Old Jim* and *The Wonder Hat*. Works on novel called "The Book of Mexico."

1922 In Greenwich Village January through April. "Where Presidents Have No Friends" published in *The Century*. Returns to Mexico at request of President Obregón, who appoints her American curator of "Mexican Popular Arts and Crafts," a state-sponsored exhibit designed to tour the U.S. While writing and researching exhibition catalog, becomes devoted admirer of artists Diego Rivera and Xavier Guerrero and caricaturists José Clemente Orozco and Miguel Covarrubias. Exhibit opens in November in Los Angeles, but bureaucratic obstacles prohibit it from traveling further. Leaves Mexico for New York feeling dispirited and defeated. "María Concepción," her first published short story, appears in December issue of *The Century*.

1923 Abandons "The Book of Mexico" in favor of new novel, "Thieves Market." "María Concepción" reprinted in *Best Short Stories of 1922*. Returns to Mexico to commission pieces as guest editor of Mexican number of *Survey Graphic*. Story "The Martyr," inspired by personal encounters with Diego Rivera, appears in *The Century*. Begins love affair with Chilean scholar and poet Francisco Aguilera.

1924   Continues affair with Aguilera through mid-April, and
        then has amorous encounter with his friend Alvaro Hino-
        josa. When she learns she is pregnant, considers but re-
        jects abortion. Publishes two articles and a translation of
        a poem by Sor Juana Inés de la Cruz in Mexican number
        of *Survey Graphic*. In summer, joins friends at a farmhouse
        near Windham, Connecticut, then stays on alone until last
        stage of pregnancy. Male child is stillborn, December 2.
        Resolves to support herself as a freelance literary journal-
        ist and seeks reviewing assignments from editor friends.

1925   Recuperates at Greenwich Village apartment of friend
        Liza Dallett. Becomes closer to Village acquaintances in-
        cluding Hart Crane, Ford Madox Ford, Malcolm and
        Peggy Cowley, Dorothy and Delafield Day, Allen Tate,
        and Caroline Gordon. Writes 12 book reviews, mainly for
        the New York *Herald Tribune*; will continue to accept re-
        viewing assignments from the *Tribune*, *The New Republic*,
        The Nation, *The New York Times Book Review*, and other
        periodicals through the early 1950s.

1926   Spends summer in Connecticut with friends, including
        writers Josephine Herbst and John Herrmann and painter
        Ernest Stock. Contracts gonorrhea from Stock, and under-
        goes surgery for removal of both ovaries, a secret she
        keeps for the rest of her life. Moves into room at 561
        Hudson Street. Takes short-term editing job with J. H.
        Sears & Co., and under publisher's name, "Hamblen
        Sears," compiles and writes introduction to a collection of
        essays titled *What Price Marriage?* ("This book and *My
        Chinese Marriage* should have no place in the list of my
        books.") Through Allen Tate and Caroline Gordon meets
        Robert Penn Warren and Andrew Lytle.

1927   In August joins group in Boston for six-day rally protest-
        ing the pending executions of Sacco and Vanzetti. In-
        spired by Tate's financial success with a popular life of
        Stonewall Jackson, resolves to write a biography; in fall
        signs contract with Boni & Liveright for book "The Devil
        and Cotton Mather" and moves to Salem, Massachusetts,
        to read Mather papers. While consulting genealogical dic-
        tionaries, researches Skaggs, Jones, and Porter family his-
        tories. "He," a story set in Texas, appears in *New Masses*.
        Conceives long, three-part autobiographical novel called
        "Many Redeemers."

1928   Continues research in Salem. Collaborates with William
        Doyle on his play *Carnival*. Analyzes herself in private
        notes and concludes that she is personally responsible for
        all her "losses." Completes two stories, "Magic," which
        appears in *transition*, and "The Jilting of Granny Weather-
        all." "Rope," loosely based on her affair with Ernest
        Stock, published in *The Second American Caravan*. Works
        as copyeditor for the small literary publisher Macaulay &
        Co., and has brief love affair with colleague Matthew
        Josephson. Falls ill with bronchitis.

1929   Accepts invitation from friends Becky and John Crawford
        to stay with them in their Brooklyn home. "The Jilting of
        Granny Weatherall" appears in *transition*. With financial
        assistance from the Crawfords and other friends, lives in
        Bermuda from March through July; writes poems and
        several chapters of Mather biography. Story "Theft," based
        on self-analysis in Salem, published in *The Gyroscope*.

1930   Story "Flowering Judas" appears in *Hound & Horn*. In
        January signs two-book contract with Harcourt, Brace:
        receives advances of $500 for a novel ("Thieves Market")
        and $100 for a collection of stories. Returns to Mexico for
        stay of 16 months. *Flowering Judas* ("María Concepción,"
        "Magic," "Rope," "He," "The Jilting of Granny Weather-
        all," "Flowering Judas") printed by Harcourt, Brace in
        edition limited to 600 copies. Meets Eugene Dove
        Pressly, a 26-year-old American employee of the Institute
        of Current World Affairs, Mexico City, with whom she
        begins love affair.

1931   Essay "Leaving the Petate" published in *The New Repub-
        lic*. Works on "Thieves Market"; changes title to "Histor-
        ical Present." Moves to Mexico City suburb Mixcoac to
        share house with Pressly and Mary Doherty. Receives
        Guggenheim Fellowship ($2,000). At invitation of direc-
        tor Sergei Eisenstein, visits Hacienda Tetlapayac to ob-
        serve filming of *¡Que Viva Mexico!* Sails for Europe with
        Pressly on the North German Lloyd ship *Werra*, August 22.
        Arrives in Bremen, September 19, and takes train to Berlin.
        After Pressly leaves to find work in Spain, moves into
        boarding house at 39 Bambergerstrass. Meets American
        journalist and filmmaker Herbert Kline, communist poet
        and social critic Johannes Becher, and young American
        writer William Harlan Hale. Spends an evening dancing

with Hermann Göring but rejects his further advances. Works on story "Wiener Blut," inspired by voyage to Germany.

1932   Shares romantic interlude with Hale before traveling to Spain by way of Paris, a city she instantly adores. Quickly returns with Pressly to Paris ("I could not endure the thought of being anywhere else"). Renews friendship with Eugene and Maria Jolas, editors of *transition*; visits Ford Madox Ford and becomes friends with his companion, Janice Biala. Frequents Sylvia Beach's bookshop and lending library, Shakespeare and Company, and the cafés Dôme, Coupole, and Select. Becomes friends with publishers Barbara Harrison and Monroe Wheeler, and with Wheeler's companion, the writer Glenway Wescott. Battling severe bronchitis, enters the American Hospital at Neuilly at end of April. Story "The Cracked Looking-Glass" appears in *Scribner's Magazine*. In June goes to Switzerland to join Pressly, now employed by the American embassy at Basel. Abandons "Historical Present" and works on three pieces of "Many Redeemers": "Noon Wine," "Old Mortality," and "Pale Horse, Pale Rider." In Basel reads Erasmus and other Renaissance writers and, at the Kunstmuseum, deepens appreciation of European art. Essay "Hacienda" published in *The Virginia Quarterly Review*. Heavily edits Pressly's rough translation of J. J. Fernández de Lizardi's picaresque novel *El Periquillo Sarniento* (*The Itching Parrot*). Moves with Pressly to the Hôtel Malherbe, Paris.

1933   Marries Pressly, March 11; couple moves to seventh-floor apartment at 166 Boulevard Montparnasse. Attends classes at the Cordon Bleu cooking school. Sits for portraits by photographer George Platt Lynes. Meets Ernest Hemingway, Gertrude Stein, and Alice B. Toklas. Visited by publisher Donald Brace, who offers contracts for "Many Redeemers" and an expanded trade edition of *Flowering Judas. Katherine Anne Porter's French Song-Book*, a bilingual anthology of traditional French songs with translations and headnotes by Porter, published by Harrison of Paris, a fine press founded by Wheeler and Harrison. Harcourt, Brace rejects the Pressly-Porter translation of *The Itching Parrot* but offers to buy Boni & Liveright's contract for "The Devil and Cotton Mather."

1934   Rewrites "Hacienda" as a long story, printed by Harrison
        of Paris in an edition of 895 copies. "A Bright Particular
        Faith," a chapter of the Cotton Mather biography, ap-
        pears in *Hound & Horn*. Story "That Tree" published in
        The Virginia Quarterly Review. In April sends Brace six
        stories that form part of "Many Redeemers": "The Grave,"
        "The Circus," "The Grandmother" ("The Source"), "The
        Witness," "The Old Order" ("The Journey"), and "The
        Last Leaf." Exhausted and ill by May, spends six weeks at
        the Parksanatorium in Davos, Switzerland. Feels betrayed
        by Josephine Herbst upon reading her story "Man of
        Steel," a thinly disguised account of the Porter-Stock
        affair, published in *The American Mercury*. "The Circus"
        accepted for inaugural issue of *The Southern Review*,
        founded by Robert Penn Warren and Cleanth Brooks at
        Louisiana State University. Moves with Pressly to 70 bis
        rue Notre-Dame-des-Champs, a spacious cottage once
        the home of Ezra Pound.

1935   Publishes three stories in *The Virginia Quarterly Review*:
        "The Witness," "The Last Leaf," and "The Grave." Sets
        aside anger to comfort a desperate Josephine Herbst,
        whose husband has abandoned her for another woman; is
        surprised and disturbed by Herbst's lesbian advances. Ex-
        panded edition of *Flowering Judas* (now also including
        "Theft," "That Tree," "The Cracked Looking-Glass," and
        "Hacienda") published by Harcourt, Brace. Begins devel-
        oping short novel from material explored in "Wiener Blut";
        calls this work-in-progress "Promised Land." On Novem-
        ber 29, addresses the American Women's Club in Paris on
        the process of writing fiction and launches speaking ca-
        reer. Depressed by repeated bouts of bronchitis and the
        darkening atmosphere of prewar Europe, resolves to "go
        home" to Texas the following spring.

1936   Harcourt, Brace supplements advance for Cotton Mather
        biography, making possible a February departure for the
        U.S. Stops in Boston to do research for Mather book.
        Visits family in Texas and is drawn to teen-aged nephew
        Paul and niece Anna Gay ("Ann"). Travels with father
        and sister Baby to Indian Creek to visit mother's grave,
        and is moved by verse on tombstone written by father;
        spontaneously writes short poem for mother (later revised
        as "Anniversary in a Country Churchyard") and buries it

under soil at the grave. Removes from tombstone a memento: the glass-encased photograph of her mother that
her father had affixed there in 1892. Returns to Paris,
quits cottage, and moves with Pressly to the U.S. in October. Acknowledging that "Many Redeemers" is not a
novel but instead a series of shorter pieces, signs new contract with Harcourt, Brace for collection of five short
novels: "Noon Wine," "Old Mortality," "The Man in the
Tree" (a story about a lynching), "Pale Horse, Pale
Rider," and "Promised Land." Lives in New York for a
few weeks until Pressly leaves for temporary assignment in
Washington, D.C. Stays at inn in Doylestown, Pennsylvania, and there completes "Noon Wine" and "Old Mortality." Story "The Old Order" ("The Journey") appears
in *The Southern Review*. Returns to New York in December and lives with Pressly at 67 Perry Street.

1937   When Pressly accepts job with an oil company in
        Venezuela, Porter regards their separation as permanent.
        Visits Texas for father's 80th birthday. Receives Book-of-
        the-Month Club Prize for literary achievement ($2,500).
        Writes story "A Day's Work." Socializes with Glenway
        Wescott, George Platt Lynes, and Lynes's brother, Rus-
        sell, an editor at *Harper's*. Briefly resumes friendship with
        radical and communist friends: marches in May Day pa-
        rade; co-sponsors Second Congress of American Writers,
        June 4–6, in New York City; contributes a translation
        to . . . *and Spain Sings: Fifty Loyalist Ballads Adapted by
        American Poets*. Suddenly distances herself from left-wing
        social circle and embraces Southern friends Robert Penn
        Warren, Andrew Lytle, Caroline Gordon, and Allen Tate.
        Participates in Olivet (Michigan) Writers' Conference
        with Gordon and Tate, and returns with them to "Ben-
        folly," their Tennessee estate. Meets Cleanth and Edith
        Amy (Tinkum) Brooks and 26-year-old Albert Russel Er-
        skine Jr., a graduate student at Louisiana State University
        and managing editor of *The Southern Review*. Moves to
        attic apartment in the Lower Pontalba, New Orleans, and
        there begins a love affair with Erskine. Completes "Pale
        Horse, Pale Rider." Visits family in Texas.

1938   Files for divorce from Pressly, January 11. Works on "The
        Man in the Tree" and "Promised Land." Becomes more
        deeply attached to nephew Paul and niece Ann. On April 19,
        ten days after divorce from Pressly, marries Albert Erskine;

couple takes temporary lodging in Baton Rouge, where Erskine continues graduate study and editorial work for *The Southern Review*. Returns to Olivet for writers conference and meets Robert Frost (an "old bull-headed bore" but a "great poet and a good man"). Moves with Erskine to apartment at 901 America Street, Baton Rouge. "Pale Horse, Pale Rider" published in *The Southern Review*.

1939   *Pale Horse, Pale Rider: Three Short Novels* ("Old Mortality," "Noon Wine," and title story) published by Harcourt, Brace. Visits New York for opening of the Museum of Modern Art, and is feted on 49th birthday by friends and admirers. Renews friendship with cousin Lily Cahill, a successful Broadway actress. In constant demand as speaker after appearances at Vassar, Bennington, Bryn Mawr, and Shipley. Moves with Erskine to house at 1050 Government Street, where they take separate bedrooms. Meets young Eudora Welty, whom she encourages in her writing and sponsors for fellowships. Returns at the end of July to Olivet, where she meets Sherwood Anderson. Story "The Downward Path to Wisdom" published in *Harper's Bazaar*.

1940   Separates from Erskine at beginning of year. Accepts extended residency at Yaddo, an artists' colony near Saratoga Springs, New York. Story "A Day's Work" published in *The Nation*. "A Goat for Azazel," a chapter from the Cotton Mather biography, published in *Partisan Review*. In the summer, "Notes on a Criticism of Thomas Hardy" appears in *The Southern Review* and "Notes on Writing—From the Journals of Katherine Anne Porter" in *New Directions*. Lectures at Bread Loaf School of English, Middlebury College, Vermont. Meets Carson McCullers and is offended by her eccentricities. Recognizes that "Promised Land" will be a long novel; changes title to "No Safe Harbor." The Modern Library publishes new edition of *Flowering Judas and Other Stories*, for which she writes an introduction. On December 2, makes first of several appearances on CBS radio program *Invitation to Learning*, hosted by Mark Van Doren. Has brief reunion, but no reconciliation, with Erskine. Receives the first gold medal of the Society of Libraries of New York University.

1941   Story "The Source" appears in *Accent*. Inducted as member of the National Institute of Arts and Letters. Purchases house at Ballston Spa, near Saratoga Springs; names it "South Hill" and begins extensive remodeling while continuing to live at Yaddo. In June signs contracts with Doubleday, Doran for a biography of Erasmus and an account of a murder trial in 15th-century France, neither ever realized, and an abridged version of *The Itching Parrot.* Friendship with Eudora Welty, a summer resident at Yaddo, deepens. Becomes mentor to nephew Paul, an aspiring writer, and artistic patron of niece Ann, a professional ballet dancer. Writes introductions to *The Itching Parrot* and to Welty's debut collection, *A Curtain of Green.* Story "The Leaning Tower" published in *The Southern Review.*

1942   Father dies, January 23. At Erskine's request, takes the six weeks' residency in Nevada required to obtain a Reno divorce; marriage dissolved on June 19. Interviewed by F.B.I. agent about anti-American activities of friends and possibly herself. Participates in writing conference at Indiana University; meets Dr. Alfred Kinsey, who interviews her as part of his research for *Sexual Behavior in the Human Female* (1953). *The Itching Parrot* published by Doubleday, Doran. "Affectation of Praehiminincies," a chapter of the Cotton Mather biography, published in two installments in *Accent.* Attends Rocky Mountain Writers' Conference in Boulder, Colorado. Lives at Yaddo in July and August while remodeling of South Hill is completed. Lonely and miserable during fall and harsh winter. Worries about nephew Paul, who is stationed with the U.S. Army in Europe.

1943   Resigns from the National Institute of Arts and Letters to protest its practice of identifying certain candidates as "Negro." (Will resume membership when practice is dropped.) With the financial support of friends Glenway Wescott and Barbara Harrison, secludes herself at Harbor Hill Inn near West Point to work on "No Safe Harbor" and other books-in-progress.

1944   Accepts appointment at the Library of Congress as Fellow of Regional American Literature; boards with portrait painter Marcella Comés Winslow in her house on P Street in Georgetown. "Portrait: Old South" published in *Mademoiselle.* Begins yearlong love affair with painter Charles Shannon, an Army corporal stationed near Washington.

The Leaning Tower and Other Stories ("The Source," "The Witness," "The Circus," "The Old Order" ["The Journey"], "The Last Leaf," "The Grave," "The Downward Path to Wisdom," "A Day's Work," "The Leaning Tower") published by Harcourt, Brace. Returns to Yaddo. Excerpt from "No Safe Harbor" published in *The Sewanee Review*. As vice president of the National Women's Committee, makes re-election speeches endorsing President Franklin D. Roosevelt. Hospitalized in Saratoga Springs with pneumonia.

1945   Signs contract with Metro-Goldwyn-Mayer to work as scriptwriter at $1,500 a week; relocates to Santa Monica. Meets Charlie Chaplin, Judy Garland, and playwright Clifford Odets. Signs contract with Paramount Pictures to write screen adaptation of Victorien Sardou's *Madame Sans-Gêne* at $2,000 a week. Excerpt from "No Safe Harbor" appears in *Partisan Review*.

1946   Sells South Hill to friends George and Toni Willison. Buys, then relinquishes, 80 acres of mountain property in High Mojave Desert. Welcomes nephew Paul, who visits California after tour of duty in France. Excerpt from "No Safe Harbor" published in *Accent*. Memoir "A Christmas Story" appears in *Mademoiselle*. In desperate financial straits due to unwise management, moves into guest wing of Hollywood house of George Platt Lynes.

1947   Works briefly for Columbia Pictures on adaptation of Chekhov's story "La Cigale." Excerpt from "No Safe Harbor" appears in *The Sewanee Review*. Meets Christopher Isherwood and Texas novelist William Goyen. Negative critical essay on the life and work of Gertrude Stein ("The Wooden Umbrella") published in *Harper's*.

1948   Friendship with Josephine Herbst suffers final rupture when Herbst publishes an attack, "Miss Porter and Miss Stein," in *Partisan Review*, and *Somewhere the Tempest Fell*, a novel featuring barely disguised, unflattering portraits of Glenway Wescott, Monroe Wheeler, George Platt Lynes, and Porter. Speaks at the University of Kansas; meets Isabel Bayley, who will become a lifelong friend. Begins yearlong appointment at Stanford, and is insulted and angry that her classes will carry no credit; becomes friends with faculty members Richard and Ann Scowcroft,

Janet Lewis, and Yvor Winters. "Love and Hate" ("The Necessary Enemy") appears in *Mademoiselle*.

1949   Receives Litt.D. from the Woman's College of the University of North Carolina, the first of many honorary doctorates. As a Fellow in American Letters of the Library of Congress, is member of the jury that awards Bollingen Prize to Ezra Pound. Teaches summer courses at Stanford. Returns to New York, where she shares an apartment with her niece Ann.

1950   Speaks at colleges and universities, and at the 92nd Street Y. "The Flower of Flowers" and "A Note on Pierre Joseph Redouté" appear in *Flair*. At Manhattan cocktail party encounters a drunken Dylan Thomas, who lifts her to the ceiling in apparent tribute. Three excerpts from "No Safe Harbor" published in successive issues of *Harper's*, October through December. Becomes close friends with protégés J. F. Powers, Peter Taylor, and William Humphrey. Begins two-year term as co-vice-president of the National Institute of Arts and Letters.

1951   Begins yearlong affair with William Goyen. Signs contract with Harcourt, Brace for "The Days Before," a selection from 30 years of essays, book reviews, and other short prose; in lieu of advance accepts in-house position as literary adviser. Speaks at Millsaps College, the University of North Carolina at Greensboro, and the Mississippi State College for Women. "'Marriage Is Belonging'" appears in *Mademoiselle*.

1952   Joins American delegation in Paris for five-week International Congress for Cultural Freedom and speaks at opening session. Retreats to secluded inn in Pont-Aven to write introduction to "The Days Before" but, tired and unconfident, finds she can manage only a brief foreword. "Reflections on Willa Cather" published in *Mademoiselle*. Returns to Paris and enjoys reunions with her French translator, Marcelle Sibon, and bookseller Sylvia Beach. Returns to New York, and moves into apartment at 117 East 17th Street. *The Days Before* published by Harcourt, Brace.

1953   Speaks at several colleges and universities. Visits Ezra Pound at St. Elizabeths Hospital in Washington, D.C. In a talk at the Corcoran Gallery, speaks out against congressional inquiries into communism on college campuses. Reads poetry on NBC radio network. Begins yearlong appointment as writer-in-residence at the University of Michigan, Ann Arbor. Excerpt from "No Safe Harbor" published in *Harper's*.

1954   Suffers attack of angina while teaching class. "A Defense of Circe" published in *Mademoiselle*. Meets and is charmed by Seymour Lawrence, editor at *The Atlantic* and The Atlantic Monthly Press, an imprint of Little, Brown. Receives Litt.D. at the University of Michigan. Begins appointment as Fulbright Fellow in Liège, Belgium. Reads "The Circus" on BBC radio. At Christmas, makes first visit to Rome.

1955   Hospitalized for three weeks with influenza; relinquishes remainder of Fulbright assignment and returns to New York in February. "Adventure in Living" ("St. Augustine and the Bullfight") published in *Mademoiselle*. Paperback selection of previously collected material, *The Old Order: Stories of the South*, published by Harcourt, Brace. Leases secluded house on Roxbury Road in Southbury, Connecticut, to work on "No Safe Harbor." Brother Paul dies, September 19. After death of Donald Brace, leaves Harcourt, Brace for Atlantic–Little, Brown, where Seymour Lawrence is her new editor.

1956   Changes title of "No Safe Harbor" to "Ship of Fools." Objects to Lawrence's calling her "woman writer" in catalog copy. Excerpts from "Ship of Fools" published in *The Atlantic Monthly* and *Mademoiselle*. Rests at Jefferson Hotel in Washington, D.C., before embarking on 15-college lecture tour. Meets Barbara Thompson, who interviews her for *The Washington Post* and becomes trusted friend. Essay "Noon Wine: The Sources" published in *The Yale Review*. Endorses Adlai Stevenson for president.

1957   With financial support from Atlantic–Little, Brown, works with few distractions on "Ship of Fools." Reads at the 92nd Street Y, New York City.

1958   Discusses Henry James on CBS television program *Camera Three*. Receives Litt.D. from Smith College and meets commencement speaker, Massachusetts senator John F. Kennedy. Vacates Southbury house. Excerpt from "Ship of Fools" appears in *Mademoiselle*. Retreats to Outpost

Inn in Ridgefield, Connecticut, for a month's work on "Ship of Fools." Spends fall semester as writer-in-residence at the University of Virginia. Meets Flannery O'Connor. Speaks at Auburn University, the University of Oklahoma, and the University of Texas at Austin.

1959   Spends spring semester as writer-in-residence at Washington and Lee University. Lectures on Mark Twain at the University of California, Los Angeles. Excerpt from "Ship of Fools" published in *Texas Quarterly*. Receives $26,000 grant from the Ford Foundation to complete "Ship of Fools." Rents house at 3112 Q Street in Georgetown.

1960   Continues to work on "Ship of Fools." Story "The Fig Tree," written in the 1920s, published in *Harper's*. Returns to Mexico to speak under auspices of the U.S. Department of State. Participates with Flannery O'Connor and Caroline Gordon in "Recent Southern Fiction," a panel discussion at Wesleyan College, Macon, Georgia. "Holiday," another story written in the 1920s, published in *The Atlantic Monthly*.

1961   Accepts invitation from President-elect John F. Kennedy to attend inauguration. Presents Regents lecture at the University of California, Riverside. Withdraws to Yankee Clipper Inn on Cape Ann, Massachusetts, to finish "Ship of Fools"; dates completed manuscript "Yaddo, August 1941–Pigeon Cove, August 1961." Seymour Lawrence launches publicity campaign for novel by selling book-club rights to the Book-of-the-Month Club.

1962   *Ship of Fools* published by Atlantic–Little, Brown to positive reviews and great commercial success. Movie rights sold to United Artists for $400,000. Turns over literary representation and business affairs to agent Cyrilly Abels, formerly her editor at *Mademoiselle*. Takes month-long vacation in Italy and Sicily with niece Ann. Purchases designer clothes and 21-carat emerald ring encrusted with diamonds. Awarded the Emerson-Thoreau Medal by the American Academy of Arts and Sciences. Deposits papers temporarily at the Library of Congress. Receives Litt.D. from LaSalle College. Long negative review of *Ship of Fools* by Theodore Solotaroff appears in *Commentary*, occasioning heated debate among readers, critics, and literary journalists. Leaves for yearlong stay in Europe.

1963   In Rome collaborates with writer Abby Mann on the screenplay for *Ship of Fools*. Receives $1,000 prize from the Texas Institute of Letters. Buys lavish furnishings in Europe. Returns home in November to the shock of the Kennedy assassination. Inducted into the University of Maryland's chapter of Phi Beta Kappa. Attends luncheon at White House hosted by President and Mrs. Johnson.

1964   After reneging on offer to purchase house in Georgetown, becomes mired in legal morass. Continues to accept speaking engagements at colleges and universities. Leases large house at 3601 49th Street, N.W., Washington, D.C. Lectures at the Instituto Cultural Norteamericano in Mexico City.

1965   *The Collected Stories of Katherine Anne Porter*, comprising the three earlier collections and four fugitive stories, published by Harcourt, Brace. Follows Seymour Lawrence to Alfred A. Knopf, Inc., and then to Delacorte Press. Signs contracts with Lawrence for "The Devil and Cotton Mather" and her collected essays and occasional writings. Film version of *Ship of Fools*, directed by Stanley Kramer and starring Vivien Leigh, Lee Marvin, Simone Signoret, and others, is box-office success.

1966   *The Collected Stories* wins National Book Award and Pulitzer Prize. Receives honorary Doctor of Humane Letters from the University of Maryland, College Park, and announces eventual donation of papers to university library. Inducted into the 50-member American Academy of Arts and Letters. Begins personal and professional association with attorney E. Barrett Prettyman Jr.

1967   Presides over first meeting of The Katherine Anne Porter Foundation, established to provide financial support to younger writers. Accepts Gold Medal in Fiction from the American Academy of Arts and Letters.

1968   Spends first week of January hospitalized with influenza. At home, receives numerous visitors, whom she entertains with lavish meals and fine wine.

1969   Moves to townhouse at 5910 Westchester Park Drive, College Park. Becomes member of usage panel for *The American Heritage Dictionary*. Begins choosing and revising pieces for her collected essays. Spends four weeks in Washington Hospital Center after falling down stairs.

Editing of essay collection completed by Lawrence and literary friends. Sister Gay dies, December 28.

1970   *The Collected Essays and Occasional Writings of Katherine Anne Porter* published by Seymour Lawrence–Delacorte. Falls and breaks hip; spends two months in convalescent home. Moves to double apartment on top floor of 6100 Westchester Park Drive. Meets Clark Dobson and John David (Jack) Horner, young men who escort her to area social events. Meets Kathleen Feeley and Maura Eichner, sisters of the College of Notre Dame of Maryland, who will guide her to a rite of reconciliation with the Roman Catholic Church on December 8.

1971   "The Spivvleton Mystery," a comic story written in 1926, published in *The Ladies' Home Journal*. Undergoes cataract surgery. Delivers keynote speech at "The Year of the Woman," a seminar at the College of Notre Dame of Maryland.

1972   Receives Creative Arts Award for lifetime achievement in literature from Brandeis University. Returns Emerson-Thoreau Medal to the American Academy of Arts and Sciences when she learns that the Academy, for political reasons, has refused to consider Ezra Pound for the same award. Heart condition worsens. On assignment from *Playboy*, takes cruise ship to Florida to write eyewitness account of Apollo 17 moon shot; the launch is "glorious" but the article never completed. Gives inaugural lecture at the newly opened Katherine Anne Porter Room of Mc-Keldin Library at the University of Maryland.

1973   Sister Baby dies, May 21. Dissolves The Katherine Anne Porter Foundation.

1974   Names Isabel Bayley her literary trustee. In private ceremony at home, receives honorary degree from the College of Notre Dame of Maryland. Revises "The Land That Is Nowhere," a fragment of autobiography written decades earlier, for publication in *Vogue*.

1975   "Notes on the Texas I Remember" appears in *The Atlantic Monthly*. Receives a rubbing of mother's Indian Creek gravestone from Roger Brooks, president of Howard Payne University, in her native Brown County, Texas. Hires retired naval commander William R. Wilkins as personal assistant.

1976   Delivers Frances Steloff lecture at Skidmore College. In
         May, travels to Brownwood, Texas, to receive honorary
         degree from Howard Payne University and attend county-
         wide 86th-birthday celebration. Visits mother's grave at
         Indian Creek. Gives final public reading, at the 92nd
         Street Y. Feeling unwell at year's end, enters Johns Hop-
         kins Medical Center for comprehensive tests.

1977   While in hospital suffers two major strokes. Returns home
         in early spring to round-the-clock nursing care. "The
         Never-Ending Wrong," a memoir of the Sacco–Vanzetti
         case, published in *The Atlantic Monthly* and then as a
         short book by Atlantic–Little, Brown. Mental abilities de-
         teriorate. When judged incompetent by psychiatrist, court
         appoints nephew Paul Porter her legal guardian.

1978   Experiences severe seizure in December. Graduate student
         Jane DeMouy becomes her friend and visits her regularly.

1979   Meets Ted Wojtasik, a young college graduate who helps
         organize her letters for eventual publication, a project
         later realized by Isabel Bayley. Receives visitors Monroe
         Wheeler, Robert Penn Warren, and Eleanor Clark, and
         calls, cards, and gifts from Isabel Bayley, Eudora Welty,
         Barbara Thompson, and other devoted friends.

1980   Moves to Carriage Hill Nursing Home in Silver Spring,
         Maryland. Friends gather for 90th birthday party. Sister
         Maura Eichner and Sister Kathleen Feeley visit regularly,
         accompanied by Father Joseph Gallagher, who hears con-
         fession and administers Eucharist ("I'm busy dying. It's
         the hardest thing I've ever done"). Dies September 18,
         with Jane DeMouy by her side. Ashes buried the following
         spring in a plot adjacent to her mother's grave in Indian
         Creek Cemetery.

Note on the Texts

This volume contains *The Collected Stories of Katherine Anne Porter*, prepared by the author and published in 1965, together with an extensive selection of the essays, book reviews, and other short nonfiction prose that Katherine Anne Porter published in books and periodicals between 1920 and 1977.

The Collected Stories of Katherine Anne Porter was published by Harcourt, Brace & World in September 1965. It comprises the contents of three earlier collections—*Flowering Judas and Other Stories* (1935), *Pale Horse, Pale Rider: Three Short Novels* (1939), *The Leaning Tower and Other Stories* (1944)—and four previously uncollected stories, "Virgin Violeta," "The Martyr," "The Fig Tree," and "Holiday," together with a foreword, "Go, Little Book . . . ," written specially for the volume. The text printed here is taken from the first printing of *The Collected Stories of Katherine Anne Porter*.

Prior to being given the order they have in *The Collected Stories*, these stories were collected in various groupings. Porter's first collection, *Flowering Judas* (New York: Harcourt, Brace & Co., 1930), was printed in an edition limited to 600 copies and contained six stories: "María Concepción," "Magic," "Rope," "He," "The Jilting of Granny Weatherall," and "Flowering Judas." "Hacienda" appeared as a small book (New York: Harrison of Paris, 1934) printed in an edition limited to 895 copies. *Flowering Judas and Other Stories* (New York: Harcourt, Brace & Co., 1935) collected the contents of the two earlier publications as well as three additional stories, arranged in the following sequence: "María Concepción," "Magic," "Rope," "He," "Theft," "That Tree," "The Jilting of Granny Weatherall," "Flowering Judas," "The Cracked Looking-Glass," and "Hacienda." The Modern Library edition of *Flowering Judas and Other Stories* (1940) reprinted the contents of the 1935 edition, with a new introduction by Porter (the introduction is printed on pages 716–18 of the present volume).

Pale Horse, Pale Rider: Three Short Novels was published by Harcourt, Brace & Co. in 1939. It contained "Old Mortality," "Noon Wine," and "Pale Horse, Pale Rider." Porter dedicated the collection to her father, Harrison Boone Porter.

The Leaning Tower and Other Stories was published by Harcourt,

Brace & Company in 1944. It contained nine stories: "The Source," "The Witness," "The Circus," "The Journey" (as "The Old Order"), "The Last Leaf," "The Grave," "The Downward Path to Wisdom," "A Day's Work," and "The Leaning Tower." Porter dedicated the collection to her nephew, Corporal Harrison Paul Porter, Jr.

The Old Order: Stories of the South was published by Harvest Books, the paperback imprint of Harcourt, Brace & Co., in 1955. It reprinted previously collected material in the following sequence: "The Old Order," a cycle of six stories comprising "The Source," "The Journey" (as "The Old Order"), "The Witness," "The Circus," "The Last Leaf," and "The Grave," followed by "The Jilting of Granny Weatherall," "He," "Magic," and "Old Mortality."

The contents of *The Collected Stories of Katherine Anne Porter* first appeared in books and periodicals as follows:

Flowering Judas and Other Stories: "María Concepción," *The Century Magazine* (December 1922); "Virgin Violeta," *The Century Magazine* (December 1924); "The Martyr," *The Century Magazine* (July 1923); "Magic," *transition* (Summer 1928); "Rope," *The Second American Caravan*, edited by Alfred Kreymborg and others (New York: The Macaulay Co., 1928); "He," *New Masses* (October 1927); "Theft," *The Gyroscope* (November 1929); "That Tree," *Virginia Quarterly Review* (July 1934); "The Jilting of Granny Weatherall," *transition* (February 1929); "Flowering Judas," *Hound & Horn* (Spring 1930); "The Cracked Looking-Glass," *Scribner's Magazine* (May 1932); "Hacienda" (New York: Harrison of Paris, 1934).

Pale Horse, Pale Rider: "Old Mortality," *The Southern Review* (Spring 1937); "Noon Wine," *Signatures* (as a work-in-progress, Spring 1936) and *Story* (in completed form, June 1937); "Pale Horse, Pale Rider," *The Southern Review* (Winter 1938).

The Leaning Tower and Other Stories: "The Source," *Accent* (Spring 1941); "The Journey" (as "The Old Order"), *The Southern Review* (Winter 1936); "The Witness" (as "Uncle Jimbilly," the first item under the heading "Two Plantation Portraits"), *Virginia Quarterly Review* (January 1935); "The Circus," *The Southern Review* (July 1935); "The Last Leaf" (the second item under the heading "Two Plantation Portraits"), *Virginia Quarterly Review* (January 1935); "The Fig Tree," *Harper's Magazine* (June 1960); "The Grave," *Virginia Quarterly Review* (April 1935); "The Downward Path of Wisdom," *Harper's Bazaar* (December 1939); "A Day's Work," *The Nation* (February 10, 1940); "Holiday," *The Atlantic Monthly* (December 1960); "The Leaning Tower," *The Southern Review* (Autumn 1941).

The section of this volume titled "Essays, Reviews, and Other Writings" presents a selection of short nonfiction pieces published by

Katherine Anne Porter between 1920 and 1977. It includes versions
of all the pieces that Porter reprinted in her collection *The Days
Before* (New York: Harcourt, Brace & Co., 1952) as well as part of
Porter's foreword to that collection. (A list of acknowledgments and
credits for previously published material that appeared as part of the
foreword has been omitted.) It also adopts the three rubrics under
which Porter organized the pieces collected in *The Days Before*—
"Critical," "Personal and Particular," and "Mexican"—adding to
them a fourth, "Autobiographical." The table of contents of *The
Days Before* appears in the Notes to the present volume, on page 1062.

The pieces collected in *The Days Before* were reprinted, many in
versions slightly revised by the author, in *The Collected Essays and
Occasional Writings of Katherine Anne Porter* (New York: A Seymour Lawrence Book/Delacorte Press, 1970). Porter began preparing her *Collected Essays* in the late 1960s, but illness prevented her
from making the final selection unassisted. Her work was completed
by a "committee of friends" chaired by her editor and publisher, Seymour Lawrence, and including Robert A. Beach Jr., George Core,
William Humphrey, Rhea Johnson, and Glenway Wescott. The contents included many essays and reviews published after *The Days
Before* and several uncollected earlier pieces, as well as much material
outside the scope of the present selection, including poems, public
letters, and three chapters of an uncompleted biography of Cotton
Mather. The present selection reprints 51 items from *Collected Essays*,
including the 34 pieces that previously appeared in *The Days Before*.

Of the remaining 25 items, two, "A Christmas Story" and "The
Never-Ending Wrong," were published as small books during Porter's
lifetime. Seventeen items are taken from posthumous collections:
nine from *"This Strange, Old World" and Other Book Reviews by
Katherine Anne Porter*, edited by Darlene Harbour Unrue (Athens:
University of Georgia Press, 1991), and eight from *Uncollected Early
Prose of Katherine Anne Porter*, edited by Ruth M. Alvarez and
Thomas F. Walsh (Austin: University of Texas Press, 1993). Six items
—"A Note on *The Troll Garden*," "No Masters or Teachers," "On
'Flowering Judas,'" "Notes on the Texas I Remember," "About the
Author," and "The Land That Is Nowhere"—are reprinted here for
the first time since their original appearances.

The following list presents a publication history of the items selected for inclusion here, with the texts chosen for the present volume noted.

"I needed both . . ." first appeared as part of the foreword to
The Days Before (1952); the remainder of the foreword, as mentioned
above, is not reprinted here. The text from *The Days Before* is used
here, under a title supplied by the editor.

CRITICAL: "The Days Before" first appeared in *The Kenyon Review* (Autumn 1943); it was revised for inclusion in *The Days Before* (1952) and reprinted in *Collected Essays* (1970). The text from *Collected Essays* is used here.

"Reflections on Willa Cather" first appeared, in much different form, as "The Calm, Pure Art of Willa Cather," a review of *Willa Cather on Writing* (1949) in *The New York Times Book Review* (September 25, 1949). It later appeared, in an expanded version and under its present title, in *Mademoiselle* (July 1952); it was collected in *The Days Before* (1952) and reprinted in *Collected Essays* (1970). The text from *Collected Essays* is used here. "A Note on *The Troll Garden*" first appeared as the afterword to the Signet paperback reprint edition of *The Troll Garden* by Willa Cather (New York: New American Library, 1961). The text from the Signet edition is used here.

"Gertrude Stein: Three Views" is a set of three items that first appeared in *The Days Before* (1952). "'Everybody Is a Real One'" first appeared in *New York Herald Tribune Books* (January 16, 1927); "Second Wind" first appeared in *New York Herald Tribune Books* (September 23, 1928); and "The Wooden Umbrella" first appeared, as "Gertrude Stein: A Self-Portrait," in *Harper's Magazine* (December 1947). All three items were revised for inclusion, under the heading "Gertrude Stein: Three Views," in *The Days Before* (1952) and reprinted, under the same heading, in *Collected Essays* (1970). The text from *Collected Essays* is used here.

"'It Is Hard to Stand in the Middle'" first appeared, as "Yours, Ezra Pound," in *The New York Times Book Review* (October 29, 1950); it was revised for inclusion, under its present title, in *The Days Before* (1952) and reprinted in *Collected Essays* (1970). The text from *Collected Essays* is used here.

"Eudora Welty and *A Curtain of Green*" first appeared as the introduction to *A Curtain of Green: A Book of Stories* by Eudora Welty (Garden City, N.Y.: Doubleday, Doran, 1943); it was revised for inclusion, under its present title, in *The Days Before* (1952) and reprinted in *Collected Essays* (1970). The text from *Collected Essays* is used here.

"The Wingèd Skull" first appeared in *The Nation* (July 17, 1943) and was revised for inclusion in *Collected Essays* (1970). The text from *Collected Essays* is used here.

"On a Criticism of Thomas Hardy" first appeared, as "Notes on a Criticism of Thomas Hardy," in *The Southern Review* (Summer 1940); it was revised for inclusion, under its present title, in *The Days Before* (1952) and reprinted in *Collected Essays* (1970). The text from *Collected Essays* is used here.

"E. M. Forster" first appeared, as "E. M. Forster Speaks Out for the Things He Holds Dear," in *The New York Times Book Review* (November 4, 1951); it was collected, under its present title, in *The Days Before* (1952) and reprinted in *Collected Essays* (1970). The text from *Collected Essays* is used here.

"Virginia Woolf" first appeared, as "Virginia Woolf's Essays—A Great Art, a Sober Craft," in *The New York Times Book Review* (May 7, 1950); it was collected, under its present title, in *The Days Before* (1952) and reprinted in *Collected Essays* (1970). The text from *Collected Essays* is used here.

Two book reviews of novels by D. H. Lawrence are presented in this volume under the heading "D. H. Lawrence." "Quetzalcoatl" first appeared in *New York Herald Tribune Books* (March 7, 1926); it was revised for inclusion in *The Days Before* (1952) and reprinted in *Collected Essays* (1970). The text from *Collected Essays* is used here. "A Wreath for the Gamekeeper" first appeared in *Shenandoah* (Autumn 1959) and was reprinted in *Collected Essays* (1970). The text from *Collected Essays* is used here.

"'The Laughing Heat of the Sun'" first appeared, as "Edith Sitwell's Steady Growth to Great Poetic Art," in *New York Herald Tribune Books* (December 18, 1949); it was collected, under its present title, in *The Days Before* (1952) and reprinted in *Collected Essays* (1970). The text from *Collected Essays* is used here.

"The Art of Katherine Mansfield" first appeared in *The Nation* (October 23, 1937); it was revised for inclusion in *The Days Before* (1952) and reprinted in *Collected Essays* (1970). The text from *Collected Essays* is used here.

"The Hundredth Role" first appeared in *New York Herald Tribune Books* (October 7, 1928) and was reprinted in *"This Strange, Old World"* (1991). The text from *"This Strange, Old World"* is used here.

"Dylan Thomas" is a set of three book reviews that first appeared in *Collected Essays* (1970). "A death of days . . ." first appeared, as "His Poetry Makes a Difference," in *The New York Times Book Review* (November 20, 1955); "A fever chart . . ." first appeared, as "In the Depths of Grief, a Towering Rage," in *The New York Times Book Review* (October 13, 1957); and "In the morning of the poet . . ." first appeared, as "In the Morning of the Poet," in *The New York Times Book Review* (February 2, 1958). The text of "Dylan Thomas" from *The Collected Essays* is used here, with subheadings ("A death of days . . . ," "A fever chart . . . ," "In the morning of the poet . . .") supplied by the editor.

"A Most Lively Genius" first appeared in *The New York Times Book Review* (November 18, 1951) and was reprinted in *"This Strange, Old World"* (1991). The text from *"This Strange, Old World"* is used here.

"Orpheus in Purgatory" first appeared in *The New York Times Book Review* (January 1, 1950); it was revised for inclusion in *The Days Before* (1952) and reprinted in *Collected Essays* (1970). The text from *Collected Essays* is used here.

Four memorial tributes by Porter to literary figures of her acquaintance are presented in this volume under the heading "In Memoriam." "Ford Madox Ford" first appeared, untitled, in *New Directions in Prose and Poetry* (1942) as one of 24 tributes by various writers published under the heading "In Memoriam: Ford Madox Ford, 1875–1939"; it was revised for inclusion, under the title "Homage to Ford Madox Ford," in *The Days Before* (1952) and reprinted, as "Homage to Ford Madox Ford," in *Collected Essays* (1970). The text from *Collected Essays* is used here, under a title supplied by the editor. "James Joyce" first appeared, as part of "From the Notebooks of Katherine Anne Porter," in *The Southern Review* (Summer 1965); it was revised for inclusion, as part of "From the Notebooks: Yeats, Joyce, Eliot, Pound," in *Collected Essays* (1970). The text from *Collected Essays* is used here, under a title supplied by the editor. "Sylvia Beach" first appeared, as "Paris: A Little Incident in the Rue de l'Odéon," in *The Ladies' Home Journal* (August 1964); it was revised for inclusion, under the title "A Little Incident in the Rue de l'Odéon," in *Collected Essays* (1970). The text from *Collected Essays* is used here, under a title supplied by the editor. "Flannery O'Connor" first appeared, as "Gracious Greatness," in *Esprit* (Winter 1964); it was revised for inclusion, under the title "Flannery O'Connor at Home," in *Collected Essays* (1970). The text from *Collected Essays* is used here, under a title supplied by the editor.

PERSONAL AND PARTICULAR: This volume collects four pieces by Porter on the craft of fiction under the heading "On Writing." "My First Speech" first appeared in *Collected Essays* (1970). The text from *Collected Essays* is used here. "I must write from memory . . ." first appeared, as part of "Notes on Writing," in *New Directions in Prose and Poetry* (1940); it was reprinted, as part of "Notes on Writing," in *Collected Essays* (1970). The text from *Collected Essays* is used here, under a title supplied by the editor. "No Plot, My Dear, No Story" first appeared in *The Writer* (June 1942); it was revised for inclusion in *The Days Before* (1952) and reprinted in *Collected Essays* (1970). The text from *Collected Essays* is used here. "Writing cannot be taught . . ." first appeared, as "On Writing," in *Collected Essays* (1970). The text from *Collected Essays* is used here, under a title supplied by the editor.

Porter's written responses to three sets of symposium questions are presented here under the heading "The Situation of the Writer." "The Situation in American Writing" first appeared, as part of

"Symposium: The Situation in American Writing," in *Partisan Review* (Summer 1939); it was collected, under the title "1939: The Situation in American Writing," as the first item under the heading "Three Statements about Writing" in *The Days Before* (1952) and reprinted, in the same manner, in *Collected Essays* (1970). The text from *Collected Essays* is used here, under a title revised by the editor. "Transplanted Writers" first appeared, as part of the symposium "Transplanted Writers," in *Books Abroad* (July 1942); it was collected, under the title "1942: Transplanted Writers," and as the third item under the heading "Three Statements about Writing," in *The Days Before* (1952) and reprinted, in the same manner, in *Collected Essays* (1970). The text from *Collected Essays* is used here, under a title revised by the editor. "The International Exchange of Writers" first appeared, as "Remarks on the Agenda by Katherine Anne Porter," in *The Arts and Exchange of Persons—Report of a Conference on the Arts and Exchange of Persons Held October 4 and 5, 1956, at the Institute of International Education* (New York: Institute of International Education, 1956); it was reprinted, as "Remarks on the Agenda," in *Collected Essays* (1970). The text from *Collected Essays* is used here, under a title supplied by the editor.

Four pieces by Porter commenting on her own fiction are presented in this volume under the heading "The Author on Her Work." "No Masters or Teachers" first appeared in *New Voices 2: American Writing Today*, edited by Don M. Wolfe (New York: Hendricks House, 1955). The text from *New Voices 2* is used here. "On 'Flowering Judas'" first appeared, as "Katherine Anne Porter: Why She Selected 'Flowering Judas,'" in *This Is My Best*, edited by Whit Burnett (New York: The Dial Press, 1942). The text from *This Is My Best* is used here. "The only reality . . ." first appeared as the introduction to the Modern Library edition of *Flowering Judas and Other Stories* (New York: Modern Library, 1940); it was collected, under the title "1940: Introduction to *Flowering Judas*," as the second item under the heading "Three Statements about Writing" in *The Days Before* (1952) and reprinted, in the same manner, in *Collected Essays* (1970). The text from *Collected Essays* is used here, under a title revised by the editor. "'Noon Wine': The Sources" first appeared in *The Yale Review* (September 1956) and was reprinted in *Collected Essays* (1970). The text from *Collected Essays* is used here.

"Notes on the Texas I Remember" first appeared in *The Atlantic Monthly* (March 1975). The text from *The Atlantic Monthly* is used here.

"Portrait: Old South" first appeared in *Mademoiselle* (February 1944); it was collected in *The Days Before* (1952) and reprinted in *Collected Essays* (1970). The text from *Collected Essays* is used here.

"A Christmas Story" first appeared in Mademoiselle (December

1946). In 1958 it was privately printed in a hardcover edition of 2,500 copies for distribution as a Christmas gift to the staff and associates of *Mademoiselle* magazine. In 1967 it was published as *A Christmas Story* (New York: A Seymour Lawrence Book/Delacorte Press), with an afterword by Porter and drawings by Ben Shahn. The text from the Delacorte edition is used here; the afterword appears in the Notes to the present volume, on page 1070.

"Audubon's Happy Land" first appeared, as "Happy Land," in *Vogue* (November 1, 1939); it was revised for inclusion, under its present title, in *The Days Before* (1952) and reprinted in *Collected Essays* (1970). The text from *Collected Essays* is used here.

"The Flower of Flowers" first appeared in *Flair* (May 1950); it was collected in *The Days Before* (1952) and reprinted in *Collected Essays* (1970). The text from *Collected Essays* is used here.

"A Note on Pierre-Joseph Redouté" first appeared, as "Pierre-Joseph Redouté," in *Flair* (May 1950); it was collected, under its present title, in *The Days Before* (1952) and reprinted in *Collected Essays* (1970). The text from *Collected Essays* is used here.

"A House of My Own" first appeared, as "Now at Last a House of My Own," in *Vogue* (September 1, 1941); it was revised for inclusion, under its present title, in *The Days Before* (1952) and reprinted in *Collected Essays* (1970). The text from *Collected Essays* is used here.

"The Necessary Enemy" first appeared, as "Love and Hate," in *Mademoiselle* (October 1948); it was revised for inclusion, under its present title, in *The Days Before* (1952) and reprinted in *Collected Essays* (1970). The text from *Collected Essays* is used here.

"'Marriage Is Belonging'" first appeared in *Mademoiselle* (October 15, 1951); it was collected in *The Days Before* (1952) and reprinted in *Collected Essays* (1970). The text from *Collected Essays* is used here.

"A Defense of Circe" first appeared in *Mademoiselle* (June 1954). It was revised for its publication in 1955 by Harcourt, Brace & Co., in a hardcover edition of 1,700 copies, as a "New Year's Greeting" to the friends of the author and publisher. The Harcourt text was reprinted, with an author's note, in *Collected Essays* (1970). The text from *Collected Essays* is used here.

"St. Augustine and the Bullfight" first appeared, as "Adventure in Living," in *Mademoiselle* (July 1955) and was revised for inclusion, under its present title, in *Collected Essays* (1970). The text from *Collected Essays* is used here.

"Act of Faith: 4 July 1942" first appeared, as "American Statement," in *Mademoiselle* (July 1942); it was revised for inclusion, as "American Statement: 4 July 1942," in *The Days Before* (1952) and reprinted, under its present title, in *Collected Essays* (1970). The text from *Collected Essays* is used here.

"The Future Is Now" first appeared in *Mademoiselle* (November 1950); it was revised for inclusion in *The Days Before* (1952) and reprinted in *Collected Essays* (1970). The text from *Collected Essays* is used here.

"The Never-Ending Wrong" first appeared in *The Atlantic Monthly* (June 1977); it was reprinted, with added foreword and footnotes, as *The Never-Ending Wrong* (Boston: Atlantic Monthly Press/Little, Brown & Co., 1977). Porter dedicated the book to her personal secretary, William R. Wilkins. The text of the book edition is used here; the foreword appears in the Notes to the present volume, on page 1073.

MEXICAN: "Why I Write About Mexico" first appeared, as a contributor's note to the story "The Martyr," in *The Century Magazine* (July 1923); it was revised for inclusion, under its present title, in *The Days Before* (1952) and reprinted in *Collected Essays* (1970). The text from *Collected Essays* is used here.

Six journalistic pieces written by Porter in 1920–22 are collected in this volume under the heading "Reports from Mexico City." "The New Man and The New Order" first appeared in *The Magazine of Mexico* (March 1921) and was reprinted in *Uncollected Early Prose* (1993). The text from *Uncollected Early Prose* is used here. "The Fiesta of Guadalupe" first appeared in *El Heraldo de México* (December 13, 1920). It was revised for inclusion in *Collected Essays* (1970) and the original *Heraldo* text was reprinted in *Uncollected Early Prose* (1993). The text from *Collected Essays* is used here, with an emendation suggested by the editors of *Uncollected Early Prose*: at page 883.3 the words "Over that painted and carved bit of wood," from the original *Heraldo* text, replace the words "They have parted a carved bit of wood" in the text published in *Collected Essays*. "The Funeral of General Benjamín Hill" first appeared in *El Heraldo de México* (December 17, 1920) and was reprinted in *Uncollected Early Prose* (1993). The text from *Uncollected Early Prose* is used here. "Children of Xochitl" first appeared in *Uncollected Early Prose* (1993); it is based on an 11-page typescript in the Katherine Anne Porter Papers, Archives and Manuscripts Department, University of Maryland Libraries, College Park, Maryland, and was given its title by the editors of *Uncollected Early Prose*. (A variant of the piece appeared, as "Xochimilco," in *The Christian Science Monitor*, May 31, 1921.) The text from *Uncollected Early Prose* is used here. "The Mexican Trinity" first appeared in *The Freeman* (August 3, 1921); it was revised for inclusion in *The Days Before* (1952) and was reprinted in *Collected Essays* (1970). The text from *Collected Essays* is used here. "Where Presidents Have No Friends" first appeared in *The Century Maga-*

zine (July 1922) and was revised for inclusion in *Collected Essays* (1970). The text from *Collected Essays* is used here.

"In a Mexican Patio" first appeared in *The Magazine of Mexico* (April 1921) and was reprinted from *Uncollected Early Prose* (1993). The text from *Uncollected Early Prose* is used here.

"Leaving the Petate" first appeared in *The New Republic* (February 4, 1931); it was revised for inclusion in *The Days Before* (1952) and reprinted in *Collected Essays* (1970). The text from *Collected Essays* is used here.

"The Charmed Life" first appeared in *Vogue* (April 15, 1942); it was revised for inclusion in *The Days Before* (1952) and was reprinted in *Collected Essays* (1970). The text of *Collected Essays* is used here.

"Corridos" first appeared in *Survey Graphic* (May 1924) and was reprinted in *Uncollected Early Prose* (1993). The text from *Uncollected Early Prose* is used here.

"Sor Juana: A Portrait of the Poet" first appeared, as "To a Portrait of the Poet," in *Survey Graphic* (May 1924) and was reprinted in *Uncollected Early Prose* (1993). The text from *Uncollected Early Prose* is used here, under a title supplied by the editor.

"Notes on the Life and Death of a Hero" first appeared as the introduction to Porter's translation of *The Itching Parrot* (*El Paraquillo Sarniento*) by José Joaquín Fernández de Lizárdi (Garden City, N.Y.: Doubleday, Doran, 1942). It was revised for inclusion, under its present title, in *The Days Before* (1952) and was reprinted in *Collected Essays* (1970). The text from *Collected Essays* is used here.

This volume collects ten book reviews written by Porter in 1920–43 under the heading "A Mexican Chronicle." "Blasco Ibanez on 'Mexico in Revolution'" first appeared in *El Heraldo de México* (November 22, 1920) and was reprinted in *Uncollected Early Prose* (1993). The text from *Uncollected Early Prose* is used here. "Paternalism and the Mexico Problem" first appeared in *New York Herald Tribune Books* (March 27, 1927) and was reprinted in *"This Strange, Old World"* (1991). The text from *"This Strange, Old World"* is used here. "La Conquistadora" first appeared in *New York Herald Tribune Books* (April 11, 1926); it was revised for inclusion in *The Days Before* (1952) and was reprinted in *Collected Essays* (1970). The text from *Collected Essays* is used here. "¡Ay, Que Chamaco!" first appeared, as "Ay, Que Chamaco," in *The New Republic* (December 23, 1925) and was reprinted, as "Ay, Que Chamaco," in *"This Strange, Old World"* (1991). The text from *"This Strange, Old World"* is used here, under a title revised by the editor. "Old Gods and New Messiahs" first appeared in *New York Herald Tribune Books* (September 29, 1929) and was reprinted in *"This Strange, Old World"* (1991). The text from

"This Strange, Old World" is used here. "Diego Rivera" collects two reviews of books about the artist and his work. "These Pictures Must Be Seen" first appeared in *New York Herald Tribune Books* (December 22, 1929) and was reprinted in *"This Strange, Old World"* (1991). The text from *"This Strange, Old World"* is used here. "Rivera's Personal Revolution" first appeared, as "Rivera's Personal Revolution in Mexico," in *New York Herald Tribune Books* (March 21, 1937) and was reprinted, as "Rivera's Personal Revolution in Mexico," in *"This Strange, Old World"* (1991). The text from *"This Strange, Old World"* is used here, under a title revised by the editor. "Parvenu . . ." was commissioned by *The New Republic* in 1931 but unpublished during Porter's lifetime; it first appeared in *Uncollected Early Prose* (1993). The text is based on a 4-page typescript in the Katherine Anne Porter Papers, Archives and Manuscripts Department, University of Maryland Libraries, College Park, Maryland, and was given its title by the editors of *Uncollected Early Prose.* The text from *Uncollected Early Prose* is used here. "History on the Wing" first appeared in *The New Republic* (November 18, 1936) and was reprinted in *"This Strange, Old World"* (1991). The text from *"This Strange, Old World"* is used here. "Thirty Long Years of Revolution" first appeared, as "Mexico's Thirty Long Years of Revolution," in *New York Herald Tribune Books* (May 30, 1943); it was reprinted, as "Mexico's Thirty Long Years of Revolution," in *"This Strange, Old World"* (1991). The text from *"This Strange, Old World"* is used here, under a title revised by the editor.

AUTOBIOGRAPHICAL: "About the Author" first appeared, as "Katherine Anne Porter, 1894–," in *Authors Today and Yesterday,* edited by Stanley J. Kunitz with Howard Haycraft and Wilbur C. Hadden (New York: The H. W. Wilson Co., 1933). The text from *Authors Today and Yesterday* is used here, under a title supplied by the editor.

"The Land That Is Nowhere" first appeared, as "You Are What You Read," in *Vogue* (October 1974). The text from *Vogue* is used here, under Porter's preferred title as evidenced by a typescript of the essay in the Katherine Anne Porter Papers, Archives and Manuscripts Department, University of Maryland Libraries, College Park, Maryland.

This volume presents the texts of the printings chosen for inclusion here but does not attempt to reproduce nontextual features of their typographic design. The editor has supplied headnotes to the book reviews, introductions, and symposium questions, datelines to the reports from Mexico City, "Notes on the Texas I Remember," and "The Land That Is Nowhere," and the titles, headings, and rubrics noted above; otherwise, the texts are printed without change, except for the correction of typographical errors. Footnotes, and datelines except those mentioned above, are Porter's own. Spelling, punctuation, and capitalization are often expressive features, and they are not altered, even when inconsistent or irregular. Except for clear typographical errors, the spelling and usage of foreign words and phrases are left as they appear in the original texts. The following is a list of typographical errors corrected, cited by page and line number: 88.27, Cornalia; 97.5, a a very; 102.21, Zócolo,; 128.22, Missus; 138.31, sittling; 149.17, rawidhe; 164.16, beach.; 168.33, Doña; 173.4, fly-brown; 178.6, better the; 186.17, Eve; 190.35, me. He; 205.4, jocky; 209.36, exactly if; 235.18, Swede."; 243.7, "You're; 258.26, an he; 291.29, strait jacket; 307.16, ouf; 337.17, Grandchildren; 395.15, splender; 399.28, ballons; 421.37, Old; 470.27, tones,with; 481.39, of; 483.10, steer's; 491.5, it?; 487.20, his agony; 501.6, them!"; 523.26, on; 559.21, miniscule; 587.18, live; 590.1, *Wingéd*; 593.29, highfalutin'; 594.14, wingéd; 619.15, how; 623.4, *Chatterly's*; 624.4, bestwritten; 634.6–7, man-and-yet and-yet-; 637.9, into here.; 656.6, lykewake; 658.21, tardily he; 659.34, (her); 662.7, male,; 665.34, dreams . . ." the; 686.4, fas; 687.7, Stendahl; 687.11, Stendahl; 687.17, Stendahl; 687.19, Stendahl,; 689.30, Steven; 696.38, by C.; 702.29, Whitman,; 704.18, *advertising in*; 709.30, system the; 712.21, foundation; 773.11, Gardens; 773.20, kind in; 774.13, of Jerico."; 778.25, victim*; 809.24, Popocatepetl which; 814.8, Weston; 816.17, Weston's; 833.25, 1691,; 842.16, O'Lochlain; 845.36, O'Lochlain; 853.18, person; 855.34, O'Lochlain; 859.36, Hayes,; 861.3, Hayes; 878.3, man either; 881.8, dusty drinks; 881.32, kind must; 883.10, Cut; 898.33, furnishing; 903.14, Villareal,; 939.10, "edgy"; 959.36, painly; 965.14, Crux; 976.1, capitol; 991.23, wearing; 996.9, beginning;; 1011.19, Moires.

Notes

In the notes below, the reference numbers denote page and line of this volume (the line count includes headings). No note is made for material found in standard desk-reference books such as *The Columbia Encyclopedia* or the eleventh edition of *Merriam-Webster's Collegiate Dictionary*. Biblical quotations are keyed to the King James Version. For references to other studies, and further biographical background than is contained in the Chronology, see *Katherine Anne Porter: Conversations*, edited by Joan Givner (Jackson: University Press of Mississippi, 1987); *Katherine Anne Porter's Poetry*, edited by Darlene Harbour Unrue (Columbia: University of South Carolina Press, 1996); *Letters of Katherine Anne Porter*, edited by Isabel Bayley (New York: Atlantic Monthly Press, 1990); *Mae Franking's "My Chinese Marriage," by Katherine Anne Porter: An Annotated Edition*, edited by Holly Franking (Austin: University of Texas Press, 1991); *"This Strange, Old World" and Other Book Reviews by Katherine Anne Porter*, edited by Darlene Harbour Unrue (Athens: University of Georgia Press, 1991); *Uncollected Early Prose of Katherine Anne Porter*, edited by Ruth M. Alvarez and Thomas F. Walsh (Austin: University of Texas Press, 1993); Robert H. Brinkmeyer Jr., *Katherine Anne Porter's Artistic Development: Primitivism, Traditionalism, and Totalitarianism* (Baton Rouge: Louisiana State University Press, 1993); Jane Krause DeMouy, *Katherine Anne Porter's Women: The Eye of Her Fiction* (Austin: University of Texas Press, 1983); Joan Givner, *Katherine Anne Porter: A Life*, revised edition (Athens: University of Georgia Press, 1991); George and Willene Hendrick, *Katherine Anne Porter* (Boston: G. K. Hall, 1988); Kathryn Hilt and Ruth M. Alvarez, *Katherine Anne Porter: An Annotated Bibliography* (New York: Garland, 1990); Enrique Hank Lopez, *Conversations with Katherine Anne Porter, Refugee from Indian Creek* (Boston: Little, Brown, 1981); Janis Stout, *Katherine Anne Porter: A Sense of the Times* (Charlottesville: University Press of Virginia, 1995); Mary Titus, *The Ambivalent Art of Katherine Anne Porter* (Athens: University of Georgia Press, 2005); Darlene Harbour Unrue, *Truth and Vision in Katherine Anne Porter's Fiction* (Athens: University of Georgia Press, 1985), *Understanding Katherine Anne Porter* (Columbia: University of South Carolina Press, 1988), and *Katherine Anne Porter: The Life of an Artist* (Jackson: University Press of Mississippi,

2005); Thomas F. Walsh, *Katherine Anne Porter and Mexico: The Illusion of Eden* (Austin: University of Texas Press, 1992).

THE COLLECTED STORIES OF KATHERINE ANNE PORTER

3.29   Carl Van Doren] Van Doren (1885–1950) was literary editor of *The Century Magazine* from 1922 to 1925.

12.8   fig-cactus] Prickly pear (*Opuntia*).

17.25   informal] The Spanish *informal* means "unreliable," "irresponsible."

17.33–34   I say to her . . . she goes quickly.] Cf. Matthew 8:9.

18.38   "Death and Resurrection" pulque shop] The death and resurrection of Christ is a common subject for murals decorating *pulquerías*, or shops dispensing pulque, a milky alcoholic beverage made from the juice of the agave plant.

20.21–22   shrine at Guadalupe Villa] The Basilica of Our Lady of Guadalupe (erected 1532–1709), in the Villa de Guadalupe Hidalgo, north of Mexico City, is sited on Tepeyac Hill, where it is said the Virgin Mary appeared to the humble Indian Juan Diego in December 1531. The shrine that houses Juan Diego's *tilma* (cloak), miraculously imprinted with an image of Mary, is the most-visited Roman Catholic pilgrimage site in North America.

21.2   Belén Prison] Mexico City prison (1880–1935) legendary for its brutality.

21.17   brasero] Small grill with a coal box underneath.

28.15–16   "*This torment of love . . . why.*"] These and other lines attributed to Carlos throughout the story parody the diction and rhythms of Salomón de la Selva (1893–1959), Nicaraguan poet and onetime lover of Porter whose poems in English are collected in *Tropical Town* (1918) and *A Soldier Sings* (1919).

29.23   St. Anthony] Antony of Padua (1195–1231), associated with the lily, a symbol of chastity.

29.29   Tacubaya] Ancient village within Mexico City.

30.39   *paseo*] Both a tree-lined boulevard and the leisurely, recreational drive or stroll one takes there.

30.39–31.1   Chapultepec Park] Sixteen-hundred-acre park on the outskirts of Mexico City.

31.24   *membrillo*] Quince paste.

32.11   *¡Ay de mi!*] Woe is me!

42.39   "The Little Monkeys"] Los Monotes, Mexico City café that in the 1920s was frequented by the muralist Diego Rivera, his wife, Frida Kahlo, and the caricaturist Miguel Covarrubias.

45.33   sou marqué] Coin of the French colonies, worth less than a penny.

47.2   Basin Street] Street bordering Storyville, famed red-light district of New Orleans.

65.8   the Elevated] One of three elevated train lines that ran north and south through Manhattan from the 1850s through the 1950s.

68.16   Ricci's] Seymour de Ricci (1881–1942), British expert in rare books and manuscripts, tapestries, rugs, and fine furniture, long associated with Anderson Galleries, New York.

68.18   Marie Dressler] Comic actress of vaudeville, stage, and screen (1868–1934).

74.26–27   since . . . Independence] Since 1821, when Mexico won its sovereignty from Spain.

74.31   Hotel Regis] Expensive hotel on the Avenida Juárez, favored by American tourists and expatriates.

76.7   the North] The north of Mexico, where revolutionary forces were under the direction of General Doroteo Arango Arámbula (1877–1923), better known as Pancho Villa.

76.8   in the old days] Between July 1914, when forces led by revolutionary general Álvaro Obregón (1880–1928) overthrew the dictatorship of Victoriano Huerta, and May 1917, when Venustiano Carranza (1859–1920) was inaugurated as the first president of Mexico under its present constitution.

81.11–12   heaven tree] *Ailanthus altissima*, also known as Tree-of-Heaven or stinkbloom.

84.10   Dinty Moore's or the Black Cat] Mexico City cafés popular with American expatriates.

94.12   St. Michael] The archangel Michael, commander of God's army; see Daniel 10 and Revelation 12.

96.25–26   Sixteenth of September Street] Calle Diez y Seis de Septiembre, named to commemorate the day in 1810 when the War of Independence from Spain began.

97.6–7   *gringa. Gringita!*]   "Gringa" and its diminutive, "gringrita," are disparaging Latin American words for a foreign-born woman, especially a light-skinned English-speaker from the United States.

98.24–26   He has . . . lonely as a wave.]   Cf. "A la Orilla de un Palmar" ("At the edge of a Palm-grove"), folk song popularized by Manuel Maria Ponce (1882–1942).

99.1   Jockey Club]   Men's cologne by the U.S. perfumery Caswell-Massey.

100.22   Alameda]   Historic park in the center of Mexico City.

101.12–13   Zapata's army]   The Liberation Army of the South, formed in 1910 by revolutionist Emiliano Zapata (1879–1919).

101.22   full charro dress]   Colorful folkloric costume (*traje de charro*) typical of a cowboy from the Mexican state of Jalisco.

102.5–6   Judas tree]   Redbud tree (*Cercis silliquastum*); in Christian folk-lore it is said that Judas Iscariot, the betrayer of Christ, hanged himself from such a tree, and since then its flowers, originally white, have bloomed blood red.

102.15   corridos]   Mexican popular ballads, cheaply printed as illustrated broadsides.

102.15   Merced market]   La Merced, the largest open-air market in Mexico City.

102.21   Zócalo]   Central square in Mexico City; also called the Plaza de la Constitución.

102.22   Francisco I. Madero Avenue]   Street named for the pro-democracy Mexican politician (1873–1913) who was a candidate for president in 1910, a year marked by widespread fraud at the polls by the incumbent administration of President Porfirio Díaz. Following the popular revolt against Díaz, Madero was installed as president (1911–13). He was executed after the 1913 coup d'etat by Victoriano Huerta.

102.22–23   Paseo de la Reforma]   Grand boulevard that cuts diagonally across Mexico City; it commemorates the liberal reforms of Benito Juárez (1806–1872), five-term president of Mexico (1858–72).

102.23–24   Philosopher Footpath]   Avenida de los Poetas, in Chapultepec Park (see note 30.39–31.1).

103.31–32   O girl with the dark eyes]   Cf. "Aquellos Ojos Verdes," Mexican popular song of the 1920s by Aldolfo Ultera and Nilo Menéndez.

104.13   Delgadito]   Skinny little one.

104.34   Paseo]   Traditional parade of automobiles and carriages in the Paseo de la Reforma (see note 30.39).

105.8   net]   *Neto*; entirely; complete and unadulterated.

105.32–33   May-day . . . Morelia]   On May 13, 1921, a riot erupted between revolutionists and Catholics at Morelia, Michoacán. More than 50 persons were killed, many by police.

106.27   General Ortiz]   Pascual Ortiz Rubio (1877–1963), president of Mexico in 1930–32.

112.27   County Sligo hall]   The meeting hall of the County Sligo Men's Social and Benevolent Association, founded in 1887 in New York City.

112.32   outland Irish]   Irish emigrants and their descendants, especially those settled in Great Britain.

113.37   Black Protestants]   Evangelical Protestants of Northern Ireland.

114.1   mizzle-witted]   Mindless, stupid.

123.11   Sons of Temperance]   Fraternal order for Protestant men, founded in New York City in 1842. One of the largest temperance organizations, it had chapters throughout the English-speaking world and thrived for half a century.

123.19–21   At midnight . . . hour—"]   From "Marco Bozzaris," by the American poet Fitz-Greene Halleck (1790–1867).

128.38   Azurea]   Line of fragrance products (perfume, face powder, etc.) by L. T. Piver, Paris.

142.17   any . . . north.]   See note 76.7.

144.36   valley of the pyramids]   In Teotihuacan, 30 miles north of Mexico City.

147.18   Oaxaca earthquake]   The major earthquake in Oaxaca on January 14, 1931, measured 7.8 on the Richter scale and left 70 percent of the city uninhabitable.

152.17   Porfirio Díaz]   Díaz (1830–1915), president of Mexico in 1876–80 and 1884–1911, was forced from office by the popular revolution of 1910–11. He died in exile in Paris.

153.2   present régime]   Administration of Pascual Ortiz Rubio (1877–1963), president of Mexico in 1930–32.

158.8   "Ay, Sandunga . . . por Diós!"]   From "La Sandunga" by Máximo Ramón Ortiz (1816–1855), popular song in the voice of a Zapotec woman grieving over the body of her dead mother. *Sandunga* means "elegance," "charm," "grace," words that describe the dead woman.

163.30   repartition of land]   Seizure and redistribution of privately owned land by the government began almost immediately after the Mexican revolution of 1910. It was accelerated with Article 27 of the Constitution, ratified in 1917, which declares that all land within Mexico is the property of the state, which has the right to transfer ownership as it sees fit: "Hence, private property is a privilege created by the Nation."

163.36   aguacate]   Avocado.

164.35   Puss Moth]   Three-seat single-wing airplane, built by the de Havilland Aircraft Company in 1929–33.

167.26   *corrido*]   See note 102.15.

170.14   Agrarians]   Peasants and others sympathetic to the repartition of land and hostile to the wealthy *hacendados* or land-owning class.

172.16   charro]   See note 101.22.

175.35   hacendados]   See note 170.14.

176.32   like Rivera's]   In the style of Mexican muralist Diego Rivera (1886–1957).

182.22–23   And the greatest . . . charity.]   1 Corinthians 13:13.

184.16–17   Ruin hath taught . . . away.]   See Shakespeare's Sonnet 64 ("When I have seen by Time's fell hand defaced . . .").

186.26   Vita Nuova]   *La Vita Nuova* ("The New Life," 1295) by Dante Alighieri (1265–1321), collection of poems with prose commentary centered on Beatrice Portinari, the idealized object of Dante's unrequited love.

186.27   Wedding Song of Spenser]   "Epithalamion" (1595) by Edmund Spenser (1552–1599).

186.28–29   "Her tantalized spirit . . . roses . . ."]   Cf. "For Annie" (1849) by Edgar Allan Poe.

186.35–36   Mother of God . . . Child;]   *Madonna and Child on a Grassy Bench* (1505–7), woodcut by Albrecht Dürer (1471–1528).

186.36–37   Death . . . knight;]   *The Knight, Death, and the Devil* (1513), engraving by Dürer.

186.38–39   Sir Thomas More's household,]   Painting (1593) by Rowland Lockey (1565–1616) in the style of Hans Holbein the Younger.

187.3   play with Mary . . . in it]   *Maria Stuart* (1800) by Friedrich von Schiller (1759–1805).

188.5   "Sic semper tyrannis,"]   Latin: "Thus always to tyrants," motto of the state of Virginia.

194.37–38   melancholy farewell . . . Granada]   "La Golondrina" ("The Swallow"), Mexican song of farewell by Narciso Serradel Sevilla (1843–1910).

200.31   Proteus Ball]   The Krewe of Proteus, a New Orleans social club that parades during Mardi Gras, sponsors an annual masquerade ball.

205.15   Tod Sloan]   American jockey (1874–1933) who, in the 1890s, revolutionized riding technique by leaning forward in his stirrups, out of his saddle, and onto the neck of the horse. His "forward mount," or "monkey crouch," is used by all jockeys today.

206.10   "Over the River"]   "(Let Us Cross) Over the River" (1876), song by Septimus Winner (1827–1902).

206.19   serpent's teeth]   See Shakespeare, *King Lear*, I.iv.287–88: "How sharper than a serpent's tooth it is / To have a thankless child!"

207.15–16   *Whoa, you heifer*]   Song (1904) by New Orleans ragtime musician Al Verger (1879–1924).

210.21   Elysian Fields]   Street in the New Orleans neighborhood of Gentilly, in the northeastern quadrant of the city.

211.18   St. Charles]   Grand hotel on Canal Street, New Orleans, a center of the city's social and political life from 1837 to 1974.

221.20   Calcasieu Parish]   Parish (county) in southwestern Louisiana, on the Texas border; its seat is Lake Charles.

241.32   stranger . . . land]   See Exodus 2:21–22.

243.38   roup and wryneck]   In poultry, roup is a respiratory illness, wryneck a congenital deformity in which the bird's neck is twisted at an angle to the body.

246.6   meeching]   Cowardly, retiring.

259.7   hand-runnin']   In unbroken succession.

267.26   Halifax]   A creek in Hays County, Texas.

274.39   gallus]   Suspender.

281.1   *Pale Horse, Pale Rider*]   See Revelation 6:8: "And I looked, and behold a pale horse: and his name that sat on him was Death, and Hell followed with him."

283.14   Liberty Bond]   Bond issued by the U.S. Treasury during World War I to help finance the war effort.

283.26   Lusk Committeeman]   Member of the New York State Joint Legislative Committee to Investigate Seditious Activities (1919–20), headed by State Senator Clayton R. Lusk (1877–1959). For a year the so-called Lusk Committee, working with police and private investigators, raided the headquarters of suspected radical organizations in search of evidence that they advocated the overthrow of the U.S. government.

285.7–8   Belleau Wood]   The four-week Battle of Belleau Wood, near Chateau-Thierry, France (June 1–26, 1918), was the first in which chiefly American forces suffered heavy casualties.

285.9   Boche]   Derisive French slang term for the German Army.

295.25   sapping party]   Group of combat engineers that advances with the front-line infantry and prepares the field of battle by digging trenches, building bridges, clearing mines, etc.

297.17   The Angel of Mons]   According to a legend fabricated by the Welsh writer Arthur Machen in his tale "The Bowmen" (1914), St. George and an angelic army assisted the British Expeditionary Force at Mons, France, during its first engagement with the German Army (August 22–23, 1914).

298.29   Hut Service]   One of many civilian support groups that provided comfort and entertainment to servicemen during World War I, establishing the model for the modern USO.

303.4–5   explosive . . . pits]   Peach pits are a rich natural source of hydrogen cyanide, the gas of which, when mixed with air at concentrations over 5.6%, is a powerful explosive.

303.28–29   Stella Mayhew]   American singer and comic actress (1875–1934) often paired, in blackface, with Al Jolson.

303.30–31   O the blues . . . disease]   First line of "Ev'rybody's Crazy 'bout the Doggone Blues" (1918), popular song by Turner Layton, words by Henry Creamer.

305.33   Over There]   The European front in World War I, a usage made popular by George M. Cohan's song "Over There" (1917).

305.33–34   Big Berthas]   Series of six powerful howitzers manufactured by Krupp arms works and used by the German Army at the outset of the war. Each fired a 420-mm. shell and had a range of about eight miles.

305.38–39   "In Flanders Field . . . row"]   Cf. "In Flanders Fields" (1915), poem by Canadian Army surgeon Lieutenant Colonel John McCrae (1872–1918).

306.11 "Tipperary" or "There's a Long, Long Trail"] Popular anthems of World War I: "It's a Long Way to Tipperary" (1912), British music-hall song by Harry Williams, words by Jack Judge; "There's a Long, Long Trail A-winding" (1915), song by Yale undergraduates Alonzo "Zo" Elliott and Stoddard King.

308.6–7 "Pack Up Your Troubles"] "Pack Up Your Troubles in Your Old Kit-Bag (And Smile, Smile, Smile)" (1915), marching song by "Charles Asaf" (the English Brothers Felix and George Henry Powell).

308.17 "Madelon"] "Quand Madelon" (1918), French popular song by Camille Robert, words by Louis Bosquet, about a Breton barmaid who refuses to kiss any one soldier because "she is true to the whole regiment."

309.28 Mumm's Extry] Mumm Carte Classique, an extra-dry white Champagne.

315.22–23 I confess . . . Paul] The Confiteor ("I confess"), spoken by the celebrant at the beginning of the Roman Rite of Mass.

315.30 Blessed . . . mild] Cf. "Gentle Jesus, Meek and Mild," in *Hymns and Sacred Poems* (1739) by Charles Wesley (1701–1788).

325.38 Armistice] On November 11, 1918, at Compiègne, France, the Germans signed an armistice agreement prepared by the Allied powers, ending World War I.

329.21 Bois d'Hiver] "Winter wood," a heavy, spicy French perfume.

329.32 Lazarus, come forth] See John 11:43.

334.34 bois d'arc] Osage Orange (*Maclura pomifera*); also known as the bodock or hedge-apple tree.

344.27 from San Marcos to Austin] About 30 miles.

403.26–27 Little Tammany Association] The Tammany Society (1789–1961)—better known, after its headquarters on 14th Street, as Tammany Hall—was the political machine that controlled Democratic Party politics in New York City in 1850–1930. In its heyday, Tammany was led by Irish Catholic immigrants who did much to advance their people's interests through political nominations, municipal contracts, influence, and intimidation. The "Boss" of the Tammany machine was a kingmaker and a popular symbol of political corruption. The Little Tammany Association was the machine's organization in the Bronx.

409.24 G-men] "Government men"; agents of the Federal Bureau of Investigation.

417.10–11   St. Veronica's] Former Roman Catholic parish in the West Village, with a church on Christopher Street.

418.7   riding . . . on the Tiger's back] Tammany Hall (see note 403.26–27) was nicknamed "The Tiger" and depicted as such in political cartoons of the day. To "ride on the Tiger's back" was to benefit from Tammany's political influence.

422.17–19   *The Duchess* . . . poems] *The Duchess* (1887) by Margaret Wolfe Hungerford (1855–1897), Irish novelist who wrote under the name "The Duchess"; Ouida, pen name of English novelist Maria Louise Ramé (1839–1908); Mrs. E.D.E.N. (Emma Dorothy Eliza Nevitte) Southworth (1819–1899), American novelist whose stories were set in the South during Reconstruction; *Poems of Passion* (1883), collection by the American poet Ella Wheeler Wilcox (1850–1919).

427.4–6   songs of Heine's] Heinrich Heine (1797–1856), German Romantic poet whose verses were set to music by Franz Schubert (1797–1828) and Robert Schumann (1810–1856).

427.6   Low German] Regional dialect of German spoken in the flat coastal and plains area of northern Germany; the dialect and those who speak it are also called *Platt Deutsch.*

433.8   *Turnverein*] German-style athletic club and community hall with auditorium, dance floor, restaurant, and perhaps a bowling alley.

436.27   *Das Kapital*] Three-volume critique of capitalism (1867–1894) by German philosopher and economist Karl Marx (1818–1883), edited and completed by his friend and fellow-Communist Friedrich Engels (1820–1895).

446.1–2   *"Mutterchen, Mutti, Mutti*] Little Mother, Mommy, Mommy.

456.4   "Heilige Nacht,"] The Austrian carol "Stille Nacht, Heilige Nacht" ("Silent Night, Holy Night," 1818) by Josef Mohr, words by Franz Xavier Gruber.

456.5   Martin Luther's "Cradle Song,"] The melody of "Away in a Manger" is traditionally attributed to Luther.

456.32   "Brother . . . dime?"] "Brother, Can You Spare a Dime?" (1931), popular song of the Great Depression by Jay Gorney, words by E. Y. "Yip" Harburg.

461.12   shot-silk] Chatoyant silk, woven with strands of two or more colors to produce an iridescent effect.

466.33   Tiergarten] Large park in the heart of Berlin, the east side of which faces the Brandenburg Gate.

470.22   "*Jawohl!*"]   "Yes indeed!"

474.31   Low-German]   See note 427.6.

477.24   Platt Deutsch]   See note 427.6.

481.21   Dance of Death]   *Der Totentanz* (1538), series of 41 wood en-
gravings by Hans Holbein the Younger.

483.9   *boîte*]   Nightclub.

485.24   *mensur*]   Duel fought between university students over a point of
honor.

504.31–505.6   "*Ich armes . . .* du verloren hast—"]   German marching
song: "What a poor devil am I, / I can't march any longer, / I can't march
any longer./ / I've lost my piccolo / From out of my coat bag / From out
of my coat bag. / / I've found, I've found the thing, / The thing that you
lost, / The thing that you lost. . . ."

505.8   "The Peanut Vendor"]   "El Manisero," Cuban rumba by Havana
bandleader Don Azpiazu (1893–1943), popularized by the Hollywood musical
The Cuban Love Song (1931).

ESSAYS, REVIEWS, AND OTHER WRITINGS

515.3   *The Days Before*, by Katherine Anne Porter]   *The Days Before* (New
York: Harcourt, Brace & Co., 1952) is Porter's selection from her essays, re-
views, and other nonfiction writings, 1922–1952. She dedicated the book to
her older sister, Gay Porter Holloway, and organized the contents as follows
(variant titles used in the present volume are set off in brackets): Foreword
["I needed both . . ."]; CRITICAL: "The Days Before," "On a Criticism of
Thomas Hardy," "Gertrude Stein: Three Views" ("'Everybody Is a Real
One,'" "Second Wind," "The Wooden Umbrella"), "Reflections on Willa
Cather," "'It Is Hard to Stand in the Middle,'" "The Art of Katherine Mans-
field," "Orpheus in Purgatory," "'The Laughing Heat of the Sun,'" "Eudora
Welty and *A Curtain of Green*," "Homage to Ford Madox Ford ["Ford Ma-
dox Ford"]," "Virginia Woolf," "E. M. Forster"; PERSONAL AND PARTICU-
LAR: "Three Statements About Writing" ("The Situation in American
Writing," "Introduction to *Flowering Judas*" ["The only reality . . ."],
"Transplanted Writers"), "No Plot, My Dear, No Story," "The Flower of
Flowers, *with* A Note on Pierre-Joseph Redouté," "Portrait: Old South,"
"Audubon's Happy Land," "A House of My Own," "The Necessary En-
emy," "'Marriage Is Belonging,'" "American Statement: 4 July 1942" ["Act
of Faith: 4 July 1942"], "The Future Is Now"; MEXICAN: "Notes on the Life
and Death of a Hero," "Why I Write About Mexico," "Leaving the Petate,"

"The Mexican Trinity," "La Conquistadora," "Quetzalcoatl," "The Charmed Life."

523.13–15   "Mr. James . . . and liked him."] These words are not by Thomas Carlyle; they are from a letter to him by the English writer John Sterling, dated December 7, 1843, published in Carlyle's *Life of John Sterling* (1897).

523.17–18   "odd legend"] See Chapter 6 of *Notes of a Son and Brother* (1914) by Henry James (1843–1916). All quotations from James used in this essay are taken from his memoirs *A Small Boy and Others* (1913), *Notes of a Son and Brother*, and the posthumous fragment *The Middle Years* (1917).

524.16–17   *Revue des Deux Mondes*] Critical monthly, published in Paris since 1829.

525.19–20   his fragment of autobiography] "Autobiography," in *The Literary Remains of the Late Henry James* (1884), edited by his eldest son, the psychologist William James (1842–1910). All quotations from Henry James Sr. (1811–1882) used in this essay are taken from this volume.

525.33–34   *faute de mieux*] For lack of something better.

527.6   Uncle Gus] Augustus James (1807–1866), brother of Henry James Sr.

527.20   Mr. Emerson] Ralph Waldo Emerson (1803–1882).

528.18   his mother's sister] Catherine Walsh (1812–1889), "Aunt Kate" to the James children.

528.25   *Charm*] *The Charm: A Book for Boys and Girls*, monthly magazine published in London, 1852–54.

529.12   Mr. Thackeray] William Makepeace Thackeray (1811–1863).

529.33   Mr. Brady's] Studio of Mathew Brady (1822–1896), known for his portraits and Civil War photographs.

531.3–5   Alice . . . whim."] Alice James (1848–1892), sister of Henry James; journal entry dated November 18, 1889, from *Alice James: Her Brothers—Her Journal* (1934), edited by Anna R. Burr.

534.16   Mr. Jenks's school] In 1853–54, Henry and William James attended a boys' school, on Broadway near Fourth Street, established by one Richard Pulling Jenks (1808?–1871).

538.1–2   Minnie Temple] Mary Temple (1845–1870), first cousin of Henry James.

539.23–25　Benjamin Paul Blood . . . in regard to it?"] Blood (1832–1919), American poet and philosopher, was a longtime correspondent with William James, whose essay on Blood's work, "A Pluralistic Mystic" (1910), concludes with the words quoted here, taken from a personal letter to James.

540.1　*Reflections on Willa Cather*] This essay is a revised, expanded version of a review of *Willa Cather on Writing* (1949), a posthumous collection of Cather's literary essays edited by Stephen Tennant. The quotations from Cather used in this piece are drawn from that collection.

540.24　Steichen's] Portrait of Cather by Edward Steichen (1879–1973), taken in 1926.

541.26　Mrs. Auld] Jessica Cather Auld (1881–1968), younger sister of Willa Cather, in *Willa Cather: A Biographical Sketch* (c. 1949), a pamphlet created by the Knopf publicity department to accompany review copies of *Willa Cather on Writing*.

544.35–36　young Mexican painter] Adolfo Best-Maugard (1892–1965), whom Porter met in New York City in 1919.

549.23　Nude . . . Staircase] *Nude Descending a Staircase, No. 2* (1912), painting by Marcel Duchamp (1887–1968).

550.17–18　Maxwell . . . *Provincials*] *The Last of the Provincials: The American Novel 1915–1925* (1947) by Maxwell David Geismar (1909–1979).

551.9–12　We must not . . . hungry roots?] Cf. "Goblin Market" (1862) by Christina Rossetti (1830–1894).

551.13　E. K. Brown . . . *Cather*] *Willa Cather: A Critical Biography* (1953) by E. K. Brown, completed by Leon Edel.

555.17　Jacob Boehme] Jakob Böhme (1575–1624), German alchemist and Christian mystic.

558.21　*Everybody's Autobiography*] Prose work by Gertrude Stein (1937) recounting her visit to America following the success of her *Autobiography of Alice B. Toklas* (1933); it is the source of all quotations from Stein used in this essay.

558.22　Kahnweiler] Daniel-Henry Kahnweiler (1884–1979), Paris gallery-owner and champion of Cubism.

559.13　Alice B. Toklas] Toklas (1877–1967) met Stein in 1907 and was her devoted partner until Stein's death in 1947.

559.20　Leo] Leo Stein (1872–1947), art collector and critic.

559.21　Sir Francis Rose] English painter (1909–1979) and illustrator of *Gertrude Stein's First Reader* (1947).

560.18   *transition*] Little magazine (1927–30) published in Paris and edited by the poet and translator Eugene Jolas (1894–1952) with his wife, Maria McDonald Jolas (1893–1987).

564.28   *Clarissa Harlowe*] *Clarissa* (1748), epistolary novel by Samuel Richardson (1689–1761).

565.35   Hetty Green] American financier (1834–1916) known as "The Witch of Wall Street" and legendary for her miserliness.

565.36   Jay Laughlin] James Laughlin (1914–1997), founder of New Directions publishers; he brought out an edition of Stein's *Three Lives* (1907) in 1933.

566.3   G.A.R.] Grand Army of the Republic (1866–1956), fraternal organization for Union veterans of the Civil War.

570.27   Santa Teresa] St. Teresa of Ávila (1515–1582), Spanish mystic and Carmelite reformer.

570.28   William Seabrook] American journalist and adventurer (1884–1945); his impressions of Stein are recorded in *No Hiding Place: An Autobiography* (1942).

575.7   *Pavannes and Divisions*] Volume of critical essays (1918) by Ezra Pound (1885–1972).

576.17–18 The poet is married] Pound married the English artist Dorothy Shakespear (1886–1973) in 1914.

577.33–34 Harriet Monroe] Monroe (1860–1936), founder and editor of *Poetry*, a monthly magazine of poetry and criticism published in Chicago since 1912.

580.11   Douglas . . . credit] Social credit, or "socred," economic theory developed in the 1920s by Scottish engineer C. H. Douglas (1879–1952), who argued that money should be used to improve society.

580.13   Ernestine Evans] American journalist and book editor (1890–1967).

582.3–4   Friends . . . Louisiana] Herschel Brickell, a scholar of Mexico, and his wife, Norma, brought Welty to Baton Rouge to meet Porter and her husband, Albert Erskine Jr. (1911–1993), in 1938.

585.22   *Manuscript* . . . John Rood] Rood (1902–1974) and his wife, Mary Lawhead, edited and published the bimonthly magazine *Manuscript* from their home in Athens, Ohio, in 1934–36. "Death of a Traveling Salesman" appeared in the issue for June 1936.

585.25   Albert Erskine] Erskine (see note 582.3–4) was an editor of *The Southern Review* in 1935–40; he was later Welty's editor at Random House.

585.30   a friend] Katherine Anne Porter.

587.5–7   a Bostonian] Edward Weeks (1898–1989), editor of *The Atlantic Monthly*, which began publishing Welty's stories in 1941.

590.15–16   Catherine Fourmentelle . . . Eliza Draper] Catherine (Kitty) Fourmentelle, a French singer; Elizabeth (Eliza) Draper (1744–1778), for whom Sterne (1713–1768) wrote the *Journal to Eliza* (written 1767; published in 1904).

590.20   Skelton Castle . . . Hall-Stevenson] Eleventh-century York-shire castle, known in the 18th century as "Crazy Castle" for the antics of its proprietor, John Hall-Stevenson (1718–1785).

590.22   Medmenham Monks] Pleasure-loving members of the "Hellfire Club" at the Cistercian abbey in Buckinghamshire, England.

593.33   his wife] Sterne married Elizabeth Lumley in 1741.

596.2–7   "From Thomas Hardy . . . prayer."] See *The Later Years of Thomas Hardy, 1892–1928* (1930) by Thomas Hardy, writing under the name of his wife, Florence Emily Hardy. This and a companion volume, *The Early Life of Thomas Hardy, 1840–1891* (1928), are the sources of all quotations from Hardy and his notebooks used in this essay.

596.27–597.18   The work . . . tremendous thing.] From *After Strange Gods: A Primer of Modern Heresy* (1934) by T. S. Eliot, the source of all quo-tations from Eliot used in this essay.

603.33   E. M. Forster has remarked] See "T. S. Eliot" (1928), in *Abinger Harvest* (1936).

607.18–19   You can read about it] See "Liberty in England" (1935), in *Abinger Harvest* (1936).

608.9–10   a mediocre book] *Boy* (1930), a novel by James Hanley, sup-pressed as obscene by the Lancashire police in 1934.

609.7–8   Virginia Woolf once wrote:] See "Oliver Goldsmith," in *The Captain's Death Bed and Other Essays* (1950).

616.21–23   Rousseau-like] In the manner of post-Impressionist painter Henri Rousseau (1844–1910).

621.14–15   *The Turn of the Screw*] Novella (1898) by Henry James.

622.37–38   "Anybody who calls . . . liar."] Lawrence, in a letter to his agent, Curtis Brown, dated March 15, 1928; published in *D. H. Lawrence: Se-lected Letters* (1950), edited by Richard Aldington.

622.38–39 "It'll infuriate . . . decent ones."] Lawrence, in a letter to his patron Mabel Dodge Luhan, dated March 12, 1928; published in *Selected Letters* (1950). In the original, Lawrence underscored the word "mean."

623.28 *Harvet Breit*] Breit (1910–1968), a staff critic for *The New York Times Book Review* in 1940–65, provided this blurb for the jacket of the Grove Press edition of *Lady Chatterley's Lover.*

624.3 *Edmund Wilson*] Wilson (1895–1972) reviewed the privately printed first edition of *Lady Chatterley's Lover* in *The New Republic* (July 3, 1929). He wrote: "It is the most inspiriting book from England that I have seen in a long time; and—in spite of Lawrence's occasional repetitiousness and his sometimes rather overdone slapdash tone—one of the best written. . . . And this one of his books, which has been published under the most discouraging conditions . . . is one of his most vigorous and brilliant."

624.7 *Memoirs of Hecate County*] Book of linked short stories (1946) suppressed as obscene by New York State and not again published in the United States until 1959.

624.14 *Jacques Barzun*] American historian and cultural critic (b. 1907); co-founder of the Readers' Subscription book club.

624.23 Mr. Schorer] Mark Schorer (1908–1977), American man of letters and professor of English at the University of California, Berkeley, in 1946–73.

624.32 Mrs. Shakespear] Olivia Shakespear (1863–1938) was Yeats's mistress in 1896–97 and remained a close friend until her death. The letter, dated May 25, 1933, was first published in *The Letters of W. B. Yeats*, edited by Allan Wade (1954).

626.9 He wrote once] See "Hymns in a Man's Life" (1928) by D. H. Lawrence, first collected in Lawrence's *Assorted Articles* (1930).

626.27 "Love . . . excrement"] From "Crazy Jane Talks with the Bishop" by W. B. Yeats, first collected in Yeats's *Words for Music Perhaps* (1932).

627.23 Swift's . . . woman] Cf. "Last week I saw a woman flay'd, and you will hardly believe how much it alter'd her person for the worse": "A Tale of a Tub" (1704) by Jonathan Swift (1667–1745).

628.7 Tolstoy once said] See *Reminiscences of Leo Nikolaevich Tolstoy* (1920) by Maxim Gorky, translated by S. S. Koteliansky and Leonard Woolf.

633.26–29 "The leader-cum-follower . . . women."] Letter to the poet Witter Bynner, dated March 13, 1928; published in *Selected Letters* (1950).

634.27–28 *The Waning of the Middle Ages*] *Herfsttij der Middeleeuwen* (1919; trans. 1924) by the Dutch historian Johan Huizinga (1872–1945), subtitled "A Study of Forms of Life, Thought, and Art in France and the Netherlands in the Dawn of the Renaissance."

636.18   strepitation] Noisiness, rowdiness.

644.5   A. R. Orage] English man of letters (1873–1934) and, from 1907 to 1922, editor and publisher of *The New Age*, a weekly review of politics and the arts.

652.7   Poetry Center] The Poetry Center of the 92nd Street Y (Young Men's Hebrew Association), New York City, inaugurated its series of poetry readings in 1939. John Malcom Brinnin (1916–1998) was director in 1949–56.

653.1–4   "This was not . . . everlasting."] From "The Lemon" (1936), story by Dylan Thomas, collected posthumously in *Adventures in the Skin Trade* (1955).

656.6   lyke-wake dirge] "Lyke-Wake Dirge" (or "Fire and Sleet and Candlelight"), 17th-century English song about the obstacles a soul confronts on the way to heaven.

659.35   stage Wendy] Wendy Darling, character in J. M. Barrie's play and novel *Peter Pan* (1904).

666.16–17   Marianna Alcoforado and The Duchess] Alcoforado (1640–1753), Portuguese nun to whom the anonymous epistolary romance *Letters of a Portuguese Nun* (1669) has been attributed; The Duchess, see note 422.17–19.

666. 36–37   E. M. Butler . . . *Rilke*] *Rainer Maria Rilke* (1941), biography by Eliza Marian Butler (1885–1959).

667.33   Princess . . . Taxis] Rilke wrote the *Duino Elegies* (1922) while visiting the Princess Marie von Thurn und Taxis (1855–1934) and dedicated his novel, *The Notebooks of Malte Laurids Brigge* (1910), to her.

669.5   Olivet] Olivet College, in Olivet, Michigan, held annual Writers' Conferences in 1936–41 at which Ford and Porter repeatedly lectured.

669.26–27   "an old man . . . writing."] The Japanese artist Hokusai (1760–1849) called himself, in his final years, "the old man mad about drawing."

669.31   "pride . . . humility."] Cf. "The Devil's Thoughts" (1835) by Samuel Taylor Coleridge (1772–1834): "And the devil did grin, for his darling sin / Is pride that apes humility."

670.14   Tietjens cycle] *Parade's End* (1924–28), four novels that chronicle the life of Christopher Tietjens, a British officer on the Western Front in World War I.

672.12–13   Eugene and Maria Jolas] See note 560.18.

673.6 "a too pained whitelwit"] See Book 1, Episode 5 of *Finnegans Wake* (1944).

675.12 Bryher] Pen name of Annie Winifred Ellerman (1894–1983), English expatriate who offered financial support to Beach, Joyce, and other friends in Paris in the 1920s and 1930s.

676.10 Hadley . . . Bumby the Baby] Elizabeth Hadley Richardson (1891–1979), Hemingway's first wife, and their son, John Hadley Niconar Hemingway (1923–2000).

676.14 her book] *Shakespeare and Company* (1956).

676.39 *beau garçon*] Beautiful boy.

679.11–13 Southern . . . War] In November 1864, while on his march through Georgia, General William T. Sherman stopped in Milledgeville, then the state capital, to set up headquarters in the governor's mansion.

685.9 *Legend and memory*] The short-story sequence "The Old Order" grew from the opening section of the abandoned novel "Many Redeemers."

686.4 *The Possessed*] Novel (1872) by Fyodor Dostoevsky (1821–1881).

686.6 Becky Sharp] The social-climbing heroine of *Vanity Fair* (1848).

687.13 Julien Sorel] Hero of Stendhal's *Le Rouge et le Noir* (*The Red and the Black*, 1830).

688.3 Hergesheimer] Joseph Hergesheimer (1880–1954), author of *Java Head* (1919) and other historical novels.

696.38 S. Sergeev-Tzensky] Sergey Nikolaevich Sergeev-Tzensky (1878–1958), Soviet writer celebrated for novels and stories set during the Crimean War.

697.21 "Add-a-Plot" cards] In "Deal-a-Plot," a parlor game of the 1930s, players were dealt cards in six categories (Character, Setting, Plot Problem, etc.) and challenged to improvise a story based on the cards' suggestions.

699.40 soluble stuff] In James's *A Small Boy and Others* (1913), his father urges him and his brother William to convert experience into "Virtue": "simply everything that should happen to us . . . were to form our soluble stuff."

713.1–2 Henry Allen Moe] Moe (1894–1975), chief administrator of the John Simon Guggenheim Memorial Foundation from 1925, when it was founded, until 1963.

716.8 Obregon revolution] See note 76.8.

716.32–34   short novel . . . reasons.] Porter customarily named "Pale Horse, Pale Rider" her favorite among her works.

735.10–11   Mayor Mary Kyle . . . Fergus Kyle] Mary Lucy Kyle Hartson (1865–1956) was elected mayor of Kyle, Texas, in 1937; Fergus Kyle (1834–1906) was for many years a member of the Texas legislature.

738.8   Sam Bass] Bass (1851–1878), deputy sheriff in Denton County, Texas, turned outlaw and was killed during an attempted bank robbery.

738.9   Right Bower] In the game of euchre, the knave of the trump suit.

739.27–28   Harry . . . Ima Hogg] Governor Hogg's only daughter, Ima Hogg (1882–1975), a philanthropist in Texas, was named for the heroine of a Civil War poem written by her uncle Thomas Elisha Hogg (1842–1880). Her three brothers were William, Michael, and Thomas; "Harry Hogg" and "Ura Hogg" are Texas myths.

740.26   Roy Bean] Phantly Roy Bean (c.1825–1903), justice of the peace and proprietor of a saloon in which he held court, escaped a murder conviction in Mexico and comfortably lived out his life in San Diego, California.

742.10–11   "There was . . . ground"] From an anonymous cowboy ballad: "There's blood on the saddle and blood on the ground,/ And a great, great big puddle of blood all around;/ A cowboy lay in it all covered with gore/ And he never will ride any broncos no more."

742.12–13   "My Love . . . Starr] "My love is a rider, wild horses he breaks" is the first line of the song "Bucking Bronco," by Myra Maybelle Shirley (Belle) Starr (1848–1889).

743.3   Nut-Brown Maid] "The Nut-Brown Maid," 15th-century ballad included in *Reliques of Ancient English Poetry* (1765), compiled by Thomas Percy (1729–1811).

749.38–39   "Birds . . . sight,"] From a children's hymn by Isaac Watts (1674–1748): "Birds in their little nests agree;/ And 'tis a shameful sight,/ When children of one family/ Fall out, and chide, and fight."

751.1   *A Christmas Story*] In 1967, Seymour Lawrence/Delacorte Press published this story, decorated with line drawings by Ben Shahn, as a small book for holiday gift-giving. Porter's afterword to this edition, dated May 5, 1967, reads in part:
    "This is not a fiction, but the true story of an episode in the short life of my niece, Mary Alice, a little girl who died nearly a half century ago, at the age of five and one-half years. The stories are those I told her, and those we sang together. The shopping for a present for her mother, my sister, in the last Christmas of this child's life is set down here as clearly as I am able to tell it,

with no premonitions of disaster, because we hadn't any: life was daily and forever, for us both. I was young, too. This is, of course, a lament in the form of a joyous remembrance of that last day I spent with this most lovely, much loved being. . . ."

Mary Alice Holloway (1912–1919) was the daughter of Porter's older sister, Gay (Anna Gay Porter Holloway).

752.4–5   Charles . . . baby]   *Adoration of the Three Magi*, in *Les Heures d'Etienne Chaavalier*, a 15th-century illuminated manuscript by French painter Jean Fouquet (1420–1481), who substituted for one of the Magi the figure of Charles VII (1402–1461).

757.26   Feliciana]   Former parish (county) in Louisiana, divided in 1824 into East Feliciana and West Feliciana. St. Francisville, the seat of West Feliciana, is situated 30 miles northwest of Baton Rouge.

757.32   Fulwar Skipwith]   American diplomat (1765–1839) who in 1803 played a major role in the Louisiana Purchase.

757.37   Graustarkian]   In the vainglorious manner of Graustark, a fictional Central European principality continually threatened with extinction by its neighbors, the setting of six historical romances by American novelist George Barr McCutcheon (1866–1928).

759.29–31   "that a man . . . confidence."]   From *A Vision* (1925, 1937) by W. B. Yeats.

760.13–14   Patrizieren . . . Amalienburg]   Houses of city council members in Basel that approximate the Amalienburg, a hunting lodge built for Charles VII in the German Rococo style.

763.34   Sully]   Thomas Sully (1783–1872), American portrait painter who, after studies with Gilbert Stuart and Benjamin West, flourished in Philadelphia.

765.2–4   Rose . . . *Epitaph*]   Rilke (1875–1926) composed this, his epitaph, during his last months: "Rose, oh reiner Widerspruch, Lust,/ Niemandes Schlaf zu sein unter soviel Lidern."

767.6   Raoul, Sire de Coucy]   The Chatelaine de Coucy (1157–1192), whose "Chanson du Chatelain de Coucy" Porter translated for inclusion in her *French Song-Book* (1933).

769.12   Laïs the Corinthian]   Courtesan at the time of the Peloponnesian War (431–404 B.C.); her beauty is mentioned by Plutarch and other contemporary writers.

769.12–13   Saint Thérèse . . . roses]   St. Thérèse de Lisieux (1873–1897), a Carmelite nun known as "The Little Flower of Jesus," is typically depicted with a bouquet of roses.

769.22–26   "A rose . . . version.)] Quatrain 116 of the *Rubáiyát* of Omar Khayyám (1048–1123), from the French version (1924) by Franz Toussaint (1879–1924).

771.35–36   rose liqueur . . . brain."] Rosa solis, praised by Dame Suddlechop in Walter Scott's *The Fortunes of Nigel* (1822): "Right Rosa Solis, as ever washed mulligrubs out of a moody brain!"

773.38–39   metamorphosed Ass] See *The Golden Ass* (*Asinus aureus*) by Apuleius (c. A.D. 123–180).

774.5–6   rose of fire . . . Vision] See Canto 32 of the *Paradiso*.

775.3–15   For the reproductions . . . *Bagatelle.*] See *La Rose dans art: Château de Bagatelle* (1938) by Jean-Louis Vaudoyer (1883–1963).

775.17–24   "A short thick body . . . Paris."] See *Fleurs de Pois* (1845), by François-Joseph Grillé (1782–1855).

775.26–27   portraits . . . Gérard] Redouté's portrait was painted between 1817 and 1823 by Baron François Gérard (1770–1837).

775.27–30   "In spite . . . apple."] See *The Art of Botanical Illustration* (1950) by Wilfred Blunt (1901–1987).

777.35   Mercier] Louis-Sébastien Mercier (1740–1814), French dramatist and writer who, in his *Tableau de Paris* (1781–88), gave a contemporary account of the French Revolution.

778.13   David] Jacques-Louis David (1748–1825), neoclassical painter sympathetic to the Revolution, sketched *Marie Antoinette on the Way to the Guillotine*, October 16, 1793.

779.25   Isabey] Jean-Baptiste Isabey (1767–1855).

781.37   Yaddo] Artists' colony, founded in 1900 by financier Spencer Trask and his wife, Katrina, in Saratoga Springs, New York.

784.12   remark of Mr. E. M. Forster] See "My Wood" (1926), in *Abinger Harvest* (1936).

785.25   *Tobacco Road*] Novel (1932) about Georgia sharecroppers by Erskine Caldwell (1903–1987).

797.26–29   "He preferred . . . world."] Elizabeth Barrett Browning to Mrs. James Martin, a lifelong friend, October 20 (?), 1846, from *The Letters of Elizabeth Barrett Browning* (1897), edited by Frederic G. Kenyon.

797.32–36   "Then came . . . cheek."] Robert Browning to Miss E. F. Haworth, a close friend, July 20, 1861, from *The Letters of Elizabeth Barrett Browning* (see above).

799.35   Butcher-Arnold translation] Porter conflates the 1879 translation of the *Odyssey* by Samuel Henry Butcher (1850–1910) and Andrew Lang (1844–1912) with the 1861 partial translation of the *Iliad* by Matthew Arnold (1822–1881).

812.14   Shelley] John W. Shelley (d. 1939), executive of British El Aguila Oil.

814.1   Covadonga Day] In Spain, a holiday in the northeastern state of Asturias, where, in A.D. 718, in the mountain town of Covadonga, outnumbered Iberians triumphed in a bloody battle against the Moors, a victory said to be achieved through the grace of Mary.

814.6–7   Sanchez . . . Gaona] Mexican bullfighters Ignacio Sanchez Mejías (1891–1934) and Rodolfo Gaona y Jiménez (1888–1975).

814.8   Hattie Welton] Adventurer, circus performer, and owner of a riding school in Mexico City.

816.9   fronton] Jai alai arena.

816.10   Alameda] See note 100.22.

826.1–2   The silence . . . Pascal,] Cf. "Le silence éternel de ces espaces infinis m'effraie" ("The eternal silence of these infinite spaces frightens me"), from the *Pensées* of Blaise Pascal (1623–1666).

827.6   Mr. Toynbee] British historian Arnold Toynbee (1889–1975), author of the 12-volume work *A Study in History* (1934–61).

830.1   *The Never-Ending Wrong*] When this essay, first published in *The Atlantic Monthly* in June 1977, was published as a small book later the same summer, Porter added the following foreword:
"This book is not for the popular or best-selling list for a few weeks or months. It is a plain, full record of a crime that belongs to history.
"When a reporter from a newspaper here in Maryland asked to talk to me, he said he had heard that I was writing another book . . . what about? . . . I gave him the title and the names of Sacco and Vanzetti. There was a wavering pause . . . then: 'Well, I don't really know anything about them . . . for me it's just history.'
"It is my conviction that when events are forgotten, buried in the cellar of the page—they are no longer even history."

830.4–5   Nicola . . . Vanzetti] Ferdinando Nicola Sacco (1891–1927) and Bartolomeo Vanzetti (1888–1927).

831.24   Webster Thayer] Judge Thayer (1857–1933), of the Superior Court of Massachusetts, was judge in both trials of Sacco and Vanzetti.

831.27   Rosa Baron] Rosa (or Rose) K. Baron (d. 1961) was National Prisoners' Relief Director of the Communist Party's International Labor Defense organization in 1925–46. She defended the legal rights of prosecuted Party members and others sympathetic to the Communist cause.

833.1   Leon Henderson] Henderson (1895–1986), in 1927 an economist with the Russell Sage Foundation, and his wife, Myrlie Hamm Henderson, raised money for the defense of Sacco and Vanzetti.

833.2   Governor Fuller] Alvan Tufts Fuller (1878–1958), Republican governor of Massachusetts in 1924–29.

834.5   *Read those letters!*] *The Letters of Sacco and Vanzetti* (1928), the source of the direct quotations from Sacco and Vanzetti used in this essay; the book was edited by Marion Denman Frankfurter (1891–1975), wife of Felix Frankfurter and his partner in the early activities of the American Civil Liberties Union, and Gardner Jackson (1896–1965), who covered the Sacco–Vanzetti case for *The Boston Globe* in 1921–26 and was secretary of Sacco–Vanzetti Defense Committee in 1926–27.

834.19   Mrs. Evans] Elizabeth G. Evans (1856–1937), of Brookline, Massachusetts, a wealthy donor to socially progressive causes who raised money for the defense of Sacco and Vanzetti.

835.5   Gardner Jackson] See note 834.5.

837.11–12   Lincoln Brigade] Abraham Lincoln Brigade, anti-Franco volunteers from the United States who fought alongside the Spanish Republican forces in the Spanish Civil War.

837.17   Bessie Beatty] Beatty (1886–1947), editor of *McCall's* magazine, wrote *The Red Heart of Russia* (1919), an eyewitness account of the Russian Revolution.

837.19   Albert Rhys Williams] Williams (1883–1962), journalist whose sympathetic reports from Soviet Russia were collected in books including *Through the Russian Revolution* (1921).

837.29–30   Frank Tannenbaum] Tannenbaum (1893–1969), political journalist in Mexican, Russian, and African American affairs; later taught criminology at Cornell (1932–35) and Latin American history at Columbia (1935–65).

837.34–35   Third International] The Communist International (Comintern), founded in Moscow in 1919, promoted the Communist cause in the West and worked toward the formation of an international Soviet republic.

840.4   "From each . . . need."] Communist slogan coined by Karl Marx in his "Critique of the Gotha Program" (1875).

841.33 AMTORG] Trading corporation serving Soviet import and export firms doing business with the United States, founded in 1924 by American entrepreneur Armand Hammer (1898–1990), the son of Russian immigrants.

841.37 ROSTA] Soviet news agency, 1918–35; superseded by TASS.

841.39 Kenneth Durant] Durant (1889–1972) became ROSTA's American bureau chief in 1919. He worked from the offices of the United Press Association, on Park Row.

842.6–8 A perennial candidate . . . honest man.] William Z. Foster (1881–1961), General Secretary of the Communist Party USA from 1921 to 1957, was the Party's candidate for United States president in the elections of 1924, 1928, and 1932.

842.15–17 Lola Ridge . . . Lumpkin] In August 1927, the political poet Lola Ridge (1873–1941) had published *The Ghetto* (1918), *Sun-Up* (1920), and *Red Flag* (1927); John Dos Passos (1896–1970) had published six books, including *Manhattan Transfer* (1925); the journalist Paxton Hibben (1880–1928) had published an eyewitness account of the famine in Russia (1922); Michael Gold (1894–1967) had founded the Communist arts magazine *New Masses*; Helen O'Lochlainn Crowe had gained notoriety as a writer on labor and social causes; James Rorty (1891–1973) was a poet and the literary editor of *New Masses*; Edna St. Vincent Millay (1892–1950) had won the Pulitzer Prize in Poetry for *The Harp-Weaver* (1923); William Gropper (1897–1977) was a cartoonist for *The Daily Worker* and *New Masses*; and Grace Lumpkin (1892–1980) had published the first of the proletarian short stories that foreshadowed her novel *To Make My Bread* (1932).

843.18 Pink Tea] Nineteen-twenties' slang term for a peaceful left-wing political demonstration.

845.33–34 Mr. Edward James] James (1873–1954), son of Robertson James, was the younger brother of William and Henry.

845.36 Jim Larkin] James (Big Jim) Larkin (1876–1947), Irish labor leader and social activist, was one of the guiding spirits of the Communist Party USA. In 1923, after serving three years of a ten-year sentence for committing acts of "criminal anarchy," he was deported to Ireland, where he became head of the Irish Communist Party and the Workers' Union of Ireland.

846.39 skew-gee] Off-course.

847.38 Herbert B. Ehrmann] Ehrmann (1891–1970), associate counsel for Sacco and Vanzetti, was the author of *The Untried Case* (1933, revised 1960) and *The Case That Will Not Die* (1969).

848.14   Felix Frankfurter] Frankfurter (1882–1965) wrote a journalistic account of the trial for *The Atlantic Monthly* (March 1927) and, years later, *The Case of Sacco and Vanzetti: A Critical Analysis for Lawyers and Laymen* (1961).

848.16   Mrs. J. Borden . . . Harriman] In 1927, Florence Jaffray Hurst Harriman (1870–1967) was known as a Washington hostess and the founder of the National Women's Club of the Democratic Party.

849.19   Mrs. Leon Henderson] See note 833.1.

852.39   "Giovinezza."] "Youth," the official hymn of the Italian National Fascist Party.

856.33   song about an Irish wake] "The Night That Paddy Murphy Died."

856.37   the first line of the Internationale] "Stand up, wretched of the earth!"

856.38–39   "*Giovinezza . . . bellezza!*"] "Youth, youth! Spring beauty!"

859.28   Mrs. Stuart Chase] Marian Tyler Chase (1897–1989), journalist and co-author of several books with her husband, the economist and social critic Stuart Chase (1888–1985).

859.36   Arthur Garfield Hays] Hays (1881–1954), general counsel for the American Civil Liberties Union and participant in several prominent civil rights trials of the 1920s and 1930s.

860.8   Baumes' Law] New York State law (1926), drafted by Senator Caleb H. Baumes (1863–1937), calling for automatic life imprisonment of any criminal convicted of three or more felonies.

861.4   the judge] James A. P. Parmenter (1860–1937), Boston municipal judge.

863.29   article by . . . Russell] "The End of the Myth: Sacco and Vanzetti 50 Years Later" by Francis Russell (1910–1989), author of *Tragedy in Dedham: The Sacco and Vanzetti Case* (1962) and *Sacco and Vanzetti: The Case Resolved* (1986).

864.21   Felipe Carillo] Felipe Carrillo Puerto (1874–1924), Porter's lover in 1920–21, was governor of Yucatán from 1922 to 1924.

865.23   "The State . . . monsters,"] Friedrich Nietzsche, in *Also Sprach Zarathustra* (1883–85).

865.26–27   Emma . . . life] *Living My Life* (1931) by anarchist Emma Goldman (1869–1940).

865.30   Prince . . . memoirs] *Memoirs of a Revolutionist* (1899) by Prince Peter Alexeyevich Kropotkin (1842–1921).

866.8   the Select]   Café in Montparnasse, Paris.

869.7   Madero revolution]   In 1910–11; see note 102.22.

871.6   La Muerte]   Death.

872.3   Carranza]   In 1914 Venustiano Carranza became the acting president of Mexico, and in 1917 the first president of Mexico under its present constitution; see note 76.8.

872.12   de la Huerta]   Adolfo de la Huerta (1888–1955) was provisional president of Mexico from June 1 to December 1, 1920, from the murder of President Carranza to the inauguration of President Obregón.

873.1   Camara]   Mexican House of Congress. Under the Constitution of 1917, the Mexican Congress is bicameral, with a Senate (*Senado*), or upper house, and a Chamber of Deputies (*Cámara de Diputados*), or lower house.

873.6   diputados]   Mexican congressional deputies (analogous to U.S. representatives).

873.17   Soto y Gama]   Antonio Díaz Soto y Gama (1880–1967), a Zapatista (see note 101.12–13).

873.24   Luis Leon]   Luis L. León Uranga (1891–1981) held several important Cabinet-level posts in 1920–28.

876.19–20   Porfirio Diaz]   See note 152.17.

876.26–27   "And their swords . . . more."]   Isaiah 2:4.

878.28–30   Waddy . . . book]   Waddy Thompson Jr. (1798–1868), U.S. representative from South Carolina, was ambassador to Mexico in 1842–44. He recorded his Mexican experiences in *Recollections* (1846).

879.7–12   Mary Guadalupe . . . Empress]   See note 20.21–22.

881.12   Tilma]   Cloak typically worn by native Mexican Indians until the 1600s. See note 20.21–22.

881.40   Teocalli]   Sacred temple of the Aztecs, built atop a terraced pyramid.

883.24   GENERAL BENJAMÍN HILL]   Although an autopsy determined that Hill (1874–1920), President Obregón's nephew and close adviser, died from complications of a stomach ailment, partisans suspected that he was poisoned by enemies of the Obregón administration.

883.30   "ships"]   Dirigibles.

883.31   Alameda] See note 100.22.

884.26   San Felipe] Philip of Jesus, the first Mexican saint, crucified in
1596 in Nagasaki, Japan, and canonized in 1862.

885.10   Reina] Queen.

886.21   canoa] Canoe.

887.4   henequen fibre] Sisal.

889.16–17   Oaxaca bowl] Traditional dark brown clay bowl with brightly
colored flower-like designs made in Oaxaca, central region of Mexico famous
for its pottery.

891.30–31   "La Adelita," . . . "La Norteña,"] Four popular songs of
Revolutionary Mexico: "La Adelita" and "La Norteña," songs about *sol-
daderas* (female soldiers from the north, allied to Pancho Villa); "La Pajarera"
("The Bird"), attributed to Manuel María Ponce Cuéllar (1882–1948); "La
Sandunga" (see note 158.8).

894.38   syndicalists] Members of the socialist and anarchist wing of the
Mexican labor movement.

895.7–10   Calles . . . Capmany] Plutarco Elías Calles (1877–1955),
Obregón's secretary of the interior, later president of Mexico (1924–28);
Adolfo de la Huerta (see note 872.12), Obregón's secretary of finance; Alberto J. Pani (1878–1955), Obregón's secretary of the treasury and secretary of
foreign relations; Rafael Zuberán Capmany, Obregón's secretary of labor and
industry.

896.23   land-reform laws of Juárez] See note 102.22–23.

897.2   *oratorio*] Chapel or other designated place for prayer.

898.4–7   Carranza . . . May, 1920.] By the end of his elected term,
Venustiano Carranza, the first post-Revolution president of Mexico (1914–
20), was unpopular with those who wanted swifter government reform. In
June 1919, General Álvaro Obregón, one of his most vocal critics, declared his
intention to run for president in the June 1920 election. On April 8, 1920, in
the run-up to the election, a worker for the Obregón campaign attempted to
kill Carranza, and the president threatened Obregón with arrest. Obregón
withdrew from the race to declare an armed revolt against Carranza; days
later, military supporters of Obregón published their plan to form a junta
that, after removing Carranza from office, would hold a free and fair popular
election. On May 21, after fleeing Mexico City, Carranza was intercepted en
route to Veracruz and killed by revolutionary forces led by General Rodolfo
Herrera. Adolfo de la Huerta was named provisional president until Decem-

ber 1, 1920, when Obregón took office after a decisive victory in the popular election.

899.6   Lupe Sánchez] General Guadalupe Sánchez (1856–1933), chief of military operations in the state of Veracruz.

899.7–8   Candido Aguilar] General Cándido Aguilar (1889–1960), Carranza's son-in-law, was governor of Veracruz in 1917–20.

899.12   *La Suerte*] Luck or fortune.

899.34   Trevino] General Jacinto B. Treviño (1883–1971) returned from military studies in Europe to join the revolt against Carranza.

903.11   Senator Fall] Albert B. Fall (1861–1944), U.S. senator (Republican) from New Mexico (1912–21) and secretary of the interior under President Warren Harding (1921–23). He led the 1919 Senate investigation into post-Revolution Mexican-American oil futures, which heightened U.S. economic fears of Mexican appropriation and nationalization of U.S. holdings there.

903.13–14   Vasconcelos . . . Villarreal] José Vasconcelos (1881–1959), Mexican man of letters and Obregón's secretary of education; Antonio I. Villarreal (1879–1944), a founder of the Mexican Labor Party and Obregón's secretary of agriculture and development.

904.10–11   Guggenheims and Dohenys] By the early 1920s, the sons of Meyer Guggenheim (1828–1905) controlled much of North American mining and smelting, and Edward J. Doheny (1865–1935), founder of PanAmerican Petroleum and its Mexican affiliate, Huasteca, controlled much of its oil.

904.22   Guffey] Joseph F. Guffey (1870–1959), owner of AGWI, a U.S. oil company with strong Mexican connections.

905.2   Esteban Cantu] Colonel Esteban Cantú Jiménez (1881–1966), governor of Baja California under Carranza and a political adversary of Obregón.

905.24   Pablo Gonzales] General Pablo Gonzáles Garza (1879–1950) plotted the ambush of Emiliano Zapata (April 10, 1919) at the behest of President Carranza and was later hunted as a traitor by the Obregón regime. He was eventually captured, tried, and condemned to death, but released on orders of President Calles. He was exiled from Mexico, and lived in San Antonio, Texas, until his death.

906.19   Zapata's horde] See note 101.12–13.

907.33   five men] General Sidronio Méndez and his sons (both officers); General Fernando Vizcaino; and General Carlos Greene.

908.36   Luis Morones] Luis Napoleón Morones (1890–1946) was Calles's secretary of economy in 1924, a position he abused for his own financial gain.

909.15   magazine] Vasconcelos published the magazine *El Maestro* ("The Master") and in 1924 founded *La Antorcha* ("The Torch").

909.23   Manuel Gamio] Gamio (1883–1960), archaeologist and one of the leaders of the indigenest movement in Mexico. Porter became friends with him shortly after her arrival in Mexico in 1920.

909.29   Jorge Enciso] Enciso (1879–1969), designer and painter, was Inspector General of Artistic Monuments 1916–20.

909.31   Adolfo Best-Maugard] See note 544.35–36.

910.17   "Land and liberty . . . forever!"] "¡Tierra y Libertad!" ("Life and Liberty!") was a revolutionary slogan popularized by Emiliano Zapata.

914.20   Oaxaca bowl] See note 889.16–17.

914.31   Emperor Maximilian's time] The 1860s.

915.13   La Cocinera] Female cook.

916.29   Pobrecito!] Poor little thing!

918.21   Musetta Waltz] Leitmotif from *La Bohème* (1896) by Giacomo Puccini (1858–1924).

919.3   Yo solita] Lonely little me.

920.4–5   "Yo te amo . . . Lindo."] "I love you, Heavenly One."

921.15   jota] Spanish dance rhythm in three-quarters time.

927.4–5   manzanilla] Chamomile.

929.1   *The Charmed Life*] The unnamed subject of this memoir is Porter's friend William Niven (1850–1937), a Scottish-born American mineralogist and archaeologist. He arrived in Mexico in 1890 to promote gold mining and the construction of a railroad, but by 1910 his interests had shifted to the Valley of Mexico, especially the area around Atzcapotzalco, where he unearthed thousands of artifacts.

936.33   Victoriano Huerta] Huerta (1854–1916) was, after a coup d'etat in which he seized power from Francisco I. Madero, president of Mexico, 1913–14. When forced from office by revolutionary forces, he went into voluntary exile.

936.38   Bertram D. Wolfe] Wolfe (1896–1977), American historian and journalist whose lifelong subjects were the revolutions in Mexico and Russia.

937.20   Pancho Villa] See note 76.7.

943.3   *The Itching Parrot*]   Porter prefaced her translation of Lizardi's novel with the following note:

"The first full translation from the Spanish of *El Periquillo Sarniento* was made by Eugene Pressly, who lived a number of years in Mexico and had made a study of the Mexican popular language and slang in which the novel was partly written, and on which its first appeal to the Mexican public was based. I edited it and revised it at great length. Ford Madox Ford then kindly read it, found it still much too long, and offered suggestions for further deletions. The final editing and cutting was done by Donald Elder, of Doubleday, Doran and Company, and at last the story has been stripped of its immense accumulation of political pamphlets and moral disquisitions, which served their purpose once, let us hope, as the author meant them to. What remains, I believe, is a typical picaresque novel, almost the last of its kind.

"For the clearing up of some knotty chronology, and some material on the life of Lizardi, I owe thanks to Dr. Rea Jefferson Spell, whose doctoral thesis, *The Life and Works of José Joaquín Fernández de Lizardi*, was published by the University of Pennsylvania in 1931. *Notes for a Biography of the Mexican Thinker*, now used as a preface to the Barcelona edition, was written in the early 1840s by an anonymous author who contributes refreshing partisanship, indignation, and sympathy to his subject, but it is a little difficult to find one's way around in.

"The first and best authority on the life of Lizardi is Don Luis González Obregón, distinguished Mexican critic and historian of literature, who wrote his first study of Lizardi as long ago as 1888. [Published by Oficias Tipografica de la Seretararía de Fomento, 1888.] Through his original researches he aroused interest in the almost lost history of Mexico's unique novelist of manners and speech, and later studies have clarified some points and disposed of others for good. To Don Luis I offer my special thanks and acknowledgments."

945.22   Morelos]   José María Morelos (1765–1815), Roman Catholic priest turned leader of the Mexican War of Independence. He was captured by the Spanish in 1815 and executed by firing squad near Mexico City.

945.32   Mexico]   Mexico City.

946.12–13   Hidalgo]   Miguel Hidalgo (1753–1811), revolutionary Roman Catholic priest known as the father of the Mexican independence movement.

946.14   Philip VII]   It was Ferdinand VII (1784–1833), not Philip VII, who was King of Spain, from 1813 until 1833, after a brief ascension in 1808 when the emperor Napoleon forced him to abdicate and imprisoned him in France for seven years.

947.2   Aldama, Jimínez, and Allende]   Juan Aldama, José Mariano Jimínez, and Ignacio Allende, fellow revolutionaries with Miguel Hidalgo.

951.9   Bustamante] Carlos María Bustamante (1774–1848), publisher and lawyer who worked vigorously for Mexican independence and afterward to block a Mexican monarchy.

953.22   Calleja] Félix María Calleja (1753–1828), viceroy of New Spain, 1813–16.

955.35–37   Blanchard . . . education."] Jean-Baptiste Blanchard (1731–1797) revised the theories on "natural" education that Jean-Jacques Rousseau (1712–1778) presented in *Émile, ou l'education* (1762).

956.5   Dr. Beristain] José Mariano Beristain (1756–1817), scholar, critic, and bibliographer of Spanish literature in the New World.

956.11–12   Torres Villaroel] Diego de Torres Villarroel (1693–1770), Spanish poet, playwright, and professor.

956.13–14   Guzman de Alfarache] Hero of *Guzmán de Alfarache* (1599–1604), picaresque novel by Mateo Alemán y de Enero (1547–1614).

966.25   Gil Blas] Hero of *Histoire de Gil Blas* (1715–47), picaresque novel by Alain-René Lesage (1668–1747).

966.25–26   Peregrine . . . Jones] *The Adventures of Peregrine Pickle* (1751) and *The Adventures of Roderick Random* (1748) were written by Tobias Smollett (1721–1771); *The History of Tom Jones, A Foundling* (1729) was written by Henry Fielding (1707–1754).

974.8   "Fantasies"] *Fantastics and Other Fancies* (1914) by Lafcadio Hearn (1850–1904), posthumous collection of stories and sketches from New Orleans newspapers.

974.21   "The Cabin"] *La Barraca* (1898), social novel set among the poor and oppressed of the Valencia countryside, by the Spanish writer Vicente Blasco Ibáñez (1867–1928).

978.10   Mr. Saenz] Moisés Sáenz (1888–1941), educator, diplomat, and Mexican ambassador to Peru, was Porter's friend in 1920–31.

978.40   Mr. Priestley's] Herbert Ingram Priestley (1875–1944), longtime professor of Latin American history at the University of California.

983.37   "*Nous . . . Gasconne!*"] "We are the children of Gascogne!", a French song of resistance of the Hundred Years War (1337–1453).

988.4   Miss Brenner] Anita Brenner (1905–1974), born in Mexico and raised and educated in the United States, wrote several books and many essays on Mexican art, culture, and history.

988.10–11   Tina . . . Weston] Tina Modotti (1876–1942), Italian actress, political activist, and photographer, met Edward Henry Weston (1886–1958) in 1918 and became his favorite model as well as his lover.

988.30–31   Syndicate . . . Sculptors] Guild of muralists, led by Diego Rivera.

990.9   Siquieros] David Alfaro Siquieros (1896–1974), Mexican muralist.

990.13   Jean Charlot] Charlot (1898–1976), French painter and muralist who spent most of his working life in Mexico.

990.14   Merida] Muralist Carlos Mérida (1891–1984), one of the founders of the Syndicate.

990.15   Dr. Atl] Mexican nature artist Gerardo Murillo (1876–1964) called himself "Dr. Atl" to signify his sympathy with the indigenest movement.

990.30–31   Orozco . . . Abraham Angel] José Clemente Orozco (1883–1949), Mexican muralist; Abraham Ángel, Mexican painter (1905–1924) celebrated for his primitive style.

990.33   Xavier Guerrero] Painter and engraver (1896–1974); co-founder, with Siquieros, of *El Machete*, the official organ of the Syndicate.

993.7   Academy] The Academy of San Carlos, founded in 1785 in Mexico City.

995.23   Preparatoria] Escuela Nacional Preparatoria (National Preparatory School) in Mexico City, where Diego Rivera and other artists were commissioned in 1921 by José Vasconcelos, then minister of education, to decorate the schools; marked the beginning of the Mural movement.

997.19   Carmen] Title character of the opera *Carmen* (1875) by Georges Bizet (1838–1875).

998.4   Mr. Morrow's town] Dwight W. Morrow (1873–1931), American ambassador to Mexico in 1927–30, built a weekend house in Cuernavaca and filled it with Mexican artifacts.

1000.4   Carleton Beals] Beals (1893–1945), Latin American correspondent for *The Nation* and author of dozens of works on revolution in Mexico and Central America.

1004.26   Archbishop Pascual Diaz] Pascual Díaz y Barreto (1876–1936), Archbishop of Mexico City in 1929–36, was often at odds with anticlerical Mexican administrations.

1007.6   1894] Porter, given to falsifying her age, was born in 1890, not 1894.

1010.1 *The Land That Is Nowhere*] See the *Tao Te Ching* by Lao Tzu (sixth century B.C.): "The long journey ends at the land that is Nowhere, that is the true home."

1010.3 a certain critic] Malcolm Cowley (1898–1989).

1010.8–9 "newspaper . . . prints] Cowley referred to Porter's early career as a "writer for several newspapers" in the second edition of his memoir *Exile's Return* (1934; revised 1951).

1011.15 Natalie Scott] Natalie Vivian Scott (1890–1957), American journalist, playwright, social worker, and university professor, was part of the artists' colony in the French Quarter of New Orleans in the 1920s and of the expatriate colony in Mexico in the 1930s.

1011.16–17 William Spratling] American professor and silversmith (1900–1967) who copied pre-Colombian designs.

1011.24 Janice Biala] Polish-born American painter (1903–2000) who lived with Ford in the 1930s in France and the United States.

1013.24–27 E. M. . . . idea'."] See "Joseph Conrad: A Note" (1920), in *Abinger Harvest* (1936).

Index

THE LIBRARY OF AMERICA SERIES

The Library of America fosters appreciation and pride in America's literary heritage by publishing, and keeping permanently in print, authoritative editions of America's best and most significant writing. An independent nonprofit organization, it was founded in 1979 with seed money from the National Endowment for the Humanities and the Ford Foundation.

*This book is set in 10 point Linotron Galliard,
a face designed for photocomposition by Matthew Carter
and based on the sixteenth-century face Granjon. The paper
is acid-free lightweight opaque and meets the requirements
for permanence of the American National Standards Institute.
The binding material is Brillianta, a woven rayon cloth made
by Van Heek-Scholco Textielfabrieken, Holland. Composition by Dedicated Business Services. Printing by
Malloy Incorporated. Binding by Dekker Bookbinding. Designed by Bruce Campbell.*